The Alchem

Who We
Once Were

J.P.Talbot

Publisher: Perihelion Imprint.

First published: 2023

Title: Who We Once Were

ISBN- 9798862243871

Previously in this series:

The Thief Fleet

A Wilful Woman

The Devil to Pay

For my beautiful, incomparable wife

Valda Joan

whose love and strength

never cease to support and inspire me.

Also for

Private J.W.Stamp

Gallipoli 1915

Signaller J.J.Power

France 1916

1987

1

"Good morning, sir. You have a letter."

I glanced up sharply from today's *Age*. "Are you quite sure?"

"It bears your name…" The club's steward replied, presenting his burnished brass salver, as baffled as I was given that I have not received more than half a dozen personal letters during the past several years; an inevitable consequence of outliving my few close friends, not that I can remember any of them addressing me with such elegant penmanship as this:

> *Ian Cribdon Esq, CMG, MC, DCM & Bar,*
> *The Macquarie Club,*
> *Collins Street,*
> *Melbourne, Australia.*

Annoyed by this uninvited reminder of the pride, pomp, and circumstance of inglorious war, I nipped a penknife from my waistcoat pocket, slit the envelope's flap, and reached for the magnifying glass I was using on a cryptic crossword in Melbourne's leading newspaper, the better to read a handwritten note below its printed letterhead:

> SOMERVILLE COLLEGE
> OXFORD OX2 6HD
> UNITED KINGDOM

3rd July 1987

Dear Mr Cribdon.

I have recently learned that our family, though not very numerous even in our ancestral heartland of Warwickshire, has a collateral line in Australia.

The Bicentennial Commission has invited me to present a series of lectures at Sydney University, and I would greatly value this opportunity to also visit you and compare genealogical notes.

Sincerely.

Frances Baxter née Cribdon
DPhil (Oxon)

"Will that be all, sir?'

"Yes. Thank you." And off he went to attend to an eminent QC and two young barristers, guests of the older man and both keen to experience the Mac's colonial charm before some upstart property developer turns us into a boutique hotel, as I believe such establishments are called nowadays.

They were four generations too late. The Macquarie's glory days were those between Queen Victoria's 1887 Jubilee and the Great War of 1914-18. A golden age when private gentlemen's clubs were essential business addresses for Australia's wool barons to receive their brokers' telegrams from Bradford, in Yorkshire, while attending to other matters in Melbourne, before returning up-country by steam train to the richest pastoral estates in the colony. An era when letters from England took a month to arrive by packet boat, unlike today's message, flown halfway around the world by jet aeroplane, almost before its ink dried.

By contrast, my earliest flights were made inside an open cockpit not much bigger than a baby's perambulator. Orbiting zig-zagged German trenches. Ack-ack shells bursting above, below, astern. Gloved fingertips tapping a Morse key, directing fall-of-shot onto enemy howitzers and ammo dumps. Hooked forefinger tugging a Lewis gun's trigger, slewing ragged bursts of fire at swarming Pfalz and Fokkers. Often in rapid succession.

It needs only a word or a name or an image to awaken memories of a fear-dried mouth and galloping pulse, above the Western Front, like now, as I limped across the foyer towards the lift cage. Its iron trellis gate clashed shut and an antique electric motor winched me aloft to the second floor where I hold a lifetime tenancy - a shrewd investment made when the club was facing bankruptcy after the Wall Street Crash of 1929 - and let myself into one of five studio apartments overlooking our Heritage Listed Garden.

The casual visitor could easily mistake mine for a monk's cell rather than an elderly gentleman's town residence, for the older we get, the less luggage we need on our annual journeys around the sun. By now my worldly goods amount to little more than a single bed, a reading lamp, a desk, a bookcase filled with dictionaries, encyclopaedias, and atlases. And on my bedside locker, a Zenith Trans-Oceanic wireless receiver, its aerial surreptitiously strung outdoors through the hole bored in the wooden window-frame, earphones looped over a chairback.

Coming from a time and place when custom and courtesy required all correspondence be acknowledged on its day of receipt, I irritably threaded a quarto sheet into my Adler portable typewriter:

The Macquarie Club
78 Collins Street
Melbourne 3000
Australia

9 vii 1987

Dear Dr Baxter.

Thank you for the letter informing me of your proposed visit and desire to compare genealogical notes.

I would assist if there were anything of a family
historical nature to impart, but regret there is none.

Sincerely.

Untrue, but I have sound reasons for snubbing a wrinkled old prune of an Oxford academic who wrongly thought she could invade my privacy without so much as a by-your-leave.

Uncapping my fountain pen, I signed *Ian Cribdon (Mr)* with two firm, black under-strokes, addressed the club's intaglio-engraved envelope, and headed back downstairs to leave it with our concierge.

Mr Perkins affixed an airmail seal and postage stamp while I consulted my watch – a family heirloom gold half-hunter by Christopher Pinchbeck, horologist to King George III – and requested him to telephone for a taxi to ensure I arrived at the Waverley twenty minutes before the first hands were dealt for this week's Bridge tournament.

2

The next fortnight passed without incident, and I was enjoying a wet, wintry Melbourne afternoon, ideal weather to be seated by an open log fire, the library's chessboard at my elbow while I tackled a *Times* retrograde analysis, when –

"I'm sorry for the interruption, sir, but there's a lady wishing to speak with you."

I glanced up, startled. "Surely you jest?"

"No sir, a most definite lady," our manager insisted, presenting her card:

Frances Baxter DPhil, FRSA, FRHistS, FBA.
Reader in Modern History
Somerville College
Oxford OX2 6HD, United Kingdom

Mr Allen knew by my silence that now was not a good time for an interruption. He gave a discreet cough. "Shall I say you are indisposed?"

This is our practiced ploy whenever anyone in Dr Baxter's trade, or a documentary tele-vision film maker, pesters me for an eyewitness account of the landing at Anzac Cove; yet another burden of being one of a dwindling handful who can still remember our disastrous Gallipoli Campaign or, as I more accurately describe it, the Anglo-French Invasion of Turkey.

I had quite enough of that stunt within moments of wading ashore through squalls of shrapnel and machine gun fire and am disinclined to relive the experience - decades later - merely to entertain prying busybodies who persist in viewing me like a museum exhibit, as remote from their daily lives as we raw infantrymen of 16 Battalion AIF were from the bowmen of Agincourt.

Mr Allen gave another muted cough. "Shall I send her away sir?"

I was sorely tempted to get back to my chess problem, but one's early lessons are not so easily dismissed – *If a man be gracious and courteous to the stranger, it showeth him to be a citizen of the world. Francis Bacon, Lord Verulam, 1561-1626* – was among the eighteen morally improving proverbs in copperplate script on the pages of my *Vere Foster's Copy Book of Plain & Ornamental Lettering.* "No."

"As you wish sir. And refreshments?"

"Only if I invite her to sit down!"

"Of course, sir."

With scarcely controlled annoyance I put away the pencil and notepad and stood to greet my uninvited visitor as her shadow fell across the waxed, wooden flooring between the hearth and one of our long sash windows that overlook Collins Street.

"It is very kind of you to see me without prior notice." The voice was young and warm and agreeable to the ear as I turned to face my intruder. The wrinkled old prune was in fact a trim, conservatively clad chestnut brunette in her mid-forties, of medium height, well featured, well formed, with enchanting dark brown eyes, not that I have reason to make such appraisals nowadays. "The tone of your reply was rather intimidating," she continued, with a modest, disarming smile. "I feared that had I phoned ahead, you would be indisposed or otherwise engaged…"

"That was very perceptive of you, ma'am," I scowled, "but as my note clearly indicated, 'family history' is not my strong suit, so I'm afraid you have wasted your time by coming here today."

"If that is your final word," she observed quietly, not at all ruffled by my gruff tone, "there is nothing more to say –"

"Quite."

"- except to explain why and how I've made contact with you."

Her verbal trap left no escape but to resume my seat and irritably gesture for her to take its companion across the firelight. "Given your maiden name was 'Cribdon,' I assumed you thought we might be distant kindred, and hoped to use your stay in Australia to learn more?"

"True," she nodded. "For if this were the case it would be a remarkable discovery, our name being so very rare, even in our home county of Warwickshire."

"How rare?"

"There are only three of us listed in the telephone directory."

"And yet you imagined you'd have better luck in Australia, half the world away from 'our ancestral heartland'?"

"Correct."

"If we're that thin on the ground," I snapped, jealously guarding my privacy, "how the dickens did you track me down?"

She remained silent as one of the staff approached with the Mac's vintage mahogany trolley, its burnished Georgian silver and fine bone chinaware proudly on display. "Good afternoon, ma'am. Good afternoon, sir. Do you wish to take tea or coffee?"

"Tea please," she replied with a gracious smile.

"Certainly, ma'am. Darjeeling? Assam? Ceylon? Oolong? Kimun?"

"Assam, with a dash of milk."

"Of course. Jersey? Hereford? Friesian?"

"Jersey." Said with an approving nod.

He selected the appropriate teapot and milk jug to complete his fussy little ritual before turning to me. "The usual, sir?"

"Yes."

I took the black, freshly brewed Java and stirred in a spoonful of un-pedigreed brown sugar from an anonymous cane-field somewhere in Northern Queensland.

"Considering the inclement weather, Mr Allen thought you might care for buttered crumpets with honey." He flicked aside a white damask napkin.

"How delicious!" she exclaimed, and in her tone of voice I heard the schoolgirl who'd won a scholarship to Oxford before making its university the locus of her life's work. Or a Six agent skilfully playing the part. Either way, I had no intention of letting this stranger pry into what little remains of my life.

"Our pleasure, ma'am," he replied with an appreciative nod. "Clover? Orange blossom? Leatherwood? Mountain Ash -?"

"Leatherwood," I interrupted. "She won't have time to visit Tasmania and sample one of the world's classic honeys in its natural state." Added by way of brusque explanation.

The trolley trundled off and we settled back in our respective seats while my inquisitive visitor cast an appraising glance around the library's ornate ceiling and Corinthian columns. "So, this is where the 'Melbourne Establishment' plots, plans, and plays?" she observed, with a hint of amused irony.

"Not any longer," I corrected shortly. "Facsimile machines and telephones mean there's less need for Billiard Room conspiracies than hitherto."

"But isn't this where Federation was decided, and why Melbourne became Australia's capital city for the next twenty-five years?" she insisted, selecting a crumpet, neatly halving it with her dessert knife before dipping a dollop of aromatic, golden honey. "It must have been an unforgettable sight, our future King George the Fifth opening your nation's first parliament." Adding, a shade too casually, "do you recall anything of the event…?"

As it happens, I did. Quite a lot. Like Spencer Street Railway Station transformed into a copy of Windsor Castle. And a triumphal arch built from eight thousand butter boxes at the intersection of William and Bourke Streets, as visible proof of our dairy farmers' loyalty to the Crown.

I also recognised her "peeling the onion" technique, starting at the outermost edges of another's life - or lie - before stripping it away layer by layer. More subtle than the Gestapo's whips and rubber truncheons in their Paris headquarters at 84 Avenue Foch, a dark and dangerous time when the counterintelligence I extracted a few miles away, by similar means to hers, was generally more reliable.

Determined to practice those skills now, I fixed her with a steady gaze. "Did not my letter say that I have nothing of value to impart, concerning our 'family history' in Australia? And yet here you are, allegedly at the behest of the Bicentennial Commission. So, pray tell me, what's the connection?" My blunt approach put her on the back foot, always the best posture in these brief encounters.

"I've been invited to present a paper that examines the socio-economic and geopolitical determinants of New South Wales' settlement in 1788," she replied, seemingly unperturbed.

"Is there any doubt?" I frowned. "The First Fleet, sent halfway around the world, to empty Britain's overcrowded gaols?"

"That is what most people believe but it is only a small part of a more complex narrative."

"How so?"

"Because they forget, or never knew, that ninety-three percent of those transported men, women, and children were hapless victims of a cruel and rapacious judicial system, and therefore –"

"'Hapless'?"

"Of course." She seemed genuinely surprised that anyone would question her judgment. "Their human rights and standards of living were abominable in England and even worse, in an Australasian convict colony where they were the Crown's plantation slaves. Some officials even used the vile racial slur," and here she lowered her voice, "'White Niggers…'"

"All the more reason to believe they would have schemed to improve their 'abominable' conditions," I remarked, quietly amused by her fear of taboo words as if they were the world's greatest threat to life and limb. Natural enough, I suppose, for timid civilians who have never stood firm against a Turkish bayonet charge, or grimly endured the Kaiser's "Hurricanes of Steel" artillery bombardments, or -

"They could not have done," she persisted stoutly. "Colonial Australia's penal system was designed to crush independent thought or action. And those who stood up for their human rights were either flogged or hanged!"

"Are you sure?" I suppressed a smile. "Some experience of life aboard a troop transport, also under strict military discipline, suggests it would not have been long before their natural leaders took command below decks. All manner of lurks would have flourished without those in authority being any the wiser. And once on dry land again," I added with an ironic aside of my own, "Sydney Town would soon have resembled Cairo after the 1st AIF – that's 'Australian Imperial Force' – landed to show Ali Baba's Forty Thieves how theft and extortion really work."

"I beg to disagree," she replied firmly. "The official records present no evidence of coordinated resistance, and none of the convicts wrote a journal or letters to prove otherwise."

"As one would expect of illiterates," I observed mildly, "but we digress. I was about to learn how you managed to collect this rare bloom of the *Cribdonia Australianus*." A wry botanical joke crafted to keep her off balance in what was becoming a lively duel of wits.

"Sorry. I was distracted."

"Indeed."

"The trouble is, it's rather a long story - "

"The interesting ones generally are."

"- but discovering such an infrequent yet familiar name was the very last thing I expected to find among my grandfather-in-law's papers."

I remained silent.

She broke first. "Don't you wish to know to whom I refer?"

"I'm sure you will tell me, when you're ready."

She was catching-onto my method. "No wonder he called you 'Our Cunning Kangaroo.'"

"Who?"

"My husband's grandfather Stephen - later Sir Stephen - Baxter."

"Ah."

"You don't seem at all surprised."

"At this stage in life, ma'am, the only cause for surprise is to awaken every morning and discover my pulse is still beating."

She had the grace to smile. "Very well, I'll be more explicit."

"That generally helps."

"Petrograd 1920..."

"Go on."

"The second attempt on Lenin's life and –"

"Enough." I raised a forefinger. "Major Baxter, as he then was, should have known better than to record such matters. But as he is no longer here, you probably feel free to write whatsoever you like, for I assume there's a report or book somewhere in the works? But be careful," I continued, with sober emphasis, "the Department of Public Prosecutions, under orders from Six, might have other ideas. And even at this remove we can make things difficult for those who go against our wishes..." I let the warning soak-in before concluding: "However, I am still very much alive and regard what he, and I, and others, may or may not have done, as sealed by an oath of silence we swore to keep forever."

"But the facts of the Martov Affair have been common knowledge since Kaminsky defected -!"

"Then why traipse halfway around the world to discuss them with me?"

"Because an entry in Sir Stephen's private journals – of which you are right, I am editing an historical monograph – implied that you 'neutralised' the Comintern agent who betrayed Cyril Downes…'"

I remained silent.

"Sir Stephen had made an earlier reference to your post-nominal initials," she continued, after vainly waiting for a response, "which I used to track you to the Registry of Medals & Decorations at the War Office. There I learned that you were later appointed CMG. A distinction awarded to those: 'Who hold high and confidential office in the service of the Empire.' After which I gained access to the Order of St Michael & St George's records, in St Paul's Cathedral, and recovered your last known address…"

If she expected me to applaud her sleuthing, she was very much mistaken. Instead, I consulted the half-hunter and read its time. "I'm flattered that someone, somewhere is taking a renewed interest in my modest achievements, but I must now bid you a good afternoon. Mr Perkins, our concierge, will call a cab." I made a discreet signal with my free hand.

"You are being most unreasonable!"

"Why? Because I decline to become a footnote in your exposé of our clandestine war against Bolshevism?"

"Yes! No! It's more than that!" she replied, before regaining her composure.

"How so?"

She hesitated. "The Cold War is thawing. Barely a month ago General Secretary Gorbachev presented his *Perestroika*, or Economic Restructure Plan to the Central Committee of the Communist Party! The Soviet Union cannot survive much longer in its present form, and when it collapses there are bound to be significant revisions of how it all began!"

"And by questioning an eyewitness of 'how it all began,' you hope to have something 'significant' to publish?"

"Yes." Said with an assertive tilt of the chin. "Is that so reprehensible?"

"No, I find it perfectly understandable."

"Then you will assist me?"

"I already have."

"How?" she frowned.

"By inferring that certain matters-of-interest resemble those countless tens of thousands of tons of unexploded ordnance littering the Western Front, decades after they were fired, but which still kill whenever the unwary examine them too closely…"

"Is that a warning?"

"You may very well think so," I replied, standing to bid her farewell with a curt nod. "Good afternoon, ma'am. And goodbye."

3

The Mac's manager approached on felt-soled house shoes, to see her off the premises while I sat down again, reached for the chessmen, and resumed my afternoon's pleasure.

He returned a couple of minutes later. "I'm sorry to disturb you again, sir, but Dr Baxter instructed me to give you this…"

Scowling at his second interruption, I took another of her confounded cards and turned it over to see written, in a firm, clear hand: *V.I.L & Icicle. I shall be at Rydges' Hotel, St Kilda, two more nights. Phone 8530-8888.*

Mr Allen sensed my sudden concern. "Is there a problem, sir?"

I ignored his respectful query. There was no way he could have understood my disquiet that an unknown Englishwoman knew of those three initials' association with that codename. Instead, I shoved her card into my waistcoat pocket and glanced up sharply. "A cab. If you please."

With that, I left the library and ascended to the second floor to collect my Burberry gabardine coat and grey woollen muffler, as well as a sable Borsalino fedora that - like its present owner – is still in fair shape even though he originally traded it for a tin of black-market sardines and five pre-war razor blades, in German Occupied Lyon.

The porter assisted me into the waiting taxi and stood back, aware of how much I dislike tipping for every minor service; it demeans both the donor and the recipient. Besides, the Mac' has a tradition of generous Christmas gratuities for its members of staff.

"Where to you go Miztuh?"

"Monash University, Clayton Campus." For one moment I thought I would have to map read for this Indian immigrant, but quickly realised that he was familiar with the route as we drove out of town through Malvern and Oakleigh while he proudly spoke of a son studying Electrical Engineering at the same institution, before mentioning his daughter's Dental Studies. I listened politely but my mind was focused on more immediate concerns as I paid off the taximeter and rounded it up to the nearest five dollars.

"T'ankew!"

"Dhyanyavad," I replied from my limited stock of Hindi phrases and, borne along by the ebb and flow of young people in all shapes and sizes, colours, and creeds, made my way to the University's Special Collections Department where, a few years previously, I had deposited – among other things – the draft *Basmachi Report*, a scrapbook of illustrated articles for *Anglers' World*, my surviving Great War diaries, and various items of correspondence to and from my old chief Sir John Monash.

Glad to get out of the raw weather, I fronted the reception desk. "Good afternoon," in my haste I had neglected to telephone ahead, "is Dr Thorpe on duty?"

The young girl glanced up from sorting a stack of library cards. "Who shall I say's calling?"

"Ian Cribdon."

Her look of surprise was overtaken by one of puzzled excitement. "Not the Mr Cribdon, who actually knew General Monash?"

"That depends on what you mean by 'knew.' I was only a junior officer on his staff, during the last few months of the war."

"What was he like?"

"Very demanding, as am I. Dr Thorpe, if you please."

"Um. Yes. One moment!" She hurried away behind a glass screen and returned a short while later. "'Jan' will see you now. This way, sir."

I tapped my way after her, down a short corridor towards a plain door that gave no hint of what, on the other side, was nicknamed Aladdin's Cave. Janice Thorpe was rather tickled by this description of her workplace, for it was she who, largely unaided, had transformed what had once been the academic equivalent of an untidy bowerbird's nest into an international research centre where all items, no matter how trivial, were meticulously catalogued for visiting scholars to examine.

I found it impossible to imagine what anyone would make of my archived bric-a-brac. Like the brass cufflinks cut from the striker ends of four Turkish Mauser cartridge cases, manufactured on Gallipoli for one shilling a pair by enterprising army engineers in their Shrapnel Gully workshop dugout. And -

"This is most unexpected!" A well-groomed, well-formed, well-featured woman of middle years interrupted my wandering thoughts as the young receptionist tiptoed away and quietly shut the door behind her. "To what do we owe the pleasure?"

"Oh, I happened to be passing by, and thought it was time to pop in and see how things were going," I smiled across her desk where several recent acquisitions were being sorted, including someone's Nobel Prize gold medallion encased in a clear Perspex cube, currently serving as a paperweight before going on public display.

"As you can see, busy, busy, busy," she smiled back, gesturing around at her crowded shelves, and filing cabinets, "but never too busy to record your, ah, reminiscences for our Audio Archive…"

"I commend your persistence." I loosened my coat and settled into the visitors' seat, hat on lap. "But, as we have previously discussed, you would find my memoirs very dull and repetitive."

"Oh please! Let me be the judge of that."

"No." I held up a hand. "It is very kind of you to say otherwise, but I know what's worth conserving, and what is not. However," I continued, about to cast my lure, "as a consolation prize, I do have another's personal effects that might be of interest…"

"Oh? And whose might they be?"

"Lucinda Cribdon's, famed in her day as the 'Antipodean Nightingale,' Australia's first lyric soprano to earn an overseas reputation." The gleam in Dr Thorpe's eyes told me that she'd seen the bait. "My great-aunt's *affaire* with the Grand Duke Pyotr Romanov did nothing to restore his dynasty's fortunes after the Crimean War. And there was that business with Napoleon III, an enigmatic little man with an insatiable appetite for exotic mistresses…"

"Heavens! I had no idea."

"Few have," I shrugged. "Like other performers who attained fame and fortune during the 1840s, '50s, and '60s – before phonographs and moving pictures immortalised their performance styles – Lucinda Cribdon is now largely forgotten."

"And yet there is material, relating to her, still in your possession?" Janice Thorpe insisted, lips parted at the prospect of scoring an archival jackpot.

"Yes," I replied, continuing to jiggle my lure "Stored at Pickford's. Three cabin trunks and two portmanteaux stuffed with theatrical memorabilia and posters, newspaper cuttings and business letters." I made it sound as if these were of trifling importance. "Oh, I nearly forgot!" Said with a snap of the fingers. "There's the autographed score that Jacques Offenbach composed for her to perform in one of his lesser-known operettas, *La Belle Australienne*, a musical romp set during the Ballarat goldrush." I smiled reflectively. "She also used to get quite choked when playing unpublished pieces by Franz Liszt, dedicated to '*Geliebte Lucinde...*'"

"This is, astonishing!" My curator was well and truly hooked, now, as she recovered her composure. "You may be sure we will conserve your bequest with the utmost respect and care. Indeed," she added, a shade too innocently, "there is no reason, funds permitting, why Monash should not house the Lucinda Cribdon Study Centre..."

We were both old hands at this polite game of cat and mouse, put and take, lunge, and feint. I had revealed a previously unknown treasure trove of primary source material that she was eager to curate, plus I had sufficient money of my own, to endow a specialised collection without it making a hole in her department's slender budget. It was now time to name my price. "Very well, we can discuss this at a more opportune moment, but today I wish to focus upon those things you already have."

"Yes?"

"I need your assurance that they will be held, under seal, until fifty years after my death."

"Of course. It's in our Memorandum of Understanding."

"True, but I need especial reassurance." I paused. "There's an Englishwoman, claiming to be an 'Oxford historian' allegedly attending a conference in Sydney, said to be researching certain events which I may have witnessed. However, I am not convinced by her story, so I want your word of honour that if a 'Frances Baxter' or someone similar, approaches Special Collections, you will insist that you hold nothing more than proof copies of my travel guides, and then inform me how she or they respond..."

"Yes, of course."

"And for my side of our bargain, I shall see that you get Lucinda Cribdon's memorabilia, in the fullness of time."

"Thank you," she smiled, aware of how adroitly I'd played her. "I don't wish to seem ghoulish," she added, "but I am looking forward to studying them. In the fullness of time."

"Good." I read my watch and got ready to stand. "There being no further business, our meeting adjourned at –"

"One moment." She turned and tapped her speakerphone's keypad. "Narelle? I'm taking the rest of the afternoon off. Professor Wharton will be around later for his Jervis Bay material. When he does, tell him we'll have its index compiled by Friday morning."

"Righty-ho," the loudspeaker replied with, I assume, the amplified, slightly distorted voice of my young receptionist.

"Thank you. Goodnight."

Janice Thorpe faced me again. "It's raining; I'll drop you off on my way home."

I blinked with quiet astonishment, never having associated her with the idea of home. Instead, I had unconsciously, unreasonably, unfairly assumed that she was a permanent fixture in Aladdin's Cave. Not quite the sort of exhibit a cleaner might flick with a feather duster, but almost.

"There is no need to look so surprised," she announced, stepping around the desk to retrieve her coat from behind the door. "I do have another life when I'm not serving behind the counter of this old curiosity shop."

"I never thought otherwise," I fibbed, reaching for my stick and hat. "May one enquire where you enjoy that other life?"

"Caulfield."

This prosperous postcode suggested rather more than a one-bedroom flat with only a gas fire, a goldfish bowl, and a wireless set for company. I shook my head. "It's very kind of you to offer, but you'll be going too far out of your way to drop me off in Collins Street. Telephone for a taxicab, I can easily –"

"No. I insist."

A lifetime of attentive listening has tuned my ear to detect even the faintest message hidden inside an otherwise casual remark. This woman had something to impart, but not here, not now. "Oh, very well, if you insist."

"I do. Come along. If we hurry, we'll miss the worst of the traffic." Then, instead of leading me out through the main entrance, she turned left, down a long corridor stacked with cardboard cartons waiting to be catalogued and pushed open a fire exit that led onto the senior staff's parking area.

I am not sure what I expected her vehicle to be, probably one of those tinny little Japanese sedans that are so popular nowadays, but certainly not a mustard yellow sportster.

"Mind your head." She assisted me to settle into the bucket seat and buckle up, before slipping behind the wheel herself, keying the ignition and blipping the throttle.

To my further surprise and relief, she drove well, using a rally driver's crisp, confident flicks of the gear stick and deft taps of the brake to weave past a convoy of motor lorries, an increasing number of other cars, and several daredevil motorcyclists racing each other to win premature death or paraplegia on this slick wet tarmac.

She broke our silence, eyes fixed beyond the swishing windscreen wipers. "I needed to speak without being overheard."

"'Overheard'? By whom?"

"Walls have ears and universities are stagnant pools of spite and malice no less noxious than Pope Alexander Borgia's Vatican."

"You disappoint me," I replied, after a moment's reflection. Never having needed to attend a university, I had the outsider's impression of such places as cloistered temples of amicable Higher Learning. "On second thoughts," I continued, "men and women, the world over, are predictably devious, scheming, selfish opportunists, given half a chance. So, what is it you wished to discuss?"

"Do you believe in meaningful coincidence?"

I weighed her question: "As when two people, some distance apart, share a similar thought or intention, at much the same time?"

"Correct."

"Within reasonable limits. Yes. Why?"

"I was planning to phone you tomorrow morning, instead of which you made contact this afternoon."

I weighed this statement as well. "What was it you were hoping to speak about…?"

"An unscheduled interest in your affairs."

"The Oxford snoop has already made contact?" I frowned.

"No." The Porsche braked to a smooth halt at an intersection, exhaust burbling with restrained power, and waited for the traffic lights to change. "Academician Yevgeny Alexandrov, of the Political Science School at MSIIR, has requested an itemised index of your papers."

"'Misery'?"

"Moscow State Institute of International Relations. Recently described by the US Secretary of State as 'Russia's Harvard,' except that Harvard doesn't teach its curricula in fifty-six foreign languages."

It required a fair amount of self-control to maintain a pretence of calm detachment. "How very odd. And did he happen to mention why such an illustrious establishment is interested in a minor footnote like me?"

"He claims that you spied on V.I.Lenin and was an agent for the Soviets' Commissar for War, Leon Trotsky, during the Basmachi Rebellion. He believes we have your original notes…"

I remained silent as the red lights turned green and she flicked stick, catapulting us from a standing start. "Well? Did you?"

"I may have done."

"And are those among your sealed papers?"

"It is possible."

"So how do I reply to his request?"

"Tell him that all will be revealed in the year 2037, or '38, or whenever I've shuffled off this mortal coil fifty years previously."

"I can't do that!"

"Why not? It's the truth. And truth, in my experience of international affairs, is a rare compliment to pay another person."

"I'm sorry, that won't do," she insisted. "It's a matter of academic courtesy, you understand?"

"In other words, you might need to touch 'Misery' for a return favour?"

"That's one way of putting it. Yes."

"Oh, very well then," I conceded. "Refer him to the *Times* newspaper archives at London Bridge. My political despatches for the 1920s and '30s were filed under the telegraphic address 'Icicle,' a play on my initials 'I.C.' Always assuming they weren't 'burn bagged' in Battersea Power Station's furnace, as the Bank of England does with its old paper money."

"I'm not sure that is what he has in mind."

"You can also tell him: '*Lutsche polbukhankii khem osustviye na vsekh.*' He'll understand…"

"Which is more than I do! What does that mean exactly?"

"'Half a loaf is better than no bread at all.' A wise old Russian proverb."

She fell silent and I was in no mood to elaborate as we entered Melbourne's Central Business District, slowing to a halt at my end of Collins Street. The Mac's porter hurried down the steps with an opened umbrella, ready to assist me, before recovering my stick and hat. "Thank you, Mr Wells."

I turned, leaning nearer the Porsche's lowered window. "And thank you ma'am. Don't look so downcast! Lucinda Cribdon's memorabilia will be worth many a bakers' dozen fresh loaves," I quipped, "compared with my stale old crusts that, nowadays, are hardly worth feeding to the ducks in Treasury Park."

4

I entered the Mac's lobby with a realisation that I had promised Special Collections rather more than might be safely delivered, even after my death. With this and much else on my mind, I decided against taking the evening meal downstairs, and instead requested a light supper of buttered toast and scrambled eggs be sent to my room at eight o'clock sharp.

As previously noted, my bedsitter apartment is modestly small, but when I helped rescue the Mac' by buying a life tenancy - cash down, no questions asked - my room was half as large again. At that time, the early-1930s, I had been tasked to monitor Japan's ambitions in China and East Asia and needed a secure base where I could stand well back, clear my head, and get a broader perspective of what was being done by the *kabuki* actors of Japanese foreign policy, and what was being whispered behind the *noh* masks clustered around the Chrysanthemum Throne.

My old hometown of Melbourne - still a grimly Calvinist citadel where everything shut for Sunday's Sabbath Gloom, later ironically described by the kinema actress Ava Gardner as "the perfect place to make a film about the end of the world" - suited my purposes.

I would disembark from the steamer at Sydney's Circular Quay, an expensively suited *taikun* on business from the Orient. After paying for a single night in a nearby hotel, I would switch the tailored cream linen jacket and trousers for a clerk's two guinea readymade in blue serge, stowed in my anonymous suitcase, and exit via the back alley loading bay, to catch the overnight express train to Victoria. Thus, anyone tailing me during the previous months abroad, would still be hunting in New South Wales long after I'd gone to ground five hundred miles away. All of which might seem excessively cautious in hindsight, but I have never doubted that it is better to be safe than sorry in a business where there is no margin for error.

Anticipating more East Asiatic assignments, I gave orders for my new base's antique plumbing to be replaced by a proper lavatory and shower modelled on those at the Peninsula Hôtel in Hong Kong. The Mac's management huffed and puffed at such "modernistic vandalism," claiming that if a chamber pot, and a pitcher of warm water from the kitchen were sufficient for Australia's first Prime Minister, Sir Edmund Barton, they were good enough for the mysterious Mr Cribdon, which explained the club's recent scrape with insolvency.

A sharp reminder of who had put up his share of the funds that kept their place going, settled the argument and it was not long before the same firm of plumbers was busy in our syndicate's adjacent bed-sitting rooms, but not before I'd got them to wall-off and install a photographic darkroom's sink, drain, and running water. Another distribution of five-pound notes ensured that the management committee remained largely unaware of my illegal alterations.

Only those who have fought in shadow wars can understand the addictive quality of secret hiding places, and of our need to always have one in reserve, as I slid the floormat back, drew a concealed bolt, and swung the wardrobe on its hidden caster wheels to reveal my darkroom's doorway, through which I stepped to click on the light.

There was no reason to believe that anyone else had ever been in here, but I still checked for evidence of unauthorised entry. My cameras – a Leica 2 with 50mm Elmar lens, and a sub-miniature Riga Minox that, over the years, has snapped a fair number of documents on fingernail squares of film – remained exactly where I'd left them, as were the enlarger, developing tanks, and shallow white enamel trays.

The jars and bottles of chemicals above the sink were stale and now little more than sentimental reminders of the hours once spent processing cassettes of 35mm Kodak Panchromatic and printing half-plate images for my Intelligence reports, or fishing magazine articles, depending on who or what had commissioned that assignment. This evening, however, there were more immediate matters to consider and decide as I unlocked a steel cabinet clearly marked:

Negative Film Store
Open with Care

Tucked behind its stacked contents was a sweat stained courier's vest whose pockets still held three hundred Silver Certificate American dollars in fives and tens; twenty old-style Bank of England five-pound notes; and a small purse of gold sovereigns. Also, a manilla envelope containing my passports, one of which is still valid although, like the vest, there is little chance I shall need it again.

Finally, on the lowest shelf, a cardboard lingerie box - *Au Bon Marché, 24 Rue de Sevres, Paris* printed across the lid in *art nouveau* swirls of faded green ink from a bygone age – tied with pink legal tape, its knot pasted over with a solicitor's paper seal inscribed, in rusty brown ink, *Memoirs of Miss Lucinda Cribdon. Dec'd 27th February 1918.*

For intensely private reasons the contents of this box had remained unread for sixty-nine years. Now, and only because of the bargain struck with Janice Thorpe, was it necessary for me to decide whether to include them among those other papers held in storage at Pickfords, or not.

I was afraid of what this confessional might reveal of the woman who loomed so largely in my earliest years. Her confidence and indomitable pluck had inspired me through many a rough patch in later life, and I had no desire to revise my opinion by learning of her inevitable human flaws and frailty, at this late stage in the game.

But assuming I do go ahead and deposit this box at Special Collections, then, as her custodian, I must be sure the Antipodean Nightingale's posthumous reputation remained unsullied, which is the very least I can do in return for her amazing generosity to an orphaned waif.

My darkroom is also a secure cellar where I can pour an occasional nightcap, certain that it has not been tampered with in a trade where a few micrograms of ricin, or botulinum-e, can mimic a variety of natural deaths. Not everybody in my former line of work was that prudent, but then I have never been seduced by the kinematic imagery of glib, boozy, womanising Intelligence officers.

They exist and I encountered quite a few in the Service. Boastful extroverts who claimed that copious quantities of grog and indiscreet pillow talk were the best ways to reveal another's secrets. For some it was also the worst way to leave a boudoir, dumped inside a laundry hamper, blood-soaked bed linen concealing the body of evidence on its way to an industrial incinerator.

Saint Joshua, our unofficial patron whose name commemorates the leader of twelve spies sent by Moses to reconnoitre Canaan, rarely protected fools for long. MI6's informal Latin motto, *dubito ergo sum* was coined three thousand years later, but I'm sure those Ancient Hebrew agents would've understood their Aramaic equivalent of "I doubt therefore I am." Or, more colloquially: "It's the second mouse who gets the cheese…"

I poured a tot of single malt, added a splash of water from the darkroom tap, and took the lingerie box to my desk where there was better lighting.

"'Here's a pretty how-de-do.'" I raised the tumbler in an affectionate salute to the memory of a bogus great-aunt first met the day before my Papa, "'Champagne Charley' Braithwaite," was hanged at Darlinghurst Gaol for murdering Mama and his younger brother Albert, dropping the final curtain on an especially sordid *cause célèbre* of the 1890s.

I polished my reading glasses and, with some hesitation, reached for a pair of scissors to cut the tape. That done, I lifted the lid and breathed a ghostly scent from the withered sprigs of lavender left in the box to preserve four or five quires of foolscap, by now the colour of pale cigar leaf. For one fleeting moment I knew how Howard Carter must have felt when he first peered inside King Tut's tomb.

The title sheet - decorated with Indian ink curlicues around the twin masks of Tragedy & Comedy, framed by sundry obsolete national flags half of which flew to the left while the rest flew to the right – was boldly inscribed in a very familiar hand:

The True & Unvarnished Account
of
My Amazing Life & Times
by
Baroness Lucinde Cribdon "Le Rossignol"

Then, in ragged blocks of text composed on the large-font typewriting machine she'd taught herself to use at an advanced age, because of failing eyesight,:

Act 1

As the handsome young Mr Irving, not yet Sir Henry would
oft remind me: Start with a Bang! Shake the Dress Circle
awake! Advice strictly adhered to during my many years of
triumph upon the world stage, and now shall employ by
announcing that the Antipodean Nightingale who charmed
the crowned heads of Europe, and turned many a lesser one,
was born Dorcas Brown, daughter of Captain Jeremiah
Brown of Nantucket, the United States of America, in whos
manly arms my widowed mother, Caroline Stoat née Cribdon
found bliss full solace!

There is no reason to think he would not have returned as pledged, to marry and assume a commanding role in his father in laws business ventures but for his tragick end, witnessed by another whaler, also fishing the Antarctics icy wastes, as a terrible black storm engulft them both, from which the good ship Ezra Hayes ne'er emerged again!

Alas! The brave young captain was not to learn that five months later a baby daughter first saw the light of day in Sydney Town, for whos reputation he was posthumously and illegally married to my mother by the intervention of my maternal grandfather, Mr Joseph Cribdon JP, whos many charitys had garnered the highest encomiums from our colonys eklesiastical establishment!

Nearly seventy years after her death, the voice, the diction, the vivid vocabulary, the florid exclamation marks, were as strong and distinctive as they had ever been in life.

I have known many women but never another like this wholly unrelated great-aunt who arrived, unannounced, at Corunna Downs where the Braithwaites ruled over a pastoral kingdom of tens of thousands of acres, to take Little Willy Braithwaite off their hands. This must sound preposterous to the modern ear, but things were done differently in an age when, as we were constantly reminded: "Children are to be seen, not heard!"

There was also my family's eagerness to get rid of me and if a rich, assertive, elderly stranger was willing to do the job at no cost to them, with no questions asked, why quibble? Nor was he likely to object. Throughout his imprisonment at Corunna, Little Willy had been made aware that his relations, without exception, regarded him as a vulgar cuckoo chick in their regal nest.

Not that one can entirely blame them. It must have been quite upsetting when their second eldest son briefly returned home after marrying Miss Maggie Stubbs, a London Cockney on tour with Fitzgerald Brothers Circus. This self-regarding family of colonial grandees instantly despised their low-class daughter-in-law, a feeling she reciprocated in spades.

I have purged most memories of those formative years, but some poignant images persist. One is of a sunny afternoon outside our chaotic rental, close to Sydney's inner-city bars where Papa upheld his nickname's reputation, and the brothels where he had most likely caught the syphilis that was hastening his alcoholic decay.

From somewhere nearby, Mama had pinched the bicycle she was trick riding up and down the street, alternately balancing on the handlebars, pedalling backwards, or hand-standing on the saddle, linen bloomers hitched above the knee while the Rocks' other urchins chased after her, cheering and waving their grimy caps.

Later, as we shared three penn'orth of fried fish and chips and watched the Paramatta paddle steamer splash past thickets of brigs and schooners moored at Circular Quay, she turned to me with one of her achingly sad smiles. "That were such fun Bill! I not 'ad a lark like it in yeers..."

A fortnight later, "Champagne Charley" staggered home earlier than expected to find Mama and Uncle Bertie - a genial soul who would tip me a trey, colonial slang for a silver threepence, to go outside and play – still in bed together. Outraged by this stain upon the family honour, or so it was declared at his trial, Papa brandished his 0.44 calibre British Bulldog pocket revolver - a common fashion accessory for the natty city gent' in those days - and shot them both dead.

My last memory of him is of a dishevelled, incoherent drunk, defiantly waving his empty pistol and shouting wild threats at the sky even as four constables threw him into their horse-drawn police van.

Any reasonable jury would have committed him to an asylum for the criminally insane, but it was his misfortune that the Braithwaites were on the wrong side of colonial politics at the time, making this a golden opportunity to humble a family who had comported themselves like transplanted aristocracy since the arrival in New South Wales of our patriarch, Captain Nicholas Braithwaite, a Waterloo Veteran of the Rifle Brigade.

Here he briefly became the protégé of the convict colony's leading Exclusive, Captain John Macarthur of the notorious Rum Corps, whose young son - Ensign Edward Macarthur of the 60th Foot – Braithwaite had befriended at the Siege of Corunna in 1809. That is until Captain Braithwaite married a colonial ladies' maid whose parents were involuntary passengers aboard two of the First Fleet's eleven ships and, through her, bred up a rival albeit "convict stained" dynasty.

Meanwhile, the offspring of a later ill-starred marriage was snatched from Sydney's cruel streets and hidden away on the Braithwaite's pastoral kingdom where there was no chance of him heaping further shame on the family name if a newspaper reporter from the gutter press found him wandering hungry and alone, up a fetid alley or laneway.

Their enlightened self-interest never extended to the boy himself, of course. In every regard he was the living embodiment of Bad Blood, the sort of animal who, had he been a black sheep, would have had its throat slit in the butcher's yard, to prevent it contaminating their pedigree Merino flock.

Thus, when a woman of evident means came to relieve them of the little brat, claiming to be a distant theatrical associate of his murdered mother, his aunts, and uncles, and cousins could scarce restrain their joy as they bundled Little Willy aboard her carriage, even quicker than he'd seen his father being tossed into the Black Maria.

I have often wondered what life would have been like, had not this providential rescue taken place. My uncles would have kicked me out at the earliest opportunity, to become an itinerant shearer tramping the bush tracks of New South Wales and Victoria, drinking my wages at sly grog shanties until killing some other lout in a drunken fury. Thereafter, hanged like my father or, if lucky, breaking rock in a prison yard for the next twenty years. Instead of which, I was restored and made whole by a remarkable old lady to whom I shall be forever indebted.

5

Thinking back on that first day's events - now almost nine decades ago - I can recall no more than a kaleidoscopic jumble of impressions until arriving at Redfern Railway Station, where my escort, or keeper, or owner, or whatever she was summoned a porter to stand guard while she went to the telegraph office, returning a few minutes later, followed by another porter pushing a trolley laden with luggage that he stowed aboard a reserved 1st Class compartment. The stationmaster doffed his cap, bowed, and pocketed a half-crown for services rendered; the porters got a zac – slang for a silver sixpence - apiece.

"'Here's a pretty how-de-do!'" she observed, seating herself opposite me, with what was to become a very familiar quotation from Gilbert & Sullivan's *The Mikado*. She then took an ornately enamelled Fabergé cigarette case from her royal blue Hussar's dolman jacket, worn above a matching, elegantly tailored riding skirt. Flicking it open she selected a Sobranie Black Russian cigarette and struck a wax vesta on the heel of her dainty button-up boot. "So," she exhaled slowly, "what's to be done with you now m'lad?"

I goggled with shock, never having seen a proper lady smoke before, at the same time experiencing a giddy premonition that my life would never be the same again.

"You look half-starved, and I'm famished. Here, give me a hand with this." She directed me to a large hamper, ordered from Anthony Hordern's grocery store in George Street that morning, and showed me how to undo its tricky latch before throwing back the lid. "Ah ha! Just what the doctor ordered."

She began briskly unpacking what I later recognised was a cold roast pheasant and *salade niçoise*; crisp bread rolls and freshly churned butter; blueberry compote and cream; condiments and cutlery, china and glassware of a quality and quantity I had never seen at home, and certainly not at Corunna Downs where I'd shovelled my tucker off a dented tin plate on a bare trestle table outside the fieldhands' shed.

Wonder of wonders there was an earthenware bottle of ginger beer for me, and a litre of Apollinaris table water for her. "They import it from Bad Neuenahr in the Rhine Palatinate," she explained, spreading a linen napkin on my lap to stop any drips or crumbs from further soiling my grubby knickerbockers. "A delightful place. You must visit one day. Avoid the *Kurhaus* casino though. Their odds are too deuced long."

I had not the foggiest idea what she was talking about. Nobody had spoken to me like this before. Instead of condescending baby talk, or sneering asides, or angry snarls, she addressed me as if I were an adult equal. Later, after we got to know each other much better, I realised that never having raised a child of her own - while working in the theatre for much of her life - she only had the one manner of speech that was applied freely to everyone, regardless of age, or class, or location.

"Come along, eat up." She broke the pheasant with beautifully expressive fingers and passed me a leg to wolf down. It must have been obvious to such an astute observer of human behaviour that table manners and polite conduct had bypassed "Champagne Charley's" squalid lair. Nor had there been much hope of improvement from a Cockney trick cyclist when her husband was away, bludging off other flotsam and jetsam gentry by promoting dodgy get-rich-quick betting schemes, and yet this amazing little lady never once reprimanded me.

Instead, she taught by example, and long before our train steamed through Bowral, and the guard came forward from his van to light the oil lamps, I had learned how to split a dinner roll and spread butter without scattering bits of crust all over the place. And rather than swig ginger beer from the bottle, I found it amusing to drink from a glass and get bubbles up my nose. We both laughed at that and tucked into our impromptu picnic the best of chums.

I must have dozed off because, when the guard returned to collect our foot warmers – small copper tanks that held about a gallon of hot water drawn from the locomotive's boiler – I awoke to find myself sprawled along the seat, under a tartan travel rug.

"Sleep well?"

"Yuss fanks m'um."

"The correct expression is ma'am, as in ham, not ma'am, as in farm. But not to worry, we'll deal with that later. Here, let's finish these blueberries, then we'll ask the guard to make two mugs of his delicious cocoa." Which he duly did in return for another coin from her ample stock of silver.

It was well after midnight before the train finally sped down the gradient from Wagga to Albury on the Murray River, nowadays the sleepy state boundary that unites New South Wales and Victoria, but in the 1890s still a patrolled frontier that divided two rival colonies of the British Empire.

I did not to know it, yet, but this was the notorious Break of Gauge where the narrower English railway coming down from Sydney, met the wider Irish railway coming up from Melbourne, and for that reason we all had to get out into bitterly cold and windy darkness, dispense more silver for our luggage to be unloaded, and then pass through a barrier to the other side of the platform where the last section of our journey began.

"Anyone would think we were leaving Prussia and entering Russia," she observed with an irritable sniff as we approached Customs, before abruptly laying a hand on my shoulder. "Stop. It's time we got rid of this 'Little Willy' nonsense."

"M'um?"

"'Ma'am,'" she corrected absentmindedly, a seasoned actress improvising a scene by looking around for cues. Luckily there was a large promotional sign for a well-known patent medicine on the nearby fence. Something had recently dented its brittle yellow and black enamel surface so that, from a certain angle, instead of reading "Iron Jelloids for Men!" it seemed to read "Ian Jelloids…"

"That'll do the trick! Firm, strong to the ear, acceptable at all levels of Society. Now, listen," she bent closer. "If anyone asks for your name as we go through that gateway, you are now and henceforth ever will be 'Ian Cribdon' and I your aunt, taking you away for the holidays. Understand?"

"M'um'am."

"Come along. Follow on."

And that is how little William Charles Braithwaite was abandoned in New South Wales and young Master Ian Cribdon took his place in Victoria, thanks to a damaged advertisement for men's virility pills.

It was late morning before our train finally clattered over Flinders Street viaduct and jolted to a hissing, wheezing, grinding halt among the corrugated iron sheds and dilapidated marshalling yards of Melbourne's main railway station.

The city still had to endure a few more years of this steamy muck and muddle before its replacement by the present majestic building that, until the Great War at least, housed a first-class restaurant and ballroom with resident dance band. There was also a telegraph and postal office; a gymnasium and steam baths; a newsagent and chemist shop; a well-stocked reading room; and a nursery-crèche for the intercolonial traveller's young family.

However, on this morning, my new relative hardly paused as she led me and two porters through the ticket turnstile, straight onto a paved area where a rank of hansom-cab horses shuffled about, tossing their nosebags, waiting for hire. Standing apart from them, in solitary splendour, was a burgundy red phaeton drawn by two matching grey ponies, not that I yet knew what such an equipage was called, of course.

Aunt Lucinda pointed and the porters stowed our various items of luggage - the Braithwaites had donated one of their children's old topcoats which otherwise would have gone to the Aboriginal Mission, plus a flour bag to carry my spare shirt, three socks, a soiled pair of drawers, and the neckerchief that doubled as a snot rag - then paid off our assistance and climbed aboard the box seat. "You sit with Mr Harris," she commanded, reaching for the whip, and releasing the foot brake.

An elderly, bewhiskered man in a groom's uniform of green velveteen jacket, brown corduroy britches, and black leather gaiters threw me a surly look, unimpressed at being driven through town by a woman, accompanied by a scruffy little guttersnipe; in time he would mellow and entertain me with blood-curdling tales of his years inside Pentridge Gaol, but not today.

Melbourne's famously fickle weather had decided to welcome us with one of its sporadic sunny spells as we trotted off, wheeling to the right, past the city morgue – conveniently close to the Yarra River's frequent suicides – and crossed the recently completed Prince's Bridge in fine style.

Though nobody could have known it at the time, the first horseless carriages would soon begin displacing horse-drawn ones like ours, but for the moment it was still possible for a colourful Bohemian to crack her whip, slap reins, and relish the looks of stern disapproval on men's bearded faces as we spanked past them in high style, iron-shod wheels growling over bluestone cobbles.

Well within living memory all this had still been virgin native forest where bushrangers bailed-up mail coaches, though nowadays no more than remnants of cleared bushland remaining inside the Royal Botanical Gardens, over to our left, as Aunt Lucinda kept her ponies in perfect alignment, hooves striking in unison along the Saint Kilda Road.

"Count Czerny, best driver in Hungary, showed me how it's done, on Vienna's *Ringstrasse*!" she laughed over one shoulder, tightening the reins to steer our carriage up a tree-lined road skirting the Gardens and Government House, though to call it a road was a bit of a stretch, being little more than a wide country lane despite a renewed spurt of building along its verges.

Government House itself originally stood alone, in solitary splendour atop a low rise on the Yarra's South Bank, from which the Lieutenant Governor had enjoyed a cooling sea breeze off Port Phillip Bay while the rest of the town sweltered and stank downwind, in summer. His pastoral idyll ended once the goldrushes at Ballarat and Bendigo got underway, sparking three decades of breakneck expansion from minor colonial outpost to the largest city in the Southern Hemisphere.

Crafty speculators claim that a rising tide floats all boats, but this only holds true until the tide goes out again, stranding gullible investors high and dry, as happened when Marvellous Melbourne's building boom collapsed a few years before my arrival. Sadly, not only did numerous private schemes fail but essential public works also stopped when London's banks foreclosed their loans, bestowing the sarcastic nickname "Marvellous Smellbourne" on a crowded city whose incomplete sewerage system still required the services of nightsoil men and their pungent "honey carts."

A hailstorm of bankruptcies flattened the market for real estate but, as always, one person's adversity is another's opportunity for those who keep their wealth in cash or readily convertible assets, thus enabling them to snap up bargains like the one we were approaching along a gravel track optimistically named Grange Road.

Tralee House stood foursquare on a trim, three-acre block overlooking dairy farms on Yarra's other, northern bank, a mute memorial to an immigrant Irishman's dream before his timber and building supply company crashed along with many another's.

My surly companion hopped out and held the wrought iron gates open for our carriage to pass before climbing aboard for the final one hundred or so yards through rose beds and ornamental cherry trees being tended by a gardener and his lad.

Mr Harris assisted his mistress to alight, unloaded our things where they would be collected later, and took the reins, restored to his proper dignity on the box seat as he trotted away to the stables and coach house.

"Come along now!" Aunt Lucinda gripped my elbow and gave it a sharp tug to stop me gawping around, open-mouthed.

As we approached the main residence, a tall, sinewy woman clad in severe black bombazine bobbed a formal curtsy.

"Good afternoon, Mrs Harris. Ian is my great-nephew. He will be staying with us. Please arrange for our luggage to be taken in. And tell cook to prepare hot beef sandwiches with English mustard."

"Ma'am." The housekeeper gave another studied curtsy and stood aside as I was towed past, numbed by the novelty of it all.

There is a persistent belief that domestic interiors of the Victorian era were cluttered with over-upholstered furniture carved from dark brown timber decorated with fretted brass work and, indeed, many were but not all, Tralee House being a rare exception as I later discovered.

Returning home to Australia from a wider, more cultivated world than the average Melburnian had yet experienced, and with a sharp eye for effective stage settings, Aunt Lucinda lost no time ridding her latest residence of its potted palms and aspidistra plants, stag head trophies and stuffed finches mounted on music boxes that tinkled a cruel mockery of birdsong. She then ordered the shamrock green wallpaper be stripped off and its bare plaster sealed before overpainting with a warm white finish, as were all the doors, architraves, and window frames.

"Too many productions are ruined by excessively detailed scenery; it distracts attention from the players," she once told me, with another of her habitual glances at the nearest mirror, of which there were about two dozen dotted around the mansion. "Our public pays good money to see us, not a ruddy backdrop!"

An unintended consequence of her touching vanity was that Tralee House remained light and airy, lifting the spirits on even the dankest and darkest of days. So much vacant wall space was also a natural setting for the crates of strange, splodgy canvases that somehow felt as if they had always belonged in these now well-lit rooms and corridors.

It was only later, after I had been scrubbed and polished and could be shown to the neighbours without embarrassment, that I saw just how radical a transformation she had wrought. My little playmates remained trapped by their parents' late-Victorian excess, and wherever there was a square yard of available wall in their homes it was sure to display a framed lithograph entitled *The Fighting Temeraire*, or *The Death of Nelson*, or *England Forever!* exhorting us to do or die for the Empire.

Smeared dabs of Impressionist oil colour by as yet little-known French artists with dubious morals and unpronounceable names, were no part of semi-rural Toorak's little world as the sun set on our nineteenth century. Not that Aunt Lucinda cared tuppence what anyone thought of her taste, as she had already made abundantly clear during our first few hours together.

6

One of the housemaids brought us a tray of hot roast beef sandwiches on hearty slices of buttered wholemeal bread, the like of which I had not seen or tasted before. Years later, going up the line to Pozières, when other men in my Lewis gun section were grumbling about their bully beef and biscuit rations, I only had to fry a couple of slices on my little Primus stove to be transported by imagination's magic carpet, back to Tralee's glass conservatory that first afternoon of my new life.

"Good?"

"Mmph!"

"Try not to speak with your mouth full. One bite at a time is quite sufficient."

She was right, of course, but so was I for there was no way of telling when this abundance would vanish in a puff of green smoke, like a djinn's phantom banquet in some cautionary tale from *The Arabian Nights*, leaving me abandoned on my nest of stolen potato sacks up a disused sewer pipe off Sydney's cruelly misnamed Playfair Street.

Nowadays, with the impending celebration of our Bicentennial next year, a whole industry of historians and newspaper writers has sprung up to eulogise pre-Federation Australia as a land of openhanded mateship for the energetic immigrant. Maybe so in the Outback, but Australia's inner-city streets and lanes were brutal battlegrounds of gang warfare. Small wonder that those of us from there, who managed to reach adulthood, have never taken our good fortune for granted. Always within us there lurks an innate readiness to duck, weave, and vanish at a moment's notice.

Those who think this attitude unduly paranoid should consider the fact that if a few days in a London slum factory changed Charles Dickens' worldview forever, what else might he have written - or not - had he spent his early childhood ratting food scraps off market stalls and from their waste barrels? Thus, every instinct was urging the young waif, who used to be me, to stuff his guts while he still could, to be in better trim when fighting for his next feed on Sydney Cove's heartless docks and alleyways.

But for the fact that this amazing little lady was watching me so intently, I would have pinched the sandwiches and stuffed them in my pocket; it was less easy to see a way of stealing the hot sweet tea being served from a silver teapot and drunk from fine bone china. I did, however, snaffle three lumps of sugar while Aunt Lucinda was distracted by something happening in the orchard outside.

She turned away from the window and summoned her housekeeper instead. "It is time we took my nephew to the bathroom."

"Ma'am"

"Come along, Ian. And take that slice of beef from your sleeve."

We trooped up a rather grand staircase and entered a spacious room, tiled from floor to ceiling, in the centre of which stood a white enamelled cast-iron bath filled with hot water, resting on what looked like huge cat's paws, one at each corner.

"Mrs Harris has boys of her own; she understands these things. I'll be outside, looking for something you can wear."

The door shut and the fearsomely tall woman, in long black dress and yellow oilskin apron, rapped out orders in a voice that many a sergeant major would have envied.

"Jacket, off."

I promptly obeyed.

"Shirt, off."

That grey rag fell to the tiled floor.

"Knickers, off."

The same.

"On the newspaper, stand!"

I mutely obeyed as she whipped out a comb and scissors from the apron pocket and gave me the closest haircut I had yet experienced, all the while muttering under her breath at what she saw crawling across my scalp. She then hastily bundled the newspaper around my greasy hanks of hair, to be burnt on the garden bonfire, along with my clothing. "Bath. In. Now!"

I had some idea of the correct drill, having experienced weekly washes in a galvanized iron pail while Mama dribbled warm water from a kettle, and wiped me down with a wet flannel.

Fearful of the nameless punishments that would befall me if I disobeyed, I stepped over the bath's rim, flinching at the rush of heat up my spindly legs.

"Sit!"

"Owww...!" An invisible sponge, rubbed on a tablet of carbolic soap dipped in pumice powder, attacked my naked neck and shoulders.

"Stand!"

The abrasive sponge stormed across the rest of me without mercy, without respite.

"Sit! Head down! Eyes shut!"

Coal tar shampoo oozed across my scalp, kneaded, and scraped, squeezed, and squished by relentless fingers and thumbs. Mrs Thomas Harris began her working life as a brothel laundrymaid scrubbing grimy bed linen, I later learned, and had been waging war on germs and dirt ever since then.

"Out!"

Resistance was futile. I stood on the bathmat while a heated towel wrapped me up and mopped me off. The sparkling clear water of a few minutes ago was now a scummy broth the colour of sewage pouring into Sydney Cove at the bottom of Argyle Street.

Aunt Lucinda held out a nightshirt several sizes too big. "Here, put this on, and follow me."

I padded along the corridor to yet another white door, ominously marked Sick Room, in effect Tralee's own private hospital, an essential feature of all well-to-do households at a time when a simple cold, untreated, could quickly lead to pneumonia and death.

"Good afternoon, Doctor, this is Ian. Ian, this is Doctor Levine, our family physician. As was his father and grandfather before him. Say hello."

"'Ello."

The compact, dark-bearded man gave me a piercing look. "How old are you?" his voice was equally dark and serious, with just the hint of a foreign accent. Much later, over chess games played in German, I learned that although also born in Sydney he had chosen to train at the Charité in Berlin where, after completing his internship, he married a local girl. "Well?"

"I don', I don' –"

"We think he's about five or six."

"Hm." Dr Levine eyed me with grave misgiving. "Nightshirt off, please."

Aunt Lucinda helped me untangle its loose folds.

"Stand on stool." I obeyed, facing him directly. "Open mouth and say 'aaah.'" I felt a dry wooden spatula depress my tongue while he peered around inside and checked my teeth. "Take a deep breath." I felt a cold stethoscope exploring my chest. "Breath out. Turn around. Deep breath." The ruthless examination continued until every square inch of me had been probed and prodded, percussed, and pinched. "Stand down."

Aunt Lucinda was watching intently. "Well...?"

"His teeth are surprisingly good for one so malnourished; eyesight, satisfactory; lung function, good; liver function, adequate. No evidence of rickets, again surprising. Both testicles descended. No sign of rupture."

"But is he, clean?"

I found this question quite odd, given that I had just been boiled and scrubbed to an unfamiliar glowing pink. It was only years later that I made the connection between this mysterious remark, "Champagne Charley's" affliction, and understood her concern.

"So far as one can tell. Yes."

"And his bumps?" Aunt Lucinda was a great believer in phrenology, the tactile interpretation of a person's skull to determine their innate character.

"There is no sign of cretinism. His 'Mount of Retention' is pronounced, indicating good memory. His brow is tall and well formed, indicating a deep thinker. His 'Mount of Empathy' is not so good, suggesting a tendency to introspection and melancholia."

"That's a relief!" She paused significantly. "And the other matter we discussed...?"

"A prudent course of action, given his circumstances."

"Very well, proceed."

Our family doctor motioned me onto the examination couch. "Lay down and look up at the ceiling." Aunt Lucinda moved behind me, fingertips resting lightly on my bony little shoulders while he busied himself Down There, as Mama used to say in hushed and anxious tones.

I assumed he was checking my "tentacles" again. Instead, there was a gentle tug, a quick snip, and the pressure on my shoulders relaxed. "You are a brave young man," she announced, with an encouraging smile to keep me distracted while Doctor Levine finished Down There. "You won't understand yet, but one day you will do, and be glad."

An experienced woman of the world, she was not wrong, although I only realised it years later when an epidemic of venereal disease struck down thousands of young Australian soldiers carelessly roaming Haret el Wasser, Cairo's notorious red-light district, winning their VD & Scar, ironic Digger-speak for the infinitely rarer and vastly more honourable VC & Bar.

Meanwhile, back in Tralee's Sick Room, I was so emotionally numb after losing a mother, a father, a name, an identity, the loss of a foreskin was the least of my concerns. I could have had a limb amputated without chloroform and felt nothing. Instead, I swallowed a cloudy mixture from a conical medicine glass before being tucked into the Sick Room's white, iron framed hospital bed, after which Aunt Lucinda drew the blinds and quietly shut the door behind her.

34

7

A knock on my door alerted me to the fact it was now eight o'clock and that I had been daydreaming rather than editing the Cribdon Papers. I thanked the maid for my supper and locked up after she'd left. I have always been fond of eggs scrambled with chopped parsley, provided sufficient cream and pepper are beaten with them. The Club's chef knew my tastes and never failed to deliver, and tonight he had thoughtfully quartered the slices of toast - wholemeal, freshly baked - which enabled me to resume reading Aunt Lucinda's erratic typescript, while eating.

Act 2

My Dear Grandpapa, Mr Joseph as the Upper Orders called him, or King Crib as the rest whispered behind his back, was a former cavalry serjeant who came to the colony in its very earliest days. Of moderate build and dark vizage he could be the very soul of generosity and yet, in the blink of an eye, reduce grown men to whimpering wrecks by a single glance, such was his aura of dread full command!

Not that I, or my half-brothers and sisters, saw this side of his adamantine nature. For us he was the indulgent grandparent who would take time off from his many business ventures to tell of Red Indians encountered in the forests of America while fighting the Rebels. Or would carve a hollow reed and make a flute upon which he would finger strange and haunting melodies, one of which I played on Dear Franz piano only to hear it promptly transcribed as a Hungarian Rapsody!

I likewise recall an occasion when Grandpapa was in a particularly jovial mood, hearing him sing a ditty that began: Im a Romany rye, Im free as the sky, I live in a tent and I dont pay no rent, thats why Im a Romany rye! Cher Jacques elaborated it later as my patter song in Act Two of La Belle Australienne where I am mistook for a female bushranger!

Grandpapa was particularly fond of me, perhaps because of my hair, which was auburn and reminded him of Grandmamas before she took to wearing an outrageous red wig, or perhaps because he had hoped that my deceased

Papa, the Captain Brown, would command the fleet of trading schooners owned by the firm of Jos Cribdon & Co!

An especial treat was to be taken for a walk from our residence in George Street, where I dwelt after the death of Mama, to see the garrison on parade at Hyde Park barracks!

It was an indication of the respect with which everyone held him, that even the highest gentry, driving in their carriages, would raise their hats as they passed by, we marching along the pavement, Grandpapa with his stick carried like a musket to show me how it was properly done while I strove to keep up!

This universal esteem was always a puzzle for in no regard did he affect grand clothes or manners and betimes, he could appear quite shabby and unkempt even though I knew he had great sums of money. On one occasion he took me into the bedchamber he shared with Grandmama, removed a leather bag of guineas from under their pillow, and taught me how to count to one hundred, in gold coins!

After we finished playing with them, he said something quite comical tho spoken in a sombre tone: When I croak, get here first, and nab the georges afore them others ramp me gaff and bludge the boodle. I assumed he referred to my half-brother and sister. Im not sure of the reasons for this, tho perhaps it had much to do with Mamas unfortunate first marriage to Zebediah Stoat, a Methodist agitator transported for sedition, who established himself in the colony as a jobbing printer of prayer books and devotional tracts!

I remain unsure of what attracted them, for there were traces of great former beauty on Mamas features, as I vaguely recall, whereas Mr Stoat was said to have been a scrawny little fellow whose earnest Christian faith could not halt the galloping consumption that bore him aloft on angels wings or so he hoped!

It was reported that Mama had been much desired in her youth and was even the subject of gossip when love notes were found linking her name to that of young Edward Macarthur, shortly before he was sent to England, to obtain a commission in the Army!

I suspect this had much to do with the fact that his father was Captain John Macarthur, the Squire of Camden, a pastoral magnate, and master of all he surveyed, whereas her father was of more common clay, albeit of great influence in Sydney Town!

The tender young hearts of our Colonial Romeo & Juliet were torn asunder by the unrelenting enmity of the Cribdon Capulets and the Macarthur Montagues, and it was later claimed, as Captain John was finally borne to an asylum, that he broke free of his bonds, leant from the coach window, and hurled wild imprecations at that d--d cur Crib!

Nor was their hostility confined to the menfolk alone. Grandmama had the highest opinion of herself and was not disposed to defer to Mrs Elizabeth Macarthur, regardless of her husbands position on the governors council, when their paths crost, which was not often, for both made sure their circles of acquaintance ne'er overlapt!

All that was put behind us upon going to Grandpapas estate, a few days removed from the noise and smells of Sydney Town. The gypsy caravan of carts and carriages, as our menage moved up from the coast, must have been an amazing sight as we plodded along Paramatta Road, led by Mr Joseph mounted on his favourite steed, the famous Tarleton, out of Saracen Maid, by Moghul, a stallion that cost 1000 guineas to bring from Bengal! At the time this was a prodigious sum of money to pay for a horse but proved to be a sound investment as it established the famous Montichella bloodline of cavalry remounts for the Indian Army!

Our first nights stop was always at the Barley Mow tavern, where we would be greeted with the greatest affection and readiness by the owner, Old Ben, his roly-poly wife Bessie, and their brood of flaxen haired grandchildren, lively as crickets and always good for a lark! Strangely I never knew their family name, for it was as if they were family, with Grandpapa and Old Ben laughing uproariously at private jokes as they reminisced about olden times!

The following day, after settling our stable and lodging accounts, despite protestations to the contrary, for Grandpapa was scrupulous in such matters, we would set forth to the mountains. This was a perilous part of the journey, there being escaped convict highwaymen in wait to rob the unwary traveller, and yet they did not molest us tho we must have presented a tempting target for such bloodthirsty desperados!

Grandpapa would oft ask Old Bens advice and was always assured there would be no trouble, tho how he could be so certain remained a mystery. I had my suspicions, of course, an inn such as his must have been a prime location for Gentlemen of the High Toby to obtain fresh horses, fence their ill-gotten gains, and learn of any troopers in the district. Old Ben was surely aware of such nefarious arrangements under his roof, but there seemed to be a silent code of understanding among these old settlers!

The Montichella homestead, its name derived from an Aboriginal word, I think, overlooked some three and one half thousand acres of fine land. Unlike his adjacent squires, who raised sheep for wool, and cattle for salted beef, Grandpapa bred horses of superior quality. These were the foundation of his trade with India, as the vessels that transported the mounts thereto, would return laden with cottons and calicos, exotic spices, and chinaware from farther afield. Goods that would then be sold through a network informally named Our Thing by Grandpapas business associates!

The homestead itself was a magnificent two-story residence he said reminded him of a palace in America during the war. This was Grandmamas domain in which she ruled over a staff composed of convicts and free, not that it was possible to tell who was who as the men were equally drest in smock frock shirts, open at the neck, trousers sewn from imported dungaree cloth, and brogan boots made on the estate from locally tanned hides. The women wore frock skirts of serviceable grey linen, white aprons that Grandmama insisted were changed every day, and if working outside, a sun bonnet or woven reed hat!

Whereas I adored Grandpapa, who could be wondrously earthy when we were out riding the paddocks, myself on a small pony, while he spake of putting stallions over mares, and managing his brood stock to ensure they never sickened, Grandmama was more distant. She could not pass a mirror without looking at her reflection and declaiming lines from some antick melodrama, or singing in a fine clear voice, old favourites such as Cherry Ripe and Under the

Green wood Tree, songs that later enabled me to establish my reputation as Europes leading lyric soprano!

Of Grandmama, little more need be said for tho everyone embellishes the truth, to make tolerable their passage through lifes Vayle of Tears, her embellishments knew no bounds! Had I not been of a somewhat skeptical turn of mind, even for one so young I might have believed her tales of success on the London stage in which she imagined herself creating a character named Lady Lucinda Lively, from whom she oft quoted at great length!

In later years, treading those same boards, I made enquiries of the oldest players by asking if any could recall someone answering to her description, but none did. But I must not be too harsh! Her improvised coaching, memorised recitations, and insistence I speak clearly, with colour and texture, were to stand me in good stead when, at the age of fifteen years and three months, I found myself thrown upon a heartless world!

Grandmama having predeceased him by a year, Grandpapa lost interest in life, particularly as his old enemy Captain Macarthur was now also dead. His passing was swift, the housekeeper finding him reclined in bed one sunny morning, the cameo portrait of his late wife gript by fingers stiff and cold!

By the time this news reached me at Miss Kendall's Academy for Young Ladies, in Paramatta, my Stoat half brother and sister had ransacked the house and taken everything of value, especially the bag of Grandpapa's guineas. It was made abundantly plain that I was not welcome, they unconvinced that my posthumous legitimation had altered the fact that I was born a bastard and thus unentitled to any share of the estate!

Grandpapa had anticipated their response, some years earlier, while smoking his pipe in Montichellas apple orchard as we watched the sunset. He had been telling me of the times when Governor and Mrs Macquarie would stay as his guests, to inspect fresh carriage horses for Government House, both men sharing memories of the American War, tho of vastly different stations in the Kings Service!

Quite suddenly he turned to me and said: Dont fire all your bullets. Always keep a few back to fight another day. When I asked what he meant by this, he pointed his pipestem at the homestead and its outbuildings and said: I could lose the whole b----y lot, and still not be down and out. When I queried this, he replied: Can you keep a secret? An empty question for he already knew my lips were, in his own colourful phrase, tight as a ducks a---s which is watertight!

He led me over to the gardeners shed, they having ceased their daily toil and took me inside. Whereupon, having shut the door, he lifted one of the paving stones to reveal a cavity within which lay a small metal box filled with gold pieces. "I got tons more hidden in case her ladyship and me got to bolt and start some place anew. He hesitated a moment before adding: You remember them others in the townhouse bedroom. Could I forget! Theres a loose floorboard under, insides a watch, a special wedding present to her ladyship, worth a good 20 quid. Like this lot, its yours if you stuck for the readys!

That time had come! Being at Paramatta I was within a few miles of Montichellas garden shed. I made haste across country and waited until dusk before recovering my inheritance and concealed it about my person. Likewise, in due course, the watch, a handsome gold half-hunter, until I was able to secure a passage aboard one of our schooners, outward bound for Madras. From thence, by various ways and means, I made my way to the capital of the British Empire and the start of a most amazing life, as shall be revealed!

My eyelids were heavy. It was long past the hour when I normally tuned into the BBC's shortwave bulletin from London, but I had already learned one item of news this evening: the most likely reason for Aunt Lucinda's puzzling concern for a rejected orphan: she and I were two of a kind.

8

I overslept and was greeted with smiles of relief from the Macquarie's staff when I eventually came down to a late breakfast.

The Mac's *chef de cuisine* had trained at the Savoy in London, later than my stays there but we still had several acquaintances in common, and I would enquire after his family if I happened to be present when he went off duty, an amiable arrangement that ensured my meals were always as requested. This was the keyword in our dealings, for whereas other members gave orders, I'd pulled enough cookhouse fatigues at Blackboy Hill in Western Australia, and at Mena Camp in Egypt, to identify with all who work in hellishly hot and steamy kitchens.

"There we go sir," the chef himself delivered my tray, now that the morning rush was over, "I trust it is to your satisfaction?"

"That is never in doubt Mr Keane," I replied, shaking out my napkin. "How's Cheryl?"

"One more year to go."

"Then she will be a civil engineer? You must be proud."

"We are. Very."

"Please remember me to her and, if I'm still here, do let me know when she graduates; I wish to present a token of my regard, to mark such an auspicious occasion."

"That's very generous, sir."

"Not at all. It is what we used to do," I replied, tucking into the grilled kippers with a hearty appetite that masked an abiding sense of loss that, as a young widower, I had never seen a daughter blossom into the wonder of womanhood.

I do not use this phrase lightly, having always enjoyed female company, not only for the normal, healthy, male reasons, but also for the pleasure of their agile minds and intuitive ability to see multiple sides of any question. Perhaps because of my peculiar upbringing, under the tutelage of one remarkable old lady, I have never regarded such behaviour as "fickle" or "flighty," but rather as the natural complement to my own masculine, linear, nuts-and-bolts view of the world –

"You have a phone call, sir," a young waiter interrupted.

I glanced up, caught daydreaming again. "For me? Surely not!"

"Front Desk's holding."

"Oh, very well then." I laid my napkin on the seat, to show I would return. The concierge had placed his extension telephone on a low table, along with a notepad and pencil. I reached for the handset. "Ian Cribdon."

"Frances Baxter." Her voice caressed my ear.

"Oh." My voice cooled. "How may I be of further assistance?"

"By accepting a sincere apology for my discourteous conduct yesterday afternoon," she replied simply.

"Accepted ma'am. I regret that your visit was unfruitful."

"It is kind of you to say so," she replied with what sounded like a contrite smile. "By way of an *amende honorable*, would you be my luncheon guest, before I return to Sydney?"

"Ye-es," I replied, after a wary pause, by no means convinced that I was hearing the real purpose of this call, "provided you allow me to choose the location, and then tell me what you know of our rare family name..."

She paused, assessing my counteroffer. "If that is your wish, then yes, of course."

"Then one o'clock. At the Macquarie."

"One o'clock it is."

"Good." I hung up, never one for elaborate endings.

The chef had seen me go and kept my breakfast on the hotplate until I was ready to resume. "Thank you, Mr Keane, that was very considerate. Oh, by the way, I shall be having a luncheon guest, a lady out from England. Will that be convenient for your staff?"

"A pleasure sir. We'll do her proud."

I then glimpsed Mr Allen. "'Dr Baxter' will be my guest at one o'clock, for preference in the Phillip Room, if that's convenient?"

"Of course. I'll make the necessary arrangements."

This left me with little more to do except finish breakfast, return to my quarters and make a battleplan, for I had no doubt that she of the warm and seductive voice was scheming to captivate what she mistakenly imagined to be a sentimental old buffer. For what reason had yet to be revealed, though I'd have bet a pound to a penny that her apology was a *ruse de guerre*. Which suggested that others, higher up Six's totem pole than she, had recently discovered that Icicle was still alive, was still of sound mind, and therefore likely to recall certain actions in Petrograd and Central Asia best forgotten now that London was recalibrating its relations with Moscow.

With much else to ponder, I chose as my uniform for today's skirmish the bespoke, dark grey three-piece Saville Row single-breasted suit with a blue silk tie and plain, finest thread Egyptian cotton shirt by Budd of Piccadilly, then went down to the foyer to greet an adversary who, as expected, was equally punctual in her timing.

No warm-blooded male could fail to notice the subtle change from yesterday's business attire, and it was not just the merest hint of lipstick, or the signature fragrance, or her artfully relaxed hairstyle. Mr Allen was equally impressed by the company I was keeping as he showed us to the nearest of five enclosed areas off the main dining room, each named after an early colonial governor. Arthur Phillip, the first; John Hunter, the second; Gidley King, the third; William Bligh, the fourth; our club's namesake, Lachlan Macquarie, the fifth. Each with its individual tone, but all sharing the same air of quiet distinction that encourages easy conversation.

"The salmon was taken from Tasmanian waters yesterday," he announced, handing us monogrammed, leatherbound bills of fare; the Mac' uses sturdy English to describe its services rather than mimicking the Continental flimflam of less confident establishments. "May I offer drinks while you consider your choices?"

I looked across at my guest. "Wine?"

"Too early in the day."

"How about Polly with a squeeze of lemon, to refresh the palate?"

"Sounds intriguing!"

I glanced up at Mr Allen. "Polly and zest, if you please."

42

We were ready to order – the salmon for her, the Beef & Guinness pie for myself - by the time a steward brought a chilled bottle of Apollinaris table water, two glasses, and sliced lemon.

"Heavens! It looks just like it does in the old *Illustrated London News* advertisements," she exclaimed, inspecting what was, for me, a familiar bottle with its triangular red trademark. "I didn't know it was still available?"

"If one knows where to shop," I replied shortly.

"But didn't the Second War damage their brand somewhat?" Said with a knowing smile. "I'd have expected you to order a French water, like Perrier or Evian, instead of a German product..."

"Why?" I scowled.

"Those." She looked pointedly at my jacket's left lapel. "I recognise the Legion of Honour, of course, but not the other..."

Annoyed at being caught off guard so soon in our encounter, I squinted down at a slim pink and grey ribbon with *officier* rosette beneath the better-known crimson stripe. Preoccupied by thoughts of how to interrogate this disturbing young woman, I had neglected to remove my *agrafes boutonnières*, worn recently for the French Consul General's Bastille Day reception. "Just a bit of nonsense instituted by General de Gaulle during the war," I replied shortly. "Nothing special."

"I beg to differ," she said. "Please tell me what it signifies. An historian needs to know -"

"Stop regarding me as if I were a ruddy museum exhibit!"

"Sorry, sir."

I recovered my poise with a sip of the refreshingly crisp water. "Very well, ma'am, it's the Resistance Medal. Everybody got one."

"*Vraiment?*" she enquired sweetly, slipping into French. "That must be why I have never seen it before, even during my postgrad' year at the Sorbonne..."

"Where I assume you had no reason to hobnob with rough old veterans of *La Résis'*," I grumbled with, I hope, equal fluency before reverting to English. "Now, you are about to tell me what you know of our rare surname."

"Yes, though I trust you will help me in return," she replied, not in the least fazed by my gruff tone.

"How so?"

"By explaining how, and why, and when a twig of what is, at best, a bonsai version of any normal family tree, got transplanted to Australia. Once that's established, I can return to the Warwickshire Records Office and, hopefully, answer some puzzling questions."

I noted her dry sense of humour. "What about your father? He must know or knew?"

"Dad was killed, in February 1942."

"Oh...?"

"Fleet Air Arm."

I considered the date and made an informed guess: "'The Channel Dash'?" Her eyebrows shot up. "How do you know?!"

"It was also my war." I was unusually terse for I am still moved by, and identify with, the Royal Navy Swordfish torpedo bombers who launched their suicide attack on two *Scharnhorst*-class battleships and the heavy cruiser *Prinz Eugen* as the German battle squadron raced up the English Channel, escorted by a flotilla of flak-ships and squadrons of *Luftwaffe* fighters.

There was not one chance in ten million that half a dozen wood and fabric biplanes, almost identical with the machines I knew in France twenty-five years earlier, could beat such odds and yet their aircrews never flinched or turned aside, skimming the waves into a storm of tracer, cannon fire, and ack-ack from which none emerged except as blazing wreckage.

I raised my glass in silent tribute to their immortal memory and wondered if my predictable reaction was the reason why Six wove it into this woman's background story when they briefed her, probably at a safe house in rural Buckinghamshire, at the far end of the Metropolitan Line from Central London. "What of his parents?" I persisted. "Old letters, postcards, family Bible?"

"They were factory workers in Birmingham, and before that, farm labourers. Not the sort who got or kept many letters or cards." She seamlessly hinted at a bred-in-the-bone shame, the common response of many raised in class-infested 1950s' England before the Swinging Sixties made it fashionable and, for some, immensely profitable to aspire downwards as popular entertainers. "Dad joined the Navy as a wireless operator/air gunner, to get away from it all."

"Hm." I recognised the Shared Experience, an essential convincer in every conman's toolkit. Six knew I'd been an observer/air gunner in the Royal Flying Corps, making it a natural hook to attach her to someone similar in the Second War, further lowering my guard and making us chums.

I was about to disabuse her of this fanciful idea, but our luncheon was on its way from the servery. Mr Keane had indeed done us proud. As its robust bill of fare implied, the Mac' eschews *la nouvelle cuisine*, best described as "Picasso on a plate," where the cook arranges five peas, two stalks of asparagus, one ounce of seared steak, and has the cheek to call it a meal.

My unwelcome guest was delighted with her honey-glazed salmon, wild mushrooms, and char-grilled red peppers on a bed of Basmati rice. "The club is your home now, is it not?" She enquired, elbows tucked in, knife and fork correctly held in the old style.

"Yes. We're convenient for the theatre and concerts whenever I need a change of scene."

"And when you don't?"

I ignored her question and posed one of my own. "This paper you're presenting. Where's it to be given?"

"Sydney University's Darlington Campus," she replied, without hesitation. "Your Bicentennial has revived British interest in Convict Transportation."

"Really?" I frowned "And what attracted you to such an arcane subject?"

"The obvious social injustice that forced men, women, children into slave era colonisation, of course."

By God, she was good! Her modishly modern responses were crisp and word perfect, I noted, with memories of recruiting similar talent from the Royal Academy of Dramatic Art, so that a prepared script and improvised lines would flow naturally if one of our agents was trapped by the Gestapo.

I envisaged this woman's likely stage career, before the prospect of a regular salary and the promise of a Civil Service pension lured her away from predatory theatrical agents and their erratic fees, and instead focused on her current performance. "During my years in Britain, albeit a long time ago, one only had to mention Australia to hear the chains clink in an Englishman's imagination."

"I, I'm sorry to hear that."

"One got used to it." I stabbed the beef pie's crisp crust. "Of greater interest, now, is where we Cribdons fit into your societal jigsaw puzzle. Thus far you've told me very little."

"And you've told me even less," she shot back, politely but firmly.

"For the simple reason that I hardly know anything myself." Untrue, but I've always played my cards close to the chest.

"But surely your parents would have told you about themselves?" she frowned.

"Both died when I was too young to take much notice."

"I'm sorry."

"I'm not. It was my good fortune to be brought up by a great aunt descended from the original Cribdon to land on our Fatal Shore…"

"Oh?" She leaned forward in much the same expectant way as my curator had, the previous afternoon.

"Here's a clue." I prepared to cast a verbal lure. "Check the eighteenth-century military muster rolls when you return to England." I placed my cutlery aside and took another sip of water. "Some papers, recently unsealed allege that Sydney Town's earliest merchant king, a Joseph Cribdon, was a sergeant in the British Army during the American Revolutionary War. Maybe, if you exert Oxford's influence to discover his Record of Service, assuming it wasn't used to light a sentry box brazier long ago, you might recover his physical appearance, conduct, place of birth, and next of kin."

"Thank you!" She reached into her bag, a classic Hermès unless my eye was much mistaken, and took out an equally expensive leather notebook to jot down the details; Six's Wardrobe Department was not doing things by half measures! I read this as an indication of how seriously Control was running her op'. Because had she been what she claimed to be, then Sir Stephen's grandson must have inherited his grandad's Midas Touch to afford such accessories for such a wife…

Baxter himself was legal counsel and close colleague of Sir Arthur Stanhope, Chairman of the Asiatic & Pacific Trust Bank during our underground wars of the 1920s and '30s, and thereby knew when and where a political breeze was about to become a destructive gale and would hedge his bets accordingly. If only I'd been blessed with a young family to raise, I might also -

"You mentioned 'papers'?"

Distracted, I glanced up. "Say again?"

"I said, you mentioned recently unsealed papers?"

"Just an old lady making sense of her life." I shrugged. "Nothing of consequence."

"A pity."

"Indeed." I returned, with effort, to the present. "Of more immediate concern though, is your reference, yesterday, to Major Baxter's diaries and journals. May I enquire which aspects of 'V.I.L' they touch upon, and the context in which they mention 'Icicle…'?"

"It's still too early to say with exactitude," she replied, cagily rationing her information, much as I was doing with mine in our undeclared bidding war, "we're still collating Sir Stephen's records –"

"'We'?"

"One of my doctoral students and I."

Mr Allen saved me from further comment as he approached with his bills of fare tucked underarm. "I trust that was to your satisfaction, ma'am? Sir?" She smiled, I nodded. "Then may I offer a selection of puddings or cheese, coffee, tea, or liqueurs?"

"How's the Sir Edmund?" I enquired.

"Exactly as he would have wished on such a wintry day as this."

I turned to my guest, for the Mac' has a strict rule about who settles the bill on such occasions, a necessary requirement if we are to retain our legal status as a private members' club. "Are you game to try a colonial classic? The Mac's plum bolster is still made to its original recipe of dried fruit soaked in Port wine. Australia's first prime minister would often order it when conducting cabinet business in this very same *salle particulière.*"

"How could an historian possibly decline such a culinary adventure?" she replied with an enchanting smile.

I turned away. "Two Sir Ed's if you please Mr Allen. And afterwards we'll take coffee in the library."

9

Silence is rarely thought of as an interrogation tool, mostly because of kinema's need for constant agitation to keep its audiences engaged with preposterous tales of bedroom romps, car chases, gunfire, and espionage. This has spawned a belief that one can always bluff, or bully, or bash a reluctant witness into revealing the secret plan, or cypher, or hiding place. Whereas a professional interrogator knows exactly where and when to jab thorns of fear and doubt into his subject's imagination, and then patiently allows them to fester in silence until the subject is ripe for confession. Therefore, the longer I waited the more certain this woman would break. In the meantime, a more urgent concern was my old spymaster's indiscrete journal entries, and Six's unwelcome attention -

"May I ask a personal question?" she interrupted in a politely level tone of voice, after the waiter had finished dispensing our drinks and returned to the servery.

"You may ask, but I am under no obligation to answer."

Ignoring my curt tone, she continued: "Do you have children?"

Momentarily nudged off-balance I recovered my poise. "No. Why?"

"Then you don't know how persistent they can be when trying to learn of their antecedents," she replied simply. "Ours are now old enough to appreciate the irony of a mother who can tell them what Napoleon ate for dinner on the eve of Waterloo and explain at great length why the emperor Augustus tended his own vegetable garden, but who knows practically nothing of what their grandfather did for a living."

"Which accounts for your interest in we Australian Cribdons?"

"Yes."

"Then I wish I could be of more assistance, but you've exhausted my stock of knowledge."

"On the contrary," she replied, leaning forward, "your reference to a Sergeant Cribdon in the American War of Independence, is a promising lead I shall follow, once home again. However, I believe you can help me now," she continued, with a beguiling smile that did not fool me for one moment. "It's not only we who have lately emerged from nowhere. My husband's origins are nearly as obscure until Sir Stephen lit up the scene, figuratively speaking."

"Really." Said with feigned indifference.

"You cannot imagine how frustrating it is to live in the shadow of such a patriarch. A larger-than-life enigma with a whole column of public achievements in *Who's Who*, but a father who left no more than a handful of holiday snapshots as proof there ever was a warm and affectionate human being inside his oil portrait of a sternly bewigged and gowned King's Counsel," she concluded, watching me closely. "You do see where I'm coming from?"

"No."

"Then allow me to elaborate," she insisted. "Have you heard of St Serendipity?"

I blinked, blindsided by her second verbal ambush in less than a minute; "I'm unsure of your meaning, ma'am."

"I mean the 'Library Angel'," she replied. "The one who illuminates a key word or phrase as we plough through mind-numbing reams of documents."

"Very poetic," I shrugged, "but what's he, she, or it got to do with me?"

"Because I felt the saint's presence when I first saw your name associated with Sir Stephen's and learned there was still an eyewitness who knew him in pre-*Who's Who* days," she replied, leaning further forward. "Hopefully a colleague who will help me to decipher the enigmatic figure who looms so largely in the children's search for their roots…"

I was getting her method. From a charming invitation to become her scholarly friend, to gossiping about General Monash's chief intelligence officer, to revealing his and my connection with Petrograd in 1920, was one conversational trapdoor I had no intention of stepping upon. Instead, I shook my head: "I'm sorry. As remarked at our initial contact, family history is not my strong suit."

"I'm not," she smiled back, not the least discomforted, "simply being here with you today enables me to visualise the society that Sir Stephen alludes to in his journals, but which no longer exists in our ruder, cruder world." Said with an artfully humble smile. "You are my 'Rosetta Stone' which, as you recall, was the key to understanding Ancient Egypt's written language –"

"Stop viewing me as if I were a museum exhibit!"

"Listen, please," she insisted patiently. "With the deepest respect, I've been granted the privilege of conversing with an authentic Edwardian gentleman. One who, like Sir Stephen, endured the hecatomb of 1914-18 and lived to tell the tale." It was many a long year since an attractive woman had given me such a bewitching smile. "You cannot imagine how it feels to be speaking with an actual participant in events I've only read about. A time traveller who still speaks of 'honour' and means it. A man whose most emphatic curse is 'ruddy,' rather than the foul-mouthed spew that nowadays passes for emphasis." She stopped short and leaned even further forward, her eyes appealingly fixed on my face. "You are a unique discovery, Mr Cribdon. Please don't shut me out…"

"Why not?" I am not easily seduced by honeyed words.

"Well, in addition to Sir Stephen's journals I'm editing the British Cabinet's July 1914 memoranda, for wider publication," she replied, easing backwards, "but mostly what I see and feel are faded, typewritten paragraphs and pencilled marginalia. Whereas, to fully comprehend the temper of that fateful time, I need to visualise living, breathing, thinking statesmen and, in imagination, hear their voices as they unwittingly make the decisions that will destroy their world and its civilisation, forever! Their manners, their codes of conduct, are the keys to unlocking much that we later generations cannot understand," she persisted, pleading with me now.

"Why not?" Repeated grimly.

She sat up straighter, as if addressing a seminar, and ambushed me yet again. "What does 'History' mean to you?"

I sensed that our roles were about to reverse. Obliged to respond or risk appearing a dim old fogey, I searched my memories of a private tutor and his lessons from a *Cambridge Shorter English History*, with its steel engravings of battles unlike any I would soon experience. "King Alfred burning the cakes?" I thought aloud. "King John signing Magna Carta? King Charles and the Ship Money - ?"

She stopped me with a raised finger. "In other words, a catalogue of disjointed events and individuals, long gone and mostly forgotten?"

"I didn't say that!"

"But that's how you and numerous others regard History," she contradicted with a sharp, sideways glance. "No wonder so few comprehend the importance of: 'To know what will be, one must study that which has been.'"

"Says who?" I enquired suspiciously.

"It's the subtitle of my *History as Pathology*."

I felt an abrupt shiver of recognition, having last heard this phrase in Egypt, during the Great War. Spoken by an eerily similar young woman elucidating Leopold von Ranke's dictum that History's purpose is the discovery of "how things really were," or "*wie es eigentlich gewesen*" in its original German. A language we happened to be speaking, despite the risk of denunciation as enemy spies.

"In it I warn against viewing bodies of historical evidence through the distorting lenses of personal emotion and cultural bias," Frances Baxter continued, unaware of my silent confusion, "but rather, with the disciplined detachment of a pathologist. Only instead of saws and scalpels to dismember a problem, our tools are interrogative pronouns – Who, Where, What, How, When, and Why – with which to establish causation and context."

Whoever coached her for this op' had done a first-rate job, I realised, recovering quickly. "That may be so, ma'am, but what is the true purpose of your second visit?"

"I've just told you!"

"With respect, I think not." My tone was cold and calculating now. "Nobody flies halfway around the world, under the pretext of finding their children's origins, while simultaneously competing with academic rivals for a vacant slot on a publishers' list. So, when you return to London you may tell whoever despatched you that Ian Cribdon is a doddering old dinosaur, with selective memory loss, who wishes to be left alone, in peace and quiet."

If I though this would unsettle her, I was much mistaken: "The cyclical undertows of History flow darker and deeper, are longer, and stronger, and exert a far greater influence on the human condition than mere academic rivalry." A cryptic response said with sudden intensity and feeling.

I cocked a sceptical eyebrow. "And only a few hours ago I was assured that your world of Higher Learning could have taught the Borgias a trick or two..."

"For many, it still does," she was forced to concede, after a moment's hesitation.

"What makes you an exception to this general rule?"

She hesitated again before responding. "I am well published. I have tenure. My husband is a generous benefactor."

"And what, pray, does 'Mr Baxter' do for a crust...?"

"James is a merchant banker. In the City."

I stirred my coffee. "So, what prompted an attractive and intelligent woman to spend the best years of her life in a scholarly equivalent of sixteenth-century Rome...?"

Her hesitation was much longer this time. Finally, with measured reluctance, she replied: "Like our children, needing to learn of their origins, I needed to learn why my mother spent the best years of her life raising an only child, on a War Widows' Pension."

"And what did you find?"

She looked away. "That it was not as simple as the outbreak of war in 1939, or the 'Peace Treaty that ended all Peace' in 1919. Because the more I study their primary sources, the more I find myself drawn into an imagined arcade of mirrors whose tantalising reflections of Challenge & Response retreat ever deeper into an indistinct, greenish blur." She looked up, sharing a sad smile. "Betimes I wonder if that was a reason why Bismarck chose to proclaim his Second German Empire in the Hall of Mirrors at Versailles, as well as to avenge Prussia's humiliating defeat by Napoleon at Jena?"

"And the point you're trying to make?" My tone was terse as I restrained memories of that other young woman, who once spoke to me, of similar matters, in a similar tone of voice.

"Very well, let's examine our question from a different angle," she insisted, unaware of the turmoil inside my chest, "it being an informal corollary of Newton's Third Law of Motion that: 'For every political action there's an equal and opposite military reaction,' which reflect back-and-forth as they recede ever further into the distant past."

"I'd say that's a fair description of the Dialectic," I observed, still reminded of similar discussions, so very long ago, and now far away.

Her look of astonishment was wonderful to behold. "You are familiar with Georg Hegel's thesis?!"

"Better than that." I returned to the present with a heavy heart. "I was *Redaktor Propagandii Angliskogo Yazka* for Leon Trotsky, the Bolsheviks' Commissar for War. Seated across the table from him, and Lenin, and Karl Radek, it was impossible to escape their fervent declarations of Dialectical Materialism's inevitable triumph on the 'Long March of History.'"

Frances Baxter could barely restrain her excitement. "What you are saying, and the way in which you're saying it, are the other reasons why I'm here this afternoon!"

"I don't, understand?"

"A familiar condition for historians," she conceded. "We strive to appear confident of our facts and firm in our judgements, but these are often little better than informed guesses glossed over with footnotes and bibliographies longer than the Book of Genesis. But imagine if we had H.G.Wells' Time Machine, and could return to the past where one could question your King Alfred or King John or King Charles? Then, by apprehending their moods and motivations, we might yet learn how to steer humanity from Past to Future, while avoiding the worst of war's reefs and famine's shallows!"

"Good luck with that." I was unimpressed.

"You're missing the point," she insisted. "'Those who forget the lessons of History are doomed to repeat them!'"

"A commonplace expression," I snapped, furious with myself for revealing my work as an editor of the Bolsheviks' English Language press releases. It was time to call an immediate halt to this meeting with a nosy stranger or risk further inadvertent disclosures. "Enjoy your stay in Melbourne but Sydney is where you may find that which you seek, in the Mitchell Library."

"That's it, then?"

"Correct." I stood with effort, at the first attempt.

"I, I can't say that I am not very disappointed," she also stood, "but after reading Sir Stephen's diaries and correspondence, I understand why his MI6 colleagues were so reticent."

"Then we have nothing more to say." I gave a slight bow. "Permit me to escort you outside."

She gripped my wrist with a surprisingly strong, well-shaped hand, unwilling to concede defeat. "Please call me Fran'." Said with a beguiling smile. "James does..."

"It is kind of you to invite me into the family circle, as it were, but by your reckoning I am an historical artifact. A dusty relic from a bygone era where first name familiarity indicated a level of trust that could only be earned after the most testing acquaintance. Or stringent enquiry…"

10

We walked together across the foyer where Mr Allen had relayed an earlier, covert signal to Mr Perkins for a taxicab to be waiting outside. She turned at the head of the Mac's steps overlooking Collins Street. "Sir Stephen also wrote extensively of your discretion…"

"He had good reason," I observed enigmatically, leaning on my cane to ease an aching right leg. "Oh, one final question -"

"Yes?"

"What did Napoleon eat on the eve of Waterloo?"

"I wondered when you were going to ask," she smiled and, to my astonishment, added a wicked wink. "Answer my questions and I shall answer yours." She then gave me a resounding kiss on both cheeks, moved under the porter's umbrella, and stepped confidently into the weather.

I acknowledged her parting wave as the cab sped off and turned in time to catch the ghost of a smile on Mr Allen's face. "I'll bet you never expected that, sir."

"You'd win, hands down," I agreed ruefully. The last person to address me in this French manner had been President de Gaulle, on the courtyard at Les Invalides, when we veterans of the Jupiter Line were decorated for our service to Free France and Allied Victory.

Moody and unsettled, I returned to the library, glad to be quit of "Frances Baxter née Cribdon." Or whoever she really was. A waiter had already cleared away our coffee cups: if only he could have cleared the lingering trace of her signature fragrance! The confounded woman had subtly imprinted her presence upon the one room where I most often seek the solace of solitude. Henceforth it would be difficult to take my accustomed fireside chair and not imagine her seated opposite me, charmingly fishing for an eyewitness account of the Soviet Union's early years during Lenin's blood-soaked social experiment.

Upon reflection, it was clear that her heart-warming yarn about children seeking their ancestry, and of being raised by a war widow parent, were verbal decoy ducks. Likewise, her tale of an heroic, working class father was cunningly crafted to hook my memories of a previous war. As for being a history professor, any competent actress could have assumed that role after coaching at whatever is the modern version of our Second War training school near Amersham, in the Buckinghamshire countryside.

So, was this intriguing young lady being run by my old opponents on the KGB's side of the Iron Curtain? Or had Six tasked one of its own to investigate me, aware that it could be awkward if a man who'd fought in Whitehall's dirty wars against the Bolsheviks, went public just as Britain was preparing to reset its relations with a post-Soviet Russia?

Deep in thought, I went up to my quarters and double-bolted the door before taking a long nap from which I awakened refreshed and better able to focus on drafting a telegram that read: Confirm dod Cribdon Fleet Air Arm 120242 STOP Query James Baxter merchant banker London STOP Query textbook History as Pathology. ENDIT Icicle. Addressed to a news agency in which I had a sizeable shareholding, it would be telegraphed to Fleet Street first thing tomorrow morning.

I then dialled International Enquiries at the Central Telephone Exchange to obtain Somerville College's number, and set my alarm clock for 2230 hours, by which time the day's work should have begun in Oxford.

All I now had to do was restrain my impatience, and how better to do that than in the spirited company of the Antipodean Nightingale? Accordingly, I retrieved her cardboard box and resumed editing Aunt Lucinda's typescript as she was about to erupt onto the world stage.

Act 3

My initial impressions of London were unfavourable, perhaps reflecting Grandmamas recollections of the extended visit she and my then young and, I suspect, heartbroken Mama made some thirty-odd years earlier!

Their ostensible reason had been to negotiate with a shipping agent following the loss of two cargos, tho why Mr Joseph himself did not make the journey, I cannot imagine. Yet it demonstrates the highest degree of trust he had in her judgment that he encouraged her to go on his behalf. However, my sense of the matter is there was also another purpose, matchmaking!

Did poor Caroline, bereft by the departure of her beloved, secretly hope to meet him again in England? Alas, that was not to be for the gallant young Edward was already serving in Lord Wellingtons army on the Iberian Peninsula! Even if it had not been so, I very much doubt that Grandmama would have allowed such a suit to prosper. Instead, once her business was satisfactorily concluded, she leased a house in Londons fashionable quarter where, amply funded by Grandpapas other ventures, she set about finding a suitable husband for their daughter!

One would have thought that an attractive young lady with a fortune of three thousand pounds a year, would not have remained long on the shelf, but it would be wrong! To hear Grandmama retell, the mere mention of Sydney Town elicited sneerful allusions to Botany Bay and the prison hulks moored in plain view on Old Father Thames!

Visits to the theatre were equally unproductive as, I suspect, Grandmama entertained vain hopes of reviving her phantom career upon the stage, and all came to naught. Frustrated by her reception in London, she moved to Bath, then still the capital of fashionable England, where she became acquainted with a retired admiral and former governor of New South Wales. In later years she would speak fondly of him as the only one with whom she could converse freely about the Colony, from which one may deduce that her matchmaking fell upon deaf ears!

There was one sympathetic woman in whom she could confide, a Reverend Mr Austen's grown daughter visiting from Hampshire, the aforesaid retired naval officers own county. The three of them would meet at the Pump Room, take the waters, and gaily comment upon the passing scene. Admiral Phillips, for such was his name, would laugh with good humour at the phantastical tales these two imaginative women wove from the most trivial incidents!

There was an occasion when Miss Austen introduced her brother, one of Nelsons captains, and Caroline might have become Janes sister-in-law but for the clarion call of duty beckoning him away to Britannias briny realm, where further glorious deeds awaited his stout heart and eagle eye!

Eventually, defeated by England's snobism and the fact of her provincial manners after so many years away from The World as she termed it, Mrs Catherine Cribdon and unwed Miss Caroline, left Home to return home and, in the fullness of time, Holy Deadlock with Mr Stoat the Printer!

Upon reflection, I have been harsh in my opinions of Grandmama. Clearly a frustrated woman of many talents who found solace by confecting fabulous stories of earlier, imagined success on the London stage, I owed her an immense debt of gratitude that, in later years, I repayed by adopting Lucinda as my own nom de theatre, an homage to her expert tuition in the ways of the world without which an innocent young girl would have soon found herself undone, with naught to show for it but heartbreak, misery, and worse!

One of her most frequent counsels ran thusly: Clad in buckskin britches or ragged breech cloth, all menfolk rise equally to the occasion, upon that we may depend! The significance of this I shall leave to others experience of the world, be that much or little, but suffice it to say, under her guidance I learned many artful and pleasing ways to satisfy a man's lusty urges without, at the same time, getting myself with child or the pox!

As she would oft remind me: Heads trump Hearts in the game of life. Men trifle a few coins for their amusement, but

we womenfolk gamble our entire fortune on every throw of
the dice! Hence tis better to conceal than reveal our hand,
for by wagering too much, too soon, we risque quenching the
fire of desire. Whereas by playing our lowest card, with
hints of higher value provided our opponent comports
himself as a gentleman ought, we ofttimes win at devilish
long odds without hazarding our Ace!

Her sage counsel was of the greatest service during nearly
two years of travel and travail between Sydney Town and
London where I arrived with but five of Grandpapas guineas
and his pocket watch, of which I had grown very fond, and
would not have parted from even under the most
straightened circumstances, such as now befell me!

At which point I must have fallen asleep, for the alarm clock's impatient
rattle found me still seated at the desk; 2230 hours in Melbourne, 0930 hours
earlier in the day at Oxford; time to see if I still had the knack, for which I paid
a quarterly subscription to a confidential phone re-directory service in
Newcastle upon Tyne, for those odd occasions when I've needed to seem as if
calling from Britain, rather than overseas. I dialled its number, waited for the
automated cues, identified myself and entered the verification code.

"Good morning. Somerville College." Calm, manicured tones that could
have been spoken in the next room, not by a woman halfway around the world.
"How may I help you?"

"Good morning, ma'am. William Braithwaite of Braithwaite & Braithwaite.
Solicitors." Aunt Lucinda's elocution exercises were much in evidence. "Doctor
Frances Baxter if you please."

"I'm afraid that is not possible."

"But I was assured she's on your staff?"

"That is true." The guarded response made me wonder if I was speaking
with a secretary in Oxford, or with one of our own, manning an "echo
switchboard" patched onto Somerville's number for operational purposes.

"We need to speak. Where can she be contacted?"

"I am not at liberty to divulge such information."

"Of course," I frowned into the receiver, "but when we corresponded, she
mentioned a forthcoming journey to Australia for their Bicentennial..."

"Then you will understand why she is unavailable. Is there a message I may
take?"

"Yes. Say that William Braithwaite called and will do so again later."

"Is that Braithwaite with an 'e' or without?"

"With."

"Thank you. Good day." The line clicked off and I sat back in my chair,
unsure if I felt relieved or disappointed that Frances Baxter was still a person of
interest. But not too much interest, a lifetime's experience warning me never to
let sentiment cloud my judgment.

11

By next morning, the weather had improved sufficiently to allow a gentle amble two blocks along Collins Street, three up Swanston, followed by a left turn into Little Bourke Street, keeping well away from the kerb, ears cocked for a car or lorry accelerating behind me.

Eventually I reached the Telegraph Office and sent off my enquiry to England. Depending upon its complexity, I might get a reply next Monday or Tuesday. On the other hand, it might be a bit longer before my reconnaissance of the intriguing 'Dr Baxter' was complete. Until then, I would continue to tread carefully, as if Melbourne 1987 was Paris 1943.

So now what? Instead of returning to the Mac' or feeding the ducks from my favourite bench in Treasury Gardens, I decided to award myself a wary day of people-watching, much as Aunt Lucinda's "Admiral Phillips" had done at the turn of the previous century. He had chosen Bath's Pump Room, I chose what until recently had been Buckley & Nunn's Arcade Tea Room but with still enough wood panelling and brass fittings to imagine a more leisurely age, as I hung my hat and gabardine on a peg and limped across to a corner table, back to the wall, a clear line of sight up and down the crowded hall.

The shop's new owners, David Jones, had retained its old-time waitresses with their bobbed hair, starched white caps, black dresses, and sensible flat-heeled shoes, one of whom hurried nearer, tugging her order pad on its length of string, from her pinafore pocket. "Sir?"

"Bushells' Billy Tea, strong as you can brew it, with a spoonful of condensed milk. And a hot bacon and egg sango with lashings of tomato relish." I smiled kindly as she struggled to match an expensively suited old toff with this knockabout shearers' breakfast.

"Um." She recovered with commendable speed. "Mug or cup? Sir."

"If you've got an enamel pot in the kitchen, that will be abso-blooming-lutely marvellous. But if not, I'll settle for the breakable sort."

She could barely control a grin. "I'll see what we can do."

"G'donya Luv," I winked and prepared to enjoy my day-release from the Mac's dignified calm. No doubt Mr Keane would've happily obliged had I put in similar order this morning, but it would not have tasted half as good, any more than DJ's toasted sandwich would come within cooee! of those many I'd chomped in the West Australian Outback, fossicking for gold, pulling sandalwood, trapping rabbits to eat as well as to earn a few pence by selling their dried skins to hatters who stripped the fur to make felt headgear.

I briefly wondered how we could whip up some woodsmoke to complement my stroll down Memory Lane but gave that idea away; too many other customers would start wailing for the fire brigade to come and rescue the poor dears.

It's a curious fact, of a curious life, that while most men of a similar age to mine are subsisting on gruel or mashed potato, I can still fit in most food that fits on a plate. Not many oldsters still have most of their teeth, and even fewer bear the invisible scars of hunger in Sydney's dockside slums during the twilight years of Queen Victoria's reign.

Today's entertainer, probably a Conservatorium student earning his rent money, pulled up the piano stool and settled down to challenge the chatter of gossip and clatter of crockery. Most of his repertoire was foreign to my ear, though I did recognise a tune from *My Fair Lady*, but his jaunty style struck rich chords of recollection. In a heartbeat I was again seated on the floor of the Music Room at Tralee House, listening to Aunt Lucinda tickle the Bechstein's ivories while reminiscing about faraway faces and places.

She was a talented player, not surprising with Franz Liszt among her distinguished lovers, and the voice was still firm and clear as she encouraged me to laugh and clap along with her breezy tunes, some of which I already knew after hearing Papa hiccup their smutty versions as he staggered home from the pub, using me as his guide dog.

Aunt Lucinda was a naturally gifted teacher who invited my immature opinions on a wide range of subjects, during our frequent conversations. Paying close attention while I aired them and, when required, suggesting alternative viewpoints for my youthful consideration. Thus, I learned by association not by compulsion, most unusual in an age when loving parents still routinely whipped their offspring as if they were disobedient puppies. "Spare the rod and spoil the child!" was a commonly heard phrase around many a polite dinner table.

Apart from her short stint at Miss Kendall's Academy, I doubt if she spent another minute inside a classroom. Having thriven by quickness of wit and memory, she knew how to impart the basics of almost any topic with speed and precision. An intuitive pedagogue, generations ahead of her time, she saw that I already knew *A Frog He Would A'wooing Go* and encouraged me to sing-along once we had replaced its lewd lyrics with Standard Received English.

From frisky frogs it was but a short hop to *The Little Hero*, and *Throw out the Lifeline*, and *The Village Blacksmith*, all eight verses, my particular favourite with its stirring images of "brawny arms strong as iron bands," and a final exhortation: "Each morning sees some task begin, each evening sees it close, something attempted, something done, has earned a night's repose!"

Aunt Lucinda was not just having fun with the noble thoughts of village blacksmiths, or the missionary zeal of lifelines thrown to "tempest toss'd men, baffled by waves of temptation and sin," she was also teaching me to use clean speech and remember that sentences don't blunder along on their way to mumbled nothings, but must proceed in an orderly manner to crisp, clear, concise conclusions.

From there I graduated to reading and writing, but not by reciting the alphabet, for that was never her way. Instead, I was thrown in the deep end and asked to look at a text while singing the memorised verses. A short while later and I could declaim, straight off the page: "Jesus is able! To you who are driv'n, farther and farther, from God and from Heav'n -!"

A couple of weeks later found me copying whole sentences in block letters while reciting them aloud. Correct longhand needed some tuition from a professional writing master, but eventually I managed to scribe morally uplifting mottoes in a neat copperplate. Quite an achievement for a rescued street urchin, much baffled by waves of temptation and sin.

The aroma of fried bacon was particularly evocative of the Westralian Outback as my waitress delivered the halved sandwich, a sprig of watercress perched on top, and an enamel mug of strong, sweet tea. "Here you go sir."

"Thanks. You're a legend."

She hesitated. "We don't get many orders like this..."

"You probably don't get many customers like me," I replied, with a respectful smile.

"If only! It'd be tons more interesting." And with that she hurried off to wait at another table.

A French author, Proust by name, once wrote a book that began with him dipping a biscuit in a cup of chamomile tea, a scene that evoked delicate and refined impressions of Parisian High Society at about the time I was pinching goods off wheelbarrows in Sydney Central Market.

For me, DJ's plain enamel mug triggered the sights, the smells, the sounds of Albert; not Queen Victoria's husband but a wrecked town in Picardy. Once more I was standing in line at the Salvo's canteen hut, waiting to gulp hot, sweet tea before giving the order to fall in and move out. It was summer 1916 and by now I was a full sergeant with my own section of Lewis gunners to care for.

Our original West Australian battalion had bled out on Gallipoli's crags and gullies the previous year, and those of us who survived had been reassigned to train-up fresh battalions of volunteers from across Australia.

A Brisbane milkman was my Number Two with an unofficial speed record for clearing stoppages and resuming aimed fire. A miner from Broken Hill was my top magazine carrier and back-up man. His mate, also a miner, was a demon with the entrenching tool when we had to dig-in fast. A 'roo shooter from somewhere beyond the mythical Black Stump had attached himself to our little gang and loved nothing better than a spot of freelance sniping during the odd quiet spell. Good mates mostly. A warrior breed our nation will ne'er see again.

"'That alright for you sir?" The waitress had paused on her way back to the kitchen, worried that something might be wrong with my untouched order.

"Yes. All good. Thanks for asking." And to prove her work was appreciated, I attacked my tucker between swigs of tea that raised eyebrows among the surrounding townswomen - long white gloves, floral hats, stocking seams vertical from heel to hemline - but all was not good inside the brain's bone box where the dead abide.

Half of our new battalion's strength were hasty reinforcements from English training camps on Salisbury Plain, a few dozen miles across the Channel; keen little Diggers, apprehensively eager to see what "It" was like. Our officer commanding, "Lucky Larry" Taylor – so called because he'd twice been grazed by Turkish bullets, first on the chin, second on the nape of his neck - had returned from Division HQ. It was now his sergeants' turn to share Divvy's glad tidings of great comfort and joy at this, our last chance to confer as a group.

I looked around, checking numbers. There was not a regular soldier among us. The bloke on my left had been a Melbourne tram driver until eighteen months ago; the one on my right was an orchardist from Northern New South Wales; the two on his right were wheat farmers from the Eyre Peninsula in South Australia; my enlistment papers had me down as a West Australian bush worker; Lucky was a Queensland country bank manager whose only previous military experience was as a trooper in the South African War.

Transplanted Poms and Pats, Taffies and Jocks, and yet already a recognisably different race. It wasn't just our sturdier build and relaxed bearing compared with the weedy conscripts now filling the British Army's devastated ranks. The difference was etched on my brother-sergeants' solemn, attentive faces. Ours was a workman's attitude to war. We had been given a job to do - it could have been clearing scrub, or fighting a bushfire, or drafting cattle - so the sooner we got it sorted, the sooner we could take a spell until the next job came along.

Lucky spread his map on a vacant canteen table and called us to order with a summary of the previous stunt in which we had been a warm-up act for the Big Show on our left flank. For their part, the British 48th Division were under orders to distract the enemy while we hopped across No Man's Land to secure the strategic hillock at an insignificant little village astride the Albert-Bapaume Road.

With Pozières in the bag, all we then had to do was enfilade the Hun trenches with mortar and machine gun fire, signalling a general advance against the demoralised Fritzes that our planners confidently predicted would either be throwing up their hands in surrender, or turning tail when they saw massed British bayonets storming over the wire.

Sadly, no-one thought to tell the Kaiser's 117th Guards Division of their role in this grotesque pantomime. Instead of fleeing in panic, the East Prussians stood their ground and fought to the death. Theirs and Ours. Years later, an official on the Imperial War Graves Commission told me that Australia lost more men – killed, wounded, missing in action - taking Pozières in six weeks, than our casualty list for eight months of battle on Gallipoli.

And now, after a short spell, allegedly to rest and retrain, a second stroke of genius had appeared on Lucky's map. Today's stunt was another attack on Mouquet Farm, inevitably nicknamed Moo Cow, about half a mile from Pozières' village cemetery. All we had to do now was hack our way through dense thickets of barbed wire; clear an unknowable number of deeply entrenched dugouts that had repulsed earlier attempts to dislodge them; establish strongpoints of our own and restart the stalled Somme Offensive, before Winter stopped play until next Spring.

It no longer matters whether our commanding officer believed this blithering nonsense or not. Captain Taylor's luck ran out a few hours later, leaving his men mired in muck and misery, but we all knew this last briefing bore no resemblance to reality, not that I was paying much attention, being more concerned with our rations and equipment for the work ahead, rather than with HQ's macabre fairy tale.

It was my corporals' duty to check that all water bottles were filled before reporting back to me. Meanwhile, I'd snaffled a case of Geeveston Fannies from a Tasmanian comforts' shipment, to ensure that every man had at least one in his pocket. Fear instantly dries the mouth and there is nothing in the world like a crisp apple to get the juices flowing again, thus conserving clean water, of which we never had enough.

I also needed to make certain my ammunition carriers had inspected each round before loading their Lewis gun magazines; too many of the new Mk-VII cartridges were being assembled by clapped-out machinery in England; badly seated primers and insufficient cordite charges were guaranteed stoppages when least needed.

And there was the constant fret over our new-fangled Mills bombs and their rifle grenade fuzes. When employed as hand grenades and lobbed across the short distances of trench warfare, a seven seconds' delay was far too long; a quick Fritz could return the gift in time for it to land among us or airburst overhead.

Our bombers, as grenadiers were then called, were handpicked men who could be counted upon to remain steady enough to cook-off three seconds, after releasing the arming lever, before bowling a live bomb into an enemy trench or machine gun nest.

My reo's also needed careful handling if they were to get through this, their baptism of fire. I had earlier scrounged a stack of old newspapers to pad our recently issued Brodie steel helmets, while reminding these nervy new chums that it was also their issue of bum fodder and -

"All clear, Sarn't Cribdon?

I had no idea what Lucky wanted me to acknowledge but, in the best tradition of armies everywhere, I nodded. "Y'sir."

"Very well, gentlemen, let's go." And go we went. Back into something no word can ever describe. Except "It…"

12

A white-gloved hand gripped my shoulder while the other one held a glass of water under my trembling chin. "I'm calling an ambulance -"

"Sod off! I gotta keep up with my lads!"

"No. I'm a nurse. You must go to hospital -"

"You would say that Sister," I giggled.

She glanced towards her alarmed friends, shook her head, and sat down beside me. "I served in Egypt and Palestine," she explained, quietly. "Not your war, I know sir, but the symptoms never vary..."

"Sorry to be a nuisance." I sat up taller.

She released the grip. "I know someone at Heidelberg who can help. Let me give him a call, please."

I took deep breaths and managed a smile. "You mean well, and I thank you for it. But we both know, once I go into the Repat' Hospital, the only way I'm coming out again, is inside a wooden box."

"But they'll look after you properly! Your family can visit any time, and there are lovely gardens -!"

"My dear," I patted her wrist, "I still have work to finish in the short while left to me, and that will not get done if I'm being wheeled around in my pyjamas, scheming extra biscuits off the tea trolley."

"Seriously," she insisted, "I think you should at least go in for a check-up."

"It will tell me nothing I don't already know. However, I shall be most obliged if you would arrange a taxicab."

"Where to?"

"The Macquarie."

"You mean, the club?"

"Yes, and before you protest that it's not a suitable retirement home for an old geezer, our medical facilities are second to none. Most consultant specialists of note are also members. We get along famously well. I'm their pet patient. The slightest cough and The Royal Alfred's Emergency Department snaps to attention," I smiled. "Alright, that's a bit of a stretch, but you get the idea?"

"I still think –"

"Do me a favour, please," I interrupted. "On your way to the telephone, kindly ask that waitress to come over here."

I could sense that, true to type, all she really wanted to do was to stick a thermometer up my backside and dress me in Hospital Blues. "Very well. If that is what you really want -"

"It is."

My waitress presented herself a short while later. "Sir?"

"Please give this to the pianist, with my compliments." I handed her the folded message I'd just written. "There's a tip in it for him, and here's yours." I added a second two-dollar banknote.

"Thank you, sir!"

"On the contrary, thank you, ma'am."

To my delight and surprise the young lad knew *Roses Are Blooming in Picardy*, a more sedate choice than *Tipperary* or *Mademoiselle from Armentières*, for today's genteel lunchtime audience.

I must have recalled Aunt Lucinda describing her cheeky exits at Jacques Offenbach's *Théâtre des Bouffes Parisiens*. Because, after paying my tab, I draped the gabardine coat like a stage magician's cloak, stuck the fedora on the end of my stick, and twirled it overhead as I paraded from DJ's Tea Rooms, a bewildered ex-army nursing sister fussing around me until we reached the waiting taxi.

Minutes later, the porter assisted me from the cab as Mr Allen hurried down to help. "Shall I call Dr McKenzie, sir?"

"No, thank you. Just a bit too much, excitement, for one day. That's all." We had reached the top of the steps and paused a moment while the porter held the doors open to let us pass.

Mr Allen took his hand away from my elbow but kept close in case I stumbled again. The dining room was well attended, as one would expect at this hour, leaving me a good choice of seats in the library.

"Is there anything you'd like me to get for you?" The manager was still evidently in two minds about calling our resident medico.

"A glass of water will do fine," I settled into a chair overlooking Collins Street. "Thank you."

It was waiting for me, on a side table, when I awoke about twenty minutes later, much refreshed. My Bridge partner, the former Mr Justice Hartigan, had also seen me come in, curtailed his lunch, and was now seated opposite, clearly concerned. "Are you feeling alright Ian?"

"Just a bit puffed." I reached for the glass and downed half in a single draught. "Lord! I needed that."

"That's not all you need," he frowned. "I saw McKenzie a few minutes ago and –"

"Thanks for your concern, Tom," I interrupted politely, "but I'm going to be here a while longer. There's unfinished business, needs my attention."

"I'll hold you to that!" He glanced around at the Mac's Corinthian splendour: "This old place would not be the same without you." These few words were the nearest he had ever come to expressing friendship. For although we complemented each other at the card table, we had never complimented each other away from it. Natural enough when one is as reserved as I am, and the other still has the *gravitas* of a former Federal High Court judge, which makes us two oddly matched old chaps whose only common interest is a shared love of Bridge.

He began to stand, as if about to leave, then changed his mind and sat down again. "Look. I'm going up to the farm for the weekend. Why don't you come along? My manager says the trout need attention, and people tell me you were a notable fisherman, so maybe you can show me how it's done?"

Aunt Lucinda's papers also needed my attention. I was even planning to send out for a roll of 35mm Ilford FP4 panchromatic film, to see if my vintage Leica could still catch those fleeting images of unaware strangers that used to be a speciality of mine. These were the things I really wanted to be doing this weekend. As for the fishing? I could not remember when I last wetted a line.

The trouble was that my inner ear had detected something deeper and darker than a concern for my welfare. Tom Hartigan had recently lost a wife - to my way of thinking this commonplace evasion of death's finality equated her with a mislaid door key – and there was an audible note of pleading in his voice.

"It'll be fun," he insisted. "I'll phone ahead. The housekeeper is expecting me. An extra mouth to feed won't be a problem."

No stranger to the dangers of loss and loneliness, I felt the stirrings of worry. Aunt Lucinda's memoirs would have to wait until Monday. "Alright," I agreed after a further moment's thought. "Give me five minutes to get my kit together."

"Thank you." Not often does one see such a look of relief on another's face. "It will be fun," he repeated, more to reassure himself than me, and stood. "I'll have them bring the car round to the front."

It was not good to hear a man of his former power and authority reduced to begging for my meagre company as I turned away and went upstairs to pack a leather valise with shaving gear and some spare clothes.

A sage green Range Rover had parked at the Mac's reserved kerbside by the time I returned to ground level. Tom Hartigan helped me aboard and then got behind the wheel. "Thank you, Ian, I really appreciate this." And off we went, onto the Freeway through Melbourne's younger and younger suburbs, out to Ringwood before turning north into the Yarra Ranges.

He drove with exaggerated care and made a particular point of setting the cruise control as we approached each roadside speed sign. "Whoever booked me for a traffic offence would be the hero of every police canteen in Victoria," he explained with wan humour, having noted my interest from the corner of his eye. "There's no love lost between those who do the dangerous and dirty work of apprehending a villain, and we bigwigs who toss the case because of a legal technicality. Bagging an ex-High Court Justice would be sweet revenge."

"You're serious?"

"Very," he replied with a grimace. "What made it particularly galling, when I presided over lower courts, was that we were often on the same side, emotionally speaking. It fairly stuck in the craw to acquit some lowlife you knew was guilty as hell, while sworn to strictly uphold the Law for fear of an even greater evil afflicting society if we didn't. *Fiat justicia, ruat coelum.* 'Let justice be done, or the heavens fall.' Cicero," he added, pronouncing that Ancient Roman orator's name as "Kickeroh," in the Classical manner.

I had no idea of what he was rambling on about, but it passed the time, and I was starting to enjoy the change of scene as our diesel Rover throbbed past forested slopes of soaring gums, and over bridged gullies of tree ferns that had not changed much since their remotest ancestors became coal.

"Irene and I nearly bought a place here when we first married," he announced as we approached Lilydale's country town main street. "Nellie Melba is also buried over there."

"'*Addio senza rancor,*'" I followed his line of gaze up to our left. "'Cheerio, no hard feelings.'"

"Sorry, what was that?"

"The inscription on Dame Nellie's tomb," I had noted the "also" in his statement. "Mimi's aria in Act 3 of *La Bohème*. It would have been 1903 or '04 when *la prima donna assoluta* rehearsed the part at our place," I continued, hoping to distract a bereft widower with my gossip, if only for a short while. "As you know, it's set in the Latin Quarter at a time when my grand aunt was becoming established in Paris. Melba, a much younger woman, also a soprano though dramatic rather than lyric, was keen to be coached for what was still regarded as a *risqué* role."

"Good heavens, you are a dark horse!" Tom chuckled. "I never took you for an opera goer."

"There was no way of avoiding it," I replied with a modest shrug. "Artistes and performers of every kind were forever camping at Tralee House on their grand tours of 'The Aw-stray-yun Caw-lunnies,' as Britons still regarded us, even after Federation."

"Did you feel any artistic inclinations?"

"I did a bit of drawing and painting, cartoons and landscapes mainly, some portraits, but a war got in the way, and by the time peace broke out, all had changed, myself included…"

"A familiar tale." He fell silent and concentrated on the road as we took the B360 towards Healesville, a region altered beyond recognition since last I motored here; orchards and vineyards now dotting what used to be mostly cleared forest and dairy pastures. "We shan't be much longer."

"No hurry, no worry, I'm enjoying the ride." As indeed I was. And if I was on Six's watch list, a sudden disappearance from the Mac' had much to recommend it.

"Ah, home at last…" Tom Hartigan slowed a few hundred yards short of a bridge across the Yarra, little more than a creek this far inland from its mouth on Port Phillip Bay and turned hard right up an immaculate gravel entryway heading south.

I have never been a farmer, but even I could see that Akilinos Estate was a model of its kind; ruler straight fences; neatly treed shelterbelts; abundant water from an irrigation dam somewhere behind them, keeping the pastures a rich and lively green.

Surrounded by such obvious expense and attention to detail, the single storey homestead could not be anything less than an architectural gem as we rolled to a halt at veranda steps flanked by ornamental terracotta urns overflowing with red and orange portulacas.

Memory slipped a cog, as it so often does these days, and for one anxious moment I relived my initial appearance at Tralee House as a tall woman of indeterminate age stepped forward to help open the car door for me. However, unlike the formidable Mrs Thomas Harris, this housekeeper was clad in denims, a blue work shirt, and was happy to see us. "Here," she insisted, taking my valise, "let me help you with that."

Tom made the necessary introductions. "Norah, meet Ian Cribdon, Bridge partner *extraordinaire*. Ian, meet Norah Birtley, Fixer Supreme. If there's anything you need, ask and consider it done."

We shook hands and went indoors, out of the evening chill, to be greeted by a cheery log fire blazing inside a substantial granite hearth below a ceiling of exposed beams and mountain ash planks. For someone raised in the airy lightness of Tralee House, this rural elegance should have felt heavy and oppressive, but the overall balance was restored by a rich display of artworks on every wall, except where French windows opened onto the gardens beyond.

Tom noted my interest in the nearest piece, an Impression of mists and dappled sunlight, possibly of a forest glade somewhere in the nearby Ranges. "You like it?"

"Yes. Very much," I replied, still absorbed. "Watercolour is an unforgiving medium. Every brushstroke counts. There's no removing the pigment once it's down. Unlike oils, of course."

He turned his back to the fire, warming cramped limbs after the drive up from Melbourne. "D'you reckon the artist was any good…?"

"Yes. A sure hand, with a sharp eye for composition."

"What about that one, over there?" He pointed to the opposite wall.

I stood back to study a more recently framed work that echoed Van Gogh's *Sunflowers*. "Same hand but there's a lack of confidence; pastels are not his thing." I then peered closer to read the artist's initials: I.H. '84.

"Care for a drink?" He assumed an affirmative answer by turning away to prepare measures of Scotch from a fine selection of top shelf labels on the sideboard. "Single malt or blended?"

"Is that a 19 Year Balvenie?"

"It certainly is," he nodded, "and allow me add what a pleasure it is to be with a man who instantly recognises quality…"

"Likewise." I added a good dash of Perrier water to my glass and waited for Tom to finish pouring himself three fingers, neat.

"It is very good of you to come." He continued, with an awkward cough. "I know you're always busy with some mysterious project or another, and yet you've dropped everything you were going to do, today, to oblige me." He hesitated, about to say more, but instead raised his glass. "Cheers."

"Cheers."

Mrs Birtley interrupted our companionable silence. "I've put Mr Cribdon's bag in his room. Now, will you be dining here tonight, or at the cottage?"

"Here," Tom replied. "Ian and I have things to discuss, and he'll probably want to turn in early. But tomorrow, by all means, let's dine at your place."

"Okay," she nodded, "Reg' dropped a stag on Black Bluff last weekend. We'll do barbecued venison with all the trimmings."

"Splendid." He turned. "How about you Ian?"

"I second the motion, but for tonight, two slices of toast and a poached egg will be quite enough. It's been a long day."

13

We took our drinks onto the veranda where two wickerwork chairs, lap rugs neatly folded, faced an orange sunset filtering through haze from a distant Forestry Department burn-off.

"Norah and Reg' are good people." Tom Hartigan took his accustomed seat; I took the other one, its woven base less stretched by a lighter person, and waited. "I'm not sure how I could keep going without them," he added, after another pause.

"Your farm is a credit to all concerned," I replied, briefly distracted as the first 'roo of the night loped from a patch of remnant bushland.

"Their work, not mine. The Family Trust pays our bills."

"All the more reason to feel pleased with what you, and they, have done by combining your strengths." I was determined to keep the mood positive.

"Maybe." Tom studied his drink. "Actually, the original plan was to sell-up and buy a cottage in Provence. It would've been a new beginning, somewhere Irene could have learned regional cooking and continue painting, while I kept a few beehives and read all the books I've not had the time to do before." He hesitated. "Then she fell ill."

"Ah…"

"Quite." He turned. "You've lived in France, haven't you?"

"A bit."

"D'you think we'd make a go of it?"

"Depends," I replied cautiously, aware of the difficulty he was having with their past and his present. "What you've just said about her love of cooking, and evident artistic talent, I'd say there was a fair chance she would have won acceptance by a people who have much reason to be cautious with foreigners. I'm sure that, in time, they'd have welcomed her into their homes, she might even have become *Tante Irène* to the children, but what of her husband?"

He frowned. "How do you mean?"

"Those books he was going to read; are they in English or French?"

"English, of course."

"Might it not be better if he bought the local newspaper and subscribed to *Le Figaro Littéraire*, a solidly conservative publication, which he then worked on with the aid of a dictionary, in the local *estaminet*? Polite enquiries about correct pronunciation, or exact meanings would help break the ice as he put aside his former position in the world and, instead, built a simple footbridge across the social divide, to connect with less exalted folk?"

"Is that how you learned French?" Deliberately or otherwise, he avoided answering my question.

"No, but it was a handy pretence whenever I needed to give the impression of not understanding what was being said around me."

"How did you learn then?" he persisted.

I paused, always wary in matters personal. "My great-aunt and I spoke three languages a week; French was Monday's excursion into the world of her many and varied experiences."

"And the other two?"

"German on Wednesday, Russian on Saturday."

"Good heavens! She must've been clever!"

"Yes," I agreed with feeling, "especially at a time when women were not supposed to have an original thought in their pretty little heads. Of course," I concluded, "as a professional performer of the first rank, she had to deliver the goods in whichever language the show required, though oddly enough we never did much Italian; *bel canto* was not her style."

I suppressed a laugh at the thought of her interpreting the Mad Scene from *Lucia di Lammermoor*; the audience would have been convulsed by fits of laughter, and the orchestra would not have fared much better; High Comedy was always the Australasian Nightingale's strongest suit. "But what about yourself?" I returned to the present. "Is it wise to be moving to France so soon after your wife's death?"

He seemed to jolt. "How did you guess?"

"I didn't have to. You told me."

"The devil I did!"

"Sorry to disagree, but all I had to do was listen to what was not being said…"

"Hmph!" He eased back and resumed studying the sunset. "With an ear that sharp, you would have made a formidable opponent at the Bar. Instead of which, you were a newspaper correspondent, were you not?"

"Hardly!" I chuckled, "That's too grand a title for my time as a plain bread and butter journo' on the *Kalgoorlie Miner*. I might've gone back to it, after the war, but instead I went fishing and wrote about that instead." Adding, with a touch of wry humour designed to distract my host from any further enquiry: "Fish are less demanding company than humans, and never sue for libel."

It failed. Mr Justice Hartigan was now in witness examination mode. "Your post-nominal initials are evidence of a good war."

"That all depends on how one defines 'good' doesn't it?" I replied with controlled annoyance, noting the evasive switch of focus, away from his uncertain future and onto my vague past. "Very little happened between 1914 and 1918 that any normal person would call 'good,' or wish to be reminded of…" I allowed him enough time to take the hint before concluding: "The reasons for that you may deduce from your own experiences of the Second War."

He frowned. "Who says I have any?"

"Oh really, Your Honour!" I teased. "Even if I hadn't looked you up in *Who's Who*, with more success than you must have had when looking for my non-existent entry, I would still have made the connection between Akilinos in Victoria, and Akilinos in Greece."

"But -?"

My raised finger silenced him. "This is not an Aboriginal placename. With an 'Ak' prefix, meaning 'sharp' or 'steep,' for example 'acute angle' in Euclid's *Geometry*, it is unlikely to occur outside the Hellenic world. Further narrowing the search, there's a village of that name in Crete, destroyed by the Hun for helping Australian and New Zealand troops escape to Egypt. Joining those dots, one may reasonably assume you were among them, heard later what happened to the villagers, and commemorated their sacrifice when you bought this property."

I feared that I might have overstepped the mark as Tom Hartigan hunched lower on his seat. "'A plain bread and butter journalist'?" he grunted. "Pull the other leg!"

"I didn't mean to offend! Today's been –!"

"No offense taken." He looked up again. "You're right, of course. After the war I did go back, to thank them, but found it blown up, after fifty hostages were shot for 'aiding the enemy.' I then contacted the other escapees, those who survived later action, and organised a fund to rebuild the local school. We still send a substantial amount, on each anniversary, to show they're not forgotten."

"Good."

I'm not sure he heard me as he continued speaking to the encroaching dusk. "When Australia's time of trial and tribulation comes - as come it must, as come it will - may we be even half as resolute as those Cretans were in '41." He glanced back at me. "One old fellow saw a Jerry paratrooper landing in an olive tree. Before the fit young man could untangle his harness, the shepherd attacked with his crook and beat the invader to death. Others fought a guerrilla war with rocks, and knives, and shotguns, and the more savage the reprisals, the more ferocious their resistance. Is it any wonder I admire them so much?" He took a long breath and tried to make light of his next few words. "Perhaps that is where I should go, instead of France, to end my run?"

"Perhaps," I observed, quietly. "On the other hand, maybe you should just sit tight and let the dust settle before taking such an irrevocable step?"

"Too many memories."

"Memories are life's shadows," I reminded him. "They dog our footsteps, no matter how fast we run to get away from them –"

"You've not lost a wife after thirty-four years of marriage!"

"I was never that fortunate." It required immense self-control to remain calm behind my enigmatic reply. "However, this does not mean I have not known heartbreak, or never lived an unfulfilled life."

Embarrassed, he looked away. "Sorry. That was uncalled for." He looked back. "Another drink?'

"No thanks, I've had quite enough. In fact, I might've had a touch too much. It's best I go and lay down for a few minutes before dinner." I managed to stand without too much effort.

"Of course. Take it easy, there's no rush." He also stood. "We'll drive around the property, tomorrow morning, and catch a feed of trout."

"I look forward to that."

"As do I. Here," he reached out to help as I wobbled slightly, finding my balance, "let me show you to your room."

14

What I'd meant to be no more than a brief doze, extended into the early hours of next morning. Someone - perhaps Tom, or Norah Birtley, or both - had covered me with a quilt and left a dimmed light on.

The homestead was deathly quiet now and I had no way of telling the time, having long ago stopped wearing a luminous wristlet watch. As for Aunt Lucinda's bequest - the gold half-hunter wedding present to her grandmother from an unknown admirer – that was left in its waistcoat pocket when I changed into a more comfortable pullover, slacks, and tweed jacket.

Half-awake I rolled over and groped for my wireless set's earphones, intending to tune into the BBC's Foreign Service or Radio Moscow's local news, as often done when sleep eludes me. They were not here, of course. Annoyed by an unwelcome break in my settled routines, I rolled back the other way and glared up at an unfamiliar, darkened ceiling.

This was not how I had planned to spend the time, awaiting a reply to my reconnaissance of the intriguing "Frances Baxter." Instead, everything was conspiring to revive images, names, events I'd hoped were dead and buried, so that I could enjoy my dwindling stock of days in peace after a lifetime of wars and rumours of wars. But within the space of a few hours, that one mug of tea at DJ's had exhumed the decaying horrors of the Western Front, as if a random shell had struck one of our many improvised cemeteries.

Tom's insensitive questioning had not helped, for which I owed him no thanks, but the real culprit, the *fons et origo* of my resentment was that confounded Baxter woman, or whoever she really was...

With any luck, my agents in England would report a shabby, self-serving academic fraud or one of Six's operatives reporting on my clarity of mind and intentions in this new world of *Perestroika*. I could then shove her down the Soviet Memory Hole that Eric Blair described with astringent irony, during our conversations over cups of dandelion coffee and unsweetened Bath buns, in the British Broadcasting Corporation's staff canteen, during the early days of the Second World War.

"She has no right to interfere in matters that don't concern her directly!" I heard myself complaining aloud, as if he were present, although tuberculosis had long since taken him to join those other wraiths who haunt my graveyard of regrets. How does one lay such lively ghosts once they begin their *danse macabre*? I don't know, never having been able to stop their capering grimaces after a single word, or image, or even a smell triggers a vivid avalanche of impressions, as when Tom had briefly spoken of Greece and the Greeks.

In a heartbeat, I was again standing at the larboard rail of a crowded troop transport. In the distance, gilded by the rising sun, the snow-capped peaks of Mount Olympus; nearby, the Dardanelles, a narrow seaway that divided Europe on our left-hand side, from Asia on our right; and dead ahead, the rocky Isle of Lemnos.

"That's Helen of Troy's place, over there." One of my ghostly tentmates aimed his pipestem towards the Asian coastline. "'Much have I seen and known, and drunk delight of battle with my peers, far on the ringing plains of windy Troy..." Adding, by way of explanation: "Ulysses, talking about the big fight they had, all because of her and that young twerp Paris, thousands of years ago."

"He may be your Lysses," our other tentmate grinned, hand cupping briar pipe, always good for a quick play on words, "be buggered if he's my Lysses!"

The three of us – Harry, a timber cutter from the dank forests of Southwest Australia; Percy, a knockabout prospector from the arid Murchison Goldfields up north; and myself, a sandalwood puller from the Big Sky country east of Kalgoorlie – were one half of 16 Battalion's machine gun section.

An orderly room clerk at Mena Camp had saved time by typing us collectively as "HIP" on Daily Routine Orders, which inevitably gave rise to a sardonic "Hooray!" whenever it was our turn to demonstrate a training drill. Not that we cared, if anything it spurred us to outperform every other gun team, not just in our battalion but the rest of 4 Brigade as well.

We were a good balance of worldly wisdom and youthful vigour. The two older men were well into their thirties and had knocked around a lot, whereas on paper I had just turned twenty; a swaggering, self-important D'Artagnan matched with Harry and Percy's sober and steady Athos and Porthos, not that we saw ourselves in that light.

The Three Musketeers was an amusing work of fiction, unlike the *Vickers 0.303-inch Machine Gun Training Manual (1914)*, we had memorised from cover to cover and could have quoted in our sleep, rare as that soon would be, with Percy our Number One, leading the way, cradling the gun, action-ready in twenty seconds.

Harry, Number Two, carrying its tripod, cross head, and elevating screw across his sturdy shoulders.

Myself, Number Three, trotting beside them with the condenser's rubber hose, canister of coolant water, and offset funnel; spare gun-barrel, flannel patches and cleaning rod; toolkit and oiler; insulated gloves and hemp packing thread; stowed in their canvas bag slung across my back.

Numbers One, Two, and Three were also required to carry 250 rounds of ammunition apiece, a Webley & Scott 0.455 revolver holstered on our webbing belt, together with an entrenching tool and water canteen.

Our rolled groundsheets were strapped to knapsacks containing, among other essentials, a wound dressing and iodine ampoule; a spare shirt, fresh socks, foot powder; ration biscuits, bully beef, apricot jam; Oxo cubes, tea, and sugar; mess tins, eating irons, jack-knife; cigarettes, matches, and a small bundle of firewood split from discarded *Fray Bentos'* packing cases.

Officially designated Light Infantry but laden like beasts of burden, we begrudged every round spent, knowing that someone – usually the nimble young chap who used to be me, if our supporting riflemen were otherwise engaged – would have to bring up another couple of belts in box magazines which, between them, held barely sufficient ammunition for one minute's sustained firing.

The popular image of a lone machine gunner, grimly hammering away, was rare in my experience of the business. We were trained to think like marksmen, sniping with thumbed flicks of the trigger bar, unless the enemy launched a wave attack that required a sustained barrage to beat it back. Consequently, we not only hoarded our stock of cartridges we also extended our gun barrel's life, even as we murderously shortened tens, scores, hundreds of other lives.

The Maxim, from which the Vickers evolved, first saw limited service in the Soudan and South Africa a few years earlier, making us the first British Colonial troops to employ it on an industrial scale.

Percy, Harry, and I were innocents abroad, too rapt with mastering these exciting new skills to understand the pain and loss we were inflicting upon unknowable, uncountable, unimaginable numbers of grieving widows and orphans, mothers, and fathers, who haunt me still.

15

"Good morning, Ian. You slept well?"

"Yes," I lied. Then, changing the subject: "What's on today's agenda?"

"First stop, the Cottage, for breakfast." Tom rubbed his hands with forced enthusiasm, unconsciously telling me much about his own state of mind this morning. "Then, drive with Reg' on a tour of inspection. Finally, up to the dam to see if we can catch lunch. Sound alright?"

"Sounds great," I lied again. In truth, all I wanted to do was stay on the veranda, stare aloft at a wintry blue sky, and imagine myself climbing ever higher above cottonwool tufts of cumulus cloud, an RE8's wooden-bladed propeller slamming its icy slipstream against the back of my fur collared shoulders. And never return.

Instead, I sensed that Tom had more down to earth reasons for showing me his domain. An ex-army nursing sister had correctly diagnosed my condition, yesterday, and I could feel a similar darkness in Tom today. Common decency required that I tag along regardless, ready to catch when he fell off his own fraying tightrope.

We walked in silence around the well-kept orchard and potager garden on our way to the farm manager's quarters, Akilinos' original homestead before someone – almost certainly Irene, the daughter of a wealthy merchant dynasty – decreed a more imposing residence for a Justice of the High Court.

Tom's face relaxed as we entered the older building through a mudroom crammed with gumboots and raincoats ranging in size from youngsters' to grown adults,' and went through to the kitchen where the family was taking breakfast. Having the boss drop in like this seemed like a regular occurrence as Norah cracked more eggs and layered the cast iron skillet with shredded potato fritters that are, I believe, nowadays called Hash Browns.

"Reg'," my host stepped ahead, "allow me to introduce an old friend, Ian Cribdon. Up from the Big Smoke to get a breath of fresh air."

I am well into the usual definition of old but did not realise until now that Tom Hartigan had, so to speak, put my name on his greetings card list as I turned to reach out and –

"Are you alright Mr Cribdon?!" Norah Birtley moved quickly. "Here, sit you down!"

"Thanks." I was grateful for her assistance. "Not used to, so much fresh air," I quipped, propping my face on an elbow, managing a wry chuckle. "Ah, that's better!"

Tom was not fooled. "For a moment I thought you'd seen a ghost?"

"Nah, don't believe in 'em." I sat up straighter and smiled around, aware that a guest's foremost duty is not to cause a fuss and be politely attentive to others' needs.

Tom had guessed rightly though. His farm manager was an outdoorsman of middle height and early middle years, one of the lean, sinewy breed I thought Australia would never see again after Gallipoli, and Palestine, and the Western

Front. Add a dark Kitchener moustache and Reg' Birtley could have been Percy Black's twin brother.

"Do you want to lay down for a few minutes?" His wife was still deeply concerned for my wellbeing.

"It's kind of you to offer, ma'am, but a mug of brewed tea, some condensed milk if you have any, and I'll be right as sixpence."

"'Sixpence'?" The family's' daughter joined our conversation.

"Five cents," Tom replied, seeking to be helpful. "They went out of circulation when decimal currency came in about twenty years ago."

"Yes, I know that, but what exactly does it mean, said this way?" she persisted, a naturally inquisitive teenager.

"Good question." He turned to me. "What exactly does it mean in this context?"

"More than most can imagine nowadays." I shared a reflective smile. "Maybe a double serve of fish and chips, or a pint of beer, or a packet of gaspers in the Sergeants' Mess."

I could have added the silver coin sewn behind my observers' half-wing brevet, a lucky charm that others on our squadron also wore over their hearts, to avert the Fokkers' Evil Eye, but kept this to myself, not wishing to be thought gullible or superstitious. Instead, I shrugged. "Mostly it was a trifling amount with which one could buy a few comforts, which probably accounts for the origin of this phrase, not that I've given it much thought until now."

"'Gaspers'?" This young lady had a commendably tenacious curiosity.

"'Wee Willy Woodbines,'" I replied, anticipating her likely response. "A cheap smoke with a ferocious nicotine kick."

"Ugh!"

"Julie, really!" Norah Birtley wagged a reproving finger.

"It's alright," I intervened. "She won't have many more opportunities to converse with a remnant dinosaur."

"'Dinosaur'?!" The family's son - about the same age as I was when Aunt Lucinda rescued me from Corunna Plains - sprang awake and leapt into the adults' conversation.

I shared a sad smile. "You are in the presence of a time traveller from a distant realm where our thoughts and language are as incomprehensible as a dinosaur's grunts and growls would be now." This risked becoming a self-pitying moan, so I lightened the mood by clawing air while uttering a comic snarl. "That's how a Blue Spotted Tyrannosaurus Rex says 'g-g-g-good morning!'"

"Wow!"

Their father, the Alpha Male as I believe anthropologists call them, was watching my antics with an understandably cool eye. "'Sergeants' Mess'?"

"Dino' speak."

Tom correctly saw that I had no wish to go any further down this track and stepped in with a question of his own. "You reckon it'll be any good up at the Dam this morning, Reg'?"

"No reason why not. I took a one kilo rainbow on a Tassie Devil spinner a couple of days ago and have been feeding 'em worms and maggots."

"Splendid. We'll be into that."

"You fish too?" Reg' looked me in the eye, another of Percy's traits.

"A long time ago."

Minutes later, Norah finished packing a picnic basket, stowed it aboard the farm's light lorry, and waved as we drove off to inspect stock troughs and fencing while Tom and his manager discussed a consignment of Angus steers booked for the local abattoir. Such matters were as far outside my range of experience as the jokey dinosaur talk had been to the children. Of more immediate concern, though, was the prospect of spending the rest of the morning squelching around a muddy waterhole, luring tame trout to their deaths.

This held as little appeal for me as it had been when *Reichsjägermeister* Hermann Goering - clad in green tights, medieval leather jerkin, Robin Hood cap perched on pomaded hair - murdered a stag fed on doped oats at his Carinhall Estate in North Brandenburg.

Not that I have anything against fishing, as such; one needs a fair amount of guile to outwit a cunning old trout or salmon. And I have spent many a pleasant day in various parts of the world, disguised as an angler. A Hardy's Palakona rod and tackle bag my only field cover. Monitoring freight train movements or covertly photographing strategic railway bridges while surveying rivers and waterways for their depth, width, and currents, by using the rod and line as units of measurement.

On those inevitable occasions when a suspicious local official questioned what I was doing, a sample copy of *Anglers' World* featuring one of my illustrated articles, usually did the trick. Its convincer, an inflated estimate of the number of wealthy foreign sportsmen who would soon be attracted to such a beautiful and friendly region as my questioner's home province, all keen to exchange their British pounds and American dollars for local marks, or zloty, or schillings, or -

"Do you need a hand getting down?" Tom's query snapped me back to the present as the Toyota Hilux parked alongside a neat wooden summerhouse, its veranda overlooking a shallow valley's landscaped views.

"No. I'm fine." I was determined to retain my independence for as long as possible by using the walking cane as a third leg to assist the dismount. "There!"

"Good man."

I'd been wrong. The irrigation dam was not a muddy hole but, rather, an enchanted lake created by the previous owner when he dammed a spring-fed creek to flood the valley. That done, no expense had been spared to craft six acres of water with reed beds and shade trees, miniature coves and headlands mimicking Nature at her fairest and finest. The chalet's interior was equally delightful and a strong reminder of the *sommarstuga* that was once my forest home in Sweden. Tom looked around its light timber walls hung with Scandinavian folk art and brightly woven fabrics. "This was the main reason why Irene wanted us to move here, but to get it we first had to buy the rest of the property."

"You did well."

"Thanks for reminding me, but without her, it's just another expense. After all," he added glumly, "we never own land, do we? At best we borrow it for our brief stay. Then along comes some other fool, who changes everything around, and we might as well have never existed."

I was saved from commenting on this bleak truth as Reg' Birtley halted at the doorway and peered inside. "If it's okay with you gents, I'll be getting back to work. Give us a call on the two-way when you need a lift home. Have fun."

"Thanks," his boss replied, "we shall."

"A good bloke," I observed as the Toyota drove off. "What's his story?"

Tom had begun sorting through an extensive, expensive collection of rods and reels. "Originally from Victoria but working as a motor mechanic in the

Northern Territory when he got called-up for National Service. After returning from Vietnam, he rather lost direction until meeting Norah, my bookkeeper, who encouraged him to do a Farm Management diploma at the Technical College. His practical skills, her accountancy, and their combined work ethic were too good for me to let go." He squinted along a rod, aligning its rings, then glanced my way again. "Why?"

"He's the spitting image of a mate who got skittled at Bullecourt, in '17," I replied, quietly. "For a moment it felt like Perce' had come to collect me."

Tom was clearly troubled to hear this. "Then you do believe in ghosts?"

"Only in private." I hesitated, before adding an explanation he could flesh-out from his own experiences of war. "Three of us trained on the Vickers. Percy Black was our Number One and, coincidentally, first to get It. Harry Murray, Number Two, got It next, in a civvy car crash, much later. I was Number Three and am still waiting, though clearly not for much longer."

"McKenzie says you're in fine shape for a man your age!"

"Gordon is a professional optimist, that's what he's good at, but thanks for the concern."

"No, thank you..."

"What for?"

"The reassurance about ghosts." He steadied his voice. "I still feel Irene's presence." Mr Justice Hartigan, avenging terror of all villains and scofflaws, was close to tears. "I swear, if she gave me the word, I'd put a gun to my head and join her. But then, you think, this is, all in my head?"

"That is my experience," I replied, uncomfortably aware of my promotion to the thankless rank of Wise Old Man, master of life's murkier mysteries. "However," I continued, frowning, "another subject I am also qualified to advise upon is the clean-up after a violent suicide. Take my word for it, Tom, there will be no sympathy or thanks if you do top yourself. Only contempt and disgust."

"Yes, yes of course, of course. But tell me, please, how do you cope with, your ghosts?"

"Ritual." I looked away sharply. "Come along. The fish are getting impatient."

We sorted our tackle and Tom chose a spinning rod with assorted lures; I selected a similar rod but tied a float rig, Reg' having thoughtfully left a Vegemite jar of earthworms with the two-way.

A creaky right shoulder meant that my days of flogging bodies of water, with a fly line, were now but a distant memory. All I really wanted was an excuse to sit by myself, on the jetty, while Tom tried his luck farther around the lake. Instead, he dithered about while I baited up, then propped his rod against a nearby fencepost and joined me on the jetty.

"Unless you're just going to stand there being ornamental," I grumped, irritated by his presence when I had hoped to be left alone, "take the weight off your feet." I gave a curt nod at the other wooden bench, bolted to the planked deck, and flicked my bait at a promising patch of shady ripples before giving my line a twitch, drawing the float away from a partially submerged log.

We settled into an alert silence and listened to the lazy slap of wavelets against the jetty's pilings while a family of moorhens fossicked around muddy shallows nearby. Tom eventually cleared his throat. "What did you mean by 'ritual'?"

I wound the reel, threaded another worm, and flicked it farther out, away from a shoal of minnows who had quickly stripped my first cast. "'Not sure the answer would make sense to anyone but myself."

"Try. Take your time. We've got all day."

"Hm." That tone should have warned him to back off.

My float kept nervously bobbing around; the minnows were not giving up easily; this was not how I wanted to spend a weekend in the country. Past experiences of helping the desperate rarely ended well. The helper all too often becoming a lightning rod for the other person's anger and resentment. "There is no one-size-fits-all answer," I finally replied.

"Please. Tell me straight."

"No." One of the privileges of old age is the right to refuse whenever we choose, and if that offends the listener, too bad.

Tom stiffened. "There's no need to take umbrage."

My patience, already worn thin after yesterday's episode at DJ's, could take no more. "You want it straight?" I looked him right in the face. "Very well, I lied to you before breakfast!"

"What -?"

"Last night's sleep was anything but 'good'!"

"There's no need to be so damn' touchy!" he snapped back. "You're not the only one who gets bad nights!"

"Perhaps not, but I have much longer experience of them!"

Tom flinched and recovered his composure. "I'm sorry."

"Meh! Close ranks. March on."

He hesitated before essaying an informed guess. "The War?"

My voice darkened. "Yes."

"You were in the trenches, weren't you?"

Something about his commonplace query, one often asked by the next generation of soldiers, triggered an angry response out of all proportion to the question itself. "Why do you people always think those were the only place we diced with Death?!"

"I didn't mean -!"

"D'you really want to know what happened last night?" I glared, ignoring his interruption

"I'm sorry -!"

"You're sorry?! I've had seventy years of sorrow and it's not done me a bloody bit of good! Not when I can still see a young man jumping to his death rather than be burned alive in the sky! Ripe with hopes and dreams of a long and happy life until the moment my bullets punctured his aeroplane's petrol tank -!"

16

My host tactfully retired to the summerhouse, returning a few minutes later with mugs of hot tea and two slabs of rich fruitcake.

"Sorry to fly off the handle." I moodily stirred the condensed milk he had remembered to add. "It was uncalled for. I must be getting old and crotchety."

"No, you're not." He resumed his place on the jetty.

"Can I have that in writing?" The quip failed to lighten the leaden gloom inside my head. "Anyhow, change of subject," I continued, between chomps of cake. "Yesterday, when you hoped Australians would be even half as resolute as the Cretan Resistance. What prompted that remark?"

"'Not sure the answer would make sense to you or anyone else…'"

"'Try. Take your time. We have all day.'"

He had the grace to laugh. "It's not the 'what', but the 'who' that concerns me."

"Oh…?"

"Last week, I had lunch with Don' Horne. He's still fuming at the way his readers misunderstand *The Lucky Country*."

I frowned slightly, remembering a book that caused quite a stir when it was first published. No great surprise, given that it condemned Australia as a first-rate country blessed with every natural advantage, governed by second rate buffoons, none of whom deserved their good fortune. "I'd have thought he would be glad anyone still cared enough to misunderstand him, twenty-odd years later," I said. "What's his problem?"

Tom sat forward hands planted on both knees. "We met to discuss the Bicentennial Celebration, next January, and both agreed that it must reflect Australia's attainments in the Arts and Music, Engineering and Science. People need to be reminded that, at a time when our population was no larger than many a large European town, Australians had garnered a host of international awards in every field of learning and intellectual achievement, so clearly there's nothing second-rate with Australia's brainpower."

"Just our leadership?"

"Precisely! For example, take the current Prime Minister, a pushy Red braggart best known for breaking the World Beer Drinking Speed Record while fooling around with a Rhodes' Scholarship at Oxford -!"

"But didn't I read somewhere that Bob Hawke finished his degree as well as that notorious 'yard of ale'?" I queried fairmindedly.

"A consolation prize B.Litt.," Tom sniffed, "nothing that requires intellectual rigor or originality of thought."

"Maybe so, but he still did better than me," I shrugged. "My only academic distinction is an unofficial record for the shortest attendance at Melbourne Grammar School; about three hours, barely enough to qualify as an Old Melburnian, if I ever wished to."

"Really?" His bushy grey eyebrows shot up. "Do tell!"

"No." I was annoyed with myself for failing to keep my ears open and my mouth shut. "Anyhow, what were you saying about the upcoming Bicentennial of European Settlement?"

"In a word, it's all rubbish," he snorted. "No wonder Don' is thinking of writing a sequel entitled *Getting by on Luck*. Millions of dollars allocated to show the world that we really are a feckless mob of sporty boozers who 'stop the nation' once a year, to learn which horse has won the Melbourne Cup!"

"That's a bit harsh."

"Not harsh enough," he scowled. "How else can one describe the freak show that will soon be touring every capital city, and many a country town, exhibiting Bradman's cricket bat, Ned Kelly's armour, Phar Lap's heart pickled in formalin, as inspiring national icons?"

"That's got to be someone's idea of a prank -!"

"Would that it was," Tom announced with grim emphasis. "These are exactly what are being promoted as representative of 'Australian Values' by a committee incapable of differentiating between meretricious and meritorious! One, moreover, with too much money and not enough imagination to review an impressive list of world-class achievements since Old Mother England shipped her unwanted, unwilling outcasts to Botany Bay!"

He drew breath. "A bizarre freak show will soon be celebrating two hundred years of 'larrikinism' and drunken misbehaviour unless we intervene now!" Mr Justice Hartigan had resumed his place on the High Court and was ripping into a lower court's flawed judgment. "We are determined to raise the Bicentennial's tone so that our youth can aspire to more than sun, sand, and sin!"

"Good luck with that." I rebaited my hook after yet another minnow ambush. "Meanwhile, back in the real world, what's the Cretan Resistance got to do with Australia's 'time of trial and tribulation…'?"

"Everything," His scowl darkened. "Sooner or later, our smug, self-absorbed 'Lucky Country' will experience another invasion and conquest."

"'Another'?" I queried, casting farther out. "I didn't think the Japs got this far in 1942?"

"Don't be absurd," Tom snapped, "of course they didn't. But read the local map, 'Yarra,' 'Dandenong,' 'Mooroopna.' Tribal names their original speakers must have thought were eternal, as recently as five or six generations ago! Barring a nuclear attack, the port city we call 'Melbourne,' in honour of Queen Victoria's first prime minister, will still be here for the Tricentennial in 2088, but I wouldn't bet on it having the same name. Mao City more likely!"

"So, what's the link with Crete's Resistance…?"

"Not 'link,' lesson.," he replied, chin tilted defiantly. "One taught by a proud people who fought against overwhelming odds and chose to die with honour rather than live with shame. Brave men and women who knew, to the marrow of their bones, that unless something is worth dying for, it is not worth living for! But when I look around at today's polyglot, ragtag, tattooed, disfigured 'Australians,' I fail to see even a glimmer of that invincible Cretan spirit." He hesitated before concluding with a moody shake of the head: "China, or whoever, will have an easy conquest. Because, as always: 'The strong take what they want, the weak give what they must!'" He paused, regaining his breath before elaborating: "Thucydides, *The Melian Dialogues*."

I winced, having first heard this bleak truth spoken at Baroness Bjerkholm's manor house near Jönköping, where a bumptious young *Hauptmann* Goering had never ceased parading his opinions for all to hear, if not to share.

"You surprise me Tom," I reeled my line in and began removing the float and lead shot, in the hope that a more natural delivery would do the trick. "A man in your profession should have more faith in the Rule of Law and –"

"That is the one immutable rule," he interjected sharply, "all the rest are pious hopes inscribed on paper! Never forget, behind every judgment handed down in court, stands a policeman with pistol, handcuffs, and truncheon, ready to enforce the verdict in case a convicted felon imagines that his compliance is optional!"

"So much for the theory of 'Free Will,'" I thought aloud, making time to frame a more useful comment by casting as far out as the bare bait would carry, letting it sink of its own accord and seeing the water heave, moments later, as yards of line stripped from my reel.

"We're on!" It was many a year since I last heard myself calling this as my rod's tip whipped, bending almost double, taking the strain.

Tom was inspired to get busy with his own rod, after we finished dispatching my two-pound brownie. I watched him hurry off to a shaded spot farther around to the left, then turned and took our lunch into the chalet.

I was now of an age when gloomy predictions, like those my younger companion had just spoken of, can be seen in a clearer light and with it comes an understanding that the future will take care of itself as it always has done in the past, for they are one and the same when pared down to their essentials.

I well recall Mr Schuster, the father of my boyhood friend David, reading King Solomon's words aloud from his family's version of the Bible: "Unto all things there is a season and a time for everything under the heaven; a time to be born, a time to die; a time to sow, a time to reap. What has been, is what will be, and what has been done, is what will be done, for there is nothing new under the sun..." Wisdom I only understood much later, but even as a youngster I felt its gravity and truth.

Born and raised in the high noon of Britain's imperial power, when it seemed the sun would never set on the British flag or the Royal Navy's global reach, by my twenty-fifth birthday the German and Austrian, Russian, and Turkish empires were as one with Nineveh and Tyre.

In my middle years, I helped defeat the Third Reich and observed the conquest of Italy's colonies in North Africa. Of the three Axis powers, Japan alone retained an emperor, in name only, after his armed forces surrendered in August 1945.

It was a Pyrrhic victory for all except one of the victors, triggering as it did the decline and fall of Britain's colonial empire, along with those of France and Holland, Belgium, and Portugal, the last two in the Congo and Mozambique. And assuming Frances Baxter was correct in her reading of current political trends in Russia, it would not be long before the ramshackle Soviet empire also fell apart.

Even the mighty United States of America, by any measure a colossus bestriding the world, had better be more careful after their recent defeat in Vietnam. Another overseas misadventure, on a similar scale, and Washington could soon find itself sharing Leon Trotsky's "Dustbin of History" with all those other geopolitical has-beens.

I ticked fingertips. Twelve extinctions in seventy-odd years; not a bad tally for one lifetime. And yet, despite their previous glory, each had proved that King Solomon was right when he concluded: "All are of the dust, and turn to dust again..."

I packed away the borrowed tackle, my reputation as a fisherman secure, even if it has inevitably dwindled since *Anglers' World* went out of business, although a trickle of royalties from my guidebooks continues to prove that I am not entirely forgotten.

"What d'you say to these, eh?!" Tom interrupted my wandering thoughts as he bustled though the open doorway, proudly displaying a nice pair of rainbow trout. "Didn't I promise it would be fun today!"

Norah had packed our lunch basket with everything two old codgers could possibly want, including a chilled half of Bollinger. My host lit the gas barbecue and insisted on demonstrating his skill as a chef by grilling fillets of trout brushed with a rosemary twig dipped in olive oil, a twist of pepper, a pinch of salt, and a squeeze of lemon. All too fussy for a man, like myself, accustomed to frying his catch on a shovel blade or roasting it over a campfire's embers, impaled on a twig, but it was obvious to me that Tom felt a third person present at our improvised feast, and was keen to prove that nothing had been lost of her culinary art.

"Cheers!" We clinked glasses and tucked into the potato salad and coleslaw.

After a while he set down his eating irons and settled back in the camp chair, replete. "Didn't I promise it would be fun today?" He was still seeking my reassurance.

To the extent that I am able, I reached out to give support and encouragement. "You've got a splendid homestead, Tom, one in a million. You have every reason to be proud and happy with what you've achieved…"

"Every reason, except one."

"Point taken," I agreed, quietly.

"Then, you, understand?" he persisted, looking hard at the plain gold ring on my small left finger.

"Yes."

"Not easy, is it?"

"No. It's not." I gripped the chair arms and stood with moderate effort. "Come along, your fish must be thinking we've forgotten them."

17

The afternoon shadows were lengthening by the time Reg' Birtley collected us from the Dam. Tom was more subdued than he had been earlier in the day, as we drove down to the Cottage to unload our catch. From there we dutifully obeyed Norah's instructions to make ourselves scarce while her husband lit the barbecue, she tossed the salads, and we ambled back to the Big House for drinks on the veranda.

"Good health." Tom raised his tumbler of Balvenie single malt to which I responded with a finger of the same Scotch, topped up with Perrier water. "It has been a good day, hasn't it?"

"Definitely." There was no mistaking another widower's need for support, surrounded by so many reminders of happier times.

We fell silent and watched dusk filling the estate's hollows and dells, clefts, and ridgelines. In imagination I flipped open my sketchbook and selected a 4B pencil to depict a nearby stand of trees, when Tom gave an awkward cough as we elderly men tend to do when preparing to revisit the past. "It's a rummy old world…"

"Mm?" I felt sure he was about to resume our earlier talk of ghosts and coping with loss, but instead it was another conversation he needed to revisit.

"Assuming the Chinese do colonise us, they'll read 'Akilinos' on the map and not suspect its origins any more than we know the true meaning of 'Yarra,' or 'Dandenong.'" He stared into his empty glass. "It'll be like we were never here."

I laid aside my imaginary pencil and caught his eye. "Tom, a word to the wise. Firstly, go easy with the grog. Secondly, the enemies you should be concerned about are already entrenched among us."

He blinked. "Who d'you mean?"

"Take note," I continued in a flat, cautionary tone. "'A nation can survive its fools, but it cannot survive treason from within. An enemy at the gates is less formidable than the traitor who moves freely behind them. His sly whispers are heard in the halls of government, for the traitor appears not a traitor. He speaks in accents familiar to his victims and appeals to the baseness deep in the hearts of all men. He corrupts the soul of the nation, working secretly in the night to infect the body politic so that it can no longer resist his stealthy poison. A murderer is less to fear…'"

"Says who?!"

"Cicero." I deliberately pronounced that ancient Roman orator's name as "Sisseroh," having no pretensions to a Classical Education, except that informally acquired while teaching myself Latin at St Mary's parish church in Kalgoorlie, by memorising Father Declan's sonorous prayers in their original tongue. "Allegedly recorded sometime after the Catiline Conspiracy drowned in its own blood. Whether or not he wrote it or a more recent, more perceptive author, I'm in no position to say, but in all other respects it rings ominously true…"

"Good Lord." Tom sat up straighter. "You attended Melbourne Grammar for less than a day? And never went up to university? Where on earth did you learn all that?!"

"Petrograd, mostly"

"Do tell!"

"There's nothing more to tell," I replied, firmly closing the door on a time and place. "Meantime stop looking to Peking for future threats when there's treason aplenty in our nation's capital, already."

"Meaning?" Said in the severe tone of a man accustomed to judging others. "I am not very patient with opaque riddles."

"Very well, Your Honour, return in imagination to the Second War, during which Australia emerged as a middle-ranking industrial power capable of building the Mosquito fighter-bomber, to pick but one example of advanced manufacturing skills." I paused for him to picture the thought. "Now show me anything more complex than an electric toaster, 'Made in Australia.'"

"Your point being?"

"That persons of trust and authority conspired, with foreign interests, to ensure that Australia reverted to the export of cheap raw materials which we now buy back, at great expense, as the essential goods we once made for ourselves. I'd say this was a clear case of industrial sabotage and political treason, wouldn't you?"

He stiffened. "I've never thought of it that way before, but surely -?"

"Few ever have," I interrupted, finger tapping the chair arm to emphasise what I was about to say, "that is why treason triumphs. For when it does: 'None dare call it treason.' Another quotation that every thinking person should read, mark, learn, and inwardly digest, as the *Anglican Book of Common Prayer* counsels us to do with other matters of existential importance..."

Mr Justice Hartigan was not about to let this witness stand down. "Don't be offended Ian, but I've never thought of you as a Conspiracy Theorist."

"I'm not. There was sufficient Conspiracy Fact, in a former life, for me to recognise the parentage of those Benevolent Bolsheviks who hoodwinked Australia into signing the United Nations' Lima Declaration, eleven or twelve years ago."

"And what, exactly, are we speaking of?!"

"An international agreement that dismantled Australia's factories and shipped them to low-wage Third World countries, thinly disguised as 'humanitarian aid...'" I let him to mark, learn, and inwardly digest this fact as well. "Once you have identified who these deluded creatures are, and whose interests they secretly serve, you'll have solved many an otherwise baffling mystery."

"Oh, come now! No sensible businessman would ever do a thing like that!"

"True," I nodded in agreement. "That is, until international tariff agreements and market manipulations force him out of business -"

"But why?" Tom interrupted. "It doesn't make sense!"

"True again," I nodded once more, "but only while we deal with normal, common-sense people in a normal, common-sense world. However, that world is a vastly different place, viewed through the spiteful, jealous, destructive, disruptive prism of Marxist activism. At which point, it all becomes powerfully clear –"

"Not to me!"

"It would, had you been in Petrograd, during the summer of 1920 -" I stopped short and abruptly changed subject. "Tom, believe me, high matters of state are invariably decided by cold hearts and cool heads before being baited with sentimental tosh for an emotional public to swallow whole.

"The frothy AgitProp activists we see chanting slogans and waving their placards on the streets, are the modern equivalent of Lenin's *Poleznyii Idiotii* or 'Useful Idiots.' Gullible idealists who imagine that after they've overthrown the existing social order, by promoting minority grudges and grievances, their new masters will permit them to erect fairy-tale castles of rainbow splendour in its place."

"But -?"

"That is not the way the world wags or ever has done since Cain ambushed Abel in the Garden of Eden," I continued. "The last thought inside many an Old Comrade's head, forced to his knees on the Lubyanka's cellar floor, an NKVD executioner's pistol prodding his bowed neck, must have been that the Czar's corrupt rule wasn't so bad after all."

"But surely -!"

"Every revolution - the American, the French, the Russian, the German National Socialist, and whatever comes next – needs its cadre of hardmen to destroy rivals, enforce discipline, and liquidate Idiots who are no longer Useful. These are usually the same political innocents who believed the Party's promises; 'Bog Paper' is a tradecraft expression that best describes their fate..."

"Stop right there!" Tom raised a warning finger. "I know of whom you speak and most strongly disagree with your description of them as deluded or gullible. Those I have worked with are, without exception, highly intelligent men, and woman, educated well above the average. Idiots they are not! I hate to say it, but you are wrong!"

I let my gaze rest on the darkening woodland scene before responding with audible weariness. "Tom, the more schooling a person has, the easier it is to warp his opinions and twist thoughts howsoever we please. Why else are Comrade Marx's disciples so contemptuous of the poorly educated *Lumpenproletariat* they pretend to serve, but who as Trotsky himself assured me, are: 'Wet logs on the bonfire of revolution'"?

"I beg your pardon!"

"Whereas, by stroking the egos of the intellectually ambitious while, at the same time, declaring in awestruck tones how wonderfully clever they are, we mould them like clay in a potter's hands..."

"That is so, patronising!"

"No. It is the political equivalent of Newton's Universal Law of Gravitation." I studied my own hands, quietly folded in their lap, before looking up again. "Useful Idiots have only a limited utility in the rough and ready world of *Realpolitik*. As the Red Guards demonstrated when they massacred seven or eight thousand Baltic Fleet sailors whose courage and faith had, earlier, rescued the Revolution from defeat -"

"But not in a democracy like ours!"

"Really?"

"Really!"

"Then what is 'democracy'?" I enquired. "Is it not the popular delusion that every citizen has an equal voice in the running of his or her country? In truth, it is the disciplined minority who decide - in secret - what the undisciplined, befuddled majority will do, when given their marching orders. Or else!"

"Or else, what?!"

I felt it was time to end on a conciliatory note. "Tom? Advise your clever friends that it is a fatal error, common to all *intelligentsia*, to imagine that the

Long March of History can be halted at their behest. They should think very carefully before undermining a charitable society that tolerates their sulks and tantrums. Not only is it ungrateful to 'bite the hand that feeds,' the Law of Unintended Consequences is also the Great Leveller, one that never fails to strike down the unwary," I reminded him, with a sober frown, before concluding: "*Gulag otdayet predatelyam bol' i smert* which, roughly translated, means: 'The concentration camp rewards treason with suffering and death.' As true now as it ever was in Stalin's Russia when *Narodnikii Komissariat Vnurennikh Del'* arrested those Old Bolsheviks who stormed the barricades in 1917 but who, nineteen years later, had outlived their usefulness.

"Nobody will ever know how many tens of thousands were shot by order of Comrade Yagoda," I continued, leaning forward to make my point. "Who was then shot by order of his successor, Comrade Yezhov. Who suffered the same fate by order of his successor, Comrade Beria. Who in turn was sentenced to death by a *Politburo* chaired by Comrade Khruschev. Who amazingly expired of natural causes a few years ago, in a Moscow retirement home for senior *Nomenklatura*."

"That may be so in a barbarous society like the Soviet Union, but not in a democracy founded upon the Rule of Law!"

"You hope," I replied, sadly, aware that our vastly different experiences of the world made further discussion fruitless. Even so I could not let the matter drop without one final attempt to inform and alert: "Tom? Revolutions of every stripe mimic the Ancient Roman god Saturn who ate his own children, to prevent them conspiring against him. Expressed simply: Monday's Radicals are Wednesday's Moderates, are Friday's Enemies of the People, are executed on Sunday."

Mr Justice Hartigan had regained his composure. "Why are you telling me all this?"

"As wise old colleague was wont to say on similar occasions: 'Think about it, and report what you discover,'" I replied with an inoffensive smile.

It was Tom's turn to lean forward, determined to have the last word. "During my time on the High Court, we heard matters of State Security *in camera*. Usually there was a 'Mr Smith' from Secret Intelligence to assist our deliberations. However, unlike the popular image of that 'James Bond' chap, our man was an unremarkable individual who arrived by taxi, never in a flashy sports car. But when he spoke, there was a tone of voice, a choice of subject matter, an analytical style of address, that immediately gave his game away. Which tells me that your guidebooks and articles for *Angler's World* were window dressing. I can only guess what else you were doing in the shop behind them, but we've known each other long enough to drop the pretence -"

"You two!" Norah interrupted, calling across the rose garden. "Dinner's ready!"

18

We took our places *en famille*; Mother seated nearest the servery, Father at the other end of the kitchen table, their two children seated opposite Tom and me. All refreshingly formal in an age of gobbled snacks and what I believe are called Tele Vision Dinners, an impression strengthened when Reg' bowed his head to thank the Lord Jesus for His many blessings.

Norah looked up, smiling, and urged us to get started on the venison. I took my time, in imagination teasing out the backstory that connected a knockabout bush mechanic, with a disturbed Vietnam veteran, with this sober Victorian paterfamilias. I sensed the common thread was his choice of a wife, probably the devout follower of some born-again Christian sect who had restored his faith, in every meaning of the phrase.

I could not help wondering if Percy Black was somewhere in his family's bloodline, the resemblance being so uncanny when Reg' glanced past his boss and fixed me with a piercing look I remember well. "'Hope you don't mind me asking, but what did you mean, telling the kids about a Sergeants' Mess this morning...?"

"Oh, just a bit of historical colour," I replied lightly. "'Mess' was an apt name for our grubby corner of the canteen hut where a few pence would buy half a pint of slosh and five Woodies." Adding, artfully: Much the same as your war, I suppose?"

"Yeah. Much the same."

I sensed an opportunity for him to open, now that we had established a common ground of experiences in uniform, a breakthrough I planned to develop once we were free to chat after dinner. Instead, Tom thought he was helping when he proudly announced that tonight's guest had been decorated with a Distinguished Conduct Medal at Gallipoli, a second one in France, and later still a Military Cross in the Royal Flying Corps.

Our conversation dropped stone cold dead. The MC is an officers-only award, which meant there was no way a conscripted Other Rank, like Reg' Birtley, would open-up to a member of the often despised, always distrusted Officer Class. For a moment there had been a good chance of building trust, while I wore three ghostly chevrons on my sleeve, but none now, with imagined pips on my shoulder.

I could have strangled Tom for his insensitive interjection; happily, the family's daughter was unaware of this. "We're doing Gallipoli." She spoke as if it were a core subject, like Maths or Chemistry. "What was it all about?"

"Julie! Enough!" In that moment I heard echoes of discord whenever a more recent war was alluded to at this table.

"It's all right ma'am," I smiled, "that's a question I've been asking myself for many a long year and am still no nearer to finding an answer that makes sense. As for the Dardanelles Campaign itself," I continued, facing young Julie again, "you'll get bonus marks for your essay if you mention that it was fought on a far wider front, and for much greater issues than our cramped little Anzac Cove beachhead."

"Why was that?" Julie persisted.

I glanced at the other end of the table, seeking Reg's silent approval, before answering. "We-ell, without becoming too complicated, most people are unaware that the French and the British, the Indian Army and the Newfoundland Regiment, the Russian Navy too, were also invading Turkey, as well as the Australian & New Zealand Army Corps."

"'Invading'?" the young girl frowned.

"That's what it's usually called when one foreign army, or in this case several foreign armies, attack another country," I explained, aware that I was going against the grain of a popular myth. "However, for a variety of reasons you can nut out for yourself, it was doomed from the start. A familiar situation in more recent wars," I added, with another sidelong glance at Reg' Birtley's intent face. "Yet even at the worst of times there were compensations. Trapped under fire one soon learns who can be trusted and who can't." I paused, aiming the next sentence at her father: "Luckily, I had two good cobbers, Harry Murray and Percy Black…"

Disappointed by the last name's lack of impact on Reg', I concluded my brief excursion into a bygone era. "At war's end, Harry was a one-pip colonel and Australia's most highly decorated soldier, but even he said that Percy Black, a Westralian gold prospector originally from a small town only a few miles from here in Victoria, was 'the coolest, bravest man I have ever known…'"

There was still not a flicker of recognition as I restated my old mate's name and details. It was worth a shot. Folk wisdom asserts that only a wise man knows who his father was; it requires supernatural clairvoyance to know what mischief grandma got up to as a flirty teenager.

Resigned to my loss, I focused instead on an excellent homecooked meal just as the young son took his chance to quiz me about something overheard a few moments before. "The Flying Corps means you flew?!"

"A bit."

"I saw a film about the Red Baron and -!"

"Alan!" Dad's voice would have stripped the bark off an ironwood tree at ten paces. "Mr Cribdon does not want to be reminded of such stuff." Reg' was quick on the uptake, no doubt thanks to a lot of "stuff" he had no wish to be reminded of himself.

"Ohhh!"

Touched by the young boy's misplaced enthusiasm, I held up my hand in the universal sign of peace. "It's alright by me, Reg', if it's alright by you. Curiosity is natural in the young. How else are they going to cope with later life?" I interpreted the father's silence as assent, before glancing back across the table and dipping a conspiratorial wink. "So, tell us about the film."

Young Alan now had an adult's permission to talk at table, a rare treat in this household. "Well, there was a German pilot, Rickoffen, who flew a red plane, which shot down heaps and heaps of…" The young lad wilted under Dad's roasting glare.

"Indeed, he did," I agreed, with a nostalgic half-smile. "Not that our paths crossed except once, at his funeral, which is probably why you and I are speaking now. A plodding 'Harry Tate' was just the sort of prey he preferred to hunt." I saw the lad's bewilderment and elaborated: "That's rhyming slang for an RE8 reconnaissance-bomber. The real Mr Tate was a music hall comedian at a time when laughs were in short supply."

"You a pilot then?!"

"No, I was required to do rather more than sit in the front seat and drive."
I felt an old familiar urge to defend the honour of we undervalued Brethren of
the Single Wing whenever anyone compared us with our chauffeur whose
alleged superior status was rewarded with a two-winged brevet at the end of
training. "You could say that I, and others like me, were the reason why those
so-called aces became 'famous' in the first place..."

"How?" Reg' Birtley was closely monitoring this conversation.

"Well, among our several duties, observers were tasked with making aerial
photographic surveys of Fritz's trenches, troop movements, and supply dumps;
map-read for pilots who frequently hadn't a clue where we were; and register
our artillery's counter-battery by transmitting Morse signals from an open
cockpit not much bigger than a baby's pram."

I deliberately left out any mention of aerial gunnery, knowing it would
prompt questions I had no wish to answer. Instead, I gave a self-effacing smile.
"Meaning we either flew straight and level, for much of the time, or else orbited
enemy lines, spotting 'fall of shot.' In either case, easy prey for ack-ack on the
ground, and Fokkers in the sky."

Norah winced.

"That is not what you think you heard, ma'am," I explained evenly.
"Anthony Fokker was a Dutch designer of notable fighter aeroplanes for the
Imperial German Flying Service. But I'm sure you've heard all this before," I
concluded, with another modest smile. "So, allow me the opportunity to thank
you Reg', and you Norah, also you Julie and Allan, for allowing me to share
your family meal. It's a rare pleasure at this end of my life."

I was finding it harder to conceal my annoyance. Not at my hosts, of course
but at the persistent hero worship of pilots like von Richthofen and, to be fair,
his opposite numbers on our side, for I can become quite tetchy whenever ill-
informed praise is heaped on those high-scoring aces of the Great War.

The popular impression of fighter pilots as gallant Knights of the Sky
jousting above the Western Front's ignoble filth and squalor conceals a grim
truth; their sole purpose was the destruction of observation biplanes like my
lumbering RE8 and, earlier in the war, the FE2, itself little better than a manned
box kite with a pusher prop'.

I was too close to the action to see how unevenly matched we were at the
time. It was only later, on a visit to Germany during which my old neighbour in
Sweden insisted I accompany him to the *Gedenkmuseum Richthofen* at
Schweidnitz, that I saw evidence of what I had long suspected; more than half
of the Red Baron's eighty kills were reconnaissance twin-seaters. He was the
falcon; we were his sparrows.

My host at that time was in high spirits as he recounted his own victories
while commanding *Jagdtstaffel Richthofen* after the Ace-of-Aces was shot down
by an Australian Lewis gunner firing from the ground, for nobody could ever
accuse Hermann Goering of excessive tact or sensitivity.

"Are you feeling alright?!" Tom was clearly worried as he unintentionally
derailed my train of thought.

"Couldn't be better." I managed to smile. "Carry on talking. I'm happy to
listen."

19

"I'm awfully sorry Ian," Tom apologised, "I think I rather put my foot in it, back there." We had finished dinner and, as good guests ought to do, left the Cottage soon after the last dishes were cleared away.

"How do you mean?" I enquired, without breaking step towards the Big House, cane tapping along a footpath dimly lit by our borrowed electric torch.

"Your war record; I thought it might help; the look on your face said otherwise."

"You meant well," I shrugged. "Besides the children won't mind. One day they will be able to tell their grandchildren how they met the pilot who shot down 'Red Baron Rickoffen' at Gallipoli, for such are the vagaries of memory."

"That's very decent of you. I feared it might've spoiled something you were setting up."

We paused at the veranda steps. "Am I that transparently devious?"

"One cannot partner at Bridge for as long as we have, and not get a good idea of how the other person's mind works," he replied simply.

"Guilty as charged," I chuckled. "I should know better than to try bluffing one of Her Majesty's principal justices."

"True." He lit the way for me to go ahead. "So, what was it you were trying to discover?"

"A personal matter," I replied, pausing again at the head of the steps. "There's a chance your manager might be related to that old mate of mine, killed in '17."

"Percy Black?" Tom opened the French doors and stepped aside while I limped past.

"Yes." I paused as the doors shut and my host went ahead to light the fire and pour drinks. "I owe him an immense debt of gratitude; this might have been a way to repay it in some small measure."

Tom put the matches back on the mantelpiece. "How?"

"Well," I began cautiously, "you have to imagine me as a cocky young know-all before arriving at Blackboy Camp, a few miles inland from Perth," I explained, setting the scene. "Opinionated, brim-full of self-importance, an accomplished *habitué* of billiard halls, slick with the false shuffle and palmed ace, it would not have been long before I was up on a charge and earning the first blot on my military record."

"But clearly you did not," Tom frowned, joining me nearer the fire, glass in hand, "or else you would never have been thrice decorated or commissioned."

"Correct. So now you know why I owe Percy so much." I finished pouring a measure of Perrier over a finger of Scotch and raised my drink in silent salute to the immortal memory of Major P.C.H. Black DSO, DCM.

"Sorry, I don't. What do you mean?"

"It's painfully simple," I grimaced. "He gave me a proper thumping after I'd cheeked him, for he was one hell of a fighter. He then picked me up, dusted me down, and explained several home truths about life as an adult before inviting me to be Number Three on his gun."

"Phew!" Tom surveyed the crackling firelight through his drink's amber glow. "Quite a story, but what's the connection with our Reg'?"

"Their appearances are identical. If there were a connection, I wanted to say how proud Reg' and his children should be to have such a fine gentleman on their family tree…"

"Hm, you may be right, but we'll never know."

"Why is that?"

"He was raised at St Joseph's Orphanage near Kinkumber. The nuns picked 'Birtley' from a telephone book. Our Mr Reginald has come a long way."

"Thanks to Norah?"

"Very much so."

"Well then, should he ever mention feelings of loss, or of lacking a proper family name, suggest it could be 'Black'," I replied. "Percy often spoke of his parents migrating to Victoria from Northern Ireland, with a sizeable brood of children, so there must be surviving relatives, if Reg' asks around."

"You really think there's a connection?"

"I'd bet a pound to a penny it being so."

"Then I'll have a word with Norah, she'll know how to handle him."

"As I imagine she always does," I remarked, neutrally.

"Meaning?"

"You and I, at the end of our wars, were hailed as 'heroes,'" I stared into the fireplace as kindling flames licked thicker logs. "He came back to be reviled at student demonstrations organised by Australia's homegrown traitors. Even the Returned Services League gave them the cold shoulder. It was not our nation's finest hour."

"'Traitors'?" Tom was not sure he had heard me correctly.

"Correct." I reached for my cane and leaned forward to give one of the logs a poke before it fell into the hearth. "As said earlier, whenever you see young people getting frothy over some fashionable grudge or imagined grievance, you can bet there are *Agitatsiya Apparatchikii* in the shadows, supplying the banners, the slogans, the money, the stage management. For nowadays there are few if any Percy Blacks to straighten-out the young before they get too bitter and twisted." I glanced up again. "Crowds are easily swayed by appeals to their hurt feelings. But regardless of whatever the placards are proclaiming, the real object of that stunt is sure to be something quite else…"

Tom remained thoughtfully quiet before finally glancing up and breaking the silence. "I envy you."

"Meaning…?"

"A lifetime of adventure is something most of us can only dream of."

"Steady on! It was by no means 'roses, roses all the way.'"

"Of course not, nobody's life is." He looked around at the material evidence of success as a Queens Counsel before ascent to the High Court and Australia's highest honours. "I didn't want any of this; others wanted it for me. I just tagged along to please her family."

"Tom," I cautioned, "Scotch is best sipped with water, not gulped neat, like lemonade. Please don't spoil a memorable weekend by becoming sentimental."

"In other words, drunk?"

"I didn't say that -"

"It's what you inferred."

I shook my head. "I've lived and worked and served with enough drunks to know it's not your style, however there is a lesser level of boozed sentimentality."

"And that's where you think I am?"

"Not yet, but be careful."

"'Careful'?" His was not a happy laugh. "That's all I've ever been. One could say that only now am I making up for decades of abstinence during which I was 'sober as a judge' in every meaning of the phrase. Now that I am no longer one, and alone, with time on my hands, I can allow myself some indulgence." He swirled his tumbler and peered at me over the rim. "D'you know what I most wanted to be in life?"

"No."

"A train driver."

"Most boys do," I observed drily, "after they've learned the limitations of life as a pirate of the Caribbean."

"I am not joking!" He recovered his composure. "My maternal grandfather told such wonderful stories of how good it felt to haul out of Sydney Central, leaving the city far behind as he sped his passengers through the Blue Mountains. To be like him, a master of flying pistons, and wheels, and connecting rods, with the roar of steam and the rush of wind in my ears, thundering through the night, would have been the very height of bliss. And at the end of my shift, to joke, and chaff, and be at ease with other men of my class and kind…"

"Tom. Don't glamourise the Proletariat. Only those who've had an easy start in life can afford such luxury."

He wasn't listening. "Instead, I did all the 'right' things. Dux of Scotch College, then up to university. A good First, followed by Articles with a leading law firm. I was the archetypal golden hamster on his little treadmill, running ever faster and faster to remain on the same damn' spot!" He recovered himself again. "The only time I have ever felt truly alive was on Crete, with Jerry hunting me from village to village."

He waved a careless hand at the rich furnishings and trappings of worldly success. "Irene wanted this. I went along with her, just as I've gone along with everyone, to please them. But eventually even she realised how pointless it was and agreed to start again, in rural Provence. And then she died, leaving me alone in a ridiculously expensive brick and timber box that feels more like a tomb than a home."

"Tom, enough! That's whisky talking. I don't wish to hear your maudlin apologies in the morning -"

"Ian. Be careful. I can easily take offense," he replied with a leaden frown, "although I shan't, for I know you mean well, but don't presume upon our friendship." He put his glass on a small side table. "Change of subject. Where did you learn to fish so expertly?"

"Long story short," I shrugged, "by a lake in Sweden, during the summer and autumn of '19."

"What in Heaven's name prompted you to go there?"

"'War weariness,'" I replied simply. "The Swedes had stayed neutral during the previous five years, which told me they were the only sensible people in a world gone mad, and God knows I needed sane company."

'Did you find it?'

"Yes, thanks to a local businessman who loaned me his summerhouse, one very similar to yours up at the dam. Not that I caught many fish at first. I'd have gone hungry had I depended on what the lake was supposed to have in abundance, though fortunately he left a motorbike in the shed so I could do my ration runs to the nearest town."

"What changed?"

For a moment, I hesitated. No great harm would have been done had I broken a redundant oath of secrecy and told the truth for once, but the camouflage of a lifetime is not easily cast aside. Instead, I retold a well-rehearsed cover story: "One of his business associates, apart from being a keen angler, had just returned from Russia and was also in need of sane company. We got along famously well; it was he who taught me how to tie lures, make casts, and feast like a king from Vättern's teeming perch, and char, and trout."

"1919?" Mr Justice Hartigan was back on the bench, questioning a witness. "Wasn't that the Russian Revolution?"

"No, by then it had become their Civil War."

"So, what was a businessman doing among mad anarchists and bomb-throwing Bolsheviks?"

"'Fishing in troubled waters' by seeking to profit from others' misfortune, like buying Fabergé jewellery from impoverished aristocrats."

"How did you become involved?"

"He discovered I spoke a bit of Russian. His was only basic so we teamed-up and returned to Petrograd for more black-market contraband."

"How did that work out?"

"Badly. The Red Terror was getting into its stride. Not a good time or place to be a shady foreigner doing dodgy deals. We bribed our way back over the Finnish border, reached Stockholm, and cut our losses. I returned to the lake, a poorer and wiser man; he returned to Berlin's underworld and disappeared."

Tom fell silent. After a short while he looked up again. "What an exciting life you've led." The aching sadness in his voice was painful to hear. "Nothing like that ever happened to me…"

"Then count yourself lucky. But speaking of time," I finished my drink and reached for the cane, "it's been a long day; I need to 'consult the pillow,' as they say in Madrid."

"Don't be in too great a hurry to get started." Tom also stood and shook hands. "We've still got lots more to see and do tomorrow."

20

Something happened to Tom during the night. Rather than doing what was planned for today, he insisted we go back to Melbourne, claiming that the drive would be easier on Sunday, there being fewer heavy lorries and tankers to contend with. As his guest and passenger, I could hardly disagree, though I can spot a feeble excuse as well as any other man.

There was no way I knew the real reasons for wanting to get away from Akilinos so quickly, but if prompted I would hazard a guess that some memory of his wife and their lives together had overwhelmed him during the early hours of the morning. Thus, after finishing a muted breakfast at the Cottage and saying our farewells, we walked back to the Big House.

The Range Rover was still where it parked on Friday. Then, just as we were about to climb aboard, Norah hurried across from the rose bed, a raincape gripped around her shoulders, a pair of secateurs and a bunch of fresh red blooms in the other hand, their stems wrapped in aluminium foil. Tom shared a sad smile. "Thank you."

"We do hope you'll both be back soon," Norah replied reassuringly, "the kids can't stop talking about Mr Cribdon." She was still waving goodbye in my rear vision wing mirror when we turned down the track.

As is often the case after a spell in the country, nobody felt like talking on the return drive to the city, only pausing once, at Lilydale where Tom left the highway and drove up Victoria Road to the town's hilltop Lawn Cemetery.

"Wait here," he said, backing out from the driver's seat, gripping the roses and an umbrella. "I won't be long."

"Take all the time you need," I replied, also dismounting. "There's someone here I haven't seen for a long while."

We parted company at the head of the asphalt path, and he continued along a familiar route to a memorial plaque that, I later learned, reads:

Irene Elizabeth Hartigan
Beloved wife of the Hon. Thomas Hartigan AC, MC
1918-1985

I meanwhile paced the other way, recalling Aunt Lucinda's elocution lessons artfully disguised as parlour recitations. *Grey's Elegy Written in a Country Churchyard* seemed particularly appropriate today as I picked my way downhill towards a raised enclosure within a privet hedge. Here I removed my hat, as if about to enter church, and ascended six broad steps to confront a massive stone block inscribed:

Dame
Nellie Melba
G.B.E

Planted foursquare atop a paved plinth on which was carved in a triumphant Trajan font:

ADDIO SENZA RANCOR

I have always felt there needs to be a comma after the first word, and an exclamation mark at the end of this line from Act 3 of *Boheme*, for the Helen Mitchell I first knew as youngster – myself, not her - was never less than emphatic in everything she undertook.

Hot sparks of artistic temperament flew during her rehearsals at Tralee House. Both she and Aunt Lucinda were perfectionists, each of whom held strong opinions on how a musical phrase should be sung, so it was not surprising that the two rarely agreed. And yet, just as a knife blade needs a whetstone and buffing wheel to perform at its best, their abrasive sessions at our Bechstein piano helped further cut and polish Melba's already acclaimed voice and delivery.

I have often asked myself why this impressively famous woman acceded to the advice and admonitions of a - by then - faded luminary. Perhaps it was her tacit acknowledgment of the Antipodean Nightingale's trailblazing career that prepared the operatic world for Melba's stunning debut a generation later?

I have read accounts of how tight-fisted she could be, some ascribing it to her Scottish heritage, and how she was not above sabotaging a rival's chances in the opera houses of Europe, but as the mother of a boy herself, she never minded me sitting in a corner of our Music Room, sketchbook on lap, silently observing as I worked at my pencil studies.

In hindsight I think she suspected the true relationship between Lucinda Cribdon and a previously unknown "nephew." It probably tickled her sense of the dramatic to imagine me as a rescued street urchin, like the youngsters whose chorus opens Act 3 of *Boheme*.

Standing bareheaded before the tomb, fifty-six years after her state funeral, it dawned on me that I am probably one of the last remaining persons to remember Melba at the peak of her vocal powers before those later, money-grubbing Farewell Performances became an unkind joke.

I also recognised how privileged I'd been to share time with her during the Golden Age of our young nation's brief history. Decades during which Europe's preeminent artists and performers competed to appear in Melbourne, then the largest and wealthiest city in the Southern Hemisphere, brought here by Aunt Lucinda's old friend and business partner the American entrepreneur James Williamson, before going on to Sydney and New Zealand.

A select few were always glad of the invitation to rest and recuperate at Tralee House. Celebrities like *Le Rossignol's* young protégée in Paris, Sarah Bernhardt; the dazzling American actress Maxine Elliott; and the London D'Oyly Carte Opera Company on their frequent Australasian tours for the J. C. Williamson theatrical empire. None of whom minded in the least when a precocious young boy strode up to them and held out his autograph album - now sadly lost - for them to inscribe.

A lifetime later, standing at Melba's tomb, my wisps of white hair damp and forlorn on this grey and mournful day, those distant memories seemed bathed in eternal sunlight, especially one balmy afternoon when someone proposed an impromptu skit on our croquet lawn.

As might be expected, Aunt Lucinda forgot that she was supposed to be retired and got peals of happy laughter for her comic interpretation of Ruth, the aged nursemaid whose original deafness is the cause of much confusion in Gilbert's topsy-turvy libretto for *The Pirates of Penzance*. Followed soon afterwards by a buxom Melba parodying *The Major General's Song* in a fruity contralto that had her audience in stitches.

None of which seemed remarkable to me at the time. These were not Famous Names to be dropped in conversation, these were our family friends having fun, just like anyone else. But of course, they were not just anyone else, and only later did I understand their human need to be accepted as fallible men and women in the most demanding of professions, while briefly shielded from their fickle public's unblinking gaze.

"*Addio, senza rancor!*" I bowed and replaced my hat. "'Cheerio, no hard feelings!' Rest well, ma'am, and thanks for all the memories…" Then, cane tapping ahead, I returned to the carpark as lowering skies began to weep.

Tom had already returned and was seated behind the wheel. He reached across to unlatch the passengers' door and waited till I was settled in, seatbelt locked. "Family?"

"An old friend," I replied, wiping rain off my face and neck, before my collar and shirt got too wet.

"How fortunate you are." He reached to key the ignition, then changed his mind and leaned forward, arms across the steering wheel, brow resting on his wrists. "In Law, one does not have friends." He spoke to the instrument panel. "Colleagues and rivals aplenty, for both terms may be freely interchanged and lose not one scintilla of meaning. Enemies too, among the villains one puts away, or among those defendants for whom one failed to secure an acquittal when pleading their case. And there are always the crooked politicians, the acerbic newspaper columnists, the devastated lives, we must deal with."

He straightened with effort, pushing backwards while gripping the wheel with both hands. "I think it was W.S.Gilbert who wrote: 'A policeman's lot is not a happy one…'"

"Yes. *Pirates of Penzance*. Act 2."

"A judge's lot is not particularly joyful either." Still speaking to himself, Tom turned away and stared through the rain-streaked side window. "One must contain such dreadful things, professional secrets, kept forever on pain of disbarment. Spanning the whole putrid rubbish dump of human sin and error, from high crimes and misdemeanours to sordid acts that no decent man, raised like you and I were, could possibly imagine."

I said nothing.

"It is alleged that one cannot touch tar without at least some of it sticking to the fingers; it's the same when dealing with crime and punishment. At least my grandfather could go home at night to wash off the railway's dirt; his grandson was never that lucky."

"Tom. Stop. I don't wish to hear any more."

He took no notice, still facing the window, warm breath condensing on cold glass. "During the six years of our partnership at Bridge, I have never known you to gossip or speak ill of others, not once. This tells me you can be trusted to keep a confidence, just as others mightier than I, have trusted your high and confidential services for the Empire. After all," he added, with a sad smile, "that CMG didn't pop out of a Christmas cracker, did it?"

"No comment."

"You really are the very soul of discretion," he continued quietly. "That's why I respect and value your trust in me, or else you would never have spoken, as you did at the summer house, yesterday."

"Which has nothing to do with today." I was necessarily sharp for I had no wish to pursue this subject any further.

"On the contrary, I believe it does." He turned from the window and looked at me in profile. "Do you know what I did, last night?"

"Of course not!"

"I also killed a young man, ripe with unfulfilled hopes and dreams. Only, instead of bullets, I used my bare hands -"

"Stop right there!"

"We were on Crete." He disobeyed my command. "I think the chap must've been a rear echelon clerk or storeman, hunting for souvenirs of the recent battle. Looking for somewhere to relieve himself, he stepped behind a thicket of bushes and almost fell into the cave where local villagers had hidden myself and nine others, until a boat could be found for our escape to Egypt."

I remained silent.

"In a moment he was going to bolt and raise the alarm. As the senior officer present, I gave him a friendly smile, raised my hands, took two paces forward as if about to surrender, and launched the best rugby tackle I have ever done, slamming him flat on the ground. There was no question of us keeping a prisoner, nor could I let him go. My foremost duty was to those brave civilians who were risking everything to assist us. And so, I strangled him."

"Difficult."

"Quite." He paused, gathering his thoughts. "It would not be long before someone noted his absence and sent out a search party. Equally certain was that the bruises of manual strangulation are a self-evident cause of death. So, after recovering his body, the villagers would be rounded up and shot. And even if we did lose the corpse down a ravine, those same villagers would still soon be murdered."

Tom had no reason to say more. This was a scene that played many times in Occupied France. "What action did you take?" I asked.

"I searched his haversack. He'd been souveniring spent cartridges and charger clips, stuff he could send home to show that their son, or brother, or husband was a frontline hero. The one thing an army post office was never going to let him send back to Germany, was an unexploded Mills bomb, the sort you must have encountered many times in the army?"

"Many times."

"Then you can imagine what happens when a grenade explodes high under the chest of a strangled serviceman, dumped in a gully alongside his bag of bits and pieces, as corroborative evidence?"

"Yes."

"It was getting dark and there'd soon be a roll call. We had to move fast, dragging him as far away as possible from our cave. As the senior officer present, it was my duty to run an improvised string - bootlaces, rifle pull-throughs, knotted strips of rag - away from the grenade and behind cover. A sharp tug, sufficient to release the unpinned firing lever, and 'whoomph!' I then recovered the string, making sure the pin was where a field investigation team would expect to find it, on their dead soldier's left thumb, and dived back into the cave almost before the echo stopped rolling around the valley."

"Well done."

"Thank you." He straightened. "It saved us and saved our village, for a while longer, when Jerry's military police concluded that one of their own had been messing about with enemy ordnance and blown himself up."

"And the moral of this story is?" I sensed there was more yet to come of his confessional.

"I finally told Irene about it a few minutes ago," he replied, quietly. "I used to dread the thought of her imagining what these gentle hands, these loving fingers, had once done to another living person, when -"

"Spare me the love story." I was necessarily curt. "What of the others in the cave? They witnessed what you did. Some would've known you had forfeited all rights under the Geneva Convention, by faking surrender to kill an enemy. I wouldn't have given tuppence for your chances if, when captured, one of them had blabbed to the *Feldgendarmerie.*"

"None did. We swore a solemn oath to keep this among ourselves and, by the end of the war, those of us who got through, went our separate ways."

"Good." I nodded approvingly. "However, you are still withholding evidence. Thus far all I've heard is a commonplace incident that, in France, we'd have shrugged off with '*c'est la guerre,*' an inevitable consequence of war."

"Very perceptive." He reached for the ignition key again. "There is more." He hesitated. "Twice, during my years presiding over a lower court, it was my melancholy duty to pass a sentence of death. On both occasions there was no question that the accused was guilty. Each man had committed a vile, coldblooded murder. But, as I looked at their terrified faces, staring back at me from the dock, I saw the contorted features of a dead German lad condemning me for his murder, as he still does. Frequently."

The engine fired up and we resumed our journey in silence, except for the diesel's rumble and the windscreen wipers' rhythmical swish-swash-swish until we parked at the Mac's main entrance, where Tom helped me dismount and tried to smile as he gave a tense handshake.

"That was awfully decent of you, to listen." He turned away as the porter, holding an open umbrella, hurried down the steps to carry my bag. I asked that it be kept aside while I went through to the Club's library where, unsettled by the grave confession I'd just been burdened with, I sought to distract myself only to find that another member had already done the *Times'* cryptic crossword.

Irritated, I sat nearer the fire to get warm while skimming today's *Age,* noting how some fat-arsed politician was planning a Vietnam Veterans' welcome home parade, fifteen years after the last Digger packed his kitbag and boarded a troop transport. I had a fair idea what Reg' Birtley and other men of his experience would say to this begrudging recognition of their part in that unhappy, unpopular, unwinnable war.

I chucked the newspaper aside and searched the magazine rack for *Punch,* but its satirical sketches of modern Britain meant nothing to me. This venerable publication's glory days were over, making it obvious to my author-publisher's eye that it was struggling to recover costs from dwindling subscriptions and anaemic advertising revenue. This further depressed my spirits as I've always had a soft spot for *Punch,* not the least because it paid five guineas apiece for my cartoons of life in the Royal Flying Corps.

One of my most popular contributions depicted a smartly uniformed staff officer, newly arrived in France, staring at wing fabric ripped by ack-ack fire, and asking: "Aw, I say old chepp! What caused thett?!" To which the RE8's observer - clad in sheepskin boots and baggy Sidcot suit, Lewis gun slung across one shoulder – scathingly replies: "Moths." Similar cartoons, equally unfunny to the modern eye, paid my Mess tab.

Uneasy and alone, I slumped by the fire, staring into the flames, Tom's experiences on Crete striking sombre chords of memory. I had made the right choice at the end of the Great War. Rather than resuming civilian life in Australia, I'd stayed behind in a Europe that was about to enter one of its most turbulent and exciting periods of the past two thousand years, whereas most other servicemen returned to the stifling routines of our smug little outpost of Empire, a hard ask after the intensity of shared dangers in uniform.

The Returned Services League did its best to restore purpose and meaning to tens of thousands of uprooted young men, many of whom had smuggled home the souvenired pistols and other battlefield trophies that tooled an upsurge of violence and suicides, once booze and brawls no longer filled the void.

Horrible as the years between 1914 and 1918 were, there had always been a sense that we were part of something bigger than ourselves. War gave heightened meaning and colour to otherwise drab lives, and for those of us who survived, it became the defining point of reference in a post-war world of perpetual doubts and uncertainties.

Time and again, men and women have proven they can endure extremes of hardship if only the effort gives them purpose, the human hunger for recognition and reward being as fundamental as our need for food and drink, friendship, and love. But when those are snatched away, or denied, the pain of living can soon become an unbearable burden.

This, I sensed, was Tom Hartigan's predicament after mandatory retirement from the High Court on his seventieth birthday, followed by his wife's death. It was no surprise that the poor chap was reduced to seeking my modest company to keep his demons at bay, but for how much longer could he hold out? From personal experience, I knew what his next step was likely to be unless given a reason to halt at the brink.

Reinvigorated, with a renewed sense of purpose, I limped over to the library's writing desk, selected an octavo sheet of headed notepaper, and uncapped my fountain pen:

The Macquarie Club
78 Collins Street
Victoria 3000
Australia

Dear Tom.

Thank you again for a most enjoyable time in your ever-welcome company.

Akilinos is truly delightful, and I look forward to another visit soon, especially now that Spring is nearly upon us, surely the best season for such splendid trout-fishing?

Do, please, give my kindest regards to Norah and Reg', Julie and Alan, when next you speak with them.

Yours aye.

Ian

I folded the note and addressed an envelope to Tom's unlisted town residence – there being always the risk of a revenge attack from some villain he'd put away - and gave it to the concierge with instructions to make sure a bicycle courier delivered within the hour.

I then went through to the dining room and treated myself to lemon sole with spring potatoes, Greek salad, and a good glass of Moselle that put me in a much happier frame of mind as I retired to my quarters, locked the door, unpacked my valise, and got ready to retrieve Aunt Lucinda's papers.

21

However, I had not been wholly honest with Tom in my brief note. The truth is, I was not looking-forward to spending more time in his company, watching him drink more than I thought prudent, reminiscing about the past as old men do with their dwindling stock of days.

It is one thing to meet every week or so at the Waverley where conversations are limited to card play, the weather, and today's headline story in the *Age*, but not when one is a guest under that other person's roof. The experiences of a lifetime have proved that the risk of voicing an unguarded confidence or secret increases in direct proportion to the warmth of a host's welcome and surroundings, unless one is especially watchful.

Conversations tend to mimic the bidding phase of Contract Bridge in which one partner reveals his hand, hoping for a similar or better from the other person, as when Tom's confessed to strangling a German soldier on Crete, after my earlier anger that told of an aerial battle above the Western Front. Without asking outright, he was in effect inviting me to put aside my caution and become a trusted confidant during our final few years.

This is an appealing prospect, but I have my reasons for maintaining an amicable distance from inquisitive others. Why then did I send such a deceitful note, I asked myself as the Mac's antique lift hauled me aloft to the second floor? Certainly not because I sought to deepen our acquaintance, but rather because I'd glimpsed in him the painfully familiar symptoms of a bereaved husband's loneliness and despair, having more than once loaded my service revolver and stared into its unblinking eye.

Thus, if a few kindly fibs and a vague promise of happier times ahead gave Tom cause to pause, I'd repaid my debt of gratitude and could focus on more immediate concerns, like the lingering memory of Frances Baxter's two short visits.

Whether she was what she claimed to be - a senior Oxford academic - or an operative from Six checking-up on me, remained to be seen. But regardless of that outcome, this confounded woman had inveigled herself into becoming my shadow's *anima*, as Carl Jung would have analysed during our sessions at his Swiss clinic, had I known her then.

Determined to bolt and bar memory's door, I returned to the present, retrieved Aunt Lucinda's memoirs of life, love, and loss in the previous century, and resumed editing them at the page marked with a wire paperclip.

Act 4

Having finally arrived at the very heart of the British Empire as the sister of Captain G.N. of the East India Companys Madras Artillery, it was time to consider the future, he with no further need of my services while in pursuit of an heiress with a fortune of 1000 per annum, the very least an officer of his tastes required to establish him in Society!

However, aware that I wished to free myself of our liaison, the gallant Captain put an Oriental substance in my drink when I was otherwise engaged, and upon recovery found myself pledged as a gaming debt in a house of ill repute off Piccadilly!

During the six months or so of my bondage, and one may interpret that word according to ones experience of life, I beheld the supposed cream British aristocracy satiating their lewdest appetites by -

I reached for a pair of scissors and clipped several paragraphs from the following three pages, not that I was shocked or surprised by what I was reading; Playfair Street had accustomed me to far worse depravities than a drunken father, a predatory uncle, and a compliant mother. But I was now the custodian of the Antipodean Nightingale's posthumous reputation and had no intention of funding The Lucinda Cribdon Study Centre for it to become an early-Victorian sadomasochistic peep show.

Frances Baxter would have been furious had she seen me destroying primary evidence, arguing that historians need to know how a cabinet minister sought relief after the Parliamentary session in which he amended the Vagrancy Act 1824 by raising the penalty for prostitution to six months in gaol, with hard labour. Or learn why Lord so-and-so paid young sailors for rough trade, several of whom then disappeared, presumed deserters, or were murdered by "a person or persons unknown," as was routinely found by London's City Coroner forty-odd years before Jack the Ripper piqued the public's imagination.

She was right, of course, but so was I, for no way was the memory of my benefactress going to be tainted by sordid speculation when some grubby "investigative journalist" – in my day all journalists were expected to investigate! – exposed the cruel realities of nineteenth century England's White Slave Trade.

I laid the scissors aside as this young but by no means helpless Colonial girl prepared to escape from her gilded cage in Jermyn Street:

My fellow soiled doves were of a class where warm beds, gaudy clothes, and sweetmeats were enough return for the indignities heaped upon them by gentlemen who were anything but gentle, and men who in their lusts were lower than animals, but whose high connexion with the Interest, an inner circle of powers behind the throne, entitled them to do as they pleased!

I was made of sterner stuff and steadfastly refused to comply. In the normal course of events this would have had me whipt in the establishments torture chamber while those same gentlemen paid to witness such punishments, but I had inherited my grandmamas spark, impudently bargaining with the bordellos madam, the only inmate ever to do so!

Rather than indulge her clients with my body, I charmed them with racy songs that inflamed their bestial urges. For lack of a more polite description, I became the hors d'oevre that wetted many a nobles appetite before the main course was served in an upstairs bedchamber!

I had, of course, an ulterior motive. By displaying my talents to a wide assortment of men, I was confident my reputation would reach the ears of some theatrical impresario, and thus it came to pass when the proprietor of the Lambeth Supper Club, not yet Nuttley's Music Hall, heard me perform Does Yer Muvver Know Yor Out Again Ternight? A ditty I had recently composed, based upon a sarcastic tune whistled by Montichellas convict labour when their overseer passed them by!

Mr Stubbs pressed his ardent attentions upon me, declaring he wished for my services as a singer, et cetera. When I explained my doleful condition, he agreed to speak with Madam, the upshot being, some days later I was informed that Captain G.N.s debt had been met and I was now free to work at the Supper Club!

My new protector was under the erroneous impression that he had bought a mistress as well as a fresh act. I disabused him of this idea by entering negotiations that fixed my fee at two guineas plus five percent, with one new song per week, for half a year!

Alas, poor Mr Stubbs! This was not what he bargained for, but I smoothed his ruffled feathers by predicting a torrent of silvery half-crowns and golden half-sovereigns pouring into his cash box, when I trod the Club's rickety boards!

I found composition easy, having often heard Grandmama improvising verses to commonplace tunes, and it was now that my piano lessons at Miss Kendalls Ladys Academy proved their value. Mr Stubbs had bought a rather fine Broadwood at a bankruptcy sale and placed it to one side of the stage, hoping its silent presence would add tone to his threadbare presentations, so imagine his amazement when I sat down and banged out a new song!

Muvver remained a great favourite because it could be sung in Cockney, which is not very different to the low speech of Sydney Town. However, my Spank You Very Much, Naughty Boy! soon became a popular if vulgar riposte on the streets of London. Twenty years later, revisiting England, it was still possible to encounter an impudent wink and Spank You Very Much when someone responded to a small favour!

Dear Reader! Pray do not think I pandered only to the lowest appetites, profitable though they were. My equally popular dramatic recitations were meant to instruct and uplift the listener, and my devout hope is that A Village Maid, Sore Betray'd prompted many a rake to mend his ways by taking heed of the death, by drowning in the village pond, of an innocent young babe and its abandoned mother!

Tho barely eighteen years of age, I soon relieved Mr Stubbs of the drudgery of managing a small theatre, for an extra five shillings per week, and saw to it that all need full repairs were made to the stage, that new scenery was painted, and the dressing room was divided down the middle by a curtain, so that male and female acts could make up in decency!

Among the several hopefuls I auditioned was Eliza Gilbert, a spoilt Irish girl who later gained notoriety as Lola Montez, with her nasty Spider Dance. A more teachable aspirant, though, was Harriet Howard the daughter of a Brighton bootmaker who until recently had been the mistress of a leading jockey!

Desperate to earn an independent income, no matter how slight the sum, she presented herself to the Supper Club and pleaded for entry into the profession. Truth to tell, her talents were small, but she had a trim figure and pleasing features that were sure to delight the Quality I attracted. The fact that she was female and auburn haired should have made us rivals, but instead we become firm friends and I saw to it she got parts appropriate to her abilitys!

One may question my generosity in a business notorious for spite and jealousy, but whereas other English girls were whey faced creatures who looked down their beaky noses at me for flaunting my Colonial Difference, (and the more they did so, the more I laught at them!) Hetty had the fine high colour of a country girl and an earthy wit I could play off. Soon our banter as Miss Push & Miss Bush at Gentlemen Only smoking concerts was the talk of the town, and further augmented Mr Stubbs fortune. Ours too, for I renegotiated our contracts to include three guineas for each new song or monologue!

It was at one of these Smokers that Hetty attracted the ardent interest of Major Martyn of the Guards and left the profession to become his mistress and, in the full-ness of time, bear him a fine son. Unlike Captain G.N., Major Martyn, tho married, was a true gentleman, and settled a generous annuity upon mother and babe!

I was sad to see her go but we stayed in touch, by means of the new penny post. It was fortunate I did so because, unbeknown to me, Mr Stubbs had squandered our takings on an ill-considered venture. Not to put too fine a point on it, he was declared bankrupt, confined to the Millbank Debtors Prison and his business sold for a pittance to Mr Nuttley, with whom I soon fell out!

Alas, the fault was mine! Had I been meek and submissive, in a word more English and less Colonial, he might have adopted the plans I had for next season. Instead, I found myself back on the street with only my savings and wits betwixt me and hunger!

Meanwhile Mr Stubbs was encountering much the same problem and I felt honour bound to ease his sad lot. To this end I spake with his keeper and arranged for him to be served one hot meal a day that I paid for by weekly instalments in advance. Clearly this was only a stop gap and the poor fellow needed more substantial support than I could provide!

To attain it I sent a note by post to Hetty in St Johns Wood and her reply invited me to take tea that very next afternoon. An omnibus conveyed me to Regents Park on the edge of Town where the horses were watered and I walked the last half-mile along a dusty lane to a charming villa set amidst bowers of fragrant herbage!

Here I was welcomed at the door by a man of modest build with the melancholy gaze of a dreamer and foreign features. His English was courtly tho heavily larded with a medley of accents. Hetty was delighted to see me and introduced her latest conquest as Louis, pronounced Loo-ee in the French style, and presented his two naturally acquired sons who were playmates for Major Martyns young boy!

In short order we arranged for Mr Stubbs to be fed thrice daily and for a solicitor to examine his affairs to such good effect that he was set free a few weeks later, by which time Hetty and I and the three children had accompanied Louis on his return to France, where he soon ascended the throne of his famous uncle Napoleon the First!

This last paragraph was a Right Royal Showstopper in every meaning of the phrase, and I was sorely tempted to keep turning the pages of an account that read more like a romantic novel than the memoirs of Australia's first internationally acclaimed performer. Instead, I put away the manuscript for the night, as my eyes were aching after reading its faded, erratically written typescript.

22

Getting damp and chilled at Melba's tomb had been foolish and before long I was feeling quite seedy. As a preventative measure, I self-medicated with a shot of Scotch, two aspirin tablets and, to block a recurrence of malaria, a pinch of quinine sulphate before going to bed. But despite these measures, by late next morning I had a temperature and wheezy cough.

McKenzie wanted to rush me into a private room at the Royal Alfred, knowing how strongly I felt about the Heidelburg Repatriation Hospital, to which I told him - in no uncertain terms! - that I was perfectly comfortable where I was and just needed a few days of rest to sweat-it-out.

After a heroic tussle in which I got the rough edge of his dour Scots tongue, in response to my own rather gruff tone it must be admitted, Gordon contacted a nursing agency to provide 24-hour attendance and arranged for oxygen cylinders to be delivered at set intervals, along with regular shots of penicillin to knock out my lurking pneumococci.

There is nothing new that can be said about a heavy cold, every person who has ever lived has experienced at least one in their lifetime, but for me its most common feature is boredom. Not that I have ever been a particularly patient patient, and well remember becoming notably rebellious at 1 AGH in Egypt, after my first evacuation from Gallipoli.

The incoming draft of nurses was warned about my attitude when I overheard Gordon telling them I was "a tough old bird who needs a firm hand." He also left an assortment of pills and potions to keep me in a contented doze for the next few days, during which a flutter of concerned young women took care of my every need, for which I was most grateful.

Confined to bed at the Mac', staring up at its familiar ceiling, gave me ample time to review the Cribdon Papers. Much remained to be edited but at least I had solved one puzzle that had haunted me for more than eighty years, namely, why did a wealthy Bohemian go out of her way to care so much for a snotty-nosed little orphan? The answer, I suspect, was a shared background of childhood rejection plus her loyalty to "poor Mr Stubbs…"

I'm not sure how common a surname that is in England, but it would not surprise me if at some future date the unfortunate Maggie turned out to be his granddaughter, making me the great-grandson of a bankrupt London music hall owner, on one side of our peculiar family tree, and a knighted President of the Legislative Council in New South Wales - descended from a couple of First Fleet convicts - on the other. As V.I.Lenin was wont to remind me, in his Irish-accented English: "Everyt'ing connect' wid everyt'ing!"

In truth, all this was no more than idle speculation by an invalid with too much time on his hands and not enough work to keep them busy, but in due course I was able to sit up in my chair again, put on the earphones and stalk the wavebands, hunting mysterious Numbers Stations with their automated voices intoning strings of five-digit code groups.

There was no way I could decrypt their contents, of course, or know from which side of the Iron Curtain they were being transmitted to agents in the field.

But hearing them revived memories of tuning into the BBC on a clandestine wireless set, at 2115 hours GMT, and waiting for the muffled "V for Victory" dum-dum-dum-dum thuds of a Zulu drum.

This famous callsign always preceded the announcer's *"Ici Londres...!"* followed by his carefully enunciated, twice repeated *messages personnels* which, in translation were gibberish like: "Grandma wore her blue hat on Sunday," or "Five plus five make twelve." Baffling to the Gestapo's *Übertragungsabhörhörer* radio location vans but, every so often, a previously agreed phrase would alert me to the next moonlit delivery of parachuted cash with which to bribe Vichy officials and buy identity papers for escaping Allied airmen.

Like Tom and his Cretan interlude during the same war, my work in Occupied France was the last time I have felt so alive, even though I was borderline famished and frightened for much of the while. Since when, it's been a solitary downhill shuffle into life's twilit dusk. Although, recently, there have been gleams of autumnal sunlight since the intrusion of an intriguing Oxford academic, or whatever she really was. The trouble being, with every passing day, Frances Baxter was becoming more of a worry for I had yet to receive a reply from England, confirming her story. Or not.

My caution must seem excessive in peacetime, but one never took anything or anyone at face value in my former life, which is why I can speak of having a former life; less cautious souls ended theirs handcuffed to a wooden post at the wrong end of a rifle range.

This and similar gloomy thoughts were interrupted on Thursday morning when my nurse answered the door and stood aside for Tom Hartigan to enter bearing a small package wrapped in expensively decorated paper. "Thank God you're up. I'd have called sooner but wasn't aware you were ill. Here!" He held out the gift. "I know you're not into flowers, and grapes are such a cliché, so I thought a Glenfiddich Reserve Single Malt would be more to your taste."

"That is very, very thoughtful." I glanced past him and gave today's nurse a nod that she correctly interpreted as permission to go down to the Mac's Dining Room, for morning tea.

Tom moved the nurse's chair nearer the window, using the movement to run an eye over my few possessions and, no doubt, wonder what secrets were hidden behind such deliberate simplicity.

"So, what's new," I enquired, having used the chair trick myself many a time, "what's news?"

"I'd have thought you would be more abreast of current events?" He cast a pointed glance at the Zenith's antenna and earth wire. "Perhaps I should be the one asking you?"

"Oh, you know how the world turns," I replied, "the more things change, the more they remain the same. But reading between the lines of Radio Moscow's bulletins, I wouldn't bet on the Politburo staying in business much longer, now that Gorbachev is General Secretary..."

Tom ignored my artful distraction and took a deep breath. "Thanks for the note. You can't know how much it meant to me." He abruptly got to his feet again and put out a hand to shake. "Get well soon old friend. You are right. Spring is just around the corner. We have lots more fishing to do. You and I together. For years to come. I hope." With that he spun on his heel and left as quickly as he had arrived.

I was still decoding his tongue-tied message when today's nurse returned bearing a telegram. "The porter said you'll want this straight away, sir."

"Thank you. I'll attend to it presently." Tom's voice had quaked with barely suppressed emotion and I could sense that mine also risked betraying my innermost feelings.

It was no exaggeration to say that the course of what little remained of my life would change, one way or another, moments after opening this innocuous, buff coloured envelope.

Feeling a mortal fear that hope deferred was about to become hope destroyed, I summoned-up the pluck to reach for the paperknife on my desk.

The first part of the telegram was brief and to the point:

> LEADING SEAMAN HENRY CRIBDON
> (FAA 64359) OBSERVER/AIR GUNNER STOP
> KIA 120242 STOP NOK MARY FRANCES
> WALSH ENDIT

These few words and their abbreviations spoke of a wartime pregnancy conceived in love but never legitimised by marriage, though that was clearly intended before the young father was killed in action on the 12th of February 1942, leaving his Next of Kin with probably no more than a few pounds in his savings passbook. Miss Mary Walsh never qualified for a War Widows' Pension. Instead, she'd raised their daughter in secret shame. And alone.

Its next part was more explicit:

> JAMES RODRIGO BAXTER CHAIRMAN
> ASIPAC FINANCE CORP (CAP £250M)
> STOP DOB 051138 VALENCIA SPAIN STOP
> EDUC HARROW & KINGS COLLEGE STOP
> POSTGRAD ECOLE POLYTECHNIQUE PARIS
> STOP MARRIED DR FRANCES BAXTER NEE
> WALSH DOB 070842 COVENTRY STOP
> CHILDREN 1S + 1D ENDIT

Its last part was the convincer:

> HISTORY AS PATHOLOGY BY FM BAXTER
> PUB OXFORD UNIVERSITY PRESS 1979 STOP
> 375PP HARDCOVER ENDIT

"Bad news -?!" The young nurse darted forward to assist me.

The dressing gown's sleeve was the only thing handy to mop my flowing tears. "Oh no, my dear. Quite the opposite -!"

23

Gordon McKenzie telephoned every morning, clearly hoping that his patient had relented during the night and now needed an ambulance. Instead, my attendants could only report rapid improvements until early the following week, when I was at last able to dress myself and go down to dinner.

Passing through the lobby I stopped to speak with Mr Perkins, the crossed keys on his lapels evidence that the Mac's concierge knew everything and everybody of consequence in and around Melbourne. "May I ask your advice?"

"Of course, sir."

"What do you know about those cassette recorder things? The sort where one can speak one's mind onto a small spool of tape?"

"I know exactly what you mean," he replied with an attentive smile. "I have one of my own. They're very useful when learning another foreign language."

"Heavens!" I blinked, wishing such equipment had been available when I was struggling to conjugate French irregular verbs. "Where can I buy one?"

"I'll make enquiries." The fact that Melbourne's shops were closed at this hour didn't seem to trouble him. Forty minutes later, as I returned from the Dining Room, he caught my attention and placed a colourfully printed cardboard box on the reception desk. "Panasonics have excellent recording quality and are very simple to operate, but if you do have any difficulty, give me a call, though I doubt you will need to."

"That's very kind of you to think so."

"Not at all. The invoice is under its lid, trade discount of course. You will also need these," he added, putting a carton of blank cassettes alongside the bigger box.

I took the lift upstairs and eagerly unpacked my purchase. He was right, assembling this kit was no problem for a man who used to repair as well as operate a Sterling Type 52 spark-gap transmitter, in the sky, while artillery pounded mud a couple of thousand feet below his reconnaissance biplane's undercarriage struts.

I felt quite pleased with myself when the cassette tape slotted into place and its lid snapped shut at the first attempt. Still following the instruction booklet, I plugged into a wall socket, pressed Start, and the tape began to roll. Now all I had to do was speak into the microphone, record a short message, and press Playback. There was just one hitch, I was inexplicably lost for words until a familiar phrase sprang to mind: "'Ici Londres! Les Français parlent aux Français...'"

When rewound and played back, it was a fair impersonation of *Radio Londres'* wartime announcer with his nightly bulletins of "Frenchmen speaking to Frenchmen" that preceded the signals those of us in the field were awaiting, nervously aware that the Gestapo's radio location vans would be triangulating our positions.

I played around for several minutes, test-recording a variety of recitations that ended with *The Village Blacksmith*, before putting the microphone aside, selecting a sheet of headed notepaper, and uncapping my fountain pen:

The Macquarie Club
78 Collins Street
Victoria 3000
Australia

4 viii 1987

My Dear Frances.

I stopped short, eerily aware of the date, exactly seventy-three years since the British Empire declared war on Germany and all hell broke loose in every meaning of this trite expression, not that we knew it at the time.

Our patriotic rush to enlist was driven by the belief that unless we moved quickly, the war would be over by Christmas. The promise of two guineas, or forty-two shillings a week, made us additionally keen to sign-up for an all-expenses-paid overseas adventure.

Wearily shaking my head at our innocence, I resumed writing:

> *After much thought I have acceded to your wish to hear*
> *an Edwardian's voice, the better to understand what was said*
> *in the Cabinet Room at 10 Downing Street, during those fateful*
> *July days 73 years ago and, to do so, shall recount a few personal*
> *anecdotes you may find of interest.*
>
> *However, as mentioned when we discussed Sir Stephen's*
> *papers, much will be left unsaid. Not that what I am forbidden to*
> *reveal are nowadays more than minor historical footnotes, but a*
> *King's Commissioned Officer's word of honour, once given,*
> *cannot be rescinded or broken.*
>
> *I shall consider my duty done if, at the end of listening to me,*
> *you feel the texture of a bygone age, as remote from today's world*
> *as that of King Alfred, King John, and the unlucky King Charles.*
> *Or know Champollion's thrill of discovery when deciphering his*
> *Rosetta Stone…*
>
> *With my deepest regard and sincerest wishes for a long, happy,*
> *and fulfilled life with your husband and children.*
>
> *Ian Cribdon.*

Whether or not I shall use this draft as a cover note for the box of tapes my executor will send to Oxford, after my death, remains to be seen. But at least it got me underway as I selected another sheet of paper to outline a script, for I am still enough of a professional travel writer to sketch an orderly structure before composing an article, especially one written for Dr Frances Baxter née Walsh, the illegitimate daughter of a heroic observer/air gunner.

1903-1912

24

If allowed only one word to define the world I grew up in as a young adult, it would be Duty. Everything we were required to do, from polishing the insteps of our shoes to correctly holding a dinner fork, was governed by an urgent sense of duty to become Proper English Gentlemen. The fact that we were born and raised half the world away from Home made it even more essential to adopt the imagined values and standards of Old Mother England, to fully qualify as Sons of the Empire, not that everyone believed this.

Those of Irish Catholic descent were notably reluctant, given their homeland's centuries of English rule, but in general there was a strong undercurrent of loyalty that surfaced every year on May 24th, Queen Victoria's birthday, when schools closed, flags flew, and brass bands led horse-drawn floats displaying portraits of Lord Nelson and the Duke of Wellington framed by local produce, culminating with firework displays for the public and balls at Government House for our local gentry.

Although nowadays it is fashionable to mock these unashamed displays of patriotism, and to vilify them for covert political purposes, an identifiable threat lurked in the shadows of our sunny, confident Young Australia.

At the time of which I shall speak, there were fewer than five million of us, mostly concentrated in Sydney and Melbourne, with the rest unevenly scattered around the edge of a landmass nearly as large as the United States of America. Meanwhile, along our northern horizon, slunk the Yellow Peril with only the Royal Navy's grey battleships between us and the tens of millions of fiendishly clever Orientals lusting after innocent White maidens, or so the popular press warned us, for nothing sells newsprint better than a strident fear campaign.

I can picture the shudder of virtuous indignation when Frances eventually hears me describing this, but it's not what her generation believes now that should concern an historian; rather, it is what we believed then, that informed our actions at the turn of this twentieth century.

Eight decades and two world wars later, we have arrived at a unique moment in time where all are nagged and scolded to celebrate Cultural Diversity even if it means betting against four thousand years of recorded human folly. The pious hope being that the more diverse and foreign another's origins and beliefs, the more readily he or she will abandon them in a secular society where anything goes, and nothing matters anymore.

This beguiling myth is only sustainable during an unparalleled Age of Abundance in which even the poorest Australian has access to more goods, more healthcare, more nutritious food than most of the Kings of England enjoyed in their heyday. But a time must come when ancient tribal loyalties and stern ancestral gods again decide who lives, who dies, and who cares, during the next Age of Dearth.

For those of us who learnt grammatical English before the slovenly yowl that nowadays passes for language, the antonym of diversity is unity, without which no group of people – be it a small family or a large nation – resembles anything more than a pile of crushed rock pretending to be solid concrete.

Macauley's *Lays of Ancient Rome*, a frequent recitation at a time when such homely entertainments were still popular, had one memorable stanza that defined an Edwardian's ideal conduct:

> Then out spake brave Horatius,
> The Captain of the Gate,
> To every man upon this earth,
> Death comes soon or late.
> And how can man die better,
> When facing fearful odds,
> For the ashes of his fathers,
> And the temples of his Gods?

Though sneered at and disparaged now, it was this fierce pride in our race and ancestry that stiffened our resolve on Gallipoli's arid crags and kept us firm amidst the Western Front's scenes and horrors unimaginable to later generations.

Assuming Tom is correct in his reading of current trends and given that Australia must one day fight for her very existence on home ground, I find it hard to imagine how our current, polyglot confusion will find the inner strength and fortitude to unite against a more ruthlessly disciplined invader.

I shan't be here to see how the Lucky Country fares when our Traitors Within throw open Brave Horatius' gates to the next wave of conquerors, but experience of life and death in Occupied France gives me hope that at least some *collaborateurs* will pay dearly for their treason.

However, it is more likely that the new Master Race will default on its false debt of gratitude to these traitors. "First to the barricades; first to the guillotine!" I remember Trotsky chortling after his Red Guards massacred the thousands of Kronstadt sailors whose armed support saved the Bolsheviks from defeat. Those poor deluded fellows had believed his panicked promises when the Red Revolution was about to drown in its own blood and imagined their simple faith would earn them special consideration afterwards, which in a macabre way it did.

Meanwhile, during Australia's brief, expansive, self-confident decade before the catastrophe of 1914 overwhelmed us, Aunt Lucinda decided that to become a Proper English Gentleman I must attend a Proper English School or at least an acceptable replica, like Melbourne Grammar, a few streets away from Tralee House.

Its hefty fees were no obstacle for a shrewd businesswoman with a thumb in many a lucrative pie, but there remained one knotty problem, my lack of a birth certificate or even a recorded date of birth. Not surprising, given Papa's frequent flits between cheap lodging houses. Besides, a birth certificate's half-crown registration fee would have been better spent on booze or bread, in that order.

Aunt Lucinda duly announced that it was high time we rectified this omission if I was to be enrolled in a proper school and consulted her clairvoyant, Madame Vestris, who for one guinea drew up my astrological chart with the assistance of Big Chief Black Eagle – on the Other Side, we were solemnly assured – and a pack of tarot cards.

Twenty minutes later she – or they if we include her Spirit Guide - announced that 21st June 1903 would be my ninth birthday. According to them,

2 plus 1 equal 3, on the sixth (3 plus 3) month of the 3rd year of the new century, thus making me 3 plus 3 plus 3 years of age.

As a bonus, June 21st falls on the cusp of Gemini and Cancer, two auspicious birth signs, as well as marking the Southern Hemisphere's winter solstice, after which the days grow longer and brighter, proof positive of a long and radiant life for young Master Ian.

I looked suitably impressed, even after mentally adding-up her 3's and discovering that she'd skipped one of them, otherwise I would soon have turned 3 plus 3 plus 3 plus 3 or twelve years of age. Impossible to believe when the true figure was probably somewhere between seven or eight, give or take a few months.

My new birthdate settled, thanks to Madame Vestris' wonky arithmetic, it was time to acquire a more suitable cover story than that of a reformed Artful Dodger, if I was to pass muster with the headmaster of Victoria's preeminent boys' school. For this I needed the assistance of Aunt Lucinda's vivid imagination as, together, we spun a colourful yarn that disposed of my fictitious birth certificate by losing it when a gang of *dacoits* sacked my family's bungalow on the wooded slopes of the Himalayan foothills.

Clad in a sober grey Norfolk jacket and britches, stiff white Eton collar, black stockings, and glossy black shoes, I stood to attention while the Reverend Doctor Blanch inspected me with the mordant eye of a sergeant major on defaulters' parade.

When asked who my parents were and what they did for a living, I manfully replied that both were now dead, having succumbed to fever at a small Assamese town where Papa managed the tea gardens, and Mama performed Good Works for grateful native women. Subsequently I'd been privately tutored at Darjeeling, by a Mr Smith, before becoming the charge of my great aunt, here in "Aw-stray-yuh."

A gifted mimic, I gave a satisfactory performance in the King's English, so there was no need to recall a memorised map of North-Eastern India or repeat a few bogus Nepali phrases, memorised just-in-case; boys matured quickly on Playfair Street, and I was already a proficient chameleon.

The upshot of this solemn pantomime meant that I was now cleared to enter Melbourne Grammar's hallowed halls on the first day of term, where the procedure was very similar to my later experiences as an army recruit.

Schoolmasters and their toady prefects marched about, barking orders, assigning us to "houses" that roughly equated to a battalion's companies. Living in Toorak meant I was shoved into Bromby House. Boys from South Yarra found themselves in Rushden House; those from Malvern got Morris House, I think. There were two or three others, but I never had reason or opportunity to learn their names

Anyhow, by the time the new intake had been chivvied and bossed around, it was time for recess. Warily alert, I followed my new schoolmates onto a rough patch of turf where others were already playing improvised games of Tag and Football.

The only cloud on this sunny scene was Bromby's Head Prefect, leading a chorus of bullies surrounding another of today's intake. The boy in question was what used to be called "delicate," being somewhat pale and frail, and thus natural prey for a power drunk, almost adult, six-footer.

Despite what has been previously said about Playfair Street's lack of fairness there was an unwritten code of conduct on the Rocks. Simply put, if we had to bash a cove, then make him your own size or bigger, for only a yellow-

113

bellied dog picks on girlies or little 'uns. There was an equally unwritten rule for these alley brawls: Distract, Disable, Destroy.

"Oy! You!! Bum Face -!!!"

Distracted, the prefect spun around, glaring.

"Yeah, you! Pick on someone y'r own size!"

He lunged to grab me. "'Foul mouthed little bugger! You'll get the cane-!"

I swayed, ducked, and rammed him straight in the guts. Disabled, he sprawled on the ground whereupon I put-the-boots-in, one to the groin, other to the head. Luckily, I failed to hit my second mark squarely and only ripped his face open instead of Destroying him.

No way was this going to be shrugged off as a schoolyard scuffle. A gang of excited prefects hauled me before the headmaster who heard them in furious silence, neglected to question me, and reached for his fearsome cane while two grinning louts attempted to tug my trousers down.

Instead, I hacked the Head's shins, nutted the nearest thug with my knee, and gnawed someone else's fingers to the bone. The rest jumped clear as I sprinted into the memorised labyrinth of corridors, across the playground and over the fence, my skills as a reformed barrow-thief much in evidence.

Dusty and dishevelled I eventually jogged up Tralee House's gravelled drive and let myself in through the tradesmen's entrance, hoping to wash and brush up before reporting to Aunt Lucinda, instead of which I bumped into her on the bathroom landing.

Beckoning me into the office where she wrote her correspondence and kept the household accounts, she invited me to sit down and tell my side of the story. That done, she cocked an amused eyebrow and observed, in French, this being Monday: *"Merde alors! Que ferons-nous avec tu maintenant?"*

How very true! Like her, I had not the shittiest idea of what we were going to do with me now. The only thing certain was that young Master Ian Cribdon had just completed his first and final day of formal schooling.

114

25

Aunt Lucinda took command of the situation by hiring English Language, Geography, and Modern History tutors from Scotch College, all of whom showed signs of apprehension when we first met, suggesting that my reputation had reached Grammar's rival establishment.

Mathematics were assigned to a penniless undergraduate who, in later years, became a full professor at Yale University and a Nobel Laureate to boot; that I have remained numerically vague, apart from basic arithmetic and geometry, was not due to his lack of passion for exponential polynomic equations.

She had already noticed my natural gift for pencil sketching and arranged for one of our frequent guests, Arthur Streeton, to give me tuition whenever he set up his easel at the end of our garden overlooking the Yarra, which soon evolved into an informal apprenticeship to this leading exponent of Australian Impressionist landscape painting.

Such skills as I ever had with the human figure and portraiture were learned from another of our distinguished visitors – for Aunt Lucinda delighted in Bohemian company, kept a good cellar, and always laid a generous dinner table – Arthur Streeton's older friend, Tom Roberts.

However, one needs more than book learning and heightened artistic sensibility to qualify as a Proper English Gentleman, so among other life skills, I was coached in tennis and enrolled at a boxing academy to learn the Marquis of Queensbury's Manly Art of Self-Defence.

I secretly regarded this exercise with contempt, there being no way I would have lasted five seconds on Playfair Street had I stood there puffing my chest, posing like a bareknuckle pugilist; in the real world one either sprints for cover or, if cornered, fights dirty with any weapon to hand, be it a broken bottle, a chunk of brick, or length of iron pipe.

However, skipping about a boxing ring, swapping padded punches, helped me become an attentive dance partner, and even sharpened my eye at snooker though, at first, I had to stand on an upturned apple box to get clear shots across Tralee's full-size table.

This was another required social skill because, in those days, a billiard saloon was the one place where gentlemen of all sorts could mingle amicably, perform well, and conduct private business, be it shady or otherwise.

In fact, I was chalking my cue and taking instruction from Mr Jem Sykes, a professional player at one of the establishments in which Aunt Lucinda had cannily invested money, when through the bay window we both noticed a very smart landau drawn by two matching greys, a liveried driver up front, another servant behind, bearing a message.

"Oh ho! That tha's a tiggy gig an' no mistake..." Mr Sykes dipped a knowing wink. "Any'ow, we're about done for t'day. Ten more swervers an' givvem y'best!"

Swerves only look difficult but are in fact quite simple once a player learns to strike the cue ball so that it spins around an opponent's snookering shot before kissing the object ball.

Completed to our satisfaction, we formally shook hands before putting away our cues, brushing the green baize, and reverently lowering its fretted tin cover so that all would be ready for our next match.

Aunt Lucinda had written a brief reply and was about to give it to the liveried messenger when I entered the hallway. The servant bowed and returned to the carriage that by now was facing down the drive towards our Grange Road gates.

"Here's a pretty how-de-do!" She tweaked a cream card from its matching envelope to display a Mr & Mrs Leon Shuster's monogrammed invitation to take tea with them tomorrow at 4pm.

"Must we?" I moped.

"Of course. It would be discourteous not to."

"But who are they?" I was still shy in company, fearful that something I might inadvertently say or do would expose me as a fraud.

"'Shuster's Surely Shone Shoes Surely Shine!'" she replied with an amused chuckle, quoting a catchy advertising slogan that proclaimed how each pair of Shuster's shoes was wax-polished, by hand, before leaving the factory. "I can't imagine what we've done to deserve such attention; it's a mystery: 'The game's afoot, Watson!'" She was also an avid follower of Sherlock Holmes' adventures.

The next afternoon, at 3.30 sharp, Aunt Lucinda led me to our burgundy phaeton, Mr Harris in all his finery on the box seat, it being inappropriate for a lady to be seen driving herself to a visit of this nature.

I still remember that sunlit, golden day similar in mood to the rural scenes that our friend, Mr Streeton, had built his reputation upon by painting *en plein air* at Heidelburg, east of Melbourne. And I especially remember Aunt Lucinda seated opposite me, every inch the woman of international *chic*, cream lawn gown imported from her couturier in Paris, an Italian lace parasol warding off the redhead's curse of freckles, for she insisted that we drive with the top down. "See and be seen," she declared as we began to move. "If not, you might as well be dead."

I grumped and continued to sulk. This afternoon could have been spent barefoot and carefree at the end of our garden, fishing the Yarra or chucking stones at little boats woven from reeds. Instead of which I found myself wearing the ridiculous Eton collar, Norfolk jacket, and surely shone black shoes, all because some silly adults had taken it into their silly heads to share a silly dish of tea -!

Mr Harris eased our ponies from a stately trot and walked them up the driveway towards a two-storey pile that proudly proclaimed New Money by combining elements of a German *Schloss,* an English Tudor manor house, and a Gothic Revival chapel set in a geometrical garden modelled on the one that Louis XIV ordered André le Nôtre to lay at Versailles; the amiable Mr Roberts having informally expanded my artistic education well beyond perspective drawing and genre composition by feeding a precocious appetite for knowledge, allied with what used to be called a "flypaper memory."

A maid opened the iron-hinged, mock Medieval front door, bobbed a curtsy, and stood aside as we entered. She gave another nervous curtsy before leading the way deeper into a suffocating maze of ornately carved mahogany furniture; gloomy paintings of armoured knights pining after blonde maidens;

alabaster urns taller than I was at the time; mummified game trophies and glass domed displays of wax flowers.

Mr and Mrs Leon Shuster awaited their guests in a Music Room large enough to double as a private concert hall, and between them stood the pale little boy I had last seen being bullied at Melbourne Grammar.

"It is very kind, of you, to accept our invitation, so promptly." Mr Shuster's voice spoke of another time, another place, another language, and reminded me of our family doctor's.

"On the contrary," Aunt Lucinda replied with all the aplomb of an international charmer, "My nephew Ian and I are delighted to make your acquaintance…"

"It is kind, to say so." Mr Shuster was clearly uncomfortable with what he was about to add: "My son desires, to apologise." He gave a sideways nudge. "David…"

The young lad stepped forward, took a deep breath, and held out his hand as Proper English Gentlemen were required to do on such occasions. "I'm awfully sorry I caused you so much trouble."

"No, you didn't." The words escaped before I had time to think or return the proffered handshake. "That slimy sod needed a good bashing!"

"W-wh-what?!"

Mr Shuster took over from his stunned son. "You were expelled! You can go not to *shul*! Why then such a mad thing?!"

I glanced at Aunt Lucinda for guidance, but she replied with the merest hint of a shrug and was, I think, rather enjoying the scene as it developed. "Well," I replied, puzzled that an adult needed such a self-evident answer, "someone had to teach the rotten dog a lesson he won't forget in a hurry."

"And for that, you put him in, hospital?!" Mr Shuster was flustered, baffled, shocked.

This was news to me, though upon reflection I knew it must be true, for whenever there was a stoush in Playfair, or Argyll Streets, someone generally got carted off on a ladder or on a stretcher, if sufficiently alive to make it worth calling the local First Aid Volunteers.

David's father was not yet finished although he was finding it harder to continue. "Tell us, is it true, you used, bad language, at him?"

"Of course." This question baffled me as much as his previous one.

"But why?!"

"To make him turn, so's to boot his nuts," I replied, surprised that an adult didn't know how to fight.

Aunt Lucinda smothered a laugh and later told me it was as good as a play to see a protective Jewish family's confusion as this raw whiff of Sydney's lowlife pervaded their genteel Melburnian home.

There being nothing further that could be politely said on the subject, David was told to take me into the garden and play while the grown-ups became better acquainted. And so began the deepest friendship I have ever known, one that changed the course of my life at a time when RFC aircrews rarely survived more than a couple of weeks over the Western Front.

All of which lay ahead of us, in an unimaginable future, as we strolled among disciplined shrubberies and rigid borders crammed with plants of every shape and size, hardly any of which I recognised though David did, and not only by their popular names but by their Latin taxonomies, too.

A lonely, only child, glad of someone his own age to share with, he excitedly described the experiments he was conducting in his little greenhouse, analysing the chemical composition of different types of soil, and then making comparisons of growth by germinating identical seeds in separate pots under controlled conditions.

His laboratory notebook was neatly written-up and its working sketches weren't bad either, though I was able to improve their perspectives, as in fact I was doing when another maid called us in for fruitcake and lemonade.

The adults had also been having a fine old time, judging by the peals of happy laughter as my aunt gave the Shusters' concert grand a hearty workout with her variations on the *Infernal Galop*, better known as the *Can-Can* from her old colleague Jacques Offenbach's *Orpheus in the Underworld*.

26

We were eagerly invited to return next week, myself to play with David, and Aunt Lucinda to play with the amateurs who practiced at Hochheim every Thursday afternoon.

Describing them as amateur implies that they were no more than enthusiastic beginners having fun, but even my relatively untrained ear could tell that these academics, and surgeons, and manufacturers like Mr Shuster, were serious musicians. None of them could have known it then, but the sun was setting on their cosy, companionable little world. Clockwork gramophones were displacing the family piano. Soon there would be fewer and fewer middle-class harmonists and their musical *soireés*.

Melba happened to be visiting Tralee House on the same weekend as one of the Shusters' regular Sunday Concerts. Aunt Lucinda reached for pen and paper to send an apology, when our distinguished friend suggested that we all go together instead; Nellie never could resist an opportunity to amaze and delight an audience, be it large or small.

David's parents gawped, there is no other word to describe their response as the world's leading operatic soprano made her entrance, sharing theatrical gossip with the Antipodean Nightingale. I doubt if any of the other invited guests even dared to imagine she might honour us with a few notes from the voice that commanded hundreds of pounds a performance at London's Covent Garden Opera House.

Seated alongside me, surrounded by the Shusters' awestruck neighbours and business partners, Melba hummed her approval as the ensemble creditably performed chamber works by Mendelsohn, Brahms, and Smetana. Aunt Lucinda then enlivened the occasion with Liszt's Second Hungarian Rhapsody, after which she winked at Nellie for it was clear to me that they had cooked up something special.

There was an audible rustle of excitement as Melba advanced to the piano, struck a pose, and launched into the *Jewel Song* from Gounod's *Faust*, Aunt Lucinda at the keyboard. To call it a sensation is a gross understatement. Women wept, men leapt to their feet and applauded wildly, including one debonaire fellow whom David called Uncle John, and who sometimes played duets with my aunt. When the gasps and applause finally tapered off, he elbowed his way through the admiring crowd, gave Melba a big hug and appointed himself her escort for the rest of the evening.

I later learned that both he and she were raised in Richmond, just across the Yarra, where they had been childhood sweethearts. After graduating as a commercial lawyer and civil engineer, Mr Monash became a business associate of her father, David Mitchell, a canny Scot and one of the few building contractors to stay solvent after the Melbourne Property Crash of 1891.

Ignored by the adults, who now only had eyes for tonight's surprise guest of honour, David and I loaded our pockets with jam tartlets and went upstairs to explore the mysterious bedrooms, leaving trails of pastry crumbs as we pondered the strange things couples were whispered to do to each other under cover of darkness.

I never liked the place; to use a modern expression, it gave me the creeps. Whereas Tralee was light and airy, Hochheim always felt dark and constricted, stuffed with every ornamental extravagance that money could buy. David never said a word against his smothering homelife, but I think we both shared the same opinion, for he was always keen to come over and play among my more relaxed surroundings.

The Shusters' coachmen would always deliver him scrubbed and polished, clad in his Sunday best, for Mr and Mrs Shuster were under the fond delusion that he and I would now spend the afternoon seated in the library, earnestly improving our minds by poring over Aunt Lucinda's extensive collection of illustrated travel books and encyclopaedias.

The truth was usually otherwise, for the first thing he wanted to do was nip upstairs and change into clothing that my aunt thought was more suitable for stalking through undergrowth, on safari in a make-believe African jungle; or for climbing trees; or for netting tadpoles; or for chucking stones at reed boats; or for stripping off at our swimming hole and diving into the Yarra.

Even at that early age, David was a naturally gifted and fearless swimmer whereas the best I could manage was a laboured breaststroke. He tried hard to teach me the Australian Crawl, recently developed by his sporting hero, Dick Cavill, the first man to swim one hundred yards in under one minute, but I preferred to keep my head up and never really got the swing of his head-down, torpedo style of ploughing through water.

Then, tired but happy, we would troop back to Tralee House where Aunt Lucinda made sure that David was bathed, and combed, and brushed so that his parents would never suspect that their precious only child had enjoyed a blissful afternoon of unfettered freedom.

Those were the balmy days of Summer, but at other times of the year, when the sky was grim and grey, I would attempt to repay his athletic coaching by revealing the billiard table's tricks and traps, but just as I was not a natural swimmer, David lacked the necessary hand-eye coordination, when sighting a cue, that I had in natural abundance.

Aunt Lucinda would sometimes take us on a conducted tour of her private gallery, drawing bright and breezy word pictures of Bohemian Paris – carefully editing the spicy bits – when describing and discussing the artists whose colourful canvases enlivened her rooms and corridors, but whose names, thus far meant little or nothing to most Australians.

The series of sketches by someone with a quirky monogram "THL" were my favourites. Their bare structures and mastery of empty space – it takes true genius to make a swept pencil line suggest a crowded circus arena – became the foundations of my own later style.

On alternate weekends it would then be my turn to visit David's home, an event I looked forward to with mixed feelings, for I could never warm to the place. I should have shown more understanding, for what I saw as a gloomy mishmash of heavy furnishings and heavier artwork, Leon Shuster cherished as proof of how far he had come up in the world.

Despite being my friend's father, and although he would in all probability have given me the shirt off his back had I asked for it, I could never warm to him, either. The reason was painfully simple; I had detected an unmanly tremor of fear when he exclaimed: "You were expelled! You can go not to *shul*! Why then such a mad thing?!"

He could not have known how I felt about school after my brief brush with it, any more than I understood how superstitiously in awe he was of those with letters-after-their-names. Men who had clearly succeeded in a classroom and then at university. Ours was a dialogue of the deaf and, in hindsight, a great personal loss for I would have learned much from his courageous story as a teenage immigrant on the Victorian goldfields.

The son of a shoemaker – *Schuster* in German, a new surname he adopted for his new homeland, after dropping the "c" to appear less foreign – he ran away from home and got aboard a cargo schooner outward bound from Bremen to Port Phillip, at that time the most remote destination on the planet.

With barely a word of English he then joined a band of other hopefuls and set off for Bendigo to seek his fortune. Somewhere along the track, as they entered the hill country near Mount Macedon, one of the prospectors lost the heel of his boot. Young Leon improvised a cobbler's last from a wooden stump, scrounged a hammer and tacks and made a repair for three pence.

That was as far as he got to the goldfields. Instead, he established his workshop in a shanty halfway inland, the ideal location to serve diggers hurrying up country, or trudging back to the coast. In either direction there were always plenty of boots or leather gaiters to fix, although it was never easy money.

A bushfire burned him out, and bushrangers cleaned him out, at which point he acquired a Navy Colt revolver and, with it, a fierce determination to defend his cashbox. But throughout these many trials and tribulations, his business continued to grow, with others now repairing workmen's boots while he concentrated on crafting bespoke shoes for Melbourne's business leaders and their ladies, at his rented premises in Little Collins Street.

His first wife had died of cholera leaving him childless. Now in middle age, moderately prosperous and in need of a boy so that he could proudly proclaim "L Shuster & Son" in silver foil on his shop window, he sent back to Germany for a wife and committed, sight unseen except for one albumen paper print, to young Hannah Goldfarb

He thought he was importing an obedient *Hausfrau* who would deliver a brood of loving children, keep the servants in order, and have his slippers ready after a hard day's haggle behind the shop counter; instead, he got a dragon who had learned bookkeeping at night school while holding down a day job in the packing room of a Frankfurt silk merchant.

It mattered not that her command of English was poor; numbers have the same value in any language. And if Mr Shuster thought that her arrival meant he could now spend more time practicing the violin and reading the scholarly books he hoped would compensate for the lack of letters-after-his-name, he was sadly mistaken in this as well.

Iron Hannah restructured his firm just as Marvellous Melbourne hit its stride, and she more than anyone else made sure that it strode forward in tens of thousands of pairs of Shuster's Surely Shone Shoes, their latest patterns express delivered by clipper ship from Europe which meant, because of the six-month difference between seasons in the Northern Hemisphere and those in the Southern, that the wives and mistresses of Melbourne's millionaires always wore the latest fashions.

The latest machinery was also imported, from the United States where they understood the marvels of mass production better than anyone else, to keep pace with the demand for quality footwear. Bigger machines meant a bigger factory; then a tannery; then a warehouse, with its own railway spur line supplying stores across Victoria, New South Wales, as far north as Townsville in Queensland. And counting every penny, of every shilling, of every pound, every minute of every day was Mrs Leon Shuster *née* Goldfarb, an apt name for such a shrewd and tenacious businesswoman.

This side of the business was kept well hidden, of course, David's mother astutely choosing to lead from behind by encouraging her slightly bewildered husband to take all the credit for their good fortune. The Crash of '91 could have ruined them, but it was she who slashed the firm's wages bill, made swingeing economies in every department, and created the cheaper product lines that kept their company afloat while others sank around them.

I pieced together this inspiring story from David's occasional remarks as we imperceptibly grew out of childhood. Several times he asked about my family, but I was able to truthfully tell him that both parents were dead and that I didn't remember all that much about them.

This was not entirely true, but was sufficient to salve my conscience, as it would have been hard to lie to my dearest friend. Not that I'd have had any qualms about doing so, if necessary, for I was always fearful that Hochheim's door would be slammed in my face if his people ever learnt the sordid truth of my origins.

In hindsight, I don't think there was much chance of that happening. David was a precious only child who was acing every other student at Melbourne Grammar. Not only was he precociously bright, and clearly destined for the highest academic prizes, but also excelled in the swimming pool and would soon compete at the 1912 Olympic Games in Stockholm.

Classroom distinction, coupled with sporting prowess, protected him from the teachers' sarcasm and jealous jibes. Meanwhile the dark legend of how a tormentor had nearly been killed on his first day of school, made lesser bullies wary as he ascended through the ranks to become a prefect himself.

For this alone Mrs Shuster was grateful to me. Then there was the fact that I spoke reasonably fluent German and could comment on the day's news while translating the *Herald*'s lead stories and political commentaries, whereas her spoken English remained thick and awkward. Eventually I discovered a kindly, shy woman hidden behind her grim Teutonic exterior, a caring mother who doted on David and, by extension, myself as well.

It delighted her to see him reviewing his homework by teaching me the highlights of that week's studies at school. Neither of us could have guessed it at the time, but I was laying the groundwork for a career in Intelligence by observing him elucidate complex subjects while I memorised them, word-for-word.

27

Pausing to review my draft script, I notice several areas that need to be pruned before recording them tomorrow morning. Given all goes well, I shall then spend the afternoon deciding what to tape the following day, and days thereafter, until I run out of material. Or time.

I must keep in mind that Frances only wants to study my voice patterns, not be forced to sit through hours of idle chit-chat describing my informal education as it continued to follow Aunt Lucinda's *Pygmalion Plan*, several years before Mr Shaw gentrified his Cockney flower girl in a stage play.

Besides learning how to behave correctly at a billiards table, the young Edwardian was expected to play Euchre, Whist, and Bridge with dignified calm, politely alert for the bottom draws and false cuts, culling and stacked hustles that I was also being taught to recognise, by a professional card sharp in Aunt Lucinda's employ.

And there was the question of deportment and appearance, for which a gentleman had to know how to choose the best tailor, order fine wine, select a good cigar, make pleasing conversation in mixed company, and be an attentive partner at tennis.

This being 1910, the Age of Men, we were also required to qualify as Two Barrels Two Birds shotgunners and firmly Seat the Saddle when riding in town or country. Acquiring these skills was a delight, unlike my compulsory etiquette lessons. No healthy young man should ever be expected to memorise the correct procedure for hailing a cab when escorting a lady, or understand its subtle variations for a wife, or a fiancée, or a family friend, or an acquaintance.

Then there was the oppressive list of gaffes that must be avoided at all costs. For instance, in the unlikely event of ever being presented to the King, or Viceroy, or Governor General, one must not offer to shake hands or begin the conversation; the initiative must always come from Him.

It was also considered bad form to cut bread at dinner; one "broke" crusty bread rolls, buttering each sippet as required. And table knives must never be held as if they were pens or used to carry cheese to the mouth, nor were they to be crossed with their fork on the plate when that course was finished.

There was a multitude of other social tripwires for the unwary and doubtless these would seem absurd nowadays, when it is quite acceptable to socialise in blue dungaree trousers and tea shirts printed with advertising slogans, as if one were a reincarnation of the old sandwich-board man. But having a mutually agreed code of dress and behaviour meant that friends and strangers could meet and converse in a civil, civilised, civilising equality.

If I had to describe Edwardian manners and protocol in one pithy phrase, it would be Tactful Awareness of Others' Feelings. We learned by observation that a tactful person instantly senses the prevailing mood and responds with politeness and understanding, regardless of the place, the company, or even the provocation.

The hallmark of a gentleman, we were told, is that he never spoke to shop assistants or servants as if they were inferior beings; only the insecure upstart needs the reassurance of arrogance. Instead, we were expected to maintain a genial dignity and display a gracious kindness, regardless of the company we were keeping at the time, and who can argue against this, especially in today's ruder, cruder world?

I observed this behaviour whenever Vida Goldstein took tea in Tralee House' conservatory. Hers is a name now largely forgotten, which is a great pity, for with the wisdom of hindsight she was a goodhearted soul, even if most Australians regarded her as a Communist ratbag.

In any event she entered my circle of acquaintance at about the same time as I began sketched portraiture; Miss Vida, as she preferred to be known, did not mind me sitting nearby with pencil and pad while she hotly debated politics with Aunt Lucinda. And yet despite their differences in age, and backgrounds, and views of the world, they remained firm friends.

Similarly, the fact that her name was the feminine form of David attracted me to this handsome, rather bossy woman who would often exclaim, in Spanish, "¡Viva la Vida!" as she girded up her loins to launch some new campaign of social reform. And yet, despite her Jewish surname, Vida Goldstein was mostly of Scotch-Irish descent and had matriculated from Presbyterian Ladies' College long before my arrival in Melbourne.

A particular conversation remains fresh in the memory, one that I shall certainly tape record to show the Fair Frances that not all nineteenth century woman – regardless of their ridiculous whalebone corsets and exaggerated bustles – were submissive playthings for men's cruel amusement.

I clearly remember an afternoon's wistful, autumnal sunlight gilding the birch trees on Tralee's riverbank when Miss Vida arrived earlier than usual and more than usually determined to put the world to rights.

Unless I've muddled the dates, this must have been shortly after she returned from America, where this feisty Australian lady had lectured the United States Congress, hammering it with statistics to prove the need for Female Suffrage, before returning home and trying for our Senate as an Independent candidate, the first woman in the British Empire to stand for election to a national parliament.

Although failing to win a seat, she did garner fifty thousand votes that she and her supporters now wanted to form into a political party by launching a new magazine – I think it was called *The Australasian Women's Sphere* – for which she needed seed capital; Aunt Lucinda was an obvious touch, always good for a donation whenever an orphanage or hospital, homeless shelter or striking picket line needed a helping hand.

I recall my aunt signing the cheque with a flourish and then pausing, a quizzical smile on her sharp, birdlike features. "Do you seriously believe that political agitation makes any real difference in the greater scheme of things?"

"Of course!" the younger woman announced with an assertive tilt of the chin. "Now that women have won the vote in Australia, it is our duty to continue the struggle until we win power!"

"Who says we don't already have power...?"

"I do." Announced with another determined flick of the chin. "One only has to step inside Parliament to be overwhelmed by whiskers and beards, top hats and frock coats!"

"True enough," the older woman agreed with a reflective nod, "but is there not a risk of mistaking the appearance of power for its more subtle substance?"

"How do you mean?!"

"You are right," Aunt Lucinda continued. "One half of the population is unrepresented, meaning that our womanly concerns are decided by men with no idea of what they're talking about. But does that mean we are powerless...?"

"Yes!"

"Then I must respectfully disagree."

"What?"

"My grandmama had a rich treasury of insights that she would ofttimes share." The raised finger silenced Miss Vida's imminent interruption. "One especially went like this: 'For some inscrutable reason The Great Anatomist created women with physically weak bodies, for which He or She or It gave us brains in compensation thereof. But female brains without masculine brawn are poor, feeble things indeed! That is why men were created. However, without our brains to direct its exertions, their brawn remains little better than a bowl of cold pork jelly. Therefore, a woman's role in the Great Topsy Turvy Drama of Life is to provide the brains, a man's part is to provide the brawn, and provided both recognise and respect their needs for each other, all do prosper. But if they don't, they won't.'"

I'd been sketching Miss Vida's expressively clenched fists, for as every portraitist knows, facial features are relatively easy to depict but fingers are fiendishly hard to draw if they are not to appear as funny little sausages.

Neither woman noticed my ears prick up at this subversive stratagem in what was then called the "Battle of the Sexes," a brutal domestic war in which most of its casualties were cowed wives with bloodshot eyes or bruised cheeks, missing teeth, or broken bones. Or murder by an insanely jealous, drunken, diseased husband.

"No! She was wrong! For change to have meaning, women must seize the reins of power!"

"Spoken like a man..."

"Of course! That's the only way we'll beat 'em at their own game!"

"My dear, listen carefully," Aunt Lucinda leaned forward to pat Miss Vida's trembling wrist. "Wild talk of snatching reins from men's hands tells me that you are riding at a fence you can never jump, because in any physical contest we are certain to get the worst of it, unless armed with a dagger or a pistol, and are prepared to use 'em."

"Might is not right! Violence is never the answer!"

"In theory," Aunt Lucinda smiled. "In practice, Might makes the Right by which weaker parties must rub along as best they can, or suffer the consequences. And if that means leading from behind, as Mrs Shuster does so adroitly with her husband, so be it. After all," she concluded, "do you seriously think they would have prospered in a man's world had she humiliated her husband by publicly 'seizing the reins of power'?"

"That is so underhand, so unworthy!"

"No, my dear, it is just another example of womanly wiles weaving their wondrous web to advantage all."

"No! It's the mentality of a slave!" Miss Vida's expressive fists punched air as if addressing a crowd of thousands. "Women must be properly educated to seize our rightful place in the world!"

"Hm." My aunt's forefinger stroked a reflective smile. "And for that to happen, you feel it necessary to snatch the political reins from our menfolk?"

"Yes!"

"Then I am much afraid that you are still confusing the appearances of power with its substance. Whoa! I'm not finished yet." The finger lowered slowly. "For example, what would you say if I told you that two women reformed the French education system, so that other women – who still don't have a vote, unlike the one you recently achieved for us in Australia – could become expertly trained teachers and midwives, lawyers and doctors?"

I am probably one of the few persons who ever saw Vida Goldstein stumped for words.

"It's true," Aunt Lucinda continued, with an arch smile. "One of them was Her Imperial Majesty the Empress Eugénie de Montijo, a staunch advocate of women's rights, and also the wife of my good friend Louis Napoleon, a lady with whom I still exchange Christmas greetings for old time's –"

"Yes, yes, but who was the other?"

"The one they called '*Le Rossignol*' or in English, 'The Nightingale.'"

"Obviously a courtesan or high-class prostitute," Miss Vida sniffed. And to show that her French lessons at the Presbyterian Ladies' College had not been forgotten: "*Une grande horizontale.*"

"You may very well think so, I could not possibly comment," my aunt smiled again. "But to continue, the Nightingale heard of a talented young woman – Mlle Julie Daubié – whose sex prevented her from taking the *baccalauréat*, or high school certificate, without which she could not proceed further. Remember, at the time of which I speak, the standard of women's education in France was barely sufficient for them to add-up a butcher's bill or read the notice boards forbidding them to pee in the street.

"Her mysterious benefactrix happened to know that the Empress was deeply concerned with all matters charitable. For instance, when the City of Paris gave a wedding present of six hundred thousand gold francs to buy a diamond necklace, Her Imperial Majesty devoted every centime to the establishment of an orphanage for abandoned baby girls, in the Faubourg Saint-Antoine.

"Meanwhile our two heroines put their heads together and agreed on a plan of action to change an unjust schooling system. The crusty old fossils at the Ministry of Worship, which at that time still controlled national education, were shocked rigid when they learned of it and did everything possible to thwart this challenge to their inflexible rule.

"Poor things! They had no idea what they were up against, even though one of the women in question was born a Spanish grandee of three armorial quarterings, a superior caste that mere mortals provoke at their peril. The Empress also chaired the Imperial Cabinet's meetings whenever her husband was otherwise engaged, and later represented France when the Suez Canal opened in '69.

"But to continue. In the fulness of time, with a gracious word here, and a sympathetic smile there, Mlle Daubié got her cherished diploma to go on to greater things, as indeed did many another Frenchwoman in the years to come, for the greater glory of *la Patrie* and the Empress Eugénie, ably assisted by the sweetly singing Nightingale…"

Miss Vida frowned. "And the moral of this story is what?!"

"Think about it, my dear," Aunt Lucinda advised with an enigmatic smile, releasing her cheque. "Tell me when you find the answer."

28

My further education in the wily ways of wondrous women continued every Wednesday afternoon at Madame Jourdan's Academy of Dance, on the corner of Chapel and Oxford streets in the neighbouring suburb of South Yarra. Here, gawky young boys and bashful young girls would pair off to trip, trudge, or trample through the Boston Two Step or Veleta Waltz.

Nimble footwork came naturally to me, and I was often called upon to demonstrate a particular step pattern, my face tantalisingly close to Madame's fragrant bosom. The memory of Uncle Bertie's fatal adventure with Mama was never far from my mind on these occasions, a stern warning that such disturbances spelt "Death!" in dripping blood red letters.

Because of the peculiar circumstances of my upbringing, I had acquired an adult's knowledge while still only a child and this conflicted imbalance gave rise to intense doubts and anxieties. On the one hand I relished putting my arm around a strange girl's waist and whirling her across the Academy's waxed wooden floor; on the other hand, I knew this was as far as it must go. Even at that early age, I could have taught Dr Freud a thing or two about repressed sexuality and the male psyche.

It was not necessary to find a dying mother and murdered uncle, in bed together, to learn caution in such matters. Salvarsan had only just been introduced and was not yet widely available as a treatment for syphilis, an endemic disease in the first decade of this century. Its leprous features and the shambling gait of *tabes dorsalis* common sights on the streets of Melbourne, and both very familiar to "Champagne Charley's" frightened little boy.

Not much escaped Aunt Lucinda's attention and I am pretty sure she knew what was happening better than I did. Matters came to a head at about the time when she presented me with an ivory handled Solingen razor and watched closely as Signor Grillo - an Italian barber who bicycled around Toorak attending to the families in our grander residences - showed me how to shave without lopping off an ear or cutting my throat.

Our tailor had already taken my measurements and returned for the fittings of my first adult morning suit in finest dark grey worsted. I must confess that I failed to recognise the young dandy posing in the cheval mirror. Of slim build and medium height, I cut quite a dash in a four-button jacket; starched wing collar and white bib shirt with gold studs; black Marcella bow tie; grey waistcoat buttoned up except for the bottom one, always left undone out of respect for our rather tubby King Edward VII.

The following week I found myself promoted to the Academy's Intermediate Class, no longer a junior but not yet a full-blown adult, where the young ladies were decidedly more dangerous than the girls I had previously squired. Not to put too fine a point on things, I often found it hard to concentrate on my footwork.

It was about now that Madame introduced Miss Maeve X, allegedly requiring a few intermediate lessons before the debutante ball season. At first glance there was nothing especially striking, except for her richly burnished, chestnut brunette hair swept up in the then-fashionable Gibson Girl style, and the creamy complexion I later came to associate with those of West Coast Irish descent. But – oh! - her enchanting eyes. Deep brown, bright with good-humoured mischief, living proof of an ancestor washed ashore in Galway after the wreck of the Spanish Armada. Even more remarkable, though, was the fact that she seemed to respond to my tongue-tied feelings.

Meanwhile, it was not long before Madame began calling on us to demonstrate the more intricate moves, becoming in rapid order her star pupils for Maeve was clearly an accomplished dancer and I a quick learner, so much so that we were soon ready to enter a major ballroom competition at the Richmond Oddfellows' Hall.

It happened that our coachman was suddenly indisposed, and Aunt Lucinda had an onset migraine that prevented her coming along to that night's gala occasion. Instead, I was entrusted with two half sovereigns and some loose silver and sent off on my own in a cab to the address where Maeve lodged with a girlfriend, while both studied shorthand and typewriting at Stott's Business College.

As a couple we did well, coming fourth in a field of twenty-five, after which everyone was invited to stay for a light supper. Maeve, however, hinted at a much better idea and we made a quiet exit, hailed a cab, and settled into the hansom's snug gloom, her head resting on my proud young shoulder as the horse clip-clopped along gaslit Bridge Road.

Another hallmark of the Edwardian gentleman is that he was the soul of discretion whenever a lady's name was mentioned in conversation, as I have just demonstrated by masking her identity even though beautiful young "Maeve" is now sadly no more than an old man's fading memory.

Suffice it to say that we spent many a delightful afternoon at her place, the girlfriend always busy elsewhere. I was never hoodwinked by this astonishing good fortune and later had every reason to be grateful to Aunt Lucinda for orchestrating such a skilled and happy initiation into the arts and joy of love at a time when I could have bitterly turned inwards upon myself.

We remained friends long after our *affaire* reached its natural conclusion, last meeting at Flemington Racecourse the year that *Evening Peal* won the Melbourne Cup. I'd been invited there by Oswald Syme, the publisher when, to my surprise and delight, Maeve and her husband of many years – one of Victoria's prominent industrialists – entered the *Age* newspaper's private enclosure, where the four of us shared a most convivial luncheon.

29

Meanwhile, David and I were inevitably growing apart as our lives took divergent paths. For me this was a time of incremental change as I trained to become a Proper English Gentleman; for him it was about to become the momentous shift from schoolboy to adult.

The Shusters were not overt in their displays of religion, for much the same reason as that dropped "c" from their name, even so they were loyal and generous benefactors of the East Melbourne Synagogue, making it the logical place for their son's Bar Mitzvah.

If I thought that my list of social gaffes was onerous, I had yet to learn of the 600-odd obligations that David was preparing to shoulder for the rest of his life, a crushing burden, even for such a conscientious student. In a moment of exasperation, he confessed to finding Hebrew illogical, unlike his beloved Linnean taxonomy with its orderly Latin names for every known plant. I could only agree. As a working language, the Bible's original Semitic tongue lacked vowels and was written right-to-left with twenty-two characters that, to my unlettered eye, resembled bent nails and twisted wire staples.

Mr and Mrs Shuster kindly included my name on their guest list, allowing ample time to choose an appropriate present for such a high and holy occasion. Aunt Lucinda asked around and learned that the ideal gift should be serious, of lasting value, and have a personal touch. In default of which a gold watch, or a set of cufflinks and shirt studs, or a sum of money in multiples of 18, which was considered an auspicious number, would do almost as well.

The big day arrived for Mr Harris to drive me across town to the synagogue in Albert Street where I took my place in the congregation, head covered like every other male in this distinguished company. Nearby sat Mr Myer the millionaire importer and retailer; also, Mr Monash the civil engineer, commercial lawyer, and reserve commission army officer; and Professor Sir Philip Rothstein of the University's medical faculty, all of whom I had met before at the Hochheim concerts.

Everyone was politely attentive to my needs but there was no question that I was the odd man out, just as they themselves wore an indefinable air of otherness that set them apart from Melbourne's frowning Presbyterianism. This cast me as the Outsiders' outsider, not that I minded, having learned early in life to live by myself, even if it has not always been easy living with myself.

Not so David, the cynosure of every eye, he performed with assurance and style, even reading passages from his version of the Old Testament with inflection and meaning. I was impressed and could not help noticing a stir of interest among the more aware seated around me and, in imagination saw Mr Leon Shuster grow another six inches by the time his son finished, probably envisaging a famous rabbi in the family.

After so much solemnity came gaiety and high spirits and sprightly music as the womenfolk joined us for a banquet at which many speeches were given and toasts responded to; it made me happy to see David so poised and confident in such company, not that anyone expected less of him.

The various gifts and tokens were paraded for inspection on a nearby table for all to admire. Mine stood well to the back, being bulkier than the gold watches, and cuff links, and slim envelopes. I was glad, not wishing to draw attention to myself when the time came for David to thank us.

He then began formally inspecting the gifts one-by-one, without naming names of course, until he came to mine, still anonymously wrapped in a dark burgundy paper. Intrigued, he broke its red wax seal and exposed a black japanned metal box with leather shoulder strap, the weatherproof shell for a polished oak case that in turn housed the Zeiss field microscope Aunt Lucinda had ordered from Germany. There was even a small, exquisitely crafted toolkit for any adjustments that needed to be made while paddling up the Amazon, or crossing the deserts of Central Asia, or camping on Arctic tundra.

I watched his fingers reverently stroking the burnished brass work, the fine steel rack and pinion gears, the engraved platinum vernier scale of a proper scientific instrument, unlike the second-hand school model in his greenhouse laboratory. He then read the inscribed silver plate attached inside its lid:

Sciencia et Cultura pro omne.
Ian Cribdon

It is my sincere hope that the other guests imagined he was weeping for joy at receiving their presents, but I doubt if Iron Hannah was fooled for one moment. Surrounded as she was by proud Jewish mothers who constantly bragged about "My Son the Doctor!" or "My Son the Lawyer!" she had no intention of apologising for "my boy the botanist," an activity she equated with sentimental ladies pressing flowers in their journals. This was something he could always do for a hobby after a hard day's work performing miracles of surgery, or dazzling juries as a King's Counsel barrister earning hundreds of guineas *per diem* for doing so.

She never openly criticised me for such a disruptive gift, but her attitude changed and my invitations to Hochheim became less frequent as Melbourne Grammar's brightest of the bright spent more time at his greenhouse bench, dissecting plant tissue and peering at stained cells sandwiched between thin slips of glass.

Quite early in the piece, while we were still inseparable friends, he had insisted on bringing the microscope over to Tralee House where our grape vines were suffering from downy mildew and set up a field laboratory in the tool-shed. I volunteered to be his dogsbody assistant, collecting specimens, and running errands while he examined leaves at the microscope's highest magnification, all the while commenting excitedly in what for me was a foreign language. The upshot was his first published scientific paper:

Differentiated Oomycete Parasitism
with reference to the
cellular morphology of Plasmopara Viticola

His fieldwork was warmly reviewed in the *Proceedings of the Royal Society of Victoria* by A.J.Ewart, the recently appointed Foundation Professor of Botany at Melbourne University, a considerable achievement for a young man who had yet to finish high school. But even this promise of greater things to come was not enough to dispel the disapproval of a mother who could see her dreams wilting like the blighted leaves in our vineyard.

Matters finally came to a head when David was selected for the 1912 Olympics' swimming team a few months before my imagined eighteenth birthday. This sounds rather grand to the modern ear, but at that time the Games were still little more than an amateur athletics carnival, with no million-dollar product endorsements for winning an event. If Shusters' Shoes had not paid for his travel and lodgings, David could never have gone to Sweden, and I suspect this was a covert bribe to change his mind about studying plant pathology.

As this year's recipient of the Governor's Gold Medal for coming top in our state-wide matriculation exams and having carried off every academic prize that Melbourne Grammar could bestow, there was not a medical or law school in the British Empire that would not have hurriedly rolled out the red carpet, had they seen him coming their way. I'm sure it was only jealousy and prejudice that blocked a Rhodes Scholarship, but how does one prove a sly whisper and a furtive nod three quarters of a century later?

Aunt Lucinda and I motored down to St Kilda docks when the time came for David to leave for Europe, Mr Harris at the wheel of the Vauxhall tourer he had taught himself to drive, sort of, and was now garaged in the coach house where the phaeton used to be, although every so often he would forget and snarl "whoa there!" instead of hauling the handbrake.

My aunt was starting to fade, and she needed an ebony walking cane to get around. Thankfully her mind was as sharp as ever, although she had been somewhat distracted for quite a while and I often caught her watching me with a questioning, preoccupied look. However, her odd behaviour was furthest from my mind as we drove past the partially finished Luna Park funfair, its grinning Mr Moon ticket gate seeming to mock a silent, anxious crowd gathered to watch the Olympians go aboard *RMS Osterley*.

The Orient Steam Navigation Company's flagship - *en route* from Wellington to London via Sydney, Melbourne, Hobart, and Perth - was assembling members of the Australasian Team at every port of call. It would be another decade before Australia and New Zealand competed as separate nations. In hindsight the Australasians of 1912 foreshadowed the Australian & New Zealand Army Corps of 1914, just as that morning's subdued mood was an eerie premonition of grim things to come.

By tragic coincidence the world's latest and largest ocean liner had sunk on her maiden voyage earlier in the week. Details were still sketchy as the telegraphic news agencies cabled their hourly bulletins from New York, the nearest port of arrival for those passengers and crew who managed to reach a lifeboat. There have been films, and novels, and endless arguments over *Titanic*'s loss in the decades since then, but I can only speak of its effect immediately after the event.

The death toll of more than fifteen hundred stunned a public not yet accustomed to casualty lists from a war where twenty-three thousand Australians would soon be killed or wounded capturing a heap of rubble that used to be a village on the road from Albert to Bapaume. However, it was not only the startling number of dead that gave *Titanic* her heightened significance to a generation firm in the belief that steam and steel, grit and determination, British engineering and human ingenuity, had conquered Nature.

It was obvious to every thinking man, that if a stray iceberg could destroy what was built to be an unsinkable luxury hotel, with every modern convenience, then something was very wrong with the world! That it could have had the insolence to drown millionaires in 1st Class, with the same indifference as it had drowned scruffy migrants in Steerage, was outrageous! Such blatant disrespect for the proper rules of conduct sparked Questions in Parliament and unleashed a pack of angry letters to the *Times* demanding Answers!

It was notable that Melbourne's daily newspapers glossed over much anxious sobbing and crying on the quayside, a time when everyone should have been in high spirits, to avoid jinxing *Osterley*'s onward voyage. Her captain certainly did his best to dispel the gloom by ordering the ship's orchestra to play lively ragtime tunes as passengers and their guests hugged and parted, perhaps for the last time.

Mrs Shuster was notably absent as we took our leave of David. Her husband alone had accompanied their boy and his luggage in a cab that ought to have been draped with black, funereal crape, so mournful was Mr Shuster's tired old face.

Apparently, there had been a terrible scene at Hochheim the previous night in which Iron Hannah called upon every manipulative weapon in her formidable armoury, hoping to force her son to change his mind about sailing to Stockholm.

Her knowledge of geography was vague at best. In imagination the Indian Ocean, the Mediterranean, the Atlantic, the North Sea, the Baltic were one and the same and crowded with lurking icebergs, all with evil designs on her precious only child.

When her wheedling threats failed to budge him, the distraught mother fell back on what should have been an infallible stratagem, the Hysterical Swoon. It spoke volumes for David's resolution that he was still standing with us on the quay that grey morning, albeit pale and downcast.

"Good luck old chap!" I grinned reassuringly as we shook hands. "Let's see you add another gold medal to the collection."

"One can but try."

Something in his listless tone told me this was not going to end well. A sportsman about to compete at the highest level needs all the emotional support he can get if he is to go the distance against other elite athletes at the peak of their form.

Because of our closeness I immediately sensed that something said or done the previous night had punched the heart out of him, and so it proved to be when he withdrew from the Finals of the Men's 1500 metres Freestyle, citing a stomach disorder.

30

That evening I bathed and dressed for dinner, as was the custom at Tralee House, for quite often there was a visiting artist, or actor, or old friend to share gossipy news from a wider world than Melbourne could then offer, but tonight we dined alone.

"It's been an odd sort of day," Aunt Lucinda thought aloud, raising a spoon to her lips. "In fact, it's been an odd sort of week," she added, absentmindedly sipping the chicken consommé that was a great favourite at our table. "There is a feeling of thunder in the air…"

I blinked, unsure if she was speaking with me, or with one of the invisible friends who accompanied her these days. A smugly ignorant youth, I thought it an amusing eccentricity, unaware that the time would come when I too would only have ghosts to converse with. Like now.

"There was the same sense of an impending storm in '67," she continued, distracted by something or someone unseen.

"Oh?"

"Strange though, because everything began so well," she elaborated with a reflective frown. "His Imperial Majesty had decreed a second and larger *Exposition Universelle*, to amaze the world with our progress since the previous one in '55…"

Trying to discover the key to this brooding monologue, I coughed lightly into my fist. "And were they amazed?"

"Of course." She set the spoon down. "Nobody knew it at the time, but that April was the last flowering of *La Belle Époque*. The tens of thousands of chestnut trees that Baron Haussmann's gardeners had planted along his new boulevards, were laden with blossom as kings and rulers from every corner of the world rode in procession to the opening ceremony on the Champ de Mars…"

"That must've been quite a sight." I was at a loss to say anything more original; it was rare for her to reminisce so spontaneously, and I was uncertain where this was taking us.

"Oh, it was indeed a sight! Prince Jérôme, an old friend, secured me an uninterrupted view of the proceedings from a seat next to the Imperial Box. Louis Napoléon himself made certain I received a *laissez-passer* granting privileged access to the Exposition at any time during the next seven months, one I availed myself of at every opportunity, there being so much to see among the many thousands of exhibits from more than forty different countries. Why, it almost felt as if one were inside an incarnated encyclopaedia!

"Thrice I went up in M'sieur Giffard's balloon to view it all from above. And yet," she hesitated, "charmed as our happy, carefree throngs of visitors were, by lively tunes from *Maître* Offenbach's latest operetta, *La Grande-Duchesse de Gérolstein*, it was that monster Bismarck who most perceptively interpreted its three-act plot of militarism gone mad, when he observed: '*C'est tout-à-fait ça!*' Or, more colloquially: 'That's the way the world wags…'" She hesitated again before concluding: "Among all the emperors and kings, grand-dukes and princes assembled in Paris that summer, he alone had the foreknowledge to hear the approaching rumble of thunder…"

"Summer storms must be pretty common in Europe," I thought aloud.

"Don't be such a numbskull! Learn to distinguish between figurative and literal imagery." She broke her bread roll with an impatient twist of the wrist. "The Prussians, with their customary lack of tact, chose to display a monstrous artillery piece at this celebration of peaceful commerce and industry. Victor Hugo, our most eminent writer, ridiculed them as 'uncouth barbarians hatched from a cannon ball.'" Then, cruelly mimicking his words in a theatrical Frenchman's mincing accent, she continued: "'Zeez enormous shells, 'urled from zee gigantic Krupp cannon, will no more stop Progress zan soap bubbles blown from zee mouth of a leedle child…' *Imbécile!*"

Aunt Lucinda controlled her anger. "His 'soap bubbles' were damned soon raining death and destruction on the very same people who laughed so gaily at Berlin's 'Paris Gun'!" She was about to add something else before abruptly changing her mind and concluding with an enigmatic: "*Plus ça change, plus c'est la même chose…*"

I was not at all sure what instance of Unaltered Change she was referring to, but by now I was sufficiently attuned to her moods to realise that she rarely spoke of the past without it serving some deeper purpose, now and into the future.

I also knew that she was closely following events in the Balkans where a coalition of minor nations, led by Montenegro and Serbia, were about to fight the Ottoman Empire over some ancient grudge provoked by the Austro-Hungarian annexation of Bosnia & Herzegovina, whatever and wherever those were! None of which had calmed her fears that such Ruritanian squabbles might yet boil over.

Once, after I'd aired my shallow opinions by declaring that such events were empty historical gestures, she tartly replied by paraphrasing Pericles, the Ancient Athenian statesman: "Just because you don't take an interest in History doesn't mean that History won't take an interest in you -!"

My aunt never missed an opportunity to remind listeners that her arch-villain, Bismarck, had predicted a major European war more than thirty years earlier when he said: "We are like men smoking in a powder magazine. One spark will set off the explosion that will blow us all to pieces. I cannot tell when it will occur, but I can say what and where. Some damn' foolish thing in the Balkans…"

Seeking to allay her fears, I leaned forward reassuringly. "The Siege of Paris happened yonks ago. The modern world has moved on since then!"

"You hope."

"No, seriously," I insisted. "David's been reading a book which proves, beyond any shadow of doubt, that conflict between the Great Powers is now impossible.'

"He hopes."

"No, seriously! You see, it all has to do with finance, and international credit, and the fact that everything is so interconnected through trade that everybody would be bankrupted within a week of declaring war. Therefore, it's unthinkable as well as impossible."

A scornful glance deflated my wide-eyed innocence as she summoned the parlourmaid for our next course, braised lambs' kidneys on sautéed potatoes, like the fresh peas and other side vegetables, also grown in Tralee's kitchen garden.

Age had not dulled her appetite, nor had it diminished her powers of shrewd observation. "Apropos of David," she neatly halved a spear of asparagus, "he looked rather sallow this morning. Any idea what's troubling him?"

I dabbed lips on a starched linen napkin and reached for the glass of Polly that accompanied our meals. "His Ma kicked up a terrible stink last night. Doesn't want him to drown!"

"A natural concern," Aunt Lucinda replied, with a disapproving frown at my cocky tone and slangy speech, "also a very common mistake. The more we cling to the ones we love, the more certain we are to lose them. Best we cut them loose, to sink or swim by making their own ways in the world…"

This seemed like a very insensitive remark, so close to the *Titanic*'s loss. "What's that got to do with David?"

"He's not the one I'm thinking of, my dear," she replied with a reflective smile. "It's time we discussed your future. What do you see yourself accomplishing, during the next four or five years…?"

"Well, Jem - Mr Sykes - thinks I'm ready for the State Championships, and after those, the Nationals in Sydney. And then –"

A raised finger stopped me mid-sentence. "Is that how you see yourself as an adult? Frequenting billiard saloons? Wagering for a livelihood?"

"Why not?" I protested defensively. "I'm good at it, the company is amusing, and I've begun a series based on those Lautrecs." I nodded towards my favourite circus sketches, framed on a nearby wall. "You'd be astonished at the rich variety of expressions to be seen around a billiard table!"

"No, I would not," she observed acidly. "That particular artist had much to teach *un aspirant*, like yourself, but the only thing to be learned from his way of life is that disease and alcohol invariably lead to a dishonoured grave…"

Without speaking the forbidden name aloud, I sensed it was not Henri de Toulouse-Lautrec but, rather, "Champagne Charley" Braithwaite she had in mind.

The next few weeks passed quickly as I trained hard for the 1912 Victorian State Championships. Meanwhile, David sent laconic postcards from every port of call until reaching Sweden, later in May, at which point they stopped, so I naturally assumed he was now too busy winning medals to have the time to write home.

For most *Argus* readers those Olympics were, at best, a rich man's jamboree somewhere near the North Pole. In fact, the only news I can recall seeing was a brief mention of the Australasians competing at Stockholm, wedged between an account of a charity ball in aid of the Soldiers' & Sailors' Help Society, and the previous day's County Cricket results telegraphed from England.

It was here that Fanny Durack won Australia's first gold medal in the swimming pool, although the nation only got to hear about it a week or so later. The sole reason I can remember her now is because of the nickname we gave to a statue of the Virgin & Child, leaning forward atop the partially destroyed spire of Albert Cathedral, seemingly about to dive into the street as we tramped towards the overlapping roars of artillery; the plunging shrieks of shellfire; the tacker-tack-tack of machine gunnery; the whipcracks of rifle fire that awaited us, just over the hill.

Such indifference must sound strange to the modern ear, given the extravagant worship of sporting gods and goddesses at the recent Olympics in Los Angeles, but like much else, ours was a simpler world before the Great War turned everything upside down. Then, at last, in early-September, a welcome note from David:

Kung Karl Hotel
Birger Jarlsgatten 21
Stockholm

3rd August 1912

Dear Old Goliath Slayer.

The Games were a bit of an anti-climax but an excellent chance to meet chaps from all over and I have decided to stay a while longer.

Jena University is doing great work on Cytoplasmic Microscopy, under Prof. von Erwald so I shall attend his lectures, to learn more and polish my German which, I now realise, is less than correctly fluent.

As ever.

D.

The reference to Goliath was his way of commemorating our first encounter at Melbourne Grammar, and the bashing I gave a prefect who stood head and shoulders taller than either David or myself, but for the rest of his message, it might as well have been an encoded wireless signal from the Moon.

In due course I replied, knowing that he would have left a forwarding address at the hotel, and with ill-concealed pride told of the intricate strategies played to win a top ten ranking in the Victorian State Titles, though not quite high enough to qualify for next year's Nationals.

Aunt Lucinda coolly marked the occasion with an inscribed silver cigarette case, but with a noticeable undercurrent of concern for the fast company I was keeping in Melbourne's shadier billiard saloons.

Matters came to a head as Christmas 1912 approached and Mr Meyer decorated his storefront windows with illuminated Nativity scenes, and drifts of cotton wool snow for an automated marionette of Good King Wenceslas to wade across, bearing food, and wine, and winter fuel for the Poor Man at St Agnes' Fountain.

The fact that our local midsummer temperatures were hovering around one hundred degrees Fahrenheit did nothing to lessen his customers' nostalgia for their grey and frosty Home on the far side of the Equator.

Aunt Lucinda invited me to join her for lunch under the trellised grape that overlooked the Yarra, languidly flowing its last couple of miles to Port Philip and the Southern Ocean.

After we settled down, the maidservant unpacked a picnic hamper containing the very same fare as I had wolfed aboard that train ride from Sydney to the Victorian border, all those years ago.

By now I had acquired sufficient social grace not to swig ginger beer from the bottle, or mangle crusty rolls while my aunt broke the cold pheasant with fingers knotted with age and arthritis.

"Ian, my dear, do you remember the last time we partook of a picnic like this?"

"Yes. Vividly."

"As do I," she nodded. "It seems but yesterday that you were a snotty nosed little waif of no account, but despite such an unpromising start you have turned into a quite presentable young man…"

"Um. Thank you.'

"Yes indeed, thank me," she echoed with the ironic, bantering tone that I later came to associate with France and the French. "Mr Sykes says that you have what it takes to do well in the Nationals, if not next year, then most likely in 1914 or '15. After which, provided you've learned to pace yourself better, you can reasonably expect to turn professional –"

"That's what I intend doing!"

"Hm." She absentmindedly buttered a piece of crust. "Well, if that is your destiny, so be it. Follow your star, I did. However," she continued in a darker tone, "be aware that the public is a cruel and fickle paymaster. It will demand more and more of you until there is nothing left to give, at which point you will be cast aside without a second thought."

"Yes?"

"Oh yes," she replied with heavy emphasis. "You must learn to pace yourself better. Without maturity and cunning inside here," she leaned forward and tapped my forehead, "talent alone is never enough."

"Meaning?" I scowled defensively.

"Take a break. Put your cue aside, the world is far larger and more complex than a billiard table. Knock about a bit, and when you're ready, come back refreshed."

"But -!"

"I have connexions and am entrusting you with a letter of introduction plus a small travel allowance to ensure its delivery to an address in Western Australia. Your berth has been booked aboard a freighter whose name, I'm told, translates as *Good Fortune* –"

"But it's almost Christmas!"

"Quite." She cocked an expressive eyebrow. "If you are ever to secure a place in the public's affection, be ready to move at a moment's notice, regardless of the date, the time, the inconvenience. Lord Luck rarely beckons twice."

"But I've arranged -!"

"As have I," she interrupted drily. "When you can place two hundred and fifty pounds, in gold, on this table, I shall double the sum so that you have sufficient stake money for the Nationals, assuming you still wish to compete." Concluding, with a theatrical flourish: "Opportunity awaits! Grab it by the throat -!"

1912-1914

31

The only throat grabbed was mine as I endured bouts of seasickness aboard a Japanese tramp steamer, laden with coal and corrugated iron, battling against westerly headwinds on the Great Australian Bight. It was no help that *Yoshi Maru*'s cook believed the only rations a European could stomach were scorched mutton cutlets and lumps of boiled potato, not that I was in any state to disabuse him of the idea. However, being confined to a bunk afforded me plenty of time to brood over being so rudely thrust out upon the world, unable to even say goodbye to Maeve who had returned home to Bathurst for Christmas.

The only other saloon passenger was a dour Scots engineer in his late-30s, under orders to extend a railway line through country he had hoped never to see again; Walter McMurdo was the first but by no means the last man I was to hear reciting *Ode to Westralia*:

> Land of forests, fleas, and flies,
> Blighted hopes and blighted eyes,
> Art thou hell in Earth's disguise, Westralia?

Soon enough I would discover the truth of its other verses:

> Land of politicians silly,
> Home of wind and willy-willy,
> Land of blanket, tent, and billy. Westralia!

Continuing:

> Land of brokers, bummers, shifty clerks,
> Nest of sharpers, mining sharks,
> Dried up lakes and deserts stark. Westralia.

Ending:

> Land of humpies, brothels, inns,
> Old bag huts and empty tins,
> Land of blackest, grievous sins. Westralia....

Meanwhile, I improvised a sign language that told the cook my European stomach was quite happy with boiled rice, fish, and pickled red cabbage, after which we got along famously well, to such an extent that he prepared a Christmas dinner of noodles, red cabbage of course, and *gyoza* dumplings made with ingredients I thought it best not to enquire about. McMurdo and I sat down to this feast, raised cups of *sake*, and solemnly toasted our chef, Hiroshi, a cheery soul who was doing his best to oblige his guests.

Perhaps it was his noodles, or the mysterious dumplings, but whatever the cause I felt much better the following day and expressed a wish to explore the ship, sketchpad and wax crayons at the ready. This was a highly irregular request, especially for a *Ketojin* or "Hairy Barbarian," Japan's equivalent of our

"Yellow Peril," but a three-quarter portrait of Captain Ishihara, posed masterfully on the bridge of his command, did the trick.

I was still not well enough to spend much time below decks studying the play of light on sweaty, half-naked stokers heaving coal from bunker to boiler, or depicting crewmen at ease in the foc'sle. This meant regular retreats aloft to my roost by the lifeboat, a sheltered alcove where I could breathe easier without being drenched by spray or battered by the unrelenting headwinds.

This was my first sea voyage and therefore nothing to compare it with. During the next couple of decades, I would experience all the world's oceans and most of its seas, some of which - like the Mediterranean and Aegean – I got to know well and mostly enjoy, but I could never say that of the Southern Ocean, a wilderness of bottle green combers and flying spume that encircles the Antarctic's icy wastes from Cape Horn to Cape Horn.

Even on the sunniest of days there was still a fearful sense that one had abandoned the warmly familiar World of Man and entered the coldly indifferent World of Nature, an emotion intensified by the occasional, wandering albatross skimming the rolling cliffs of water, hunting squid one thousand miles from the nearest rocky nesting site.

The *Titanic*'s fate was still fresh in my mind, and whereas a good number of her passengers had been saved after she went down in the busy North Atlantic route, there would be no rescue if *Yoshi Maru* foundered on the Southern Ocean. Marine radio transmitters were not yet mandatory and small shipping companies, working on slim margins, were in no hurry to add the expense of specialist equipment and trained operators, so it would probably be weeks before anyone noticed that we were overdue, by which time it would hardly matter.

I was secretly relieved when Captain Ishihara finally made landfall, his first after dropping Port Phillip's pilot at Queens Cliff, even if it was no more than a low coastline draped with curtains of rain.

The P&O shipping line's coaling station at King George Sound was a welcome sight as I clambered off a leaky lighter and plodded ashore. Until now I had only known two cities – Sydney as an alley rat, and Melbourne as an aspiring toff – so I had nothing else by which to measure this remote but strategically important settlement on the far edge of nowhere. Fortunately, my Scottish travel companion had been here before and set about hiring one of the pony traps that did service as local taxicabs, but only after we agreed to split the fare fifty-fifty.

Deal done on a handshake, we loaded our baggage and hunched under the canvas dodger as a dejected pony toiled up a gravel track that curved around one of two granite hills between which huddled the small town of Albany; though unaware of it at the time, I was entering an emotional state nowadays called "Culture Shock."

Less than a fortnight earlier I had swaggered up Swanston Street, blazer unbuttoned in the summery warmth, straw boater cocked over one eye, a jaunty young man-about-town with not a care in the world; past electrically lit, richly laden store windows; jostled by crowds of Christmas shoppers, tradesmen, and errand boys; deafened by the grind of iron-tyred cartwheels and the impatient clang of tramway cars; elated by the heady pace and pulse of Marvellous Melbourne at its most sophisticated and cosmopolitan.

Now, roughly three hundred-or-so hours later, I found myself clad in a tweed travel coat, newsboy cap pulled low against the dismal weather, jolting down a mostly deserted street of meagre little shops fronting what, until recently, had been a creek bed. Though I didn't realise it yet, this smug little township was a bright beacon of prosperity and culture, mirth and enlightenment compared with many another Westralian settlement or mining camp dotted across a wilderness half the size of Europe.

Our pony managed to keep its downhill balance on slick wooden paving blocks and cobblestones and pulled up short at a modest railway station close to the western end of the Trans-Australian telegraph line which, together with the P&O coal store, were the main reasons for Albany's existence at all.

A pencilled note, thumb-tacked to the locked door, announced that a mixed goods and passenger train would depart for Perth, Western Australia's only city, at 6pm sharp for which purpose the ticket office would open one hour beforehand. Signed: *Station Master*.

McMurdo and I consulted our pocket watches and agreed there was no point waiting under an open porch for the next four hours. With only one suitcase to carry, I volunteered to take his engineer's satchel of drawing instruments and leather tube of drafting paper, while he carried the rest of his luggage and led the way to a nearby coffee palace.

An historian, like Frances Baxter, must have encountered this rather quaint term in old books and newspapers but, as an Englishwoman specialising in European geopolitics, it is more likely that she won't understand its origins. Therefore, when I record this episode, I shall add a brief explanation of how and why the Christian Women's Temperance Union established coffee palaces and temperance hotels in each of Britain's Australasian colonies.

Television and kinema dramas portray our quarrelsome, hard-drinking Colonial Era Australians as lovable larrikins with hearts of gold but coming from a time when the breed was all too common, I am qualified to say that they were often vicious, drunken brutes, and that to go unarmed on the streets after dark, was to throw dice with the Devil.

Albany's alcohol-free oasis promised a welcoming refuge on such a miserable day, and we were both grateful for the dining room's log fire to warm chilled fingers while the rest of Australia, farther north, sweltered through summer heatwaves and bushfires, for such are the vagaries of climate on an island continent.

"Will yous be eatin'?" The tone was surly and suspicious.

We turned to see our host framed in the doorway, arms folded across his barrel chest. "That all depends upon what ye have to offer," Walter McMurdo replied with a defiant scowl of his own.

"Mutton chops. Mashed taters. Boiled beans. Steam cabbage. Irish stew. There's spotted dick for sweets. It's all writ on that there card." His thumb jabbed at one of the dining room's several unoccupied tables.

"Aye, well, we'll start wi' a pot o' tea then."

"That's extra thruppence. Each."

Walter glanced in my direction. I nodded back. He glanced at the manager. "Right. Off ye go. An' quick about it!"

We took a table nearest the fire, and I tried an amused, worldly smile. "Charming fellow, eh?"

"There're more where that came from." He studied the grubby menu for a few moments, then flicked it aside and looked up. "This is Westralia an' we're Tuthersiders."

"I beg your pardon?"

"You and I just got off the boat from t'other side o' Australia."

"So?" I persisted, an opinionated young man who still believed he had the right to an answer for every question.

"Westralians hear me speak and know I am a foreigner o' no account. On the other hand, they see and hear in ye the sort they resent the most…"

"Come off it!" I laughed. "We're all Australians now!"

An engineer by instinct as well as by training, he took his time drafting an reply. "Not so many years ago here was still an independent colony wi'in the British Empire, like Jamaica or -"

"As were we all," I interrupted.

"Aye, but ye are not all on the wrong side of one thousand miles o' trackless desert!" he snapped back, not used to being corrected when delivering an opinion. "These 'Sandgropers' as they call th'selves, feel closer to Old Mother England than they've ever felt for the pushy folk o' Sydney or Melbourne. And who's to blame them?"

"Sorry. I'm lost. What do you mean?"

"Pay attention." He leaned nearer, the better to emphasise what he was about to say. "Until recently, yon' ex-convicts and starvation farmers were outcasts, marooned on one million square miles of semi-desert governed by threadbare English gentry. Then, without so much as by-ye'r-leave, everything they'd toiled to build was swept aside when a raggedy breeked prospector stumbled across the motherlode near Kalgoorlie, unpenting a flood of Tuthersiders, every Jack and Jill wi' only one thought in mind, t'get rich quick and get back home on Tutherside, quicker…'"

"But if these people were so miserably few, surely they would've been glad of fresh company?" I was still viewing the world through the eyes of a Melburnian city slicker.

"Not when tens o' thousands of 'Wise Men from the East' outvoted the locals in a referendum to choose a'tween remaining a proud, self-governing British colony, or surrendering their independence to be a lesser part of an Australia ruled by Melbourne. Perhaps only a Scot, ruled by London, would fully understand?" He added with a curt gesture of dismissal. "Here's our tea. I'll be ordering fresh meat, no' kitchen scraps boiled as 'Irish stew.'"

"Likewise," I agreed, having arrived at much the same conclusion.

32

By stretching our drinks with a jug of hot water, and by dragging out the meals, we managed to rent four hours of warmth for two shillings and ninepence apiece, during which McMurdo shared his previous experiences of what was effectively, for me a foreign land, before stepping out into the rain.

Back at the ticket office, I dipped a sovereign from my waistcoat pocket to pay for a single seat to Perth, receiving in exchange a half crown - British money still legal tender although Australia had now begun minting our own coinage - two silver florins, a sixpence, and a few coppers change. The inevitable travel and living expenses were eating into my small stock of capital with which I had left Melbourne and were further incentives to make haste with Aunt Lucinda's letter to Mr Alan Sharples, 251 Hannan Street, Kalgoorlie.

During the years ahead, I would suffer far worse train journeys than the one from Albany to Perth, bad as it seemed at the time while our locomotive shuffled and shunted from one country siding to another, dropping off baskets of fish frosted with crushed ice, or picking up an occasional passenger to slump beside us in the lamp lit carriage.

McMurdo grunted awake during the early hours of the morning and gathered his things together when we jolted to a halt at a place whose name ended "-in," like many another settlement I was soon to know.

Glimpsed through smoke grimed glass, Narrogin on a moonlit night seemed little more than a huddle of railway workshops with an adjacent barrack block for the tracklayers and maintenance crews; I assume there was a small township nearby, housing the mechanics' families and quarters for salaried staff, like Walter McMurdo.

We shook hands and I watched through the window as he trod from darkness to darkness through a pool of yellow gaslight. Betimes he had been grumpy and cantankerous, yet I sensed he meant well, with an older man's awareness of a younger one's immaturity and need to grow up fast. But now that he was gone it was all up to me as the Great Southern Railways' overnight goods train wheezed and panted, iron couplings snatching and clanking, resuming our irregular canter northwards through the night.

I must have dozed off on my slatted wooden bench, for the next thing I remember was blinking gummy eyelids as dawn broke over mile after mile of featureless bushland along both sides of the track. Then, with increasing frequency, this gave way to farm blocks cleared by ring-barking tall timber and burning-off the undergrowth to raise a few bags of wheat on parched and rocky soil. Even with my lack of knowledge, it was not hard to imagine the backbreaking toil needed to repay money borrowed from the speculators who financed this railway by taking up hundreds of square miles of Crown Land for resale to hopeful new settlers.

The locomotive eventually shuddered to a halt, a couple of hours after daybreak, and stood mournfully hissing on the outskirts of a one street settlement that reminded me of my first railway journey with Aunt Lucinda, when we'd changed trains to cross from New South Wales into Victoria.

Beverley was the last stop on the privately owned Great Southern Line; to finish our journey we must now transfer to the West Australian Government Railway. Luckily none of their staff seemed to be in any great hurry, much to the relief of we male passengers lining up at a corrugated iron trough, and no doubt that of the ladies too, behind their wooden picket fence.

A minute or so later the stationmaster sauntered along his platform, whistle lazily spinning on a brass chain as he twirled it backwards and forwards around his forefinger and leaned against the latrine's doorpost. "Any o' yous wan' brekkie?"

"My bloody oath!" someone growled, accompanied by grunts of agreement all round.

"Come on then."

We trooped after him, across the vacant gravel street and into a steamy dining room where the rival companies' train drivers and firemen were amicably tucking into free breakfasts - compliments of the management – as their reward for delivering hungry customers to the Railway Hotel.

During our journey north, once the daylight became sufficient to get a clearer view of things, I had fished out my pocket sketchbook and jotted a few quick images to illustrate a first letter home. Now, waiting in line to order a meal, I turned a fresh page and with a few deft strokes caught the likeness of our handsomely moustachioed stationmaster.

"Oy!" A bony finger prodded my shoulder. I spun around and confronted the young, ginger haired commercial traveller I'd seen piling his sample cases aboard the luggage van at Albany. "Tha's clever," he grinned, pointing at my sketch. "Y'do much like it?"

"Some," I replied warily.

"Tell you what!" The cheery grin expanded. "Do me a pitcher and I'll shout brekkie. It's a surprise for the girlfriend." It was a surprise for me, too, as I had never thought to earn a casual breakfast this way before. "Look," he continued, "grab us a table and I'll fix the orders." He winked. "The firm's pay'n' fr'it!"

I was happy to comply and in due course pencilled a fair likeness of his open, uncomplicated face, inscribed *To Elsie with all my love Kev'*, framed inside a wreath of hearts, and roses, and lovers' knots tied with elaborately flowing ribbons.

"Cor! Thanks mate," he chuckled, carefully putting it away. "I know one bloke's gunna get lucky t'night...!"

"Glad to oblige," was the best I could think of to say before shovelling up my plate of fried ham, eggs, and mashed potato, washed down by gulps of hot tea as the WAGR train crew got ready for work and we passengers got aboard.

Commercial travellers are gregarious souls, outgoing and curious, for whoever heard of a shy salesman? My new companion was no exception and clearly enjoyed meeting people and making contacts as we settled into our seats while the Government's locomotive coupled-up.

I accepted his card and learned that Kevin Fitzgerald represented a Perth firm of wholesale chemists as he reached forward again, this time offering me his opened packet of *Navy Cut*.

"Thanks." I selected one and returned the favour by striking a match for his cigarette, and then my own, as men did in those days.

"So," he whiffed smoke from the corner of his mouth, "what brings you to our part of the world?"

"We've heard a lot about you in the East."

"All good I hope?"

144

"Mostly," I replied, with a tactful nod.

"Yair, well, there's tons of bulldust talked about yous Tuthersiders by the older sort here, but take no notice o' them," he insisted, leaning further forward. "If you want my opinion, free and for nothing, business 'as never been so good, not with all them new customers and stuff come over from the Yeast…"

"Glad someone approves of us." I took a token puff and, as courtesy demanded, gave his brand a glance of approval.

"So, you'll be staying long in Perth…?"

"Can't." I'd already begun to roughen my speech, the better to merge with these new surroundings. "Gotta get to Kalgoorlie."

He cocked an eyebrow. "You not thinking of having a shot at prospecting, are you?"

"'Might." I have always played life's cards close to the chest.

"Don't," he announced firmly. "Jus' don't, it's a mug's game. The easy stuff's long gone. Though to be fair," he added, upon reflection, "there's still some nuggets to be had. Why, only last week, a bloke come in with a real biggie; three hundred ounces! The newspaper said rain must've washed it down a gully. Lucky bastard."

"Tha's gotta be worth a tidy bit?"

"Four quid an ounce the paper said!" He gave a dreamy sigh. "I'd be made for life with only 'alf as much…"

"Blood'oath." I might have said more except that our locomotive gave a throaty whistle and everyone either jolted forwards or backwards, depending on which way we were facing as the train moved off on the last eighty or ninety miles of track into Perth.

I have always been that indispensable other half of any conversation, the attentive listener. Kev', as he insisted that I call him, was by contrast an assertive, self-absorbed talker. Happy to confide his hopes and dreams, worries and woes as our train huffed across the forested escarpment that overlooks Perth's coastal plain.

By the time we reached the city's outskirts, I had the detailed plans for his wedding to Elsie Muldoon at St Brendan's parish church. I was also privy to every move in his plot to outflank Ray Plunkett - 29 years old, Church of England, married to a posh telephonist - and snatch old Mr Richards' job instead.

Hopefully this would coincide with The Wedding, by which time the firm's warehouse manager would have been sacked – his haemorrhoids were giving him strife and he was forgetting stuff – meaning a raise of ten shillings a week for the victor. More than enough for the new Mr & Mrs Fitzgerald to get a building society loan for a nice little villa in Nedlands, wherever that was.

Office politics were not his only ticket in life's lottery. The other one was *Greased Lightning*, a greyhound of which he had a five pounds half-share. With a bit more training, he assured me, *Greasy* was a dead cert' to win back every penny lost thus far to Perth's backstreet bookies.

I shan't record these homely vignettes of Australian life before the Great War; it would never do for Frances to imagine I was mocking simple folk. I do not want her to think of me as a conceited snob brought up among Melbourne's merchant kings and higher professionals. Besides, she doesn't need to know how and why I secretly envy the stoical dignity and courage of a husband who slogs away at a job he can barely tolerate, brings home an unopened pay packet, helps raise the kids to the best of his limited ability, and loves his missus as they grow old and infirm together.

Meanwhile, in stark contrast to Albany's miserable weather, a few hundred miles south, Westralia's capital was enjoying an absolute cracker of a summer's day as we pulled into Perth's modest Central Railway Station where I helped Kev' load his laxative pills and patent hair lotion, shampoo powder and fake French cosmetics aboard a goods trolley. After which he stuck out a hand and gave my one a hearty shake. "It's real good talking to a bloke who don't interrupt all the bloody time! You sure you can't stay a bit longer? I get Sunday off. I know Elsie would be thrilled to meet you. We'll show you the town, maybe catch a steamer down the Swan to Freo' for a bonza time on the beach. Whaddya say...?"

I was tempted to accept his kindly offer. I certainly felt the need to catch my breath and get my bearings after being unceremoniously thrust from the comforts and certainties of Tralee House, but in all conscience I could never bludge off a young couple saving up for their first home. This meant, if I did stay until Sunday, my purse of sovereigns would be significantly lighter by the time I caught a train the following day. "Love to, mate, but gotta keep going. You know how it is." I tapped the side of my nose. "Business."

"Yair." He winked back. "'Early bird catches the worm,' eh?!"

"Too right," I agreed, nearly adding: "'But it's the second mouse gets the cheese...'" Instead, I hefted my suitcase. "See yuh."

"See yuh!" he replied with a cheery wave and set off for the exit, pushing an iron-wheeled trolley, while I headed for a Travellers' Aid Post run by the Salvation Army.

The Sallies were old friends in a non-denominational sense, Aunt Lucinda was always good for a cheque at Christmas, and few things delighted her more than a brass band banging along at full blast. I clearly remember her ordering our carriage to stop, one afternoon, when Melbourne Citadel's bugles and drums were marching up Bourke Street. As the parade passed, Salvation lassies rattling their tambourines, she turned to me with a wistful smile: "It's hard to imagine now, my dear, but I used to shake *le tambourin* - and do the splits! – as *La Belle Australienne*..."

Smiling at this and other fond memories of a most remarkable old lady, I approached a door decorated with a large wooden placard painted in the standard Salvo's Blood & Fire crimson lettering:

CLEANLINESS IS NEXT TO GODLINESS
HOT WATER, SOAP, CLEAN TOWEL
3d

I paid my three pence and went into a vacant cubicle where a bloke could shave, change, and spiff up before hitting the town. That done, my next task was to stow the suitcase and topcoat in the station's Baggage Room; the day was getting warm, and muggy, and my tweed suit was uncomfortable enough without further layers of clothing.

Whistling a chirpy tune, I strolled across to the ticket office and learned that the Eastern Goldfields' Railway ran an overnight passenger service to the curiously named Kalgoorlie, with stops along the way to deliver mailbags, replenish the locomotive's coal bunker, and refill its water tank.

Even hearing the name Eastern Goldfields' Railway spoken for the first time was enough to quicken the pulse of an eighteen-year youth under orders to return home with a minimum of two hundred and fifty pounds at the end of his adventure. Just repeating those magical words aloud, "Eastern, Goldfields,

Railway," seemed to double and redouble the buttery yellow sovereigns in my waistcoat pocket.

Stifling a yawn, I decided to look around Western Australia's only population centre of any consequence, and I must confess that my initial impressions were not favourable after the brisk pulse of Melbourne. No matter how one viewed the scene, Perth was more like a sedate country town than the capital city of Australia's largest state.

Disappointed, I hopped across the ruts and potholes of an optimistically named Wellington Street and reached a debris field of demolished workshops and tenements where a noticeboard assured me the new Central Post & Telegraph Office would soon be built. Two years later, revisiting Perth on a 24-hour leave pass from Blackboy Hill army camp, I found that the initial contractors had only managed to excavate a large pond and then gone broke when their steam pumps couldn't keep up with the flooding groundwater.

That hole, and countless thousands of other muddy craters, still lay ahead of me in an unimaginable future as I wandered about town, window-shopping for the next hour or so before taking lunch at the Palace Hotel. After which I found a deep leather seat in the reading room, draped a copy of the local newspaper across my face, and passed out, utterly exhausted.

33

I nearly missed the night train but managed to scramble aboard with seconds to spare, found a corner seat where I could roll my overcoat to make a pillow, stuffed it against the window, and dozed until about midnight when we pulled into a siding to replenish the locomotive's coal and water. This was our cue to pile out and crowd the station tearoom where saveloy sausages with mashed potato and gravy, meat pies with mashed potato and gravy, and corned beef fritters with mashed potato and gravy, were the chalkboard specials.

I have no idea which one I ordered or how much it cost. After two days and two nights on the go, at the end of a troubled sea voyage, all I wanted to do was go up to my room at Tralee House, drag a blanket over my head, and sleep the clock around. Instead, I was still blearily awake when our train clanked into Kalgoorlie later that morning.

Several of the passengers were newcomers like me, eager young men seeking their fortunes on Western Australia's fabled goldfields. Others were weathered, older men in sober, serviceable suits, returning from business on the coast. Or navvies clad in brown corduroys, grey flannel shirts, canvas jackets and hobnailed boots grimed with ochre dust and grit. This last group had clambered aboard at the refreshment stop and was a maintenance crew for the newly constructed pipeline that brought water up and over the ranges from a reservoir near Perth, before starting across four hundred miles of arid mulga country.

Peering through the carriage window, I was surprised to see that Kal', as everyone around me called the place, was not the romantic Wild West town I had imagined. Acres of corrugated iron roofing were evidence this was no longer the frontier tent city where, only sixteen years earlier, one quarter of the population had died of typhoid fever between January and December.

That was the official figure so the true number must have been much higher in outlying settlements and bush camps where conditions were even more squalid; unsurprising when the only clean water was distilled from brackish seepage and sold for five shillings a gallon at a time when eight shillings was a good day's wage for a workman elsewhere.

Yawning, drugged with tiredness, I dragged my suitcase from under the seat, dumped my coat over one arm, and stumbled into the waiting crowd. Disoriented, desperate to find an hotel room where I could get some shut-eye before setting off to find Mr Sharples, I barely noticed the small urchin who got under my feet, forcing me to halt for a couple of moments while he disentangled and -!

I spun around, scanning the crowd, but my experiences of pulling the same trick, to momentarily distract passengers boarding the ferry at Sydney's Circular Quay, told me that my purse had already flicked from the knuckler to her sparrow, a women's touch being defter than most men's, before the gang split. I'd been dipped by regular finger smiths, for only a booby glances behind to see if his mark has twigged it.

Anger and shame and humiliation were the least of my emotions at being taken so readily after my own apprenticeship as a buzz cove. Years of soft living and stern admonitions to become a Perfect English Gentleman had dulled those formative experiences among less-than-perfect Australians, but as Aunt Lucinda had ofttimes reminded me: "'Crying over spilt milk ne'er poured it back into the jug.'"

In the same manner, snarling over stolen money would never put it back in my pocket, no matter how much I wished otherwise. Equally true, going to the police and reporting my gullibility would only brand me as a chump and do nothing to improve the situation.

Instead, cursing under my breath, I found a nearby bench and counted the small change in my trousers' pocket; these four shillings and eightpence ha'penny would now have to keep me alive in a strange town until I could find work; a tall order by anyone's reckoning. However, I consoled myself by thinking that Mr Sharples should be good for a few ideas once we became better acquainted.

Very much awake now, I approached the nearest porter and asked for directions to Hannan Street which, as I later learned, is named after the Irish prospector who found a nearby clay pan studded with alluvial nuggets – many the size of hens' eggs - triggering a goldrush that rivalled the Klondike's at about the same time. I then left the station and, a couple of hundred yards later at the end of Wilson Street, stopped in my tracks, quite overwhelmed by so much open space and harsh sunlight.

Whereas Melbourne's inner-city lanes tended to be gloomy chasms overlooked by office buildings, four or five storeys high, with scarcely enough shoulder room for a Hansom cab to overtake a handcart, Kal's main street was spacious enough for a bullock team to turn, and not only bullocks. I had seen camels at a circus but had never imagined them harnessed to a sulky, or a baker's cart, or plodding along in convoy, saddled with galvanized iron water tanks, outward bound for a remote mining camp.

At that moment I was reminded of my first train journey that began with Aunt Lucinda lighting a Black Sobranie while wondering aloud what was to be made of me. A decade or so later I felt the same eerie premonition that my life was never going to be the same as it had been, half an hour ago.

"Good day." I approached a local lounging against a wooden electric power pole, probably waiting for a friend. "I wonder if you could help me, please..."

He stared me up and down. "Whad'dya'wan'?"

"I believe this is Hannan Street. I need to find number 251."

He sucked a tooth. "Sharpie's?"

"If that's Mr Alan Sharples, yes."

"Over there." He gave a barely perceptible nod. "Past the York. Join the queue."

"Thank you." I could see a York Hotel across the street and kept going diagonally, weaving between turbaned Afghans leading yet more camels, and half a dozen loose-limbed bushmen trotting past on their tough little brumbies, before taking cover at one of the telephone poles that ran up the centre of this vast main street, waiting for a flock of bicyclists and a couple of motor lorries to pass the other way.

The bystander's parting remark made no sense. I was the only one taking an interest in *A. Sharples General Dealer & Broker*, displayed in gilt paint above the narrow storefront sandwiched between a locksmith's and a Japanese steam laundry. Suitcase gripped in one fist I used the other to try opening the door while peering inside an unoccupied office through its side window.

"'Y'lookin' for Sharples?" A man of middling height and age called from an adjacent veranda.

"Yes! I've come rather a long way and need to see him soon!"

"Ah, well then," he suppressed a grin. "Pop round the corner." He nodded further up Hannan's. "Cassidy Street. Number 46. Y'can't miss it."

"Thank you!"

"G'luck…"

Heartened by his reassurance, I hurried past an ironmonger, a haberdasher's, and a tailor's shop, before turning the corner into Cassidy Street. He was right, no one could possibly miss Number 46's ornate brick façade that partially hid the plain corrugated iron shed behind it. A black, horse-drawn hearse, parked outside, showed that Alan Sharples was also in the funeral business. He seemed to be doing well, I noted with some relief, entering a vestibule hung with purple crape, its walls decorated with advertisements promoting cast-concrete, readymade tombstones with catalogue names like *The Glamorgan*, *The Harp*, *The Bonny Doon*, and *The London Town* for those dying far from Home.

"Good morning, sir. How may we be of assistance?"

I turned. A sad-eyed man, wearing a rubber apron, had come in from the rear shed, bringing with him a whiff of the formaldehyde I recognised from David's laboratory experiments. I reached out for a handshake, relieved my journey was over at last and that I could now get some rest. "Mr Sharples?"

"No."

"Oh. Well." The hand fell to my side. "Where can I find him? I have an important letter, from Melbourne…"

"Are you family?"

"No, but my aunt knows him well."

"I se-ee." He ran bony fingers through thinning hair. "Then I'm afraid you must inform her that Mr Sharples, having shot himself last night, was unable to receive her communication."

Not sure I was hearing correctly, and with an abrupt void in the pit of my stomach, I asked for clarification.

Apparently, it was a common story on the goldfields. Alan Sharples had borrowed beyond his means to finance a mine that produced only a few ounces of gold before petering out. Unable to repay his creditors, and about to be declared bankrupt, he chose Death before Dishonour as gentlemen were expected to do before our slaughter on the Western Front rather devalued such vain gestures.

"You have come far. May I offer a cup of tea?"

"No, thanks.".

"Will you be staying long?"

"All depends, now." I was edging towards the door.

"Do you have anywhere to stay?"

"Yes," I lied. At which point I turned tail and bolted.

Eventually I slowed down, leaned my suitcase against a veranda post, and sat down on it to take stock of a situation that could not have been worse, or so I imagined at the time.

I shall suppress these next several days in my tape recordings for Frances. No man worthy of the name wants to be thought of as a mug, least of all by an attractive and intelligent woman. I would also be ashamed to reveal that my first instinctive reaction, after being robbed, was to think about dipping a few pockets on my own account; one's earlier self is only ever damped down, never entirely extinguished.

Hunched outside a pawnbroker's office, shoulders slumped, chin on fists, the only thing that stopped me from resuming a life of crime was the lack of recent practice. There was a good chance I would muff my first dip, be collared by an angry crowd, and hauled up before the local beak. It was not nobility of spirit or a belief in honesty as the best policy that stayed my hand, but the very real prospect of spending the next month in clink before being run out of town with a police record shadowing me as a criminal Tuthersider.

Instead of which I was now stuck on the far side of Australia with only a few shillings in my pocket and no clear idea of where to turn next. To be fair, we must not be too harsh with that anxious young man; fear, thirst, hunger, lack of sleep can unsettle even the sturdiest mind.

Slouching back to the railway station, I hoped to find the porter who had assisted me earlier, but he was busy in the goods yard, stacking boxes aboard the overnight Perth Express. However, the ticket clerk, a Cockney Londoner with no reason to tease or taunt a Tuthersider, listened to my request.

"You come to the right place Guv!" he winked. "The missus does a bit o' letting out, on the side, so to speak." He gave another conspiratorial wink. "It's not payday so there's a bit o' room out the back…"

"Thanks," I replied, trying hard not to sound puzzled by his enigmatic hints. "But I feel it's only fair to tell you, I'm a bit short of the readies, just for the moment…"

"Tell the missus Albert sent you." With which he drew a rough map in my sketchbook and sent me a couple of blocks down Wilson Street, before turning hard right into Hay Street. Anyone familiar with Kalgoorlie will immediately have a fair idea what trade Albert's wife was associated with, not that she herself was a prostitute so far as I could tell, but there were ancillary services that included plenty of washing, and ironing, and sewing if a brothel was to attract the better class of client.

Thus, a day that began with the theft of almost all my cash, had continued with crushing news at an undertaker's, ended up on a wire bedframe in a dosshouse, serenaded by player pianos tinkling sentimental melodies in nearby bordellos.

34

I had forgotten what it felt like to wake up flea-bitten, before joining the queue of other dossers at the dunny, after which I nipped into the laundry for a cold shave and quick rinse. Luckily there was no mirror where I could see my reflection, but I could smell the rest of me ripening in Kalgoorlie's desert heat, unlike Perth's steamy coastal warmth, and Albany's rainy, Antarctic chill; I had experienced the full extent of Southwest Australia's summer weather during the past couple, or three, or was it four days? On top of all else, in a popular expression of the day, I no longer knew if I was Arthur, or Martha, or Neither.

Determined to keep up appearances for as long as possible, I cadged a small piece of breadcrust, moistened it with spittle, and rubbed most of the grime off my starched collar. Afterwards, I bought the whole slice from Mrs Albert, with an appealing look at a pan of beef dripping on her kitchen table.

The tin mug of chicory essence "coffee" cost a further one penny, but at least I was now fed and watered, ready for whatever the day ahead had in store for me, starting with one of the dossers forcing the brass locks on my elegant leather suitcase.

"Excuse me old chap," I lisped in my Perfect English Gentleman tones, "that article of luggage is mine, don'cha know?" The Distractor.

He turned, toothy sneer exploding into an agonised shriek as I gripped his jacket lapels and snatched his face into a full head butt, the Disabler. Following through with a brutal knee to his groin, the Destroyer.

He was probably as surprised as I was at how swiftly I'd reverted to a more primitive self. Still ruefully shaking my head at such a display of bad manners, I collected the overcoat that had been my pillow, wished everyone else a good morning, and left them staring down at their writhing mate as I set off to seek my fortune on Kal's unwelcoming streets.

The suitcase tagged me as a new chum, so I went back to the station and booked it into the Luggage Room, together with my overcoat, as if planning to leave on the next train. Instead, I set off to forage the gridwork of roads and laneways north of Hannan Street, targeting the backyards of hotels, pie shops, and bakeries.

Previous experience had taught me that commercial kitchens usually save spoiled food and unsold scraps, to be collected after-hours by someone raising a backyard porker; with good luck and shrewd timing, a fly cove can subsist quite well on buckets of pigswill.

I can picture Frances' disgust if I were to include these details in my taped memoirs, for they would throw a most unflattering light on the realities of Australian life before the Great War. However, if I did it would illuminate the universal truth that whereas a well-fed man can have many problems, the hungry man has only one. It would also prove how quickly a fastidious Toorak toff can adapt to hostile conditions when push comes to shove.

An only child herself, I wonder if she has ever invented a little brother or sister to share her sorrows? It would be interesting to compare notes, not that we shall, but if we did, I would have to confess to a dark and dangerous half-brother who has been my companion for many a long year. Melbourne Grammar imagined it was expelling Little Ian Cribdon the unruly, orphaned son of an Assam tea planter, but it was Basher Billy Braithwaite, his faceless phantom who destroyed a prefect, jobbed the headmaster, and outran his enforcers.

And as I had just demonstrated, the switch from one identity to the other can be triggered in a heartbeat and result in serious damage, a trait I am not proud of, although upon occasion it has proved useful. Indeed, I can still remember Carl Jung's nods of approval as I described how Aunt Lucinda had balanced the Shadow, as he called it, during my weeks at his clinic.

With tonight's grub sorted, my next priority was to find a shed where I could camp until I was in funds again. After trudging up and down more gravelled backstreets, checking out the stables and carters, wheelwrights and coachbuilders, blacksmiths, and iron foundries, I eventually discovered a snug hide among the barrels stacked behind Kalgoorlie's Brewery & Ice Works.

None of those trades was going to deliver me a quick two-fifty quid and return ticket to Melbourne, even if I had the necessary skills, so instead I plodded back to Hannan Street's commercial centre and took a hunger-sweaty break by leaning against the Town Hall's noticeboard.

Among the Local Council's dire warnings against burning domestic rubbish, and running unlicenced boarding-houses, was a part-time job at the Municipal Dog Pound, (uniform provided) and the Sanitary Department's opening for a Rat Catcher, (wage negotiable.) It says much for my then state of mind that I seriously considered applying for both jobs as a stopgap until something better turned up.

Instead, shoulders back, chest out, newsboy cap at a jaunty angle that belied my true feelings, I continued tramping up Hannan Street, checking hotel billiard rooms to gauge the level of competition. On balance most players were fluky amateurs betting rounds of drinks, though some games had ten-pound notes on the table; trouble was, covering such bets was far beyond my means at present.

My footsore pace quickened when I noticed a cluster of men staring at a nearby shop window. I inched to the front and saw the very same nugget that Kevin Fitzgerald had sighed over on the train, tantalisingly close, displayed on a red velvet cushion behind an iron grille.

Gold's high density made it seem rather unimpressive. However, an ornately lettered card alongside it more than made up for that by informing everyone that Mr Samuel Madorsky, Licenced Bullion Buyer, had paid £1,250 for this specimen. Other prospectors, with large or small quantities to sell, could depend upon the fairest price, guaranteed by daily telegraphic communication with London. Cash tendered in strictest confidence.

I stood transfixed, mesmerised by a dull, misshapen lump of yellow metal, but there is a mystical quality about raw gold that does the strangest things to men's brains; with fewer than four shillings in my pocket, after last night's doss, I was defenceless against a violent attack of Gold Fever.

Thinking back from our present day, I can understand why persons of Frances' age and experience will never experience this strange affliction. The coins in their pockets are intrinsically worthless copper or nickel tokens, and the sums in their bank accounts are anonymous bookkeeping entries. Even her husband's hundreds of millions of pounds are no more than abracadabra arithmetic, not solid, tangible bullion. Only the few of us who still remember a world before the Great War, can recall the confident ping of a spun silver coin, and the honest heft of a gold sovereign on the palm of our hand.

Spellbound, I shuffled aside to make room for the next dreamer in our excited crowd. I had seen enough to know that half this lump of gold, even a quarter of it would return me home in triumph with money to spare for the pearl necklace I would lovingly clasp around Maeve's beautifully naked neck. How to get from here to there was still unclear, but at least I now had a target, which is half the battle won.

This newfound optimism soon evaporated as sweat as I slogged up to the top of Hannan Street, through roasting heat bouncing off the roadway, and had to call a halt again, this time in the Spiritualists' Reading Room that shared its address with a clairvoyant, who did not seem to be overworked. I'm not sure if it was an attempt at humour, or whether it was meant as written, but the card pinned to Madame Barnett's door told me that she was "Closed Due to Unforeseen Circumstances," leaving the Reading Room unattended, not that there was much worth pinching.

Weary and dejected, I kicked off my shoes and leafed through a recent copy of *Ethereal Realms*, a magazine that arrived at Tralee House by mail every month; Aunt Lucinda was an avid student of ghosts and apparitions and shared her discoveries in frequent correspondence with Sherlock Holmes' author, a fellow explorer of the Spirit World.

Not that an opinionated young twerp like myself believed in the supernatural, but then I have never made a precarious living in the theatre, a workplace where superstitions run rife. Some, like never bringing a peacock's feather on stage, made sense because of their similarity to the Evil Eye. Others, like jinxing a production by whistling backstage, were less obvious, even to Aunt Lucinda as she coached me in theatrical lore and customs. Tactfully, she never once asked me to accompany her to a séance, aware that I had no wish to awaken the dead in my past.

Roughly refreshed but footsore and grumpy, I resumed my reconnaissance of Kalgoorlie by crossing over Hannan Street and trudging down its long and dusty left-hand side, past tobacconists and stationers, fishmongers and oyster bars, tailors, dressmakers, butchers, and auctioneers. All the trades and services that were the mainstays of Australian town life early this century.

Hungry and parched, the shimmering midday heat finally got the better of me as I sought a patch of shade to sit down and rest. The Shamrock Hotel & Skating Rink seemed like my best chance of avoiding sunstroke, but first I had to spend three of my remaining pennies to buy the glass of lemonade that allowed me to enter the Winter Garden and take stock of an increasingly grim predicament.

My first duty was to inform Aunt Lucinda that her correspondent was dead. I tore a page from my sketchbook, to compose a brief message that would fit inside a prepaid, a tuppenny envelope, the next time I passed the General Post Office in Hannan Street. At which point I thought it a good idea if I read her letter first, in case something else required immediate attention while I was still in Kalgoorlie. A quick slit with my pocketknife and I took out a folded note, handwritten in dark green ink:

Tralee House
Grange Road
Melbourne

16ᵗʰ December 1912

Dear Mr Sharples.

Pray accept my sincere thanks for your excellent advice to
subscribe £1,000 in the Paynes Find share float. This
realised a nett profit of £657/10/9d when my broker
recently offered these shares on the Melbourne Change!

I gave a low whistle. It was unfortunate that Alan Sharples had not been as perceptive when he bet his own hand on the Nullagine Lease.

Turning now to a more personnel matter, the bearer of this
missive is my nephew Ian who has the makings of a useful adult
but of late has become intolerably full of his own importance!

People say this is the nature of youth everywhere but having
invested much time and effort into his formation I have no
wish to see it go to waste. Unless a man of your experience can
shew him that money does not grow on trees but must be
earned by sustained effort, I fear he will become a layabout ladys
poodle instead of making his mark on the world!

I confide this in strictest confidence knowing you will do all
that is need full!

Lucinde Cribdon
Baronne de l'Empire

I, was, furious! "*Layabout ladys poodle*" indeed?! The nerve of the woman to speak of me in such a condescending manner! I had a good mind to go straight back and have it out with her -!

My pride badly stung, the first impulse was to write a hot, angry, accusatory letter in reply. However, I had not forgotten the wise old proverb that warns how eavesdroppers never hear good of themselves, a stern reminder that I had broken the golden rule of polite conduct by reading another's correspondence without first asking permission.

Chastened, I drafted a pencilled reply:

Dear Aunt Lucinda.

Arrived in Kalgoorlie.
Mr Sharples shot himself the previous night.
Will notify address presently.

Reviewing this staccato news, I saw it was too stiff and hinted that I had read her message and been deeply hurt. Better by far to let my temper cool before expanding it into a longer, more informative, less abrasive letter, possibly accompanied by a cartoon of myself ogling the pretty young skater who'd just caught my eye as she pirouetted around the rink, in the style of those *Cirque Fernando* sketches on Tralee's dining room wall.

Their finished oils and lithographic prints are now in the world's major private collections and public galleries, but to my way of thinking, Lautrec's smudged pastel strokes best convey the creative vigour of nineteenth century

Montmartre, especially his cheeky self-portrait winking at *Le Rossignol* as she turns a revealing cartwheel in an imaginary act.

"G'day."

Momentarily distracted, I looked up at a tall, burly man, thumbs hooked through his waistcoat's armholes. "Er, good day."

"You new in town?"

"Yes."

He nodded at my unfinished cartoon. "That what you do for a crust?"

"Sometimes." What else could I say?

He stuck out a fist. "I'm Jonno, the manager."

"Ian Cribdon." I politely returned the handshake. "Glad to meet you." As indeed I was, this being the first glimmer of acceptance by anyone local.

He pulled up a chair, spun it around, and sat opposite me, brawny arms folded atop its back. "So, what brings you to Kal'?"

A good question and I was not entirely sure of the answer, but I knew when to blend fact with fiction to achieve a given end which, at this moment, was a refill for my empty lemonade glass.

"I'm freelancing for the *Age*," I replied with confident modesty, if there is such a phrase "The editor wants me to do a series on the 'Real Westralia,' but it's got to be something more than 'land of blighted hopes and blighted eyes,' which is how people see you, over in the East."

"Hn! You'd never think we were the same bloody country…"

"Good point." I slipped easily into my new character as a roving reporter. "Would you mind if we quoted you?" I continued, flipping a fresh page in my sketchbook, as if about to take dictation.

"Go for your life, it would make a change, them bastards showing an interest."

"Fair's fair," I observed wisely. "It's time we stopped describing Westralia as the home of 'bummers, brokers, shifty clerks,' and began recognising the importance of your miners. I mean, just up the street there's a chunk of gold worth twelve hundred quid…"

"Yair, well, don't get too steamed up." He had detected a worrying note of excitement in my voice. "There's plenty enough other villains, without getting mixed up with prospectors, so just you mind your step."

"Too late." I breathed an apologetic sigh. "I got dipped last night."

"Oh?"

"Picked clean," I elaborated with a rueful grimace. "Lucky, I still had enough for a telegram to Head Office. Trouble is it's Friday," I concluded with a resigned shrug. "The newspaper's paymaster won't be back till Monday. It'll be a long and hungry weekend, waiting for the cash to come…"

He gave me an appraising look and scratched his chin. "You not et yet."

"It was breakfast, or telegram, not both."

He straightened up. "Stay here."

Five minutes later he returned with a tray from the hotel's kitchen. Never were fried sausages, potato scallops, and a poached egg on buttered toast, more gratefully received. "Thanks," was the best I could mumble between mouthfuls washed down with a mug of hot tea.

"Slow down," he cautioned. "It don't look good for business, you chundering all over the floor."

This was sound advice, and I tried remembering my table manners as he turned the cartoon around to study it more closely. "Who's this for?"

"My aunt," I replied, chewing more carefully now. "The other side's a message, saying the contact she gave me, shot himself a couple of nights ago."

"Sharpie."

"Yes."

"Useless bloody drongo." There was no place for sentiment in this town. "Still, that's his problem. Yours is earning bed and board between now and Monday. Got any ideas?"

There are times when it's best to look baffled and let someone else take the lead. " No. Got any suggestions?"

He re-examined my cartoon and then looked up again. "You good at painting?"

"It depends on what you want," I replied warily, looking around at the skating-rink's tired decor. "If you've got a brush and a pot of colour, I can help freshen things up."

"Nuh! I mean painting. Proper painting. Pitchers."

"Oh. Well then, what've you got in mind...?"

"Finish your tucker. I'll be in the bar when you're done."

A few minutes later, rested and refreshed, I joined him in a large, rather empty space, it not yet time for the knock-off shift at the West Kalgurli Mine to come in and rinse the dust from their throats.

"The Nat's got a huge, big Klowee over their bar," Jonno explained. "The Shammy needs one too. Trouble is the Eyetie painter who promised to do a pitcher only got started before shooting-through with me best barmaid! I mean, is it any bloody wonder the Nat's getting all the trade when all I've got to show is this -!"

He pointed up at an expanse of wall plaster above a landscape mirror elaborately decorated with gilt harps and shamrocks promoting Tullamore Dew which, in turn, reflected a colourful parade of bottled spirits flanked by beer kegs draped with wet towels to keep their contents cool.

The wayward Italian artist had made a bold start on a reclining female nude, by her appearance *d'après* the Sistine Chapel's chubby cherubs before becoming more intimately connected a real woman and eloping with her to Perth. Fortunately, Tom Roberts had taught me the rudiments of perspective and portraiture. With any luck, something might yet be salvaged from this frenzied daub.

"Hmm." I puffed cheeks and shook my head. "That horizontal intersects the primary diagonal, and its secondary hues are unbalanced..." I was confecting technical nonsense, on the run to give an impression that I knew what to do, and how to go about it.

"Yair, well, whatever, but can it be got right?" Jonno was aware of how many punters the rival establishment's "Chloe" was pulling while the best he could offer them to look at was an advertisement for Irish whiskey.

"It'll take time..."

"You in a hurry to get somewhere?" he countered shrewdly.

"No, but I'm not going to rush off and leave a bodged job behind!" I replied, as if defending my artistic integrity and reputation, of which there was not a shred.

"Right. Here's the deal. Take your time. Just finish that there pitcher right and I'll see you get free board and lodgings. Three square meals a day, clean bedding, and your own room. Laundry too, and a wash bowl," he added, conscious of my fragrant aroma as well as the grubby linen. "Wha'dya say?"

157

I wanted to sob "done!" but instead asked, "what paints and brushes do you have, or were they pinched as well?"

"Over here." He led me behind the bar and dragged out a wooden crate filled with jars of powdered pigments, plus a jumble of sponges and fresco brushes.

"Ri-i-ight." Without having served one day of an apprenticeship in this most demanding of artforms, I was being invited to step up as a journeyman and deliver a masterpiece. So far as I could see, my only alternative was to roost in the brewery's barrel yard and steal pig swill. "My case is at the station. You fix me a room with good light, and half a dozen big sheets of brown paper, and I'll get stuck into the job."

"Thanks mate!" I had just taken a massive load off his shoulders and dumped it on my own, but such is the blind confidence of youth that I did not feel its weight at all.

35

On my way back from the station, I made a point of stopping at the National Hotel, on the corner of Wilson and Hannan Streets directly opposite the Town Hall where, only this morning, I had considered applying for a rat catcher's job.

To celebrate my good fortune, I breasted up to the bar and called for a pot of the local bitter which earned me some coarse chaff as a Tuthersider, the ten-ounce glass of beer or "pot" in Melbourne being a half-pint "middy" in Western Australia. I took it all in my stride. I wasn't here for the company but, rather, to study the rival Chloe's main attractions and decide how I might improve upon them.

Amazing breasts and startling nipples were obvious requirements, likewise generous hips with a whisp of silky gauze across her lap as the Greek goddess of fruitful harvests lolled awkwardly on a bed of wheat sheaves. The artist had got that detail right even if the rest of his composition lacked *éclat artistique*, as Aunt Lucinda would have announced with a dismissive sniff.

It took me less than ten minutes to decide what needed to be done to correct this omission, after which I cheerfully strolled the short distance down Hannan's and checked into the Shamrock.

Jonno was as good as his word and had organised a cubicle with northern light and a stack of brown wrapping paper on the bed. The height of luxury, however, was a pail of warm water, a bowl, a tablet of Lifebuoy soap and a fresh towel on the washstand. I stripped and gave myself a trench bath, as they would soon be called by millions of other young men, before putting on my only fresh clothes and returning downstairs.

"Good?" he called across the bar room.

"Tops," I replied, joining him as he served a thirsty miner.

"Y'know, I been thinking." He leaned forward tattooed arms crossed. "You still gotta make a quid. So, you do me the best job you ever done, and I'll put the word out you're a famous M'lb'n artist, come over from the Yeast to do me a Klowee. And as a special favour to the Shammy, you're open to do a few pitchers for blokes to send home, faces and suchlike. Y'reckon a couple of bob each sounds good?"

I reckoned that two shillings for five minutes' sketching sounded very good indeed, and so began my working life on the Western Goldfields, painting a nude enticement on the wall of a public bar.

It was my good fortune to have taken notice when Arthur Streeton and Tom Roberts critiqued each other's work during their weekend stays at Tralee House; this gave me the confidence to brush three layers of lime wash and egg white over the previous artist's ground and begin again.

While these base coats were drying, I drafted a selection of classical poses modelled on Botticelli's *Birth of Venus*, Velazquez' *Rokeby Venus*, and Ingres' *Odalesque*, each with enough exposed skin and suggestive shading to revive the weary drinker after his twelve-hour shift underground, shovelling gold ore into a skip

Jonno reckoned we were on the right track and gave me a matey punch on the upper arm to prove it. I then showed him a supplementary sketch of Maeve's gloriously naked neck and shoulders, seated at the end of our bed, smoothing on a black stocking, face turned towards the viewer in three quarter profile, lips parted as if about to speak, a merry twinkle in her eyes. Her other charms were artfully concealed, which made them even more enticing to the thirsty imagination.

The Shammy's manager stared and stared again before slowly letting his breath escape. "What, a, corker!"

If I do record this episode for Frances, I shall have to explain that "corker" was high praise before the Great War and came from a popular song that began: "My girl's a corker, she's a New Yorker, I'll do anything to keep her in style…"

Numerous parodies were sung in the trenches. "My girl's a corker, she's a streetwalker, I caught everything from her!" was the least vulgar as we competed to add new stanzas, up and down the line in a defiant, bawdy version of *Ten Green Bottles*. Poor old Fritz never did understand Australian troops any more than I expect an enlightened, modern English academic to feel the terror that dwelt inside our steel helmets as we jeered at imminent death and injuries.

Meanwhile, back in that Golden Age we thought would never end, but soon would be gone forever, I set to work transcribing Maeve in thick strokes of crayon across sheets of brown paper. Jonno wanted a few changes, some of which I allowed, others I strictly forbade; as the artist-in-charge, my word prevailed. Besides, I hadn't molested his barmaids or taken sly slurps from the cellar, unlike his previous artist-in-residence, so was worth keeping sweet.

I had hoped to get everything finished for a Foundation Day unveiling ceremony, but the preparations for marking Australia's First Settlement, in January 1788, got in the way. This gave me an opportunity to rethink my composition and make corrections before beginning the painstaking task of pricking holes along every half-inch of every line, big or small, until the cartoons – in the original Italian sense of master drawings on thick paper – could be lightly glued to the whitewashed panel above the bar.

By the time I was ready to "pounce" a calico bag of soot along every line, creating a tramway of little black dots that I could then link up with strokes of sepia paint, I was exhausted; on the other hand, I was also exhilarated.

Without a day's formal training, just close observation of our nation's two greatest living artists at the peak of their powers, I was making a fair fist of the job myself. It must be said these were far from ideal conditions to work under and I soon understood Michelangelo's cranky behaviour as he slaved away at the Sistine Chapel's ceiling.

Every night, after the last client staggered into Hannan Street and Jonno locked up, we cleared away the bottles and barrels and laid short planks across the gap between their shelf and the bar. I would then place a couple of chairs on those and lay more planks between them to improvise a scaffold, before climbing up to resume work.

I could only do so much by hissing yellow gaslight before my eyes blurred and itched, at which point I had to pull everything down, leaving the bottles for Jonno to check their contents when he came back on duty in the morning. After which I would rummage around the kitchen for an early breakfast, go up to my cubicle, and sleep through into the afternoon.

A quick wash and shave, then downstairs again for a light lunch before opening for business as prospectors and miners came in to have their pictures "took" by this famous Melbourne artist. By setting-up shop near the skating rink, I also earned a steady flow of silver florins by drawing sentimental keepsakes in the style of the one recently designed for Kevin & Elsie Fitzgerald.

Truth to tell, I was heartsick, and this added an especial poignancy to my work for others. Applying layers of colour to Jonno's Klowee aroused memories that fired my determination to earn sufficient money to speed back to Maeve's loving bed.

I was not the only lonesome young man on the Goldfields and there were abundant opportunities for a quick release of tension. The Shamrock earned a steady number of spotters' fees from establishments in Hay Street, plus had its own informal stable of girls ready to service the clientele. As a resident insider, I qualified for a trade discount, so to speak, but the memory of "Champagne Charley" Braithwaite's horrible end was never absent on these occasions.

Another, more wholesome tension, was building up in the main bar as day followed day and nobody could see what was happening behind the bedsheet hung over my work-in-progress. A natural showman, Jonno was delighted; our version of a strip-tease act was poaching the Nat's drinkers who were now piling into the Shammy to learn how much longer to go before All Was Revealed.

Too much work and not enough play makes Jack a dull boy and I was in danger of becoming a very dull lad indeed, even as my stash of silver grew in its secret hide under the washstand. In an attempt at clearing the brain and sharpening the eye, after nights perched on a plank, I went into our billiard saloon to set up a frame and get a bit of solo practice. Jonno happened to be passing through after helping unload the brewers' dray in his backyard and paused to watch me snapping pocket shots off the cushion. "Not bad."

"Thanks." I sighted my cue and cockily sank a tricky red.

"'Reckon you could show the locals a thing or two?"

"Maybe."

"'Tell you what. There's a promising young lad I know. He's alright, but needs a bit o' polish…"

Flattered, I straightened. "'Glad to help. Bring him on."

"You stay here. Let's see if I can find him…"

Something in Jonno's tone should have alerted me. Instead, I continued a one-man display of flashy cue work, my mind on other matters, like finishing Maeve's beautiful face in egg tempera, fresco-secco, to retain its full depth of colour in a smoky public bar, and to give my work permanence long after I sped home to the real woman.

"Ah, Fred, meet Ian, the bloke I been telling about."

I turned to shake hands with a rather quiet, reserved, middle-aged man, whose other hand was resting lightly on the shoulder of a young fellow standing beside him, presumably his son.

"Ah, Ian," Jonno said, "this is Wally, the one I told you about."

I shook hands again, this time with a youth a few years my junior.

"'Reckon you can polish 'im a bit?" Jonno continued, with a questioning look in my direction.

"Sure," I replied, in imagination taking over where Jem Sykes had left off with me. "Let's set up a frame and he can show us a few shots. I'll go from there."

"Sound alright to you, Fred?"

"Always ready to learn something new," the proud father replied, letting go of his son.

I busied myself setting-up the balls, yellow through black, and then stood aside to chalk my cue while young Wally chalked his.

"Tell you what Fred, let's add a bit o' spice," Jonno remarked, scratching his chin. "I'll bet you a quid, your player can't break one hundred afore mine does…"

The older man hesitated before, reluctantly as I thought, accepting the challenge. "Done."

Jonno then turned to me. "You game for a quid?"

"Sure," I shrugged, in imagination a strong contender for the 1913 or '14 National Championships, about to educate a local yokel from beyond the mythical Black Stump that is the outer limit of civilization, for we East Coast city slickers.

Magnanimously, I let the youngster break, expecting the balls to scatter wildly before I took over, popping them in rapid order to gasps of jealous admiration. That delusion dropped stone cold dead when young Wally's first stroke sank a red, returning the white cue ball exactly to the tip of his waiting cue as if he had thrown a boomerang.

At this juncture I should have settled my bet and crept off. Instead, I stood rooted to the spot and watched a magical display of skill, as if this nondescript youth had cast a spell over the balls; making them bend to his will by telepathy and deft clicks of the stick; pocketing colours faster than I could tally the score. Had we been playing a formal game, he would probably have broken a maximum with the greatest of ease, instead of which he took pity on me and stopped at one hundred.

I counted out ten florins and watched Fred stroll away with his son, chuckling, as Jonno turned to me with a tight expression on his usually open face. "That was the best bet you ever lost."

"Uh?" I was still in shock.

"Soon you was going to take all the bunce you made with them there pitchers, waltz down the road to Billy Weston's Billiard Saloon, and blow the bloody lot!" I flinched. The man was psychic. "You still don't get it," he continued with heavy emphasis. "This is the Goldfields. Nothing's the way it looks. That old digger you seen in the street, ratting durrie stubs to roll a smoke, could be a millionaire tomorrow if his lease comes good today. And the swell you seen lighting his cigar with a fiver, will be back on the bones of his bum when his luck turns bad. So, think about it, and while you do, I'll bet you another pound to a poke in the eye, young Wally will be a Number One, like his dad and his grandad afore him, and you're the sort of pigeon they pluck for laughs. So don't say you not been warned!"

It was as well that I did not take up Jonno's wager. Walter Lindrum eventually retired as the uncontested World Billiards Champion after breaking more records than any other player in history, several of which I believe still stand.

36

Two days later and we were ready for the grand unveiling. Jonno had done a splendid job of promoting the event and, by six o'clock that evening, it was standing room only in the main bar, our street windows crammed with excited faces peering in to witness The Greatest Show in Goldfields' History, as my patron persisted in calling it.

This was not what I had volunteered for. In my innocence I had thought it would be a simple touch-up of another artist's botched mural in exchange for free meals and a clean bed. Instead, I had been promoted as Michael Angelo's most famous assistant, sent out West special, to do the finest Klowee in Kal' -!

I prayed for the earth to open and swallow me up. Even the most experienced artist knows fear on an opening night, and that is after a working lifetime of public scrutiny. I was none of these things. Foolishly I had stuck my head out and very soon it was going to be brutally chopped off by men who detonated dynamite, deep underground, for a living. And I had already sensed that an angry mob of Outback Australians could have taught Gengis Khan a thing or two about vengeance, pillage, and destruction.

Meanwhile I knew that Maeve's left instep needed stronger Cerulean Blue to emphasise its curvature; her hair was not right, either and I should have brushed more Venetian Red to complement the Emerald Green chosen to tint her eyes, their lustrous dark brown not showing too well in yellow light.

I stood paralysed with fear as Jonno handed over to "His Worship H.W. Davidson JP -! Mayor of Kalgoorlie -! The Best Bloody Town in the whole Bloody World -!"

My world was about to collapse in ruins. There was nothing I could do to prevent it as Mr Davidson reached up to tug the cord that would open a clothes-peg, release the bedsheet, and complete my humiliation.

Eyes squeezed shut, I wished myself far, far away as the linen swung aside over kegs and bottles. Nothing happened. Nobody moved. Instead, there was an electric tension in the air, as if a violent thunderstorm was about to break. Then, someone in the street outside, shattered the silence. "Faaakinell!"

The entire room erupted with cheers, whistles, and clapping hands. Maeve's sideways glance, half-smile, and suggestive wink covered up a host of technical errors. Nobody cared a hoot about those while they could indulge every red-blooded man's fantasy of waking up in a four-poster bed, its rectangular lines framed the image, to find a nakedly beautiful young woman pulling on her black stockings after a night of unbridled passion, as coy lady novelists used to describe a good healthy romp.

Upon second thoughts, this minor triumph is unlikely to appear on Frances' tapes. Although great fun to remember, I must be careful with my posthumous reputation, just as I have been to safeguard Aunt Lucinda's after her captivity in a Jermyn Street brothel. Besides I have no intention of revealing just how stinkingly drunk I got as rough men shouted me shot after shot of rum while thumping my back and pumping my hand.

The following day, much the worse for wear, I came down to a later breakfast than usual. Jonno diagnosed a monster hangover and prescribed two Aspirin tablets with Seltzer water. "There's a bloke wants to see you," he added, taking back the empty glass.

"Uh?"

"Could be another job."

"Uh."

A short while later a shadow fell across my table. I looked up blearily and saw a middle-aged chap who could have stepped straight off the pages of *Country Life*, with a dark spike beard, a monocle screwed into the left socket of piercingly blue eyes, clad in tweed Norfolk jacket, knee breeches, woollen stockings, and polished brogues. "Uh?"

"Cedric Shaw." The tone was clipped, fri'fully upper crust English. "May I join you?"

"Uh."

"You've drawn quite a crowd," he remarked, stood stiffly to attention, "as well as quite a mural."

I peered sideways from the dining room to the main bar where drinkers, three-deep were staring up at the wall above Tullamore's mirror; Jonno's investment in free bed and board was paying handsome dividends. "Uh."

"So, what's your story young fellow?"

I groggily gathered my wits together, up to every trick these rock spiders use to prey on homeless young men. "What's it to you?"

"I'm told you're a good worker."

"So?"

"My crew is down one man. Poor chap broke his leg. Can't wait for it to mend. We cast off the day after tomorrow. His berth is yours."

I laid my cutlery aside and fixed this weird creature with an icy sneer. "Sod off! I'm nobody's bum boy."

"Never thought you were," he snapped back. "Disgusting habit. Chloe's good though. Splendid thighs. Top marks. You're now at a loose end."

I resented his abrupt manner, as if he had taken elocution lessons from a telegraph printer and tilted my chair backwards with an air of calculated disdain. "I shan't be for long…"

"Correct. Report to Malloy's Livery Stable. Good day Mr Cribdon." And with that he turned on his heel and marched off.

A while later, lunch completed, I strolled to the cubbyhole where Jonno did the hotel's accounts. He stoppered his inkbottle, shut the cashbook, and glanced up. "Well?"

"That queer cove." I jabbed a thumb in the general direction of Hannan Street. "When did they let him out of the loony bin?"

"Don't you ever listen at what I tell you? Didn't I say the Goldfields is where nothing looks like it is?!" he challenged, arms folded, their tattooed anchor, hula girl, and palm tree on display.

"Yeah, but -?"

"That's Mr Shaw. Just back in town. You're in luck."

"What?!" I spluttered. "He's a spider!"

"Not him," Jonno growled. "There's no straighter ge'man on the Goldfields. I wouldn't have given your name if I thought different. Besides, I owe'm a favour and his crew needs a steady worker."

"What?!"

Jonno almost smiled. "You never done a Klowee in your whole bloody life. That *Age* story is bulldust too. There was no money on Monday nor ever was going to be, I checked, but that still didn't stop you giving it a go. Not like Spaghetti-for-Brains who could only think of rootin' me bar girl. You kept your mind on the job, nutted out the problems as they come along, and stuck at it till the job got done proper. Mr Shaw liked that too."

"I tell you he's a spider!"

Jonno nearly decked me for this gross insult. Instead, I was curtly informed that my eccentric visitor had been a Royal Naval officer until some disagreement with higher authority made him retire ashore in Western Australia. Kalgoorlie being as far from the sea as it was possible to travel and still buy a good cigar, he had come inland, made, and lost a couple of fortunes, and was well on his way to making a third by pulling sandalwood.

"Maybe so," I interrupted, "but I know sod all about sandalwood!"

"You'll soon get the hang of it." Jonno stood up to his full height of six feet three inches. "It's that or go hungry. You're off the premises."

"Uh?!"

"You done good, but I want you out o' town."

"But -!"

"Tons o' blokes been asking for you to do more Klowees and I don't need no competition. Besides, I'm doing you a favour," he continued soberly. "It's best you keep away from Billy Weston's, because if you don't, you'll soon be skint again, with bugger all chance of making the readies to get back to that girl of yours..."

"Uh?!"

"Come off it!" he grunted. "Nobody does a Klowee like mine and not have a real girl in here," he tapped his forehead. "You got two choices, Billy Weston or Mr Shaw. The one'll pluck you clean inside ten minutes. With the other, you'll make better than wages..."

"How?" I demanded with the prickly pride of youth. "What's sandalwood worth?"

"You still don't get it," he scowled. "Didn't I say nothing looks like what it is?! Mr Shaw don't go hundreds of bloody miles into the Mulga just for stink wood! It's the stuff the stumps pull up, specially if they're working a dry gully or quartz gravel..."

I caught my breath. "Gold?"

"Why else would a bloke risk dying of thirst or getting speared by the Blacks?" he replied. "Mr Shaw knows his way around. Got a finger in all sorts of pies and could easy give the game away, but he likes going bush. Says it reminds him of being on a ship, navigating terror firmer instead of water. As for you," he concluded, "shovel up your kit, I want you gone, quick smart. Molloy's is a couple of lanes back, out along Dugan Street."

37

Dusty and dripping with sweat, I halted in the livery yard's gateway and peered around at a cluster of iron sheds, feed lots, and a forge where the blacksmith and his hammerman were shaping red-hot bar iron into a horseshoe on their clanging anvil.

"Welcome aboard Mr Cribdon." Seen by the full light of day, this eccentric Englishman looked more than ever like our new Sailor King, George the Fifth as portrayed on the recent Coronation posters and souvenir teacups. "Step aft. Lively now!"

I followed into one of the sheds that doubled as an office. "Thank you, Mr Malloy, that will be all."

"Sorr."

The yard's proprietor went off to attend to something outside while Mr Shaw took his place behind the cluttered desk. "Pull up a seat young fellow. What has Mr Johnson told you?"

"Nothing." I heard myself echoing this man's brisk speech.

"Good. Best we start with a clean slate." He sat forward, elbows on the yard's untidy paperwork. "Item. This is your first voyage. You will sign-on as a probationer and attend to such duties as I or other crewmen may assign. In return you will receive a one fourteenth share of nett proceeds when we pay-off. Given you then wish to sign-on again, and have met with the crew's approval, you will be rated a full one seventh."

I felt rather like Jim Hawkins of *Treasure Island*, being interviewed for a cabin boy's job aboard a modern-day pirate ship.

"Item. You will keep yourself, your dress, your equipment in good trim. You will respond cheerfully and promptly to all commands. In the event of an attack, you will look to your front with whatever weapons are to hand, confident that your shipmates are looking to theirs.

"Item. When in town and off duty you will never gossip or disclose matters you may have observed or learned of while in the field. Should you do so I shall soon hear and you will be discharged forthwith.

"Item. This being your trial voyage, you will not be required to invest a share in our enterprise. That will come later, assuming you toe the line and keep up to the mark. However, your present dress is unsuitable for work." I thought this a bit rich, coming from a man dressed for the Australian Outback like a cartoon huntin', shootin', fishin' squire. "Mr Malloy!"

"Sorr?"

"Ready the gig."

"Sorr!"

"Follow on Mr Cribdon. Lively now!"

The stablemaster steadied a pony trap while Mr Shaw and I got aboard then, with a quick flick of the whip, we trotted back into town where our first stop was the Union Bank. I dutifully followed inside while the manager hurried to greet us, not quite bowing, and scraping the ground with an imaginary plumed hat, but very nearly so.

"Mr Jenks. This is Mr Cribdon. He wishes to open an account."

"Of course, of course! Come this way gentlemen, please!"

We went into a back office where Mr Jenks fussed around, getting his papers together. "So, ah, Mr Cribdon? How much do you wish to deposit?"

"Well, I, er –"

"Twenty-seven pounds." Mr Shaw glanced my way. "Mr Johnson says that's what you've earned from your character sketches and portraits."

At this I snapped out of my trance. "I take exception to your tone sir!"

"Enough." He raised a finger. "Your savings will be as safe here as if they were in the Bank of England, augmented by what you earn with us. Stop dithering!"

I counted-out the gold sovereigns I had just exchanged for my hoard of silver at the hotel's till.

"Sign on the dotted line, here, sir…" Mr Jenks offered me a pen and printed form. "Name and address at the top, if you please…" I dipped ink and complied, using Jonno as my temporary mailbox. "And here is your passbook. You'll see that I have entered your deposit so that every time you make another, it will –"

Mr Shaw adjusted his monocle and silenced the manager with a firm look. "What's his rate of interest?"

"Well, er, two percent."

"Piffle! Mr Cribdon is a commercial client, not some blasted factory lad saving pennies to buy his sweetheart a new bonnet!"

"Yes sir, of course sir. Three percent."

"Hmph!" He turned to me. "You happy with that?"

"Um, yes."

"Splendid." He turned away and shook hands with the manager. "Keep up the good work Mr Jenks."

"Of course, sir. Thank you, sir!"

"Come along now, Mr Cribdon. Sharp's the word, swift's the motion, like all the fishes in the ocean!"

I had not the slightest idea what he was talking about as he untied the pony from its veranda post, and we got aboard for a short trot up Hannan Street to Lazarus & Co.

"You are most very welcome gentlemen. How can my humble establishment be of service this beautiful afternoon?"

"Mr Cribdon needs the full outfit."

"Gladly." Mr Lazarus twitched a tape measure from around his neck. "This way if you please, sir."

Twenty minutes later, I studied my transformed self in the shop's full-length mirror. A reflected young man of medium height and build clad in cotton drawers, singlet, and grey socks; hobnailed Blücher boots and rawhide gaiters; dungaree trousers; grey flannel shirt, brown corduroy waistcoat and blue denim canvas jacket; bright red neckerchief and a broad-brimmed felt hat, shared my puzzled smile.

Still shaking my head with quiet bemusement, I buckled the leather straps around a mackintosh groundsheet, blanket roll, and oilskin riding coat, spare shirt, socks, underclothes, and a knitted Balaclava helmet. I thought this last item rather odd, as if we were going to the South Pole with Captain Scott instead of venturing into hot, desert country. "Look, this is all very interesting Mr Shaw," I frowned, "but your friend Jenks took my last quid!"

"Your friend Mr Johnson anticipated the need." He turned to the tailor. "Put it on Shamrock's account."

"Of course, sir." The shopkeeper straightened again. "A prosperous voyage Mr Shaw!"

"They generally are, Mr Lazarus. They generally are." He then drove back to the stable yard and beckoned me to dismount with my suitcase, into which I had by now packed most of my city clothes and follow him to the office.

"You won't need shaving tackle. Where we're outward bound, water is scarce and beards less trouble. Your paper, pencils, and journal will fit into a saddlebag, along with the various other items you will require and acquire as we proceed," he pointed to one hanging on a nail by the doorway. "Keep that greatcoat." He nodded at the one I had worn when arriving in Albany and had kept in anticipation of cooler weather as summer gave way to autumn. "Days are still hot as Hades, out in the Mulga, but you'll find the nights are as cold as a witch's tit. Leave the rest. Mr Molloy will take good care of it, won't you?"

"As if t'were me own loyf!"

"Quite so." Mr Shaw was reaching up to a rough-sawn plank shelf off which he dragged his own swag, strapped inside a sailcloth groundsheet, and a small black tin trunk. "Get your case up there, Mr Cribdon, and we'll be on our way."

Mr Molloy gave me a hand to heave it onto the same shelf and made certain I took the saddlebag out to the pony and trap where he shielded his eyes and looked up as Mr Shaw and I got aboard. "How long d'y'tink ye'll be away d'is toy'm?"

"Hard to tell. Depends on what we find. Send out a search party if we're not back in eight weeks."

"Same track as before d'en?"

"No. Nor'nor east to Leonora and Lake Darlot, then due east to Banya and beyond. We'll mark the track."

"New country…"

"The best sort." Mr Shaw flicked whip and off we went, the trap's iron-shod wheels sending up a fine spray of grit and dust as we headed out of town towards a patch of bushland, somewhat to the west of Kal's ominously well-stocked cemetery, where a cluster of improvised stockyards and humpies had been wired together among the sparse, scrubby acacia trees that are the Mulga.

One of these yards had recently been repaired and now held about twenty camels, draft animals for our German wagon, a copy of ones the Lutheran settlers originally brought to South Australia. Parked alongside it was a lighter spring cart, similar in appearance to the General Service wagons I would later see by the hundred in France, ready to haul our day-to-day equipment and supplies.

"Gather round gentlemen!" Mr Shaw beckoned his crew to move closer. "We have a new hand, Ian Cribdon. He'll be taking Mr Gorse's berth. I'm sure most of you have already seen his other handiwork at the Shamrock. His new job is to prove he's as good in the bush as he is with the brush -!"

"We ort'a get some ripper bedtime stories then!" one of the crew grinned as the others laughed with the dry, laconic rasp I would soon associate with these Australians of a now extinct race.

"Later!" Mr Shaw joined in the laughter. "But first up, let's do the honours." He began leading me around the semi-circle of bearded, weathered outdoorsmen, pausing at each one in turn. "Mr Patrick Donovan. First Mate."

I returned the callused handshake. "Delighted to meet you."

"Hmm." The tone told me I was very much on probation.

"Mr George Smith. Cook Quartermaster."

By now I was getting the measure of my companions and used fewer words to return a less grinding handshake. "G'day."

"Mr Karl Steiner. Mechanic & Carpenter."

I resisted the temptation to show-off my German. "G'day."

"Mr Joseph Mullins. Driver."

"G'day."

"And last, but not least, Mr Ahmed Khan. Cameleer."

I blinked. Lean and sinewy, chiselled leathery features framing grey eyes atop a dark blond beard dyed with henna, this was the first Afghan I had seen close-up, although I had often read about these fierce tribesmen in boys' adventure tales.

I tentatively shook hands. Then, perhaps from some dimly remembered yarn set on the Khyber Pass, I lightly touched fingertips to my chest and gave a slight nod, a salute he returned with equal gravity.

"Your task, Mr Cribdon, is to make yourself useful to each and every one of these gentlemen, as and when required." Mr Shaw eyed his Number One. "Mr Donovan? Set him to work."

"Aye aye…"

I do not have the vocabulary or skill to depict the following days and weeks and months in a manner that Frances could relate to. Instead, I should perhaps gloss over them with a few light paragraphs, but this would not do justice to a vanished world that historians of her time and place need to be aware of.

She says she wants to hear my voice, the to better understand the frock-coated grandees who strode around Whitehall during the July Crisis of 1914, making the fateful decisions that will unwittingly destroy their class and its way of life forever. But there were other Edwardians, at the farthermost reaches of the Empire, ones that London's choices would also destroy. These were the hardy, inarticulate men I shall give voice to when the time comes for me to describe life in the Outback before the Great War.

I shall make it easier for her by authorising Special Collections to allow early access to my journals, for I doubt if she or any of her Oxford colleagues has ever tied a camel pack, or stitched a broken harness, or shot a kangaroo for meat, or forge-welded a broken axle on a rock anvil, or dug an emergency well, or mastered any of the dozens of other tasks we had to accomplish if we were to return alive from what was still a largely unexplored wilderness.

These still lay ahead of me as I carried wood and water for the cook; learned how to feed camels while checking for chafes and sores that could become serious issues at the worst possible time; and assisted Karl Steiner attach new chain to the windlass that would pluck whole trees from the ground, for unlike mulga, sandalwood does not coppice or regenerate from its stump but must be replanted from seed.

At dinner call I was issued with a tin pannikin into which went potatoes, fried meat, boiled peas, and gravy; an enamel mug for stewed tea; a knife, fork, and spoon. These eating irons were now my responsibility to keep clean and bright for morning inspection; though I did not appreciate it yet, Jonno was not wrong when he said I was in luck to get this berth.

At the time it seemed improbable that bloody-minded bush workers would let themselves be called "crew," and "rated" alongside a "Fuck'n Ghan!" who had an equal share in the enterprise.

It felt equally absurd to describe a trek into the Interior as a "voyage," but these terms were second nature an ex-Royal Navy officer for whom Near

Enough had never been Good Enough aboard a battleship, and who now required the same exacting standards when fitting-out a land expedition.

Under his calm authority, we implicitly trusted each other to complete our various tasks. In sporting terms, we were a premiership team, and our morale was equally high, unlike other gangs of pullers who were often slovenly, sullen, argumentative, a danger to themselves and everyone around them.

Not that Mr Shaw ever yelled or threatened. A look of cool reproof was sufficient to make sure the work was put right immediately because, despite his unapologetic Englishness - a fact that should have set us against him - Cedric Shaw had the rare gift of inspiring the best in men. This should not be taken as an unconditional endorsement of his kind, for I still have my full share of Australian scepticism when meeting polished strangers, but fair's fair and things must be told the way they were.

A knockabout life has taught me that everyone embellishes the truth to make tolerable their lonely trek through our Vale of Tears, but at the time of which I am thinking there was no way to tell if Mr Shaw's carefully measured stories of active service in the Soudan, Egypt, and China were based on actual events or were a colourful blend of others' tales. Notwithstanding this possibility, one thing I did gain from his entertaining anecdotes in the months ahead, was an awareness of a much wider world than Melbourne could then offer an impressionable young man.

Meanwhile, as that first evening merged with nightfall, and manic kookaburras cackled in the surrounding trees, and Kal's streetlamps glimmered a mile or so away, we gathered around the campfire, and yarned about things that meant nothing to me yet. Eventually Mr Donovan got to his feet and addressed the Chief, as we called Mr Shaw among ourselves: "Lights Out? Kit Day tomorrow."

"Quite so. Proceed." He also stood and briefly glanced my way. "Where did you learn how to greet Mr Khan in that manner?"

"I, I read about it, somewhere. Why, was it the wrong thing to do?"

"Quite the reverse. He appreciated the gesture. Few of our kind are so perceptive. Sleep well, Mr Cribdon."

38

Heavy dew settled across my face and bare head, blanket, and greatcoat, during the early hours of the morning. Cursing fluently, I dug inside my saddlebag pillow, tugged the woollen Balaklava around my ears, and tried getting back to sleep in a scrape near the fire's embers. This should have been easy but, for some reason, sleep eluded me. Probably because I had yet to learn that one is always more wary and wakeful, resting in the open, than when safely tucked up indoors.

That night was the first of many in which I would peer up and marvel at the southern constellations, sparkling like crushed diamond dust from horizon to horizon, the desert's bone-dry atmosphere making it seem as if it were possible to reach up and touch them with a fingertip. A city dweller since birth, except for three miserable months at Corunna Downs, I had never had much reason to take notice of the night skies when there were brighter, more colourful lights in Mr Myer's store windows, or along the Royal Arcade between Bourke and Little Collins Street.

Kal' was subtly different in ways I could not yet put into words, but there was already an uneasy sense that life could take an abrupt turn at any moment unless I kept focused on the fact that all this was just an interlude, a way to see a bit of the world and make enough money before sprinting back home to Melbourne.

All I needed now was a decent nugget. Just one, a fraction the size of that specimen in Madorsky's window, would be enough to return with a stock of frontier stories to prove to Maeve what a dashing adventurer I was, while tactfully omitting any mention of her nude portrait on the wall of a miners' pub.

The recent past had shaken my confidence and I needed the reassuring certainty of old friendships to restore balance. In no order of priority, I wanted to share time with kindly Arthur Streeton, listening to his tales of Bohemian life in London while deciding whether I should also try my luck as a colonial artist in England.

Another traveller I needed to see was David. When next we met, he would, in his modest way, probably talk me through a scrapbook filled with snapshots of Sweden, and photos of him working alongside Professor von Whatsisname.

And when asked what I had done, apart from a creditable performance in the State Championships, I would just as modestly show him a newspaper account of the huge nugget I'd unearthed in the trackless deserts of Westralia. Guided by a wild band of frontiersmen. Led by, a renegade, British. Naval officer. With a dark. And. Dangerous -

"Wakey-wakey, rise and shine!" Mr Smith's toecap nudged my ribs. "Hungry men, it's brekky time!"

I laced my boots, pulled on the greatcoat against dawn's piercing chill, and set to work rebuilding the fire before filling the billycan from our water cart while the cook-quartermaster arranged his pots and pans on the supply wagon's tailgate.

I still thought of cooks as useful servants who kept order in the kitchen, downstairs, while matters of importance were decided in the study or drawing room, upstairs. I could not have been more wrong and under the Chief's guidance quickly learned that a clean, innovative camp cook is worth his weight in gold and needs to be treasured accordingly. Without him taking care of the Inner Man, morale sags, tempers fray, and soon everyone is at everyone else's throat. In the longer run, health suffers and, in extreme cases, death follows soon after eating contaminated food.

George Smith was a master of his craft and had, perhaps not surprisingly, learned it in the Merchant Navy where rations were notoriously meagre. Turning them into halfway edible meals without inciting mutiny aboard a windjammer, required skills of the highest order.

Porridge oats, dried apple, and raisins had been left soaking overnight, and after a quick boil were the first serving but not before Mr Donovan checked our eating irons for cleanliness.

I blinked as the Chief led by example and stood in line to pass inspection and get fed. Gone was the tweedy English squire of yesterday. Today, clad in dungarees, corduroy vest, hobnailed boots, and gaiters he was an Australian bushman from top to toe; only the monocle and trimmed beard remained of his former self.

The rest of breakfast was a slab of fried mutton on a wedge of damper made from flour, water, and baking powder, cooked in a Dutch oven over hot coals. Vitamins were still largely unknown, and balanced nutrition was only spoken of among vegetarian food faddists, so it's little wonder that outlying camps and expeditions often suffered from chronic sickness and debility, constipation, or diarrhoea.

We were lucky to have a leader trained in the Royal Navy where anti-scorbutic rations had been standard issue for over a century, hence the earthenware demijohns of Bickford's lime juice on our stores' inventory. Issued daily in a mug of water, these soon became a welcome treat and preventative medicine combined, the farther we tramped across gibber plains into desolate breakaway country.

Our rolling stock had to be kept in tip top order and correctly laden, a task that fell to Joe Mullins, a gloomy old bushman from the back blocks of Queensland where he had shorn sheep, ridden countless miles of boundary fencing, and trapped wild dogs for the government bounty. Later, and already getting on in years, he had volunteered for the South African War in which he served as a Service Corps wagon driver.

I eventually got to know him better and realised his gruff manner was defence against a world that foolishly looked down on illiterate bush workers. This should have been apparent much earlier when we first gathered to sign "Ship's Articles," as the Chief called our formal agreement to share and share alike. Everyone else, including Mr Khan, either inscribed or scribbled a signature except for Joe who made a shaky cross, witnessed by *Lt Cdr C.W. Shaw DSO RN*, to please a decent old man who only wanted his mark to look as important as everyone else's.

As the camp's dogsbody my task was to assist everyone check their equipment before helping stow it aboard the carts. I was surprised to see just how much gear was needed, ranging from the Chief's medical kit and sextant case to Karl Steiner's toolbox and tackle, the cook's sacks of rice and tins of Maconochie's mixed vegetables, to the carpenter-mechanic's adze and crosscut saw. In effect we were a self-sufficient expeditionary force.

What I had not thought to find were five Winchester rifles, a pair of Webley revolvers, and a well-used hammer shotgun with packets of ammunition for each calibre. Mr Shaw noted my interest and paused from packing them away. "You shoot?"

"Just clays and the occasional rabbit."

"So, you can be depended upon to supplement our snares by potting larger game? Splendid! With luck these won't be needed for any creature more threatening than the 'roos we'll take for fresh meat." He patted the nearest rifle's walnut stock. "Now, hitch a camel, go to the railway yard's hydrant, and refill Furphy." He dug around in his trousers' pocket. "These should do the trick."

I palmed his two silver half crowns, sensing a test to see how quickly I responded to the unfamiliar, and how far I could be trusted to deliver results without anyone looking over my shoulder, so instead of muddling about with unfamiliar bits of saddlery I set-off to find someone who did. "Mr Khan?"

He paused from splicing a halter rope and glanced up. "Yiss?"

"When convenient, kindly show me how to hitch a camel to the water cart." I had unconsciously begun copying the Chief's polite, direct form of address in situations where others might have snapped a command.

"Yiss."

Ahmed Khan was a man of few words although, as I later discovered, he had learned to speak and read quite good English as a *Havildar* - the equivalent of Sergeant - in the Queen's Own Corps of Guides on the turbulent North-West Frontier between tribal Afghanistan and British India. If their name sounds slightly comic to modern ears, conjuring up as it does images of young ladies erecting tents and learning First Aid, let it be known that the Corps of Guides was the gold standard of courage and discipline by which all other units of the Indian Army were measured, as I saw for myself during the early 1920s.

How and why such a veteran came to be in the Westralian Outback was never explained, not even when we became better acquainted while he taught me to converse in basic *Pashto*. Thinking on it now, I suspect that vengeance – *Badal*, in *Pashtunwali*, the Pathan Code of Honour – was somewhere in his past. However, such questions are best left unasked when dealing with proud and prickly tribesmen who can sustain a blood feud across many generations.

All of which was to come later, but today he focused on showing me the correct way to select and harness a moderately tame ox camel - the bulls are dangerously unpredictable, especially in the rutting season - and between us we got it between the shafts of our cylindrical water cart with its iconic: Good Better Best, Never Let It Rest, Till Your Good Is Better, And Your Better Best, embossed in cast iron below the J.Furphy & Sons' trademark.

As it still held a few gallons, we transferred these to a smaller galvanised tank under the wagon driver's seat, for every pint counted, even on the edge of town. The Furphy could now set-off laden with potable water, though soon enough this would become a shandy of whatever we bucketed from soaks and *gnamma* holes along the way.

"*Hooshtah!*" Our cameleer gave my charge a smack on the rump and left me to get on with it, proud as Punch to be entrusted with such an important job, but even a castrated camel has a mind of its own as I discovered long before we finally rumbled to a halt, sweating, and swearing, at the railway siding.

The yard foreman strolled over. "Water?"

I controlled the urge to sarcastically enquire if he thought ours was a dunny cart and nodded instead. "Yeah."

"Five bob."

He pocketed the two silver coins and pointed me over to the locomotives' water tower where I unlatched the cart's circular lid while he swung a canvas hose and filled my tank to the brim.

Some experience of the world's wicked ways told me that one hundred and eighty gallons of the Railway Company's water allowance had just leaked from a broken main or mysteriously evaporated in the hot sun. Given that similar water had cost five shillings a gallon, only a few years earlier, today's load was a bargain.

I arrived back at camp as the waning sun cast oblique shadows across surrounding bushland. Determined to show that I was now an effective member of the crew I made an utter botch of unhitching the camel before trying to tether it to the others' picket line. Fortunately for me, if not my pride, Ahmed Khan was on hand with a pair of hobbles to keep the beast steady while I managed to finish the job.

Crestfallen, I turned just in time to catch the Chief giving me a resolute frown and to hear his sage advice: "*Festina lente*, 'hasten slowly.'" Adding, in a phrase I later learned can be attributed to the emperor Augustus: "'That which is done well, is done quickly enough…'"

And thus began my apprenticeship as a cameleer, apropos of which, although the correct name for these creatures is dromedary, nobody ever called us dromedeers, not that it mattered as days merged into weeks, and weeks into months during which I became adept at handling imported Indian beasts as well as our locally bred draft animals.

The former were usually more vicious and temperamental than our Westralian-bred camels. They were also smaller in stature, more liable to mange and were forever getting septic sores I had to treat with sulphur and turpentine salve. Being so narrow in the chest, these wounds tended to ulcerate between the forelegs and brisket, never the easiest places to work on while trying to restrain a camel swarming with fleas and flies in dusty heat.

The local breed had a fuller configuration, being deeper chested with well-sprung ribs, and were better adapted to our feed and conditions, although the Indians generally had more stamina and required less water, hence what we gained on one we lost on the other.

Ahmed Khan was a hard taskmaster and therefore a good teacher in a business where inattention to detail can easily lead to disaster when hundreds of miles from the nearest settlement. As already noted, he was a man of few words but many surprises, not the least being the presence of a tall, raw-boned Irishwoman and their two redheaded boys.

When I innocently wondered where his other three wives were, having seen him kneel at dusk, facing Mecca, he gave a rare laugh and assured me that having one like "Kafflin" was enough for any man to handle. This I could well believe, having witnessed their ding-dong rows in which she gave as good as she got, and yet never once did they come to blows so one must assume that this oddly matched couple shared a deep and abiding affection, each for the other.

It could not have been an easy arrangement, especially for her. Racial tensions were always simmering, and even when those were not about to explode, the ancestral hatreds of Protestant and Catholic could burst into flame at the slightest provocation. These ancient religious wars were further subdivided as chapels and churches, tabernacles and tented revivalists did battle for wayward souls.

As if all that were not fuel enough for spontaneous combustion, there remained the constant friction between we Tuthersiders and the now outnumbered Sandgropers whose bar room brawls frequently spilled into Hannan Street, with snarling drunks kicking and belting each other senseless.

Even during our basic training at Blackboy Camp, and then in Egypt *en route* to Gallipoli, and later still in France, these smouldering feuds could detonate at any moment, especially behind the reserve lines where two pints of plonk – Digger speak for *vin blanc* - cost one franc, the equivalent of a shilling.

Meanwhile, during these twilight years of peace on the Goldfields, Mrs Kathleen Khan bullied, badgered, and blarneyed her way around, over, or through life's slights and slurs. Yet despite all she treated me kindly enough, which was as much as one could hope for. It probably helped that when not pulling sandalwood and scratching for gold, I took it upon myself to repay her husband's language lessons by improving their boys' handwriting as well as teaching them how to draw comic characters for fun.

Both lads were quick learners and could have done well if only they had learned to control their equally quick tempers, which was entirely predictable when one considers the likely offspring of a bareknuckle Biddy and a Pathan warrior. It was no surprise to learn, much later, that both young men had lied about their ages and joined-up in 1916.

Jamal, known as Jim, died of wounds at Ypres the following year; Malek, known as Mick, was killed by a sniper's bullet at Montbrehain five weeks before war ended in November 1918, coincidentally on the same day as the citation for the second bar to his MM was published in the *London Gazette,* one of only a handful of Australian soldiers to be awarded three Military Medals for separate acts of valour during the Great War.

I shall do justice to them and their story when the time comes to enshrine the memory of two otherwise forgotten Diggers who stood up for a country that looked down on their parents.

39

Shortly after first light, that last morning in Kalgoorlie, the carts were hitched-up and our campsite swept as cleanly as possible, under the circumstances. The First Mate then marched over to the Chief and reported that all men were present and correct; that the latrine bucket had been emptied at the regulation depth, by me; and that every item of equipment had been accounted for. Sah! Pat Donovan's service as a troop sergeant major with the South Australian Mounted Rifles, during the Second Anglo-Boer War, ensured that our column always began the day on time and in good order.

The road north from Kal' to Leonora is most likely an asphalt highway nowadays, unlike three quarters of a century ago when it was still no more than a rutted bush track linking an archipelago of campsites littered with rusted tins, broken bottles, and hunks of sundried dung.

My first night out was spent on one such rubbish dump, but only after we'd shovelled the worst of it aside. I soon learned that, as a matter of habit, our team always burned, bashed, buried its empty tins in the latrine pit, unlike most other pullers and prospectors heading up-country. I ascribe this unusual conduct to the fact that except for myself, all the rest had served in an army or in a navy - Royal or Merchant - and understood the need for good order and discipline.

Karl Steiner fitted this pattern exactly, being raised in a land where *Ordnung und Disziplin* were strictly enforced at every level of society. The youngest son of a foreman mechanic at the *Benz Motorwerke* in Mannheim, he had completed his compulsory military service in a Pioneer battalion digging fortifications, grading roads, and building bridges; hard training that was of the greatest value in the Australian Outback.

Hungry for adventure and, I suspect, determined to get as far away as possible from a tyrannical homelife in an increasingly militaristic homeland, he jumped ship at Fremantle and made his way to the Goldfields where he began saving money to buy a one-way ticket for the Girl Next Door, and to open a bicycle repair shop in Perth.

He was the team's youngest member until my arrival. A good-natured fellow, we got along well. It helped that I could translate for him as his English was still limited, though naturally I was always careful to include everyone else in our conversations, to avoid any suspicion of gossip or back-biting which can so easily fester when foreigners begin chattering among themselves.

Karl repaid the favour by introducing me to tools and equipment I never knew existed or had thought were needed. Such mechanical aptitude as I have shown in later life, from reading a micrometer to shim a Lewis gun mount, to estimating the placement of gelignite to bring down a truss bridge and stall a *Wehrmacht* motor convoy, were his legacy, never imagining that one day it would be turned against his own countrymen. Of such are the sorrows of history.

However, we had more immediate concerns on that first evening out from Kal' as the crew tossed a coin to roster our guard duties through the dark hours ahead. Mine was the first shift with Joe Mullins, for which I was issued the double-barrelled Greener, loaded with buck shot, while Joe glumly thumbed cartridges into one of the Winchesters. I thought this was all a bit excessive and disputed the need by declaring that the last bushrangers had been hanged more than twenty years earlier.

"If only we could say the same 'bout them Black bastards out there!" Joe replied with a scowl at the encroaching shadows.

I flinched at his snarling hatred. Usually, when referring to Aborigines by a variety of casually mocking nicknames, the ones we had in mind were those lazily camped under a tree at the western end of Hannan Street or prowling Kal's back lanes where the elders would cadge tea and sugar from distracted *wadjilla* housewives while the youngsters pilfered anything not chained up or nailed down.

Their behaviour was annoying but hardly a threat to life and limb, and no reason for deadly force, or so I thought having heard Vida Goldstein rage often enough against *The Native Question & What Must Be Done,* a then popular pamphlet proposing castration as the Final Solution for the Native Problem.

Brimming with an eighteen-year old's righteous indignation, I demanded to know Joe's reason for his hostile attitude, to which he simply growled: "A'cause they eat their babes…"

I lost no time telling him what I thought of such lurid slanders, by spluttering that Australia was a twentieth century nation where there was no place for obscene, defamatory talk of infanticide and cannibalism -!

His sneering laugh cut me to the quick as he replied with a detailed account of things seen and heard while boundary riding the inland frontiers of New South Wales and Queensland.

I frankly disbelieved his laconic accounts of unwanted half-caste infants being roasted to obtain their "body oil" for black magic; of slain enemies being butchered for their kidney fat; of things, indescribably vile, done to women and girls.

These horrific slanders could only be an initiation rite to test the new chum, and it certainly seemed that way as the rest of our crew gathered around to watch Joe stoke my anger with ever more outrageous tales of grotesque cruelties.

The Chief finally saw it was time to step between us with a calming smile. "Thank you, Mr Mullins, you've made your point. Our young friend still has much to unlearn." He then faced me, no longer smiling. "We are now in another world, Mr Cribdon. One in which thinking like a Melburnian gentleman will, most likely, attract a spear to your guts or a *waddy* to the back of your skull."

"B-But you heard what he said?!"

"Of course."

"It's, disgusting!"

"The truth is not always welcome to our more refined ears…"

I hesitated. "You're saying, what I've just heard, about them eating babies, and those things they do to their womenfolk, are true?!"

"Why else do you think the church missionaries are kept busy saving young lives and patching-up their unlucky mothers?" He paused, eyeing me closely. "It is a fatal mistake to romance the Aborigine as Nature's Gentleman. That's for sentimental city folk to believe in the safety of their withdrawing rooms while policemen patrol well-lit streets outside."

He shared a sad smile. "*Lex Talionis* - the ancient law of revenge and retribution, red in tooth and claw – is alive and well, just beyond your safe city limits, ever ready to strike down the unwary. Indeed, I would wager a pound to a penny that some unfortunate's 'man meat' is being consumed within a day's march from where we stand at this very moment."

"Never." I shook my head, convinced this was a sadistic tease.

"As you wish," he shrugged, "but don't be too quick to dismiss another man's hard-won experience just because it fails to accord with your version of how life ought to be led. Meanwhile," he concluded, "keep that gun ready and be prepared to use it. If forced to do so, make every bullet count. Warning shots in the air are taken as signs of weakness and will only encourage further predation."

I must tread warily if recording this and later conversations. Frances is of a generation that imagines it has rediscovered the Noble Savage and agonises over the loss of his Primitive Eden. I can truthfully say there was precious little nobility amidst abundant savagery during the first years of this century, and there is no evidence it ever existed if one believes the Aborigines' own unedited Dreamtime Stories that unashamedly tell of abduction and rape, blood feuds and warfare, revenge and sorcery. And of the need to limit a tribe's hungry mouths during frequent seasons of dearth and famine.

I shall have to refresh my memory before deciding how much more to reveal, and how much to suppress. Fortunately, I have always kept sketchbook journals. Those that have survived the wear and tear of a life on the move are now housed in Special Collections, so a telephone call to Janice Thorpe will be quite in order if I do decide to revisit these last two years before the Great War.

However, some memories leap to mind unaided, like the sombre change of mood as our little caravan of carts and camels left the Leonora Road and headed eastwards into the arid breakaway country and miraged salt lakes between Mount Yaboo and Bungarra Rocks.

Three or four months earlier, the most sky I had ever had reason to notice was a crimson sunset at St Kilda Pier where I finished an oil colour, inspired by Turner's *Fighting Temeraire,* of a Tasmanian steamer on Port Phillip Bay. For all practical purposes I was still a self-absorbed townie, more inclined to look down at the pavement for stray coins, than upwards at the narrow slots of grey blue above Melbourne's bustling street life.

Westralia changed my outlook forever, and in ways I would find hard to explain to a much younger Englishwoman if we were to meet again. Although now a long lifetime ago, I am still no nearer to finding words to evoke the West's immense skyscapes and lonely desert winds, or to say how deeply these affected me.

God knows, I tried hard enough! Firstly, in a letter to Maeve, written by a brash young frontiersman who claimed to be doing amazing deeds for King & Empire; and secondly a few years later, when I wrote *Boolya's Hoard,* an adventure yarn in the same vein as Rider Haggard's *King Solomon's Mines,* only set in the Australian Outback instead of Africa, while recovering at 15 AGH in Alexandria,

In it my youthful equivalent of the wily old hunter Alan Quartermaine, saved his comrades from a deadly ambush by cannibal tribesmen; crossed a trackless waste in search of water, carrying a wounded Aboriginal girl on his back; discovered a fabulously rich goldmine; and eventually returned home to a thinly disguised Maeve's passionate kisses. I managed about thirty pages of this treacly tosh before wisely concluding that a novelist's life was not for me.

Old age brings its inevitable aches and pains to the failing body, but sharper pangs by far are those inside the head whenever reminded of the heedless, hurtful things said or done while yet an arrogant young fool; at such dark moments I still find myself squirming with embarrassment.

Meanwhile, our crew had made camp in open bushland with abundant sandalwood to pull, dock, and stack during the next several days. As there were no chores needing my immediate attention, I decided to climb the granite flanks of an adjacent ridge, to clear my head, for I was still in a prickly mood after that run-in with Joe.

Halting for breath at the top, I stared northward, awestruck by an endless expanse of quartz gravel plains, ochre clay pans, and sunblasted cliffs that reached far beyond the cramped confines of my little world.

In imagination, I was the sole survivor of a plague that had killed every other person on Earth and knew how H.G. Wells' *Time Machine* pilot felt when he landed at his most distant future point, the sun a dimming cinder, our planet a cooling rock lost in the inky void of Space.

This insight struck me with an emotion I have never shared with anyone except Carl Jung during my time at his clinic. There is no way I could confess it to Frances and still retain her respect, for any man with normal human feelings should have been terrified by such a bleak vision, but in my case it had quite the reverse effect.

An equally intense flash of self-discovery revealed that I would often be in a crowd but never of a crowd. Other men need human company and the support of companionship to function at their best, but for whatever reason, I would always be the outsider –

"You have just earned three black marks."

Startled, I spun around. The Chief stood about five yards back, rifle underarm as if about to shoot game on an English estate. "What?!"

"Leaving camp without telling anyone. Going unarmed in hostile country. And being so preoccupied, you never heard me approach." His frown froze me. "A Blackfella could have crept up and clubbed you to death with the greatest of ease."

"If there were any. Look -!" I gestured at the wilderness.

"Wrong." He shifted the Winchester to his other arm. "They've been tracking us ever since we left the road. There could be one behind that rock," he pointed, "and with their ability to spear a playing card at thirty paces, you would be dead moments later." He turned away sharply. "Come along. There's work to be done before they send their old gins to spy on us. As for your conduct, Mr Cribdon, I expected better of you."

Chastened, I followed, determined to stay more alert in future. It was a humbling lesson, at the time, but one that thirty years later would stop me from walking into a Gestapo trap at the Gare du Nord.

His prediction about spies being sent to the intruders' camp came true that same afternoon. I was watering our camels from the Furphy after refilling it from a soak dug at the foot of the granite incline, when two grimy, wrinkled, naked Aboriginal women shuffled in from the surrounding bushland, mewling and croaking as they drew nearer.

The Chief and First Officer were old hands at this game and had worked out a response on previous expeditions. Mr Shaw marched forward with a stick to trace a firm line on the ground between our camp and the women while Mr Donovan reached into the supply cart and retrieved a cavalry bugle that I had often wondered about.

Stiffly at attention, he brought it to his lips, elbow horizontal to the ground, and let fly with *Boots & Saddles*, its brazen call clanging into the distance.

Meanwhile the Chief scribed mysterious, meaningless squiggles and circles in the dirt before solemnly breaking the stick in two, turning his back on the terrified gins, and tossing one half over his right shoulder, the other half over his left. He turned again as both women fled.

"It's the kindest thing we can do for these poor people," Mr Shaw explained when I later quizzed him about this peculiar performance. "It is a fatal mistake to allow their women into the camp, for if they are not spying on us – like that couple we've just seen - they are often being pursued by vengeful menfolk," the Chief continued sadly. "An unthinking Whitefella is likely to try stopping the buck beating his lubra over the head, at which point both will turn on him for interfering in their domestic squabble, and he'll be lucky to escape with only a few bruises."

"But -?"

"It is an even more serious mistake to invite them to share food, or skylark around as soft-hearted travellers do, seeking to be friendly, never realising that the native's mind is not responsive to such overtures," he continued, determined to teach me the realities of life on nine tenths of Australia's still largely unexplored landmass. "Restraint is not in his vocabulary: 'Give him an inch and he'll take a mile.' Especially when his fellow tribesmen appear to share the silly Whitefella's bounty. At which point their anxious host will see his entire stock of rations gobbled up unless he calls an immediate halt, which inevitably leads to anger, and resentment, and bloodshed -"

"But what has this got to do with breaking sticks and playing bugles?" I interrupted, still under the spell of Vida Goldstein's reforming zeal.

"Because one thing the native fears even more than an empty belly, is the 'Boolya Man' and his bull roarer. In Africa we called them witch doctors," Mr Shaw added with an understanding half-smile. "Here the names differ but their followers' superstitious dread is just as powerful, especially when he's twirling a 'roarer overhead, summoning-up the ancestors." He paused again, eyeing my reaction. "Our noisy mumbo jumbo says we are powerful Whitefella Boolya Men, with a spirit army of our own, and must be left alone, which is surely best for all concerned..."

His pious fraud seemed to work, for none of the natives came near us during the next five days at Boolya Rock, as the Chief named it on his precisely drawn route map, plotted with daily sextant shots on the march.

During our time there we ranged out with the windlass, pulling, and cutting sandalwood, always with a sharp eye on the subsoil dragged to the surface on torn roots. By the time we finished working this patch, and the Chief had planted replacements from his sack of sandalwood nuts brought up from Kal', our wagon was half-laden with yard long billets, ready for the manufacture of Chinese joss sticks and, as a bonus, between us we had fossicked thirty ounces of raw gold that were now stored in a padlocked strongbox below the supply wagon's bench.

After some debate and tossing of coins it was agreed we should stay another few days and try our luck on a nearby creek bed where we took turns shovelling gravel into the dry blower, a portable arrangement of graded sieves which, when shuffled back and forth, winnowed dust and worthless mullock from the heavier, richer pay dirt.

This sounds simple enough but was, in fact, devilish hard work for much sweat and little gain. But such are the ways of prospecting, just as we were about to chuck it as a bad job, George Smith unearthed a lode of pea-sized nuggets that eons of winter rainstorms had washed downstream from a weathered quartz reef in the surrounding hills.

None of them came anywhere near rivalling the monsters that regularly appeared in Madorsky's window but that did not detract from their hypnotic power as our cook weighed the gold on his kitchen scales, using copper pennies as units of measurement, after which the Chief entered the total on a tally slip, we then checked to confirm fair play.

This one discovery, alone, more than paid for the entire expedition and put a smile on our faces as we moved along to fresh woodland, where we completed loading the wagon before heading back to Kalgoorlie.

40

Nobody was aware of it yet, but the market for sandalwood had peaked, now that yet another civil war in China was giving that unhappy nation's worshippers more urgent matters than joss sticks to spend their money on.

The Great War would briefly revive the trade when the Australian Army Medical Corps ordered gallons of sandalwood oil as a treatment for gonorrhoea, but like so much else, this bleak prospect lay in an unimaginable future as our broker's cheque was ceremonially cashed at Mr Jenks' Union Bank, after which we retired to his back room and divvied up the proceeds.

Though only a dogsbody probationer, I deposited thirty-six pounds in my savings account while retaining eight pounds seven shillings and fivepence for living expenses, thus I had every good reason to feel proud of being well on my way to presenting Aunt Lucinda with a plump bag of sovereigns, as tangible proof of how wrong she had been in her reading of my character as a layabout "ladys poodle"! And for me to claim the other half of my stake money when I turned professional.

Business concluded to everyone's satisfaction, the Chief invited us to join him for lunch at the Shamrock where, with characteristic thoughtfulness, he ordered a lamb pilaf and mixed green salad for Ahmed Khan while the rest of us tucked into grilled pork chops and roast potatoes, buttered carrots, and steamed cabbage. With the wisdom of hindsight, I know who was eating most sensibly for our climate, but at the time I was famished for salty, crunchy, oily tastes after nine weeks of 'roo stew and tins of Carrot & Bean Medley.

Regardless of what was on our plates, all were in fine spirits by the time we popped the bucket of iced champagne – plus a bottle of Mr Khan's favourite tipple, Kalgoorlie Aerated Waters' lemon fizz – and clinked glasses to toast the conclusion of a successful voyage.

I had been forewarned to make myself scarce when the time came for the rest of the crew to vote on whether I could remain aboard, so knew what to do when the Chief caught my eye and nodded towards the main bar next door.

I strolled out to see if my Klowee's novelty had worn off yet. Obviously not, for Maeve's saucy wink was still enthralling thirsty miners, assisted by tinkly ragtime tunes from the coin-operated pianola Jonno had bought at a bankrupt's auction during my absence. He beckoned me over. "How's it going? Making a quid?"

"I'm putting a bit away."

"Uh huh." He sucked a tooth. "Keep it up and don't let Billy get his fangs stuck in, or you'll wind up skint again…"

"No chance of that," I lied, secretly shaken by Jonno's insight. Feeling lucky, I'd been planning a five-pound flutter at Weston's Billiard Saloon.

"Yeah, well –!" He was about to add a further warning but stopped short when one of the waiters came in from the dining room to escort me back.

"Welcome aboard, Mr Cribdon." This, plus firm handshakes all round, told me all I needed to hear, for truth to tell I liked being with these men, just as I was beginning to feel at-home in the Outback.

A heartfelt, "Thank you gentlemen, mates all," was the best reply I could manage at short notice, but it appeared to be enough, judging by the pounding fists that made our cutlery and chinaware jig about on the tabletop.

The next item of business was to decide if we should try another, quicker prospect before the weather got too hot, for although the nights were still cold enough to lay a thin crust of ice on a mug of water, the sun was developing a noticeable sting as the days lengthened.

I was not the only one feeling lucky and by general agreement we decided to have one more shot at Yerilla before giving it away until the cooler months, next year. This proved to be a good move and I was able to add a further fifty pounds to my savings before we finally called a halt, but not before agreeing to team-up again in autumn.

Ahmed and his camels then headed south, laden with supplies for a new mine at Norseman; George Smith became the Shamrock's second cook during the holiday season; Karl Steiner hopped the train for an appointment with the German Consul in Perth; Joe Mullins got a job at the Brewery, maintaining their delivery wagons; which left only the Chief, Mr Donovan, and myself, to sort ourselves out.

"Got plans for Summer?" the somewhat older of the two other men asked me with a shrewdly enquiring look.

"Not yet," I shrugged. "I've done a few cartoons the local paper might take. And there are letters that need answering before I get too involved in anything else. Why?"

"Well, if you're stuck for digs, there's a spare room at my place," Mr Donovan concluded. "One quid a week, all found."

This startled me as I had always seen him as inherently remote and disapproving, certainly not the type who would turn his home into a lodging house. I suspect this was a plan hatched between himself and the Chief, to distance me from Weston's shark pool.

One pound a week for bed and board was a bargain on the Goldfields, even if the room was likely to be a lean-to shed, and the food whatever slopped out of a pot, so I collected my suitcase from Malloy's and hitched a lift to an address in Keenan Street, scribbled on an empty Rizla packet.

I was wrong. The Donovans – his wife Dulcie was the local piano teacher - lived in modest comfort and employed a daily maid to help around the home. I was also wrong in my opinion of the man himself. On duty, our First Officer was a strict disciplinarian, but off-duty he was a charming fellow with a fine baritone voice whenever he and Dulcie hosted a musical evening for their friends and neighbours.

These rekindled fond memories of the Shuster's soirées as did David's handwritten note, redirected by Aunt Lucinda, before being mislaid in an upcountry postbag:

Hochheim House
Toorak Road
Melbourne
3rd June 1913

Dear Old Goliath Slayer.

Germany was an eye-opener in matters social
as well as scientific. The research underway at Jena
is world class, however I found it odd to be among
so many heel-clicking uniforms of all styles and colours.

Fortunately, while at the Games, I met some really
decent chaps from Cambridge, one of whom is reading
Biology at Gonville & Caius, and the work they are doing
at the Cavendish is equal to anything in Kaiserland.

That's all my news for now, what's yours???

D.

These few lines unsettled me. A young genius was considering attendance at one of the Empire's two most prestigious universities. After which, with a family fortune behind him and his own considerable personal charm, a distinguished career and the highest honours were guaranteed in the decades ahead.

Contrast this golden future with a bearded cameleer's prospects; palms callused from wrestling with halter ropes; arms muscled from digging up creek beds; fluent in blistering curses learned while swatting clouds of bushflies drinking his salty sweat. It was easy to see who was riding high, and who was not. Of more immediate concern, though, was Maeve's response to my most recent multi-page letter. Ominously there was no address, and it was undated.

My Dearest Ian.

You express yourself so well that I can easily
imagine myself in the "Great Outdoors."

Sadly, I must forego that pleasure as I shall
soon be moving to London where Mr Syme
of the Age is expanding his telegraphic news
bureau, for which the Secretarial College
has recommended my services.

I shall always remember our times together,
with great fondness, but I am happy to
part in the knowledge that you are doing
great things against daunting odds and
will assuredly emerge a stronger, better man.

Affectionately yours.

There followed Maeve's real name and initials. The expression "Dear John Letter" had yet to be coined by American servicemen during the Second World War, but hers was a good example of the earlier Australian version.

41

Maeve's note wounded my pride, and I seriously considered a hurried return to Melbourne, as noonday temperatures inched above one hundred in the shade for diehard traditionalists planning to celebrate Christmas 1913 with roast dinners and boiled plum puddings.

Fortunately, common-sense prevailed - for me at least - and rather than catching an eastbound steamer at Albany I walked into the *Kalgoorlie Miner's* office to show the Managing Editor a folio of my drawings, emerging shortly thereafter with an offer of fifteen shillings apiece for local character sketches, plus six par's of text for him to sub' into shape.

Cedric Shaw was the obvious start for my career as a roving reporter and several days passed before I got a reply apologising for the delay, having just returned from business in Esperance on Westralia's south coast, with an invitation to luncheon that same afternoon.

Beard trimmed, best shirt ironed, jacket sponged clean, I bustled into the Shamrock's dining room, sketchbook, and pencils at the ready, eager to make a start even before the main course was served. Instead, Mr Shaw lowered his soup spoon and raised a finger, cutting me off mid-sentence: "Never start an interview, or an investigation, or an interrogation with a direct, personal question," he began, with a note of severity in his voice. "Not only is it bad form, it puts your subject immediately on the defensive."

"But -?"

"Pay attention." The frown deepened. "Everyone, without exception, prevaricates and, upon occasion, resorts to barefaced lies when threatened by a stranger's curiosity."

"But how else do we scoop the real story?" The brief exposure to journalism was already evident in my speech.

"Enjoy your meal." He resumed lunch by spooning up his bowl of mulligatawny with a distinctive to-and-fro dipping action I would later observe among the gentry at English country houses.

Crestfallen, I complied willingly enough having acquired an appetite for this tasty concoction of Indian pepper, chicken, rice, and diced vegetables.

Mr Shaw eventually dabbed lips with a linen napkin and eased back in his chair, monocle focused on me again. "When stalking a tiger, one should never charge into the undergrowth, blindly hoping to make contact unless also willing to be mauled. Better to peg out a dead goat and let the prey come to you..."

"W-what?"

He ignored my hesitant query. "The same rule applies when stalking that most elusive and dangerous of animals, Man. Mixing metaphors: 'Softly-softly, catchee monkey...'"

"Uh?"

"Abrupt enquiry immediately makes a person wary, just as you would be if I were sufficiently ill-bred to ask outright what your father did before he died or was killed." I must have flinched because he gave a knowing nod. "Whereas, if I were to obliquely enquire about your name and its origins, for you are the only Cribdon I have met anywhere in the world, then little-by-little you could be coaxed into revealing all that I wished to learn."

"Um."

"There are two ways of achieving this," he continued, ignoring my muted response. "*A priori* and *a posteriori*, both derived from the Latin, as I'm sure you have already gathered. The first means 'from what comes before'; the second means 'from what comes after.' Thus, an *a priori* argument works forward from cause to effect, or from a general rule to a particular case. Whilst an *a posteriori* argument works backward from effect to cause, or from a particular case to a general rule. Or, in other words, *a priori* is an argument by deduction, and *a posteriori* is one by induction..."

"I-I'm sorry, what the hell are we talking about?!"

"Your future, for there is no way a man of your nature and character will be content to pull sandalwood until old and spent like Mr Mullins."

"I might!"

"I think not." He turned, waiting for the next course to be served. "Thank you, Mr Jones, that will be all for the moment." He faced me again. "There is a foolish misapprehension that it's 'weakness' for one man to ask for another's help or advice. Consequently, far too many go through life pushing doors marked 'Pull,' so to speak, becoming ever more envious and frustrated when others, no better endowed than they, seem to be having all the luck..."

"And the connection with writing a newspaper story, is what?" I enquired, a young man with more than a touch of defensive suspicion in his voice, unsure of where and why this older man was leading him.

"The highest compliment one can pay another person is to ask for their advice or opinion," he replied simply. "Chances are good that if it's a matter close to his or her heart, you won't be able to shut them up for the next half hour. And if you can't turn that into several column-inches of newsprint, you'd better reconsider your choice of career."

Confused, I looked down at my plate of grilled steak, steamed peas, fried potato scallops, standard lunchtime fare on the Goldfields, Summer, or Winter.

My host's subtle, supple advice was the very reverse of everything I firmly believed that Real Men needed to attain success in life and love. Steely eyed, inflexibly brave, morally upright, the young heroes of G.A.Henty's popular Victorian adventure stories – with rousing titles like *Wulf the Saxon*, or *Under Drake's Flag*, or *For Name and Fame* – never asked for anyone's advice or permission. British grit and a smart uppercut to the villain's jaw were all that a decent, clean-limbed chap needed to get ahead in life!

Somewhat wiser and much older now, I see all too clearly the damage such authors inflicted upon generations of readers by their depictions of brightly coloured, unrealistic ambition. If only I'd had the talent, I would have liked to put the record straight by holding up fictional mirrors in which young readers could view themselves without romantic distortion and learn thereby that wishful thinking, alone, is never enough to make a go of life.

Meanwhile, back in that lost Age of Innocence, the Chief smiled with a mature man's understanding as I struggled to collect my confused thoughts. "Cheer up! 'Hasten slowly...'"

"As you keep saying!" I snapped peevishly.

"Then there must be a good reason for it," he replied, not in the least offended. "Now, I suggest we postpone the rest of our talk until we finish our meal, after which I shall sit in half-profile while you sketch my features and enquire what advice I would give to other young hopefuls seeking their fortunes on the Goldfields."

Some minutes later, Mr Shaw tilted his head, the better to appraise my sprightly character sketch of him wearing a peaked naval cap, monocle aglint, cheroot nipped between finger and thumb. "Is this really how I seem in public?"

"Not in so many words," I explained. "Cartoons are not meant to be photographically exact or lifelike."

"Of course," he agreed, "for if they were, I would insist you erase these golden oakleaves from my cap; only full commanders and above are entitled to such splendour."

"Which you were not?" I enquired, already copying his seemingly casual, oblique questions.

"Hardly!" he chuckled. "I was damn' lucky to retire honourably with two and a half rings on my sleeve, after pleasuring an admiral's delicious young niece!"

I crouched forward. "May I quote that?"

"Most certainly not! Tact and discretion mark the gentleman from the cad, as much as they differentiate the professional journalist from the ha'penny hack, and don't you forget it."

Chastened, I slumped back. "My only experience of life at sea was crossing the Bight." I glanced up. "Seriously, why does anyone in their right mind pick such a wet and miserable job?"

He shrugged. "There was not much else a fourteen-year-old lad, burdened with a name that sounds ominously like 'Seashore,' could do by the time the Royal Naval College finished thumping him into shape. It was not all bad though. Truth to tell, I miss the Senior Service more often than it misses me." He returned the sketch before adding by way of explanation: "There are joys that a landsman will never know…"

"Like?"

He smiled reflectively. "Like commanding a destroyer, twenty-five knots on the dial, her boilers at full head of steam, knowing you've taken a miscellany of individuals and of them crewed a superbly-tuned Greyhound of the Deep." He savoured the moment. "No man worthy of the name will ever know such pride and fulfilment hunched over a ledger, scratching away his life with pen and ink."

"If you say so," I frowned, "but Kal's one hell of a long way inland…"

"381 statute miles, 331 nautical." His crisp reply was evidence of the exacting standards Queen Victoria's navy had thumped into her officer cadets.

"But surely, if you'd wanted a change of scene, why come here, of all the godforsaken places on Earth?" I persisted

"Why does anyone?" He shrugged. "The lure of lucre. Not that it took long to learn that a prospector's luck rarely lasts for long, as I saw with poor old Paddy Hannan after the big miners moved into town. But by then I'd become strangely attached to the place and its colourful cavalcade of men, and women, old, and young, from every corner of the globe. To paraphrase Dr Johnson's opinion of his London, one and a half centuries ago: 'The man who tires of Kalgoorlie, sir, is tired of life!'"

I eased forward again. "Can I quote you this time?"

"Go ahead, it's a catchy headline."

Something in these words alerted me that, among his several business interests, Mr Shaw had money in our local newspaper. Jealous rumours called him one of the wealthiest men on the Golden Mile, a shrewd operator with a thumb in many pies, including the Shamrock Hotel where he kept a suite of rooms - his cabin, as he called them - on the upper floor overlooking Hannan Street. Yet, for some unknown reason, instead of choosing to lead a life of idle ease he preferred to lead a ragtag crew of sandalwood pullers into our still largely unknown Never-Never Country.

I steadied my nerve. "Um. Would you mind if I asked a personal question...?"

"That all depends on what it is," he frowned, "and whether or not it has any bearing on the feature article you are writing for *The Miner*."

"I believe it does."

"Proceed."

"Rumour says you're not short of the readies, with interests all over the show, and yet you go out with us, pulling sandalwood and fossicking for gold. Why?"

"I enjoy the company."

"But the flies, the dust, the sweat, the heat?!"

"Believe me, Mr Cribdon, such discomforts are as nothing compared with those inflicted upon young lads at the Royal Naval College..."

"I-I'm sorry, I just don't get it."

He cocked his monocle's eyebrow. "Oh?"

"Well, whenever I hear others talking about what they'll do once they've made their pile, it's either go home to the Eastern States, or go Home to England and buy a country manor." I paused, studying his impassive face with its uncanny resemblance to our new king, George the Fifth. "I imagine you could do both, instead of which you do neither. So, why...?"

"Why indeed?" he thought aloud. "One could argue that navigating the Outback is not so very different from navigating the ocean, except that here we have more landmarks and fewer opportunities to drown. And yet, regardless of their difference, there is the same thrilling sense of boundless horizons awaiting discovery."

"I still don't get it."

"Robert Herrick did," the Chief remarked drily: "'Attempt the end, and never stand in doubt, nothing's so hard that search will find it out.' Though I'm pretty sure he adapted this from Terence's: '*Nil tam dificiliest quin quærendo investigari possiet*,'" he added, reflectively. "Both express the same exhilarating challenge of manly endeavour and of fresh discoveries, rather than poodling around the fleshpots of Sydney, or foolishly playing the *nouveau riche* English squire to amuse ennobled neighbours."

I leaned forward, intrigued by this glimpse of the Chief's inner world, not yet understanding all his frequent Latin tags, though in no way did I feel he was putting-on-airs to impress a callow young follower. "Can I quote that?"

"No." His tone was final.

"Correction," I insisted. "Not 'the fleshpots of Sydney' but, 'nothing is so hard that search will find it out...'"

"Why?"

"Because I reckon that's the best advice a bloke can give anyone new, on the Goldfields, and down on his luck." I spoke from personal experience.

"Hm." He weighed my proposal before giving a curt nod by way of reply. "And I reckon we'll make a journalist of you yet, Mr Cribdon. Proceed."

42

Until now, I had no idea that a year could pass so swiftly. Twelve months ago, almost to the day, I'd been confined to my bunk, seasick aboard a tramp steamer, outward bound for a place I had never heard of, but which would soon be my new home. An even greater surprise was the speed at which I'd adapted to this alien way of life.

No longer an overt Tuthersider, I had adopted the dress, the manner, the speech of a Sandgroper, sauntering up Hannan Street as dusk settled over our town; hands in pockets to frustrate lurking finger-smiths; chiacking with acquaintances among the jostling crowd of other Christmas shoppers enjoying the evening's cool.

Mr Myer's lavish displays seemed curiously remote and unreal as I stopped to admire Montgomery Brothers' electrically lit store window, its stiff mannequin dummies clad in the Latest London Fashions; I felt immensely proud of Kal's determination to keep up with the rest of the world amid what was still a savage wilderness.

Until a couple of decades ago, the tens of thousands of square miles around Kalgoorlie – "Place of Silky Pears" to its local tribesmen - would have been much like Boolya Rocks and those other gravel beds I had dug into, sweated over, and sworn at frequently. Then, in a matter of months, the discovery of gold nuggets - many the size of billiard balls, a few considerably larger - changed everything forever.

It is impossible to tell how much gold was taken during those chaotic early years, but assuming a likely figure of half a million ounces, this amount would have struck over two million sovereigns at the Royal Mint, according to the School of Mines' instructor I interviewed for a newspaper article.

These were the bait that lured the butcher, the baker, the candlestick maker to risk everything and set up shop in a ragged tent or brushwood shanty until bricks and corrugated iron could be hauled up from the coast, by bullock cart and camel train, before the Eastern Goldfields Railway Company saw sufficient reason to float its shares on the London Stock market.

The magical velocity of coins, the fuel of credit, powered the exchange of goods and services that transformed a grove of silky pears into Westralia's largest, wealthiest, most vibrant town outside of Perth.

It was my good fortune to be there when a second commercial boom got underway as work began on a railway line from Kalgoorlie to Port Augusta, one thousand miles east, across the waterless Nullabor Plain, attracting a fresh influx of thirsty, spendthrift tracklayers and navvies from Russia, and America, and Africa, the equal of our local miners for hard drinking and hard living. And yet, on this Christmas Eve of 1913, there was surprisingly little friction as the Season of Peace & Goodwill fulfilled its promise for the last time that many would ever know again.

I held Montgomerys' door open to let a couple of happily gossiping housewives go first, then followed inside and headed straight for the haberdashery counter where I had earlier spotted a sturdy pair of leather braces, marked down for a quick sale. These were a present to myself, after deciding no longer to hitch my trousers with a tightened belt, it being more sensible to leave the waistband slack in this climate.

The second purchase was an exquisitely embroidered Brussels lace handkerchief in a presentation box decorated with a romantic engraving of Gaasbeek Castle. From memory I tendered ten shillings for both items. The money and sales docket were placed in a metal cylinder, loaded onto spring-loaded trigger, and shot – pinggg! – up one of the overhead wires that connected an elevated cashier's desk with every sales point on the floor.

Within the minute it returned – ponggg! – bringing my change and a stamped receipt that freed me to go across the street to the Miners' Aid stall where, for a small donation, a young girl gift-wrapped the handkerchief's box with silver paper and red silk ribbon.

I finished my shopping with a stroll down Hannan's to Beale Brothers who, as well as selling pianos, ran a busy side-line as picture framers. The previous week, I'd left a folio of portrait sketches at their workshop, and they had done a first-rate job with polished cedarwood mouldings and a lightly textured, grey cardboard matte; the Chief and Mr Donovan, Karl Steiner, George Smith, and Joe Mullins would receive their presents at tomorrow's lunch.

Only Ahmed Khan would be absent, as he was out of town, delivering stores to a mining camp north of Kookynie. Instead of his solo portrait I had composed a family group - Mum and Dad in the top corners, their two boys below them - each set inside an ornamental medallion copied from the book of Persian architecture in Mrs Donovan's little library.

Happy with the Beales' handiwork, I paid well and asked for each piece to be wrapped and individually named, to prevent confusion before returning to my lodgings in Keenan Street.

A quick wash and brush up, followed by a light supper, and I was ready to attend Midnight Mass at St Mary's, on the corner of Brookman and Porter Streets. Dulcie Donovan – DeeDee to her friends - cuddled up to her husband, he expertly handling the reins, as one would expect of a former cavalryman, while I lolled in the back of their pony and trap until we briefly stopped to give a lift to Kathleen Khan née Riley - KayKay to her friends - at which point I sat up straight and delivered my present for her and the boys to open later.

The Donovans were childless and, I suspect, both saw in me a substitute son who might, with a little coaxing, be persuaded to cross over to Rome. Not that anyone ever put the hard word on me, but I could sense an unspoken desire to see this restless young heathen find stability and comfort in the tight embrace of Holy Mother Church.

When Dulcie eventually asked me why I accompanied them to Mass and yet took a back pew, I replied that I enjoyed hearing her play Bach fugues on the organ and liked studying the interplay of light and shade on colourful vestments as Father O'Meara went about his business. But no way in Heaven or on Earth was I going to subscribe to the dogma of Papal Infallibility, with its blind obedience to whatever the Pope told his followers to do with their lives. I was already too private a person to surrender my independence just to earn a baptismal medal and another assumed name, though said more tactfully than that, having no wish to hurt a kindly, concerned, decent woman.

Mrs Donovan was also a strictly traditional Christmas cook, one who regarded toiling over a hot stove as character-building mortification of the flesh, especially when the air outside shimmered with the sun's summer heat bouncing off rock-hard ground.

I suspect that her husband was not wholly convinced of the need for this as he carved the baked ham while she heaped our plates with roasted potatoes, steamed cabbage, and boiled carrots. Fortunately, we were sufficiently aware to make the necessary nods and noises, regardless of what we thought privately.

The parish priest was this afternoon's guest of honour and repaid the favour with a sonorous Latin benediction; Joe Mullins, seated on my right, responded with his own muttered version of Grace: "Two. Four. Six. Eight. Dig in. Don't wait -!"

If I do recount this scene for Frances, I shall redact his sardonic mockery, typical though it was for a now extinct race of Australians. Men like Joe and others of his breed were tempered and hardened in a world that later, softer people cannot begin to imagine. Even I find it hard to recall, and that's with some experience of life in the Outback before the Great War turned everything upside down and inside out.

Their dry, raspy, biting sense of humour accurately reflected a time, and a place, and a society we shall never see again. Many will argue that's progress, but I'm so sure. On balance I feel we've lost more than we have won, measured in national pride and spirit, courage and initiative, grit and determination.

The Chief remained seated – Royal Navy style when taking the Loyal Toast - and addressed our hosts with his customary gracious, well-chosen words before inviting us to charge our glasses. What Monsignor Declan O'Meara really felt while saluting "His Majesty the King Emperor!" remained a mystery, there being no way of telling if his other hand's fingers were crossed in the dark folds of his soutane.

Dulcie Donovan and the maid had prepared enough to feed twenty hungry men, not just our small gang, and was puzzled when we mopped our brows and declined second helpings by protesting that we must leave enough space for the hot mince pies and plum pudding. This prompted our guest of honour to excuse himself by saying that he had other parishioners to visit on this Holy Day holiday.

Everyone else retired to the music room where our presents were neatly arranged on the sideboard. My sketches were a great hit with all except George Smith who was still on duty in the Shamrock's kitchen; he would have to wait until closing time tonight before unwrapping his parcels and packets.

The mistress of the house was equally delighted with my choice of a Brussels lacework handkerchief; its exotic box told of faraway cities where a frustrated Outback piano teacher might once have achieved fame and fortune as a concert pianist. This is not idle conjecture. I had noticed several clues and cues during my stay at this address. Especially the *Frankfurt Hoch Conservatorium & Music Academy 1905 Admissions Guide* tucked among her sheet music.

Her husband straightened his waistcoat and stood to attention beside the upright grand piano while she got ready to accompany him in the recital they had been rehearsing for the past week or so. As already noted, Pat had a fine vloice and it was a delight to hum along with *O Come all ye Faithful*, and other old favourites.

There was an unstated social obligation that we each now contributed something to the entertainment. Karl led the way and got a huge round of applause with *Holy Night, Silent Night*, sung in its original German.

The Chief also had a pretty good throat as he launched into a ballad of his own devising, its tune roughly based on *Hearts of Oak*:

A wet sheet and a flowing sea

A wind that follows fast.
And fills the white and rustling sail
And bends the gallant mast, my boys!
While like the eagle free
Away the good ship flies, and leaves
Old England on the lee...!

Dulcie Donovan was not the only one of us present today with unfulfilled dreams of what life might have been.

Joe Mullins was a real surprise. Although illiterate, he had memorised *Christmas Day in the Workhouse* by ear. Not only that, but he also now recited its many verses with a choked, angry passion that made me wonder if he identified with the pauper who:

Rose midst silence grim
For the others had ceased to chatter,
And trembled in every limb.
He looked at the guardians' ladies,
Then eying their lords he said
I'll eat not the food of villains,
Whose victims cry for vengeance
From dark unhallowed graves.
Great God it does but choke me
For this is the day she died -!'

The best I could manage, after such an epic blast at Victorian England's notorious Poor Laws, was my old standby *The Village Blacksmith*, with appropriate gestures to show arms like iron bands, concluding with:

Thus on the flaming forge of life
Our fortunes must be wrought!
Thus on its sounding anvil shaped
Each burning deed and thought!

It was sheer coincidence that the next course, about to be served by the maid, was a plum pudding the size of a soccer ball ablaze with burning brandy. By now the sun was setting and the air cooling down as a late breeze flowed over the wet hessian curtains hung from water-filled gutters around the roofline. This dropped the temperature sufficiently to restore our appetites for a token mouthful of pudding and nibbled mince pie.

I took mine onto the veranda, with the rest of the menfolk, leaving Mrs Donovan and the maid to clear the table while her husband brought out a tray of tumblers, his soda siphon, and Jonno's gift, a bottle of *Four Crowns* whisky.

The ways in which we each took our Scotch said much about who we were and where we hailed from. Mr Shaw poured two fingers, added a shot of soda, and waited for us to fill our glasses; Joe Mullins took his neat; Karl was teetotal and took a half tumbler of the carbonated water instead; Pat Donovan took his dram fifty-fifty as did I.

The Chief leaned forward to clink glasses. "It has been a good year for our enterprise, gentlemen," he eased back, sipping appreciatively, "1914 promises to be even better."

His second in command cocked an enquiring eyebrow. "You've got something special in mind?"

"Uh huh." The tone of voice said that more would be revealed once we settled down with the conversation ebbing and flowing at an easy pace. Meanwhile, our individual preparations for a relaxing smoke also said a great deal about who we were.

The Chief lit one of his Burmah cheroots, imported directly from Rangoon in bundles of twenty-five, and stretched out on a recliner.

Joe Mullins unlaced a shabby tobacco pouch, made from the tanned scrotum of a Western Grey kangaroo, and thumbed black shag into his clay pipe.

Karl struck a wax vesta and treated himself to a *Dreipunkt* cigarette, posted up-country from a speciality tobacconist in Perth.

Pat Donovan rolled a slim durrie from a one-ounce tin of *Afrikander Smoking Mixture*; he said the illustration of an oxcart printed on its orange lid reminded him of ambushing a Boer supply column on the Veldt.

I loaded my briar with a generous pinch of rubbed *St Bruno Flake* and eased out on a Queensland Squatter, the once-popular form of reclining chair with swivelled arms on which a man could rest his weary legs without removing his boots, in case he needed to leap back into the saddle.

Our confusion of smoky aromas discouraged the mosquitoes that otherwise congregated on the damp hessian, thirsty for human blood as well as water.

Frances will most likely lecture me *in absentia* on the evils of nicotine, as is the modern fashion, not that it will be any concern of mine by then. In anticipation of her disapproval, and because I feel it is important that historians know the Why, as well as the What of their subject matter, rather than viewing the past through the prismatic lens of modern prejudice, I shall try to describe the importance of tobacco in men's lives at the turn of our century.

Smoking in those days was a companionable, masculine ritual, equivalent to the Red Indians' peace pipe ceremony. Offering one's tobacco pouch to another bloke, or accepting a cigarette from his opened packet, established a common bond between strangers. Often, by striking a match to share a light, a man could strike up a casual conversation that might lead to a lasting friendship.

The cost to our nation's health was spoken of by medical missionaries to Australia's working poor, but their warnings fell on deaf ears among men who were more likely to die from a septic scratch, if working in a stable; or be killed by a falling tree, if cutting timber; or crippled by a host of lung diseases, if breathing rock dust and dynamite fumes, underground. Their chances of reaching a ripe old age were iffy at best, even when they had never puffed a coffin nail or sucked a gasper in their entire lives.

Tobacco and its amiable rituals brought a small measure of comfort to hardworking men for whom the daily grind meant keeping one jump ahead of the rent collector, if lucky, before their worn-out bodies finally broke down.

"Next year, I marry!" Karl announced with a proud smile.

"The girl's on her way then?" Joe asked between easy puffs.

"Yes. Ingrid says yes. The Consul says yes, all her papers in order are, to leave the *Reich*. I sent money for the ticket!"

"When's the Big Day?" Pat Donovan enquired kindly.

"After one more – you say, 'voyage'? – for the gold, for the house, for the shop."

"Shop, eh?" It was the Chief's turn to show interest in the other young man's future. "Selling what?"

"Bicycles *und Motorwerke*. I know the automobile!"

"A garage, eh?" The Chief nodded approvingly. "Good plan. There're going to be a lot more cars and lorries on the road before we're all much older." He whiffed fragrant smoke at the veranda's corrugated iron roof. "Let me know when you're ready and I'll see you get the right place at the right price."

"Thank you, sir!"

"No," the older man smiled back, "thank you Mr Steiner. A young nation needs young men with ambition and a young family to feed. You'll do well."

1914

43

I saw in the New Year with my sketchpad and crayons, observing tipsy revellers blowing toy trumpets or twirling wooden rattles, weaving up and down Hannan Street until the Post Office clock tolled midnight, at which point everyone linked arms, sang *Auld Lang Syne,* and wished each other the best of luck for 1914.

Pat Donovan shook me awake, seemingly minutes after I dragged a blanket over my bleary eyes and reminded me that we were going on an excursion this morning, for which an early breakfast awaited our urgent attention.

The mystery deepened after we'd eaten. He went over to a locked cupboard and took out a rifle I had not seen before. The Winchesters we carried in the Outback were light, sporty lever-actions, ideal for dropping a 'roo or warning off Blacks, but this firearm was ominously different; a factory new, bolt-action repeater with blunt, brutal lines; a blued steel box magazine jutting ahead of its trigger guard.

"You seen one of these before, Icy?" With the initials I.C. this was my inevitable nickname.

"No. What is it?"

"SMLE," he pronounced it Smelly, "the Short, Magazine Lee Enfield." Adding: "Tons better than them Lee Metfords we had in the Transvaal, though you'll still see a few on the range today. Anyway, chop-chop, time and tide wait for no man!"

With that he slung a leather bandolier of cartridges, shouldered his rifle, gave Dulcie a peck on the cheek, and headed into the yard where their pony and trap stood waiting. I climbed up beside him, steadying the new rifle between my knees while he handled the reins and, with a flick of the whip, set off out of town.

Kal's mullock dumps and head frames fell astern as we clip-clopped parallel with one of the several narrow-gauge railway lines linking the outlier timber camps that cut boiler fuel and pitprops for the mines.

After a couple of miles, we turned right, joining other sulkies and carts, traps and wagonettes going in the same direction through remnant scrub, each filled with men from every other rifle club in the district, all converging on the Osborne Range for its Inaugural Invitation Shoot.

Pat Donovan had to attend, as Vice-Captain, but I was far less certain of my place in today's event. Left alone, I would have preferred to be writing-up my journal. The discipline of putting my thoughts on paper helped keep them in order, for there was still one unresolved question uppermost in my mind a week after the Chief queried what my plans were for the coming year.

Earlier in our acquaintance, I must have told him that I planned to get back to Melbourne with two-fifty in gold. I might have added how much I ached for Maeve. But of late, our muscular, masculine, Outback life had edged her from memory's crowded foreground. So, instead, I told him that I wouldn't mind having another shot at Mount Wundana where, earlier in the year, we had successfully fossicked east of Pindin.

196

There was no need to question my choice. Each of us, in our own way, had fallen under the spell of that rocky escarpment's crystal-clear night skies; its dawn winds soughing through the desert oaks' dark green needles; its immense vistas of ancient, dried-up lakes and riverbeds that, Ice Ages ago, brimmed with running water from the once-verdant Great Victoria Desert.

My tone must've hinted at more than I cared to admit, even to myself, because he snapped me a piercing look. "No, you don't, Ian." This was the first time he'd spoken my given name.

"But -?"

"You don't belong there."

"I beg your pardon?!"

"Only mystics, madmen, and messiahs are drawn to such places," he continued, with firm emphasis. "You are too young to be any of those. A lifetime of choices awaits; don't blow your chances." The regret was plain to hear as he concluded with an enigmatic: "Bob Scott never knew how lucky he was to die at the South Pole while still at the top of his game."

He noted my puzzled surprise at hearing anyone refer so casually to Captain Scott, the Empire's latest tragic hero since his glorious death on the Ross Ice Shelf the previous year. "We were at Dartmouth," the Chief explained simply, "and both served aboard *Boadicea* on the South Atlantic Station. Fate dealt us much the same hand of cards; the only difference, he played the king. I played the joker."

"Which is the highest trump in Euchre," I quipped, determined to lighten the mood, for truth to tell it disturbed me to hear a man I so respected, confessing to human weakness and -

"Wake up Dreamy Dan!" Pat Donovan's sharp words of command snapped me back to the present as he reached for his rifle. I jumped down after it and peered around at a sprawl of mess tents, marquees, and cooking fires.

The impression of an army encampment was heightened by young cadets in uniform, as were men of my age in similar khaki. Later I learned that today's shoot qualified towards their annual Militia training requirement. There were even several of Pat Donovan's generation sporting Boer War slouch hats, in his case still with its South Australian Mounted Rifles' badge and Light Horse plume of emu feathers proudly erect.

"Lively now! You'll have to sign in."

I dutifully followed over to the largest tent where a trestle table had been set up, behind which sat another of the old brigade, minding the attendance register.

"Ah, Charley, this is Ian Cribdon, the bloke I was talking about."

"G'day."

"G'day," I returned a brisk, noncommittal handshake.

"You shot three-oh before?" the older man frowned.

"No. Just clays and small game."

"Hm. Well. I s'pose we'd better get your name down." He handed me a pen while glancing over my shoulder. "Keep an eye on him, Pat, we don't need no cowboys."

"He's solid."

"If you say so." Charley was not convinced. "Next!"

We walked across to a nearby fire where an earlier detail was brewing gallon pots of tea, took a couple of enamel mugs off a table improvised from ammunition boxes, dropped one penny apiece into a glass jar, and joined the queue.

"Refresh my memory," Pat said, turning to me again, "how old are you now?"

"Going on twenty. I think. Why?"

"That means you're due for call-up," Pat observed with a thoughtful chin scratch. "When you get the word, register as a bush worker, that way nobody'll expect you to polish boots and attend regular parades." It was apparent to whom he was referring. The uniformed lads around us were townies – clerks and shop assistants mostly - and thus able to attend compulsory drills and lectures in a large shed behind Kal's Town Hall.

"I'll sign you up as a club member." He finished with the kettle and stepped aside to let me take my turn. "It'll count as training when the authorities check your record."

"You reckon they might?" I queried, filling my mug with hot, sweet tea the colour of molasses.

"My fuck'n oath they will!" Off the leash of Dulcie's loving care, a man among men for the next few hours, Pat was free to speak his mind howsoever he chose to. "We'll need every bloody rifleman we can muster when the Peril gets here." And with that he strode off to oversee the duty roster, leaving me to enjoy my drink by the cook's fire.

Less palatable was his allusion to a sinister phrase that resonated with every Australian since our newspapers began parsing Old Mother England's sly Naval Agreement with Japan, and I must be careful if I do record this incident for Frances, two world wars later.

In what used to be our characteristically gruff, colonial way, Australians abbreviated The Yellow Peril – Kaiser Bill's colourful description of China, which now included Japan, as *Die Gelbe Gefahr* – to simply the Peril. And perilous it most certainly was after the Imperial Japanese Navy sank the Russian fleet at Tsushima and the Mikado's army conquered Manchuria.

It was fortunate that Gilbert & Sullivan wrote their Japanese musical comedy when they did. A generation later and the world no longer laughed so readily at little brown men with fans and strange haircuts, mincing about in flowery robes on the stage, but who instead wore Prussian blue uniforms and fired Mauser rifles with deadly effect on the battlefield.

Nowadays, even to hint at the Yellow Peril would have me burnt in effigy by Progressive zealots, so I may have to remind Dr Frances Baxter that an historian's duty is to recall the past as it truly was - in von Ranke's original German: *Wie es eigentlich gewesen war* - rather than reconfigure it to suit current fads and fantasies. This should also persuade her that although my formal education is nil, I have picked up a few useful scraps of knowledge along the way, ones that might be worth listening to.

Meanwhile, back in those dwindling years of a peace we thought would never end, I became sufficiently adept at interpreting foreign news – with Aunt Lucinda's expert tuition - to understand how seriously the South African War had revealed Britain's isolation when the Dutch and Germans, French and other nations began cheering the plucky little Boers' early successes.

It didn't matter that the final victory was Lord Kitchener's at the head of half a million British troops from every corner of the globe. Nothing could fudge the fact that an empire upon whose flag the sun never set had been seriously challenged by a few thousand farmers – *Boer* in Cape Dutch – defending their rustic way of life. The unspoken question, now, was how victorious would Britain be if challenged in Europe by a major industrial power with a modern army?

The Royal Navy, for its part, discreetly made plans to bring the Pacific Fleet back home to British waters if - or when - a European war broke out, entrusting the Imperial Japanese Navy with a responsibility to protect Britain's farthest-flung dependencies.

To mollify these anxious Overseas Britons, London sent a military delegation led by Kitchener himself, to inspect our defences. David invited me to attend the review at Victoria Barracks when his honorary Uncle John – by now Colonel Monash – showed the visiting British officers what Australian troops could do. We must have made a good impression, for although the delegation's technical report was scathing, no fault was found with the quality of our part-time soldiers who were described as "magnificent specimens of manhood!"

The upshot was a by no means universally popular Universal Training Scheme for all physically fit males between eighteen and sixty years of age, and the establishment of an armaments factory at Lithgow in the foothills of the Blue Mountains, far enough inland to be safe from naval gunfire and invading Japanese marines.

A dark shadow fell across my fist and half-empty mug. Startled, I glanced up. "Yes?"

"Jack Morgan." The older man stuck out a miner's gnarled fist. "Range Safety Officer. I'd better show you the ropes." And thus began my introduction to field musketry by learning to strip and name the Smelly's parts from muzzle crown to brass butt plate, a drill that would become instinctive for many hundreds of thousands, during the next few years.

Then, once I could tell the difference between an extractor claw and a bolt head - and could demonstrate that I knew how to remove, clean, and replace the traveller spring from its ten-round box magazine - I began loading, cocking, dry-firing distinctively marked dummy 0.303 Ball cartridges, all the while belly-down on a separate practice range, well away from the main event with its steady thump-thump-thumping of aimed fire.

I much preferred to crouch upright, shooting off-hand, or resting my rifle on a rock or against a tree trunk, unlike the refined torture of a cricked neck, bony elbows scraping gravel, aligning the rear sight's notch with the blurry foresight blade with the distant blob I was told to imagine was a charging Asiatic with evil designs on White Australian maidens.

Jack shared some of the discomfort by laying prone beside me; squinting into a prismatic tube that allowed him to view my sight picture; patiently coaching my trigger release and breath control; at the end of which I was utterly exhausted without firing a single round of live ammunition.

"Jesus, mate -!" I gripped his wrist to haul myself upright. "Are soldiers really expected to crush their balls and bugger their elbows, all at the same time?"

"No," he grunted, "if you want to stand up, go ahead, it's your funeral. Johnny Boer was always happy to oblige."

I got the picture. "Point taken."

"Good man." He shouldered his rifle, but not before getting me to draw the bolt and visually check the magazine was empty before proving, by touch, that the chamber was unloaded. This I did by poking my little finger up-the-spout, as he termed it. "Right. Let's get some tucker. Then we'll see how much you've learned."

Gerry Mason, Kal's wholesale butcher and, also, a club member had supplied trays of pork sausages, beef rissoles, and rump steaks sizzling on steel plates outside the mess tent, while the morning's final detail of marksmen finished their shoot from the 500 yards mound.

Despite my raw elbows and stiff neck, I was curious to learn more. Apparently, it was the cadets' duty to manage the target frames from inside a covered trench while live fire cracked overhead, with an occasional ricochet or bullet splash to liven things up.

At the end of each detail a cadet signaller lowered the red flag, to indicate that all firing had ceased and that it was now safe for another cadet, at the other end of the range, to semaphore the scores to Pat Donovan, who noted them in the range log before his signaller flagged the butts to patch and make ready for the next detail.

"How's it going?"

I turned sharply. The Chief was standing behind me, clad in his country squire tweeds, naval spyglass poised to resume reading semaphored signals. "Oh, not too bad."

"A bit of a change from potting kangaroos."

"You can say that again!" I responded with all the shallow bounce of youth. "Like, imagining the bullseye as a Jap's head!"

"Uh huh." He adjusted focus and peered downrange. "Personally, I've always aimed at the heart and lungs. Even if you're not spot-on, three inches up or down, left or right doesn't affect the outcome."

"Oh." I didn't know what else to say, intuitively sensing that it would be bad form to enquire who, when, where, and how many he had shot in this manner. Instead, I gave one of my dismissive shrugs that had become an irritating personal habit. "Well, let's hope it never comes to that, eh?"

"Indeed, let us hope, though 'hope' has no place in a planned operation," he replied drily. "Killing another man, regardless of his colour or intentions, is not a task to be entered into lightly or easily forgotten."

"But what if the Peril does invade us?" I persisted, determined to make adult conversation.

"Then all this will have counted for nothing." He lowered his telescope and glanced around at the men, the rifles, the chests of cartridges.

"How so?!"

"A word to the wise." He faced me again. "The sole purpose of an armed force – by land or by sea – is to warn off rivals. You'll notice I don't say 'enemies,' for by the time things reach that pitch, it's far too late."

"But I thought -?"

"Such a policy of armed prudence is best expressed in the Royal Navy's motto: *Si vis pacem para bellum*," he continued, ignoring my startled interjection, "which as I'm sure you've already translated, means: 'If you wish for peace, prepare for war.' And you will also notice we say 'prepare," which doesn't necessarily mean 'make,' unless a rival has seen weakness or doubts our will-to-win..."

I pondered these sombre observations before glancing up from the ochre gravel. "So, what if the Japs do invade us?"

"Then we are honour bound fight to the last man and to the last cartridge. 'For how better can men die, than facing fearful odds, for the ashes of their fathers, for the temples of their gods...?'"

"We'd beat 'em!"

"I wouldn't count on it." Mr Shaw hesitated, distracted by things unseen. "We trained their navy, Germany trained their army, and the Japanese are smart learners. I can't speak for their army, but I do know that their naval college at

200

Etajima is modelled on ours at Dartmouth, the only difference being its curriculum is twice as hard, and its discipline twice as harsh."

"In other words, you think they could beat us?" I scowled.

"They sank the Russian fleet a few years ago..."

"But we can't just stand down and surrender!"

"Nobody said we should," he replied with an older man's sad, understanding smile. "Although rather late in the day, if this is the best we can do," he glanced around at the straggle of men in their baggy khaki uniforms, gathering at the mess tent, "it's better than nothing. In the longer run, though, I'd be more concerned about China's intentions."

"The Chinks?" I queried incredulously. "They're nothing!"

"At present," he agreed. "However, those brave men who defended the Taku Forts, also to their last man and their last cartridge, were something quite else, believe you me!" He paused again, selecting his words carefully. "With firm discipline, consistent training, modern weaponry, and more inspired leadership than a corrupt and crafty old Dowager Empress, China will again amount to 'something...'"

"Again?" I blinked, unsure of his meaning.

"The Royal Navy requires its officers to be *au courant* with wider issues than our strictly professional duties," the Chief replied with one of his enigmatic smiles. "My appointment to Admiral Bridges' staff, aboard *HMS Glory* on the China Station, afforded me opportunities aplenty to learn the Celestials' story insofar as a Foreign Devil, like myself, is able to..."

"What did it teach you, sir?"

"That the current nadir in their fortunes is but one of several during the past four thousand years," he replied simply. "Each defeat has invariably given rise to another epoch of great power and achievements that those teeming millions of proud, industrious, resilient people have never forgotten. Any more than they have forgotten the humiliation heaped upon them during the Second Opium War – well within living memory - when we and the French, looted the Summer Palace before burning it to the ground." He eyed me closely, as if reading my thoughts. "'*Fu zhai zi huan...*'"

"What on earth does that mean?!" I laughed uneasily, thrown aback by this sudden turn in our conversation.

"It's an old Cantonese proverb that roughly translates: 'A son must restore the family's honour that his father lost," Mr Shaw explained in a sombre tone now. "I shan't live to see the Dragon wake from its slumber, as allegedly warned against by Napoleon, but you may be sure the day is coming when China will be an immensely more formidable adversary than those cardboard barbarians you'll be shooting after lunch. Speaking of which," he brightened again, "we'd better hurry up and join the queue, or else there'll be nothing left for us to eat."

After lunch, I did my best to apply Jack Morgan's lessons by awkwardly thumbing two clips of five rounds apiece against the stiff magazine spring, closed the bolt, set the safety catch, and awaited further orders.

"Shooters! Identify your targets -!"

I squinted across two hundred yards of weedy gravel and blinked thirsty bushflies from moist eyeballs.

"Aim -!"

I released the safety catch, cuddled the stock to my cheek, concentrated on breath control, and took-up the trigger's first pressure.

"Ten rounds! In your own time! Fire -!"

The Lee Enfield has a hefty kick unless tucked firmly against the shoulder. I flinched at first but kept shucking hot brass, thumping shot after shot downrange. Fortunately, I'd stuffed scraps of four-by-two cleaning flannel in my ears or else I'd have been deafened by the time it came to: "Cease fire -!"

Much to my surprise, when all the scores were totted up, I hadn't done badly. I was nowhere near the top, of course, but neither was I rock bottom as might have been expected. Even Charley, who had been so dubious when I signed-on, gave a warmer handshake than his earlier greeting. "You'll do." He peered at the sketch I was preparing as today's outright winner was chaired off the range, borne aloft on the shoulders of four teammates. "Tha's clever. Who's it for?"

"*The Miner* wants a report and a picture." This was not strictly true, but I intended filing a story anyway. As for my line drawing, halftone photographs were still a novelty on the Goldfields. Our region's principal newspaper knew it was cheaper to spend a few shillings on a local art teacher, rather than staff a photoengraving studio, whenever it needed to etch a cartoon or illustrate a news item.

Charley gave a respectful nod. "So, you're a journo'?"

"Sure am." I was not about to decline the promotion.

"Hm." He straightened. "I'd better see you get a proper list of names and scores. Blokes like to see 'em spelt proper. Not like that fuckwit the paper yewster send out..."

"Thanks. I'll see they're done right."

"Onya mate. Oh, by the way, we shoot every weekend. I know you'll be gone bush with Mr Shaw, but while you're around, stay in touch." This I did and not only for the extra half-crown earned by filing chatty, informative reports under the by-line *Bullseye*.

Frances and her generation of more tender-hearted, enlightened souls would recoil with horror if I were to confess that I relished the smell of hot gun oil and burnt cordite, not yet identifying them with anything more serious than the good-natured chaff and comradeship of other men as we lay shoulder-to-shoulder, punching holes in targets that ranged up to nine hundred yards away.

44

The days were becoming noticeably cooler as the sun rose later and set earlier; soon it would be time to go-bush again. Sadly, Karl would not be coming with us now that Ingrid had arrived from Germany with her glory box of household linen and other essentials for a new life in a new land.

Both were devout Lutherans at a time when that church was still thin on the ground in Westralia. However, the Chief arranged for an itinerant pastor to bicycle the hundred miles up from Norseman and conduct a service at Molloy's Livery Stables, swept spotlessly clean for the occasion.

Karl was a lucky fellow, as indeed was his fiancée, childhood sweethearts for as long as both could remember. He was a hardworking and thrifty mechanic, she was a hardworking and thrifty dressmaker, and both were ideally matched. Her knowledge of English was almost non-existent, so I made myself available as an interpreter, with Karl's permission of course.

Their wedding day could not have been more auspicious. A crisp, clear Kal' morning with a hint of autumn in the air. The bride had been lodging at the Donovans' since her arrival in Australia, chaperoned by Dulcie, and was driven to the ceremony in their trap, its bodywork trimmed with bunches of everlasting daisies and sprigs of green wattle. Pat dismounted and helped his wife, as matron of honour, get out first and fuss about with the hem of the bride's dress, so that Ingrid would not trip as she stepped down.

The Chief had volunteered to stand-in for her father and was determined that the wedding photograph would show her family, back home in Mannheim, how well their eldest daughter had done by going halfway around the world to wed her *Mann*.

Not for the first time I felt as if we were in the presence of our new king because of their uncanny resemblance. Clad in a naval officer's dress uniform – with a decoration I later learned was the Distinguished Service Order worn on a medal bar with the Queen's Soudan Medal, the Khedive's Soudan Star, the Egypt Medal, and Chinese War Medal with Taku Forts clasp – it was as if His Majesty had personally graced the occasion when Lieutenant Commander Cedric Shaw escorted the blushing young girl into the improvised chapel where the rest of our crew had assembled.

George Smith looked quite dapper in his new, second-hand suit; Joe Mullins had put on a clean flannel shirt and dungarees; Ahmed Khan wore a white *shalwar kameez* and black waistcoat, while his wife sported her Sunday dress topped-off with a black lacquered straw boater, with artificial red cherries decorating its brim.

Pastor Liebig conducted the service in German, after which we were all invited to sign the Gothic lettered certificate, including Joe who made a determined effort to draw his name. We then all got aboard our various vehicles and paraded in triumph up Hannan Street, past smiling, waving strangers to the

Shamrock Hotel where Jonno had laid on a feast under the shade of a quondong tree in his back yard.

Flushed with excitement, Karl and Ingrid thanked each of us for our gifts and best wishes. One envelope, I suspect, contained the paid-up lease on a small shop and living quarters in Maritana Street, to which, after a decent interval, they retired for their honeymoon.

The Chief watched the new Mr and Mrs Steiner drive off, alone in Jonno's borrowed gig, then lit a cheroot and shared a wistful smile with the rest of us gathered on the hotel's pavement veranda. "Dear God in Heaven, grant them a long and fruitful, and happy life together..."

Meanwhile, Karl's substitute was Ezra Gorse, the man I replaced after he broke his leg, last year. Although he never did me any harm that I know of, I never warmed to the man; his eyes seemed too close together, like a rodent's; and there was a sense that he was forever secretly telling himself smutty jokes.

The Chief must have felt this also, for he was less than enthusiastic about enlisting the fellow, but time was short and experienced bush mechanics were in short supply as we assembled our kit for an extended prospect nor'west beyond Menzies and the Kurrajong Ranges.

At first, we were sceptical, being sufficiently experienced to know what map references like Ephemeral Lakes and Dead Camel Hill were likely to mean, on the ground. Whereas we were very familiar with the country beyond Boolya Rocks, where there was still an abundance of sandalwood and a good chance of finding sufficient pay dirt to return a profit. However, the Chief's counterarguments were equally good and potentially more profitable.

A man of his background and training never did anything without extensive research, as was apparent during our briefing. His initial statement was to remind us that Kalgoorlie and Coolgardie were not the be-all and end-all of the Eastern Goldfields, as he had ascertained during a recent visit to the Surveyor General's Office, in Perth. Here he'd learned that more than fifty gazetted townships, and perhaps twice that number of camps, had briefly flourished wherever there was surface gold to be found. Then, just as quickly, abandoned when rumours and reports reached them of richer strikes elsewhere.

"These finds are by no means exhausted." He tapped a large-scale survey map on the back of Molloy's office door, the better to keep our route secure from prying eyes, simply by hanging a coat over it. "In most cases they've barely been touched for the past decade or so, during which time the Indian Ocean's cyclonic rains have continued to scour those gullies and flats..."

There was no need to say more. We were all familiar with Madorsky's window and its frequent displays of nuggets that varied in size from a duck's egg to a man's boot, mostly found in eroded creek beds and gullies.

As on our previous expeditions, we assembled at the Cemetery Camp as it was commonly known, for a final equipment inspection before our plodding column of camels and carts set off along the Leonora Track, roughly parallel with the Northern Railway line.

Passenger-freight trains gave mocking toots as they chuffed past on their way to Menzies, clean-shaven townsmen and their wives or girlfriends leaning from opened windows, keen to view a pioneering scene that was becoming somewhat rare on the Goldfields.

I made several sketches, intending to compose a genre work entitled *Then & Now* with elements from Turner's *Rain, Steam, Speed* and Tom Roberts' *Evening Train to Hawthorn*, but nothing came of it.

Decades later, I still find it impossible to disentangle my true feelings before a catastrophic event, from those imagined or remembered afterwards. But of one thing I am sure, we were no longer the same happy band of brothers. Lively, good-humoured chaff had been replaced by extended moods of glum introspection. We ought to have been excited at the prospect of new country, but the spark was just not there despite everything the Chief did to rekindle it and lift our spirits.

If asked for a reason, I would have peevishly replied that Ezra Gorse was our Jonah although the man himself did nothing overt to earn such harsh criticism. There was no need to. It was his misfortune to be one of those sad individuals who suck the emotional oxygen from his surroundings and replace it with a dank fog of doubt and uncertainty.

It did not help that water was tightly rationed and small game notably absent as we worked our way across a moonscape of abandoned digs and shallow workings.

Sandalwood was also less abundant than expected, as we trudged towards the Ranges and finally made camp at a *gnamma* holding a few hundred gallons of last year's scummy rainfall.

It was far from ideal, but better than nothing as a base from which to prospect the dry creek, downstream from a quartz outcrop.

The Blacks had been dogging our heels for the past several days. That night, standing sentry with the shotgun, a pocketful of Eley buckshot cartridges ready for quick reloads, I listened to the hypnotic drone of chanting and rhythmically clicked sticks away in the middle distance.

"Them buggers is up to no good," Joe Mullins growled from his post behind the shadowy ration cart. "You keep both eyes peeled…"

The droning chants must have stopped sometime after Ahmed Khan relieved me at midnight, for by the time I awoke, all was quiet except for the usual dawn chorus of birds chortling in the low scrub.

I revived our fire and filled the kettle for a brew; Ahmed attended to his camels; the Chief and Pat Donovan stood at the cart's tailgate, planning the day's work. Only Joe remained on edge; gnawing his corned beef and damper behind the Furphy's water tank barricade; one eye on the surrounding bushland, the other on his rifle, propped against the cart's wheel. "This's when them fuckin' Boors use't –"

The scream stopped him mid-sentence. Then another, closer, followed by angry yells as a terrified young girl fled into the clearing and ran towards us. It was all over in seconds. One of her kinsmen hurled his boomerang as if she were a hunted kangaroo, wild meat to be brought down with shattered leg bones, pitching forward as yelling menfolk swarmed over her, clubbing, and bashing with animal fury.

Something about the scene overrode the Chief's ironclad rule of non-intervention in Aboriginal family quarrels. Ever the English Officer & Gentleman, Mr Shaw strode forward to defend a lady in distress. "Belay there! Halt, I say –!"

The first spear landed just below his rib cage, the second one caught him in the shoulder as he went down.

"Yous rotten bastards!" Joe cranked his Winchester and laid down a barrage, matched by Ahmed's more considered shots. Pat emptied his revolver, dropping at least one attacker. I let fly with both barrels, confident of finding targets in that melee, and followed up with a second volley.

The Blacks scattered, leaving their dead and wounded where they'd dropped.

We dashed from cover, still armed for there was no telling what else the enemy had in mind as Pat Donovan knelt and managed to draw the spear from Mr Shaw's back; a glancing blow, off the shoulder blade, meant it was quite shallow and –

Two shots banged behind us. We spun. Ezra Gorse was making up for his lack of involvement, earlier, by despatching the wounded now.

"No!" Pat Donovan took command. "Get me a saw!"

The bush mechanic was about to obey when Ahmed ran up, having assessed the situation, and found the right tool for cutting off the spear's barbed head protruding through the Chief's left side.

I steadied our patient. George Smith gripped the spear's shaft to immobilize it while the saw wore its way through wood the thickness and consistency of an iron bar. "Thank you. Gentlemen." The Chief was now barely conscious but still aware of what was happening around him as the unspeakable Gorse chambered a third cartridge to shoot the wounded girl as well. "Stop! Stop. Stoppp…"

Havildar Khan knew what to do and he did it very well.

45

None of this must appear on the tape recordings that Frances will receive after my death. Infinitely worse massacres were about to drown the world in a flood of blood, but nowadays a defensive skirmish in the West Australian Never-Never Country at the start of this century, would be more fiercely condemned than the Great War itself, by sentimental, muddle-headed city folk.

The spear had pierced the Chief's liver, and nothing could be done to stop it bleeding out. We laid him on his swag and did the same for the wretched Ezra Gorse, whose skull had been smashed in with a rifle butt. This left only the girl to deal with.

She could not be abandoned to the tender mercies of her family. Nor could she be expected to walk with broken legs. Although atrociously bruised and lacerated, by the greatest of good luck the fractures were contained, or else I would not have bet on her lasting more than a couple of days before gas gangrene killed her, as often seen later, on the Western Front.

Between us we pooled sufficient medical skill to make splints, improvise a stretcher from two bush poles and a chaff bag, and get her aboard the wagon after dumping most of our hard-won sandalwood. Throughout it all she bore the most excruciating pain with a courage and fortitude that earned our highest admiration, unlike the savagery and cowardice of her despicable kinsmen, as we grubby white aliens debated what to do next.

Joe Mullins surprised everyone by stepping forward. "I done this when the missus took crook." Somehow, we had never associated this solitary old cove with hearth and home, or of being the caring kind. "She'll need a bit o' looking after, special, so's best leave 'er to me." A task we were glad to hand over to him.

Our next duty was to the dead. Clearly there was no way we could take them back to Kalgoorlie, or even Menzies, not in this weather, knowing how quickly dead camels bloat and putrefy. It was my idea that we go uphill, having earlier seen how these mesas – or *kopjes* as veterans of the South African War often called them - usually had a weathered hollow at the summit, some containing a decent depth of pebbly soil.

We carried the Chief and then dragged the other body by its heels, up a short incline to the crest, strewn with cobbles and larger lumps of rock, before going back to collect our spades and a pickaxe, Pat's bugle, and the *Book of Common Prayer*, read aloud every Sunday morning.

Ahmed, meanwhile, volunteered to stand guard at the camp while we scraped two shallow graves, the Chief's symbolically a couple of yards farther uphill, to disassociate him from Ezra Gorse. Their bodies just fitted, barely twelve inches below ground level.

We took a breather before tidying up, George Smith and Joe Mullins standing to one side of the Chief's grave, myself, and Pat Donovan on the other as our new leader leafed through the prayers, looking for something a layman could respectfully say.

"Um. 'O God of Grace and Glory, we remember our mate, and thank you for giving him to us, to know and to love on our earthly pilgrimage. In your boundless compassion, console we who mourn. Give us faith to see in death the gate to eternal life, so that in quiet confidence we may continue our course upon earth, until we are reunited with those who have gone before. In sure and certain hope of the Resurrection to Eternal Life through our Lord Jesus Christ, we commend to Almighty God,'" Pat blinked a tear, "the straightest ge'man, who ever, drew breath!"

"Amen," we agreed with heartfelt emotion.

"Um. 'We commit his body to the ground. Earth to earth, ashes to ashes, dust to dust.'" Pat wiped a wrist across his eyes. "Right-o, fill it in."

We shovelled what little soil there was before erecting a cairn of decent sized rocks, as a marker for the search party who would eventually collect his bones for proper burial, in the meantime protecting them from dingoes and wild dogs. Then it was Ezra Gorse's turn.

Pat kept the Prayer Book shut and looked upwards at what seemed to me like a vast, overarching canvas of Winsor & Newton Azure Blue sky stroked with Cremnitz White cirrus cloud. "Ah. You listening, God? None of us got on much with this cove, but that don't mean he wasn't a sort o' mate. I can't say we'll miss him. It wasn't good the way he topped them poor sods who couldn't fight back, so you could say he got what was coming. Whatever, he's your business now, if you've got room up there. He was a creepy bugger, down here, but if there's anything in your Resurrection stuff, give him another go, so's he comes back in better shape, next time around. Um. Amen."

"Amen," we agreed before shovelling and stacking his grave.

Pat damped lips and smartly swung the bugle from rest to present for the *Last Post*. This was the first time I heard these proud, plangent tones ring out, though soon enough they would become very familiar. Pat motioned us to remain still while he silently counted to sixty, before sounding *Reveille*.

The Royal Navy would have conducted an officer's funeral with more pomp and ceremony than we could manage on a barren hilltop, but even had this been Westminster Abbey with a full male choir and solemn organ music, it still would not have come anywhere near expressing our profound sense of loss and grief as we trooped back to camp.

"Right-o. Gather round, gents." Pat Donovan beckoned us closer. "I reckon we're done here. Time to report back to Menzies, so we'd better have something to tell 'em."

After a brief discussion it was agreed that I should take down the following dictation, it being thought that my neat handwriting would make our story look more convincing:

> *To whom it may concern.*
>
> *We, the undersigned, do solemnly and sincerely bear witness to the fact that while at a prospect three day's march north-west of a line from Dead Camel to Mount Peperil, a band of Blacks chased one of their lubras into our camp, with intent to maim or kill her.*
>
> *Mr Cedric Shaw, ably assisted by Mr Ezra Gorse, endeavoured to calm the situation, but tragically the aforesaid gentleman was speared, while the latter was bludgeoned to death by a person or persons unknown.*

*Seeking to avert further tragedy, warning shots were
fired and the Blacks fled. Thereafter, Mr Shaw died of
his wounds and both gentlemen were subsequently
buried under cairns atop the hill we have named
Mount Cedric.*

*Signed:
Ian Cribdon
Patrick Donovan
Ahmed Khan (His Mark)
Joe Mullins (His Mark)
Geo. Smith*

"Thank you, gents." Pat folded the document and carefully put it away.
"This'll do the trick..." Our crew's new leader was determined to continue
following correct procedures, starting with a proper disposal of personal effects.

Ezra Gorse's bits and pieces were listed by me, emptied into a flour bag and
tied-up with a labelled string, its knot sealed with dab of melted saddlers' wax
from our harness repair kit. The Chief's small metal travel chest was next on the
wagon's tailgate, where its contents were duly witnessed.

I catalogued his daily journal; his brass sextant by Dolland's of London; his
watch keepers' telescope by Negretti & Zambra, also of London; his well-
thumbed copy of *Norie's Mathematical Tables*; his ebony parallel rule and
polished steel dividers; his purse containing twenty-three pounds, twelve
shillings and sixpence in gold and silver; his tin canister humidor containing
nineteen Burmah cheroots; and a slim leather wallet that opened to form a
desktop picture frame for a sepia-toned studio photograph of a poised, very
attractive young lady clad in the style of forty-odd years previously, and thus
far too old to have been the Chief's wife or sweetheart.

"She's a corker!"

"My oath!"

"Too rich for my blood ..."

I tactfully closed the wallet and, as I did so, noticed a faded red silk tassel
attached to a dance card tucked behind the framed portrait. Lavishly printed in
gold ink, the card commemorated a visit by HRH the Prince of Wales to
Farnwell, country seat of the Earl and Countess of Lowestoft, 19th May 1867, to
mark the eighteenth birthday of their daughter the Honourable Lady Isobel
Keswick.

One did not need to be Sherlock Holmes to identify the "P!" who claimed
Lady Isobel's last dance of the evening. A shrewd idea of how these things work
- thanks to Aunt Lucinda's adroit coaching – strongly suggested that our Chief
was born sometime in February 1868, probably at a discreet *hôtel de
l'accouchement* for unwed noblewomen near Paris.

Many years later, conversing at the Athenæum with a senior courtier from
Buck House, as he familiarly termed Buckingham Palace, I enquired if there was
an especially trusted officer who took care of unexpected royal pregnancies.

"'Unexpected'?" he chuckled. "Hardly! Not with every ambitious mother
in the land eager to cast her daughter at every prince casually swimming by! To
think otherwise would be like giving the cellar keys to an alcoholic and claiming
to be shocked – shocked! - by what inevitably eventuates."

"So, there is such an arrangement?"

"Of course." He shared a lofty smile. "Even if the said daughter fails to hook a prize fish, as most are fated to do, there are still plenty of consolation prizes in the pond..."

"Like?" I was intrigued by this glimpse behind the curtain that normally screens the Royal Household from prying commoners' eyes.

"Schooling at Eton, if the baby's a boy; Cheltenham Ladies' College, if it's a girl," he replied. "And afterwards? For the daughter, ample opportunities for a suitable marriage. For the son, a commission in the Armed Services, or for the more studious a place at Oxford or Cambridge. And for those of a more spiritual bent, there's always an RP..."

"'Harpy'?" I asked, imagining this to be an insider's joke. "What on earth has a mythological half-human bird of prey got to do with hushing up a princely bastard?"

"R, P," he corrected, stressing each letter. "Royal Peculiar, those ecclesiastical appointments that devolve from Buckingham Palace, rather than Lambeth Palace, the Archbishop of Canterbury's residence lower down the pecking order," he continued, quite enjoying this chance to display Britain's ancient and secretive Powers behind the Throne.

"For instance, the Collegiate Church of St Peter, better known as Westminster Abbey; the Queen's Chapel at St James' Palace; the Chapel Royal of Hampton Court; the Chapel of St John the Evangelist in the Tower of London. All those and more, answerable only to the Sovereign, with lots of 'jobs for the boys.' Or sons."

Since that meeting, whenever I examine the silver effigy of King George V on the obverse side of my DCM, I always give it a respectful extra polish in memory of a very gallant English gentleman who was almost certainly His Majesty's illegitimate half-brother.

Meanwhile, before breaking camp the following morning, we took turns at climbing the hill to pay our final respects. Ahmed accompanied me while Joe and George Smith guarded the kit. During the night, I had used my penknife to inscribe a packing-case lid with the Chief's rank and name, and a line from Tennyson's *Ulysses* that had recently become famous:

To strive, to seek, to find, and not to yield

This was the epitaph Terra Nova's crew left on Captain Scott's grave in Antarctica, and most appropriate, I thought now, for another naval officer's grave in the arid wastes of Western Australia as my companion prostrated himself in prayer and I nailed the board to a wooden stake.

A saddened, much reduced expedition eventually led its camel train down Shenton Street and reported to Menzies' Police Station. Here we deposited our affidavit and detailed instructions for a search party to recover the dead on Mount Cedric. I can't be sure it was ever done, able-bodied men had rather a lot on their minds during the next four years, after which the Outback's pre-war dead, in their lonely graves, no longer mattered so much.

Topsy mattered greatly, though. This was the name given by Joe to the young girl in his care, and it was an astonishment to see him gently spooning broth into her battered little face; cheerfully wiping her bottom clean; patiently changing her dressings; tenderly brushing away the flies as we jolted back to civilization.

Obviously, there was no way we could keep her. Instead, Pat led us to the Australian Inland Mission's recently established hospital and explained our predicament. Fortunately, he knew the matron, a tough old army nurse who had also served during the South African War and this earned us a brief hearing, but no more.

It was not that her establishment was callous or indifferent, just overwhelmed by atrocities like Topsy's and chronically underfunded, despite the sporadic sums raised by church fêtes and raffles and meagre Sunday collections elsewhere in the country. Luckily, we were able to toss enough in the hat to pay for a young native girl's care.

"What'll happen to her now?" I asked, troubled by a deal that would have enraged Progressives like Vida Goldstein, had we been in Melbourne.

"If she's lucky, and lives, they'll find a place for her in the laundry or kitchen. If not," Pat concluded, sadly, "God only knows."

46

Ahmed gave me a verbal message to take home to "Kafflin," informing her that he'd won a contract to supply the new mine east of Leonora; its postscript, so to speak, were two ten-pound notes, his share of the sum raised by selling our wagon, watercart, and supplies to a New South Welshman who reckoned he could turn half a million acres of saltbush into a profitable pastoral lease.

The wagon's few remaining sticks of sandalwood barely paid for our night's accommodation and breakfasts at the Railway Hotel, after which we shook hands and wished each other good luck. Then – hooshtah! - Ahmed's camels dwindled away into the distance, leaving us standing on the rusty outer fringes of a corrugated iron township.

"Top bloke."

"Solid."

"Yeah."

We tramped back to the station and caught the 10.35 down to Kalgoorlie, covering in a little over two hours a distance that took us a week's travel and travail, more than two months earlier.

"What a rotten, stinkin' shame!" Joe announced, staring out of the window as we chuffed along, wrapped in a sorrowful silence broken only by the track's rackety-clickety-clack. His was a fair description of the way we all felt, The Chief's death affected us badly, and it was not just that we had lost a serious sum of money, we had lost a good mate, and in my case much more.

It is generally agreed that youths - about to become young men – need an older, wiser man to guide them at this critical juncture in their lives, especially if brought up in a household of women as I was. For how else do we learn the unstated rules of conduct, the Tao of Warrior & Defender, Provider & Lover?

This is too often dismissed as shallow Hero Worship but, in my case, it went far deeper than that. Cedric Shaw was the inspirational alternative to a drunken, syphilitic wreck who murdered my mother; the Mystical Father that Carl Jung later psychoanalysed at his clinic, when I was at my lowest ebb.

It was raining hard by the time we reached Kalgoorlie. This seems at odds with previous impressions of heat and dust, but Kal' is one of those places where, when a storm rolls in from the Indian Ocean, it can dump inches of water within the hour, flooding the land for miles around.

Pat had providentially telegraphed ahead to let his wife know we were on the morning train. Thoughtful as ever, she hitched the pony trap, raised its canvas dodger, donned oilskins, and drove down to the station to collect us. Somehow, we all squashed aboard as she then trotted across town, dropping off George Smith at his lodgings, and Joe Mullins at his tin humpy, before driving Pat and myself back to Keenan Street where a packet of letters awaited me on the dressing table in my bedroom.

Aunt Lucinda's green inked writing was becoming shaky, and uncertain, but her mind was as sharp and inquisitive as ever. These I put aside for later enjoyment, having spotted one with a British postage stamp:

Gonville & Caius College
Trinity Street
Cambridge

16th May 1914

Dear Old Goliath Slayer.

*You have been much on my mind of late, and I do
hope that all continues to go well with you and your
fellow adventurers in that Wild & Woolly Westralia so
eloquently described in your most recent letter.*

*My adventures are of a more contemplative, less physical
nature than yours, though not without
moments of discovery. How could it be otherwise
when seated at the very same table, in the very same room
as the one occupied by Dr Edward Wilson during his
time at Caius (pron. "Keys") long before going with
Scott to the South Pole?*

*Sat here now, overlooking Harvey Court, (named after
the famous anatomist who wrote De Motu Cordis to
describe the blood's circulatory system, while he was
personal physician King Charles I), one is so alive to
deeds others have done before us, deeds that we are
honour-bound to emulate in our turn.*

*The very air we breathe invigorates and encourages one "to
strive, to seek, to find, and not to yield," a noble phrase that
should be graven above the Cavendish's entrance, instead of
"Laboratory of Physical Chemistry."*

*I'd love to show you around and introduce some splendid
chaps who are not in the least snooty with Colonials. I'm
sure they would be thrilled to speak with an authentic
Australian bushman.*

As ever.

D.

I was not in the least thrilled with these changes to my oldest, closest friend, and certainly did not like being told to pronounce "Keys" for a word that can be easily spoken as written! I read this as another linguistic booby-trap set by the English to keep their lower classes in baffled subordination, like pronouncing Featherstonehaugh as "Fanshuh," Cholmondley as "Chumli," and St John as "Sin Gin," although I used to get wry amusement from this last one, when much younger and could playfully offer it with tonic water, ice, and a wedge of lime to earlier versions of Frances Baxter.

Less amusing was the idea of being put on display like some newly discovered primitive organism, an amusing human specimen for other privileged sons to picture in my natural habitat, chewing a gum leaf, bottle corks dangling around hat brim, snarling monosyllabic profanities at the flies.

Not to put too fine a point on it, I was jealous, for no way could an out-of-work cameleer and sandalwood puller hope to reconnect with a young genius who saw himself as the natural successor to centuries of great scientific discovery.

I was still moody and withdrawn when Dulcie summoned me to the dinner table and enquired of her husband and myself what our plans were, now that the Shaw Crew was no longer in business. There was an anxious undertone in her voice; a piano teacher's fees are not much, at best, and rarely regular. I memoed myself to pay another five shillings a week rent.

Mrs Donovan was painfully aware that her husband was now on the wrong side of forty, and though in his own words "fit as a mallee bull," had led a hard life. There was also a piece of Boer shrapnel lodged in his left thigh, near the sciatic nerve, and this made him grumpy on cold mornings. His body's wear and tear were starting to show in other ways too, like the audible grunt whenever he got up from a seat, too quickly, and the irritable flashes of annoyance whenever a job failed to meet his exacting standards.

"Don't you worry about that, Love." His great paw reached across the table and reassuringly enfolded her slender, muscled, pianist's fingers. "Something's bound to turn up."

She glanced my way. "And what about you Ian…?"

"I'm thinking of writing something like King Solomon's Mines but set in Westralia. I've also applied for a job as the *Age* correspondent on this side of the country." Both declared with all the arrogant, insufferable confidence of youth. "That alone will be worth another pound a week, plus expenses."

"Hm. Well. Before we lose you to bigger and better things, we'd better get this lot to Madorsky's." Pat laid our linen, underweight sample-bag on the table. "Then we can divvy up and you can take Mr Khan's share to his missus when you deliver her message tomorrow." I was quick to note how Pat was adopting the Chief's formal style of address, although there was no longer a crew to command. "As for m'self," he concluded, "I'd better get down to Perth, with Mr Shaw's box of tricks, for his solicitor to see everything's shipshape."

As is so often the case with inland storms, by the time I awoke next morning, yesterday's rainclouds were crossing the Great Victoria Desert on their way to South Australia, leaving bright winter sunshine and thirsty soil to soak up the puddles.

We had previously arranged to meet Joe and George when the gold buyer's shop opened, and both were already waiting there as the Post Office clock struck nine.

"A pleasure to see you again gentlemen." Madorsky paused, counting heads. "I trust our friend Mr Shaw finds himself well…?"

"No."

"No?"

"The Blacks got him." Pat's voice was stone cold flat.

"Ay!" Madorsky spread both hands, their palms expressively turned upwards. "No, not him! Not the Chief! How?!"

"Icy's wrote it up. It'll be in the paper. So, what's this lot worth?" Pat dropped our meagre haul on the counter under which, out of sight but never out of mind, lay a sawn-off shotgun.

"Is not, good news." Madorsky kept shaking his head as he loaded the gold scales' pan with yellow grains and flecks of colour. Weighed in troy ounces, multiplied by the overnight spot price telegraphed from London, we had made a little over seventy pounds or about a tenner apiece. Good news it was not.

"Will you, carry on, the business?" he enquired with a shrewd glance as Pat pocketed our cheque and we got ready to visit the Union Bank.

"Might do. There's a lot to think about first. See yuh."

As was our custom, we used Mr Jenks' office to cash the earnings and split them seven ways, setting aside an equal share for the Chief's estate, and one for the Public Trustee to hold until someone claimed Ezra Gorse's things.

"Let's get a drink."

We tramped down to the Shamrock and fronted the bar below Maeve's enticing wink.

"Ah, g'day gents!" Jonno was polishing a glass. "Didn't expect you back so soon -!" He stopped short, sensing our dark mood. "Where's Mr Shaw?"

"Back there," said with a northward tilt of the chin. "Speared."

"Fuck no -!"

"Fuck yes." Pat slapped a half sovereign on the beer mat. "Schooners all round and have one for yourself."

Jonno pulled five 15-ounce glasses, shoved the money back, and waited till we all had a drink in our fists. "The Chief."

We clinked drinks. "The Chief."

Pat, ever the sentimental, bighearted Irishman beneath his hard shell, blinked a tear and looked around, as if searching for a familiar face. "Good luck, mate, wherever you are. They d-don't come no better than you was…"

We drank to that as well.

Jonno eventually broke the silence. "Now what?"

"Well, seeing as you've got the room keys, we'd better go and check there's no stuff in his kit he wouldn't want the people back Home to find."

This remark puzzled me. Later, in Egypt and France, I learned the reason why, whenever the Chaplain removed blue postcards and other incriminating evidence that a fallen hero had been human after all, before sending his effects home to a grieving family. If the bloke was one of mine, I would add a personal letter of condolence and tuck it inside the *New Testament* we were issued with on embarkation.

Meanwhile, as the last sand grains of peace trickled through an hourglass, we were blissfully unaware of, George and Joe, Pat and I followed Jonno upstairs to Mr Shaw's cabin overlooking Hannan Street. This felt wrong, as if invading a private sanctum, but nonetheless we all went in.

By now I'd been elected our scribe and record keeper, and dutifully listed every item as drawers and cupboards were emptied onto the simple, iron-framed bed. For a man of some wealth, Cedric Shaw had been surprisingly frugal, judging by the sparse furnishings and lack of ornamentation; to recoin a phrase, one may take a boy out of the Royal Naval College, but you will never take the Royal Navy out of the man that boy grew into.

The only evidence of his earlier life was the navy-blue uniform, neatly stowed in an officers' metal trunk, together with his commissioning parchment – signed: *Victoria R.I.* – and a leather case containing the decoration and campaign medals last seen at Karl and Ingrid's wedding. An enigma to the end, I was pretty sure I knew the reason why, but kept it to myself; we orphans respect each other's secrets.

Everyone present signed-off the list and arrangements were made for Mr Shaw's room to be cleared, his possessions put into storage, and a Perth firm of solicitors informed of their whereabouts.

"Well, that's it, gents." Pat took one last look around before leading us downstairs again. "Good luck Joe, stay in touch. You too George," he added, with another handshake. "Tell us when you're on cookhouse duty so's I know when not to eat here." His laconic joke eased the pain of parting.

I still had one further duty to perform and set off for Ahmed's place out by the racecourse. Kathleen Khan was busy at the laundry trough when I walked round to the back yard and presented her husband's share of our slender earnings.

A tough, pioneering Biddy, she flicked soapsuds from her elbows and listened in silence to my edited account of the skirmish, probably wondering how much longer it would be before another traveller called, this time with news of her own man's death by sickness, or accident, or ambush.

"Thanks Ian, 'tis good o' ye. Now, back t'work."

My last visit for the day was to the Steiners' Maritana Street home and shop. Here at least things were going well. Our local fishmonger's motor lorry was up on blocks, outside, while Karl lay on his back underneath, adjusting the Albion's drive chain sprocket.

Wiping his hands on a wad of cotton waste, a young man in his natural element of oily machinery, Karl led me through his bicycle shop to meet the missus, happily kneading a batch of scones in a kitchen as spotlessly neat as only a proud *Hausfrau* could possibly keep it.

Their smiles faded when I told of the news. We shared our commiseration, and after a decent interval I left, but not before inspecting one of the new Raleigh roadsters on display; unless a better job turned up, and soon, I'd be doing a lot more newspaper reportage in and around Kal', for which I was going to need a reliable bike.

"I give it for you, two shillings the week?" Karl was already a businessman who understood the lure of hire purchase and the power of compound interest repayments.

"Let's see what's in the bank first," I replied, "then we'll talk cash."

"*Prima!*"

On that confident note I headed off to file my story at the *Miner*'s office and printery.

47

The newsroom staffers were naturally concerned; Mr Shaw had been a popular local figure, a generous donor to Kalgoorlie's benefit clubs, and always good for a fiver on any subscription list.

I hung around for a bit, watching the compositor set my copy with dull grey slugs of type for tomorrow's edition, then drifted back into the street. On the way through I swiped a paper off the stack of unsold yesterday's news awaiting collection by a butcher or greengrocer needing cheap wrapping material.

My pace quickened as I strode towards the Town Hall where a large banner proclaimed: *Melba! One Night Only!* There was no need to say more. The world's most famous singer was coming to town, and I intended to use the occasion to communicate with the *Diva*.

The bloke in the box office gave me a pitying look as I fronted his brass grille. According to him, every ticket had been snapped up within minutes of going on sale. A blow-in from the bush, like myself, had Buckley's chance of getting within cooee of this evening's concert. Unquote. However, a shilling, tantalisingly near the man's itchy fingertips, revealed that Nellie had taken a suite of rooms at the Palace Hotel and was not to be disturbed at any price.

I crossed back over the road and walked up a couple of blocks to the Palace, ordered a middy of Hannan's Lager, and sat down to write a brief note in my sketchbook.

From memory, it asked Madame Melba to kindly assure Madame Cribdon, that her nephew Ian was in good health and making his fortune on the Goldfields. I also asked *La Prima Donna Assoluta* to relay my new address – 21 Keenan Street, Kalgoorlie – the next time she spoke to *Le Rossignol*. This last detail was a crafty ploy to invite a response without appearing to ask for one.

That done, I folded the note, sketched a lively cartoon of Aunt Lucinda at the piano, a Black Sobranie cigarette cocked at its accustomed angle, on the back, and beckoned the barman to step closer. "They tell me you've got Melba hidden upstairs."

"So?"

"See she gets this." I laid my message on a damp beer mat.

"Oh f'fuckssake!" he sneered. "I'd like two bob for every masher what's got the hots for Her Nibs!

"Glad to oblige." I slipped a silver florin under the folded cartridge paper; now he could not take one without picking up the other.

"Yeah, well, I might look into it…"

"'Might' my arse!" I recovered the two-shilling piece. "You want this, then you gunna run upstairs, give Madame Melba's manager this note, and tell him an old family friend says *'toi toi toi'* for tonight's performance!"

"Eh?!"

"It's a secret code," I glowered. "We'll know if it doesn't get delivered."

"Er, um."

I replaced the tip. "Go -!"

He fled as I finished my drink and headed back to Keenan Street. For one moment I had considered saying *"in boca al lupo"* instead – literally "in the wolf's mouth" – a nonsense charm from the superstitious world of Italian opera, one that Melba would have understood perfectly, but its German equivalent was easier for a barman to remember and just as effective at averting bad luck on Opening Night.

Footsore and weary after hoofing around across town, I kicked off my boots, flopped on the bed, and skimmed the stale newspaper acquired earlier. Perhaps because of my lack of formal education, I have always been addicted to the printed word; jam tin label or sonorous passage from the King James Bible, it makes no difference as I parse its grammar, spelling, and syntax, regardless of time or place.

"Oh, bloody hell...!" Prominent on Page 3, below the fold, was an embarrassingly familiar advertisement for Dr Nilsson's patent cough mixture:

> When coughers seek a soothing balm
> Their lungs to ease, their fears to calm
> They note as wiser ones procure
> A bottle of Great Nilsson's cure!
> It ne'er needs reason to bind
> Logic to the shrewdest mind
> Hence many proofs do all assure
> The fame of Nilsson's wond'rous cure!

That I can still recite this doggerel is because it earned my first professional fee of one guinea, in a competition sponsored by the manufacturer. Woeful stuff now, but a fair indication of the higher standards of public literacy before the Great War.

My attention wandered further up the page to the report of a Russian count robbed of five thousand pounds' worth of jewellery on the Paris Express. And then to an adjacent report of the excitable woman, claiming to be Australian, recently arrested for trying to break into Buckingham Palace where she hoped to sell King George a pair of houses as investment properties.

By comparison with these entertaining squibs, a foreign news cable from the Balkans reported on the political venom and conspiracy associated with that unhappy region. It seemed that some young fool had taken a pot-shot at an archduke, and the Austrian Emperor was gloomily resigned to the loss of yet another member of the Imperial Dynasty when informing his army and navy: "The Almighty has demanded this immeasurable sacrifice from me and the Fatherland."

As I later learned, the Habsburgs had not been having much luck since the execution by firing squad of Franz Josef's younger brother, Maximilian, fifty years earlier in Mexico. Followed by the murder-suicide of his eldest son the Crown Prince Rudolf, and the Baroness Maria Vetsera, at Mayerling in the Vienna Woods. Followed by the assassination of his melancholic wife the Empress Elizabeth, in Geneva. Followed by the death of yet another younger brother, the Archduke Karl Ludwig, after drinking typhoid-contaminated Holy Water from the River Jordan.

I stifled a yawn, more interested in a cable from London, reporting The World Peace Conference at which the keynote speaker had presented irrefutable scientific evidence that a major European conflict was impossible. Norman Angell's name was very familiar after David bought his best-selling book, *The*

Great Illusion, and then ear bashed me at great length with its impressive statistical data.

Twenty-four years later, in Vienna, during Germany's annexation of Austria, I interviewed the aging Prince von Lauten zu Klosterberg an eyewitness of the Archduke Franz Ferdinand's funeral, after the Heir Apparent's assassination in July 1914; the Prince's aching sorrow, spoken in the beautiful German of *Alt Wien* rather than the Prussian snarl of *Neu Berlin,* has haunted me ever since then.

According to him, the ruling Habsburgs, with their inbred disdain for lesser dynasties, denied the archduke his full burial rites because his equally murdered morganatic wife – the former Countess Sophie Chotek von Chotkow und Wognin - was of inferior rank and thus barred from the Imperial Crypt, much as she had been snubbed throughout her married life at court. Meanwhile, a delegation of one hundred senior members of the old nobility, including Sophie's relatives, were ordered to wait outside under rainy skies. As if all that was not ominous enough, the steamboat carrying the two coffins up the Danube to Artstetten Castle, nearly capsized as a violent squall swept down the valley. "It was, as if Heaven itself, was warning us," von Lauten lamented.

Sadly, that warning was ignored, and not only by Austria's fossilized aristocracy. The Emperor Franz Josef's chief of staff, Field Marshal Konrad von Hötzendorf, described by those who knew him best as combining furious energy with unfathomable stupidity, had already tried a couple of dozen times to launch a war against Serbia; at each attempt he'd been thwarted by the more realistic Archduke Franz Ferdinand. A Serbian assassin's bullet finally removed this defender of the peace, and von Hötzendorf seized his opportunity to flex Austria's military muscles by making fifteen imperious demands.

The Serbs, an independent sovereign kingdom, could have rejected this arrogant *démarche* with contempt but instead offered to submit their case to international mediation. Hötzendorf's furious stupidity now boiled over and he ordered Austrian Navy's gunboats to steam down the Danube and bombard the Serbian capital, Belgrade, into submission.

Slavonic Russia, bound by treaties and ties of blood to the South Slavs, mobilised. Germany, already in a state of chronic nervousness that mirrored the Kaiser's hysterical paranoia and seeing a threat to its borderlands from the Tsar's empire, less than a week's march from Berlin itself, mobilised. France, bound by treaty to assist Russia, and itching to repay the humiliation of 1871, mobilised. Britain, whose maritime trade routes were under increasing threat from Imperial Germany's High Seas Fleet, mobilised.

Not that I was aware of these machinations until much later. Such diplomatic jousting belonged to a remote, Ruritanian world of international bluster that had no relevance to the grit and grime of everyday life on Westralia's Eastern Goldfields as I stifled another yawn, let the paper slip from my fingers, and dozed off.

An hour or so later, I awoke with a start as someone kept urgently tapping on my bedroom door. "Message for you!" Dulcie stood aside as I came out on stockinged feet and padded onto the front veranda where a bicycle courier waited, receipt book in hand.

I signed, tipped the young boy a trey – slang for threepence - and went back inside, opened my pocketknife, and slit a rather posh envelope addressed in elegant copperplate script.

"Good news?!" Dulcie was anxious for any sign of an upturn in her family's fortunes, no matter how small or remote they might seem.

"Wait a bit, Love," her husband intervened with a kindly touch of the hand, "give the boy a chance..."

I opened the envelope and shook out a promotional postcard of the diva playing Gilda in *Rigoletto*, on the back of which was scrawled, in a different hand:

Supper! Melba

Pat and Dulcie's jaws dropped when a ticket to this evening's concert also fell on the table, and not just for a cramped squat at the back of the auditorium, but in the front row, one of a few reserved for local notables.

"W-what? I mean, how?" Dulcie was stunned.

"An old family connexion," I said with commendable modesty, despite the urge to boast. "She's a friend of my aunt in Melbourne."

"Whew! You are a dark horse!" Pat puffed cheeks. "We'd better get you togged up for such a grand occasion; I'll lend you my best suit."

"Thanks, no need."

"But you can't sit with the mayor and all them others, dressed like that!" He gave me an up-and-down look of stern disapproval.

"I won't be." My fingertip steered the ticket towards him. "Sorry there's only one, but I could try and put the hard word on for another –"

"You don't want to hear Madame Melba?" Dulcie was aghast at what amounted to sacrilege in her tight little world of high art and music.

"No need to. I've heard it dozens of times before, rehearsed with my aunt. Let someone else enjoy *Lo Hear the Gentle Lark*." Besides, I'll pop round and see her afterwards.

"What?" Pat was bewildered by my indifference.

"I'll bet you she opens with *Lark*," I continued, trying to leaven the moment. "Then at some point she will be *Comin' Through the Rye*, sung in dialect to charm her fellow Scots. Concluding with *Home Sweet Home*. And for encore, Tosti's *Goodbye*, with herself at the keyboard."

My two older friends watched in awe as I took the postcard and left them to decide who should enjoy this most special of treats, not that I had any doubt that Pat would insist on his wife going instead, and so it was. Clad in her Sunday best, wearing the pearls that her fiancé had bought in Ceylon while returning from the South African War, she looked proud as a queen, seated beside him on their pony trap, trotting off to the concert.

I felt a warm glow at being able to delight and surprise a decent, hardworking couple who had shown far more kindness than my twenty-five shillings a week rent entitled me to expect. Pat eventually returned home, having arranged to collect Dulcie after the show, and found me replying to correspondence, under the gas lamp that lit their dining room table.

"Thanks mate." He sat down opposite. "The missus walked on air, going in, and you should've seen the faces of those who couldn't get a ticket. Bloody amazing."

"Glad to help."

"That aunt of yours must've been a bloody amazing woman too."

"She still is," I glanced at her most recent letter, the one I'd been replying to, "and in her day, as famous as Nellie."

"Dinkum?"

"My oath. Paris, London, St Petersburg, they all fêted *Le Rossignol*...'"

"Well, I never!" Still shaking his head, he unpouched his tobacco pipe and chomped it for a cool suck, being strictly forbidden to smoke indoors. "Still, with them sort o' contacts, you won't be needing to fossick and pull sandalwood much longer, will you?" He frowned. "Had any luck with the *Age* job yet…?"

"No. Not yet."

"So, you'll probably stay a bit longer and work at the *Miner*…?"

"I hope so."

"So do we," he replied, clearly wondering who else he could rent my room to. "It's all gone bad recently. Nothing's the same without the Chief." Pat blinked a damp eye. "A man can't expect his wife to earn the readies that buy their grub and pay the bills. Not that we haven't got a bit put aside for a rainy day," he added, defensively, "but a bloke's got to pull his weight or else he's just a bludger, and that's no good."

I sensed the unspoken question and nodded in sober agreement. "'Like me to keep an ear open for jobs around town, while I'm working for the paper?"

"If you don't mind."

"Mind? Of course not! That's what mates are for."

"Yair. True." He stood, with a stifled grunt. "Speaking of same, I'd better get that suit. Then you can come in when I pick up the missus."

His dress shirt and jacket fitted well enough, but the suit's legs needed shortening with safety pins, and the waistband had to be taken in at the back, but I passed muster by the time we trotted back down Hannan Street.

The crowd was twenty-deep around the Town Hall doorway, struggling to buy one of Melba's autographs at one shilling apiece, all proceeds going to the local Hospital Fund. "Make way for a newspaper reporter!" I gasped, shoving to the front.

John Lemon, Melba's general manager and accompanist, was controlling the flow of traffic as the lady herself busily signed programs, tram tickets, even a starched collar. He glanced at my postcard invitation, then at me again. "Are you, Ian Cribdon?"

I understood his doubts, having just caught a glimpse of myself in an ornamental mirror; bearded, suntanned, with fists roughened by manual labour, I was more like "The Wild Man from Borneo" than a spruce young toff from Toorak. "I certainly am, and I'm really looking forward to catching up with all the news from home…"

My rounded vowels and well-modulated tone convinced him that I was not an imposter. "Ah. Good. It's a madhouse here. Better get to the hotel and wait. We'll be done in about twenty minutes."

"Thanks. See you there."

Back at the Palace I ordered a thick beef sandwich with plenty of hot mustard, a firm favourite since that first meal at Tralee, well-aware of what "Supper" signified on my invitation.

It is no accident that Melba's posthumous reputation now largely rests upon her connection with thin slices of dry toast and a rich confection of peaches on ice cream, the former meant to counteract the latter. Generously proportioned, my old family friend was trapped in a perpetual tug o' war between appetite and girth, and tonight would be no exception.

As so it proved to be when the *Diva* made her grand entrance, accompanied by a fawning entourage of local worthies, eager to bask in her reflected glory as she graciously held court. I flicked open my reporters' notebook and began collecting names for tomorrow's puff piece in the *Miner*.

Melba noticed me skulking around and probably assumed, from my shaggy appearance, that I was an Anarchist bomb-thrower about to write his name in the history books. A quick word with John Lemon, then a nod and a smile as she beckoned me to approach The Presence. "Ian?" she announced with all the panache of a monarch addressing a loyal retainer. "I nevvuh would have recognised you…"

"Indeed, ma'am, there have been times recently when I have hardly recognised myself," I replied, inclining my head in humble submission. "Kindly inform my aunt that I'm doing well, learning new skills every day, and hope to be home soon."

"Of course." My audience was at an end as other admirers came forward to worship The World's Greatest Voice refreshing herself with dry toast and a bowl of chicken broth, more like courtiers witnessing Louis XIV's *souper royal* at the Palace of Versailles, during the 1680s, than an after-show snack at Kalgoorlie's Palace Hotel in 1914.

Later, once her public had been dismissed, this old family friend granted me an exclusive interview for *The Miner* to syndicate, and a printed programme inscribed:

> *To Dulcie Donovan.*
> *With fond regards for a fellow pilgrim on Music's æternal quest.*
> *Melba.*

I also received a nine-carat gold tie pin bearing a monogrammed NM, one of several kept in a leather cigar case that John Lemon had in his jacket pocket, ready at a moment's notice for Madame to star in one of her spontaneous investiture ceremonies.

48

Dulcie was overcome with emotion when I presented Melba's autographed programme, next day at breakfast, and soon this framed memento had pride of place alongside the imitation marble bust of Beethoven on her piano lid, where young students could draw further inspiration from its presence.

Sid' Hocking, the *Kalgoorlie Miner*'s Proprietor & Managing Editor was equally impressed when I filed *Supper with Melba*, on the strength of which I was promoted to Social Correspondent, with an extra three shillings a week in my pay packet, plus instructions to hire a dinner suit on the newspaper's account, and permission to use the Reporters' Room typewriter instead of filing handwritten copy.

A week or so later, I was seated at this still unfamiliar machine, pecking away with two fingers, writing-up a Masonic lodge dinner, when Sid' burst from his office, clutching a sheaf of overseas cablegrams, a sickly blend of concern, fear, and excitement on his face.

"Wha'sup Boss?" our Turf Correspondent enquired, glancing over the *Western Form Guide*, an aptly nicknamed "racehorse" cigarette – hand rolled shreds of tobacco no thicker than a pencil lead - glued to his bottom lip.

"It's war...!"

"War? You mean, them Japs is here at last?!" A fellow member of the Rifle Club, this is what he'd been training for and dreaming of, for the past several years. "Good-o!"

"No. Germany..."

"Uh?"

"Germany."

"What the fuck've they got to do wiv us?" The office boy was keen to sound adult, ready for the next reporter's job to fall vacant.

"'Don't, rightly, know." Sid' recovered his composure and tossed the cables for us each to grab one. "Special Edition, midday!" Not that there was much for a journalist to do except cut, paste, and sub' London's official story.

The Times, owned by Lord Northcliffe, a virulent anti-German whose post as Britain's Director of Information would later inspire Josef Goebbels' Ministry of Propaganda, was already shaping British and Imperial public opinion with screamers like:

Great Armies Move!
Germany Invades France!
Royal Navy Ready!
Kaiser's Guilt!

And, most fateful of all for our guileless readers:

Australian Fleet & 20,000 Men Join the Fray!

I watched the comp's lock-up their type before sending the finished chases through to the Machine Room, then snitched one of the first copies off the press and went home, making a detour through Maritana Street and dropping into Karl's bicycle shop. "G'day mate, heard the news?"

"No. What?"

"Read this." I left Karl to translate the Special Edition's headlines for Ingrid while I went off to boil the kettle.

"What means it?" He stomped into their scullery, flourishing the front page, his wife in tow.

"I can't say, but things could get sticky." I switched to German so both could understand what I meant by that. "You are subjects of the Kaiser, citizens of the Reich, and technically now at war with Australia –"

"Quatsch!" Hard-headed, practical Karl was having none of this nonsense, even from Good Mate Jan, as he insisted in calling me. "We want nothing of the Kaiser! Why else we here in Ozzy? I pay my bills, exactly! I make business, good! I am at war with, nobody!"

"Let's hope you're right..." A frequent guest in this kitchen, I knew where the teapot was kept, and prepared a brew for my two friends who, I suspected, would soon be needing it.

Karl remained sturdily indignant, denying any possibility of trouble, but Ingrid was more attuned to potential dangers for her new family, marooned as they were in a strange land half the world away from Mannheim. "What can we do, Jan?"

Ian "Toorak Toff" Cribdon hadn't a clue but it never takes much to summon Basher Bill Braithwaite from his dark lair. "All the money you've got in the bank, get it out, now! Gold and silver, not banknotes," he instructed them. "Stash it where the cops can't pinch it."

"No." Karl shook his head. "That is, unofficial, dishonest."

"Nein! Es ist Umsichtig!" In blunt terms he was told that it is prudence, not dishonesty, for everyone to suspect Authority.

Sadly, this upright, hardworking man had never learned the realities of life on Sydney's streets and within days, fuelled by the xenophobic hysteria of London's cablegrams to the *Miner*, Karl's shop was looted by a loyal mob and his remaining assets stolen by the police, while he and Ingrid were confined to the railway goods yard along with fifty or so other Enemy Aliens collared across the Goldfields.

I called an emergency meeting of the Chief's old crew at our usual table in the Shamrock's beer garden, where we could not be overheard, and explained the situation as I saw it from my vantage point in the Newsroom. "Karl and his missus are our mates. We're honour-bound to do everything we can for them."

"Right," Pat agreed with emphasis. "I say let's break 'em out and go north to that cave near Boolya, till the stink blows over."

"Nah." Joe disagreed. "Wundana. There's better water there."

"You're both thinking wrong!" George, the old merchant seaman, had other ideas. "There's tons o' German boats calling at Esperance for copper ore and stuff," he announced. "It'll be dead easy to get 'em aboard one and took back home!" He dug around his pocket and slapped two sovereigns on the table. "That's my share of the ticket."

"Nice try, mate," I replied, sadly, for it wasn't a bad plan, "but the way I'm reading the news, no German ships will be leaving Australian ports until further notice."

224

However, something about the two gold coins awakened memories of days on the run and needing to hide my loot from the Rocks' knuckle men. I found another two quid in my purse and put them alongside George's contribution. "Who's next?"

The other donations, mostly in silver, gave us a working capital of eight pounds for Karl's escape fund, Ahmed being away on another of his freight deliveries.

I explained what had to be done next, got a vote of approval, and set off with Pat to the Union Bank where, after much persuasion, for Mr Jenks was under telegraphed instructions to prevent a bank run by nervous depositors, our money was exchanged for the sixteen half-sovereigns we then took back to Keenan Street

While Pat was changing into his Light Horse uniform, proud evidence of service in South Africa, I rolled the small gold coins – each about the size of a trouser button - in a strip of the waxed lead foil used to keep tobacco fresh and asked Dulcie for her oldest kid leather glove.

"You really are a dark horse," her husband chuckled, watching closely as I cut off the glove's thumb before sewing the small cylinder of gold inside, leaving four inches of greased cotton ribbon dangling from one end. "Is this what they teach you at them posh schools over East?"

I shook my head, checked the seams were tight, and stood. "Now let's find Karl."

This was not difficult. All we had to do was to follow the jeering catcalls behind the railway station. Pat marched up to the nervous Militia corporal whose section was standing guard, bayonets fixed, facing a crowd of drunken patriots. "Orders to interrogate the Steiners!"

"Sah!" Dazzled by the polished brass crown on Pat's tunic sleeve, conditioned to obey orders behind an ironmonger's counter, he nearly fell over in his haste to let us into an enclosure that already stank of overflowing latrine buckets and insufficient personal hygiene, there being only one water pipe, rationed to one hour in the morning, one hour at night.

Karl, never the most flexible of men, was rigid with rage, not surprising given the shock of being treated worse than a criminal by townsmen and women who, less than a week ago, had been his neighbours and valued customers. Other men would have broken, but I sensed an indomitable hatred stiffening his pride.

This prompted a quick change of plan. So, while Pat pretended to copy answers on a clipboard, at the same time slipping the prisoner two slabs of chocolate and fifty cigarettes, I approached Ingrid

"Why, Jan, why this to us?" Her eyes were raw red with crying. "If only the Chief was here! He would do what is right -!"

"Listen," I interrupted, keeping my voice down in case the patriots denounced me as a spy for speaking in German, "here are sixteen gold pieces. God willing, they may help buy freedom, or food, or medicine before this *Schrecklichkeit* ends. We must now assume you will be searched and more property stolen –"

"No!"

"Yes." My fierce scowl underscored the warning. "Your only way to keep these safe is stick 'em up your *Arschloch* or in your *Fotze*," I continued, using language I would never have spoken to a woman in less desperate circumstances.

She blushed as I explained how the soft leather suppository could be plucked out before defecating, or whatever. "You are a good man."

"Karl's our mate. You look after him."

Pat touched my shoulder and pointed at the gateway. "Time to go."

I winked reassuringly at her husband's sweaty, staring face, stamped my foot and yelled: "Then blame the fuckin' Kaiser -!"

The boozy bystanders gave us a rousing cheer and slapped my back as we marched past, onto the street again.

49

There have been many times since then in which I have questioned this shameful episode, so at odds with our sunny self-image of friendship for all, and I believe the most likely answer can be found among the nervous tensions that began to simmer after the Anglo-Japanese Naval Treaty of 1902.

Consciously or otherwise, we became increasingly fearful of foreign invasion against which we could only mount a few thousand rifles, a puny weekend militia, and a miniscule professional army now that the Royal Navy had, in effect, abdicated its defence of Australia to Japan. But History is a trickster. Instead of the nearby Yellow Peril it was the remote Prussian Militarism, imagined in newspaper cartoons as a bloodthirsty gorilla, *Eine Pickelhaube* on its brutish head, that triggered Australia's these spasms of heedless hatred.

They were not only evident in Kalgoorlie's goods yard but right across the nation, especially in South Australia, a state settled by Lutheran migrants. Here, second generation citizens with German surnames were being arrested on suspicion of signalling to mysterious airships said to be hovering above Hahndorf, ready to land an invading army in the Barossa Valley.

Adding to this confusion was the official announcement that Japan was now Britain's ally, which led to an immediate about-face on the rifle range where the Peril was redrawn as the Brute with spiked helmet and upturned Kaiser Bill moustache.

I believe it fair to say that War Fever infected everyone including those most passionately opposed to it, like Miss Goldstein and her Women's Peace Army, a contradiction in terms if ever saw one, as the nation raised 20,000 troops for the First Australian Imperial Force. Men already registered, like me, were automatically expected to volunteer by reporting to the Drill Hall on Wilson Street.

Pat Donovan – increasingly down in the mouth, with no income and little hope of earning one soon - needed no further incentive to enlist. Bluffing our way into Kal's improvised internment camp, wearing his old uniform, the embodiment of power and status, was good enough reason for an unemployed bushman to join up again.

His wife hid her fears and tears as best she could when he cheerily reported that he was now acting-sergeant of C-Squadron in the Seventh Light Horse Regiment, under orders to report to Claremont Showgrounds in Perth and start putting young recruits through their paces.

Neither he, nor I, nor anyone else could have foreseen what lay in wait for us beyond the firestorm of rumours and assertions as more and more reports of Hunnish Frightfulness in Belgium inflamed an already angry and confused public.

I thought I knew better than to get swept up by hysteria, firmly convinced the war could not last long and would be over by Christmas, Norman Angell having mathematically proved that nations' stocks of sodium nitrate, essential for the manufacture of explosives as well as agricultural fertilizers, would soon be exhausted after the first shots were fired in his hypothetical war.

David had used these data to persuade me that a British naval blockade would strangle exports from Chile, the primary source of this essential raw material, and that any large-scale war would run out of puff long before it really got going. Unfortunately for him, and for me, and for tens of millions of others, German science proved *The Great Illusion* to be an even greater illusion when the Kaiser's chemical industry began catalysing nitrates from freely available air.

Meanwhile, confident that my help would never be needed but unwilling to shirk my duty as a Son of the Empire, I joined the Drill Hall queue and passed the time by listening to what the other blokes were saying around me.

Some were keen as mustard to join Lord Northcliffe's newspaper crusade for Civilization & Decency against the Teutonic Thug. Others were just as eager to get away from a nagging wife or pregnant girlfriend. Others were simply bored with their jobs and wanted a bit of excitement. Others, lean and bony, the gaping soles of their boots held on by rawhide thongs, reckoned that six bob a day, with free tucker and clothing, was worth a go. And then there were those homesick Britons who saw enlistment as a return ticket to London or Glasgow, Cardiff, or Dublin.

I eventually shuffled through the door and found Jack Morgan, our rifle club's Safety Officer, manning the reception desk, looking rather splendid in his Militia uniform. "G'day Icy! I wondered when we'd be seein' you. They got your name?"

"Yeah. Six months ago."

"Ri-i-ight." He trailed his pencil down a long list of available men. "Ah, here we are! There's only one Cribdon, so it must be you." He handed me a cardboard file containing the paperwork I had completed on registration and pointed to another queue at the back of the hall. "Good luck mate!"

A few minutes later, after being weighed and measured, I dropped my strides, as trousers were informally known, and coughed hard while one of our local doctors, a white coat over his reserve officers' uniform, groped me for signs of rupture. He then checked my teeth, thumped a stethoscope across my back and chest while telling me to breathe in, breathe out, breathe in again. And finally scribbled his signature on the printed form a clerk had been annotating in my file.

Apparently, I was considered fit enough to join a smaller crowd in the hall's annexe, where the Ladies' Patriotic Fund was serving mugs of tea and cheese sandwiches until enough of us had assembled for the next phase of induction.

A roll call was checked against our files, after which we shuffled into line while a recruiting sergeant, sent up from Perth for the occasion, held a Bible aloft and got us to raise our right hands before leading us through a massed mumble. From memory, my contribution was: "I, Ian Cribdon, do solemnly swear that I will be faithful and bear true allegiance to His Majesty King George, his heirs and successors, according to law, so help me God."

I then dutifully signed my attestation on another printed form, not yet aware that a soldier's Record of Service routinely acquires dozens of sheets of paper in duplicate, triplicate, quadruplicate, and returned to the reception desk where Jack Morgan took my file, rubber-stamped a travel warrant, and presented it with a flourish. "Congratulations, you're one of us now."

"I am?"

"Kal's quota's just about full up." He flicked his few remaining unstamped warrants. "Get your stuff sorted and be back tomorrow morning, nine o'clock sharp."

My next task was to inform Sid' Hocking that his Social Correspondent would not be coming to work tomorrow morning. I can't say he took it well but having done so much to promote the war effort, he could hardly complain when a member of his staff volunteered for service. He walked me to the cashier and watched her count out my wages before escorting me to the street where we silently shook hands.

The Union Bank was still open for business. I spoke with Mr Jenks and arranged for two hundred pounds to be transferred to Aunt Lucinda's account in Melbourne, with the balance held over until I knew how much the Army paid its men.

I then walked down Hannan Street to the Post Office, bought a stamped envelope, and returned to my lodgings where I could sit and compose my thoughts with pen and ink. Dulcie Donovan said nothing when I mentioned that I too had enlisted; just gave me a sad nod, went into the kitchen, and shut the door.

21 Keenan Street
Kalgoorlie

10th August 1914

Dear Aunt Lucinda.

The Union Bank has transferred £200 into the Tralee
House account at the Bank of Melbourne; not the full
sum I promised, but events have rather overtaken me
this past week, so can we delay the final £50 until
I know what the Army's wages are?

From the above you will see that I depart for camp
tomorrow morning. There is an awful lot of tosh said
about this "war," but I very much doubt if our weekend
warriors will be ready to leave Australia before it's all over
in Europe, for which see the analyses in David's book by
N.Angell. Speaking of whom, should you happen to meet
or telephone D's parents give them my regards.

I am looking forward to a change of scene, so this fuss
could not have come at a better time. I enjoy working on
newspapers and, in a few months, once this nonsense is
over, will return to Melbourne and join the Age, after
gaining sufficient experience to make a good reporter.
I shall use my spare time in camp to learn Pitman's Shorthand,
which will be most useful.

Hoping all goes well with you.

Ian

Aunt Lucinda's Last Will & Testament instructed her solicitor to include this selfish, emotionally cramped letter with my other correspondence from Egypt and France, wisely foreseeing its value as humbling evidence of my painful passage to adulthood during the next few years.

Dulcie said hardly a thing at dinner while Pat briefed me on what to expect tomorrow. "And you'll have to get rid of that beard," he concluded, "except for a moustache. Best whip it off now, rather than wait for the camp barber to butcher your chops."

This sounded like good advice. Later, after helping to wash and dry the dishes, I took my razor, soap, and a bowl of warm water into the laundry shed that doubled as a bathroom and lathered up. Maeve would not have recognised the face that emerged from behind its mask of thick, dark whiskers; I had changed a lot and not necessarily for the better.

The cheeks were flatter, the mouth was harder, the eyes were deeper beneath a brow the colour and texture of lightly tanned leather. I kept the moustache for a few moments longer, quite admiring its rakish, debonaire look until a ghostly image of "Champagne Charley" Braithwaite filled the mirror, at which point quick flicks of the razor removed both the man and the memories.

I did not sleep well, and it did not help when Dulcie began practicing piano scales during the small hours of the morning. She looked dreadful at breakfast. Pat, meanwhile, had taken refuge inside his old uniform, its brass warrant officer's crown replaced by a sergeant's chevrons, the orange, black, and gold ribbon of the Queen's South Africa Medal, along with the green, white, and orange ribbon of the King's South Africa Medal, in pride of place above his left breast pocket.

"Take care," she said in a husky voice. "I shall pray that St Christopher protects you, both." She then presented each of us with a small silver medallion on a neck chain. I still have mine. The other was probably returned with her husband's effects some months after Major Patrick Aloysius Donovan DSO MC was killed leading his Light Horsemen against the Turkish trenches at Nazareth, on the road to Damascus, a few weeks before the war ended.

Tight-lipped, he drove us in their pony trap to the Drill Hall, where Dulcie gave him a last despairing hug. She was not alone. Other wives and girlfriends were also parting from their husbands and sweethearts. The Kalgoorlie Prize Brass Band filled-in time by playing tunes from *A Gaiety Girl* while waiting to lead us by an indirect route to the railway station once we'd answered the roll call and shuffled into line.

Those in their Militia uniforms were put at the head of the column to create an impression of order and discipline for the expectant crowds; the rest of us were a mixed grill of tag-alongs. Many were dressed in their Sunday best, with ties, starched collars, and straw boaters, laden with suitcases as if going on holiday or applying for a job in Perth. Others travelled lighter.

After two years of pulling sandalwood and fossicking for gold, I could easily stow life's essentials in a rolled oilskin coat and blanket slung across my back, leaving both hands free, rather than carry my old leather suitcase. A sugar bag, looped on my knife belt, held a pint sauce bottle of cold tea, a wad of corned beef sandwiches, and eight ounces of peppermints to freshen the mouth.

I had also chosen to wear my more serviceable work clothes of wide-awake hat, flannel shirt, corduroy vest, dungaree trousers, leather gaiters and hobnailed boots, in case there weren't enough army uniforms to go around, or better still if a quick victory in Europe meant that our services were no longer required.

The band struck up with a rousing *Soldiers of the Queen*, fifteen years too late for the Boer War but a good tune to march into this next one, and off we went, trampling each other's heels until an exasperated sergeant could establish a semblance of order with his hoarse, "Lef', ri', Lef', ri', Lef' -!"

The crowds clapped and cheered and flapped their handkerchiefs as we tramped down Hannan Street, swinging right into Lionel, then right again up Hay where one of its many knocking shops had draped a bedsheet banner across the front porch, with *Good Luck Boys! Hurry Back Soon!* scrawled in carmine lipstick, sparking a predictable chorus of whoops and coarse banter. Finally, back on Wilson, we swung left for the last hundred yards to the railway station.

In contrast with the brothels, just left behind, this building was draped with red, white, and blue bunting above its main entrance. Most likely left over from the Coronation three years previously, as I could see no other reason for *God Bless King George & Queen Mary, Long May They Reign*, in twinkling tinsel script along the facade.

The bandsmen strutted to a halt and fell silent while Kalgoorlie's Mayor wished us Godspeed in our noble crusade! To show the world what real men! Goldfields' men! Are made of -!

I was more interested in the goods yard, hoping to catch a glimpse of Karl and Ingrid but as I later learned all Enemy Aliens had been transported to their internment camp on Rottnest, a rocky, fly-infested island some miles off the sandy, fly-infested coast at Fremantle.

It is quite possible the same train that took them into captivity was waiting for us now, being shabbier than the usual passenger express, with slatted wooden 3rd Class seats for about two hundred men, plus goods wagons for the officers' horses and crates of equipment from the Drill Hall.

The locomotive driver kept tugging impatient toots on his steam whistle, chivvying us aboard our dogbox compartments. The band struck up *Onward, Christian Soldiers* as the last door slammed shut. The engine responded with laboured puffs and hisses, clanks and jolts, and off we went to war.

50

Two years' hard yakka on the West Australian Goldfields had toughened me into a traveller able to adapt to pretty much any situation, like now, wedged into a corner seat with bundled swag and tucker bag, not yet knowing what a rare luxury this was soon to be as our steam train chuffed and snorted away from Kalgoorlie's lengthy railway platform.

Later, in France, I would become one of forty other troops crammed inside a wagon built to carry that number of men, or eight horses, or any combination of both, squatting on a damp bed of unswept straw and dung, propped against our rifles. But today the other young men around me were too excited by the novelty of their surroundings to settle down. I nearly came to blows with one noisy little number who kept yelping about the Belgian Atrocities and how many Huns he was going to bayonet by way of revenge -!

When I demanded how many Germans he knew or had worked with, he screeched that he was glad he never had! I then told him, in no uncertain terms, to stop believing newspaper headlines, and dismissed him as one more casualty of Lord Northcliffe's venomous propaganda war.

Sadly, he was right, though I only discovered this years later, retracing General von Kluck's trail of destruction through Belgium where whole towns and villages of this harmless little neutral country had been looted, torched, and hostages shot; seven hundred men, women, and children in Dinant alone. And of those who escaped his firing squads, many more died later as slave labourers in the Ruhr's factories and coalmines.

I still squirm with embarrassment when I recall chanting, to the tune of *The Girl I Left Behind Me*: "Kaiser Bill is feeling ill, the Crown Prince he's gone barmy! We don't give a fuck for old von Kluck, or his chicken army! Cock-a-doodle-doo, they'll make fine stew! Enough for me! Enough for you!" Chorus: "*Mein Gott! Mein Gott!* What a bloody rotten lot are the Kaiser's infantry-y-y!" as 48 Battalion AIF and a million other marching men clad in khaki, and *horizon bleu*, and *Feldgrau*, converged on the Somme's swampy, meandering river valley.

Nowadays it is fashionable to portray the Great War as an obscene waste of precious human life, and for high-minded Progressives to sneer at our unashamed pride and patriotism, but the Prussian Brute was a real and present danger at the turn of this century. Anyone who doubts it should read a history of Occupied Belgium, to understand what Occupied Europe would have been like, had not the Australian Army Corps' depleted battalions spearheaded a drum roll of victories that climaxed the Allies' Hundred Day Offensive during the Summer and Autumn of 1918.

Meanwhile, four years previously, we civilian recruits sped through isolated railway settlements with lonely Outback names like Southern Cross, and Burracoppin, where tiny groups of schoolchildren dutifully waved flags and handkerchiefs as our train carried their daddies and uncles and older brothers into that unimaginable future.

Halfway down to the coast, we slowed to a halt at Merredin where more coal and water were loaded aboard while the local Patriotic Fund plied us with sausage rolls and gallons of hot tea. The inevitable consequence of their generosity became apparent well before Kellerberrin, in the heartland of Westralia's Wheatbelt, when one of my companions groaned that he was bursting for a leak.

This was not so easily done, given that the Army had commandeered suburban rolling stock without a dunny cubicle in lieu of which every compartment had been issued with a galvanised iron pail. The only problem was, ours had been taken out to empty at Merredin and then left behind when we scrambled aboard as the train began to move. In the event I grabbed his collar in time to stop him from becoming Kalgoorlie's first Fallen Hero when the slipstream flung open the door he had released to piss outside.

Frances does not need to hear this. Suffice to say it was a great relief when we finally detrained on the spur line at Helena Vale Racecourse in the foothills of the Darling Range, a few miles east of Perth. Here I said goodbye to Pat Donovan, who had been travelling in the SNCO's reserved compartment, as he got aboard for the rest of his journey to the Light Horse training camp at Claremont Showground.

Dusk was falling fast, and we infantry recruits still had a way to go before reaching Blackboy Hill. This meant a hard trudge up a bush track that never seemed to end. Those recruits wearing their best shoes and Sunday suits were soon in poor shape. The rest of us, mostly bush workers, put our heads down and slogged it out.

I had no idea what to expect as we tramped past a makeshift guardroom and sentry box. Maybe a larger version of Kalgoorlie's Drill Hall. Or perhaps a mosaic of huts with whitewashed kerbstones, like the barracks that Pat had described from his time in the South African War.

Instead, lines of tents straggled among the mostly uncleared undergrowth and standing timber. Luckily it was still late winter and the ground damp, or else, with so many open campfires, the whole show would have gone up in flames long before we arrived.

I never could fathom why the army failed to requisition the racecourse and grandstand, downhill, for our training area; perhaps the West Australian Turf Club felt that cancelling its 1914 Summer Calendar was one sacrifice too many for the war effort? Instead, 11 Battalion, recruited from Perth's landed gentry and townsfolk, had been tasked with transforming a rocky hilltop into a functioning army camp.

We newcomers failed to appreciate what a miracle of blood, sweat, and foul language this was until it was our turn to pitch in with pick and shovel to dig more latrines and drainage ditches from rusty brown laterite. This hardened our mutual dislike in the weeks and months ahead. Soldiers are necessarily tribal and, in this case 11 Battalion, already considered itself socially superior to we rough, unlettered bushmen of 16 Battalion.

Meanwhile, halted on a parade ground that largely existed in imagination, bewildered and footsore, my companions gawped and gossiped while a harassed, elderly lieutenant told us to find a tent, remember its number, and wait for the cookhouse bugle.

It was obvious to me that Kalgoorlie's volunteers were not expected yet, and that those in authority were inventing an army on the run. This was not strictly true. The First AIF was an astonishing feat of arms given that Australia - a nation barely thirteen years old since Federation in 1901 - had never organised anything on this scale before but would soon be sending a fully equipped army corps into battle, 10,000 miles from home.

I checked out several tents but did not care much for the muddle inside them, or what it told me about the men I would be sharing with, so instead I found a sheltered patch under a banksia tree, set up camp for the night, and broke out my own eating irons and tin mug which was fortunate as, by the time my segment of the queue reached a steamy, smoky field kitchen, there were no more mess tins for today's draft.

Even those earlier in line were sharing forks and spoons to scoop their tucker from the emptied canisters of vegetables that our cooks had stewed with chunks of worn-out oxen, sold to the Commissariat as prime beef.

As a bonus ingredient, every bug, beetle, and moth in the district was orbiting the overhead carbide lamps, many singeing their wings and tumbling into the open cooking pots below; it was an astonishment that none of us died of ptomaine poisoning during the next several days.

One of our older recruits was having trouble with his stew. From where I stood it looked as if he had lost his teeth and was trying to chew with bare gums; how he passed the strict medical examination was just one puzzle among many. Fortunately for him, I always carry a sharp knife as a matter of course, so it was only a matter of moments to approach and volunteer to cut his meat into smaller bites.

"Fanks." He was clearly embarrassed by having to depend on another man for such a basic task.

I left him to get on with it and went off to secure my lair for the night, ready for the inevitable thieves who would soon be sliming around for what they could pinch from we confused newcomers.

51

Only one prowler disturbed my rest during the night, although his scream must have awakened many another in the small hours before Reveille. Not that an experienced bushman – such as I had grown into since leaving Melbourne - needs a bugle to tell him when to get up and get the day going.

I was still buckling my swag's straps when a twig cracked. Turning sharply, ready to deal with this latest intruder, I found the bloke I'd helped the previous night, unlit pipe clenched between nutcracker jaws overhung by a drooping black moustache, studying me intently.

Unsettled by his sudden appearance and penetrating gaze, and for lack of anything better to say, I quipped with what I imagined would be taken as a joke: "Why, if it isn't the old toothless tiger himself -!"

His fist landed a mighty punch to my upper chest. I hit the ground and my shadow-half bounced up, straight into another knock-down followed by another bounce, followed by progressively less agile bounces as I got well and truly pummelled.

Although clearly annoyed, he was only sparring for it was equally plain that I was up against an accomplished fighter, whereas at best I was no more than a furious street brawler. He could have easily knocked me cold, but instead he stood off at arms' length and systematically dropped me into a panting heap. Only then did he remove his pipe that had been bobbing up and down in time with his punches. "Don' get cheeky wiff me, young ffella."

"I meant it, as a joke!"

"Iff only a joke when I larff," he replied, barely out of breath, although lack of teeth was badly affecting his speech. "Any'ow," he continued, dusting his palms before giving me a hand up, "one good turn defferverff anuffer. I come over to ffee how you waff getting along." He eyed my roost. "They won't let you kip like thiff muff longer. Come on, anuffer bloke wanff to meet you."

"Uh?"

"Hop to it!" I was reminded of the Chief and his brisk mannerisms, and for that reason obediently slung my swag and followed up the line while this strangely compelling cove gave me several painful home-truths about the proper codes of conduct in a man's world.

The army had already issued its available stock of bell tents, the sort that accommodate eight men sleeping in a circle like fingers on a clock dial, feet to the central pole, kit piled alongside them. To make up for this deficiency, three-man bivouac shelters had been improvised from railway wagon tarpaulins thrown across bush poles. My sparring partner halted at one of these bivvies and turned: "The nameff Perffy Black. Whaff yourff?"

"Ian Cribdon."

We shook hands.

Another mature man, a few years younger than Percy, stooped from their bivvy and eyed me before glancing at his mate. "This the cove?"

"Yeff."

He turned, hand out. "Harry Murray."

"Ian Cribdon."

We gripped work-worn palms.

Nowadays, when adult sportsmen who should know better, hug and prance around like excited little children in a kindergarten sand-pit, it must seem rather odd that we Australians were once so reserved. But ours was a harder, leaner, tougher world than today's amazing Age of Abundance. Friendship in those straightened times was often a matter of financial, or social, or physical survival and had to be tested over time, not frittered away on casual acquaintance or wasted upon silly displays of shallow emotion.

I inspected their quarters, relieved to find that all was "shipshape and Bristol fashion," as the Chief would have required it to be and accepted their invitation to share an unoccupied patch of bare ground. The three of us were destined to become an unofficial unit during the next seven weeks of fatigues and foot drill, fatigues and musketry, fatigues and bayonet fighting, fatigues and lectures, fatigues and route marches, fatigues and jerks, as we nicknamed our PT instructor's physical training.

On that first morning we lined up at the QM Store and were issued with one blanket apiece; one pair of shoddy, ill-fitting dungarees that stained our legs dark blue; two thick grey flannel shirts; two pairs of long woollen drawers; one pair of boots and two pairs of socks; a ridiculous floppy white rag hat; and an ornamental cube of soap that had to be shown, unused, at our frequent kit inspections. Our civilian clothing was then stuffed into hessian wheat bags, labelled and, soon afterwards, stolen.

During the next week we gradually accumulated uniforms consisting of a belted Norfolk jacket made from serge cloth dyed the colour of stale pea soup, with four roomy outside pockets and a smaller fifth one, inside, for a bandage rolled around an ampoule of iodine; breeches cut from cheap corduroy, buttoned at the knee; and puttees, narrow strips of khaki fabric, that we learned to wind around our lower legs. Greatcoats, hats and badges, singlets and shirts, mess kits and enamel mugs continued to arrive in dribs and drabs, dumped off at the Quartermaster's Store by horse cart or motor lorry.

Though we didn't know it at the time, we were being closely watched by a cadre of professional officers and NCOs seconded from the British Army, around whom Australia was building an expeditionary force to defend the Mother Country. Matters came to a head one morning when a short list of names was read out on parade, and those of us on it were told to fall out while everyone else marched off to their respective duties.

Harry swapped a questioning look with Percy, who swapped it with me, unable to think of any military offence that could have booked us a place on today's defaulters' parade. Not that it seemed very probable as almost every man, except for me, was a sober, attentive adult in his high-20s or even higher-30s, and thus unlikely to be crimed for youthful misdemeanours.

One of our British NCOs, a lugubrious staff sergeant with a Kitchener moustache and medal ribbons from every colonial war of the past twenty years, addressed us in a thick regional accent. "Ri-i-ight, yoos loocky lads! Let's see what sort o' fooking mess yoos c'n make o' Mr Vickers -!"

Puzzled, we trooped after him into the lecture marquee where a line of wooden benches faced two central tables on which stood "Mr Vickers" and his twin brother, each with a toolkit, spare barrel, and canvas belt of inert drill rounds.

"T'battalion's only got yonder coople! Tha' means only t'best o' yoos can be troosted wi'em! Mah job is to find 'oo gets t'specialist pay! So, eyes open, gobs shut, an' let's get started -!"

Staff Enoch Armitage was a weapons instructor whose blunt Geordie manner and crushing Northumbrian sarcasm would never do in today's world. There was nothing sensitive or understanding about his rote learning and snap questions, nor should there have been when teaching men how to load, fire, and service a machine gun in the heat of battle. Time was of the essence, and he had only one hour in which to pick the battalion's top talent, and then start training those who remained seated after the others were dismissed.

Never were our extra six pennies a day more dearly earned as we split into two competing teams of three men apiece and began dismantling each Vickers, chanting the parts and their functions as we laid them out, in order, on the table, before reassembling our gun, again and again and again, timed by the demonic Staff Armitage.

That evening, crouched inside our shelter, Percy revised today's training schedule by quizzing and being quizzed from the manual he had borrowed from our instructor. If I had not already guessed it, I would soon have realised that my elderly tentmate was a naturally gifted leader of men. Not that anything in his background as a carpenter in Victoria, or as a prospector on the Murchison Goldfields of Westralia, hinted that Percy Charles Herbert Black would ever amount to anything out of the ordinary, but "cometh the time, cometh the man" as my Aunt Lucinda had frequently reminded me.

The same could be said of my other companion and, in time, good mate Henry William Murray. Of the three of us, Harry was the only one with even a skerrick of military experience, after serving in a Tasmanian volunteer artillery unit before moving to Westralia where he worked for a while as a farm labourer, then as a bicycle courier pedalling mail and messages between Kalgoorlie and its outlying settlements, before going south to cut railway sleepers in the rain-drenched forests around Manjimup.

52

Next morning, we gathered in the marquee, ready to strip the Vickers yet again only this time wearing blindfolds to accustom us to working in darkness. Then, after a short period of familiarisation, Staff Armitage began mixing the parts, forcing us to identify and locate each component by feel alone while everyone else jeered and thumped the tables to annoy and distract us. Machine guns need machine men, intelligent robots able to function under the most extreme conditions, and this is how the army fashioned us.

Percy was Number One on Gun; Harry was Number Two; I, being the youngest and most agile, was Number Three. However, at any moment our instructor would shove aside whoever's thumb was on the trigger bar, bawl "Stoppage!" or "Reload!" or "Range 800!" or "Flank attack left!" so that his replacement could take over, address the problem, and resume stuttering make-believe fire.

Across the civilised world, tens of thousands of other men like us were being machined into interchangeable spare parts for Industrial Warfare. Then, one morning towards the end of the week, we were ordered to take our guns to the firing range in a nearby gully where fifteen white painted steel plates, roughly the profile of an adult man, stood in line at the 200 yards mark.

We flipped a coin. 16 Battalion's other crew won the toss and settled down to blow away the steel plates. This was the first time any of us had fired a Vickers. The noise was deafening, exciting too, with gravel and ochre rock dust boiling around the targets, hot brass spilling from the gun's ejection port.

Four plates survived the hailstorm of lead and copper. Then it was our turn, after the targets had been propped up again, with Percy on the trigger bar, Harry feeding the quarter belt of 0.303 Ball ammunition, myself on standby.

"Identify your target!" Pause. "Fire -!"

Tap-tap! The first plate spun as Percy's thumb flicked-off two rounds. Tap-tap! Another plate jumped. And so it went, from left to right, in rapid order, until the final plate was destroyed in a grand finale squall of bullets.

"Fook me dead...!" Our instructor wiped a sweaty hand around his neck. Thirty aimed shots had accounted for fourteen targets, with the fifteenth plate ripped apart by the remainder of our allowance. How, and why, and where, and when Percy had acquired such intuitive skill, was yet another mystery hinted at by this gentle yet quietly fierce man, if one can allow such a contradictory image.

Later that day, in the Wet Canteen, Enoch Armitage shouted each of us a middy of Stirling Lager and declared that he had rarely witnessed such deadly marksmanship with a machine gun, even at the Battle of Omdurman, sixteen years earlier. Adding, that given the chance, an average trainee will rip through a belt, intoxicated by the reek of burnt cordite and the hammering recoil in his clenched fists, but in an unremarkable Australian prospector from nowhere special, he had met the Master.

Our commanding officer thought to so too, promulgating his congratulations in Daily Routine Orders, along with the award of our MG cuff badges and 24-hour leave passes to enjoy the bright lights of Perth. This we promptly did by hitching a lift in a motor lorry heading back to the railway station, after delivering a load of corrugated iron and barbed wire.

A couple of suspicious MPs examined our papers when we got off the train at Perth Central. Thinking back on it, we must have been an iconic tableau of the period, three footloose Diggers, slouch hats tilted back, with pay in our pockets and enough free time to spend it unwisely.

My first impulse was to order a slap-up feed at the Palace Hotel in St George's Terrace, for truth to tell our camp rations were skimpy and the itinerant pie sellers were doing a roaring trade on their pitch outside the camp's guard hut, but I was outvoted by the other two who claimed they had a better option. Grumbling, I tramped along beside them through Forrest Place, still a work in progress, past Boans Brothers' Emporium.

This used to be familiar name across Outback Westralia, for where else could we send a cheque or postal order and a shopping list – often laboriously pencilled on cardboard torn from a packet of Cooper's sheep dip - and, a week later, drive the sulky down to our nearest railway halt for a parcel, perhaps containing a pair of work boots, a dozen rabbit traps, a set of wire strainers, a box of Eley shotgun cartridges, or similar essentials?

Meanwhile, still in an Age of Blissful Innocence - now lost beyond recall - we turned left into Murray Street and, couple of blocks later, reached the Salvation Army citadel, an imposing redbrick fortress complete with ornamental turrets and fake battlements.

I grimaced at the prospect of dining there, much preferring the idea of crisp linen napkins and silver service to erase the memory of cookhouse stew and boiled spuds dumped in my mess tin. Nor did I hold back on my opinion of voluntarily feeding with down-and-out dossers. Not that I had anything against the Salvoes, as such, but I'd already had enough of one army's idea of a square meal without wasting precious time on another's meagre offerings.

The two older men were more familiar than I with the citadel's layout, from their previous visits as civilian workers, and shared knowing chuckles as they prodded me along a corridor towards the dining room where I was happily proved wrong. The tables were clean, the service was cheerful, the place was light and airy, the tucker was good, and the price was right, at ninepence for three courses and unlimited tea.

This put me in a happier frame of mind for the rest of the day and our overnight stay, Harry already having booked three curtained cubicles in the second-floor dormitory. At fourpence apiece - including fresh linen, hot showers, soap, and clean towels – this was decadent luxury after the raw conditions at Blackboy Hill.

A grandmotherly Salvationist at the reception desk gave us a map of Perth, marked its main features, and warned us against going anywhere near Roe Street. The name meant nothing to me but reading between the lines I am sure we were being viewed as brutal, licentious, lustful soldiers, ripe for mischief and therefore moral trophies to be snatched from Satan's snare.

Disappointingly for this popular image of randy troops on the prowl, instead of visiting the brothels we went on a shopping spree at Boans', looking for those little necessities that were not army issue; it was here I bought the hikers' Primus stove that was still giving excellent service years later, trout fishing in the mountain valleys of Afghanistan.

We then made a beeline for the Museum where Percy was keen to look at old things and learn how they worked; Harry chose the adjacent Library, having heard that it was giving away surplus books to men in uniform; whilst I headed for the West Australian Art Gallery, awkwardly sandwiched between the old City Gaol and a more recently built Jubilee Hall that resembled a brick and plaster pudding mould.

I had no great hopes of finding anything of value in this provincial collection. Most likely a few amateur daubs of trees and grazing kangaroos by local artists; perhaps a spiritually uplifting *genre* piece by Holman Hunt or Gabriel Rosetti, donated by a colonial worthy to earn a place on the New Year's Honours List at Government House; and invariably a folio of still-life etchings, *d'après* Rembrandt, bequeathed by a rich merchant who didn't know what else to do with them.

To be embarrassingly frank, I was a Tutherside art snob. However, it didn't take long to realise that a discerning eye had assembled some very choice works in this farthermost corner of the British Empire. One piece especially caught my attention, *Down on His Luck* by Tom Roberts' friend, Fred McCubbin, also a frequent visitor at Tralee House, with others of their self-styled Heidelburg School. I had long admired his artistry but was unaware that he had done this hauntingly evocative portrait of a lonely swagman slumped on a fallen log in a forest clearing, moodily staring at a dying campfire.

Two years earlier and I would have dismissed it as sentimental tosh, *passé* even before our Queen Empress Victoria departed the scene, but now knew better having often enough sat on similar logs, similarly dispirited, staring at similar fires in the reign of our thoroughly modern King Emperor George the Fifth.

I made detailed sketches of the subject's hands, his right one holding a twig to poke the grey embers, his left one cupping a bearded chin as he contemplates an uncertain future before unrolling his swag and bedding down for the night. I then made an overall drawing to fix its dynamic structure and colour balance, keen to share this discovery with my two mates when we met again in about an hour's time, at our previously agreed rendezvous.

53

Harry was already seated on the street bench nominated as our Point Zero, another military phrase that was by now part of our everyday speech, engrossed in one of three books donated by a sympathetic librarian. He glanced up as my shadow fell across the page. "Strewth, Icy, these Greek coves lead complicated lives!"

"How's that?" I replied, wondering if he might be referring to the Greek fishermen I used to yarn with, at St Kilda, back home in Melbourne. Or others like the proudly moustachioed proprietor of Pitsikas' Oyster Bar in Hannan Street, until I glanced over his shoulder and saw that he was tackling a parallel translation of Homer's *Iliad* in English, Latin, and Classical Greek.

This would have stunned most observers. Rough soldiers were not expected to be interested in anything higher than racing form guides, or divorce court scandal sheets like *Truth*, but not in this case, Harry's mum having secretly fed his hunger for knowledge after her husband dragged him out of junior school to work on the family farm in Tasmania.

"Y'see," he continued, leaning forward, "there's these three goddesses, and a golden apple which the boss god presents to a bloke who sounds French, but isn't, named Paris." Harry was rapt by this ancient tale of murder and deception, rape and revenge. "Paris then gives it to one of the goddesses, named Aphrodite, and declares her to be the prettiest, but only after she's promised him that the most beautiful woman in the world will fall in love with the poor chump. I mean, Blind Freddy and his deaf dog can see this won't end well!"

"Uh huh." I sat down, puttied legs outstretched, familiar with the plot after copying Rubens' *Judgment of Paris*, to improve my dry brush technique.

"Now comes the tricky part," Harry continued with an infectious grin. "The most beautiful woman, *et cetera*, happens to be married to the King of Sparta, who swears vengeance when the young Trojan prince bolts with Queen Helen. The King then does what any decent bloke would do, go after the missus with an army, and for the next ten years the Greeks and the Trojans dingdong on the ringing, windy plains of Troy, getting nowhere! That is, until a shrewd cove named Odysseus, comes up with the bright idea of building a wooden horse the Trojans can drag into their city, as a war trophy. The thing is, the Greeks fill it with crack troops, waiting for darkness and the chance to open the city gates and let their mates in..."

"Which duly happens, and the whole show goes up in flames," I concluded.

He blinked. "You've read the book?"

"Nope, but lots have, looking for a good story to paint, or write music."

"Really?" Harry's thirst for knowlege was unquenchable. "Who?"

"Oh, Peter Paul Rubens is one artist who comes to mind." I scratched my chin. "As for the music, Hector Berlioz composed a bloody great five act opera called *Les Troyens*. And another Frenchman, with a German name, Jacques Offenbach, wrote a saucy operetta entitled *La Belle Hélène*."

"Strewth," Harry gave an admiring nod, "you learn something new every day! But what's really got me stumped is the time it took 'em to win the fight. I mean, ten years?!"

"Sounds feasible," I thought aloud, noticing Percy heading our way with purposeful tread. "England and France fought a Hundred Years' War, once, but they didn't have 'Mr Vickers', just bows and arrows, swords and lances."

Harry frowned. "You think ours could last that long?"

"Not a chance." I shook my head. "A pound to a penny says we'll still be here when they call it quits in Europe. Nobody'll need us then."

"You reckon?" he frowned.

"That's the way it looks."

"Bugger. I was hoping to see a bit of the world."

"Too bad," I replied, with the swaggering self-assurance of a city bred know all. "There's a book by Norman Angell you really should read." I waited while Harry fished a pencil stump from his tunic pocket and got ready to write on the back of a cigarette packet. *The Great Illusion*. It's heavy going in places but a bloke like you will get through it easy."

"How's it go?"

"Well, basically, England, and France, and Germany are so connected by banking and commerce, once they've used up their reserves of credit and raw materials – like Chilean nitrate, needed to make explosives – the war will grind to a halt. And at the rate the newspapers say men and munitions are being used up in Europe, that can't be delayed much longer…"

"Hm, I s'pose that's a good thing, for them," he replied, more than a shadow of regret in his voice as Percy joined us.

"Now what are you two bookworms up to, eh?" he enquired, the new false teeth evident in his clarity of speech.

"Icy reckons the war can't last much longer and we won't be needed in France."

"Is that so?" Percy, the oldest of our little gang, cocked a sardonic eyebrow.

"That's the way it looks," I replied defensively. "There's a stack of scientific evidence proves it can't. Why, are you keen to get Over There?"

"My oath!" He shifted my small parcel and plonked down between us. "I've just seen a crossbow," he aimed a finger at the museum. "They were hot stuff once, with dead simple triggers, in countries like France. I reckon they must've got some real big collections, so I want to see what else they've got!"

"Happily, I don't have to go that far. Here, take a squiz at this." I flipped my sketchbook open to display Fred McCubbin's masterwork.

Harry peered uncertainly. "What is it?"

"A painting, called *Down on His Luck*. Come on, I'll show -!"

"Ma-a-ate." Percy laid a calming hand on my shoulder. "I don't need no bloody picture to tell me how it feels to be down on my luck. Nor does Harry, I'll bet…"

"Me too!" I snapped, proud of my hard yakka in the Outback. "But just look at this composition!" I swept a fingertip across the sketch. "And the brushwork is top notch, especially in its foreground detail, but you've got to see it, to really understand!"

"Whoa, take it easy, Percy soothed, "the only pictures I want to see are showing at the Empire Palace." He nodded back towards the centre of town. "I reckon we've earned ourselves a bag o' chips and a good laugh."

I couldn't dispute that even if I did feel that Fred McCubbin had more to show us than, well, whatever the kinema was offering a few yards down the street from our base at the Salvoes' citadel.

The main feature turned out to be a recent Charlie Chaplin flick, but first we had to sit through a series of shorts, including one of last year's Kalgoorlie Cup, for which a resident pianist improvised tunes to match the strolling bystanders in their Sunday best, pointing and smiling at the kinematographer cranking film through his camera, before quickening to a frenzied gallop as blurred horses raced across the screen above his head.

By contrast, the Italian tightrope walker was almost sedate, escorted by a tinkly version of Elgar's *Salut d'Amour*. Then came a prettily dimpled girl, urging her pack of miniature terriers to dash through a maze of hoops before jumping aboard toy fairground rides that whirled them round and around. Finally, a caped magician pulled a white pigeon from his top hat, sneezed a shower of playing cards, and vanished in a smoky flash of trick photographer's magnesium powder.

Harry passed me our paper bag of chips and I dug out a crunchy, salty handful as two young hopefuls - he dressed as Pierrot, she as Columbine - tried excruciatingly hard to amuse us during the interval.

Years later, Sam Goldwyn assured me that nobody ever goes broke underestimating the public's taste. Putting his money on this act would have proved him wrong with wheezers like: "Why must you never share secrets in a garden? Because the potatoes have eyes, the corn has ears, and the beans 'stalk'!" And just before tripping off the stage to a tepid patter of applause: "A burglar broke into a lawyer's house, the other night, and the lawyer robbed him!"

The lights dimmed and it was the Little Tramp's turn to raise a laugh at which he was more successful than the preceding act, judging by the guffaws erupting around my pool of silence. Sadly, I've never warmed to Charlie Chaplin's brand of humour, not even when staying at Douglas Fairbanks' mock Tudor mansion in Hollywood, where the world's most celebrated comedian was our next-door neighbour and would often hop over the garden fence to share a meal.

However, watching him play a dishevelled drunk who staggers into buxom ladies, twirls a cane that pokes someone else in the eye, collides with a hotel bellboy whom he then kicks up the bum, before finally diving under a bed while an irate husband brandishes a revolver, reminded me too much of "Champagne Charley" Braithwaite's fatal misadventure.

Nonetheless I have always remembered that day and those mates with affectionate nostalgia, albeit tinged with melancholy, for we all knew the spell would break once we returned to camp in a few hours' time.

Until then, we tucked into a hearty evening meal; sang-along with rousing hymns by the Salvation Army choir; luxuriated in hot showers; and finally crashed out on real beds, not the Australian Army's coarse blankets, thin groundsheets, and lumpy greatcoat pillows.

54

The pace had quickened, even during our short absence, and it was not just the news that a combined force of New Zealanders and Eastern States' battalions was sailing westward to join 11 and 16 Battalions for our voyage to France.

Westralia's main newspapers were busily publishing posed halftones of recruits with previous Militia experience, to puff the myth that the rest of us were battle-ready warriors. What they did not report was the professional cadre's furious despair over our chaotic route march to the racecourse where we were supposed to practice an embarkation drill on a grandstand that, for the purposes of this exercise, became a make-believe troop transport.

The local mums, and dads, and children lining the road, waving, and cheering, proudly imagined that we were off to fight the foe as eight half-companies trudged past, leading a column of horse drawn GS wagons laden with kitbags and rations, ammunition boxes and miscellaneous items of equipment that included a field kitchen and a cobblers' bench to repair our boots on campaign.

Percy and 16's other machine gun corporal made very sure our weapons were correctly stowed on the first wagon, both men determined to keep their sections ahead of, rather than a part of the riffraff traipsing behind us.

A member of the Macquarie Club's staff recently used a colourful expression that sounded like: "Trying to herd kangaroos…" If so, that was an apt description of the scene at Helena Vale that morning in the Southern Spring of 1914, as rowdy recruits skylarked around the grandstand, placing fake bets, and cheering imaginary horses past the winning post, as if this was a weekend's sport. Our NCOs and officers eventually got a grip on us so that a pretended embarkation for overseas duty could proceed roughly according to plan.

All of which was sadly predictable when trying to control men for whom discipline continued to be a matter of choice. If an order seemed reasonable, we would go along with it, but if it was not, we would not. This was hardly surprising, given that several recruits had been union organisers or shop stewards, so it was not unusual to see a group of soldiers down tools and discuss a command before taking a vote. This happy-go-lucky attitude kept the Regimental Police on their toes, and there were mornings when the defaulters' parade was longer than the line of sickies and malingerers queuing outside the Regimental Aid Post.

The pot boiled over next morning when our Commanding Officer marched onto the parade ground to confront his battalion. The mood was sulphurous, and I could hear union agitators murmuring behind me. The temptation to call down the Wrath of God must have been immense but Lieutenant Colonel Pope, a railwayman in real life, was canny enough to recognise the volatile human material he was dealing with. Instead of enraged threats, he made a speech that in its way equalled Napoleon's rallying cry at the Battle of the Pyramids. From memory it went something like this:

"Soon you will be in France where you will be fighting alongside the finest regiments of the British Army! Professional soldiers whose battle honours were won centuries before Australia existed!

"You will be closely watched and cruelly judged until you can prove you are better disciplined! Better fighters! Better men than they will ever be!

"I know you can do it! You know you can do it! We are Westralians and anything others do well, we always do better!

"From now on! Whenever you see a mate dragging his feet! Or looking like a sack of spuds dressed in khaki! Or needing a poke to get his chin off the ground! You will put him right! You will back your mates, and they will back you, for that is the West Australian spirit!

"You are going to make bloody sure 16 Battalion is not only the best in the Australian Army! You will make it the envy of the English! The terror of the Huns! The wonder of the world! And you can count on me, your officers, your NCOs, to back you every inch of the way while you're doing so -!"

There followed what used to be called a pregnant pause before one Outback growler bawled, "three cheers for Good Old Popey...!" A rolling barrage of cheers and shrill whistles agreed with him.

Harry, Percy, me, and the other machine gunners, were paraded on the right flank, some distance from the riflemen, under the watchful eye of Staff Armitage. I caught the look of shock on his face as an excited mob of soldiers had to be restrained from chairing their colonel off the parade ground, as if he were a winning jockey or boxer.

Events like this should have forewarned our commanders that when we did eventually catch up with the Brigade of Guards and other hard-core British regiments on the Western Front, there would be serious adjustments of attitude by all concerned.

Meanwhile, at Blackboy Hill, the change of mood was immediate. Every man now knew exactly what he had to do, to smarten up, to pay attention, to make sure his mates did the same. In the best possible sense, 16 Battalion AIF became a self-disciplined, self-respecting, self-regulating championship team.

This does not mean that our NCOs and RPs didn't have to crime some backsliders, but they were now far fewer and universally despised by the rest of us labouring hard and long to pack equipment and stores and get them down to Helena Vale railway station, for the final stage of our journey to Fremantle and embarkation.

My faith in Norman Angell was ebbing fast. Nothing in the local newspapers suggested that Europe would run out of money or Chilean nitrates before we arrived there. Reports of British and French, German, and Austrian, Russian, and Serbian armies digging-in for the Northern Winter, preparing for next year's Spring offensives, suggested that our war might last a bit longer than anticipated.

It was about then that I got another of David's beautifully handwritten letters:

Gonville & Caius College
Trinity Street
Cambridge

10th August 1914

Dear Ian.

Everyone here is so exhilarated and relieved that the long wait is over. It feels as if a summer storm has broken, washing the stale air clean and bright again.

This seems perverse when describing something as destructive as war, but our tired old world must be purged in the flame of battle so that a newer, better one can arise from its ashes, like the Phoenix.

I shall soon find this out for myself. Being an Officers' Training Corps cadet, I expect to be sent to France, as several others have already done.

Meanwhile, (strictly entre nous,) I am secretly engaged to a girl at Girton College. My Mary is so beautiful and intelligent I cannot believe my luck! Her people are Scottish grandees of the highest rank, hence our need for chaperoned discretion.

As things stand it's by no means certain they would welcome the son of a Jewish shoemaker into their illustrious clan. However, I shall strive to win sufficient distinction on the battlefield to prove my worth, unlike that Stockholm fiasco.

D.

Postscript: What price The Great Illusion now?!?

Not much, I thought, so at least we were agreed on this point although I could not help noting my demotion from Dear Old Goliath Slayer to the more formal Dear Ian. I assumed this was inevitable, given the exalted circles he now moved among, and yet for some reason Harry's recent description of Homer's Paris as a poor chump, stuck in my mind.

Not that I was upset or jealous for there was never anything in our friendship to suggest that David was less than straight as a billiard cue, but until now I had always regarded him as a laboratory hermit whose only sex life was that he shared with plants and soil microbes.

The discovery that my friend's heart was as vulnerable as any normal young man's, delighted me. However, it was also a matter of concern for I had a nagging fear that he was setting himself up for an emotionally crushing fall, many times worse than Maeve's tactful note, when the fateful moment came for him to meet his prospective parents-in-law on their ducal Scottish estate.

55

One week later, 16 Battalion detrained at Fremantle railway station and formed fours. Then, rifles sloped, marched with new-found pride and discipline through crowds of cheering wives and sweethearts, wistful old men and eager youngsters, up Market Street before wheeling right, along another street whose name I missed while the town's brass band led us towards Victoria Quay where two steamers were busily winching aboard laden cargo nets of stores and bales of horse fodder.

In my innocence I thought that all we had to do now was collect our kitbags, piled in alphabetical order on the cobblestones, and tramp up the gangplank of His Majesty's Australian Transport *Ascanius* as if she were *Yoshi Maru*.

That was my mistake. Two years ago, I had still been a footloose civilian, now I was the lowest face on the military's totem pole and, like hundreds of other privates crowded around me, an expendable item of equipment for an impersonal machine to shunt around until either consumed in battle or declared surplus to requirements at war's end.

That was the Army's mistake. A high percentage of my colleagues were bloody-minded Australians who, until only a few months ago, had either roamed the Outback or prowled inner city laneways. These were not the sort of men to respond quietly when told to sit on their kitbags and wait. And wait. And wait. Inevitably someone began singing: "O why are we waiting, when we could be fucking -?!" to the tune of *O Come All Ye Faithful*. Others, myself included, groused that our officers were so useless they couldn't organise a piss-up in a brewery let alone beat the bloody Kaiser -!

That was our mistake. Impatient, ignorant, ill-informed, we were blind to the miracle of improvised organisation happening around us. It was only much later, after a stint on the Staff, that I realised what a towering achievement our First AIF was, after London's declaration of war on Germany and an exchange of telegrams committed Britain's two most remote dominions to raise a combined expeditionary force of twenty thousand Australians and eight thousand New Zealanders, ands then send them halfway around the world in fewer than one hundred and fifty days, go to whoa.

The recruitment of riflemen and gunners was relatively easy; far more complex was their organisation and admin'. I once tried enumerating the number of departments that kept our small part of the Western Front operational, during a rare pause in Ludendorff's March Offensive of 1918.

My incomplete list broadly began with the Secretariat, to write and circulate the movement orders and personnel files without which no army can effectively function for more than a day or two.

Then the Commissariat, to indent, buy, and supply previously unimaginable tonnages of food, clothing, and ammunition.

Then the Paymasters' Corps, disbursing millions of pounds wherever Australians were at war by sea, land, or air, while held accountable to Treasury, in Melbourne, for every shilling spent overseas.

Then the Corps of Royal Engineers' sappers and pioneers, building encampments, digging latrines, boring wells, laying water mains, grading endless miles of roads and railway tracks.

Then the Veterinary Corps with its farriers, blacksmiths, saddlers, who kept tens of thousands of mules and horses hauling the GS wagons and gun limbers that also needed skilled wheelwrights and cartwrights.

Then the Signals' Corps' linesmen, telegraphists, motorcyclists, and bicycle dispatch riders; postal clerks, carrier pigeon handlers, messenger dog masters

Then the Army Medical Corps' hospitals staffed by doctors and nurses, laboratory staff and mortuary attendants, dentists, and dental technicians.

Nor should one forget the chaplains of every denomination, plus army schoolmasters for the many illiterates in our ranks, all of whom depended in one way or another upon cooks and kitchen hands, butchers and bakers, and the scores of other ancillary skills, trades, and services.

That both nations' governments - one in Melbourne, the other in Wellington - were able to deliver an effective fighting force by Christmas, using no more than a skeleton staff of regulars to flesh it out, showed a sturdy confidence impossible to imagine in today's world of timid oversight committees tangled in their own sticky cobwebs of restrictive regulations, but that was the way we rough and ready Colonials got things done in 1914.

"16 Batt' MG Section!" A harassed NCO was striding up and down with pencil and clipboard, scanning the confused mass of faces. "Front and centre, wherever the fuck yous hidin' -!"

His was a reasonable concern, given that not a few troops had skipped off into town to sink a drink or catch up with family; the MPs were still collaring strays, weeks later.

We machine gunners shouldered our kit and broke ranks. "Here!"

"These'r y'billetin' chits." He shoved six squares of green cardboard, each with a printed letter and number, into our grabbing fists. "Tha's your line, over there." He pointed. "Move!"

We moved as directed and joined the battalion's HQ company of signallers, medics, and other specialists tramping up one of three gangplanks; a cursing caterpillar of sweaty soldiers; rifles and bayonets, leather bandoliers and pouches, haversacks and groundsheets, greatcoats, and kitbags, thumping and tangling as we shuffled aboard.

This is how someone smuggled a live joey all the way to Egypt, as a unit mascot, one that we kept alive on pinched horse feed. Unlike the eight thousand other Australians we left behind on Gallipoli, this young kangaroo lived to a ripe old age in Cairo Zoo.

Two of the Provost Marshal's crushers scowled like dyspeptic gargoyles alongside a young subaltern checking the muster roll. Names and numbers ticked we were pointed towards one of *Ascanius'* crewmen detailed to show the government's passengers to their quarters. Freo's cheering crowds had imagined us as virile young heroes off to war, but once aboard the troopship it was obvious the crew viewed us differently.

This was quite understandable. Until the Australian government commandeered her a few weeks earlier, *Ascanius* had been a first-class passenger liner freighting refrigerated cargoes for the Blue Funnel Line, one of Britain's oldest and proudest shipping companies. A firm of this nature was never going to welcome aboard two thousand citizen soldiers eager to carve their initials on every polished wooden surface, and equally keen to souvenir any of the ship's fittings that could be unscrewed or wrenched off her bodywork.

Nor were *Ascanius'* crew thrilled by having to accommodate the equivalent of a small country township in what were already cramped conditions. Though we didn't value them at the time, HQ's green cards were our tickets to the relative luxury of hammock space on the lower main deck, adjacent to a partitioned area booked for the SNCO's Mess.

Immediately above us, in every meaning of the phrase, the battalion's commissioned officers were quartered in the saloon deck staterooms, while down below the bulk of our troops were roosting in holds usually stacked with frozen New Zealand lamb and chilled Australian cheese, for the British market.

Ventilation was already a problem and could only get worse once we entered the tropics. The officers' mounts did not know how lucky they were to be stabled on the airy, after well deck in stalls padded with coconut matting, each attended by its groom. This was a top perk. A smart cove could always look busy with his horse's curry brush when the less privileged were being detailed to mop up seasick, or vomit, or empty the latrine pails into scupper chutes.

None of which was evident yet, as we blundered about the cramped space that was to be our barracks for the next month, improvising hooks to hang kit, and in some instances stabbing a bayonet into a gap where it would support a reasonable weight. Meanwhile the MG corporals had been called aside and issued with their briefing sheets.

"Right-o gents. Gather round." Percy held the floor and read the rules that, in theory, governed our every action from Reveille at 5.30 ack-emma, to Lights Out at 10.00 pip-emma, Army-speak for ante-meridiem and post-meridiem timekeeping.

When questioned at the end of his recital, we all nodded as if we understood what the hell was expected of us, and then shoved onto the promenade deck where hundreds of others were waving and blowing kisses to friends and family down on the quayside as the final platoon tramped aboard and *Ascanius'* remaining gangplank cleared away.

Squashed together, between Harry and Percy, leaning against the rail, we watched with varied degrees of indifference while others wept and waved, for none of us had close family and such friends as we would need in the months ahead were already with us.

I had posted a parting note to Aunt Lucinda a couple of days earlier, informing her of my likely moves, and another to David who may well be in France by now, trying to win a medal that would compensate for his failure at the Olympics in Sweden. So far as I was concerned, my social debts were paid and I could now turn my back on the past.

Such callow indifference would probably strike Frances and others of her kinder, softer generation as cold and heartless if it were to be recorded, and I am of two minds about doing so. On one hand there is a natural reticence about revealing too much that might adversely affect her memory of me. On the other hand, I feel it my duty to inform a working historian how we Men of 1914 truly felt about ourselves and our world, before Australia's political myth-mongers draped us with the Anzac Legend's cloak of invisibility.

"'Bet you don't know what *Ascanius* means." Harry gave me a friendly poke in the ribs.

"It's the name of this bloody boat," I replied, puzzled by such a daft question.

"Nope," he chuckled. "What about you Perce'? Got any ideas?"

The eldest of our little gang scratched his chin and gave the matter deeper thought. "It's a fancy name for pox, piles, or pimples."

"Nope," Harry repeated, always glad to share a fresh nugget of knowledge. "I've been reading about the Trojans. There's a bloke called Ascanius who gets away as Troy burns, and makes it to Italy with his dad, Aeneas, where they set about building the Roman Empire that their direct descendant, Julius Caesar, really got going. How's about that, eh!"

Percy's sardonic grump was lost in the throaty blare of the steam siren on the funnel above us, ordering the wharfies to cast off their mooring lines before the troopship's massive bronze propellers began ponderously churning Fremantle's dredged channel, nudged towards the open sea by a fussy little tug boat.

56

Crushed against HMAT *Ascanius'* portside railing, shoulder to shoulder with my mates of 16 Battalion, I don't recall feeling anything out of the ordinary, although others round me were more emotional as they realised this might be their last sight of home. My main concern was a rumbling belly; its last meal had been a skimpy porridge, bread, and jam breakfast at Blackboy Hill Camp, and it was now mid-afternoon.

I shall elaborate on this for Frances. People in her line of trade lavish attention on the grand sweep of politics and strategy but are notably lax when it comes to the stuff that really matters to a soldier, like his rations and accommodation. Perhaps these are considered too vulgar for academics to care about? But I shall insist they do matter a great deal and are often the brittle apex upon which the inverted pyramid of Victory or Defeat wobbles until chance tips it one way or the other.

Overcrowded troopships like *Ascanius* became bywords for filth and discomfort and would make a fine lens through which to examine this neglected aspect of military history, given that life aboard was an unrelenting struggle against squalor and disease, lethargy, and discontent. How could it be otherwise when the heads, as latrines are called at sea, were insufficient at the best of times and regularly blocked up, forcing men to either stand with their backs to the wind and aim over the stern, or take sly squats in dark corners, during the night? One had to be very careful where to tread and being sentenced to the Sanitary Squad was a punishment to be equally avoided.

Strictly rationed water meant that laundry was more of an ideal than a reality, and within days our sweat-sodden shirts and cotton drawers stank, not that it seemed to bother the lice, or chats as they were informally known. Crushing the little buggers between our thumbnails, while yarning with other blokes, gave rise to the expression "having a chat," or "chatting with a mate."

Our battalion commanders – plural now that the 11 Battalion, plus a South Australian contingent, were crammed in with 16 Battalion – did their best to keep us frisky by ordering jerks every morning on the promenade deck, followed by close-order foot drill, and bayonet practice against old mailbags stuffed with cleaning rags slung between the lifeboat davits.

There were also the inevitable lectures from pamphlets or cheat-sheets entitled *Why You Must Salute Officers*, and *Why You Must Keep Your Feet Clean*, both doomed to failure; the former because saluting never sat well with Australians, and the latter because it was well-nigh impossible with only two quarts of water, per man, per diem, that included our cooking and drink allowances.

All of these, and other delights, awaited us as we steamed from the Swan River onto Gage Roads where *Ascanius* had orders to lay at anchor with the other troopship, HMAT *Medic*, until our armed escort arrived from Albany after shepherding the main convoy westwards from Melbourne.

Meanwhile each mess table drew lots to see who would collect the first evening's rations from the galley. This was a doddle as the cooking range had yet to be fired-up, meaning that our initial meal afloat consisted of ships' biscuits and mousetrap cheese washed down by warm tea slopped from a galvanised bucket. Not everyone enjoyed this scratch picnic as bouts of seasickness honked and puked around us even though the ship was only gently rocking about on the Roads' enclosed waters.

I was not convinced by the cooking range story. A whiff of fried sausage had leaked over the partition that separated us from the SNCO's Mess; I could only imagine what treats the Commissioned Officers were enjoying in their stateroom quarters above us. However, I was sufficiently aware of the world's wickedness to realise that by keeping us semi-starved, we would be forced to patronise the purser's canteen if we wanted anything more than the equivalent of basic prison fare.

It was equally plain that we would have to queue for so long that a man could faint from hunger before reaching the counter. However, as Aunt Lucinda had oft reminded me, "in adversity is opportunity," and here was a golden opportunity that I could exploit while others wasted their time by grumbling about the iniquities of army life.

I quickly shook hands with the ship's purser, Mr Owens, a genial Welshman who recognised a kindred spirit when I explained my plan. Our contract sealed with a wink and a nod, I now had authority to present an itemised shopping list earlier in the day, at full price less a five percent commission for my initiative; Harry and Percy got trade discounts, of course.

Then, at suppertime, while the other companies were milling around, I collected a box of hot meat pies, savoury biscuits, cigarettes, and chocolate at the canteen's back hatch, for our mess table. As a bonus, two bottles of tomato sauce fell into my open tunic pocket as I brushed past them and became the exclusive property of 16 battalion's machine gunners.

I believe the current phrase is "win-win" and this certainly described my life as a freelance grocer aboard Ascanius. The lads got what they wanted, when they wanted it, without having to jostle hundreds of other men in the queue. Mr Owens – under orders from his skipper, Captain Chrimes, appropriately pronounced "Crimes" – made handsome profits for the ship's officers' syndicate, by fiddling the margins between wholesale, retail, and whatever the cook's thumb on his galley scales could steal from the government's ration allowance.

Next morning, our blankets rolled, hammocks stacked, we tramped on deck to greet our first dawn afloat with star jumps and press-ups led by a former circus strongman clad in dazzling white singlet and tennis slacks, tightly waxed mustachios quivering with compressed energy.

Ablutions were chaotic, not surprising with only one enamel bowl and one gallon of water to share between twelve men, several of whom were trying to shave with cutthroat razors; fortunately, I had taken Pat Donovan's advice and bought myself a new-fangled Gillette with two packets of spare blades.

Breakfast porridge was then bucketed from the galley, ladled into our mess tins, and slurped up before each company got-fell-in on its allotted patch around the promenade deck.

Kit inspections completed, Daily Routine Orders were read out and sentries posted to guard the rifle racks, the officers' quarters, and off-limits areas of the ship per DROs, while the rest of us got-fell-in again for our smallpox, cholera, and tetanus jabs; even at this early stage of our army lives, we were already conversant with, and conversing in, the military's clipped phrases and initials.

Processed at the Sick Bay we then formed yet another queue for our pay book; our dead meat ticket, as the stamped aluminium identity disc was soon to be known; and our pocket edition of the *New Testament*, courtesy of the British & Foreign Bible Society.

Someone in command had the bright idea that now was a good time for the compulsory VD Lecture, introduced by an embarrassed and ill-prepared padre. The poor fellow bluffed his way through the ordeal with high-minded references to motherhood and dire warnings of God's vengeance upon all whose sinful lusts sullied the sanctity of innocent Australian maidens. A more worldly-wise medical orderly then came straight to the point with his Chamber of Horrors, a gallery of gruesome photographs that told the love lives of shrivelled anatomical specimens gleefully plucked from a glass jar of formalin by a long pair of tongs and held out for our closer inspection.

There was a noticeable loss of appetite when the midday dinner pails arrived, and I scored an extra issue of "mutton stew." This item may have fooled city recruits, but others, like me, who had trapped and fed on rabbits in the Outback, instantly recognised the pale, stringy flesh, and toothpick rib bones of Australia's cheapest frozen meat. Not that I minded much, being rather partial to curried bunny, but was troubled by thoughts of what the cooks might be planning to disguise as "beef stew".

Our afternoon's lecture sessions had barely got underway when we sensed a quickening of excitement as *Ascanius'* crew hurried to their posts and coloured bunting streamed up her signals gaff. Nobody gave the order to Dismiss. Instead, everyone – officers, NCOs, other ranks alike – crowded the portside rail to watch a grey warship steaming towards us, its Aldis lamp impatiently blinking Morse-encoded instructions.

Ascanius' stokers had been raising their boilers' pressure for the past several hours, probably forewarned by wireless telegraphy, so within a short while she was able to take-up position behind our escort. Naturally we expected to see the Royal Navy's white ensign leading the way, but instead were confronted by the Imperial Japanese Navy's battle flag.

I was not the only man baffled by a Rising Sun banner that, until recently, had decorated cartoons and posters warning of the bucktoothed, bespectacled, evil yellow dwarves threatening our northern shores. And yet, just as Australia was about to go to war against a European nation that only two or three months ago had been a valued trading partner, Japan was no longer the Peril but, instead, Our Loyal Ally.

This was my first encounter with *Realpolitik*, a foretaste of later dealings with spymasters like Sir Stephen Baxter, best summed-up by Lord Palmerston's axiom when he was Queen Victoria's Foreign Secretary: "Nations do not have permanent friends, or permanent enemies, they only have permanent interests..."

I was still pondering this rummy turn of events as our little convoy steamed onto the Indian Ocean, Rottnest Island off our starboard bow, unaware at the time that Karl and Ingrid Steiner were watching HIJMS *Ibuki*, HMAT *Ascanius*, and HMAT *Medic* pass within sight of their internment camp.

57

Our second day at sea was a muddled extension of the first as exasperated officers and NCOs discovered the truth in a phrase attributed to General Bonaparte, before he crowned himself Emperor of the French: "Order! Counter-order! Disorder!"

The coast of Western Australia was no longer in sight and with every passing hour we were another thirteen nautical miles farther away from home. Ours was now a tight little village of three ships, steaming together across an otherwise empty subtropical sea of foam-crested waves, funnels billowing dark clouds of soot and sparks against a glassy blue sky, Lascar stokers heaving ton after ton of coal into the hungry furnaces.

Something about these striking images reminded me of Aunt Lucinda and David's honorary uncle, John Monash, playing their four-handed piano version of Debussy's *La Mer* at one of the Shusters' Sunday Concerts. Not for the first time in recent days, I wished it had been possible to pack my oil colours and some canvas boards, but instead I made do with quick pencil sketches to set these shipboard scenes in case there was a chance of developing them later.

Frances will find these drawings in my journal of the month-long voyage to Egypt via Ceylon and Aden, assuming I authorise its posthumous release from Special Collections. I may do so, for although descriptions of sea travel are invariably boring, my account of life aboard the First AIF's convoy has some flashes of humour and moments of drama, especially after we joined the main convoy three days out from Fremantle.

I felt an immense swell of pride as we went on deck for our daily dose of jerks and saw three columns of troop ships majestically ploughing in line ahead, across several square miles of seaway. Forty-eight converted freighters and liners, escorted by the British cruiser HMS *Minotaur*, our cruisers *Sydney* and *Melbourne*, and Japan's *Ibuki*, were carrying Australia and New Zealand's new armies halfway around the world to France, or so we believed at the time.

None of us ever forgot the sight and sound of *Sydney* giving three warning blasts of her siren as she swung away on a northerly course, signal flags flying, smokestacks billowing, and there was not a man among us who did not cheer himself hoarse a few hours later, when she returned in triumph after sinking the German commerce raider SMS *Emden*.

God knows we needed all the uplift we could get to counteract the dismal conditions below decks. *Ascanius'* condensers were designed to make sufficient distilled water for her engine room boilers, plus a small margin for the crew and occasional passengers; they were never meant to cater for the additional equivalent of a small Australian country town.

There was no way of avoiding the fact that with barely sufficient fresh water to drink, even with supplementary tanks on deck, it was not only our clothing that stank, and the nearer we got to the tropics, the stinkier we became. It didn't help much when surly crewmen rigged hoses and improvised canvas baths amidships for us to caper around in the nude, trampling our laundry.

Soap and seawater instantly curdle and trying to raise a lather only left us feeling even more horrible than before. Skin infections like scabies, and ringworm, and impetigo spread rapidly, and it was not long before the medical orderlies were daubing our groins, armpits, and faces with copious amounts of red mercurochrome and gentian violet antiseptics.

With caustic Australian humour we called these lurid splashes of colour our tribal warpaint, accompanied by Tarzan yodels as we stripped off our khaki serge after morning inspections, and made ourselves comfortable for the rest of the day.

It must've been quite a sight, platoons of semi-naked young men in grubby vests and drawers, bare feet encased in beetle-crusher boots, performing close-order drill; bayoneting stuffed mailbags; squatting around little groups while attending lectures on French military history, the importance of cavalry, and Prussian Frightfulness, to name but a few of the compulsory subjects.

The medical officers had far more serious problems to cope with as they battled to contain an outbreak of measles for which 11 Battalion's sappers hurriedly built an isolation hospital on the poop deck. In best army tradition this was where we machine gunners practiced firing at targets bobbing astern on towlines. I never could fathom what value this had in the context of land warfare, although liaising with the South Australian signallers was useful training as they flagged our orders from the bridge, but I am very sure it did nothing to raise the spirits of those penned inside the hospital's wood and canvas shelter a couple of yards away from us.

The common cold was a real killer. Ashore one can pop an Aspirin, rest easy, and let Nature run her course; not so when crammed into a poorly ventilated ship with hundreds of other coughing, sneezing, feverish patients. Very soon the medics were fighting a full-blown epidemic of pneumonia that, in an age before antibiotics, often meant death when otherwise healthy men drowned as their lungs choked with fluid.

Ascanius logged her first – but by no means last - casualty a week after leaving Fremantle, when one of 11 Battalion's lads was discharged from hospital sewn up in a blanket, with a few pounds of coal at his feet, and laid on a grating amidships under an Australian flag. Our padre performed the Last Rites. A firing party discharged three volleys. The huddled bundle tilted over the side, splashed, and vanished astern.

Jerks by themselves were never going to slow our rapid loss of condition, so while the weather stayed reasonably cool, boxing, wrestling matches, two-man wheelbarrow races, tug o' war and skipping rope contests were added to our daily PT programme.

These were imagined by our commanding officers to be good, clean, wholesome fun, but for a nation that will bet on two raindrops sliding down a windowpane, every competitive sport is a challenge for the committed punter, of whom we had many.

Few things are easier to corrupt than a boxing match, as I learned when Percy refused to go into the ring after being offered twenty quid to throw his fight. Other men were less scrupulous, or more trusting as the ship's illegal bookmakers wagered hundreds of pounds in cash and IOU chits.

The coins and banknotes were secure enough, but IOUs needed guarantees of payment in full; this service was contracted out to professional knuckle men who had learned their dark arts protecting the brothels and backstreet bookies of Sydney and Melbourne. Happily, little violence was ever needed, the certainty of a measured dose of pain being sufficient to keep most debtors reminded of their obligations to *Ascanius'* gaming syndicates.

My little grocery business signalled that I was a prime cove, as we described those making a sly quid on Playfair Street, which earned me a warm invitation to visit a secret casino, and I agreed, more out of curiosity than with any thoughts of making a killing at cards.

That night, after the bugler sounded Lights Out, I was escorted down into the bowels of the ship. This area was off-limits to all except her crew. Armed sentries were posted to impose this order, but sentries are only human, and all humans have a price, so there was no trouble entering the foc'sle where the stokers bunked. Two pounds, a serious sum when converted into rupees and sent home to India, rented us a table and several square feet of floorspace for the next several hours.

A previous distribution of cash to the Master at Arms and his petty officers of the watch, allowed a couple of dozen sweaty, swearing, young Australians to crouch under a caged electric light bulb, throwing dice, betting High or Low on drawn cards, and guessing the fall of two tossed pennies, well into the early hours of next morning.

Army Regulations strictly forbade gambling aboard troop ships, and equally prohibited alcohol, but words alone were never going to stop a couple of thousand bored, restive, thirsty citizen soldiers from doing and getting what they wanted. I knew of at least one firm that was nursing flagons of homebrewed hooch deep inside the horses' feed store. Until these were ready for sale, we had to rely upon the gallons of grog smuggled aboard by enterprising crewmen.

My entrance ticket to the casino was a one-shilling glass of quite drinkable *arrack* from the Lascars' *Serang*, or native foreman who was managing their side of the business, after which I settled down to study the action. The banker caught my eye and winked. "Y'gotta be in it to win it!"

"No show mate," I replied with my natural Sydney snarl, "I'm only in on m'birthday…"

"When's that then?"

"Thirtieth o' February."

"You'll keep," he grinned and made a fair fist of an undercut shuffle for the next faked deal.

At times like these I have always been grateful for Aunt Lucinda's coaching. Large amounts of money were in play, and I saw nothing that could not have been cheated to advantage had I put my mind to it, but a finely honed survival instinct warned me to steer well clear of anything associated with debt collection.

A marked man could easily be nudged down a steep flight of stairs, or crimed for a theft he'd never committed, and that is before going into action where and when anonymous bullets ricochet all over the place. As Pat Donovan once remarked, reminiscing about his service in the South African War: "A surprising number of unpopular officers and NCOs must've had their backs turned to the enemy when they got knocked over…"

58

Recalling my initial meeting with Frances Baxter at the Macquarie Club, I clearly remember her referring to Australia's First Fleet of unruly, unwilling colonists whose two hundredth anniversary will shortly be celebrated. I equally remember responding with a flippant remark that compared their conditions to those aboard a crowded troopship in 1914, little realising how close to the truth this was now that I've had time to reflect upon the First AIF's convoy of which I was one small part.

Both events have an elegant symmetry; Britain sent out a workforce of convicts who may or may not have been hardened criminals as we understand the phrase today; one hundred and twenty-something years later, Australia sent back an expeditionary force of free men who may or may not have been driven by a patriotic urge to help Old Mother England in her hour of need.

There is no way of telling, but I'd bet a pound to a penny that Frances' first captive Australian settlers were just as cunning and resourceful as their descendants were, steaming into the hot and humid tropics. Even the Provost Marshal's crushers gave up looking for trouble and turned a blind eye to all but the most serious military crimes, like striking a superior officer, or stealing from another soldier.

Surprisingly little theft was ever reported, not because of excessive honesty among men who regarded all government property as fair game, but because our light-fingered brethren were given every chance to repent of their sins when held over a latrine bucket, long enough for them to inhale its rich fragrance, before being shoved in and held down to the slow count of five.

This belief in Rough Justice *versus* Deference to Higher Authority was another difference between we sturdy Australian volunteers and the weedy British conscripts we eventually fought alongside in France. Those brave little men from the mines and mills of Northern Britain possessed undoubted grit and courage, and yet they always seemed to be waiting for permission to act rather than running a quick eye over the situation and getting on with the job.

I often wondered if this was a fault of Britain's bred-in-the-bone class system, itself an offshoot of an Industrial Revolution that demanded group obedience on the factory floor, at the expense of individual initiative and "go" in the Outback. However, what I did soon discover is that we were their argumentative, assertive, bloody-minded opposites.

Not that Australia has ever been a classless society, as Frances' convicts would be the first to agree, with their overburden of guards, and magistrates, and governors, but at least some of them must have found that adversity, in a new country, presented a world of fresh opportunities for the nimble and daring chancer.

Whereas the physical distance between a Melbourne banker and an itinerant shearer, tramping the back blocks of Victoria one generation after transportation ended, was immeasurably wider than that between a convict and his master, but at no time was there an insurmountable barrier of class and birth that prevented a man from striding across the social divide, provided he had ambition, and stamina, and a lucky touch.

Men like Sir Sidney Kidman showed it could be done. The nation's uncrowned Cattle King eventually held more than one hundred pastoral leases or roughly three percent of Australia's landmass; not bad going for a farm boy who started out with five shillings and a horse that was blind in one eye.

The Australians of my day still had that vital spark. We were never brilliant at forming-fours or obediently marching in step, but when pinned down by enemy fire, we would find ways to keep going forward and engage the enemy, rather than hunker down and wait for help. Even at the very end, when our exhausted battalions were hardly more than skeleton companies, those incomparable soldiers were still game to rally for one final push through the Hindenburg Line.

Not that every man in our army was a native son. At one point a good half of the Fighting Sixteenth's strength consisted of Poms and Pats, Jocks and Taffies trying to get home again. Other Britons were West Australians by choice, like our commanding officer Mr Pope who I believe originally came from London. That said, there must have been something in Australia's air that quickened their spirits, for once in khaki and trained-up there was no difference in their confident bearing, or breezy attitude to life in general, and higher authority in particular.

All this was yet to be revealed as our convoy crossed the Equator, reached Ceylon, and anchored at Colombo's Lunapokuna coaling station. Any hopes that we would be let ashore, to experience this self-styled Pearl of the Orient, were quickly dashed. Nor were the fruit sellers' bumboats allowed to get in the way while coal barges freighted hundreds of tons of fuel for the next leg of our voyage to France.

Coaling ship is the dirtiest, hardest, most punishing work devised by man, and yet there was no lack of volunteers among our troops to help the crew heave sacks of anthracite into *Ascanius'* bunkers, tempted by the promise of a freshwater shower, a bottle of beer, and extra pay, accompanied by 16 Battalion's scratch band of musicians tootling and banging a medley of popular tunes on the foredeck. Instead, I bought a pack of blank postcards from the canteen at one ha'penny each and set up shop selling sketches of imaginary tropical scenes at sixpence apiece, for others to send home when the mailbags went ashore, and our convoy raised steam again.

The transit to Aden, on the southwestern coast of Arabia, was not without incident. Two Lascars died of heat stroke, inevitable given the conditions those poor beggars had to work under in the stokehold, and were buried at sea with as much decency as time and place allowed. We passed the hat around for their families in Bengal, though how much of it ever reached them after passing through Captain Chrimes' pocket, is anyone's guess.

Conditions on the troop decks were not much better. By now we were taking turns sleeping out in the open to get at least some rest every alternate night, which endeared us not to the crewmen who still had to go about their duties while tripping over semi-naked men sprawling, snoring, farting, cursing on every available flat surface.

It was no surprise that our morale drooped and there were instances of rabbit stew, or boiled tripe and turnip being thrown at mess sergeants by men who would have killed for the mythical fried mutton chops that were alleged to be part of a private soldier's one shilling and fourpence a day ration allowance; sergeants and warrant officers fed rather better on three shillings and three pence; our commissioned officers must have thought they were dining at the Ritz with mess allowances of six shillings a day.

A brave attempt to jolly us along was *Cooee!* a mimeographed newsletter composed and edited by the Padre, which put out an appeal for anyone with talent to step up and form a concert party. With two thousand men to pick from, it was not long before Captain Peterson, 11 Battalion's Entertainments Officer, was auditioning jugglers and acrobats, harmonica players, parlour vocalists and comedians.

High Jinks on the High Seas delivered something for everyone, including a sarcastic, sing-along version of the bawdy *Good Ship Venus* that began: "T'was on the good ship *Ascanius!* By Jove, you should've seen us!" Sturdily accompanied by our fifes and drums. "The figurehead was a loaf of bread the captain wouldn't serve us -!" And a barnyard impersonator with his menagerie of quacking ducks, mooing cows, barking dogs, and clucking hens expressing shock and amazement at what Dirty Bertie and Flirty Gertie were doing behind the haystack.

Thinking back on it, I wonder if historians truly understand the importance of bands and bandsmen in military life? Not only on parade, or on a march, but also on the battlefield - in my war - where many were killed or wounded as stretcher bearers, several of whom were highly decorated for their courage under fire, including at least one Victoria Cross recipient. I must remember to make this point in my next recording for Frances.

Despite Captain Peterson's best endeavours, the grumbling continued unabated as we sweated our way across the Indian Ocean until, in the small hours of the morning about three hundred miles out from Aden, *Ask Any of Us* - as we had nicknamed our vessel - rammed the next troop ship in line. Luckily, HMAT *Shropshire's* overhung stern meant that our main damage was confined to buckled steel plates above the waterline, while her twin screws were sufficiently set-back to escape the full impact, or else she would have been towed the rest of the way to Egypt.

What might have happened, had we struck elsewhere on *Shropshire's* hull, no one knows. It is quite likely that one or both of us would have been so badly holed that no pump would have held back the inrush of seawater, and yet there was surprisingly little panic or confusion even as the two ships crunched and ground together in total darkness, splintering their port and starboard lifeboats.

In a preview of our steadiness on Gallipoli and the Western Front, every man performed the Birkenhead Drill and coolly assembled at his emergency station, wearing kapok lifebelts and, for most, little more than a towel loincloth. Thoughts of *Titanic's* last minutes passed through many a mind as *Ascanius* kept venting steam with long, mournful blasts of her siren, while we awaited orders to abandon ship by hopping over the side, as there were now insufficient lifeboats to go around. But somehow both vessels managed to pull apart, assisted by searchlights beamed from ships passing by in column-ahead formation at reduced speed, without either vessel taking on too much water. Most astonishing of all, *Ascanius* managed to keep up with the rest of the convoy, even with gashed bows.

59

Like many another man who grew up in the age of boys' adventure stories, I expected that my first sight of Africa would be of a dense jungle improbably teeming with gorillas and lions, tigers, and elephants. Instead, as our convoy passed the British protected island of Socotra and entered the Gulf of Aden's inbound shipping lane, Africa's north-eastern cape – the Horn – was close enough for us to see the scrubby hills and barren cliffs of Somaliland on our left-hand side.

Harry joined me at the rail and squinted into the thick, bluish veil of stifling heat: "Buggered if I know how they did it..."

"Who?" He had broken my wistful daydream of a cool, overcast day at the riverside end of Tralee's Garden, casting for black bream.

"The Ancient Egyptians." Harry was as ready to talk about pharaohs as he was to discuss the fall of Troy. "That's Ophir," he pointed at the rocky wilderness, "where they got their gold, and silver, and ivory, and jewels. Though to look at it now, you wouldn't think it possible, would you?"

"Nuh."

"Some writers say it's where the Queen of Sheba came from with frankincense and myrrh, peacocks and apes for King Solomon. Though why he'd want those has me stumped. I mean, no decent bloke could stomach eating monkey, though maybe it was luxury food to show who was king and who was not?" He winced. "Me? I'd settle for a thick slice of roast peacock, with mashed spuds, peas, and gravy..."

"And a pot of Stirling Lager to wash 'em down." I accepted the implied invitation to take a seat at one of our phantom feasts.

"And ice cream for afters."

"Strawberry or vanilla?"

"Chocolate." He grinned nostalgically. "There's an Eyetie bloke in Manjimup makes 'em perfect. Every time I'd go into town to collect the wages, I'd treat myself to a jellatty, as he called 'em. I reckoned I'd earned it, cutting sleepers for Wagger..." This was our standard pronunciation of WAGR or West Australian Government Railways.

"Hard yakka," I agreed, no stranger to hard work myself, much reminded of pulling sandalwood in the harsh, dry country five hundred miles north of Harry's rain sodden jarrah forests.

"Blood oath." He shook his head at the memory of unrelenting toil with axe and maul and wedges in Westralia's Sou'west, even more dank and gloomy than his native Tasmania. "You reckon there'll be ice cream in Egypt?"

"If their climate's anything like this, they must live on the bloody stuff." I wiped a hand across my sweat freckled brow.

"Nuh, it can't be that bad." Harry was the eternal optimist but, in fact, the saturated heat was even worse by the time we reached Aden where we moored off Steamer Point while water lighters refilled our galvanized tanks amidships. This sounded enticing, but the water was so highly mineralised that it was fit only to rinse faces, brush teeth, and quick wipe-overs.

The port itself must have been a volcano that, long ago, ejected two unequal hills of cindery grey rocks marking the harbour's outer entrance. The small one to our left was called Little Aden; the larger one on our right was Big Aden; not the most original names for such significant landmarks. It was from here that the British Residency and its small garrison defended this bleak outpost of the Indian Empire, especially its telegraph station, a crucial link in London's business dealings with the Raj.

Unlike Colombo, local bumboats were allowed alongside so that we could haggle for strings of dates and native curios. Apart from these, there was no other reason to stay once our mail went ashore, and the convoy was soon heading back onto the Gulf, in single column, bound for Bab el Mendeb.

Only much later did I learn that this translates as "Gateway of Tears," in Arabic. An apt name for the chokepoint between the Arabia on our right, the recent Italian colony of Eritrea on our left, and the tiny British island of Perim in the middle. And thus, ideally placed for salvage operations in congested and stormy waters frequently battered by sirocco-like gales off baking hot hinterlands to port and starboard. The island's strategic importance was also recognised by the Turks who, a few months later, launched an attack from nearby Yemen and briefly established a toehold before the garrison company of Sikh Pioneers won a brisk little battle on the beach.

Meanwhile, and for the next fifteen hundred miles, we were never out of sight of Africa's ochre brown deserts and Arabia's sunblasted cliffs, shimmering in daytime temperatures and humidity that defy description. The nearest I came to managing it was in a letter to Aunt Lucinda, when I said that the Red Sea reminded me of Tralee's laundrymaid boiling our linen, in midsummer, with all the doors and windows shut tight.

Regular sandstorms added to our misery by lashing the convoy with grit and dust that got into our hair, and eyes, and every mouthful of rations.

I've heard claims that the word "posh" comes from a P&O clerks' short form of Port Out, Starboard Home, when First Class passengers would book cabins on the shaded side of the ship going out to India down the Red Sea and book the other side when sailing home again, up the same accursed stretch of water. I seriously doubt it; conditions aboard *Ascanius* were equally horrid and torrid, regardless of whichever side of the ship we sheltered on.

A more immediate puzzle was the actual name of this dreadful place. The waters around us were a sufficiently transparent ultramarine for one to see stingrays and sharks darting off as the shadow of our keel passed over them; the sky above stayed an oppressive dove grey with touches of raw umber at the edges; the landscapes on both sides were uniformly cardboard brown streaked with sepia shadows. Nothing was even vaguely red in colour or hue.

I mentioned this to Harry as we sweltered in the noonday shade, lectures and drills being now restricted to early morning and late afternoon, whereupon he immediately brightened up. "It's probably something to do with the compass."

I blinked. "Say again?"

"The Ancients knew a lot about such things, just by watching the sun," he elaborated. "Of course, they didn't have words like North, South, East, or West, so instead I'll bet they used colours."

"You're joking!"

"Nope." He shook his head. "Think of it this way, when you're north of the Equator, like we are now, and looking south, the sun is hot on your face. Wait long enough and it gets red with sunburn. So, to a Roman or Greek, where we are now is south of Rome and Greece and is therefore the Red Sea. However," he continued, warming to his ingenious theory, "in the Northern Hemisphere, facing north, back to the sun, the face is colder, and since colder means darker, as in evening or night, they called the sea, north of Turkey, Black."

"Strewth." I was impressed and used his own well-worn phrase: "You learn something new every day!"

"I reckon," Harry was always glad to share the fruits of his not inconsiderable intellect. "There's also another couple of seas named after colours," he added, reflectively stroking his chin, "the Yellow, and the White, but I'm not sure yet what they mean…"

"Nor me neither," I concurred. "We'd better check 'em out next time we're near a library."

"Yeah, let's do that."

Not that we ever did. Very soon we had more urgent matters to occupy our minds. It was only much later, lunching at the Royal Geographical Society in Kensington, that I learned how large areas of the Red Sea are periodically affected by reddish brown algal blooms; that the White Sea is covered by ice for much of the year; that the Black Sea was regarded as unlucky by Ancient Greek traders because of its vicious storms and ferocious native tribes; and that the Yellow Sea is so-called because of the vast tonnage of pale silt carried downstream by the Huang He to the Gulf of Bo Hai.

I recall this incident not to mock the memory of a good mate and comrade in arms. A frustrated academic whose formal schooling ended at the age of twelve, but rather as an instance of how naturally inquisitive humans respond to a lack of factual knowledge by making-up plausible stories that fill the gap. Perhaps this is the foundation of religious myths, legends, and dogmas? Scientific theories, too?

I'll run this thought past Frances at my next recording session, though I shall never hear her considered response, which is a great pity for I sense that it would have been a stimulating and enjoyable exchange of views.

Meanwhile, with the Great War less than three months old, our convoy continued cautiously picking its way up the Gulf of Suez – the Red Sea's north-western branch, the other being the north-eastern Gulf of Aqaba - exchanging signals with liners, and freighters, and warships heading down the southbound navigation channel. Only the native feluccas and other small craft felt free to flit around as they pleased, seemingly blind to the risks they ran by cutting in front of a 5000-ton cruiser like the *Sydney*, who with the *Ibuki*, were now our escorts, *Melbourne* having detached for other duties at Colombo.

We were not aware of it at the time, but the Libyan sand dunes to our left and Sinai's rocky hills to our right were still technically part of the Ottoman Empire, although Egypt itself had been garrisoned by Britain since the 1880s, to keep a firm grip on the Suez Canal. Now, with Turkey a German ally, wherever we looked was enemy territory, making the Canal a prime target for Turkish troops garrisoned in Palestine.

We machine gunners were given orders to take up positions on the bows, one Vickers covering the port side, the second Vickers covering our starboard side, in case something happened. Not that anyone in authority seemed to know what that something might be, but kitting-up got us back into trim as fighting men with a purpose in life as we watched over limpid blue waters alive with skittering shoals of flying fish, chased by dolphins hunting a quick snack.

Ominously, the nearer we approached Port Suez at the head of the Gulf, the murkier those waters became until, by the time *Ascanius'* screws stopped churning dense whorls of fermenting black filth, we already had a fair idea of what other delights awaited us among the ancient sights and smells of Egypt or, as we inevitably nicknamed the horrible place, "Egg Whipped."

Australians used to have a talent for ironic double-talk, probably an echo of our recent convict past when work gangs spoke in Flash or back-slang, and as we lowlife still did in Sydney, the better to hide our "pots and pans" from police spies and snitches. Thus, Port Tewfik on the eastern bank of the Canal's entrance, inevitably became "Port Two Fuck," while Suez on the opposite bank was, for equally obvious reasons, "Sewers."

Apart from their miserable huddles of grubby grey harbourfront buildings overlooked by a rocky escarpment, all else was a sun-bleached wilderness devoid of charm or much vegetation, with precious few signs of life apart from the odd vulture orbiting the native quarters.

"Strewth," Harry muttered, leaning against the rail beside me, "is this what they mean by 'The Mystic Orient'?"

"Nah. It's more like something out of Scheherazade's *Tales of One Thousand & One Frights*," I replied, trying to lift our spirits with a jokey play on her *Tales of One Thousand & One Nights*.

"Who?"

"A local princess who stayed alive, for a thousand and one nights, even though her husband, the prince, planned to chop off her head, next morning."

"Dinkum?"

"That's how it's written," I replied with an exhausted shrug.

"Bastard savages…"

"Yeah."

At which point our conversation lapsed into gloomy silence as a raft of turds drifted past, under attack from a hungry shoal of *al-bultiu*, a local breed of tilapia we would later smell being grilled on wayside stalls in Cairo.

60

I must be careful when describing the common soldier's lot in Egypt, vintage 1914, while speaking to an enlightened Englishwoman of 1987, or '88, or whenever my recorded voice is eventually heard in Oxford. Even so, I feel it my duty to recount events as I witnessed them, believing that historians have an equivalent duty to record events and people without fear or favour, "warts and all" as Oliver Cromwell is alleged to have replied when his portrait painter asked how the Lord Protector wished to be remembered by posterity.

It won't be an easy path to tread without stepping on easily offended toes, and yet there is no other way to describe the Egypt that we of the AIF knew, as other than a festering cesspit of iniquities. Later, after Mena Camp was built and we got to know the country better – or worse, depending upon one's viewpoint - one medical orderly best summed up the prevailing mood by predicting: "When God's finally 'ad a gutful o' people and reckons the world needs a good enema, to flush 'em out, Gyppo Land is where He'll shove the fire hose…"

And yet for me at least, there were redeeming features if one cared - or dared - to explore away from Cairo's more recent European avenues, and instead enter its ancient *souk* of narrow laneways where crowded stallholders yelled their wares and frequently came to blows while poaching a likely customer.

This was not to everyone's taste, given that solitary British soldiers were fair game for robbery and the occasional stabbing. However, my early life, foraging Sydney's docks for whatever could be pinched from a cart or cargo net, had taught me that urban survival largely depends upon pace and posture.

An anxious look and furtive slink are blood in the water for city sharks. Whereas a confident stroll, lightly balanced on the balls of the feet, head up with a distant smile, hints at dangerous uncertainties that give the average lout cause to pause. In this manner, I eventually spent quite a few hours exploring Cairo's backstreets, observing, and recording their kaleidoscopic sights and smells,

On one trip I might watch a coppersmith annealing sheet metal over a charcoal brazier, before tap-tap-tapping it into kitchenware on a tiny anvil. Standing still, outside his smoky cavern of a shopfront, mobbed by excited children. Both hands shoved in my breeches' pockets – a prudent measure with so many apprentice finger-smiths targeting this alien being, for so I must have seemed – none of them ever suspected the small block of cartridge paper and stub of 4B pencil in my right pocket, as I blind-sketched the keystrokes of drawings I would later develop from memory, back in camp.

On another visit I might stop awhile to study the various types of camel saddles and harness; richly decorated with tinkly brass bells, garish tassels, and blue beads to avert the Evil Eye. These never averted mine; fingertips flicking the hidden pencil until forced to squeeze aside as the animals themselves, laden with fruits and vegetables and fodder from the Nile's rich alluvial soil, swayed past, gracefully placing their broad pads with each lurching, forward step.

It was on these explorations that I learned to appreciate the local music. Frequently, I would sit by myself at a pavement café's circular zinc table, just large enough for a *demitasse* of Turkish coffee and saucer of salted pumpkin seeds, watched by curious Cairenes bubbling their *hookahs* while I let the rhythmic tap of a finger-drum and the scribbling, nasal quarter tones of something like a clarinet, transport me in imagination to the legendary splendour of Harun al-Rashid's Baghdad, as if flying Aladdin's magical carpet.

I was always generous with my praise and *mukafa'a* or gratuity, in scrappy Arabic, whenever an itinerant street band serenaded this curiously different *Ustrali*. But all that still lay well in the future as hopes wilted that we would soon be sailing onward to a cooler, greener, more fragrant land. Instead, shrivelling in the Gulf's rancid heat, we swung at anchor off Port Two Fuck and awaited our turn to enter the Sewers Canal.

Apparently, it was just wide enough for single vessels to transit the hundred miles or so of desert between the Red Sea and the Mediterranean, and this required precisely timed instructions telegraphed from Port Said, releasing convoys from each end so that they would bypass on the Great Bitter Lake.

The first suspicion that we might not soon be quit of this fetid rubbish dump came with the news that the Canadian Expeditionary Force had arrived in England and was now wintering in what should have been our billets on Salisbury Plain, prior to crossing over to France in the Northern Hemisphere's springtime of 1915.

The second indication was a sombre lecture outlining the political situation in Egypt and a warning of another revolt fomented by German gold and Ottoman agitators. It seemed quite likely we would be staying a bit longer and might see action against howling mobs of protesting civilians when the British military government finished replacing the pro-Turkish Khedive with a more compliant ruler.

Confirmation came when we learned that our pay would now be given in *piastres* – instantly dubbed "disasters" – worth tuppence ha'penny apiece, of which 100 made an Egyptian pound. These circulated as silver coins of 20, 10, 5, 2, and 1 piastres, further subdivided into smaller coppers called *millemes*, or $1/1000^{th}$ part of a pound. There were even smaller half and quarter *milleme* coins, hungrily snatched up whenever comparatively rich and well-fed Australians chucked them away as worthless "pocket shrapnel," which should have told us a lot about the *fellahin*'s wretchedness and the cause of his frequently hysterical rioting.

A subsequent lecture did little to improve our understanding of the place. Solemnly entitled *Intercourse with the Natives*, it gave us one of our few ribald laughs since leaving Fremantle. What the presenter meant to say was the need for a firm hand when dealing with hordes of beggars whining for *baksheesh*; the need to repulse the brazen advances of local women who were diseased *bints* of the lowest sort; the need to stay away from bars and similar places of shady entertainment where the stranger was liable to be drugged and robbed; and the importance of hard bargaining for even the most trifling items or services, in a land of cheating children and their predatory parents.

"Cheer up!" I gave Harry a friendly poke in the ribs.

"What's to cheer about?" He scowled and glanced up from sewing a lance corporal's chevron on his tunic's sleeve. "This is the first time I've been anywhere different, and if this's what's meant by overseas travel broadening the mind…" He did not need to complete the sentence; we all felt much the same.

Ascanius eventually joined a plodding line of steamers at sunrise, two days later, the Canal Company's pilot holding our speed at eight knots to minimise the wash of bow waves on fragile earthen banks, following a railway line northward across the desert to Port Said.

An armoured train clattered past, heading in the same direction, pushing a sandbagged wagon, its 37mm pom-pom autocannon manned by turbaned Indians. These saluted smartly as we waved and shouted the "coo-oo-ee!" that would soon echo across Cairo, and Paris, and London, and wherever else Australian soldiers stayed connected on unfamiliar streets.

Our little convoy exited the Canal at nightfall and moored off Port Said's western breakwater, dominated by a statue of Ferdinand de Lesseps, the French engineer who oversaw its construction during the 1860s. His name and story were familiar to me, having often heard Aunt Lucinda speak of banqueting with him when the Empress Eugénie officially opened the Canal, the culmination of France's decades-long *mission civilisatrice* to the military and commercial crossroads of Africa and Asia.

"And by Jings didn't those pashas, and beys, and bimbashis need civilising!" She chuckled at the memory of her duties as a *dame d'honneur* handpicked to play a leading role in what nowadays would be called a Diplomatic Charm Offensive.

According to her, Napoleon III spared no expense to impress the Turkish viceroy, who repaid the compliment by drowning several hundred of Port Said's beggars and cripples - tied up in sacks aboard one of his gunboats, heading out to sea as the Imperial yacht approached land - about to be drowned like unwanted kittens, so that his honoured guests would only experience a refined and elegantly modern Egypt.

This, and other lurid word pictures, did nothing to improve my opinion of the place or its people during the next day of waiting at anchor. Then, as a purple dusk settled over this ancient land, *Ascanius* cast off and steamed westwards, portholes blacked out, lights dimmed, essential precautions while Austrian U-boats still openly traversed neutral Italy's Straits of Otranto, outward bound for Allied shipping lanes in the Eastern Med' and Ægean, or inward bound to refuel and rearm at Pola or Trieste on the Adriatic's Illyrian coast.

We approached Alexandria next morning, led through a minefield behind which Britain's Mediterranean Fleet rode at anchor, line upon line of battleships and cruisers, destroyers and torpedo boats, oilers and colliers, fleet auxiliaries and ocean liners converted into hospital ships. As we did so, several native craft began taking a close interest, quite likely hoping to sell useful information to *Taskilat Mahsusa*, the Ottoman Intelligence Service.

Their conduct was not unreasonable, given that the average Egyptian had no reason for loyalty to his aloof *Inglezi* occupiers. Things might have been different had France not gone to war with Prussia in 1870, and lost, leaving the door ajar for Britain to buy a majority shareholding in the Suez Canal Company and, with it, *de facto* rule of Egypt.

French talent and culture in nearby Syria transformed dowdy Beyrouth into a sparkling Paris of the Middle East, so perhaps they could have waved the same magic wand over Cairo? A futile speculation; history only records what was, not what might have been.

My two mates joined me at a rail overlooking the wharves, and office buildings, and trading houses of Egypt's most cosmopolitan city. "That's where the Pharos stood," Harry announced with a sideways tilt of the chin towards the outer harbour's palace fortress of Ras el Tin. "Not pharaohs, but *Pharos*, Greek for lighthouse, one of the Seven Wonders of the Ancient World," he elaborated, "more than four hundred feet tall!"

"Four hundred, eh?" Percy reamed the dottle from his briar pipe and rubbed a pinch of tobacco between calloused palms. "Where's it now?"

"An earthquake knocked it down."

"Hm." Percy loaded the pipe bowl and cupped a match over it, cheeks puckered. "They must've had some bloody good tackle to lift bricks and mortar that high." He flicked his dead match into the harbour just as one of 11 Battalion's lads dived over the side and swam through surging muck and flotsam towards the nearest dockside boat ladder, the first but by no means last thirsty Digger to break bounds and go in search of a cold beer.

"More than four hundred, you say?" He continued, reflectively trickling aromatic smoke while performing deft mental arithmetic. "Divide by three, that's one hundred and thirty-three yards. Divide by twenty-two, equals..." He opened his eyes. "A whisker over six cricket pitches, top to bottom." He puffed contentedly. "Y'reckon there's a museum where we can see how they got it done?"

I shall tape this laconic yet revealing conversation to record two men who, though now largely forgotten, were legends in their day. Harry Murray the self-taught scholar, and Percy Black the talented bush mechanic. An honour to serve with and a privilege to be their friend.

61

The regimental police were kept busy during the couple of days we remained in Alexandria, as other thirsty men either swam ashore or pirated one of the bumboats allowed alongside to sell fruit and trinkets, easily done amidst the confusion of unloading horses into quarantine and winching bulk stores, including one million rounds of 0.303 cartridges, onto waiting lighters.

Every effort was made to smarten the rest of us with haircuts, showers, and shaves now that clean water was being piped aboard; luxuries that did much to restore our morale before getting orders to disembark.

At their best, armies are greater than the sum of their parts; of such was the AIF by late-1918, but only after four years of hard lessons learned. This was certainly not the case in late-1914 as barely trained officers and NCOs struggled to build order and discipline on shaky foundations of muddle and mistakes. Often the results were hilarious, sometimes tragic, occasionally fatal, but with the charity and clarity of hindsight there is no way I could have done half as well as they did with such a chaotic scrum.

We had yet to find our land legs after one month penned inside a cargo liner as, buckled and strapped in full field order, we stumbled down the gangplanks like drunken sailors and dumped our kitbags on requisitioned donkey carts. These were supposed to follow when we marched off to the railway station, rifles sloped, bayonets fixed in a display of naked power meant to overawe the local natives; Allah alone knows what they really thought as companies of armed *ferangi* tramped past like an out-of-step millipede, many of our faces blotched with coloured antiseptics.

Those in authority had correctly judged that raw Australian troops would not yet know how quickly stolen equipment can vanish up an Egyptian side alley. For that reason, British military police in starched khaki drill, red caps square on shaven skulls, revolver belts a dazzling white, were detailed to keep an eye on the carts and our kit. I can't imagine what the Mother Country's hardmen thought of their Colonial Cousins; in a phrase common at the time, our appearance would have made the Sphinx weep.

The Egyptian Railway Administration's antique rolling stock was another sight to behold, as evidenced by the cast iron plate bolted to our loco's rusted water tank:

Swindon Steam Locomotive
Engineering Works
1854

Instead of being retired to an industrial museum, or sold for scrap, this early Victorian relic with matching wagons and carriages, looked as if the railway company had discovered it up an abandoned siding and then found a gullible Australian purchasing officer to take it off their hands, for cash.

Clambering aboard and getting sorted took us a while longer, during which time exasperated MPs kept collaring strays investigating a nearby advertisement for *Pyramiden Lager Bier*. Eventually, after much huffing and puffing, the carriages jolted and banged together as our vintage railway engine wheezed off along the track that ran across a low spit of land between Lake Mareotis and the Mediterranean Sea.

It was late autumn, thirty degrees north of the Equator, but the sun was still a blindingly hot reflection off acres of lakeside saltpans. It did not help that our third-class carriages only had slatted wooden shutters, most of which were either broken or jammed open so that grit and saline dust blew over everything and everyone inside.

Compounding the misery, we were back in our khaki serge tunics, flannel shirts, cord breeches, cloth puttees, and hobnail boots, the colonel having reasoned that the sight of us in shipboard undress would have irreparably harmed the Empire's reputation for ruthless fighting men.

As if all that were not enough aggravation for one day, the Australian Army Service Corps had neglected to issue travel rations. The more experienced had guessed might happen and, not before long, *Ascanius'* canteen's locked door was picked, whereupon we filled our water bottles with lemonade and crammed our haversacks with plunder; sweet revenge for the previous weeks of extortion by Captain Chrimes and his merry men.

I traded half a bar of chocolate for a packet of Huntley & Palmer cheese crackers, and five cigarettes for a tin of Cornish pilchards in tomato sauce. Harry, Percy, and I then pooled our loot and enjoyed an impromptu picnic lunch while other little gangs did much the same thing, up and down the carriage, or went hungry depending on how enterprising they'd been, earlier in the day.

It was a massive relief when our train left the saltpans behind and began shuffling southward through lush fields of grain, and cotton, and sugar cane, and what Harry thought must be tobacco, having seen similar crops growing near Manjimup in Westralia.

Like much else we would soon discover about this land, its fertility was an illusion, the encroaching Western Desert never more than a couple of miles away from narrow strips of green that had miraculously sustained a great civilisation for upwards of four thousand years.

"Jeezus!" one of our battalion's other machine gunners, a wheat farmer from Pingelly in real life, was crouched at a gaping window, oblivious to the flying bugs and insects that ranged in size from pinheads to bottle corks, scooped aboard as our train panted along. "Them bastards must be getting fifty bags to the acre!" He pointed as a patch of grain, smooth as a ripple of golden velvet, inched past and fell astern. "How the fuck they do that then?!"

"They don't." Harry glanced up from book on permanent loan from *Ascanius'* library. "The Nile does."

"Uh?"

"Every year it rains upstream in Africa. Tons of mud come roaring down to flood these lowlands. Once it drains away, the locals seed their next crop on fresh soil."

The other man's laugh was cruelly dismissive. "Get away!"

"It's a fact." Harry was sure of himself. "They've been farming like it since the pharaohs. That's why Joseph, in the Bible, was sent down to get corn from Egypt when his brothers were doing it hard on the family farm, up north, in Palestine."

"You gotta be joking!"

"No. I'm reading about it."

Percy also got ready to support our friend, if this argument got heated, but there was no need as the other gunner slumped into baffled silence. Instead, Corporal Black offered an observation of his own. "I know sod all about Joseph and flooded fields but take a squiz at that!" He pointed as we rattled past a village of mudbrick houses, surrounded by shaggy date palms, where two elderly men clad in grubby white nightshirts, were hauling down one end of a pivoted beam while the other end tipped what looked like a sack of water into an irrigation ditch. "That's the way! Keep it simple. Don't get too clever."

At least someone was enjoying the journey and gleaning fresh knowledge, for I most certainly was not. My mental pictures of Egypt had formed on wet and wintry afternoons, seated inside Tralee's heated conservatory, while Aunt Lucinda tended to her prized orchids, and I copied coloured lithographs from David Roberts' *Sketches in the Holy Land & Syria*.

These once-fashionable, orientalist illustrations were originally published on subscription for wealthy connoisseurs, about seventy years earlier, by an adventurous Scot who travelled up the Nile to Nubia. His dreamy *Arabian Nights* images of Bedouin camped at desert oases, or wandering among ancient ruins, bore no resemblance to the overcrowded squalor and overpowering stench of an Egypt I needed to get away from as soon as possible, by resuming our voyage to France's green and pleasant land.

Memo to self; I must be less critical when recording these scenes. People and customs change over time, and I sincerely hope that Egyptian life has changed for the better since the Great War, for it could hardly be worse.

Eventually our train ground to a halt at dusk, while there was still enough light to see minarets silhouetted on the skyline of a city much as it had been since Saladin built his great fortress at *al-Kahira*, as Cairo was then known, which I believe translates as "Victorious," in Arabic. The Citadel was his celebration of Saracen power.

Eight hundred years later, it was performing a similar role as the headquarters of a British Army of Occupation. That was not the official title, of course, London preferring to pretend that its troops were a benevolent presence, protecting the Suez Canal for whichever oriental despot sat on the throne, be he a corrupt Turkish viceroy or an obedient sultan. Not that either man doubted who ruled the rulers after British and Indian forces destroyed Urabi Bey's rebel army at Tel-el-Kebir in 1882.

Hungry, thirsty, exhausted, Australia's contribution to this imperial drama tramped into the Citadel's lamplit maze of courtyards where the garrison was under orders to make us welcome; sweaty sock cheese, stale bread, warm cocoa, and hard veranda decking were our first taste of the Middle East's fabled nightlife.

Next morning, grumpy and gummy eyed, we fell-in to escort our kitbags back to a railway spur line where another elderly train was waiting to take us the last few miles to camp. I am not sure any of us cared much, one way or the other. What we needed more than anything else were barracks to stow our kit, a good feed, and sleep. Instead, we detrained at Mena, last stop on the suburban line to an hotel that was once a hunting lodge, though how anyone caught anything except crotch itch and sunburn on this naked expanse of sandy gravel, was beyond my limited understanding.

Our officers lost no time shifting into the building, accompanied by a chorus of groans and hisses. This was as close to mutiny as I can remember during four years of war, and I was as guilty of venting my frustration as any other AIF private. It was only later, by then a staff officer myself, that I understood the urgent need for a table, a typewriter, and a telephone so that plans could be made, daily routine orders issued, pay sheets tallied, local purchases receipted, and rations indented per muster roll.

While Colonel Pope and his opposite number in 11 Battalion were establishing their workplace, our NCOs were marching us towards the Pyramids not far from Mena itself, before halting about halfway and ordering us to link our rifles' piling swivels in bells of five apiece. These improvised markers formed our camp's notional main street until enough lumps of limestone could be gathered to trace the rest of the bivouac's lines.

It was a pity about the tents. There were none, nor would be until a new shipment arrived from England, for ours were lost in transit between Broadmeadows Camp and Melbourne Docks. The wonder is that so little else went astray, given the haste with which the Australian Government rushed to war for murky political reasons I only discovered much later.

The British Military Government in Egypt was also scheming behind the scenes, in their case for the overthrow of a pro-Turkish Khedive and his replacement by the more amenable Hussein Kamel Pasha. The arrival of several thousand rowdy colonials, masquerading as soldiers in transit to France, could not have come at a worse time and it was clear that nobody in authority had any idea what to do with us.

We knew nothing of this, but I strongly suspect that we were neither wanted nor expected to stay long, hence the bare stretch of ground on which we had to rug up and sleep in the open for the next two weeks of bitterly cold nights and scorching hot days, sharing our bedding with sand fleas and scorpions, blankets dragged over our heads and faces whenever the next choking sand storm hissed in from the desert.

This was fair enough for prospectors and bush-workers accustomed to kipping under the stars in Westralia, but at least our dirt there was comparatively clean. Not so in Egypt, where hardly any rain falls to compost the human and animal dung being constantly added to millennia of powdery filth. Septic throats and croupy coughs, inflamed eyes and suppurating ulcers, skin rashes and digestive ailments were the least of our problems and, very soon, an average of three men a day were dying. Mostly from chest infections that nowadays would be cured with a few shots of penicillin.

The army's true heroes were our medics who had to cope with all of this, plus the inevitable injuries of camp life that ranged from the banal to bizarre. A fair example of the latter was the young lad who dropped his breeches behind the hessian windbreak of B Company's latrine. Lighting up a cigarette, he flicked its burning match into the pit he was perched above, not knowing that the Sanitary Squad had just sprayed a mixture of paraffin and petrol to smother its seething wads of maggots. The rest of his war service was spent flat on his face, waiting to be shipped home to Australia.

Fortunately, the British Royal Engineers had anticipated our desperate need for water and moved quickly to run a galvanized iron pipeline up from the Nile, through a chlorinator, and out to a line of standpipes; without these we could never have made it through that first horrible day, even if the nominally cold water was sickly warm by the end of it.

The AIF was equally fortunate to have sergeants major like ours, a former British regular turned publican and backstreet bookmaker, who immediately sized-up the situation, told us how and where to build a rough field kitchen, then left us to get on with the job. He returned a short while later with two Egyptian peasants bowed under bundles of palings stolen from Mena's backyard fence. A couple of piastres, a threatened kick up the bum, and a snarled *"Imshi!"* repaid their efforts.

Our sun-warped planks were immediately hidden from envious eyes and fuelled the low trench fire warming a mess of curry powder, bully beef, tinned vegetables, and crushed ration biscuits. Revolting stodge but, for famished men at that time and place, a feast.

The trouble was, we only had one dixie, a puzzling name I thought referred to the American Civil War until Harry told me that it came from *degci*, the Hindi word for cooking pot, as we laboriously scraped ours clean before boiling tightly rationed water for a brew.

Later, tormented by thirst on Gallipoli, nobody ever complained about swigging curried tea through a scum of beef dripping, often with overtones of lamp oil from the tins that carried our water up from the beachhead.

There is an irritating torrent of tosh every April 25th, the anniversary of our landing at Anzac Cove, whenever some sanctimonious twerp describes that disaster as "Australia's coming-of-age," for which I blame Charles Bean the Official War Correspondent and his political handlers, fishing for widows' and orphans' votes during the 1920s and '30s. Whereas, in my opinion the transformation from Colonies to Commonwealth began five months earlier, at Mena, as West Australians and New South Welshmen, Queenslanders and Victorians, Tasmanians and South Australians were forced to put aside our tribal differences and build an army camp from scratch.

Australia's symbolical stride into adulthood happened to coincide with my own twenty-first birthday, give or take a year or two, a fact that I have often reflected upon as my own body continues to age and my nation grows older if not wiser, at much the same pace.

62

Besides daily fatigues, and the posting of armed sentries to warn off thieving natives, there was a war to win, and for that our feet needed hardening after weeks of easy living aboard ship. To achieve this, the General Staff decreed that we should be marched through sand dunes to our training areas, rather like racehorses exercising on a beach.

As a result, otherwise fit men soon broke down with torn tendons, or twisted knees, or ruptures, while others succumbed to sunstroke and the odd touch of malaria. Influenza and pneumonia also returned to thin our ranks, not surprising when clad in sweaty wet serge uniforms; it would be some time before we adopted the British Army's sensible cotton drill shirts, Bombay bloomers as their baggy knee britches were called, and those seemingly comic but practical Wolseley pith helmets that replaced the many slouch hats blown overboard, during our voyage from Fremantle.

It was now almost midwinter and yet the local midday temperatures still nudged one hundred degrees Fahrenheit. If any work was to be done, it had to start early with Reveille at 0400 hours followed by three hours of exercises before returning to camp for a prison rations' breakfast. After which the day's work continued until knock-off at 1100 hours, only resuming late in the afternoon. For the rest of the day, we found whatever shade we could and grumbled.

As machine gunners we were assigned a squad of riflemen to hold a defensive perimeter while we engaged the enemy with aimed fire in less than thirty seconds from demount. This was easier said than done, rifles being relatively light and quickly actioned, whereas the Vickers with its tripod, tools, water, and belts of ammunition tip the scales at well over two hundred pounds on a good day.

Usually, we towed these impedimenta on a Boer War trek cart with the marching infantry, but such an arrangement was never going to work once we began trudging over sandhills and along rocky gullies; it was now that my work as a sandalwood puller proved useful.

At my suggestion, the battalion's Machine Gun Officer indented for ox camels. I then picked the best pair and devised padded rope harnesses to carry a Vickers, with its water can and two magazines, on one flank of each pack-animal: our tools, tripod, and another couple of magazines, on the opposite side.

Percy, Harry, and I were immediately dubbed The Three Wise Men, from our resemblance to Biblical pictures of the Three Magi leading camels to Bethlehem, but it was my quick-release harness that became standard issue when the Imperial Camel Corps was raised to fight in the Sinai Campaign.

There was no lack of practice at mounting a gun and firing imaginary belts of ammunition – indicated by me twirling a wooden football rattle - in support of the infantry's frontal attacks against lines of flags marking imagined enemy positions. Columns of men would advance by company, by platoon, by section, firing make-believe volleys by shouting "Bang! Bang! Bang!" at the target flags, before rushing forward to bayonet the finish line's sandbags.

We were in a good position to assess these antics and it was not long before all agreed that bayonet charges were not the most intelligent use of firepower or manpower . A century previously, when muzzle-loading muskets often misfired, it was a different story, but none of us saw much point turning our bolt-action rifles into the modern equivalent of a Zulu assegai, especially when a slew of machine gun bullets could topple a row of steel silhouettes at two, three, four hundred yards, in two, three, four heartbeats.

"*Ça c'est magnifique, mais ce n'est pas la guerre, c'est de la folie!*" I growled to myself at the conclusion of one such dummy attack, in imagination emplacing my gun on an adjacent hillside with its murderously clear field of fire.

"Eh?" Harry's ears pricked up.

"'That's magnificent, but it's not war, it's madness...'"

"Who says?" My friend never missed a chance to enlarge his stock of knowledge.

"A French general, observing the British Light Brigade charging 'Into the jaws of Death.'" Aunt Lucinda had made sure that Tennyson's heroic poem was on my list of recitations. She had also added quite a lot of background colour from what she later learned of that fatal day on Balaklava's battlefield, conversing at Court with Marshal Bosquet after his triumphant return from the Crimean War.

"Hmm." Percy unfolded from behind our Vickers where he had been sitting on a spare ammo box, boots wedged forward. "I wonder who else thinks that as well...?"

Not many. The only previous military experience anyone had was on the open plains of South Africa, hunting unfriendly farmers, and for a brief while longer that is how we kept rehearsing for this war against a major industrial power.

Then reports arrived of actual conditions on the Western Front. Bayonets were still fixed, but now the infantry attacked shallow trenches behind imitation barbed wire made from string tied to wooden pickets, and all the while our Vickers kept rattling its make-believe support.

Playtime ended with the start of more realistic training. In the language of the day, our battalions were to be "inoculated" by exposing the troops to the sights and sounds of battle. To heighten the realism, MG sections were ordered to aim a stream of bullets one yard above lines of men hugging the ground. At the word of command, we would then elevate and thrash a beaten zone of plunging machine gun fire one thousand yards ahead of the infantry, who were imagined to be confidently advancing under a protective hail of friendly shot.

That was the theory, but in practice it was the formula for a massacre until Corporal Black respectfully reminded our officer commanding that a projectile's trajectory is affected by temperature and resultant air density, serious considerations when attempting precision marksmanship on a baking hot desert. A more careful reading of the ballistic tables raised our fixed aim to five feet instead of three, above the prone infantry.

I cannot speak for other gunners, but I do know that Percy further elevated above the likely height of panicked men jumping to their feet, when our signallers flagged the order to commence firing. Luckily there were no squibs as we hammered hundreds of rounds downrange, for that would have meant a badly primed cartridge and corresponding drop-short bullet, with still sufficient terminal energy to kill had it struck one of our own.

Marching back to camp, we heard 11 Battalion singing *Tipperary*, a music hall ditty brought to Egypt by recent British reinforcements, and soon to become the iconic Great War song. As already noted, 11 City of Perth Battalion and 16 Bushman's Battalion were recruited from opposite poles of Westralian society, so our rivalry was intense, and Mr Pope let it be known that we needed a distinctive song of our own

I had once written an advertisement for Nilsson's Cough Mixture, so composing a new song in Egypt should not be too difficult. In the event it took a bit of effort, but by juggling words that rhymed, and getting the cadence right, 16 Battalion was soon proudly marching to *The Man Who Broke the Bank at Monte Carlo*, played on a harmonica while the rest of us gave full voice to its new lyrics: "As we march along these Gyppo roads with an independent air! You can hear the Huns declare, 'Keep the Aussies over there! For we've heard they're rough, we know they're tough, and we poor sods have had enough! They're the men who've come to beat the bloody Kaiser-r-r -!"

Though I do say so myself, we sounded impressively menacing on our night-time excursions through the city streets, hundreds of hobnailed boots crunching in step with a brief rest for char and wads - tea and corned beef sandwiches - at the Citadel before marching back to Mena, led by our markers' lanterns.

There was more to this than the mere hardening of feet and strengthening of leg muscles. Tensions were rising as the date approached for the installation of a new ruler, Khedive Abbas Hilmi being conveniently absent in Constantinople, thus saving London the bother of killing him locally after a botched assassination attempt in the Turkish capital.

Our shows of force were also explicit warnings to the Egyptian public that any rioting, fomented by spies and nationalist agitators, would not be viewed kindly when the new puppet ruler was paraded through his capital, flanked by a squadron of Indian lancers and British dragoons.

63

Numbers 3 and 5 Brigades AIF drew the short straw and fifty rounds per man before lining the street from Abdeen Palace to the Opera House, as honour guards for the new Sultan when he nervously drove past his new subjects in an open carriage.

Their other duty, apart from watching for rooftop snipers, was to keep the sullen bystanders tightly pushed back, making it harder for an assassin to aim his pistol or throw a bomb. The British Army's contribution to this festive occasion, apart from the ceremonial horsemen, was to stand-easy, out of sight but not out of mind, ready to respond if the natives failed to cheer their new master, the latest in a long line of foreign puppet rulers since the emperor Augustus overthrew Cleopatra, the last Egyptian monarch, a couple of thousand years earlier.

As luck would have it, 16 Battalion drew the long straw and a rare day of light duties that we machine gunners were determined to enjoy by climbing the Great Pyramid and seeing the Sphinx, neither of which we had done yet. "Come on. Let's go before it gets too hot!" Percy and I filled our water bottles, snaffled some ration biscuits, and set off after Harry who was impatient to view this sole survivor of the Ancient World's Seven Wonders.

A swarm of hawkers touting fake antiquities and erotic postcards, grubby packets of nuts and trays of dusty honey cakes, materialised from the sand dunes like *djinn* as we left camp. By now every soldier had mastered at least two words of Arabic – *imshi!* or "fuck off!" and *mafeesh* or "no more" – underlined with a cuff, or a punch, or a kick, or all three in rapid succession.

Not that it made much difference. Like the annoying clouds of flies that accompanied them everywhere, these touts would fall back a short distance, mewling and muttering, before pushing their luck again.

I admired their desperate tenacity and, with memories of an earlier self, recognised kindred spirits struggling to earn a crust. I also knew we would never get rid of them unless a firm bargain was struck first. "*Maan, yatahdat, al'inglezi?!*" I demanded, scanning a frieze of crumpled brown faces that portrayed a wide range of human emotions from low cunning to downright stupidity. "Who! Speaks! English?!"

"Me-Me-Me!" A young lad broke forward, stood to attention, and comically saluted, *ferangi* style. He was one of the newsboys who brought the *Egyptian Gazette* into camp every weekday morning, Artful Dodgers easily bribed to shout insults at unpopular officers or NCOs: "Speshul! Speshul! Captain Shitface Big Fuckuh! Reedollabahtit! Speshul! Speshul!"

Percy swapped questioning looks with Harry as I put on my most menacing scowl. "Right-o Abdul," all Arabs were Abdul, "listen good. You tell them," I pointed at his followers, "we want things, we tell you, you tell them. No more! *Tafahum?*"

"*Nem sayidi!*"

"You do, you get, *athnyn qurush!*" I held up two fingers to indicate the number of *piastres* he would earn, plus undoubted commissions from his keepers, provided he kept them from bothering us.

"Jeeze, Icy, you're a dark horse!" Harry grinned as Abdul self-importantly dismissed the crowd and attached himself to us, proud as a lord to now own three rich *Ustrali*. "Where the hell did you learn all that?"

"Oh, here and there," I shrugged modestly. Here, was Egypt; There, was Playfair Street, the misnamed heart of Sydney's harbourside slums.

Abdul's skills were soon required when a plump brown slug of a man with a red *tarboosh* atop a slick of greasy black hair, dark blue *djubbeh* coat worn over his striped *galibaya*, demanded five disasters apiece for the privilege of climbing "his" pyramid. Strictly speaking it was "their" pyramid, for behind him stood half a dozen squinty enforcers disguised as official guides, also in red flowerpot hats with dull brass badges, but without a *djubbeh* over their grubby nightshirts, which I assume was the boss man's uniform.

Some experience of how the world wags told me that these ancient monuments were profitable real estate, fought over by rival gangs since at least the time when Alexander the Great was anointed a living god by the local priesthood, pretty much where we stood now. A flurry of angry shouts got us the Special Friends' discount rate of seven and a half disasters for all three, including the use of a rope up the Pyramid's nearest corner.

I gravely acknowledged Abdul's assistance and told him to await our return, before we began climbing, often needing the rope as we clambered from one yellowish limestone block to another, each about a yard from top to bottom, many studded with fossilized seashells some of which Harry souvenired with his army jack-knife's marlin spike.

We had earned a breather by the time we reached the small flat area atop this, the tallest of three pyramids on Giza's plateau. The equivalent of one shilling and sixpence, a large amount of sweat, grazed knees and bruised elbows, were a trifling price to pay for such a stunning panorama, I thought, reaching into my haversack for sketchbook and pencils.

Egypt's intensely blue sky was still crystal clear from horizon to horizon; the *simoom* would not start blowing its billowy clouds of filthy grit until later in the morning. Thus, we were able to look eastwards, beyond the black snake of the Nile and its green ribbons of irrigated cultivation, to the bare Mokattam Hills and Arabian Desert. Or westwards, to the sand dunes and *wadis* of our training area and Libyan Hills, behind which the Sahara stretched all the way across North Africa to the Atlantic Ocean. Or downwards at Cairo's mudbrick sprawl, crowded around the Citadel and Mehmet Ali's great mosque.

"Bloody hell -!" Harry shielded his eyes, the better to see a vulture majestically riding the air currents nearby. "That's Nekhbet!"

"What's a neck bet?" Percy reached for the briar pipe in his tunic pocket. "And if you say it's a hot tip for the Melbourne Cup, you're one month too bloody late."

"There's no need to get shitty just because you didn't win the battalion sweepstake!" Harry was inclined to be gruff whenever anyone seemed to be knocking him down a peg.

"Whoa there!" Percy held up a hand in the universal sign of peace.

"Well then!" Harry jabbed his thumb skywards. "For your information, that bird, there, is Nekhbet, the vulture goddess of Upper Egypt. The pharaohs worshipped her for good luck and good harvests!"

"And umpteen hundred years later she's still on the job?" Percy's eyes twinkled as he loaded his pipe.

"'Hundreds'? Bloody thousands!" Harry shot back. "This pyramid we're on was built four and a half thousand years ago, as the tomb for Khufu, who took twenty years to do it!"

"Not by himself he didn't," Percy retorted drily, shielding the lit match.

"Of course not! He had thousands and thousands of slaves to shift more than two million blocks, each weighing more than two tons!"

"Is that a fact?" Percy wagged the match out and trickled smoke while I completed a quick sketch of both men in profile, like bantam cocks sizing each other up.

"Alright, let's round the numbers and call it two million over twenty years. That's one hundred thousand per annum, divided by three hundred and sixty-five." He clicked tongue, frowning at an imaginary blackboard's chalked sums. "That's two hundred and seventy a day, twenty-four-hour shifts, non-stop, for twenty years. Still rounding numbers, that's a bit over eleven blocks an hour, or one every five and a half minutes, for twenty years, night and day, with no down time. Right?"

"Ri-i-ght."

"Well, if you believe that, you really must think the moon is made of green cheese!" He shook his head in mocking disbelief. "F'Chrissakes, we'd be busting our guts to do half as well with steam shovels and machinery…"

"They had thousands of slaves!"

"I don't care how many bloody slaves they had the numbers say it never happened." Percy cracked a sardonic chuckle. "There's no way this thing got built in so short a time, using two million stone blocks."

"But the books say -!"

"Books say what writers want 'em to say," Percy grunted. "Numbers tell it like it is. Two plus two is four, always has been, always will be, no matter how you write it in any language." He paused, challengingly. "The only way Cuckoo got this job done, in that time, was to use fewer blocks."

"He couldn't have!" Harry was infuriated that anyone would dare doubt the printed word. "There are over two million!"

"Balls." Percy Black - carpenter, bush mechanic, gold miner - was, in imagination, rolling up his sleeves. "If I had to build a pyramid, I'd start by sticking four posts in the ground and use a cord line to check their squares and diagonals were spot on. Then I'd build corner pillars where the posts were, and link those with four courses of stonework, breast high, to make a shallow box.

"Your Ancient Egyptians were not stupid, they'd never waste time and effort by filling it with two-ton blocks of dressed stone when all they had to do was shovel the rubble inside, then add enough sand to bring up the level before raising the next course, sloping inwards as they climbed.

"As for getting those blocks in place," he glanced over the edge of our small platform, "this wall's a readymade ramp. I'd use it to keep hauling up more stonework and more filler, in skips or baskets, getting narrower and narrower, quicker and quicker, till we reached the top."

He drew on his pipe and eyed the vulture overhead. "Oy, Neck Bet! You've been around long enough to know the score. What's right, numbers or words?"

Harry remained silent, like me awestruck by the uncluttered elegance of our friend's mind and mathematical clarity of thought.

When I share this conversation with Frances, I shall ask her to check the latest theories on how the Great Pyramid was built. Assuming her academic colleagues have finally discovered that it really is a gigantic sandcastle sheathed in stone, she can reliably inform them that Corporal P.C.H. Black, service number 170, 16 Battalion, 1st Australian Imperial Force solved their ancient riddle in less than three minutes, shortly before Christmas 1914.

The sullen thud of a distant field gun startled us on the way back to ground level; I immediately thought the revolt had broken out and that we were about to be attacked by a mob of rioting *felahin*. Percy shook his head and kept counting as the thuds continued at a steady pace until they stopped. "Twenty-one. The Royal Salute," he remarked, climbing down to the next level of dressed limestone blocks. "Probably for his nibs the Sultan, poor bastard."

"Why's that?" Harry enquired, joining us.

"Would you live here when there's the rest of the world to pick from?"

"Yes."

"Then more fool you." Percy reached up to give his mate a hand. "The sooner I get to France and that Hundred Years' War kit that Icy talks about, the better."

Abdul hurried forward as we clambered off the last course of blocks and sorted ourselves out. "*Effendi?!*"

"Now, the Sphinx," I replied firmly.

"*Nem effendi! Follo'!*"

This we did by trudging around the corner, across an ancient rubbish dump until we came to the partially buried trunk of a massive, half-human lion.

Percy was curious; Harry was enchanted; I was annoyed to see how badly its face had been pocked by French musket balls during Napoleon the First's *mission civilisatrice*. Meanwhile, a tipsy Tommy on the Sphinx's weathered shoulder, was entertaining his mates with a British Army barrack-room ballad I had not heard before: "The sex life o' the camel, is queerer than anyone finks!" he bawled. "At the height o' the mating season, 'e tries to bugger the Finx! But the Finx's arse'ole is bunged with the sands o' the Nile! Wot accounts for the hump on the camel, and the Finx's dirty ol' smile -!" At which point Tommy lost his footing and tumbled, still gagging with laughter, onto the gravel below.

Abdul tugged my sleeve. "Wot he say?!"

"Egypt, good place," I lied. "Egyptians, good people.'"

"Yiss! Yiss!" The young lad agreed. "Now, photo! My uncle!"

I was not sure if this meant my promotion to honorary membership of his clan, or that the seedy cove sidling towards us with an ancient bellows camera, really was an uncle. Not that it mattered, and I saw no point in being churlish by dismissing him.

Instead, I stood between Harry and Percy, the Sphinx leering over our heads as Uncle burrowed under his black cloth, groped around to remove the lens cap for a couple of seconds, and processed the snapshot in a portable darkroom the size of a suitcase.

We each bought a copy at one disaster apiece. I recently found mine being used as a bookmark in an old copy of *Murray's Guide for Travellers in Transcaucasia & Persia*, clearly signed in pencil by all three of us, which is probably why the memory of this day is so strong.

I also remember feeling quite disturbed at the time. It did not sit well with me that, when surrounded by such evidence of a great and glorious past, these modern Egyptians were reduced to pimping their pyramids and flattering foreign invaders who held them in contempt. Which was probably the reason why I sketched a whimsical cartoon of the photographer and presented it as a gift from one creative artist to another. It was obvious the poor fellow got more kicks than thanks in his precarious trade, for he kept bowing and wept tears of gratitude.

Abdul had been watching at my elbow, intrigued by how a curved stroke can express so much. I flipped a fresh sheet of cartridge paper and sketched the Sphinx, except for its face, while Harry and Percy went off to fossick for bits of ancient pottery and the entrance to a hidden tunnel said to end at the stone lion's mouth, through which Ancient Egyptian priests were supposed to have uttered their prophesies.

Meanwhile, I gauged Abdul's proportions by holding up my thumbed pencil and superimposed his features onto the Sphinx. The overall effect was rather dull, so I twitched an eyelid, added a cheeky grin, and tilted a slouch hat with the AIF's sunrise badge, at a rakish angle.

"There you go."

"Yiss!" He grabbed it as if I were giving him the keys to *La Banque d'Ègypte.* "Yiss! Yiss!"

It was getting hot, and I was not the only one exhausted after so much extended effort as we trooped back to camp where Percy insisted on paying our guide's fee in full. Rarely were two disasters better spent. During the weeks ahead, our tent got the first and cleanest copy of that day's news. Our laundry was taken care of, though by whom and where I have no idea, except that it was always promptly returned clean and ironed. And if we needed any errands or small purchases, Abdul would nip off and return with the correct change, less a trifling commission.

True to type he also managed a mythical "sistuh," embellished by obscene grins and lewd gestures. Much to his surprise, this failed to entice any of us, and although the hallmark of a gentleman is to always maintain a genial dignity with servants, I rather forgot myself and left Abdul in no doubt what I, and Percy, and Harry, thought of his disgusting proposal.

Baffled, he slunk away, and only made a tentative reappearance the next morning, during our eleven o'clock break, fearful he might have lost a lucrative contract. Instead, we welcomed him affably and bought our regular newspaper as if nothing had happened. Encouraged, he pointed at the headline and looked up at me. "What are, this?"

"'What is this?'" I corrected.

"What, is, this?"

"'German Troops Repulsed.'" I tapped a finger left to right, unlike the Arabic script's leftward flow, and repeated each word while he echoed it. That done, he resumed his newspaper round, chanting "Jernan Trups Repulzt! Reedollaboutit!" and outsold every other newsboy.

64

Reveille moved forward one hour on Christmas Morning, allowing the cooks to prepare a more lavish breakfast than our usual bread and jam, porridge, and tea. As a bonus, training was suspended and a limited number of leave passes were issued to mark the season of goodwill to all men, except the Huns and Turks, of course.

We then filed past Colonel Pope to receive an attractive brass box containing tobacco, matches, and a greetings card from Princess Mary whose profile was embossed on the lid, together with the names of Britain's allies; some were familiar, like France and Russia, but few if any of us knew what Montenegro and Serbia were doing in our fight, or even where those places were on the map.

This handy little gift slipped easily into a tunic's breast pocket. Mine stayed with me throughout the war and is now archived with my other souvenirs, somewhere in Monash University's Department of Special Collections.

Meanwhile, back in Egypt on that first Christmas Day of the Great War, the battalion's Chaplain did his best to convince our church parade that God so loved the world that he impregnated a simple village maiden engaged to be married to the local carpenter. As one of 16 Battalion's medical orderlies chuckled nearby: "Try tellin' that to 'er dad...!"

The Padre was a decent sort and showed sincere concern for the welfare of his unruly flock. I think he was also missing his own family, for he spoke with deep feeling once we got to the guts of his sermon, namely the need to stay pure in thought and deed so that when we all returned home, crowned with the victor's laurels, our parents and wives and sweethearts would have no reason to be ashamed of our conduct overseas.

"Best o' luck with that...!" The medic's work included writing-up record sheets for the battalion's "Short Arm Inspection" at which anxious young men would drop their britches so that rubber gloved fingers could poke and prod their aching groins and weeping sores.

"- in the name of the Father, the Son, and the Holy Ghost. Amen."

"Amen," most of us responded as a matter of habit before a goodly number went forward to take Communion while the rest made a beeline for the cookhouse and our share of the fried eggs, bully beef fritters, and real toast, washed down by mugs of sweetened pineapple juice from a Queensland comforts shipment.

My two mates urged me to join them in a cricket match against 11 Battalion's machine gunners, but I was in no humour to play games and had a valid leave pass to account for my lack of enthusiasm. This high value perk was payment for a charcoal portrait of the Orderly Room Sergeant wreathed in Allied flags, a pyramid in the background, after getting Pat Donovan's message offering to meet in town.

As luck would have it, yesterday was my turn to join two hundred other naked men sloshing about in Mena Hotel's swimming bath, a privilege the officers enjoyed every day but one that we Other Ranks only got every week.

Reasonably fresh and less fragrant than usual, clad in my number one khaki, boots polished, I passed muster at the guardhouse gate and joined a throng of other young men heading for the tram stop outside Mena's Greek Restaurant; the banter and jokes around me were clear warnings that our medical officers would soon be prodding a fresh crop of aches and sores.

If I were to develop this scene for Frances, it would not be to suggest any superior moral strength on my part, but rather as a fond tribute to Maeve – my youthful Melbourne dance partner - for sharing tender delights that were not for sale in a Cairene bordello. I must have seemed a strange and lonely sight, surrounded by raucous Diggers - the mocking nickname we would soon give ourselves, burrowing into the ground under enemy fire - several of whom cheerily invited me to join their brothel crawl. Not wanting to be thought a kill joy, I winked back and confided that I'd already lined-up a day of hot mischief.

"Onya cobber!" they grinned back.

"You too," I replied with another knowing wink. "But remember, if you can't be good, be careful. And if you can't be careful, be good..."

We then piled aboard the tram, and I fell silent, mentally sketching scenes through the empty window frame as Cairo's squalid outskirts merged with more substantial streets, approaching the English Bridge that connects the river's west bank with Gezireh Island, and gave the Zoo a wistful nod. Percy, Harry, and me had recently visited the battalion's smuggled kangaroo, now hopping around its own little enclosure, a long way from home like the rest of us, though in more agreeable surroundings than ours.

Whoever designed Cairo's Zoological Gardens left an abiding memorial to his skill by artfully blending exotic trees, date palms, floral beds, and shady grottoes, all linked together by colourfully patterned mosaic pathways kept reasonably clear of fallen leaves and palm fronds by lethargic sweepers. Not that I blamed them for their lack of pep in Egypt's torpid heat; as Noël Coward would later sing at his private recitals in Hollywood, only mad dogs and Englishmen go out in the noonday sun.

The Great Nile Bridge completed my crossing to the East Bank where I jumped off the tram, ignoring my companions' shouts that Haret El Wasser was still another three stages up the track, and set off along the Corniche; the Eternal Nile on my right hand, modern European mansions on my left; overtaken by tinkling, horse drawn *gharris* and splendid *equipages* mingling with elegant limousines and sporty roadsters, their sun roofs folded back, the better to see and be seen by everyone who was anyone in Cairo's High Society.

The *fellahin* toiling on their landlord's muddy fields were probably no better off than their remote ancestors had been under the pharaohs, but Egypt's twentieth century upper crust were clearly enjoying the good life under foreign occupation. Turkish or British, both armies required local goods and services easily swindled with fake invoices and arithmetical conjuring tricks.

I strode up the steps of Shepheard's Hotel, not yet off-limits to ranks other than commissioned officers, and entered the palatial foyer of Egypt's oldest, most celebrated watering hole. *"Je m'appelle le soldat Cribdon,"* pronounced "Kreebton" as I introduced myself to the Concierge. This was not just a brash young man showing off, this was a proud young patriot determined to show the world that not all Australian private soldiers were barbarians who smashed up bars and brothels for fun. *"Est-ce qu'il y a un message pour moi?"*

"Un moment m'sieur..." English defended the Suez Canal, but French powered the cogs and wheels of Middle Eastern commerce. *"Ah, oui,"* he

glanced up from his card index and pointed, *"le sergent-chef Don Ovan est là-bas..."*

"Merci de votre aide." I returned his polite nod and strolled into Shepheard's famed Bar & Grill like a gentleman of means and leisure.

Pat was seated alone at the far end, nursing a tall glass of dark beer, moodily staring at a mirror like the one in the Shamrock, in Kal', except that this was fringed with tinsel and garish paper chains, the bar's manager doing his best to promote Christmas cheer among his many and varied customers.

Pat looked up, glimpsed my reflection in the mirror and stood, hand outstretched. "Good to see you again mate. Thanks for coming."

"Likewise."

We exchanged firm grips.

"What's your poison?"

"Scotch and soda. Enough of one, plenty of the other." No way was I going to drown my sorrows in Dublin stout, not in this climate, even if Shepheard's Grill was being kept relatively cool by an overhead punkah fan and evaporative screens on its windows.

Pat clicked fingers, gave the order, shoved a silver coin across the bar, and waited for me to collect my drink before leading the way to a corner table.

"Cheers." He raised his glass in salute and, like the veteran sergeant major he was once more, after promotion to his former rank, inspected my appearance. "So, they've made you a machine gunner, eh?" He read the wreathed MG badge on my right cuff, much as I was doing for the restored crown on his sleeve. "Army life must suit you."

"You're not looking so bad yourself," I replied. Tanned, taut, trim, clad in a cavalryman's twill uniform of finer cloth than an infantry's baggy serge, my old friend and colleague cut quite a dash in his light-horseman's polished leather accoutrements and emu plumed hat.

One of Shepheard's legendary waiters ghosted up with a bowl of salted cashew nuts, compliments of the manager who knew he would soon recover this trifling cost when our dry throats tabbed more drinks.

"Suk'ran jazilan." I was and still am a firm believer in Aunt Lucinda's rule that when travelling abroad, everyone, regardless of their place in society, is an ambassador for his or her nation and must behave with gravity, dignity, and courtesy when dealing with the locals, irrespective of colour, creed, or their place in society.

"Afwa'an effendi," the waiter bowed and took a respectful step backwards, before ghosting off to generate more thirst among these peculiar *Ustrali,* so like *Inglezi* in appearance, and yet so unlike them in other ways.

Pat cocked an amazed eyebrow. "What's all that mean?"

"'Thank you very much.'"

"Strewth! You talk the local lingo then?"

"A few words," I shrugged modestly. "Enough to get along. French is more useful though."

"You talk that too?"

"A bit."

"It must be difficult!"

"The grammar can be," I agreed cautiously, "but dozens of our words are the same. For instance, this table is still spelt t-a-b-l-e in French; the only difference is that it's pronounced 'tah-bluh.'" I shrugged again. "You speak French every day -"

"Never!

283

"Then where d'you think 'rendezvous,' 'morale,' 'camouflage' come from?" I began ticking fingertips. "'Bivouac,' 'picket;' 'infantry;' 'cavalry,' 'artillery,' 'volley;' 'trench,' 'reconnoitre,' 'attack;' 'corporal,' 'sergeant,' 'lieutenant,' 'colonel;' 'brigade,' 'battalion,' 'bayonet,' 'barricade -'"

"You mean, they're not English?"

"French words, every one of 'em."

"Well, I never!" Pat reached for his Guinness and took a deep draught while he pondered this amazing revelation. "Thanks for telling me. It'll be handy if we ever do get to France."

"You mean we might not?" I seized on the note of doubt in his voice, aware that senior NCOs have a bush telegraph system that is often better informed than their commanders'.

"It looks likely."

"How?"

"German engineers are building a railway across the desert from a place called Guzza, so's the Turks can attack the Canal in force, and they've already probed our forward defences." He trailed a fingertip round and around the glass's damp rim. "Light Horse is tasked to harass their supply lines, like we did with the Boers, to stop their artillery getting within range of our ships..."

"Ships?" I frowned. "In a desert?"

"Think about it," he sat forward. "Sink one big freighter in the Canal and it's all over, Red Rover, for supplies and reinforcements from India and the Far East. GHQ's staff can't talk of anything else," he added, emptying his glass, and clicking fingers for a refill. "I'd say the way things are shaping up, you'll find more use for that Gyppo lingo, here, than any amount of French, in France..."

This grim prospect did nothing to lift the foggy gloom that had been dogging my heels for several days.

"Chin up!" Pat dug into the bowl of nuts. "You'll soon be dead."

"It feels like I already am," I grumbled, opening my purse to buy the next round. Aunt Lucinda had telegraphed ten guineas as a Christmas present, and in my current frame of mind I felt like blowing the whole bloody lot if it would make me feel any better about the past twelve months.

"Go on..." Pat, older and wiser, sensed what was really troubling me.

"Well, remember what you and me, Joe and George, the Chief and Karl were doing at your place? This time last year?"

"Too right I do..."

"Who'd have thought, then, everything would go arse-up so quickly? Not just for us, but for the whole bloody world!"

"'You'll never know you're happy till you're not,'" he concurred as the waiter scurried nearer. I stacked enough disasters on his tray to pay for the next round plus a hefty tip to keep him attentive.

Pat stared into his glass, as if searching for answers in its depths. "I reckon it's the same for being lucky, and not knowing it. I mean, there was you and your pictures; the Chief and Karl with their songs; Joe with his *Christmas Day in the Workhouse*; and not one of us knew how lucky we were, at the time, or how soon our luck would go bad..."

Pat abandoned his search and looked across the marble topped table instead. "Every night, the missus prays that God will somehow fix things up." My old friend did not sound convinced. "She told me so, in a nice long letter, in a parcel with a big fruitcake, and thick socks, for the cold weather, in France."

His gaze was moist with more than booze. "'I'll never know what she saw in a bushman, like m-me. She's much cleverer, and does foreign lingo, like you.'"

"Really?"

"My oath." His pride was touchingly evident. "She taught herself German, from a book, because she wanted to go there and do piano, once I'd made our fortune. All we needed was one lucky strike and we'd have had buckets of money to do whatever she liked..." His smile was achingly sad,

"You'd have gone with her?" I asked, intrigued by this unexpected insight into an older man's private world.

"O'course!" He seemed puzzled that anyone would ask such a question. "I'd have kept an eye on things and seen she'd nothing to worry about while doing more piano. Fair's fair," he insisted, "she looked after me, with her lessons and stuff, when I was down on my luck. It's only right I'd do the same for her, once we were in funds. Then, just as we'd cracked it, a bloody war gets in the way!"

"Cracked what?"

He took a deep breath. "The Chief's lawyer wrote saying there's one thousand pounds, for Dulcie to go to Germany and do piano. Instead, I'm stuck here, fighting the bastards!"

He took another deep breath. "The poor girl's not travelling well. She never says so, but I can tell. The church ladies give as much support as they can, but as she says, it's not like having a husband around the place, even if he does drop breadcrumbs on the floor under his seat at the dining table." He tried to laugh but it didn't fool me. "I thought this stunt would be like South Africa, but it's not, not with a missus to look after."

I was not sure where this melancholy monologue was going, or if indeed it was going anywhere. One thing was certain, though, I was not the only glum soldier in Egypt this Festering Season.

He took another, deeper breath. "Who would have thought, when she was cooking that dinner at our place, we'd be getting shickered in a Gyppo pub, a year later?"

"Not me mate."

"Nor me neither," he grunted. "And who would have imagined dead-straight honest Karl in jail, for being a Hun, and him just m-married." This sentimental, bighearted Irishman blinked back another tear. "The m-missus says his bank sold the shop for thirty quid, ground value, after some cranky s-sod shoved paraffin and burning rags, through the letterbox." He stared up at the punkah's canvas sail, gently wafting backwards and forwards, probably driven by a little boy hidden out of sight, tugging its cord like a bellringer. "Nothing's gone right since the Chief got knocked -!"

I sensed where this would end up unless someone more sober applied the brakes. "That's as maybe," I interrupted severely, "but one thing you may be sure, he'd have been down on us like a ton o' bricks if he'd heard us moaning."

"But -?"

"I'm not finished." I raised my finger, an unconscious habit acquired from Aunt Lucinda. "He gave me a right royal reprimand at Boolya. Not that he ever shouted or swore, it was all in his disappointed tone of voice. I've never forgotten it, or him."

Pat nodded unsteadily, trying to focus his eyes. "I know. I know. Sometimes I see him, with me, on inspections. Back straight as a ramrod, checking everything's shipshape. A p-prince among men."

"Me too. He's still here," I tapped my forehead. "Always will be."

Fortunately for us, Pat was an amiable drunk, unlike the popular image of an enraged Paddy challenging any ten men in the room to come outside and fight, so I had no trouble curtailing the drinks while he was still sober enough to walk to the lavatory, where he promptly parked himself inside a vacant cubicle while I returned to the Concierge.

"*M'sieur?*" He remembered me with a professionally bland smile.

I briefly explained that the servant of *le sergent-chef Don Ovan* had failed to book a Christmas luncheon, leaving us desolated, as Shepheard's Hotel was famous for its hospitality, a fame that reached as far as Western Australia where the *M'sieur Ovan* was a wealthy goldminer. And yet, without a second's thought, he left all that behind when the bugle call of duty summoned him to honour and glory! And how did I know this? Because he was also the owner of a very big newspaper of which, until recently, I was the parliamentary political reporter, before also hearing the clarion call of duty for King & Country -!

His interest quickened: "*Vous êtes journaliste? Un chroniqueur?*"

I modestly acknowledged both titles, adding that I naturally understood how full the dining room must be on such a day as this, and how unreasonable it would be to expect his staff to prepare an extra table for a pair of late guests. However, I was quite certain that such a famed establishment would have at least one *salle particulière* in which unscheduled foreign dignitaries could dine and take their ease…?

This sounds disgustingly shallow, translated into English, but I am quite sure that Frances will understand how well it worked in French, when I share the scene with her at tomorrow's recording session.

Whether or not he believed this outrageous lie is immaterial, a sovereign – already worth more than its face value in the *souk*, now that wartime paper scrip was rapidly replacing honest gold and discredited Turkish banknotes - secured us a curtained alcove off to one side of the main dining room, and the undivided attention of two servants.

While Abdul One and Abdul Two were preparing our table, I went back to the lavatory and found Pat in somewhat better shape than before. "Come on mate. Time to wash and brush up."

"Why?" he blinked.

"It's Christmas Day and I haven't had a decent feed in months. We're about to put that right –"

"Whoa." Alert now, his raised hand stopped me mid-sentence. "Most of my pay goes home to Dulcie; I've got to be careful."

"No worries," I grinned. "I drew *Kingsburgh* at 20-1 in the Melbourne Cup sweepstake." Untrue but honour was satisfied so far as Pat was concerned. "You and she fixed last Christmas' dinner; this one's on me. Come along, best foot forward."

We must have been a strange sight, a pair of oddly matched Australian troops strolling through a dining room packed with prosperous civilians and senior British Army officers. A full colonel gave me his frostiest glare as I brushed past, quite upset that two servants had been diverted from their other duties to escort Pat and myself to our private dining area.

Never were ten guineas blown to greater effect. We toasted the Chief in vintage champagne, tearfully reminisced about our other mates, and tried to recall campfire yarns from a world that was already fading into myth and legend. Meanwhile, Shepheard's *table d'hôte* lived up to its international reputation for excellence and we partook of everything before concluding with cigars and cognac. The only hiccup was when Pat tried to lead everybody - brass hats and millionaires alike - through *Good King Wenceslas* but fortunately Abdul Two was on hand to help me get him back under cover.

We were both merrily tight, myself rather less so, as Pat had already been hitting the grog before I arrived. Therefore, as the most clearheaded of the two, I arranged for a discreet exit, after settling the bill and lavishly tipping the Abduls.

Like all good *salles particulières* this one had a private doorway so that Egypt's merchant kings could dally with their concubines without anyone else being any the wiser. I steered Pat out through it and down a long corridor to a discreet courtyard where our *gharry* waited at the kerb. "*Maadi! B'sret al'an!*"

"*Nem effendi!*" The cabby flourished his whip and off we set at a brisk trot towards Cairo's leafy outer suburbs.

The fresh air soon revived Pat who insisted on showing our driver how to hold the reins and steer his bony nag, at speed, through Cairo's chaotic traffic. How we survived the journey I shall never know. The driver, a diminutive soul with an ingrained stare of despair on his grimy little face, stopped pushing against a six feet two inches Light Horseman and resigned himself to Allah's mercy, offering only the occasional, timid direction.

Eventually, by some miracle we reached Maadi, described by homesick Englishmen as "Surrey with Sunshine" although it was more like an Indian Raj cantonment with imported bungalow architecture, transplanted shade trees, and manicured lawns for English expatriates. The contrast between the cavalry's quarters amidst such splendid surroundings, and our shabby tents on the gravel plain at Mena, was evidence that the army's mounted gentlemen still regarded themselves a sabre cut or two above we peasants who fought on foot.

The cabby helped me unload Pat a short distance from the guardroom, out of sight while he tidied himself up, after which he shoved a fistful of disasters into our driver's open palm and strode away with barely a wobble.

"*Madha turid effendi…?*"

"*Mena.*"

"*Nem effendi!*"

I let him get on with the job while reclining on grubby, threadbare cushions, staring sideways with marked indifference. Cairo's charm had long since faded, assuming it ever had any. I was not thrilled by the prospect of fighting a war in this rancid armpit of the Middle East as I paid-off the gharry and marched into camp along the afternoon's lengthening shadows.

1915

65

1915 began with a bang, two hours after sappers of the Royal Engineers stealthily clambered up the Great Pyramid on New Year's Eve, guided by the light of a full moon, or else they would most likely have broken their necks. Then loaded a signal rocket on the apex platform, four hundred and fifty feet above ground level, lit a slow fuze and were back in camp by midnight, when their prank whooshed high above Mena and detonated with a thunderclap that had the rest of us scrambling for our weapons, ready to do battle with the Turks.

It was four months premature and much else was to happen before our wishes were granted. During the first three of those months, we trained hard for war on the Western Front, especially after the rest of 4 Brigade arrived early in January aboard the Second AIF convoy to leave Australia.

From now onwards the tempo quickened, urged along by Brigadier General Monash, David's honorary Uncle John and Aunt Lucinda's piano partner in a civilian life that already belonged to a bygone era. In those days he had been a prosperous businessman, lawyer, and civil engineer; a pioneer of reinforced concrete and a respected figure in Melburnian Society, despite Old Money's cool disapproval of his pushy self-promotion.

Being a Jew did not help in our sternly Presbyterian town, but now that he wore the crossed sword and baton "nail scissors" insignia of high military rank, his relentless determination to get-ahead became the driving force that would eventually make 4 Brigade the gold standard by which all other AIF units were measured and found wanting.

My first experience of this new doctrine was a TEWT - Tactical Exercise Without Troops – when we MG specialists marched to a recently built sandbox, under an improvised awning, where the Brigade Machine Gun Officer directed imaginary fire against miniature enemy positions until our response was as automatic as our weapons.

At the other end of the scale, senior officers like Colonel Pope were drilled in battalion manoeuvres under every condition likely to be encountered in France, including imaginary snowstorms, and pelting rain, umpired by a commander who had overseen the construction of roads and railway viaducts across the Victorian Alps, in all weathers, overcoming every obstacle that stood in his way.

General Monash won his earliest battles on the unforgiving terrain of boardrooms and budgets, time sheets and hired labour, and as I later learned, saw his military appointments – starting with 4 Brigade and culminating with command of the Australian Army Corps - as engineering projects of which he was the site manager, coordinating everyone and everything on the master plan.

Still in Egypt, another innovation was the extended compass march, by night as well as by day, for companies led by their captain; then at platoon-level, led by a lieutenant; and finally, at section-level, led by NCOs who were expected to step up to the crease once the officers were bowled out by enemy fire. In practice, privates were also required to take command and lead whoever was left of their mates.

The purpose of all this sweat and toil was finally revealed at Heliopolis aerodrome when we paraded for the Commander in Chief who, to a chorus of cheers, assured us that we were fit and ready for service in France. Sir George Reid, a roly-poly senior Australian politician now based in London, followed up with a pompous bellow of platitudes that matched his top hat, frock coat, pinstripe trousers, and white spats cruelly cartooned in my next letter home.

Meanwhile, unless we were out on yet another training scheme amidst sand dunes that doubled as snowdrifts, and swarms of yellow locusts that served as mock blizzards, Abdul the News kept delivering our morning papers, I kept teaching him to read headlines in English, and these kept us abreast of whatever the Official Censor wanted us to believe.

For instance: "Royal Navy Attacks Turks!" and its sub-paragraphs describing the bombardment of some decrepit forts on the Gallipoli Peninsula – inevitably nicknamed "Galloping Polly" – artfully glossed over the three Allied battleships sunk during their latest futile attempt to force the narrow straits between Europe and Asia.

None of us imagined how profoundly such news would shape and, for many, end our lives. At the time of which I shall briefly speak to Frances, there was no way that we simple, trusting soldiers could have known the whys and wherefores of our political masters.

Britain's covert strategy to control the Middle East's oilfields, now that the Royal Navy was phasing out its coal-burning battleships and replacing them with oil-fired dreadnaughts, would only be grudgingly revealed long after one war ended and the next one was about to begin.

I shall not dwell long upon the Dardanelles Campaign. If she wishes to learn more, there are numerous books and articles on the subject, and I see no point adding my penn'orth of fuel to that funeral pyre of empire. Even at this distance the memories are too raw, which is strange for I've come to terms with my experiences of the Second World War and can even look back on some with nostalgia, but never on our landing at Anzac Cove.

It infuriates me to hear politicians bleating stale platitudes about "Noble Sacrifice" whenever the nation pauses to celebrate Anzac Day. True, this now encompasses every other Australian war since 1915, but for the dwindling few who can still recall that ill-fated campaign, April 25th should be the occasion when cold, clear, analytical lessons are reviewed to ensure the same mistakes never happen again. And by that I do not mean feeble whines about the "futility of war" but, rather, a sober recognition that if one must fight - having exhausted all honourable alternatives - then it must be ruthlessly fought and won as if General Monash and his staff were still in command.

Sadly, that was never on the cards after London handed General Sir Ian Hamilton its poisoned chalice of a plan to invade Turkey in thirty days' time, after the Royal Navy's bombardments had given the Turks and their German allies five months' notice of an impending attack.

None of this was apparent to us at Mena Camp during that eerily quiet March of 1915. I only learned the details much later, interviewing Sir Ian himself, an urbane, cultivated, likeable man who had no more hope of success than we did. What he told me would indeed have made the Sphinx weep.

For instance, maps are basic equipment on the most elementary army exercise, let alone a frontal attack on the Ottoman Empire, but the only ones that the Mediterranean Expeditionary Force had to work with were some Admiralty charts and a French survey made for the Crimean War, in 1853. To make good this deficiency, a junior staff officer was sent around Cairo's bookshops with a bag of money and orders to buy up every available copy of Murray's *Travellers in Constantinople, Bosphorus, Dardanelles, Brousa & Plain of Troy*.

Allegedly this was his second attempt. The first shopping trip is said to have netted a box of misprinted *Baedecker's Guides* which, when opened, contained maps of the Rhine Valley. I am very sceptical, knowing a bit about editing and publication, but even if untrue it illustrates the shambolic state of MEF's planning and organisation.

Meanwhile, *Taskilat Masusa*'s agents, deeply embedded at every level of Egyptian society, made it inevitable that Turkish Military Intelligence knew of Britain's need for these guidebooks within minutes of their purchase. This guaranteed that its Station Chief in Cairo would courier his report to Constantinople shortly thereafter. As for the correct maps, when eventually found, they were fifty years old and planimetric rather than topographic. According to them, the Gallipoli Peninsula was dead flat from shore to shore.

I feel nothing but pity for our Military Intelligence. They were handed an impossible brief and given one month to achieve what, for the next war's Normandy Landings, took well over a year and an incalculable number of man-hours to set in motion and, even then, it came perilously close to failure.

I feel less charitable about the arrogant fools who wrote and issued our ridiculous orders in London. The political head of the Royal Navy at the time was Winston Churchill, an ex-cavalry subaltern, so if one were to seek the worm in the rotten apple that was the Dardanelles Campaign, one need look no further than this man's impulsive character and previous employment before entering politics.

When I speak of it to Frances, I shall begin by confessing a personal bias, never having warmed to the fellow during those occasions when our paths crossed during his years in the political wilderness. These meetings usually took place at country house-parties where, out of courtesy to my host or hostess, I was careful to edit any mention of Gallipoli whenever he quizzed me about my war service.

I could not forget that it was he who ordered the seizure of two neutral Turkish battleships under construction at Vickers-Armstrong's Tyneside yards, largely paid for by penny subscriptions from patriotic Turkish schoolchildren, kerbside collection boxes, and peasant women selling their hair to Parisian wigmakers.

How this insane act of piracy played into the hands of the Sultan's pro-German ministers, after the Kaiser donated two battlecruisers as replacements, is best left to the verdict of history. I can only say that it required superhuman self-control not to head-butt Churchill's pink, puggy face on behalf of eight thousand Australians buried in Gallipoli's gullies and ravines.

I shall put it to Frances that training horsemen for the cut and thrust of mounted combat does not qualify anyone to direct a ponderous fleet in the Eastern Mediterranean, 3,500 miles away from Whitehall, if only because dreadnaughts and cruisers fail to respond as quickly as a horse to the prick of its rider's spur.

Anyone with any understanding of human nature can easily envisage how an impatient, impetuous young man - as Churchill was at the time – overrode his cautious advisors and galloped ahead of prudent naval officers trained to think of nautical miles steamed per ton of fuel, or the adverse effects of bad weather on maritime strategy, or the impact a single torpedo might have on the British Empire's precarious balance of power in the Middle East.

Although, with the wisdom of hindsight and the rueful realisation that I was also once an impatient, impetuous young man who would most likely have behaved in much the same manner – given the same opportunities – ought not the senior politicians who appointed him to the Admiralty, shoulder the blame for their tragic misjudgement?

Sadly, I shall not live to learn her reply, though it would be interesting to know what a professional historian makes of my introduction to the pride, pomp, and circumstance of inglorious war.

66

As thought precedes action, so rumours precede orders, and both were wildly circulating around Mena Camp in late-March. Something big was brewing but not even the sergeants' bush telegraph knew its precise details, a golden opportunity for the AIF's bookies to hedge thousands of pounds on France as our next destination, or Britain, or Turkey, an obvious trifecta for the serious punter of whom there were many.

In retrospect it should have been obvious where we were going but not at that time or in that place, given that even those few who had paid attention to their geography lessons, at school, would have been hard pressed to find Turkey on a blank map of the world.

It was indicative of GHQ's porous security that what we imagined was a top level, hush-hush operation, was in fact common gossip on Cairo's streets, as we discovered after winning a 24-hour pass for acing all other machine gunners at an inter-battalion speed and accuracy trial.

Harry wanted us to take a felucca trip up the Nile to Karnak, to see the monuments he was reading about, until I proved just how far it was by showing him the illustrated tourist brochure I was copying from to decorate my sixpenny postcards.

In the end we compromised by taking the tram into town and hopping off at our usual stop, near the Egyptian Museum's distinctive, two storey, ochre red building where Percy Black was determined to resume his search for proof that he was right about the Great Pyramid's construction; "There's got to be a blueprint in here somewhere -!"

Harry Murray was equally determined to continue his inspection of the larger-than-life statue of Thutmose III, carved in rose granite as highly polished as a rifle bore, while wondering how they did it with only copper chisels.

All I wanted to do was tuck into a bowl of ice cream at Groppi's on Soliman Pasha Street, not far from the Museum. However, to oblige the other two I curbed my impatience by strolling around dusty halls and alcoves, translating their badly lit, poorly presented labels on displays of pottery and stoneware, scarabs, and oil jars, and of course the obligatory unwrapped mummy for tourists to gawk at.

The recent outbreak of war had not discouraged a conducted tour of middle-aged, moderately rich, and still neutral American couples jostling past me to gather around an opened coffin where their guide put on an entertaining display of ignorance by announcing: "We are now in the presence of Queen Cleopatra -!"

The poor devil was doing his best to feed a family and I saw no point drawing attention to the mummy's label that read: *Une Princesse de la Dynastie IV, ca 2,600 á 2,400 avant J.C.* His clients had paid good money and come a long way to be amazed and excited, none of whom would have thanked an Australian soldier for spoiling their fun.

One couple was doing that without any help from me or anyone else. His name was Myron, hers I think was Louella, and they owned a furniture factory and a big new house in Cleveland, Ohio, which she was pining to see again. "F'Goshsakes, My'ron, I am so through with your morbid 'culture!' I want no more of it -!"

One could only sympathise with her plight. I was also from a new country of clean skies, and vivid colours, and found Ancient Egypt's grubby browns and dull polychromes no more appealing than Modern Egypt's teeming beggars and scheming shopkeepers. I was also in accord with her distaste of death on display, like a freak show's two-headed calf.

Moments later the group hurried off to see "Mark Anthony's sword!" leaving me alone with the anonymous princess. A quick sum on the back of my sketch pad placed her time of death at about four and a half thousand years ago, or roughly the age of Cuckoo's pyramid if Harry had his dates right.

"Pardonner leur ignorance, Votre Altesse..." For some reason I felt it my duty to apologise aloud, in her label's language, for others' crass behaviour.

This dried up bundle of bones and parchment skin had once been a young woman of high rank, perhaps even a daughter of Khufu himself, and I felt it was disrespectful - as well as distasteful - for ignorant strangers to giggle at her shrivelled body.

Years later, on my way back from Afghanistan, I was befriended by Max Mallowan at the Babylonian site that he and his team were excavating for the British Museum. Over dinner in his tent, I felt sufficiently at ease to remark that I had once spoken - in French - to an unknown princess of the Fourth Dynasty and had seen her thoughts projected as living pictures, inside my head.

Max's wife intuitively understood what I was inexpertly trying to say and would not let the matter drop. "What did she show you Ian...?"

"Well, it was almost kinematic," I replied with an embarrassed laugh. "In colour too. Not as dusty brown 'Death Cult' exhibits but as lush fields and golden crops along the bountiful Nile. As abundant game, and fish, and birds. As sunny days and balmy nights. As cheerful music on flute and harp, and merry songs. As beer and wine, bread, and honey cakes. And in that moment, I glimpsed how sweet life must have been in Ancient Egypt. And why my unknown princess could not bear to leave it behind. And why she believed that, by preserving her body, she would be able to relive its joys and pleasures forever, in the Afterlife..."

Max nodded understandingly as Agatha leaned forward to pat my wrist and advise me to write down such a poetic passage. I did not, of course, but I am pretty sure she did, for there are echoes of it in her novel *Death on the Nile*.

Percy Black finally gave up looking for the Great Pyramid's blueprints; Harry Murray was no nearer discovering how a pre-industrial civilization could shape one of the planet's hardest rocks, using one of its softest metals; and both agreed with me that it was high time we tucked into generous serves of Groppi's famous ice cream. The manager recognised us from previous visits and shared a sad smile as we took our accustomed table against a riot of richly decorated Oriental tilework that doubled as a wall. "I sorry we no see you more."

"Eh?" Percy frowned. "You're banning us?" This was quite possible, given the rowdy behaviour of other AIF troops, far from home and off the leash of a wife or sweetheart.

"No, no, no! You good Ozzies!" Mr Demitrios insisted. "But soon you in Constantinopolis! I have cousins, will look after you!"

"Whoa!" Percy could have been calming a frisky colt. "How d'you know where we're going? Even we don't!"

"No, no, no! Everybody know you must soon be at the Hellespont," I noted the Classical Greek name for the narrow channel that the Franco-British navies had failed to force thus far, "then Bosphorus, then Byzantium..."

"You're dead wrong mate!" Harry chuckled. "Everybody knows we're going to beat the Kaiser in France."

"No, no, no." The manager wagged a reproving finger. "I know is *Tourkiye*. Everybody know is *Tourkiye!*"

"Steady on -!" Percy re-joined the conversation. "How d'you know we're going to Turkey?"

"A high officer was talking of it to his lady," Mr Demitrios explained. "A colonel so must be true!" At which point he summoned a waiter to take our orders and hurried off to welcome some well-to-do travellers who, by the appearance of them, were Italian businessmen keen to sample the Egyptian version of their own nation's favourite refreshment.

"He's got that wrong," Harry insisted, elbows on table, drawing us into a conspiratorial huddle. "I've been reading about how the Secret Service spreads furphies like this so's Germany switches its army away from France. And once they've done that, we'll land the knockout punch when and where they're least expecting. It's called 'strategy.'"

"So, you reckon this 'everybody knows' is just a load o' bulldust?" Percy sounded far from convinced.

"Of course! Bloody hell, if it was real, and the Turks knew we were coming, there'd be no surprise, and that's the other thing plans need if they're going to work, surprise!"

Percy was still not persuaded: "What d'you reckon Icy?"

"Don't know," I replied, hesitantly, "but it makes a kind of sense. I mean, what the colonel cove was doing must've been part of a bigger plan to deceive the enemy." Then, as my imagination warmed to the story: "that woman was probably a German spy sent to seduce him, but I'll bet he'd got her measure! It's called the Double-Cross..."

I blush to recall such credulity. My only excuse is that like countless thousands of other young readers of William Le Queux's espionage novels, I had acquired an exaggerated respect for the British Secret Service's omnipotence and cunning. It was only after the Great War, and by now a small part of it myself, that I discovered just how underhand, undermanned, underfunded MI6 really was during those inter-war years of Pacifism and faith in a whimpering League of Nations.

Percy might have persisted with his line of questioning, but the waiter was hovering around, waiting to deliver three bowls of vanilla ice cream sprinkled with crushed green pistachio nuts.

We took our time savouring velvety mouthfuls of bliss before topping off with two cups of tea, one black coffee, and a selection of the *baklava* and *kanefeh* sweets for which Groppi's was renowned. Coincidentally or on purpose, I'm not sure which, the building itself was shaped and decorated rather like a large wedge of wedding cake at the intersection of two streets.

Replete and relaxed, we split the bill, settled our account, and strolled out into the afternoon's fetid heat. This was the cue for waiting *gharri* drivers to lash each other with their whips as they competed for the custom of three wealthy *Ustrali*. The losers backed off, spitting, and croaking as we hopped aboard the victor's rickety cab. I jabbed his shoulder. "*Khdna 'iilaa yimka!*" This last word was my phonetic version of "YMCA."

"Nem effendi!" he grinned in gap-toothed triumph, translating Young Men's Christian Association as code for European pederasty. Determined to earn a fat commission by supplying three rich Australian soldiers to a male brothel, he walloped his nag and off we went,

I surmised this somewhat later, in the meantime happy to loll on his soiled cushions as we jingled towards al-Azbakeya before taking a sudden turn to the left. "Oy! Wrong way!" I jabbed him again.

"Yiss!"

"Wrong fucking way!" Percy chimed in.

"Yiss!" the driver grinned over one shoulder, whipping his horse to a quicker shamble.

"Turn this shit cart around!" Harry added, grabbing the reins.

Too late. We had entered the maw of Haret El Wasser, Cairo's infamous red-light district, and were heading deeper into its bowels where the stench of overflowing gutters and moral corruption was even worse than in the adjacent downtown area. Shamefully we were not the only AIF in the area as our driver lurched to a halt at a garishly painted shopfront and leered at us. "Nyce boi! Cheep boi!"

"Listen good Piss Brains!" Harry snatched the whip and began using it, firstly on the bordello's pimp who had rushed out to drag us inside, then on the bony rump of the *gharri*'s nag. "Get us to the 'Y' or else I'll chuck you over the side and do the job m'self!"

"Yiss, yiss! Boi, boi!"

"Uskut!" My earlier feelings of contentment vanished as I added a newly learned curse: *"Ibn homaar!"* Effectively telling this loathsome offspring of a donkey to shut up!

In hindsight I am glad we saw the "Wozza" when we did. A few days later, on Good Friday, three thousand Australians, New Zealanders, and Tommies burnt it to the ground as their parting gift before going to war.

The cabby persisted in exposing us to further perversions as we threaded through side alleys until finally arriving at al-Gormhoreya where we paid him the basic fare, showed our leave passes to a couple of glowering British MPs stationed at the door, and entered a YMCA that felt like Paradise after our brief excursion through Hell.

The Chaplain had a good memory for faces and recognised us at once when we signed-in for the night by booking three cubicles, plus the full service of showers and dry-cleaned uniforms. "How's it going lads?"

"Ah, pretty good, all things considered," Percy replied suspiciously, always on guard against Soul Catchers, being only one generation removed from Ulster and its dour religion.

"Well, be assured we shall be praying for you and your brave comrades…"

"Uh?" I blinked.

"It is a noble mission you are embarking upon," he continued with an earnest frown. "Yours is the New Crusade that will overthrow the Turk and, in God's good time, liberate the Holy Land."

Percy stiffened. "What?"

"But first Constantinople must be freed and Christ's rule restored by cleansing the Hagia Sophia of its abominable Mohammedan presence –"

"Says who?!"

"Why, it's common knowledge," the God Guesser shared a knowing smile, "but the Lord will protect you." He then made the sign of the Cross and strolled off to console some other blokes who were placing sly bets on a brisk game of ping-pong in the nearby recreation room.

"I need a beer." Harry led the way half a block up the street to the Soldiers' Recreation Club where they had a wet canteen, and we could see what fresh attractions were on the pin-up board. His pick was the American Cosmograph Theatre where they were screening educational travel shorts and the latest Chaplin comedy, which instantly turned me off, while Percy seemed to have lost his appetite for further adventures and opted to play a friendly frame on a vacant snooker table, instead.

We chalked our cues, he won the draw and crouched, pipe jutting from the corner of his mouth, breaking the triangle of red balls with a well-aimed shot. I could have pocketed at least two but held back to match my friend's pace. He was not fooled and gave me a penetrating look. "You're a shrewd young cove. Where'd you learn?"

"There's a table at my aunt's place," I replied, sighting my cue.

"Not at home?"

"It is home." I sank a tricky red.

"Ah..."

"Long story short, Mum and Dad drowned when the Manly Ferry capsized," I lied with a shrug of weary resignation. "Aunt Lucy took me in." I then potted the yellow ball.

"No brothers or sisters?"

"Nope."

"Lucky bugger," he grimaced. "Our place swarmed with 'em; I couldn't get away quick enough."

He probably intended to say more but the Rec's manager was heading our way, beaming with reassurance. "Good luck lads!" He shook our hands. "You show them Turks what's what! We'll be thinking o' you."

"Uh, thanks."

Percy's breath escaped in a low, slow whistle as the chirpy little chap bustled off to encourage someone else. "And I'm thinking Harry had better be right about the Secret Service..."

67

Abdul the News got quite emotional when we pooled our loose change in a khaki handkerchief, knotted the corners together, and presented it to him, together with a portrait sketch and inked thumbprint attached to a letter recommending his services To Whom It May Concern.

The following day, after striking our tents and loading the GS wagons, 4 Brigade marched off, its segmented columns of troops snaking across town in one final show of strength, towards Cairo's main railway station. Here the assembled steam engines gasped and wheezed while harassed Army Transport Officers, strode up and down the platforms, clip boards tucked under red and green ATO armbands, allocating men and equipment to carriages and open wagons with letters and numbers chalked on their sides.

The Service Corps got it right this time and issued us with ration packs of tinned sardines and doughy slabs of Egyptian bread, though by now we were sufficiently experienced travellers to stock-up beforehand with plenty of dried fruit and biscuits. Those were generally too sweet for me, so I went for pistachio nuts and *bastima*, a local beef jerky that reminded me of the 'roo biltong that George Smith used to make for on-the-track snacks.

We machine gunners were parked aboard a goods van, alongside a pair of surly MPs armed with service revolvers, standing guard over the brigade's ironbound pay chest. Their attitude was understandable, Military Police are nobody's friends and, as rear-echelon wallopers, felt awkward in our company. We pretended they didn't exist, made ourselves as comfortable as conditions allowed, and watched the world go by. So far as I was concerned, Egypt had lost any allure it might once have had, and I was not in the least sad to be quit of the horrible place.

"What d'you reckon France will be like, this time of year?" Harry remained firmly convinced that the Kaiser had been hoodwinked into moving his forces eastward into Asia Minor.

"You'll find out soon enough, if we ever get there." Percy was equally convinced that he was wrong.

I'm not sure what my feelings were. Probably the numb indifference of every soldier who has awoken to the truth that he is just a numbered name with as much control over his destiny as a dead leaf has on a mountain rivulet.

Our train shuffled into Alexandria after nightfall and panted to a halt on a floodlit quay alongside a captured German freighter pressed into service as a makeshift troop transport and now the focus of much orchestrated confusion - if one can allow such a phrase - as stores, and wagons, and field kitchens were winched aboard and stowed below. This left we new arrivals to fend for ourselves until roll call the next morning, by which time the MPs had further reason to organise manhunts throughout the nearby brothels and shebeens.

Matters did not improve when most of us eventually got-fell-in on the quayside to answer our named numbers before trudging up the gangplanks and dispersing to chalked areas on the ship's filthy decks.

Of the voyage itself, the less said the better, except to note that its washing, cooking, and messing arrangements were unspeakably bad; God only knows what cargo the Germans were carrying aboard this miserable tub until a few months ago, for there was not a square inch that did not crawl with vermin.

Once safely out at sea with the rest of the convoy, and now with no chance of loose talk informing the enemy of our plans – as if they didn't already know! - we were officially informed that our destination was Lemnos, a small island about sixty miles from the Gallipoli Peninsula.

I must be careful when speaking of these days to Frances. My language can become extremely coarse whenever I try describing what we were about to attempt in late-April 1915. As for maintaining secrecy and surprise, any half-alert Turkish lookout with a telescope on Sari Bair's peaks along the peninsula's western coastline, could have logged every ship inbound for Lemnos on a reasonably clear day.

I have spent a lifetime trying to make sense of this campaign, but even at its very beginning, thanks to Aunt Lucinda's frequent discourses upon history and geography as lived by one shrewd old lady, it was obvious that London and Paris had given Constantinople sufficient warning to prepare the defences of Islam's heartland, over which the Sultan ruled as Allah's Shadow on Earth and Commander of the Faithful.

The Y's chaplain had called us modern crusaders, a figure of speech for him but not for an enemy who had declared our invasion a *Jihad* or Holy War, with its promise of Eternal Bliss for those Faithful who died fighting the Infidel Crusaders. In other words, we poor deluded chumps.

I doubt if this signified anything in London, where some buffoon wrote a leaflet telling us how spineless the Sultan's troops were after they were repulsed during a recent raid on the Suez Canal. One passage sticks in my mind:

> Turkish soldiers, as a rule, manifest their desire
> to surrender by holding their rifle butts upwards
> and waving these or rags of any colour. An actual
> white flag must be regarded with the utmost
> suspicion as a Turk is unlikely to have access to
> a garment that clean.

If it is true that "Every victory is won before it is fought," as the Chinese general Sun Tzu wrote when emphasising the need for meticulous planning on campaign, then it's corollary is equally true: "Every defeat is decided before battle begins."

As an example of such ageless wisdom, one needs only to read the overweening arrogance on display in London's ridiculous little leaflet. This, I firmly believe, goes straight to the heart of our failure at Gallipoli, a disaster matched by the Turks' other crushing victory, at Kut al Amara, south of Baghdad.

The only good thing I can remember of that ghastly voyage across Homer's Wine Dark Sea – as Harry kept reminding me - was cashing the betting slip written by a battalion bookie with whom I had fluttered a quid on Turkey, at a time when France was still our dead cert' destination.

Not that I had any special inside knowledge, but I have generally found that it pays to spread one's bets whenever punters are certain of a result, because Lord Luck is a notorious trickster.

These two pounds, plus the earnings from my postcards, meant I was quite well-off after the last pay parade many of us would ever attend, a few hours before we landed on Lemnos. I was not the only man left scratching his head at being paid in the enemy's currency, upon receiving a fistful of ornately decorated Ottoman banknotes that looked for all the world like miniature prints of Persian carpets.

Apparently, the islanders had only been Greek for a couple of years, following the Royal Hellenic Navy's victory at the Battle of Lemnos, and many still preferred their familiar Turkish money, another detail I viewed as a vote of no-confidence in our immediate future.

The Australian & New Zealand Army Corps commander, General Birdwood, clearly believed the Turks would soon be waving their rifle butts when he told us: "The reason you were all paid in Turkish currency is so that once you have won the battle of the beaches, and are on your way to Constantinople, this money will give you something to live off. But there must be no haggling in the villages you pass through, as all prices will be fixed by the Commissariat."

Seventy-odd years later, I still believe that one could search the entire history of warfare and not find a more glaring example of misplaced optimism than Birdie's blithe self-confidence.

There was an alternative possibility, one I shall take to the grave along with many another secret, for even if it could be proved, what good would be done by revealing it now? In essence, a senior officer in the Pay Corps must've cut a deal with an equally corrupt official at *La Banque d'Ègypte*.

Turkish *piastres* were being withdrawn from circulation, after the Khedive's overthrow, and nothing would've been easier than to fake the destruction of now-worthless paper money before exchanging it - under the table - for an agreed sum per bundle. All that then had to be done, to realise a handsome profit in pounds sterling, was confect a story that would allow the troops to be paid with this rubbish shortly before we went into action where many were bound be killed, or too traumatised to understand the swindle played upon us.

Of more immediate concern, however, was the limited issue of 0.303 Ball ammunition and the insufficient number if pressed steel, five-round charger clips needed to reload rifles in the heat of battle. Fortunately, this did not directly affect machine gunners as we got used to wearing holstered Webley revolvers, with all our other clobber.

Not that we were home and dry, for there was still a critical shortage of the fabric belts that fed the Vickers, and I did not relish the prospect of fumbling about with loose cartridges, tied-up in brown paper packets of ten rounds apiece, loading the belts by hand while being shot at and shelled.

68

Our convoy passed through Lemnos' outer boom defence and, one-by-one anchored off Mudros, the island's only town of any consequence, shortly after sunrise the following day.

The harbour itself reminded me of Aden, though far less arid and forbidding. Indeed, at this time of year - the brief Ægean springtime between stormy winter and scorching summer - it was translucently beautiful. The surrounding hills, misted with heathland flowers, framed a body of sapphire blue water unlike any I had seen thus far. And in the distance, the snowy peaks of Samothrace were aglow as the sun rose from beyond Troy, and Helios drove his blazing chariot overhead, towards the western Underworld from whence he would emerge in the east again, tomorrow morning.

I had more to worry about than Ancient Greek myths, even though Harry insisted on expanding my education as we leaned against the rail and marvelled at the vast armada of British, French, and Russian warships, tramps and colliers, fleet auxiliaries and troop transports, anchored across the roadstead.

There were also pre-war luxury liners, fitted out as hospital ships, last seen at anchor in Alexandria. And HMS *Ark Royal*, the world's first seaplane carrier which, even as we watched, lowered one of its flimsy machines into the water, prior to it taking off on a reconnaissance flight over the Dardanelles.

Though we didn't realise yet, one of the humblest vessels was arguably the most important, an oil tanker converted to freight water from Egypt, without which we could not have survived for more than a few hours on Gallipoli's parched crags. Even at this distance in time it seems paradoxical that all the high hopes and plans of the British Empire hinged upon one unremarkable vessel doing its duty, and those several others that would, in due course, be hauling fresh water from as far afield as Malta and France.

The many and varied units of the largest invasion fleet in history, until D-Day twenty-nine years later, ranged in size from commandeered Thames paddle-steamers to majestic battleships of which at least one had been mauled during the Royal Navy's most recent attempt to force the Straits.

Her hull was badly bashed and one of her funnels leaned over at a drunken angle while naval artificers, with spluttering oxy-acetylene torches, strove to patch her up for another shot at the impossible. For those of us with imagination, the realities of war had just taken a giant stride closer.

A flotilla of barges had been assigned to take us ashore, but to reach them we first had to clamber down slack rope ladders, bumping, and thumping against sheer iron plates. Not easily done when laden with field kit tipping the scales at seventy pounds that, for many, was half their own bodyweight. One poor blighter lost his grip just as the barge eased away, creating a gap of about one yard wide through which he plunged, straight to the bottom of the harbour. A diver recovered his body, next morning, and a new drill was hurriedly devised for the actual invasion, now only a few dozen hours away.

In the meantime, we battered and bruised survivors landed on Lemnos, formed fours, and tramped up the beach under the curious gaze of earlier Allied arrivals. French Zouaves in tight blue coats, baggy pantaloons, and pipeclayed gaiters; British Tommies in Bombay bloomers and pith helmets; Gurkhas in kit much like ours, except their hats were not cocked-up at the side; smartly turbaned Sikhs and Punjabis of the professional Indian Army; Russian marines in blue pea jackets and horizontally striped *telnyaska* shirts; *Evzones* of the island's Greek garrison, clad in tasselled black fezzes, short kilts resembling a ballet dancer's tutu, and hilarious, upturned shoes with pompoms that wiggled as they marched. The Newfoundland Regiment's cod fishermen and lumberjacks had yet to join this motley crew.

We, by contrast, were a drab lot and hungry, not having eaten much since leaving Mena Camp. It took a lot of persuasion to keep us together long enough to claim a straggle of tents before attacking the nearest cookhouse. Its staff's angry threats and anguished pleas were of no avail as we organised a monster brew of hot tea to wash down hunks of bread and jam, fried sausages, and mutton chops liberated from the officers' pantry.

Some optimist called the British MPs to come and deal with men who had just burned down Cairo's bars and brothels, but when the Redcaps arrived and found several hundred famished Australians hacking into their tucker with jack knives and sharpened bayonets, they quickly agreed that their services were required elsewhere. Afterwards, Mr Pope gave us a pro-forma wigging but the twinkle in his eye said he thought otherwise, and thus was born the legend of Digger initiative and "go."

There was no time for sightseeing with Z Hour ticking ever closer. During the past several months we had trained hard for war on the Western Front. Now we had to unlearn everything and replace it with disembarkation from a mother ship, at sea, into boats as varied as steam pinnaces, towed barges, and rowed whalers, of which there were barely enough.

Given everything went according to plan, these would ferry us to the shallows through which we would wade ashore and pile our kit behind a convenient sand dune. Bayonets would then be fixed, a whistle blown, and an unspecified number of Turks would begin waving their grimy undergarments.

We could then take a rest until enough other men and munitions, wagons and mules, horses and field artillery had assembled to begin our victory parade up an unknown, rugged peninsula; along the Sea of Marmora's equally rugged and unknown coastal road; before finally laying siege to the Ottoman Empire's capital city, about one hundred and fifty miles from our landing beaches.

If I were recounting this for Frances instead of reminding myself of its salient points, I would suppress the undignified sarcasm, but nothing will ever suppress the fact that the only men who really knew what the hell they were doing for the next eight months were the Turks, valiantly defending their homeland, to the last man and the last cartridge.

Allied post-war histories have done a splendid job of whitewashing the epic muddle that was Gallipoli, and I applaud their efforts, because until recently there were still too many widows and orphans believing that their menfolk fell as heroes on the field of honour, rather than as soft tissue targets who got in the way of a stray bullet or random shell fragment, ignorant to the last of where, why, and what they were doing.

None of us suspected the bleak truth yet, although some of the older men were slow to share our youthful enthusiasm as we charged a line of quaint windmills, each with multiple arms and triangular sails, near an olive grove behind Mudros; the similarity with Don Quixote's tilt at phantom giants was not lost on me, either.

One benefit of these antics was the chance to spend our Ottoman Bank disasters on fresh eggs and vegetables, bought from the local farmers over whose properties we trampled. Later, in secluded corners and hollows, like the veteran bushmen many of us were, we cooked up this fresh food to counteract the constipating effects that 3B - Biscuits & Bully Beef – were having on our guts, especially in dry weather, with tight water rations. This is another indelicate detail I shall spare Frances, for fear of being thought a nasty old man, although I do feel that historians should realise there is a lot more to fighting a battle than the blowing of bugles and the beating of drums.

Next morning, alerted to the fact that a machine gun team could be crippled by an enemy sniper if his single shot left two survivors doing the work of three, it was decided to adopt the British army's six-man structure by augmenting ours with three semi-trained volunteers. This overdue improvement gave me extra water and ammunition carriers who, at a pinch, could man the gun when the rest of us got knocked out. We shook hands, tried to remember names, and for the purposes of quick identification dubbed them Four, Five, and Six.

The other half of today's training program consisted of learning to scramble in and out of landing boats, over, and over, and over again. This was not popular, but it had to be done quickly, and soon, as we found out the following day.

I think it was the 21st or 22nd of April and the weather had turned foul overnight, with blasts of horizontal sleet ripping down from nearby mountain peaks, still capped with last winter's snow. This was our cue to halt all outdoor training and, instead, crowd into prefabricated huts for pep talks by company and platoon officers under orders to share Brigade HQ's glad tidings of great comfort and joy.

I can no longer recall what I felt or thought at the time. Within a few dozen hours the cocky, confident young fellow who used to be me would be dead. Not in any physical sense, but deep inside where his spontaneity and warmth used to be. I believe it to be a universal truth that anyone who survives even a few hours of combat will never be the same man again. Henceforth he is a stranger to that earlier, better self whenever their paths cross in the dark and echoing hallways of memory.

I would like to be able to assure Frances that I believed in what we were about to do, for it would raise the tone of our one-sided conversation instead of imagining her politely listening to a misanthropic old curmudgeon's recorded voice, but I can't. For no matter how one paints a word-picture of the Dardanelles Campaign, nothing will ever conceal the fact that it was an epic blunder from start to finish.

69

"What d'you reckon, Icy?" Harry was seated on one side of me, Percy on my other, sharing the thick fog of tobacco smoke, sweat, and damp serge as HQ's briefing paused for Any Questions?

Never one to give an opinion without due thought, I peered across several rows of heads and reviewed what the chalkboard had told us thus far, especially its coloured diagram of what looked like a grossly misshapen wet stocking dangling from a clothesline. This was supposed to represent the Gallipoli Peninsula, separated from Asia Minor by the Dardanelles, a dozen square miles of water that had already exacted a fortune in money and men's lives, and was by no means finished with us yet.

The Allied navies had finally realised that millions of pounds worth of battleships could not break through, unaided, and now required we shillings-a-day soldiers to do the job instead. To achieve this, five landings were scheduled within the next few hours, starting at the stocking's heel on the west coast, and working around to its toe on the east side; these were Y Beach, X Beach, W Beach, V Beach, and S Beach, collectively known as Cape Helles. Constantinople, our ultimate objective, was roughly where the neck would be if the stocking were being worn by a very long and unattractive leg.

Concurrent with these attacks, a diversionary raid was about to be launched by the French at Kum Kale, opposite Helles, on the Asiatic side of the Strait, with Anzac Force launching our simultaneous diversion at Z Beach, about twelve miles up the west coast from Y Beach.

"Well?" Harry persisted, as someone in the front row stood to ask the Signals & Intelligence Officer a rambling question that nobody else could follow.

"It's too complicated." I turned to my other friend. "Like you said, on Cuckoo's Pyramid, words can mean whatever you want them to mean, but numbers represent cold hard facts…"

Percy spoke around his briar pipe. "Like?"

"Nothing adds up. It's a dog's breakfast. And even when we've beaten the Turks, down there on the beaches, it'll be a bloody hard slog up the road to Constantinople." I pointed at the Peninsula's rough outline.

A bloke in the second row stood to air much the same thought. Lt Wilton, 16 Battalion's SIO, calmed the murmurs of agreement by reassuring us that the planned attacks were bait to trap the Turkish army into defending these beaches – he rapped the chalkboard with his knuckles - at which point a crescent of battleships stretching from the isle of Imbros to the mouth of the Straits, here and here, would shell them to smithereens, here. Furthermore, Brigade's Signals & Intelligence Officer had told him that one of *Ark Royal's* aeroplanes saw large numbers of enemy troops milling about, probably in the early stages of a panicked withdrawal, just before the weather closed in.

"It will be like when they raided the Canal and ran away," Mr Wilton declared, before informing us that our role, though subsidiary, greatly mattered in the greater scheme of things.

After landing at Gaba Tepe – his knuckles rapped again – we Australians and New Zealanders were going to entrench ourselves on the high ground, here, here, and here, ready to enfilade any Turkish reinforcements who may be heading down the Peninsula, here. Or, more likely, harass those fleeing northward from Cape Helles, here.

The advancing Allies, comprising French Zouaves and Senegalese on the right wing, here; the British 29th Division and field artillery in the centre, here, would then march up the peninsula, neutralising the coastal forts as they went, allowing the navy to pass through the Dardanelles, enter the Sea of Marmora, sink the ramshackle Turkish Navy and shell Constantinople into submission.

Meanwhile, on land, contact would be made with Anzac Force, here, and from then onwards Anzac would be the left wing of a triumphant advance that would occupy the Turkish capital, open the channel for supply convoys to Russia, and end the war. "Any further questions…?"

Percy began to stand but thought better of it as we were dismissed to our lines. Hats pulled down, waterproof groundsheets dragged across shoulders, we squelched off to the Salvation Army's canteen shed where I secured a table near the potbelly stove while my mates bought three mugs of hot sweet tea, thick with condensed milk, a complete meal by itself.

"What were you going to ask him, Perce'?"

He glanced my way. "Your question. How far to Con's Tin Opal and how long before we get there."

"We'll soon find out," Harry chipped in confidently.

"I hope you're right."

"You don't sound sure?"

"I'm not." The oldest of us unlaced his tobacco pouch. "You, and me, and Icy know that when talking of times and distances in the bush. It's double and add half, and if lucky, we're only one hour and a mile out." He finished loading his pipe, struck a match and lit up, lost in thought.

I was feeling lucky now. The mail orderly had earlier delivered a bag of letters and small parcels that had been shunting between Port Suez, and Cairo, and Alexandria, before catching up with us on Lemnos.

One letter, from the Union Bank in Kalgoorlie, showed a good balance plus interest since the last one six months ago; a wrapped copy of *Cue Ball*, the Victorian Billiard & Snooker Guild's quarterly newsletter, might as well be reporting life on Mars, so far removed was its news from my present world; and a Christmas card signed Elspeth MacCracken (Miss) – a pupil at Toorak Primary School, a short distance down the road from Tralee House - informing me that Mrs Fenner had told the class to draw these cards for local men enlisted in the army. Mine was of a kookaburra on a sprig of golden wattle, with a scroll in its beak, wishing me a Happy 1915.

I put her thoughtful little gift inside Princess Mary's brass box and promised myself to reply once I'd attended to other personal mail. David's clear, precise calligraphy was a welcome sight, as always, but I put that envelope aside for the moment and turned my attention to Aunt Lucinda's typewritten letter, proudly demonstrating her new skill:

Tralee House
Grange Road
Melbourne

18th February 1915

Dear Son.

My thoughts are with you and your comrades
whose exploits fill the newspapers here.
I have never been easily fooled and am not
now as what is reported must be a pale
reflection of the dangers you confront.

My own experiences of war are few but the
Siege of Paris and the Communes Terror allow me to understand
what you are at and convince me that Bismarck must be beaten.
Keep this in mind and be strong.

Despite all I believe you were born under a
lucky star and will make your mark in the
world as did I, it being an amazement that I have
played a leading role on lifes crowded stage for as
long as I have.

The news at home is much the same as before tho sad to report Mrs
Harris death. At least she is now at peace with her husband, a man
whose troubled past never evidenced itself in his long years of
service for me. I miss them both, as loyal domestics are not easily
engaged these days.

Arthur Streeton called recently to inform me that he has joined the
Army Medical Corps with Tom Roberts and expects to be sent
abroad soon.
When I protested, they being too old, he replied one must do ones
bit.

My bit is turning Tralee House into a Red Cross
hospital for the sick and wounded arriving at
St Kilda and Dr Levine is directing it for me.

Adieu Dear Son. Your loving aunt who regards
you as the boy she once had but lost to the
croup.

I am not ashamed to confess a lump in the throat; this was the first time she had addressed me so intimately and possibly the last. The wistful, elegiac tone and the lack of her lively exclamation marks were a warning that we were unlikely to meet again in this life.

Seeking a happier distraction, I studied David's envelope for clues, but there were no censors' seals or initials on its flap to indicate it came from a military base, for the stamp was standard British issue and cancelled at a country post office:

Gonville & Caius College
Trinity Street

Cambridge

2ndnd February 1915

My Dear Old Friend.

I am sorry that I have not replied to your letters and
postcards from Egypt but feel ashamed when I compare
what you are doing in the war, and what I am not.

The other chaps in my O.T.U have gone to France and
some have won promotion and distinguished themselves at the Front
while I languish here, awaiting my call to arms.

I cannot prove it, but every instinct tells me that the
College is using undue influence to prevent me doing what I must.
They have even offered a fellowship and pecuniary advantages I do
not need.

I gave your best wishes to M and I told her what a "bonza cobber"
you are, and a machine gunner to boot! She knows how we met at
Melbourne Grammar and delights in such glimpses of a sunny,
carefree land Down Under, so unlike Scotland's grim, granitic
Calvinism. Often, we think what fun it would be to chuck it all and
elope to the Goldfields you so expressively described, there to start
afresh as plain Mr & Mrs Smith.

I adore her in every way but we both know how impossible it would be
for a civilian student to ask her father (the colonel of a Highland
regiment in France,) for his daughter's hand in marriage; for me that
would be one rejection too many.

Unless this resolves itself soon, I am going to return home,
enlist in the Australian Army, win a medal, march up to "The
Laird" with it pinned on my chest and demand his immediate
consent a la Goliath Slayer!

Between ourselves I am fed-up with pretending to be the Perfect
English Gentleman, forever attentive to others' whims, while
being politely snubbed in return by those who are Proper
English – or Scottish – Gentlemen.
Who knows? One day you will be leading your camels across the
Outback to find "Mr & Mrs Smith" camped out, botanising, for
I am sure there must be a myriad of plants awaiting taxonomic
classification &c.

I would like that very much, and so would M, who is equally
fed-up with the way things are, and would gladly chuck all the
vanities of rank to assist with my fieldwork.

Please continue writing and sending your cartoons, even if I am
less forthcoming, as I'm sure you will understand. This has not

been an easy time for me, or for Mary, and we can only cling to
what we share, while awaiting happier days.

   D.

"Good news?" Harry enquired as I returned David's letter to its envelope.

"An old mate's got girl fever," I replied, reaching for my mug of tea.

"He'll get over it."

"That what you've done?" I enquired, setting the mug down, and warming a bruised shoulder nearer the stove.

"Uh."

"'Whut dusna kull yuh, tuffens yuh,'" Percy growled from his corner of the table. Timeless wisdom spat out in the gritty, grating, quarrelsome Ulster accent he'd sought to escape after leaving Victoria to seek his fortune as far away as possible from the Blacks' family home.

70

Next morning's weather could not have been a more welcome change. The contrast between yesterday's driven sleet and today's mild breezes, tinged with the scent of thyme and wild herbs on nearby hillsides, lifted the spirits and made one glad to be alive.

From horizon to horizon, a Winsor & Newton Cerulean Blue southern sky brushed with wispy strands of Seashell White cirrus cloud, flecked here and there with touches Gainsboro Grey shadowing, made me itch for a box of oil colours, an easel, and a large rectangular canvas. Instead, all I had was my pocket sketchbook and a stubby 4B pencil to make the preparatory landscape drawing. With luck I would return to Lemnos, one day, and complete it before going on to depict the Sporades and Thracian Sea's legendary isles through fresh, Australian eyes.

The local men's weathered features were an intriguing mixture of breeds, not surprising given the ebb and flow of invading tribes and nations across the Ægean and across the millennia. Clad in top boots, baggy breeches, sheepskin coats, and astrakhan hats, they could have easily doubled as the Bandits' Chorus from *Maid of the Mountains*.

We glimpsed none of their womenfolk whom history had taught to keep well away from strange soldiers by staying inside solidly built farmhouses, whose narrow doorways and tiny windows were easily barricaded.

Our training, such as it was, was over. There was no point pushing any harder. If we didn't know our stuff by now, we never would. Better to conserve our strength and use the time remaining to get our affairs in order. Mindful of this and much else I went back to the Salvos' canteen, bought three stamped envelopes, three sheets of paper, and found an unoccupied table.

My first letter was to Aunt Lucinda, of course, thanking her for all she had done to transform an orphaned Oliver Twist into a fair copy of Pip, the youthful protagonist in *Great Expectations*. This was a great favourite of ours at Tralee House, and ideal for theatrical games in the conservatory whenever it was too wet to play outside. Her Magwitch, the transported convict and Pip's invisible benefactor, was hair-raising in its realism and showed why the immortal Sarah Bernhardt had chosen *Le Rossignol* to coach her dramatic roles.

My next farewell was to David. I did my best to reassure him that "peace hath her victories no less renowned than war," as someone once told Oliver Cromwell, and that he should be grateful "Keys" wanted him to stay alive. I added a few unsavoury details of army life, sufficient to give him reason to rethink, before concluding that we'd be on Gallipoli by time he read this, and if I got the knock, please keep a kindly eye on my aunt.

My third and final note was to E. MacCracken (Miss), Toorak Primary School, Canterbury Road, Victoria, but first I took her card from my tobacco tin and studied the drawing of a lively kookaburra perched on a sprig of wattle. Its lines were firmly inked, the pastel colours well balanced, she had promise and I rather wished I could help as I had helped the Khan boys, back home in Kalgoorlie.

Instead, I wrote a friendly note of thanks for her kind wishes and assured her that such gestures mean a great deal to soldiers about to go into battle. I then added that if she read my name in the newspaper's list of casualties, would she please go up the road to Tralee House and show Miss Lucinda Cribdon this letter and accompanying picture.

I now needed a mirror. Fortunately, there was one over a washbasin near the door that led out to the latrines. Above it was stencilled, in the Salvation Army's standard-issue Blood & Fire red lettering:

Ye Are Created
In God's Image!
(Genesis 1:27)

I studied my version of the Divine and sketched a reasonable self-portrait without cartoonish quirks, just the sober features of a young man in uniform, Rising Sun badges on his tunic collar, looking straight back at the viewer with a questioning half-smile. I signed and dated it – *Ian Cribdon, Lemnos, April 1915* - before returning outside and trudging uphill through muddy hutments.

A few yards short of the Army Post Office, I saw a padre setting up shop in a nearby hut where he and 11 Battalion's quartermaster, a Perth solicitor in real life, were getting ready to witness last-minute wills revoking those made before we embarked at Fremantle.

I hesitated a moment then went inside to bequeath my savings account and accrued army pay to young Elspeth, with a request that she use it to further her artistic studies. Not a great sum, these days, but at the start of the Great War one hundred and thirty quid was more than many a workman's yearly wages.

When I speak to Frances about this time and place, I shall ask her to imagine the Mediterranean Expeditionary Force as if it were a massive steam locomotive at a railway platform. Its huffs and hisses telling us that all is ready to move, but not until the guard blows his whistle do the connecting rods inch forward, the first actions in a quickening series of reactions that will drive the machine onward.

It's a laboured analogy, and she may not even remember seeing such an engine, but this is the only way I can convey the mood at Mudros that springtime morning, as nineteen thousand men of the British 29th Division – the Old Incomparables - filed aboard their transports. Line after line after line of soldiers heavy with rifle and pack: the last remaining units of Britain's pre-war Regular Army; as doomed to extinction as their comrades – the Kaiser's misnamed Old Contemptibles - had been the previous Autumn, in Belgium and France.

Some estimates put the number of vessels on the waters of Port Mudros at over two hundred, and from memory that seems likely, but during the next day and a half the number dwindled as company after company, battalion after battalion, brigade after brigade formed up and steamed away to their battle stations.

For some, like 29 Division, escorted by the super-dreadnaught HMS *Queen Elizabeth,* this was the isle of Tenedos, within striking distance of Cape Helles. For others, like Anzac Force the following day, it was Imbros, within sight of Gaba Tepe.

Years later, I hosted John Masefield the poet and novelist to a Sunday Roast at Simpson's in the Strand, during which I reminded him of a piece he published about us, in 1916. For a moment I thought I had overstepped the mark, so bereft was the look upon his face. Then he began to declaim, softly, as if to himself alone:

"'On Mudros, in fine weather, a haze of beauty comes upon the hills and water till their loveliness is unearthly, it is so rare. Then the bay is like a blue jewel and the hills lose their savagery, and glow, and all the marvellous ships in the harbour are transfigured.

"'And in the bay are more ships than any port of modern times. The transports, all painted black, lay in tiers, well within the harbour, the grey men of war nearer Mudros. Now in that city of ships, so busy with passing picket-boats and noisy with the labour of men, the getting of anchors begins. And ship after ship, crammed with soldiers, moves slowly out of harbour, into the lovely day, and feels again the heave of the sea.

"'No such gathering of fine ships has ever been seen upon this earth, and the beauty and the exultation of the youth upon them makes them like sacred things as they move away. And the sailors on the other ships cheer and cheer till the harbour rings with cheering. And as each ship crammed with soldiers draws near the battleships, the men swing their caps and cheer again, and the sailors answer, and the noise of cheering swells, and the men in the ships not yet moving join in, and the men ashore, till all the life in the harbour is giving thanks that it can go to death rejoicing.

"'And presently all are out, and the sun goes down with marvellous colour, lighting island after island and the Asian peaks, and those left behind in Mudros trim their lamps knowing they have been for a little brought near to the heart of things...'"

John never set foot on Lemnos or came anywhere near the Dardanelles during the Great War, but the mind's eye of a master poet saw and felt it all in exquisite detail.

Meanwhile, the departure of the 29th Division was the first stroke of that imaginary locomotive's connecting rods. From now onwards there was no going back, no turning aside, nor did any wish to as 16 Battalion paraded for our final rollcall.

Then came the last-minute issue of a combination pick and shovel, with detachable wooden helve, rolled in an empty sandbag, strapped across our knapsacks. Some impulse made me pinch another half dozen bags, instinctive greed at the time but soon to be of vital importance.

We then exchanged our Australian slouch hats for the British Army's peaked trench caps - mine had earflaps buttoned on top, rather like Sherlock Holmes' deerstalker - supposedly to keep our identity secret. Whether or not this was true is irrelevant now. I certainly found the trench cap less liable to blow off in Spring's blustery weather, quite serviceable in Summer when worn with a neck cloth, and comfortable always on my close-cropped scalp, but like our other headgear useless against shrapnel or Mauser bullets. It would be another year before the Brodie "salad bowl" steel helmet was added to our schedule of equipment.

There had been occasional glimpses of Brigadier General Monash during the past few weeks, but only at a distance, usually with an adjutant in tow while they inspected training sites, and he dictated orders. Today he paused long enough to address each battalion in turn, not yet the trim, articulate, commanding figure he would become in France, but still a plump civilian businessman in uniform, striving to strike a martial note with staccato sentences:

"Officers and men. The King wishes you every success in the knowledge that you are constantly in His Majesty's thoughts and prayers. He knows we are undertaking one of the most difficult tasks any soldier can be called upon to perform. Your victory will win imperishable glory for Australia!

"Lord Kitchener lays special stress on this operation, the success of which will be a crippling blow to the enemy. It will not be easy until we have dispossessed the Turk of his positions and secured our own.

"Every effort will be made to bring up transport as often as possible, but the ASC may not be able to get their wagons up to our lines for some while. If this should happen, you must not think that your wants have been neglected.

"You have been issued with three days' rations. Husband them carefully, likewise your water and ammunition. Do not blaze away at shadows! Make every shot count! Good luck!"

Colonel Pope led three cheers and gave the order for HQ Company – followed by A, B, C, and D Companies – to embark aboard *Haida Pascha*, the same verminous tub that brought us from Alexandria.

Number 2 Brigade had already left Port Mudros and was steaming ahead in convoy, to secure 1 Brigade's gains and consolidate the beachhead.

Numbers 3 and 4 Brigades were our designated rear guards, tasked with holding the Turks at bay while Artillery, Transport, Supplies & Support came ashore.

April 25th happened to be Sunday and thus far we had been spared a church parade, but now there was nothing more to do except brood, so those in authority thought it was the right time for the God Guesser to annoy us.

Grumbling, we got-fell-in on the waist deck and waited for our sergeant major to give the order for "Cafflicks-n-Jooz!" to fall out; Nonconformists who were promptly collared to assist the cooks while the rest of us stood-easy and let the Padre's disheartening sermon wash over our heads.

"Well, boys, I know you're going into action today, and that many of you will never see another sunrise, having done your duty! However, take comfort from General Hamilton's stirring words that in conjunction with the navy, you are about to solve a problem that has puzzled many. That you will succeed, none can doubt, and in so doing defeat the Abominable Turk! The whole world is watching your progress! Therefore, be worthy of the great feat of arms entrusted to you -!"

"Balls," Percy muttered alongside me.

"Amen," Harry replied, which was as close as we three got to a religious experience that day.

I said nothing. The Devil Driver's morbid musings were less of a worry than our shortage of prepared ammunition belts. More than seven minutes of sustained fire and we'd be reloading them by hand. I had already discussed this with my opposite number on 16 Battalion's other machine gun crew and had agreed to pool our manpower and resources once entrenched among the dunes of Gaba Tepe's gently sloping beach.

"- God's infinite blessings be with you boys!"

Spiritually refreshed we lined up with mess tins for beef and vegetables boiled in a slop of gravy powder, plus two ships' biscuits the consistency of roofing tiles. I ate my share readily enough, but other men were less keen, nervously puking over the rails or crowding the ship's heads as the thunder of battle grew ever louder and nearer.

The super-dreadnaught HMS *Queen Elizabeth* beat the big bass drum in a Bedlamite band of bangs and crumps every time her fifteen-inch guns punched a salvo of one-ton shells through a gigantic belch of dirty brown smoke. Impressive and seemingly invincible, but such ordnance requires only a moderate elevation to sink another battleship on the same horizontal plane and is therefore useless for shore bombardments that need plunging fire, to penetrate underground bunkers and smash trenches.

Inevitably, many of the battleships' shells roared straight over their targets, like monstrous express trains, and some probably splashed into the Dardanelles on the far side of the peninsula. What we needed now, more than anything else were monitors, or shipborne howitzers, able to lob high explosives up, over, and down onto the enemy, from directly above.

When I speak to Frances at our next recording session, I shall give only a thumbnail sketch of these days, starting from when *Haida Pascha* anchored in Port Mudros until our escort, HMS *Ribble*, laid alongside, off the landing beaches, waiting for eight hundred riflemen to clamber down onto her deck, line up at their chalk marks and wait for the destroyer's crew to haul in a string of lifeboats, whalers, and lighters onto which fifty troops apiece climbed, stumbled, and fell. We machine gunners had the Devil's own job getting our unwieldy weapons and kit aboard a barge laden with ammunition, water, and supplementary stores.

A steam pinnace hitched up, tooted its little tin whistle, and began gamely towing these clumsy craft against the same uncharted current that had, in today's pre-dawn murk, landed the first wave of troops on the wrong beach.

Now, instead of Gaba Tepe's relatively easy hinterland, Anzac Force was committed to breaking out from a nameless cove enclosed by sandstone cliffs a mile or so farther north, atop of which the Turks were furiously digging in, determined to defend to the death their Faith and their homeland against we latter-day Christian Crusaders.

The Allies' triumphant march up the Gallipoli Peninsula stumbled and fell at the first obstacle and, despite our best efforts, never got up again during the next eight months of bitter fighting against a courageous and righteously fanatical adversary.

71

In the years that followed, increasingly younger Australians would ask me what Gallipoli was "really like" whenever the nation paused to commemorate the anniversary of our landing at Anzac Cove. I would pretend to misunderstand their question and talk about the Aegean's springtime weather instead. Only once did I tell a stranger what really happened on that golden, sunlit afternoon in April 1915.

An eventful decade had passed since then and I was to all intents and purposes a seasoned civilian traveller with a profitable line in popular fishing guidebooks to exotic lakes and rivers around the world, but behind the public mask I was a Veronal addict again.

A colleague's wife was quick to recognise all the danger signs and promptly arranged for me to consult a Swiss doctor doing good work with ex-soldiers in my condition and insisted upon accompanying me to make sure I didn't jump train between Paris and Zürich.

A tenacious little Frenchwoman, she was still at my elbow as we changed over at the *Hauptbahnhof* of international banking's capital city, and caught the light rail to Bollingen on the lake's upper north shore where we were met by a bespectacled, severely formal man an inch or two taller than I, moustache clipped, voice likewise: "*Mme le Médecin* Martel-Baxter?" He enquired with a heel click.

"*Oui,*" my keeper replied in an equally brisk manner, "*d'accord.*"

"It is an honour to meet the author of *Chromo Therapeutic Modalities for the treatment of Repressed Traumatic Sequelae.*" Announced with another heel-click.

"Likewise, for me to meet the author of *Psychology of the Unconscious.*" Announced with a curt Gallic nod.

Their professional courtesies completed, both medicos now took notice of me. "This is the patient of whom you wrote?"

"*Oui.*"

Frowning, he extended his right hand. "Jung. Carl. *Doktor.*" The clasp was firm, the bow precise, for in such matters the Swiss are even more Germanic than their northern neighbours.

"Cribdon. Ian. *Nichts.*" I replied, always quick to raise a barrier of ironic humour in strange company.

"*Nichts,* as the English 'Nothing'?" He seemed relieved that we could converse in his native tongue. "I think not. Everybody has a mind, a soul, a subconscious, and those are most definitely 'something.' We speak of them later. Come!"

Stephen Baxter's wife shepherded me aboard the waiting limousine and sat with me sandwiched between herself and Jung while his chauffeur drove us uphill to a handsome residence with what used to be called "million-dollar views" of Lake Zürich, its wooded hillsides, and craggy fells.

And so began my reluctant exposure to psychoanalysis by one of its founding fathers. He and I were never close, often a problem when the patient becomes emotionally dependent upon his therapist, but something in my case notes presented by *Mme le Médecin*, prompted Jung to allocate me a plain, north-lit room, with instructions to paint a series of Great War pictures.

I hotly resisted the idea but, little-by-little, found myself experimenting with mixed media, like gluing cigarette stubs onto cardboard pharmaceutical packets retrieved from the Clinic's wastepaper bin. Another experiment consisted entirely of torn-up *Hundert Billionen Mark* banknotes, worthless after Germany's hyperinflationary crash a couple years earlier, pasted over a broken sheet of plywood salvaged from the fuel heap. The oils I mostly applied by brush or spatula, but sometimes with my fingers. Often, I was so engrossed that I barely noticed *Herr Doktor* or heard him querying this or that colour or detail.

After a week or so of this childish playing around, I progressed to more traditional media and painted several realistic canvases, three of which caught his attention. The first was an Impressionist coastline reminiscent of Claude Monet's *Christiana Fjord*, with ghostly launches and rowing boats straining to reach the shore under a dying blue sky splashed with what seemed like white chrysanthemums.

"Flowers?" Jung asked, pausing on his way back to the Consulting Room.

"Shrapnel."

"And that is what…?"

"Imagine a bloody great shotgun shell!" I snarled. "Chuck it at the sky with a timed fuze! Watch it arch over! Hear it fire three hundred lead slugs at we poor sods below!"

"And you are there now…?"

Yes. I am. Crouched aboard a barge being towed shoreward. Squalls of shrapnel beating down, pocking the sea, splintering woodwork, puncturing a water canister inches from my face. Stuttering machine guns are reaping Death's harvest as our tug chugs nearer and nearer the beach. Shellfire is blowing apart entire craft, every man aboard either killed outright or drowned by the weight of his kit. And I am mortally afraid.

"This follows next?" Jung's manicured finger reached past me to touch a nightmare composition of pale rubber masks in a bathtub of diluted red wine.

Yes. It does. I am staring over the side of the barge, about to land through a hailstorm of rifle fire as we run aground on a reef of dead men. A cobbled pavement of watery faces is staring back at me through the shallows into which I must now jump, stumbling over blubbery bodies, losing my balance, choking on bloodstained seawater. Even as I flounder clear of them, more dead and dying await me, strewn like drifts of seaweed across the beach. And I am mortally afraid.

"Here is somewhere?" The finger tapped a Cubist landscape of cinder grey shapes framing a tight black triangle defaced by crimson streaks. It could have been an abstract by Picasso or Metzinger but is in fact my vision of Shrapnel Gully, a narrow creek bed up from the beach to Monash Valley and a scrubby knoll soon to be named Pope's Hill.

Here is where a scratch team of 16 Battalion's machine gunners, New Zealand infantry, and strays from all over, will patch a gaping hole in our defences for the next days and nights of relentless counterattacks.

Here is where Percy Black will be shot through the hand and lose part of his left ear but keep on firing.

Here is where Harry Murray's face will bleed from flying chips of rock and ricocheting metallic fragments as he feeds belt after belt after belt into our gun's reeking breech, only pausing to plug the Vickers' water jacket by hammering spent cartridge cases into a pair of gaping entry and exit bullet holes.

Here where I will lead a charmed life, dimly aware that a burning whiplash has grazed my neck. As Three-on-Gun I am its operations manager, directing Four, Five, and Six to scrape dirt into their individual sandbags while I fill the half dozen pinched earlier, stacking them along the parapet even as they jolt and leak under the impact of enemy fire.

Even with Percy's thrifty double-taps we are burning up ammunition at a furious rate. I grab Five, point over the hilltop's edge behind us and lead the way downhill again, tumbling through scrub the texture of barbed wire, puttees, britches, tunic, skin ripped, Turkish marksmen banging away from their hides on adjacent hilltops, aided by the waning moon and our warships' searchlights probing for targets to shell.

Down through Monash Valley, shoving past shadowy reinforcements moving up to the front, we report to the beachmaster who directs us to Anzac HQ, a shallow dugout, its doorway draped with groundsheets to conceal a pair of paraffin lamps.

Somewhere along the way, a faceless stranger has taken command of my bruised and bleeding body. He confronts Captain Margolin, raps out a name and number and announces that he has come to organise supplies of water and ammunition for 16 Batt's guns.

There is not yet an inch of spare rope on the beach, but there are dozens of rifles the dead no longer need. Five and the stranger search for them, aided by rippling muzzle flashes and the wandering searchlights, stripping slings, linking their brass lugs, making one continuous strop.

Meanwhile, Margy – the troops' nickname for this stern, gruff, Russian Jewish disciplinarian who, until recently, ran the general store at Collie in the forest country south of Perth – is assembling supplies that more reinforcements will dump where Monash Valley forks around the foot of Pope's Hill.

The stranger claws his way back to the crest, sniper rounds splashing rock and dirt, secures his end of the webbing to a thorn bush and signals Five to start sending up boxed ammo for both guns.

It is as well they do, for soon the Turks will fire star shells and fling forward waves "Allah! Allah! Allah!" yelling men, their bayonets slashing, stabbing, slashing, stabbing -!

Percy keeps his thumbs hard down on the trigger bar; Harry keeps feeding belts; the stranger, with Six and Four, keeps reloading them by the light of the hissing, swaying, descending parachute flares. Five will be found next morning, shot dead on the slope where he was retrieving a two-gallon canister of water.

Unbeknown to these men on the frontline, those on the beach at Anzac HQ are planning an immediate withdrawal. This as-yet nameless cove is a death-trap. Best to call it off now, swallow a humiliating defeat, and conserve the men for later. Instead, Churchill and Kitchener remain adamant; General Hamilton remains compliant; and the defenders on Pope's Hill remain defiant, holding the line long enough for those in authority to regain their nerve and postpone the inevitable until December, by which time the Allies will have suffered one quarter of a million casualties. For nothing.

72

The anonymous stranger and I remained uneasy comrades in arms, even after being withdrawn from Pope's Hill and sent down to the misnamed Rest Camp. Here we swam between showers of shrapnel while several more of 16 Battalion's battered survivors fell to Abdul the Terrible, for there were few places one could hide from enemy snipers dug in along the surrounding ridges.

We always knew who it was; his signature headshots at extreme range were a dead giveaway, in every meaning of that phrase. On the other hand, he could have been she - Abiha the Terrible? - when rumours began circulating of Turkish women flushed from snipers' nests and bayoneted. One was claimed to have a box of match grade ammunition for her scoped Mauser, a stack of rations, and a basket of carrier pigeons to report our movements to the Turkish artillery spotters.

I never met anyone who witnessed these early versions of Soviet *zhenskiye snayperii*, and to this day I am sceptical. Turkey 1915 was still a strictly male dominated Muhammadan society, unlike Stalingrad 1942, a time and place where Russian women were as ruthlessly accurate as any marksman in the Red Army. However, it is worth noting, if only as an example of "Trench Whispers," for whenever troops are cut off from news and left to their own devices, they soon make up stories to suit every occasion.

These flourished on the Western Front where the mystical Flare King could be relied upon to report exactly what the Kaiser had just told Little Willy, the Crown Prince, about how badly things were going for the Fatherland, or predict the exact day when it would end in Allied victory, and many another morale-boosting furphy.

Meanwhile, at Rest Camp, we continued to dig graves, spread chloride of lime, act as stevedores for a procession of barges landing mules and fodder, Indian Army mountain-guns and limbers, GS wagons and equipment of every description.

Not surprisingly the bullet graze on my neck became septic and had to be swabbed with gentian violet, padded with gauze, and bandaged until I was ready to choke.

The only good thing one could say about Rest Camp were the opportunities to pilfer as we unloaded Q Stores' boxes and bundles. Harry, Percy, and I once shared a memorable feast of tinned roast pheasant – Officers' Only tucker - Dundee fruitcake, and a real novelty for my friends, a one-pound tin of Beluga caviar.

Initially they were unimpressed, declaring it was just swanky fish paste when spread thickly on ration biscuits, but after I told them to take smaller bites, and let the oily, flavoursome eggs dissolve on the tongue, they began to understand why civvies paid twenty shillings for a four-ounce jar of the stuff we were scoffing by the spoonful.

Meanwhile the enemy's shot and shell continued raining down on our positions until one morning when the gunfire slackened. So, either they were running out of ammunition - unlikely with tens of thousands of tons of German munitions pouring into Turkey along the still technically neutral Bulgarian railway system - or else the Sultan's gunners were stockpiling for The Big Push.

Neither rested nor refreshed, we remnants of the old 16 Battalion were ordered up to the front, through Shrapnel Gully, along Monash Valley – mercifully enlarged and deepened by now - to stiffen 15 Batt's positions between Courtney's and Quinn's Post. We didn't know it yet, but this was the hinge point where Turkey's 19 Division was preparing to deliver the killer punch that would roll up Anzac Corps and drive us back into the sea.

Alerted by aerial reports of massive enemy concentrations in nearby gullies, we stood-to at 0300 hours instead of the usual 0330, while I made doubly sure every belt it was possible to scrounge or pinch was loaded, for I did not need a repeat of our desperate fight on Pope's Hill, the previous month.

The Turks' preparatory bombardment was unlike anything endured thus far. All their stockpiled high explosive shells now thundered down as dawn broke, shrill bugle horns sounded, and wave upon wave of insanely brave men broke against massed volleys of rifle fire, and the murderous rattle of our Vickers.

Percy's outstretched legs baked under a mounting hillock of hot brass; Harry fed the gun's greedy maw; I topped-up its coolant jacket with the urine collected downstream from our skimpy water rations; Four, New Five, and Six reloaded belts, revolver holsters unflapped for a last-ditch defence.

The next thing I remember was a medical officer in blood-spattered apron, trying to dig a shell splinter from my naked right thigh. A fraction to the left and I would have bled out from a torn femoral artery; a further couple of inches and I would have been singing *castrato* in the Choir Eternal.

He grunted at an assistant who plonked a flannel cone over my mouth and nose, dribbled chloroform from a bottle, and I knew nothing more until a nursing orderly checked my pulse to see if I was dead yet, aboard a converted luxury liner, *en route* to Alexandria.

Most people believe that Florence Nightingale reformed the British Army's medical establishment in 1855, but I can assure them there was still much room for improvement when I eventually arrived at Cairo railway station, sixty years later, clad only in scraps of uniform encrusted with dirt, dried blood, and vomit.

A couple of lethargic Egyptian workers dragged my stretcher off the train, and dropped it to the ground, alongside everyone else's in the blazing sun; Miss Nightingale's patients, landing at Scutari during the Crimean War, would have felt quite at home.

Sometime later a convoy of lorries rolled up and took us to 1AGH, Heliopolis, a grand hotel that promised much but delivered little. An overworked, undermanned staff of AAMC doctors and nurses, assisted by untrained local European women and unwilling Egyptian sweepers paid a few disasters a week to disturb the dust, were waiting to admit us to 1 Army General Hospital which included the adjacent Luna Park fairground.

What should have been a straightforward procedure was complicated by the lack of case notes. These had been left behind on a train that was now steaming back to Alexandria for another load. Things began to improve, once the Australian Army Medical Corps got to grips with industrial scale death and injuries, but it was our misfortune to be among the first evacuated from Gallipoli, a campaign meant to be a walkover against a demoralised enemy and therefore tightly budgeted to limit the cost of medical supplies.

Fortunately, someone on Lemnos had thought to tie a cardboard luggage label to the identity disc each of us wore around our neck; on it was written our details and a summary of treatments given or deferred. A harassed medico and nursing sister eventually reached my stretcher, inspected the label, and booked me for immediate x-rays; apparently there was reference to a suspected shell fragment close to an artery.

With so many palatial hotel rooms to choose from, those in authority thought the Radiography Department would function best inside a dodgem car shed powered by a belt-driven generator hooked up to a petrol engine of uncertain age or ancestry.

My scans were developed in a hand basin and, shortly afterwards, an exhausted orderly prepped me for surgery inside Lunatic Park's ticket office, just across the fence from the Heliopolis Club's spacious tennis courts, polo stables, and swimming pool.

I remember vomiting awake in a recovery ward that until recently had been the Haunted House of Africa's first purpose-built funfair. When judged fit enough to move, another orderly wheeled me to an indoor roller-skating rink where six hundred or so other patients sweltered under a glass roof; an insane design feature in a climate like Egypt's, especially now that spare parts, to fix the broken evaporative cooling system, were no longer available from Germany.

That said, we had nothing but praise for the European medical staff who worked tirelessly to keep us more-or-less clean and never too hungry, but the same can never be said for 1AGH's administration. It required scant knowledge of the world's wickedness to sense that someone was selling our rations and Red Cross parcels on the black-market.

Of equal concern was the lack of ventilation in summer temperatures of 100 degrees Fahrenheit, despite the large number of electric fans said to be stored in one of the palace's many empty rooms, but nobody could find an authorising officer to sign for their release. One veteran of Britain's many colonial campaigns said it reminded him of an incident during the Zulu War when an armourer sergeant refused to break open his padlocked ammunition boxes, after mislaying the key, without getting a superior's written permission, even as the *impis* were about to charge.

One of our medicos took matters into his own hands, forced the door, and distributed the fans wherever they were needed, namely everywhere. The fairground's fragile wiring overloaded, the main fuse box exploded, and the screaming match that followed, in the AAMC Medical Director's office was clearly audible at the far end of the building.

None of this ever appeared in Australia's newspapers, of course. With a war to win and civilian morale to sustain, the Official Sensor only allowed good news to escape from Egypt. However, experienced Diggers soon learned that glowing accounts of splendid meals, clean sheets, and caring angels smoothing our rumpled pillows, were written in reverse-code.

Death dogged us from the battlefield and continued thinning our ranks. In those days there were no antibiotics to treat infected wounds and one became inured to an expiring "kaaa-ah-kkk..." from a nearby bed, generally at about 0400 hours on the skating rink's illuminated wall clock. Then would come the shadowy squeak of trolley wheels, muttered thumps, and bumps, before the wheels squeaked back to the mortuary.

Aunt Lucinda was right; I was born under a lucky star and had been gifted with unusual powers of stamina and recovery by someone in my murky bloodline. Whether or not he or she was a Braithwaite, or a Stubbs, or an anonymous tumble in the hay, was beyond my ken if not my kin. But for whatever reason, the wound on my right thigh was swift to pucker and heal, its pus and lymph draining though a rubber tube into the bucket under my bed. Barring a relapse, I would soon be able to start moving around again.

In a sense this came quicker than expected when Dragon Woman, a humourless veteran of the South African War recalled for nursing duties in Egypt, marched up to read my temperature chart and, instead, scowled at an official note pinned to my papers. "Hmph."

"What's the trouble, Sister?"

"You're for the Sergeants' Ward."

"Oh?"

"And you've got a DCM."

I later learned that Captain Margolin added my name to his list of those recommended for a Distinguished Conduct Medal, together with Percy Black and Harry Murray, for our defence of Pope's Hill.

Neighbouring patients reached across, shook hands, and wished me luck as a couple of AAMC orderlies trundled my bed past the funfair's roundabouts, left at the helter-skelter, and into the Ghost Train pavilion that doubled as our SNCO's ward. Here the food was better, conditions less cramped, and we got rather more attention than the privates I left behind on the skating rink.

A few days more I was able to sit-up and sketch cartoon portraits to stop myself from going mad with boredom. It was at about this time that One and Two popped in to see how I was getting along.

I must say they looked very spruce. Both were sufficiently recovered from their injuries to be let out in freshly ironed khaki drill uniforms; both wore their walking wounded armbands stencilled with a red crown; both had single pips on their shoulder straps, marking them as second lieutenants commissioned in the field; and both sported the DCM's crimson and dark-blue ribbon.

"G'day Icy!"

"G'day, sir?" I replied, putting aside my sketchbook.

"Balls!" Percy grinned and pulled up a chair so that he could sit one side of the bed, Harry the other, while they loaded me with oranges, strangely absent from the hospital's scale of rations; a new briar and two ounces of St Bruno, it being safer to smoke a pipe in bed as there was less chance of hot ash setting fire to the mattress; plus, a lemonade bottle that knowing winks told me did not contain lolly water.

I felt infinitely better for seeing them here. These men were the last of my training camp mates, and although other patients around me were chirpy and accommodating, it is never a good idea to form close friendships in a business where nothing and nobody lasts for long.

Harry, true to form, had searched Cairo's second-hand bookshops until he found two abridged copies of *Caesar's Gallic Wars*, in parallel English and Latin, one of which he now gave to me. "It's a bloody good read."

"Eh?"

"The way I see it, normal stories are written like they all happened in the past. Y'know, 'He said this, she did that,' but not Julius Caesar! His stories read like you're really there." He picked a page at random, determined to prove the point. "'Our soldiers, being hard pressed on every side, are dislodged from their position with the loss of six centurions, but the Tenth Legion, posted in reserve on level ground, blocks the Gauls in their eager pursuit and thrusts them back while the cavalry attack both flanks,' and so on, and so forth. You'll enjoy it."

I have never been a great fan of Caesar's self-promoting propaganda, but I treasured Harry's goodhearted gift and still consider *De Bello Gallico* an excellent bedtime read; half a dozen paragraphs, in the original, are enough to get anyone, anywhere, ready for sleep.

"Come on mate." Percy stood and eyed my other friend, "they're waiting for us." Then, glancing down at me. "It's 'investiture parade,' for medals and suchlike. You'll get yours once you're on your feet again. We'll catch up on Lemnos. The gang needs you back, quick smart."

73

I shared my oranges with the other sergeants, some of whom were quite shocked that a pair of "ossifers" would come all this way from their posh hospital at Mena, just to laugh and joke with a lowly Other Rank.

"It won't be long before you get pipped," one of them mumbled jealously.

I said nothing. Perhaps I should have told him that, from my first day in khaki, I had sensed that sergeants enjoy the best of all possible worlds, with sufficient authority to shape and lead their own sub-units, but without the distractions of commissioned rank. By keeping my head down while doing a solid job within the battalion machine gun company, I managed to hold onto my cherished three chevrons well into following year.

One advantage of being in hospital and nearer the centre of things, is that my next batch of mail finally caught up with me the day I limped back from the Physio' with the assistance of a cane.

Assuming I mention this episode to Frances, I shall suggest that her students research Army Postal Services, the undervalued rear-echelon clerks and sorters who sustain frontline morale.

The pulse quickened when I saw the small bundle of letters on my bed where the postal orderly had chucked it on his way through the ward. Two were instantly recognizable – Aunt Lucinda's and David's – but the other two were intriguing mysteries.

The first, a large envelope, contained a photograph of solemn little girls in identical knee-length pinafores, buttoned boots brightly polished, one row seated either side of an unsmiling older woman, the other row at attention behind them. Written on the back in pencil: *I am next to Mrs Fenner.* This evened the odds to fifty-fifty, when identifying young Elspeth McCracken. Her attached note was touchingly naive:

> *Dear Mr Cribdon.*
>
> *Thank you very much for your kind letter*
> *and lovely picture.*
>
> *We have it in our classroom and think of*
> *you and all your brave comrades all the time.*
>
> *I hope your weather is warm and that you are*
> *safe and well. The weather here is very wet and cold.*
>
> *E. McCracken (Miss)*

Still smiling wistfully, I put it aside and opened an unfamiliar green, *Postes & Tèlègraphes d'Egypte* envelope:

CONGRATULATIONS UPON THE AWARD

OF YOUR DISTINGUISHED CONDUCT
MEDAL STOP ON BEHALF OF MALVERN
CITY COUNCIL AJWELLER (MAYOR)

I assumed this meant that something must have been recently published in a newspaper and that I was now an authentic local hero, whatever that meant in real terms; perhaps free tram rides up and down Toorak Road? Chuckling at this whimsical idea, I opened David's letter from England:

Gonville & Gaius College
Trinity Street
Cambridge

1st July 1915

Dearest Old Friend.

Please accept my most sincere congratulations on your recent promotion and award.

I shall complete my research for Prof. Punnet before reassessing the situation.

D.

Reading between these few lines, I sensed that David would soon be volunteering for the realities of war, and that my queasy descriptions of camp life had failed to make a lasting impression. His brief note saddened me. I would not have wished my experiences, thus far, upon my worst enemy let alone someone who regarded me as his dearest old friend.

Hoping for something to cheer me up, I opened Aunt Lucinda's typed letter, sent before my name appeared in the local press. It failed to lift my spirits. Her mind was misting over, not surprising as she was now well into her nineties, though that is about where I am now, and I don't think I've gone doolally just yet?

The burden of her message was a sumptuous *dîner à deux*, the previous evening, with Franz Liszt at Bad Neuenahr. The fact that he had been dead for almost thirty years, and their *affaire* would have been at least another thirty before that was of no account. The good old dear was reliving her glorious encounter with one of Europe's most dashing charmers, most talented composers, most handsome pianists, a man of impeccable taste bewitched by the Colonial Difference, as she coyly described her own undoubted charm and wit.

Much could be read into this letter and the previous one for that matter, with its reference to a dead child, but I preferred not to, firmly believing that one's secrets should die with us. Instead, I limped across Lunatic Park's parched dirt and cracked concrete pathways, heading for the Red Cross canteen where we could buy the contents of our stolen comforts' parcels.

I ordered a mug of tea and picked up a copy of the *Egyptian Gazette* to check on progress, if any, at what was now officially known as Anzac Cove. Civilians reading this official bulletin would have imagined everything was going splendidly, but soldiers with any knowledge of the ghastly place knew otherwise.

My snort of contempt carried some distance because the bloke seated further down our trestle table, also reading the same paper, glanced up and nodded. "Yeah, what a steaming heap o' bullshit..."

"My oath," I replied, with feeling, "but least they spelt the names right. Speaking of which, mine's Ian Cribdon. 16 Battalion."

"Bill Proctor. Otago Rifles." He made no attempt to reach out and shake hands. "Were you, that lot, on Pope's Hill?"

"Uh."

"Thanks."

"What for?"

"Your MG's covering fire." Adding, after a moment's hesitation, "not that it did me much good." His gaze dropped to what was not under the table, and for the first time I noticed that he was propped up in a wheelchair.

We became friends during the next couple of weeks, before he was repatriated to New Zealand and whatever a legless farmer can do to feed his young family. There was no chance a double amputee would go AWOL, so Bill was granted a permanent pass for two, himself and anyone willing to push the chair, empty the can under his seat, and wipe him clean. Inspired by old Joe Mullins' unselfish concern for a crippled Aboriginal girl I volunteered for the job, reckoning it was the least one could do for a cobber.

This not only got him out of Lunatic, I got more exercise than Physio' could allocate time for. We would slowly trundle around the edge of the aerodrome and chat while watching the aeroplanes – BE2Cs if my memory is correct – fly east to patrol the Canal Zone, and westward into Libya where they were keeping an eye on Senussi tribesmen agitated by Ottoman agents and German gold.

One of our excursions ranged as far as Maadi Camp where Pat Donovan was preparing his Mounted Infantry for this other war in the Western Desert, a now forgotten campaign that prefaced T.E.Lawrence's later adventures in the Hejaz. I wangled the trip by drawing a sweetheart portrait for a Signals Corps sergeant i/c the Transport Pool where, earlier, I had noticed a motorbike and sidecar that nobody seemed to be using much.

By unbolting most of the sidecar's bodywork, it was possible to rope Bill and his chair to its chassis. I then scrounged two pairs of goggles and off we roared through Cairo's leafy suburbs, regally waving to flummoxed European civvies in their pith helmets and tropical whites as we thundered past, hooting with laughter.

Pat welcomed us with a huge grin and made certain that Bill Proctor got a slap-up luncheon in the canteen before showing him around the camp, like the honoured guest he was. Then, as we rested under a palm tree's shade, I took out my sketchbook and drew the two of them merrily clinking beer bottles, the very best of chums. Bill was intrigued to see how a few pencil strokes could depict so much, and during the next week or so, before he embarked for home, I coached him in simple perspective drawing. To my surprise, given the extent of his injuries, he had a good eye and a steady hand.

We kept in touch while he reported progress at an art school in Wellington and told me of his dream to earn a living as a magazine illustrator. Instead, the missus walked out on him, taking their son with her. It was only much later that I learned how he then folded a couple of house bricks inside his pinned up trouser legs, rolled his wheelchair to the end of the Cook Strait Ferry pier, and finished what the Turks began.

Meanwhile the Great War ground on with no end in sight. Every able-bodied soldier in Egypt, including convalescents like myself, was needed back at the Dardanelles where one last throw of the dice, to break the stalemate, was being planned amidst the usual porous lack of secrecy.

The Medical Board pronounced me fit for Light Duties; the hospital returned my brass tobacco box and other personal items salvaged from the rags of my old uniform; Q Stores issued new kit and within a few hours I was on the train to Alexandria. One good thing about it, as a sergeant I was now entitled to a carriage with upholstered seats instead of the slatted wooden benches of my previous rail journey.

It's hard to tell, seventy-odd years after the event, what I really thought at the time. Probably relief at escaping from Heliopolis' macabre fairground; apprehension, certainly, for now I knew what lay ahead of me; and a gnawing fear that I had lost my nerve. We might develop these themes when next I speak with Frances, for she doesn't need to hear any more descriptions of body lice and trench warfare.

Luckily the troop transport was an improvement on the muck and muddle of a few months ago. HMT *Southland*, a former transatlantic passenger steamer soon to be torpedoed on another run across the Ægean, was a fair example of the new system and most troops were able to land reasonably fed and rested after we anchored off Anzac Cove and waited for a steam pinnace to tow us ashore, before backloading the sick and wounded.

I no longer recognised the place. In my absence Gallipoli had grown like a malignant ulcer. The bare hillsides and slopes I knew in April were now honeycombed with dugouts and gouged by miles of communication trenches. The beach itself looked as if a gigantic shipwreck had strewn its cargo up to the foot of the cliffs where its survivors had built huddles of Robinson Crusoe shelters from scraps of flotsam while awaiting rescue.

Despite the thousands of lives lost, the millions of pounds spent, the Sultan's snipers still held the high ground, and his artillery still peppered the beachhead with shrapnel and HE.

74

I am strongly tempted to call a halt at this juncture. Frances only wants to hear an elderly Edwardian's voice describing his vanished world and its quaint customs, and Heaven knows I've said enough for her to form an opinion of those! If I were to continue in this vein, she would have to endure yet another account of a war that destroyed my generation physically, emotionally, and spiritually, and is that what she wants to do with her time?

Every year, on the anniversary of our landing at Anzac Cove, some fat-arsed, speechifying politician brays that Australia was born, as a nation, on the beaches of Gallipoli; if true, it was more of a backstreet abortion than a properly managed delivery.

I have no desire to record my small part of this disastrous episode in our nation's story, for no sane person wishes to be remembered for stories of dirt and disease and death in all their ghastly manifestations. But if I were to inflict them on Frances, I should have to find an acceptable way to describe the nauseating stench that greeted us, hundreds of yards offshore, as we approached a wooden jetty built while I was away.

It was not just the familiar, cloying stink of Allied and Turkish dead melting in summery heat beyond the wire. And even when it was possible to bury them in shallow graves, dug by exhausted fatigue parties, a regulation 24 inches of sandy soil tossed on top was never enough to suppress the cadaveric gases leaking from our crowded cemeteries. But that was the merest trifle compared with the fermenting reek of open latrine pits.

During my absence, tens of thousands of other rancid, unwashed men had come and gone, leaving their residues behind them, mostly at the bottom of long drops where maggots flourished, and flies bred by the million. These boiled out of the bog pits like thick clouds of angry black smoke whenever we perched on the horizontal crossbars, like chooks in a hen house, off which those too weakened by dysentery would sometimes slip, fall, and drown.

An enemy gunner popped me a Welcome Back puff of shrapnel as I disembarked and started up the beach, peering around at unshaven wraiths clad in ragged scraps of Allied uniform; some in tattered AIF tunics, others in Tommy bloomers with their backsides cut out; some wearing slouch hats in advanced stages of decay, or peaked field service caps with cloth puggarees roughly stitched around the brims, or turbans if they were the Indian Army's Sikhs and Rajputs.

"G'day mate," I approached the one bloke who seemed more alert than the rest, "any idea where 16 Batt's hiding these days?"

"Follow the signboards Sergeant," the Beachmaster replied with a frosty sniff. "And please don't salute, it only draws Abdul's attention to these." He tapped the three strips of gold braid worn above his shirt's left breast-pocket, rather than prominently on his shoulders where a Royal Navy commander would usually display his rank.

"Sir." I continued picking my way over filthy, unwashed sand, the Ægean being virtually tideless; between store dumps and mounds of fodder for the mules and donkeys corralled nearby; past regimental aid posts filtering patients into a sandbagged field hospital, conveniently near a gully crammed with wooden crosses.

16 Battalion HQ was a dugout roofed with curved planks retrieved from a wrecked lifeboat. An orderly corporal gave me a weary glance and ducked around a blanket curtain to announce my arrival.

"You fit again?" Captain Margolis enquired in his dark, thick, menacing voice.

"Yes sir."

"Report to Mr Black in Training Gully."

I found Percy farther along the beach, under camouflage netting and thus reasonably out of sight from direct fire, where he had established a machine gun school. Always slim and trim, he was now gaunt and bony.

"Glad you could make it," he said as we shook hands and sat with our backs against a rockface. "Whoo! Thanks…" The four ounces of Latakia tobacco I'd bought at Zamalek's in Garden City, Cairo, was much appreciated as he loaded his pipe and brought me up to date.

Harry had been posted and was now 13 Batt's MGO; as for 16 Battalion itself, we were now mostly half-trained reinforcements, keen lads but ill-prepared for war. Three had already failed to understand what the

HEADS DOWN!
SNIPERS ACTIVE!!

notice boards were telling them to do. In predictable, civilian displays of defiant bravado, each had peered over the sandbagged parapet to see what all the fuss was about, moments before a 7.92mm Mauser bullet - approaching at just under three thousand feet per second - informed their mates instead.

The camouflaged machine gun school served two purposes. Firstly, the need for more gunners now that we had cadged another two Vickers from a Royal Navy Armoured Car unit, who were never going to use them in this terrain. The second purpose only became apparent when Percy led me to the head of the gully, nominally the butts where our guns were tested, only to find there was also a tunnel, dug and deepened by the Sappers. This was part of a network of underground shelters for the British and Indian reinforcements arriving by night, whose presence must be kept secret from Turkish spotters and German reconnaissance aeroplanes, until the last moment.

The afternoon's shadows were lengthening, our preferred time to move in semi-darkness, when the variable shadows were most likely to confuse a sniper's aim, as I took a relieving party with bundles of picket posts and rolls of barbed wire up to 16's MG position on Russell's Top, facing the Chessboard and Battleship Hill, if memory serves me right. This fragile strand of trenches and rifle pits became my responsibility when I took-over the Vickers and its stock of ammunition.

The Turks, less than fifty yards away, heard us talking and for a bit of a lark gate-crashed the party with a salvo of broomstick bombs that wobbled overhead and randomly exploded several pounds of black powder and scrap metal. Wickedly primitive, these improvised mortar bombs were usually spent artillery cases attached to long poles and contained scrap material stuffed around a fragmentation charge and contact detonator. We never knew what the next delivery would bring; I've defused duds that included a broken alarm clock,

327

rusty nails, and crushed ration tins, even blunt gramophone needles that left terrible wound tracks.

One of my reo's copped a chunk of broken bottle on his jaw and was evacuated to the beach we had only just left, while the rest of us stood-to, anticipating an attack, but things settled down again except for the random crack of bullets passing overhead, echoed by the distant thumps of their discharge.

If Frances were to ask me to describe Gallipoli in a single sentence, I would reply with a single word: Thirst. All else, the rotting flesh; the blowflies that encrusted our food so that we ate with one hand over our mouths, little fingers furiously scraping these unwelcome dinner guests off our mess tins; the maggots and body lice; the indiscriminate death and injury; were as nothing compared with the refined torture of a parched throat on a scorched hilltop in late summer.

It was not lessened by a diet of ships' biscuits, dried vegetables, and salty corned beef that slithered from its tin on an ooze of melting fat. If we were lucky, we might get an allowance of one quart of water per man, per day, often brought up in unrinsed two-gallon petrol or paraffin tins, the last leg of a journey that began nine hundred miles away, at a pumping station on the Nile.

This allowance was barely sufficient to sustain sedentary work in the shade, at this time of year, with nothing to spare for personal hygiene. However, the Vickers cooling system was an even greater concern. While topped up with condensate, we could defend our sector, but if it ever boiled off, the barrel would warp, the action seize-up, and we'd be using our revolvers to hold back the Turks.

The Vickers was sacrosanct, a mechanical deity with everything and everyone subordinated to its insatiable demands. For all practical purposes they were irreplaceable. At a time when Germany had been producing fifty a week for the Kaiser's army, only twelve a week were being made in Britain, and even after America's arsenals began churning them out by the hundred, there were never enough machine guns to meet our needs.

Meanwhile every sip of water mostly evaporated as sweat, leaving a few ounces of dark brown urine for emergency coolant. The urge to drink the gun's dedicated reserve of water had to be resisted, even when maddened by thirst. This was not hyperbole. I am convinced that more than a few of our casualties were men who lost their minds and woozily invited a sniper to end the misery of thirst.

75

A couple of days later, I stabbed another hole in my belt; what had been gained in hospital was rapidly falling away, and not only weight but also my general condition. I could already feel the first belly rumblings of the Trots, unavoidable when every bite of bully beef or dollop of apricot jam was shared with swarms of flies hatched on the corpses a few yards away.

It was now early August, and we sensed a quickening in the air. The brass hats were said to be planning a multipronged offensive to break the deadlock and resume the Allies' triumphant march on Constantinople before winter set in. To achieve this, they were going to launch coordinated attacks at Cape Helles as well as up the coast at Anzac Cove, to distract and confuse the Turks while fresh divisions landed, by night, at Suvla Bay another five miles north of us.

If I do speak with Frances about this madness, I shall have to explain what these terms meant. Starting with a brigade of four battalions, each of which was roughly eight hundred strong, led by a lieutenant colonel, or in total three thousand effectives commanded by a brigadier general. Four brigades comprised one division of twelve thousand troops commanded by a major general. And three divisions, roughly speaking, made up an infantry corps which, with Engineers, Signals, Pioneers, and Artillery, could amount as many as fifty thousand personnel under the command of a lieutenant general.

An historian of her experience will immediately spot the fatal flaw in Suvla's grand design. Such an unwieldy force as Kitchener's New Army volunteers and part-time Territorials, shipped straight from England, was never meant for an offensive campaign of this nature. Their training, such as it was, had prepared them for static warfare on the Western Front, where dogged resistance and a gritty determination to hold ground, were the correct mixture. Hence, these newcomers were simply incapable of dash and initiative while awaiting orders from commanders who were just as bewildered as their baffled troops.

It is easy to be wise after the event. It took me fourteen years to fully understand the Suvla Bay fiasco, and then only after revisiting the battlefield and climbing Hill 971 for the first time without being shot at. From here I saw the second glaring error that should have been obvious to anyone who has ever compass-marched soldiers across broken country at night.

Darkness disorients all but the most expert pathfinder. Timing and distances rapidly lose their meaning as doubts and wild guesses muddy the mind, so that one is lucky to arrive anywhere near the designated target by daybreak. And yet this was the task handed to a mixed grill of relatively experienced Anzacs, the always tough and professional Gurkhas, and Lord Kitchener's anxious new volunteers.

We spent that day cleaning weapons, checking ammunition, lightening our kit, and stitching white patches of cloth to our tunic's right shoulder. This was meant to keep us in touch with the man in front as we assembled in column of route along the beach, at sunset.

Ahead of us lay about four miles of dry gullies, and tangled undergrowth, and crumbling gravel slopes, before a righthand turn into an allegedly shallow valley where we were supposed to assume an attacking formation, storm Hill 971, dislodge the Turks, and establish a position that would command Sari Bair. All in pitch-black darkness, for by then the silvery crescent of a waning moon would have set.

Meanwhile the British IX Corps would be simultaneously wading ashore, ready to advance inland at first light. They would then liaise with our force, cut the peninsula at its waist to stop reinforcements reaching the Turks at Cape Helles before we outflanked them, and silenced the guns that were still blocking the Allied navies' passage through the Straits.

This was a massively tall order, even at the best of times, one that would have needed much more than its quota of good luck, experienced troops, and competent leaders, none of which we had.

I have never understood why Suvla's protected bay was not our primary target in April, rather than ineffectually scattering troops in penny packets, hither and thither as target practice for the Turks, before finally deciding to do so, months later. By which time it was all too little, too late, and destined to become a textbook example of how not to fight a battle.

In the event we fought our way to 971's summit, got pushed back, and spent the rest of the day pinned down on its lower slopes until we could have another crack at it under cover of darkness, with much the same result, and by next morning we had done our dash.

Colonel Pope got orders to withdraw and detailed a rear-guard of riflemen to cover our one remaining MG section as we kept scything wave after wave of Allah! Allah! Allah! heroes, determined to finish us off with the bayonet. This they nearly did as our remnants, plus stragglers from the King's Own Loyal Lancaster Regiment, pulled back to 13 Battalion's defensive perimeter.

The Battle of Sari Bair rumbled on without us; of 16 Battalion's eight hundred or so effectives who marched out from Anzac Cove, fewer than two hundred trudged back. The other three battalions were similarly thinned. Our brigade of South and West Australians had ceased to exist, except on paper.

This did not mean we could rest on our laurels, or lick our wounds, or do any of those other tiresomely clichéd things. There was work to do at Number One Outpost, where Sikh troops had cleared the scrub blocking their fields of fire, strung coils of barbed wire, and dug a network of communication trenches, which gave us a grandstand view of the New Zealanders' disastrous attack on Hill 971.

The only way to lessen a steady flow of casualties from sniper fire and shrapnel was to dig ever deeper underground, and those of us who were not on the fire step got stuck in with pick and shovel, extending and improving the trench system. As the NCO i/c our Vickers I was reasonably fortunate in this regard, not that I would have been of much use.

The wound in my thigh had never entirely healed and helping to carry a machine gun, its tripod and elevating gear, water cannisters and supplies, plus boxes of ammunition belts across sawback ridges, at night, had not improved matters. My belly cramps were also in full flood.

Captain Margolin scowled at the mess dribbling down my bare legs, scribbled a chit, and ordered me to report sick forthwith. I made it most of the way down to the beach, and when my knees folded, a ration party carried me the rest of the way to the forward dressing station.

Dr Isaacs, one of Melbourne's leading specialists and a viola player in the Hochheim amateur orchestra, was now an AAMC major and fortunately on duty when the orderlies hauled my stretcher into Admissions. He could never have recognised me under my bearded crust of filth, but Cribdon is a rare enough surname for him take notice and book me for priority evacuation.

This was well-intentioned but the facilities on Lemnos were equally chaotic and swamped by casualties from Suvla. There were never enough tents or marquees and hundreds of us spent the next several days on bare ground, covered with waterproof sheets that kept being blown away on the fierce winds that sweep down from the Anatolian Highlands.

Anaesthetics and wound dressings were also in short supply and there were rumours of amputations that would not have been out of place on Waterloo's battlefield, a century earlier, and on two occasions I saw nurses ripping up their cotton and linen garments to improvise bandages and slings.

I could easily have dropped my bundle, as many did, but word had rattled down the chain of command ordering specialist NCOs be returned to Egypt where there was a better chance of survival; riflemen are expendables in the arithmetic of war, but we specialists had the skills and experience needed to train replacements. Even so I was nearly buried at sea, as were other patients in transit to Alexandria, but there was still enough pulse on my wrist to make it worth the trouble of admitting me to 15 AGH.

I didn't appreciate it at the time, but this Army General Hospital was the exact opposite of the other one at Lunatic Park. Someone had finally got a grip on things by commandeering a recently built secondary school at Abbasia, one of Alex's more affluent suburbs, and appointed Colonel Herbert James CB CMG to be its commandant.

A ramrod straight RAMC veteran, he brought a lifetime of practical experience to the job. This included quelling an outbreak of bubonic plague in Hong Kong; treating wounded Chinese troops during the Sino-Japanese War, for which he was decorated with the Order of the Double Dragon by the Emperor in Peking; and command of the Royal Army Medical College at Millbank, in London.

These facts were unknown to me at the time, but much later I made it my business to learn who this remarkable man was, before sending a letter of appreciation to his address in Southern Rhodesia, where he had gone to live in retirement.

There was never any nonsense about electric fans or stolen comforts parcels while Colonel James strode the wards. Under his command, 15AGH became a briskly efficient workshop for the repair of broken soldiers, unlike the tragic shambles at Heliopolis. It was indirectly due to his unbending professionalism that I began making a good recovery once my bowels had settled down and the wounded thigh was properly attended to.

Abbasia was officially a British military hospital and therefore most of the staff were also British, a collective noun encompassing Scots, Welsh, Irish, as well as English. It followed that a large proportion of the nurses were graduates of hospital schools in the United Kingdom, or Red Cross trainees enrolled as Voluntary Aid Detachments, whose VAD initials were immediately translated as Very Adorable Darlings.

It was an astonishment to see the former Queen of Portugal, or Lady X, or the Honourable Y, or Miss Z the shipping magnate's daughter, cheerfully emptying bedpans, delivering meals, or changing wound dressings that stank of blood and pus and frequently crawled with maggots.

By any measure, regardless of birth, these were the flower of our generation's womenkind and many would die of infectious diseases, or be killed in action, or murdered by the Hun - like Nurse Edith Cavell - before the war ended.

Jealous rumours claimed that the prettiest were reserved for the Officers' Ward at the far end of the hospital, but we NCOs were not entirely deprived of Adorables, one of whom bore a striking resemblance to Maeve, my dance partner in Melbourne, with the same burnished chestnut hair, the same creamy complexion, the same beautifully proportioned face, the same merry twinkle in enchanting dark brown eyes of unfathomable depth.

It came as no surprise when I eventually learned that her noble family held estates in Southwest Ireland, although she herself had been schooled at Cheltenham Ladies' College before planning to continue her education on the Continent. Then, just as she was about to take up a place at Berlin University to study German Language & Literature, war broke out and, instead, she volunteered to travel farther afield where among other previously unimaginable skills, she learned to blanket bath an Australian machine gunner recovering from a rough trot at Sari Bair.

There was no point either of us being bashful. She found it hard to keep a straight face whenever a certain anatomical feature, with an inflexible will of its own, stood up to greet her. However, far from being affronted or indignant, she continued to sponge my groin and wounded thigh with diluted carbolic disinfectant as part of her daily rounds, even though this was a chore that any other VAD could easily have handled.

Her surname carried a lot of weight at the highest levels of Society and there are relatives alive today, so if I do mention our idyll to Frances, I shall be discreet in the Edwardian manner. Given that we met, laughed, and loved in Alexandria, a city founded by Alexander the Great, and that the feminine form of Alexander is Alexandra, of which the affectionate diminutive is Sandra, this will, I believe, sufficiently protect a distinguished family's reputation from smutty gossip.

76

I found myself regaining a zest for life whenever Sandra wheeled me to the Physio' and she would quite often wheel me back to Recreation Room if the *Simoom* was blowing outside. And when it was not, onto an open terrace from which in those days one could glimpse the sunlit Mediterranean to the north; the city's market gardens to the south; and east to where the Delta's rich, alluvial cotton fields began.

She had dozens of other men to attend to and, like all Adorables, was under the watchful eye of a Matron held strictly accountable for their virtue by Colonel James who famously disapproved of "sparking." Thus, our meetings had to be brief and formal though pleasantly frequent, for she enjoyed my company as much as I enjoyed hers.

Most of her other patients were Tommies, until recently farm labourers and factory hands, downtrodden casualties in a centuries-old class war that had trained them to humbly squirm whenever "a proper lady" spoke in her cut crystal English accent. Australia, on the other hand, is a much younger society and far less respectful of authority, which may or may not be a good thing, depending upon one's point of view. Thus, I always greeted her with cheerful chaff whenever our paths crossed, as happened one afternoon when she prettily marched up to my terrace sun bed and presented a slim packet of letters.

"Shall I read them for you?" This was a standard ploy that gave VADs official permission to sit and talk while helping a wounded hero whose eyes were giving him a spot of bother.

"Only if you've got time," I winked, making room for her beside my chair, "as the swagman said to the barmaid..."

"Oh, I'm sure we can spare a few minutes," she smiled back, accepting the invitation while examining the topmost envelope's English postmark. "What beautiful hand script!"

I noted her unconsciously direct translation of *Handschrift*. "Yes. It's my oldest friend's."

"Then let's see what he's got to say, shall we?" And with this she took a pair of bandage scissors from her apron pocket and neatly slit open the envelope. "'Gonville & Caius College,'" I also noted her correct pronunciation, "'Trinity Street, Cambridge. Dear Old Goliath Slayer. I have satisfactorily finished my work for Professor Punnet. The die is cast – alea iacta est! – and instead of returning home to Melbourne or signing-up for the AIF at Australia House in London, I have applied for a commission in the Royal Flying Corps. The examining medico says I am A1 and there is no reason why they won't accept me for training. I have yet to tell the Old Folks, but I am sure you of all people will understand my reasons for taking this step. When next we meet, we'll both be wearing the King's uniform! Take care, old friend. As ever, D.'"

Sandra replaced the letter in its envelope and cocked a quizzical eyebrow: "'Dear Old Goliath Slayer'?"

"A schoolboy nickname," I shrugged. "A play on David & Goliath. Nothing special."

"No. You're wrong. It's much more." She was serious. "He seeks your approval."

"How the hell did you nut that out?" I sat up straighter.

"I-I just can," she replied, before continuing. "Like most letters, his is greater than the sum of its parts. The choice and order of words reveal their writer's character as clearly as his thoughts. One senses he is simultaneously writing another, parallel message, as if wanting you to intuitively grasp what he's unable to tell you directly…"

I am disinclined to believe that the Irish, and Celts generally, possess Second Sight but there was no denying an uncanny echo of Maeve's ability to read another's thoughts and occasionally foretell events she could not have known beforehand.

"Ah! This looks interesting." She opened Aunt Lucinda's letter, addressed on an irregularly pecked typewriter. "'Tralee House, Grange Road, Melbourne. My Dear Son. I am told you have distinguished yourself in battle. Be not too brave lest the candle of life be snuffed out prematurely. When I told Cher Jacques of your deeds in Turkey, he replied that war is only glorious when set to bright music upon the stage, and that I should buy you out immediately ere worse betide. I have never bought a person tho' I suppose the price will be high as everything else is these days since Bismarck trampled our fair land. O the shame. I so hate the brute. He was recently seen leading his Prussian barbarians through the Arc de Triomphe which he defiled by asking a bystander for a match to light his cigar, so insouciant and unmindful of where he was. O God how I hate him and all he stands for. Show no mercy to the Prussian when you meet upon the field of battle. Take care Dear Boy. Lucinde, Baronne de l'Empire.'"

"Whew!" Sandra recovered her breath and gave me a most gorgeous, wondering smile. "'My Dear Son'?"

"Only in her aged imagination," I mumbled, acutely embarrassed to hear such sentimental tosh read aloud.

"Do tell!"

"Nothing much to tell." I shrugged. "Aunt Lucinda took care of me after my parents died when I was young. Now, what's in that little parcel?" I pointed at a brown paper packet nestling in the one womanly lap, of all the womanly laps in the world, I most wished to burrow under and explore.

I can't be sure if Sandra's mindreading skills intercepted my thoughts, but she did seem a trifle flustered when undoing the packet and taking out a handwritten note, tightly rolled inside a khaki scarf tied up with a blue hair ribbon.

She composed herself and flattened the crumpled sheet of lined paper, cut from a school exercise book. "'Dear Mr Cribdon. Thank you for your kind letter. Mrs Fenner read it to the class, and they were happy to hear it. I have knitted this for you, trusting you find it of use. The weather here is getting warmer so your weather must be getting colder. Yours respectfully. E. McCracken. Miss.'" She paused and glanced my way again. "Isn't hers a lovely gift?"

"S'pose so." I was gruffly defensive. "The girl's got talent. Sent me a Christmas card drawn in pastels and Indian ink. She gets my savings and accrued army pay when I'm skittled. I've asked they be invested in decent art materials and lessons from a good teacher."

"And yours is, a loving gift." I sensed that my Adorable was starting to view me through fresh eyes. "Are you an artist, yourself?"

"Only an amateur," I mumbled evasively, "but I have friends who are the real thing. Um, got a pencil…?"

She fished around her apron pocket and found one.

"Thanks." I turned over David's letter and completed a lightning portrait sketch on the back of its envelope and, by so doing, revealed feelings I dared not put into words.

"This is, so beautiful!"

"Yes." I looked up. "You are."

"Heavens!" She blushed and looked down at her fob watch. "Matron will be wondering where I've got to!" Standing abruptly, she smoothed her long khaki-drab, tropical uniform skirt and hurried away.

77

Sandra gave me a wide berth for the rest of the week, during which time I learned to bathe and shave myself again and began walking with the aid of a cane around the school grounds, now tightly packed with bell tents and marquees as more and more casualties landed from Gallipoli.

My preferred stop on these walks was the Coptic Christian Chapel, just across Ahmed Badawi Street from the school gates, on loan to the British as a place of quiet reflection and private worship. It was not only relatively cool and quiet, inside, the chapel was also one of the few places in Alex' where a soldier could get away from the Army without being crimed for going Absent Without Leave.

Something about the building and its purpose reminded me of St Mary's in Kalgoorlie, and of the way that Pat, and Dulcie, and I would attend Mass; they for the good of their souls, me for the pleasure of organ music and the play of candlelight on Father Declan's vestments while I memorised his Latin pronunciations.

I was still enveloped in a mist of nostalgia for that lost world of peace and contentment when Sandra quietly sat down beside me in the incense-fragrant gloom. "Hello."

Startled, I turned. "Oh! Hello."

"I saw you come in…"

I hesitated. Then: "'I'm awfully glad you did."

"Why…?"

"I've been thinking a lot, of old friends, back home, and need a good 'gee up.'"

"Is that what I do for you…?"

I remained silent. A week or so previously I'd come across Sandra's debutante portrait photograph in an old copy of *Country Life*, part of a consignment of illustrated magazines sent out to Egypt by the British Red Cross Comforts Fund. The young woman I'd been cheerily and cheekily chaffing was, in fact, the eldest daughter of the Fifth Earl of a domain whose identity I shall protect by giving it the fictitious name of Nobury. My favourite nurse was the Honourable Lady So-and-So who, according to the photo's paragraph, had shelved her plans to study aboard and was now training to become a VAD.

"Well…?"

"Yes." I looked up. "I like you. A lot."

"'Like…'?"

I hesitated, summoning up the courage to continue. "If things were different, if we were different, I'd use a different word, but they're not different, and we're not different, so I can't, and I won't."

"Why not…?"

I studied her finely boned profile, imprinting my memory with every adored shade and line and texture. "Because I'll soon be back on the Peninsula where my luck's bound to run out. And when it does, I don't want to go, having hurt someone, like you, by saying, or worse, doing, something, silly."

"Would it be, 'silly'?" She persisted gently.

"That's a hard call," I replied with marked reluctance. "You're the only decent thing left, up here," I tapped my forehead.

Sandra reached out, took my right hand, kissed its leathery palm, and gently held it to her left breast in the most lovingly sensual manner imaginable. I kept it there long after she took her own hand away, lost in the wonder of its soft curvature, gentle warmth, and eager pulse of her beating heart.

"We get a forty-eight hour leave every month," she said, finally. "I'm taking mine this weekend and will be staying at the residence we Adorables have leased for our personal use..."

"Won't it be, crowded?"

"Not if I make the necessary arrangements."

I sat up straighter, stunned by the amazing gift that had been quite literally handed to me. "If I'm hearing what I think I'm hearing, I had better wangle a couple of overnights at the Y."

"What a splendid idea!" She shared an arch, upper-crust English smile. "Perhaps we could arrange to meet in town? Do let me know when you're free, won't you?"

What followed next is nobody's business but ours. Suffice it to say, a sweetheart portrait for someone's missus and kids on the family farm in Victoria, got me the required rubber stamps for a convalescent's permission to leave hospital and lodge at the YMCA in Abdul Hameed Street, close to Alexandria's fashionable beachfront area.

I showed my pass to a pair of Redcaps at the Y's door, signed in and paid for two nights' appearance on the guest register, then limped outside again and waved my stick to hail a *gharry*. The driver assumed I needed to visit the notorious brothels of *Rue des Soeurs* – described by one wag as the Mediterranean Fleet's principal navel base - and took it rather amiss when I told him, in my rough Arabic, that I wanted a quite different address, and that if he played me false, I'd shove his head up his horse's arse till he croaked -!

Sandra was seated on a spacious balcony between two ornamental orange trees in large terracotta pots, overlooking a rather grand and leafy street. She pointed downstairs and mimicked a door knock. I waved back, paid off the driver, and had barely reached the head of the steps when the door opened and a female servant of indeterminate age and origin, silently beckoned me through.

I never enquired, for that would have been ungentlemanly, but I suspect that Lady X, the Honourable Y, and Miss Z the shipping magnate's daughter had clubbed together and leased this fine residence, furnishing it with their familiar Maple & Co tables and chairs, Liberty fabrics and curtains, to create an island of well-bred calm amidst Egypt's septic squalor. Sandra herself was wearing a floral cotton shift, her form deliciously free of the stiff and starched hospital uniform. The silent maid was dismissed with a nod and for the first time we found ourselves alone in each other's company.

"May I call you Ian?"

I suppressed the hoary Outback joke of being happy to be called anything except "Late for Breakfast," and instead gave her a correctly measured bow. "I shall be honoured." Then, straightened: "May I call you 'Sandra'?"

"Of course." We shook and held hands for longer than etiquette allowed. "Now," she looked me up and down, eyeing the khaki drill tunic, the breeches, the puttees, the boots, "let's get you into something more comfortable."

I followed her into a generously proportioned bedroom where she indicated a kaftan on the dresser and left me to strip off. I noticed three identical pairs of men's leather slippers - Small, Medium, and Large - lined up beside the bed, mute evidence that other Adorables also received friends in this discreet home-from-home.

Sandra had returned to the balcony and was taking the evening breeze off the Med', one street away, when I re-joined her. She smiled. "Better?"

"Yes. Thank you." I eased into a high-backed wicker chair alongside hers and released a heartfelt sigh of contentment.

"Drink?" She nodded to what looked like a large bronze Roman urn, probably excavated during the Khedive's rush to bankrupt Egypt by turning a tenth century Arab *souk* into a nineteenth century European metropolis, filled to the brim with an assortment of bottles on ice. "I understand that Australians are rather partial to beer. I'm not sure what sort you prefer, so I got as many different kinds as I could."

"It's true, we are," I replied, testing her words for any trace of patronising condescension, but found none. "A schooner of bitter works like magic on a dusty throat after a day's hard yakka down a mine, or drafting cattle, or cutting timber sleepers," I explained, leaning forward to sort through the various labels.

"Did you yacker and draft?"

"Not as such. Mostly I trapped rabbits, pulled sandalwood, and fossicked for gold. Ah! Tonic? And gin? Let's leave the beers for later. These'll do the trick now. May I fix you one?" I glanced up again.

"Please do." She set out the glasses and sliced a lime while I mixed the spirits and aerated quinine water. Our only available ice was in the urn and stank of chlorine, vital in a land where typhoid, and dysentery, and cholera, and Allah alone knows what other contagious horrors lurk in every open drain, so we agreed to pass on that.

"To us." I raised my glass.

"To us…"

78

Dinner was unlike anything I imagined it would be. Instead of sharp handclaps to summon servants bearing heaped platters and bowls, as I believed these displaced English toffs lived in their Surrey-with-sunshine enclaves, Sandra led me into a neat little kitchen equipped with every modern appliance one could hope to find in the Year of our Lord 1915, including a new Vulcan gas range and a varnished oak McCray icebox like the one at Tralee House.

"Why so surprised?" She asked, whisking half a dozen eggs in an enamel bowl.

"Well, I thought you'd have *khadam* doing this sort of thing," I replied awkwardly. "Aren't British expats supposed employ mobs of native servants, hopping about at their beck and call?"

"Not in this household," she replied firmly. "We were all raised surrounded by domestics of every description, from boot boys to butlers, gossiping and conspiring behind our backs. You cannot imagine how liberating it feels to be doing things for ourselves!" She flourished the whisk for effect. "Now, be a darling, hand me the pepper while I slice these asparagus spears."

I did as she requested and watched her taking the slender green stalks from the saltwater that had kept them fresh while sterilising the inevitable local microbes. In due course I learned that Cheltenham Ladies College's enlightened curriculum made sure that its young ladies knew how to cook, sew, iron, and generally look after themselves, be they a foreign princess, an earl's daughter, or an industrialist's heiress.

Sandra had baked the pastry shell in an open flan dish earlier this afternoon, into which she now poured the seasoned egg and cream before prettily decorating it with a lattice of asparagus and thin strips of cheese. "There!" She popped it in the oven and set the timer. "Half an hour at three-fifty should be about right. Now," she straightened, "I know exactly what you need, young man!"

She led the way into a tiled bathroom, very much like the one at Tralee House, where the mute maidservant had filled a large, white enamel bath with hot, muskily aromatic water.

Sandra was not wrong, this was exactly what a battered and bruised soldier needed more than anything else in the world as I stripped off and stepped over the rim, groaning with pleasure as I sank up to my neck in wondrous warmth while she went away to attend to something outside.

"Better…?"

I must have dozed off, for when I opened my eyes again and looked up, she was looking down at me with an appraising smile. "Bloody marvellous," was exactly how I felt, before I could check my tongue, not wishing to offend her ears with coarse language.

Still smiling, she let the shift crumple to the floor and daintily stepped into the opposite end of the bath, her superb legs outstretched between mine, toes playfully, artfully, teasingly pleasing me.

We took our dinner in loving silence, and never did a quiche taste better, or a chilled Chablis refresh so well. Afterwards we sat out on the balcony between the ornamental oranges, inhaling their heady perfume, holding hands, watching the crescent moon rise above Alexandria's *El Kornesh* seaside promenade as fireflies glowed among the palm trees' drooping fronds.

Sandra was still intrigued by Aunt Lucinda's letter and its references to that arch villain Bismarck. I told her what little I knew of the older woman's life abroad and mentioned the conversation with Vida Goldstein, at which my aunt had spoken of plotting with the Empress Eugénie to open higher education for all Frenchwomen.

"I never knew that! What a progressive thinker she must be!" Sandra had fought for women's rights, as a Suffragette, before volunteering to assist in an even bigger fight. "Then she really is an Imperial Baroness?"

"I s'pose so." I was not usually impressed by such kickshaws, but since becoming aware of Sandra's own exalted ancestors, I was starting to pay more attention. "There's always a Christmas card from the Empress, exiled in England since Napoleon III died. Why?"

"Because I would dearly love to see her!"

"So would I." Said with feeling, for I had no wish to see Gallipoli or hear gunfire, ever again. I stopped short, resolved not to think of the war during these few unsullied hours together. "She's a good sport. I only wish I'd asked more about her early days in the colony and learned why she was on first name terms with everyone-who-was-anyone in Paris, during the Second Empire. But what about yourself?"

Sandra was not easily deflected. "Do tell me, what is a sandalwood puller? What does 'fossick' mean? And why does the adopted son of a baroness choose to do such things?"

I found myself telling her of David - she had already met him, in a sense, by reading his letter - and of my abortive trip to Kalgoorlie, a name she insisted I write on a scrap of paper for her to look up on an atlas, later, it sounds so outlandish.

Some details were improved for dramatic effect, like finding gold nuggets the size of emu eggs, and wild brawls on Hannan Street that made Westralia sound more like a kinematic picture of America's Wild West than a sedate former-British colony.

Other events were blanked out, like the massacre at Mount Cedric, and my nude mural of Maeve, on display in an hotel's public bar. But overall, I think she got a reasonably truthful picture of who and what I was, except for the fever-stricken tea planters who had long since replaced a murdered mother and hanged father.

"But who is this 'Chief' you speak of so warmly…?"

"'The straightest ge'man on the Goldfields,'" I chuckled, mimicking Jonno, the Shamrock's manager, "though at first, I thought him a regular queer cove. Ex-Royal Navy, who came up to Kal', made and lost couple of fortunes, and was well on his way to making a third."

"'Was'? What happened…?"

"Killed. In an accident."

"Really?" She seemed to be looking straight past me to check something."

"Yes."

"Ah…"

"Why?" I frowned.

"You cared for him a lot."

"I still do." There was a catch in my throat. "The Chief was a prince among men."

"Indeed," she smiled enigmatically. "Now, it's my turn to share with you the rural delights of Counties Clare and Limerick." Which she did by accompanying me in imagination on horseback, for I had the feeling she was an accomplished rider as we trotted around her ancestral estates, unwittingly teaching the social codes that would later allow me to pass muster at English country houses, seemingly inattentive as high matters of state were spoken of in billiard rooms or on salmon beats.

The *Country Life* article had already told me that her father was a prominent figure in the Protestant Ascendancy, but it was she who added that he was also an enlightened landlord whose Catholic tenants enjoyed free access to a cottage hospital and dispensary; good housing by the standards of the day; a marriage dowry for their daughters; and an alms house for the aged.

Not that these benefits earned him any lasting gratitude. The Old Pile, as Sandra flippantly called their castle, was sacked and burned by the Fenians during the Irish War of Independence, as I later discovered when writing a series of articles on lake fishing in Eire.

Her mother, the niece of a former Viceroy of India, had been a celebrated beauty painted by Sargent. Ardently pursued by Edward, Prince of Wales, she had tactfully kept him at arm's length and instead became the chatelaine of many thousands of Irish acres where, among her other benevolent causes, she became a leading figure in the St John Ambulance as well as an enthusiastic patron of Henry Vere Foster's non-denominational primary schools. It was no accident that her personal motto, strictly adhered to, was *Noblesse Oblige*, or Privilege entails Responsibility.

The others in Sandra's immediate family were an older brother presently serving with the Royal Dublin Fusiliers, somewhere in France, and a younger tomboy sister, semi-secretly planning to abscond from CLC and join the VADs, once she had earned her Red Cross Certificate.

Despite my innate Australian distrust and scepticism, nourished by *The Bulletin*'s acerbic cartoons of chinless British aristocrats visiting "Aw-stray-yuh," I secretly envied her family. This had nothing to do with the pomp and ceremony that accompanies high rank but was simply an orphaned outsider's awareness that such people know who, and what, and where, and why they are. And with that comes the easy confidence these gifts bestow on those fortunate enough to be born with them.

Our soft murmurs and gentle laughter tapered into silence as a sea mist chilled the night air. It was time for bed, but not for sleep.

79

The *muezzin* atop nearby Abad El Rahman Mosque awakened me with his thrice-repeated call to prayer, each slower than the last as they ascended heavenwards. It was still dark outside and yet, like birds awakening in a forest, across this ancient city the same call – *salat al fajr* – echoed and re-echoed to greet the dawn. I had heard it often enough on Gallipoli when the Turkish defenders would halt the war at regular intervals. It says much for our peculiar relationship that we would ease the shooting and shelling, so as not to interrupt their devotions too much. Then, once they were done, it was back to business. Peculiar indeed!

Sandra was still fast asleep, her breath gently fanning the hairs on my chest, fragrant and fresh, warm as satin, nakedly smooth as silk beside me. I doubt if there was a prouder and happier young man on the planet that morning as I offered up my own silent prayer of thanksgiving, to Maeve, for revealing those things that had enabled me to amaze and delight another beautiful young woman.

Eventually she awoke, gave me a drowsily contented smile, and insisted on preparing a breakfast we then shared, propped up on pillows while planning the day ahead. Originally, we had intended to pack a picnic lunch and go boating on Lake Mareotis to look at the flamingos and pelicans, but the weather had other ideas, this being the start of what passes for a Rainy Season on the Egyptian coast. Not that either of us required much persuasion to stay exactly where and how we were.

Came Monday morning we bade a reluctant farewell to *Chez Adorable* the VADs' nickname for their private address, pronounced as in French, and made our way to 15AGH where I found myself on the Duty Sergeants' roster as a first step back to full duties, during which someone noticed that mine was a field promotion and I therefore needed to attend a course on the duties of a Senior Non-Commissioned Officer.

In tandem with this was a half hour session in the gymnasium, rebuilding my physique with barbells and Swedish drill, steadily increasing until I was sweating through a full hour in the morning as well as Physio' in the afternoon.

My time here was ending. Sandra knew this as well and wangled a second 48-hour pass while I slipped a one pound-note to another sergeant to take my place on the roster. I then bribed an Orderly Room clerk to stamp my papers and signed in at the Y before hailing a *gharri*. This time I brought a small amount of luggage that remained unopened while we took our bath before taking an elegantly prepared yet simple meal on the balcony.

The following morning, I unfolded an easel, set up a prepared canvas, opened a box of oil colours borrowed from the hospital's Recreation Room, and showed her my sketchbook's work notes of the original on David's envelope. Her portrait was my goodbye present after two amazingly beautiful, unforgettable weekends, for the way I saw it, our *affaire* had reached its natural and inevitable conclusion.

Two travellers from vastly different worlds had met, merged, and found their greatest delight in each other, but there was not one chance in ten million that an Australian infantry sergeant and a British earl's eldest daughter would ever amount to anything more than a joyful wartime fling.

After breakfast, she changed into the long, tropical service uniform frock and white apron I'd first seen her wearing. The Red Cross on her breast made a powerful focal point as I composed form and shape, light and shade, tone and texture, hues, and colours from my previous drawings.

It is no exaggeration to say I worked like a man possessed, applying the brush and spatula with an assurance I have never attained since then. We took a break for luncheon and a loving nap, after which I added a few touches to the portrait and signed-off with: *Icy Alexandria '15.*

"I-I shall treasure this, forever. One day you will be as famous as Sargent, because I shall make sure you get all the right introductions!" She meant it, never realising that his golden age of aristocratic portraiture was being blown to bits on the Western Front, even as we spoke.

Decades later, I read in a *Daily Telegraph* weekend supplement that Sandra's portrait had been acquired from a private collector and put on display at the Imperial War Museum, in London. Shortly afterwards, *VAD Nurse of the Great War* was selected as the artwork for an exhibition catalogue and posters. I never acknowledged my role and have allowed art historians to puzzle over *Icy Alexandria* and the heartfelt passion an unknown painter felt for his anonymous subject.

The following week I was discharged as fit for Active Service and reported to Movements, dreading another tour of Gallipoli. Had I possessed Aladdin's lamp, my only wish would have been for a loan of his magic carpet, so that Sandra and I could fly to a remote tropical isle where we could turn our backs on the war and start anew in our equivalent of David's "Mr & Mrs Smith..." Instead, I got orders to report at 5 Training Establishment, one hundred and seventy miles southeast of Alexandria.

My belovèd risked the hospital matron's wrath by walking me to the Transport Pool where I had arranged to hitch a lift with a convoy that would drop me off at Tel El Kebir before continuing down the road to Ismailia.

"Be careful." She kissed my open palm. "When all this is over, we shall go away, together."

A wonderful prospect but impossible, given the odds against it ever happening. I had lost the power of speech and reached for my kitbag, but still she held on tight, tracing a forefinger along my palm's creases before placing a small, very old bronze *ankh* - the Ancient Egyptian symbol of life eternal – on them and folded my fingers around it. "You have a long lifeline and I know you are well protected..."

"How so?" I managed to ask without my voice quaking too much.

She glanced up with another of her inscrutable smiles. "That first night, when we spoke, I felt a presence I thought was His Majesty's. It was not, of course, but someone very similar is taking good care of you.

I shivered. At no time had I ever mentioned the Chief's appearance or voiced my suspicions about his paternity.

The crisp and sunny late-winter's day raised my spirits, riding atop a stack of camouflage netting aboard one of fifty lorries in convoy as we crossed the Rosetta and Damietta branches of the Nile, before heading down through the oases of Tanta, and Benha, and Zagazig towards the sprawling military base that we Australians had inevitably nicknamed "Keg o' Beer."

I jumped off at its sandbagged guard post, showed my papers to an MP sentry and was directed to the Sergeants' Mess where an orderly escorted me into a larger adjacent hut. Mr Mess President – a grizzled warrant officer, similar in style to Pat Donovan - was taking lunch with about twenty other instructors before returning to their various duties and classrooms. He stood, inspected the crimson and navy-blue ribbon over my left breast pocket, then the wreathed MG proficiency badge on my right cuff, and formally shook hands. "Welcome aboard, Mr Cribdon."

"Thank you, sir."

Most of the peacetime rituals that used to be a feature of Officers' and SNCOs' Messes, like dining-in nights at which regimental bandsmen played while candlelit silver trophies gleamed on damask laid tables, no longer applied. Those that had survived wartime austerities were generally at the level one would find in any respectable household, like Tralee House, and I had no trouble fitting in.

The only hiccup was my belief that talkers mostly repeat what they already know, whereas listeners often learn something new. This meant that while other sergeants and warrant officers yarned and drank, I remained their attentive bystander nursing a middy of beer, the bystander who knew when to smile, when to chuckle, when to laugh at the right moment.

Some resented this and thought I was putting on airs; 16 Battalion's epic defence of Pope's Hill was already the stuff of Digger legend. Thus, any man who fought ashore during those first desperate hours was, by definition, a national hero with or without a DCM to stake his claim to immortality.

Being solitary by nature, I did not greatly mind what people thought of me and soon had more pressing concerns when fifteen other MG specialists assembled for Number 1 Course on the newly introduced Lewis Gun. Rumour had it that whoever came top would be held back as an instructor for subsequent intakes and I was determined to be that one, having lost all appetite for Gallipoli, or any other horrible place where strangers went about carelessly killing each another.

I wrote the required thank'ee note to Sandra shortly after arriving at Kebir, in which I told her how much I treasured our time together and wished her all the very best for a long and fulfilled life of future happiness; the model response of an Edwardian gentleman closing the door on an *affaire* that had been sweet and intense while it lasted, but which was now over. Finished. Done with.

Such formality would strike today's young people as very odd, if what I see in the Mac's Tele Vision Room is any indication of their current standards of behaviour and courtship. There are times when I think that Cole Porter must have been clairvoyant when I heard him playing a piano duet, with Noël Coward, as they mockingly crooned: "In olden days a glimpse of stocking was looked on as something shocking, now Heaven knows, anything goes!"

However, by renouncing her affection I knew I was saving us a world of heartache, for it was plain to me that an Anglo-Irish peer of the realm, Knight of the Most Illustrious Order of St Patrick, Knight Grand Cross of the Most Venerable Order of St John, member of His Majesty's Most Honourable Privy Council, was never going to welcome an Australian cartoonist into his illustrious, venerable, honourable family. Nor, truth be told, did I want to be any part of his toffy-nosed circus.

Sandra was an intelligent, engaging, adorable young woman doing her bit for King & Country in a military hospital, but how engaging and adorable would she be once returned to Court & Society as depicted in *Country Life* and *The Tatler*?

I am too thin-skinned to meekly accept, from an enraged patrician father, that I was the colonial swineherd who stole his daughter's virtue and besmirched the family escutcheon! For the sake of my own self-worth and male pride it was best that I be the one who nipped our romance in the bud, to save myself the humiliation of having an irate earl do it for me, and for what I would most likely do to him in return.

It was therefore with very mixed feelings that I read her prompt reply in the next APO delivery. She had misinterpreted my farewell note. Her letter sparkled with a puckish good humour and elegant puns. Written during the quiet hours of night duty, she seemed glad to chat *in absentia*, and concluded by hoping that all was well with me. She didn't quite say, "Please stay in touch," but her intention was plain enough.

This was not what I had planned! My head sternly warned against responding, but as so often happens in the great gamble of Life & Love, heart trumped head and I fooled myself into believing that it would be quite safe if I played the Disinterested Friend card with a sketch of trainee Lewis gunners in a comic muddle, and a humorous account of our daily routines. After all, only an unspeakable cad would pleasure a beautiful young lady in bed, and then cut her as if she were a half-crown streetwalker!

I should have listened to common-sense but, instead, found myself eagerly looking forward to her letters and postcards with their astute observations and searching queries on a wide range of subjects. I had already marvelled at how her mind had honed its formidable edge on the dense thoughts of Germanic philosophers like Johann Fichte. It was she who first explained his dialectical triad – Thesis, Antithesis, Synthesis – by quoting the original text while frying our breakfast eggs, before explaining how Georg Hegel had developed Fichte's original proposition.

I had never, ever dared to hope that one day I would find intellect, and beauty, and kindness so perfectly balanced, but now that I had, it was a terrifying experience. No way could I play the Disinterested Friend. I had to be with Sandra, all of Sandra, and nobody but Sandra, for evermore. And it was not just her obvious physical charm, there was also a supernaturally intense attraction, impossible to define or resist.

I have long held a private theory that men and women are the equal halves of a greater whole, and that our main purpose in life is to search for and cherish that one whose half most completes our own unfinished self. It was my tragedy to have found that Mystical Other on the far side of an unbridgeable social divide.

Despite all, during the next several weeks, my often whimsical, sometimes illustrated replies were written by the hissing glare of a Tilley lamp in such a way that she could bind them in a folder as if they were weekly instalments of a Dickens' novel. Here they joined *Boolya's Hoard*, an improbable adventure yarn based on *King Solomon's Mines*, that she had implored me to share with her.

My daylight hours were spent with a different sort of love. It sounds obscene to speak of the Lewis gun in this manner, but whereas I had operated the Vickers as if it were a lathe on Death's assembly line, the Lewis was more like a precision hand tool a man could become attached to as he hugged and lugged it around the battlefield.

Its advantages were obvious within moments of seeing one for the first time. I knew straightaway that we ought to have had these automatic rifles for the attack on Hill 971. Relatively light and man-portable, half a dozen Lewis gunners would have stalled the Turkish counterattacks and secured our position atop that accursed ridge. There was even a chance we might have won the Suvla stunt if only I'd had enough of them, enfilading the enemy's positions, instead of relying upon a Vickers' indirect barrage fire.

These insights redoubled my efforts to master Colonel Lewis's "Belgian Rattlesnake," so called because although designed for the United States Army, Belgium's *Fabrique Nationale* was the first to recognise what a revolutionary weapon it was, soon followed by Birmingham Small Arms Company who took over the manufacture when FN's Liège factories were occupied by the Kaiser's army the previous August.

Our course was the first to handle one, brought out to Egypt by a BSA technician promoted to temporary lieutenant on the General List. He was not an inspired instructor, but he did his best to follow the army's systematic method of demonstrating a function, explaining its components, leading us through repeated practice sessions, before consolidating our knowledge with verbal and written examinations.

We had been issued with notebooks and pencils, and I suspected these would be marked at the end of the course, and thus made very sure mine was neatly written-up with expanded drawings of every item on the List of Parts, from butt plate to radiator casing front clamp, via feed operating arm, cartridge guide spring, gas regulator key, and so on for eighty-five interconnecting pieces of machined steel, brass, and aluminium. Recalling how Percy had used a Vickers' training manual for after-hours' revision at Blackboy Camp, I borrowed a Lewis Gun manual and organised informal quizzes for the rest of my course, determined to be seen as instructor material.

Classroom theory done and dusted the time came to test our skills by firing at piles of discarded mudbricks along the banks of an ancient canal that used to connect the Nile with Lake Timsah when Pharoah ruled the land. Here we fired magazine-pans of ammunition from standing, kneeling, prone positions, fire-and-movement crawls from one sandbag to the next.

We were by not the first soldiers to use this ochre gravel for the purposes of war; I souvenired several Martini-Henry cartridge cases the desert winds were winnowing to the surface, relics of the battle fought here thirty-five years earlier when Britain took control of the Canal.

No doubt, had we dug deeper, we would have uncovered bronze arrowheads, and below them the sharpened flints and sling stones that even earlier warriors had shot or flung to conquer or defend this strategic neck of land between Asia and Africa. What future generations will make of our squashed, copper-clad lead slugs never occurred to us as noisy fountains of grit and dust pulverised an ancient slave's hard labour.

After a fortnight's intensive training we were awarded our LG cuff badges and results. I came first by several percentage points but no instructors' posting followed, instead we packed our kit and RTU'd. In my case Zeitun Camp was the Unit Returned To.

By now Gallipoli was a lost cause and secret plans were underway to evacuate the dreadful place by the end of the year, hence no more reinforcements were being fed into the meat grinder. Instead, as our depleted battalions withdrew from Lemnos, we old hands were under orders to flesh them out with new drafts from Australia.

1916

80

Our evacuation from Gallipoli, completed during the last week of 1915, was a humiliating defeat that still resonates across the Middle East, regardless of how often newspapers reported the cunning ruses that hoodwinked the Turks into letting us escape without loss. For men like me, those comforting stories were at best a thin slap of whitewash that concealed one quarter of a million casualties, with nothing good to show for eight months of bitter fighting.

It did not help that our arrangements to receive the new drafts from Australia were atrocious even by Egyptian standards, with never enough tents, never enough water, never enough of anything needful, and for me a bleak reminder of conditions when the 1st AIF arrived in this accursed country.

As if all that were not enough official bastardisation to contend with, the standard British Army ration allowance of eight pence halfpenny, per man, *per diem*, was meagre at the best of times. Now, with market prices doubling and the Egyptian contractors' shameless theft, it was at famine level. Not that it mattered greatly as there were no cookhouses to feed the incoming troops, only fire pits lined with steel tie plates and track fittings pinched from a nearby railway yard, to heat the unappetizing slop in our dixies.

Fuel for the campfires was another fret. With few woodlands of any value on the Nile Delta, and none on the Western Desert or Sinai, all firewood used to be shipped down the coast from Turkish Lebanon to Turkish Egypt, until the outbreak of war put an end to this trade. Now, except for broken packing cases and ammunition boxes, we had to depend upon imports of kindling and brushwood from Cyprus and Greece, to heat the troops' skimpy rations.

Some enterprising lads with access to petrol, filled empty ration tins with sand, poured on a cup of fuel, struck a match and, if they didn't blow themselves up, brewed hot drinks for our increasingly damp and chilly nights in the desert; I preferred my less-dramatic Primus stove.

Corrupt Egyptian contractors were not the only criminals making life difficult; city magistrates, back home, were giving their hard cases the choice of jail or enlistment in the AIF. Those of us already in uniform felt that if these rancid specimens were not wanted in Australia, then sure as hell they were not wanted in our ranks!

I am happy to report that the regimental crushers were merciless when double-marching these alley rats before our Officer Commanding, on their ways through to the guardhouse or a military prison's even harsher regime. I have often felt they were the ones responsible for those later, sadly true reports of mistreatment, robbery, and murder of German prisoners, that tarnished the AIF's reputation on the Western Front.

Frances will no doubt protest at my implied approval of rough justice, when she eventually receives these tape-recorded cassettes, so I had better explain that an army stands or falls on trust or lack thereof.

While there's a belief that one can count on mates doing the right thing, and while they can count on you to look after their interests, it's a winning team. But if an NCO lets the canker of distrust and disobedience infect his unit, without taking immediate action to restore the balance, everyone suffers. As a reformed sneak thief, myself, I recognised all the opening moves and acquired an occult reputation for stopping crime before it got started.

Our stay in Egypt, between evacuating Gallipoli and embarking for France, is an unrecognised campaign that opened early in January 1916 when orders were given to strengthen the Canal's defences against Turkish raiding parties. GHQ still had no idea what to do with twenty thousand restless Australians. Deploying us in the Sinai Desert, on the far side of the Suez Canal, seemed like the quickest way to evaporate our unruly spirits. This began with orders to entrain aboard open railway wagons – thirty men apiece, kit and weapons stacked along the centre, eyes squeezed shut against flying sparks and soot – for a miserable journey to Ismailia.

Detraining at Moascar on the outskirts of that filthy, flea-bitten town, we marched to a pontoon bridge spanning the Canal from its west bank to east, where a military road was being built inland. Sweating and swearing we marched past gangs of Egyptian labourers and camels humping panniers of broken rock from nearby quarries, while Royal Engineer sappers and Pay Corps clerks kept a tally of loads and quantities.

A further couple of miles up country, tucked among steep, razorbacked sand dunes, we stumbled into Number 1 Staging Camp and found, as usual, too few tents and too little of anything except heat and flies, discomfort, and sickness. I continued ahead with a reconnaissance party to check the frontline defences, an extended chain of sandbagged strongpoints linked by communication trenches, eight miles into the wilderness that Moses roamed while plotting to massacre the Canaanites.

Three Turkish army divisions, one hundred miles farther north, were planning to do much the same to us, by recapturing Egypt and cutting the British Empire's spinal cord between Suez and Port Said. I was sceptical of their chances. My men were in no great shape after tramping only a few miles across this same terrain; it was hard to see how the Turks were going to erupt from Sinai's mirages and dust devils, fighting fit and fit to fight, without months of preparation that our reconnaissance aeroplanes would surely have seen coming.

We emplaced the Lewis guns with interlocking fields of fire, to support a stretched line of riflemen. The main force was held in reserve, together with the Vickers' section and a couple of 10-pounders manned by Sikhs of the improbably named Hong Kong & Singapore Mountain Artillery, keen to blast away with shrapnel when the footsore Turks eventually plodded into range.

Our ground reconnaissance was entrusted to a second exotic unit, the Bikaner Camel Corps, recruited and paid for by General Sir Ganga Singh a warrior prince who commanded his own private army of tough Rajastani *sowars*. Instantly nicknamed the Buccaneers, these mounted infantrymen had proved their worth in China during the Boxer Rebellion, and later during the conquest of Somaliland, and would soon thrash their current enemy in a brisk little battle at Waadi Hilumi.

Sir Ganga himself was a most gracious and enlightened host during my second visit to India in the 1930s. As I learned then and will share with Frances, notable among his many achievements was the banning of child marriage that hitherto amounted to domestic slavery spiced with rape; the promotion of higher education for women; and the excavation of a major canal system that turned seven and a half million acres of arid wilderness into fertile farmland for his people.

I shall suggest to her that Sir Ganga's life and deeds are rich material awaiting a serious biography because, to the best of my knowledge, nobody has ever written one in English. Assuming she takes the hint, an excellent focal point will be Sir William Orpen's imposing oil-on-canvas of world statesmen signing the Versailles Treaty in 1919 where, standing immediately behind the leaders of France and Britain, she will find a handsomely moustached senior British officer proudly wearing a turban - General Maharaja Sir Ganga Singh GCSI, GCIE, GCVO, GBE, KCB, GCStJ - representing India's immense contribution to Victory.

Of course, none of these events would've seemed even remotely possible, four years earlier in Egypt, where every couple of days fresh troops were sent up the line and the previous draft brought down to resume training, it being vital for morale that we maintained a sense of purpose and discipline.

It was here that we learned to wear the Phenate Hexamine "bogyman" gas mask. As practical Australians we regarded the idea of a Turkish chlorine attack on a windswept desert as a huge joke, knowing that any gas released would likely blow back onto the enemy or disperse, long before reaching our lines. The more worldly and imaginative among us promptly nicknamed these baggy protective hoods "Ansells," from their resemblance to the thin rubber prophylactic sheaths made by Eric Ansell in his Richmond factory, across the Yarra from my old home in Toorak.

Then, just before we were driven insane by the twin scourge of sand fleas and thirst, Brigade marched us back to Ferry Post where we took over the Canal's inner defences. These amounted to a line of earthworks built from dredged spoil reinforced by countless tens of thousands of sandbags, its southern flank anchored on Lake Timsah's farthermost shore, while the northern one connected with the Canal a mile or so above Ferry.

It was here that we emplaced MG sections at Benchmark and Ridge Post, both regarded as lucky numbers for troops whose main duty, apart from swimming and fishing, was to keep watch on local feluccas with their graceful triangular sails, or wave to steamers and warships as they passed by in convoy. These were often close enough for passengers to reply by throwing chocolate, cigarettes, and tobacco wrapped in newspapers, which passed the time very pleasantly for a fortunate few. Life was less agreeable for the rest of us, accommodated as we were in ragged tents that let everything in and kept nothing out.

Systematic training was impossible, now that we also had to provide sentries for a large ammunition dump on the west bank. In addition, we manned the ferry transporting horses, mules, camels, troops, back and forth whenever the pontoon bridge was swung aside. And when the bridge was open again, we were expected to police its traffic by checking civilian passes and luggage to ensure that no Ottoman spy or sympathiser smuggled arms and explosives into Egypt.

The worst job of all was having to replace the Native Labour Corps whose sticky fingers itched to get stuck into the hundreds of tons of supplies being landed at Ferry Post. We had earned the nickname Diggers on Gallipoli, because of our prowess with pick and shovel, now we became Wharfies lumping ration boxes and ammunition cases, engineering equipment and medical supplies, onto light railway wagons that chuffed away into the distance where an attack on Gaza was being stealthily stockpiled.

In between these chores there were endless coils of barbed wire to unload from the barges and carry away on tent poles slung between our bruised shoulders. And when that loathsome task slackened there remained thousands of iron water pipes to shift, each one coated with a tar compound that smeared our naked skin like the proverbial on a pauper's blanket.

Although committed to leading by example, as is every NCO's duty, I was soon as exhausted and fed up as any other man in the army. It did not help that the first anniversary of our landing at Anzac Cove coincided with this low ebb in our lives. Elsewhere the AIF was holding commemorative parades to honour veterans of that disastrous campaign, not that we outliers needed a reminder of those we'd left behind on the Peninsula.

To mark the occasion, I snaffled a crate of *Pyramid Lager* while another couple of blokes ambushed a tray of sausages, also in transit to the Officers' Mess. We then vanished behind a sand dune where our Officer Commanding, a rare survivor of the slaughter at Lone Pine, found us merrily unbuttoned when he popped over to share a hot snag', a warm beer, and a toast to fallen comrades.

81

It was about then that I got a brief note from Sandra, saying she was on embarkation leave and hoped we might be able to catch up before she left Egypt. My head sternly warned me to stay away. Nothing good could possibly come from stoking the feelings damped down with camp gossip and cartooned letters. But, inevitably, heart trumped head in life's greatest gamble.

Young and ardent, I was as much in love with Sandra's mind as I was with the rest of her enchanting self. It is no exaggeration to say that I burned to be with her again, to listen, to talk, to test ideas stimulated by our correspondence. The thought of sharing her other delights was not wholly absent, of course, when I wangled a 48-hour pass before sending a cautious telegram accepting her invitation.

I drew a clean set of khakis from Q Store, and a new pith helmet to replace the old wreck I'd worn since losing my trench cap on the way to 1AGH; our iconic slouch hats were still only seen on newcomers while we Originals waited for fresh uniforms to arrive from Australia.

After collecting six weeks' accumulated pay, I tapped into the sergeants' bush telegraph and organised a lift in an otherwise empty staff car returning to the Transport Pool in Alexandria. This gave me ample time to weigh my options as we sped along the desert road, horn honk-honking to overtake crawling artillery trains, plodding ranks of infantry, and trotting detachments of cavalry while I lolled on the back seat, cheekily impersonating a senior brass hat reporting to GHQ.

Sandra's note was waiting at the Y's reception desk and told me to come straight to *Chez Adorable*. Whistling a happy tune, I signed in, shouldered my haversack, and directed a *gharry* to my favourite lamp-lit street. The mute maidservant promptly responded to my door knock. I hesitated for only a moment, relishing the rich aroma of whatever it was that Sandra was preparing for dinner, then bounded upstairs, two steps at a time, casting aside all pretence of friendly restraint.

Sandra greeted me with a fond smile, a warm embrace, and a loving kiss before leading the way to our accustomed seats on the balcony where we usually took our ease before bath time games began, but not this evening. Instead, I turned sharply as footsteps approached us and saw an elderly man in spotless whites, a chef's toque firmly seated on balding head. "What the deuce -?!"

"*Gnädiges Fräulein,*" he gave Sandra a courtly bow, "all that you commanded is done. I await further orders."

"*Danke, Anton. Ein paar minuten mehr bitte.*"

"*Zum befehl, Exzellenz.*" He bowed again and withdrew.

I knew that she had planned to study in Germany, but we had agreed not to speak that language in case a third party overheard it and denounced us as spies, something too easily done in these times of heightened fear and suspicion. "Who the devil is that?" I frowned.

"*Maître* Anton Wehrli," she replied. "César Ritz, Auguste Escoffier, and he established the Savoy Grill as London's premier supper rooms. In fact, it was

Anton who prepared my parents' wedding breakfast after their marriage in the Guards' Chapel," she added. "Why?"

"That's as maybe," I countered, "but what the hell is he doing here?"

"He was *chef de cuisine* for the Khedive, whose ouster coincided with Anton's wish to return home to Switzerland," she explained simply. "However, he's agreed to stay on at the Montaza Palace for a short while longer, to train the new king's staff and, as a family favour, prepare meals for me, on special occasions."

"Say again?" I blinked. "The Khedive's head cook owes you a favour?"

"Strictly speaking it's my father he's indebted to," she conceded. "There was a spot of bother at the Savoy, six thousand pounds went missing and some famous reputations were badly dented, but Pa' knew that Anton was straight as an arrow and took care of things," she added, with a modest shrug that implied great privilege equals great power as well as great responsibility. "And before you ask," she continued, "this special occasion is my way of thanking you for so very, very much…"

"Glad to oblige." Said with more than a dash of defensive irony.

"You see, there's less need for me now that we've finished with the Dardanelles, and Australian army nurses are replacing us," she explained, reaching out to pat my wrist, "so I've volunteered for the Channel hospital ships where the need is greatest. But, please continue writing and drawing, even though I shan't be able to reply as frequently as I would like to." She hesitated before concluding: "Conditions on the ships, and ambulance trains, are a bit hectic: I won't have much free time between transfers."

By now I had sufficient experience of battlefield evacuations to know what she spoke of. The implication that the Western Front's casualties were even worse than ours had been, and that she would soon be toiling among them, affected me badly and I would have said more except that *Maître* Wehrli was about to serve our first course, a poached duck egg in roasted onion consommé that redefined the meaning of superb.

By unspoken agreement we finished the first course in silence and waited for the second in quiet anticipation. Although it was late springtime there was a noticeable chill in the night air, perfect for the hearty Swiss dish that was about to be served.

"*Züricher Geshnetzeltes und Rösti.*" Announced with a measured bow.

"*Danke Anton, ich bin mir sicher, das absolut exquisit ist.*" And absolutely exquisite it most certainly was!

Aunt Lucinda only engaged the best cooks, but none of them could have prepared sliced veal and sautéed kidneys in white wine, cream, and demi-glace sauce, like the dish before me now. *Rösti*, the traditional shredded potato pancakes of the Bern region, lightly fried in seasoned butter, made the perfect accompaniment, as did a Kreuzberg '09 from Bad Neuenahr, in the Rhine Palatinate.

"I have often felt you must be psychic." I raised my glass to salute this most remarkable young lady. "Now I know for certain…"

"Why is that" she smiled back

"Because of all the vintages in the world you might have chosen, this is the one that could have come straight from Tralee's cellar…"

She accepted my compliment with another gracious smile. "It was really as simple as one plus one makes a pair, namely your fascinating aunt and Franz Liszt." A raised finger stopped me from interrupting as she concluded: "What you've said of their passionate stay at Neuenahr, suggested that her vintner would have imported many a case of this delicious red, to remind her of those happy times, long ago..."

I would have pursued this uncanny insight, except that two bowls of pistachio ice-cream and fresh strawberries, perfectly matched in colour and texture, were about to appear on our table.

Shortly thereafter we took our coffees onto the balcony and waved goodbye as a motor taxi drove our chef back to Montaza's kitchens where a lavish banquet was in preparation for the new king's state visit to Alexandria.

"Such a delightful man," Sandra observed with an endearing smile as we sat down on our accustomed wicker chairs between the blossoming orange trees in their terracotta pots and watched fire-flies glow among the nearby palm fronds, stirred by a gentle onshore breeze.

"And a culinary wizard to boot," I agreed sleepily, "but surely, he must've learned some English? Working in London?"

"Of course," she smiled in the semi-darkness. "He speaks quite fluently, albeit with a heavy accent. Why?"

I searched for the right words before cautiously replying: "Didn't we, um, agree that German was *Verboten*?"

"Not among old friends. Besides," she added with a mischievous chuckle, "*Mann muss eine lang Nase immer machen* to nosy little spy hunters!"

I was quite shocked to hear this pungent phrase, literally: "One must always pull a long nose." Which roughly translates as cocking a snook at authority, an action more aligned with our easy-going Australian troops than the Kaiser's obedient subjects, so I was naturally intrigued to learn where she might have overheard such a subversive expression.

"In Germany of course," she explained. "'Pa' arranged for me to spend summer with an academic family in Berlin, to see if I still wanted to go there instead of Cambridge."

"And did you?"

She took her time, forming a considered opinion, before replying: "It was an unsettling experience, but one that stiffened my resolve to discover how, and why, Bismarck imposed Prussia's abominable Second Reich on those formerly jovial, independent German kingdoms, principalities, and Free Cities of the Hansa League."

"'Unsettling'?" Two years into a war against the abominable Prussians and their Turkish allies, I could find a stronger description than that!

Sandra nodded, after another reflective pause. "It felt as if I were living two parallel lives. Remember," she continued, turning to look at me, her face softly lit by a gas streetlamp a few yards beyond the balcony's railing, "I'd been schooled to regard Germany as *Das Land der Dichter und Denker* - the homeland of poets like Annette von Droste Hüsthoff, of philosophers like Johann Fichte - in luminous contrast to stuffy old England and dreary old Ireland."

She paused, aware that such opinions bordered on treason, before concluding with a sad smile: "Instead, it felt as if Wagner had composed one of his interminable operas, with *Dr Jekyll & Mr Hyde* its subject, and then coerced the newly-minted *Reich* into chorusing its menacing libretto."

She sensed my disapproval but persisted with her lonely vindication of the most reviled people on earth, at that period in history. "Inside their family circles one could not wish to find more cultivated and agreeable hosts. All were amateur musicians of high standard; all read widely; all thought deeply on matters of consequence; most were decent, honourable men and women.

"And yet, whenever venturing outdoors, it seemed as if they felt obliged to wear a ferocious mask. Heels would click like gun shots; everyone would bow like clockwork toys whenever I was introduced as *Die englische Gräfin*, though of course that is Ma's title, and everyone conversed - if one may describe it so - by barking like vocal wolfhounds. One had the feeling that a Grimm Brothers' wicked witch had cast her evil spell over the entire nation, condemning it to strut about on an invisible parade ground…"

"Hardly the sort to thumb their noses at authority," I observed drily, unimpressed by her fond memories of homelife in Hunland.

"Certainly not the older generation," she agreed with weary forbearance, "but there was one young student who used to visit, hoping to improve his English for the *Abitur* examination. He claimed to be a Social Democrat, but I suspect he was a secret Communist from the way he mocked Germany's gimcrack colonial empire in Africa, the Pacific, and China. All very exciting and mildly dangerous when one is abroad for the first time." Her wistful smile faded to sadness. "I wonder where he is, now? Or even if he still is, now?"

I shrugged indifferently, having long since lost any sympathy for the strangers whose munitions and allies had tried killing me on numerous occasions and would be trying again soon, in France. "And yet you still wanted to study their language and literature?" I frowned. "Why?"

"Because German is so, enthralling," she replied simply.

"Eh?!" My shell-shocked ears had obviously misheard her.

"Don't look so stunned, Darling! I know you speak it quite well, but if only you could open your heart to German's elegant syntax and logical grammatical structure, you would find much that is, truly wonderful…"

"Bloody hell."

"Please don't scoff. I am serious!"

"That's what worries me!" I shook my head in disbelief. "German syntax and grammar, enthralling and wonderful? I've heard everything now -!"

"No, you have not!" she interrupted firmly. "Take for example a substantive compound noun like *Verschlimmbesserung*. As you know, *schlimmer* means to make something worse, and *besser* means to make something better. In other words, this conjunction describes a good intention with a bad outcome!" She paused, studying me closely. "Now, where in all of our misty, imprecise English language can you find such a concise way to express such a complex sentiment?"

"I hope I never have to!"

"And that, my dear, is where we must agree to disagree," she concluded with a reproachful shake of the head. "You are content to muddle along with the same old vocabulary of slipshod, Anglo-Norman words and phrases sprinkled with foreign borrowings that, as Humpty Dumpty says in *Through the Looking Glass*, mean whatever you want them to mean. I, on the other hand, prefer a language and culture that is systematically building its own great universal library of science, and art, and music that any literate, enquiring mind can access and work within!"

Debating the finer points of German grammar was not what I wanted us to be doing on this, our last night together: "You can't be serious?" I asked, with an incredulous half-smile.

"Never more so," she replied with a challenging frown. "You have no idea how infuriating it is to 'converse' with drawling male cousins who never complete a full sentence. Idle young fellows barely capable of starting one! And even if they do reach a vague conclusion, leave me wondering what it was they were trying to say in the first place. 'Ay wot? Don'cha know, ol' chepp? Haw! Haw!!'

"Whereas, conversing with my German friends," she continued, regaining her composure, "our thoughts develop in an orderly, systematic manner. And if perchance a word or definition doesn't yet exist, it is permissible to construct a new one, and for everyone to understand what's being said. Try doing that in English!"

"I've no need to," I snapped back, a peevish, ardent young fool, "and never with your 'friends'!"

"But -?!"

"Now you listen to me!" It was high time I asserted my male authority. "The orders that torpedoed the *Lusitania*, that shot Nurse Cavell, that sacked Luvain, were each and every one given in your 'wonderful' bloody German!"

Like the great majority of men and women of my time and place, I had fallen prey to Lord Northcliffe's screeching headlines and lurid despatches from Occupied Europe. Lady Sandra Nobury was one of the few sane exceptions to his venomous rule. "Yes!" she declared proudly. "And in every abominable act I see the dark fears that compelled it -!"

"The Huns? Fearful?!" Northcliffe's editors had done a splendid job of seeding our imaginations with half-tone pictures of spike-helmeted brutes goose-stepping their way to world conquest.

Sandra ignored my disbelieving snort. "Only a barbarian can fail to admire the homeland of Beethoven! Of Friedrich Fröbel, the pioneering genius of kindergarten education! Of Alexander von Humbolt, polymath *par excellence*! Of Leopold von Ranke, the pioneer of modern historiography! Of countless other towering figures in every field of art and science!"

"Try telling that to the *Lusitania*'s passengers -!"

"If I could, I would, for even they would understand, once they knew the reason -!"

"What reason?!" My laugh was cruelly disdainful.

"'Geography determines destiny'!"

"Says who?!"

"Napoleon!"

"When?!"

"When half-a-million of his French soldiers raped, burned, and pillaged the German heartland during their abortive invasion of Russia! And did so again when, as a defeated rabble, they plundered their way back to France, across the same devastated wasteland! Hanging! Shooting! Torturing defenceless German peasants to disgorge what little remained of their food and fodder! Chased by an even more rapacious Cossack horde! Horrors that Germany has never forgotten!"

"Nah! All that happened yonks ago!" I announced, distancing myself from Europe's feuding follies behind a screen of flippant Australian slang.

"One hundred and four years," she announced with haughty precision. "Almost within living memory!"

"Not mine!" I responded with a petulant, childish remark that laid me wide open to the most scorching five minutes of my young life.

There was much more to Sandra than mere physical charm and kindly warmth. There was also a formidable intellect and strength of character that pinned me against the wall, so to speak, while she shredded my shallow opinions with references to an earlier conversation in which she'd declared that an historian must think and act like dispassionate pathologist when confronting a body of historical evidence, and bravely seek factual truth no matter how disturbing it may be for his or her preconceived beliefs, rather than rewrite the past to cowardly conform with whatever happens to be someone else's fad or fantasy.

It was thanks to her lucid, spontaneous, geopolitical tutorial, that I began to decode centuries of European history which, until then, had been no more than a catalogue of disjointed events and individuals, long gone and mostly forgotten.

And saw the crucial importance of the English Channel as a defensive moat that doubled as Britain's highway to a worldwide commercial empire upon which the sun never set.

And understood why, with three flanks covered by the Atlantic, the Pyrenees, the Mediterranean, France could regard Central Europe as her *terrain de manœuvre* for more than two centuries of trampling petty German city-states, principalities, and kingdoms that lacked natural frontiers, except for the Rhine and the Alps, both of limited value against invading foreign armies.

And grasped why that unhappy nation's destiny has always been decided by its geography, and why its people have always been in a state of fearful tension on the North German Plain – stretching as it does between the Lowlands and Muscovy –a natural battleground for French, Spanish, Austrian, Russian, Swedish, Dutch and British armies, before, during, and after the genocidal Thirty Years War of the early-1600s.

"Blenheim! Leuthen! Eylau! Leipzig! Hochkirck! Zorndorf! Scores and scores of devastating conflicts fought on German soil!" she concluded defiantly. "Is it any wonder its people feel the need to be armed to the teeth, with threatening enemies on every side, and why *Einkreisung* – encirclement – looms so largely in their collective imagination?!"

"Maybe so, but what's any of this got to do with the "Rape of Belgium'?" I mumbled uncomfortably.

"Work it out for yourself," she replied in a voice abruptly drained flat. "I am so awfully, awfully tired, of trying to make sense, of a world gone mad." She took a despairing breath. "When this is over, I shall return to Berlin, doing whatever I can, to prove that Britain and Germany are natural allies, not enemies, and that all this has all been a dreadful mistake." She hesitated one last time, before tentatively adding: "Perhaps we can both go? You and I, working together…?"

"What?!"

"I've never asked before, out of respect for your privacy, but how does a fossicking sandalwood puller come to speak German at all?"

I scowled defensively. "Our family doctor qualified at the *Charité*. We'd discuss all sorts of things, in German, whenever he, and I, and my aunt played *skat*, which was quite often."

"You surprise me," Sandra leaned forwards. "I can't imagine *Mme la baronne* enjoying a German card game, given how much she detests Bismarck, after the disaster of '71…"

"Actually, in her own words: 'To play a leading role on the world's great stage, one must charm in French, command in German, and bewilder in Russian!' Thus, we only spoke French on Mondays, German on Wednesdays, and Russian on Saturdays," I explained shortly.

"What an astonishing lady!" my own astonishing lady exclaimed with a delighted handclap. "I would dearly love to meet her!"

"No more than she would love to meet you," I replied before concluding, with more than a hint of yearning: "I owe her an immense debt of gratitude..."

"I know."

"How?"

"You are a good man, Ian Cribdon, but there is more to you than plain goodness." She hesitated, picking her next words with care, aware of how prickly I can be in matters personal. "For most men it's a question of innate nature, but in you I see evidence of caring nurture. Perhaps that's your attraction?" She paused, gauging her progress thus far. "Remember, if it were not for this horrid war, I would be expected to dance the night away with inarticulate Guards' officers or hobnob with country squires, in Town for the Season, whose only interests are yelping dogs, galloping horses, and dying foxes. Whereas, with you, my dear, there will always be fresh horizons we can explore together..."

"What's that got to do with my aunt?" I was becoming defensively gruff again.

"Everything and nothing," she replied enigmatically, examining my face closely. "Everything, because in you I see her affectionate handiwork. You have never had a single day of formal schooling and yet converse widely and well in at least one of three foreign languages; you draw and paint with flair; and when required, comport yourself as a gentleman to the manner, as well as the manor, born." Her eyes sparkled, as they always did in our punning word games. "You clearly come from a richly cultivated family background, and it would be an honour to thank your aunt, in person, for what she's done, for us..."

"But."

"But what?"

"That's the 'everything' half," I frowned. "What's the 'nothing'?"

She hesitated. "I am aware of a great darkness within you, even before this dreadful war added more to your grievous burden, and yet I don't feel in the least threatened by it. Because, come what may, I know you will always be there for me," she reached out to touch my chest, "as I shall always be here for you." The same finger lightly touched her breast.

I squirmed, tortured by memories of a syphilitic father's homeward shuffle, and of the sunny afternoon Mama bled to death alongside her murdered brother-in-law. I had every reason to fear losing this radiantly wonderful woman's respect, if she ever learned, the sordid truth, about me. "And what does this fanciful tosh actually mean?" I glowered.

"It means, just as David's letter was greater than the sum of its parts, your words reveal more than –"

"They're not as revealing as they could be!" I shouted angrily.

"As one would expect of a gentleman," she replied with a wise smile. "*Boolya's Hoard* is less restrained. Likewise, your hero Darcy Shaw. The way he rescues that poor abused Aboriginal girl from the bushrangers, then carries her across the Outback to the AIM hospital at Mackenzie, tells me much about their author's own depth of character.

"Also, when Darcy confronts Ezra Gorse and feels not the slightest twinge of pity after searching the dead man's pockets for evidence of how he swindled the camel driver's family out of their share of the goldmine!"

She rested chin on fist. "There is much more to you than meets the eye, Sarn't Cribdon. But what I've seen thus far, I admire immensely –"

"Halt!" My hand flew up, as if signalling troops on the march, struggling to restrain the raging tumult beneath my ribs. "You know! I know! We both know! It is impossible! For this! To go! Any further! There is no future for someone like you! Attaching herself to someone like me! And yet my only wish, my only desire, my only ambition is to be your loyal, your loving husband! The father of your children! The guardian unto death of our family!"

My unscripted, impassioned, heartfelt words kept tumbling out. "God knows, if things were different, if we were different, I would be the happiest, the proudest man in the universe! But we are not, nor ever will be, and I feel so utterly wretched, to be so near and yet so far from the one person I respect, I cherish, more than any other, or ever will do -!"

She silenced my anguished cries with a finger lightly touching her lips, then, with infinite grace and tenderness, reached for my trembling hand.

82

Early next morning, I carried her kit down to the waiting *gharri*. She looked so neat, so complete, so elegant even in a drab tropical VAD uniform, I knew this was one image that would remain with me, vivid and true, until my final breath.

"Please," she smiled, "do stay in touch. If only by postcard."

"No." I looked away. "Not a good idea."

"Why not?!"

"Because all that was said last night, holds true today, and always will do." I looked up from the dusty ground and faced her squarely. "What we've shared here can never be equalled, can never be repeated, because you are about to return to a family, to friends unlike any I've known or, to be frank, would be comfortable with, any more than they'd feel at ease, with me."

"But -!"

"I know who I am, and what I am, and where I fit into the greater scheme of things," I persisted quietly, overriding her objection, "and you don't belong, any more than I belong in your world. Therefore, it's best we call it quits, and go our separate ways."

"So, this is, the end…?"

"Yes"

She said nothing more. Instead, taking both of my hands, she kissed each palm before placing her own between them, as if in prayer. It was another fifteen years before I decoded what had seemed like a spontaneously loving gesture of farewell, and then only after studying an illuminated missal in El Escorial's medieval library, depicting a knight as he pledges his fealty to the King of Aragon by placing his hands between those of his overlord, exactly as Sandra had done with mine.

The *gharri* driver flourished his whip and the ramshackle equipage lurched away towards the docks. I turned, went upstairs, collected my kit, and never again set foot in *Chez Adorable*.

The rest of that dreadful morning was spent slumped on one of the stone plinths that line the seaward side of *El Kornish*, staring far beyond the moored battleships and cruisers of the Mediterranean Fleet, my vision blurred by bitter tears of regret. I must have looked so bereft, so down on my luck, that not one of Alexandria's teeming, persistent beggars dared approach me for *baksheesh*, lest I give him the Evil Eye instead.

Eventually I found my way to Central Transport Pool and hitched a ride to Ferry Post, much to the surprise of my messmates who had not expected me to return until the following day, bringing the latest hot gossip.

"Nah," I grunted, "just some personal stuff needed sorting." I did not elaborate. None of my brother sergeants would have believed me had I told them how I had just spurned the most beautiful, the most intelligent, the most loving woman any man could ever desire, or even dare to desire.

Instead, I cruelly banished Sandra from my world and, in her place, built the reputation of a rock-hard NCO. The implacable judge of all things slack and slovenly. A demon for by-the-book discipline on the firing range. The one hundred percent perfectionist with a caustic tongue for those less motivated. Grown men had every reason to tremble whenever young Sarn't Cribdon inspected their weapons and equipment.

Even so, I was never knowingly harsh or unreasonable in my judgments and asked nothing of any man that I could not do myself. If a Digger was a willing lad but a bit slow to grasp some element of training, I'd take him aside and unpick the problem, often with an explanatory diagram in my sketchbook, until a sudden grin of comprehension wiped away his anxious frown: "Gee! Thanks, Sarge'!" At such moments I would not have swapped my three chevrons for a Field Marshal's baton.

Meanwhile, our Postal Orderly had delivered an envelope to my tent, David's distinctive handwriting on the address panel, along with a rubber-stamped military post-box number in the upper-right corner, plus cancellation marks from Malta, Lemnos, Cairo, and Alexandria, tracing its erratic tour of the Near East before finally reaching me in the Suez Canal Zone.

Badly in need of a friendly word after much emotional turmoil, I slit the envelope to see what my oldest friend was doing these days:

No. 3 Flying School
RFC Hainault Farm
Essex

3rd December 1915

O Goliath Slayer!

At last, I can look the whole world in the eye, knowing that I am now doing my bit for King & Country!

One might think the RFC wanted us to learn to fly as soon as possible, but the first two months were spent on foot drill, PT, and subjects as arcane as the science of aneroid barometers, the theory of carburettors, and sail making (!) that taught us how to stitch thin cotton fabric over bare wooden ribs and spars.

As a consolation prize (?) we were given ten rounds each and told to shoot them from a Lewis gun at a plywood model of a Hun 'plane, on an old tricycle pulled across the range. Those of us who passed these elements of Military Aeronautics were then sent to various flying schools of which mine is No 3 near a village about ten miles from London.

I am naturally impatient to get into the air but first must learn to manoeuvre on the ground, for which we waddle around the aerodrome in "penguins" a flightless bird that best describes those machines whose wings have broken off on landing but whose engines are still capable of spinning a prop' with sufficient thrust to push us along. This is harder than imagined, for if one moves the throttle (accelerator lever) forward too fast, the propeller's increased rotation

risks tipping the whole rickety contraption over, often with
fatal consequences.

This being winter, the weather is bad and flight
training only happens when there's a break in the
clouds, so driving a penguin is the nearest I've got
thus far to emulating the birds! (Or as an Australian
should that be "emu-lating" our own flightless fowl?)

Flying attracts decent chaps from all over and I now
count a Rhodesian tobacco farmer, two Americans
pretending to be Canadians, and a DO (District
Officer) from Malaya, among my colleagues.

And to think, only a few months ago I was content to sit
by myself and stain microscopic slides of plant tissue?
Goodness! How times change, and we with them!!

Do, please, let me know how things go with you and your
gallant mates, whose exploits fill whole pages of the
newspapers sent from home.

As ever.

D.

I noted M's continued absence and my return to favour as a giant slayer even if our experiences were by now on vastly different planes, in every sense, unaware that mine was about to veer off in a new direction.

Our nation's hometown newspapers had done a splendid job of burnishing the Anzac Legend and for the next year there would be no lack of volunteers eager to join our ranks. These fresh reinforcements now enabled extra battalions to be raised by taking experienced veterans from an Original, like 16 Battalion, and raising a new one, like 48 Battalion.

Which is why, one week later, I was closely inspecting a section of newcomers on Kebir's gritty parade ground. Several were almost twice my age but so intoxicated were they by heroic reports of Gabe Tepe and Lone Pine, Quinn's Post and Pope's Hill, that someone like me was automatically regarded as a bemedaled demigod.

Young and easily flattered I was not about to disappoint them by failing to puff my chest and growl like that mythical breed of sergeant who chews broken bottles and farts molten glass. "Ten-shun! Prepare to meet Mr Lewis! The select few who reach his highest standards will qualify for this and specialist pay!" I tapped the LG badge on my cuff. "The rest of you will bash gravel with the common herd! That is your choice! Your future! My decision…" Heavy pause. "Squa-ad! Ri-ight turn! Qui-i-ick march! Lef' ri'! Lef' ri'! Lef' -!"

And so, for the rest of my time in Egypt, I became a full-time weapons' instructor training back-up crews of Lewis gunners, one of which aced the brigade when the time came to test their skills on the range. It was as well we did, what we did, when we did, for soon afterwards we got orders to break camp, route march to Serapeum and entrain for Alexandria where three troopships awaited us.

One, the White Star-Dominion Line's *Canada*, had served during the South African War and, for the first months of this one, had housed Britain's enemy aliens until an internment camp could be built on the Isle of Man. Now, she was once again pressed into service as a squalid, overcrowded transport; in a classic military muddle, my section's names were on her manifest while the rest of 48 Battalion marched aboard the larger, twin funnel liner *Caledonia*.

Our destination was, of course, an official secret, not that it stopped every bootblack and barman in Alex' from knowing exactly when and where we were going; GHQ could have saved everyone a lot of bother and published a sailing notice in the *Egyptian Gazette*.

Memories of the *Lusitania*'s sinking, the previous year, and of many another ship torpedoed since then, were uppermost in our minds as the convoy steamed out at dusk and headed westward towards France, smokestacks belching sparks and smoke, propellers churning a phosphorescent wake visible for several miles astern

83

I shall not bore Frances with an account of this voyage. Like many another in wartime there was heavy emphasis on boat drills and the wearing of life jackets at designated assembly points. As well, there were the usual physical jerks, short arm inspections by medical officers, and pamphlet lectures on trench warfare that, as we were soon to discover, bore little resemblance to reality.

Meanwhile, riflemen were kept busy stabbing their bayonets into sandbags stuffed with rag, and we machine gunners were kept equally occupied by stripping and reassembling our weapons. For this I either blindfolded my men or scattered the parts under a blanket they then had to fumble for, matching the pieces by touch, distracted by their mates' jeers, timed by my wristlet watch.

Fortunately, *Canada*'s gangplank was still connected when an APO lorry raced along the wharf and offloaded a stack of mailbags mislaid in a warehouse for the past umpteen weeks. Our MP detachment volunteered to sort and deliver the letters and parcels throughout the ship, under the gargoyle glare of their provost marshal, as we steamed towards Malta.

I made sure my men got sufficient free time to catch up with their news from home; mine I took into our Sergeants' Mess, the old passenger freighter's Second-Class saloon, and gave myself a break from shepherding clumsy soldiers on the jam-packed decks above.

Cue Ball had finally noticed that Private Ian Cribdon was now serving in the Army, under the headline *Snookering the Hun!*

E. McCracken (Miss) politely thanked me for the illustrated book entitled *Wonders of Egypt & The Holy Land* that Mrs Naylor had read to her class during Bible Studies.

Aunt Lucinda was still happily wandering around her museum of memories, simultaneously conversing with her grandfather, Sydney Town's first merchant king; a mysterious Captain Brown; an equally unknown Caroline Stoat; and the Empress Eugènie, whose husband was determined to bed one of her ladies in waiting, the scoundrel!

A real surprise for me was the letter from Sid' Hocking, my old editor on the *Kalgoorlie Miner*, offering one guinea apiece for articles describing the overseas adventures of an AIF soldier. I had more than a few thoughts on this subject but kept them to myself and instead put the offer aside for further consideration.

David's correspondence was always a good read and his latest letter described finally getting out of a penguin and into a real aeroplane, the Maurice Farman Longhorn, so called because of the extended wooden skids that were supposed to stop it from flipping over onto its back if landed at too steep an angle.

Apparently, flying lessons consisted of keeping both hands and feet on the controls while mimicking his instructor's movements in the back cockpit; all other directions were given by poking the student's shoulder with a cane and shouting above the rattling roar of an air-cooled engine peculiar to the Rumpety Bumpety Dump, a nickname that described the Longhorn's unpredictable behaviour every time it hit the ground. Thus far he had survived three hours of brutal landings and take-offs and was looking forward to going solo as soon as England's springtime weather eased its sporadic windy showers.

"You've got bigger balls than me!" I thought aloud, preferring to take my chances with random shells and bullets, rather than be trapped inside a rats' nest of wire, wood, and fabric that either caught fire while taxying for take-off, or fell out of the sky before bursting into flames upon impact with the ground.

"Eh? Whassup?" a fellow sergeant asked, glancing over his copy of *Truth* with its titillating tales of divorce court frolics.

"An old cobber's gone and joined the Flying Corps."

"Fuckin' Suicide Club."

"My oath!" I shoved upright, stuffed the letters in my tunic pocket, to be answered later and went outside to catch a breath of fresh air on this involuntary Mediterranean cruise.

Other Ranks, NCOs, and Officers generally kept themselves segregated but there was an informal zone amidships where friends and neighbours could meet without counting the number of pips or chevrons on the other's uniform. Percy Black and I had agreed to catch up here at what would have been a mid-morning smoko had we still been in civvy life.

My old workmate and mentor was leaning on the rail by a lifeboat davit, watching the convoy's two other ships ploughing along in formation, aboard one of which – I think she was the *Marathon* – Harry, the third member of our original HIP team, was still 13 Battalion's MGO.

Percy turned as I joined him. "Remember the last time we did this? Going into Lemnos…?"

"Uh huh."

"Seems like a lifetime ago." He squinted into the distance. "I'd no idea what was ahead of us then and be-buggered if I do now…"

We lapsed into a reflective silence and watched the steamers' funnels trailing plumes of dense grey smoke, a dead giveaway to every U-boat within twenty miles, as I later learned.

"Ah, forgot to tell you." Percy glanced my way again. "While on the pips course, in Cairo, I bumped into an old mate of yours."

"Who?"

"Paddy Donovan, Light Horse Regiment. Told me a lot. He reckons you should stick your hand up for a commission. I reckon so too, and will put in a good word, if you like?"

"Thanks, but no thanks."

Percy made time to think by taking out his pipe, unlit because of the fire hazards aboard ship, and chomped it for a cold draw. "You don't strike me as the sort who dodges responsibility."

"All depends," I replied. "A couple o' dozen men, with all their cares and woes, are plenty enough for me to handle well. Besides, I enjoy helping recruits learn stuff they've never done before, like back there, on Kebir's range."

"You'll be helping even more, with pips."

"Nuh." I shook my head firmly. "If I come out of this war, more or less intact, and still a sergeant, I'll have no reason to grumble."

After this we yarned a while longer, comparing his experiences on the Murchison Goldfields and my time fossicking the dry country north of Leonora, the sort of talk that takes a bloke's mind off what he knows lies ahead. By contrast, the battalions' fresh reinforcements kept frothing around us, excited by the prospect of seeing action at last.

"Them poor bastards had better enjoy the peace and quiet while they still can," Percy concluded, casting a sardonic glance in their direction, before stowing his pipe and straightening away from the rail. "Anyhow, duty calls, I'm today's Mess Officer."

"And that's another job I'm happy to let others do," I grinned.

"Maybe. But don't forget what I said."

We went our separate ways, me aft to direct a live fire drill peppering an empty barrel bobbing astern on a towrope.

84

The convoy anchored off Valetta, Malta's capital city named after Jean de Valette, Grand Master of the Knights of St John whose epic defence of the island, in the mid-1500s, marked the high point of the Ottoman Empire's westward expansion. I wished Harry had been with me so that I could have been the one sharing these nuggets of historical information, for once, instead of which I spent what little spare time I had, scribbling replies to my earlier letters.

Then, once the mailbags were safely away in the same launch that brought the pay chest and several high-ranking passengers aboard, the convoy raised steam and headed into the narrow straits between Sicily and North Africa, a notorious hunting ground for enemy submarines based in the nearby Adriatic.

Two Royal Navy destroyers made a brave show of dashing around our flanks, rather like excited terriers on a rabbit warren, hoping to alarm and confuse any U-boat's periscoped view of the world until we were safely past the isle of Pantellaria and approaching Tunisia's Cape Bon, dimly silhouetted on our port side.

By next morning we were in the clear with only the faint smudge of Sardinia to the northeast, holding a steady course for landfall at the French naval base of Toulon where another pair of escorts, flying the *tricoleur* this time, joined us for the last leg of our voyage by cautiously leading the way through a defensive minefield.

Approaching Marseilles, we paraded by companies to exchange our silver piastres for their equivalent in grubby paper francs; 25 centime coins with holes punched through their centres, rather like nickel washers; and assorted bits of copper change.

Aunt Lucinda had originally fired my appetite for languages by reading *The Count of Monte Cristo* in its original French, enacting each character with every dramatic gesture in her considerable repertoire. Thanks to her I still have indelible impressions of the betrayed hero, Edmond Dantès; his heartbroken betrothed, Mercedes; and that slimy villain, Danglars.

With their story in mind, I sketched Château d'If as we passed by the prison island immortalised by Alexandre Dumas and dedicated it to *Mme la baronne Lucinde Cribdon*. For added effect I depicted the moment when Dantès, wrapped in a shroud, pretending to be a corpse, is thrown into the sea, from which he will escape and by the end of the novel reveal himself to be the fabulously rich Count of Monte Cristo.

There was only one problem with her method of teaching an impressionable young lad; the French he learned to mimic was more suited to the florid melodramas of French Theatre, circa 1850, than the grim realities of Wartime France, circa 1916, as I soon discovered when buying fresh fruit at a country railway station somewhere between Auxerre and Paris. The wrinkled peasant's look of puzzled contempt told me that I was an affected freak gabbling something that must have sounded like: "A bounteous day unto thee sweet lass! Forsooth, vend me yonder apricocks -!"

It was a useful lesson and another reason not to put my hand up when the call went out for interpreters, preferring instead to relearn the language from scratch by conversing with *poilus*, tradesmen, and minor officials, absorbing from them a more authentic vocabulary during the months ahead.

All was not lost though. I continued sketching aspects of a golden summer's landscapes as we shuffled past at no great speed on tracks that were no longer safe or sound, given that so many railwaymen had been conscripted for the French Army's own overstretched transport system. In the coarse slang of the time, *fixer quand baisée* was now the accepted rule for maintaining tracks and rolling stock, like much else during a time of deepening national crisis.

Seen through Westralian eyes, France was an amazingly rich and beautiful country, with her verdant fields and meadows, vineyards, and orchards unlike anything in our arid homeland. However, one curious feature aroused the anger of others around me, and that was the number of women, some young and very pretty, doing heavy manual labour on the farms and roads. "Tha's not right!" I heard one of our men grunt to a mate. "I'll bet their fellas're down the pub, like them Gyppos, leaving the missus do all the hard yakka. Lazy pricks!"

I said nothing, having already guessed the truth when our convoy disembarked at Marseilles and an honour guard of third-tier French reservists presented arms for inspection by our brigadier. The contrast could not have been more pitiful and revealing. On one side of the quay, lithe young Australians, lean and muscular, average height five feet ten inches; on the other side, paunchy veterans of the Franco-Prussian War, peaked *képis* on balding heads, clad in baggy red britches and old-fashioned navy-blue coats, armed with the Chassepot rifle and needle bayonet of half a century ago.

Few young Frenchmen were enjoying a lazy time in any pub these days. Most of those we glimpsed through the slid-open side doors of our *quarente huit* wagons, as an asthmatic locomotive panted northwards through summer's heat, were either wearing *horizon bleu* uniforms, or on crutches, or in wheelchairs, and these were the lucky ones. A quarter of a million of their generation had been slaughtered and a further half million wounded during the first three months of a war that still had another two years to go.

In those days, rail travellers arriving in Paris from the south would normally get out at the Gare de Lyon, cross the city by taxi or omnibus, and resume their journey at the Gare du Nord if, like us, they were going through to Rouen. This was never on the cards for thousands of young Australians with exaggerated ideas of the saucy delights on sale in the French capital. Instead, smelly, and dishevelled; bedding straw and dirt stuck to our uniforms, weapons, and webbing; we dismounted from wagons built to carry forty men or eight horses and formed up in the middle of an industrial wasteland.

A volunteer group of local women – at least half of them wearing a black arm band – earned our eternal gratitude by improvising a canteen where we drank imitation coffee sweetened with saccharine tablets and chewed our way through grey bread rolls stuffed with synthetic meatloaf smeared with *substitut de guerre* mustard; Argentine corned beef was no longer so bad after all.

There were no latrines so, with another couple of NCOs, I collared a work party and organised a battalion bog on the far side of a coal heap, so that our residues would eventually get shovelled into a boiler, which was better than the alternative. As time went by, we became quite notorious for our ability to adapt and adopt without waiting for permission from higher authority, unlike our British cousins.

An intricate network of wartime feeder-lines looped around the western outskirts of Paris, serving the factories and armament works that now covered countless acres of what until recently had been orchards and market gardens. It was here that I began to sense the gargantuan scale of war on the Western Front compared with the Dardanelles' sideshow, as we resumed our journey past hundreds upon hundreds of open wagons laden with materiel, artillery pieces, and high explosive shells; some heading in the same direction as ours, while the bulk went to Verdun where the need was greatest.

Infantrymen traditionally grumble about the army's blunders and bungles, but in truth it was a miracle anything got done at all. With increasing experience, I came to understand and respect the rear echelon staff who kept millions of men supplied with tens of millions of tons of ammunition, and food, and stores, as well as they did.

I became aware of just how fragile this mighty enterprise was as our trains shuffled northwards, nose-to-tail with other cargoes of men and munitions. The way I viewed it, we resembled an inverted pyramid poised upon an apex of railway tracks and switches. Disrupt those and there was no chance that the horse-drawn carts of previous wars, or even fleets of modern motor lorries could transport the vast stocks of food and fuel, ammunition, and general stores we saw dumped in ever-larger quantities, as we neared the Western Front.

I was in unconscious agreement with a former Chief of the Prussian General Staff who ordered more railway lines for the rapid mobilisation of his troops, either to attack or defend-in-depth, instead of increasing the number of static fortifications as had been the case in former centuries. So serious was von Moltke that only the brightest and best of his War College graduates were assigned to the *Militäreisenbahnhauptamt*, a mighty mouthful for the ferociously efficient Officer Corps of the Chief Department of Military Rail Transport.

France belatedly learned her lesson after the humiliating defeat of 1871, during which Prussia deployed fresh troops at an average speed of thirty miles per hour against straggling columns of exhausted, footsore Frenchmen. At the outbreak of this war, an army of coolies had been hastily recruited in Indochina and brought over to Europe where squads of slender Annamese, wearing their distinctive conical bamboo hats and blue tunics, tirelessly shovelled the ballast that an incessant rumble of iron wheels shook from between loosened wooden sleepers, as we clanked past.

This was all very exotic and exciting for young Australians who had never been abroad, and in many cases never travelled more than a few miles from the local footy oval. I shared their amazement at the variety of humans swept up by a world at war. During our hesitant, halting northwards crawl, we often passed trainloads of coal black Senegalese from French West Africa, or leathery-featured Algerian *spahis*, or dark-bearded Moroccan *goumiers* heading the opposite way, into Verdun's crucible of horrors.

The British Empire was no less varied in its manpower and soon we no longer took much notice of Scots in their Balmoral bonnets, Indians in their various styles of turban, New Zealanders in their lemon-squeezer hats, Canadians and Newfoundlanders in their forage caps, South Africans and Rhodesians in headgear like ours.

We had already served alongside Gurkhas at Gallipoli, the Hong Kong & Singapore Mountain Artillery and Bikaner Camel Corps in Egypt and would soon be swapping badges and cigarettes with troops of the British West India Regiment, gunners of the Bermuda Militia Artillery, and Britain's oldest allies the Portuguese, in their curiously corrugated steel helmets. Eventually contingents from Russia and Siam, Italy, Brazil, and the United States would join us in the trenches.

It remained swelteringly hot all the way north from Marseilles, but as we approached Rouen – some distance up the Seine from the main Channel port of Le Havre – the sky clouded over, and we arrived in a thunderstorm, pelted with torrential rain. Groundsheets buttoned across shoulders, hats pulled down, rifles sloped, most of the battalion tramped off, following a young British officer on horseback.

He was alleged to know the way to our billets among the endless lines of barrack sheds and tents, cookhouses and workshops, hospitals and casualty clearing stations that made up one of the largest military bases on the planet, but he did not. I missed the first but by no means last instance of Australian insubordination on the Western Front when our rain soaked and frustrated troops heckled that poor, flustered schoolboy lieutenant. Instead, I quietly detached my men and kept them under cover, aware that summer storms never last for long.

Then, once the towering clouds had rumbled and banged away towards the English Channel, and the evening sun broke through again, I offered to assist the ASC troops who were struggling to unload a GS wagon from the flatbed end of our stationery train.

There was more to this than the unaffected mateship that comes naturally to Outback Australians, and even to some city slackers. By now I was a sufficiently experienced soldier to understand the crucial importance of good relations with the Army Service Corps whose shadowy influence extended in every useful direction, from free travel to shares in all the good stuff that inevitably falls off the back of a lorry.

I sought out their sergeant, introduced myself as a cashed-up client, and made certain that our battalion's Lewis gunners would henceforth get first pick of the contraband on our brigade's internal black-market; one's earliest experiences of street life are never entirely forgotten. "Thanks mate," I said as we shook hands to seal the deal, "you're a legend."

"You too, Cobber," he replied with an equally firm handshake. "Stay in touch."

I turned, spotted Captain "Lucky Larry" Taylor heading our way and brought my men smartly to attention. "Sah!"

"At ease Sarn't." The look of utter weariness and frustration on his face reminded me of the reasons why I was content to look after a handful of men, well, rather than run myself ragged trying to keep tabs on two hundred. "There's been a bit of a mix up, nobody knows where to put us tonight. You lot stay put and don't move. I'll send a runner once someone knows what's happening."

"Sah!"

"Good man." He returned my salute. "Carry on."

And carry on we most certainly did, assisted by our new ASC mates who, as I'd suspected, were diverting rations intended for the Officers' Mess. I meanwhile traded four tins of corned beef for buckets of hot water from a nearby locomotive, not only to brew plenty of hot strong tea but also to make sure my men got a good wash, shave, and clean up after three days and two nights of camping on horse dung. I was proud of our little gang and there was nothing I would not have done for them, and they responded by giving of their best, both on the parade ground and on the field of battle.

Summer evenings linger longer in the northern hemisphere's higher latitudes, and we had plenty of twilight to enjoy a feast of tinned ham, Jacobs' crackers, and baked beans heated over my Primus stove, topped off by tinned peaches sprinkled with vanilla custard powder. Gruesome stodge in civilian life but the stuff of dreams in a world of hard-tack army rations.

A stiff glug of Dewar's Scotch from the Service Corps' secret cellar was the perfect nightcap before climbing back into one of the wagons and laying my groundsheet on a stationary floor for the first time since embarkation at Alexandria.

85

Lucky's runner trotted up shortly after daybreak and had no trouble leading the way as we marched through a maze of hutments to 4 Brigade's lines where each battalion was assembling for roll call. We took our place with HQ company, answered names and numbers, and got an approving glance from the sergeant-major when he saw how neat and tidy, shaved, and clean our MG section was compared with the scarecrows standing alongside us.

I must not be too hard on the rest if I do mention this to Frances in our next recording session. Unlike we Lewis gunners, the riflemen had spent a miserable night roosting wherever they could find; some under lean-to shelters by a transport pool's workshops; others in the soccer field's pavilion; and others by doubling-up with British units like the Durham Light Infantry and Norfolk Regiment, who were themselves billeted in cramped quarters.

Our officer commanding, Colonel Leane did not hold back when letting fly with a short, sharp commentary aimed squarely at our deficiencies. A strict, upright, firmly opinionated leader, I was never sure what my feelings were for him.

Undoubtedly brave and determined, he ended the war a brigadier general with an impressive row of decorations earned under fire, but there was always a perception that he favoured his family to the exclusion of everyone else. This was hard to deny when his adjutant was a younger brother, and three more brothers plus six nephews also served in the same unit. For this reason, ours was mockingly known as the Joan of Arc Battalion, being Made of All Leanes, a laboured pun on the saint's nickname, Maid of Orleans.

Our mass bollocking duly delivered we were then told to prepare for a de-louse followed by medical and dental inspections, but first there was a session in the shearing shed where a line of barbers' stools awaited, manned by chirpy Cockneys who delighted in scalping us in thirty seconds flat, followed by an equally swift shave with an open razor.

Sardonically baa'ing and bleating we flocked to one of several communal shower baths, plumbed into a commandeered brewery boiler house by the Royal Engineers, where our soiled shirts and drawers were chucked into the trolley baskets and then wheeled to a nearby brew vat of boiling soapsuds before repair and reissue to the next draft of troops bound for the Front.

Scrubbed and hosed off we split into five columns and paraded in the nude, except for the identity discs worn on a string around our necks, past a board of medical officers who checked us for the pox, ruptures, irregular heartbeat, weak eyesight, rotten teeth, and those like myself with recently healed wounds.

Having survived their poking, and prodding we padded through an adjacent clothing store for new-old underclothes, shirts, and socks before returning to the change area where our original boots, tunics, and britches hung on nails along the wooden plank walls.

One tealeaf was caught with his hand inside a pocket not his own, copped a memorable bashing, and was not mourned when Fritz sniped him a few weeks later; this will sound cruel to Frances' gentler ears, if I mention it, but ours was cruel work, at a cruel time, in a cruel world.

The RSM passed the word that all subordinate NCOs had a meeting with him in the Salvation Army hut at 1200 hours. An old school regimental sergeant major who had seen action in the Soudan, South Africa, and the Northwest Frontier of India before volunteering for this latest clash of arms, Mr M'Ginnis was not inclined to mince words when it came to laying bare our faults and failures.

There was much audible squirming and shuffling before he finished with the announcement that we had twenty-four hours to get the battalion up to scratch or else he would be addressing newly appointed non-commissioned officers at tomorrow's meeting -!

Suitably chastened, I joined the hurried exit, for while I knew that my men were several cuts above the rest, nobody escapes the Wrath of God when a deity like RSM M'Ginnis hurls his thunderbolts.

"Sarn't Cribdon."

I turned. "Sir?"

"Here."

"Sir."

"Are your men ready for action?"

"No sir."

"Why not?" he growled.

"They performed well enough at Kebir, but I'll only know how good they are, under fire. Till then I'm withholding judgment. Sir."

"Hm." He pondered my words. "Very well. Make sure they are. We don't have much time. There's a big push coming." He read the DCM ribbon above my left breast pocket. "You're solid but the reo's are a worry. It's one thing to stand shoulder-to-shoulder with your comrades while the shot and shell are flying. It's another matter to hold your ground alone, with maybe a loader, beating back an enemy charge. Have your lads got the ticker to fight to their last round?"

"I'm making bloody sure they have."

"Good man. Proceed."

"Sir." I left the hut and strode back to our billet with much on my mind. Not least was the huge number of sandbagged blast barriers enclosing our stores and Nissen hutments. This seemed very odd, given that the Front was over one hundred miles away, and to the best of my knowledge no German artillery piece could fire a shell half that distance.

Two nights later, I saw the reason why when a Zeppelin droned down the coast from its base near Brussels, reached the mouth of the Seine, turned sharp left, and dropped three tons of aerial torpedoes - as bombs were still called - onto the British staging areas near Rouen. Bombing was still an inexact science and most of the load exploded randomly, doing little harm, although one fuel dump continued to belch black smoke for the rest of the week.

Our ack-ack was fast and furious and futile. Machine guns jabbered madly, and pom-poms punched shell-after-shell up the wavering beam of a searchlight at what looked like a silver-painted salami sausage before the airship disdainfully turned around and droned back to Belgium.

86

It was an enlightening experience to see what a serious threat of demotion can accomplish in just one day of intensive drill and kit inspections by motivated NCOs. The change in our battalion's attitude and bearing was evident when we paraded for Colonel Leane's caustic appraisal – if not approval - before being handed over to the Trench Warfare instructors.

I thought we knew all there was to know about modern combat but quickly realised that Gallipoli belonged to the nineteenth century compared to the Western Front, if the battle training ground - laid across hundreds of acres of neighbouring farmland - was any indication of what lay ahead of us.

It was here that we learned how to employ the recently introduced Mills grenade; left thumb hooking pull-ring; right fist gripping cast iron "pineapple"; roll knuckles apart. Split pin, clear! Arming lever, clear! One, two, three, toss -! Thudd...

Learned how to cut through barbed wire, wearing clumsy leather hedging gloves.

Learned how to bridge the thicker entanglements by running duckboards and trench ladders across them.

Learned how to shoot and manoeuvre through clouds of tear gas wearing the new box-respirator instead of our superseded bogyman PH helmets, all the while staring through celluloid eyepieces that inevitably misted over with sweat and condensed breath whenever the nose clip slipped off our sweaty, greasy skin and we no longer exhaled through the mouthpiece bitten between our teeth.

I dealt with this problem by trading five cigarettes for a roll of adhesive dressing tape, pinched from a hospital store, and showed my men how to stick a patch over their nostrils for the clip to grip.

The battalion's reinforcements were less frothy by the end of their first week of battle training, and downright flat by the end of the second as 4 Brigade assembled in the Blue trenches for a demonstration frontal attack against the replica German, or Red trenches, that extended for half a mile in breadth and about the same distance in depth.

Salvoes of Brocks' rockets were to simulate artillery cover while our bombers – as grenadiers were then called – cleared the enemy's dugouts with thunder flashes and the rest of us blazed away with blanks at straw bag Fritzes before the obligatory bayonet charge.

Concealed trip wires were set to randomly tangle the attackers who remained where they fell, so that the stretcher-bearers could practice their casualty clearance drills.

Meanwhile, the umpires were sending runners with written messages, and revised orders by flagged semaphore signals, that our platoon commanders had to respond to quickly and, if they tripped over, it was down to we NCOs to take command and keep the show moving forward.

An unscripted touch of realism was supplied by the weather. For the past week Rouen had sweltered through hot summer days, but all that changed when a frontal low moved in from the Atlantic and rain bucketed down just as we were due to hop over the bags and charge across a replica No Man's Land.

This was excellent preparation for what was to come during the months ahead, not that we appreciated it at the time as meticulously rehearsed manoeuvres degenerated into adult mud wrestling matches with company, platoon, and section leaders struggling to stay in touch with their exhausted men.

Valuable lessons were learned and shared at our debriefing sessions. We had trained hard to keep sand and dust out of our machine guns on the peninsula and in Egypt; now we knew that liquid soil penetrates the smallest aperture, clogging the breech block and recoil spring until they can be stripped and cleaned, a near-impossibility in battle.

To address this problem, I suggested we repurpose the discarded Ansells, and within a few hours our Lewis guns had improvised, snug-fitting breech covers.

The open-bottomed magazine pans were another disaster-in-waiting whenever our loaders, who of necessity had to crawl or lay prone alongside the gunners, dragged them through the muck in canvas buckets.

These lads earned their extra sixpence a day specialist pay, given they also had to carry gas masks, full battle order, water bottles, entrenching tools, revolvers for personal defence and, like the rest of us, were about to wear an extra one and a half pounds of Brodie steel helmet apiece. Comfort was never a word one associated with infantrymen during the Great War.

All evidence to the contrary, our rehearsal was passed as satisfactory. It had to be for there was no more time to train now that the Big Push was about to kick off. France was fighting for her very existence at Verdun, five months into what would become the longest battle in history when it eventually froze to a halt in November's blizzards, and unless the pressure was eased by drawing the Kaiser's troops northwards to defend German gains in Picardy, she must soon collapse through sheer exhaustion, bled bone dry.

It was to avert this disaster that khaki caterpillar columns of Britain's New Army and the Empire's volunteers began tramping eastwards from Normandy, and southwards from base camps at Étaples and Bailleul, and assembly areas like Calais. Seen from the air we must have resembled tributary brooks and rivulets of men, sluggishly flowing into the Valley of the Shadow of Death that was the Somme.

We footsloggers had only the vaguest idea of what was at stake as platoons, companies, battalions, brigades inched along timetabled routes, following signposted tracks maintained by coolies of the Chinese Labour Corps. Tough little peasants, trotting along with bamboo poles on their shoulders, balancing baskets laden with ballast from nearby gravel pits. And where these were absent, acres of woodland felled for the corduroy logs needed to cross soft ground, all the while overtaken by motorcycle despatch riders and staff cars, ambulances and lorries, horse artillery and ponderous traction engines towing squat-barrelled howitzers. Everything and everyone inward-bound for the Front.

Ten years later, I drove my new Citroën C3 tourer up to Normandy, nominally to write a series of articles promoting the region's superb chalk stream fishing, but in truth I needed to lay the ghosts of 1916. This I did by retracing what I could remember of our track between Rouen and Albert, only to discover that hardly a thing remained to show where once a million men marched into battle.

Cows grazed where farriers once shod thousands of draught horses and trimmed the hooves of tens of thousands of mules; where immense stores of hay and sacks of oats fed them; where the Veterinary Corps kept them going until the poor beasts could give no more, at which point their hides were stripped for the tanneries, their meat butchered for human consumption, their bones crushed to make nitro-glycerine explosive.

Nothing remained of the improvised villages that briefly sprang up every twelve miles or so, where the Royal Engineers had bored deep wells and installed the steam pumps that supplied a host of men and mounts with water, twenty-four hours a day, seven days a week.

These trampled patches of mud and commandeered barns, identified only by official numbers and the troops' ironic nicknames, were where we bivouacked until cleared to march to the next staging post, and at every one I would call my men aside and inspect their feet, for no way was I going to let them limp into battle. This was not just a figure of speech, especially for those of us who had worn out their more supple Australian leather boots and been issued with the British Army's hobnailed clodhoppers.

Initially they grumbled but soon saw the point of sitting on groundsheets, unlacing boots, pulling off sweaty woollen socks so that I could check for blisters and infected toes. And when these were revealed, I would take a pair of nail clippers, a small bottle of iodine, and the roll of adhesive plaster from my haversack, and help the bloke put things right. At the same time, I inspected their boots for loose soles or gaping seams, and when required got them repaired by the cobblers who, with the medics and cooks, the blacksmiths, and wheelwrights, were keeping us on the move.

After a man got my nod of approval, he would dust his feet with medicated talcum powder, pull on fresh socks, and tuck the previous pair under his knapsack straps where they flapped dry before being swapped around at the next halt. Not every NCO was as conscientious, but this was my infantryman's version of the farriers' working motto: "No hoof, no horse..."

Meanwhile, at higher levels of command, there was rarely anything haphazard about troop movements during the Great War, although it often seemed that way to us. MPs on horseback monitored the flows of traffic, ready to alert the nearest breakdown gang whenever the track had to be cleared, or where more ballast was needed to repair potholes into which draught horses could flounder up to their bellies, and laden GS wagons sink above their axles, unless quickly filled. On one occasion I witnessed an emergency repair when a lorryload of tinned bully beef was tipped into a patch of soggy ground, to improvise a solid road base.

The pre-war railway line from Rouen to Amiens was reserved for the vast tonnages of shells and heavy equipment needed at the Front and, in a macabre exchange, for evacuating thousands of wounded men. Light-gauge railways fanned across the countryside like steel cobwebs, linking supply dumps, seemingly without number as we marched, and whistled, and sang from "Hyde Park Corner" to "Whitehall", from "Soho" to "Shithouse Corner," getting ever closer to the guns' surly grumble.

I still remember lorry tyres piled in heaps almost as large as a cottage; hundreds of red, two-gallon petrol tins stacked alongside transport pools; mobile workshops where flaring oxy-torches dismantled wrecked vehicles to keep others running. And always the insistent clank and clamour of war, and the occasional buzz of aeroplanes, mostly ours though once we jeered a black-crossed Fritz falling from the sky, dragging its smoky plume into an abrupt whoomph of flame behind a nearby ridgeline.

Somewhere between "Old Kent Road" and another staging post the Tommies called "Piccadilly," we briefly halted beside a field on which were parked several oddly shaped, rhomboid steel boxes on cogged tracks, draped with camouflage netting.

Naturally I asked a sentry what they were and was relieved to hear that someone in authority had finally learned the lessons of Gallipoli. Apparently, these machines were self-propelled water tanks to keep us supplied with that most essential ration as we advanced deeper into enemy territory. Had I got much closer, I would have seen that what I thought were hosepipe nozzles, protruding from the sides of these strange contraptions, were in fact stubby gun barrels.

A decade later, with hawthorns in blossom and larks warbling above ripening wheat that rippled like green velvet in the breeze, I returned to the spot where I first saw a Mark-1 tank and found nothing to show that great empires once fought here.

Sometime in the distant future, archaeologists like Max Mallowan and his charming wife will fossick for the rusty traces of our moment in history, only to discover that Caesar's legions left a more permanent legacy when they laid a military road nineteen hundred years earlier. One that still cuts across the chalk downs from Albert to Bapaume through an insignificant little village called Pozières.

87

The Big Push was well underway by the time our element of the Australian 1st Division crossed the Somme at Amiens and followed the Ancre from Corbie, up a shallow river valley towards Albert that, for centuries past, had been no more than a sleepy market town. All that abruptly changed with the outbreak of war so that now, two years later, its gap-toothed skyline of smashed houses and gutted public buildings had the misfortune to be overlooked by a low escarpment, from which Fritz's artillery enjoyed a clear view of our positions, making them death pits much like those on Ypres Salient, farther north in Flanders.

Years later, after the dust settled, I tried making sense of this time and place in my life, but with limited success, rather like the campaign itself. One thing I did learn, however, was that far from being a single battlefield the Somme comprised several distinct, overlapping battles, any one of which at any other time would have been considered a major engagement with its own corps of historians retelling their versions of events. Instead, because of the sheer weight of fighting along our fifteen-mile front, Beaumont-Hamel and Delville Wood, Pozières and Mouquet Farm, blurred as-one in the acrid fog of war.

All that remains in the public memory are flickering kinematic images of the Kaiser's machine gunners silently massacring Kitchener's New Army on 1st July 1916 after which everyone's luck ebbed and flowed until mid-November, when ice and snow stopped play at the start of the worst European winter in half a century.

At this point I must pause and ask myself, does the enchanting Frances Baxter really want to hear any more of this depressing stuff? There are hundreds of books and newsreels on the subject, and the Imperial War Museum – aptly housed inside a former lunatic asylum – is overflowing with artifacts and dioramas that give a fair impression of life and death in the trenches.

If she were to ask my frank opinion, I would have to reply that the Great War for Civilisation - as our Victory Medal solemnly proclaimed it to be - was in fact the end of civilisation as we Edwardians understood the word. All that followed - the Roaring Twenties, the Great Depression, the Second World War - were perplexing spasms for those of us who remembered a more settled, orderly, and confident social order, so perhaps now is the right time to sign off and pack away my tape recorder?

Upon reflection, easier said than done. An old man's memories are like the snagged thread of a knitted garment, one thought unravels another, and then another, and then another, and won't stop unravelling until the last inch of thread casts loose.

It certainly felt as if the short thread of my life was about to end during July, and August, and September of 1916 as we fought to dislodge Fritz from his hilltop strongholds between Basentin Ridge to the south and Thiepval farther north, with Pozières a hedgehog defence of machine gun nests, midpoint.

A furious bombardment had hastened Albert's destruction two weeks before we arrived at what little was left of that now uninhabitable town, the stink of burnt explosive still heavy in the air, even out on the brickfield where our battalion bivouacked alongside camouflaged British artillery.

This was a mixed blessing. On one hand we could trade rations and cigarettes with the Tommies; on the other hand, Fritz's artillery had our coordinates tabbed on his Hate Map. Every morning at 7.30 ack-emma, regular as clockwork, he would fire a salvo five-point-nines in our direction. Being so predictable, we took cover in the excavated clay pits five minutes earlier and waited for the clods of dirt, iron shards, and copper drive bands to thump back to earth before getting on with the day's work.

The Sergeants' Mess was a haven of relative peace and tranquillity inside an abandoned tool shed, re-roofed with tarpaulin pinched from a nearby railway siding. Here we could snatch a bit of shuteye on an old sofa rescued from somewhere in the ruined town, or wistfully daydream about the placid routines of daily life in Australia whenever the Postal Orderly pedalled past on his bicycle, dropping off packets of letters and small parcels.

As happened the day I returned from a meeting with the battalion's MGO. The switch to Mk-VII spitzer cartridges from the earlier, round-nosed Mk-VIs was causing concern on the eve of battle, and he wanted reassurance that my men were aware of the required adjustments to our magazines' feed tracks.

It was a welcome distraction to find mail waiting for me on the Mess' table, another piece of furniture salvaged from someone's wrecked home. David's handwriting was familiar, as was Elspeth McCracken's neatly printed envelope, also Aunt Lucinda's, but the fifth letter was a mystery with its distinctly foreign hand script.

Frowning, I snapped open my jack-knife to slit the envelope, and took out a sheet of paper bearing the ornate letterhead of Shuster & Son, framed by line engravings of their warehouse and Melbourne factory, alongside a mainline locomotive with smoke belching from its chimney, about to load boxes of footwear for delivery up and down Australia's Eastern States.

The note itself was carefully handwritten with Continental crossed-7s and upswept-1s in royal blue ink

7 May 1,916

Our Most Dear Ian.

Forgive me that I write you thus but it is felt we must ask a generous act.

It is not good a German name to have these days, even for loyal citizens of King George, and the Collins Street, home shop of Shuster & Son has been stricken in the window by bad men who know not what they do.

For this end I have my Davids photograph put therein, he in His uniform so proud! Also that of you medalled, from Cairo to dearly loved Mme Cribdon, for you we also regard as a son. As she told us, you can both now stand guard on our home shop window.

People here think war is good for trade but I know it not. They think I am making money for the making of army boots,

*but I am not. The government tells me to make them for 3/- a
pair, but that is not so if they are to be of quality, thus I give 9d
of my own pocket, to make the job good. Shuster & Son never
made rubbish and will not now start!*

*Please to give approvement for your photograph to stay,
just as you stay in our hearts always.*

Blessings of Leon & Hannah Shuster

I am not ashamed to confess to a lump in the throat and a prickle in the eyes
as I re-read this distant echo of happier times.

There was a similar emotion while reading Elspeth McCracken's thanks for
my postcard from Alexandria, depicting an imagined Great Lighthouse, one that
prompted Mrs Walsh to tell her class a story about Alexander the Great cutting
the Gordian Knot. However, what really brought me close to tears was to read:
"My Daddy wants to do his bit and has joined the army. He tried before but they
told him he was too old but now he is young enough. His name is Eric John and
he worked in a bank. When you meet him, tell him we think of him lots and
lots."

Shaking my head, only too aware of what the poor chump had volunteered
for, I opened Aunt Lucinda's ever-welcome letter from home. As in her previous
ones, the years tended to slip and slide around, so that a sentence beginning
with Dr Levine's rehabilitated amputees in Tralee's gardens, could as easily end
with a description of *Le Rossignol* winding bandages for the wounded, or singing
patriotic airs to sustain the French garrison's morale during the 1870 Siege of
Paris.

Most touching of all was her insistence that I proceed directly to an address
in that city's outskirts and introduce myself to young Alexandre Dumas by
reminding him that she co-wrote the stage adaptation of *La Dame aux Camélia*s
an*d* would have played the heroine, Marguerite, but for her contract with *Mâitre*
Offenbach for whom she was in rehearsal as Manuelita in *Pépito*.

David's letter dealt strictly with the here and now as he told me of his solo
flight across London to Farnborough aerodrome, during which he blipped his
Avro trainer's engine in salute above Buckingham Palace, before returning to
base via Hounslow Heath. Shortly afterwards he was awarded his pilots' badge
and expected to soon join a squadron in France.

Meanwhile, the battalion Intelligence Officer, Captain Latimer, was waiting
for us in the brickfield's kiln shed when our section, platoon, and company
commanders assembled early the following day. With only the briefest of
greetings he flicked aside a groundsheet, rather like a conjuror revealing his
Next Amazing Trick and directed our attention to an impressively detailed clay
model. of the battlefield between Albert and Pozières, north to Beaumont-Hamel
where the Newfoundland Regiment had been decimated on its first day of
battle, and south to Delville Wood where the South Africans and Rhodesians
were grimly defending a wilderness of shattered trees stumps.

It was now Australia's turn to try knocking Fritz off the highest ground on
the East bank of the Somme, and from there turn his left flank at Thiepval on the
far side of what used to be a little valley of no consequence to anyone but local
farmers who formerly shot hares for the pot, on a few dozen acres of rough
grazing.

This was tall order and Mr Latimer did not even bother to sugar the pill
when he reported how German field engineers had spent the past several

months tunnelling ever deeper into a thick bed of chalk, sheltering their troops from all but the heaviest howitzer fire.

One *Schwerpunkt* dominated the escarpment's glacis, laced with hedges of barbed wire strung on corkscrew steel posts, saw-tooth rifle pits and machine gun nests' interlocking fields of fire. As further proof that Fritz meant business, his fall-back line was studded with flamethrowers, gas projectors, and *cheveaux de frise* of iron spiked wooden logs at waist height.

Codenamed Gibraltar, this reinforced concrete blockhouse, and its maze of underground galleries was modestly described as a tough nut to crack, but until someone did, there was zero chance of capturing the enemy's OP on Windmill Hill.

Gibraltar was our designated target, but first we had to march up the old Roman road until bearing right at a mine crater, one of several blown under the old frontline, during the initial attack. Then angle left up a shallow depression about half a mile long, named Sausage Gully, so-called because of the Royal Artillery's observation balloons tethered above us like bloated blood puddings with chubby tail fins. Finally halting at a chalk pit where we would be met by guides from the battalion we were to relieve, during the short hours of summer darkness.

It seemed quite straightforward and attainable as the IO's billiard cue pointer traced our route up a length of string pegged by matchsticks across his model. Questions asked and mostly answered, we synchronised watches and dispersed to brief our individual units and distribute the identification ribbons that every man tied to his right shoulder strap, to complement the coloured patch roughly stitched on the back of his tunic. As one further insurance against mistaken identity in close quarter fighting, we prepared to roll our sleeves up to the elbows.

The battalion's cooks laid on a farewell feed of corned beef hash and pancakes, bread, and jam, at the same time issuing three-day ration packs of beef and biscuits.

There being no need for money from now onward, we pooled our loose francs and centimes, knotted them in a handkerchief and entrusted it to the Padre; whoever lived to win this informal lottery would drink-up for those who didn't make it back. The Sin Shifter also promised to post the letters we handed over for safekeeping before falling-in by companies to answer many a soldier's final roll call.

There were no whistles or songs as we marched out into a beautiful summer's day, passing under the Virgin & Child atop the basilica, leaning forward as if to bless the columns of khaki clad men, passing by in light battle order.

Infantry: pouches stuffed with five-round clips of rifle cartridges and a pair of Mills' grenades apiece; gas masks on chests; steel helmets tilted forward, shading solemn, determined faces.

Signallers: bearing folded semaphore flags and coils of telephone wire, carrying pigeon baskets, leading messenger dogs.

Stretcher bearers: shouldering canvas-rolled poles and Red Cross satchels of bandages, wound-dressings, tourniquets.

Sappers: laden with ladders and wire cutters, Bangalore torpedoes and brushwood fascines.

Lewis gunners: awkwardly hauling knotted tow ropes, like Arctic explorers dragging sledges, loaders shoving coffin-shaped carts like macabre baby perambulators.

Even had we felt like whistling or singing, nobody would have heard us above the hurricane howl of artillery as every British and Australian gun along our sector pounded the enemy with high explosives and shrapnel, phosgene, and tear gas. The air encasing us throbbed with madly colliding shock waves. The ground beneath our boots quaked like jelly. One of my men dropped dead when his overworked heart could take no more of these pulsating body blows.

Shoving through a sluggish stream of ambulance lorries, ammunition wagons, field artillery pieces, most of the battalion reached Chalk Pit where, at last, we could dump the handcarts, give our weapons one final clean, and check our drum magazines one last time.

By some miracle of organisation, insulated dixies of hot tea sweetened with condensed milk reached us in time for a dinner of fish paste sandwiches, wrapped in newspaper, packed inside salvaged McConachie's M&V boxes. More welcome still were the stoneware jars stamped SRD, which officially meant Special Ration Distribution, initials sarcastically interpreted as Seldom Reaches Destination, although enough Navy-strength rum reached our tin mugs to light a happy glow in many a cold belly.

Our guides were late, unsurprisingly with Fritz throwing everything he had back at us. It was not until the early hours that we awoke from wherever we'd slumped, struggled to our feet, and stumbled along broken duckboards, following the guides' dimmed blue lanterns, augmented by hissing parachute flares and Very lights, mostly German.

As we joked at the time, the Kaiser must have won the contract to illuminate No Man's Land, but there was little to joke about as we entered the shattered trenches from which the battalion would attack at dawn, under a covering barrage that was later reported as the heaviest in the war, thus far.

Any recollections of what happened next belong to the faceless stranger first encountered on Pope's Hill. He led a charmed life here as well, except for the inevitable nicks and grazes from splintered flint blasted from the chalk by exploding Bangalore torpedoes - lengths of iron piping packed with TNT - our sappers were detonating under unbroken wire.

When one of his crews was knocked out, he grabbed their gun and ammo bucket and continued uphill, reaching a shallow crater just in time to open fire over its rim as ghostly, gas-masked, coal-scuttle-helmeted shapes charged from behind a salvo of smoke shells.

88

We barely noticed the reinforcements passing our remnant battalion as we tramped back to Albert, but the looks of fascinated horror on their faces said they'd seen us alright.

Days and nights of bombardment, machine gun fire, and grenade battles had killed many, wounded more in body and soul, and left the remainder as little better than ragged automata, drugged with exhaustion.

Roll call revealed the extent of our losses; 48 Battalion had ceased to exist as a fighting unit. Bad as this was, the first order of business was to rebuild morale by leading my men into the bath hut where the Royal Engineers had rigged field showers heated from a nearby kiln.

Quit of our filth, and sweat, and bristles we queued for fresh uniforms; the old ones either burned or, if repairable, contracted to a religious order near Amiens, who specialised in stitch craft.

The cooks had drawn rations for a full battalion and today we got triple issues of tucker in our mess tins. After wolfing my lot, I told the lads to find a roost and lay up while they could, for it would not be long before Leane the Keen would be striding around, snapping orders left, right, and centre.

Anticipating his probing questions, I stripped our Lewis guns, noted those needing refurbishment, signed them over to the armourers, and made a beeline for the Sergeants' Mess where I knew of a dark corner with a thick layer of straw.

I was wrong in my assessment of Colonel Leane. RSM M'Ginnis must have cautioned him against going too hard, too fast, too soon because instead of more foot drill, more bayonet practice, more lectures on the importance of discipline, he authorised two days of light duties during which we were free to play cricket, kick a footy ball, and in my case go fishing in the Ancre. Although I had no tackle it doesn't take much skill to bend a pin, hook up a worm on the end of few yards of cobblers' thread tied to a stick, add a cork float, and doze in the shade of a willow tree.

I am not sure who was most surprised, myself or the plump two-pound redfin perch flopping around on the bank. Big enough for a tasty snack, I dispatched it and lit a low fire in a hollow between the tree's buttress roots. Busy doing this, I didn't notice Captain Taylor contentedly puffing his pipe as I pushed a stick through the fish's gills to begin toasting it over the hot coals.

"What's it they say about you can take a man out of the Bush, but you can't take the Bush out of the man?"

I glanced over my shoulder and came to attention. "Sir?"

"Stand easy." He removed his pipe and inspected its bowl for a moment. "I've had my eye on you, Sarn't. You care for your men. There are vacant ranks to fill. I want to put you up for a commission. What d'you say?"

I shook my head. "With respect, thanks but no thanks."

"Why?" he frowned. "Better pay, better conditions."

"You've just put your finger on it," I replied, relaxing slightly. "I do care for my men. We're family. But it wouldn't be the same if I got too high and mighty."

My own kith and kin had rejected Little Willie Braithwaite, and although Aunt Lucinda gave him a new name and a loving, lavish home, it was only in the army's lower ranks, sharing danger and discomfort with brothers-in-arms like Percy Black and Harry Murray, that I had acquired an identity I felt justifiably proud of. All the better pay and better conditions in the world could never compensate me for its loss.

"Hm." Lucky considered my reply with the close attention of a country bank manager assessing a farm loan. "Very well. Have it your own way. But if you change your mind, let me know."

"Thank you, sir."

"And you'd better turn that fish around before it burns."

Our free time ended abruptly the following day with the arrival of fresh reo's, straight off the Folkestone ferry at Boulogne and route-marched to Albert; inexperienced, undertrained, but needed to bring our units up to strength. My task and that of all remaining NCOs was to ensure they learned the basics of trench fighting, and for the next week we hammered them hard.

Meanwhile the capture of Gibraltar had cleared the way for other AIF battalions to fight their way into the village until they too ran out of puff, left flank dangerously exposed to the German redoubt at Mouquet Farm, a short distance north of Pozères cemetery where the 94th Jäger Regiment had taken a terrible beating at our hands.

My home battalion, the 16th West Australian, suffered equivalent losses during its brief occupation of the farm before being driven back over its trenches and barbed wire entanglements by machine gun and artillery fire, gas shells and grenades. It was now the rebuilt 48th's turn to counterattack and make Moo Cow Farm - as we inevitably nicknamed the accursed place - a British strongpoint.

Major Percy Black, DSO, DCM, had led the previous stunt and was i/c this one as well. By now an AIF living legend, his name alone inspired the best in a man, and I felt honoured to be on his team once again.

Meanwhile, Lucky called his sergeants to order in our corner of the canteen hut, one of the few relatively undamaged buildings left in Albert. The master plan was deceptively simple; Division HQ had assigned a battery of Stokes mortars to keep Fritz's head down while we got through the wire, cleared the forward trenches, and bombed our way into the old farm's cellars and more recently dug underground chambers.

"All clear on that, Sarn't Cribdon?"

My attention had wandered as, in imagination, I distributed a crate of pinched apples to save my raw, inexperienced troops from emptying their water canteens when fear dried their mouths, as it would, and soon. "Yes'r."

"Very well, gentlemen, let's go."

And go we went until the last thing I remember was of leading my gunners through a gap in the wire, at which point something among the welter of explosions flung me arse over heels backwards.

What followed remains to this day a nightmare of hobnailed boots leaping across my body. Of being stabbed with a syringe of morphia in a casualty clearing post. Of an improvised x-ray laboratory, somewhere behind the lines, that confirmed how a shell splinter had shaved my tibia halfway down the leg, but mercifully without shattering the bone or destroying the connective ligaments, or else amputation would have been the only course of action.

Normally I would have been admitted to one of our base hospitals in Northern France. Instead, for reasons never explained, I was booked for treatment in England. Perhaps being an NCO Lewis Gunner & Weapons Instructor - of whom there were never enough, given our rates of attrition - got my papers rubber-stamped Class 1 Expedited Evacuation. Not that I was in any shape to fathom this rummy turn of events, taken aboard a hospital ship to Folkestone, where I was unloaded into a grossly overcrowded ambulance train.

Our doctors, nurses, and orderlies were heroic figures at the Front and no less so when striving to do their utmost in moving carriages built to carry two hundred patients though often laden with half as many again, stretchers stacked one above the other or laid on the gangway floors as mine was, splattered by others' leakage, blood, and vomit.

Exhausted medicos and VADs kept stumbling over us as the train hurried through the night to reach Clapham Junction where more staff were waiting on a gaslit station platform, ready to sort the living from the dead on a seemingly endless conveyor belt of sick and injured, dead and dying from the battlefields of France. The former to a convoy of motor ambulances for delivery to hospitals dotted across London, the latter to a line of covered lorries for burial in suburban cemeteries.

Slipping in and out of fevered awareness I was eventually unloaded at 3LGH, a converted orphanage near Wandsworth Common, after three days and nights in transit. By now, my uniform was a plaster cast of congealed muck and had to be hacked off in slabs by using a pair of tailors' shears.

The contents of its pockets were bagged and tagged while a couple of orderlies wheeled my naked body into a nearby sluice room on an iron meshed trolley and began gently washing me down with a bucket of warm water doped with carbolic acid.

An RAMC captain then carefully peeled the blood encrusted first field dressings from below my right knee, releasing the familiar smell of gas gangrene, identical to the stench of corpses rotting on the wire in No Man's Land.

Three other medicos quickly assembled, frowning at my temperature chart, and nodding while they discussed how the shell fragment must have embedded a scrap of puttee cloth, each fibre of which would have swarmed with necrotic microbes from the indescribable filth of trench warfare. This would not have shown on the x-ray and was easily overlooked by their overworked colleagues on the frontline; amputation was now the only option, given the speed with which septicaemia can gallop up a limb and into the viscera.

All but one of them agreed and were about to send me through to the surgical ward. The exception was a young fellow with ginger hair and freckles, who insisted that I was the ideal subject for an experimental treatment he was developing. By sheer persistence he wore the others down, on the proviso that once the infection reached my knee, the leg would be "disarticulated" – it's curious how such words spring to mind, decades after they were last heard spoken – without further delay.

Accordingly, I was wrapped in blankets and wheeled to a converted pantry where conical flasks of brownish liquor lined the shelves and was prepped for immediate treatment. Not that I was in any fit state to note such details at the time, and only later discovered that the CIBL, on my AF-1220 record card, was medical shorthand for Continuous Infusion of Beta-Lactam.

Apparently, this was a mysterious brew of moulds that were being filtered and drip-fed into a test group of four other men, each bed hooked-up to an elaborate array of tubes and inverted glass bottles that I was soon plumbed-into, although by now I was long past caring what anyone did to me.

The next week or so remain a fever swamp of tangled images through which specialists appeared and disappeared like white-coated wraiths, keenly discussing my temperature chart as its numbers fell and my blood pressure stabilised. Not everyone was so fortunate. Twice the curtains around neighbouring beds were drawn, the apparatus disconnected, and a trolley trundled away to the morgue.

It was only years later that I made the connection and realised how an anonymous genius at 3LGH had pre-empted Alexander Fleming and Howard Florey by more than two decades, not only by isolating a primitive form of Penicillin but also by using it to successfully treat war wounded, of whom I was one of his lucky handful.

Meanwhile, the fever abated and, even more incredibly, my bloated, blackened calf muscle continued to shrink and regain its natural colour whenever the dressings – soaked in yeasty sludge - were changed.

Our medical staff were not the only heroic figures on a military hospital's totem pole, the chaplains were also untiring in their efforts to assist our recovery, as happened shortly after I was moved to one of 3 London General Hospital's open wards while still feeling rather sad and sorry for myself.

"Hello old chap…"

I opened an eye and focused on a tall, diffident padre wearing the white dog collar and black-buttoned tunic of his corps. "Uh?"

"I see they've got you down as coming from Melbourne. That's my hometown as well. Is there someone there you would like me to write a letter to?"

"Nuh."

"Still hurting…?"

"Uh."

"Pain can be a sign of God's Grace…"

I said nothing, for had I spoken the poor fellow would have copped a blistering earful of the filthiest curses.

"I know from experience." He seemed to be reading my thoughts. "I used to be an arrogant young fool until one day at Grammar where I was bullying some harmless young lad. Another young chap jumped to his defence by attacking me." His scarred cheek twitched with a sad, lopsided smile. "Put me in hospital for quite a while during which I realised that I had brought it all upon myself. I am quite certain that my attacker meant to kill me but instead, through God's Grace, he gave me the chance to discover that I had been spared for a higher calling than the downward spiral of degradation I was then upon." He made the Sign of the Cross. "Let me know if there's anything I can do for you."

That was the last I saw of him. I heard later that he had been posted to a battalion in France where he was awarded an MC & Bar for repeatedly going out into No Man's Land to rescue the wounded and console the dying, before being killed at Bullecourt, along with Percy and three thousand others of Australia's finest.

I sometimes wonder if he recognised my uncommon surname, put two-and-two together, and used our chance meeting to make amends for the bullying that provoked my street brawler's counterattack. I shall never know but, in the meantime, I was becoming quite an authority on military medical establishments and judged Wandsworth to be a humane example that many another could have learned much from.

Not that it was ever slack or casual in things that mattered. One could almost hear the bedpans rattle with apprehension when Colonel Bruce-Porter made his daily rounds, accompanied by the equally attentive Matron, and woe betide any nurse – stood to attention by the dressing post - who failed to keep the red stripes on our grey woollen blankets in line with every other blanket along her side of the ward.

Although unaware of it at the time, I was still riding a winner that began at 15AGH Abbasia after the shambolic skulduggery of 1AGH Heliopolis, when I discovered that 3LGH richly deserved its fond nickname of The Happy Hospital, thanks largely to Bruce-Porter's inspired leadership. A top physician in civilian life, he would be twice decorated and then knighted for his work at Wandsworth and 40BGH in Baghdad, by war's end.

Diggers and Tommies were originally pitched in together, but it was not long before our more relaxed attitude to blanket stripes undermined the British Army's notions of good order and discipline, and we soon found ourselves banished to a line of huts on the farthermost corner of the orphanage's grounds, with our own RAAMC staff to tease and chaff, as happened one morning while I was waiting to be wheeled over to the Hydro Pool. "Hello there, young Ian!"

Startled, I nearly dropped my copy of *John Bull* with its weekly serve of patriotic hatred for the Frightful Hun and looked up. "Well, I'll be blowed! Arthur! What the blazes are you doing here?!" A superfluous question, really, when the subject is clad in khaki with a corporal's chevrons and a Red Cross orderly's badge.

"Smike" Streeton was Australia's foremost landscape artist and a frequent guest at Tralee House. Now nearing fifty years of age he could have honourably sat out the war in Sydney or Melbourne, but instead had enlisted in the Medical Corps, caring for the wounded, and taking us to our various appointments, as he did today while bringing me the latest news from home.

Aunt Lucinda was in good health, though apt to confuse our current war with her earlier Franco-Prussian one. Tralee House was a convalescent home for the Class Two repats, its lawn dug up and turned into a vegetable garden to supplement their rations. As for the city of Melbourne, a pall of Calvinist gloom hung over it like a fog as the newspapers published ever-lengthening casualty lists.

On a lighter note, Arthur promised to introduce me to the Chelsea Arts Club as soon as I was up and about again. An established member, like our other friend Tom Roberts who at sixty years of age had also volunteered and was now working in 3LGH's Dental Store, he regarded the Club as an island of sanity in an ocean of madness.

It was he who introduced me to the editor of *The Wandsworth Gazette*, our hospital's magazine, and very soon I was drawing cartoons and decorative borders for such dated, questionable humour as: "Child: Mama, can I take my best doll to Heaven when I die? Mother: No dear. Child: Can I take my second-best doll? Mother: No dear. Child: Then I'll go to Hell with my golliwog -!"

I felt great affection for the Royal Patriotic School's children who regularly visited us with bunches of flowers, and gifts of knitted socks and bed caps. These young nippers were the army's orphans or neglected offspring whose asylum we now occupied, and for whom we laid-on afternoon treats which generally included a sing-along concert, and sometimes a conjuror who was happy to amaze and delight for a cup of tea and a slice of cake in lieu of his stellar performance fees at the Palace Theatre on Charing Cross Road.

My comic drawings of cartoon animals were also in great demand as prizes for our little games and contests. However, it was my *Wandsworth Race Day* sketches that I think most caught the spirit of who, and what, and where we were, with their sprightly vignettes of Australian patients scooting wheelchairs around the larger of our two Recreation Rooms, as if it were Flemington racecourse, cheered on by punters and bookies waving their sticks, crutches, and bandaged stumps.

89

It is often claimed that luck – good or bad - comes in threes, as happened a few days after I began rehab' by gingerly pedalling a static bicycle in the Gymnasium.

Exhilarated after completing an imaginary quarter-mile bike ride, I limped back to the ward and found a packet of mail, redirected from Brigade HQ at Amiens, tossed on my bed, David's letter uppermost with news of his maiden artillery-spotting sortie over enemy lines. Its tone was more sober and restrained than his previous news, and I could tell that war was no longer a brave adventure to compensate for his self-defeat at the Stockholm Olympic Games. For some reason, M was still absent, and I sincerely hoped it was not evidence of things more serious.

Aunt Lucinda's letter was her tardy, slightly confused response to my much earlier one informing her that I had fallen for a young lady of high birth and intelligence while in Egypt. Drawing upon her own rich experience in affairs of the heart, my aunt counselled us to cherish each moment and live for each other in a whirlwind of loving discoveries, concluding with a strict injunction to wine and dine Sandra to the very best of my ability. For which purpose a sum of fifty pounds was being deposited in my Melbourne account, to be drawn upon by telegram from the London & Commercial Bank's overseas desk, as required.

Profoundly touched by this gift but relieved that it no longer mattered, I opened Miss E. McCracken's polite note enclosing an Indian ink drawing of her pet Maltese terrier, *Patch*. Its lines were confident and deft, their artist demonstrating real promise for an eleven-year-old, and I resolved to discuss this with Arthur Streeton, when next we had a chance to talk.

Thus far nothing but good luck, now for the bad, delivered on a plain postcard addressed directly to 3LGH, sent the previous afternoon from VAD Headquarters in Clerkenwell:

72hr change over.
Shall visit tomorrow.

There was no need for a signature! Her distinctive handwriting was proof that my movements were being tracked by the Honourable Lady Sandra Nobury's VAD spies! There was more than enough pain in my body, in my mind, in my life, without this wretched woman adding more by disobeying my orders to leave! Me!! Alone -!!!

And as if all this was not sufficient ill-fortune for one day, Arthur entered the ward with a worried look. "Now then young fella'm'lad, what've you been doing that you oughtn't?"

"Say again?"

"The Boss wants to see you."

"Why?"

"Don't know," he frowned, "but you'd better get your skates on, toot sweet."

I shared his concern. It must be a matter of importance. The hospital's Commanding Officer was not the sort who would take it into his head to chat with an obscure AIF sergeant, one of the many hundreds of patients under his lofty care, so I concluded it might have something to do with my rare recovery from septicaemia which was exciting a lot of interest among the staff, whenever they studied my charts, and I'd overheard talk of more extensive laboratory tests.

I was as baffled as the medicos were and, as I'd earlier noted in Egypt, often made me wonder if somewhere in my murky bloodline was an ancestor endowed with unusual powers of stamina and recovery. I had no way of telling, of course, nor did it matter much as I paused outside the Commandant's office, straightened my Hospital Blue's jacket, cream flannel shirt, and red tie before reporting to the Orderly Clerk: "Ian Cribdon. The Boss wants to see me."

"'Colonel Bruce-Porter,'" I was sharply rebuked as the fussy little man led the way to another door and gave it a reverential knock.

"Enter!"

"Sergeant Cribdon. Sir!"

"Pass!"

"Sir!"

He stood aside and firmly shut the door behind me. "Three One Five, Cribdon. Sir."

"Ah, yes, stand easy, stand easy." The Commandant smiled, rose, and walked around to my side of the desk to cordially shake hands. "Permit me to be first to congratulate you Mr Cribdon."

"Sir?"

"His Majesty the King is graciously pleased to approve the award of a bar to your Distinguished Conduct Medal." He presented the *London Gazette*'s official communiqué. "It also gives me the greatest pleasure to welcome you into our ranks."

"Sir?" I blinked, again, not sure if my shellshocked ears were hearing him correctly.

"Your field commission has been gazetted, with immediate effect."

"Oh."

"Your kit is being moved to an appropriate ward. Carry on and, ah, keep up the good work."

"Oh. Yes. Well, thank you sir."

The abrupt change of address nearly spared me the pain of Sandra's visit, but her spies were still on my trail or else she could not have found the way to an otherwise empty officers' ward – its other patients scattered throughout the hospital for their medical appointments - where I was hunched alone on the edge of my new bed, glowering at the brown linoleum floor.

A lack of response forced her to take a short step backwards: "What's the problem?"

"You."

"What?"

"I ordered you to stay away!" I snarled. "But since you're here, let's get this bloody thing sorted!"

"W-w-what?!"

I ignored her confusion and led the way out to the Officers Only sunroom, although today its grimy glass roof and windowpanes were streaked with autumnal rain.

Service in the ranks had not entirely erased my manners as I positioned a wicker chair for Sandra to be seated, before taking another one across the small circular table with its overflowing ashtray and crumpled copies of the *Times*, then crouched forward, about to reprimand her as if she were defaulting Other Rank -

Instead, it was she who struck first with all the innate authority of an aristocrat born to rule over a large household of servants and retainers: "I am willing to make some allowance for your present attitude, Ian, but tread carefully," she warned in a menacingly calm voice. "So, what is your problem?"

"These, for starters!" I chucked the official communiqués across the table and half-turned, pointedly giving her the cold shoulder.

"'His Majesty the King.'" Her voice trembled slightly as she began reading the first one aloud; I did not yet know that the Duke of York was her godfather before becoming heir to the throne. "'Is graciously pleased, to approve the award of a bar, to the Distinguished Conduct Medal of 315 Sergeant Ian Cribdon DCM, 48 Battalion, AIF, for initiative and leadership at Pozierès.'" The tremor became more audible. "'Sergeant Cribdon's prompt action with his Lewis gun was decisive in halting an enemy attack that, had it succeeded, would have imperilled the gains of previous days and nights of battle. His conduct throughout inspired all who witnessed it.'"

She blinked back a tear and looked up at me. "I am, so proud -!"

"Read the next bloody one!"

"Oh. '315 Sergeant Ian Cribdon DCM & Bar, 48 Battalion AIF, to Second Lieutenant, with immediate effect...'"

"The sneaky bastards!"

"No! You should be proud of that as well!" she exclaimed, instinctively viewing my promotion from her higher rung on England's vertical ladder of power and privilege.

"Well, I'm not!" I yelled, facing her again. "Pips are the last bloody things I need!" My coarse words and violent speech were signs of how close I was to the edge.

She flinched as if I had struck her. "But -?!"

What followed next is best forgotten as I raged at the Army, at her unwelcome intrusion into my life, at the loss of my little gang even though most of them were already dead or soon would be. All the pent-up pain and perplexity of the previous days, weeks, months, years since enlistment overwhelmed me as she stood around the table and laid a comforting arm across my quaking shoulders. Under its gentle weight, I toppled over, buried my face in her lap, and howled my heart out.

A passing ward sister dashed in to quell the commotion. I dimly remember Sandra saying that she was not only my girlfriend but also a nurse on the casualty trains and therefore accustomed to dealing with such matters, after which the older woman left us alone as gentle fingers resumed stroking my head and neck.

Visitors were required to leave at four o' clock sharp but it was well past the hour before my personal VAD finally parted at the ward door, with a kiss on the cheek instead of her earlier, ignored handshake.

"You really are a lucky young devil." The voice behind me was infused with all the pain of a man who, as I later learned, was trapped inside a sterile marriage. "If only there were a lady, like her, who cared that much, for me…"

I shot an angry glance up and around at an intruder from one of Ward O-6's adjacent cubicles for senior officers, a mature chap with the clipped moustache and tightly buttoned manner of a professional British Army officer. "Phillip Grenville." He held out his left hand, the right one tucked back in its sling after today's visit to the physiotherapist.

I returned the awkward handshake. "Ian Cribdon."

"Australian?"

I stiffened, ready to rebut a sly reference to convicts and other strange animals. "Yes."

"Then may I say how glad I am to make your acquaintance?"

"You may."

"One day, I hope to visit your country, assuming Fritz spares me that long," he added, with the wry tone of one who knows that life at the Front is a constant lottery in which a stray bullet, or whirling shell fragment, can be just as fatal as an aimed shot.

"Why?"

"Because I intend to see what it is that makes your men so different."

"'Different'?" In those days I was overly sensitive to the condescending attitudes a certain class of Englishmen had for their "Colonial" cousins.

"Vastly different," he emphasised. "You have a spark we are in danger of losing. If I can learn where it comes from, I shall bring some back, like Prometheus, to rekindle Britain's spirit."

I blinked with astonishment and, as is my wont on such occasions, took cover behind an ironic quip. "Be careful what you wish for. Getting chained to a rock, an eagle pecking your liver for breakfast, is a steep price to pay for a spark."

He chuckled, relieved to hear that I understood his figure of speech and had played it with a quick flick of humour, and so began one of those enduring friendships that meander like underground watercourses, every so often breaking through the surface of events before disappearing again. Of more immediate value, however, was his subtle tuition in those things a newly minted officer and gentlemen needs to be aware of.

It was during these sessions I learned that Phillip Fitz Clarence Grenville was the fourth generation of what used to be called a Military Family. His father was Lieutenant General Sir John Grenville, and his mother's kinsmen - almost without exception - had attained high rank, including one of Queen Victoria's field marshals. The only broken link in their iron chain of duty to the Crown was a granduncle who amassed the family fortune by manufacturing the guns, in Birmingham, and the explosives, in Scotland, that his male relatives employed elsewhere to extend and defend the British Empire.

It was a foregone conclusion that a young man of my mentor's temperament and background would enter the Royal Military Academy, Woolwich, and from there pass into the Corps of Royal Engineers. By the time we met at 3LGH he was a brevet lieutenant colonel, wounded in the arm and chest at Ypres, and wisely using this enforced break to study for the General Staff Selection Board.

As for myself, I was happy to pose questions from a crammers' guide, and in the process gained a deeper knowledge of the professional army's innermost workings. Grenville, as he preferred to be called in his distantly British way, repaid the favour by arranging for Gieves & Hawkes, the military tailors, to send their senior fitter to take my measurements.

The AIF's eight pounds' kit allowance was the cause of much resentment and bitterness for newly commissioned Australians, when compared with the British Army's fifty pounds' allowance for the same uniform, meaning that our pittance fell far short of Saville Row's bespoke service. However, I have always been careful with my money and had a profitable side-line with published cartoons and souvenir portrait sketches.

As I grew accustomed to a promotion that so clearly delighted Sandra in her pestering postcards from Rouen, where she was currently based, I became equally determined to be as well presented as any of her noble relatives in uniform, when the time came to end our *mésalliance*. Though, with any luck, I would be passed fit for light duties and posted to a training battalion before her next Home Leave.

90

The postcard I most dreaded receiving, had been sent yesterday and arrived this morning at the same time as a note from Harry – now Captain H. W. Murray – congratulating me upon my promotion and second DCM, which crossed in the mail with mine congratulating him for the DSO awarded after his epic fight at Mouquet Farm. Sandra's message was mercifully brief:

72 hour pass!
Tomorrow?

I remained undecided for a couple of hours before telegraphing an equally curt reply to VAD Headquarters, suggesting we meet for lunch at the Criterion in Piccadilly, Grenville having assured me that its service was first rate and the bill of fare as good as wartime rationing allowed.

He also insisted on using his family connexions to get us a pair of matinee seats at His Majesty's Theatre, in the Haymarket, where *Chu Chin Chow* had recently opened to enthusiastic revues, since when tickets of any kind were unobtainable well into the New Year, so how he managed to wangle two at short notice, remains a mystery.

Scheming a leave pass from 3LGH was easier and only required a portrait-sketched Christmas card to get me the necessary rubber-stamped signature. Officially I should still have been wearing Hospital Blues in public, but having paid for premium service, the tailors had come up trumps with a pre-war quality wool and silk barathea twill uniform that I was determined to show off, irrespective of anyone's rules or regulations.

Grenville insisted on loaning me his Sam Browne belt instead of the glossy new leather item I had just bought, arguing that its slightly worn appearance would help disguise a raw, single-pip subaltern. The real reason, I suspect, was his need to imagine something of himself squiring a beautiful young lady for a night on the town, instead of an empty marriage to a woman who never once visited him in hospital.

I buttoned my trench coat against the sullen weather and put on a well-worn slouch hat - our distinctive headgear from sunny Australia, widely regarded as a beacon of hope amidst the deepening gloom of England's third wartime winter - and reached for my cane, needed whenever the right leg gave me a spot of bother.

I broke a Bradbury – the new ten-shilling note, signed by John Bradbury, Chief Cashier if the Bank of England, that replaced half-sovereigns when gold was withdrawn from circulation at the outbreak of war – to pay for the taxi ride across London from Wandsworth to Piccadilly. This allowed me ample time to review my plan of attack because, as the man in our mismatched duo, it was my duty to end it before we became the subjects of public comment and objects of private ridicule.

It was only much later, with the wisdom of hindsight, that I saw the error of my foolish ways, but one must not be too harsh when judging that prickly young fellow; Edwardian gentlemen were, by definition, bound by codes of conduct that, even as we continued to obey them, were fast becoming redundant.

My conflicting emotions redoubled as I entered the Criterion and saw Sandra in the Ladies' Lounge, skimming a copy of *The Tatler*, quite likely recognising the grandees preening themselves on the pages of England's leading Society journal. She herself was clad in a drab black VAD overcoat, a Red Cross armband on its left sleeve, wearing a frumpy cap that resembled the top of a cylindrical Royal Mail pillar box, determined to be seen as engaged in serious war-work, unlike the socialite butterflies fluttering for *The Tat's* photographer.

Her eyes sparkled as I made a grand entrance, rather tickled by the rustle of interest among several other women, some awaiting their escorts, others hoping to pick-up a lonely officer for the weekend.

"Hello."

"Hello." For a moment, it felt as if we were meeting all over again, in the Coptic Chapel, except this time she offered me her hand. "I'm glad you came."

"Not at all," I returned the handshake with a formal bow," I'm glad you accepted my invitation," I lied. "Shall we go in?"

"Yes. Let's."

I got a good look at ourselves in the cloakroom's mirror when the attendant gave me our numbered tin discs. There was no question about it, we were a handsome, iconic couple for that time and place. She in her unadorned blue-grey uniform frock, without the white apron of course. Me in tailored khaki, with a dark blue and crimson ribbon and silver rosette above the tunic's left breast pocket; the gilded brass A of an Original Anzac on my shoulder flashes; wound stripes on the right cuff below two inverted overseas service chevrons, the red one for service at Gallipoli. Every inch a proud young warrior who had won the finest and fairest of British womanhood, except that he was trying his utmost not to -!

Sandra remained oblivious to the raging tumult inside my chest as she paused and glanced around the crowded dining room. "Nothing's changed, and yet everything is so different now…"

"Meaning?" I was unsteadily brusque.

"Meaning, that although the ambiance is not what it used to be in peacetime, the décor is exactly as it was when Mrs Langtry smuggled me into a meeting of her Actresses' Franchise League, claiming I was Tinker Bell's understudy in *Peter Pan* at the Duke of York's," She explained, with wistful smile. "A theatrical in-joke," she continued, "because, to suggest a fairy, one only needs coloured lights and tinkly notes from the orchestra pit, not a real junior at all," she elaborated, trying hard to make conversation. "Pa' was furious when I told him with whom I had joined the Suffragettes, especially when I impudently added: 'Life belongs to the living, and he who lives must be prepared for change!'"

"Says who?" I scowled, struggling hard against the gravitational pull of her wondrous warmth and intellect.

"Wolfgang von Goethe. *'Das Leben gehört den Lebenden –'*"

"Shh!" I grabbed her arm and linked it with mine as an elderly waiter approached to show us to the table Grenville had reserved.

It was unlikely that a decorated Australian officer and a strikingly beautiful Anglo-Irish nurse would ever be denounced as German spies, but I was not willing to run the risk at this low point of the war, with casualty lists filling entire pages of Britain's daily newspapers. Even to speak of Germans or

Germany, except with spits, and snarls, and curses, was dangerous at a time when patriotic Britons were allegedly stoning "sausage dog" dachshunds, in the street.

Sandra fell silent while the Criterion's chefs did their best with what little they had, but there is only so much anyone can confect from potatoes and turnips, cabbage, and dried beans. The meat course may have been rabbit, or cat, or dog, disguised by thick onion sauce; the fish was probably caught in the Thames or one of London's gravel pit reservoirs; the fowl claimed to be chicken but was just as likely pigeon snared on a rooftop in nearby Trafalgar Square or seagull netted at Southend-on-Sea.

The British public never knew it at the time, or else their morale would have sunk even faster than the Kaiser's U-boats were sinking Britain's merchant fleet, but the Ministry of Food now held fewer than six weeks of essential supplies, under armed guard in secret locations around the country. I later learned that the government had printed Emergency Ration Books to replace the ones civilians already needed to buy a bread allowance adulterated with chaff and powdered chalk.

We, of course, were unaware of this and kept chatting impersonally about our various experiences since parting in Egypt. My resolve to maintain a coolly proper distance wavered and it required a supreme effort to stay focused on what must be done. By tacit agreement neither of us spoke of the war. Instead, she asked me how I was getting on with *Boolya's Hoard*, and when I said I hadn't given it any thought recently, began telling me of another Australian novel, *Robbery Under Arms*, that she was reading a few pages at a time, between long spells of duty.

I had enjoyed it as a boy but did not have the heart to tell her that railway lines and telegraph wires had put gentlemen bushrangers out of business, long before the turn of our century. Her obvious delight in its vivid descriptions of dangerous young men riding across endless, sunlit plains in search of adventure, obliquely hinted at her own constricted background and one possible reason why she was romancing my imagined origins.

Our reconnection in Ward O-6 had prompted me to ask 3LGH's library for a copy of *Debrett's Peerage*, the official studbook of Britain's bluest of blue bloodlines. After looking-up her pedigree, it was clear how centuries of service to the Crown, and intermarriage with other great families, had affected a free-spirited young person with a mind of her own. I was flattered to think that such an attractive and intelligent woman would seek my company, with its aura of daring exploits in a plainspoken land far from the inherited burdens of honour and duty, but I was not fooled for one moment by -

"I intend to go there one day."

I returned to the present. "Go where?"

"Australia, of course!" she chided with a tentative smile. "Since meeting you, I've seen how different Australians are, and want to learn what it is that makes you so."

"'Different'?" This ominously familiar word has multiple meanings in English, and I needed to be sure of her intention.

"For instance, I love the way you say: 'C'mon, let's give it a go!'" she continued. "Too many of our menfolk look for an excuse to do nothing when challenged to try something new." She hesitated, perhaps aware of sounding disloyal to her own tribe. "It must be all that sunlight that makes you so confident."

"What's sunlight got to do with it?" I scowled defensively.

She remained quiet as the waitress collected our pudding plates – the apple turnover with margarine and corn flour mock cream was as good as could be expected – and took orders for a hot drink of roasted dandelion root and chicory essence.

"Well?" I persisted, once the young girl was out of earshot.

Sandra took her time before replying. "I feel that sunlight, or lack of it, has much to do with national character. For instance, in Britain and Ireland, the atmosphere tends to be cool and misty, there are few sunlit vistas, so we are inclined to view the world through a grey filter." She was revisiting a conversation we'd had the previous year in Egypt, at the same time rekindling feelings I needed to quell if our *affaire* was to end honourably, and soon. "I suspect that climate shapes the vague, moody English language, and explains why we rarely give direct answers but, instead, assume the other person understands our oblique replies…"

As if to prove her point she paused for comment before, disappointed by my silence, continuing. "Perhaps, this's why I am so attracted to the logical structure and clarity of that, ah, other North European language? Though come to think of it, their climate is hardly any different from ours, so it can't be weather alone. In any event," she concluded, trying to brighten up again, "be assured that I am determined to explore Australia's fascinating new world."

I dared not open my mouth in case it was the heart - not the head - that replied as our mock coffee was delivered, taken black, unsweetened, and the reckoning settled with generous gratuities all round.

"Are you sure you're feeling alright?" she asked with a worried sideways glance as we left the table. "We can catch a taxi back to Wandsworth, if you like?"

"No. I'm fine."

"You seem very, preoccupied…?"

"I said I'm fine! It's the old bone box." I irritably tapped my forehead.

"France…?"

"Australia," I lied again, handing over our cloakroom tokens. "The Originals are going home on convalescent leave, but I'm a specialist MGO and there are never enough of us for the training battalions, so there's no chance I'll be on a boat soon -" I broke off to acknowledge and tip the elderly attendant as she handed us our coats. I held Sandra's open for her to slip into. She turned with a smile, imagining she had found the cause of my grumpy mood. "I'm glad."

"Why?" My tone was anything but glad.

"It will be so much easier to stay in touch, while you're in England, or France…"

The confounded woman still hadn't got the hint and I was at a loss to see how to part with the least pain for me. For her. For us!

91

London's drizzle had eased sufficiently for us to take the short walk from Piccadilly, down Haymarket to His Majesty's Theatre, during which I twice switched my cane to the left hand while returning salutes from non-commissioned ranks unable to duck into a convenient shop front, or up a side alley, as we approached them.

Sandra was clearly thrilled to be escorted by such a gallant young chap even if he was infuriatingly vague about their destination, until all was revealed when she saw the queue waiting at His Maj's box office, in case a few matinee tickets fell vacant at the last minute.

"It was nice thought, Darling, but *Chu* is sold-out until next February, so there's no chance we can just walk in -"

"Y'reckon?" I shook off my inner darkness and cocked a questioning eyebrow.

"Of course. See how many are ahead of us!"

"'C'mon, let's give it a go.'" I forced the cheeky grin of a daredevil Digger on leave in the Old Country and gripped her arm.

Protesting strongly, she accompanied me up the steps and into the foyer where - "Ta dah!" - I flourished a pair of tickets from my tunic pocket; deposited our things in the cloak room; bought an illustrated programme; and gave a silver threepence to the usherette who led us to a pair of seats in the very front row of the Dress Circle.

"You never cease to amaze!" she laughed delightedly. "We may die of many things, but boredom will never be one of them -!"

"Hear, hear!" An elderly gentleman, seated with his wife behind us, gave my shoulder an approving pat. "You take good care of this young lady, m'boy!" Adding, with a courtly nod in Sandra's direction: "As I'm sure he will, ma'am. One can tell he's the right sort!"

What threatened to become an embarrassing encounter stopped as the lights dimmed, the orchestra struck up a twinkling, orientalist overture and the fire curtain lifted to reveal a lavish banqueting scene in Old Baghdad where Kasim Baba, brother of Ali Baba, was preparing to welcome a fabulously rich Chinese merchant, Chu Chin Chow, little knowing that his guest was really Abu Hassan, chieftain of the Forty Thieves, in heavy disguise.

This musical mishmash of an *Arabian Nights* pantomime bore no resemblance to the Middle East that Sandra and I had recently experienced. Not that it was ever intended to, with a chorus of scantily clad female palace guards described with sly humour by one newspaper critic as "more navel than military in appearance," delighting every soldier and sailor in the audience.

Such tuneful tosh was just what Tommy Atkins and Jack Tar needed to lift their spirits before returning to the Western Front or anti-submarine patrols off the stormy Western Approaches, which accounts for the play's record run of five years.

Abu Hassan was played by the broodingly handsome Oscar Ashe, a fellow Melburnian who, like many another Australian, found fame and fortune overseas. During my own later years abroad, I would frequently encounter our richly talented diaspora at the highest levels of industry and finance, science and politics, art and music, in numbers out of all proportion to what one would expect from such a tiny and remote nation.

Given we then had a population smaller than many a European capital city, Australia gave birth to such diverse celebrities as Dame Maude McCarthy, Matron-in-Chief of the British Army throughout the Great War; Errol Flynn the swashbuckling kinema actor; Sir Howard Florey who led the team that developed the first broad-spectrum antibiotic drug; Sir Hubert Wilkins, a South Australian country lad who became a pioneer aviator, climatologist, and Arctic explorer; Suzanne Bennett – Lady Wilkins in private life - the Broadway actress and celebrated portrait painter, born in a North Victorian prospector's hut; and Eileen Joyce the international concert pianist, raised in Kalgoorlie's twin-town of Boulder on the Eastern Goldfields. And those were but a few of the many notable expat' Australians I could name.

I can become quite cranky whenever the ignorant sneer and rattle imaginary chains to denigrate my land and my people. At such times I firmly remind them of Australia's outstanding achievements in every field of human endeavour where, to use a boxing expression, we consistently punch above our weight! And, as Frances will hear in tomorrow's tape-recorded conversation, I shall never apologise to anyone for anything in my nation's short history!

Nor do I despise those unruly, unwanted First Settlers who triumphed against unimaginable odds, much as their great-grandsons did during the Summer of 1918 when our skeleton battalions smashed through the Hindenburg Line, igniting a roaring bushfire of Allied victories that only ended when the Kaiser abdicated, and his broken army threw in the towel.

Not that any of this was on my mind that afternoon at His Majesty's as Sandra snuggled up to keep warm in a barely heated theatre, coal being needed more for industry and the Royal Navy than for civilian entertainment, and hummed along with the show's hit song, *Any Time is Kissing Time*, with its haunting refrain: "Youth is the time for loving, so poets always say. Surely 'tis so, you ought to know, any time is kissing time…"

The interval was a welcome opportunity to take a break, stretch the legs, mingle at the crowded bar. The French *horizon bleu* uniforms I recognised immediately. Three other officers, in Bersaglieri green and black, were Italian and probably on liaison duties with the War Office in nearby Whitehall. I even spotted a couple of Russians in their distinctive snuff brown tunics, most likely part of an Allied purchasing commission, as I grandly suggested to Sandra that we crack a Dom Perignon, but instead of champagne she asked for Malvern Spa water.

Our mutual surprises had been frequent in Egypt and she was still delivering them now. I should not have been too surprised because, except for that Chablis and a couple of G&Ts in Alexandria, I don't remember her ever touching alcohol, and yet she was far from being a killjoy or wowser, as we say in Australian.

My aching admiration for her redoubled as I turned away from the bar, carrying two glasses and a bottle of Malvern, in time to see a willowy chap in Coldstream Guards' uniform, the three pips of a captain on his cuffs, wafting through the crowd towards us, a drink of some kind slopping over his fist.

"What-ho Sandra!" He used her correct name of course. "Splendid show, ay wot!" Then, with a dismissive glance in my direction: "Who are you?"

She beat me to it. "Meet my very dear friend Ian Cribdon."

"Oh. Aw-stray-yun." Said with the infuriatingly muffled drawl a certain type of Englishman affects.

"Too bloody right I am. Who are you?"

Sandra felt the air crackle with male pride and stepped between us. "Ian, this is George Ffoulkes-Manley." Adding by way of explanation: "He was in my brother's year at Eton."

"Yes, so I was, by Jove! How's Jimmy getting along? Dublin Fusiliers, ay wot? Should've joined the Guards, like his Pa'."

"James has a mind of his own," there was an unusually sharp edge to her voice, "as well you know!"

"Ah yes, so devilish hard to keep track these days. You heard Brigade put me up for an award? Fell just short of the mark but better luck next time!" This last remark was aimed squarely at the inch and a quarter of coloured silk ribbon above my left breast pocket.

"Come along, Darling," Sandra tugged my sleeve, "we must be getting back."

"See you after the show!" he warbled above the din of voices and clinking glassware as we turned our backs on him. "Supper? Drinkies -?"

"Jesus wept," I groaned, "do the Poms really breed 'em like that?"

"Don't be too hard on the poor chump," Sandra replied with an understanding smile.

"Poor? He must be loaded, with that double-barrelled moniker!"

"And don't be too quick to assume things are always as they seem to be," she cautioned, pausing at the foot of the crowded stairway. "His people may be substantial brewers who imagine they can buy their son an entrée into Society, but the harder they try, the more he's called 'Faux-Manly' behind his back -'"

"Hn."

"It is cruel, and wrong, and impolite to make fun of another's name," she continued, with a determined frown. "If only George could stop pretending to be what he's not, and instead start being what he is, we might yet see a decent young man emerge."

"Hmph!"

"Tch, tch, tch," she wagged a reproving finger under my nose. "You know my taste better than that! Come along, we mustn't miss the final act."

Minutes later, the curtain rose to reveal the seductive female spy, Zahrat, telling Ali Baba how to gain entrance to Hassan's secret treasure cave. As soon as she's gone, he exclaims "Open Sesame!" fills a sack with plunder and makes good his escape. Kassim notices his brother's sudden good fortune and just as quickly says the magic words, only to be ambushed by Hassan, who knifes him.

The thieves' chorus then marches on-stage, brandishing silver-painted plywood scimitars, announcing their intention to raid the Baba Palace and recover their missing loot, before marching off again.

A trick with the lighting reveals Ali's cocksure son, Nur, cajoling Zahrat - a beautiful young slave girl - into his bedchamber with sweet words and erotic references to *Rahat Loukoum*, better known as Turkish Delight.

Using this sugary hanky-panky as cover, the charming Zahrat stabs Hassan in the back, kills his gang with boiling oil, and everyone else lives happily ever after.

It says much about Britain's moral climate in those perilous times that we laughed at theft and deceit; cheered two murders, three if the original Chu Chin Chow's is included; and guffawed when a slinky temptress scalded forty men to death. I may develop this theme as an Edwardian's proof that as times change so do the ways people respond to them. And that much puzzling behaviour - even in the recent past - cannot be decoded unless its context is understood first.

Meanwhile, the actors sprang back to life for their curtain call before the orchestra, down in the pit, struck up the National Anthem that everyone got to their feet and sang with fierce loyalty, turning an otherwise drab little tune into a rousing hymn of defiance against the Kaiser:

> God save our gracious King
> Long live our noble King
> God save the King!
> Send him victorious
> Happy and glorious
> Long to reign over us
> God save the King!
>
> Continuing:
> O Lord God arise
> Scatter his enemies and make them fall
> Confound their politics
> Frustrate their knavish tricks
> On Thee our hopes we fix
> God save us all!
>
> Concluding:
> From every latent foe
> From the assassin's blow
> God save the King!
> O'er him Thy arm extend
> For Britain's sake defend
> Our father, prince, and friend
> God save the King!

I wonder how many others can still remember singing these patriotic verses without hesitation or embarrassment? Our number dwindles daily. Soon none will be left to tell of the British Empire at its pinnacle of pride and power.

I had earlier arranged for a cab to be waiting. Petrol was strictly rationed with most of it reserved for military transport and essential services, as a result many of Victorian London's Hansom cabs had been dragged out of retirement by bony nags branded US - Unfit for Service - at the Army Veterinary Corps' remount depots.

"Thanks sport." I tipped the doorman a shilling.

"Ta ever so much Guv'nor!" He touched his peaked cap's brim and was about to say more when a heavy hand thumped my shoulder.

I spun around to find Ffoulkes-Manley's watery blue eyes staring down at me from what he imagined was a lordly eminence. "Where! D'you shink you go'nk! Wiff m'girl!"

The temptation to snot this opinionated twerp was immense and it was only Sandra's shocked expression that stopped me from using the crowd as a blind to knee his nuts. Instead, I flicked his fingers off my sleeve. "Go away."

"I'm! Your shuperior off'cer!"

"Go away. Sir."

"You can't! Shpeak to me, like that!" He lurched forward. "Shiss m'girl! I'm taking. To shupper!"

I looked up at the cab's driver on his sprung seat behind the passengers' box. "'Got any idea where these coots roost?"

"Wellington Barracks, mos'ly," he replied, scratching a bearded chin against his whipstick.

"How much to take him there?"

"'Alf a crown."

"Make it three bob, you'll need to clean up after he –"

"Don't shpeak of me! Like that, you Awshrayun, arooph…!"

I stood well clear as he chundered into the gutter and reached up to deliver the now downwardly adjusted fare of two shillings and sixpence, then scanned the tight circle of amused faces and picked a couple of Tommies from the crowd. "Right-o lads, shove him in the cab and here's a bob for slosh and gaspers." I displayed a shilling, one day's pay in the British Army's lowest ranks, and watched the grinning privates wrestle a drunken Guards' officer into the box before slamming its hatch across his bony knees.

"Thank you, gentlemen."

"Fank'ser!"

A patter of applause concluded this impromptu entertainment as Sandra and I watched what should have been our cab rattle off towards the Household Brigade's barracks, oil tail-lamps fading into the dank murk.

I caught the doorman's eye again and beckoned him nearer. "Sorry about the mess. He's not having a good war."

The doorman nodded. "The missus an' me got two boys in France and one in Palestine. Don't you worry 'bout nuffink. I'll see it gets cleaned up proper."

I was about to ask for the most direct route from the Haymarket to Buckingham Street, in the blackout, when a lighter hand than the previous one touched my shoulder. I turned sharply. The old chap who had been sitting behind us was standing behind me now, his crimson-lined opera cloak flung back as if he were Mandrake the Magician with a black silk topper tilted over one eye. "That could have been most unpleasant, but you handled it well," he said. "If I'm not much mistaken, you also gave him your cab. So, what's next?"

"Thank you for asking, sir," I replied, my protective right arm around Sandra's slim waist as the exiting crowd jostled past us, "but the walk to Buckingham Street will help clear our heads."

"'Walk'?" He frowned. "Nonsense! My wife and I will consider it a privilege to take you there directly." He put a gold whistle to his lips and blew three mellow notes, as if summoning a gun dog. Instead, a Rolls Royce Silver Ghost emerged from the gaslit gloom, pale streetlamps reflected on gleaming royal blue coachwork, parting the crowd as if he were Moses and they the Red Sea.

During our leisurely drive towards the City of Westminster's Adelphi District, I thought it wise to decline dinner at the Dorchester by explaining that my nurse and I had to be back at the hospital by midnight, and that we had arranged to have supper *en chaperon* with her brother in his chambers.

"That's a pity," our host observed, reaching for the voice tube to send an order to the uniformed chauffeur in the forward cabin, "I was rather hoping we might become better acquainted. Ah! Slow down Jenkins, Number 14 must be quite near." He sat back and glanced my way again. "When the war's over, you may like to consider working with us." He handed me his card:

Sir Alfred Stanhope KCIE
Chairman
Asiatic & Pacific Trust Bank
1 Lombard Street, London EC3
Telephone: 738
ABC Telegraphic Code: ASIPAT

"I'm flattered you should think so, sir, but numbers are not my strong suit," I replied hesitantly, before lightening the response with a quip: "As we say in Outback Westralia: 'One, two, three, big mob...'"

"Maybe so," he chuckled, "however ours is not that sort of bank. We employ others to reconcile balances, call in overdrafts, audit accounts. Our business demands a more personal chemistry and intuitive *comme il faut* when negotiating loans to, and bond issues for overseas governments and corporations. Bookkeepers I can employ any time; less often do I meet a man of your evident parts." He paused lightly. "Do let me know when next you're in Town. You too, ma'am," he added, turning to address Sandra who was conversing with Lady Stanhope.

Jenkins held the door open for us to dismount and then resumed his place behind the wheel where, instead of trying to reverse in this narrow, seventeenth century street he drove straight ahead onto a temporary gravel track past an ancient gateway and disappeared into the enveloping darkness.

92

"You lied about my brother!" Sandra was furious, though I could only discern her faint outline amidst these unlit shadows.

I trapped the fists pounding my chest and chose the next words with studied care. "One day soon you will meet and marry a man of your own rank and place in the world, but for that to succeed your character and reputation must be above reproach, which it will not be if prurient gossip connects you to a fly-by-night nobody from the Colonies."

"How dare you presume -!"

"I dare because I care." I released her trembling wrists. "A tipsy Guardsman doesn't have to be the only lovelorn swain who saw you out with a soldier this afternoon."

"But -!"

"And as if that were not bad enough, we've just driven with a couple who probably know everyone who's anyone in London, if not the Empire, and for some strange reason I've been offered a job. They won't forget driving us to a private address that such worldly folk will assume is *un lieu de rendezvous illicites* unless I've thrown them off the scent with a more convincing story…"

"You are so, devious!"

"Yes, I am. Fortunately for you." I lowered my voice. "Alex' was as free and pure and full of joy as any love can ever be. I shall treasure our memories until my final breath, be it soon or be it late, but now we're in England and must go our separate ways. Whoa! I'm not finished." I raised a cautionary finger even though it was unlikely she could read the gesture. "If against all odds I get through the war and we meet again, let it be as good friends, which we will not be if I've cost you 'a suitable marriage…'"

"Stop!" She stifled a sob. "I don't want to hear, anymore! I am so tired, so wretchedly tired, I can no longer think straight. Stop, please stop -!"

"As you wish. Now, let's go inside, organise a bite to eat, and get some zeds, because you're not the only one who no longer knows whether he's Arthur, or Martha, or Neither. Then, tomorrow, when the brain fog clears, we'll sort this thing, once and for all." I struck a match, found the bell pull, gave it a firm tug.

Moments later the antique street door creaked open on its dry iron hinges, spilling yellow light down worn sandstone steps, at the same time silhouetting the housekeeper's stocky figure as she bobbed a curtsy. "Lieutenant Cribdon, sir?"

"Yes. Colonel Grenville has kindly offered us his quarters."

"I am fully informed of the arrangement sir. This way if you please." She stood aside as Sandra and I entered the ground floor of a town residence originally built in the late-1600s. Since when, someone with wealth and taste had incorporated electric light, gas, and running water, while still managing to leave the original décor largely intact.

It needed no great imagination to picture Sandra's forefathers in their periwigs and embroidered *justaucorps* coats, seated around a table in this very same room, plotting to overthrow King James the Second and sell the vacant throne to his Dutch son-in-law, William of Orange.

"And this is, what?" Sandra was trying hard to get her bearings.

"The male equivalent of *Chez Adorable*, except that it's in Central London, and the family property of a friend at Wandsworth."

"Will you be taking supper now, or will I show you the facilities first? Sir? Ma'am?"

"Let's do that first," Sandra, more accustomed than I to handling English servants, took the lead by answering the housekeeper's question with a dignified smile as we ascended three additional floors by means of a tight staircase through the dining room; the library-cum-sitting room, with a piano and half-size billiard table; to the bedchamber above.

"I trust you will find all to your satisfaction, ma'am. There is fresh linen and aught else you require in the dresser." She indicated a fine old campaign chest of drawers made of teak and a lighter coloured wood, probably camphor, and plain brass bindings that had seen a lot of active service during the past century or so.

"Thank you, Mrs...?"

"Blane," the elderly woman replied, her shoulders back, chin up. "Since a girl, have I faithfully served the Grenvilles. My husband, Mr Thomas Blane, is the General's batman in Salonika. Doing his bit for King & Country as do I here for the family's young gentlemen."

Recalling her simple words, I hear echoes of a world impossible to imagine nowadays, of an age when lifelong service to a great family was as proudly declared as if it were a coveted order of knighthood.

"Thank you, Mrs Blane." Sandra knew the exact tone of voice to use when acknowledging senior rank and status in another's household. "And should we require further assistance?"

"The sem'phore is right there by the door ma'am." The housekeeper indicated a brass and porcelain handle which, when tugged pulled a steel wire that jingled a bell and flipped a numbered flag on a signals panel in the servants' quarters.

"Very well then, and supper. As soon as possible?"

"Yes ma'am." Mrs Blane curtsied and bustled off.

Sandra slumped on the antique four-poster bed, awakening awkward memories of Maeve's mural in a Kalgoorlie public bar. I, meantime, reconnoitred the room, opening drawers and peering behind the lavatory door to check where things were.

"Why have you brought me here?" Her voice was weary beyond measure.

"Not for what you may think," I replied, turning to squat on my haunches, the better to look up at her shadowed face. "What we must say, what we must do, cannot be said or done in a noisy restaurant or a crowded theatre. And because I have no home in London, and yours is across the Irish Sea, Phillip Grenville has kindly loaned us a calm, well-ordered place to put our affairs in order."

Sandra was on the point of replying when Mrs Blane returned to announce that supper was ready in the ground floor dining room.

Approaching the table, from the foot of the stairs, it was evident that someone in the family had a country estate with abundant wild game as well as a home farm that was rarely, if ever, visited by the Food Ministry's inspectors with their powers to prosecute farmers and confiscate their unregistered livestock. Mrs Blane's country fare pork and hare terrine, baked apple tart with real clotted cream, charcuterie board and cheese platter were a reminder of how well some Britons fed before the war.

Tired and replete we went upstairs again, shut the bedchamber door and swapped questioning looks; neither of us had brought so much as a toothbrush. In the event, there was no need, for not only was the campaign chest filled with freshly laundered nightwear, the renovators had contrived to squeeze a shower and lavatory into the corner where once stood a commode and washstand. Here we found fresh soap and safety razors, toothbrushes and tooth powder, combs, and bay rum hair tonic, neatly arranged in a mirrored cupboard over the sink.

"That's yours." I pointed at the four-poster. "This's mine." I nodded down at the truckle bed - meant for children or servants - that wheeled from under the master and mistress's more extensive one.

"No. Please don't. I feel so cold. So very cold. And tired."

Without another word we shed our day clothes, climbed aboard the four-poster, and fell into an emotionally exhausted sleep, wrapped around each other for warmth, like some dear old Darby & Joan married couple.

Neither of us awoke with any great urge to get next day started and I was content to postpone the inevitable for as long as possible, even though her soft, sleepy breath on my neck aroused awkward memories of our first awakening, in Alexandria. Instead, we dozed together, listening to rain falling on the tiled roof, gurgling along the eaves' gutters, before dropping through cast iron drainpipes to the street below.

Eventually, I had to get up, after which I padded across hand sawn oak floorboards to a casement window overlooking what, in peacetime, were Westminster's fashionable Thames Embankment Gardens but was now a misty village of Nissen huts housing the overflow from Whitehall's enlarged ministries.

I had ot yet to recognise it, but Britain had two distinct armies in this, the first total war of modern times. One, clad in khaki, was fighting on a Front that reached from the English Channel to the Persian Gulf and India, where German agents and Islamic preachers were agitating the Pathan border tribes more than usual.

The other army, clad in civvies, served on the Home Front. Hundreds of thousands of women typists and telephonists, messengers and despatch riders, lorry drivers and delivery clerks, mechanics and machinists conscripted into the Ministries of Supply & Munitions, Treasury & Pensions, Recruitment & Manpower, Rationing & Food, Mining & Industry, Fisheries & Agriculture, Admiralty & Blockade, Cabinet Office -

"A penny for your thoughts?"

Startled, I half-turned. Sandra had also needed to get up and was now standing beside me, wrapped in a loose blanket. I resisted the urge to slip an arm around her waist and instead pondered the enigma that was, for me, London. "I can't be the only 'Son of the Empire' who imagined our capital to be the largest, the grandest city in the world, only to feel disappointment when we discover it's no bigger or better than Port Melbourne...?" I queried, nodding across the wintry roofscape towards the East End's dockland of cranes and belching smokestacks.

Although today was my first exposure to this scene, en vérité, its muted greys and smudged bluey greens were a familiar sight on the walls of Tralee House where my aunt enjoyed a fine collection of Monets, several of which depicted the foggy Thames at twilight, some with ghostly ships moored to indistinct quaysides, others of Tower Bridge and the Houses of Parliament.

"First impressions are not always true." Sandra tried to snuggle up. "One day, we'll walk through Hyde Park from Kensington to Berkeley Square, in Autumn when the trees are ablaze with red and gold, then you'll understand. I know!" She brightened. "We'll hire a rowboat, explore the Serpentine, and pretend it's the Yarra!"

What must be done could be deferred no longer as I caught a tight cough in my clenched fist. "Won't your husband object to a threesome?"

She drew back. "Who said anything about, 'husband'?"

"I did. Last night. When I reminded you that a time is coming when you must marry a man of your own rank and place in the world."

"'Must'?"

Her tone warned me to back off, instead I continued, hoping she would see that mine was the only sensible course of action for a couple in our predicament. "I've read a lot recently, and one of the things I've learned is that a woman of your class has an implicit obligation to produce 'an heir and a spare.' No ifs. No buts. No exemptions -"

"Is that how you see me?!" Her explosive anger was terrifying to experience. "As a pedigreed brood mare?!"

I had forgotten that, only a few hours previously, the Honourable Lady Sandra Nobury had told me of her recruitment into the Suffragettes. Since when she had matured into a resolute young woman determined to shape her own destiny without any man's permission, as she reminded me now with brutally blunt words that beat about my ear like a boxer's blows.

Some men would have shut her up by shouting her down, others would have biffed her into silence, but I bit my tongue, not that I could have got word in edgeways as she furiously unburdened fears and feelings I never knew of until now. Finally, she threw herself face-down onto the bed and smothered her wracking sobs in the pillows.

I eased alongside her, propped on one elbow, and gently stroked her neck and hair, much as she had done for me, that chaotic afternoon in Ward O-6.

"It's, so unjust!" Her words were muffled but their intent was clear as she rolled over. "You men, are legally entitled, to the lion's share! Of everything! We women, are your chattels, and ornaments! To be used, or abused, as you please!"

I broke into a shivery sweat as memories of poor little Maggie Stubbs, shot dead by an insanely jealous husband, burned across my mind like a magnesium flare swaying downwards on its parachute over No Man's Land.

"Darling!" Sandra sat bolt upright, frightened by what she had unwittingly triggered. "I didn't mean you personally!"

"It's, nothing." I struggled to get my breath back. "You're right. The world is unequal, is unjust, is unfair. It always has been. It always will be. So, perhaps there's a reason?"

"How can there be?!"

"Steady on," I cautioned, trying to steady my own tumbled, jumbled thoughts. "As Aunt Lucinda is wont to say: 'For some inscrutable reason the Great Anatomist made women with weak bodies that He, She, or It compensated for by giving us strong and supple brains,'" I began. "'However, even the best of brains is powerless to achieve much without muscle power, which is why brawny men were created. Similarly, without female wit and wisdom, masculine brawn is no better than a bowl of pork jelly. Therefore, everyone's role in the great topsy-turvy drama of life, is to respect and rebalance our unequal halves. And once paired off, men and women alike, work as one by sharing each with the other, and caring each for the other.' Or words to that effect."

Sandra had drawn up her knees and was sitting forward, chin resting on them. "Is that what you, yourself, believe?"

"Yes." I recovered my balance. "It fits a theory I've been working on for some time."

"And does your theory account for inequalities of birth, and rank, and all that 'heir and spare' nonsense?"

"Yes. It does."

"How?"

"Because in the end, everything boils down to family honour –"

"That irksome burden!" she interrupted with an angry toss of the head.

"You don't know how lucky you are to have it!" I snapped back. Afraid to say any more, I shut up, slid off the bed and stood silhouetted against the window. "Come on, let's see what's downstairs in the pantry. I'm so hungry I could eat a racehorse and chase the jockey for afters!"

My breezy Australian exaggeration lightened the mood, and it was a more relaxed couple who found Mrs Blane up to her elbows in bread dough, by the look of it real wheaten flour, probably smuggled into London from the Grenvilles' home farm.

Trained since girlhood to be the attentive, discreet family servant, there was nothing in this elderly woman's manner to suggest that she ever gossiped about the young gents and their girlfriends for whom she kept house; if anything, I detected a wistful awareness that these brief, illicit encounters were the last happy memories many of us would take to an unmarked grave in a collapsed dugout, or as unrecognisable gobbets of meat and bone scattered around a shell crater.

Sandra and I sat at the kitchen table sipping mugs of real Ceylon tea, not the more usual *Union Jack* dried raspberry leaves, while Mrs Blane prepared a pre-war English breakfast of smoked ham, scrambled eggs, and field mushrooms fried in butter, with delicious toast and Fortnum's Dundee marmalade to follow. She then bustled off to attend to something upstairs as we revelled in these robust, half-forgotten tastes and textures.

I briefly nipped outside to the backyard, to check on the weather, and just as quickly nipped inside again. "It's not looking good."

"Very well." Sandra refilled our mugs from the blue enamel teapot. "I vote we take these to our room, and let the day do as it will…"

"If that is your wish." I hoped she felt the lack of warmth in my reply, for I was determined to make a quick, clean break, once we were alone again.

93

Fortunately for my plans, Mrs Blane had lit a cheerful fire in the library-cum-sitting room, its blazing billets of seasoned beechwood further evidence of a countryman supporting his London relatives through times of rationed scarcity.

I went over to the billiard table, chalked a cue, and potted a few balls to steady my nerve. Sandra, meantime, sat at the piano and reflectively fingered an arpeggio scale before striking up that old hymn tune - *There's a Friend for Little Children, above the Bright Blue Sky* - to accompany the VADs' unofficial anthem in a beautifully clear voice:

> There's a home for tired nurses,
> above the bright blue sky.
> Where matrons never grumble,
> and colonels never pry.
> Where all our little sorrows,
> are drowned in cups of tea.
> And all these ruddy bedpans,
> rest eternally…

Still half-smiling at its droll imagery, she stood and came over to see what I was doing. "You are very good…"

"Number Eight in the Victorian State Championships." I sighted another tricky jump shot with back spin. "Not quite up for the 1913 Nationals, but who knows what 1914 might have been if only the Kaiser hadn't put the kibosh on things?"

"And assuming he hadn't," she persisted, watching me closely as I crouched, cue poised, "might you have turned professional?"

"Maybe." I hopped the cue ball over a snookering red to sink another with a finely kissed cannon shot. "Billiard saloons attract a host of colourful characters and I'd begun a folio of sketches, *d'après* Lautrec's *Cirque Fernando*."

"Really?" She was impressed. "Will you resume your art studies instead, when the war's over?"

"No idea." I rested my cue and straightened. "It's a bad luck magnet, to talk of life after the war. Best to ignore the future. Then it's no great loss when Fritz decides we don't have one."

Sandra averted her face. "And yet you must have some faith in a future, to speak of a private theory that, presumably, looks forward to happier days 'sharing each with the other' and 'caring each for the other'? And does this, theory, say anything about, our sharing and caring…?"

I took a deep breath. "Yes. It does."

"And…?"

I took an even deeper breath. "Here is where we must go our separate ways and never look back."

Her face lost its colour. "W-what?"

"It's over."

"How, how, how dare you cast me aside as if I were a, a, a shopgirl of no account -!"

"I dare because I care -!"

"Hah!"

"I promised, in the Coptic chapel, never to hurt you -!"

"What are you are doing now?!"

"Being cruel to be kind –!"

"'Kind'?!"

"One day you'll know I'm right!" I sobbed. "No way in the world would I part if you were anyone other than who and what you are!" Tears stung my eyelids. "But you are who you are, and what you are, and because of the duties, the obligations, the responsibilities that come with such an inheritance, I am ordering you to do the right and proper thing for yourself, for your family, for your class, and for God's sake leave me alone -!"

Shocked, she stared at me disbelievingly. "You are, serious?"

"Yes." More than anything else in the world, I ached to devote the rest of my life to this woman and at its end share the same grave until the end of time itself, but such a romantic folly could never be. One does not marry an individual, one marries an intricate network of relationships, and after reading Sandra's lineage in *Debrett's Peerage*, I knew with absolute certainty that her people and mine had nothing in common.

"This is rubbish!" She stamped her foot. "I thought you Australians had freed yourselves from superstitious awe of birth and titles -!"

"That may be true but it also irrelevant!" I replied with an angry jut of the jaw. "Of greater concern are your family and friends, and from what I've read, none of those would ever welcome me into their magic realm! You would be forced to choose between remaining part of it, or earn their disdain by staying apart from it, wed to a nobody from nowhere! And that is one gamble I will never allow you to take -!"

"Don't I have any say in the matter!?" she demanded with a haughty glare.

"You'll do as you're bloody well told!" Two years of ordering men to follow me into the fog and flame of battle had tempered my tone and today she got it hot and strong -!

"Then damn you, Ian Cribdon! Damn you! Damn you! Damn you!" With that she spun on her heel and marched downstairs from where Mrs Blane called a cab.

Much later, the housekeeper found me hunched in the darkest corner of the room, like I'd been gut-shot, which is how I felt. "Would you like me to bring you some chicken broth sir?"

"No, thank you, ma'am." I slowly looked up. "But if you've got a pen, ink, and paper, I'd be most grateful for those."

"As you wish sir."

Eventually I regained sufficient strength to sit up at the writing desk and compose my thoughts:

My Dearest.

I regret nothing we have ever done or said.
You will remain, to my dying breath, the finest, the
most decent person I shall ever know, so why did I
cruelly reject your love and affection?

*To understand this, you must remember I am a very
ordinary man caught up in extraordinary times that have
taken me from my former place in life. I have no
distinguished ancestors and therefore no inborn
obligation to honour their memory and continue
their line unbroken. You have.*

*There are many who claim Amor Omnia Vincit -
Love Conquers All - and imagine this refers
only to physical desire. However, there is a higher
love, one associated with those Roman virtues
on your family's escutcheon - Gravitas, Dignitas,
Veritas - to which I now add Genitas.*

*As I'm sure you already know, this is the duty of
a patrician lady to mother the next generation of her
gens, or noble lineage, for which she earns the same
respect and authority as her paterfamilial husband.*

*You may think you are free of this ancient obligation
and can choose whomsoever you like, but Sanguis
Crassior Aquae - Blood is Thicker than Water - and
you could never rest easy knowing that you had betrayed
your ancestors by marrying a lesser man than they were.
Similarly, I could never live with myself knowing I'd
brought dishonour upon you and your name.*

It is therefore right and proper we go our separate ways.

Your loyal and faithful friend.

Ian Cribdon.

Among the advantages of never having suffered a formal schooling, was
the freedom to browse far and wide in public and private libraries while other
boys sat listless and bored in their stifling classrooms.

The visual strength of Latin words has always attracted me, which is why
I taught myself to read that unquiet dead language, much like French in some
respects, and another reason for my attendances at church with Dulcie and
Patrick Donovan, where I memorised the pronunciation of Father Declan's
sonorous Latin Masses that spoke of Faith & Redemption while this secret
barbarian heard the tramp of Caesar's legions conquering Gaul.

There was, of course, a fair amount of swagger in my display of informal
scholarship. Likewise, a touchy male pride that insisted I be remembered as a
man who could have competed on equal terms with any other in Sandra's world,
had he chosen to do so.

All things considered, though it hurt like hell, I knew I'd made the right
decision and was now free to turn my back on the past and get on with what
little remained of my future.

Firmly resolved to henceforth wipe Sandra from my mind, I re-read the
letter, made a few minor corrections, addressed the envelope, and went
downstairs to the kitchen. "Is there a post-box nearby, Mrs Blane?"

"Why, yes sir. On the corner of Adam Street."

"Then may I presume upon you for a stamp?"

"Certainly sir." She searched the kitchen dresser for an old tobacco tin and gave me two green halfpenny postcard stamps, to make up the penny postage rate for a full letter.

"You're very kind." I affixed them to the envelope and tucked it inside my tunic. "I can't stay any longer, but as evidence of my sincere gratitude, please accept this to buy some comforts for your gallant husband."

She blinked with astonishment at the crisp new one-pound note on her kitchen table. "Oh no sir, that's far too much!" As indeed it was at a time when many a factory worker earned just one pound a week, and a scullery maid might think herself wealthy if she pocketed twenty shillings a month.

"No ma'am. It is far less than what I - what we - owe you for much kindness and attention." I shrugged into the trench coat, reached for my hat and cane, determined to be remembered as a man of means.

"Shall I call a cab as I did for the young lady sir?!"

"No thanks. A walk in the rain will clear my head."

Old age is a horrible place to revisit the errors of youth and I flinch even now, remembering my conduct then, viewed across the gulf of seventy years during which the world and its manners have changed beyond all recognition.

Young people today would never behave in such a stiff-necked way, not when they can barely exchange names before rutting like beasts in a barnyard, if kinema films and tele-vision shows are to be believed.

I would not expect Frances to understand an Edwardian's "Death before Dishonour" attitude to affairs of the heart, if I were to share it with her, which I probably shall not.

94

"Hello old chap." Grenville was seated in the Sunroom, misnamed at this time of year, and glanced up from the *Manual of Field Fortifications* he was preparing for his Staff College Selection Board. "You're back earlier than expected. Had a good time?"

"Brilliant," I lied. "*Chu* was an absolute hoot from go to whoa."

"Glad to hear it," he smiled wistfully, doubtless imagining subsequent delights. "When next in Town, and needing a quiet place, have a word with Mrs Blane and give her my regards. I'm sure she'll oblige."

"That's jolly decent."

"Not at all. Oh, by the way, a Corporal Streeton is looking for you. Apparently plans are afoot to organise a bit of a do for the kiddies."

"Good old Arthur!"

"You know him then?"

"Oh yes," I smiled. "He's longstanding family friend and often sets up his easel at the river end of our property."

"And now he's here? How extraordinary!"

"Indeed," I agreed. "As Australia's foremost landscape artist, he could have remained at home, painting canvases at one thousand guineas apiece, and nobody would have thought any the less of him. Instead, he volunteered to be a Medical Corps' dogsbody…"

"Well, I'll be dashed!" Grenville sat forward in his chair. "This's exactly what I mean about you Australians being splendidly different. I mean, the most unprepossessing fellow can turn out to be someone of note. I really must come and visit you! Fritz permitting, of course."

"Please do. It'll be great to show you around, but be prepared for surprises," I cautioned, paraphrasing Jonno's warning to me, a lifetime ago, "the shabby old digger, fossicking for spent durries to roll a smoke, could soon be a millionaire if his lease comes good. And the blow hard, shouting drinks for everyone while he lights his cigar with a ten-pound note, could be back on the bones of his bum by the end of the week, when some rival pulls a swifty…"

"By Jove," Grenville chuckled, "what a vigorous language you have as well!"

"You'll soon get the swing of it," I promised, heading out of the door and down the corridor to the RAMC Registry to see where Arthur was, finally catching up with him at the Dental Stores, sharing a pot of war economy tea with Tom Roberts while the latter sorted boxes of false teeth.

Arthur glanced around as I came in: "Ah ha, young Ian! Just the man we need to see!"

They weren't to know it, but these were just the men I needed to see after the blackest day in my short life. Apparently, it was Christmas in a week's time and volunteers were needed to paint sets for a pantomime, to entertain our little friends, the military orphans.

In the event it was amazing just how much we accomplished in only a few days, patients and staff, officers and men working together to put on a comic pastiche of *Jack on the Beanstalk*, *The Goose that laid the Golden Egg*, and *Dick Whittington's Cat* that confirmed 3LGH's nickname of The Happy Hospital.

It could not have come at a better time for my tortured soul as I immersed myself in painting, and carpentry, and the making of dozens of coloured paper hats for a young audience who were ecstatic when Widow Twanky – played by a burly RAMC sergeant with a magnificent Kitchener moustache - lost her bloomers while being pursued by a make-believe goose played by our Chaplain, who in turn was being chased around the larger of our two recreation rooms by a senior medical officer disguised as Dick Whittington's ginger moggy.

Later that day, we adults were treated to that timeless farce, *Charley's Aunt*, presented by a travelling theatre company doing-their-bit at troop camps and military hospitals. This was my first meeting with Noël Coward, still only a young lad but already a polished performer in the role of Charley Wickham, an Oxford undergraduate and one of a pair wildly in love with two young heiresses under the watchful eye of an elderly guardian. Needing to find a sympathetic chaperone, they persuade another Varsity chum to dress up as Donna Luisa d'Alvadorez, a cigar-smoking aunt from Brazil, with predictably hilarious complications before true love conquered all, unlike it does real life.

Our Christmas mail never arrived when an Austrian U-boat torpedoed the passenger freighter from Alexandria to Marseilles, so I have no idea what Aunt Lucinda, or Miss McCracken, or anyone else was thinking of as 1916 merged into 1917.

Fortunately, this did not apply to mail from France, and David's letter was a rare tonic with its hope of catching-up in London early in January.

1917

95

My New Year's present was a travel-warrant from AIF HQ, in Horseferry Road, with orders to report to Cambridge University for the Knife & Fork, a crash course in polite behaviour and table manners that all newly commissioned second lieutenants, promoted from the ranks, were required to take before joining an officers' mess. The implication being that, unless we were properly house-trained, we would remain uncouth oafs who ate with our fingers, slurped tea from a saucer, and picked our teeth with a dinner fork. Not that it was ever stated quite so bluntly but the intention was clear enough.

I telegraphed my revised schedule to David and suggested we meet at his old stamping ground before boarding an overcrowded troop train. An hour out of London it began to snow and never let up, requiring work-parties of troops to go ahead, shovelling the way clear, one hundred yards at a time.

Somewhere in the middle of the night we halted at a railway siding and coaled the locomotive, bucketful by bucketful, then recharged the water tanks with melted snow, gallon by gallon, before creeping onward through swirling grey murk until finally arriving in Cambridge the next afternoon.

A few of us got off here while the bulk of the troops continued towards the Norfolk coast where they were being deployed against an imagined invasion from across the North Sea, presumably covered by what remained of the Kaiser's High Seas' Fleet after its recent mauling at the Battle of Jutland.

This irrational fear greatly assisted the German war effort by keeping four fresh divisions of British troops on the Home Front, defending England against a phantom threat at a time when every man was needed on the Western Front.

The stationmaster read my movement order and directed me up a slushy, ill-kept road past the University's Botanic Garden until eventually I reached a cluster of huts on the banks of a narrow river in full flood.

Everywhere I looked, the ground was speckled with unfamiliar birds feasting on worms driven to the turfed surface by rising water levels. These soggy grey surroundings further deepened my depression as the realisation of what I'd lost by rejecting Sandra's love and laughter, continued to erode my spirits. Even so, my irrevocable decision was clearly the only sensible course of action for a couple as divided by caste and background as we were.

Meanwhile, unaware of it at the time, my new surroundings were the famous Backs, so-called because some of the oldest colleges backed onto them and were, in Springtime, the setting for much upper-class tomfoolery during the May Week balls that ended each academic year.

I heartily despised the place, with its assumption that we who had distinguished ourselves in the ranks - several others on the course were also decorated veterans – were unfit company for the young toffs of the University's Officers' Training Corps, until we had learned not to wipe our snouts on the tablecloth or belch at the end of a meal.

To be fair, there was some useful stuff other than this insulting waste of time and its equally nonsensical sword drill that we were expected to master. For instance, as King's Commissioned Officers we were required to take our place on courts martial, and for that we had to learn the correct procedures by role-playing their various characters in those sad little dramas.

There was also good value in the simple housekeeping arrangements of running a company of upwards two hundred ill-assorted men, to ensure the correct allocations of kit and pay, messing and accommodation and, by implication, how to wangle seven days' compassionate leave for their hasty wartime marriages.

Much of this we, as NCOs, had already learned from hard, practical experience but it was timely to be reminded of it in a systematic manner. However, what really provoked a heated discussion was the lecture by a retired major general who had given much thought to his years of service that probably began during the Zulu War.

From memory, the nub of his advice was as follows: "Should you ever be called upon to perform a task that looks like certain death, and yet honour and duty demand you do it, then you must not hesitate. On the other hand, unless your duty demands it, you must not rashly expose yourself to needless danger.

"There are many sorts of vanity, and among them is every man's natural pride in his courage. However, such 'pride goeth before a fall,' as when a man exposes himself to danger, hoping to show the world how brave he is.

"As officers you hold your lives in trust for your country, to be spent if necessity demands the sacrifice, but never to be thrown away in a pointless display of bravado. The ruling factor must always be the good of the cause, never forgetting that a trained officer is not easy to replace, and should therefore not perform dangerous duties that can be delegated to a private.

"It may be argued that the private's life is as dear to him as the officer's is to himself, but that is not the point. A trained officer is of more value to his country, and harder to replace, than a private. This is not an excuse for cowardice but rather a sober assessment of risk and reward in the calculus of victory.

"During the recent Russo-Japanese War, a certain Japanese colonel best summed it up when he told his troops, just before leading an attack: 'Some of us will not be so fortunate as to give our lives for the emperor today, but do not seek to give them unnecessarily, for they will be needed later.'

"When all is said and done it is your duty to lead from the front, and if that path leads to death, then you will have repaid the debt of honour you owe to your King. But until then be thrifty with your life and those of your men, 'for they will be needed later...'"

Frances will never understand the rawhide thongs of Duty & Discipline that bound my generation. The best analogy I can think of is to compare them with the British Empire's fabled bullion reserves made evident by the gold and silver coins in our pockets, seemingly as immutable as the Law of Gravity until August 1914.

The next fifty months of a world suicidally at war debauched centuries of accumulated faith in the established social order, much as they destroyed the Empire's accumulated wealth, until by 1918 our lofty ideals had sunk until they were on par with the grubby paper promises that had displaced honest coinage.

Only those of us who survived the Great War know the confusion and guilt we've secretly borne ever since then. I for one still bow my head with shame whenever I recall how sternly I sacrificed Sandra's happiness on the altar of a foolish belief that it was my duty to do so.

96

David's postcard arrived in time to save me from a surly act of insubordination that, at the very least, would have earned me a severe reprimand, the weather having done nothing to quell my foul mood. The wettest, greyest winters in Melbourne were a passing nuisance compared with a dank and dismal January in Cambridge, surrounded as it is by reclaimed bogs and fens. As for the curved corrugated iron Nissen huts, appropriately nicknamed "igloos," these were barely kept above freezing point by potbelly stoves fed with damp sticks and substandard coal.

David used his university connexions and money from the Shusters' generous allowance to book a private room at the *Eagle*, a quaint old pub in the middle of town, where he suggested we meet for dinner. I then told Mr Mess President that I would not be dining-in tonight but instead was going to meet a schoolmate, on leave from France, and marched off before he could recover his composure.

Frankly, I could not have cared less what my final marks were, assuming I got that far, and would have gladly told the Army where to shove its commission if challenged to account for my increasing flashes of anger and resentment. The possibility that I was approaching the end of my tether, after two years of active service, coinciding with a time of immense personal distress, never once crossed my numbed mind although something must've been apparent when David stood to greet me with a questioning frown. "Hello old chap! My word, you have changed..."

This was not surprising. We last saw each other on St Kilda's quayside when he was about to embark for the Stockholm Olympics while still a Melbourne Grammar prefect and I a conceited young colt, about to be broken-in on the far side of Australia. The years since then had thumped both of us into better shape as two adult men sized each other up.

My oldest and dearest friend was barely recognisable in the distinctive, high-collared RFC uniform, his pilots' wings and lieutenant's pips proudly on display. The man himself was now a lithe, athletic, six-footer. At another time, in another place, David Shuster could have won worldwide fame as a broodingly handsome kinema idol, the living embodiment of elegance with dark eyes, a slim moustache, and an indefinable air of mysterious otherness.

He was the pedigreed thoroughbred from his brilliantined hair to his polished black shoes, whereas I was the feral brumby from my cropped scalp to my brown leather boots. Even so I caught envious glances at the ribbon above my left breast pocket, and the gilded brass A on my shoulder flashes, making it painfully apparent that he was still smarting over his failure to compete in the Finals of the 1500 metres Men's Freestyle at Stockholm.

This saddened me more than I could possibly say. David was so supremely gifted, with a soaring intelligence to match, he should never have needed anyone's token of approval, least of all a scrap of coloured silk and a silver disc not much bigger than a half-crown that any fool can win, provided he's in the wrong place, at the wrong time.

"Only the best will do on such a special occasion," he announced with a flourish, breaking my introspective train of thought by retrieving a Krug 1910 from its bucket and ricocheting the cork from ceiling, to wall, to floor. "Well met, O Goliath Slayer!"

"It's, ah, kind of you to keep reminding me of that incident," I acknowledged cautiously, accepting a generous measure of the Shusters' favourite fizz, and raising it in salute before inviting the bubbles to work their magic, "but Melbourne Grammar is half the world away, and we've both grown up a lot since then…"

"True," he conceded thoughtfully. "Very well, henceforth I shall loyally address you as 'Dear Old Golly'!" He raised his glass. "For even as I can never forgive a snub or insult, I shall never forget a kindly act such as yours, at a time when I was, vulnerable."

I pondered his enigmatic confession while he continued with an imperceptibly forced smile. "We read an awful lot about Anzac, and Gallipoli, but what was it really like?"

I answered with a few word pictures that no reputable newspaper or illustrated magazine would dare to publish.

"Oh." It was his turn to ponder layers of meaning before brightening again. "Egypt must've been alright though?"

"If you like sin, sand, and sunburn," I quipped, gaining time to fathom what was on David's mind, for I sensed that all was not well.

"I suppose you climbed a pyramid?" he continued, inviting me to help myself from the platter of pre-war quality cheese and biscuits.

"As one does." I used my jack-knife to pare a wedge of ripe cheddar. "'I've even got a picture of myself and a couple of mates with the Sphinx. Some of our lads riding camels in the background. Tourist tosh but good fun."

"You didn't?"

"Ride a camel?" I grimaced. "Bloody hell no! I had my fill of those flea-bitten brutes in Westralia."

"Of course. I forgot." He looked into the fireplace and gave its logs a pensive stab with the iron poker. "You always were always the adventurous one. Ever ready to tackle a fresh challenge. I envy that gift…"

"Come off it, mate!" I protested strongly. "You know stuff, and do stuff, and think stuff I can't even pronounce the names of! Why," I continued encouragingly, "if ever we got into a pissing contest, you'd beat me by a yard!"

My deliberate vulgarity did the trick. David laughed and went over to the door to order up the first course of our dinner, a hearty, ox-tail soup ideally suited to the grim weather outside. Ample funds and the right connexions ensured that our next course, grilled rib eye beef with buttered potatoes and all the trimmings, was another example of pre-war British cuisine at its finest, as was the rhubarb tart, a pudding that requires serious amounts of black-market sugar to counteract its acidity.

Conversation always flows best after a good meal, by which time everyone has had time to relax and reflect. This was certainly the case with David and I as we ordered up another Krug and stretched our legs towards the glowing hearth.

Ticking fingertips – 1912 to 1917 - we were astonished to discover that it was a few weeks over five years since last we spoke, and yet it seemed like only yesterday as we gathered up the loose threads of our lives and began weaving them together again.

I enthralled David with a modestly truthful account of my time in Westralia, omitting the native massacre and nude Klowee, of course. The Chief held centre stage as a larger-than-life leader, pulling sandalwood and fossicking for gold, assisted by a colourful cast of swashbuckling characters.

Even the months at Blackboy Camp, and life aboard a troopship through the tropics to Sewers and Port Two Fuck, had acquired a romantic aura by the time I finished embellishing them with a few artistic flourishes. There was more to this than a natural human urge to show off; David and I were sufficiently attuned for me to sense that he was troubled and therefore, as a friend, it was my duty to lift his spirits with comic exaggeration.

The concluding thumbnail sketches of Anzac Cove and Pozierès were perfunctory as I brought our conversation full circle and enquired after his own adventures thus far. "'Last I heard, you were either waving to the King, as you flew over Buckingham Palace, or making a first flight, over enemy lines?"

"The latter." He eased forward and stared into the fire's glowing coals. "*Un très* dicey stunt…"

"I've never been up in an aeroplane," I persisted with an encouraging smile. "What's it like?"

David the scientist took his time choosing words before David the pilot replied. "It all depends on whether someone is trying to kill you, or not. Subtract Fokkers and Pfalz from the equation, add a crystal-clear sky and towering, snowy peaked cumulus clouds, and you would not wish to be anywhere else in the universe."

He began smiling again. "The freedom to swoop and play like a bird, thousands of feet above the ground, can only be experienced, never described. 'O, he flies through the air with the greatest of ease, that daring young man on the flying trapeze! When asked how he does it, he is sure to reply, 'nobody knows but me…!'" This brief snatch of a once-popular song described a youthful Icarus freed of all his earthly cares and woes, and I envied him more than words can say.

"But restore the Fokkers and Pfalz, and instead of an open sky substitute cloud cover the colour and texture of steel wool from which, at any moment they will dive, spitting bullets, there is nowhere in the world you'd less want to be…"

"'Dicey' indeed."

"Quite." He looked up. "But what really sticks in my craw is the lack of understanding by those who should know better." He was scowling now. "Too often it seems as if we are fighting on opposite sides of the same bloody war."

"I'm sorry, you've lost me."

"No more lost than I am, frequently," he replied with sudden heat. "The sooner we get our own squadron up and running, the better for all concerned!"

"I'm still lost."

"Alright," he replied, regaining control. "Point One. Don't believe a word you read about the Flying Corps; it's a shambles from top to bottom once you get behind the scenes. The brass hats persist in snowing us with orders and counter-orders, making it up as we blunder along!"

"Perhaps they are?" I remarked, determined to be fair-minded.

David gave me a startled look. "What?"

"I mean, how long has anyone been fighting a war in the sky? Three years? And how long have men been fighting on sea and on land? Three thousand?" I shrugged. "It's an astonishment that things work as well as they do."

David blinked with surprise. I did not have the heart to tell him that it was not my original idea but, rather, the distillation of several chats with Grenville as we prepared for his Staff College Board.

"That's as maybe," my oldest friend grumped after a few moments' reflection, "but the first thing I'm going to do, once we're free, is insist on systematic coordination between pilots and observers instead of our present haphazard arrangements!"

He gathered his breath. "I frequently fly with a total stranger in the rear cockpit, some gormless Air Mechanic Second Class who volunteered to fire-off a few rounds with a Lewis' on the station range and is now rated an aerial gunner! Or it's another officer whose sole ambition is to become a pilot himself. Not with us, of course, but on a scout squadron, for that's where the medals are once he's logged the necessary operational hours and can be shipped back to England for training. At which point, whatever he's learned of telegraphy, and gunnery, and navigation is lost, and we start all over again!"

David's hands flew apart in exasperation. "It's like playing Snakes & Ladders with our lives and machines! As for the AM2, I have probably never seen him until we climb aboard, and I may never see him again, and yet for the next two or three hours I must entrust myself to an obedient lump who keeps mumbling: "Sorree suh…""

I gave a puzzled laugh, never having heard David so het up before, and was intrigued by this crack in the shell of his normally studied composure "So what's getting your own squadron got to do with, well, sorting things out?"

"For starters we'll be all-Australian with no 'Clueless Claudes' mucking us around with their class-conscious antics that have no place in the air, where all are equally vulnerable, regardless of rank or birth!" he snapped back, further revealing a coarser grain than I had thought I'd hear from such a refined young man. "Then we can start putting things right, like pairing pilots and observers as a team, not sitting apart like bloody strangers in an omnibus!"

"That doesn't make sense," I interjected, aware of how and why we cross-trained our Lewis gunners and their loaders.

"Agreed." He regained his composure. "Fortunately, change is in the air, literally! For political reasons you won't find in any newspaper but which I've heard on the grapevine, our government has raised an independent Australian Flying Corps to match an equally independent Australian Army Corps."

"Oh? And when's that due to happen…?"

"Well, according to Uncle John's sources," he replied, indirectly referring to General Monash, a close family friend in peacetime, "the first unit is *en route* to England for advanced training. But it will be some while before they're ready for overseas duty, hence the need for an all-Australian experimental flight like ours, to gain the practical experience we can share when the others eventually join us in France -"

"Whoa!." I raised my hand. "Back up for a moment. What 'political reasons…'?"

"They're, ah, rather murky."

"How?" I persisted, instinctively starting to research a feature article for the *Miner.*

"Well, in a nutshell, Japan is now our ally and yet little more than three years ago they were the Yellow Peril. Consider this: why the change of heart?"

"Don't we have a Naval Treaty, or something?" I frowned.

"No."

"But I thought -?"

"London has, we don't," David elaborated in a hard, flat voice. "Australian interests count for nothing in England. They never have and never will."

"But aren't we all fighting the same enemy?" I persisted. "Our Empire versus the Kaiser's?"

"You suppose wrongly."

"Sorry mate, I'm lost again. What exactly d'you mean?"

"Given Japan emerges victorious, they're going to want rather more than a telegram thanking them for their attendance, which is all that Australia can expect unless we've promoted our own interests first!"

"Like what?" It was my turn to frown.

"German New Guinea, for starters. Unless we grab it before the Japs do, they'll be within canoe-ride of Northern Queensland when next they get the urge to do to us what they've already done to China and Corea, namely occupy and colonise!"

"Strewth…" Such cloak and dagger conspiracies were no part of my still-limited experience of the world. "So, what's having an Australian Flying Corps and an Army Corps got to do with poking a stick in the Japs' bike wheel?"

"Everything," David replied in the same hard voice. "While we remain blended with Britain's other imperial troops, Australia will have no identity when the prizes are given out after the war. However, by fielding our own forces, London is being constantly and consistently reminded that we are paying our way and have earned the right to be heard at whatever passes for a peace conference. Unofficially it's called the 'Blood Debt…'"

"Surely not!" I chuckled, seeking to gently deflate the bubble of such fanciful nonsense. "We're kith and kin -!"

"'Nations do not have permanent friends, or permanent enemies, only permanent interests.'" This was by no means the last time I heard a wiser man than I abbreviate Lord Palmerston's First Law of Geopolitics. "Unless we can demonstrate that the Australian war effort in the air, and on land was of greater value than Japan's contribution at sea, England will shrug us off without a second thought. Take my word for it. I know their sly and duplicitous ways!"

"Oh, really!" I laughed with disbelief.

He steadied himself before replying. "You've only fought alongside Australians, men you can rely upon to stick at a job, and get it done properly. I, by contrast have only fought alongside caste-infected snakes who smile to your face even as they prepare to bite your throat!"

David's hatred shook me, especially when I recalled his early letters from Cambridge that spoke so warmly of the British; it was evident that something very painful, very personal, very profound had turned him against them. "Well, I'm sorry to hear that, mate, but there's not much I can do to put things right."

"Actually, there is." He sat up straighter. "Are you looking forward to joining a new battalion at the Front?"

"Like hell I am!"

"Then how about the Australian Flying Corps…?"

"Uh?"

"You're one of us, weigh less than eleven stone, are a qualified Lewis gunner. Put your hand up for an observers' course and it can be fixed."

"Are you, serious?"

"Never more so," he insisted, "I need you in the back seat, working together, like we have always done in the –"

"What about the 'Suicide Club'?" I interrupted. And why am I supposed to swap a possible knock, on the ground, for a dead cert' when the wings fall off?"

"It's quicker," he replied simply. "Until then you'll earn an extra thirty-five shillings a week, sleep between clean sheets, eat hot breakfasts, and after a day's work – quite a few of which are spent on the ground because of bad weather - dine in the Mess." He raised an eyebrow. "Is that how it was at Mouquet Farm...?"

I looked away before looking back again. "No, but there's something else that concerns me greatly."

"What?"

"This sudden rage against the Poms. When you first came to this bloody country you couldn't stop singing their praises. Now you talk like they're all arseholes."

"That's none of your business!"

"Wrong!" I snapped back. "If I'm to leave the ground in a machine you're driving, I need to know you've got your mind on the job!"

"It's, nothing."

"Wrong again." I reached across and tapped his chest. "I don't care if you get shitty with me for saying so, but I've noticed that 'M' no longer sends her best. So, is it still Rainbows & Roses on the Love Front, or not?"

"You, devil."

"I've been called worse. Try harder."

He turned away and began reluctantly describing how Lady Mary Strathallan invited him home to meet her family. Instead, what should have been a happy occasion with any normal people, became a humiliating disaster as grimly polite parents made it clear that, in his own words: "I was as welcome as a bastard on Fathers' Day -!"

This once common expression was further evidence of his roughened manners as he continued describing that - no matter how brilliant a Cambridge scholar he was, and how dazzling his academic prospects, or even how rich his people were - there would never be a seat at their lordly table for a Colonial Jew.

"Without anyone saying it, I knew they viewed me as a rag picking *Shmutter* from the ghetto and forbade further contact with their precious, pedigreed daughter -!"

There was much more in a similar vein but eventually he calmed down and even managed an exhausted smile. "What about yourself Golly? Didn't you say you'd had a bit of luck in Egypt?"

"Oh, just a refreshing fling with a nurse, nothing serious," I lied, selfishly relieved to have rejected Sandra before her people rejected me, an opinion he confirmed with a tight smile: "How very wise of you."

"Why so?"

"Because the one thing I've learned is that it's a mistake to commit one's life to a woman."

"That's a bit drastic!" I protested. "When you find the right one, you'll think differently -!"

"I did. There won't be another." His words fell like clods of earth on a coffin lid. "While there's war, I shall do my bit. When it's over I shall return to the Cavendish and thereafter devote my life and fortune to Soil Science."

"Uh?!"

"The knowledge of that which an ignorant majority call 'dirt,' never understanding that what they despise and desecrate, is a nation's richest treasure," he continued stiffly. "There's a primitive tribe in Africa that calls their soil 'Mother of All...'" He paused. "I leave it to your good sense, to decide which of us is truly primitive and stupid." He paused again and took a deeper breath. "Soil, good soil, rich soil, productive soil is the foundation upon which great civilisations rise and flourish. And without it, decline and fall."

"Bloody hell…"

David cocked an ironic eyebrow. "That's the general reaction whenever I broach the subject. The soil's bounty is taken so much for granted that nobody notices or cares as it depletes and degrades – like Rome's North African granaries, now deserts - until it's too late to wish it back."

"Hm. I haven't thought that way before," I admitted, with reluctance.

"In common with everyone else," he added, "myself included although, as you know, I've always had a bit of a thing for plants and how they work."

"What changed your mind?" I asked, curious to learn more about an unknown side of this man, one of a small handful I have ever befriended.

"Oddly enough, flying above the trenches." He sat into the firelight, chin resting on his clenched right fist, lost in thought. "I began noticing the multiple colours and textures of subsoils thrown up by shellfire, and yet within a short while green plants of every description were re-establishing themselves on what should be sterile, lifeless muck. You see," he continued, starting to brighten again, "textbooks teach us that soil is just ancient rock, weathered over millions of years, which is true up to a point, but there's a missing link, and I know what it is!"

"Go on…" It was a relief to see him happy again.

"You remember that wonderful microscope you gave me?"

"Yes."

"Well, one night I was studying a grain of basalt sand, a commonplace rock, Ca-Mg-O6-Si2, formed by the rapid cooling of volcanic magma, when I noticed something rather strange. This inert, inorganic fleck was host to a clearly visible microorganism, *talaromyces flavus*, which as the name suggests, is a filamentous fungus -!"

His enthusiasm was so strong that someone like me, who had not understood a single word, or letter, or number thus far, was swept along by the thrill of discovery.

"I had a strong feeling that if only I observed it long enough, perhaps by time-lapse photography, I would see the basalt dissolve and disappear. But not by any impersonal weathering, as conventional wisdom tells us, but by the digestive juices of a living bacterium! And if so, what happens to the magnesium, the silicates, the other constituent elements?"

"No idea!"

"They can't vanish," he replied, sitting back. "That would defy the Laws of Conserved Mass & Matter foreshadowed by Epicurus when he wrote: 'It is impossible for anything to come from what is not, nor can it be destroyed,' or words to that effect. Instead, I predict they are exuded as water soluble, sub-microscopic nutrients that sustain *talaromyces* before itself becoming food for more complex life forms. These, in their turn, feed others, rung by rung, higher and higher up the Ladder of Life."

"Sounds feasible," I conceded, based upon my very limited understanding of chemistry.

"The Prophet Isaiah put it most pithily: 'All flesh is grass,'" David continued. "This being so, the Animal Kingdom depends for its very existence upon these mysterious little moulds and fungi sustaining Earth's mantle of vegetation! And in that dazzling moment I saw 'the world in a grain of sand,' and with it the work I was born to do!"

"Mate," I sighed patiently, "you're probably right, I can't tell, but is it worth rejecting the hope of a good woman, just to share the rest of your life and money with microscopic moulds?"

425

"Yes." His eyes had acquired a fanatical glitter of certitude I would observe years later, in the back room of a Munich beer cellar, discussing watercolour landscapes with a still relatively unknown political agitator awaiting his cue to go upstairs and harangue a throng of loyal followers. "Yes!"

Eventually I limped the short distance back to camp and, cane tapping ahead through rainy darkness, sought out Mr Mess President to apologise for my earlier behaviour.

A veteran of the South African War who had involuntarily exchanged his left arm for a DSO at Mons, in the first month of this one and been relegated to training duties, Major Warren surprised me with a kindly nod. "Quite understandable, Mr Cribdon. It's been a long and bitter struggle, and we are far from finished yet. We need to stay in touch with our friends while we still can, so why don't you invite him to dine with us tomorrow night? I'm sure we'll all benefit from hearing of his experiences piloting an aeroplane."

"Thank you, sir. I'll send him a note."

"Please do. And a word to the wise…"

"Sir?"

"Pace yourself more carefully. I see from your record that you've been through rather a lot, but as I've just said, it's not over yet. Remember: 'You will still be needed later…'" He paused again. "I am recommending an instructors' posting, to give you the maximum chance of recuperation before a return to frontline duties…"

"Thank you, sir."

The following day, after morning parade and before our first lecture – *Maintaining Unit Morale* - I sent a runner to the *Eagle* with a formal invitation for David to join our Mess.

It was a matter of great personal pride to be seen alongside such a fine, upstanding man, elegantly trim in his RFC tunic, when I introduced him to Mr President and my course colleagues that evening. Most of them were on detachment from British regiments and, despite my best efforts, still regarded Australian troops as rude, crude, brawlers with bayonets. It must have come as something of a shock to shake hands with an urbane, poised Old Melburnian. David's self-control was immaculate, and I saw no sign of last night's hatred for the very men he was now affably chatting with and listening to attentively.

Afterwards, when we were seated in the best-heated igloo, he held the floor with a witty, descriptive account of a reconnaissance pilot's war above the battlefield, being careful to differentiate his duties from those of the escorting pilots in their single seaters, like the recently introduced Sopwith Pup, whose exploits were making them household names in the illustrated newspapers and magazines.

Without denigrating these self-styled "Knights of the Sky," David was careful to stress whose aerial photographs, and artillery liaison, and bombing raids were of direct assistance to our men in the trenches, a point well taken by an audience who themselves would soon be back under fire in France.

He ended by borrowing my remark the previous evening, the one about a need to understand that, whereas wars have been fought on land and sea for at least three thousand years, aerial combat was little more than three years old. In this short while it had evolved from firing a pistol at enemy aeroplanes, to machine-gunnery, night-navigation, and long-range bombing sorties, and in every one of them Britain had the Hun on the run!

David modestly acknowledged their patriotic applause. Later, as I escorted him back to the *Eagle*, he asked: "How did it come across?"

"Bloody brilliant, especially the bit about 'the Hun on the run.'"

"Total tosh," he grimaced in the light of a dim gas lamp as we turned into Benet Street. "Brother Fritz is miles ahead of us in engineering and design, but I know how to beat him, and will do so once we have an independent squadron to test new ideas and disprove old ones."

"Isn't that a bit ambitious, for a two pip louey?" I observed cautiously

"No. I know I'm right." He paused in the pub's doorway and faced me again. "Paired crews for starters. Then I'll work on improved petrol filtration; and magnetos with non-corrosive contacts, like the platinum ones Fritz already has. I also have an idea for a mechanical blower that automatically steps-up the carburettor's air intake as we gain altitude and lose barometric pressure. But first things first, you and me working together as a team, what d'you say…?"

"Yes." The word escaped before common sense could intervene, such was my confidence in his judgment, towering intellect, and absolute certainty whenever he undertook a task.

"Thanks Golly, you've just taken a huge weight off my mind. Leave ends tomorrow so I'll be away early in the morning but will keep you posted." He hesitated, searching for the right words. Then, with a slightly embarrassed laugh: "I am so awfully glad to see you again, Ian."

"Likewise, David."

We shook hands and parted.

97

My course finished the following Friday afternoon and, true to his word, Major Warren recommended I be assigned to a training unit; Horseferry Road agreed and ordered me to report to Étaples, a few miles down the Channel coast from Boulogne, on-exchange with a British unit.

After a reasonable night's rest in the War Chest Club, just across the road from AIF headquarters, I presented my travel warrant at Victoria Station and was directed to a junior officers' carriage where I tossed my valise onto the overhead luggage rack, before squeezing between a couple of freshly baked subalterns in their brand-new uniforms.

Of the ten of us in this compartment I was the oldest by a few years and the only foreigner. The other nine wore cap and collar badges of assorted English line regiments and were studying me with nervous curiosity that I acknowledged with a neutral nod before doing what every veteran soldier does whenever he gets the chance to snatch a bit of sleep.

I had already seen enough of my companions to be unimpressed. Although of equivalent junior rank, the gulf between us was unimaginably wide. These youngsters would have still been in middle school when I enlisted on the Goldfields. Now, three years later, after ninety days at an Officers' Training Unit, they were on their way to the Front; "like lambs to the slaughter" is a tiresome cliché but in their case, it was the sober truth. Fortunately, none of them could see inside my head or else they would have been considerably less frothy as they chattered among themselves, wondering what "It" would be like, and how soon they would be able to meet up with old so-and-so, gone ahead from school.

I was reminded of the 29th Division embarking at Lemnos, the last intact force of a professional army that once garrisoned a worldwide empire and saw, in these pallid, pimply schoolboys, clear evidence of just how swiftly Britain's manpower was being destroyed.

Gallipoli's "Old Incomparables" had been sturdy, country-bred fighters, steady and loyal to the end, which came soon enough for many of them on the blood-drenched beaches of Cape Helles. Their proud regiments had been replenished by the eager young volunteers of Kitchener's Army who, in turn, were massacred on the Somme the following year. This year's drafts were weedy conscripts for whom sixty-three inches was now the official minimum height for a British infantryman.

God alone knew who or what would be fighting next year's battles, assuming we lasted that long. Probably Bantams - named after the plucky little gamecock - hardly taller than the Lee Enfield rifle they were unable to carry any distance.

Those stunted children of Britain's industrial wastelands - millworkers and colliers from the age of twelve - did the best they could with what little they had. Many served as message-runners, arguably the most lethal job on the Western Front, or in tunnelling companies, digging mines beneath enemy trenches where they were often counter-mined, or gassed, or fought horrific underground battles with spades and pickaxes.

Siegfried Sassoon once told me how he found a couple of Bantams stuck in a patch of mud. A caring officer, he scooped them up, tucked one under each arm as if they were sandbags, and carried them to dry ground. I've sometimes wondered if Jack Tolkien's Hoppits were inspired by his experiences with these brave little souls on the Somme? I rather wish I'd asked if his characters were Bantams in disguise now that his stories are becoming better known.

Meanwhile, aboard the troop train, I reflected on the past several weeks since rejecting Sandra. Though painful to recall, our final break had been for the best and I looked forward to immersing myself in army life again, with its disciplines, drills, and procedures that leave no time for brooding regrets.

Eventually we jolted to a halt at Folkestone and, senior officers first, then our lot, then the rest, proceeded aboard one of the Southern Railway's cross-channel ferries pressed into war service. Dazzle painted with irregular shapes and shades of grey to confuse the U-boats who were still getting through Dover Straits' minefields, we were escorted by a couple of converted steam trawlers - armed with two-pounder pom-poms and racks of depth charges on their transoms - during the four hours or so it took us to make the crossing to France, thread between freighters waiting to unload, and dock at Boulogne.

Only captains and above were allowed into the 1st Class quarters below, while we Joes - as the lowest ranked Junior Officers were contemptuously called by the men we were supposed to lead and inspire – crowded the after deck overlooking the troops themselves, huddled in their life jackets, shoulder-to-shoulder on every square inch of available space. Not for the first time, I was reminded that to be a sergeant is to enjoy the best rank in the army, as I became increasingly familiar with its worst.

The Great War's one-pip lieutenants were held in no regard by anyone. Corporals and below detested them; sergeants and warrant officers despised them; captains, majors, and above considered them battlefield tourists who would most likely get killed before learning to do anything useful. Only the brass A's on my shoulder flashes, and the silver rosette on a grubby scrap of crimson and blue ribbon, earned me an occasional nod of respect and recognition.

The drizzle on England's side of the Channel became a steady downpour as we stacked our lifejackets, ready for the next contingent of homeward bound troops to put on, and disembarked; senior officers first, then our lot, under the hostile glare of troops who were already being yelled at by NCOs in blue armbands, prior to marching off into the late afternoon's sodden gloom.

The town itself was once again a military camp. Caesar began the custom when he assembled his legions here for the invasion of Britannia. Eighteen hundred years later, Napoleon's massed his *Grande Armèe* along the cliffs overlooking Boulogne, which was as near as he or his army ever got to England. Now it was our turn to return the favour by disfiguring every available tree or wall with divisional signs and arrowhead notice boards while armed MPs hunted deserters and shirkers, up and down the town's fetid back alleys.

A transport officer spotted me looking lost and beckoned, then ticked my name off his master list and stamped my papers to prove that I was now officially in France, finally directing me to one of several lorries filling-up with other subalterns.

The more exalted ranks enjoyed staff car rides for the last leg of their journey to Étaples. The troops would route march these same twenty miles tomorrow morning, as part of their introductory toughening-up before battle training began at the infamous Bull Ring. Unaware of what other delights awaited us, we arrived at a sprawling maze of tents and barracks, drove over a substantial river bridge, and were delivered to our quarters an hour or so after dusk. My initial impressions were not bad, except that nobody had anticipated our arrival so there was no food and insufficient bedding for the night.

The inexperienced moped and moaned at the iniquities of army life. The rest of us did what we'd done many a time in the trenches; Assess, Adapt, Adopt. This, for me, amounted to firing up my pocket Primus stove to heat a tin of M&V - meat and vegetables that were mostly chunks of carrot and turnip buffered by shreds of mutton – with a sprinkle of Keen's curry powder from the small tin kept inside my haversack, ready for such emergencies. A ship's biscuit, poked inside a spare sock and pounded to gritty dust with the butt of my revolver, nicely thickened the improvised stew.

After I'd cleaned my mess tin and eating irons in an adjacent latrine, I claimed one of the hut's vacant bunks, rolled my coat to make a pillow and drifted off, reasonably content with the world.

98

Any lingering contentment evaporated as I got to know Étaples better. The largest British army camp on the Continent, there were rarely fewer than eighty thousand troops in transit or being patched up in the two-dozen field hospitals of this sprawling cantonment.

Such large numbers told only a small part of the story. What mattered most was what happened here, and why it acquired such a dismal reputation. It never helped that at its heart huddled the ancient fishing port of Étaples where the river Canche dribbles into the English Channel. Once an important commercial centre before the harbour silted up, its most notable feature now was an eighteenth-century slum where chamber pots were routinely emptied into the gutters of Paradise Lane, as the main street was sarcastically known by our troops.

Many of the villainous faces I saw skulking around the marketplace and along the quayside, and sketched from memory, would not have been out of place wearing *le bonnet rouge* as they jeered their former lords and masters *en route* to the guillotine, trussed and bound aboard a nightsoil cart.

Meanwhile, a few hundred yards across the same river were the splendid villas and seaside mansions of wealthy industrialists from Lille and landed gentry from Pas de Calais. In stark contrast to the pre-Revolutionary decay on the east bank, these buildings were of contemporary design and boasted every modern convenience on a landscaped promontory that had, until recently, been a private hunting preserve.

An English linoleum manufacturer from Leeds saw its potential for development, formed an Anglo-French syndicate and began adding luxury hotels, golf courses, tennis courts, cycle tracks, a casino, and grandly named the new town Le Touquet Paris-Plage. He also made a thumping great profit for himself and his shareholders, as rich Parisians travelled the short distance North to sample the delights of *le weekend anglais*.

All of which changed with the outbreak of war. Common soldiers were confined to the squalid East bank where tent lines, barracks, workshops, store dumps, and the infamous Bull Ring training area were situated. By contrast, officers enjoyed varying degrees of comfort at Le Touquet, on the West bank. To make sure that no ranker ever entered the Forbidden City except on duty, MP detachments guarded the river crossing, checking papers while fawning on us and snarling at our men.

It came as no great surprise, a few months after my posting to the Flying Corps, to learn that this festering pustule finally burst as thousands of troops went on strike for better conditions. Order was restored after the ringleaders were shot, but morale failed to respond.

My initial impression was confirmed when, on the first morning, I met the Senior MGO, an alcoholic one-pip-colonel who had as much knowledge of machine gunnery as I had of astrophysics. How, and why, he got the job was never explained. I assume he wangled a cushy number at the beginning of the war and dug in behind a barricade of desks and filing cabinets, until peace broke out or Fritz drove the British army into the sea, in which case he was ideally placed to hop aboard the first rescue boat.

I took my instructions, signed out a copy of a much-amended training manual with a pack of grimy teaching-aid cards, and was told to go to a numbered hut where it was thought I might find someone keen to learn how to operate a Lewis gun. Eventually I reached the end of a long line of identical wooden sheds and discovered seventeen men under the command of a lance corporal, smoking and playing cards on the floor, after shoving their wooden benches and trestle tables to one side.

It would have been fatally easy to threaten and bluster as this mixed grill of Tommies lethargically shuffled to attention. Instead, I shrugged off my wet trench coat in such a manner that everyone got a good look at the DCM ribbon and wound stripes, visible proofs that I was not just another Clueless sent to make their lives more wretched than they already were. "Right-o gents, gather round."

In short order I resumed the instruction schedule developed at Kebir. A training model gun had not yet been issued to our course, so I memoed myself to make good this deficiency and made do with blackboard drawings supplemented by personal anecdotes of what happens under fire when a machine-gunner fumbles or forgets. Something must have clicked because when I returned from lunch, towing a Lewis gun cart containing the full schedule of parts and equipment, plus a bucket of dummy magazines, all the tables were properly aligned, and the lads sat smartly to attention as I came in.

They were not a bad crew, I met worse during the next month, but as an Australian MGO on-detachment I had a novelty value that held their interest as we became better acquainted. Not that I was ever their New Best Friend, as they quickly discovered when one Smart Aleck thought he could cheek me. At which point Sarn't Cribdon pounced from behind his officers' camouflage and kicked him off the course, much to the delight of his mates who had already formed a similar opinion of the silly twerp.

By the end of that week, classroom drills completed, they were safe enough to be taken to the range where we began all over again, this time with a functioning gun and live ammunition. The boozy half-colonel wafted past and seemed happy with the noise we were making whenever dust and grit furiously fountained on the target butts. His deputy, a much steadier major, invigilated the final examination and signed off my first course as Very Satisfactory.

Captain Murray's brief note from 16 Battalion HQ at Bullecourt was, however, anything but satisfactory, and tipped me over the brink of a very dark place:

Dear Icy.

Sad to report Percy got the knock last Wednesday. Fritz had us pinned down and the attack was in trouble. Percy volunteered to lead a party forward, find a gap in the wire and get things moving again.

As you'd expect, he succeeded, and we got through but somewhere along the way he didn't make it.

I went back but haven't been able to find him yet.

I know you'll share my feelings of loss, for there never was a braver man or more inspired leader.

Harry.

This was the sober, heartfelt opinion of another inspired leader, recently awarded a Victoria Cross for supreme courage and initiative under murderous fire. A friend who would finish the war commanding a machine gun battalion, the most highly decorated officer in the British and Imperial armies.

99

Hard work is the best medicine for a man in my condition and I had settled into a routine that was getting consistently good results when, one morning, an admin' runner found me demonstrating the correct procedure for stripping a Lewis gun's return spring; it seemed my presence was required at the STO's where I fronted up to the Senior Transport Officer and collected a travel warrant, with orders to report forthwith to Number 1 School of Military Aeronautics.

Nobody ever shed a tear upon leaving Étaples and I was no exception to the rule when I hitched a lift to Boulogne where I caught the ferry and arrived in London later that same afternoon.

The abrupt transition from War to Peace was an unsettling experience, especially for those troops on ten days' leave from the trenches, many of whom still had mud on their boots and the Front's stench on their damp serge uniforms. These worn and weary men kept milling around the platform, rifles slung, some with souvenired coalscuttle helmets hooked over bayonet scabbards, trying to get their bearings in an alien world of civilians.

I briefly considered taking up Grenville's offer of a night's stay at Mrs Blane's but quashed this as a bad idea. Sandra had largely been absent from my thoughts, in France, and I had no wish to reopen this wound now that I was back in Blighty. Instead, I caught a cab to the War Chest Club, organised a feed, a hot bath, and turned in early, ready for a quick start, next morning.

Paddington Station was less crowded with khaki when I showed my travel warrant at the ticket gate, the following day, and got aboard the Great Western Railway's 8.15 train to Bristol, stopping at Slough, Maidenhead, and Reading where I was due to get off.

I was the only soldier in a compartment filled with amiably curious middle-aged men who seemed to be mostly commercial travellers or skilled craftsmen returning to their factories in the Midlands, and my pronunciation of local place names inevitably drew some good-natured ribbing. It seemed that Slough, a pretty market town beyond the outer fringes of London's urban sprawl, was called "Slaow" not "Sluff." A short while later, as we headed up the Thames Valley, I thought it best not to enquire where Maidenhead got its name from as we paused there to board more passengers.

My travel companions cheerfully corrected me when I spoke of needing to get out at Reading, as in reading a book, when I should have said "Redding." These and other linguistic oddities made David's early letter, from "Keys," less pompous than I'd thought at the time.

Peering through the window as we chuffed through picture-postcard scenes of quaint farmhouses, lush meadows, and green woodlands unlike anything in Western Australia, I realised this was my first real sight of the England that poets wax lyrical about. Robert Browning's *Home Thoughts from Abroad*, which begins with "O to be in England, now that April's there!" made more sense, now, than when Aunt Lucinda included it in my repertoire of recitations, alongside Brave Horatius and the brawny village blacksmith.

My companions were a cheery lot, even if they did tend to fret about convicts and kangaroos once they discovered that my uniform was Australian. Some remembered relatives who had gone out to the colonies, decades ago, either voluntarily or because the local magistrate allegedly convicted them of stealing a chicken or handkerchief or some equally trivial item, except to its previous owner.

The more venturesome quizzed me for details of life Down Under as they insisted on calling my homeland, while wondering if it was too late to take the plunge and emigrate to more sunshine and wider opportunities. I assured them it was never too late to have a go, provided a man was willing to work hard at whatever luck threw his way and illustrated it with anecdotes from the Goldfields and city life in Melbourne, including a description of how Leon Shuster founded his family's fortune with a threepenny boot repair on a bush track in Victoria.

They seemed genuinely sorry to see me leave when a bit over an hour after leaving London we arrived at Reading where I shook hands all round. A young Australian soldier had brought a whiff of romance and adventure to their cramped lives, and perhaps one or two broke free after our chance meeting. If so, I hope it worked out well for them in our more optimistic, freer, bigger land on the far side of the world.

Reading was, and for all I know still is, a pleasant county town with picturesque old buildings and churches, some of whose interiors I sketched during my few days of sightseeing until the Observers' Course got started. I soon learned that it was famous for three B's - Beer, Bulbs as in flowers, and Biscuits – the tasty sort made by Huntley & Palmers, not the anonymous dog food in our ration packs.

A ticket collector clipped my travel warrant and volunteered to telephone the Flying Corps depot and let them know I had arrived, a friendly gesture and much appreciated when, about twenty minutes later a Crossley tender chugged up to the station forecourt. I chucked my kit into the back and sat alongside the driver, a sullen young aircraftman with bad acne, my left leg jammed against the brass fire extinguisher, right leg wedged against the fuel tank as we drove back into town.

Number 1 School of Military Aeronautics was based behind what looked like an old Tudor gateway that I later learned had been built only a few years previously. The bequest of a prominent local family, Wantage Hall accommodated students at what was then an Oxford University extension college, until the Royal Flying Corps commandeered their dormitories and adjacent buildings.

This meant that for my first time in uniform I would not be sleeping in a dugout, or under a groundsheet, or on the floor of a goods wagon, or in a barracks, or on a hospital bed. Even the junior officers' quarters at Le Touquet amounted to no more than an unlined wooden shed with an adjacent dunny and cold-water shower. Wantage Hall, by contrast, was the Savoy at its most splendid.

Even the permanent staff members were decent, friendly chaps, compared with the morose ogres at Étaples, when I presented myself at the Adjutant's office. "Welcome aboard Mr Cribdon," he smiled. "You're a few days earlier than we expected but I'm sure you'll find plenty to keep yourself busy until things get started. You're in Room 5 with Mr Laurie. He's Canadian so you'll have a lot in common."

I saw no point informing Captain Deedes that Australia was on the opposite side of the Equator from Canada, was considerably hotter for most of the year, and that we therefore had precious little in common except loyalty to the Crown. "Thank you, sir."

"Mess Call is at 1800 hours; Prep' & Revision from 1900 until Lights Out at 2200; Reveille at 0600." He made this sound like a Spartan hoplite's bootcamp, little realising what decadent luxury eight hours of uninterrupted sleep was for anyone coming from where I'd been for these past few years.

Room 5 overlooked the quadrangle that now doubled as our parade ground and physical training area. My cellmate, so to speak, was sitting at the open window, enjoying the tranquil view, puffing a briar pipe. He turned, stood, and stuck out his free hand: "Frank Laurie."

"Ian Cribdon."

We shook and eyed each other up and down as men do. Half a head taller than I was and somewhat broader in the shoulders, I judged him to be an outdoorsman in his late twenties.

A likeable, talkative sort, it wasn't long before I learned that he was not Canadian at all but came from Montana in the United States. At the outbreak of war, he trekked across the nearby border, enlisted with Princess Patricia's Light Infantry, and went into the trenches at Frezenberg Ridge the following year. Later, he was recommended for a commission and, later still, accepted for pilot training in England.

When I asked why a neutral American would get himself mixed up in the British Empire's quarrel, he said that he had read about the Belgian Atrocities and felt that the only decent thing a red-blooded son of a gun could do was to step up to the mark and fight the Filthy Hun!

Well, maybe. By now I had acquired a sufficiently wide knowledge of men on the Westralian Goldfields – Land of the Wanted & Unwanted - to wonder if there might not be a faded Reward Notice on a wall, far away, with our Mr Laurie's description printed under another name.

Not that it was any of my business who or what he was leaving behind; it's an unusual man who doesn't have some awkwardness he would rather lose. And if Frank, for we were soon on first name terms, wanted to reinvent himself as a fighter ace, best o' luck! Meanwhile he volunteered to show me around, having used his time since arriving yesterday afternoon, to recce Wantage Hall.

Next morning, after a leisurely breakfast in the Mess and with no official duties for the rest of the day, it was he who suggested we take the opportunity to snaffle a couple of bicycles left by students when they were evicted by the RFC. These were now stacked in a shed behind the gymnasium. Hobnail boots and puttees are not the best kit for a bike ride, but Frank had also found a cache of tennis togs as he insisted on calling them, determined to acquire the style and language of a pukka British officer as quickly as possible.

Looking quite sporty in white slacks, tennis shirts, Plimsoll shoes, we prepared to explore Reading and its surrounds. I packed a sketchbook and pencils in my haversack, together with brown paper bag containing four slices of grey bread smeared with margarine and a jam that was mostly sugar beet pulp and artificial strawberry flavouring; Frank chummed the Mess cooks for similar rations so that both of us were set up for a day of high adventure.

We could not have chosen a sunnier, more idyllic morning to cycle out through our mock-Tudor gateway and set course towards the town's western outskirts.

If Frank really was from Montana, he would have been more used to log cabins and sod huts than urban bricks and mortar; as for myself, I nowadays felt more at home with the Goldfields' corrugated iron and sackcloth shanties, rather than Marvellous Melbourne's pink granite civic pride. Thus, neither of us had much by which to judge what we now pedalling past, though later I learned that Reading has several architectural gems predating the English Civil War, and some fine examples of Georgian public buildings that predated Britain's settlement of Australia.

None of this mattered greatly as we wove our way between and around the horse-drawn drays, and bakers' carts, and delivery vans that were still indispensable for town life during the first decade or so of this century, Frank at the controls of his imaginary Sopwith, stuttering audible tacker-tacker-tack! machine gunfire as his bike swung past slower targets,

The fun faded as we flew in formation around a corner and landed near the walls of Reading Gaol on one hand, the remains of what I assumed was a Civil War castle, on the other. Only later I did learn that it was a great abbey until Henry VIII of Six Wives fame stole its money, split its lands among his henchmen, and let the locals to tear down the rest for their personal use.

Frank took a close interest in Reading's prison fortress, wryly comparing it with a more modest structure called Lincoln County Jail where he'd once stood at the back of a large crowd, watching three men being hanged from the main gate's horizontal beam, for bank robbery.

He continued plotting imaginary escape routes over, under, and through the Gaol's east wall until I finished sketching the abbey ruined gateway for my next letter home to Aunt Lucinda, at which point something triggered an urge to keep moving and off we sped, over a bridge and onto a canal towpath that led westward, out of town by water meadows and market gardens.

A group of Women's Land Army girls, scything cattle fodder on one of the paddocks, restored Frank's good humour when we stopped to exchange a few pleasantries and, in his case, set up a possible date, as he termed a casual tryst.

By now it was getting on for lunchtime and my right leg was reminding me that it needed a rest, when we happened upon a thatched, two storey canal-side inn with a most unusual name, *The Cunning Man*. At one time it must've been a thriving business but was nowadays somewhat run down, rather like the canal system itself, ever since the Great Western Railway Company offered quicker, cheaper, more reliable freight services between Bristol and London.

For lack of anything better to do, we parked the bikes under an old pear tree and went inside the pub. Our host, as he kept referring to himself in the third person, was an ex-bargee who had walked his tow horse up and down the Kennet Canal footpath before coming ashore; the way he told his tale one would have thought he had roamed the Seven Seas with Sinbad the Sailor before retiring to dry land and late marriage. An amiable, uncomplicated soul, he insisted we try his Old & Mild.

Seated outside on a rickety bench we sipped tankards of this cloudy brew and swapped questioning glances; both of us came from lands where beer is clear and cold and crisp, not dark, and warm, and thick. I could see the point of drinking it as a comforter on a snowy winter's day, but Old & Mild was not my idea of a thirst-quencher. Frank, however, rather liked this soupy English ale and was full of praise for it when our host wandered out to join us, business being slack now that most of the district's young men were in uniform.

He asked where we were from and we told him, but I am not sure it registered on a mind that had spent its formative years walking a barge up and down the narrow strip water that passed along the bottom of his overgrown garden. I envied his simplicity, for there are worse ways and places to pass the time between birth and death as we swapped fishing yarns, during which he told me - in elaborate detail - of the monster pike he once took from a reedbed on the other side of Burghfield Bridge.

A couple of swans waddled up the bank, hunting for crumbs while Frank and I munched our jam sandwiches. When I mentioned that I came from Western Australia where all swans are black, the publican shook his head in solemn disbelief, probably thinking I was one o' them there leg-pullers from the Anty Podes, heered much tell o' recent like.

Frank had a more urgent matter on his mind when, in his own frank manner, he enquired if any of the local girls was hot to trot now there was a shortage of local boys to fill the gap, so to speak...?

The Cunning Man's licensee gave a cunning wink, tapped the side of his nose, and said he would be happy to discuss the matter when the young ge'man come back later...

Meanwhile, as our conversation meandered along these highways and byways of imagination and desire, several RFC training-machines had been buzzing up, and around, and down again beyond a distant line of trees, prompting Frank to suggest we head over there on the way back to Wantage Hall, to get some idea of what to expect when our courses began next week.

Restored and refreshed we biked towards the School of Military Aeronautics' aerodrome in the grounds of a rather grand country estate, where an aeroplane I was about to learn was the Avro 504 basic trainer, was being refuelled from a dump of petrol tins. Its pilot frowned suspiciously as we wheeled our bicycles nearer to get a better look; for aught he knew we were the Kaiser's secret agents, sent on a sabotage mission. "Are you in the Corps?"

"We sure as heck are!" Frank replied with an infectious grin, hand outstretched as he gave his name, rank, and number.

The other man warmed somewhat, acknowledged the greeting, and began showing us around the Avro, reciting its performance figures. His attitude cooled upon learning that I was only going to train as an observer, but Frank was the clearly right sort of chap, full of beans, destined to become another gallant Knight of the Skies.

Inevitably, I suppose, the instructor asked if my companion would like to get a foretaste of the game, as he termed it. Three other 504s, parked a short distance away, had completed their flight tests, and only this one needed to be signed-off, making now the ideal moment for a joy ride.

"You betcha life I do!" Frank was the happiest man I'd seen in a long time as the instructor handed him a spare leather helmet, goggles, and a set of overalls, for even at an altitude of one thousand feet, an aeroplane's slipstream can be piercingly cold.

"Good luck mate!" I called out as he climbed into the front seat, most probably previewing his first victory over the Western Front, having flown an imaginary Sopwith down Reading High Street.

An airman mechanic stood to one side of the Avro's toothpick skid, gripped the propeller blade, and began winding it over to suck fuel-air mixture into the 100-horsepower *Gnome et Rhône* rotary engine's nine cylinders.

The instructor, seated behind Frank, gave a thumbs-up to signal the ignition switch was on. The mechanic gave one final flick and smartly stepped aside as the Avro began taxiing, trailing its distinctive mist of castor oil lubricant, before turning into the light breeze, indicated by the aerodrome's drooping windsock and, after a brief run, lifting into a beautiful, late-afternoon sky streaked with wisps of cadmium orange cirrostratus.

The climbing machine alarmed a nest of larks, one of which trilled aloft as the biplane passed overhead; since then I have never heard Vaughan Williams' *The Lark Ascending* without being reminded of that rare moment of rural peace in a world at war.

Did I feel a twinge of envy that Frank was up there instead of me? Of course, but I felt equally glad for his sake when the Avro droned out across flooded gravel pits we'd noticed earlier from the pub garden, and performed several figure-of-eight turns, one shakier than the rest as my new companion got his first taste of piloting an aeroplane.

Then, about twenty minutes later, the Avro puttered back, engine blipping, wheels skimming roughly mown paddock, settling down, starboard undercarriage strut abruptly folding, lower wingtip ploughing turf, fuselage flipping over, Frank and his pilot struggling to unbuckle their seat harnesses as a roaring belch of orange flame engulfed them both.

Two days later, I gave evidence at the Court of Enquiry and heard how a slack mechanic had failed to replace the cotter pin in a half-inch castellated nut. The vibration of repeated landings and take-offs had loosened it until that final circuit and bump when the retaining bolt fell out and eleven hundred pounds worth of flying machine got struck off the school's equipment schedule.

I learned much from this accident. Like, always accompany the pilot on his ground inspections before getting airborne. Some became quite shirty, believing that I was undermining their alleged superior status, to which I would politely remind them that two heads are better than one, and that we both held the King's Commission and were equally responsible for His Majesty's property, our lives especially.

It helped that I was a machine gunner by trade, accustomed to checking components by feel as well as by sight, under battlefield conditions. Three times later, in France, I found defects hidden under impacted grease and grot that could have been fatal, once airborne, had I not discovered them first by manual inspection.

As an Australian I never once apologised, backed down, or assumed something was right just because a higher-ranked Englishman imagined it was.

100

I drew the short straw to be OIC at Frank's funeral. It was felt this was the right thing to do, as I was the only person who had known him during his brief service in the Royal Flying Corps and, as a bonus, I could be Officer in Charge of the instructor's funeral as well.

Depending upon how one looked at it, I was lucky that so many others had crashed previously, for by now there was a well-established procedure. Instead of searching *King's Regulations* for the correct drill, all one had to do was send a note to the Adjutant at Brock Barracks on Oxford Road, requesting the presence of a firing party and bugler in Reading Cemetery at 0900 hours next day – the Flying Corps having recently abandoned the Army's ack-emma timekeeping and had instead adopted the Navy's 24-hour clock – and leave it for the Royal Berkshire Regiment to do the rest.

Our adjutant signed-over seven shillings for me to distribute as gratuities when I borrowed a ceremonial sword to go on Frank's coffin, together with his Princess Patricia's forage cap. The flying staff took care of the partially cremated instructor before we chocked both coffins on the back of a lorry and secured two Union Flags with cord tie-downs. I squeezed in front with our chaplain and off we drove with six officers as pallbearers in close pursuit, crammed aboard the school's Ford patrol car.

Our cortege eased to a more sedate pace at the cemetery's ornamental gateway and proceeded up the middle of a kite-shaped expanse of grass and headstones until we reached a new plot where the RFC and local military hospitals were, by now, regular customers. Row upon row of them.

Two open graves awaited us, wooden planks, and webbing strops in place as the bearer party unloaded their coffins and laid them in position for me to recover the swords and caps. Someone else neatly folded the flags, ready for the next funerals, while I checked the names painted on each pine plank lid to ensure they corresponded with the white crosses being hammered into the ground by one of the attendant gravediggers.

The chaplain recited the Burial Service with hardly a glance at his *Book of Common Prayer*. The coffins sank into the ground. The six-man firing party presented arms and discharged three volleys of blanks. The bugler sounded the *Last Post* followed by *Reveille*, after which I distributed the seven shillings, thanked everyone for their attendance and drove back to camp, our God Guesser merrily chattering away, trying to dispel my sombre mood.

If I do tell Frances about this commonplace episode during the Great War, I shall have to explain why I did not abandon the RFC and return to a safer job at Étaples. It was never that simple. Not only was I obliged by bonds of friendship to support David on the AFC's experimental flight, I had no guarantee of remaining on the staff for much longer.

Last year's Big Push had been along the Somme; this year's even bigger offensive was about to be unleashed farther north, in Flanders. There was every chance the casualty rate would be proportionally higher and that I would soon find myself promoted to replace a company MGO killed on the frontline, where my somewhat limited mobility would not restrict an ability to direct batteries of Vickers' guns from their static emplacements.

David had been right, life in the Flying Corps was cushy until one's number came up, as Frank Laurie had just demonstrated, and there are worse ways of being killed than in a crashed aeroplane. Whichever way one looked at it, we were all bound to get the chop sooner or later.

The following Monday thirty-six young men formed fours on the parade ground where we were ordered to tuck squares of white card behind our cap badges and regard ourselves as Cadets (P) or Cadets (O) until further notice. One of David's early letters after enlistment had described his first two months here as nothing but vigorous foot drill and time-fillers before getting anywhere near an aeroplane. That was late-1915, we were now into 1917, and the technically, tactically superior Imperial German Air Service had already shot down more than two hundred of our machines, this one month alone.

The need for even half-trained aircrew, in France, was greater than ever and the tempo in England was correspondingly quicker than David had known. Split into two flights P and O - initials that had nothing to do with the famous shipping line – we marched off in opposite directions and were thrust straight into classroom work that included subjects as diverse as Mechanics and Basic Engine Repairs, Theory of Flight and Meteorology, Dynamics and Ballistics, Electrical Theory and Wireless Telegraphy, Morse Code and Semaphore.

This last item seemed odd in the context of aerial warfare, but the Type 52 Sterling wireless set could only transmit signals, not receive them. If our colleagues on the ground needed to reply, their options were limited to a blinking Aldis lamp, or cloth panels pegged out in encoded patterns, or wagged flags.

These days and then weeks were my first experience of sitting at a school desk, learning by rote, and I found it irksome after acquiring information at my own naturally quicker pace. However, persistence pays, and I learned not only a lot of vitally useful information I also learned to curb my impatience with slower minds.

As observers it was expected we would spend much of our time in the air directing artillery fire, and my introduction to this was a large, cardboard and plaster model of trenches and their rear areas, displayed on the gymnasium floor, rather like one we studied before Pozières. Only now, electric light bulbs randomly glowed to indicate shell bursts that I, crouched inside a laundry basket suspended from the roof rafters, reported with alphabetical clock-dial references to mark the make-believe fall of shot. This was done by tapping a silent Morse key, to accustom us to not being able to hear its usual clicker-click above the roar of an aeroplane's engine.

Those of us who passed Basic Training were then sent to Brooklands, near Weybridge, to hone our skills in wireless telegraphy, map reading, and writing observation reports inside the open cockpit of an FE2 pusher biplane, one thousand feet above Surrey's North Downs.

After an intensive fortnight of this we moved to the Aerial Gunnery School at Hythe where our training began with bumpy rides along a narrow-gauge railway track in a mock-up fuselage, shooting a Winchester 0.22 repeater at static plywood models of German aeroplanes, no great challenge for an experienced game bird shooter and 'roo hunter.

From there we graduated to the unshrouded Lewis gun, with its ninety-seven round "stew pot" magazine instead of the shallow, forty-seven round "frying pan" I was accustomed to in the trenches and commenced live firing at canvas drogues towed behind a modified DH6. It was now that my skill with a billiard cue became apparent when quickly and instinctively estimating angles of deflection and points of impact above the English Channel.

A detail sure to intrigue Frances is that we never wore a restraining harness, unlike the chap in the front seat. The nature of our work meant that we had to crouch about when firing at oblique targets, or swivel on a spindled piano stool to key messages, decode signals, or plot a course on the map board.

This was fine enough while the pilot flew straight and level, or if there was not too much turbulence, but if he had to take evasive action there was a fair chance the observer would be flung to his death. As happened on several occasions unless we grabbed the Scarfe ring's gun-mount with both fists, wrapped our ankles around the piano stool's pedestal, and held on for dear life.

At the completion of our training, had we been pilots, the Air Council would have authorised us to wear our proficiency badge. However, because of what I shall charitably call the Royal Flying Corp's class-conscious confusion, we trained observers were regarded as probationary players who still had to earn a place on the team by surviving a given number of operational hours before being grudgingly allowed to sew on a very plain, unadorned Winged-O.

This looked as if its designer had ripped the wing off a dead pigeon, for inspiration, and was often sarcastically referred to by others as the Flying Arsehole. By contrast, a pilot's brevet was an RFC monogram framed inside a crowned laurel wreath borne aloft by a pair of stylish, outspread wings. Our humble place in the Flying Corps' order of battle could not have been more explicit, even though it was our eyes and brains the Huns were trying to kill as we exchanged fire, or directed artillery bombardments, or navigated for our chauffeurs, fooling around in the front seat.

The only exception, at the time of which I shall speak, was an immediate award to the top two graduates of each course. My notebooks had always been favourably commented upon, with their scale drawings and neat penmanship, and I am sure it was these rather than any great ability in the sky that tipped the balance in my favour when selecting one of the two winners in this insulting lottery.

With my sharply honed Australian sense of fairness, I felt it reeked of ingrained English snobbery, was fundamentally spiteful, and did nothing to build morale when and where it was needed most. However, David's congratulatory letter was warm in his praise and eagerly looked forward to me joining him on the strength of D-for-Dingo Flight, XIII Squadron RFC, at Le Hameau in Picardy, as soon as possible.

101

By now my kit included a fur lined leather helmet and goggles, elbow-length gauntlets, sheepskin knee boots, and the recently introduced Sidcot flying suit, named after its inventor, Sidney Cotton, an Australian pilot in the Royal Naval Air Service. All of which required a bulky kitbag as well as my officers' valise, meaning I had both hands full on the hitched lift to Dover Priory railway station.

I'd been feeling a bit seedy these past few days, with a dull headache and achy limbs, none of which greatly surprised me, given the exhausting pace of the last three months coming on top of Étaples, Mouquet Farm, and Pozières. I was long overdue for some serious leave and hoped that my summons to Horseferry Road meant that AIF headquarters had been keeping a tally of my entitlements before joining Dingo Flight.

Squashed aboard a train filled with troops returning home from Flanders via Calais, I found my numbered seat in an officers' carriage with its characteristic fug of damp uniforms, stale tobacco, and unwashed bodies. Those around me were mostly dog-tired and nodding off, which I didn't mind as the headache was not going away and I was in no mood for idle chitchat.

The locomotive puffed and panted, clanked, and jolted into Charing Cross Station a little before noon. I remained seated while everyone else scrambled onto the platform. Clammy sweat freckled my chest, arms, and neck. Somehow, I got my kit off the luggage rack. Stumbled out into the fresh air. And keeled over.

What followed assumed a nightmare quality as a passing RAMC captain took my pulse while I lay on the concrete platform, looked at my tongue, estimated my temperature, which must have been on the wrong side of one hundred degrees Fahrenheit, and ordered six troops to improvise a litter while he strode ahead to commandeer a place aboard one of several ambulances collecting patients in the station yard.

It was my good fortune that he picked one about to drive off across Trafalgar Square, up the Mall, past Buckingham Palace, with another consignment of wounded to King Edward VII's Hospital for Officers in Grosvenor Gardens. I lay on its floor with my bags, vomited copiously from malaise and motion sickness, and was the first off before the stretcher cases could be moved.

My Good Samaritan RAMC medico must've had a blank casualty clearance ticket in his tunic pocket, on which he scribbled his name, unit, time, and *Meningitis? Instanter!* before tying its string tag to my identity disc.

Meningitis is still fatally swift unless treated immediately, which in those days amounted to very little as a team of VAD nurses in grey linen neck-to-ankle typhus overalls propelled the stretcher trolley to an isolation ward where my uniform was stripped off and sent to the fumigator.

I was in no condition to appreciate it at the time, but one of London's leading consultants then made a grand entrance, stethoscope worn like a badge of high rank across the front of his spotless white coat, a matron and ward sister in anxious attendance as he gravely examined me from the soles of my feet to the crown of my cropped scalp. "You're a lucky young fellow."

That was not how I felt as he turned away to deliver his verdict. "Varicella. Bed rest. Fluids *ad libitum*. Light diet, light clothing, standard treatment. He'll soon be right as rain."

The itching became worse during the afternoon and by nightfall I had a fine crop of watery blisters across my shoulders, chest, and belly, though only a few on my face or other extremities. One of the VADs – a finely featured lady of a certain age, with a thick gold wedding ring on her left third finger and thus unlikely to arouse awkward memories of another person, in a similar uniform - appeared with a bottle of calamine lotion and a wad of cotton wool to cool my burning skin.

"'Varicella'?" I croaked.

"Chickenpox."

I felt humiliated to be laid low by a childhood complaint. She read my thoughts: "There are serious complications in adults. Lay still, young man. You're in the right place."

As indeed I was, King Edward's being founded when army officers were still expected to pay for their own medical treatment, unlike non-commissioned soldiers. The South African War exposed the obvious inequity of this system and prompted the future King Edward's mistress - Lily Langtry the prominent actress and Suffragette - to campaign for a hospital where officers could receive medical attention without going into private debt for their public service to the Empire. Its proximity to Buckingham Palace, plus royal patronage, meant that our treatment was never less than the best available.

My formidable VAD reappeared the following morning and, while she was swabbing blisters, I overheard a senior member of staff respectfully address her as "Lady Grenville." This is not a particularly common surname and so I took a punt: "Permit me asking, ma'am, but are you by any chance related to Colonel Phillip Grenville?"

An eyebrow twitched imperiously. "D'you know him?"

"We shared the same ward at 3LGH. I owe him a great debt of gratitude. Please give my regards when next you meet."

"Shall do," she replied briskly, and finished daubing me with my pink war paint, as I jokingly called the calamine lotion.

Good food, good nursing, and abundant rest meant I was making a good recovery when Grenville himself popped in to find me in the sunroom overlooking Grosvenor Gardens, sketching a vase of purple and blue delphiniums on the window ledge.

He looked quite dapper in his Number One uniform and even a little excited, something most unusual for this stiffest of stiff-upper-lipped Englishmen. When I commented upon it, he bashfully confessed to having just come from an investiture at the Palace where His Majesty had bestowed my friend with the CB's intricately enamelled neck badge and crimson ribbon.

One peculiarity of the British honours system is the length of time that can elapse between an act of valour or meritorious service and the gazetting of its award. This is the moment when one may begin officially wearing the ribbon although the medal itself can take a while longer to arrive if it is to be ceremonially presented – like Grenville's Companion of the Most Honourable Order of the Bath - rather than signed for as a registered packet, as I did when my DCM eventually caught up with me at Kebir's APO.

Grenville was very concerned about my state of health and asked if I had any relatives or friends in England with whom I could spend a convalescent leave. Learning that I had neither family nor friends in the Old Country, he gave a firm smile and promised to put that right as soon as I was up and about again. He then gave an equally firm handshake and strode downstairs to the car that was waiting to whisk him back to Woolwich where he was now attached to the Royal Military College, preparing Royal Engineer officers for their duties on the Western Front.

As one would expect of such a man, he was as good as his word, and I assume the VAD relative had been keeping him posted of my progress, for he was waiting downstairs in the hospital's entrance hall when I was discharged from King Edward's to begin a week's convalescent leave.

Every inch the English country squire in Norfolk tweed jacket, plus fours, and brogues, this was the first time I had seen Grenville out of khaki and was strongly reminded of my first meeting with Cedric Shaw at the Shamrock Hotel, half the world away and what, by now, felt like several lifetimes ago.

"Good to see you up and about Cribdon," he said, beckoning for a porter to carry my kit out to an open Austin Tourer, its ML plates indicating a privately-owned civilian vehicle on Military Liaison duties and therefore entitled to extra petrol coupons. By some stretch of imagination these duties included taking me for a ride in the country as we motored across Chiswick Bridge, and then again across the Thames at Twickenham, heading southwest through Surrey towards Hampshire.

The towns, and villages, and hamlets we passed through were familiar names I'd flown over during my navigation course at Brooklands, but it was fascinating to see what such quaint locations as Farleigh Wallop, and Brown Candover, looked like at ground level, as we whirred along country lanes that decades later would become traffic-jammed highways.

"We're going down to the Cottage!" Grenville announced tweed cap reversed, peering ahead through motoring goggles, the windscreen only partially deflecting bees and bugs zipping between banks of wayside wildflowers. "You like to fish?! Let's see what you make of our beat!"

"Thanks!" I called back, reaching around to take my goggles, and flying helmet from their bag on the seat behind me. "It's jolly decent to make such an effort on my behalf!"

"Not at all! Enlightened self-interest! One day I shall visit Australia where I'm sure you will be a most engaging and informative host!"

"I look forward to it!"

"As do I -!"

Our conversation lapsed. It was a hard to keep talking above the exhaust's rumble and slipstream's whistle. I was quite happy to sit back and watch a country unlike anything I'd seen before. My homeland, the one that Grenville was so keen to visit, largely consists of map references like Mount Desolation and Dead Camel Creek, mute evidence of a much harsher, crueller terrain than England's green and pleasant land.

Though I didn't know it at the time, I was witnessing twilight's last glimmer on an ancient world in which sheaves of grain were still gathered by the armful; where conical haystacks were still thatched with pagan symbols to ward off lightning strikes; where hedgerows were still husbanded by successive generations of hedgers and ditchers; where roadmenders still camped in lonely sheds, patiently raking, and patching their assigned lengths of gravelled track.

We slowed at a crossroads in the middle of which stood a white painted wooden post and fingerboard directing us towards Winchester. Grenville now revealed a fine baritone as he turned right to follow the sign: *"Domum, domum, dulce domum! Dulce, dulce, dulce domum! Dulce domum resonemus…!"* He stopped singing and cast a sideways glance at me. "Any idea what that is?"

"Home Sweet Home, in Latin?" I replied, remembering the times I'd heard Melba practicing something similar, in English.

"Good guess, but not quite! It's the *Wykehamist Song,*" he explained, with a reflective smile. "*Dulce Domum* can be translated as 'sweet home,' of course, if one treats *domum* as a neuter noun. But on the other hand, it might also be the accusative case of *domus,* which infers an adverbial 'sweetly homeward,' not that either one greatly matters," he chuckled, "both fit today's journey!"

I had not the foggiest idea what he was going on about; my self-taught Latin was more like a Roman legionary's version of Pidgin English than his classically polished grammar.

Only later did I learn that Winchester College is one of England's great Public Schools and has been since the Middle Ages when it was founded by Bishop William of Wykeham, hence Grenville's reference to Wykehamists as its students still called themselves. Though as he drily remarked: "You can always tell a Wykehamist, but you can never tell him very much…" In the event his grammatical conjuring tricks told me a great deal, though only an outsider could have sensed their importance.

Grenville's *dulce domum* was the unintended key to those foggy ambiguities of aristocratic English that so infuriated someone I never wished to think of again, and inspired her love of German's crisp, concise, clarity. We plainspoken Colonials often felt the same way whenever conversing with Englishmen who were grandmasters of a drawled, opaque speech designed to keep themselves Up, their lower classes Down, and we foreigners Out. And yet little more than three generations earlier, the world's first industrial empire had been built upon the blunt talk of mechanics like Watt, and Stephenson, and Arkwright, pioneering geniuses who expressed their thoughts in plain, uncompromising Anglo-Saxon that left no room for vague ifs, buts, or maybes.

Some made great fortunes, married into the upper gentry, and sent their sons to schools like Winchester in the mistaken belief they would thereby become Proper English Gentlemen. This was a fatal delusion, for not only did the boys learn to despise their fathers' gruff, provincial manners, they also imbibed the values of an imaginary Classical Age by parsing Cicero's speeches in old Latin, and Pericles' orations in an even more ancient Greek.

Meanwhile, on the other side of the German Sea, as we used to call that body of water between Norfolk and the Netherlands, the forces of modern science and engineering were doubling and redoubling in Essen and Düsseldorf, and farther south in Mannheim and Augsburg, where inventors of international stature like Diesel and Maybach, chemists like von Baeyer and von Liebig, were national heroes and models for ambitious young lads to emulate and excel.

Schooled in hard mathematics and rigorous laboratory method, taught in a language that is steady and firm as I had often been reminded by someone in Egypt, this new generation of Germans were decades ahead of their English relatives who, with few exceptions, were happy to enjoy the fruits of an earlier generation's grimy sweat and toil.

Frances Baxter will likely disagree with me, if I share this insight with her, but I am convinced that muddled miscommunication underwrote the July Crisis of 1914 that destroyed my generation after a couple of pistol shots, up a side street in a provincial Balkan town, triggered their avalanche of disasters.

France and Germany were traditionally hostile neighbours; Imperial Russia had recently bound herself by treaty to assist Republican France in the event of war with Germany; Imperial Germany was equally bound to support the Austro-Hungarian Empire in the event of war with the Serbs, who were under the protection of their brother Slavs, the Russians. In effect, Central Europe was a seething witches' brew of mutual suspicions, marinated in ancestral hatreds that risked boiling over at the slightest provocation.

The only undeclared hand amongst these festering feuds, plots, and conspiracies was Britain's; would London take part in a Continental war or would the British watch to see which way the cat jumped? This was a concern that exercised many an anxious mind in Paris, and St Petersburg, and crucially in Berlin as the *Reich* braced to knock-out France via Belgium before the Czar's massive, ill-equipped armies steamrolled their way across the Polish border, not seven days' march from Germany's capital, as they had done a century earlier at the end of the Napoleonic Wars.

The Kaiser notoriously dismissed Britain's land forces as a "Contemptible Little Army!" but at least one adult in his entourage of flunkies should have reminded him that Britannia still ruled the waves, and that the Royal Navy was ready and able to escort convoy after convoy of loyal Overseas Britons hastening Home from the farthest reaches of the globe. Convoys not only of manpower but also immense stocks of raw materials and foodstuffs mined, harvested, and manufactured across the British Empire. Most ominous of all for the Kaiser's Ruritanian patchwork quilt of minor kingdoms and duchies, was the looming threat of a ruthless naval blockade that would, during the next five years, starve to death three quarters of a million of his wretched civilian subjects.

This stern warning should have been the duty of Britain's Secretary of State for Foreign Affairs, Sir Edward Grey, a kindly soul, coincidentally schooled at Winchester where, no doubt, he also learned to sing the confused grammar and woolly logic of a dead language. Small wonder this amiable birdwatcher and keen fisherman was unable to express himself with crisp, concise, clarity. A Kalgoorlie barman would have made a better fist of the job: "One toe over the Belgian frontier, matey, an' the whole British Empire's gunna be on top o'yuh like a ton o' bricks -!"

Instead, Sir Edward politely hemmed and hawed, parsed and paused, penning elegant, elliptical memoranda that baffled his staff as much as they confused those anxiously watching the course of events from Berlin, St Petersburg, and Paris until, at the eleventh hour, he finally addressed Parliament and clarified Britain's position. By which time the Kaiser's armies were kitting-up for their march on Paris and the second German triumph in forty-three years, or so they firmly believed.

This is not to say there would not have been a Great War elsewhere, but hopefully not in Flanders, or on the Somme, or at Verdun, if only Grey by name, grey by nature, had been capable of acting like a Twentieth Century statesman instead of thinking like a Roman senator debating the trifling affairs of some distant *colonia*.

Now, two years and several months after his Olympian blunder befell us, Grenville and I were driving southwest, if my recently acquired skill of reading the sun for directions was correct. This was not as simple as it might seem for an Australian born in the Southern Hemisphere where the sun rises on our eastern right-hand side, when facing its northward Equatorial arc, and sets in on our western left-hand side. This caused endless confusion in England and France where the sun rose on our eastern left-hand side, facing the sun's southward arc, and set on our western right-hand side. Unless we kept a sharp eye on the compass, one could easily wander off course and arrive at the wrong destination, as several disorientated Australian aircrews discovered after landing at German aerodromes on the wrong side of the Western Front.

Grenville was, however, familiar with this route as we continued motoring past signposts to villages like Monks Wood and Bishop Sutton, ecclesiastical names that spake of an England long before King Henry VIII looted the monasteries to reward his Tudor New Men.

"Ah, *dulce domum!* Home sweet home at last..."

The Austin changed gears and swung right once more at a sign pointing up a lane to another quaintly named village, Itchen Stoke. However, before we could reach it, Grenville slowed left at a farm gate where I hopped out to hold it open, as passengers do on West Australian wheat or sheep properties.

The Cottage was not what I had expected. Instead of a thatched dwelling with honeysuckle twined around the porch, as romantic novelists had led me to believe was always the case, we braked at the entrance of a substantial Elizabethan manor house overlooking lush water meadows dotted with a breed of sheep unlike any I had seen before. A housekeeper, rather like Mrs Blane in appearance, stood to attention in white pinafore and frilled bonnet as we approached. Meanwhile, an elderly bewhiskered man I later learned was her husband, unloaded our bags and prepared to follow us indoors.

"Welcome 'ome zirr." She bobbed a curtsy. "Ge'man."

"Thank you, Mrs Godwin. Allow me to introduce my friend, Mr Cribdon." I got another curtsy and realised what an odd sight I must have been in britches and tunic, fur-lined helmet pulled down around my ears, goggles pushed up. "He'll be staying with you for a few days, and I know you will take very good care of him."

"You won't be a-stayin' then zirr?"

"Sadly not. Duty calls. I must leave tomorrow morning but shall return in a few days' time. Now, let's show him to his room, then we can see what's for luncheon."

My bedchamber was a simple but sunny whitewashed plaster and bare timbered attic, with a dormer window through which I enjoyed a view across the meandering River Itchen towards a small village and some low hills folding into the distance.

It says much about my state of mind that, even as I surveyed this peaceful landscape, in imagination I was directing Lewis gunners to enfilade enemy positions along those commanding heights, and didn't hear the door open behind me. Grenville had to give a couple of polite coughs to get my attention. "Now let's see if we can find something more comfortable for you to wear..."

An old oaken armoire stood in one corner of my room, filled with neatly stacked shirts, underwear, and clothes for most everyday occasions.

"You're about Ronald's size. Here, try these on." Grenville hauled out a set of tweeds and a comfortably soft, blue flannel shirt.

"This is all very generous," I smiled uncertainly, "but won't he mind a stranger wearing his kit?"

"No. He'd be glad to help."

Only later did I learn that my host's younger brother had been killed leading his men into action at Le Cateau, three weeks after the outbreak of war

102

A farmhouse meal was just what I needed after a hospital diet of pearl barley broth, mashed potatoes, and steamed cabbage. By contrast, Mrs Godwin's cob loaf with real butter, dry smoked ham, and pickled onions were the stuff of dreams, especially when taken with a pint of homebrewed ale drawn straight from the pantry keg.

"Good?" Grenville laid his cutlery aside and glanced across the kitchen table as I hoed into my share of this feast.

"Bloody brilliant." For one unguarded moment I was an Australian in polite English society, then I heard the housekeeper's muted gasp in the background. "Um, very nice, thank you."

Frances will find this episode quite hilarious, living as she does in an age when the coarsest language is bantered between men and women without raising a blush or an eyebrow; I shall certainly include it in tomorrow's recording session as an example of how wildly the pendulum of acceptable behaviour can swing in one long lifetime.

It will help her to better understand we Edwardians and our world if I then explain how aghast London's theatre critics were when a reformed flower girl, in George Bernard Shaw's improbable play *Pygmalion*, forgot her elocution lessons and exclaimed "Not bloody likely!" Tepid stuff nowadays but, in 1913, the subject of furious letters to the *Times* denouncing "That sanguinary adverb…!"

Grenville, a soldier himself, understood even if Mrs Godwin felt the need to busy herself elsewhere, and nodded his approval. "'Nothing like a spot of country fare and country air to buck a chap up after a rough trot. Now, it's your call," he continued, "but I'm thinking we might tie a fly and go for a walk along the river. The morning rise is over, but I know a few spots where fish can still be taken, if approached in the right manner. What d'you say?"

"I can't imagine anything better."

"Good. That's settled then."

We finished our meal, stacked the dishes, and went through to a gun room that not only housed several braces of London twelve bores by James Purdey, and a pair of Rigby's deer rifles from an earlier era, but also a lovingly curated collection of split cane rods with matching reels and lines.

Grenville noted my awestruck indecision at such an abundance of choices and amiably suggested the right rig for this afternoon's excursion, including a well-worn anglers' vest that I suspect might have also belonged to Ronald, from the way he eyed its fit, and nodded to himself.

We exited the kitchen garden and set out across the nearest meadow, livestock scattering as we approached them. Grenville glanced sideways. "I believe you have quite a lot of sheep in Australia?"

"Mobs of 'em," I replied. "The wool clip underpins our economy. It's said we ride on the sheep's back. Which may be true, but they're nothing like yours," I added, mentally comparing these plump, blocky animals with the bony creatures grazing our sparse rangelands.

"Better…?"

"Hell no! Blind Freddy and his deaf dog could tell your lot are in better shape than anything we graze on saltbush."

"Interesting." He fell silent as we continued pacing ankle-deep through lush green feed, I think secretly pleased to hear my enthusiastic opinion of his livestock. "We've been breeding Hampshire Downs for almost a century," he continued. "That's when we first crossed Old Hampshires with Southdowns, to improve carcass weight, plus a touch of Wiltshire Horn for the fleece. How d'you think they'd go in your part of the world?"

"'Can't say, I'm no grazier, but you sound like one?"

"I am." The words reflected an inner pride and satisfaction. "The Empire only requires we give of our best years. Assuming Brother Fritz allows me to retire, I shall return like Cincinnatus, though not to my plough but to the tupping fold where I shall assist Matthew as we to continue strengthening our bloodline."

"'Matthew'?"

"Godwin; Mrs G's husband and first-rate flock master," he announced, as if reviewing a crack regiment on manoeuvres. "What he doesn't know about breeding would not cover my thumbnail. Of course, the Godwins have worked this land for as long as anyone can remember. Probably since Winchester was the capital of Saxon England, if their name is anything indication."

"This land?" I queried, looking around as we approached a stile over the meadow's riverbank fence.

"Strictly speaking, for only the past three generations," Grenville corrected himself. "An earlier Matthew came up from Vernalls near Lyndhurst, after his master left the Navy and retired to live in Bath. He found employment here and, to our good fortune, settled down with his family. Ah, thank you."

I assisted him across the stile by holding his rod case and woven wicker creel until he reached the other side, at which point I passed them over with my own and joined him on a well-maintained path stretching for about half a mile of the Grenvilles' river frontage.

I've known more challenging waters than this one, camped in the high country of Northern Victoria where I first fished the Snowy River's tumbling rivulets and Mitta-Mitta's tributaries. By comparison the Itchen was tame and uninteresting as we cautiously positioned ourselves downstream from a stand of alders.

I was about to learn that this river, and the better-known Test a few miles away, are two of the finest trout and salmon runs in Britain, their sparklingly pure water sprung from deep chalk beds under several of the villages passed earlier in the day.

Grenville coached me as we studied the passing swirls and whorls for signs of life, and then demonstrated what he meant by deftly flicking a shaggy, nondescript lure under an overhanging branch where it was immediately ambushed by a splendid pan-sized brown trout who wrongly assumed that a careless insect had lost its footing and fallen into the stream. And thus began my lifelong love affair with the Itchen.

That evening, Mrs Godwin presented our catch at the dinner table as six lightly grilled fillets on a bed of buttered new potatoes, with minted peas fresh from the garden.

"Try this." Grenville offered me an unlabelled wine bottle. "Tell me what you think of it…"

I filled my glass, admired the contents' greenish golden hue, sniffed appreciatively, and let a generous mouthful play with the tastebuds. "Bon plonk! It looks like Hock but isn't. What's the secret?"

"Stinging nettles." He shared one of his rare smiles. "A great favourite in the country at this time of year. It's only young and doesn't keep long, but then we don't keep it for long," he added with a wry chuckle. "Another seasonal favourite is bramble wine, best enjoyed beside the fire on a dismal winter's day. It also makes an excellent *digestif* after a hearty meal of jugged hare washed down with elderflower 'champagne...'"

I had always believed that England's squires were boneheaded buffoons who populated Australia with convicted innocents, not amiable gentlemen who relished plain food and drank wines made from wayside weeds. Doubtless there were country magistrates harsh in their judgments, and in due course I was to meet their modern equivalents in the city's self-styled High Society who were, almost without exception, recently enriched social climbers hungry for the reassurance of arrogance.

The first Grenvilles might well have behaved in a similar manner after 1540, the year in which Thomas de Grenouille, a French lutenist at Hampton Court, dedicated a book of *Chansons de Amour* to *Hys Most Puisante & Auguste Majestie*, with flattering references to the King Henry's own composition *Greensleeves*. M'sieur Grenouille was also an adroit schemer, as I would read in the family's library, for not only did he gain the King's favour he also gained a manor that formerly paid a quitrent of five gold angels *per annum* to the Bishops of Winchester.

Life in a new land, with new land, required a new name. Had he directly translated his old French one, these new English gentry would have been Frogs in every sense of the word. Instead, he opted for the more aristocratic Grenville, and for more than three centuries, successive generations of his line either served the Crown at court, or on the battlefield, or farmed their Hampshire estate, acquiring the innate poise that treats all comers with the same genial dignity and gracious kindness that my Aunt Lucinda insisted upon in our Melbourne home.

I was starting to feel at ease in their company, and even found myself edging closer to an understanding of their tightly knit world in which a senior army officer could look forward to working alongside a farm labourer, without in any way compromising his own dignity, grace, and kindness.

The city's *nouveaux riches* needed to flaunt their new riches with costly wines and ostentatious toys, but a well-grounded countryman like Grenville was sufficiently sure of himself to delight in homebrewed beer. His choices spoke of an unaffected self-confidence that an outsider, like me, could only envy.

"Something's a bit of a puzzle," I said, finally, breaking our affable silence.

"Oh? What?"

"Why the urge to see my part of the world? 'Land of forest, fleas, and flies; blighted hopes and blighted eyes; art thou Hell in Earth's disguise? Westralia!'" I glanced around the timber-panelled dining hall with its centuries of family *bric-à-brac* artlessly displayed. "Frankly, if I had a place like this, be buggered if I'd want to go somewhere like that!"

"Fair comment." He set his glass down and dabbed lips with a starched napkin before continuing. "The scenery is unimportant, it's who lives upon it that concerns me, and how you've got to be the way you are, and in so short a while."

"Oh?" I tested his words and tone of voice for any hint of condescension. "And how are we...?"

"You be the judge." He paused, assembling his thoughts. "I'd been stretchered out and was awaiting my turn for an ambulance, when one of your battalions marched past. Another one, British, had already gone through, moaning that sentimental twaddle *Tipperary*, with its long, long way to the sweetest girl they know, but not your lot. There was a spring in the Australians' step, a gleam in their eye as they challenged the enemy with their version of *The Girl I Left Behind Me*: 'Kaiser Bill is feeling ill! The Crown Prince he's gone barmy! We don't give a fuck for old von Kluck, or his chicken army!' Every man had an air that was almost a swagger, and in that moment, more than anything else in the world, I wanted to join their ranks."

He paused, blinking a damp eye. "By God, Cribdon, they were magnificent!" There was an embarrassed catch in his voice as he concluded. "It would have been the greatest honour in the world to fight alongside them, even though I knew what they were going into, as did they. Yet go they went, heads held high, proud as kings, daring Fritz to do his worst -!"

"Phew..."

"That's not what you expected to hear?"

"No. It's, well, I'm not sure what to say!"

"Well, I say, be ready to show me around when I do come to Australia," he continued, regaining his accustomed poise. "You see, for me, the puzzle is that a fair number of those chaps would have been British born, perhaps even recent migrants indistinguishable from their brothers and cousins in our battalions. And yet something in your country air had already worked its magic, for they were no longer the same men." He paused to steady his voice. "Good fortune permitting, I shall learn much from your wool industry, and as I do, see if I can also learn what it is about your country that sparks this spirit and, if possible, bring it back home, for Heaven knows we shall need it after Victory..."

"Why is that?" I frowned.

"Britain's fittest and finest are either dead or broken in body and soul," he replied simply. "What's filling our ranks now are those who didn't step up until compelled to. If we are ever to amount to anything again as a nation, as an empire, we shall need to recoup all the energy and initiative we can muster by reaching out to, and learning from, our overseas brethren."

He hesitated before continuing in a more reflective tone. "Life's a rummy thing. Only three or four generations ago, Old Mother England was still transporting her ne'er-do-well children to the Australasian colonies, little knowing that the alchemy of distance would transmute them and their bloodlines into those superb warriors I saw on the Menin Road." He paused yet again, watching me closely. "Does that answer your question?"

"Yes. I think it does."

"Good. Now, it's my turn, and I do hope you won't mind if I tactfully enquire what happened to that beautiful young lady who visited you at 3GH?" Grenville began simply. "And before you answer, please don't suspect my motives. I'm a married man, not happily but nonetheless duty-bound to behave honourably. Thus, I have no ulterior motive except the natural concern one may express for a friend's wellbeing."

Grenville had given me time to assemble a concise answer. "We agreed to go our separate ways." Announced with a defiant flick of the chin.

"Ah." He steepled his fingertips, the apex of a triangle formed by elbows planted on the chair's armrests. I waited for him to enquire why, but instead he remained quiet, waiting for me to make the next move.

Being young and impatient it was I who broke first. "Don't you wish to know what happened?"

"When you are ready to speak." He was a natural interrogator.

"She didn't dump me!"

"No?"

"No." Said with an emphatic scowl. "It was my decision. She protested, but I knew it was the right and proper thing to do."

"Why?"

I countered his question with one of my own. "Didn't you recognise her?"

"Not particularly."

"Well, you might have seen her photo in *Country Life*, about three years ago," I explained, adding her true name, title, and lineage.

"Oh."

"Oh indeed!" I snapped peevishly. "No way in the world was I setting myself up to be snubbed by her people!"

He pondered my reasons before delivering judgement. "May I congratulate you, Ian? It takes a profound understanding of the human condition to make such a heart-wrenching break. I was less prescient, aimed too high, and have paid for it ever since." He coughed drily before continuing in a heavier voice. "I have a sufficient private income from the family trust fund, plus whatever my rank allows, but it was never going to be enough for the spendthrift daughter of a viscount. And there was one further complication I had not foreseen…"

"Oh…?" It was my turn to play the waiting game.

"My wife worships at the temple of Sappho whose cult, as you may or may not know, flourished on the Isle of Lesbos, hence no heirs and successors. The fund bribes her with five hundred pounds *per annum*, paid quarterly in arrears, provided she keeps up appearances while living a life of secret depravity." He hesitated. "Ours is a squalid arrangement that would never have been, but for my blind ambition to 'get ahead.'"

"Can't you sue for divorce?"

"Good Lord no!" He recoiled from the thought. "That would dishonour our name forever."

"I'm sorry."

"Don't be. I'm only telling you this in strictest confidence in case there are times when you wish you had persisted with the Honourable Lady Sandra; believe me, you've saved yourself a lifetime of grief! Now," he stood, "I spy an unopened Dalwhinnie on the sideboard; let's draw its cork and toast your superior judgment."

103

Mrs Godwin, her husband, and I stood at the main door as the Austin set off on its return journey to Woolwich; the manor was now mine until further notice.

"Oi'd better be gettin' back t'work," Matthew announced, solemnly replacing his old cloth cap.

"An' mind you be cuttin' that there firewood a'right,' his wife admonished, straightening from her curtsy, "or there's no cookin' done!"

I nearly asked if I could tag along and help, for I knew they were short-handed with so many labourers called up by the army but decided against pushing myself forward too soon, having sensed that a gruffly reticent countryman like Matthew Godwin must be approached with unhurried observation, as if he were a trout in the nearby river, especially when the observer was an unknown foreigner like myself. So, instead, I went up to the bedchamber, checked the pencils and sketchbook in my haversack, and set out to explore the surrounding meadows and woodlands, after promising to be back for the midday meal.

I needed to be alone. There was much to think about, and it was not just England's alien landscape and its puzzling people, or even my host's stark warning against unequal marriage. The previous evening, after dinner, Grenville had taken me on a guided tour that included his family's portrait gallery of bewigged, dumpling-faced Georgian gentry; minor Regency rakes; and sepia-toned photographs of whiskery Victorian gentlemen posing with muzzle-loader shotguns and immense salmon rods.

None of the portraits were by Gainsborough, or Reynolds, or any artist of note. At a guess they'd been done by itinerant limners who dabbled in portraiture as a side-line to their stencilled decoration of houses unable to afford the latest wallpapers from *ancien régime* France.

The Grenvilles had been necessarily frugal until recent times. Most English landowners were, unless a coal seam ran under their property, or a railway company needed to buy a right of way. And thus it was for my friend's family until an inventive granduncle in Birmingham patented a rifle-boring machine, invested its royalties in a Scottish factory making smokeless powder and nitro-glycerine, and upon this floodtide of cash floated a family fortune that allowed his previously threadbare military relatives to begin marrying up the social ladder.

That much was obvious to anyone with an eye for detail, as happened when my host showed me his parents' photographic wedding portrait of a young Captain John Grenville proudly at attention in an ornately frogged tunic, a knighted lieutenant general's attractive daughter in flowing white veil and flounced dress by his side.

Of more immediate concern to me, however, were its two adjacent, more recent photographs; one of Philip Grenville himself as a newly commissioned Royal Engineer, fifteen or so years earlier; the other of a handsome young fellow, clearly related, in the uniform of a Territorial Army subaltern, a band of black crepe around his picture frame.

Grenville spoke with surprising freedom and fondness of his dead brother, which was rather uncomfortable for someone of my origins and temperament. It felt unsettling to be among people who were openly proud of their ancestors. The puzzle, for me, was what part I was meant to play in their family saga, for Grenville did not strike me as the sort who would reveal so much, so soon, to a stranger, unless there was good reason.

I paused in the shade of an oak tree that was probably an acorn when Monsieur de Grenouille reinvented himself as Master Grenville, and surveyed the nearby Itchen, placidly flowing down its vale towards Southampton Water and the English Channel.

An early morning mist had burned off and we were in for another warm day as I began making notes for a landscape in the style of John Constable. The Cottage, as Grenville persisted in calling it, was notably lacking in landscapes among its collection of paintings. This was something I intended to put right as I packed up and returned to the manor where Mrs Godwin diffidently served a bowl of mutton broth accompanied by man-sized hunks of crusty, home baked bread. "Oi hopes that a'right zirr...?"

"It is very welcome, ma'am" I replied in my most appreciative tone,

She almost blushed. "Whoi, tha's koind."

I spooned a sample taste, smacked lips, and nodded approvingly. "So, tell me, what did Ronald enjoy most?"

"Oo, the young master were never fussy so long as it were good homecook food!" Her face beamed before suddenly crumpling. "Such a lovesome young m-man. We do all miss 'im so!"

What followed were heartfelt reminiscences of a happy lad who loved fishing, and rabbiting, and learning country lore from her husband; who grew into a bright young man studying estate management at the Royal Agricultural College until war broke out; who was killed twenty-one days later by a machine gunner like me. "M-master Ronny were never a sodjer! He were a farmer, born an' bred!"

I finished lunch and went upstairs, got out of his clothes and back into my khaki before going down to the library where, earlier, I had noticed a writing desk on which Grenville had left a note:

> Please feel free to use whatever you need to
> enjoy our beat. In the meantime, may I
> suggest this book as a practical guide to
> our local conditions?

Alongside it was a first edition of *Fly Fishing* by Sir Edward Grey, inscribed:

> To my very good friend John Grenville
> for many happy hours on his river at
> at Hampton Rise. "Dulce domum."
> E.G.

I flicked through it then sat down and selected a sheet of headed notepaper, dipped ink and dithered around with ideas for a newsletter but, truth to tell, I had lost my appetite for correspondence, not that I now had all that many people to correspond with now. Aunt Lucinda? David? Miss McCracken? Harry? There used to be another, but she no longer mattered.

Furious with myself for sloth and indecision, I laid the pen aside and reached for *Fly Fishing* again, hoping that something in it would ease the chronic ache under my ribs, Grenville having thoughtfully tabbed a page that led me straight to the heart of the matter:

> Let the season be about the beginning of June and the angler be at the Itchen, and let us consider a day's fishing which shall be typical of many days this month.
>
> The wind shall be southwest and balmy with light clouds moving before it, between which gleams of sunshine fall upon the young leaves and woods, for there are many fine old woods by the water meadows.
>
> Granted these two conditions it will follow there will almost certainly be a rise of trout at some time during the day, though it is very improbable there will be one before ten o'clock with the most likely rise between eleven and twelve.
>
> Desiring earnestly not to miss a minute of the rise, and leaving a fair margin for uncertainties, the angler is best advised to be at the river by half-past nine, where he should be at the lowest part of the water he intends to fish and there sit down to watch some part known to be a good place for free rising trout.
>
> The first sign of the coming rise will be a few flies upon the water either olive duns or some near relation, and the angler should tie his lure in like manner.

My host had not only tactfully told me how to fish his water, at its best, he had also introduced me to an angling classic that would, in time, become a model for my own *With Rod & Line on Distant Waters* guidebooks.

I took Sir Edward's counsel the next morning and began my study of the Itchen's secret runs and rills, assisted by a river warden who at first thought I was a poacher from the Winchester garrison until he got close enough to read my uniform. "You be the Gren'lle ge'man I heered much about a't Pos' Office," he announced, respectfully doffing his cap.

"G'day." I reached out a hand. "Ian Cribdon."

The elderly bloke was flummoxed by an openhanded Australian greeting and bobbed his chins instead. "Um. Oi'm Russell."

I assumed this was an English social codesign that we must remain on master-servant terms whenever he stopped by to see how I was getting along, and to share news of what he and other wardens were doing to keep their river in pristine condition.

It came as a shock to learn that what I thought of as a wild stream was, in fact, as carefully tended as an herbaceous garden, its water weeds dredged, predatory fish plucked out, and new stock introduced from the hatcheries. It was an even greater surprise for him, however, when I described the untamed rivers and lakes of Northern Victoria and Tasmania's Central Highlands.

"Well, Oi never!" I am sure he thought I was pulling his leg and went on his way, shaking his head.

Regardless of whether I caught myself a bush tucker meal, or not, these few days were an idyllic pause in a war that still had more than a year and a half to run. There was always something new to delight the eye and keep the pencils busy, be it a brightly plumaged kingfisher, or the fluffy yellow flowers of an elder bush on the riverbank, or the play of cloud-dappled sunlight on distant meadows.

Russell was humbly tongue-tied when I presented him with a sketched portrait on my last full day at Hampton Rise. By then I had also persuaded Matthew and his wife to sit in the walled garden while I smoothed the wrinkles on their weathered features and watched shy, wistful smiles of remembrance for the lusty young couple they once were.

During the afternoons, while the trout rested, I would either help Matthew – he had finally decided I could be trusted to fix a fence and repair a gate – or catch up on belated correspondence before walking into the village to the General Store that doubled as the local Post Office.

My letter to an outlandish name like Toorak caused no end of palaver as the postmistress tried estimating the correct rate to an address unimaginably far from rural England, until war broke out. A bygone age when a postcard to London had probably counted as the day's big event. Standing in line with sad-eyed housewives clutching their laboriously handwritten letters and occasional comforts parcels to sons and husbands on active duty, I saw just how scarce menfolk had become as the war ground on in France, and Italy, and Salonika, and Palestine, and Mesopotamia, and the Northwest Frontier of India.

Britain's womenfolk were doing their best to keep up appearances, but an observant outsider could tell that something had broken, and even when the authorities later tried to patch it up with post-war ceremonials and pompous platitudes, the break remained visible on local war memorials and in tens of thousands of empty fireside chairs.

I was ready to go when Grenville collected me late in the morning, the following Friday, no longer the tweedy squire but once more a senior officer of the Royal Engineers, the cherry red ribbon of a CB worn in pride of place above his tunic's left breast pocket.

I saluted smartly and returned his firm handshake as he ran an appraising eye over my appearance. "Looks like our country air and country fare have done you a power of good," he nodded approvingly. "I wish you could enjoy more, but it's maximum effort in Flanders. Home leaves are being cancelled left, right, centre. Ah, thank you, Matthew." He acknowledged the older man helping to load my kit on the back seat. "How did Mr Cribdon go?"

"As like 'e was born to it zirr," the flockmaster replied with a solemn nod. "Mark'ee they got p'culiar ideas where 'e come from, but 'em zeem t'work," he added grudgingly. I think this referred to the time I twitched a sagging fencepost, bushman style, by cutting a forked branch and using it to improvise a windlass.

"Good man. Now," he faced me, "it's time we were on our way."

I warmly shook Matthew's hand. His wife bobbed a curtsy and then, to everyone's surprise, gave me a big hug. "Do take care zirr! Come back safe!" This had nothing to do with the envelope containing a one pound note she would later find on her kitchen dresser, for I could hardly treat Grenville's staff less generously here, than I had at his family's Buckingham Street address.

Summer rain had fallen earlier in the day and the Austin's canvas roof was still clipped down tightly so there was no need to wear my flying helmet and goggles for the return trip to London. It also made the ride a lot quieter and allowed for some conversation as the miles rolled past.

"Did you find Grey useful?" He pitched his voice above the engine's rumble.

"Absolutely!" I replied. "Most days, more than enough for a feed. Out of the water, onto a twig, over the fire. Swaggy style."

"'Swaggy'?"

"Swagmen. Itinerant shearers. Humping their blanket roll from Queensland to Victoria. Following the seasons."

"What a marvellously virile breed you are," he chuckled. "I do so look forward to meeting them!"

"That's as maybe," I cautioned, not wishing to romance my people too much. "Just be aware that Swaggies can be quite fragrant in hot weather."

"No doubt," he agreed, "but when this war's over, those of us who've survived will no longer be troubled by body smells…"

"Any idea when that might be?" I queried, wondering if he had privileged access to Intelligence.

"It all depends."

"On what?"

"The rain."

I blinked, studying his profile for some trace of humour, but found none.

"This year's Big Push is laying the groundwork for next year's final offensive," he continued. "Messines proves we can do it. Our next target, Passchendaele Ridge. Trouble is," he added, a Sapper trained to think of subsoils and topography, "the Yser is marginal marshland at the best of times, even without shellfire churning up its drainage systems."

He paused, watching the road ahead as a rabbit dashed across from one patch of undergrowth to the next, before concluding: "Had it been my call, I'd have attacked in late winter, early springtime, while the ground was still frozen solid. Still, fingers crossed, this fine weather will hold sufficiently long for us to take the high ground and establish next winter's frontline…"

"Hence, 'maximum effort'?"

"Yes."

We fell silent, alone with our individual memories of the Western Front, and did not speak again until reaching Basingstoke and a pub with the intriguing name *Hammer & Tongs*, possibly the site of an old forge. Here we took a break over pints of Wartime Economy bitter ale and a plate of cold beef sandwiches, while keeping a close eye on our car in case a thief tried pinching the spare petrol tin strapped to its running board.

"I have no idea what awaits me at Horseferry Road," I began, after clearing my throat, "but from what you've said it won't be long before I'm back in France, so this may be the last opportunity to say how much I value all that you've done to make my stay in England an unexpectedly enjoyable experience…"

His eyebrows shot up. "Why 'unexpected'?"

"Well," I hesitated, "and please don't take this personally, but Englishmen have a certain reputation where I come from, and it's not always positive."

"With good reason," Grenville agreed with surprising candour, opening a sandwich to inspect how thinly the cook had contrived to slice a joint of rationed beef. "We can be pretty obnoxious among ourselves as well as in our dealings with others."

He glanced up again. "That's another reason why I find your company so refreshing. It's not often one can converse freely with an intelligent, objective outsider, secure in the knowledge that it will go no further."

"Oh?"

"You listen, you think, you say only as much as is necessary, as I first observed when preparing for the Selection Board" he continued. "These are rare qualities in a world that relishes scandal and gossip. They are even more rare when allied to broad knowledge and experiences such as you clearly possess. One can only conclude that Melbourne Grammar attracts some remarkably inspired schoolmasters..."

I acknowledged his compliment with a nod and let the matter drop.

104

We slowed to a halt at 130 Horseferry Road, AIF's London headquarters and clothing depot for muddy, bedraggled Diggers on leave from the trenches. A borderline slum in peacetime, though only a short walk from the Houses of Parliament and Westminster Abbey, nowadays it teemed with whores and pimps drawn like foxes to a hen coop by thousands of virile young men with accumulated pay in their pockets, and sufficient time to spend it unwisely before returning to problematical futures in Flanders and Picardy. The local Bobbies had pretty much given up on the horrible place and were glad to leave law enforcement to our MPs, ex-Sydney knuckle men, brutally effective with the truncheon and handcuffs.

Grenville joined me on the pavement. "I know it is bad form to speak of life after the war," he began simply, "but should you ever consider pursuing a career in England, do let me know." He trapped a dry cough in his clenched fist. "There are some splendid girls in the county. Well read, well bred, good families. I'll be delighted to make the, ah, introductions." We briefly shook hands. "Stay in touch."

"Thank you, sir," I replied with my best Brigade of Guards salute, the sort that quivers as it snaps over the right brow, determined to show a couple of gawping Diggers how such things are done properly. I detected a twinkle in Grenville's eye as he returned an equally crisp salute before driving off towards Woolwich.

AIF HQ was an old drill hall roughly partitioned into offices that opened onto a crowded central walkway. The first thing one noticed upon arrival at the Enquiries desk was the incessant clatter of typewriters churning out the orders, indents, and requisitions that a modern army needs to function as it burns through immense stockpiles of everything from bullets to bully beef, men to munitions. The typists were mostly English women, with a few expat' Australian girls doing a job that was a prized perk, given its opportunities to fraternise with eager, well-paid young men.

The desk itself was manned by a Chelsea Pensioner with a black tricorn hat, his red coat displaying a rich fruit salad of campaign ribbons. The first one - in yellow and crimson - commemorated his service as a bugle boy in the Second Opium War.

"'Ere you go. Sah!" I took the printed card and filled it in with my name, number, rank, and XIII Squadron RFC. He filed the card, stamped my papers, and pointed me through to an adjacent warehouse converted into a luggage store where soldiers could dump their kitbags. There was also an armoury to secure the troops' rifles and officers' side arms until their return to France.

Service revolvers were prized booty and more easily smuggled out for a backstreet deal than a Lee Enfield rifle, so I took the precaution of stowing my Webley in the rolled-up Sidcot that was itself stuffed into one of many hundreds of similar kitbags on the stacked shelves.

I kept my valise and went through to the Paymaster's before joining a slow queue of other men at the APO, in case there were any letters for me. I was in luck, but this congested hallway was never meant to be a reading room so I crossed Horseferry Road to the AIF's War Chest Club - funded by patriotic donations from Australia - to book a bunk for the night and find a quiet corner where I could catch up with news from home.

The top item in my packet was a buff-coloured notification that I was on embarkation leave and must report to Movements, every morning by 0900 hours, to learn if I was on the following day's Departures. In effect I might still be cooling my heels in London a week from now, or landing in France the day after tomorrow, depending on how badly things were going Over There.

David's letter ached with exhaustion. Our squadron's twin-seat RE8s were operating every flyable day, registering artillery fire, bombing railway junctions, strafing supply columns behind German lines. "Boocoo dicey stunts," even with scout escorts, of which there were never enough against the Huns' superior strength as the RFC's reconnaissance bombers fought their ways home from these daylight sorties. Weaving through ack-ack and ground fire. Under constant threat from above and behind. Losing ten, twenty knots of already limited ground speed to the prevailing westerly winds. Petrol tanks down to their last gallon, engines sucking fumes, ofttimes gliding the final stretch. Staring past a stationary propeller blade. Sweating a dead-stick landing inside the aerodrome's perimeter hedge, or not, depending upon how the dice were falling that day.

And yet, according to David, the official opinion of RE8 aircrews was that we were the airborne equivalent of delivery van drivers. Dull, unimaginative tradesmen less deserving of recognition than the top-scoring scout pilots in their nimble Sopwiths, idolised by popular newspapers and on the kinema screen. Not the most inspiring picture of what lay ahead, even if my oldest and dearest friend tried to lighten the mood by saying how much he looked forward to catching-up and matching-up, as he put it, with me in the back seat, himself in the front, and both of us bashing the Boche.

Aunt Lucinda's letter was a surprisingly lucid reply to my much earlier one informing her of the decision to dump Sandra, though not put so bluntly. In plain language she told me not to be a young fool, and that in affairs of this nature one must obey the heart's yearning not the head's warning, and although breaking-up is painful, the pleasures of making-up are sweet beyond measure. A point underscored by a restrained account of how she and Franz Liszt survived a furious clash of temperaments at Bad Neuenahr, after which he pursued her to Vienna where all was forgiven and forgotten midst showers of flowers, *et cetera*.

In my case I knew she was wrong! It was one thing for two celebrated performers to recover from a lovers' tiff, it was quite another matter for a prickly young Australian soldier to submit to the sneers of a belted earl and his toffy nosed family! David would have been icily polite with his Mary's people, but there was no way I could have kept my temper, despite the Icy nickname -!

Young Elspeth's letter was a welcome contrast as she thanked me lots and lots for showing her drawings of *Patch*, her Maltese terrier, to Mr Streeton and Mr Roberts. Both artists had written warm and encouraging comments that she was now applying to a more ambitious series of birds and animals in her parents' back garden. Meanwhile, Daddy was sending home lots and lots and lots of picture postcards from Egypt that she was scaling up and copying in poster colours, for the school's patriotic mural.

This left only one more envelope to open, addressed in an agonisingly familiar hand. Angered by its writer's disobedience, I furiously crushed the accursed thing in my fist and hurled it at a nearby rubbish bin, then strode off to the canteen's dining room where I found a vacant table in the officers' enclosure and gruffly ordered a ninepenny luncheon. I have no idea what it was except that it was warm enough and edible enough to shovel up and keep down.

The waitress cleared my table and asked if I wanted a cup of tea, one ha'penny extra if sweetened. I must have nodded for she tilted a stewed brew from the gallon pot of boiled bramble leaves on her trolley, stirred in a spoonful of beet syrup, and handed it over. "There you go sir."

"Uh." I barely noticed, drenched with grief as the emotional scar tissue, so painfully grown over my heart's bleeding wound, threatened to rip open again. It hardly mattered that I had refused to read what was inside Sandra Nobury's wretched envelope. The fact that it had been sent at all was cruel proof of her determination to keep tormenting me! The trouble was, unless I confronted my fears, I would be haunted by cowardice, during what remained of my life.

With extreme reluctance, and against my better judgment, I trod back to the rubbish bin, fished out her crumpled ball of paper and smacked it flat on a wooden tabletop. Cursing fluently under my breath, I stabbed a forefinger under the flap and plucked out her bloody, bloody, bloody note posted yesterday at VAD Headquarters:

Dear Ian.

Colleagues at King Edward's have kept me informed of your recovery, for which I am much relieved and glad.

You will soon be in France. If this note reaches you before then, please can we meet for dinner?

S.

The blasted woman would not stop pestering me! She even admitted to spying on my movements! Fortunately, I could pretend the letter got lost in the post, a common occurrence in wartime, but something in her gentle entreaty prevented such a vile, deceitful act. One I could not live with, no matter how brief this must be at a time when the Flying Corps' aircrew attrition rate was nearly fifty percent per fortnight.

Resolved to have it out with her, once and for all, I left the Club; declined the company of a whey-faced girl with too much rouge and not enough clothing under her garish, harlequin kimono coat; and dodged through the traffic, back to AIF Headquarters' Post & Telegraph office.

A quick flick through the *London Telegraphic Directory* revealed the Voluntary Aid Detachment's code - Voladlund – that I pencilled on a blank form before adding, in firm block letters,

CRITERION 1900HRS TONIGHT IC

Honour was satisfied. With any luck the telegram would not reach her in time, I told myself as I got ready for this evening's brief encounter, just in case it was delivered and read. Rather than unpacking the Saville Row dress uniform, worn for our previous meeting at the Criterion, I signalled my extreme displeasure by not changing out of my baggy serge Norfolk jacket, cord breeches, coarse woollen puttees, and beetle crusher boots - there being no need for a topcoat at this end of a warm summer's day - before leaving the War Chest Club and hailing a taxi by raising my cane.

"Where to mite?" the Cockney driver grinned with what he imagined was an Aussie accent, anticipating a generous tip for delivering me to a better class of brothel than this grimy corner of Westminster had to offer.

"The Criterion. Piccadilly."

"Good-o bonza!"

I slumped on the seat, careful not to let any small change roll out of my pockets and into the cunningly contrived gap between the cushion and backrest, and silently cursed my weakness; I should have left her bloody letter in the bloody rubbish bin -!

Now, assuming she got my signal in time, I'd be stuck with her company, and all the emotional barricades raised during the past months might not be high enough, or strong enough, to keep her at a safe distance. I might yet find myself saying, or worse, doing something incredibly stupid and pointless -!

"'Ere you go Cobber," the driver announced with another linguistic flourish.

I paid off the taximeter; added a modest tip for trying to make an overseas visitor feel welcome, suggested he shout an occasional "Coo-ee!" to attract more Australian customers, and entered the Criterion's rotating glass door, exiting left towards the Ladies' Lounge.

I was deliberately early so I could later tell myself, with a clear conscience, that I had hung around until seven o'clock before nipping off to the Anzac Buffet for a hot meal, a game of billiards, and -

"Hello." She put aside the *Country Life* and stood to greet me with a formal handshake.

"Hello." I was shocked by her changed appearance. The cheeks were drawn and there was a haunted look, around the eyes, that I had seen on other faces in the trenches. Her grey uniform frock and frumpy pillar-box cap only made matters worse. "Thank you for coming. Would you mind awfully if we went somewhere else?" she continued. "I've seen the menu and it's not very good tonight."

"Sure. Whatever."

We went out into the street and waited for either a vacant motor taxi or one of the resurrected Hansom cabs to growl around the Shaftesbury Memorial Fountain - incorrectly called the Statue of Eros - and pass within hailing distance.

"I hope you are keeping well."

"Not too bad."

"Varicella, wasn't it?"

"Chickenpox."

"I'm sorry. It must've been very uncomfortable."

"No need. I've got over it."

"You're on embarkation leave, are you not?"

"Yes. Notified today. I'll soon be gone."

"I, I've never been up in an aeroplane." She was struggling to make conversation with a grimly unresponsive young man. "What's it like?"

"Cold. Draughty. Deafening."

"But it must be wonderful to see the clouds so close?" she persisted.

"Depends. Cumulus, not bad, till you lose sight of the ground."

"That must be, frightening?"

"I've known worse." I broke off, stepped forward, stuck two fingers in my mouth, and let fly with a shrill whistle. "Oy -!'"

The cabby hauled reins, iron horseshoes skidding to a halt on Piccadilly Circus' wooden paving blocks. "Where to Guv?!"

"Ask her." I held the cab's flap door open for Sandra to go first, after she had given the address of her preferred restaurant, by the sound of it somewhere in Mayfair. Fortunately, I had plenty of cash after drawing my accumulated pay, and there were several hundred pounds in my personal account, so I was good to go for whatever two meals were going to sting me this evening.

There is not much spare room in a Hansom. This can be wonderful on occasions like Maeve's amazing kisses after the ballroom competition at Oddfellows' Hall, but not now as Sandra and I sat in our respective corners, me facing away from her, watching the passing scene. When she was ready to talk, I was ready to listen, until then I preferred my own company.

We left London's café district and clip-clopped into the increasingly privileged area beyond Hyde Park. The way I read it; she was planning to give me a hard time at one of those posh supper clubs where a glass of cheap fizz costs as much as a bottle of top-shelf champagne elsewhere.

How a baggy-arsed Digger was going to fit into their dress code was not for me to say, or care about, as our cab's tired old nag shambled to a halt at an anonymous, black-lacquered door, its brass furniture kept parade ground bright by the club servants in what must have once been a patrician's town house.

I hopped down, gave the driver some silver, told him to keep the change and go easy with poor old Dobbin, then looked around, fists on hips, getting my bearings in a twilight made longer by British Summer Time, recently introduced to conserve coal for industry, and so that farm labourers could work more daylight hours per day.

Berkeley Square was not unlike the Place des Vosges I would sketch in Paris, years later, absent the Henri Quatre colonnade and fashionable boutiques. Instead, a plain wooden fence – the original iron railings had been cut up and carted away to make munitions early in the war – were keeping the common herd at a distance.

"Come along. We'll be late."

"What for?"

"Dinner."

Curious to see how her vengeful stunt would play out in the next minute or so, I followed under the club's replacement wooden archway with its as-yet unlit oil lamp and tramped up a short flight of granite steps.

The servants were evidently under orders to keep a sharp eye open for mug punters; my escort didn't even need to knock before the door swung open and a maid bobbed a curtsy. "Good evening m'lady."

"Good evening, Doris." Then, turning to me: "Come along."

The maid relieved me of my slouch hat as I entered the rummiest supper club imaginable, my boots echoing on waxed timber flooring. The management had contrived to theme their business with all the casual trappings of an authentic aristocratic residence and had clearly paid a packet for a pair of reproduction Gainsborough portraits in the vestibule.

These were brilliant copies of an eighteenth-century couple - he in military scarlet with the blue ribbon of the Garter across his chest, she in the height of fashion for her time and place in Society - I realised, pausing to take a closer look at their masterly brushwork and convincing *craquelure*. "Strewth! They're as good as the originals…"

"How reassuring," Sandra observed, without breaking step. Lost in admiration of the anonymous copyist's skill, I followed her into the club's dining room, only to find that it was not. Instead of attentive waiters, poised to kick me out, only three persons were present as my sketchers' eye froze the scene.

Centre: a tall, middle-aged man, clean-shaven, neatly trimmed hair, white-tie dinner suit and cream piqué waistcoat. Right: a strikingly handsome woman of about the same age, hair *a la grecque*, grey silk evening gown, single rope of pearls. Left: a fresh-faced young fellow in uniform, captain's pips on tailored cuffs, Royal Dublin Fusiliers' collar badges -

Sandra laid a restraining hand on my clenched fist. "Pa'. This is Ian."

The Earl of Nobury, a disguised title of course, gave me a most cordial smile and advanced to shake hands. "Thank you for coming, Mr Cribdon. This is a pleasure I have long anticipated. Ever since our daughter began speaking of you."

My jaw dropped. My fist relaxed. My shoulders straightened as I found myself responding to a firm, dry, welcoming handclasp.

"Permit me to present my wife, Claire."

"Ma'am." The deportment lessons at Madame Jourdan's, in South Yarra, were much in evidence as I bowed.

"And our son, James."

"Sir." I stiffened to attention.

"Oh, come off it!" Sandra's brother grinned, open hand thrust forward. "*En famille* it's Jim. And yours?"

I blinked, baffled, bewildered. "In the battalion, it's Icy. Otherwise, Ian. Plain, unadorned Ian."

"May I call you that?"

"If you wish."

"We'll have ample time to become better acquainted later," Lord Nobury intervened with a charming, unaffected smile much like the one that stole my heart when I first saw his eldest daughter emptying bedpans and cheerfully wiping soiled bottoms in a stinkingly hot Egyptian hospital ward. "Dinner is about to be served, so if you wish to rinse your hands, I'm sure Sandra will show you the way..."

She led me to a white painted door similar in shape and appearance to the Sick Room's at Tralee House, only this one opened into a somewhat dated Victorian lavatory, in the original sense of a place to wash and spruce up, with polished copper piping and ornate, polychrome glazed tiles. I had no need to brush my hair, having chosen to keep it cropped short under a steel helmet, but the face certainly needed a refreshing splash. I ran cold water, bent over the basin, then straightened and reached for a linen towel while examining my image in the mirror, Sandra standing behind me in the doorway as I addressed her reflection. "Why?!"

"You mean, why did I entice you here?"

"Yes!"

"Would you have come, had you known?"

"Oh, for pity's sake!" I snapped, turning to face her. "I don't need any more distress! Look at me! A knockabout Digger who will never belong in surroundings like these -!"

"I am looking at you," she interrupted firmly, "and what I'm seeing I admire more than ever." Then, turning away, she led me into a pleasantly intimate family dining room – I later found a grander formal reception area upstairs – and took our places; the Earl seated at the head of the table, facing the

465

Countess at the other end, his son and heir on the right hand, myself, and the Lady Sandra on his left.

The eldest of we three men closed his eyes, head bowed. "O most gracious God. Bless our family and friends that they might be safe in these times of great peril. Protect our monarch and nation and keep us ever mindful of our duty to serve others, for the greater glory of Your Son, Jesus Christ. Amen."

Romantic novels and boys' adventure stories, in Australia, had led me believe that British nobles only dined off haunches of venison served on gold plate. Well, maybe once, but not in this household and certainly not in wartime. Their potato and onion soup was delicious but well within a civilian's scale of rations. Apparently, it was a great favourite at Buckingham Palace where His Majesty insisted that he and Queen Mary were issued the same basic food allowance as their subjects.

The other surprise was just how relaxed my dinner companions were when not on public display. This was made very evident by the little jokes and pet names as our conversation ebbed and flowed, the others always making sure to include me by asking my opinion on a wide range of topics, listening intently when I replied, after weighing the pros and cons of whatever was under discussion.

By the time our main course was served – cauliflower and bean casserole with a few ounces of meat to make the gravy – I was starting to feel more at ease, given my secret fears and insecurities. True, it flattered me that a man of superior rank and birth was finding it hard to keep his eyes off the Winged-O and DCM worn below it. James' tunic was bare except for a red-white-blue ribbon of the recently gazetted 1914 Star, although he had been fighting in France, on and off since first leading his men into battle during their epic fight at Mons. A noble's son evidently no longer qualified for an automatic decoration in today's British Army.

The war was only mentioned once and that was when Lord Nobury asked his son a veiled question about the Dubsters' morale, and whether they had settled down after last year's rebellion in their home city? I had read about the Dublin Easter Uprising in the Egyptian newspapers and had a fair idea what he was referring to when the younger man replied that his Fusileers were in good heart, all things considered.

His father frowned at such lack of confidence, whereupon Jim elaborated with something rather surprising and prophetic: "When the war's finished, we're finished." Questioned further, he raised the spectre of demobilised Irish veterans joining the Fenians to establish a republic and attack the Six Counties, by which he meant the Protestant Ulstermen of Northern Ireland, who were themselves grim fighters on the Western Front, a prospect fraught with bad choices and worse outcomes.

"There's no putting the Independence genii back in the bottle after last year's botched business," the younger man concluded sombrely. "This is our Twilight of the Gods, our Götterdämmerung as Sis' would say," he added, with an enquiring glance in Sandra's direction.

I am certain that Lord Nobury did not approve of such talk at his dinner table, or of the reference to his eldest daughter's former plans to study German Language & Literature in Berlin, but was too courteous to pursue the matter while a guest was present,

The bread-and-butter pudding lightened our mood. Cook had saved her stale crusts for such a special occasion, though instead of butter she'd used margarine, and instead of imported currants or raisins, the dish was layered with rings of dried, homegrown apple sweetened with dabs of honey.

Recalling this moment in history, long ago now, I wonder if Frances will understand my obsession with food if I try to explain it? Probably not, familiar as she must be with superior markets – as I believe they are called - laden with colourful tins and boxes and packets of exotic edibles from every corner of the globe.

Two housemaids cleared the table while we proceeded to the withdrawing room where, in the custom of the time, we took a dish of tea and resumed our conversation. Neither Lord Nobury nor his son was a smoker, unusual for men of their day, and I was not yet a nicotine addict so there was no need to leave the ladies.

The Countess, Lady Nobury, had remained quietly observant throughout all this, scrutinising my every word and gesture, for she was without doubt a formidable *grande dame* behind her gracious exterior.

"Mr Cribdon" she smiled, just enough to keep me at ease, "Sandra tells me that you have worked in the 'Outback' of Australia?" She pronounced our name correctly.

"Yes ma'am."

"Please correct me if I'm wrong, but are not the distances immense?"

"Yes, they are," I agreed. "Five hundred miles between Nothing Much and Even Less is not unusual," I added, risking a whiff of laconic Aussie humour.

"Astonishing." She leaned forward. "So, what happens if you fall ill, or one of your workers is injured, and you are far from a St John's dispensary?"

I weighed a several options before choosing one to reply: "There's usually a medicine chest in our kit. But if the problem can't be fixed, and the patient is still alive, we'll try to get him or her back to an AIM bush hospital."

"'Her'?" she frowned. "There are injured women in the 'Outback'?"

"Some." I hesitated before elaborating with an edited account of Topsy's journey to Menzies.

"Good Lord -!" the Earl exclaimed as I finished on a suitably modest note.

"Lionel?" his wife interjected firmly. "We must do something about this."

"Yes, of course m'dear, but dashed if I can see what!"

"Think positively," she commanded. "It is fortuitous that Ian is in the Flying Corps. There is an obvious connection between aeroplanes and casualty evacuation. Why, only the other day I saw in *Daily Graphic* how we are using them for this very purpose in Palestine," she continued. "If one had been available at Mount Cedric, that poor girl would have been spared her terrible ordeal, and instead of six days on a camel cart would have been in hospital within the hour!"

Events would soon erase this chance remark, and much else besides, but there was no way that John Flynn - founder of the Australian Inland Mission - would have known how an Anglo-Irish noblewoman foretold his Royal Flying Doctor Service by more than a decade.

It was getting late, and I had to be at Movements by 0900 hours tomorrow or risk being charged with going AWOL. The Earl shared my concern and said he would make a phone call from his study.

He returned a few minutes later, during which time Sandra spoke with her mother while her brother and I compared experiences of war in France. "You may relax," his lordship smiled. "They're not expecting you tomorrow. Our home is yours for the night."

105

My protests were politely brushed aside, and Sandra's brother showed me to a guest room, with its own shower cubicle and toiletries cabinet, not unlike the one at Grenville's town house overlooking Embankment Gardens. "Sleep well old chap."

"Thanks. You, likewise." I shut the door and stood, back hard against it, surveying my latest roost in a stranger's house.

If only I'd had the gumption to destroy Sandra's letter, unread, I would not have fallen so easily into her trap! But there was still time to escape by knotting bed sheets, hopping through the window, and hitting Berkeley Square on the run; I'd memorised the route and reckoned I could reach the War Chest Club before it shut at 2359 hours -!

Ashamed to have even considered such a bizarre plan, I stripped and folded my uniform on the dressing stool, dipped clove oil toothpowder on a damp finger and rubbed it around my mouth and gums. That done, I sorted through a drawer of freshly laundered nightwear; thus far all I seem to have done in English homes was dress in others' clothing, I thought without humour, trying on a pair of striped flannel pyjamas that resembled prison garb.

The summer night was still warm as I switched off the overhead electric light and lay on top of the sheets, staring up at a darkened ceiling. My room's blackout curtains stopped pale gaslight entering from the Square's shielded kerb lamps two storeys below, much as they were keeping the household's brighter lights contained within.

These and other Air Raid Precautions were strictly enforced, even though the Thames ran straight through the heart of London, a silvery target marker for Zeppelin navigators on even the darkest of nights. The only beneficiaries from blackout regulations, that I could see, were the manufacturers of white paint needed to mark edged pavements, lamp poles, and other trip hazards.

Sleep was difficult. Sandra's presence, a few paces down the corridor was, disturbing. The poor darling had looked so worn and subdued at dinner. She had seen too much, smelt too much, felt too much on the hospital ships and trains. Battle fatigue was no longer confined to we men on the frontline.

More than anything else in the world I yearned to comfort her, as she had comforted me in my darkest moments, but that was unthinkable under her parents' roof. Dangerous, too, for my determination to escape immediately after breakfast and be on the way to France as soon as –

There was a hesitant tap at the door. My heart skipped a beat as I padded across to see who was there. "Yes!"

"Good, you're awake," her brother replied quietly, "may I come in?"

I answered by switching on the light, opening the door, and stepping aside. "What's the problem?"

"I need your advice."

I cleared the dressing stool, so he could sit down, and perched myself on the end of the bed. "Shoot."

"I'm putting my hand up for the Flying Corps. Pa's not happy and wants me to go on the Staff; only son and heir, and all that rot." His laugh failed to convince me. "Perhaps you could have a word? Tell him what it's really like, and put his mind at rest?"

"Are you asking the right bloke?" I replied cautiously. "I'm only a 'One Wing Wonder,' and newly fledged at that. You need someone with more experience."

"Well, couldn't you at least try?"

"I could, maybe, perhaps string a few words together if you arranged an opportunity, before I take off in the morning," I replied with even greater caution, "but why the Flying Corps?"

"I've had a gutful of the trenches, and the air above them looks, clean."

"Understandable. Anything else?"

"That's it. Though of course," he added, quickly, "I must do-my-bit."

He was lying to me and fooling himself. Something in his manner reminded me of Frank Laurie's thirst for fame and medals, only to be killed before he even got started. Not that I blamed James for wanting to get out of the PBI - Poor Bastard Infantry – but I felt equally sure the RFC was not the right billet for the next Earl of Nobury as I reached for my tunic and took out David's most recent letter. "This's from my best mate, a pilot on XIII Squadron. Read it. Make your own mind up."

"Thank you!" His eager smile faded long before he returned the letter. "'Boocoo dicey stunts' indeed."

"Still keen?"

"Ye-es."

"Right-o, fix the meeting and I'll tell your dad what I've learned thus far, then you'll both have some idea of what's at stake."

"Thanks, it's awfully decent of you -"

"No, it's bloody stupid of me." I contradicted, replacing David's letter in my tunic pocket. "You've done your bit longer than most. The experience gained makes you of greater value alive, on the Staff, than you will ever be, smashed to bits or burnt to a cinder."

"But I've nothing to show for it!"

"Listen mate. You're still breathing; millions are not. That is one hell of an achievement."

"You don't understand – !"

"My bloody oath I do!"

"How?!"

"That's none of your business."

He blinked, unaccustomed to plain speech from a stranger, then began smiling again. "I'm not surprised that Sis' is so fond of you. It's rare to meet such a straight man. I-I don't know how to put this, more tactfully, but I do hope you both, somehow, find a way of staying together…?"

"Not a snowflake's chance in Hell."

"But why not?!"

"Strictly speaking, that is also none of your business." I paused, trying to suppress the turmoil inside my chest. "It would be different if Sandra were my sort. The Battalion Chaplain would've done the deed in Alex', quick smart. But she's not my sort, and I'm not her sort, so that's an end to the matter."

"But can't you -?"

"No." I could have been addressing a dim recruit. "She has duties and obligations I can never match or ever want to. I know who I am, what I am, and where I fit into the greater scheme of things. None of which includes rah-rah-rahing around Town in a frock coat and pinstripes, sporting a monocle and spats."

"Steady on!" James snapped me a frosty glare. "I take grave exception to the cartoon caricature of what you think we are!"

"Good. It'll make it easier to part in the morning. Now, I need to get my zeds," Digger speak for a cartoonist's Z-Z-Z thought bubbles when depicting someone asleep. "G'night."

106

"I've arranged things with Pa'," James said as we went through to breakfast the next morning. "There's a Cabinet meeting at Number Ten but he can spare us a few minutes."

"I won't waffle. 'Stand up, speak up, shut up.'"

"Thank you."

"No, thank you. It's the least I can do for so much kindness. Speaking of which," I continued, taking my place at the table and noticing the empty chair beside me, "where's Sandra?"

"She's not feeling well."

"Hardly surprising," I thought aloud, passing a spoon through my bowl of unsweetened porridge, "given what she's seen and done..."

We were the only ones present this morning, the Countess preferring to take breakfast upstairs, to discuss the day's household arrangements while her husband got ready for Downing Street.

"You have a blackboard?" I asked, putting my spoon aside for a moment.

"Yes, I think so, in the nursery, upstairs."

"Any chance of borrowing it for ten minutes?"

"It is ours."

"Of course, not thinking straight. Too much rattling around the old bone box." I rapped knuckles on forehead and tried to laugh.

James summoned a maid, gave instructions, and looked back at me. "You are serious? About leaving today?'

"There's a war to win and they can't do it without me," I joked, striving to lighten the mood. "Besides, a good guest knows when it's time to go or, as my great-aunt, a notable performer in her day was wont to remind me: ''Tis better to exit the stage five seconds early, while your public is still shouting 'More!' than to linger one moment longer, when their ardour begins to cool...'"

"Is that how you see us?" he frowned. "As an audience?"

"'All the world's a stage,'" I reminded him, "'and one man in his time plays many parts.' Sometimes it's Fearless Freddy the hero; ofttimes it's Sir Jasper Grasper the villain."

"And who are you playing today?" Sandra's brother persisted with a shrewd sideways glance.

I hesitated before replying awkwardly. "I'm Pierrot, the mute outsider in *la commedia dell'arte*. Condemned by fate to love his Columbine from afar..."

Her brother slowly, wonderingly, shook his head. "You really are a most complex, erudite man! And we used to think of Australians as, well, a bit rough around the edges -"

"Not all." I spread War Economy plum flavoured apple pulp on my piece of toast. "Some of us were house-trained as puppies and no longer chew slippers or piss on the drawing room carpet." I glanced up. "Ah, thanks Luv, put it over there by the wall. And you brought chalk and duster too?" I smiled at the housemaid. "Good thinking."

"Fank'ew'ser!" And with a hurried curtsy she fled, overwhelmed by a simple compliment, nearly colliding in the doorway with Lord Nobury clad in sober dark grey for his ministerial duties.

James and I stood and spoke together. "Good morning, sir."

"Good morning gentlemen." He consulted his watch and returned it to the fob pocket before looking my way. "I believe you have something to tell us?"

"Yes." I motioned him towards a vacant seat from which to see the blackboard I was standing beside. "Aircrew duties are unevenly shared between pilots and observer/air gunners," I began without preamble. "I shall briefly detail their individual tasks before examining their combined duties, in the air and on the ground. Concluding with an assessment of the current situation, as seen from one man's necessarily subjective viewpoint."

It felt natural to slip back into my weapons instructor's role. The current and next Lords Nobury could have been recruits learning to strip a Lewis gun though today I was detailing the required steps for service in the Royal Flying Corps, towards the end of which I became aware of another person in the room as I wrapped-up with the usual: "Any questions?"

The elder Nobury shook his head. "None. I only wish our Cabinet meetings were as concise and productive. What about you, m'boy?"

"It looks like quite a challenge."

"Indeed!" James' father turned to me. "Now. We'll be seeing you at dinner?"

"No sir. I must get going. You've all been very kind, but my kit is at the War Chest, and there're things to sort at AIF HQ before joining the squadron." I was lying through my teeth. In truth, I was desperate to escape before my resolve weakened any further.

"Pity that." Her father reached out his hand. "Well, it's been a pleasure meeting you, Mr Cribdon. Do please call again, next time you're in Town."

"Thank you, sir." I returned the handshake. His was a most generous invitation but one I had no intention of accepting as he and his son left the room, deep in conversation.

I rubbed the blackboard clean and put everything back in its place as Sandra approached with hesitant steps. "I am." She cleared her throat and tried again. "I am, sorry you're leaving. I did so hope, we might spend. A little time, together?"

Thus far I had managed to avoid looking at her directly but something in her pleading tone made me turn and never have I seen such heartbreak in another's eyes. A leaden groan welled up from my innermost depths as I slumped on the nearest chair and sobbed scalding tears of bitter remorse. Without another word, she sat down beside me and cradled my head in her lap, as if we were back on Ward O-6.

I think I heard a maid enter the room and leave quickly. Time passed before I was able to sit up straight again. "Sorry. Bad form."

"There's no need to be. I, I'm glad you still care –"

"Care?! Jesus Bloody Christ I have never stopped caring! That's what makes all this so bloody, bloody hard!" I blubbed.

"Can't we, just enjoy, today?" she asked softly, stroking my cheek now. "The army's not expecting you yet."

"You don't understand!" I exclaimed, wiping my eyes. "It's not that easy!"

"Then let us try understanding together." She wiped away her own tears. "Do you remember me once saying, how much I'd love, to show you Hyde Park? And go boating, on the Serpentine?"

"Yes! Vividly."

"Then why don't we 'give it a go'? Just you and me together...?"

I nodded in dumb agreement, and she hurried upstairs, returning a few minutes later, changed back into uniform, not wishing to be seen as a soldier's pickup but as his equal in service, and joined me at the by now authentic Gainsboroughs. Exchanging shy, excited smiles, we stepped out into the cloudless perfection of a sunny morning.

"This way." She led diagonally across Berkeley Square's shady little park to where it intersects with Fitzmaurice Place and Charles Street, down which we turned, strolling side by side through the heart of Mayfair, overlooked by other nobles' town houses, clubs, and private banks.

For once it was I who had to salute first as splendidly tailored majors, colonels, and above emerged from their homes or paid off taxis. Their looks of frosty disapproval amused us greatly as a one pip lieutenant, in baggy Australian serge the colour of stale pea soup, a strikingly beautiful VAD on his left arm as if supporting a convalescent patient, acknowledged their presence with the relaxed wave for which we were notorious in pukka British military circles.

Sandra turned left into Chesterfield Street, shortly afterwards turning hard right into Curzon Street before finally arriving at Park Lane which, as the name suggests, marked the end of bricks and mortar and the start of a royal park, or did until recently.

Any hope we had of finding a quiet place to be alone was dashed, now that lumberjacks of the Canadian Forestry Corps were logging Hyde Park for the war effort, closely followed by units of the Women's Land Army hoeing and weeding vegetable gardens on the newly cleared ground.

A searchlight aimed skywards from scaffolding astride the arch at Hyde Park Corner a short distance away. The arch itself was draped with power cables from the electrical generator on a converted bus chassis and hung with telephone lines connecting a sandbagged bunker to Anti-Aircraft Command at the War Office in Whitehall. A web of similar wires radiated across the park, linking batteries of ack-ack guns mounted on six-wheeled trailers, one of which was parked close to the bandstand we were strolling towards.

"This is not what I hoped for." Sandra slowed to view what was once London's most popular pleasure ground.

As if trying to revive that time of peace and plenty, a scratch team of military bandsmen was doing its best to cheer up a clump of glum civilians while, a few yards away, gunners of the Royal Artillery racked shells, ready for the next daylight attack by *Gotha* bombers, menacingly large twin-engine biplanes that earlier in the week had killed or wounded five hundred East Enders in a bungled raid on Woolwich Arsenal.

"Listen!" I raised a finger to catch her attention. "That's our song." The band's medley of tunes from *Chu Chin Chow* had reached *Any Time Is Kissing Time*, played as a waltz. A gammy right leg meant I would never again be as spry on a ballroom floor as once I'd been, but this was no reason not to give it a go now. "M'lady?" I made an elaborate bow, my slouch hat sweeping the ground before her, as if it were a courtier's plumed headgear from a more gracious age. "Pray grant your humble admirer the honour of this dance!"

"What -?"

Arm around slim waist, I walked her into the one-two-three, one-two-three, one-two-three waltz time, increasing its tempo as she got the rhythm and gave me a most enchanting smile. Then, as if we were hero and heroine of a Regency romance by Elinor Glyn, the popular lady novelist, she entered the spirit of our private game: "Fie, Mr Cribdon, you are too forward! You ravish my senses! O Sir! I tremble for my virtue ...!"

We burst out laughing with all the spontaneous joy of young love, to such an extent that neither of us paid heed to the applause as a crowd of pale, shabby, wartime Londoners forgot their troubles and clapped an anonymous Digger and his nurse tripping the light fantastic while the bandmaster quickened his beat to match our steps.

We slowed to a stop. I removed my hat again and, with another flourish, bowed to my partner who replied with the full curtsy of a debutante presenting herself to the King. Then, hand in hand, we skipped away towards the Serpentine's lakeside café as our band struck-up *He's a Jolly Good Fellow!*

"You dance extremely well Darling!" Her eyes were still sparkling when I brought over our tray from the cash register, gingerly balancing two cups of coarse black tea and a couple of slices of doughy seedcake. "Where did you learn?"

"Madame Jourdan's in South Yarra. Why?"

"Because it is further evidence of that unknown world I shall explore with you, and every time we make a new discovery, enter it in the journal of our adventures together."

"You are, serious?"

"Oh yes," she smiled. "Very."

I was tormented by conflicting discoveries of my own. On the one hand, David's crushing humiliation by a Scottish nobleman's family, and Grenville's dire warning about marriage above one's station in life; on the other hand, Sandra's wondrous warmth, and wit, intellect, and kindness. Mine for the taking, mine for the keeping. If only I dared, if only I could!

We finished our snack in companionable silence and continued strolling along the lakeside path, hand in hand, towards a boat pen where, for one shilling and a small deposit, an attendant shoved us off on our own make-believe voyage of discovery around the Serpentine.

Sandra sat in the stern, smiling to herself, fingers lightly trailing in the greenish water as we splashed along, for I was a hopeless rower. "Do you remember when we nearly went boating on Mareotis, in Alex'...?"

"Cheeky!" I grinned back, missing my stroke as one oar blade dug water while the other skimmed rippling wavelets.

"I never imagined that any woman could feel so fulfilled, so complete as I felt, that first morning," she smiled. "And do you remember what you told me, our last evening at *Chez Adorable*...?"

"What?" I frowned.

"'Nothing less than a lifelong future together will do, for my only wish, desire, ambition is to be your loyal and loving husband, the father of your children, the guardian unto death, of our family...'" She paused before continuing in a much quieter tone. "My only wish, desire, ambition is to be your loyal and loving wife. The mother of your children. The protectrix unto death, of our family..."

"Stop!" I let go the oars and stared at the inch or so of water slopping around my boots. "You ask, too much!"

"No, I don't," she disagreed firmly. "This is the twentieth century. A modern woman no longer must wait for the man of her choice to go down on bended knee and beg for her hand in marriage!"

"You don't get it!" I despairingly looked up again "We can't."

"Is it my family?" she frowned. "Do you still think of us as pinstriped fools in frock coats, monocles, and spats, rah-rah-rahing around Town?"

"No. You. They. Embody every kindness, a man, could want."

"Then what's your problem?"

My tongue froze, my guts felt as if they were about to drop. Pope's Hill, Pozières, Mouquet Farm were as nothing compared with what I must now do. Summoning up every remaining scrap of courage I looked her full in the face. "I lied to you."

"O God, you are already married."

"No. Worse."

"What?"

"My people were not tea planters."

"Uh?!"

Hesitantly, sparing no sordid detail, I told of Maggie Stubbs' murder; of "Champagne Charley" Braithwaite's trial and execution; of my life on the streets; of the shame heaped upon me at Corunna Downs; of my rescue by a bogus great-aunt. "So now you understand, why there can be no future, for us," I concluded sadly. "And why, though it hurt like hell, I had to say those things and do those things, to stop you making a terrible mistake..."

She looked away into the middle-distance as our boat continued drifting until gently nosing to a halt in a reedbed, only then did she look back. "Thank you. This explains everything."

"No. Thank you. I have never told anyone else, nor ever shall. Our days and nights, together, were luminous, and beautiful, beyond compare. I only ask, in years to come, if I come to mind, you won't judge me, too harshly?"

Smiling now, she shook her head in mock dismay. "Ian Cribdon, my dear, dear husband, for such an intelligent and worldly man, there are times when you can be astonishingly slow on the uptake..."

107

Young and ardent, my first thoughts were of how quickly we could get a Special Licence - very popular with soldiers needing to marry while on leave - as Sandra and I began walking back through the park towards Mayfair.

Not that anyone's paperwork or stamp of approval were needed except for appearance' sake. In a single breath we had become husband and wife in that little rowing boat, each pledged to the other for eternity. And the strangest thing was our shared belief that we had been together before, in ages past. And for the first time in this life, I also felt fulfilled and complete.

"It's not that simple," she cautioned with a knowing smile when I mentioned the Special Licence. "I still have a few more weeks aboard *Winchelsea* before taking up a training appointment at Clerkenwell."

"Can't you cut it short? God knows you've done enough already!"

"Would you shirk your duties?" she frowned. "No. I thought not. Besides, before our engagement can be formally announced in the *Times*, family and friends must be told, and sufficient notice given to secure the Guards' Chapel. And, of course, I must first ask His Majesty's permission."

"Say again?" I blinked.

"I am His godchild," she replied as if this were an everyday event. "It would be disloyal as well as discourteous to announce my marriage without informing the Palace beforehand."

"Phew...!"

"Don't worry Darling," she raised my fist to her lips, "He's a sweetie. The Queen is another matter," she added, "still a very *Korrekt* German princess. The war can't be easy for her, with so many kinsmen fighting on the other side..." Neither of us had any inkling that King George was about to change his patronymic from Saxe-Coburg-Gotha to the politically less dangerous family name of Windsor.

"So, when do you think we can get on with the job?"

"As soon as Pa' arranges the details."

"Speaking of whom, how do you think he'll take the news...?"

"That, my dear, is something you must find out for yourself," she replied with a mischievous wink.

"Thanks a lot!"

We eventually arrived back at Berkeley Square half an hour before dinner. I gave my hat to Doris the maid just as Lord Nobury strode across the hallway, about to take his red despatch box upstairs. "Ah, you decided to stay after all. Splendid!"

"Thank you, sir. Um, there's something I wish to ask, when it's convenient."

"Of course. No time like the present. Come along."

I followed upstairs to the second-floor landing and His Lordship's study, a spacious, room with long sash windows – not unlike those in the Macquarie Club's library, now I come to think of it - overlooking Berkeley Square's miniature parkland.

"Those ancient plane trees, down there, are my assurance that all goes well in the World of Nature, even as the suicidal World of Man goes stark raving mad," he mused aloud, standing at the window, arms folded, lost in thought.

I used the opportunity to read the room for clues that might help me better understand the grandee who could be about to become my father-in-law. The many hundreds of books appeared to be well-read volumes, not decorative shelf fillers. The official papers and red despatch box on his desk told of a man engaged in high matters of state. The silver-framed family photographs spoke of a happy homelife and –

He turned around, as if reading my mind. "'Recognise anyone else in here?"

"Sir?"

"Look over to your left."

I shifted and realised that I was standing near the only oil portrait in his study. Signed Thos. Lawrence PRA, it depicted a young woman of the late Regency Period, clad in an Arabian gold, green, and crimson *abaya* cloak, a jewelled turban and peacock's feather on her beautiful head.

"Well, I'll be -!" I checked my tongue. But for the paint's obvious age, I could have sworn that Sandra had posed for her portrait after being fitted out by a theatrical costumer. "Incredible. Who is she?"

"The more interesting of my grandmothers," he replied, joining me as I admired this former President of the Royal Academy's bravura brushwork and rich palette of oil colours. "One could say she is the reason why my wife and I have always understood, if not always approved of, our daughter's independent spirit.

"As for the Lady Caroline, her father was governor of Gibraltar. I suppose its proximity to North Africa – on a clear day one can see Morocco across the Straits – fired her enthusiasm for all things Oriental. To which end, while still hardly more than a girl, she scandalised Society by eloping with the skipper of a brig smuggling contraband hither and thither around the Mediterranean.

"After sundry adventures she returned to England, married Sir Andrew Fyffe the banker, for whom this portrait was painted. Sadly, he was killed a couple of years later when his carriage overturned on the Brighton Road. His untimely death left Lady Fyffe a wealthy widow, free to resume her travels of the Syria and Turkey where she learned Arabic sufficiently well to transcribe the more exotic, frankly erotic *Tales of One Thousand and One Nights,* decades before Burton's unexpurgated edition. It was then she met and married the First Secretary of our embassy in Constantinople, dying there while giving birth to my mother who, in the fullness of time, wed George Augustus, the Fourth Earl."

"I am saddened to learn of it." And I was.

"Yes. A great loss," the Fifth Earl Nobury agreed, sitting down behind his desk. "Now, what is it you wish to speak about?"

I hesitated, summoning up my courage for the second time in one day. "I wish for permission to marry your daughter. Sir."

He gave a reflective nod. "I can't say it comes as a surprise. She has never lacked for admirers, and you are by no means the first young hopeful to try his luck. So, what have you got to say for yourself?"

"Well," I began, cagily, "we have known each other since I was admitted to 15GH Abbasia, during which time we have corresponded regularly and are in broad agreement on much that matters."

"For instance?"

"Female Suffrage, 'Votes for Women.'"

"Are you for, or against?

"In principle, I'm in favour." I wondered if I dare go any further with this member of the War Cabinet, but in for a penny in for a pound, I continued: "However, I feel that by crudely agitating for the appearances of power, the more strident Suffragettes devalue the real power that women already exert…"

To my surprise and disappointment, he ignored this cue for me to share Aunt Lucinda's cool riposte to Vida Goldstein's heated argument at Tralee House. Instead, he frowned. "Do you love her?"

The suddenness of this commonplace question immediately raised a red flag. I wondered how many other young hopefuls had sunk their chances with extravagant declarations of undying love, one of the tritest expressions in the English language. "No sir."

He blinked, taken aback, as I meant he should be. "Why is that?"

After a few more seconds of reflection, I replied: "Those things that Sandra and I share, and agree upon, are more enduring than mere 'love.'"

"How so?" He eased forward, the better to hear me clearly.

"It's not easily put into words," I said after another thoughtful pause. "It is what it is, a feeling of certainty, of unity when we are together. And the knowledge that something vital is missing, when we're apart."

He weighed each word before continuing: "What are your prospects? Can you afford to keep my daughter…?"

"Yes sir. There are five-hundred and thirty pounds in my savings account, earned by freelance writing and the sale of cartoons to *Punch*, plus my accrued army pay. I am also a beneficiary in my great aunt's will, who is not without means or property in Melbourne. However, I consider it improper to anticipate another's death, just as it is unlucky to speak of life after the war. But assuming I get through, my prospects will be whatever Sandra and I make of them, for she will be the equal partner in our marriage."

"For instance?"

"I could begin formal studies at the Royal Academy; Arthur Streeton and Tom Roberts will sponsor me. It's a very competitive field but I'm confident of making a name for myself as a painter and illustrator. On the other hand," I concluded, waiting until the end to play my ace, "Sir Alfred Stanhope, of the Asiatic & Pacific, wishes to discuss employment when I return to civilian life…"

"Does he by Jove?!" His Lordship sat further forwards, both hands flat on the desk's leatherbound blotter. "Do you see yourself in banking?"

"Not until recently," I replied after further consideration, for I sensed that he and I shared the same dislike of glib answers. "As I informed Sir Alfred, I am not particularly numerate and the prospect of totting up an accounts ledger does not greatly appeal."

"What did he say to that?"

"According to him: 'We employ others to reconcile balances, call in overdrafts, audit accounts. Rather, our business requires a more discreet personal chemistry and intuitive *comme il faut* when negotiating loans and bond issues with foreign governments. Bookkeepers I can employ any time; less often do I meet a man of your evident parts…'"

Lord Nobury sat back, finger lightly tapping the despatch box lid as if about to make a point at 10 Downing Street. "Sandra showed me your letter. What did it mean when you told her that she might think she's free of her obligation to honour *Gravitas, Dignitas, Integritas*, and can choose whomsoever she wishes, but 'blood is thicker than water'? And what did you mean by saying that she could never rest easy, knowing she had betrayed her ancestors by marrying a lesser man than they were?"

"Exactly as written. Sir."

"And yet here you are, asking for her hand in marriage?"

"Yes. I am."

"Why?"

"Because she does not consider who we are to be an impediment, and by so doing gives me every incentive to live up to her standards and equal those earlier men in her family!"

He pondered these last few words before slowly and deliberately getting to his feet again. "I feel this calls for a celebration, don't you?"

Decades later, the Seventh Earl allowed me access to the Nobury Estate's Muniment Room where, for one last time, I read my letters to his grand aunt. He also showed me the correspondence between the Fifth Earl and his old Grenadier Guards' comrade, Sir Ronald Crauford Munro Ferguson, Australia's Governor General writing from Government House Melbourne, the nation's capital until the 1920s. In it His Excellency spoke warmly and at length of the Baroness Lucinda Cribdon's impeccable social standing, public benevolence, and private business acumen.

108

My belovéd wife, in fact if not yet in name, was waiting anxiously as her father and I came downstairs together. She blushed with excitement as I dipped a conspiratorial wink, took her hand, and walked into the withdrawing room where Lady Nobury just happened to be reading a book, the Honourable James Nobury just happened to be reading today's *Daily Telegraph*, and both just happened to be awaiting our arrival. Her ladyship glanced up sharply. "Well?"

"Ian has kindly consented to join our family, m'dear."

"I am so pleased." She proceeded to give her daughter a warm embrace before offering me her cheek for a light, dry buss.

James was fairly bubbling at the prospect of having a man of his own age and experiences to converse with and confide in as he pumped my hand. Then, turning: "Good pick, Sis'!"

The housekeeper summoned her staff, from cook to scullery maids, to hear their employer announce our news, after which everyone raised their glasses of Bollinger '94, the year of Sandra's birth, especially laid down for this occasion as she and I stood side by side, hand in hand, giddy with happiness.

After dinner, and shortly before we retired to our various rooms, Lord Nobury made a similar phone call to last night's one, only this time he was not smiling when he returned. "You're on tomorrow's draft. Ten o'clock, Victoria Station. I've arranged for your kit to be waiting. We'll get you there in plenty of time."

"Thank you, Sir." There was not much else to say, now, except "Good night."

It was unlikely to be a good or restful night, staring up at the darkened ceiling. Too much had happened too quickly. Small wonder I found it impossible to doze off, although I must have done so, for the next thing I remember was Sandra, warm and fragrant and satin smooth under the sheets beside me.

We parted shortly before dawn and the next time we met, with loving smiles, was at breakfast. Afterwards Lord and Lady Nobury took their leave on the doorstep, thinking it best that the young people, as they called Sandra and James, should accompany me to the station in a Wolseley staff car summoned from Whitehall's transport pool.

Its official plates cleared the way as the government chauffeur drove us onto the station's forecourt and parked while harassed police constables and railway staff redirected other traffic around us. James shook hands after returning my salute, tactfully leaving Sandra to accompany me alone to the RTO's where I collected my bags and travel warrant before approaching Platform 3's iron gates where stony-faced MPs ensured that only authorised personnel boarded the train.

"It won't be long! Then we'll be married -!"

"We already are!" I reminded her, leaning out of the carriage window. "We always have been -!"

"I know! But the family likes a bit of fuss! We mustn't disappoint them!"

"We shan't!"

"Take care Darling!" she insisted as others also reached up for one last touch, walking alongside the train as it began inching forward. "Write soon! Write often -!"

During my last visit to London, several years ago now, I made an intensely personal pilgrimage to Victoria Station, late one wintry night. Only a handful of passengers stood about in the foggy gloom, waiting for a last service to the suburbs, but in my mind's eye that echoing emptiness was thronged with khaki-clad ghosts. One small group was performing a muted clog dance in hobnailed boots while a chum's muffled mouth organ squawked a popular music hall tune, doing their best to reassure wraith-like wives and sweethearts that every man of them would soon be home again, safe and sound, for good.

Half a century earlier, I'd piled my kit onto an overhead luggage rack and squeezed between a Service Corps' captain, and another Joe promoted from the ranks, sporting an MM ribbon and Norfolk Regiment collar badges. There were eight of us and, unlike my last trip to France, we had all been Over There and knew what awaited us, the Third Battle of Ypres by now a ghastly slogging match drenched with unseasonal rain and storms, our side grimly determined to wrest Passchendaele Ridge from the Hun before winter set in.

Cigarettes were ritually shared, but conversation was scrappy and superficial, each man alone with his hopes and fears as the train picked up speed through London's south-eastern outskirts, trailing smoke as we entered the County of Kent's verdant hop fields and orchards, iron wheels hurrying us down to the Channel Ferry.

I was in no mood for talk. From grumpy, lovesick young man to the gloriously radiant prospect of a married lifetime with Sandra at my side, of myself at her side, was a wealth of happiness I had never imagined humanly possible to find. Even the thought of conversing with Cabinet Ministers and other grandees at my father-in-law's townhouse, no longer daunted me; Little Willy Braithwaite had been stripped of his malign influence and banished forever.

Eventually, it would be my turn to interview some young hopeful, though who and where were as unknown as any future can be. Perhaps inside the summerhouse of a picturesque country manor very much like the ones we were passing now. Converted into a working artist's studio, with good north light. Rich with the aroma of turpentine and oil paints. Surrounded by commissioned portraits and landscapes of Britain's great country homes. Or perhaps I would question my prospective son-in-law in the oak-panelled study of an imperial banker, the grave and careful custodian of millions in foreign bonds and securities.

There was no way of telling what the decades ahead held in store for Sandra and me, except that they would be good, and abundant, and fulfilled.

The prospect of growing older and wiser together was curiously comforting as I imagined us still holding hands, still smiling lovingly as our children took their places in a world made whole by a Great War that ended all war. Even though, by then, those hands would be wrinkled and we slower of gait as we completed our long walk together, through life's dusk, into its nightfall.

I freely confess to having a vivid imagination, but this has always been tempered by a fair amount of hard-headed realism when evaluating first things first, like our imminent wedding in the spiritual home of the Household Division and immortal regiments like the Grenadiers and Coldstream Guards.

I was going to need much moral support to get through a ceremony that was bound to be a glittering occasion; Grenville would be at ease in such exalted company, and David would of course be my best man in his trim RFC uniform; I could not imagine better choices when it came to making intelligent conversation with peers of the realm and ministers of the Crown, afterwards.

The only problem was how to break my good news to a man who had been so cruelly snubbed and humiliated by similar folk. Still, it would be sweet revenge when Mary's parents read his name in *Country Life*, or *The Tatler*, or both, with a photographic report of the wedding, and discovered what a golden prize they had spurned.

I memoed myself to include a young, single woman of high character and intellect on our guest list, one who would complete David as much as Sandra completed me. I devoutly hoped so, for I owed him an immense debt of gratitude and friendship as I looked forward to catching up again during the next few days.

The list already included one woman of formidable strength and character, *La Baronne Lucinde*. I had no idea of civilian shipping arrangements in wartime, but given the ceremony was unlikely to take place in under two months, this gave us plenty of time to arrange a passage from Melbourne after receiving my telegram, always assuming her health was up to extended travel.

It would also be a chance to meet her old friend, the ex-Empress Eugènie, whom we should also invite to the Guards Chapel, as evidence that Sandra's new Australian family was not without connexion in high places.

The train finally slowed, hissing, and clanking onto the railway pier and that marked the end of this stage of our return to the Front, and of my happy daydreams.

The RTOs had their embarkation drills down pat after nearly three years of war and, by now, one and a half million movements through this one port alone; briskly emptying the carriages per duplicated clipboard sheets; armed men falling in by platoon and company; tramping aboard the ferry; collecting their kapok lifejackets as they stepped off the gangplank. We Joes crowded the afterdeck, dusted with soot and sparks, the vessel casting off, steaming into the English Channel, port and starboard paddles churning ahead, slapping waves in unison, escorted by a pair of armed trawlers to deter the frequent U-boat attacks in these perilously narrow seas.

109

A watery sun illuminated our embarkation at Folkestone but, by the time we reached Boulogne four hours later, the western sky was Turneresque and deeply troubled. An approaching stormfront's streaky overlays of chrome lemon, crimson lake, burnt sienna, and billowing charcoal, were reminders of Turner's masterwork *The Fighting Temeraire*, often displayed with other patriotic prints, like *England Forever!* and *The Death of Nelson*, in my little playmates' homes along Grange Road.

Artistic appreciation would be the last thing on many a soldier's mind when this weather reached Flanders during the early hours of tomorrow morning, I thought to myself as the outline of Cape Gris-Nez emerged from coastal haze on our port bow while, dead ahead, lay the Liane's river-mouth and Boulogne's port since Roman times.

Troop transports usually got priority over inbound freighters laden with munitions and materiel, horses and fodder, machinery and spare parts, coal, and petrol, but not today as we joined the queue awaiting a tug and its string of lighters to carry us ashore, an uneasy reminder of the landing at Anzac Cove and our first clue that the British offensive in Flanders was faltering.

Until recently, I'd had the infantryman's contempt for rear echelon shirkers, which is how we thought of the ASC's clerks and storemen, cosy and dry in their billets behind the frontline. However, assisting Grenville to prepare for his Selection Board had broadened my perspective; I now saw what an intricate machine the Army was, and how success or failure hinged upon the prompt and accurate delivery of paperwork up and down the chains of command, supply, and procurement.

That much was obvious, less so was the need to sustain morale and dedication among the battalions of typists and clerks as they also buckled under the relentless pressure of needing to beat the Hun at Third Ypres before the weather beat us. A weary or disgruntled man could so easily file an order in the wrong tray, or misdirect a requisition, with crucial ammunition and rations either going to the wrong unit, or not going at all. Someone wiser than I best summed-it-up at the time: "Battles are won by gunners and infantry; wars are won by lorry drivers and clerks."

The situation was even more critical at the docks where Anarchist members of the *Confédération Générale du Travail* - roughly translatable as the General Workers' Union - demonstrated their bitter resentment of British troops doing wharf labourers' work, by dragging our stores and equipment from ships' holds, letting them dangle under a steam crane's jib before deliberately smashing them down on the quayside.

In all fairness it needs to be said that the unionists were not without good reason for their anger and what would soon be called Bolshy behaviour, when one remembers how the government in Paris had recently ordered French soldiers and police to open fire on striking coalminers and factory workers in Pas de Calais, killing and wounding several hundred men, women, and children.

The prevailing mood of bloody-minded muddle was very apparent when we eventually got ashore, long after dark, and the troops marched off to a transit camp somewhere on the edge of town, leaving me at a loose end, the AIF having transferred my details to the Flying Corps who had yet to take me on-strength.

Hungry, morose, deprived of Sandra's warmth and laughter, I dropped my kit on the foyer floor of the nearby Hôtel Terminus and demanded a room for the night. This was scornfully refused with a bored Gallic shrug and curled lip, to which I responded with a barrage of fluent, filthily colloquial French.

Next morning, washed, refreshed, clad in my walking out uniform of Sam Browne belt, holstered revolver, and mackintosh trench coat, I presented myself at Movements in Rue de la Falaise, opposite the Quai des Paquebots transport pool, where nobody had a clue what to do with me.

Lost in the system, it was suggested that my papers might be on their way from London and that I should return later, but at least one member of the counter staff was kind enough to tell me where the officers' transit billets were situated in Rue des Signaux, at the other end of the road.

Here I dumped my kit and scrounged a meal before going for a walk three miles out of town, through the dank weather to a tall column commemorating Napoleon I's failed attempt to invade England. My main purpose was to report back on its present state to Aunt Lucinda, who had often told me of the glittering occasion when she accompanied Napoleon III and his Empress to inaugurate the monument in the early-1850s.

As a soldier in uniform, I was entitled to climb the 200-odd steps inside it without first buying a 10-centime ticket, and so I availed myself of the opportunity to stand atop, under the first Emperor Napoleon's imposing bronze statue; myself damp and miserable, staring northward, picturing lunchtime at Berkeley Square, seated alongside Sandra, shyly holding hands under the table.

Back at ground level I bought two stamped souvenir postcards; addressed one to my aunt, telling her that all was well with her memories; the other to Sandra, signed ICHD, our secret code for Ian Cribdon Husband Dear. After posting them in the kiosk's blue, ornate cast iron letterbox, I thumbed a lift into town on a lorry from one of several Canadian camps between Boulogne and Wimereaux, but Movements still had no idea where to send me or what I should do even if I got there, so I booked another night in Rue des Signaux and returned to Rue de la Falaise next morning, with the same result.

By now it was evident that I was being given the run-around in which an annoyance is flicked from desk to desk, in the hope that it will lose interest and go away. True, I was asking a lot to expect a search for one stray personnel file among the scores of thousands of others in circulation, as more and more men were fed into Passchendaele's meat grinder where entire battalions ceased to exist within days of reaching the Front. This much was understandable, but I was beginning to sense a much deeper level of concern, namely the venomous hatred and rivalry between the Flying Corps and the Army.

A sarcastic hint here, a jealous remark there, and it soon became apparent that those in authority resented scarce resources and manpower being diverted to what many still regarded as an overseas branch of the Royal Aero Club. In their opinion we were pampered battlefield tourists, buzzing around the sky, enjoying the view while others, less privileged, fought the real war amidst mud, muck, and misery.

The Army's lower ranks equally hated the Flying Corps for the cushy life its personnel enjoyed in a fabled world where even an airman second class could reasonably expect a hot meal and a dry bed at nightfall, unlike his corresponding number in the trenches.

None of this was helped while Britain's newspapers and illustrated magazines glorified the RFC's aces as blithe, handsome demi-gods duelling high above the Western Front's squalid violence.

Out of time, out of patience, I finally took matters into my own hands and hitched a lift to St Omer, the RFC's main base, inland from Boulogne. Here at last Admin' seemed to have a grip as it accounted for replacement aeroplanes of all types, ferried across the Channel to this converted racecourse before issue to the sixty squadrons currently serving in France.

I fronted up at the Orderly Room and explained my predicament. The staff were sympathetic, but my papers still hadn't arrived, although perhaps they had gone straight to XIII Squadron, based on a farm somewhere nearer the Front?

Eager to catch-up with David, share the good news, and ask him to be my Best Man, I hitched another lift, this time aboard a Crossley tender taking two refurbished engines from Central Workshops to Le Hameau, along the old Roman road to Devion. From there we tracked through a web of muddy lanes and crowded army encampments to a requisitioned cow paddock about six miles behind Arras.

Dismounting at the guard post I paused to mentally sketch my first impression of a frontline aerodrome's saggy brown canvas hangers and workshops; sandbagged munitions bays and petrol dump; Nissen huts and camouflaged RE8s dispersed around the field; ack-ack batteries on standby in case Fritz nipped across the frontline for quick strafe, as had happened the previous week.

Glad to be somewhere I could relate to, I fronted the Orderly Room's counter and gave my name, rank, and number, but my papers were still missing, however a telegram from London had informed the squadron that a 2/Lt Cribdon was in transit to the Experimental "D" Flight of an embryonic Australian Flying Corps.

"This way sir." The Orderly Sergeant led me to the CO's office, knocked and stuck his head around the door. "Mr Cribdon's just signed on, sir."

"Thanks, Sarge'. That'll be all."

"Sir."

I was about to formally announce myself again when Captain Roy Ellis, in real life an auctioneer from Toowoomba on the pastoral slopes of the Great Dividing Range in Queensland, waved me to a vacant chair and offered one of his cigarettes. "Good trip?"

"Eventful." I declined the offer, having temporarily stopped smoking to please Sandra. "Thus far, I'm not sure if my papers are chasing me, or I'm chasing them."

"Oh, not to worry, they'll turn up. Now, I see you have your logbook. Let's take a squizz." He flicked through the few pages that recorded my abbreviated training at Reading, and Brooklands, and Hythe, before giving me a wry smile. "You're as well qualified as everyone else we've met recently, but don't be in too much of a hurry. Learn the ropes and settle down. We're a friendly lot."

"I know."

"You do?" He cocked an amused eyebrow. "How's that?"

"David Shuster and I were at school together. His family and mine have been –"

"Then, you've not, heard?"

"Not heard, what?"

He searched for words that never came easily, no matter how often we spoke them during the Great War. "I'm, awfully sorry. Dave got the chop. On Wednesday."

When I record this episode for Frances, I shall have to explain that whereas her generation bares its soul at every opportunity and emotes over life's little mishaps, we were expected to control our feelings and never allow them to control us.

Such stiff-upper-lipped behaviour is easily mocked in times of peace and plenty, but it was what kept us steady and strong through shocks and horrors unimaginable to those fortunate to be born later than we were. Accordingly, I remained outwardly calm when Ellis informed me that David had been killed the same afternoon that Sandra and I were pledging our love on the Serpentine.

In a deadly counterpoint to our happiness, the German IX Reserve Corps had attacked the Belgian Army's precarious toehold on the Ypres Salient under cover of low cloud and driving rain, less than one hundred miles from sunny Central London. However, a short break in the weather had been forecast to reach Flanders by midday. RFC Command ordered all serviceable aeroplanes be refuelled and rearmed while their crews were briefed on the vital need to support our Belgian allies in their hour of greatest need.

The Australian flight's target was Rumbeke, nearest point to Ypres on a canal system freighting munitions from the armament factories in enemy occupied Liège farther east. A local Resistance cell had reported a new ammunition dump, identifiable by its proximity to a distinctive wharf and unloading cranes on the canal's embankment.

Ellis led a force of seven machines, and it says much about those desperate times that Brigade thought that fifty-odd 20-pound Cooper bombs had any hope of affecting a major offensive.

Things went from bad to worse for Dingo Flight soon after take-off. Fighter cover, as it was later called in the Second War, was nowhere to be seen and the lowering cloud base forced our unescorted aircraft to enter enemy airspace within rifle shot of the trenches. Mercifully the same miserable weather was hampering the *Fliegertruppen* as Ellis traced a zigzag course that masked his remaining six machines' targeted destination, until banking hard left and flying up the canal in line-astern formation, at treetop height.

By now the *Jastas* were scrambling – another expressive term we didn't have in the Great War – to intercept our intruders, Ellis still in the lead, aiming for the wharf and its adjacent ammo dump, before hauling the stick back to three hundred feet, the minimum altitude for a bomb's arming vane to spin off and cock its contact fuze.

A very Australian innovation was the white phosphorus shell on his ordnance rack, an improvised target-marker that another Australian, Donald Bennett, would later adopt for the RAF's Pathfinder Force during the Second War.

The raid was as successful as such a bomb load could ever be, leaving several fires, sporadic explosions, and general panic but at a heavy price for the surviving aircraft; battling home against the westerlies and deteriorating weather; harassed by *Jagdstaffeln* until an RFC Camel squadron broke up the party and shepherded the remaining four RE8s home to Le Hameau.

David downed one Pfalz with his forward-firing Vickers' gun, and scored a probable, his observer accounting for the third of these recently introduced single-seaters. What was not known at the time, was how badly wounded David was. He might have saved his life by landing near an enemy unit, a not unknown occurrence, and seeking medical treatment as a prisoner of war. Instead, he flew his crewman to safety, barely clearing the boundary hedge before dying at the controls as his machine rolled to a halt.

"We've put him up for an award," Ellis concluded. "Trouble is, there's only one posthumous decoration - the VC - and live British aces have priority for those, not dead Australian recce pilots…"

"When's his funeral?"

"Last Thursday. The village church has a plot for our chaps." He paused, eyeing me closely. "We like to get this sort of thing done quickly. You understand?"

"Of course." I had not forgotten Frank Laurie's funeral.

He stood. "Here, let me show you around. Sarn't Rogers will take care of your kit."

I followed as he proceeded to introduce me to other members of staff, then took me to the workshop where groundcrew fitters and riggers were rebuilding the last of the machines shot-up over Rumbeke, our depleted flight's only effective strength until replacements arrived from the factories in England.

I asked to see David's aeroplane but was told it was artillery spotting over the Salient and, with any luck, would be back soon. However, if it failed to return, St Omer would indent for another at a cost to Treasury of about two thousand pounds apiece. Not quite easy come, easy go, but very nearly so as the Empire burned through centuries of accumulated wealth in a matter of months. The war's cost in human talent and lost brainpower was not only harder to estimate, but also of infinitely greater value, and far longer duration.

Our Officers' Mess was a commandeered hay shed - the farmer had drafted his cattle elsewhere - its wattle and daub walls decorated with pictures clipped from British and French illustrated magazines. A coloured lithographic print of the King in his admiral's uniform, bedecked with medals, overlooked a crudely drawn sketch of Kaiser Bill pinned to a dart board near the bar - four planks laid across two empty beer barrels – lit by paraffin Tilley lamps hooked on chains from the rafters. A very old piano, a Red Cross Comforts Fund gramophone with burnished brass horn, and a selection of popular songs on shellac discs in their brown paper sleeves, completed the furnishings.

Everyone I shook hands with seemed glad to chat for a few moments and yet I felt a reserve that was more than the usual cool assessment of any newcomer joining a tightly-knit group of men. I soon discovered the reason why and adopted the same code of thoughtful distance myself; it is never wise to invest too much friendship in a business where new faces are constantly appearing and then disappearing, almost as quickly.

110

Sergeant Rogers left my bags on a vacant camp bed in the row of officers' two-man tents, coincidentally David's, not that it greatly troubled me. Any squeamishness I might once have felt no longer applied after snatching many an exhausted rest alongside a bloating Turk, or in a shell crater surrounded by unidentifiable bits of soldier.

My new tentmate was David's observer on that final flight - Peter McNamara - a Boer War veteran whose weathered features spoke of an outdoors life fossicking for tin ore along Tasmania's freezing cold creek lines, so it was not long before we were swapping campfire yarns and comparing our experiences of working in the bush, mine of the arid Westralian Outback, his of the dank rainforests that cover much of Australia's island state.

Unprompted, he praised David's courage, adding words like "brainy," and "quick on the uptake," and hoped that, once he had accumulated enough combat hours, he could train to become as brave and skilled a pilot as my oldest friend had been, not that I had spoken of our connection.

Workdays always began early on an RFC squadron, although it could be said they rarely ended, with groundcrews often toiling through the night to patch and prepare machines for next day's dawn patrol. There were sound mechanical reasons for getting aloft as soon as possible. As a day warms up, its air loses density with a corresponding loss of lift, always critical and sometimes fatal when an aeroplane is operating near the upper limits of weight and drag. If my memory serves me right, by subtracting the RE8's tare from its gross we arrived at a nett payload of eight hundred and seventy pounds on a good day, of which there were few during the autumn of 1917.

This final figure encompassed a two-man crew of eleven stone or one hundred and fifty-seven pounds apiece, say three hundred pounds distributed between the front and rear cockpits; forty gallons of fuel, another two hundred and fifty pounds; now add the guns and magazines, cameras and plate holders, wireless transmitter, and lead-acid battery. Meaning that many machines were perilously laden on their lumbering take-off runs.

There's a lot of tosh talked about pilots and observers being forbidden to wear parachutes during the Great War, because it was thought they would encourage us to bail-out whenever we saw a Hun approaching. In which case, apart from the insulting insinuation of cowardice, why were Guardian Angel 'chutes issued to airship crews and balloon observers?

The plain fact of the matter is that Leslie Irvin had yet to invent a compact, free-fall parachute. Unlike those larger, more buoyant aerostats, we could not afford the additional weight and parasitic drag of two bulky packs slung over the side of an already cramped fuselage, their static lines likely to tangle if we had to jump together from a spinning machine.

On an average workday, given the weather was marginally flyable and Brigade had ordered a specific stunt, we would assemble in a Nissen hut with a large blackboard at one end, a line of named clothes' hooks at the other, where the first order of business was to get into our flying kit.

This amounted to sheepskin thigh boots and a long leather motoring coat for pilots; sheepskin knee boots and padded Sidcot suit for the man in the back, whose multiple duties meant that he had to fly without a restraining harness if he was to crouch upright in a thrashing slipstream, either artillery spotting, or taking vertical shots with his camera, or returning fire against attacking enemy aeroplanes, or all three in rapid succession.

Depending upon the day's task we would be briefed, issued with maps and code sheets, and left to get on with the job; pilots by inspecting our machine; observers by signing-out our guns and double-stack magazines from the Armoury.

I closely monitored these procedures during my first active morning on the squadron, before going outside to watch a couple of 'Eights drone off into the distance, tasked with photo-runs over Zandvoorde and the Lys Canal, to take advantage of a sunny break in the early autumnal weather.

"'Looks like they've left us a spare bus," Ellis thought aloud, eying the one remaining RE8, "what say we go for a drive?"

I collected my kitbag and brought it to the Briefing Room where I found David's vacant peg and laid claim to it. Although there were so few hours in my logbook, my Sidcot had already acquired its characteristic stink of airsickness, sweat, and stale urine as I buttoned up, pulled on my boots, stuffed leather gauntlets into the overalls' side pockets, and loosely pulled the goggled helmet down around my ears.

This was only a familiarisation flight but, even so, Air Board Regulations required that all machines be armed when flying within ten miles of the Front, so I signed-out a Lewis and three mag's, loaded them aboard their trolley cart and followed Ellis to B-Bertie on the dispersal pad.

With memories of Frank Laurie fresh in mind I closely mirrored the pre-flight inspection, then mounted my gun on its Scarfe ring, locked one magazine atop its pivot post, ready to crank the charging handle once we were safely airborne.

The remaining two mag's neatly fitted their ledge boxes, one either side of my knees as I settled on the piano stool, facing aft, picturing the air mechanic behind me ponderously winding our four-bladed propeller over and over and over by hand; sucking fuel vapour into each of the V12's cylinders until, at the twelfth turn, with a thumbs-up, firing one hundred and forty horsepower of ragged spits, splutters, and smoky coughs; undercarriage wheels straining against their chocks; Ellis testing the engine's oil pressure and magneto drop before throttling back and waving chocks-away.

Seventy years older and I can still feel the tingle of nervous anticipation as we taxied out, the mechanic steadying our lower port wingtip, jolting and lurching over the tussocky paddock, turning us into the wind.

Ellis eased the throttle lever forward, exhaust stacks roaring, undercarriage tyres starting to trundle, then bounce, then skip along the runway's mown strip, until generating sufficient forward speed to overcome gravity, Le Hameau's patchwork quilt of variegated brown fields and green woodlands falling astern as we gained altitude.

He could not have chosen a more splendid day for a familiarisation flight, Ivory clouds lightly dusted with Charcoal shadows, billowing over a crystal-clear sky of Cerulean Blue. Levelling off at three thousand feet. Droning sou'west. Me with my fur collar pulled up, watching our aeroplane's rudder twitch, correcting drift. Ellis flying roughly parallel with the Front from Arras to Albert.

There was no reason for concern except for two black dots at eleven o'clock high, hurrying eastwards to Hun Land. Odd behaviour for Allied machines so I kept a close watch, waiting for them to disappear behind towering pillars of cumulus that would soon be dumping more rain on Tommy and Fritzi alike.

I can only assume that the temptation of an unescorted RE8, with its promise of an easy victory, was impossible to resist. Unsure of the correct procedure, I turned to the Gosport tube's rubber funnel over my map board and called something like: "We've got bad company! I'll sort him out -!"

My opponent, a sleek Albatros D.III, swooped astern, bouncing about on our slipstream's roiling wake, an angle of attack that promised its pilot his best chance of a quick kill –

This was likely his familiarisation flight, too, and the first time he'd triggered his guns in anger. If so, I could imagine the thrill of their clattering recoil and the daydream of a maiden victory overriding his instructor's warning that a zero-deflection approach offers the same tactical advantage to the attacked as well as the attacker -

By contrast, I was a qualified marksman who'd deployed his weapon like an automatic rifle on two battlefields, foresight blade splitting the Albatros' propeller arc, left fist locking the Lewis gun's spade grip, right forefinger hooking tight tacker-tack-tack taps -

It only needed one burst to shatter a prop' blade, or smash the Mercedes' cylinder block, or hit the pilot, to finish the job. Instead, a punctured petrol tank or broken carburettor feedpipe began spraying volatile fuel into the hot engine compartment –

The Albatros rolled away to starboard, its pilot kicking rudder, unable to sideslip the blazing inferno before throwing himself clear, preferring death on impact with the ground, to being roasted alive in the sky -

"He's done!" I called into my end of the Gosport tube as a twirling plume of smoky yellow flames followed him earthwards, then swung my gaze astern in case the second Albatros' pilot thought he was in with a chance while I was still distracted. Instead, he kept flying eastwards with bad news for someone's family in Germany.

Dingo Flight's commander completed a wonky one-eighty degree turn and set course for Le Hameau where we landed about twenty minutes later, taxied up to the workshops, and switched off. Ellis climbed onto the lower wing and jumped down to inspect damage. We had got off lightly, all things considered; fifteen random holes in our doped fabric and one shot-off starboard aileron hinge.

An air mechanic helped me dismount the Lewis gun and noticed the rime of burnt cordite around its muzzle crown. "Um, any luck, sir?"

"Uh huh." I was in no mood to crow over the death of a young man who would doubtless have celebrated mine with bottle of champagne and a good cigar in his *Offiziersmesse*. There were already too many anonymous deaths on my conscience for another to make much difference. What really hurt, though, was having to besmirch a beautiful, paintable sky with smoke and flame and scorched flesh.

"'We've got bad company,'" Ellis thoughtfully echoed my words of a short while ago. "'I'll sort him out…'" He'd ended his inspection and was inspecting me now. "Icy by name, icy by nature?" Then peeled off his gauntlet and stuck out a heartfelt handshake. "Bloody good show! See you back in the Mess."

490

I returned his firm grip and tramped off to the Armoury, the mechanic proudly towing the Lewis' cart as if it were a battle trophy, where I asked the corporal i/c if I could borrow his bench and, despite a muted grumble, proceeded to strip, clean, and oil my fired weapon. His objections stopped once he saw that I was also a tradesman and happily obliged when I asked for a pot of white paint and pencil brush to print my initials – I.C. – on the spade grip. "Do us a favour, Corp', keep this one aside for me."

"Right-o sir!"

"Now. Have we got any spare mag's?"

He fossicked around and found me a box of reasonably new magazines. I picked them over, inspecting their feed tracks before painting my initials on the best three, and told the armourer that I would return later to hand-load them myself.

111

I climbed out of my Sidcot, hung it on David's old peg, and entered the Mess to find Ellis recounting our adventure to four of A Flight's British pilots. Everyone turned to greet me with something akin to awe, so I assume he had embellished our story for they were all keen to shake hands and shout me a pint at the bar, an offer I modestly accepted before raising a glass of the local *bock* to our Sailor King's portrait, as if all I'd done was a routine daily occurrence, though of course it was anything but that.

The probability of an inexperienced observer scoring a victory on his first flight was vanishingly slim and had nothing to do with my skills as a gunner and everything to do with an inexperienced enemy allowing himself to be swept along by the thrill of the chase. A more cunning pilot would have manoeuvred up-sun and given us a quick squirt as he dived past, before pulling a stall-turn to rake the RE8's underside; Ellis and I would then have been the ones jumping to our deaths.

After a short while I took my leave, went over to the Intelligence Officer's hutch to report on the day's work, and returned to the Armoury where I spent the next half hour or so loading my magazines, inspecting each round to check that its primer was properly seated, as we'd done on Gallipoli where the Vickers' 0.303 ammunition was often sub-standard.

Supplies had thankfully improved during the past two years, for the RFC at least, who were now issued with match grade cartridges in distinctive green cardboard packets, but old habits die hard which is why some of us lived long enough to become old diehards.

An historical detail that Frances may find interesting is that I only loaded five successive rounds of Tracer per magazine, the other ninety-two rounds were 0.303 Ball. Thus, when I saw blips of burning phosphorus flicking away, it was time to switch mag's rather than wait until tugging an unresponsive trigger on an enemy machine looming closer.

Others loaded one round of Tracer to every five of Ball, for purposes of aim, but I found these a distraction and preferred to rely on my shotgun training and championship billiard play to estimate lead-distances and angular deflections.

That done, I went off to find the Transport Pool and see if I could scrounge a motorbike, with directions to St Pierre's churchyard; as it happened, I only had to putter a short distance to see a church steeple behind a line of trees.

I kicked down the bike's stand and walked through the lychgate towards a short row of fresh white crosses, aiming for the latest at the right-hand end of the line. Head bowed, lost in thought, I did not hear footsteps until a discreet cough alerted me. "Iz, uh, vrend?"

I turned. An elderly man in a priest's soutane, stood behind me. "*Oui m'sieur le curé,*" I replied, automatically responding in French. "*C'était un très cher ami...*"

"*Ah, cette guerre abominable!*" he grimaced with feeling, and so began my friendship with Father Matthieu, a veteran of the Franco-Prussian War and later service in French Indochina before entering the priesthood and, until August 1914, finding peace in the Picard countryside.

We talked of David for quite a while, the sad-eyed Frenchman glad to speak in his own tongue, for his English was as limited as his knowledge of Australia, and in due course shared several meals at the *presbytère*, prepared by his housekeeper, a poor widow with three sons at the Front, one still alive, during the few months I remained on the squadron.

After that first meeting I rode back to the aerodrome and searched the workshop's scrap heap for a flat piece of aluminium cowling. I then borrowed a scriber, a ruler, a pair of tin snips, and trimmed a six-pointed Star of David before borrowing a set of letter dies to stamp my friend's name, rank, and number in the soft, silvery metal.

Father Matthieu helped me nail this sacred symbol to a fresh wooden stake, tactfully replacing the cross when I returned next day with the star and a quarter-plate camera schemed from the Photographic Section. I then made a couple of exposures; one of David's grave, close-up, another farther away, of the local *curé* proudly standing guard beside it, like the old *sergent-chef* he still was under his clerical garb.

On the way back to the aerodrome I began wondering if our Chaplain had sorted David's things yet and went to the Orderly Room to find out. Apparently, there had been two funerals at another squadron that same day and our resident God Guesser had attended those, promising to return later, there being no great urgency as it would take several weeks for HQ at Horseferry Road to process a package to Australia. This allowed me time to check that my friend had left nothing behind to tarnish his memory, as I explained to our Equipment Officer, who agreed to oversee the inspection.

What I feared to find was not there. All the letters from Mary had either been burned or returned and her name inked from his laconic diary. More expressive were his field notebooks, filled with sketched plants and neatly written observations of soil and climate, with cryptic remarks in a private shorthand that seemed to be a mixture of botanists' Latin and scientists' German.

I have no idea what they meant but I do hope they found a receptive museum or library, for I am sure they contained the seeds of many a significant discovery that others would now make on my friend's behalf.

The only other thing of interest, before sealing his uniform, kit, and papers in a stout plywood box that originally contained a pair of Cooper bombs, was an envelope with instructions that it be forwarded to 2/Lt Ian Cribdon DCM & Bar in the event of 1/Lt David Shuster's death.

"That's me," I explained to the inspecting officer. "Permission to open it?"

"Of course, old chap. I'll, ah, look the other way."

I appreciated the courtesy, unsure of what had been on David's mind when he wrote these few words:

Dear Golly.

I hope you never read this but of late I've been much troubled by dreams, premonitions, and regrets.

Whether or not they mean anything, who can

*tell? Hopefully, after the war, we shall dine
again at The Eagle and laugh at our fears.*

*However, they feel real enough and, in the event
of them proving true, please take care of the Old
Folks so far as you can, for they regard you as
the second son they never had.*

*Despite many years in Melbourne, both feel lonely
and a long way from their childhood homes in
Kaiserland.*

*This war is proving very hard for them, and they
need a familiar, supportive presence such as
yours, as do I.*

Good luck, best of friends.

D.

112

Our riggers worked long into the night, gluing and screwing B-Bertie's aileron and wingtip back together again, while the fitters shone their electric torches through gashed fabric, tracking each bullet's path through dark corners and crevices where it might have struck the airframe, damaged a control cable, or weakened a mounting, and when found, fixing the problem.

Close behind them came the fabric workers, stitching and doping fresh patches as well as checking every square inch of surface area for minor grazes that could balloon into major rips once airborne again.

Our lives were in the hands of these weary men in their grimy overalls; I remember them still with affection and respect.

Three days later, the batman I shared with Peter McNamara awoke us before dawn by lighting our tent's hurricane lantern off his own and serving two mugs of warm tea from an enamel pail. It was still dark outside except for the sullen grumble of artillery and rippling muzzle flashes – Ours and Theirs – along the nearby frontline as we trudged through frosty grass and entered the Briefing Room's hut.

Brigade had alerted our squadron's Intelligence Officer to be ready for a despatch rider with orders for another day of maximum effort. Apparently, Gris-Nez' weather station was forecasting reasonably clear skies for the next twenty-four hours, so there was no time to waste if we were to ease the pressure on our troops dug-in among the shattered tree stumps of Polygon Wood, under constant shellfire from Fritz's heavies atop Gheluvelt Plateau.

Those men were very much our troops, the IO emphasised, commandeered billiard cue rapping the blackboard to show where the 1st Australian Division was stubbornly blocking the 50th Wurttemberg's attacks along the Menin Road's supply route. "We mustn't let them down..."

"My fuckin' oath we won't!" a gritty voice growled behind me, to which we all assented with feeling, especially those of us who until recently had also fought in the trenches.

Dingo Leader chose me to fly with him again as the other crews went into individual huddles over their maps by the hissing glare of Tilley lamps, knowing full well that today we'd be slap bang in the thick of it, spotting for British counter-batteries tasked to suppress Gheluvelt's howitzers.

Ellis knew from the entries in my logbook that this was my first live shoot, and that my training thus far consisted of seven practice runs slung from a college gymnasium roof. It was insane. It was also evidence of how desperate the situation had become as unskilled men were thrown into the sky with little more than a hope and a prayer. Even so, my pilot said he felt lucky with me covering his tail, and that with a nickname like Icy, knew he could count on me keeping a cool head when things got hot.

Dawn was barely a blush on the horizon when we tramped out to the fuelled machines and made ready, using our electric torches for the pre-flight checks before climbing aboard. It was still dark at ground level where two parallel lines of galvanised iron watering cans were positioned into the wind.

Holding about a gallon of paraffin oil apiece, rope wicks poked down their spouts, when lit these formed a wavering flarepath as the replenished squadron taxied towards them, wingtips steadied by groundcrew with lanterns, a ghostly scene illuminated by the pulsing spurts of blue flame from our engines' vertical exhaust stacks.

One by one we trundled forward and took off, climbing through misty layers of whitening grey to meet daylight at 1,500 feet, continuing in upward spirals as an escort of Sopwith Scouts joined us. Our heavier, less agile reconnaissance bombers wing-wagged greetings and set course for a frontline clearly marked by pulsing gun flashes in the semi-darkness ahead.

I had designed a set of cue cards for an observer's duties while still at Wantage Hall, each easily read in large black and white upper-case lettering; the one for today's op' was tucked under a clear celluloid sheet alongside my map and crayon pencil on its short piece of string.

I cranked the Lewis gun, by no means convinced that a thin screen of single-seaters, armed with one Vickers' apiece, could hold off a determined *Jasta*, then strapped a pair of Admiralty binoculars around my neck - rather like clumsy metal ice cream cones in my gloved fists - hooked one ankle under the piano stool, and got ready to lean over the side of the cockpit as soon as Ellis began orbiting our sector.

My task was to scan the battlefield, searching for enemy gun emplacements. Not easily done, bare face exposed to the sub-zero slipstream, goggles raised, pitting my wits against masters of disguise, decoys, and deception. Unless one was very careful a telegraph pole could be shelled to splinters in the mistaken belief that it was a carelessly camouflaged 105mm FH 98/09.

The only way to be reasonably sure of a genuine target was to be watching as its hot muzzle blast shimmered – best seen against the shadowed ground below, hence the early start - though even these were not always conclusive, for Fritz often mimicked the effect with fireworks.

Meanwhile, we kept plodding round and around as dogfights clashed overhead and ack-ack annoyed us from below. Fortunately, after more than two years' service in and out of the trenches, I could detach whole slabs of consciousness by setting them adrift like icefloes on an imagined dark, wintry sea and, instead, focus an artist's eye on the landscape scrolling below me.

The trick was to search for minor details that betrayed current occupation of a site rather than looking for big stuff. Then, whenever a gun fired, momentarily unmasking its position, trigger our camera's shutter release, crouch back into the cockpit and pencil a cross on my map.

The RE8 had an endurance of better than four hours but ninety minutes staring through binoculars while being shot at, were quite enough for anyone as we broke off and headed for home, ripped fabric flogging in the airflow.

Groundcrew moved quickly to make repairs as we taxied to a halt. While they went to work with gluepot, needles, and thread, I took our camera's magazine to the Photographic Section's darkroom before joining Ellis and the IO in his cramped office where a breakfast of hot sweet tea and toasted bacon sandwiches awaited us.

My report was still being typed when a runner brought in the enlarged prints of this morning's work, together with a whiff of the methylated spirits used to damp off the darkroom's rinse-water. These were matched with my confirmed sightings, tagged with code-letters, and handed over, plus a carbon copy of the report, to a despatch rider who roared away on his motorbike to Div' HQ's Artillery Liaison.

We were now free to lounge around the Mess and read a newspaper, or write a letter, or snatch a bit of sleep. One may take a man out of the infantry, but you will never take the infantry out of him, so I found a quiet corner, rolled my Sidcot to improvise a pillow, and dozed off.

Ellis nudged me awake about a couple of hours later. Divvy had been on the blower and given our IO today's targets; the darkroom was finishing two sets of master prints, one for me, the other for our wireless telegraphist on the ground. Each individual print overlaid with concentric circles around the enemy gun site, like a clock dial with 12 as North, 3 as East, 6 as South, and 9 as West, subdivided by five-minute increments.

The rings themselves began at 10 yards from dead centre and were scaled at 10, 25, 50, 100, 200, 300, 400, 500 yards, and then labelled in the same order, X, Y, Z, A, B, C, D. In theory all one now had to do was send a set of copies to the gunners, keeping the other set to register puffs of colour-coded smoke, and report they had fallen on B-10 or E-25 or wherever. Seldom did their first or second or third shot land on X.

The despatch rider roared off again and we awaited Divvy's call that the duplicate photo was on its way to the gunners. This was our cue for us to take off for the Salient again where, at any moment, the sky was either swarming with aircraft or was a sudden void, as if a gust of wind had scattered a cloud of midges, leaving our RE8 to beetle along on its own, feeling very exposed and lonely indeed as I lowered the wireless aerial, an iron sinker attached to forty yards of copper wire wound onto a wooden fishing reel above a fairlead hole in the deck.

My next job was to fire-up the transmitter, fingers-crossed the cold hadn't numbed its battery, and tune to frequency by keying the day's code letter until acknowledgment from the ground. Rarely did the wireless telegraphist, hunched in his dugout, get my signals first time; the miracle was that he got them at all while his receiver's cat's whisker crystal was being jolted around by the seismic thuds and crumps of incoming enemy fire. Often the only way I knew we were in touch was when ground troops laid out a large letter L made from panels of white linoleum, indicating our artillery was ready to open fire.

A red, or yellow, or green panel would then be laid inside L's elbow to which I would reply by keying dah-dah-dit, G for Go, and refer to our master print as the first ranging shot arched over the trenches and, with luck, exploded a burst of red, or yellow, or green smoke within 100 yards of the target.

Finally, a pencilled note, clipped by a clothes' peg to an endless loop of cord between pulleys in our front and rear cockpits – it being impossible for an observer's helmet to stay connected with his pilot's Gosport tube - told me that we were low on fuel and returning to Le Hameau for the second time since breakfast.

113

This was the tempo of our lives until heavy rain and zero visibility stopped play. By now we were down another three machines, our ranks were thinning fast, and I was well on the way to becoming an Old Hand.

Seven decades later, I still fail to understand what the point was of keeping an experimental flight in the front line where its aircrews were being shot down before we could impart our hard-earned knowledge to newcomers from Australia, presently training in Lincolnshire as 3 Squadron AFC. Parodying Tennyson's patriotic ode, *The Charge of the Light Brigade*, we shrugged it off and assured each other: "Ours not to question why, ours but to muddle by…"

I cannot say I was sad to be off op's until the sour, autumnal weather cleared; there were many practical lessons to mark, learn, and inwardly digest before going airborne again; some from the most unusual sources, as I discovered when taking my turn as the squadron's censorship officer, opening and reading letters to Australia or to relatives in Britain.

One obvious purpose was to delete any information that might assist the enemy; another, more covert, was to gauge unit morale and nip petty grievances in the bud before they became major concerns; a third reason was to get advance notice of an impending paternity claim or money problems.

I found it very touching to read how closely our groundcrews identified with their machines and how deeply the losses were felt. A kindly word of thanks, given by a pilot or observer, was as treasured and proudly shared as if it were an award from the King himself.

Equally informative, for me, was to learn: *"There's a new officer cove up from the ranks, a regular Deadeye Dick. Popped a Hun, first flight, with only a handful of bullets! A lone wolf who knows his stuff."*

Sandra's latest letter was the best of all. Hurriedly written at VAD Headquarters – known to its inmates as the Vadhouse – it began simply:

My Dearest Heart.

Preparations are well advanced for the happiest day of our lives, (thus far!) Pa' has spoken with HM who is delighted with the news and gives us his royal blessing. (Didn't I tell you he's a sweetie?!?)

The Guards' Chapel is ours for 26th November, a Monday, so we have the weekend to get ready.

Ma' wants the seamstress to remodel her (Ma's) wedding dress, a family tradition, but as you will be in uniform, so shall I!!!

*No doubt it will cause a bit of fuss, but this is wartime,
when such rules no longer apply as we build a more
hopeful, happier world for our children.*

*The invitations have been printed and sent out. Now
when family and friends read of our engagement it
won't come as a shock, for I am certain many of them
have given up on me ever taking The Plunge!*

*One last spell of duty on Winch' and I'll be free to
arrange my trousseau &c &c before starting with
Admin' and thus able to make a welcome home for
your leaves in London...*

Your eternally loving wife.

S

PS. I am so glad you are not flying dangerously.

And I was equally glad that I'd edited any references to my first and
subsequent flights, in letters to her VAD mailbox. However, it had been much
harder to write to David's parents:

RFC Le Hameau

12th October 1917

Dear Mr & Mrs Shuster.

*There are no words to express my sense of loss
when I learned of David's death. Truly he was
the best friend a man could ever wish for, and it is
some consolation to know that he died as he lived,
a hero to all who knew him.*

*As the enclosed photographs show, I have made
arrangements for his grave to be properly looked
after with others of our squadron.*

*I shall soon be married to a British girl of good
family, and if we are blessed with a son, he will be
called David and I shall see that he grows up knowing
what an honour it is to be named after his father's
oldest and truest friend, David Shuster.*

With my profound sympathy and respect.

Ian

I re-read this several times, making sure there was nothing in it that would connect David's need to redeem himself by volunteering for the Flying Corps, with Iron Hannah's hysterical sabotage of his chance to win a medal at the Stockholm Olympics; she could not have survived the horrifying truth of her predicament, had she known.

114

The weather finally lifted, and another three new machines flew in from the supply depot, their delivery pilots returning to St Omer aboard the same lorry that brought fresh aircrews from the ferry terminal at Boulogne.

Each of these youngsters was given an introductory lecture in the Briefing Room, half an hour's ground instruction, then turned loose with a sandbag instead of an observer in the rear cockpit, to see how well they performed circuits and bumps with an aeroplane prone to sudden stalls if its pilot failed to keep an eye on the rev' counter and airspeed indicator.

Two managed the required number of landings to qualify, but the third misjudged his approach, eased the throttle too soon, conked the engine, and crashed. This was not necessarily fatal provided the pilot hit the magneto switch and turned-off the fuel cock before impact. Failure to do so meant there was every chance a ruptured fuel line would squirt petrol and explode, as happened this time.

The brief spell of fine weather added a second Albatros, a Roland D-II, and another twelve hours, forty minutes of artillery spotting to my logbook - with different pilots, Ellis being away on a course - before rainclouds once more rolled up the Channel from the Atlantic.

This was when our Mess President discovered me conversing fluently with the local *curé*, on the strength of which I was appointed Mess Catering Officer, authorised to trade with Father Matthieu's shrewd, secretive parishioners. Entrusted with our funds in paper francs, a haversack of canteen cigarettes, and a motorbike pannier bag laden with tins of sardines and bully beef, I would return later in the day with bottles of apple brandy, farmhouse *chacouterie*, fruit jams, and other delicacies hidden from the Food Control Police.

The money and cigarettes were obvious attractions, but a surprise was how popular the beef and sardines were; I assumed that cooked meat in salty dripping, and tasty fish in olive oil, were luxury fare for a civilian population starved of fats and flavours.

Only later did I learn that our tinned foods were currency in *Le Système*, a nationwide syndicate of black marketeers who moved other, shadier goods and services from country to town, town to city, city to country, round and around, bribed along by our unopened tins of meat and fish.

An artful old soldier like Father Matthieu was delighted to facilitate his parishioners' underground commerce, and I was equally glad to help with his parish duties.

We must have made a peculiar sight, my pillion passenger holding his biretta cap in place with one hand, vestments flapping behind, like a witch on a broomstick instead of a priest on an RFC motorbike ridden by an Australian, steel helmet and gas mask slung across mackintosh coat, rattling past British convoys and staff cars, cavalry detachments, and horse-drawn field artillery.

MP roadblocks frequently flagged us down, checked my papers and Father M's *carte d'identitè* before waving us through, confident that no German spies would ever have *le cran* to hide in plain sight, disguised as such an odd couple.

Then, while *le bon curé* absolved the dying in their cottage beds, comforted the sick, and consoled grieving parents who had just received an official telegram thanking them for the gift of a son *mort pour la Patrie*, I would be haggling over a kilo of smoked sausage or a pot of *foie gras* next door.

It was after I'd returned from one of these foraging expeditions and had returned the balance of our funds to the Mess Treasurer, that my tentmate – Peter McNamara – glanced up from his newspaper and asked: "What are the odds there's another Ian Cribdon in the Flying Corps, answering to your description, about to marry an earl's daughter…?"

"About ten million to one," I shrugged. "Why?"

"This is you, then?" He tapped an entry in the *Times'* Personal Column.

"Mm," I nodded reluctantly, foreseeing any number of snide comments from the British officers on our squadron, once the word got out that their fairest and finest was about to marry an Aw-stray-yun.

"Strewth!" Peter shook his head in disbelief. "You are a dark horse!"

"What's the problem? We're only getting married. Thousands do, every day." It says much for my numbed brain that I really believed what I said. Boy meets girl, they fall in love, marry, live happily ever after, end of story. Except, of course, ours was never going to be that simple.

I was promptly summoned by XIII Squadron's CO, Major Forbes-Glynn, a remote figure who usually kept a wary distance from D Flight's piratical crew of Australians. "Good afternoon, Mr Cribdon," his moustache fairly bristled with goodwill, "what's this I hear about you getting married in November?"

"Yes sir. The 26th, I think."

"You do realise it's customary to ask your commanding officer's permission first?"

"Really?" I blinked with polite surprise. "I didn't know there was a proper drill. I've never been married before."

"Well, there is. Not that there's a problem; I'll see the paperwork goes through immediately. Now, you'll need compassionate leave. Usually it's only seven days, but I notice that you've not had much of a break recently, so shall we say two weeks?

"That will be splendid. Thank you, sir."

"It's no more than you're entitled to. Well, ah, congratulations once again and, ah, do please give my best wishes to your fiancée."

"I shall sir."

"Well! I must say all this has come as a bit of a surprise as well as an honour for our squadron," he had sufficient tact not to add, "having a Cabinet Minister's son-in-law on our strength," though I'm sure this was uppermost on his mind when he dismissed me.

Word soon got around, and it was not long before I felt a distinct change of attitude by those serving with me, a mixture of awe and approval rather than, as I had feared, jealous hostility.

This was not what I wanted. Left to my own devices I would happily have settled for a Registry Office wedding with a couple of mates as witnesses, rather than what threatened to become a full-blown Society circus.

Fortunately, our God Guesser was a good sport and signed-off a Confirmation Certificate as evidence that I was a paid-up member of his Anglican Church and therefore a suitable candidate for a wedding conducted by the Bishop of London, with all the pomp and ceremony required for such a high and mighty occasion.

115

By now, the Third Battle of Ypres resembled two punch-drunk boxers propping each other up in the ring, blindly trading blows, Passchendaele Ridge the prize at stake.

Anywhere else and this slight fold in the ground would have counted for nothing, but amidst the reclaimed marshes and flatlands of Flanders its modest elevation dominated every Allied position around the Salient and was symbolically vital as the last few acres of Free Belgium. Passchendaele's counterscarp also masked the Germans' own supply hub at Roulers railway junction, a scant six miles away.

Though we did not know it yet, defeat was an imminent prospect. Soon, five British divisions would be stripped from the Western Front to reinforce our Italian allies, who were about to be overrun by the Austro-Hungarians at the twelfth Battle of Isonzo. Meanwhile, on the Eastern Front, Russia's armies were melting away, demoralised by Bolshevik agitators, after the Czar's abdication earlier in the year. The Kaiser's armies were now within grasp of victory on both fronts, hence the need for one supreme effort by the Allies to get dug-in along that accursed ridge, before another dreadful winter like the previous one of 1916-17.

Our squadron flew dawn-to-dusk every flyable day, and several that were marginal at best, supporting the New Zealanders when they took Gravenstatel. We were still barely operational when the Canadians finally captured Passchendaele itself. During this period, I logged more hours of artillery spotting, two daylight bombing raids on Roulers railway yards, and a Halberstadt D.III, last seen spinning into the ground.

Rain and frequent squalls brought some relief to us, if not to our troops in the trenches, and were a welcome opportunity to gather my thoughts before going on leave.

Sadly, Dr Levine had advised Aunt Lucinda against attempting the voyage from Melbourne, so instead she sent her heartfelt blessings and a serious sum of money with instructions that it be lavished on my new wife. In fact, I was seated in the Mess, writing a reply describing our wedding arrangements, and was about to tell her that Sandra's brother was now my Best Man, when –

"The murderous swine!"

I glanced up. Fresh faces were forever replacing old ones. I had no idea which of B Flight's pilots was scowling at today's *Daily Mail*, delivered this morning by an RFC courier flight from England. "What's Fritz done to upset us now?" I enquired, more to be polite than with any real interest.

"Torpedoed a hospital ship, that's what!"

My mouth dried. I leaned forward. "Let me see. Please."

"Here! Look for yourself!" He skimmed the paper across the table between us.

The headlines were standard Northcliffe screamers: Hunnish Horror! Survivors Slaughtered! There then followed an account of how *HMHS Winchelsea* had been attacked nine miles out from Le Havre, late in the afternoon of Thursday 15th November, portholes clearly lit to identify her as a hospital ship, hull painted white, large red crosses prominently displayed on both sides so there could be no mistaking her purpose.

The U-boat fired two torpedoes, surfaced, and cruised around, shining a searchlight, as if admiring its handiwork, before casually machine-gunning the lifeboats.

"I say old chap! What's the matter?!" My colleague sat bolt upright. "You look like you've just seen a ghost -!"

"I hope, not." I steadied my voice. "I know someone. On that ship."

"Oh. Jolly bad luck."

My worst fears were confirmed when Major Forbes-Glynn summoned me to his office shortly before lunch. "You have, a telegram…"

I borrowed the letter opener on his desk and took out a plain printed form with hastily gummed strips of text:

REGRET TO ADVISE LOSS BY ENEMY
ACTION OF NURSE (true name and title)
ABOARD HMHS WINCHELSEA STOP
THE FAMILY SHARES YOUR GRIEF
STOP DETAILS FOLLOW STOP JAMES

Something deep inside me froze and has never thawed since that dreadful moment. Freckled with cold sweat, hand trembling, I gave the form to my Commanding Officer. "I'm afraid, there won't be a wedding, now. Sir."

He read the telegram with evident distress. "I'm most awfully, awfully sorry Ian."

A full report of *Winchelsea's* sinking brought me no comfort. Sandra had twice gone below as the ship sank, climbing aloft each time with a wounded soldier slung across her shoulders. The captain stopped her returning a third time and, instead, thrust her into the last lifeboat as it was about to cast off. It was one of those targeted when UB-34's captain, Freiherr Helmut von Grundwitz, machine-gunned the survivors.

Later, when the grotesque parody of War Crimes Trial was staged in Leipzig between May and July of 1921, Grundwitz's defence was that he was lawfully responding to provocation when someone in the lifeboats shouted insults at the Kaiser and fired a revolver; these were sufficient grounds for an acquittal typical of other contemptible verdicts.

The Rape of Belgium and Nurse Cavell's murder were never tried, which was hardly surprising with so many embittered Germans convinced that the Fatherland's only crime was to have lost the war, stabbed in the back by Jewish profiteers and Communist agitators. Frances, however, might find it historically informative to learn how a higher form of justice eventually delivered judgment after Grundwitz's return to civilian life as a shipping agent.

Millions of Germans were bankrupted by post-war hyperinflation at a time when one English ten-shilling note could be exchanged for ten billion *Reichmarks*. He, by contrast, amassed a tidy fortune in foreign currencies by trafficking white slaves for Turkish opium, selling Berlin's nastiest blue movies to American perverts, and smuggling Comintern saboteurs from Leningrad to port cities around the world.

The years passed with leaden tread and he must have thought that the world no longer remembered what he'd done. Then, on the rainy evening of the ninth anniversary of *Winchelsea's* sinking, a shadowed stranger accosted him in the unlit entrance of an apartment block where his mistress lodged at 136 Kreuzweg, a short distance from Lübeck's main railway station.

There followed a harsh exchange of words during which the stranger shone his pocket torch on a forged *Kriminalpolitzei* warrant card. Grundwitz irritably unbuttoned his topcoat and loosened the jacket underneath to reach for his own identity papers, thus clearing the way for a swift, professional kill.

The bogus *Kripo* emptied his victim's wallet and dropped it beside the corpse. Then checked the scene was clean, except for a crushed electric light bulb, and returned to the station. Here he retrieved his commercial travellers' sample case of homeopathic remedies from Left Luggage and caught the overnight express to Munich.

A week later, the city's *Gerichtsmedizine* reported that the lethal weapon was a commonplace slot-head screwdriver, especially sharpened to stab upwards from below the sternocostal cartilage. This had punctured the subject's heart and been left embedded in thick muscle to ensure that no bloodstains or arterial spray patterns contaminated the thief's raincoat or gloves, there being no evidence of fingerprints on the screwdriver's painted wooden handle.

What was not published in the local press were details of the facial bruising and broken nose, mute evidence that the victim's head had been snatched forward, burying it in the assassin's shoulder to muffle the scream detonated by a kneed groin while the other fist finished a trademark OGPU liquidation. A fact confirmed by the one-rouble banknote recovered from von Grundwitz' gaping mouth, a *smert' predatelyam* warning to any other traitor planning to double-cross the Soviet Secret Police.

116

My leave pass and travel papers were still valid, but instead of taking me to a wedding they took me to a memorial service.

James was waiting at Victoria Station. We exchanged salutes and caught a taxi to Berkeley Square. Ours was a silent understanding, it being impossible to express such profound grief without becoming disgustingly emotional. At times like these one has a duty to lead by example and not become a nuisance. Besides, others – on all sides of the war – were suffering far greater losses.

The Earl and Countess received me with great kindness at dinner where I was introduced to Sandra's young sister Margaret, hence the fond nickname Meg. A gawky schoolgirl, she kept staring at me as if I were a Martian, one of those exotic characters from the recent Edgar Rice Burroughs' novel of that name. Afterwards the family discussed tomorrow's service and offered me an opportunity to speak, which I declined, not sure how well my voice would hold up in public.

The following morning, we drove past Buckingham Palace to Wellington Barracks, site of the Guards' Chapel, already packed with mourners, many of whom had originally planned to attend a wedding service here.

Everyone stood as we entered and took our places at the front. I found it unsettling to be seated where I should have been standing with Sandra at my side. Instead, there were two vacant, highbacked chairs, rather like thrones. Curiously insensitive and cruel I thought until, behind us, I heard more scuffling and murmuring as the congregation stood again.

Standing with the Noburys, I turned to see what was going on and nearly collapsed. For a moment I thought Cedric Shaw had come to rid me of my pain, then I saw Queen Mary on his arm, both dressed in unadorned black as the royal couple took their places, facing the altar.

The Bishop of London welcomed us in the name of the Father, the Son, the Holy Spirit, and spoke of Sandra's life and courageous death; out of respect for Her Majesty, there was no mention of the Kaiser or of German atrocities.

The British Army's Matron-in-Chief, who I'm proud to say was an Australian, then spoke for the thousands of other women serving in uniform, saying that Sandra's loss - and those of her companions who had also been named in the Bishop of London's address - would remain forever an inspiring example of devotion to duty.

Her father, the Fifth Earl, recited Psalm 23 with only the hint of a tremor in his voice, opening with that familiar line: "The Lord is my Shepherd, I shall not want..."

The choristers of St Paul's Cathedral then led us through John Bunyan's rousing old hymn *Pilgrim*:

> Who would true valour see
> Let him come hither.
> One here will constant be
> Come wind, come weather.

There's no discouragement
Shall make him once relent.
His first avowed intent
To be a pilgrim.

I defiantly sang the subject pronouns as "her" in all three verses, and cared not a damn who cast startled glances in my direction, before the bishop reverently committed Sandra's absent body, yet ever-present soul, to God's infinite mercy

A Grenadier Guards' bugler sounded the *Last Post* followed, one minute later, by *Reveille*, as befitted a courageous young woman and her companions, killed in action while saving others' lives. During the Minute's Silence between these calls, I took Sandra's wedding ring from my tunic pocket.

Asprey & Garrard the Crown Jewellers had made it when I sent them the circumference of Sandra's third left finger, nibbled from the middle of our rowing boat's cardboard ticket, using the bandage scissors kept on a cotton tape in her uniform frock's lap pocket.

As the bugler sounded his final notes, I slipped the gold ring over the knuckle of my left hand's little finger, where it remains to this day.

All but two of the congregation joined the choristers in singing the National Anthem, after which Their Majesties stood and prepared to leave but not before first approaching the Noburys. The Earl bowed, the Countess curtseyed, hands were shaken and short conversations ensued. Plural, because Queen Mary spoke woman-to-woman, even as her husband was speaking man-to-man with the grieving father.

What I did not expect, though, was the Earl taking my elbow and drawing me forward. "Sir. I have the honour to present our daughter's fiancé."

The King-Emperor had such a strong presence, one failed to notice that he was quite short, about five and a half feet tall, with eyes of startling blue. He faced me with truly gracious attention. "My wife and I share your grief, Mr Cribdon, and feel it most deeply." King George's voice was firm and strong, as one would expect of a former naval officer, its timbre very similar to my Chief's in Westralia.

"Sandra was always welcome at our home, both for the pleasure of her conversation and the delight of her company." He then added words that came straight from the heart. "I would promptly give up everything within my power, if only it would turn back the clock to happier times. For all of us…"

I received the royal handshake and watched Their Majesties leave, responding with grave nods to bows and curtsies. Then it was the family's turn to lead the way, driving through Central London to the Savoy where what should have been our wedding breakfast was now my wife's wake.

I stood with James and his parents, shaking more hands, receiving condolences from peers and cabinet ministers, men of affairs and their wives, every one of them curious to inspect the previously unknown Australian soldier who very nearly married into the British aristocracy.

One familiar face registered on my deadened brain, Sir Alfred Stanhope's. "A terrible loss for you, Mr Cribdon, and for the nation." Said with quiet dignity. "Do, please, stay in touch."

117

Breakfast the following day, at Berkeley Square, was understandably subdued. Sandra's father used the occasion to assure me that this was my home in London, and that both he and her mother wished me to regard them as family. I nodded, unable to speak, and looked down at my lap to hide the tears.

Their son insisted I accompany him to a piano recital of Beethoven sonatas at the Royal Albert Hall, played by his old teacher, Donald Tovey.

I knew that Sandra was - had been - an accomplished pianist when she sang that eerily predictive: "There's a home for tired nurses, above the bright blue sky…" What I did not know, until now, was that her brother was also a talented player.

We entered the auditorium and took our seats. In my case numbly prepared to endure whatever it was attracted my brother-in-law, for that is how we had agreed to regard each other, after he saw me slip his sister's wedding ring on my finger, and realised what it signified.

The poor chap must've needed consoling company to invite someone of my lowbrow tastes, not that I was a musical illiterate, that being impossible at Tralee House. But my aunt's repertoire largely consisted of jaunty tunes by Offenbach and soulful melodies by Liszt, her hatred of Bismarck encompassing every German composer of the past three centuries, even the one with a Dutch surname, Ludwig van Beethoven.

She was not alone. The Albert Hall had become a battleground for this present *Kulturkampf* or Culture War, depending upon one's choice of language. Only a few days earlier it had staged a Grand Patriotic Concert of all-English music, conducted by Sir Edward Elgar, including the premier performance of Laurence Binyon's *Ode to the Fallen*, with its familiar verse recited at every Armistice Day service since 1919:

> They shall not grow old,
> As we who are left grow old.
> Age shall not weary them,
> Nor the years condemn.
> At the going down of the sun,
> And in the morning,
> We shall remember them.

The walls were still bedecked with red, white, and blue bunting swagged between the national ensigns of Britain and the Dominions, France and Belgium, Japan, Russia and Italy, Portugal, and Serbia, as *Maestro* Tovey bowed to his audience and struck the opening chords of Sonata Number 8, *The Pathétique*, determined to prove that music still had the power to transcend human fear and folly.

I got ready to doze as James' fingertips stroked imaginary keys, exploring what were, to my untutored ears, novel thickets of sound and rhythm. I had not the faintest idea what they were saying, of course, but by the time Donald Tovey struck the first chords of Sonata 21, *The Waldstein*, I was starting to get a sense of this new musical language.

Sonata 29, *The Hammerklavier*, drew back the curtains and let the daylight flood in, ready for James' commentary as we shared a pot of tea and a couple of sticky buns in a nearby Lyons' Corner House.

"You see, by the end of his life, Beethoven had composed thirty-two sublime piano sonatas,' he explained, leaning across the table to make his point. "These are often, and correctly, described as music's *'New Testament.'*"

"There's an *Old Testament*?"

"Bach."

At least I was familiar with that name, after hearing Dulcie Donovan practice some of his simpler pieces on the piano, at home in Kalgoorlie, before transposing them to the organ at St Mary's.

"Each defines a distinct period," Sandra's brother continued with an absorbed smile, most likely his first since *Winchelsea*'s loss and, if so, evidence of music's healing balm.

"The first you heard, *Pathétique*, is obviously influenced by Mozart and Haydn, and considered Early Period. *Waldstein* is Middle Period when Beethoven begins to experiment with new tonal textures. While *Hammerklavier* is Late Period, and so confoundedly complex it was considered unplayable by anyone other than its composer, until Liszt showed how lesser mortals could master it…"

I was unsure how to respond intelligently, so I turned the question around. "Have you mastered it yet?"

"No." He shook his head. "Maybe, when the war's over, I'll be in a better frame of mind…"

"I think I know what you mean."

"You do?"

"It's the same with painting, and illustration," I replied, on firmer ground now. "*Punch* pays me a fiver apiece for cartoons, but nothing else matters much anymore."

"Will you ever get back to your serious work?" he enquired closely.

"Don't know," I shrugged. "What about you? With the piano?"

"Not sure." He stretched these two words, as if no longer certain of their meaning. "I've composed a few chamber pieces and sketched a concerto that might amount to something, one day, but I'll never be anything more than a capable amateur."

"Stick with it." I was always ready to encourage others' artistry, even when my own wobbled, like now. "I'm sure you'll do as well as that bloke we've just heard!"

"It's kind of you to think so, but unlikely, even if I didn't have to shoulder five generations of responsibilities, when my turn comes," he added, with a sad grimace.

"Oh?"

"Jealous commoners imagine that inheriting a peerage is to be 'born with a silver spoon in the mouth,'" he explained, with weary resignation. "They are so consumed by envy that they fail to see the golden ball and chain that restricts our every choice and chance in life…"

I remained silent, reminded of striking a similar chord in what I'd meant to be my farewell letter to Sandra, and then looked up again. "Come on mate," I shoved away from the table, "we've had a good morning's listen, now let's have a good afternoon's look."

We split the bill, stepped outside, hailed a taxi – London's cabbies were always on the lookout for spendthrift Australian soldiers' distinctive slouch hats – and hopped off at the National Gallery in Trafalgar Square.

"There's something here I've wanted to see for as long as I can remember." Intrigued, James followed me until we found the gallery where *Fighting Temeraire* had been on display since Turner bequeathed it to the nation, sixty-odd years earlier.

I leaned over the kerb rope, closely studying the technical skill of a crotchety old Englishman who unwittingly pointed the way ahead for a younger generation of French Impressionists like Monet and Pissarro, Sisley, Renoir and Berthe Morisot. Voluntary exiles in London after the Franco-Prussian War and all, like their artwork, familiar names at Tralee House where Aunt Lucinda delighted in recounting their colourful lives and loves as she showed our guests around her extensive collection of their paintings.

Of *Temeraire* itself, none of the coloured lithographs on the withdrawing room walls of other homes along Grange Road, and farther afield, came within a bull's roar of the original in London. At about one yard deep by one and a third wide, *Temeraire* has exactly the right balance for its subject, not that size matters for this masterpiece, in the truest meaning of that much abused noun.

"You see the way he's positioned his subject well to the left, when you'd expect the ships to be dead centre?" I began. "And note the feeling of progression, as if the old battleship and its steam tug are moving into the mid-foreground. And see how the setting sun is equally spaced to the right," I continued, absorbed by what I saw and felt, "casting identical red reflections on the water as the sparks and flames, blasting out of the tug's smokestack, unite the composition with the merest chromatic hint. Here, let me show you." I took a sketchbook and cigar case, modified to hold a selection of coloured crayons from my tunic pocket and, with deft strokes, limned what I wanted him to share.

Instead, James ignored me and kept peering at the evidence of Turner's genius. "I have seen quite a few copies, but only now, thanks to you, do I see what his ghostly, bone white ship, and rusty tug, and blood-red sunset are telling me...."

"Which is?" I enquired quietly.

"They symbolise the inevitable, irreversible end of every glorious age. A veteran of Trafalgar, whose decks once thundered to the roar of cannon and the cheers of her crew, is now no more than a decaying hulk on its way to the wreckers' yard, there to be broken up for scrap metal and firewood..." He hesitated before intoning, more to himself than to me:

> Now the sunset breezes shiver
> Temeraire! Temeraire!
> And she's fading down the river
> But in England's song forever
> She's the Fighting Temeraire...

"Go on," I persisted, just as quietly.

"That's how I feel about our world," he replied, simply. "Three centuries of Romanovs? Dethroned in three weeks by Red revolutionaries. The Saxe-Coburg-Gothas? Forced to hide behind a new name that doesn't remind their subjects of Hun bombing raids. And for how much longer can the Hapsburgs and Hohenzollerns exist in their present form? Even if they were to win the war, they would lose the peace, overwhelmed by dark forces they've unleashed upon themselves and the world. Indeed," he concluded, "how long before we lesser dynasties must also bow to the winds of change, or by resisting them, be torn up by the roots?"

"Your point being…?"

"My point being, like Mr Turner's once-mighty man o' war, History's wrecker's yard awaits everyone, regardless," he responded, with a sideways nod. "These few square feet of painted canvas are a timely reminder that nothing lasts forever. 'Sceptre and Crown must tumble down, and in the dust be equal made, with poor crookéd scythe and spade.'"

I was in no mood for his morbid speculations. "Come on, mate, there's something else we need to see -"

"No." He turned away and resumed studying Turner's evocative riverscape. "An earl's coronet and ermine mantle must also tumble down, and in the grave be equal made, with poor workman's cap and coat. And yet, today we've heard sublime sounds that outlived their composer's brief time on earth and are seeing images that still evoke the deepest human emotions," he leaned forward to read the descriptive panel below its framed canvas, "sixty-six years after the artist laid down his brushes."

"What of it?" I frowned, unsettled by these echoes of Sandra's penetrating intellect, so agonisingly missed as the anaesthetic of her heroic death wore off.

"I'm not, sure." He turned away, reflectively rubbing his chin. "I need time to reconsider who I am, and what my purpose in life may be."

"And I need time to study Velazquez's *Rokeby Venus* -!"

"No. Let's go home. Please, Ian."

118

My next four days were spent with the Earl and Countess, James, and the young Lady Margaret as relatives and friends came to Berkeley Square to express their condolences. It was all very formal and correct, with never a sniffle or damp eye to mar the occasions.

Recalling that vanished world of restraint and good breeding, I am reminded of my brother-in-law's acute interpretation of *Temeraire* as symbolising the old, established order displaced by a newer one. Within the next decade, popular entertainments and moving pictures would sow a rich harvest of bizarre behaviours unimaginable before the Great War. By the time it became my business to visit Hollywood, epicentre of this worldwide cultural revolution, "Anything goes!" was a popular catchphrase, hiccuped with many a boozy, bootlegged wink signifying that everything had indeed gone.

And yet, only twelve years earlier in 1917, I still had to bite my tongue whenever assorted Society fossils expressed their amazement that an Australian held the King's Commission, spoke the King's English with fluency, and never once blew his nose on a dinner napkin or nibbled peas off his knife blade. Several times I had to look away and ignore an unthinking slight. Once, I came dangerously close to treating an ancient viscountess as if she were a defaulter about to be double-marched before her Commanding Officer, so determined was I to prove that my homeland was no longer a remote rubbish dump for her criminal classes -!

Fortunately, the younger set was less obsessed with chains and whips, convicts and transportation. Britain's newspapers and kinema newsreels had done a splendid job of burnishing the Anzac Legend for these war-weary Britons, and the youngsters' response when meeting a bronzed demi-god in all his uniformed glory, was very flattering. But by the fourth evening after my wife's memorial service, I'd had enough weak tea and sympathy to last me for what little remained of my lifetime.

Thus far I had not paid much attention to young Margaret who always seemed to be parked in the background on these occasions, to such an extent that I wondered if she was the dim relative everyone knows about, but tactfully never speaks of. Then, as the Duke and Duchess of Abercorn were about to take their leave, she dipped a knowing wink and murmured in my left ear: "What a frightful bore..." Her voice was agreeably modulated, and her choice of words was not those of a simpleton when she added: "I don't suppose there's room in your kitbag for a stowaway? I've got my Red Cross Certificate now and would be awfully useful at the Front..."

Her brother was not surprised when I told him later, as we took a stroll around Berkeley Square's miniature parkland before dressing for dinner.

"Meg's always been a bit of a pest," he observed ruefully. "She adores acting imaginary plays. Currently, she's the 'Scarlet Rose,' a seemingly scatter-brained English lady with a secret life of high adventure, about to rescue the Czar and Czaritza, disguised as 'Comrade Svetlana'!" he chuckled. "But don't be fooled. Those bright little eyes see everything, and the brain behind them forgets nothing…"

"She fooled me!"

"Don't worry, she's underage," he replied, mistaking my meaning. "The VADs won't take her for another year. And even if the war drags on after that, she'll stay on this side of the Channel."

"Good." I was gruff. "One loss is too many; two would be devastating." I had not forgotten the haunted look of despair on Father Matthieu's housekeeper's prematurely aged face, dreading the news that she had given her last son *á la Patrie* or, more accurately, that he had been led away by strangers and killed far from hearth and home.

"I-I'm glad you see it that way," James remarked, after a tight pause. "I, ah, wouldn't want you to think badly of me."

"Why would I?" I blinked, somewhat surprised.

"Because I've, taken your advice," he replied awkwardly, "and decided against volunteering for the Flying Corps. Instead, I'm to become an Infantry Liaison Officer, on Haig's staff. It's not what I want, but doing one's duty for King & Country, is not always what we'd like to do for ourselves. I'm not funking it!" he added with a suddenly defensive note in his voice.

"Mate." I faced him. "You've been at this game from day dot. If a cat has nine lives, you must've been issued with ninety, so don't tempt fate by chancing your eighty-ninth. How many others of the original BEF are still alive? Precious bloody few!" I gave him a long hard look. "Just look after Ma', and Pa', and Meg. In the long run, those are the only ones who matter."

"And your good opinion." He sounded relieved. "That matters. For all of us."

"Hm." I said nothing more as we left the park and went in for dinner, at the end of which I announced that I would be accompanying James back to France when his leave ended tomorrow. This came as a bit of a shock, for they knew I still had the better part of another week to run, but despite their protestations I remained politely firm.

Dog tired, needing to be a lot brighter in the morning, I made an early night of it assisted by the Veronal prescribed by XIII Squadron's medical officer. I doubt if there were many aircrew – Ours or Theirs – who didn't pop a pill to get going in the morning, and another to switch off at night. Without them we could not have done what we did, for as long as we did. Usually, I downed one, maybe two after a bad stunt, but this evening I felt so wretched – perched alone on the edge of the bed that Sandra and I had consecrated during our last night together – I swallowed three with a whisky chaser that emptied the bottle hidden inside my spare pair of socks.

Previous experience suggested this would stun me for the next several hours, but what I did not yet know was the terrible price I was about to pay, trapped by a paralysing nightmare of madly flashing coloured lights, powerless to stop giant shrimps, and crabs, and hagfish stripping the flesh off my wife's bones in the sandy depths of the English Channel. Since when, I would rather starve to death than eat a crustacean.

Next morning, barely coherent, I took leave of the Earl and Countess while their surviving daughter stood well back, staring at me with an odd look on her face, probably picturing me as the moustachioed villain in one of her imaginary melodramas.

I shared the taxi to Victoria Station and the RTO's office, where an elderly clerk struck James' name, rank, and number off the master list, but looked baffled when I presented my travel warrant. "You're early, sir. You've got another six days!"

"I know. Find me a seat, standing room in the corridor, a ride on the roof, I don't bloody care. Just get me to where I know what's what and what's not!"

In the event he found us a couple of adjacent numbers on his list, James being determined to keep an eye on me as we squeezed into a sweaty, smoke-filled compartment. "You don't have to do this!" he insisted, continuing our earlier conversation, "there's still time to go back home for a few more days -!"

"And do what?" I was trying hard to be civil. "You know I don't belong. Most likely I never did, not that it matters anymore. It's best I get away quickly. I won't be responsible for my actions if I see another Christmas decoration proclaiming, 'Peace on Earth and Goodwill to all Men'!"

I stopped short and tried again. "Sorry. That was uncalled for. Sandra's death is no easier for you than it is for me. I shall never forget what you did to welcome a stranger, from another world, but now she's gone, I'm surplus to requirements."

"Don't be ridiculous! We all like you, a lot!"

"Thanks, but even HM knows that if he gave everything a king possibly could, there would be no return to happier days. What's done is done and we must slog it out to the bitter end." Which, in my case, could not be delayed much longer.

The latest winter storm had blown itself out, but our Channel crossing was still rough enough for several hundred groggy, grey-faced soldiers to stumble ashore at Boulogne, later that afternoon, leaving the ferry's crewmen to clean up with hosed seawater and stiff brooms, behind them.

"Let me give you a lift," James said as we sorted our kit, nodding towards a waiting staff car, for such are the perks of rank and connexion.

"No thanks. I'll kip here the night and take off in the morning."

"Well, if that's what you really want," he replied, eyeing me cautiously, for I'm sure he sensed what was on my mind, "but I'm sure it will be no trouble finding a billet at GHQ..."

"Don't worry. I'll be right." We exchanged salutes and I watched him being driven off to Field Marshal Haig's General Headquarters at Montreuil sur Mer, half an hour down the coast, a short distance from Étaples of infamous memory.

I decided to have one final night of civilian life by booking into the Hotel Terminus instead of the officers' billets in Rue des Signeaux. The desk clerk recognised my face and hurriedly arranged a cot, a cubicle, and a brass token that entitled me to one five-minute wash with tepid water. I then bought a wartime economy dinner of turnip and cabbage fritters, and mashed potato, if I remember rightly, and afterwards sat down to write my thank'ee note to the Earl and Countess.

I did my best to make it not read like a voice from the grave, although that is what it was, having returned early to the Front so that an enemy bullet would find me this much sooner.

Several times in London I had loaded my revolver with a single round, and the only reason I kept unloading it was the unpleasant mess some poor housemaid would have had to mop up.

I should have sat on the balustrade of Westminster Bridge, house bricks in my pockets, pulled the trigger, and let Old Father Thames do the rest, but by inviting a Hun to finish the job now, I was leaving an unblemished name for those who still cared about such quaint niceties.

There was nothing hysterical or histrionic in my decision to call it quits. I could not have been cooler, calmer, or more collected. Once life loses its purpose, with no hope of recovery, what is the point of carrying on? Truth be told, I was rather looking forward to a momentary flash of pain and a glimpse of what, if anything, comes next.

I sealed the Noburys' letter and began another, this time to Elspeth McCracken (Miss) who by now was probably at high school. In it I thanked her for all the news from home and best wishes since her hand-drawn 1914 Christmas card. I hoped that she had found Arthur Streeton's advice useful in her art studies, and strongly urged her to visit the National Gallery in London, one day. Meanwhile I was enclosing an English five-pound note that, when exchanged for Australian coins and banknotes, should buy her a decent stock of paints and materials; my main bequest would come later, as a pleasant surprise.

Finally, instead of my usual signature, I cartooned a cheery Digger shouting "Goodbye-ee!" as he hopped over the bags, echoing a popular song that included this apt verse:

> Though it's hard to part, I know
> I'll be tickled to death to go!
> Don't cry-ee, don't sigh-ee
> There's a silver lining in the sky-ee!
> Bonsoir old thing, cheerio, chin-chin
> Napoo, toodle-oo, goodbye-ee!

The letter to Aunt Lucinda was more restrained and factual as I described Sandra's memorial service, my few words with the King Emperor, and what followed. It was not necessary to mention loss and bereavement for I knew she would read those between the lines. It concluded by saying that I had finished my leave and was returning to XIII Squadron.

David's death meant there was no one else to inform, so I bought a half-bottle of bathtub brandy masquerading as Martell *Cordon Bleu* cognac and tramped upstairs to my cot.

The following day, bleary eyed and gravel mouthed, I presented myself to Movements in Rue de la Falaise and hitched a lift to St Omer, and then another to Le Hameau where a dusting of snow had fallen during the night. This didn't seem to be hindering op's as I paused under the Orderly Room's porch and watched a machine lumber aloft, setting course for the Front as it disappeared between lowering drapes of dark grey cloud.

Admin' was accustomed to troops overstaying their leave, so having one return after under-staying his was something of a novelty. There was a similar response at the Mess when I signed-in, but I shrugged and said that wartime London was too dismal, and not having family or friends in Britain meant there was no point hanging around the wretched place.

The new faces, who'd arrived during my absence, must have thought me a queer cove to throw away half a leave; the old faces, of whom there were still some, understood and I'm glad to say made no mention of Sandra's death or her memorial service, extensively covered in the newspapers. Only civilians can afford the luxury of extravagant grief; soldiers are necessarily thriftier with their emotions.

Roy Ellis had completed his course in preparation for Dingo Flight's amalgamation with the all-Australian 69 Squadron RFC, soon to be 3 Squadron AFC, and was delighted to see me return, having just flown with one of the new observer/air gunners and, as he confessed, been scared rigid by the young man flapping about in the rear cockpit. "Thank God you're back in time…"

"In time for what?"

"The 'Gazers are forecasting a twelve-hour gap, tomorrow. It's a big stunt, maximum effort. I've hit this target before, so we'll be pathfinding for the other squadrons –"

"'Squadrons?' Plural?"

"All three. The full wing," he replied with sober emphasis. "Precise details to be confirmed, but with you covering our arse, I can now focus on my half of the job."

"Good. I'm ready."

There was much forced laughter around the Mess table that evening before we aircrew turned-in early. The unspoken wish for most others, I'm sure, was that the Allied Meteorological Unit on Cap Griz Nez - informally known as the Crystal Ball Gazers - had got it wrong and that bad weather would scrub tomorrow's stunt.

119

Our batman delivered a pail of warm water so that Peter and I could share a quick rinse and shave before an early breakfast of porridge, toast, and a fried egg in the Mess hut. Pilots and observers then paired-up, crunched across the snow, and warmed the Briefing Room with our bodily heat while the IO took his place at the pulpit, as we nicknamed his lectern.

Ellis was right, today was a big stunt; forty RE8s tasked to bomb an ammunition dump at Ingelmunster on the same canal as the one where David got his number; a coincidence I read as an auspicious omen.

Carrier pigeons, parachuted in baskets to the Belgian Resistance by night, had flown back reports of a new artillery shell being stockpiled near the canal. By all accounts it dispersed an even more toxic chemical fog than the Yellow Cross mustard gas that was now inflicting horrific deaths and injuries on the Western Front, itself a diabolical advance on the Green Cross phosgene shells that replaced the primitive chlorine munitions of early-1915.

Codenamed Blue Cross, this gaseous-arsenic compound was the satanic brainchild of Professor Fritz Haber whose artificial nitrogen fixation process had leapfrogged Germany's reliance on imported Chilean nitrates. This evil genius was now gloating that his enhanced gas attacks were "an improved form of killing," not that such a frank confession would bar him from receiving the Nobel Prize for Chemistry a year or two later.

Concentrating munitions like these, so close to the Front, plus Intelligence reports of a new gas mask being issued to *Sturmtruppen*, were clear evidence that the Huns were preparing a Christmas Surprise for the Canadians on Passchendaele Ridge. If all went according to plan, this doomed hump in the ground would again change hands under choking clouds of Haber's improved lethal gas and the Kaiser's artillery would once more dominate the Ypres Salient.

No way could our few thousand pounds of high explosives destroy several thousand tons of shells, but what we could do was blow up and disrupt a sufficiently large number by shattering the glass bulbs containing a liquid component of their binary chemical charges. Do that and it would be weeks before the decontamination squads finished their work, and the ordnance technicians could access what remained of the stockpile.

To achieve this, our armourers were loading twenty-pounders onto our bomb racks while other groundcrew shovelled snow by dawn's early light. All then formed fours and began marching upwind, downwind, back, and forth, compacting what remained of the snow with their gumboots, to mark out the runway.

Pre-flight inspection completed, condensed dew drained from our RE8's petrol tank, I settled inside the Scarfe ring's gun mount, pyjamas under my serge uniform, itself buttoned inside the padded Sidcot suit, toes aching with cold inside fleece-lined boots.

The other aeroplanes responded well to the sub-zero, oxygen-dense air, twin exhaust stacks spitting, coughing, spluttering awake, one after another, joining a chorus of undulating snarls as their pilots revved up, then down, testing electrical circuits and oil pressures before waving chocks-away and starting to ponderously waddle downwind after us, in line-astern.

Today, both lower wingtips were being steadied by gloved pairs of mechanics in greatcoats and Balaklava helmets, struggling to stay on track between shallow, shovelled snowdrifts as we led the way, doubtless cursing fluently as they manhandled our machine into the light breeze, blasted by gritty ice dust whipped up by the wooden propeller's flailing backdraft.

Overladen though we were, the frigid air offered a slim margin of extra lift as Ellis held his throttle lever hard forward, undercarriage struts grunting and shuddering, pneumatic tyres thumping and bounding along their trampled strip of frozen muck, tail skid barely clearing the boundary hedge as we roared over it.

Facing aft, I had an uninterrupted view of our aerodrome's baggy brown canvas hangars and workshops, sandbagged fuel dump and ordnance bays, Nissen huts and tent lines, as we toiled upwards, into the wintry morning sky.

Something made me cup my leather gloves as if they were a megaphone and bawl farewell at the dwindling scene: "It's so easy to go-ee! There is no silver lining in the sky-ee! Bonsoir old things! Cheerio, chin-chin! Hip-hooray, I'm on my way, goodbye-ee...!"

I had lived a rich and fulfilling twenty-something years, fuller than most men experience in their allotted three score and ten, and had beaten the odds in a gamble where many don't survive their first week, or day, or hour in action. But with my wife gone ahead, there was no reason for me to stay behind. From the moment I'd signed-on in Kal's Drill Hall, there'd been a bullet waiting somewhere with my name on it, and I was now as ready as I would ever be to welcome its blessèd release.

Oddly at peace with myself, I imagined cartooning XIII Squadron's machines as a flock of migrating birds chasing the red and yellow streamers on our outer wing-struts. Air-to-ground wireless was primitive at best, even when supplemented with Morse Code toots on our Klaxon horns. Air-to-air telephony was not even a daydream. The only communication between aeroplanes was by these coloured rags that served much the same purpose as a cavalry troop's pennons, or semaphored hand gestures that made us seem like demented tic-tac men on a gale-swept racecourse, or by Very pistol.

I loaded mine with today's recognition code and fired a single red star as two more squadrons approached from XVI Wing's other aerodromes. Both leaders fired single greens, the correct reply, and joined up as a mixed bag of Camels and SE5 scouts rose from the ground-shadow to cover our flanks.

Swivelling on the piano stool, I hunched forward and shouted into the Gosport tube's rubber cone that all were present and correct. Ellis raised his fist and punched it ahead, my cue to load two blue stars and fire Follow On to seventy-five other biplanes flying in staggered formation above and behind us.

Compared with the Second War's thousand-bomber saturation raids and their blockbuster tonnages, our show was a puny but tragic portent of things to come. By sad coincidence the Ingelmunster attack was almost fourteen years to the day since the world's first powered hop over a sand dune in December 1903, evidence of just how far and fast aeronautics had advanced, or degenerated, depending upon one's viewpoint.

The Wright Brothers could never have imagined their flimsy aerial machines riding into battle like a troop of heavy cavalry. Or foreseen our dozens of red-white-blue roundels furiously rippling on muddy green and brown doped fabric as we breasted the sky's choppy air currents.

Dull thuds of dark grey smoke greeted us over the Front, spraying a lethal pollen of iron splinters and shrapnel, largely ineffective though I did notice one RE8 starting to lag.

Tracking deeper into enemy territory, Ellis intersected the Dienze-Harelbeke Canal, our last waypoint and my cue to signal the formation with two more blue stars as he banked hard a'port to open the bombing run when, in a heartbeat, an arrowhead formation *Jasta* emerged from a misty veil of grey stratus at three o'clock -

Radar belonged to the next war. Our earlier equivalent was a network of ground observation posts and sound location horns linked by dedicated telephone lines. These had been triangulating our course and speed from the moment we crossed the Frontline, giving *Luftsreitkräfte* Command vital minutes in which to set an ambush over the estimated target area -

One-by-one the Dr-1s peeled off and dived, twin Zero-Eights raking our formation. A dazzle-camouflaged triplane tagged the squadron leader's streamers on my machine's wing struts, swooping close enough for me to see its pilot's triumphant smirk below glinting goggles -

But instead of terror, the black Iron Cross on his rudder, identical to the one on a U-boat's battle ensign, detonated an indescribable rage inside my panting belly –

Teeth bared. Howling with manic laughter. Clenched left fist swinging the Lewis gun. Right forefinger hooking juddered bursts of 0.303 Ball. The Fokker staggered and fell away, trailing oily flame -

Ellis held steady for the ammo dump; green tarpaulin covers lightly dusted with snow; control column hard forward; gravity clawing our cheeks and eyelids; bomb-release cable toggled -

Dog-fighting scouts tangled with the *Jagdtstaffel* while the rest of XVI Wing followed us down, defying furious ground fire to plaster our white phosphorus marker with HE –

One took a direct hit, adding its fuel and bomb load to the funeral pyre of Fritz Haber's Christmas surprise for the Canadians on Passchendaele Ridge -

A second DR1 dived astern, scenting wounded prey when he saw gashed fuselage fabric wildly flogging our airframe –

I held him off with thrifty tacker-tack-tacks while Ellis began hedgehopping homeward across Flanders' wintry flatlands -

The Hun pilot chased us down an avenue of poplars, not realising that our turbulent slipstream could flick his machine a whisker to one side, as happened when a wingtip clipped an overhung branch, cartwheeling him into the patrol of Uhlan lancers we'd startled a moment earlier -

Our luck held even though the RE8's engine had blown a poppet valve, a not infrequent occurrence with the Daimler V12, and kept stumbling along longer than one would have thought mechanically possible on eleven misfiring cylinders -

Rifle shots chased us across entrenched thickets of barbed wire before our engine finally conked and piled into the ground alongside a British field gun battery -

As the unsecured observer I was thrown clear, landing atop a snowdrift, skidding to a halt on my face, goggles dragged under chin, winded but otherwise unhurt. Sadly, the same could not be said for Roy, tightly strapped in, neck breaking as his head snapped forward on impact.

A couple of artillerymen helped me lift him from the cockpit and carry his body to their sandbagged position while I recovered our maps and Lewis gun.

One of the Tommies poured me a tin mug of hot sweet tea that wouldn't stop slopping over my gloved fingers, no matter how hard I bit its rim.

An ordnance cart carried Roy and me to the rear, after delivering its load of shells.

A Service Corps lorry dropped us off at Le Hameau as more snow and darkness fell.

Bruised and dishevelled, I reported to the IO and gave an account of today's action.

A couple of days later, a bearer party of myself and five pilots carried Roy into St Pierre's churchyard where pickaxes and shovels had chipped a regulation-depth grave from the frozen earth. Transverse planks removed, his coffin sank into the ground, cradled by webbing strops. A bugler sounded the *Last Post* and, one minute later, *Reveille*. Six airmen then presented arms and discharged three volleys of blanks.

The Brigade Chaplain's staff car led our lorries back to Le Hameau where we gathered around the Mess's potbelly stove and raised our glasses to another name whose face was already fading from memory, the God Guesser doubtless wondering which of us he would bury next, but the atrocious weather delayed that certainty by shutting down most op's this side of a Christmas that was anything but merry or bright.

St Omer did their best to raise morale by sending out a concert party of singers, and acrobats, and comedians who distributed small cardboard boxes of plum pudding, courtesy of the Australian War Comforts Fund. As my Christmas present to Sandra – ever present in my heart and rarely absent from my thoughts - I snaffled another three and popped one into each of three Red Cross mailbags containing POW letters to homes in Germany, but not before inscribing each box with *Fröhliche Weihnachten* and a pencilled note wishing the recipient good luck and a safe war.

In the meantime, our squadron commander had obtained Brigade's authorisation for a photo-recce of Roulers railway yards during which I tossed the mailbags, trusting that our improvised parachute drogues and yellow streamers would mark their descent and assist recovery.

It was less easy to compose a letter to Mrs Joan Ellis of Langton Street, Toowoomba, detailing her husband's last flight. Written in my neatest Italic script, I hoped it would bring more comfort than the official telegram and a typewritten "...popular fellow, greatly missed..." Letter of Condolence.

In it I emphasised the cool courage needed to hold an aeroplane steady while under attack from all sides, honour bound to disrupt the thousands of tons of poisonous gas shells stockpiled for Passchendaele Ridge, her husband's courage thereby saving countless numbers of Australian, Canadian, and British soldiers from unimaginably vile deaths and injuries.

I signed-off with my sincere admiration for Roy as a man and as a comrade, before adding a charcoal and crayon sketch of his grave in a snowy French churchyard, half the world away from Queensland's summer heat. I gave this artwork my best, knowing it would be treasured, perhaps in a family album with his snapshots of service overseas. Perhaps with the one of us standing alongside B-Bertie, grinning at the Photographic Section's camera after our first victory together.

1918

120

Then, early in January, Dingo Flight got orders to amalgamate with the embryonic Australian Flying Corps, in transit from Savy to Bailleul, the strategic railway junction and Anzac Corps' main supply base, not far from Hazebrouck.

RFC Bailleul was a weird and dangerous arrangement of three aerodromes – East, Asylum, and Town Ground – sharing the same field. Weird because there was no obvious benefit to be gained by operating three independent units from the one crowded patch of frosty turf; dangerous because there was not a skerrick of air traffic control in those days before ground-to-air wireless telephony. This meant that diverse machines would fly from all points of the compass, read the windsock's pivoted, white-painted T, and attempt to land before anyone else claimed the vacant slot.

This was inherently dicey for single seaters because, every so often, two would approach together, one above the other; the upper pilot unable to look downwards through his cockpit's plywood deck; the pilot below him too focused on the runway to look upwards; both men unaware of each other's presence until their machines ran out of height and they ran out of luck.

It is often claimed that a change is as good as a rest, but not in my case when I got stuck with the job of instructing 3 Squadron's replacement observer/air gunners, seven excited young men, mad keen to "hammer the Hun" as they laughingly imagined our work to be.

I was aghast by their lack of knowledge as well as experience. One had completed an abbreviated two-month course in six weeks. Another had yet to shoot more than one pan of ammo at a target drogue in the air. A third suffered from airsickness. All thought I was being funny when I said: "Stay alive long enough and you'll learn from others' mistakes. Get killed and others will learn from yours…"

I used to be a conscientious instructor, writing, and illustrating course notes that students liked to keep as well as read, but I could no longer be bothered to crank a Gestetner duplicating machine, or mark exam papers. Instead, I took the easy way out by telling selected yarns of war in the sky. It was not systematic, but it seemed to work well enough, whenever the weather lifted and we could resume artillery shoots and bombing raids between Armentières and wherever else Fritz required our attention.

Then, one foggy morning, an Orderly Room runner found me censoring letters in the IO's office, idly correcting spelling mistakes and dotting absent apostrophes in red ink. Stifling a yawn, I half-heard the airman mumble something about our new officer commanding – a Major Drake, or Blake, I'm not sure which – requesting my presence.

Flicking cigarette ash off tunic and cuffs, collar and tie roughly straightened, I wandered along to the OC's office, mildly curious to see what his problem was, only to learn that Major Forbes-Glynn had put me up for an award before his posting to Brigade HQ.

A chap was supposed to look happy and proud and thrilled on these occasions, but such was my numbed indifference that I could only look puzzled, the Military Cross being a decoration mostly bestowed on pilots, rarely on their perceived passengers in the rear cockpit.

This seemed to be the right time to announce that I wished to apply for flight training, much on my mind since discovering that not everyone in the driver's seat was as skilled or considerate as Roy Ellis had been.

It might be thought that having a limp could be an obstacle when piloting an aeroplane, but I had recently learned that Frank Alberry, also an ex-sergeant machine gunner and DCM, had just qualified even after winning a wooden leg at Pozières, and would soon be joining us.

The Ingelmunster stunt had unleashed an unquenchable thirst for revenge, and I was secretly relishing the prospect of watching more of my prey leap to their deaths from machines I'd set alight; was secretly chortling at the thought of more and more Iron Crossed wings crumpling under the impact of my bullets; was secretly drunk with joy as, in imagination, I exterminated more, and more, and more of the filthy swine who'd murdered my wife -!

I managed to conceal this madness and, instead, humbly informed the OC that I wished to join his exclusive Two Wings Club. Suitably flattered, for he was of course a pilot himself, he promised to have the paperwork ready to sign after I returned from Div' HQ, where I was under orders to attend a meeting at 1100 hours tomorrow.

Accordingly, after breakfast the following day, uniform brushed and sponged by my batman, gas mask and steel helmet slung over trench coat, I hitched a lift in one of the ration lorries heading down to Armentières, formerly a prosperous town famed for its woven linens, but now little more than random heaps of rubble. It took us well over an hour to cover the short distance from Bailleul, not that I was in any state to care after another night of giant shrimps, and crabs, and hagfish.

Sick at heart, I dozed as we threaded past columns of GS wagons, marching troops, and ambulances. Steam tractors towing new Mk-IVs from the railway yard, each tank chained to its individual low loader, and more ambulances. Salvage Corps lorries piled high with brass shell cases and discarded weapons recovered from the battlefield, and yet more ambulances.

The Australian Corps' positions were a continuation of the Ypres Salient, north, connected with the Arras Line, south, and officially a Quiet Sector despite its overlapping bangs, and thuds, and crumps up and down the nearby Front.

During my last visit to London, several years ago now, a well-meaning acquaintance invited me to a screening of *Oh! What a Lovely War* at the Odeon Kinema in Leicester Square. Billed as a satirical comedy, this Left-wing agitprop portrayal of my war failed to raise a smile and, a few minutes into the film, I excused myself, and went back to the Savoy Hotel.

What especially triggered my displeasure were the scenes of splendidly uniformed army brass-hats enjoying lives of elegant ease in requisitioned châteaux while their bedraggled troops endured brief lives of muck and misery in the trenches. Whereas, in an age before wireless telephony, divisional commanders often came up to the sandbagged parapets to assess the situation for themselves. And as for sheltering in comfy funk holes, when I later researched the matter for a magazine article, I was surprised to learn that more than two hundred British generals were killed in action, or gravely wounded, during the Great War.

Many were inspired leaders, like Major General "Rosie" Rosenthal, GOC 2 Division AIF who, a few nights before he was gassed, hopped over the bags into No Man's Land and captured a German wiring party, herding them back to the

Australian lines with his revolver, all the while hissing fluent Danish curses which probably terrified them more than the certainty of being shot dead if they tried to escape.

However, at the time of which I shall speak to Frances, General Birdwood was still our corps commander - genial old Birdy with whom I once shared a chirpy conversation, unaware of who he was, as we skinny dipped off the beach at Gallipoli – now recalled to London for top level talks at the War Office, leaving the Australian Army Corps temporarily under the command of GOC 3 Division, Aunt Lucinda's piano accompanist and David's honorary Uncle John.

Eventually, my Service Corps' lorry driver found his way through a maze of streets delineated by shattered shops and wrecked homes, their civvy inhabitants long since evacuated to the rear, depriving us of the mythical "Mad'mwa'zell f'm Armonteers" to serenade with our "inky-pinky-parlyvoo," and braked outside the former-Technical College, its walls pocked by bullets and shell fragments, windows patched with bits of cardboard and packing case lids, re-roofed with tarpaulin and sheets of corrugated iron.

I thanked the driver, paid my fare with five Woodbine cigarettes – Woodies were our unofficial units of currency in the trenches - and climbed down onto what had once been the school's recreation area but was now an expanse of broken brick, cracked asphalt, and shards of glass.

An MP examined my papers at the Guard Hut, saluted, and raised the striped barrier pole, letting me through the barbed wire entanglement that surrounded Div' HQ's sandbagged outbuildings and sheds.

An Orderly Room clerk ticked my name off his list and pointed me down a grimy, cheerless corridor festooned with telephone lines and emergency lighting cables that led into what used to be the Assembly Hall where other men were standing around, waiting for something to happen.

Most were infantry, with whom I felt an immediate affinity, although some were noticeably cool when they saw me arrive; I also used to believe that Flying Corps aircrew were pampered playboys who enjoyed a cushy war while we poor sods did not.

A smartly tailored captain entered, chestnut brown riding boots splendidly polished, wearing the despised Strawberries & Cream armband of a staff officer on his right sleeve. "Your attention please, gentleman," he smiled pleasantly enough. "The ceremony will shortly begin. So, greatcoats off and take your places on the chalked crosses you'll see on the floor, over there, Private Anderson J.K. your left marker."

The rest of us shuffled about in seemingly random order until the last name was called, placing a AAMC lieutenant colonel at the far end of our short parade. The aide-de-camp then walked past, pinning a small brass hook above each tunic's left breast pocket, before returning to the doorway and nodding outside.

Moments later, our GOC 3 Division entered, no longer the plump civilian brigadier general last glimpsed on Gallipoli but now an erect, commanding figure who had grown as many inches in height as he'd lost in girth during the past two years. Accompanying him was another ADC bearing a wooden tray, probably borrowed from the canteen.

"Private Anderson. Front and centre!"

The Digger marched up to Major General Sir John Monash, recently knighted for the Messines Ridge victory, exchanged a few words, shook hands, saluted, and returned to his place with a shiny new Military Medal hooked on his tunic.

Six other MMs followed, then three of the scarcer DCM – frequently awarded as a consolation prize whenever that month's unofficial quota of Victoria Crosses had been awarded - before it was the turn for five MCs, in alphabetical order, putting me first in line.

"Congratulations, Mr Cribdon. I've read good reports of your progress. Keep it up." He took a silver Military Cross off the tray, attached it to my hook, and shook hands. I took one pace to the rear, saluted, turned, and marched back to my place in the line.

"Colonel Wright…"

The senior Medical Corps' officer advanced, shook hands, saluted, and returned wearing the handsome white enamel and silver-gilt cross of the Distinguished Service Order, identical to the one I'd last seen on the Chief's naval uniform when he escorted Ingrid Bauer to her wedding day with Kurt Steiner, at Malloy's Livery Stable an eternity ago.

"This concludes today's ceremony," the aide announced after Sir John had returned our salutes and left to resume his higher duties. "You are now invited to partake of light refreshments in the adjacent room." He led the way to where another ADC was waiting to remove our medals, snap them in their monogrammed leather cases and recover the brass hooks, ready for the next investiture.

Still vaguely bemused, I pocketed my decoration and strolled into a canteen annexe where tea and coffee, fruitcake and jam tarts, sausage rolls, and hot bacon sandwiches awaited on plates and platters. The infantrymen among us immediately attacked the sandwiches and sausage rolls, leaving the cake and tarts for more refined palates to scoff. I joined in and was halfway through a bacon sango' with lashings of tomato relish when I felt a light touch on my shoulder.

Turning sharply, I confronted a taller, older man, the gilt brass crowns of a major on his immaculately tailored cuffs, the laurel green tabs of an Intelligence Corps officer on his tunic lapels, a coldly remote frown framing steel-grey eyes. "Mr Cribdon?"

"Yes sir?"

"Stephen Baxter."

We briefly shook hands after I switched the sandwich to my other paw.

"Bring your refreshments to my office." The accent was upper-crust English and fri'fully out of place in a roomful of boisterous young Aussies horsing around with their new medals.

121

Until recently, his cramped workspace had been the college janitor's cubbyhole, if a lingering whiff of carbolic soap and bleach was any indication of its previous purpose, as Baxter squeezed behind the laden desk and curtly nodded me to an upended ration box cushioned with a rag-stuffed sandbag.

"You have been brought to my notice as a person of interest." He sounded as if I were a vagrant applying for bail at the local magistrates' court. "It is alleged you have knowledge of French, and German, and Russian. Is this true?"

"A little. Sir."

He took a recent copy of *Le Soir* from a stack of newspapers next to a paste pot, scissors, and pile of bulging scrapbooks. Flicking it my way, he sat back, eyes hooded. "Front page, lead story."

I scanned dense columns of text, to get their gist before returning to the lead par'. "Ah. 'The Supreme War Council, has again, met, in cordial agreement, at General Headquarters, Versailles. Delegates, of French, British, Italian, American armies, are in, perfect accord with plans, to liberate, territories presently enslaved, by enemy forces. President Poincaré is confident that German morale is cracking and will soon be –'"

"Now this." He flicked me a somewhat older copy of *Die Kölnische Zeitung*, Blackletter Gothic is not my preferred font and I had to work harder. "Um. 'English fraud revealed! Official reports, to hand, prove English lies, concerning recent destruction, of munitions transport, disguised as, hospital ship, typical of this deceitful race!'" I was unable to control the shudder in my voice. "When our heroic commander, Freiherr von Grundwitz, surfaced his undersea boat, help to render with, his noble act was met, by storms of gunfire, from -!'"

"And this." Baxter seemed unaware of my distress as he tossed a shabby *Pravda*, by the look and smell of it, smuggled out of Petrograd inside a soiled laundry bag.

I took my time, remembering what Aunt Lucinda had taught me of the Cyrillic alphabet's thirty-odd symbols in which an English P looks like an inverted U; R looks like uppercase P; the letter A amazingly remains the same; V resembles B; and D could be the end profile of a lopsided railway wagon.

"Er. 'Comrade V.I.Lenin, denounced, Karensky as *vragy naroda*.' Enemy of the people?" I thought aloud, before continuing. 'A class traitor opposed, to peace talks, at Brest Litovsk, selling Russian blood, for foreign gold, of Anglo-French, paymasters.'" The rest is political jargon I don't get, except there's a reference to German demands for Ukraine's *zernovyye magaziny* or 'grain stores' and *ugolnaya shakhtii* which I think means 'coalmines.' Sir." I shut up and said nothing more, always wary with strangers, even when they are friendly, which this one most certainly was not.

His disturbing gaze never wavered as he recovered the copy of a Bolshevik propaganda sheet whose masthead ironically translated as *Truth*, then resumed speaking in short, flat phrases: "I disapprove of nepotism. It smacks of unearned preferment. Regrettably, I have no say in the matter. Therefore, we must get along as best we can. In your case by performing such duties as will be assigned by Sir John's MAI *en liaison avec* GHQ, namely myself -"

I had not the faintest idea what he was talking about. Nor did I care in my current state of mind. Eventually I learned that Major Stephen Baxter was not only 3 Division's Military Adviser (Intelligence) he was also Field Marshal Haig's personal liaison officer, one of a very small handful with direct access to the Commander-in-Chief. Without knowing it at the time, I was already breathing more rarefied air than most one-pip Joes ever got to sniff between 1914 and 1918.

"Your orders will vary according to circumstance," he continued in the same distant, frigid tone, "and will be executed without question -"

"One moment! Sir." I snapped awake, in no humour to be shoved around by anyone, least of all by this arrogant Pom. "There is a question, indeed there is a problem!"

"Oh?"

"I've been selected for pilot training," not strictly true but the situation demanded immediate action, "and am about to be posted to a flying school in England!"

"Really?" Said with a bored drawl.

"Yes sir. Really!"

"Then your friends in high places must have decided otherwise."

"But sir!" I jumped to my feet. "I'm not a pen pusher -!"

"Don't be impertinent!" His anger exploded like a burst of shrapnel. "You hold the King's Commission! You will obey your superiors without quibble! Do I make myself clear?!"

Unbeknown to me at the time, my opponent was a leading barrister and King's Counsel in civilian life, currently foregoing an income of thousands of guineas *per annum* to serve King & Country for a few shillings a day. Baxter KC, the righteous scourge of Britain's case-hardened villains on trial for their sins, often their lives, was never going to tolerate insubordination from anyone, least of all an opinionated young upstart from Australia.

"Yes. Sir," I seethed as he led the way down another grimy corridor, its gloom made visible by electricity from an oil-engine generating plant thumping away in the yard outside. At the end of which we entered one of the technical school's former classrooms; cracked walls hung with maps; old desks shoved together to make larger working areas for more maps and filing trays overflowing with multicoloured signal forms.

Baxter called his staff together and curtly introduced me as a probationary staff officer. In short order I then shook hands with an Anglo-Portuguese wine merchant; an Oxford mathematician; a solicitor from Manchester; a Bond Street art dealer; a Dublin-born West End theatrical director; a Scots antiquarian bookseller; and the Welsh owner of Britain's largest travelling circus, currently in hibernation until peace broke out again. All on detachment from the British Army while training-up a cadre of Australians to take over their duties.

I didn't know it yet, but these amateurs-in-uniform were pitting their collective wits against *Abteilung III(b)*, the German Army's professional Intelligence & Counter-Espionage Bureau with its twenty years' head start on Britain's puny Military Intelligence Department. But what at first seemed like fatal weakness in fact masked notable strengths, not the least being flexibility of unconventional thought and rapidity of action when sabotaging the enemy's plans or ambushing his agents in the field.

These covert actions would eventually prove decisive on an invisible battlefield of lies and whispers, decoys and deceptions masterminded by the Admiralty's Room 40 codebreakers, an elite group of scholarly cryptanalysts whose very existence remained a State Secret until well into the 1920s.

122

Until now, I had visualised land warfare as if it were an expanded chessboard of challenge and response but was about to learn that the Great War was in fact a worldwide, three-dimensional machine of which the Western Front was but one of its many springs, cogs, and levers. Though perhaps machine is not the right word, suggesting as it does an emotionless mechanism incapable of human error. Therefore, when speaking to Frances about this period of the Great War, I shall probably compare it with a ravenous, Grendel-like beast that demanded constant nourishment via an intricate network of roads, and railways, and shipping routes that formed its veins and arteries.

However, long before those could deliver hundreds of thousands of men and millions of tons of materiel to battlefronts in Europe, the Balkans, and Asia Minor, there first had to be a corresponding nervous system of cypher clerks and wireless operators, despatch riders and linesmen servicing intricate webs of copper wires and telegraph keys, synchronising every Allied movement eastwards from the Atlantic to the Persian Gulf, and southwards from the North Sea to Lake Tanganyika in German East Africa.

Much of this revealed itself as I became more aware of 3 Division HQ's responsibility for thousands of those men, and considerable tonnages of their rations, weapons, and equipment. However, at first the only thing that made sense was the help I gave to our cartographer as he interpreted the aerial photographs that other observers were now taking over German lines.

Once his coloured inks were dry, I would take their updated trench maps to an adjacent shed where photoengravers - one of whom had done time in Pentonville prison after his nearly perfect banknotes began circulating on British racecourses - made the zinc plates for a lithographic printing press housed in a nearby laundry.

Headquarters' motley crew included not only the essential cooks and clerks, driver mechanics and storemen, wireless operators, and telegraphists, but also a pigeon fancier who looked after dozens of messenger birds in their loft. And a commercial artist whose eye-catching surrender leaflets were left scattered in enemy trenches, by our raiding parties. 3 Divvy even had its own mobile kinema unit mounted on a Crossley tender, contracted to British Pathé for their biweekly *Animated Gazette,* an early form of newsreel that repaid the favour with flattering images of General Monash and his gallant Australian fighters; Baxter was a masterly fixer as well as a stern taskmaster.

These and other intriguing features became apparent as I became better known, but first I had to pass a stiff entrance exam that meant spending time in our Registry – the former chemical store of the school's textile dyeing laboratory – swotting up Imperial Germany's Order of Battle, its uniforms and badges, ordnance, transport, and communications.

I then had to complete a written paper for which the pass mark was ninety-five percent; compose an essay describing how, where, why, and when I thought the war was going to end; and speak for five minutes, on any topic, in any language of my choice.

I could easily have thrown a tantrum and demanded a return to 3 Squadron, but that would most likely have earned me a severe reprimand and possible demotion to the Sanitary Corps, where I'd have been put on display as every army's lowest form of life, the degraded ex-officer.

I also felt it was my duty to uphold Australia's honour in the company of these British strangers. The same stubborn pride stopped me from chucking the written examination, which I passed comfortably. Instead, I planned to give my talk in French, using its rich palette of accents from the most refined *haut bourgeois* lisp to the coarsest guttersnipe snarl, every shrug, every pout, every sneer, every flicked finger heaping scorn on the Air Board's training of its observer/air gunners.

I was confident that such bitter, sarcastic, mocking jibes against higher authority would disqualify me from further HQ duties and ensure a prompt return to the Australian Flying Corps, for I could see no way of avenging Sandra's murder while entangled with these rear-echelon base rats.

However, I misread my audience. Instead of earning their furious disapproval, the assembled wine importers, actor managers, booksellers, and lion tamers roared with laughter and applauded an impudent firework display of vulgar French slang. After which, a quietly amused Baxter presented me with the despised Strawberries & Cream armband, two laurel green collar tabs, another pair of pips, and field promotion to the thankless rank of Captain (Intelligence Staff) acting unpaid. None of which I ever wanted -!

And yet, despite my new Staff Corps flimflam I was still no more than a glorified errand boy being given the run-around by older men accustomed to employing bright young sparks who had yet to prove themselves worthy of hire. From early morning until late into the evening, they kept me on the hop delivering messages, filing reports, copying orders, sticking pins in maps, raiding the stationery cupboard for carbon paper and duplicating ink.

Mouth shut, eyes open, I stayed alert for any chance of escape from our GOC's Military Family, as a divisional commander's advisers and ADCs are correctly termed. In General Monash's case it was also family; two aides-de-camp, Captains Moss, and Simonson, were his nephews. Not quite as blatant as the Made of All Leanes battalion I'd served with, on the Somme, but still sufficient to fuel the smouldering suspicion of "Jewish self-interest" that pervaded our Officers' Mess.

I kept my own counsel for it was not hard to picture an anguished letter from "Iron Hannah" Shuster, written in their native German, imploring her dear friend Johannes Monasch to snatch me from harm's way after the death of her precious only son. I sensed this might be one further reason for Baxter's dislike of me, although happily I saw very little of the man from my lowly perch in the departmental totem pole.

None of which was made any easier to stomach whenever I paused between jobs and cast envious glances at the sky, watching a Camel, or SE5 or Bristol F2 drone overhead on its way to war. Up there is where I belonged; pouncing from cloud cover; guns hammering Hun after Hun after Hun until they broke-up in the air, or spiralled earthwards, out of control; not wafting around HQ, scrounging rolls of gummed paper tape and tins of thumbtacks.

Matters finally came to a head one dank afternoon when a runner summoned me to Major Baxter's office. "Take a seat Mr Cribdon." He removed his reading glasses and spoke around an unlit briar pipe before gesturing with its stem to the padded ration box. "Settling in alright?"

"Aren't you the best judge of that?" I queried neutrally. "Sir."

"Yes, I suppose I am," he agreed in a similar tone, glancing down at a green cardboard folder on his desk. "Horseferry Road has sent me this notification. It seems you are what's called an Original Anzac, long overdue for convalescent leave in Australia." He looked up. "Any reason why you haven't gone yet?"

"I am, or I was, a Specialist MGO." Announced with pride. "The training battalions have first claim on our services."

"Hm." The pipestem tapped my file. "But you are now more of a 'generalist' and thus eligible to return home for a well-earned break." He eyed me shrewdly. "That is what you want to do, isn't it?"

I said nothing. His sudden concern for my welfare could be signalling an intention to sack me in a sneakily indirect English way, and I was not game to say anything that might give him reason to reconsider RTU-ing me to 3 Squadron AFC.

"Well...?"-

"No sir."

"Come now!" he frowned disbelievingly. "You must have friends, family, eager to hear of your overseas' adventures!"

"No sir."

"What? No friends? No family?"

"Few of one, fewer of the other."

"But if you don't return home, the only alternative will be to remain on Active Service, in France."

"Yes sir."

"Is that your wish?"

"Yes sir."

"How very odd. May I enquire why?"

"You may, but it's a personal matter I prefer not to discuss."

"Ah." He eased back in his chair, testing every syllable. "I can't claim to understand your motives," he concluded, "but doubtless they answer your present needs, as one would expect from a man of such interesting parts..."

I felt the first chilly shiver of doubt, unsure how, and why, and where this devious man might be going, after all -

Baxter was leaning forward again. "Your gift of attentive silence is highly valued in our line of business. Of course, we're an unconventional lot, one that our regular army colleagues will be glad to see the back of, once we've helped win their war and can resume selling first editions, importing barrels of wine, employing jugglers and acrobats, *et cetera*..."

An abrupt flash of insight illuminated how my wary self-effacement had only deepened the very hole I was trying to climb out of -!

"It's an open secret that the War Office is uncomfortable with a volunteer army corps composed of amateur colonial soldiers whose commanders include a civil engineer, an apple orchardist, an architect, a country town solicitor, a schoolmaster," Baxter continued, seeming to ignore my confusion. "There will be an audible sigh of relief in our ranks when these gentlemen return to civilian life on their side of the globe, regardless of how brilliantly they've performed in uniform, on ours. Apropos of which," he added, as if the thought had just struck him, "what are your plans, after this war ends?"

"I have none."

"Why not?"

"It's a bad luck magnet." I scowled defensively. "Staying alive, one breath to the next, is the best we can hope for. In the trenches. In the sky."

Baxter put his pipe down and took up a pencil, hypnotically tapping it end-over-end. "Indulge me for a moment while we review the evidence."

All I could see were my fading hopes of an early Return to Unit as he continued in the same reflective tone of voice: "You are of course aware that things are not going well for us in Russia?" He glanced at a point behind my right shoulder, as if an invisible presence were monitoring our conversation, another trick designed to unsettle persons of interest facing an uncertain future, either inside a police cell or in his law chambers. "From what you understand of the situation, how do you imagine Berlin interprets the Red Revolution…?"

"Kaiser Bill must think all his bloody Christmases have come at once!" I was deliberately rude, crude, and slangy. More than ever determined to prove my unsuitability for HQ duties -!

"Why?"

"One less enemy to bugger things up!"

"Such being the case, what will he do now that his forces are no longer required on the Eastern Front?"

"Who says they won't be?"

"How do you mean?"

"That *Pravda* article. The one about Hun delegates demanding Ukraine's wheat and coal."

"What of it?"

"It's bloody obvious," I snapped back. "If I were in the Kaiser's boots, I'd grab every ton of coal I could, for my industries. Likewise, every ton of food for my factory workers at home, and my soldiers at the Front. All of whom must be losing their appetite for war, which's all I've given them to eat since the Royal Navy blockaded our meat and grain imports from places like Argentina!" I paused, hoping for an angry rebuttal, but Baxter refused to take the bait

"Assuming you're right," he conceded, pencil steadily tap-tap-tapping away, "what follows next?"

"That's equally obvious!" I pushed harder to prove myself unsuitable for duties on his staff. "Nobody volunteers their rations when they themselves are half-starved. Therefore, the Huns need to garrison the Ukraine if they're to commandeer its harvests and secure the railways moving it westwards, to the Fatherland."

I paused again, trying to estimate if my blunt opinions and abrasive manner were having the desired effect, before leaning forward myself, as if about to throw a punch: "But before they can move a single ton, they'll need umpteen miles of blockhouses and mounted patrols, defending the track against sabotage and partisan raids."

Baxter considered this point carefully. "Whom would you detail for such a Herculean task?"

"Von Mackensen's XVII Cavalry Corps. Perhaps von Below's 1st Reserve Division?"

My inquisitor gave me a sharp look. "Assuming these units are retained by *Armeegruppe 8*, for essential guard duties, what's available for redeployment elsewhere?"

"Von Francois' I Corps at Kiev," I was still citing the Order of Battle memorised for my examination. "Von Scholtz' XX Corps at Zhitomir –"

Baxter stopped me with another sharp look. "What do you consider their most likely objective?"

"Not Salonika. Not Palestine. Not Mespot'," I replied just as sharply. "Those are sideshows. France is the Big Event. So, it's the Western Front or nowhere."

"And as it can't be 'nowhere,' we must anticipate their imminent arrival at the very moment when Gough's 5th Army is being stripped to keep Italy in the war and Austria out of the Po Valley" Baxter observed, more to himself than to his grumpy young listener. "*Ergo*, all that the Kaiser needs for final victory is a successful breakthrough offensive in Artois. With a left hook where Gough's depleted troops adjoin our French allies screening Arras. Supported by a right punch to knockout the Amiens railhead. Or vice versa. Because whichever way we look at it, the Bolsheviks have just dealt Ludendorff a winning hand..."

"Sir?" I frowned.

"Come now!" he chided, with a frosty smile. "If this were your game, which card would you play? The left-hand or the right-hand?"

"Whichever is my weakest suit."

"Why?"

"Bait."

"For what purpose?"

"To draw him away from my primary objective."

"Which is?"

"The one I'm going to hammer with every bloody thing I've got!" In imagination I was fighting to free myself from HQ's clutches. "'Distract! Disable! Destroy!'"

Baxter remained silent for quite a while, pondering things unseen before revealing his thoughts again. "Once Ludendorff declares his hand – Arras or Amiens - our exhausted allies will fall back for a last-ditch defence of Paris, abandoning terrain that Fritz will occupy, confident of another decisive battle like Sedan, forty-odd years ago. As for us, we'll be dashed lucky to reach the Channel ports in halfway good order."

He shoved away from his desk. "The Western Front is about to erupt, attacked on multiple fronts by a greater armed force than any previous one in history. This is the Kaiser's best chance of winning a 'Waterloo Peace,' with which to cement Prussian hegemony over Europe and establish the German Empire as a world power." He shot me a shrewd look. "It is also our last chance to ensure he suffers Napoleon's fate, instead of enjoying the Duke of Wellington's triumph."

Baxter reached for his cap and Sam Browne belt, hooked on nails in the wall behind him. "I'm taking a short leave, to be as refreshed as possible before the onslaught." He faced me again. "You are owed more but will have to make do with what is allowed my Military Secretary, responsible for decryption, *et cetera*."

"But sir! I'm not a pen -!"

"Yes, Mr Cribdon?" His cocked eyebrow and tone of voice were stern warnings not to push my luck any further.

123

Resigned to my fate for a little while longer, I wolfed an early breakfast and went through to the Registry to sign out a current *Field Codebook*, about the same size as the *New Testament* issued to us when we embarked at Fremantle, but not as thick and more easily concealed in the couriers' linen vest worn under my shirt.

The codes were now my responsibility until signed back after our return to HQ, and another reason for the hefty leather holster and cartridge pouch on my Sam Browne. In all other regards I was travelling light, just a few personal items stowed in the canvas valise modified with a souvenired German rifle sling, in case both hands needed to snap into action.

Major Baxter joined me at the motor pool where we exchanged salutes before climbing aboard a drab green Vauxhall staff car, its canvas roof buckled down against the glum weather, 3 Division's painted metal pennant erect on the offside mudguard; rank has its privileges as well as responsibilities and I might as well partake of the former while they were still available to me.

Armentières to Paris via Peronne and Compiègne would have been a three-hour trip in peacetime, but even with the pennant and car horn honk-honking our way past plodding columns of troops, GS wagon trains, convoys of motor lorries and batteries of field artillery, it was afternoon before we reached Gare du Lyon where Baxter flashed his GHQ *mandat de voyage prioritaire*, aided by a discreet distribution of pre-war silver francs, to claim our booked berth aboard the overnight express to Marseilles.

That done, I took a Fortnum's picnic hamper into the reserved compartment, there being no certainty the Restaurant Car's galley fire would be lit during this time of perpetual shortages. Forage cap removed, khaki trench coat off, armband stuffed into my tunic pocket, shirt collar slackened, I marvelled at sitting upright on an upholstered bench after my previous railway journey, northwards from Marseilles, aboard a goods wagon built to carry forty men, or eight horses, or any combination of both.

Baxter returned with two bottles of Vichy water and two copies of every newspaper and periodical from a nearby *kiosque à journaux*. "These should keep us gainfully employed," he announced, giving me one bundle before removing his coat and slipping off the armband underneath; our green tabs were quite enough to arouse envy and resentment among the less privileged, without adding further insult to injury. My MC and DCM ribbons were the only visible proof that at least one of us used to be a proper soldier before joining the enemy, as frontline troops invariably regarded the Staff Corps.

"Please feel free to comment." Baxter said, loading and lighting his briar before shaking open a copy of *Le Temps* and going straight to its Editorial. I did the same, privately wondering how much he was able to read into the French political scene, a vipers' nest of intrigues and jealousy, even in peacetime as *l'affaire Dreyfus* proved during the 1890s. Twenty-odd years later, French politics and politicians were - if anything – even more venomous during a war that had already cost the lives of one million fellow countrymen.

I was wrong. Baxter was not only fluent he was also acutely perceptive, dissecting yesterday's furious oration by Premier Clemenceau in the National Assembly, relating it to the broader strategy of holding firm against the Central Powers – Germany, Austria-Hungary, Bulgaria, and Turkey - until the United States built-up its numbers on the Western Front.

"Incidentally, who did you say taught you to speak and read French?" he enquired, lowering the newspaper again.

"I didn't." By now I had his range. Every question was an examination of evidence, as if assembling a legal brief for or against me.

"Who did then?" he continued, not in the least discomforted.

"A relative."

"French?"

"Australian."

"Really." He seemed quite surprised. "I was not aware your nation was bilingual, like Canada?"

"It isn't." I hesitated while deciding how much, or how little to reveal. "Most of her working life was spent in France."

"'Her'?"

"A great aunt who adopted me after my parents died."

"Married to a Frenchman?"

"No but there must have been many who wished they were," I replied, luring our conversation away from my fictitious tea planters by hinting at Aunt Lucinda's life story. "She preferred the freedom of her profession to the constraints of marriage."

He laid his newspaper aside. "What did she do?"

"Sing, dance, act. Captivate half the crowned heads of Europe..."

"Really?!" He was hooked. "Pray continue!"

"It's ancient history," I shrugged. "No doubt if one were to search the Second Empire's newspaper files for 'Le Rossignol,' or 'the Antipodean Nightingale', one would find reviews for her performances in several of Offenbach's one hundred operettas..."

"Small wonder you put on such a dazzling performance t'other week," he chuckled, genuinely amused. "Tell me, is she still alive?"

"Very much so."

"In Australia?"

"Yes. The Third Republic disgusted her after the Second Empire fell and, as she would often tell me: "'Tis best to exit the profession while your public is calling for 'more!' rather than await the inevitable decline when others, younger and prettier, claim its fickle favour...'"

"A wise lady."

"Indeed. I owe her, a lot."

"I imagine you do," he thought aloud as the couplings clanked, the carriage jolted, and our locomotive began toiling along the platform, gasping, and panting through gusts of sooty steam.

I was happy to let the matter drop and turned to *Le Canard Enchaîné*, a bitingly satirical magazine recently discovered. Its title translated as *The Chained Duck*, but the masculine noun *canard* also meant a down-market newspaper, which put a vastly different slant on its acerbic editorials at a time of harsh wartime censorship and imprisoned journalists.

There was much for the soldier to agree with as the *Duck's* writers contrived to be simultaneously patriotic yet pacifist but never defeatist, with a caustic blend of cartoons and savage irony directed at the nation's mismanaged war effort.

"'All set up for a fair,'" Baxter announced, interrupting my study of a cartooned President Raymond Poincaré in his nightshirt, leering at a bare-breasted Marianne in Delacroix's *Liberty Leading the People.* "'A famous French landmark, five words, eighteen letters.' Any ideas…?"

I have always enjoyed anagrams and word games - Aunt Lucinda had often played them in French as well as English - so it was not hard to pencil a couple of trial substitutions on *Le Canard*'s margins before glancing up again. "'*La Tour Eiffel á Paris*'?"

"Hmm…." His pencil ticked letters. "By Jove!" He glanced up with an approving smile. "You're right."

Happily, I was wrong about the Restaurant Car's ability to cook a decent meal, when it served a scalding hot vegetable soup, and *fricassée de lapin chasseur* suspiciously unlike any rabbit I've shot or trapped in Westralia. Consequently, Fortnum & Mason's picnic basket remained largely untouched as we rattled southwards through the night, except when Baxter opened its half-bottle of Haig's Dimple and poured two stiff drinks, if we were to get any sleep at all, before adding a splash of Vichy to his Scotch. I took mine straight.

"*À votre santé.*"

"*À la vôtre*," I replied, clinking glasses in a nod to the Middle Ages when one's wine or beer might be spiked with arsenic or wolfsbane to kill a rival in love, or power, or both. Thus, by looking each other in the eye while exchanging splashes of drink, a man could be reasonably sure that the other person was not trying to poison him, at least not yet. "To your health," was more than a polite formula in those perilous times.

Baxter set his glass down and gave me a measured look. "You are an unusually reserved young man."

"Sir?" I affected surprise, though I knew it to be true, for I have always played life's cards close to my chest.

"Any particular reason?"

"'From listening comes wisdom; from speaking comes repentance.' An old proverb in my first copybook. Why?"

"Because most men would have enquired where we are going, long before now, but not you."

"There's no need. This train goes through to Marseilles. The label on your bag," I glanced up at the luggage rack, "bears an address in Nice, farther along the coast, so it's unlikely we'll be getting off at Auxerre or Avignon to change lines, therefore Nice it must be."

"Correct," he conceded with an appraising nod. "My wife has converted our holiday cottage into a military hospital." He drained his glass. "Now, give me a hand to pull down these bunks."

I was accustomed to dozing through the crump of shellfire, but sleep was hard to find on this journey, especially as I had no wish to reveal my Veronal addiction to a deskbound stranger incapable of understanding the how and the why and the wherefore of such matters. The Webley's bulk, tucked under my trench coat pillow, did not make things any easier as our carriage jolted along tracks in an even worse state of repair than my first experience of French rail travel, rattling northward to Rouen with 48 Battalion AIF.

France was now so exhausted, so run down, so utterly spent that *un train express* was barely able to travel faster than a pre-war *train postal*, thus it was well into the following day before our locomotive shuffled to a halt at Marseilles' Gare St. Charles.

Baxter set off to distribute more silver coins - in great demand for the black-market economy, now that banknotes had replaced honest money in circulation - while I stood guard over our kit on a dingy platform, surrounded by sad-eyed *poilus* embracing their wives and sweethearts while the troop train's impatient steam whistle urged them aboard *la charrette de boucherie*, or "butchers' cart."

It felt wrong to be still alive and standing where my dead mates had departed for Pozières, and Mouquet Farm, and Ypres -

"A penny for your thoughts?" Baxter caught me staring into the void.

"I'd be taking your money for nothing."

"Try me."

"It wouldn't make sense. Unless you'd been here. With us."

"Ah." He got the hint and reached for his valise, my cue to sling mine over one shoulder and follow, leaving Fortnum's picnic basket, emptied earlier at our improvised breakfast, the Restaurant Car now shut for some complicated reason best summed up by our steward's *"c'est la guerre"* shrug.

Baxter had bribed us aboard the *Méditerranée Express* that used to carry Europe's rich and famous to their winter holidays on the French Riviera. There was precious little evidence of that leisured age now, as we puffed through the coastal ranges, briefly glimpsing the Mediterranean at Toulon before heading inland again, through ridgeline tunnels and across soaring viaducts until re-joining the coast at Frejus.

From now onwards it was mostly a flicker-book gallery of sapphire blue seas, sunny afternoon skies, and glimpses of picturesque little towns I planned to visit, one day, in the unlikely event of surviving the war.

These dark thoughts were kept well-hidden as I searched my haversack for sketchbook and crayons, and studied the passing scene, freezing selected views before putting down lightning sketches from memory.

"Good Heavens!" Baxter was watching me closely. "I didn't know you were also an artist?"

"I'm not," I replied shortly. "Just the occasional cartoon for *Punch*." I thought it best to gloss over my sixpenny postcards and portrait-sketched bribes.

"You are too modest." He unflapped a Morocco leather tobacco pouch and loaded his briar. "I've been married to a talented painter long enough to recognise similarities when I see another at work. So, correct me if I'm wrong," he continued, speaking around his pipestem while waving out the burning match, "but it seems as if you can," puff, "mentally 'photograph' an event or place or person," puff, "and 'develop' it later?" Puff. "On paper?"

"Of course." I was surprised that an artist's husband had to ask such a question. "Turner often did. Lautrec too, with *Cirque Fernando*."

"Interesting…"

Thereafter we remained largely silent, as I continued sketching and our locomotive continued its weary panting along the Côte d'Azur towards Cannes, Nice, Monte Carlo, and Ventimiglia. But even this millionaires' playground was unable to escape the realities of war as wagonloads of men and munitions shunted eastwards to the Italian Front, and many a charming villa flew its Red Cross flag to show where a westbound ambulance train had dropped off its load of broken men.

Eventually the locomotive gasped and grunted to a brief halt at Gare de Cannes. Baxter followed me onto the platform, for I needed to stretch my aching right leg, buy a bottled lemonade, and treat myself to a wartime economy cheese baguette off a handcart doing brisk trade with other travellers. I was also keen to observe the gangs of porters in their blue smocks, bawling "*Ouvre la voie!*" as they shoved between gossiping knots of passengers and bystanders.

"Hard to believe that, almost within living memory, this was no more than a fishing village." Baxter was drawing my attention to the elegant Hôtel Colette, one of several imposing buildings fringed by shady palm trees, barely a stone's throw away.

"What changed it?"

"A senior Scottish law lord came, saw, and was conquered by the Mediterranean's warmth, colour, and vivacity. So, instead of continuing his Grand Tour, Henry Brougham ordered a villa be built at Croix des Gardes and settled there to enjoy the good life."

"Sounds like a sensible choice to me," I replied, by no means enamoured of Northern Europe's changeable weather and miserable climate.

"Quite so," Baxter agreed, with a wry smile. "Others, equally keen to escape our island's abominable winters, came, saw, and were captivated by the Riviera's sunny charms. Business boomed to such an extent, the Town Council commissioned a fine statue of milord, on the Promenade des Anglais," Baxter pointed roughly in the direction of the sea, "in a rare display of Franco-British gratitude..."

"And now we're Allies."

"More or less." He might have expanded this cryptic remark, but the guard's whistle had begun chivvying us aboard for the last leg of our journey to Gare de Nice Ville, similar in appearance but no less war-worn than Marseilles' railway terminus.

This time a grubby five-franc note was sufficient to hire a taxi for the last few miles uphill, initially between shops and tenement dwellings until we reached the crest of an escarpment overlooking Villefranche sur Mer, to the south, and the Maritime Alps to the north, their greying snow caps brushed with sunset's dusky pink.

As I would discover next morning, Baxter's holiday cottage was a substantial, extensively restored 18th century Provençal *mas* or manor house enclosed by its own vineyard, olive grove, and formal gardens, built atop the remains of a Saracen Fort, a Roman villa, an Iron Age settlement, a Neolithic campsite.

But this evening my attention was focused on a short, trim woman clad in a plain black frock, her dark hair pulled back in a severe bun, stepping forward to greet us under a lit portico lantern above which hung a Red Cross flag.

I naturally assumed she was the housekeeper until Baxter gave her a fond embrace before introducing me to his wife. "*Je te présente mon collègue le Capitaine Cribdon.*"

Jeanne Baxter's care-worn features were instantly transformed by a most enchanting smile. "*Un plaisir de vous rencontrer, M'sieur le Capitaine...*"

124

Morning sunlight blinked through cracks in the bedroom's weathered wooden shutters. I blinked back, unable to recall where the devil I was. A familiar confusion for any soldier who has spent his past several years in transit from training camps to billets, to trenches, to casualty clearing stations, to hospitals, before starting over again for a second or third time.

For a while longer, I wallowed on the decadent, civilian luxury of a feather mattress, reliving last night's family dinner and the generous measures of a full-bodied red that triggered my collapse, for I had no clear memory of climbing into bed. Though I must have been sufficiently aware to hide the codes and my revolver under the bolster pillow. Not that I'd anticipated a firearm would be needed, but I would not have put it past Baxter to test me by trying to lift them during the night.

He was a rum cove in ways I'd not encountered before. Most schemers plot and plan for their own selfish ends but I had a feeling that Stephen Baxter was engaged in a more impersonal game, one he was playing as close to his chest as my fictitious tea planters were to mine. Though I didn't realise it until much later, I'd been granted a rare opportunity to observe the contrasting halves of his complex character; in uniform, GHQ's coldly aloof Intelligence Liaison Officer with 3 Division Australian Army Corps; in civvies, a warm and loving husband who clearly adored his wife.

Being young, and callow, and in many ways inexperienced, I found this puzzling. For whereas he was the embodiment of an elegantly tall, late-Victorian English gentleman who must have cut an imposing figure in horsehair wig and black silk gown at the Royal Courts of Justice, Dr Jeanne Baxter née Martell would not have attracted more than a passing glance if noticed haggling over a string of onions in a French provincial marketplace. But, as is so often the case, appearances can be deceptive.

Eventually I would learn that Mlle Martell - a daughter of the centuries-old dynasty of cognac distillers - graduated top of her year at Montpellier Medical School before commencing an internship at the Royal Free Hospital for Women in London. Then, one autumnal afternoon, seated in Brunswick Gardens, listening to a military band playing patriotic airs before embarking for the South African War, she accidentally dropped her parasol. A spruce young barrister, striding back to his chambers in Gray's Inn Road, stopped, stooped, and recovered it for her.

"*Merci, m'sieur,*" she responded instinctively, in French, for she was still not wholly proficient in English.

"*Vous êtes française?*"

"*Mais oui! Êtes-vous français?*"

"*Malheuresement non. Je suis un Anglais simple qui respecte beaucoup la musique et la culture glorieuses de la France…*"

She must have been stunned to hear an Englishman responding with ease, and grace, and near-fluency. They exchanged names, agreed to attend a concert at Wigmore Hall the following Sunday, and six months later were married at Salignac-sur-Charente.

Thereafter she became one of the first women to be elected a Member of the Royal College of Physicians and began private practice as a consultant Obstetrician & Gynaecologist while her husband continued building his stellar reputation at the Bar. There was no reason to imagine this oddly matched couple would not have continued enjoying their very comfortable, *haut bourgeois* lifestyle but for the outbreak of war in August 1914, which happened to coincide with the children's annual visit to their grandparents' estate.

Returning to England, via Paris and Calais, the two adults were shocked to see the French Army's medical services overwhelmed by scores of thousands of casualties from the Frontier Battles. Passing through railway yards overflowing with unattended stretchers on open ground, or if lucky covered with ragged tarpaulins, or packed inside goods wagons on filthy straw like cattle on their way to an abattoir, husband and wife agreed that it was their Christian Duty to address the problem forthwith-!

Upon arriving home at Hampstead, the Baxters convened a meeting of like-minded supporters and one month later the newly incorporated French Flag Nursing Corps despatched its first ambulance unit of British trained medical staff to France, under the command of Dr Martell who had reverted to her maiden name, one that translates as "Hammer" in Old French. An apt moniker for such a dynamic force of nature as *Mme le Médecin* at a time of national crisis, one brought about by a politically corrupted General Staff and its insane belief that a spirited bayonet charge could brush aside artillery and machine gun fire; eight hundred thousand dead and wounded Frenchmen proved them wrong during the weeks before Christmas 1914.

More hospitals were needed after the Italian government switched sides and declared war against their former German, Austro-Hungarian, and Bulgarian allies of the Central Powers. Dr Martell responded by converting her family's Mediterranean holiday home into an Acute Medical Centre for casualties from the Italian Front.

It was she who recruited the Poor Sisters of Christ to cook, clean, comfort, and pray; arranged for Marie Curie to install an x-ray machine and laboratory; asked Kathleen Scott, another friend and herself a noted sculptress, to advise on the restoration of *les Gueules Cassées*.

I was about to meet these grotesquely disfigured men after going downstairs to get the day started with a quick recce of the kitchens and pantry, wooden limb workshop, and wards in their prefabricated sheds.

During my reconnaissance, I peered into the wine press cellar where Mrs Scott, widow of the Antarctic explorer, was working with Paul Darracq, taking plaster casts of these Smashed Faces.

An acclaimed sculptor and teacher in Paris, he would use them to mould pink rubber masks from lifelike copies of mangled flesh and bone, complete with false eyebrows and moustaches, new chins and cheeks, ears, and noses, in Nice. It was now that I first saw there really are fates worse than death, confronted by men who in earlier times would have mercifully died on the battlefield but whose lives had been saved - if that is the right word - by modern anaesthetics and surgery.

"The blind will never know how lucky they are," *Maître* Darracq agreed as we shared a calming cigarette in the yard outside his studio.

Still badly shaken, I eventually found Baxter on the terrace overlooking Villefranche and St Jean Cap Ferrat, clad in a blue and white striped Breton fishermen's shirt, bleached canvas trousers, espadrille sandals, and a gardeners' straw hat.

He heard me approaching and glanced around from his tripod-mounted prismatic telescope. "Sleep well?"

"Yes. Thank you, sir."

"Good." I thought I detected a note of concern in his voice. "Well now," he continued, eyeing my crumpled uniform, "We'd better get you out of those togs and into something more appropriate. My civvies won't fit, but I'm sure we can find something. In the meantime, help yourself to coffee and *petits pains*." He gestured to a nearby picnic table.

No man who has ever contemplated stealing a bucket of pigswill to get through the day, needs a second invitation to tuck into crisp bread rolls, creamy Normandy butter, and thick apricot jam made with sun-ripened fruit from the estate's orchard.

Baxter, meanwhile, had resumed squinting at a distant convoy of merchantmen steaming eastwards along the hazy southern horizon, inward-bound to Genoa, most likely laden with more men and munitions for the Italian Front. "*Hélas!* They are so unyieldingly obstinate," he observed, more to himself than to me.

"Who are, sir?"

"Those destroyer escorts," he answered, peering intently as he adjusted telescope's eyepiece. "*La Royale*, as Republican France paradoxically calls its navy, disdains to believe our Royal Navy's intelligence that Austrian U-boats have recently adapted external fuel-tanks, thus extending their patrol range well beyond eight thousand nautical miles...."

"It matters?" I was still at heart an infantryman, not yet educated to see how dependent we all were upon the Royal and Merchant Navies doing their lonely duties out of sight, often out of mind, hundreds, perhaps thousands of miles behind the Frontline.

"It will, if they persist in holding column-ahead formation as if this were a peacetime Fleet Review," Baxter replied darkly. "It's only a matter of time before Emperor Karl's submarines penetrate the Straits of Messina's minefields and attack Allied convoys in these waters..."

I shrugged, not sure if an answer was required, as he glanced over his shoulder to watch a post cart clip-clop to a halt on the nearby access track. "*Eh bien, voila le facteur!* He comes early. There must be a priority telegram. You have the codes?"

He probably assumed I'd hidden them in my bedroom and was preparing to admonish me for a breach of security, until I reached under my shirt to unbutton the couriers' vest, once the postman had finished delivering the hospital's mailbag, some personal telegrams for its patients, and an encoded *prioritaire* for Baxter.

"*À vos orderes, mon Comandant!*" This elderly veteran of the Franco-Prussian War - its green and black campaign ribbon proudly worn alongside the green and gold ribbon of the *Medaille Militaire* on his blue *Postes et Télégraphes* tunic - snapped his receipt book shut, saluted, and marched back to the waiting pony cart.

We watched him slap reins and clip-clop away before decrypting what at first seemed to be no more than a routine sports report for an office syndicate's betting pool:

WOLVERHAMPTON WANDERERS 2:3
LEEDS // NOTTINGHAM FOREST TO
PLAY ARSENAL //CLAPTON ORIENT
VS TOTTENHAM UNITED RAINED OFF //
STOCKPORT COUNTY CENTRE FORWARD
INJURED // BIRMINGHAM CITY VS
TOTTENHAM HOTSPUR AT HOME //ENDIT

Even if our rivals in *Abteilung III(b)* had understood the significance of these teams in the English Football League, they would have been none the wiser without the four-digit key that Baxter was using to unlock the code groups I was transcribing as plain text.

His deputy, the wine merchant, was keeping us abreast of *Operation Hatchet* as units of 3 Division took turns at marching up to the Front, returning after dark aboard unladen ration lorries and GS wagons. A few days later, another battalion would do the same, and so on at frequent intervals. Meanwhile, the Royal Flying Corps was under orders to let an occasional Hun reconnaissance machine escape with photographs of what seemed to be a steady flow of reinforcements from the Australian training camps in England.

Spoofing became a highly specialised artform during the Second War, but we pioneered it during the First, with bogus wireless traffic between phantom units, deliberately careless talk in Amiens' shadier *estaminets*, and doctored field notebooks accidentally-on-purpose left behind by trench raiders.

"As a matter of principle, I abhor deceit." Baxter struck a match and set fire to my transcript, watching its ash fall to the terrace's pavers before grinding it to dust with his heel. "But in times such as these, we must compromise our principles for the greater good and embrace deception, or else Fritz will know for certain that we are more thinly stretched than he already suspects we are…"

"Sir?" I queried, unsure where I fitted into his brooding monologue.

He glanced up. "Every belligerent nation – barring latecomers like the United States, and Brazil, and Siam – is at its last gasp. France has watered-down her battalions to field a full complement of regiments, hoping thereby to project the appearance of strength; personally, I doubt if Fritz is so easily duped."

Baxter hesitated before concluding: "Were I a gaming man, given our currently precarious position I'd lay short odds on the Kaiser winning this final round, once his Eastern armies complete their westward pivot." I sat up straight, startled by what sounded very much like defeatism. "But I am not a gambler," he added, as if reading my mind, "and you will notice that I said: 'currently precarious position,' not 'permanent'?"

"There's a difference?" I scowled, unwilling to be taken into his confidence, knowing it could count against me if the Aircrew Selection Board discovered I was privy to matters of value to the Hun, in the event of being forced down by engine failure behind enemy lines. "Given the way things are going."

"And how are 'things' going?" he queried with another of his infuriatingly English half-smiles.

"Bloody awful, if what I read in the local press is even halfway true!" By being deliberately abrasive and "Colonial," I kept striving to prove my unsuitability as a British staff officer.

"And what have you been reading?"

"Treason," I snapped back. "The National Assembly is no better than a megaphone telling the Kaiser that France is ready to throw in the towel!"

"True," he nodded thoughtfully. "Those hysterical tirades, urging peace at any price, are clear evidence that *La Grande Nation* is physically, spiritually, emotionally, financially exhausted after Verdun and only needs one more punch to be knocked clean out of the ring. No army's courage is inexhaustible, and those poor beggars have taken a terrible pounding from the very first day of war..."

"Are we in any better state?"

"Aren't you the best judge of that?'" he replied, turning the question. "My task is to interpret casualty reports and wireless intercepts as if they were legal briefs, sifting them for hints and clues, winks and whispers, but only a frontline officer can read his men's faces and look into their hearts." He lifted an expressive eyebrow, challenging me to an argument, but I kept silent, waiting for his next move. Disappointed, he continued: "So, how do you rate our Australian troops?"

I weighed several options before answering. "Right question, wrong bloke. You'd do better to ask an Englishman, met at Wandsworth. Phillip Grenville. Who once told me how envious he felt when one of our battalions marched past his stretcher: 'By God, Cribdon, they were magnificent! Proud as kings. Heads held high,' singing 'Kaiser Bill is feeling ill, the Crown Prince he's gone barmy, we don't give a fuck for old von Kluck, or his chicken army...!'"

I gave a dry cough. "Many of them are now dead, or crippled, and as there is still no conscription, dwindling numbers are volunteering to take their place. But the fewer who do, the greater our determination never to betray those who are marching with us, in spirit, on the road to Berlin..."

Baxter gave me another of his coolly appraising looks and was about to add something but changed his mind as a convoy of three ambulances braked on a nearby hardstanding. His wife wearily climbed down from the leading Renault lorry-conversion, still clad in her black frock under a white lab' coat, its sleeves smeared with fresh pus and blood, wearing the same haunted look I had last seen on my wife's belovèd face at Victoria Station -

We shook hands in the formal French manner, and I waited for her to take a seat before doing so myself, careful to draw my chair aside so as not to intrude while they caught up with news from home, in English, out of courtesy to their guest.

One of the letters that Baxter had sorted from today's delivery had been sent by their son, presently at Westminster School where he was in the Officers' Training Corps and, in his own words, frightfully keen to enlist on his eighteenth birthday next year.

"Damn' young fool," his father scowled, folding the letter after sharing its contents.

"But the war cannot last that long?" The anxious mother leaned forward. "It must end soon, no?"

"Yes, but few in authority agree with me." Her husband looked away at the trails of coal smoke on the far horizon. "The Ministry of Munitions is tendering for another two thousand armoured fighting vehicles, to spearhead *Plan 1919* and breach the Hindenburg Line." He looked back at his wife's careworn expression. "As ever, Whitehall's pipe dreams are more attainable on paper than on the ground, for nobody has the faintest idea where the Tank Corps can recruit that number of trained drivers and skilled mechanics."

"*Les Amèricains*?" His wife instinctively reverted to her native tongue.

"'*Timeo Danaos et dona ferentes.*'"

"Means what?!"

"'I fear the Greeks, even when bearing gifts…'"

"Greeks?! Americans?! Bah! You English always speaking stupid riddles!"

I later learned this had not been a good morning after the arrival of another ambulance train at Gare Nice Ville, and Jeanne Baxter was in no mood to humour her husband's nuanced views of the world. What I did sense, however, was the French higher education system at work, with its emphasis on critical analysis and Cartesian Logic, in stark contrast to an English public school's reliance on ambiguous ancient texts.

"You are quite right, my dear," he replied, not in the least put out. "It's our version of the cuttlefish's ink, with which we distract enemies and confuse allies alike." He stood. "Come, let's see what delights are on the menu today. Mr Cribdon has only had a few bites of bread and a *demitasse* of coffee since last night, and like the good soldier he is, our young friend places the highest priority on his 'grub.' Or should I say 'tucker'?"

125

Messing arrangements at *Hôpital Militaire 731* were more monastic than military, as one would expect with the Poor Sisters in charge of catering and a Mother Superior as formidable as the Reverend Mother Agnes. Thus, instead of segregated messing areas, every department had to sit on the same hard wooden benches and eat off the same bare trestle tables in accordance with the austere rules established by Ste Genevieve de Valençay, a sixteenth century mystic tormented by visions of Hell who, after her ascent to Heaven, performed the requisite number of miracles for an Earthly beatification.

Baxter had correctly deduced that I was more than ready for the sisters to wheel *le déjeuner* into our converted barn mess hall, but only after Mother Agnes had recited the Benediction and given everyone a sin-scorching glare. What the vegetable broth lacked in quality was made up for by quantity, and the hunks of bread served with it contained no more than the official quota of pulverised grain husks and sawdust needed to extend our rationed flour; I had eaten worse in the trenches and set-to with restrained gusto.

For all that we were supposed to dine in equal humility, without rank or distinction, it was inevitable that the cleaners and gardeners would choose to sit with their workmates; the clerical and admin' staff with theirs; and the medical staff, plus visitors like myself, with theirs

Baxter beckoned me to a vacant space beside him while his wife took her seat across the other side of our scrubbed wooden table, no longer clad in a soiled white coat but still dressed in the wartime black that all patriotic Frenchwomen had pledged to wear until the enthroned female statue of Strasbourg - in the Place de la Concorde - cast off her mourning shroud to signal the liberation of Alsace-Lorraine, a captive province of the German Empire since 1871.

She spoke to the radiographer, nodded at something the pharmacist added to their conversation, before turning, her expressive, dark brown eyes firmly fixed on my face. "Stephen says you are artistic."

"He is too kind, ma'am." Aunt Lucinda's deportment lessons were much in evidence. "At best I do a bit of amateur sketching."

"That is not his opinion," she insisted. "I studied oils and aquarelle before the war. What is your medium?"

"I've dabbled in most media, but nowadays it's easier to carry a pencil, a notebook, and a packet of crayons in the pocket."

"He says you 'cartoon.' That is, draw comic pictures."

"Er, occasionally. Why?"

"Because I regard ours a providential meeting."

"'Providential'?" I smiled uncertainly. "How so?"

"My *mutilés* are needing of your help."

"Say again?" I automatically used the army telegraphists' phrase that had embedded itself in my everyday speech.

"The special woundeds," she explained, with restrained emotion. "Those ones who never will return to war, or for many, to family. Help them. Please."

"How so?"

"I give to them art classes, to help their brains, their hands, their eyes, where they have. Another is for this afternoon but so too is the meeting I must attend. Do it for me."

"Um, I'd be, happy to," I fibbed, much preferring to spend that time alone, in a remote corner of the property, getting my own troubled mind into a semblance of order, "but I'm not really qualified –"

"Thank you, Captain." Her careworn features brightened for a moment. "I knew we could count on you. But first you must exchange that uniform for informals," she continued, becoming serious again. "My wounded ones are frightened of officers and disturb to see them, fearing they will be consigned to the trenches again…"

I was about to demand what the hell sort of army she thought we were but was stopped short by the arrival of a second boiler on its trolley, this time containing not only soupy scraps of potato, carrot, and turnip, but also chunks of a gristly meat that until recently had probably dragged many a wagonload of ammunition before becoming too sick or too weak to drag any more.

No French midday meal is complete without litres of wine, in this case a very ordinary Algerian *vin ordinaire* further watered down by order of Mother Agnes, a wise precaution in a medical establishment where nobody could afford to doze on the job. The equally determined Dr Martell then gave orders for me to be taken to the clothing store after which we agreed to meet where she would introduce me to my unwanted students.

Half an hour later - by now clad in a casual shirt, trousers, and straw sandals like Baxter's, only mine were cast-offs donated by the local St Vincent de Paul Society - I joined her at a prefabricated wooden shed that, judging from the *tricoleur* roundels instead of a Red Cross painted on its steeply pitched roof, had been an *Armée de l'Air* workshop until *Le Corps Médical* snaffled it.

"They are, so damaged. Be kind to them, they try of their best." She composed her face before looking up at me again. "You speak our tongue. This is good, for they know not yours. But art and colour speak to all. No?"

"Indeed, they do ma'am, indeed they do." Said with weary resignation. "You may count on me to do my best, whatever that may be."

"Good. Come." She opened the door and as she did so, cracked a smile, like a seasoned trouper when the curtain goes up, and announced our presence by la-la-la'ing *Le Galop Infernal* from Offenbach's *Orpheus in the Underworld*.

This jaunty little tune instantly rekindled fond memories of Aunt Lucinda seated at her concert grand, bony fingers flying up and down the keyboard as she sang along with a *risqué* version of the same tune, better known in English as the *Can-Can*.

"*Merde alors…!*" It felt as if we were stepping into Madame Tussaud's Chamber of Horrors, or the Marquis de Sade's madhouse at Charenton, or a combination of both as fifteen grossly mutilated soldiers responded to her sprightly entrance by thumping their wooden legs and crutches. Or, if they still had hands, waving their sticks like conductors' batons.

"Today, my friends, we are privileged to have with us a famous Australian artist come to learn how well we do things in France!" she announced with a dramatic flourish.

"*'Autrichien'?!*" a hulking *poilu* snarled, thinking his pink rubber ear had heard that I was Austrian and therefore one of the hated invaders of Northern Italy where, as I later learned, he had been blown up by a landmine.

"No, no, no!" she laughed, "Australia! Land of Kangaroo!" At which point this remarkable little lady began hopping up and down: "Oompity-oompity-oomp!"

None of her students had the slightest idea what she was on about. They probably thought it was a folk dance from some faraway cannibal kingdom, not that it mattered much as they gleefully joined in with their sticks and crutches.

"Il s'appelle Ian Cribdon," she continued, pronouncing my name as "Zhan Kreebton," when everyone paused for breath. "I am confident you will be excellent teachers and show him of your best. Sadly, I must attend a meeting, but shall return, I promise."

Confused, I accompanied her to the door. "What are they doing?" I hissed. "And what the blazes am I supposed to do about it?!"

She brushed away a tear. "Give to them your love."

The door shut firmly in my face, forcing me to turn around and confront as daunting a task as any in the trenches or in the skies above them. Luckily, I had acquired a fair amount of the French Army's pungent argot while conversing with Father Matthieu. "Right-o yous hairy-arsed sons o' bitches!" I growled. "What's wi'v this shit'ouse brothel o' yors?!"

These were the last words any of them expected to hear from a famous artist of dancing kangaroos. "Bugger me dead!" the one with a rubber ear and scarred face, hooted from his wheelchair. "They talk real French where yous from?"

"Yair!?" I replied with an impressive Gallic pout and flicked finger. "So, you lazy sods gunna show me yor good shit, or what then?!"

There was more to this vulgar display than met the eye. I was in danger of becoming unnerved by these grotesquely masked human wrecks and needed to regain my composure as quickly as possible, if I was to be of any use to them. And if this required foul smirks and leers, so be it as I took the nearest chair, spun it around and sat, arms folded along the back. *"Allons-y! Commençons! Vite!"*

In short order I learned that Rubber Ear had organised his little gang as a workers' cooperative. Those without artistic talent coloured-in printed outlines of bunched flowers and idealised village scenes on otherwise blank postcards, while the more inspired tried their hand at original designs, even the one who had lost both hands to a faulty grenade fuze, brushes and pencils clamped between bruised lips as he dabbed and jabbed and scratched bits of salvaged cardboard.

Something in his ferocious determination to overcome crippling disability reminded me of my Kiwi cobber, Bill Proctor at 1AGH Heliopolis, so I set this young lad a few simple exercises in perspective and shading, and in later years would often see Raoul Duclos' angry cartoons of French political slime in *Le Canard*.

However, my greatest dread was that this was a sweatshop exploiting maimed soldiers for private profit, until *Caoutchouc* - Rubber Ear's nickname – put me straight. Every centime collected by civilian volunteers, selling these cards from door-to-door, went into the hospital's Comforts Fund to send small sums home, for those who had families, and to buy good tobacco, better wine than we had just drunk, and black-market chocolate for men who – God knows! - had little else worth living for.

True to her word, Jeanne Baxter returned about half an hour later and shared a triumphant smile with her devoted followers, as I now knew them to be. *"Eh bien m'sieurs!* No cause for alarm. *Ces sales bâtards* will trouble you no more."

A chorus of thumped crutches and waved sticks greeted this cryptic announcement as we took our leave and entered her office in the main building.

"Which 'filthy bastards' won't trouble them anymore?" I asked politely.

"The army paymasters," she replied, motioning for me to take a seat, facing her across an exactly organised desktop. "They wanted to cut my patients' miserable allowance, because of work for a few francs, by the painting. Ouf! What monsters they are!"

"What did you tell them?"

"Ah!" She raised her hand as if blocking a hostile thought. "I asked for a letter of demand, to show my uncle, Proprietor of *Le Temps* newspaper…" I sensed how well this adroit and intriguing woman – in every definition of the phrase - complemented her equally adroit and intriguing husband, as she continued: "Now. You know a little of me. What of you?"

Alerted by her sudden interest, I turned the question around. "You say I know a little of you, ma'am, but there is even less of me to know…"

"Tch! Don't take me for a fool," she huffed, "Stephen speaks well of you. This is not usual. My husband does not tolerate the fool any more than I. So, *m'sieur le Capitaine*, your story *s'il vous plaît…*"

"There is not much to tell," I replied, shoving splayed fingers across my cropped scalp, a revealing sign whenever I feel cornered. "Until the war, I was just an ordinary young chap, doing ordinary young things."

"Like?"

"A bit of dancing, a bit of flirting, a bit of billiards –"

"No."

"I beg your pardon?"

"I see more," she announced with a clinician's piercing, impersonal gaze. "I observe a hardness one never got by the dance, the flirt, the play with coloured balls!"

"I had bread-and-butter jobs, of course," I replied coolly, "but nothing special -"

She crouched forward. "Name me them."

I folded my arms and returned a defiant glare. "Gold prospector. Sandalwood puller. Rabbit trapper – !"

"So! Where did you learn my language?"

"In Melbourne."

"Who instructed you?"

"I fail to see how that is any concern of yours," I snapped, irritated by her attitude, "but since you ask, my great aunt!"

"Who was?"

"*Une confidente* of Her Imperial Majesty the Empress Eugénie," I replied with a haughty, discouraging sniff that failed to throw my pursuer off the scent.

"By name?"

"*Mme la Baronne et Dame d'Honneur Lucinde Cribdon!*"

"Hm." *Mme le Médecin* Jeanne Martell-Baxter could have been reading a temperature chart but, instead, she frowned at the plain gold ring on my left little finger. "You were a married man."

I wanted to scream: "I still am and always shall be!" For there was - and still is – a profound belief that Sandra and I were One, long before we met in Alexandria, and will be again, one day soon. Instead, I snarled: "That's none of your damned business!"

"Wrong! Everything of you is my business!" she snapped back. "You pretend well but you stand at the precipice! It is my duty to hold you back, to bring you back, for if you go over, there is no coming back!"

"Uh?!"

"Never take me for a silly little woman!" She crouched further forward. "There are body pains! There are brain pains! And of the two I am concerned most with those of *la mentalité*, which is where I see you now!"

"Why bother!" I sneered defensively.

"Maybe not for you, but for my husband, I do!"

"Eh?!"

"Stephen works *en secrète* for the Victory! I know not at what, but I know him!" She took a deep breath, regaining an air of professional detachment. "He needs the intelligent *protégé* as Her Imperial Majesty needed *une confidente*, to trust with attentive silence and discretion absolute. He feels that one might be you. Therefore, I am prescribing a course of treatments, to take you from the precipice, to be of use to him and to the Victory," she concluded, reaching for her reading glasses and a pen.

"Don't I have any say in the matter?!"

"No. None."

"Blood oath I do! I've a personal matter to settle -!"

"'Personal' matters nothing in war!" she speared back. "Victory matters everything! You will trust your body and mind to me and my staff! You will do what you are told! You will feel better of yourself, of your work!" She dipped the inkwell and jotted a brisk comment on my report card before glancing up again. "Remove those clothings."

"No!"

"Obey me!"

"Why?!"

"To see that we must work with. Disrobe!"

Her manner recalled Mrs Thomas Harris, Aunt Lucinda's terrifying housekeeper, my first day at Tralee House as, with angry compliance, I peeled off except for the codebook's vest, there being no place for false modesty in army life.

"It too."

"No."

"It too!"

"No!"

"Very well! Unbutton! Stand by the window. Left profile, right, front, back!"

I stood full-frontal, fists on hips, elbows out, silently challenging her while she jotted more notes, in pencil this time, scanning me over her spectacles' top frame. After which she approached with a tape measure, a stethoscope, and probing fingertips; unbeknown to me at the time, I was about to get a Harley Street specialist's five guinea consultation, gratis.

"Lay down." She pointed to a couch and closely examined my damaged right leg before it was the fingernails' turn as she pressed each one, gauging their blood flow and recovery rate. Pulse, neck, throat, eyes, ears, scalp, glands, not a square inch remained unexplored, untouched, unknown, not even my infantryman's gnarled feet that she somehow tickled awake.

Taking her notes back to the desk, she removed her unflattering, wartime economy steel-framed spectacles, and peered at me long-sightedly. "You are in worse condition than I feared. There is much to do but prevail we shall!"

She reached for the electric buzzer on her desk and summoned a uniformed male nurse. "Jules? Escort our patient to the steam bath. Commence him immediately. Follow with the massage and the convalescent diet. I shall attend later to administer the sleeping draught."

"*À vos orderes, Madame le Medicin!*"

"Not so bloody quick!" I interrupted. "Major Baxter may be your husband, ma'am, but he is my superior officer!" Announced with heavy emphasis before facing the attendant. "And unless I have his permission to be absent from duty, your services will not be required." Said in a more civil tone.

126

Furious with myself for allowing a bossy little Frenchwoman to prod and probe and percuss so intimately, I set off to find her husband, but he was no longer on the terrace. At which point my simmering temper began to boil, never the best state of mind with which to address a superior officer when I eventually found him, seated under a jasmine pergola with spectacular views of the snow-capped Alps.

"Permission to be relieved of my duties," I demanded, slamming to a halt. "Sah!"

Startled, he glanced up from his book – *Riders of the Purple Sage*, a bestseller Western I once thought of transposing from Utah to the Australian Outback with a fresh cast of characters, after *Boolya's Hoard* limped to its unconvincing climax – and gave me a long hard look. "What's your problem?"

"*Madame le Médecin* demands that I take a steam bath and massage, convalescent food and a sleeping draught!"

"Good. I thought she might -"

"Therefore. I can no longer be responsible. For the codebook. Sah!"

"Oh, very well, give it here." He reached out, only to be given my sketchpad, instead, on which were scrawled a couple of short sentences. "What is this?"

"A receipt. For my general court martial. If the codes 'disappear.' Without proof of transfer -!"

What followed is best forgotten. Baxter, to his immense credit, listened without comment to my wild assertions before finally taking the pipe from his mouth and studying its bowl for several moments before glancing up. "Thank you, Mr Cribdon. This is why we brought you here."

"What -?!"

"Had you expressed yourself so freely at HQ, I'd have had no option but to charge you with gross insubordination."

"But -!"

"Permit me to finish." The pipestem aimed at my chest. "Now, with a modicum of luck and my wife's skills, we may yet save you from yourself -"

"You don't understand!"

"Wrong." He interrupted, with frigid certainty. "In my civilian profession, I am required understand persons of every degree, from the highest in the land to the lowest in the gutter, many of whom are even more agitated than you are. Either by what has happened or what is about to happen, in court or on the scaffold. These are the occasions when we must assume a mask of impersonal calm, but beneath the peruke and black silk gown, the lace jabot and starched linen bands, we are as prone to feelings of love and hate, sympathy and disgust as any other man."

He paused, carefully weighing his next few words. "In your case I am impressed that you have restrained yourself as well as you have, even before *Winchelsea*'s tragic loss…"

"You knew - ?!"

"Of course. Apart from the fact that not a sparrow falls without Intelligence learning of it soon thereafter, your intended father-in-law was prompt to acknowledge my letter of condolence."

"How -?!"

"His lordship originally consulted me when one of his chefs was implicated in a fraud at the Savoy Grill," Baxter continued, as if addressing an attentive jury. "In the event we settled out of court. Thereafter, Nobury and I have remained on amicable terms." He used the correct family name, of course.

I glowered at the gravelled patch between my straw sandals. "And I suppose he asked a favour to stick me on the Staff?!"

"That I cannot say."

"Then how did I get this bloody job?!" I was long past caring what anyone thought of me now.

"You are better placed to answer that, than I, coming as you do from Melbourne," he pronounced the name clearly, as if it were "Well Born" rather than our more usually mumbled "Mel'b'n," "the hometown of our General Officer Commanding." I remained silent as he continued. "You have potential, Mr Cribdon, but even the most talented individual is doomed to drift aimlessly, unless he can attract a timely touch of luck or influence. Apropos of which, I wonder if that was the reason for Napoleon's puzzling remark when considering a certain divisional commander's promotion: '*Je sais qu'il est un bon Général, mais est-il chanceux?*' Meaning, as I'm sure you already understand: 'I know he's a good general, but is he lucky?' However, I am less sure you have grasped the importance such luck plays in a greater drama than our brief lives encompass…"

"Great, small, who the hell cares?" My voice sagged as I stared up at the sapphire blue southern sky, stroked from horizon to horizon with gauzy whisps of cirrus cloud, distracted by the drone of an *Aéronautique Maritime* seaplane taking off from Nice harbour, enviously watching it climb into view before setting course towards the distant horizon. "I'm a bloody useless office boy, as well you know. Whereas, up there," I pointed aloft, "I shall make those Hun bastards pay dearly!"

Baxter prepared his briar by lightly tapping its bowl on the pergola's wooden upright post, dislodging a plug of grey ash, before responding. "Correct me if I'm wrong, but am I hearing a young man's wrath against an enemy who killed his dearest -?"

"Those sods murdered her!"

"True," he acknowledged, with a sombre nod, "but somewhat longer experience of the world than you presently have, advises me that such intense revenge is a dish best eaten cold."

I stiffened. "Hers was coldblooded murder. It will be repaid in hot blood! Hun blood -!"

"How?" Baxter cocked an eyebrow. "By destroying another five of their machines, will that satisfy your bloodlust? Or do you need ten? Twenty? Thirty? More?"

Confused and angry I said nothing as he unrolled his tobacco pouch. "Believe me, Mr Cribdon, revenge such as yours is a cancer of the soul, a foul infection that destroys its host even as he seeks to destroy –"

"I, don't, care!"

"Clearly not but others do, and it is for their sake that I now offer the following counsel: think long and hard before returning to the Flying Corps where, assuming you survive the frequent mishaps of a pilots' training school, you may, with luck, destroy a goodly number of the enemy. But your winning streak is bound to end when another man, more skilled or *chanceux*, claims your scalp." He paused, studying my face. "Is that what you want?"

"Yes!"

Baxter nipped a pinch of tobacco between finger and thumb, tamped it into the pipe bowl, struck a light and reflectively drew heat. "Very well, if that is how you wish to die, so be it." He shook out the match flame and replaced the partially consumed stick in its small cardboard box, before continuing. "Had you chosen an alternative course of action, there would have been opportunities aplenty to inflict far greater suffering on those you wish to punish…"

I glanced up suspiciously. "How?"

"That would depend upon the prevailing situation and whether or not you were still with us," he replied, reaching for the sketchpad. "In the meantime, I'll take care of the codes." He signed the top sheet and waited for me to take off the couriers' vest before exchanging it for the receipt.

"You are, in the normal course of events, a prudent young man," he concluded, riffling the book's pages, to check they were still intact, before returning them to their pocket. "It's a rare gift. But if after due consideration you still wish to return to the Royal Flying Corps, I shan't stand in your way, for only the wholehearted volunteer earns an honoured place on our secret battlefield…"

If I do record this embarrassing episode for Baxter's granddaughter-in-law, I shall risk depicting myself as an immature, self-pitying young fool. And although that is the plain, unvarnished truth, is that how I wish to be remembered by a charming, intelligent young woman like Frances?

I think not! Besides, hundreds of thousands of others, on every side of the Great War, suffered far worse pain and loss than I can ever imagine. Those poor devils in Paul Darracq's workshop would have gladly exchanged their plight for mine - in a heartbeat, had it been possible - and they were by no means the worst afflicted of our doomed generation.

Meanwhile, restored by his promise of an early return to Active Duty, I left Baxter to resume his Wild West adventure and strode back to where Jules Roux was waiting with towels, liniments, and rubbing alcohol in the hospital's improvised gymnasium.

A legendary cyclist with *Équipe Alcyon-Dunlop*, who used his record-breaking road races to research and improve the human machine as he described his own wiry frame, he set to work on my aching muscles and tired tendons after a soaking steam in the former conservatory's Turkish bath. These relaxed me to such an extent that I was only marginally aware of downing the bowl of eggnog gruel and, a short time later, the spoonful of a sugary brown mixture that knocked me out until next morning.

127

Stephen Baxter accompanied his wife on her rounds after breakfast and found me prone under a Finsen lamp, naked except for a loincloth and a pair of welders' goggles. The paradox of abundant sunlight, outside, was lost on those working inside a clinic where modern, scientific medicine required flickering voltmeters and buzzing rheostats to be correctly practiced. *Mme le Médecin* checked the dials, noted their readings, took my pulse, and gave it a severe smile before moving along to the next cubicle with her entourage of nurse-attendants, leaving Major Baxter to keep me company while I got dressed.

"Feeling better?"

"Not sure yet." I began exchanging the loincloth for a pair of cotton drawers. "Still a bit shaky."

"That's quite understandable, all things considered."

"It's kind of you, to think so," I replied with marked hesitation. "'All things considered...'"

"Oh that?" There may have been the hint of a smile, though one could never really tell what was on this man's mind. "I'm not troubled by yesterday's *contretemps*, so there's no reason for you to feel concerned today. In fact Jeanne was rather pleased when I told her –"

"'Pleased'?"

"Apparently she was trying to provoke you into a 'healing crisis,' only instead of treating a fevered body she was hoping to treat a fevered mind –"

"You mean, bossing me around, like that, was a bluff?" My resentment began bubbling again.

"That is not the expression I would have used," her husband warned. "There are occasions when it's necessary for a patient to empty his constipated mind with one massive, emotional purge *'comme on vide ses intestines.'* Her words, not mine."

"You mean her way of saying I was tricked into behaving badly!"

"Another expression I would not use –"

"Well, I do sir, and I resent being played for a fool!"

"Nobody is saying you are –"

"That's how it looks to me!"

"A word of caution, Mr Cribdon. Get off your high horse before you are thrown off." Spoken, now, in an abruptly cold grey voice that mirrored his cold grey gaze. "Trickery connotes guilty intent, often abbreviated as *'mens rea'* from the more explicit *'actus reus non facit reum nisi mens sit rea.'*"

"'Mens' what?" I snapped, peevishly twisting the word and its meaning.

"'The act is not culpable unless the mind is guilty of it,' a foundation principle of English Common Law, as are 'Presumption of Innocence' and 'Trial by Jury,'" Baxter replied, unfazed as he reached inside his shirt pocket for the briar pipe and tobacco pouch. "Setting those aside for the moment, be aware how strongly I disapprove of your ungrateful insinuation. My wife's best efforts are, and will continue to be, dedicated to your recovery…"

His rebuke stung my prickly pride. "Sorry sir." I gave a self-conscious cough and finished buttoning my trousers. "Things have got a bit out of whack recently. Would a note of thanks be in order?"

He considered the idea while loading his pipe and gave a brief nod. "Now, if you're ready, let's take a stroll in the garden; Jeanne forbids smoking indoors."

Thus far there had been no mention of a return to the Flying Corps, so I assumed he was leaving me to make the first move in which case I saw no harm in awarding myself an impromptu Mediterranean holiday before returning to Headquarters, where it would take less than an hour to settle my Mess tab, shake hands with the cartographer, and hitch a lift back to RFC Bailleul.

We paced along a gravel path through an orchard laden with fragrant peach and apricot blossoms. Unlike the bare trees up north in Picardy, where it was still late winter, these were heavy with the promise of summer's riches as bees sped from their nearby skeps, gathering the pollen that kept *l'Hôpital Militaire 731* supplied with antiseptic ointment and, I suspect, sweetened the last rites of more than a few patients by disguising the bitter taste of mercifully overdosed morphine sulphate.

His junior in rank and younger by half a lifetime, I should have waited for Baxter to broach whatever was on his mind, but I felt less constrained now that I would soon be on my way to a flying school in England. I had also recently recalled another proverb in my earliest copybook, *Knowledge itself is Power. Francis Bacon, Lord Verulam, 1561-1626,* and was keen to glean as much as possible from this modern man of knowledge and power before we went our separate ways: "May I ask a question?"

"Of course."

"Your reference to Ancient Greeks bearing gifts. Was that someone, or something, nearer our present day?"

"Ah yes. '*Timeo Danaos.*'" He pondered these few words before glancing my way again. "'Any idea to whom they allude?"

"No, but Mrs Baxter had just spoken of '*les Amèricains…*'"

"'Means what,' you think?"

"I trust you're about to tell me."

"Very well, let's begin with Vortigern." He cocked an enquiring eyebrow. "Any ideas?"

I took a tongue-in-cheek punt. "A patent virility tonic, like 'Iron Jelloids for Men!'?"

"Not even close," he chuckled, one of the few times I could remember him doing so. "Imagine, if you will, Ancient Britain after the legions march off to defend Rome from encroaching hordes of barbarians, leaving the Britons to muddle along as best they can, with Vortigern one of several warlords squabbling over the decaying scraps of empire."

Baxter revealed an unexpected talent for storytelling as he continued: "Challenged by a coalition of Pictish tribes from North Britannia, Vortigern contacts a firm of foreign mercenaries, Messrs Hengist & Horsa Ltd, for a consignment of warriors who, upon prompt delivery from the Continent, trounce the Picts." He paused. "What happened next?"

"They took their pay and went home."

"Only if the wolf haunted moors and marshes of Jutland were more congenial than the airy Weald of Kent with its remnant vineyards, hot baths, centrally heated villas, and other novelties of *architectura et cultura romanum,* no matter how decrepit those had become by the Fifth Century AD."

"You mean, they didn't leave?"

"Of course not! And for the next five hundred years, until the Normans imposed their iron-fisted Feudal Order, much of Lowland Britain was farmed by Anglo-Saxon *ceorls* whose silver coinage was of such honest weight and purity that Arab merchants chose it to trade their rich silks and rare spices along the Golden Road to Samarkand and Far Cathay." The look on his face said that his inner ear was wistfully listening to the ancient echoes of these evocative placenames before returning, with reluctance, to our modern age of tanks and aerial bombs. "Therefore, the moral of this story is…?"

"Be careful who you invite into the camp, when they come better armed?"

"Correct."

"So, what's the connection with '*les Amèricains*'?"

"Give it some thought and let me know what you discover," he replied, turning away to shield his eyes and face the hospital's sunlit buildings. "Ah! The nimble Roux speeds our way, like Aesculapius' wingéd messenger. It must be time to resume your pounding and pummelling."

I pondered his brainteaser until more pressing matters intervened, not that I found an obvious link between those crafty Jutish mercenaries and the American Expeditionary Force who, by early-1918, were landing in their tens of thousands at Brest and Le Havre, every week.

As an Australian I could relate to their carefree swagger, seeing in it a reflection of the AIF's cocksure invincibility before Turkish Mauser bullets and Krupp field guns proved we were but mortal flesh and blood after all. Watching an AEF Doughboy was rather like seeing an early photograph of oneself and wondering whatever happened to that young man who used to grin so readily at a camera lens.

If one could overlook their tendency to brag, especially those from cities like New York or Chicago, most of Our Transatlantic Cousins - as Baxter insisted on calling them - were decent blokes once they realised that we'd been at this game for the past four years, and that they still had much to learn before plunging into action for the last few months.

Every nation has a natural desire to claim the victor's laurels for its dead and wounded, on behalf of their widows and orphans, but not every nation has a kinema industry to embellish its myths and legends and then sell them to the world as Gospel Truth. A goodly number of silent movies and, later, talking pictures must have left viewers wondering what the rest of us were doing in 1918.

To be fair, the AEF's attack along the Meuse-Argonne Front was the right-hook punch that mirrored our left-fist body blows during that last round of the big fight, but only after those magnificently fresh soldiers had cut their way through barbed wire higher than a man's head and dozens of yards deep; destroyed *Hagen Stellung*'s concrete pillboxes and mantraps; cleared a further two lines of trenches; and strangled Imperial Germany's main supply route, the railway between Sedan and Mézières that, until then, had been shunting upwards of two hundred and fifty trainloads of men and munitions, per day, into the Western Front's meat grinder.

However, Allied Victory seemed an impossible outcome in early-1918, as I submitted my aching body and "brain pains" to *Mme le Médecin*'s intensive physical and psychiatric care, during which she quickly identified my Veronal addiction. Her husband was equally attentive, visiting me every morning with the daily telegrams we decoded together.

I began looking forward to these meetings, as afterwards he would invite my opinion on a wide range of topics, some of which I was qualified to speak upon, others I had to ask him to elaborate before he drove off to unspecified business in Menton, farther along the coast.

At the time I thought he was being amiably attentive, not yet recognising an Oxford Tutorial much like those that Baxter himself had experienced while reading Law at Oriel College and was now employing on an impressionable young Australian. Nor did I yet realise what a good example these were of elicitation, as we later termed it when recruiting an agent or tempting a defector.

It is impossible to recall much detail after an interval of seventy years and two world wars, but one episode remains clear in my mind, chiefly because of what it foreshadowed for countless millions in the decades ahead.

We had been debating Imperial Germany's need to keep a firm grip on Ukraine's wheatfields and coalmines, and their likely effect on the outcome of this war, when I lifted a finger to pause our conversation. "It's the third time I've heard you say that…"

"Say what?"

"'This war.' By implication there's another?"

I think he smiled. "Very perceptive, Mr Cribdon."

"But surely there can never be another, not on such a scale!" I was convinced the Great War to End All War would deliver on its promise after witnessing what artillery bombardment does to a village like Pozières.

"You're right," he agreed, with some reservation, "but only while we restrict our viewpoint to the present conflict. But if we step back and take a broader perspective, you will see that the next war's ranging shots have already been fired on a battlefield greater by far than any previous one in history…"

"That's not possible!"

"Judge for yourself," Baxter replied, loading his briar. Striking a wax vesta, he slowly waved it over the pipe's bowl and took a long puff. "Tell me." He shook the flame out. "Who wrote: 'The Communist disdains to conceal his views and aims. He openly declares that these can only be attained by the forcible overthrow of all existing social orders. Let the ruling classes tremble before the Communist Revolution! Proletarians have nothing to lose but their chains! They have a world to win…'"

"Blowed if I know. Sounds like a typical Red-Ragger!"

"Good guess. Karl Marx."

"Never heard of the chump."

"You will," Baxter promised me with grim assurance. "In fact, you have already encountered one of his more zealous disciples."

"Oh?"

"'Comrade V.I.Lenin.'"

"The *Pravda* bloke?"

"The same."

"But haven't we agreed that Russia is down and out?" I persisted. "What chance have they got to cause any more trouble?"

"That remains to be seen," Baxter observed between pensive puffs. "It's a knotty problem. One in which something as commonplace as a pistol shot might yet disrupt the best laid plans o' mice and men. Especially Whitehall's hopes of restoring the Russian monarchy by persuading Grand Duke Michael Alexandrovitch to drink from his family's poisoned chalice…"

"Sir?"

"They are deluding themselves; Karensky's Moderates are either dead or soon will be," he continued, blowing an almost perfect smoke ring. "*Ergo* the prospect of the world's largest, potentially richest nation, ruled by Bolshevik revolutionaries, is fraught with dangerous possibilities…"

I failed to see the link. His annoyingly unfinished sentences resembled cryptic crossword puzzles. Fortunately, I have always relished pitting my wits against their clue setters and attacked today's problem head-on. "How the devil can a gang of bearded, Bolshy bomb-throwers endanger 'the rest of us?"

"Let me tangentially address your question by noting that calm logic, and sober consideration of consequences, are frequently absent in high matters of state," Baxter replied, after another calibrated pause. "The greatest human tragedies can be triggered by hubris and vanity, as much as by chance or choice, since at least the time when Queen Helen of Sparta eloped with Prince Paris of Troy."

"But -?"

"For instance, the 'All Highest' Kaiser's gnawing envy of his British cousin's colonial empire upon which the sun never sets although, as some wags assert, that is only because God doesn't trust us in the dark," Baxter added, with an ironic twitch of the lips. "For whereas Cousin George is *de facto et de jure* Emperor of India and monarch of much else besides, Cousin Wilhelm can only play at being an emperor while his Ruritanian chorus of German princelings is willing to sing their praises for an upstart King of Prussia."

"But what if -?"

"It follows that the imagined glory of not only establishing a European empire, by crushing France and incorporating great swathes of Western Russia into the *Reich*, but of also acquiring a worldwide empire by default, after bleeding Britain dry in Flanders and Picardy, is most appealing to a fickle character so easily charmed by delusions of grandeur. However," Baxter continued thoughtfully, "unlike Germany's vainglorious *König und Kaiser* Comrade Lenin and his ilk know exactly what they're about as they plan the conquest of far more than a remote coral archipelago or a few tracts of tropical jungle…"

"Meaning?" I snapped, out of patience with his Dance of the Seven Veils, my private nickname for this man's intellectual striptease acts.

"Exercise your imagination and let me know what you discover," he concluded with a bland smile, quite likely reading my mind as well as his wristlet watch. "Ah, it's nearly time for your next appointment with the indefatigable Mr Roux…"

128

By next morning I was sufficiently recovered from yesterday's physio' session to perch on a low stonewall and sketch three convalescents planting spuds in the hospital's kitchen garden.

Their stooped shoulders reminded me of Van Gogh's *De Aardappelplanter* as I scratched away with a stick of willow charcoal on a pad of cartridge paper, creating an example of monochrome shading for this afternoon's art class with my Smashed Faces, blissfully unaware of an approaching vehicle until its driver fumbled a double-declutched gear change and the exhaust backfired. Charcoal and paper went flying in every direction as I spun around, but instead of charging *Sturmtruppen* it was only a sporty red Peugeot cabriolet tourer parking on the ambulance bay.

To my even greater surprise, Major General Sir John Monash climbed from behind the steering wheel, whereupon I snapped to attention, about to salute as he strode towards me, but before I could he gave a dismissive flick of the hand. "Stand easy, Mr Cribdon, we're both in civvies," his were a dapper navy-blue yachting blazer and white flannel trousers, mine were St Vincent de Paul castoffs, "and not required to acknowledge the King's Commission."

"Yes sir."

"Where do I find Mr Baxter?"

"Most likely in the pergola. Sir."

"Take me there."

"Sir."

We fell into step along the orchard pathway towards a sheltered vantagepoint with its panorama of the Alps and Mont Mournier's snowclad peak.

"Settling into your new appointment?"

"Er, yes sir."

"Good. Quicker the better."

"Sir?"

"Ah," Monash switched focus, "there you are Baxter."

My current chief got to his feet in a more relaxed manner than I had done, as we approached. "Glad you could make it, sir."

"I damn' near didn't," our divisional commander grumped, dusting his blazer's sleeve before shaking hands. "French drivers are as much a threat to life and limb as the confounded Boche!"

I thought that was a bit rich, coming from someone who had just mangled a gearbox, and got ready to take my leave but Baxter made a discreet gesture that told me to stay while he turned to our guest. "If it's alright with you, sir, I'd like our young colleague to sit-in. He's a promising junior."

I pretended not to hear this belittling remark. Only later did I learn this is an expression that two barristers would understand, General Monash being an established commercial lawyer as well as a practicing civil engineer. In his and Baxter's peacetime work, junior counsels were a KC's righthand men, the more ambitious regarding it as their first rung up the ladder of prestige, honours, and wealth.

"Certainly." Then, glancing at me. "Join us for lunch."

"Thank you, sir," though I had little idea what I was being grateful for as he and Baxter went ahead, back to the Peugeot, speaking in guarded phrases that meant nothing to me. On the rear seat was a picnic basket I was told to take over to a rustic belvedere with extensive views across Villefranche and the sparkling Mediterranean; on a day such as this, it was easy to see why pre-war millionaires had followed Lord Brougham's example and built their holiday villas along the Blue Coast.

I set the basket down at a table flanked by wooden benches, curious to overhear what Monash and his spymaster were up to, this far behind Allied lines, as I served them with cold roast chicken and crisp baguettes before attending to my own needs.

Le Salade Niçoise – what else would one choose in Nice? – was a welcome change after Mother Agnes' prison rations, stuffed as it was with anchovies, hardboiled eggs, green beans, black olives, and flaked tuna, prepared by the *Premier Chef* at Hôtel Regina where General Monash was registered as "Mr Knight." A sensible precaution, given that the *Côte d'Azur* was a prolific hunting ground for amateur spies and professional agents alike, though how anyone on *Abteillung*'s payroll could have failed to report Monash as a senior British officer in mufti, was impossible to imagine.

Erect of bearing, brisk of speech, moustache exactly trimmed, 3 Division's General Officer Commanding was the "very model of a modern major general," as Aunt Lucinda would likely have quipped from her favourite Gilbert & Sullivan operetta, had she been with us.

Apart from waiting on my superiors, there seemed to be no good reason for me to be here at all, elbows in, knife and fork daintily pecking away, one small mouthful at a time, as instructed at the Commissioning Course in Cambridge. But I was not deceived; Baxter required my presence and, as I had already discovered, he rarely did anything without a farsighted reason.

Until now their talk seemed to be a continuation of previous discussions at the Regina, and largely dealt with *Operation Hatchet's* progress and the Allied defences hurriedly strengthening Amiens railhead.

The subject then turned to the impending German offensive and our likely response, given the massive forces lining up against us, supported by the largest concentration of guns and mortars ever seen or heard on the Western Front.

"You're an artillery spotter." Monash faced me. "What should be our riposte?"

I was somewhat taken aback, quizzed by a senior officer, and needed time to think.

"Well?" he frowned impatiently.

"One moment, sir." I was determined to get my thoughts in order before replying. "No doubt there are better options if there were time to implement them. However, from what I believe I've overheard, time is not on our side, therefore one must adapt and adopt with what's available."

"Go on."

"Assume the object of this exercise is to infect the enemy with doubts and uncertainties," I continued, in the plain speech of a sergeant weapons' instructor, not the tippy-toed evasions of a three-pip base rat.

"How?"

"Disperse 'shadow guns' equal to the number of likely known artillery pieces. These need not be more than sections of telegraph pole mounted on GS axles, provided their outlines look convincing under tarpaulin covers, in transit, or under camouflage, when positioned.

"Now shuffle them around as in 'Three Card Monte.' Aerial observers are easily confused, staring over the side of an aeroplane, battered by the slipstream, staring at the ground through binoculars while harassed by ack-ack and enemy aeroplanes. It is enough that the decoys look convincing on a photoprint and worth the expenditure of ammunition to destroy them, and that our actual guns are better hidden or misinterpreted as poorly concealed dummies. Sir."

3 Division's GOC swapped a questioning glance with his Intelligence Chief, then looked back at me. "On paper, on my desk, tomorrow morning."

"Yes sir."

The two men resumed their previous discussion in which Monash clearly respected Baxter's opinions although less clear was his sarcastic reference to Australia's Prime Minister, Billy Hughes as "Captain of the Push." To my Sydney ear this sounded very much like an unsavoury gang leader, an opinion confirmed when Monash added a sour remark about the PM's "Gory Bleeders" or enforcers, another phrase familiar to every Australian who has ever recited Henry Lawson's epic poem *The Bastard from the Bush*, or its vulgar parodies.

The informal conference ended abruptly when our superior officer took out his pocket watch, checked the time, and stood: "Thank you gentlemen. Keep me posted."

I cleared the table, packed away Regina's monogrammed plates and cutlery in their picnic basket and followed the other two men back to the Peugeot where General Monash faced me one last time. "When next you write to your aunt, give her my best wishes. I attended *Orphée aux enfers* at the Monte Carlo Opera House last night. It brought back happy memories of our piano duets at Hochheim and of her many amusing anecdotes of the Offenbach Touring Company. Also remember me to the Shusters." He then added something quite unexpected, coming as it did from a senior army commander: "I utterly loathe and detest war, it is so, wasteful!" Heavy pause. "No nation can afford to lose a talent as great as their David possessed…"

I nodded dumbly and stood aside while he got behind the wheel and Baxter stooped to crank the starting handle, sparking the still-warm engine's throaty rumble. Engaging reverse gear was still a bit crunchy but our GOC's departure was rather less dramatic than his arrival had been.

129

"'David'?" Baxter queried, tugging a tuft of grass to wipe a smudge of grease from his fingers.

"A friend." My tone guarded, as always, in matters personal.

"Killed recently?"

"Yes."

"And the Shusters?"

"Friends of my aunt."

"Who played duets with Sir John at 'Hochheim,' presumably the Shusters' home address?"

"Correct."

"I was not aware that he was a pianist. Is he any good?"

"That is not for me to say. Sir."

"Quite right." He tossed the grass aside. "As is your assessment of the situation. 'Three Card Monte'? Very apt."

I blinked, puzzled by his unaccustomed praise. "Decoys are hardly novel. Fritz uses them all the time."

"As do we all," he agreed, "but you caught their essence in one pithy phrase."

"Then you think Mr Monash really does want to see my paper, on his desk, tomorrow morning?"

"You have reason to doubt his word?" Baxter countered; eyebrows cocked enquiringly. "I must say, he has never struck me as the sort of man who wastes his time by giving pointless orders."

I was at a loss for a suitable reply as he continued. "Use my study to write your report. Apropos of which, I recommend block capitals for main points and headers, though for the rest I'm sure you have a perfectly legible hand."

"I'd prefer a typewriter, if one's available."

Baxter's smile faded. "You type?"

"Yes." Touch-typing was a skill I felt justifiably proud of in an age when most men still believed that keyboards were best suited to the dainty fingertips of lady typists.

"Where and why did you learn?" He enquired suspiciously.

"The *Kalgoorlie Miner*," I replied, perplexed by the sudden chill after his warm approval of only a few moments ago. "Typed copy is less liable to error than blocks or longhand, when the comp's set-up a form and send it through to the machine room."

"But your enlistment papers said you were a bush worker," he frowned, "now you're a journalist?"

"Nothing so grand," I frowned back. "Just a stringer doing local flower shows, lodge dinners, racing fixtures -"

"Does Sir John know this?"

"My aunt may have told him before the war. Why?"

Baxter ignored my sharp response. "Do you still communicate with the Press?"

"Yes." I was increasingly baffled by the direction this interrogation was leading. "*Diggers' Doings* are worth two guineas apiece." Sid Hocking's initial twenty-one shillings per article had to be doubled before I took on his job as well as my other, official duties.

"Describe these, '*Doings*.'"

"Jokes. Comic mishaps. Amusing puff pieces. Anything that makes Overseas' Service seem like a bit of a lark for the homefolks." Until a telegram boy props his bike at the garden gate and rings the doorbell.

"You submit them to the Censor?"

"Of course."

"What else?"

I shrugged. "*Punch* cartoons are worth a fiver apiece."

"For example."

"Alright…" Increasingly annoyed by his mimicking *Mme le Médecin*'s staccato interrogations, I provocatively picked one recent sale: "Imagine a smartly uniformed Clueless Claude inspecting the ripped fabric on an RE8 after a daylight bombing raid," I began. "'Aw! I say, ol'chepp!' the staff officer exclaims, 'what caused thett?!' To which the observer, dismounted Lewis gun slung across one shoulder of his baggy Sidcot, sarcastically replies: 'Moths.'"

Baxter's frown darkened. "Is that how you see us? As 'clueless?"

"With respect," I replied, determined to exploit this sudden chance of an accelerated return to 3 Squadron AFC, "that is exactly how you are viewed by those of us who fight in the sky as well as in the trenches."

Baxter said nothing. Instead, he curtly beckoned me to accompany him to the belvedere where, by accident or by design, he took the seat just vacated by our GOC. "I could, if I were so inclined, say that it is not we who are 'clueless,' but rather those of you who ignorantly imagine our sole purpose is to orchestrate the random slaughter of foreign strangers!" He drew breath. "But I shan't, for time is of the essence and there are far greater issues at stake in what little time remains."

I felt my face warm as his reprimand slapped its mark.

"Instead," he continued, "our most immediate task is to frustrate those who are actively conspiring to undermine General Monash's authority, one whom others at the very highest levels of command have ruled to be the right man, in the right place, at the right time! Is that clear?"

"No sir." I'd recovered my poise. "I fail to see what any of this has to do with me borrowing a typewriter!"

Baxter unrolled his tobacco pouch, a sure sign that I was about to get a lecture. "Typing is an uncommon skill, one that, in conjunction with your newspaper work, might have indicated a secret collaboration with those conspirators. That aside for the moment, let us examine certain facts germane to the matter at hand."

I sensed he was, in imagination, addressing an attentive jury: "During your pre-war encounters with Mr Monash, as he then was, you must've observed his talent for ruffling feathers and treading on toes, a common trait among those born clever, but not clever enough to conceal their cleverness from others less gifted, less ambitious, less hungry for fame and glory."

Baxter paused, eying me, perhaps disappointed by my lack of response, or maybe relieved that I despise gossip. "Being of German Jewish ancestry does nothing to help his cause in Lord Northcliffe's newspapers," he resumed, "with their tediously predictable 'Hunnish Horror' headlines."

"If you say so. Sir."

"What I say is of minor importance," Baxter corrected with a sharp, sideways glance. "Whereas the opinions of Australia's Official War Correspondent carry a disproportionate weight with your Prime Minister, Mr Hughes, and his political cronies, in their ongoing campaign to undermine General Monash."

"I'm lost." As, indeed, I was. "Of whom are we speaking? And why are you telling me?"

"Last question first," he replied. "I need to be sure that you are not in unauthorised communication with Australian newspapers."

"You have my word of honour!" I was annoyed by his suspicion that I might be selling unattributed news on the sly.

"Good." Baxter seemed convinced. "As for whom we speak of, he's a certain Captain Charles Bean." Baxter pronounced it Be'an, as a Scottish surname, not a garden vegetable. "A gallant and tenacious son o' the vicarage who must've counted every shot fired since going ashore at the Dardanelles, so meticulous and lucid are his despatches, as one would expect of a fellow-Oxonian. However, he has recently taken it upon himself to play the kingmaker, for reasons that need not concern us at present."

"Why should that be our problem?" I queried sharply.

"Because he has yet to learn that political intrigue is a high stakes game for newcomers like himself and his backer. Especially when playing at the same table that fleeced Phillip of Spain, Louis the Sun King, Napoleon, and many a lesser gambler during the past four hundred years." This most English of Englishmen shared his most English of enigmatic smiles. "All of whom learned, too late, that sleepy Old Mother England wrote the geopolitical equivalent of *Mr Hoyles Booke of Compleat Card Games*."

"'Backer'?"

"Glad you reminded me," he nodded. "Mr Keith Murdoch, a stuttering, vengeful son o' the kirk from your hometown. A proud and prickly man who suffered many a snub while seeking employment on Fleet Street but who, in the fullness of time, returned to London like Banquo's ghost, as General Manager of the United Cable Service."

"So?" I countered, always non-committal whenever another man's reputation is under scrutiny.

"Because one can easily envisage such an astute, well-connected journalist relishing his 'power behind the throne' as the sole source of foreign news for the Melbourne *Herald* and the Sydney *Sun*, your country's two most influential newspapers," Baxter replied. "In another age, Mr Murdoch would have made a notable Medici *consigliere* in Renaissance Florence, or Borgia cardinal in Rome, for he has all their requisite stealth and cunning. However, such careers being no longer available, he has chosen instead to manipulate the Great Australian Public with tales of derring-do abroad, while selectively whispering into the ear of your Prime Minister, Mr Hughes, to advance his personal agenda at home..."

"Which is?"

"Ah! Another shrewd question, Mr Cribdon." The smile never wavered. "Before answering it, allow me to declare a personal interest."

"If you wish."

"Thank you." Baxter studied his pipe bowl and dislodged a plug of ash by tapping it against the chair leg. "As you have surmised from my previous remarks, Mr Murdoch is no friend of the English and is thereby promoting an independent Australian Army Corps for reasons of private 'pay back' as well as national pride and independence. But to achieve these two ends he must first sack those officers - like myself - on secondment from the British Army, all of whom he suspects of 'white anting' his masterplan, as I believe you say in Australia?"

"And are you?"

"Only when and where they conflict with greater interests than his."

"But does he really have that sort of power?" I persisted, by no means convinced I was hearing the full story.

"He imagines so," Baxter replied, moving smoothly along. "General Birdwood's promotion to GOC 5 Army leaves vacant the position of General Officer Commanding AAC which, for the previously noted political reasons must be filled by an Australian lieutenant general in a race that only one of five divisional majors general can win.

"Messrs Murdoch & Bean are doing their utmost to nobble our runner by advancing their syndicate's entry, Brudenell-White, via their connexions in the Northcliffe newspapers," Baxter explained. "A sound choice, I might add. BW is a professional officer of high intelligence, great personal charm, and outstanding ability, but not the preferred winner at GHQ and, significantly, the Palace."

"Whereas General Monash is?" I enquired, trying to untangle this skein of secret ambitions and naked self-interests.

"Correct."

"Is this my cue to ask 'why?'"

"I'd be disappointed if you did not," Baxter replied, pipe dipping into the open tobacco pouch on his lap. "Our line of work requires us to maintain a healthy, albeit discreet curiosity in all things, at all times…"

"Very well," I sighed quietly, "why is General Monash their preferred choice for GOC Australian Army Corps?"

"Good question, glad you asked." Baxter finished reloading his briar. "First and foremost, the way he took 3 Division's odds and sods and forged them into top-notch fighting force at Messines and, later, Broodseinde Ridge." He struck a wartime economy *allumette* but its head broke off. The next match was sturdier as he steadied it. "Also, Sir John's character is sound," puff, "as one would expect of a man who has amassed a tidy personal fortune," puff, "in a most unforgiving," puff, "profession."

Baxter shook the match flame out. "No amount of bunkum or blarney can excuse a collapsed railway bridge, or a drainage system that fails to flow. However, as noted earlier, when we discussed the Kaiser's vainglorious dreams of world domination, one should never discount the human factor in high matters of state. For example, Field Marshal Sir Douglas Haig, and Major General Sir John Monash, embody the attraction of opposites -"

"Can't we speak in plain English, just for once?" I interrupted, barely controlling my irritation. "Sir."

"Very well," Baxter replied, not in the least vexed by my impatience. "Your man is a pushy, self-promoting Jew of German parentage; our man is an emotionally constipated, inarticulate Presbyterian Scot.

"Your man is heartily hated by Australia's Welsh-born Prime Minister and his political toadies; our man is equally detested by Britain's Welsh-born Prime Minister and his gang of newspaper character assassins.

"Your man is an overt outsider, with all that implies, and so is ours, for it's not easy to rise to the top of a caste-ridden army, with New Money made from the sale of whisky, rather than the rents off ancestral estates.

"Similarly, both men hunger for recognition and acceptance, despite one being married to a lady-in-waiting of the Dowager Queen Alexandra, with all the advantages that must bring to the family breakfast table."

Exasperated by Baxter's socialite shadow boxing, I crouched forward. "May I ask what any of this has got to do with us smashing the Hun?"

"More than you can presently imagine," he replied, still not upset by my abrasive tone. "We – that is to say yourself, and I, and a few others – have been chosen to 'monitor the situation,' and stand ready to protect your Melburnian neighbour's interests when he takes command of the Australian Army Corps."

"'Chosen'? By whom...?"

"Humble cogs such as we have no reason to know which of the more powerful springs and levers require our obedient tick-tock-ticking behind the great clockface of public affairs," he replied suavely.

"I haven't the foggiest idea what you're talking about."

"You will, one day." Baxter cocked an amused eyebrow. "Just as I'm equally sure you will eventually appreciate the delicious irony of 'Pommy Bastards,' like myself, defending an Australian against his own people who are equally determined to sabotage his chances, for that's the way the world wags. But not to worry," he concluded, "give it some thought –"

"'And let me know what you discover'!"

"Correct. Speaking of which, I had better organise a typewriter." He straightened. "'Three Card Monte'? A good title. Succinct and expressive. You'll do well."

130

Baxter made his customary appearance next morning with our daily telegram, after which he would spend the rest of the day with General Monash at Menton while I continued regaining a semblance of physical and emotional health under the watchful eye of *Mme le Médecin* and her nursing staff.

Thus far, the only hard news in our previous signals from HQ had been the fifth one's report of an *Abteilung* agent collared bicycling around 3 Division's rear area, spying on field bakeries to count their ration loaves and thereby estimate our true numbers. Interrogated by a former London Metropolitan Police Special Duties' Officer, the terrified woman was offered two choices: cooperation or execution. Unsurprisingly she chose the former and sent her edited report to a secret post-box on the Franco-Swiss border.

"What'll happen to her now?" I asked.

"She'll be kept on a tight leash until surplus to requirements," Baxter shrugged. I assumed this meant that her shabby impersonation of Mata Hari would also face a firing squad, in due course.

The sixth, seventh, eighth, and ninth telegrams dealt with routine surveillance until I began decoding the tenth. "Superscript *Beta -*"

Baxter peered over my shoulder to inspect the priority tag. "Not before time."

"Sir?"

"Brother Fritz can't delay his opening move for much longer. Not with food riots convulsing the aptly named Hungary; Bulgaria losing heart; Turkey on the ropes; and with every passing week, more and more fresh American divisions landing in France."

"But is he ready?" I enquired. "Fritz, that is?"

"As ready as he will ever be," Baxter replied enigmatically. "He has the numbers for the next month, maybe six weeks, after which the balance of power will inexorably swing against him. Therefore, his overriding objective is to strike now, either on the Somme or in Flanders. Likewise, ours is to cover our jaw, slogging it out until he drops his guard, and we throw the knockout punch…"

My experience of trench warfare told me that whatever lay ahead would not be won by adhering to the Marquess of Queensberry's Rules but kept this to myself as we critiqued today's telegram, beginning with its superscript *Beta*, the midpoint "Standby," between *Gamma*'s "Watch & Wait," and *Alpha*'s "Action Immediate." Today's signal specifically noted *Armeegruppe Somme*'s reinforcements from the Eastern Front, and their massed artillery under the direction of *Oberst* Georg Bruchmüller, an ominously familiar name in Allied Intelligence circles.

Recalled from retirement at the outbreak of war, this comparatively junior officer had quickly earned a formidable reputation in Ukraine and Galicia where his *Wirbelstürme aus Stahl* had destroyed countless tens of thousands of Russian troops. These same Hurricanes of Steel were now poised to blast miles-wide gaps in our defences, through which lightly armed, rapidly advancing storm troops would pour, overwhelming what remained of our shattered resistance.

At which point a triumphant Kaiser would have eclipsed his grandfather Wilhelm Friedrich's victory in 1871, by defeating both France and Britain in 1918, much as his Eastern Front armies had already done to the Czar's empire the previous year.

Baxter gathered up the transcript, plus my typed, one-page report entitled *Operation: Three Card Monte*, and straightened. "I shall inform Sir John while you organise our immediate return to HQ."

I watched him stride off to the hospital's transport pool of pedal bicycles, a couple of *Corps Médical* motorbikes, and a Delage Sports Tourer reserved for himself and *Mme le Médecin* unless needed by a senior member of staff or as an emergency ambulance.

"'Here's a pretty how-de-do!'" I thought aloud, echoing one of Aunt Lucinda's familiar lines from a Gilbert & Sullivan comic opera.

Less comical was the fix I now found myself in, for whereas Baxter had our *Mandat de Voyage Prioritaire* and a purse of silver with which to bribe railway officials, I had nothing except remnant street cunning, which I read as another of his sly tests. Not that it bothered me greatly. Soon I would be flight training in England, making now the ideal moment to pop his bubble of English superiority with an Aussie farewell prank that I knew Sir John Monash would also relish, having frequently observed what an accomplished practical joker he was himself, at the Shusters' social gatherings.

The thought that he might be less eager to fool his Intelligence Chief in a time of grave national crisis, even though travelling incognito, never once entered my troubled mind. Only much later did I realise that what I was about to attempt was so grotesque, so bizarre, so ill-considered, the best anyone could have said in my defence - at my court martial - is that I had finally taken leave of my senses after three years of war.

If I do record this episode, I shall first have to explain the importance of a good practical joke in our Edwardian heyday of charades, amateur theatricals, and other homely entertainments. Assuming I do so, I shall stress that our merry japes never degenerated to whipping a chair from under someone about to sit down or covertly knotting together another's shoelaces; such spiteful cruelties were abhorrent to all but the most ill-bred lout.

On the other hand, to partake in an audacious spoof like the one played by a group of Cambridge University students a few years previously, when impersonating an Abyssinian prince and his entourage aboard HMS *Dreadnaught*, was to win a legendary reputation spoken of with many an admiring chuckle throughout the Empire.

Whistling *The Man Who Broke the Bank at Monte Carlo*, I strode up to the hospital's Admissions Desk where today's Duty Clerk – a young girl from the local Red Cross Auxiliary - gave me an eager smile and promised to telephone for a taxi while I returned to quarters for a quick wash and brush up before changing back into uniform, a staff officers' brassard returned to my upper right sleeve.

"*Où?*" the elderly driver grunted, smouldering cigarette bobbing up and down, glued to his bottom lip with dried spittle.

"*Pour la Gare, vite!*" I replied with a menacing Gallic growl, whereupon he dropped his flag, released the handbrake, and launched into a helter-skelter downhill ride, rubber horn honk-honking as we approached the railway station's crowded concourse; I could not have wished for a better arrival to impart a sense of urgency to my next move, after paying-off the taximeter.

France's six principal railway companies had been commandeered by the army at the outbreak of war and their liaison posts assigned to elderly reserve officers more suited to administration than the command of frontline battalions. One of these grey moustaches was now effectively the military stationmaster at Gare Nice Ville as I slammed to a halt in front of his paper-strewn desk and threw an impressive Brigade of Guards' salute at my peaked cap with its distinctive laurel green Intelligence Corps hatband *"Mon Colonel! Je demande l'action la plus urgente – mais secrète – au nom de Son Altesse Royale!"*

Flustered by a sudden promotion, two ranks above his majority, the best he could utter was a confused: *"Quel?!"*

This was my cue to boldly announce that a senior member of the British Royal Family would be travelling incognito to attend an emergency conference in Paris, departing this very afternoon! A situation requiring the utmost tact! Urgency! And discretion, with so many spies and assassins lying in wait for this distinguished guest of M. Poincaré, President of the French Republic!

"Ce serait désastreux!" my one-man audience predictably responded to this impudent, improvised drama. *"Que voulez-vous que je fasse?!"*

"What you must do, is rigorously perform your duty for a gallant ally and loyal friend of France!" I replied, striking a dramatic pose that would not have been out of place in an amateur production of *The Three Musketeers*. "The Duke of London is an English gentleman of the highest degree, and yet in times such as these, insists upon receiving no more consideration than any other soldier of the Allied armies! A simple compartment to Marseilles, an overnight sleeper to Paris, will suffice for His Royal Highness, myself, and his other bodyguard!"

"Mais bien sûr, ce sera fait!"

Meaning we had a deal. Now for the convincer, without which no confidence trick can be sustained for long, to which end I'd been reading his lacklustre service ribbons from Indochina, Algeria, and Morocco. *"Mon Colonel*, satisfy my curiosity. Is it true the President of the Republic honours worthy soldiers every July 14th, to commemorate *la Fête Nationale*?" His embittered grunt confirmed what I already suspected. "Then prepare for a 'surprise' notification from the Élysée Palace, because His Royal Highness is sure to acknowledge your invaluable assistance, during his conversations with *M. le Président…*"

I left the railway station, twenty minutes later, with *un Mandat de Voyage Prioritaire de la plus Haute Priorité* validated by red, blue, and green rubber-stamped seals over swirled signatures. I also had copies of the telegrams sent ahead to secure our passage in case there were any misunderstandings at Marseilles.

Baxter, in the meantime, had returned from Menton and was watching me hop off the taxi with a cocksure strut. "Any luck…?"

"Le Méditeranée, 13.25 hours, changing at Gare St. Charles for the overnighter, arriving at Gare de Lyon sometime tomorrow depending on the condition of the track, unquote," I replied, secretly delighted with my progress thus far.

Baxter consulted his wristlet watch. "Then we've just enough time for a quick luncheon."

"With Mr Monash?" Said with an anxious frown as I looked around for the other player in my farewell practical joke.

"He's not needed yet. Come along! We mustn't be late."

131

Jeanne Baxter joined us in her husband's study where she found us sharing a tray of bread, cheese, and fruit on his desk. There were family matters to settle before he returned to the Front, so I shut my ears and instead reviewed the deception played on an unsuspecting French major.

In hindsight, it felt uncomfortable to have so callously exploited an older man's shriveled ambitions, but would anything less have secured a private compartment to Paris? But for how much longer could it be sustained, absent a Royal Highness to justify such an exorbitant privilege? Playing that pivotal role had been Sir John Monash's part in our practical joke. Now, within the next hour or less, I had to – somehow! – conjure up a replacement HRH.

Baxter, meanwhile, was nodding in agreement with a point his wife had just made: "Excellent idea. I'll be back shortly." With that he stood and left the room, leaving me alone with the formidable *Mme le Médecin*.

She was the first to break our silence with a sad, apologetic smile. "I regret, we cannot extend your treatments. Take good care and you will be well again in the body. But the mind is another matter in these terrible times, with so much loss, so much sorrow to trouble it. A body wound I can see and treat, but those of the brain are never visible, take much longer, and are impossible to predict the outcome of…"

I acknowledged her veiled apology with a courteous nod.

"Thank you, for the understandment." She gathered her thoughts before continuing. "May I ask now, a favour of you?"

"That depends on what it is, ma'am."

"Support my husband. Please."

"How so?" I blinked uncertainly.

"He is an honest man, forced by war to do things dishonest for dishonourable men, but he trusts you."

I examined her request before replying in measured tones: "I am not sure of your exact meaning, but I do know you ask too much."

"Why?!"

"Mine is not a paper war." I pointed skywards: "Up there is where I must go."

She read the half-wing on my tunic and thought I was referring to dog-fighting scouts and stuttering machine guns, not a sacred space where matrons never grumble, and colonels never pry. "Please! Reconsider."

"It is not possible. I have my reasons -"

"As have I!" she interrupted with a despairing look. "They are as deeply felt as yours! I love Stephen with all my heart, for he is a good man! Others are of the blood, for I love the Land of France with every fibre of my body! As I believe you do, or you would not speak our tongue with such expression!" She recovered her composure before simply adding: "*Le Rossignol* instructed you well."

"What?!"

"You were warned never to regard me as a silly little woman," she announced by way of reply. "You were also informed of an uncle, the Proprietor of *Le Temps*, a newspaper whose archives contain much material of Louis Napoleon's regime."

"You've been spying on me!"

"*Non! Absolument pas!* I confirmed details, the better to know of your condition!" She intended adding more, but instead resumed her mask of clinical detachment as Baxter himself returned, buttoning into the plain, unadorned khaki tunic of a middle-ranking Intelligence officer.

"Righty-ho," he announced cheerily, "ready to go?"

"I'll get my kit."

"We'll be waiting outside." As both were, Jeanne Baxter behind the steering wheel, her husband relaxed alongside her as he pointed me to the rear bench seat.

Most men of my time and place would have been annoyed that another man could subordinate himself to a woman in matters mechanical, even though thousands of women in uniform were now driving staff cars, and ambulances, and lorries. Often through shellfire, by night and by day, in all weathers. Along the Western Front.

However, perhaps because of my unconventional upbringing in a free-spirited Bohemian household, I had no such inhibitions. Besides, during the past several days I'd overheard fragments of conversation which told me how *Mme le Médecin* had taken driving lessons from Dorothy Levitt, the celebrated lady motoring journalist, holder of a World Land Speed Record, inventor of the rear-view mirror and, for good measure, by Royal Appointment driving instructress to the Dowager Queen Alexandra.

Jeanne Baxter had then driven the family's De Dion Bouton on five endurance trials, one of which ran from London to Edinburgh along roads barely improved since the last stagecoach needed a week to cover the same distance. Learning of this, the Duchess of Sutherland cordially invited her onto the executive of the Ladies' Automobile Club, recently formed to rival the all-male Royal Automobile Club of Great Britain & Ireland, a network of influential connexions that would soon empower a fierce little Frenchwoman to lead the FFNC into battle in October 1914.

I was therefore in skilled hands as the hospital's Delage whirred downhill into town, only slowing as it approached Gare Nice Ville. "Hello?" Her husband half-stood, leaning forward on the windscreen's varnished wooden frame while peering around. "What the deuce -?!"

A narrow strip had been roped-off in front of the main entrance decorated with red, white, blue bunting; a scratch team of bandsmen facing a row of uniformed railway staff across an unrolled red carpet; both groups under the command of their military stationmaster.

"Uh oh..."

"Yes, Mr Cribdon?" Baxter enquired, too sweetly for my comfort.

"One moment sir, I'll go ahead and see what's happening -"

"Yes. Let's do that."

My pulse thumped as we marched in step towards the restricted area. The officer i/c saw us approach, sprang to attention and saluted, palm turned outwards at his kepi's peak. I got ahead by one full pace and returned the salute with a furious frown. "*Mon Colonel!* Who authorised this madness?! Did I not tell you His Majesty's cousin travels incognito, disguised as a simple English major?! By this display you alerted the German agent who attempted to kill the Duke of London less than an hour ago -!"

"W-w-what?!"

"By God's Infinite Mercy the filthy swine failed and paid for it with his own life! Though not before wounding my brave comrade, Captain Ellis, now in surgery at *Hôpital Militaire 731!*"

"I-I-I-!"

"Calm yourself, 'Sir Ian,'" Baxter advised with a lofty smile as he effortlessly slipped into the French of a fluently spoken *milord*. "Be not hasty in your judgment. I am confident that our gallant ally meant well, is that not so Colonel…?"

"Moreau, Your Majesty's most obedient servant!"

"Then think no more of it." Baxter had instantly transformed himself into the living embodiment of princely grace and charm. "Ah, my guard of honour? How very considerate. Come, we must not disappoint those brave fellows."

"N-no, Your Majesty!"

Stunned by Baxter's blindingly swift powers of recovery and adaptation, I followed close behind, where I imagined an equerry was supposed to be, until reaching the red carpet. Here we halted while the bandsmen struck up a spirited *Marseillaise* and a fictitious Duke of London saluted the French national anthem before glancing my way again. "Kindly collect our kit and, ah, explain the situation," said in English this time. "Tell our chauffeuse to telegraph ahead for a staff car to be on standby for rapid departure from Paris."

"Sah!"

Jeanne Baxter was observing us from behind the steering wheel, poised to interrogate me once I finished marching across Nice Ville's concourse as if it were Horse Guards' Parade, when the Household Division troops its colours for the Sovereign's inspection. "What happens?!"

"As you reminded me recently, ma'am, Major Baxter works *en secrète pour la Victoire*…"

"I fail to see the connection!" she snapped, watching her husband bestow genial words of encouragement on his guard of honour.

"I am sure he will tell you, when permitted to do so. In the meantime, he requires you to telegraph our liaison, in Paris, for a staff car to be waiting at the station, ready for a quick escape. It will also help if, when questioned, you announce that a Captain Ellis has undergone surgery for wounds inflicted when he foiled an assassination attempt on the Duke of London -"

"*Quoi?!*"

"Why? Because, if Necessity is the mother of Invention," I replied, faking an old English proverb while reaching into the car for my valise and Baxter's kit, "Deception is the father of Success."

"Bah!" she flared up. "You are like those other colleagues of him!"

"But not for much longer, ma'am." With that, I gave a polite bow and marched back to the station where my commanding officer and the stationmaster were about to step onto Platform-3 and another red carpet, this one unrolled to an opened carriage door.

Passengers who had boarded earlier were now hanging out of their windows, excited by this unscheduled glimpse of pre-war pomp and ceremony as we took our leave of Moreau, during which I think I overheard Baxter murmur "*la Légion d'Honneur*…" If so, he was indeed supernaturally quick on the uptake.

Uniformed attendants carried our bags to a reserved compartment, with its own cramped lavatory cubicle and an improvised buffet laden with gift boxes of local delicacies, a wicker basket containing a selection of regional wines, and a pair of glasses commandeered from the Hôtel des Anglais.

My commanding officer slipped me his purse of silver francs during our brief passage along the corridor, with murmured instructions to disburse them as gratuities, duly done before the elderly men were dismissed with a regal nod.

Baxter waited for the door to slide shut behind them before glancing around with a disbelieving shake of the head. "His Majesty's cousin, the 'Duke of London,' evidently travels in grander style than His Majesty's Counsel, 'Learned in Law' usually does…" Then, facing me with a baffled frown: "How the blazes did you imagine you could pull off such a preposterous stunt without my *Mandat de Voyage Prioritaire* -?!"

Our locomotive's shrill whistle delayed the answer. Carriage couplings clanked and tugged and clanked again as we began moving. Slowly, at first, through huffs of sooty steam. Gathering pace over switch points and level crossings. Starting to retrace our Riviera journey of the previous week as I reached into my tunic's patch pocket and took out a Morocco leather wallet embossed with the French Republic's coat of arms in gold leaf.

Baxter examined *le Mandat de la plus Haute Priorité,* as if it were crucial evidence for the Prosecution, before looking up again with a subtly altered expression. "You talked, Major Moreau, into issuing this?"

"No, sir," I replied, with commendable restraint, "I spoke with the Regional Director of Military Rail Transport, Brigadier General Péguy, by telephone."

Baxter returned the wallet and looked away, watching olive groves and sapphire blue seas flick past our window, like the moving images inside a child's zoetrope toy. Meanwhile, I used my jack knife to slit open a flat, cylindrical box of pre-war quality candied figs and held them out for him to take first pick, using a small wooden fork tucked under the lid.

Baxter glanced back from the passing scene and made a considered choice. "Thank you. Tell me." He continued, between thoughtful chews of sugary textured fruit. "Is being a newspaper reporter? A bush worker? The orphaned relative of a distinguished actress? All that you have ever been?"

"Why do you ask?" I frowned.

"Because what I have just witnessed would have been astonishing in our own language but persuading a senior French official to authorise his highest priority railway pass – sight unseen! – in a foreign tongue, suggests a more variegated background than your enlistment papers suggest…"

"I don't know what you mean. Sir."

"Don't play the innocent with me." Said in a cold grey voice that must've loosened the bowels of many a villain on trial for life or liberty. "I've dealt with slim customers of every description in the course of my profession, but few if any could've matched your performance today."

I leapt to my feet. "I resent that insinuation -!"

"Sit, down. Nobody is impugning your prickly sense of honour. Or accusing you of anything illicit. Merely observing an irrefutable fact," he replied, as if dealing with a fractious witness in court. "So, where did you learn such quickness of wit? And who taught you?"

"I fail to see how it concerns anyone but myself!" I was still standing, one hand gripping the luggage rack, balancing as the train thumped along its track towards Cannes.

"Allow me to be the best judge of that." Baxter spoke with frigid courtesy. "I am your superior officer and could order you to answer or face a disciplinary charge, however, I shall not. Instead, consider this," he raised a cautionary finger to stop me interrupting. "On your commissioning course, did they not tell you to 'father' your men *in loco parentis*, by looking after them to the best of your ability?"

"Yes," I replied, alert for another of this cunning man's verbal traps.

"I don't hold with such familiarity," Baxter continued, ignoring my cautious response, "but that does not mean I don't care about my subordinates' welfare." He eyed me shrewdly. "Your present conduct is therefore a matter of concern. You clearly have courage and initiative aplenty. I also suspect you are an adversary I would not care to meet up a dark alley. You are therefore richly endowed with rare and useful skills. But...!"

"But what?!" I demanded, more than ever determined to prove my unsuitability for Staff Corps duties.

"You are allowing these rich gifts to control you, not yet having learned to control them -"

"I'm lost!" Exclaimed with barely restrained derision as I shied away from further discussion of things so close and personal.

"Not yet, though you may soon be," he observed drily. "My wife sees you on the brink of a dark pit. One more step and you will be lost forever. And that would indeed be a great loss."

"With respect, sir, this's sentimental tosh!"

"With equal respect, I disagree," Baxter replied evenly. "Ours is a Manichean world of Good versus Evil; of Integrity versus Expediency; of Hope versus Despair; of Life versus Death..."

"Mani-what?" I was out of patience with his patronising sermon.

"Manichaeism, an ancient Persian belief that the world – and all we humans upon it – are locked in an eternal struggle between the forces of Light, and the forces of Darkness. A battle in which all are free to pick sides, but none are free to remain neutral," he replied simply. "Most wobble from side to side, sometimes good, sometimes bad, for men and woman are by our very nature faithless turncoats. But these are not the Devil's preferred recruits," Baxter continued with sober emphasis.

"He seeks the brave, the quick, the despairing, to take his seductively easy escape from their wretchedness and heartache, only to discover - too late! – there is no escape from the demonic legions of Hell. And yet, if only they had shown greater fortitude and forbearance, those Lost Souls would have won an honoured place among the Enlightened Ones, fighting the Good Fight that continues unto this very day. As it was for my wife's martyred Cathar ancestors during Rome's so-called Albigensian Crusade." He paused, closely studying my reaction. "'And here endeth the lesson...'"

I shook my head in bemused disbelief. "I don't buy whatever it is you're selling."

"It would be remarkable if you did, so early in the piece," he replied, not in the least put out by my dismissive snort. "Our devout hope is that you will find the courage to stay alive long enough to discover for yourself the truth of what you have just heard. But for the moment, I suggest -"

We were interrupted by another uniformed attendant, from the onboard galley this time, pushing a trolley laden with real coffee and trays of freshly baked, pre-war quality *petits fours*, savoury little appetisers for HRH the Duke of London, Sir Ian his equerry, and lesser notables travelling *Classe Luxe*.

132

My annoyance abated somewhat by the time our attendant finished serving refreshments and then pushed his trolley farther down the corridor. Baxter's improvised sermon was no more than could be expected from a desk warrior who talked of struggle and battle, on a map or on a blackboard, but who had never been shot at or returned fire himself, preferring to leave that dirty work for others to do on his behalf. Nor was I impressed by his Holy Joe impersonation, being innately suspicious of Soul Catchers, as Percy Black called the eagerly attentive army chaplains who mingled with us at kit-up, prior to our next tour of Hell's earthly Chamber of Horrors.

Those were the occasions when he and I and many another found their presence an irritating distraction. Likewise, their fervent promises of Life Everlasting for which we first had to qualify by being blown to bits, or buried alive inside a collapsed dugout, or choked to death by poisonous gas. More to my taste were - and secretly still are - those ancestral echoes of All Father Odin's Hall of the Heroic Dead where Harry and Percy, Pat Donovan and Cedric Shaw, David and Sandra are holding a place for me at their feast board.

Meanwhile, I could not fail to notice the subtle way in which Baxter warned against self-murder although his advice was now redundant, having ceased loading and unloading my service revolver the previous week. Instead, I would soon be re-joining my wife as her proud young husband, his guns' ammunition well spent, before ramming one final Iron Crossed fuselage -!

"A penny for your thoughts?"

Startled, my mind snapped back to the present. "They're not for sale."

"The look on your face said that might be the case," Baxter replied, still holding out my share of the savouries, "but there's no harm in asking, is there?"

"That all depends."

"On what?"

"Your reason for asking."

"Shall we say, a natural, human desire to make civil conversation?"

"I'd prefer we spoke of weightier matters than my private thoughts."

"As you wish. Pick a topic as well as one of these," he replied, "I'm getting tired of holding this damn' plate for you to ignore."

"Oh." I took notice of the nearest *petit four salé* which, as luck would have it, was filled with my favourite anchovy and green olive tapenade. "Thanks."

He replaced them on the makeshift buffet shelf, "Now," he faced me again, "what is it you wish to discuss?"

I wiped my fingers clean on a linen napkin and sat back. "What did you mean when you said that Mr Monash is 'not needed yet'? I thought generals were supposed to lead, not follow?"

"Correct."

"Then why is he still in Menton, fooling around at the opera instead of returning with us, to the Front?" As a captain, albeit acting-unpaid, I was only one pip below Baxter's substantive rank and therefore entitled to express my opinions without too much fear or favour.

"Fair comment." Baxter seemed impervious to my gruff tone. "Let us begin by imagining that same opera house in which the first thing we notice is a flustered bandmaster bumbling around the orchestra pit, telling his players how to hold their instruments, how to read their parts. What would be our initial impression?"

"I'd wonder what the hell any of this had to do with beating the Hun."

"We speak figuratively, Mr Cribdon." He was no longer smiling. "I'd hazard a guess you'd wonder what this village glee club was doing on the programme. However, if after we'd taken our seats, and the first violin had tuned up, the conductor strode from the wings, mounted the podium and, with a masterful flick of his baton, launched into the overture, you would instantly recognise that we were in the presence of skilled professional performers."

"And the moral of this story is?"

"To illustrate Sir John's role in his division's recent victory at Messines," Baxter replied, loading his pipe from its unflapped tobacco pouch. "For whereas many of our senior commanders are still leading imaginary cavalry charges in the Soudan or South Africa of their youth - Field Marshal French is a good example of this fatal nostalgia - your Melburnian neighbour brings a thoroughly modern, razor-sharp brain to the challenges of modern warfare."

"Go on..."

"By contrast with the previously mentioned gentleman, Sir John directs his sector of the Western Front as if it were a civil engineering project. He could be building a bridge, or a road, or a harbour in which every man and every item of equipment has its place, its time, its function. Only then is he ready to conduct every note of a colossal composition. Though instead of strings, woodwind, and brass, he conducts Infantry, Engineers, and Artillery 'as if they were Mahler's *Symphony of One Thousand,*' was how he described it to me." Baxter hesitated before conceding: "Something he does very well..."

"Hence GHQ's and the Palace's support for his promotion to GOC Australian Army Corps?" I replied, harking back to our earlier conversation on the terrace overlooking Villefranche sur Mer.

"Yes."

"And the subversive newspaper campaign by jealous rivals?"

"Yes."

"Then why is he exposing himself to hostile comment by loafing around on the Riviera?"

"'Loafing' is hardly the word I'd have chosen," Baxter replied with marked disapproval. "Like the *maestro* he is, Sir John has trained his brigadiers and planning staff – his principal instrumentalists, if you like – during these past several months of meticulous rehearsals. We are now ready to perform at concert pitch the moment he mounts the podium in a few days' time."

I was not convinced this was the whole story. "And which instrument does Intelligence play, the piccolo or the triangle?"

"Neither." Baxter prepared to strike a match, then changed his mind and shrewdly glanced my way again. "We're the 'backstage hands' an audience never sees or has reason to think about. The anonymous 'desk warriors' who prepare the maps and write the instructions for Sir John's brigade commanders to execute on the frontline. The very embodiment of 'Clueless Claudes,' would you not agree?"

"I might, if that was all you did."

Baxter feigned surprise. "You surely don't think there's more to our work than the distribution of 'bum fodder' for you chaps in the trenches to scoff at before using its paper for a more practical purpose?"

"'Please don't play the innocent with me.'" I was determined never to give an inch in our verbal tugs o' war. "I can think of no reason for you to spend whole days at Menton if all you'd done was deliver a transcribed telegram. Sir."

His eyebrows shot up in mock surprise. "But what else could we have been doing?"

"That's not for me to say," I replied cagily, "but *Abteilung* are derelict in their duty if they don't have waiters and barmen on the payroll, in France, like they have in Alex'."

"To what end?"

"For the same reason as we're probably renting similar eyes and ears in neutral countries like Switzerland and Holland, Denmark and Sweden," I replied shortly.

"Go on..." his wastepaper basket; my people reported what he'd annotated or clipped

"Speaking personally, I have never seen a more obvious senior military officer in mufti than 'Mr Knight' when he came to your place. The Kaiser's spies would've got his range within minutes of him signing the hotel register. In their boots, I'd have made damn' sure my people delivered his newspapers; my people cleaned out his wastepaper basket; my people -"

"How the blazes do you know all this?!".

"I don't, but I'll bet you do. Besides," I continued firmly, "his pencil was sharpened to about one quarter its original length when he estimated 3-Divvy's tonnage of shells, after lunch. That told me a lot."

Baxter recovered his poise. "Anything else?"

"Your regular appearances must've triggered keen interest."

"How so?"

"Fritz would be blind not to see a mysterious Englishman arrive almost every morning, bringing a report of some kind, and deaf not to overhear what was being 'carelessly' discussed when you were served a nice pot o' tea and plate of bikkies." I waited for a comment that never came, before concluding with another lick of mordant Australian humour: "I read nothing in the Huns' Order of Battle to suggest that *Abteilung* is a charity employing the handicapped."

Baxter fell silent and turned away as our train thumped along, oblivious to the passing vista of golden beaches and rocky headlands bathed in a glorious, honeyed light that never ceases to attract painters and artists to the South Coast of France. As Henri Matisse was wont to remind me, years later, whenever our stays at *le Guetteur* coincided – now returned to its pre-war identity after a brief spell as *Hôpital Militaire 731* - from whence we would paddle his canoe around Nice Harbour, amiably putting the world aright.

Baxter gave a dry cough and faced me again. "Misdirecting the Kaiser's Intelligence Service was not the only item on our agenda. We also had to decide ways and means of coping with the inevitable feuds and follies that agitate any group of men forced to work closely together during times of heightened danger and grave uncertainty."

"Oh?" I noted the abrupt change of subject.

"Put simply, your aunt's piano partner has entrusted us to be his 'Praetorian Guard,' tasked with frustrating enemies internal as well as external, thus freeing him to concentrate on 'beating the Hun...'" He paused, studying me closely. "You doubt me, Mr Cribdon?"

"Yes." I was deliberately blunt. "There's a lot more to this than you've told me thus far. Sir."

"'Yea verily, I say unto you, take no heed of the morrow, for the morrow shall take care of itself,'" Baxter reached for a copy of *Le Temps*, one of several complementary newspapers and magazines provided by the railway company for its *Classe Luxe* passengers. "'Sufficient unto the day is the evil thereof.' *Matthew 6:34.*"

"'Means what?'" I responded, irritably echoing *Mme le Médecin's* frustration with her English husband's misty mindscape.

"'Means' all will be revealed at its proper time and place." he replied, not in the least fazed by my gruff tone, retrieving a pair of reading spectacles from his tunic's breast pocket.

133

I gathered our kit as the train approached Marseilles' Gare St Charles, clanking, and wheezing past a marshalling yard crammed with wagonloads of munitions bound for the Italian Front. However, my target was much nearer to hand as I reached out to snaffle one of the unopened, complimentary bottles of red wine.

"Please don't." Baxter's request was polite, but its tone brooked no refusal.

"Sir?"

"Consider these 'le souper du roi' at Versailles." He pointed at the other bottles and a selection of mostly untouched fruits and cheeses. I blinked, unsure if this was a joke or the start of another lecture. "Every night, the royal cooks would present the Sun King with sumptuous dishes from which he would take a few morsels before retiring with his maîtresse en titre or, less often, his neglected queen," Baxter explained patiently, reading my thoughts. "Then, as soon as the bedchamber door shut behind him, dukes and marquises and counts would push and shove and scuffle over a leg of fowl or goblet of wine snatched from the royal supper table."

"Are you, serious?" Being young and Australian, I was quick to suspect this older Englishman's ironic humour, having read several historical novels in which European aristocrats feasted at elaborate banquets amidst scenes of splendid idleness. "Those toffs never did anything like that!"

"Oh yes they did," Baxter replied with a touch of melancholy. "Famished aristos fed off the king's scraps, like his pet dogs, vying each with the other for some trifling privilege that could be squeezed for a few louis d'or." He paused before concluding: "Theirs was a precarious existence long before the first bewigged head fell into a guillotine's basket…"

I was frankly baffled. "Maybe so, but what's all that got to do with us, now?"

"A great deal, once we accept that modern railway employees are no less driven by need and greed than were Louis XIV's threadbare courtiers. In fact," Baxter continued, "I'd bet anything you like; these wines and delicacies were divvied up long before we came aboard, and that every sip, every mouthful we've taken since then, has been one less for some miserably paid serveur to sell on the black-market, or smuggle home to his anxious family. Such humble folk naturally assume that His Britannic Majesty's cousin understands the rules and will leave everything behind, except for a token nibble or two." He cocked an eyebrow. "So, what d'you think they'd say if one of us 'pinched' their booty…?"

"They'd think it's what anyone would do, given half a chance!"

"Except that we are not 'anyone,'" Baxter replied severely. "Thanks to you I'm now of the Blood Royal, and thanks to me you're now a bogus Knight of the Realm, and neither of us has need to steal food."

"Point taken." I coughed into a clenched fist, annoyed at having revealed more of myself than I usually to do with strangers. "'Old habits die hard.'"

"Old habits also die swiftly and with the greatest of ease," he warned with a piercing frown. "In our business it is often the most trivial detail that betrays an enemy agent, whose assumed background, and the incidental details that validate it, resemble a knitted protective garment. Provided everything he or she does or says remains in character, there is no reason to suspect them of being other than what they claim to be. But let one thread of that garment snag, and their 'cover story' begins to unravel. For example," he continued, "imagine questioning a cigar merchant from Stockholm. A charming fellow, happy with himself and the world, fluent in every answer. There is no reason to suspect him but for one seemingly insignificant detail…"

"Which is?"

"He maintains eye contact."

"Why is that a problem?"

"Swedes modestly avert their gaze, as required by '*Lagom*,' their nation's unofficial code of social conduct," Baxter explained simply. "Whereas a German arrogantly looks you straight in the eye."

"Strewth, I never knew that!"

"You do now, but that's not all our cigar merchant's unhappy fate can teach us," Baxter continued, beginning to stand as our carriage crawled along one of St Charles' seven or eight platforms.

"Oh?"

"Never assume a new identity as if it were a wig or false nose, as actors do, before returning to their everyday lives after a performance. Intelligence is not a make-believe drama in three acts with a happy ending. To be effective we must strip off every vestige of our old selves and their bad habits – like snaffling food – and seamlessly integrate with whatever our current task requires us to become. Often at very short notice…" I sensed he was referring to our recent brush with disaster at Nice Ville railway station. "And here endeth the second lesson for today, 'Sir Ian.'"

The train ground to a halt and we stepped onto the platform where a smaller, less effusive welcome than the fanfare departure at Nice, awaited us. Baxter bestowed gracious words of appreciation on our attendant and turned away, leaving me to disburse more silver francs, an act I now realised was an example of what he had just taught me.

For the purposes of today's journey, my commanding officer was a member of the Royal Family and, as they never carry cash, neither did he after handing me his purse. Instead, equerries give out such money as may be required, a curious fact overheard while recovering at King Edward's Hospital, a stone's throw from Buckingham Palace.

Gare St Charles' military stationmaster advanced to meet us, saluted, and reported there would be a short delay while the Overnight Express got ready for its northbound journey to Paris. Meanwhile, light refreshments awaited us in the 1st Class Waiting Room…

I scented a trap, knowing how flimsy our cover story really was. An alert *Agent de la Police* could unmask us with one telegram to the British Embassy in Paris, the Duke of London being an entirely fictitious character. Baxter must've also known there was no such duchy, nor ever had been, but this did not stop him playing the unflustered embodiment of royal charm, conversing fluently with overawed French railway officials after gracefully accepting a morsel of Camembert cheese, a dry biscuit, and a few sips of champagne, with a slight nod in my direction to reinforce his recent warning.

By the greatest of good fortune nobody questioned our credentials and I like to think that we left a small group of war-weary Frenchmen with a higher opinion of their British allies than they would've had before we briefly brightened their day. At the conclusion of which, I disbursed more francs from our stock of silver - a princely sum, now that each coin was worth twice its face value in wartime scrip on the black-market - and slid the compartment door firmly shut behind our attendants.

"You learn quickly," Baxter observed from his seat nearest the window.

I shrugged slowly. The emotional drain of the past half hour – on top of the previous days, weeks, months of pain and loss – was taking its toll as I slumped on the opposite seat, eyelids drooping, unaware of aught else until Baxter shook my shoulder and said it was time to go for'ard to the dining car.

Electric light bulbs were unobtainable at this low point of the war, except through le Système, which is probably where the railway's bulbs had gone, written-off as "breakages." In their place a half-candle, embedded in a glass ashtray packed with damp sand, glimmered on each table; fingers-crossed there were sufficient soda siphons to replace the also stolen fire extinguishers, in case one of the candles fell over or a glowing cigarette end dropped into a dark and dusty corner of our wooden carriage.

Another time, another companion, and candlelight could have been quite agreeable but not here, not now, not when confronted by an artfully spiced "beef" consommé that was probably dragging a field gun until a few days ago, followed by an equally mysterious, primped-up casserole. Neither dish succeeded in raising my spirits. Nor did the wine list. Instead, I opted for Evian water to cleanse the palate and clear a foggy brain.

Baxter spooned cream into his cup as the coffee trolley trundled away, added a shot of Calvados brandy, and leaned into the wavering pool of candlelight to prevent others, seated nearby, overhearing us: "There are two qualities that distinguish Australians," he began, with a modest, disarming smile. "The first is your 'give it a go' initiative; the second is your shrewd assessment of the associated risks…"

An exhausted doze, propped upright in a lurching railway carriage, had done nothing to lighten my heaviness of heart, and I was in no mood to be flattered by this supple, subtle Englishman. "You've forgotten the third."

"Which is?"

"Our notoriously plain speech. So, enough of the blarney. What's your point?"

"Good question, glad you asked." Baxter leaned over the wavering candle flame, pipe bowl inverted and drew heat, arranging his thoughts before sitting upright again. "To answer that, accompany me in imagination to the Year of our Lord 1893."

"I'm probably not born yet."

"True," Baxter chose to ignore my muted sarcasm, "but curb your impatience as we revisit 'the City of Dreaming Spires,' where Oriel's Provost, Dr Binning-Munro, has invited a distinguished alumnus - visiting Britain in his capacity as Premier of the Cape Colony and Chairman of the De Beers mining company - to take sherry with the Junior Common Room."

I remained watchfully silent.

"Others are quizzing Mr Rhodes about business opportunities in South Africa," Baxter continued, reflectively, "but as I already know the future course of my life, I can afford to ignore their ingratiating chatter and, instead, pay close attention as our guest outlines his plans for the British Empire in which we Oxford Men are being invited to join him on its civilising mission to the world."

"That's a bit rich!"

"Several million pounds worth." Baxter shared a rueful smile. "Our first meeting, at Oriel, was my 'Road to Damascus moment,' though unlike the one in *Acts 9:3-9*," he hastened to add. "The Anti-Imperialists decried all that Mr Rhodes said, as is their wont, but I knew what he meant for we had much in common..."

"Like?" I'd remembered the Chief's lesson on basic newspaper reporting, a lifetime ago, in the Shamrock Hotel's dining room.

"We were both 'sons of the vicarage,'" Baxter replied simply. "His was at Bishops Stortford, in rural Hertfordshire; mine served a village of workers at a paper mill, and the canal bargees who supplied it with raw materials, in the same county.

"Both of us had learned, early in life, that church mice are not the only poor and needy creatures on an ecclesiastical scale of rations," he elaborated, with a touch of wry humour, "and were accordingly driven to improve our lots; he by emigrating to fame and fortune in Southern Africa; I by attending Watford Boys' Grammar School and winning a scholarship to read Law at Oxford."

All this was lost on me, of course, but nonetheless I found myself assembling material for an imagined Character Sketch in the *Miner*.

"My respect for Mr Rhodes' vision grew as we maintained a lively correspondence during the next few years." Baxter continued, reflectively trickling smoke. "His health was never robust. This gave his words and actions a luminous energy. Newspapers dubbed him the 'Colossus of Rhodes.' An apt title, for like all larger-than-life individuals, he could be impatient with dullards, as when he described certain Liberal politicians as 'poodle faking loafers.'

"Challenged to explain this harsh judgement, by others in the JCR, he replied that Britain's future lay not with: 'Pudding-faced Parliamentarians and indolent aristocratic landlords, but with energetic, ambitious Britons who had the gumption to risk all and emigrate to the South African Veldt, the Canadian prairies, the New Zealand sheep runs, the Australian Outback. And upon arrival were not afraid to roll-up their sleeves and build a new future for themselves, for their families, for the Empire...'"

"At least he was qualified to talk about that." I found myself curiously moved. "No man gets to name to a new country simply by sitting on his arse and daydreaming about it."

"Correct," Baxter agreed, "not that I knew what he meant at the time, of course. In fact, it wasn't until meeting you and your Australian colleagues, that I grasped the full significance of his words."

"Oh?" I was immediately on-guard again.

"Simply put, you are the first Australians I've met, apart from those sons of the 'Squatocracy,' as I believe you term your landed gentry, up at Oxford. And what you've taught me has been a real education, in every sense of that phase, as well as confirming Rhodes' opinion of 'Overseas Britons' as a rejuvenating force within the Empire," Baxter added, gesturing with his pipe stem. "Whereas those former chaps constantly strove to be to be more English than the English, often with comical upsets, your troops are magnificent, bloody-minded individualists; loyal to their 'mates,' devils in khaki to their enemies; quick to seize the initiative, as you yourself did at Pozières -"

"Don't sentimentalise us," I interrupted sharply.

"I'm not," Baxter frowned at my tone. "The JAG's' court martial transcripts frequently pass over my desk; we're old colleagues. But even the most wayward man deserves a fresh start in a new land, as Mr Rhodes implied when he said: 'If the British Empire is not to suffer the same fate as every previous one, each lasting an average of two and a half centuries or ten lifetimes, then we must search farther afield than London's foggy streets for its new leaders and statesmen! Instead of relying upon timid stay-at-homes, it is our duty to rally those sturdy, adventurous Overseas Britons, not all of whom have lived by the Old Country's laws, and harness their restless energy to build an enduring, worldwide confraternity dedicated to the advancement of Civilisation!'

"Otherwise," Baxter concluded, expressing his own opinion now, "Britain will shrivel like a deflating rubber balloon until she is no more than an overcrowded pair of islands inhabited by a little people whose forefathers once bestrode the globe, but who subsequently frittered away their inheritance upon ale, cigarettes, and football games."

I was far from being persuaded that this was the truth, the whole truth, and nothing but the truth. "So, the moral of this story is?" Then I caught a familiar look in his eye. "Ri-i-ght. 'Think about it and report what you discover...'?"

"Correct." He got to his feet, swaying as the train lurched along into the night. "The attendants will have prepared our berths by now; we'd better get whatever rest we can, while we can."

I can't remember who first spoke of a "Dark Night of the Soul," but I had a good idea of how they must've felt as I dozed on the cramped bunk above Baxter's in our dimly lit compartment.

He had not fooled me for one instant. Long before the start of our journey, I'd been reminded of Phillip Grenville artfully casting lures along the Itchen's shady banks. The only difference now, I was the prey that Stephen Baxter was trying to catch with seemingly innocent references to Aunt Lucinda, the Shusters, and David's honorary uncle Mr Monash.

Even his autobiographical story was, I felt, a wily half-truth. What he was hoping to gain was not for me to say. The fellow was too effortlessly superior, with his Latin tags and Scriptural quotations, for my plain taste.

Moreover, his remark about Australian students amusing other young toffs by striving to be more English than the English, had stung me badly. Not that he could've known how much time and effort had been invested moulding me into a colonial copy of the Perfect English Gentleman at Tralee House. A shallow pretence stripped off at Blackboy Camp, together with my civvy clothes, and gladly exchanged for the rough uniform and rougher manners of an infantry private.

Three years older, and much wiser, I was in no humour to play posh mind games with Major Stephen Baxter KC. Although, upon reflection, I had to confess that he had never done me any harm that I knew of. In fact, he'd gone out of his way to welcome me into his family home; most unusual in France where acquaintances are kept at the front door until sufficiently well known for a warmly familiar "*tu*" instead of the frostily formal "*vous*."

It is only now, with the wisdom of hindsight, that I realise how Baxter's oblique remarks echoed the Oxford tutorial method that stimulates individual discovery, and independent thought, by posing open questions without giving readymade answers; these the student must make for himself and, by so doing, toughen his mental sinews.

It was my youthful error to mistake this subtle teaching with the languid drawls. And incomplete sentences. That so enraged, my beautiful. Irreplaceable wife. Describing her male cousins' speech. At our little home. In Alexandria -!

Clenched teeth failed to quench the burning ache inside my chest, or dam the tears, or muffle the pillowed sobs as the Paris Express rackety-clackety-clacked through the horrid darkness of a wartime night.

The sleeping car attendant brought us a pitcher of lukewarm water, sometime after dawn. Baxter, as the superior officer, got first go. Once he finished shaving and had dressed, it was my turn, using the last pint to cool inflamed eyelids and smarten-up in the cramped lavatory cubicle, sheer luxury for a man who had often used his steel helmet as an improvised wash bowl and, sometimes, as an emergency urinal.

I scowled back at the reversed image, framed by swirls of arum lilies etched on the cubicle's *art nouveau* mirror, and made a final check of my khaki shirt, collar, and tie. Then buckled the Sam Browne, loaded holster firmly seated against left hip, and emerged, chin up, ready to confront another long and lonely day.

Baxter put aside the current number of *La Guerre Illustrée* – twenty pages of sepia halftone lies depicting cheerful *poilus* in their dry and spacious dugouts, feasting on abundant rations served by friendly cooks in crisp white aprons - and glanced up: "Sleep alright?"

"Yes sir."

"Good man." He tossed the magazine aside and got to his feet. "I suggest we get first in line for breakfast."

As it happens, we were not, but being an HRH gave Baxter precedence over a delegation of senior government officials on their way north to a ministerial conference in the capital, all of whom kept scowling at the attention lavished on a mere British major and an even lower Australian captain, until a furtive whisper informed them who we were, travelling in disguise. I should have been entertained by how well a cheeky spoof can work, when done with verve and confidence, but I was not.

"Something troubling you, 'Sir Ian'?"

"'Your Royal Highness' is most perceptive," I responded stiffly to his implied warning, given the number of ears focused on us, as the dining car attendant finished serving freshly toasted *brioche* made from real wheaten flour, spread with pre-war quality butter and a generous dollop of mixed fruit *confiture*.

How France sustained herself on such skimpy tucker until the main, midday meal, was an impenetrable mystery for a man who used to stoke up with a breakfast of fried 'roo steaks, slabs of soda bread baked in a campfire's hot coals, washed down with a mug of stewed black tea, before a hard day's yakka with pick and shovel.

"I do hope it's not too serious," Baxter interrupted my solitary thoughts. "As I said to Cousin George recently, it is vital the Royal Family maintains a calm dignity in public, no matter how distressed we may feel during these difficult days. And nights…"

"Sir?"

"We were discussing the Prince of Wales's wish to assume frontline duties with the Coldstream Guards." Baxter pitched his voice a shade higher, for those nearby to overhear and gossip about later. "Of course, there's no question that we must share the people's suffering and sacrifice, insofar as we are able to, but if HRH were to be gravely wounded, or worse yet, killed…"

I shrugged indifferently, wondering what sort of circus for verbal acrobatics this modern Machiavelli's law chambers were, for a King's Counsel in peacetime, and Field Marshal Haig's Intelligence Liaison Officer at war. "But haven't they already got a spare as well as an heir?" I added, wincing inwardly as this phrase triggered memories of an earlier, happier time and place.

"That is not the point!" Baxter was clearly annoyed by my attitude. "He has a duty to remain on the Staff where there are important tasks for him to perform. Because it is all very well for a young fellow to seek glory on the field of battle or wreak revenge for great personal loss, in the skies above, but if he was to read his commissioning parchment closely, it would remind him of His Majesty's direct, personal commands, would it not?!"

Baxter was no longer speaking about the Prince of Wales. "From memory they go something like this," he continued, sternly: "'We, reposing especial Trust and Confidence in your Loyalty, Courage, and Integrity, do hereby appoint you,' followed by your new rank, and an admonition to: 'maintain Good Order and Discipline, and to observe and follow such Orders and Directions as you shall receive from Us,' that is from the King himself, 'and any other of your superior officers!'" These last few words were especially stressed as my own superior officer shot me a steely frown. "So, what's troubling you?"

"Nothing that can't wait. Sir."

134

He slid our compartment door shut, locked it from the inside, and turned. Gone was the suavely affable Englishman. In his place stood someone quite else. Villains, on trial for their lives, would have felt clammy terror when Baxter KC led for the Prosecution. I felt an involuntary shiver myself as he spoke in the equivalent of a graven granite inscription. "All cards on the table. What is your problem?"

It took some nerve to respond frankly. "I've had a gutful."

"Of what?"

"Your insufferable shadow boxing!"

"Explain."

"That bulldust, back there, in the dining car, was not about the Prince of Wales, it was me you were getting at!"

"Correct."

"Well, I've had a gutful!"

"Stop repeating yourself."

"I'll repeat myself as often as I bloody well like!"

"You hold King's commission. You will do as you are told -"

"Wrong!" I fired back, a distraught young man, far from home and his rapidly dwindling number of friends.

Baxter's cheeks blenched. "How dare -!"

"That might wash for 'timid, stay-at-home' Poms," I pressed on regardless, "but not with 'magnificent, bloody-minded individualists' I'd have not lasted five minutes as a sergeant, if all I'd done was demand unthinking obedience from my mates as if they were your lacklustre English peasants!"

"How -!"

"Because, to get the best from Aussie troops, you must intelligently explain the situation and allow enough elbow room for Digger initiative to work its magic!" I continued, overriding his angry objections. "And then trust 'em to deal with any Fritz stupid enough to stand in our way!" I drew a deep breath before concluding. "So, once again, I've had a gutful of shifty evasion and sneaky half-truths. And you can take it as Gospel that I'm looking forward to being RTU'd to where 'Yes' means yes, 'No' means no, and 'Fuck off' means just that! Sir."

I doubt if anyone had ever spoken so bluntly to Stephen Baxter. None of those other Australians he'd known at Oxford - with their manicured English manners, comic or otherwise - could have done so. Even I was stunned by how quickly the veneer of genteel Melbourne can peel back to reveal the underlying rough-hewn armature of Sydney Town's recent convict past.

"Have you, quite finished?"

"Yes. Unless you want more."

"Don't be impertinent; it does you no credit."

"I don't want credit, I want out!"

"Very well, cite me one example of the 'shadow boxing' you find so offensive!"

"Right-o!" I was determined never to yield an inch. "For instance, when you told me that Mr Monash had entrusted us to be his 'Praetorian Guard,' tasked with frustrating his enemies internal - by which I assume he meant that Bean bloke and Billy Hughes' mongrels - as well as enemies external, thus freeing him to 'destroy the Hun'!"

"Yes."

"But when I asked how we were going to do it, what did I get? Bible babble and a vague promise that 'all would be revealed at its proper time'!"

Baxter fell silent. Instead, he resumed his seat by the window and stared out at the dank grey morning as our locomotive valiantly shuffled northwards, away from the sloping vineyards of Burgundy and onto the gentler *paysage* of Île-de-France, the last leg of our journey to Paris.

I flicked open *La Guerre Illustrée* and amused myself by rewriting the captions on several propaganda photos, noting some as cartoon material for *Punch*; reminded that he who speaks first, loses. And I was in no mood to lose to anyone. Least of all a Clueless like this Stephen Baxter cove.

He eventually spoke. "You fail to take into account the importance we place on the Australian Army Corps, and of the need to have the right man in command at this crucial juncture."

I looked up from a lying picture of cheerful patients in a multiple amputees' ward. "Who can doubt it? We're your expendables. Whenever a Pommy unit gets into strife, it's our job to rescue the poor lost lambs -"

"Wrong!" he glared back. "I had hoped for an adult understanding of the situation! Instead, all I hear are juvenile jibes and provocative sulks! And if that's the best you can do, the Flying Corps is welcome to your services; we're better off without them!"

I felt the colour draining from my face as he continued in the same cruelly cold tone. "And before you 'fuck off!' as you so eloquently put it, know this! The Australians, the New Zealanders, the Canadians, the Rhodesians, those other sturdy Overseas Britons, are all we have left to spearhead one final, decisive counterattack after the Kaiser unleashes his Eastern forces on the Western Front!

"The once-superb regiments of Britain's pre-war army now exist in name only, their ranks filled with conscripts of whom the best one can hope is that they will find sufficient inner strength to stand their ground and fight!

"You may think GHQ is careless with your lives, but that is also wrong! Sir Douglas frequently expresses his admiration for Australian dash, Australian pluck, Australian grit!

"So, while you buzz around the sky in your little aeroplane, I and others will be doing our utmost to support Sir John Monash in his great work and, by association, defend his gallant Australians against their own political leaders' jealousy, prejudice, and sabotage -!"

Neither of us had much to say after this epic clash of temperaments and it was a very subdued pair of men who got off at the Gare de Lyon, half-expecting to be met by either a guard of honour or a squad of military police. In the event a presidential aide from the Elysée Palace buttonholed us with an anxious enquiry about the Duke of London, for whom a car and mounted escort were waiting on the forecourt.

Baxter announced that HRH would be along presently, and that we were going ahead to notify the British Embassy of his arrival, after which we moved smartly in the opposite direction, searching for a Vauxhall staff car with 3 Division's pennant on its mudguard. Our luck held and we were several miles from Paris before the search for a missing HRH turned into a furious manhunt for two spies disguised as British Intelligence officers.

Baxter wisely left me alone. His reprimand had cut me to the quick and was not made any easier by the knowledge I had brought it all upon myself, a discovery that mirrored the anonymous padre's confession in 3LGH, when he'd said that "pain is a sign of God's Grace..." Maybe so, for him, but not for an insecure young man with two confusing identities - William Charles Braithwaite the orphaned slum boy, and Ian Cribdon the adopted Toorak toff - both of whom had briefly found unity of purpose and peace of mind in Sandra Nobury's loving heart.

The grief I felt then, and still do, after seven decades of wandering the world alone, wondering how my life might have been if only von Grundwitz had obeyed the Hague Convention on Hospital Ships, can never be expressed. My only meagre comfort is the knowledge that he died with "*Winchelsea!*" hissing in his left ear.

Had not David also been killed, we could have talked it through, for there was nobody else I sufficiently trusted to discuss a matter so personal. Even if I returned to 3 Squadron, it would be as a stranger because few if any would remember me now, so quickly did aircrew come and go.

Baxter sat with his back turned, looking through the side window, studying the convoys of lorries and GS wagons, horse artillery and cavalry, marching infantry, and pioneer battalions. Every man, every machine, every animal, heading to the Front.

"This is the Kaiser's last throw of war's iron dice," he thought aloud, turning to face me again. "How they fall, will decide if he is to reign as a second Napoleon, Emperor of Europe, or die a reviled prisoner on St Helena..."

I remained silent, more immediate matters on my mind as we skirted the pyramidical slag heaps and wrecked coalmines around Lens, before covering the last few miles to Armentières' shattered outskirts.

The old Technical School had copped more damage during our brief absence, after another night-time bombing raid by Gothas operating from their base near Brussels.

An aerial observer, myself, I knew that it required no great skill to target the AIF's railway yards and supply dumps. All an enemy pilot had to do was fly his compass needle westward until he intersected the Lys Canal, a distinctive silvery squiggle visible on the darkest of nights, then follow it to Lac de Hem, a large, reflective body of water slap bang in the middle of town.

Rue Jules Lebleu was still partially blocked with rubble, but our Service Corps driver managed to skirt around it and turn left at the guard post where he braked and disinterestedly watched his two passengers climb down into the raw, late-afternoon murk common on the Franco-Belgian border at this time of year,

Baxter turned, his right hand extended. "This is where we part company. It's been a memorable experience for me, but I do understand the need to avenge your loss, and devoutly hope you find that which you seek."

"Thank you, sir." We shook hands. "Um. One final question, if I may?"

"Yes, Mr Cribdon?"

"When General Monash spoke of his 'Praetorian Guard,' did he specifically mention my name?"

"Actually, yes," Baxter replied with an inward frown. "Apparently he once gave you a lesson in perspective drawing."

"Heavens, so he did!" I was astonished that anyone with his weight of responsibilities could remember such a trivial incident, years ago. "It was during the interval at a Shuster Concert. He also helped David for his, that is Dave's, laboratory notebook sketches."

"Your dead friend?"

"Yes."

"What was he like...?"

"Brainy. Loyal. Straight as a billiard cue. By any fair measure he should've got a posthumous VC for his last flight. Instead, all his parents got was a paltry 'Mentioned in Despatches.'"

"Indeed." Baxter nodded. "Ours is an inequitable system of incentives and rewards. Tell me." He continued, in a quietly interested voice. "Where did you first meet?"

"At Melbourne Grammar," I replied. "A Sixth Form bully was giving him a hard time."

"And you intervened...?"

"Someone had to."

"Yes." Baxter nodded again. "Someone always has to, though few have the moral courage to step forward when others are stepping back." He eyed me quizzically. "You seem unconvinced?"

"Sorry, what was that?"

"It doesn't matter." He brushed my distracted query aside. "I sense something else troubling you. Do you wish to share it with me...?"

I hesitated, weighing options, before clearing my throat. "A while ago, my brother-in-law said he wanted a transfer to the Flying Corps. He'd also had a gutful of the trenches and, as he said, the clouds above them, looked so clean, and inviting."

"I can imagine," Baxter agreed with yet another thoughtful nod.

"But when we last met, he said that he was now under orders to report to GHQ. 'I'm not funking it!' he insisted, afraid I thought he was using family influence to get a cushy billet. 'I still want to fly, but doing one's duty for King & Country, and one's obligation to consider others' needs before one's own, must always come first...'"

"True."

"His dilemma has set me thinking about an equivalent duty to stand by our mates, in their hour of need," I continued, awkwardly now. "I'm only a substantive one-pip of no account, whereas David's honorary uncle is in line to be a corps commander. But if, as you say, he asked for my help, albeit indirectly, I'm duty-bound to give it."

"What about your other matter?" Baxter enquired with one of his shrewd sideways glances.

"That will have to wait." I hesitated again, before concluding: "As an older and wiser man recently reminded me: 'Revenge is a dish best eaten cold.'"

It was Baxter's turn to fall silent before returning to the present. "You can still change your mind, Ian. Nobody will think any the less of you. Intelligence is a thankless task most of the time, and rarely acknowledged any of the time."

"I know."

"No, you do not," he disagreed firmly. "What you've seen thus far is only its reflection of Alice's Looking-Glass. But step through to the other side and you enter a world of dark contradictions that are often repugnant to men of conscience and integrity. And yet this is the price we must pay to defeat an even greater evil..."

"Like Mani-whatsit, the Persian religion?"

"More or less."

"Well, it can't be any worse than setting fire to some poor blighter's aeroplane and watching him jump to his death."

"That I wouldn't know," Baxter affirmed sombrely. "However, what I do know is this, if after due deliberation you decide to join our ranks, there can be no turning back. So be very sure you know what you're doing, and what your reasons are for doing so."

I felt no hesitation now. "David left me a letter, in the event of his death. Asking me to, 'take care of the old folks,' by which he meant Mr and Mrs Shuster, 'who regard you as the second son they never had.'" I dry coughed into my clenched fist. "I believe his wishes extend to their friends, like Mr Monash, of whom there are very few these days, 'for a dear old couple from Kaiserland.' Sir."

"Are you absolutely sure?"

"Yes."

Baxter shifted his bag and put out the free hand to grip mine a second time. "Good man."

Thus, a journey that began with a foolish prank that still makes me wince whenever I recall it, ended with me volunteering to remain on the Staff for reasons of love, and loss, and loyalty impossible to transcribe into plain English.

135

These tape-recorded memoirs have long outrun their original few minutes of Edwardian speech patterns that Frances wanted to hear, the better to understand our smug, self-confident world before the events of July and August 1914 destroyed it forever.

I must consider calling a halt at this point, not only because of the painful memories evoked, but also of my concern that I may unwittingly reveal the covert work begun that murky Flemish afternoon in March 1918. For even if there were a Statute of Limitations that freed me from the *Official Secrets Act (1911)*, I would still be bound by the Oath of Secrecy taken upon a King's Commissioned Officer's word of honour.

Frances's less inhibited generation would doubtless scoff at such quaint restraint though she herself would, I am equally sure, promise to respect the limits I've set on our lopsided conversations. However, historians are by their very nature nosy creatures, forever ferreting among the midden heaps of others' lives, sniffing out tantalising titbits of gossip for publication and career advantage. In this I am much reminded of Æsop's scorpion who declared, after fatally stinging the frog that was helping him to cross a river, "I can't help myself! It's the way we scorpions are -!" Or words to that effect.

My caution with the winsome Dr Baxter née Cribdon is well grounded, and I have no intention of disclosing to her, or anyone else, what I may or may not have seen, or heard, or done for her grandfather-in-law, apart from the few bland paragraphs that refer to Counterintelligence inside the one hundred and nine volumes of Britain's *Official History of the Great War*.

Our opponents in *Abteilung IIIb* were less constrained and rarely missed a chance to puff themselves as ruthless professionals and, a quarter of a century later, I recognised several familiar names in the Gestapo's senior ranks. By contrast, *Military Intelligence (Section 6)* preferred to be imagined as a scratch team of amateur players in the British Empire's worldwide Great Game, one in which only the Filthy Hun and Bolshy Swine swindled, and lied, and murdered to put runs on the scoreboard; an artful myth told by popular novelists and Lord Northcliffe's newspapers for their guileless readers to believe uncritically and swallow whole.

It was during the opening moves of *Der Kaiserschlacht* – The Emperor's Battle, better known as Ludendorff's Spring Offensive – when reports of civilian panic and military collapse were pouring in from all along our crumbling frontline, that I witnessed the iron core of Baxter's cultivated English calm, illuminated by laconic references to Joshua's spies in the Bible's *Fourth Book of Moses* aptly named *Numbers, 13:1-33*, interspersed with pithy quotations from Sun Tzu's *Art of War*.

One of that ancient Chinese general's precepts is still, in my opinion, the quintessence of an Intelligence officer's work: "O Divine Spirit of Subtlety & Secrecy! Through you we learn to be invisible, through you we learn to be silent, through you we hold the enemy's fate in our hands…"

All silence and subtlety ended with a bang at 0445 hours, Thursday the 21st of March, when ten thousand German artillery pieces and heavy mortars opened fire with a sheet lightning glare of muzzle flashes visible in Paris and as a thunderclap heard in London, seconds later.

During the next five hours, Colonel Bruchmüller's Hurricanes of Steel rained three and a half million rounds onto the British 5th and 3rd Armies, blasting miles-wide gaps through which Oskar von Hutier's storm troops led an exultant tidal wave of fresh German divisions.

During the next few days, Fritz recaptured the Somme's battlefield - lost during 1916 and '17 – and, with it, vast dumps of ordnance and supplies, together with tens of thousands of shell-shocked prisoners as General Gough's overstretched, undermanned 5th Army bulged like an about-to-burst dam wall.

The Kaiser was now as near to crowning himself Emperor of Europe as he would ever be. Strutting up and down the map room in *Das Hauptquartier der Westfrontarmeen*, crippled left hand resting on a theatrical sword hilt, right fist punching air to emphasise every staccato yelp. Imperiously ordering his field commanders to roll-up General Byng's 3rd Army, their last obstacle before Amiens' railhead, the BEF's pivot pin upon which Victory or Defeat swung like an erratic compass needle.

Lose control of these shunting yards, workshops, and locomotive turntables, and the intricate network of narrow-gauge lines that kept the British Expeditionary Force armed and fed in Flanders and Picardy, would be lost. Lose those and there would be no option but to break contact with our exhausted allies, retreat to the Channel ports, dig in, and prepare for the worst.

At which point the French Army, bled dry by its horrific losses at Verdun, would mutiny for the second time in nine months and sue for peace after a humiliating reprise of the *débâcle* at Sedan in 1871. Or so it was believed at the Belgian resort town of Spa - ironically in the Hôtel Britannique - where Wilhelm II and his military courtiers gathered to celebrate their greatest advance on the Western Front since August 1914.

Not that I or any others of my lowly rank in the Order of Battle were aware of these details until long after the Great War ended, by which time dozens of memoirs, regimental histories, and official accounts were crowding the world's bookshops or being serialised in scores of popular magazines.

It was only then we learned how General Ludendorff and his Junker toadies became so obsessed with securing their place in the Pantheon of Prussian Heroes, alongside Frederick the Great and Gerhard von Scharnhorst, that they overlooked what must have been obvious to every alert Joe or NCO on the ground, as triumphant storm troops outran their supply lines.

It was equally obvious what happened next when half-starved men, with skimpy rations of sawdust *Ersatzbrot* in their knapsacks, captured British field bakeries filled with hot loaves of crisp wheaten bread. Or plundered GS wagons laden with bacon, fresh meat, cheese, and real butter, not the *Reich*'s wartime margarine that resembled yellow candlewax in taste and texture. Or looted regimental canteens stocked with biscuits, confectionary, and tobacco of a quantity and quality unseen in the Fatherland for the past four years. Or broke into cellars stacked to the rafters with beer, wines, and rum.

The demoralising effect of such abundance on the enemy's offensive spirit was not yet evident as General Monash's previous staff lectures and training exercises snapped into action, even though the man himself was still in transit from Menton.

It was now that I saw the truth of Baxter's remark about my aunt's piano partner being an orchestral conductor of the first rank when so many other Allied divisions and brigades, battalions and companies were melting away in a confusion of exhausted men and abandoned equipment.

By contrast, 3 Division AIF was like a pack of wolfhounds straining at the leash, baying for blood. There was an electrical tension in the air, as if every man, of every rank and trade, knew what was at stake and by this knowledge became taller, and stronger, and greater than he had ever been before. Or would ever be again. Not by chance alone, of the fifty Victoria Crosses awarded to British and Imperial troops during those climactic weeks of 1918, twenty were bestowed upon Australians, a number that requires no further comment.

My preparations for battle amounted to being photographed for an all-areas *laissez passer* and taking charge of a 550cc Triumph motorcycle, together with its booklet of petrol vouchers and set of road maps. I was now equipped to move quickly, by day or by night, to any town, village, or reference point where our forces were, and once there, assess the situation by interviewing officers and men alike. I was also required to pencil-sketch, or snap with my Vest Pocket Kodak camera, matters or places of interest before returning to HQ by the quickest route, ready to type a concise, illustrated report of what I had just seen, heard, and assessed.

In effect I had resumed my former trade as an observer, only instead of an RE8's rear cockpit I was now seated astride the sprung leather saddle of a motorbike, bumping across much the same countryside as I'd seen from the sky; in our laconic Digger-speak it was "same meat, different gravy..."

At first, I was mightily miffed, coming so soon after Baxter's portentous warning about Alice's Looking Glass and the dangers lurking behind it. Tootling around on a Trusty, our fond nickname for Triumph's seemingly indestructible machine, was not how I'd imagined the Secret Service to be. Instead of false whiskers and a purse of gold with which to seduce a slinky female enemy spy – a frequent device in William Le Queux' espionage novels – I was just a glorified despatch rider of whom there were already plenty in our Divisional Transport Pool.

I would have challenged Baxter to explain this mistake except that he was now at Montreuil-sur-Mer, liaising with his colleagues on Field Marshal Haig's staff, as they countered the German onslaught, presumably the reason for his retention when other British officers-on-secondment to the Australian Corps had been sacked by our political masters.

My first inkling of why Baxter picked me for this unlikely job came early in the piece when I got orders to report on a Pioneer battalion, bivouacked among the soggy turnip fields between Neuf Berquin and Merville.

None of the fatigue parties or those manning its picket line, bothered to hide their contempt when I rumbled past, festooned with binoculars and map case, haversack and water bottle, steel helmet, gasmask, and service revolver. In appearance just another battlefield tourist playing at soldiers.

I knew what was on their minds, having often thought much the same myself, and thus realised I'd get no help or information above the barest minimum unless I first proved my credentials.

In the context of that time and place these were the MC and DCM ribbons on my tunic, worn under a mackintosh coat nonchalantly flapped wide open while I searched for my cigarette case to share around; Percy Black, of immortal memory, had earlier taught me how a *Gold Flake* or *Navy Cut*, accompanied by a lit match cupped in my hands, was a sure-fire invitation for some other man to share his news and views. And thus it proved to be, with the Pioneers. Instead of impatient shrugs and dismissive grunts, my prepared list of questions was answered in full, with understanding nods between we Brethren of the Trenches.

That done, I asked the Officer Commanding for permission to speak with his sergeants, the fount of all wisdom in any man's army, and soon spotted a couple of ANZAC veterans with the same brass "A" on their shoulder flashes as those on mine. A modest reference to the capture of Pope's Hill, and my later work as a sergeant machine gunner at Sari Bair, elicited a frank picture of their men's strengths, deficiencies, and readiness for battle.

These were briskly noted in my shorthand notebook, supplemented by snapshots of my two new mates, with a promise to send complimentary prints from HQ's Photographic Section; a promise unable to be kept until after we'd fought Fritz to a standstill, within sight of, but beyond reach of, Amiens' supply dumps and railway marshalling yards.

By accident or by design, for one could never be sure with someone as subtle as he, Stephen Baxter had prescribed the best treatment for a man in my dire emotional state, namely hard work that left no time for self-pity or regrets.

Any idea that I had been given a cushy number, running errands and messages, evaporated in sweat as I began shoving a laden motorbike through slush up to its wheel hubs, over shattered *pavé* cobblestones, into muddy craters and potholes, struggling to reach firmer ground before mounting up for another few hundred yards until starting all over again. Never the easiest of jobs, even without a gammy right leg.

French country roads were not meant for traffic heavier than an ambling farm cart on its way to market, and maybe a weekly *diligence* or stagecoach, jolting between neighbouring towns. The destructive impact of lorries and ambulances, GS wagons and steam traction engines, tanks and heavy artillery, plus untold tens of thousands of infantrymen slogging through columns of fleeing peasants with their few sticks of furniture atop a handcart, is best left to the imagination, for I lack the skill to describe it in words.

However, one scene, memorised and later sketched, caught the spirit of these desperate days. A bandy-legged peasant, pushing his invalid wife in a rickety wheelbarrow. She with a brood of chicks in a saucepan clutched on her lap. Both with the same blank stare of disbelief on their wrinkled old faces as I rode past, hot on the trail of a platoon mislaid in the Fog of War.

I shall revisit Special Collections at Monash University and ask the curator, Janice Thorpe, to retrieve my 1918 journals from her archives. Memories blur after seventy years, and I must be certain of my facts if I am to bequeath Frances with a reasonably accurate account of one man's experiences during those decisive battles that ended the Great War.

However, one fact that I have never doubted is GHQ's wisdom when it concentrated the Australian Corps on the Armentiéres Sector, roughly equidistant from the River Lys to the North, and the River Somme to the South. Viewed from the air, or on a topographic map, our lines resembled a sturdy headland holding back an onrushing tide, making it exactly the right place for Field Marshal Haig's *corps d'elite* at a time of greatest peril, when none of his staff could be sure which of our flanks – the Northern left or the Southern right – Fritz would focus on.

Intelligence was betting that *Operation Michael*, Ludendorff's opening gambit, was a decoy to draw us southward, onto a cratered Abomination of Desolation as Baxter aptly described the killing fields of 1916, with reference to the Old Testament's *Book of Daniel*. Then, with the BEF entangled on the Somme's barbed wire for the second time in two years, *Operation Georgette* would throw the killer punch westward, along the shorter Lys Line from Ypres to the coast, and knockout our crucial Channel ports.

Michael therefore had to be an elaborate diversion. For if it were not, and the Somme Line was the main German axis of attack, the distance traversed before capturing Amiens would be almost double that required to take Boulogne and Calais. And with every mile gained, von Hutier's communications would stretch and weaken even as General Byng's would compress and strengthen, a fatal misreading of mapped terrain that no graduate of the Prussian *Kriegsakademie* would ever make. Surely?

136

None of this was more than informed conjecture when 3 Division received orders to deploy northwards to Flanders where *Georgette* was expected within the next four days. We kitted-up and were well on our way north when the apparent collapse of Gough's 5th Army tempted the Kaiser's staff to commit the gravest of all military sins: the issue of fresh orders while still in contact with a shaken but not yet broken enemy.

Michael was now the main battle and Amiens the principal target for two hundred infantry divisions and their artillery. A cooler head than Ludendorff's should have reminded the Kaiser of von Kluck's fatal change of axis towards the Marne, away from Paris, during the earliest weeks of this war. And if that were not a sufficiently persuasive argument, he might have taken notice of Napoleon's furious "Order! Counterorder! Disorder!" during an earlier one.

The upshot was bewilderment for the enemy's troops and frustration for our footsore Diggers, halfway to Ypres when they got GHQ's orders to about-turn and quick march back to the Somme where things were going from bad to worse for the remnant 5th and 3rd Armies along an ill-defined, crumbling frontline between Cambrai and Arras.

General Monash had re-joined us after two days of nonstop travel from Menton and taken command at 3 Divvy's emergency HQ in a town hall roughly midpoint between Hazebrouck and St Omer, twenty miles from our old base at Armentières, now in enemy hands.

I was too busy, maintaining contact with 3's dispersed units, to notice the change of tempo when our conductor strode onto the podium and, so to speak, flicked his baton. And yet despite his evident mastery of the situation, the GOC 3 Division was increasingly the target of maliciously hysterical rumours implying that he had lost his nerve and should be bundled off to an admin' post in London, as Baxter reported while briefing me on 3 Divvy's impending move to Doullens, fifteen miles north of Amiens, where we were needed to stiffen British 10 Corps' Ancre Line.

I was stunned when he added that there might be a grain of truth in these slanders. When I queried it, with some heat, he replied by explaining how the loneliness of high command, at a time of extreme peril, can unsettle even the most steadfast commander beset on all sides by doubts and worries, his own as well as everyone else's.

"More than we can ever imagine, he knows that nothing he can do will win the war in an afternoon, but one misstep and he could lose it before sunset," Baxter explained in a sombre tone. "His is a burden that few men shoulder, and even fewer are game to confess they bore, lest it be seen as weakness. Hence his need for the attentive, discreet, loyal supporters alluded to when I spoke of a 'Praetorian Guard...'"

"I fail to see the connection."

"You soon will do." He studied my face closely. "As a consequence of that staff purge at the behest of your Prime Minister and his co-conspirators, to undermine Sir John by depriving him of our support and given my duties for

Sir Douglas *en liaison avec* 3 Division, I have no option but to order you to stand guard alone, until further notice."

"Eh?" I blinked incredulously.

"I trust your discretion." Baxter was concerned by weightier matters than my puzzled surprise. "In time of war, all face an identifiable enemy, but not all are surrounded by less visible enemies such as your family friend attracts with his unfortunate talent for brash self-promotion and, I regret to say, 'Jewish cleverness...'"

"But isn't he the preferred choice at GHQ and the Palace?" I queried, referencing our earlier conversation.

"Absolutely, now more than ever, for which reason I require you to stay alert," Baxter replied. "Pinpoint the source of these rumours and, if possible, discover who's been promised what, by whom, by way of an award, or promotion, or well-paid job after the war. And keep me posted."

I steadied my voice. "In other words, you want me spy on a brother officer?"

"Or officers, plural," Baxter frowned at my angry tone. "It's for the greater good of the greatest number. Brutus, Cassius, and Decimus are circling even as we speak, daggers drawn, and won't stop until David's honorary uncle is stabbed to death, figuratively speaking -"

"I don't buy it!" I interrupted. "What sort of hold does one newspaperman – two if you include that War Correspondent bloke – have over men of real power? For I assume we are speaking of the same people?"

"I am tempted to reply, 'think it over and report what you discover,' but time is of the essence!" he snapped back. "Firstly: Mr Murdoch sells his opinions, thinly disguised as United Cable news, to every daily in Australia where the average reader thinks only what his newspaper tells him to think. *Ergo*, our vengeful son o' the kirk wields enormous influence to shape national opinion for or against whomsoever pleases or displeases him.

"Secondly: His co-conspirator, Captain Be'an, narrowly beat him to become Australia's Official War Correspondent with its unique opportunities to select scenes, edit events, and record the official story for a post-war generation of widows and orphans. Mr M was hungry for that power, too, but has had to settle for the next best thing by enlisting Captain B as his catspaw.

"Thirdly: Your Prime Minister, Mr Hughes, is hastening from Australia to claim a seat at the conference table and charm a decisive bloc of army voters prior to next year's Parliamentary elections. But to retain power then, he needs M&B's support now. Such being the case, the Universal Law of Political Expediency says he will stop at nothing to get it. And if this requires the sacrifice of his most able general, it won't be the first or last time a man of his slippery nature has betrayed another for personal advantage." Baxter paused, eyeing me closely. "And until now you thought all the significant action was taking place on the battlefield in France?"

"Of course -!"

"That's not how *Realpolitik* works," Baxter interrupted with a sad, understanding smile. "Messrs Murdoch, Be'an, Hughes & Co are a powerful cabal of self-interests that a mere Field Marshal, or even the King himself, must handle with the utmost tact if we are to emerge victorious from this current crisis..."

I was by no means convinced by Baxter's tale of political chicanery and backstairs intrigue, which was hardly surprising for a young man inured to the worst of war on the ground and in the air, but who was still a wide-eyed innocent in so many other ways. Besides, my overriding concern was locating 3 Division's sub-units dispersed across square miles of countryside, with the time needed to concentrate them shrinking rapidly, as Ludendorff's forces surged onward, seemingly unstoppable as a swarm of locusts.

Frances is unlikely to understand what a complex mass of men and machinery, materiel, and munitions the word "Division" embodied during the Great War, so I had better to explain how Major General Monash's 3 Division fitted into Lieutenant General Birdwood's Australian Corps.

Each of the Corps' five divisions comprised four brigades apiece, which in 3's case were the 9th commanded by Brigadier General Rosenthal, the 10th commanded by Brigadier General McNicholl, the 11th commanded by Brigadier General Cannan, and the 15th commanded by Brigadier General Elliott.

Each of these, in turn, comprised four battalions, nominally commanded by a lieutenant colonel, and were further subdivided by companies and platoons until the whole pyramid of military power rested upon the aching shoulders and sweaty feet of thirty thousand private soldiers.

With reference to feet, I think it important to mention that our ability to march and fight as well as we did, during the weeks ahead, depended upon a handful of anonymous cobblers in their mule-drawn workshop carts, endlessly stitching loose soles and nailing broken heels for tens, hundreds, thousands, tens of thousands of troops on the move. This is probably one aspect of Military History that scholars of Frances' calibre have never considered, so I must bring it to her attention in our next recording session.

Meanwhile, besides 3's sixteen infantry battalions there were 3's machine gun battalion; 3's field engineer battalion; 3's pioneer battalion; 3's artillery comprising four brigades, each with twenty batteries of guns, plus seven batteries of mortars; 3's ammunition sub-park with its own dedicated transport column to deliver the countless thousands of rounds of HE, Gas, Smoke, Shrapnel, and Illumination needed to support an infantry attack or lay down a defensive barrage. And tethered high above the guns, when the Flying Corps was busy elsewhere, a baggy sausage balloon filled with flammable hydrogen gas, an artillery spotter dangling immediately below it in a wicker basket, making him one of the loneliest men on the Western Front.

Nor should one forget 3's Signals Company, with its constantly sniped linesmen whenever they crawled out under fire, to patch a broken telephone wire or lay a new line. 3's Field Ambulance with its attendant medicos, stretcher bearers, and storemen. 3's Supply Train with its farriers, blacksmiths, and wheelwrights for the scores of GS wagons. 3's Veterinary Section for our hundreds of horses and mules. 3's Driver Mechanics for our convoy of lorries. 3's Salvage Company, 3's Sanitary Company, 3's mounted Military Police. And these were by no means the totality of skilled, semi-skilled, unskilled hands who together made 3 Division AIF such a formidable fighting force.

If Frances should wonder how one very old man can remember such detail, I hope she will understand when I tell her that it was my task to maintain contact with 3 Divvy's dispersed sections during March and April 1918, a task not made any easier with telephones and telegraphs frequently broken by shellfire or sabotaged by enemy infiltrators.

I once cartooned myself as a motorcycling sheepdog, obeying the whistles of his masters at HQ where events were about to hammer us even harder as the German advance relentlessly ground forwards, and Amiens railway yards seemed about to fall. However, Fritz had not reckoned on General Monash's civil engineering flair for reading terrain off a map and improvising solutions as he rose to the challenge, minute by minute, hour by hour, supremely confident of his ability to get things done.

But first he needed to get a grip on where, and what, and how his forces were doing - especially the artillery, without whom he could only hold back the enemy as far as a rifle or machine gun bullet would strike – so without further ado he commandeered two Vauxhalls, a Ford lorry, and a couple of Sig's linesmen.

Into the cars he piled his key staff officers. Into the lorry went a table and chairs, a typewriter, several reams of blank paper and tubes of ink for the duplicating machine. Also, spools of telephone wire for emergency repairs, plus a case of field rations, for none of us could be sure where, when, or what we would eat next. The linesmen and lorry driver jumped aboard their vehicle, ready to follow wherever the brass hats took them on a wild hunt for British 10 Corps' HQ.

It was now that Baxter put my name forward to be our pathfinder, arguing that I was uniquely familiar with this terrain, both on the ground and from the air. Not that General Monash needed any persuasion, given our previous encounters, though being proposed by a British officer, and approved by a senior Australian who himself was under a darkening cloud of envy and suspicion, did nothing to enhance my reputation with the other, more recently appointed Australian staffers. Some of whom were, I'm sure, secretly wondering which East European surname my rare "Cribdon" disguised.

I had no say in the matter and besides, could not have cared less what others thought of me amidst the prevailing panic and confusion. Of greater concern was the urgent need for a weapon with more authority than a Webley revolver, in case we bumped into an enemy patrol. Accordingly, I souvenired a Lee Enfield and bandolier of cartridges off the back of a salvage lorry, then attached it down the motorbike's front forks, butt snugly uppermost against the carbide headlamp's bracket, twitched in place with short lengths of telephone wire.

A curt nod of command from the leading staff car, a kick-start for Trusty, and off we sped towards Doullens, honk-honking past clumps of worn-out Tommies plodding to the rear.

137

The Duke of Wellington is alleged to have said, upon viewing a corpse-strewn field somewhere in Spain: "Nothing except a battle lost can be half as melancholy as a battle won." To which I would add: "Or a great army in retreat," as ours was, driven back mile upon mile by the whistling thuds and crumps of advancing gunfire.

The confusion grew worse as we approached Doullens. I still had a sergeant's nose for morale and what I smelt that afternoon was the unmistakable stench of fear and despondency; if a squadron of the Kaiser's Ulhans had galloped into town during the next few hours, they would have bagged a prize haul of prisoners with barely a shot fired.

And not just the thousands of shuffling, shambling, stumbling, walking-wounded and dispirited men trudging westwards, but also the President of France, Raymond Poincare; French Premier Georges Clemenceau; French Generals Foch and Petain; Lord Milner of Britain's War Cabinet and close colleague of Lord Nobury; Field Marshal Haig with Generals Wilson, Lawrence, and Montgomery in attendance; their staffs, legal counsels, and interpreters as well.

It was all supposed to be hush-hush but not for the distraught peasants staring at Field Marshal Haig's staff car parked outside the *Hôtel de Ville*, venerating the small Union Jack attached to his Rolls Royce' radiator cap, as if it were a holy relic in a medieval time of plague. They were notably less reverential to the Panhard Lavassors parked alongside it, one with the presidential coat of arms and *tricoleur* fluttering above its windscreen frame, and another pair with the five-star, metal guidons of *Génereaux de l'Armée* stiffly erect on their mudguards.

We didn't know it at the time, these grandees were only a few dozen yards away, threshing out an emergency order that was about to combine the BEF and French Army under Marshal Foch as Supreme Allied Commander.

By comparison, a two-star Australian general was of little account, although very soon their Anglo-French Accord would stand or fall upon the decisions taken, and the orders given by this sturdy, middle-aged man clad in a baggy Norfolk jacket indistinguishable from any other Digger except for the red stripe painted around his steel helmet, and the crossed sword and baton below a single pip, on his serge cloth epaulettes.

Not that General Monash or anyone else in our flying column headquarters could have possibly imagined what the next few days were about to hurl our way as we edged between exhausted, battle-grimed men to reach the railway yard, just as the first elements of 9 Brigade were unloading from a long line of open coal wagons.

I saw Baxter lean forward and speak urgently to our GOC, seated up front with the driver. Monash nodded and my superior officer jumped down, beckoning me to kick Trusty back on its stand, and follow as he made a beeline for a weary British subaltern leading what remained of his company.

The young lad gave them the order to halt and stand easy, at which a good quarter of his men slumped to the ground, leaning forward on their rifles while he showed, on Baxter's map, where he had fought the enemy, with estimates of the casualties inflicted on both sides, and a summary of subsequent encounters.

My job was to take down the salient points in my shorthand notebook. Absent the grinding din of iron cartwheels on *pavé* slabs, the rancid stench of sweaty, unwashed bodies, and the contagious stink of panic, I could have been in the reporters' gallery of Kalgoorlie Magistrates' Court.

One of Britain's keenest legal minds kept gathering raw Intelligence for Generals Monash and Rosenthal until an agitated officer dashed up with the news that a column of German armoured cars had broken through at Hébuterne; that Hun cavalry were burning farms, shooting hostages, driving the local population towards us in a human screen; and that, as Town Major responsible for Doullens' defence, he was giving orders to evacuate -!

"You! Will!! Not!!!" General Monash's upswept hand silenced the TM's distraught babble. "You will barricade the streets! You will emplace sharpshooters!! You will do your duty and fight to the death, yours, or theirs, whichever comes first!!!" He abruptly turned away and faced us instead. "What is your assessment of the situation, Mr Baxter?"

"Grave but manageable," my chief replied in a coolly dispassionate voice. "The 2nd Liverpool Irish bloodied the 15th Silesians at Bavincourt, one of eight reserve regiments that now comprise von Hutier's vanguard while his first line troops regroup for the push into Amiens.

"Concerning armoured cars, petrol supplies from Romania have been increasingly tight since last December. I estimate there are too few vehicles to be a serious threat, except as recce' units. Ditto their Marienfelde lorries, which are barely sufficient to keep the field guns fed with adequate but not abundant quantities of ammunition.

'Furthermore, given the boggy nature of the terrain here, here, and here," a manicured index finger flicked his map board as the two generals leaned closer, "I see limited opportunities for hostile deployment and close artillery support. We can therefore expect a succession of leapfrogged infantry attacks on a narrow front – here and here - along the embanked road from Arras. Sir."

"Thank you, Mr Baxter," Monash replied with a triumphant smile, "and I see opportunities for decisive action!" At which the three men crouched over a larger-scale map spread across the bonnet of the nearest car and, with red crayon, deployed 9 Brigade's available strength as two wings – left and right - angled like a ferret net pegged on a rabbit warren.

The wings' volley fire would funnel the German column onto our contact zone where the Lewis gunners and support riflemen lay in wait. Assuming Fritz was still game after such a mauling, and assuming our ammunition was now spent, bayonets would be fixed. Withdrawal was never an option.

While these orders were being written up and signed, I finished tightening Trusty's drive belt and stood-by to lead the way to Mondicourt where Brigadier General McNichol was enrolling stray Tommies as his brigade's auxiliaries after a short, sharp re-motivation course from this stern headmaster of a Victorian boys' grammar school, in peacetime.

Further orders given and signed for, we sped onwards to Coutourelle where British 10 Corps were believed to be headquartered, only to be redirected to Corbie. Halfway there we wrongly learned that Corbie had also fallen and that HQ. was last heard of at Montigny, where we eventually arrived after dark, rain-streaked headlamps sweeping past remnants of 10 Corps miserably camped around an abandoned château inside which Lieutenant General Congreve VC and Brigadier General Hore-Ruthven VC were studying maps, collating Intelligence reports, issuing orders by candlelight as we tramped into what must have been a grand salon or ballroom, before the war.

I don't know who exclaimed it first as both generals turned to see who these muddy strangers were, but I shall never forget words that still make me shiver with pride: "Thank God! The Australians are here -!"

Meanwhile, my shorthand skills had not gone unnoticed which meant no sleep that night after General Congreve finished briefing our commander and allocated a telephone line for 3 Division's latest temporary headquarters.

I stayed close to General Monash, pencil poised, noting his queries, requests, and demands as clear evidence of impending collapse was laid bare on a billiard table spread with maps, despatched reports, and rough estimates of reserve forces.

Congreve's men had held the line between Bray-sur-Somme and Albert until mid-afternoon, before being outflanked and forced to give ground, worn down by four days of continuous fighting. "I'm afraid we've left the paddock gate open," the senior British general admitted ruefully. "The Huns have the bit between their teeth; if not reined in tomorrow, they'll be shelling Amiens railway junction the day after." He rapped the map with a handy billiard cue. "What you must do, Monash, is slow them sufficiently for our chaps to resume the fight."

"Slow them be damned!" our commander growled. "I'll stop the bastards!"

Congreve must have heard it too for I glimpsed a gleam of satisfaction as he continued: "The Ancre and the Somme, here and here, are your anchor points. Get as far up their valleys as you can. There's a line of old trenches from Méricourt to Sailly-le-Sec, here and here. Fortify them. There's just a chance the Huns don't yet realise they've got a clear run all the way to Villers-Bretonneux."

We returned to our room and set to work; for me this began by threading the typewriter with a waxed duplicating stencil and transcribing General Monash's dictated orders. Signed copies were then passed to our despatch riders who set off, after midnight, to locate General Cannan's 11th Brigade and McNichol's 10th so that a trap, like the one at Doullens, could be set on the Corbie-Bray Road.

I then typed an urgent request for General Byng's commandeered London buses to scoop up as many of our troops as General Rosenthal could spare and hurry them at Franvillers where 3 Division HQ relocated next morning.

On the way there, General Monash saw me wobbling along on my motorbike, terminally exhausted, and promptly loaned me his bedroll with strict instructions to find a quiet corner while others set up shop in our latest country manor HQ.

I missed the next several hours of high drama, visible from Franvillers' plateau, looking east where the advancing German horde was being harried by a shrinking number of Tommies supported by a handful of tanks fighting stubborn rear-guard actions.

I also missed the moment when sixty London buses chugged along the lane with a battalion of General Cannan's 11 Brigade, veteran fighters who kitted-up, formed fours, and crossed the Ancre at Heilly to secure the opposite bank.

Historians rightly make much of General Gallieni's decision, in August 1914, when he ordered hundreds of Paris taxi drivers to transport French troops to the Marne, in time to deflect von Kluck's advance and change the course of the war. I shall tell Frances that an equal, belated credit must be given to the far fewer London bus drivers who took our Australian troops to the Ancre and changed the course of the war in March 1918.

Not that I knew it at the time; bleary-eyed, swigging hot sweet tea from a borrowed mug; watching more buses arrive, from 10 Brigade this time, before ponderously chugging away for another load of men and weapons. Soon afterwards, yet more buses began delivering a battalion of General Rosenthal's 9 Brigade, now that Doullens had stabilised.

What impressed me most, though, was the attitude of our officers and men as the orders I had typed and duplicated passed down the chain of command. There were no bellyaches or grumbles, normal for hungry and tired soldiers, just the solemn recognition there was serious work to be done, and that they had been chosen to do it as they marched off with their distinctive stride, chins up, proud as kings, exactly as my friend Phillip Grenville saw them at Ypres the previous year.

I believe this was in part due to the way French civilians had taken us to their hearts when their own army was slaughtering a generation of husbands and sons. They must have sensed something different in the bearing of these lithe strangers from a faraway land, a spirit, a strength, an air of invincibility that inspired confidence and hope impossible to find nearer home.

Old women and young children, fleeing the enemy's advance, stopped, and stared, and burst into spontaneous cheers of *"Vive l'Australie!"* when they saw us marching past the other way. It was at Heilly that a Digger famously promised a tearful local woman, in his Trench French: *"Finnee retreat madam! Boocoo Aussies eesee!"*

What took place next deserves to be commemorated as equal to the Spartans' immortal defence of Thermopylae - the Gates of Hell - against the might of the Persian Empire. Twenty-five hundred years later, a scratch team of transplanted Poms and Jocks, Pats and Taffies, led by a civil engineer whose commanders included an architect, a schoolmaster, an insurance manager, a country solicitor, stood their ground and fought the German Empire to a standstill.

I was uniquely positioned to follow the course of events from my end of a mahogany Louis XV dining table, typewriter clattering orders and requisitions as if we were putting out a Special Edition of the *Kalgoorlie Miner*.

Our improvised staff work paid off. By early-afternoon of March 27th there were better than five thousand men in position, with 44 Battalion defending the Somme bridges, after a forced march to occupy Corbie before Fritz did.

The enemy was not about to give up easily though, probing every gully and fold in the ground to get at us, but General Monash had their measure, emplacing his Lewis gunners and riflemen where they would inflict the maximum punishment.

Credit must also be given to the anonymous armourers and storemen who anticipated our needs by sending a busload of 0.303 Ball and Mills' bombs with the first convoy, ensuring that every man who came thereafter was fully armed when he joined the fight.

What developed amidst the thickets and reedbeds of the Ancre's shallow valley was a classic soldiers' battle, in which victory hinged upon the dash and initiative of individual privates and corporals, but there was only so much a rifle or even a Lewis gun can do against flamethrowers, light mortars, and 77mm field guns.

Other troops would have dug in and waited for reinforcements but not so our lads. Nimble as crickets, these bushmen 'roo shooters and weekend rifle club volunteers` relentlessly biffed the enemy with fire-and-movement marksmanship, winning sufficient time for 3 Divvy's artillery to gallop up, unlimber, and thunder into action with HE and Shrapnel.

138

Our GOC basked in the reflected glory of his men's stunning achievement as congratulations flowed in from every level of command, including a treasured telegram from the new Generalissimo, Ferdinand Foch. Consequently, there were fewer muted calls for General Monash to be sacked, not that his enemies ever gave up conspiring his downfall, any more than the Kaiser had given up capturing Amiens. At best, 3 Division had won breathing space to slow the retreat and steady a lot of badly shaken troops, which was the best that anyone could have hoped for at this critical juncture of the war.

A few days later, Baxter found me refuelling Trusty from a two-gallon tin of petrol before setting off on another tour of inspection. "Ian? Permit me to introduce our colleague, Mr Be'an…"

I turned sharply to face a rather diffident, scholarly, bespectacled captain with a despatch rider's satchel and binocular case slung criss-crossed over his trench coat.

"Charles? Allow me to introduce my young protégé Mr Cribdon, of whom we have spoken…"

"Indeed, we have!"

Puzzled, I wiped oily fingers on a rag and cautiously returned an enthusiastic handshake. "G'day."

"Major Baxter has told me how well you led them along unfamiliar roads, in pitch darkness: 'As if he were back home, on the Westralian Goldfields, tracking bushrangers -'"

"Eh?!"

"I am thrilled to make your acquaintance and look forward to hearing of your more recent adventures," he continued, with a significant glance at my working uniform's grubby Winged-O and ribbons, "but I have an appointment to interview General Monash, for the historical record, and we must not keep such a high and mighty chap waiting, must we?"

"Sure. Whatever." I was unsure of his exact meaning or tone of voice as I watched Captain Bean hurry off, then turned to confront Baxter. "'Bushrangers'? What the hell was that all about? No way could I have tracked any in Westralia. The last one was hanged, years ago, in Queensland!"

"Really? I was not aware of that," Baxter replied, with an inward frown. "More to the point, neither was he, which indicates how far he's strayed from his roots, and maybe why he is so keen to reconnect with them?"

"Perhaps. But that still doesn't explain why you've put me in such an awkward situation."

"All in good time," he cautioned mildly. "I hope to have the answer when you return, for by then an assortment of kaleidoscopic images will have assumed a coherent pattern and I shall be more certain of their meaning…"

Previous experience of this man's infuriatingly vague English manner had taught me that further argument was pointless, so instead I returned to the Orderly Room and signed out today's worksheet. That done, I rumbled off to appraise the network of emergency roads behind our neighbouring forces –

Major General MacKay's 5th Division, and our old Gallipoli mates the New Zealanders – who, with 3 Divvy, manned the Somme's northern flank, forcing von Hutier to bash away at easier targets farther south.

Hours later – backside numbed by the iron framed saddle's merciless thumping, gum booted legs bespattered with slush and muck of every kind - I reported to the château's icehouse, disused since the outbreak of war stopped the shipment of ice blocks from their winter ponds in Norway.

The nature of 3 Division's Intelligence work meant that we kept our distance from other staff. This not only eliminated the risk of strangers overhearing loose talk or seeing maps and scale models that were Authorised Eyes Only, it also bestowed a flattering air of mystery and intrigue on our green collar tabs, whenever we dined in Mess.

"Good trip Ian?" A routine question that never expected more than a grunt for its answer as Baxter sat forward to receive my report. "Take the weight off your feet. And help yourself." He nodded at his tobacco pouch conveniently left open on the desk between us.

"Thanks." I slumped onto one of several French Army camp chairs that had informally joined the Australian Army during the past few days, dug my pipe from a tunic pocket. knocked it against a chair leg and greedily loaded with a pinch of Baxter's Signature Blend of rare tobaccos by Robert Lewis of St James Street, a short distance from Berkeley Square of blesséd memory.

While I was performing this comforting ritual, Field Marshal Haig's Liaison Officer & General Monash's Military Advisor (Intelligence) estimated our road network's carrying capacities, an essential prerequisite when planning large-scale deployments of men and materiel. This he did by overlaying the detailed battalion reports he had already received, with my broader, current assessment of conditions in an imagined game of "three-dimensional chess," as he described these intricate moves. Pausing, he glanced up and removed his spectacles to rub weary eyes. "Are you quite sure we need this much ballast at Pont-Noyelles?"

"Another fifty tons of gravel will never go astray on that floodplain." I struck a match, laid it over my pipe bowl and drew the flame downwards. "The country, thereabouts, is as flat as a tack, with river silt umpteen yards deep. One good downpour of rain and it'll be marshland again." I shook the match out and savoured a wonderful first puff of richly textured contentment impossible to imagine in today's world of finger-wagging scolds. "Speaking of which, the Labour Corps' ganger reckons they'll need a minimum twelve-inch thickness of woven branches to float the new roadbed, here and here."

Leaning forward, I tapped my pipestem on Baxter's map. "The trouble is. there's not a skerrick of vegetation nearby. However," I continued, pipestem tapping again, "up here, between St Gratien and Fréchencourt, there's an old hunting preserve with any amount of hedging and undergrowth ready to cut and carry. I suggest we mobilise the Pioneers, detail half a dozen lorries, and solve Mr Wu's problem at one go."

"I'll have a word with Transport." Baxter jotted a line on his notepad before sitting back, both eyes shut, easing their strain. "If only our Mr Be'an were as easily solved, or satisfied…"

"Is this my cue to ask what the kaleidoscope has revealed?" I queried, by now familiar with this man's oblique thought processes.

"I'd be disappointed if you didn't." He sat forward and began loading his own pipe, a sure sign that I was about to get a lecture on some arcane topic. "As always, our work requires a lively curiosity tempered by caution and restraint. But the short answer to your question is that the kaleidoscope's beads are still jigging around, and I'm deuced if I can see our Mr B's reasons for allying himself with an arch-schemer like the vengeful Mr Murdoch, in their campaign to unseat General Monash…"

"Isn't it obvious?" I retorted. "As you've said yourself, the GOC can never resist a chance to blow his own trumpet, like that telegram from Marshal Foch he keeps waving about? And didn't you once tell me: 'It's the curse of the clever to tread on others' toes without meaning to give offence'?"

"Thanks for the reminder." I was not sure if Baxter appreciated hearing his own words echoed by a subordinate. "However, Charles Be'an is the one who most concerns me most, at present." It was his turn to light up, ease back in his seat, eyes wide open, shrewdly alert now.

"Why so?"

"He's the key to a riddle that has kept me perplexed for some while." Puff. "Trouble is, I am too close to the subject and can't see the wood for the trees, so to speak." He shared a rare, rueful smile. "You remember we once spoke of those Australians up at Oxford? The ones forever trying to be more English than the English?"

"What of 'em?" I was intentionally curt.

"Mr Be'an is one." Puff. "After reading Law at Hertford College, some years after I took my degree at Oriel, he returned to Australia where he briefly practiced on the county court circuit before becoming a roving rural reporter for the *Sydney Morning Herald*." Baxter took another thoughtful draw from his pipe. "At the outbreak of war, this obscure scribe soon became Little Jack Horner by sticking in his thumb and pulling out the plum job as Australia's sole Official War Correspondent. And with it, immense power to shape public opinion. Who, we must therefore ask ourselves, nominated him from among several dozen more experienced journalists? And whose interest does he now serve by way of gratitude…?"

I shrugged, irritated by Baxter's predictable shadow boxing. "What I don't get is why you told him about me chasing phantom bushrangers."

"We needed to pique his interest sufficiently for him to seek you again." Baxter huffed an almost perfect smoke ring. "So that when he does, you will discover his agenda, and keep me informed."

"I don't like it."

"As you have already made abundantly plain," he frowned. "However, there are numerous things I don't like doing as I go about my business upon His Majesty's Secret Service. But done they must be and done they shall be. Kindly bear this in mind and attend to your duties while others attend to theirs."

140

I was far from convinced of the need to spy on a fellow Australian but was spared that unpleasantness when encroaching enemy guns began pounding Franvillers with HE and Gas.

General Birdwood, now in his final days as GOC before assuming command of Gough's battered 5th Army, promptly gave orders for 3 Division's HQ to evacuate and fall back on Bertangles, six miles west of St Gratien, and about the same distance north of Amiens, where 3 Squadron AFC and 48 Squadron of the newly created Royal Air Force shared an aerodrome.

Our new headquarters was an elegantly proportioned, mid-18th century, three storey château that I believe still belongs to the Counts of Clermont-Tonnerre, as were two previous castles on that site, during the Middle Ages.

I puttered along on my motorbike behind General Monash's staff car, through the parkland's stone-pillared gateway, down a long gravelled drive to the foot of the main entrance steps and watched our GOC stride up them to salute an aristocratically erect woman clad in mourning black from head to heel, her young boy standing to attention at her side, now the twelfth Count de Clermont-Tonnerre, after his father was killed in action a few days earlier.

General Monash's command of French was sketchy, and the Dowager Countess' knowledge of English did not seem to be much better, so it was fortunate that Stephen Baxter was on hand as an interpreter, the grieving noblewoman greatly relieved to see the husband of her colleague in the French Flag Nursing Corps, *Mme le Médecin* Jeanne Martell, and to accept his promise that we would take good care of the ancestral home during our occupation.

She probably found this hard to believe, given the Australian troops' reputation as souvenir hunters of anything not nailed down, boarded up, or hidden, so it was Baxter who suggested that General Monash order a detailed inventory be made of every room's furniture and fittings, and then make each one the personal responsibility of a subordinate officer with strict orders to court martial any man pilfering even the smallest item of private property. This had the desired effect after a couple of tealeaves got ninety days detention in Étaples infamous military prison, after being collared with a silver inkwell and paperknife engraved with Clermont-Tonnerre's crossed keys coat of arms.

No less dramatic was the effect these lordly surroundings were having on our General Officer Commanding, a man already endowed with more than his fair share of male vanity, of whom the fortunes of war had briefly made a master of all he surveyed, and the fortunes of peace would return to a modest suburban house in Melbourne, a few streets away from Aunt Lucinda's property on Grange Road.

It was inevitable that he would revel in his new role as Lord of the Manor, with its unique opportunities to parade what many considered to be vulgar displays of captured German weapons, whenever notables like Field Marshal Haig and His Majesty visited Bertangles, during the weeks ahead.

Meanwhile, across the surrounding parkland, sappers bored wells and laid water mains; pioneers dug latrine trenches and built sandbagged revetments for ack-ack batteries; pioneers bolted sheets of curved, corrugated iron Nissen huts over prefabricated wooden flooring; linesmen raised poles and strung miles of telephone wire that connected 3 Division's switchboard to every other comm's hub along the Western Front.

This change of pace and shift of focus afforded me too many opportunities to brood over what might have been. Twice I awoke believing I had spoken with my dead wife. Absurd, of course, but the tear-soaked pillows told a different tale.

Another matter troubling me was the lack of news from Tralee House. I'd written several letters and postcards to Aunt Lucinda, but had received no replies, which was most unlike her. For a while I thought they must have been aboard one of the mail liners recently torpedoed in the Mediterranean, but eventually a letter from Australia got through the U-boat blockade:

Baldock, Harrison & Quinn
60 Queen Street
Melbourne
Victoria

2nd March 1918

Dear Captain Cribdon.

It is with regret that I must inform you of the death of Madame Lucinda Cribdon, at her Grange Road home on Wednesday the 27th day of February.

She was in fine spirits to the very end, though with increased frailty as one must expect of a lady approaching her one hundredth year.

After generous bequests, the residue of her estate will be prudently invested and held in trust, its interest equally shared by the Eugenie Napoleon Orphanage in Paris; Melbourne University's Music Department, for studies dedicated to the memory of Franz Liszt; and yourself.

I have the honour to remain, sir, your attentive servant.

Henry Baldock

Saddened but not surprised, I returned the letter to its envelope, announced that I would be back later to help with sorting I-Section's Map Library, and went for a walk to clear my head. Solitary by nature, I have never had more than a handful of close friends, and the list was growing shorter the longer I lived. Lost in thought, I paced through the park gates, absentmindedly returned a sentry's salute, and trod the short road past estate workers' cottages to RAF Bertangles, on a neighbouring paddock.

Headquarters had reciprocal hosting rights with the Air Force Officers' Mess which entitled me to prop up their bar at the *Plough Inn*, gallows humour in a business where three, four, five, six machines could be shot out of the sky and ploughed into the ground before breakfast, as would soon happen when 48 Squadron's Bristol F2s dive-bombed the Somme bridges at Corbie.

Small wonder I'd been viewed as a reincarnated ghost when 3 AFC's Mess President greeted me upon arrival, I with the hope of finding someone from Dingo Flight who remembered David Shuster and Roy Ellis, but there were none, nor had been for quite a while.

Everyone was politely baffled when I spoke of XIII Squadron RFC's Experimental Flight. From where they stood, I must have seemed like a reincarnated veteran describing the Battle of Waterloo.

The Royal Flying Corps itself was rapidly fading into history as our khaki uniforms were replaced by Royal Air Force Blue, an economy measure to use up the huge stocks of Czarist uniform cloth abandoned in Bradford's warehouses, after the Bolsheviks reneged on Russia's War Debt.

However, today, instead of moodily nursing a second, or third Scotch at the bar, I trudged across rough tussocks of turf and approached the FCO's open-sided canvas pavilion by the aerodrome's windsock. "G'day. Mind if I watch?"

"Go ahead." The Flight Control Officer glanced up from his desk with its clutter of binoculars, pencils, logbook and loaded signal pistol, ready to fire a volley of red flares if two machines began landing on convergent approach paths. "Be glad of the company. Things are a bit quiet."

"'Knock on wood,'" I cautioned the younger man, as everyone seemed to be these days, recalling my own rostered duties at Le Hameau; logging the departure times of machines taking off for the Front and those that returned, tattered, and torn, engines coughing dark smoke.

The FCO's field telephone jingled impatiently. "Controller." Pause. "Zero eight zero?" He reached for his binoculars and stood outside to scan that quadrant of the sky, phone lead trailing as he held the handpiece with his other hand. "Got him..." Another pause before signing-off with an exasperated: "Stand down, f'Chrissakes! It's only a Camel." As it proved to be. The humped outline of a Sopwith's machine guns' cowling clearly visible as another squadron's aeroplane thumped to a bumpy halt, probably lost, if my experience of the average pilot's navigational skills was any guide.

"Bloody ack-ack gunners," the Flight Controller grimaced, reading his wristlet watch before logging the new arrival. "Never happy unless banging away at –"He stopped short as an ambulance lorry raced off the Coisy road and braked in front of a canvas hangar. "Sick Bay's over there." His thumb jabbed in the opposite direction. "Do us a favour." He glanced at me again. "Go and put 'em right."

"Sure."

I reached the ambulance as half a dozen excited Diggers, two wearing Red Cross armbands, were unloading a laden stretcher. "Nailed the bastard!" one chortled as he saw me approaching.

"Which one of millions?" I retorted drily.

"The Red fuckin' Baron –!"

Not sure I'd heard correctly I followed inside the hangar and watched the medical orderlies dumping their load across two wooden trestles as the realisation of what they were doing sank in.

Less than a couple of hours ago, this untidy sack of blood and bone had been the Ace of Aces, victor of eighty aerial battles, Officer Commanding

Jagtstaffel von Richthofen, but now was no better than any common soldier rotting on the wire in No Man's Land.

His flying boots, gloves, helmet, goggles and much else had been souvenired within moments of the first Australians reaching the wreckage of his crimson Fokker triplane. All that remained now were his unbuttoned Sidcot – highly prized loot taken from unlucky British aircrew - worn over a pair of blood-soaked silk pyjamas.

Rigor mortis was tightening the neck muscles, spreading downwards and outwards towards the extremities. Soon the corpse would be stiff enough to prop up for the squadron photographer to take a death mask snapshot.

I flicked open my sketchbook and caught the likeness of surprisingly peaceful features, their chin bashed on impact with the Dr-1's instrument panel, but otherwise largely intact. This was not the face of the Fatherland's *Rächender Engel*, or Avenging Angel immortalised on thousands of propaganda postcards, but of a decent young chap, his better nature consumed in the fires of war as were countless others of our generation.

By now the word had got around. Soon every man and his dog were hurrying to catch a glimpse of this moment in history. I'd seen enough and went outside in time to greet my old CO, Major David Blake, who took charge and oversaw von Richthofen's funeral at Bertangles Cemetery, the following day.

Six pilots carried Our Gallant Enemy, as one of the wreaths described him, to the graveyard where the Brigade Chaplin conducted a non-denominational service. There is a photo of the event. My face is one of three grouped on his left-hand side, in the second row.

141

Military funerals were no longer worth a second glance at this late stage of the Great War, and yet the memory of von Richthofen's angered me for several days thereafter: I suspect the main reason being that Gallant Enemy wreath which perpetuated the myth of pilots as Knights of the Sky jousting high above the sordid squalor of the trenches. The fact that pilots were chosen as coffin bearers, with no thought that other, equally mortal aircrew had died at the Red Baron's hands, did nothing to lessen my simmering resentment.

Concerning Richthofen's alleged gallantry, more than half his kills were lumbering reconnaissance bombers like my RE8, or obsolete biplanes like the earlier DH2, itself little better than a powered box kite. In his eyes, we outgunned Tommies were game-park stags. But even against such easy prey, our noble hunter still required his *Jasta* to fly a defensive screen while he bagged another trophy for his collection of engraved *Ehrenbecher* silver goblets, lovingly fondled – sixteen years later - by triumphant Hermann Goering during our private tour of the *Richthofen Gedenkmuseum* at Schweidnitz. Tact and awareness of others' feelings were never my old acquaintance's strongest suit.

Meanwhile, 3 Divvy's HQ was now operational and open for official visitors, like the nosy Captain Bean, hurrying to intercept me as I strode across the yard towards HQ's transport pool in the Château's stable block, tasked to report on an emergency causeway across one of the Somme's tributary streams. "Mr Cribdon! A moment of your time if you please?!"

I let him catch up and pointedly read my watch. The overlapping thuds and crumps of Bruchmüller's artillery pounding the British 8th Division at Villers-Bretonneux - Germany's last obstacle before Amiens' marshalling yards and railway workshops - were an urgent reminder that gossip was not on today's worksheet as *Operation Michael* approached its climax. "If you must."

Australia's Official War Correspondent kept pace. "I've been hoping we'd meet again -"

"Why?" I had not meant to be rude, but this obvious question had a mind of its own. Besides, I was in an especially foul mood after another night of crabs, and shrimps, and hag fish.

It says much for his innate courtesy that Bean chose to ignore my ill temper. "Why? Because I need your opinion. And before you interject again, I should add that Major Baxter speaks highly of your skills and wide knowledge, even though you're not a Varsity man."

I ignored this patronising compliment. "'Need'?"

"Yes."

"How?"

"A cadre of promising young men is being recruited to play leading roles in Australia's post-war future," he replied simply. "We older chaps see it as our duty to set you on the right path by establishing a common point of reference, as I believe you airmen say when planning an attack?"

"Yes. We do. As for the rest, I've not the foggiest idea what you're on about." Bean was nearly twice my age but, with equivalent rank, he and I were empowered to speak as equals.

His response was not what I expected. "'Australia takes her pen in hand, to write a line to you, to let you fellows understand, how proud we are of you. The man who used to hump his drum, on far-out Queensland runs, is fighting side-by-side, with some Tasmanian farmer's sons. The old state jealousies of yore, are dead as Pharaoh's sow, we're not State children anymore, we're all Australians now!'"

"You wrote that?" I scowled.

"No. A friend. Andrew Patterson."

"Hm. I never saw any evidence that the Ancient Gyppo's were big into pig breeding," I thought aloud, "but the general idea's not too bad."

"Thank you. He'll appreciate the compliment, for you are exactly the sort of chap we have in mind for the United States of Australia," Bean replied, with an approving nod. "Look, I don't want to detain you any longer than necessary, but those clouds are telling us it's about to rain again. Would you mind awfully if we took shelter for another minute or two?" He pointed to the stables' open doors.

"So long as you don't mind me getting ready."

"Of course not."

We got under cover just in time. I wheeled Trusty from its stall, vacant now that the estate's horses were on campaign as officers' mounts in the French Army, kicked down its rear stand and searched the tool pouch for a socket spanner.

Bean watched me remove the spark plug and wire-brush its nickel alloy electrodes. "Why are you doing that?" he enquired, peering short-sightedly through his glasses.

"French lamp oil has a higher volatility index than their bloody petrol." I blew carbon dust from the spark gap. "I'm experimenting to get a hotter burn."

"How?"

"By dissolving 0.303 cartridges' cordite, in acetone from the fabric workshop, to extract nitro-glycerine." Explained with a curt, sideways glance. "Why?"

My interrogator failed to reply at first, but when he did, I detected a note of wistful envy in his voice. "The thing I most admire about you bushmen, is your ability to 'nut out' problems in ways that would never occur to a city dweller…"

"There's not much choice," I replied shortly, wondering what he hoped to gain by buttering-me-up as I ran a thumbnail around the plug's screw threads prior to scraping my 4B pencil to deposit a thin coating of graphite between the plug's steel shank and the cylinder's cast-iron head. "It's fix or fry, in the Never-Never, when things go bung on a hot day."

"And that exactly defines the can-do spirit our Australian troops have in such abundance!" Bean exclaimed. "Don't you see?! What you've described so succinctly as 'fix or fry' is what must be recorded for posterity and celebrated, if we are to remain an outpost of Western Civilisation amidst Asia's teeming millions!"

I said nothing. Instead, squatting on gum booted heels, I set the plug and applied sufficient torque to firm it in place without jamming the cylinder's brittle metal threads. Then it was the ignition lead's turn for a quick clean and tighten. Finally, I stood, faced him, and cleared my throat. "You believe that guff?"

"Of course." He seemed surprised that anyone could doubt his word. "Australia is barely seventeen years old since Federation. We were an adolescent in the British Empire's great family of nations until recently. But thanks to men like yourself, we've 'Come of Age'!" He caught his breath. "You must see that, surely?"

I am sceptical of flattery; there is always a hidden price tag. "No. I don't."

"Very well, allow me to elaborate," Bean replied, striking a determined pose. "Australia's actions in the Great War will be our nation's foundation legend, our *Iliad*, though greater in scale than anything Homer imagined for his Heroic Greeks in their war with Troy! I shall write such an epic story that generations unborn will thrill to read of Gellibrand, and Hobbes, and Brudenell-White, our Agamemnon, Odysseus, and Achilles!"

"And which 'Testicles' moniker does 3 Divvy's boss get?" I replied, adjusting my steel helmet's chinstrap while lapsing into the Outback's laconic monotone that comes naturally where mouths are kept shut against pestering bushflies. Today it was a pose crafted to tickle the romantic imagination of this bespectacled, bookish cove.

Bean hesitated, unsure of himself or perhaps unsure of me, before giving a guarded answer: "General Monash's actions at Messines, and the Ancre Battle, will be recorded fully, but of greater importance are the exploits of Australia's other military leaders, and the inspiring examples they set for our nation's future readers and leaders." He paused, eyeing me anxiously. "You do see that, don't you?"

"Not especially." I shook my head. "You're wasting breath talking to a plain sergeant dollied up as a Clueless Claude. I'm just an ordinary bloke whose only concern is staying alive in the here and now, not fretting over a future that probably won't come!" I humped Trusty off its stand and got ready to mount, draped in my wet-weather gear hung with gasmask, binoculars, haversack, and battlefield clobber.

"Wait! One more question!"

"Alright," I scowled again, "but make it quick. I've got work to do."

"Look, don't get the wrong idea," Bean blurted, with an anxious smile, "General Monash is highly regarded, but he remains an enigma for we lesser mortals, and hard to describe in ways that an average reader will understand. So, speaking as a plain soldier yourself, helps me to help them understand him. Please?"

I scratched the nape of my neck where the helmet had worn a slight callus. "How?"

"Paint me a word picture of Monash that an average reader will immediately grasp."

I recognised a trap that I just as promptly sidestepped by scratching my chin and looking perplexed. "I don't know. I'm not sure. I mean, what does any three-pip know about his divisional commander?"

"True," Bean agreed patiently, "but you must've seen him strutting around Headquarters, putting on airs, and overheard what other officers think of such brassy conduct?"

"Sure. He's not everyone's favourite uncle."

"How so?"

"Well, I mean, he can be pushy, and doesn't mind treading on toes, but maybe that's what generals have got to do, to win battles?" I concluded fairmindedly.

"You're saying he's not popular among his staff…?"

I scratched my ear this time. "Well. I can't speak for all. But like I say, he's not everyone's favourite uncle."

"Hm. 'Not everyone's favourite uncle'? That's one way to describe him," Australia's Official War Correspondent thought aloud. "Tell me Mr Cribdon – or may I call you Ian? – would you say that Monash's Teutonic background and, ah, exotic religion are matters of concern among your brother officers...?"

"Fair's fair!" I chuckled artlessly. "He can't help where his folks come from. As for that other thing, Sam Madorsky, on Hannan Street, always paid a fair price whenever we took our gold to his shop. So, what's the fret?"

"Yes, yes of course!" Bean hurried to cover his tracks. "I don't wish to imply that your friends and associates were less than honourable, but General Monash's position is somewhat anomalous. Indeed, I'm sure you can imagine how such a vulgarian would appear on the pages of Australia's *Illiad*, and can imagine the adverse impression if a backstairs conspiracy were to place Monash in command of the Australian Corps? And can we be sure that future generations of Australian readers and leaders will feel inspired by an autocratic German Jew preening himself at the head of our young nation's army?"

"Hm, that's a curly one," I conceded.

"Exactly so. Which is why we are taking steps to ensure that only the right sort of chap leads Australia to victory by embodying the sobriety, the dignity, the gentlemanly conduct so lacking in You Know Who..."

"I think." My chin was getting quite a workout as I resumed scratching it. "Well, I mean, I think I see where you're coming from. But be buggered if I can see what an ordinary bloke like me can do much about it!"

"Correspond." He reached into a pocket and presented his card. "My APO box number is uncensored. Tell me whatever you wish to, confident it will go no further."

"Aw, thanks!" I took the engraved, white pasteboard oblong and reverently tucked it under my mackintosh coat.

"Tell me, Ian, what are your plans, after the war?" he continued, as if the idea had just struck him. "It can't last forever, then you'll be back to doing what you did before. It won't be easy to forget that once you were a highly decorated officer as you tramp the back blocks of Westralia, turning your hand to whatever will earn a meal and a bed for the night..."

"My oath," I agreed, shoulders slumping.

"But it doesn't have to be that way,' Bean continued with what I believe was sincere concern. "I know people who can put decent, honourable work your way."

I looked up from my muddy gumboots, with a hesitant smile. "Dinkum?"

"'Dinkum.'"

"Then count me in!"

"Good man," he smiled, adding "good luck!" as I kicked Trusty awake and rumbled off into the weather, justifiably pleased with my performance as I passed through the park's gateway and set course for Le Querrieu, having just demonstrated that false whiskers and a purse of gold are not the only ways of getting inside an adversary's head and taking control of his mind.

142

I got back to HQ by mid-afternoon, typed-up my report and delivered it to Baxter's office in the château's pantry, at the back of the building where few unauthorised personnel had reason to go.

"Thank you, Ian." He pushed up his reading glasses and parked them on a balding, domed forehead. "A profitable trip?"

"I've known better," I replied. "Those bloody tank transporters are playing merry hell with the roads."

"Indeed. But take comfort from the fact that roads are neutral participants in war and don't discriminate between us or Brother Fritz. Besides the longer his lines of communications extend along such horrible tracks, the harder it is to maintain momentum," Baxter replied with an imperturbable smile. "Think of Napoleon's *via dolorosa* to Moscow."

"I'd rather think of our *via triumphalis* to Berlin!" I responded, by now accustomed to playing his word games in which, with increasingly frequency, I gave as good as I got.

"All in due course." He nodded approvingly at my neat riposte, "But first, share with me what the inquisitive Mr Be'an wanted to hear this morning -"

"How the blazes do you know we met?" I blinked.

"Ian, take heed: 'Not a sparrow falls without Our Father's knowledge.' *Matthew 10:29*, or in matters less Heavenly, Intelligence knowing soon thereafter."

"Point taken," I conceded grudgingly. "Right-o. First up, he's swallowed the hook you baited with that bushranger tale. 'I've been hoping we'd meet again!' When I asked 'why?' he said that he and others were recruiting a cadre of bright young men to lead a 'United States of Australia' after the war."

"And how does he propose doing that?" Baxter sat forward, elbows on desk, chin resting on laced fingers.

"By writing a history of the Great War as Australia's *Illiad*, 'to be our young nation's foundation legend,' only larger in scope than Homer imagined for his 'Heroic Greeks in their Trojan War.'"

Baxter's eyebrows shot up. "Nobody can ever accuse him of excessive modesty, can they? Pray continue!"

"He then anointed three divisional commanders as modern versions of Agamemnon, Odysseus, and Achilles. When I asked which moniker he had mind for General Monash - suggesting 'Testicles,' a joke that went over his head - I was told that future generations of Australians would not care to read of a 'vulgarian German Jew' leading our army to victory. I then asked what he wanted a 'plain sergeant dollied up as a Clueless Claude' to do about it? To which he replied: 'Correspond.'"

"How?"

"He gave me his card, told that its APO box number is uncensored and, by implication, invited me to relay malicious gossip overheard in the Mess."

"May I see it, please?"

I took Bean's card from my tunic pocket. Baxter reached for it, lowered his glasses, and read the engraved inscription with a secret smile before – "Abracadabra!" – making it vanish. I gasped with astonishment as he casually turned his open hand over and over to prove there was nothing there, before plucking the card from behind my left ear.

"'The speed of the hand deceives the eye!'" he announced in a fruity, stage magician's voice. "'Now you see! Now you don't!'" Before concluding, in a much colder tone: "And that, in a nutshell, is the nature of our business."

This was my first inkling that he was a talented amateur magician whose greatest joy, after a hard day in court, had been to perform conjuring tricks at the birthday parties of his children's excited little friends.

"Was there anything else?" he continued, retaining the card.

"Yes. He dangled the prospect of a well-paid job after the war."

"Provided you spy on General Monash?"

"Yes."

"Then we mustn't disappoint him."

"How?" I frowned suspiciously.

"By developing a lively, albeit misleading correspondence, of course."

"Now look here!" I snapped back. "No way am I going to snitch on my aunt's friend!"

"Nobody is asking you to," Baxter replied blandly, "others shall do it for you. To the untrained eye, one typewriter's font looks much the same as any other –"

"But what about my signature?!"

"'In My Father's house are many mansions,' *John 14: 2*," he replied. "Meanwhile, in a less Divine realm, His Majesty's Secret Service provides temporary accommodation to those who would otherwise be wasting their talents in Pentonville Gaol or Wormwood Scrubs."

"I don't like it!"

"Ian. How often must I tell you, liking or not liking an order is no part of our duty as King's commissioned officers?" He cocked an eyebrow, challenging me to dispute the truth of his remark.

"Maybe so," I scowled back, "but there is still one outstanding matter to settle!"

"Oh?"

"What the hell did you mean by telling him I was, 'not a Varsity man'?!"

"Ah ha!" Baxter chuckled. "He picked up on that. Splendid!"

"Not for me it's not!" I snapped back. "I resent being portrayed as an ignorant, gum leaf chewing 'Bastard from the Bush'!"

"Nobody is implying you are." He was no longer smiling. "If I had thought so, you would not be here today."

"But -?"

"The fact that your mind is not constricted by the straitjacket of a formal education, and that you draw upon a wealth of experiences I cannot begin to imagine, have conferred upon you a degree *summa cum laude* from the University of Hard Knocks," he continued. "As for my dismissive remark, which you impulsively misinterpreted, it was Be'an who was being tested and found wanting." He reached for a red, Top-Secret file on his desk. "Speaking of which, you did well today."

143

The teenage conscripts of Britain's 8 Division were not doing nearly so well at Villers-Bretonneux, inevitably nicknamed "Veeb" by we Melburnians in a nostalgic tribute to our local beer - Victoria Bitter - commonly known as VB. Pounded by artillery fire; drenched with mustard gas; under ferocious attacks by von Hutier's storm troops; those weedy young lads had no choice but to fall back for the last-ditch defence of Amiens.

Their retreat was particularly galling for our 4 Division's battle-hardened veterans who had fought the Germans to a standstill, earlier in the month, and then handed over to the Poms. Now, within the next few hours, Fritz would begin shelling the BEF's crucial railway junction. Nobody in command on either side of the war doubted that *Der Kaiserschlacht* had reached its tipping point; Victory or Defeat teetered on a knife's edge.

If I were asked to nominate one instance of the Monash Touch, I would pick the recapture of Villers Bretonneux by Brigadier General Glasgow's 13 Brigade and Brigadier General Elliott's 15 Brigade, on the night of the third anniversary of our landing at Gallipoli, an auspicious date not lost on those two commanders.

Ordered by HQ to launch a conventional dawn attack, led by tanks under a creeping artillery barrage, it is said that Bill Glasgow told his British opposite number, in no uncertain terms, that as this was an Australian stunt it would be won the Australian way, before Fritz could consolidate his position -!

By the misty gloom of a full moon, unable to reconnoitre in the time available, the two brigades moved up and launched a pincer attack, storming the town with bayonet and grenade in a pitched battle lit by parachute flares and star shells.

By dawn Villers-Bretonneux was ours again and would remain so for the rest of the war, a feat of arms described by both Haig and Foch as impossible to believe, even with the evidence of one thousand caged prisoners, scores of machine guns and 77's, and *Mephisto*, one of a handful German A7Vs to engage in history's first tank-on-tank battle.

It is alleged that Hindenburg tearfully informed a furious Kaiser that our counterattack had choked the *Reich*'s last hope of a decisive victory on the Western Front. Not that it stopped Ludendorff from trying again and again with *Georgette*, *Yorck-Blücher*, and *Gneisenau* in Flanders, but from now onwards Fritz was running out of puff, bravely, stubbornly, grimly winning time to dig in behind the Somme Valley's natural defences where another vision of hell awaited us in August.

My minor role in these events was cut short when Trusty's front wheel hit what I though was a puddle but was, in fact, a shallow, rain filled crater that sent me tumbling, though not far enough to escape the motorbike landing across me. Fortunately, the fuel tank's cap remained in place or else I would have most likely burned to death.

Some passing Tommies improvised a carry-all with their rifles and a groundsheet and took me to the nearest RAP. Here an overworked MO ticketed me for evacuation on the next convoy. Instead, I bluffed my way out of the Regimental Aid Post, hitched a lift aboard a ration lorry, and clocked in at the Château next morning.

Baxter gave one startled glare and strafed me for failing to take better care of myself. He then summoned our Chief Medical Officer who conducted a proper examination that revealed cracked ribs with severe subcutaneous contusions and localised haematomas; Lord Luck had been my pillion passenger the previous evening.

With all the invincible confidence of youth, I assumed this meant two or three weeks of light duties, chest strapped with elastic bandages, but Baxter had other plans, and nothing was going to stop him from putting them into immediate effect.

Despite my feeble protestations, I was despatched by ambulance to Boulogne, carried aboard the ferry and met at Folkestone by another ambulance with orders to drive straight to King Edward's Hospital. By now I no longer cared which of the army's numerous medical repair depots it dumped my exhausted body and numbed brain. However, I was still sufficiently aware to realise that, for the first time ever, I'd been allocated a private cubicle.

This was a privilege strictly reserved for field rank officers, not substantive one-pip Joes. When I said there must be a mistake, the ward sister frostily assured me that King Edward's was not in the habit of making mistakes, and that orders had been given to afford me every opportunity to rest and recover. Naturally I asked: "By whom?" Whereupon she silently pointed upwards, the universal codesign for influence in high places, and left me wondering if Baxter's connexion with Lord Nobury had anything to do with this rummy turn of events.

Next morning, badly knocked around but fit enough to wolf a pre-war breakfast of real coffee, toast, bacon, and scrambled eggs, I was visited by a youngish staff captain wearing the same laurel green collar tabs as those on my grubby tunic, now waiting for a drycleaner to collect it with the rest of my uniform.

"Mr Cribdon?"

"Yes?"

"Geoffrey Clarke." We shook hands. "Stephen Baxter told me to liaise with you."

"Oh?"

"I was his junior at the Bar," Clarke explained, before continuing: "It is his opinion that you will recover quicker, and return to duty sooner, if you have meaningful work to occupy your mind. Therefore, I am to provide you with newspapers and magazines, English and Foreign," he patted his bulky briefcase, "returning at the end of the week with others. In the meantime, you are invited to complete an 'analysis of the news-behind-the news...'"

"One moment -!" I nearly tipped over the breakfast tray as I owched sideways to try and stop him placing a substantial pile of newsprint on my bedside table, plus an exercise book, a pair of scissors, a box of pencils, and a recent edition of Langenscheidt's *English-German Dictionary*.

"The Stationery Office will deliver a typewriter and copy paper this afternoon," he continued imperturbably. "Meanwhile, if you require anything else, telephone me on Extension 35 at the War Office."

"But -!"

"Good day. Get well soon."

Exasperated, I watched him go before letting fly with a gnarled spray of curses, for it required no great powers of imagination to see Baxter pulling strings. Even in a London hospital, there was no escaping the man's pervasive influence, which made me feel more than ever like a desert traveller trapped in quick sands, drawn ever deeper into depths from which there was no escape.

Fortunately, the Honourable Lady Caroline Grenville was still on King Edward's staff. She read the Admissions' List, saw my uncommon surname, and made it her duty to keep applying icepacks while I took deep breaths despite the acute discomfort. "Pump those lungs, young man! Keep those airways open! I don't allow pneumonia on my ward!" And by Crikey she meant it.

Although only a VAD, the lowest face on a wartime hospital's totem pole, I quickly sensed that the Hon' Caro' - as Phillip Grenville warily called his relative by marriage - was the sort of woman that veteran matrons tried not to cross, and senior medicos dared not provoke. I also had a strong feeling that even the bugs and germs dived for cover when they saw her marching their way, for I was showing definite signs of improvement after only two days of her strict regime treatment.

The source of her formidable strength of character was not hard to fathom, once we became better acquainted. The youngest daughter of a marquess, she married a millionaire arms manufacturer and climbed the Matterhorn in an age when lady mountaineers still wore long tweed skirts, hobnailed boots, and chic felt hats.

After conquering all the Alpine peaks worthy of her attention, she turned to ocean canoeing and wrote the first guidebook to describe the Outer Hebrides from wavetop height on a stormy Atlantic day; it was her example that largely inspired my own later efforts in a similar line of work.

I enquired after Phillip Grenville, adding that I hoped to spend a few days at Hampton Rise, if my convalescent leave permitted it. To which she replied, in a characteristically firm voice: "He'll enjoy that. Pam' too. Runs the farm like clockwork. War Effort y'know."

"'Pam'?"

"Wife."

"So, they've, ah, patched up their differences...?"

"Gad no! Couldn't be happier!"

"But I thought they were irreconcilably estranged?" I wondered how else one could tactfully refer to a Lesbian *ménage à deux*.

"Oh. That one," the Honourable Lady Caroline sniffed. "Bad blood. The Zepp' did us all a favour. Better orf dead. His new un's a good filly. Good stock. Good breeding. Good pick."

I later learned that one of the last Zeppelin raiders had randomly dropped a three hundred pounder on the artists' studio where Phillip Grenville's first wife and her lover had moved some weeks earlier.

With the end of this week approaching, I thought it best to make a start with Baxter's homework assignment. By now I had some idea of how his mind worked, though I was still unsure why he wanted a written commentary on current European events, as seen through the eyes of a young, self-taught Australian journalist.

One clue was his reference to "news-behind-the-news," itself prompted by something I'd said on the train to Nice, when describing my job with the *Kalgoorlie Miner*: "'News' rhymes with 'skews.'" I was trying to sound like a fictional, hardboiled city reporter. "Objectivity is by definition impossible to sell -"

Challenged to support this shallow, callow argument, I replied that stories are shaped by the reporters' subjective viewpoints. Or, as Sid Hocking the *Miner*'s Owner-Editor had taught me, my first day on his newspaper: "Nail your end par' and lead with a catchy intro'."

"In other words, you're saying that the perceptive reader must first consider the storyteller-behind-the-story," Baxter queried, though I am sure he already had the answer, "and identify his 'slant,' as I believe you call it, before addressing the story itself?"

"That's one way of looking at it -"

"Some would say it's the only way," he retorted, concluding with an apt quote from his frequently consulted Sun Tzu's *Art of War*: "'To discover an enemy's intentions, survey the field of battle through his eyes...'" Now, some weeks later, I had a feeling that my powers of perception were about to be tested by a thick stack of *Times, Telegraph, Daily Graphic, Le Temps, Le Figaro,* and *Das Berliner Zeitung* on my bedside table.

Fortunately, I have always been attracted by acrostics and cryptic crosswords – quite likely because my own life itself has been so problematical - and launched a logic attack on this latest puzzle by sorting the newspapers into six chronologically ordered heaps.

I then gave each masthead its own page in the exercise book and composed an index of headline stories, from the oldest date to the most recent edition. Now I could cross-reference news' items in Britain, and France, and Germany, searching for patterns by asking myself the Who? Where? What? How? When? Why? that influenced their writers' choices.

Apart from our sole victory at Villers-Bretonneux, my improvised newspaper archive recorded nothing but Allied disasters; small wonder that Field Marshal Haig was compelled to issue a *Special Order of the Day* that concluded:

> There is no other course of action open to us but to fight it out. Every position must be held to the last man. There must be no retirement. With our backs to the wall and believing in the justice of our cause each one of us must fight on to the end. The safety of our homes and the freedom of mankind depend upon the conduct of each one of us at this critical moment.

Since when, things had gone from bad to worse to worst; Messines falling to the Germans on the 10th; Hazebrouck on the 12th; Bailleul on the 13th; Passchendaele, of infamous memory, on the 16th; Kemmel Ridge on the 17th; Bethune on the 18th.

Baxter did not need reminding of these, nor did he need my ill-informed opinions, so instead I trawled for those seemingly trivial fillers that lurk deep inside every newspaper. A good example of my random catch was *Das Berliner*'s one paragraph account of an agreement between Neutral Holland and Imperial Germany, for increased shipments of sand and gravel, delivered by canal barge to Occupied Belgium.

My own experiences, inspecting frontline transport systems, spun these few words into evidence that the enemy was repairing his rear zone roads, laying new ones, and adding to an already formidable array of reinforced-concrete machine gun pillboxes.

Assuming my analysis was correct, this could only mean that Fritz was buying a fallback insurance policy by strengthening his defences in case *Georgette*, or *Yorke-Blücher* faltered. An opinion noted in my Appreciation of the Situation or ApSit, one of several acronyms routinely used in I-Corps' Eyes Only signals and memoranda.

Thus far I had been left alone to get on with my work, except for the discreet attentions of King Edward's staff, and my afternoon sessions with the physiotherapist that coincided with piano recitals by students from the Royal College of Music, in the adjacent Music Room, a most agreeable and relaxing coincidence.

Then, one morning, shortly after breakfast, I heard the tramp of many feet approaching my private ward. Two junior probationary nurses reached me first and quickly draped a dressing gown over my pyjamas, straightened the bedding, and toed the bedpan out of sight as Matron herself appeared, leading a phalanx of ward sisters and specialists escorting today's visitor, clad in the black frock coat and grey pinstripes of a very senior public figure.

Lord Nobury turned to Matron and shared a gracious smile that awakened aching memories of another face, in another hospital. "Thank you, ma'am. Mr Cribdon and I need a few minutes alone."

I was, of course, also standing to attention. Nobury gestured me to be seated again at the desk as the crowd dispersed, shutting the door behind them, and perched himself at the end of my bed. "We must be brief. Cabinet adjourned at midnight." He read his pocket watch to check the time. "We resume at eleven thirty and I yet have to inform the Palace." He eyed the stack of clipped newspapers and my pencilled notes near the typewriter. "I see you are as aware of the situation as we are."

"Sir." Truth be told, I still had no idea what a Minister without Portfolio did at 10 Downing Street, not yet realising that he was the go-between a constitutional monarch, forbidden to meddle in parliamentary business, and a popularly elected Prime Minister who needed to stay sweet with the Palace. Or, as I later overheard him described: "Lionel Nobury is Cabinet's ambassador to the Crown, and the Crown's ambassador to Cabinet…"

"Baxter tells me you knew General Monash before the war." He came straight to the point.

"Only by sight," I replied defensively, "and not all that often."

"Quite so," He seemed to be reading my thoughts. "I would not usually ask you to comment upon another man's character unless he was present to defend his reputation, but in these perilous times I must. For only the Australians and the Canadians still have the numbers, the means, and the stamina to hold the enemy at bay while we reconfigure our forces. It is unfortunate that the Fifth Army needs Birdwood. His promotion decapitates your corps at the very moment when we least need ambitious rivals stabbing each other in the back."

Nobury paused, eying me closely. "Baxter says that you are also aware of the conspiracies and intrigues, *pro et contra* Sir John, mostly *contra*, in the Australian press. What you cannot yet know is that your Prime Minister is about to join the War Cabinet with a letter of dismissal in his briefcase, should Sir John Monash get acting command of the Australian Corps, based upon his seniority *vis-à-vis* four other divisional commanders.

"This is an internal political matter, normally outside London's remit, but that does not mean we are indifferent to its outcome," he continued. "If necessary, ways will be found to change Mr Hughes' mind. But before Cabinet intervenes, we must be sure that the man we've backed is the best candidate at this time of extreme crisis for the Empire and, in no small measure, Civilisation itself.

"I only know of Monash by hearsay, and from what I've read of his conduct at Messines and the Ancre, but in all other respects he is a blank sheet. You, however, knew him in civilian life when his true character was not yet cloaked in khaki and gold braid," Nobury concluded, ignoring my startled look. "I wish you to disregard the animosity that his ancestry and faith inevitably attract and, instead, share with me your impressions of the man himself."

"But I was only a child!"

"Children have a clarity of vision that sees through adult deceits and deceptions."

"Sir! You ask too much!" I sat bolt upright. "I despise gossip! I consider it bad form when one gentleman speaks of another behind his back -!"

"Your sentiments do you credit and are what I expect of you." He paused heavily. "However, much depends upon your frank observations."

"Is that an order?"

"Only if you choose to make it so," he frowned back. "I would prefer to hear your plain, truthful opinion, freely given. Secure in the knowledge that your identity will never be revealed. For which you have my word of honour as a Queen's Commissioned Officer and Peer of the Realm."

"Those are too grand," I countered with all the prickly pride of youth. "The word of, Sandra's dad, is good enough, for me."

He looked up at the ceiling, composed his features, and looked down again. "You have it."

What followed was, I believe, a fair and balanced word picture of Aunt Lucinda's piano partner and David's honorary uncle during a time of peace and plenty now beyond recall. I then added some personal impressions of Brigadier General Monash training himself and his troops in Egypt, before applying the lessons learned, on Gallipoli. Culminating with his confident mastery of the battlefield when all around him were panicking at Doullens.

144

Two days' later, Geoffrey Clarke knocked on the cubicle door and let himself in. "Good afternoon, Cribdon. Feeling better?"

"Yes, thank you, Clarke." Even after three years of fighting alongside the English, I still found their armlength courtesy hard to take after the honest informality of Outback Australia. "What's new?"

"Nothing good, I'm afraid. It's all in here," he added, unlatching his briefcase to deliver a fresh batch of newspapers. "So, this is your report?" he continued, itching to know what was on the twenty foolscap pages, bound in cardboard recovered from the hospital's salvage bin, and addressed

EYES ONLY
Major Stephen Baxter.
3 Division HQ Australian Corps
France
EYES ONLY

all four sides sealed with signed strips of adhesive wound-dressing tape.

"Ah, can't be too careful, can we?" Clarke attempted a light-hearted laugh, examining the seals before handing over a plain envelope. "With the compliments of the gentleman in question."

"Thank you." I was not duped by his affability and waited until the door shut before slitting the envelope with my nailfile. The note was undated, handwritten in I-Corps' dark green ink:

> *Ian.*
>
> *Events proceed apace with Messrs Porridge &*
> *Vegetable striving to advance their favourite,*
> *Broody Black, once Our Feathered Friend flies off*
> *to his new perch.*
>
> *Their machinations continue unabated and gain*
> *traction in unwanted, unwonted quarters.*
> *I shall soon be in London and will discuss these*
> *matters en privé.*
>
> *S.B.*

Another thing that grates with me whenever dealing with a certain type of Englishman, is his addiction to schoolboy humour of which Baxter's note was a fine example with its thinly veiled reference to a Scotsman, Keith Murdoch, as

Porridge; Charles Bean, as *Vegetable*; Brudenell White as *Broody Black*; and General Birdwood, as *Our Feathered Friend*.

I replaced his cryptic message in its envelope and began to index this latest batch of newspapers, but my heart was not in it today. Instead, I outlined a cartoon for *Punch*, modelled on a then-popular advertisement that rather cruelly showed a bull looking at a jar of Bovril while mournfully thinking "Alas, my poor brother…" Only, in my version, it was the Kaiser mournfully staring at a pile of skulls, and saying "Alas, my poor Empire…"

It was neither entertaining, nor witty, but the best I could manage in my current state of mind. The sights, the sounds, the smells of wartime nursing in King Edward's had rekindled heartbroken memories of my murdered wife. There were often moments when I glimpsed her from the corner of my eye, but when I spun around, she was gone. Fortunately, I had a private ward or else it would have been difficult to maintain a properly composed face in public.

Another wretched day dawned. Bathed, shaved, breakfasted, I grimly set to work analysing reports from the crumbling Austro-Hungarian Empire, as reported in a recent copy of Vienna's leading daily *Die Presse*, for which I needed to keep dipping into the *Langenscheidt* dictionary with Baxter's engraved bookplate on its flyleaf.

An hour or so later I was interrupted by a young nurse bearing a basket of hot-house grapes, unimaginable luxuries for most Britons, even in peacetime. "These're for you sir!" She bobbed a curtsy and fled, before the temptation to beg for one overcame her sense of propriety, leaving me alone to read the handwritten card with its discreetly embossed earl's coronet centred at the top.

> *My Dear Ian.*
>
> *Fruit can be such a cliché, ordinarily, but my sincere hope is that these will hasten your recovery in our more straightened times.*
>
> *Claire Nobury.*

I was deeply touched by her gift, for until now she had kept a polite but cool distance from her late-daughter's unconventional choice, who proceeded to open his sketchbook and compose three jaunty figures striding arm-in-arm across the page. Left: a jolly Jack Tar. Centre: a radiant VAD nurse. Right: a cheeky Tommy Atkins. Overhead: a solitary RE8, its goggled observer pointing towards the rising sun. Entitled: "Comrades in Arms!"

I replaced Lady Nobury's card with my sketch and took the grapes down to the Nurses' Rest Room where I knocked, asked for permission to enter, and placed the basket on a table cluttered with illustrated magazines, sandwich plates, and teacups. And in that moment, I solemnly swear I heard a gentle voice singing:

> There's a home for tired nurses,
> Above the bright blue sky,
> Where matrons never grumble,
> And colonels never pry.
> Where all our little troubles,
> Are drowned in cups of tea,
> And -

One of several young women present sprang forward. "What's the matter sir?!" Unable to reply, I stumbled past her and fled upstairs to weep alone.

After which I should have known that Fate's fickle finger was about to poke me in some new direction because, instead of Geoffrey Clarke returning with another bundle of English and Foreign newspapers, two days later, it was Baxter himself who strode into my cubicle.

"I've just popped over for a short while," he announced, leather gloves and forage cap tucked underarm; Sam Browne belt, shoulder strap, brass fittings, lustrously polished by his batman; tailored tunic and trousers cut from the finest khaki barathea; every inch the very model of a modern major.

"How?!" I was not sure if my shellshocked ears were deceiving me. Like hundreds of thousands of other soldiers, I had only experienced dawdling French *quarante huit* troop trains and vomitus Channel crossings. For all of us, without exception, popping over to England for a short break was never on the cards.

"Air Force courier flight," Baxter replied as if all he had done was hail a passing taxi. "Bertangles to Hendon in little more than two hours. Absolutely amazing! As are the views you airmen enjoy," he continued, smiling reflectively. "When the war's over, I shall learn to fly. It looks like fun." I said nothing; "fun" not being a word I associated with flight or flying. "But enough of that," Baxter continued. "Let's get you home."

"'Home'?"

"As of now you are officially convalescent, and this room is needed for the chap waiting outside on a stretcher."

I gathered my few belongings, shoved them into the valise and limped downstairs, changed from pyjamas into the Hospital Blue flannel uniform that Walking Wounded soldiers were officially required to wear in public. It also unofficially entitled us to free bus rides, free kinema tickets, free seats at park bandstand concerts, but only once to my knowledge did it extend to free travel in a cabriolet Rolls Royce Silver Ghost.

"Good afternoon, Jenkins," I recognised Sir Arthur Stanhope's chauffeur as he held the door open for Baxter and myself to get aboard a sunlit rear seat, the car's roof folded back so I could enjoy open air and unimpeded views after close confinement in King Edward's, "this is a most pleasant surprise!"

"Likewise, sir. Sir Arthur has placed us at your disposal."

Baxter leaned forward. "Merton Lane, Hampstead, if you please."

"Merton Lane, Hampstead it is," Jenkins replied, confirming that he'd heard the address correctly before gliding away from the kerb and setting course for North London. I restrained an urge to regally wave to pedestrians as we progressed through Belgravia, not sure that Baxter would appreciate the prank any more than Cairo's disapproving European expats had, in their pith helmets and tropical whites when Bill Proctor and I roared past them on an army motorbike and sidecar.

I looked away as we approached Marble Arch. The memory of that magical day on the Serpentine was too raw, too painful, too personal as we drove up Finchley Road - between Lord's Cricket Ground and Regent's Park - before taking a sharp right through a tangle of lesser streets to reach Highgate Road. Another hard left and, as if by one of Baxter's conjuring tricks, we were driving through a picture postcard English countryside of heathland, lakes, and woods on our left, Millfield's stately homes on our right.

The Rolls' gearbox slicked down a cog and we entered a narrow lane, shaded by mature oak trees. Baxter leaned forward again and tapped our driver on the shoulder: "'Next entrance. On the left."

Jenkins slowed at a white, five-barred gate hinged between two sandstone pillars, swung open by an elderly gardener and his lad, forewarned by telephone from the hospital. Both doffed their caps and bowed as we purred past, up a curved gravel driveway towards a two storeyed neo-Georgian residence set in its own miniature parkland, not unlike Tralee House in style and size.

Its similarity to my adopted home, in Melbourne, eased the pain of more recent memories, for I have long admired those young architects who rebelled against the fake Gothic battlements, stained-glass gloom, and mock-Medieval interiors of an earlier Victorian era. Instead, drawing their inspiration from Georgian simplicity enhanced by electric lighting, hot running water, and flush sanitation.

"Welcome to my humble abode." Baxter took my valise and led the way up a flight of steps much like those at Château Clermont-Tonnerre. His ironic humility did not fool me for one moment. In his shoes, pausing to survey my domain, I'd have had every reason to review - with immense satisfaction - my progress from a poverty stricken country vicarage to this discrete display of wealth and power.

"Mrs Williams?" He was speaking to a cheerfully chubby Welshwoman. "Captain Cribdon will be our honoured guest while recovering from his injuries." Then, to me: "Mrs W is our cook-housekeeper, as indispensable as her husband, Mr W our gardener and odd job man. I am confident both will be most attentive to your needs. Meanwhile, arrangements have been made for Jenkins to take you back to King Edward's for check-ups. But if you do need help beforehand, Mrs W will call next door."

"I hope that won't be necessary, for I don't want to put her to any trouble," I explained courteously, "but how would calling next door make things better?"

"Sir Andrew Crawford is our friend," Baxter replied. "He's also Physician-in-Ordinary to His Majesty. You'll be in good hands should anything need urgent attention."

My eyes popped. "Your neighbour is the King's medico?!"

"Mm." He smiled reflectively. "Jeanne and he used to go at it hammer and tongs, over Sunday luncheon, honing their skills on each other's stock of knowledge. Though, in strictest confidence, she considers his Ob's & Gynae' somewhat dated. Still," he brightened, "that won't be a problem for you, will it? Here, let me show you to your room."

Its similarities with Tralee House extended to the generously proportioned interior spaces, their creamy-white walls and well-lit areas hung with choice original canvases, mostly *d'après* Manet and Renoir.

There was also a surprising homage to Berthe Morisot, the largely forgotten female Impressionist whose portrait of *La Baronne Lucinde* in sumptuous, Second Empire court dress - painted shortly before my aunt's departure aboard the Imperial Yacht *L'Aigle* for Egypt, where the Empress Eugénie officially opened the Suez Canal - held pride of place in Tralee House.

The portraits and landscapes in Baxter's collection were more recently dated and mostly initialled JMB; the one in my airy, second-floor room, an evocative oil colour of a sun-drenched olive grove, the Maritime Alps a shadowed purple in the background. Clear evidence of its artist's nostalgia for

Mediterranean warmth and colour, after marrying and establishing herself amidst England's muted greys and greens.

Valise unpacked, my dry-cleaned and freshly pressed khaki uniform hung in the clothes' closet, I returned downstairs to find Baxter in conversation with a grave, middle-aged man. "Ah! Ian. Permit me to introduce, Mr Henderson, our tailor." We shook hands. "I trust you won't take offence," he continued, "but I can't help noticing that you don't seem to have civilian clothes...?"

"True enough," I agreed. "My civvies got stuffed into a wheat bag, at enlistment, and probably pinched soon after. Why?"

"We'll need you out of uniform for a short while."

By now I was sufficiently attuned to this man's methods to interpret his polite observation as a direct order and patiently submitted to Mr Henderson's tape measure while Baxter added the occasional approving comment. There was nothing much I could add to the conversation. Men's fashions had moved on from those I knew as a Melburnian city slicker, before being unceremoniously tossed into a rougher world of work boots, leather gaiters, denim trousers, and oilskin coats.

The upshot of all this fussing around was an agreement to cut and deliver a plain business suit in navy blue worsted, with a three buttoned, single-breasted sack jacket; half dozen white bibbed shirts with detachable collars and cuffs; black socks and black patent leather shoes. Kit that an ambitious young City clerk would wear as he ran messages, delivered documents, and schemed to bed the boss's daughter.

I watched Mr Henderson climb aboard a pony trap and set off down the driveway. "That's one hell of a drive back to London," I thought aloud as he disappeared behind a clump of flowering rhododendrons.

"If it were his intention," Baxter agreed, "but why pay the exorbitant rents of Saville Row when one can establish a similar shop closer to where your clients live, at a fraction the cost and with none of the inconvenience of travelling up to Town every day?" Adding, with a rueful chuckle: "If only my profession allowed me that privilege! Anyhow, let's go into the conservatory while Mrs W prepares an early dinner."

I followed and made myself comfortable in a wicker chair, watching Baxter set out two spirit glasses and a dark bottle with a plain label that told me nothing except that it was unlikely to be SDR firewater in this setting.

Baxter, as he so often did these days, read my mind. "Gray's Inn stopped being a public tavern six centuries ago, but we benchers see no reason why our cellar should not be kept amply stocked with the very best." He poured a finger of rich amber spirit into each glass and motioned for me to choose one.

Aunt Lucinda's coaching in the subtle art of tasting came to the fore as I closely examined the colour, swirled the nose, then allowed a sip to develop on the tongue before slowly breathing out. "Strewth Almighty. This one's out of the box..."

"Is that Australian for 'good'?" Baxter enquired anxiously.

"Oh yes, very, very good," I replied, awestruck. "What's its story?"

"'Réserve familiale Martell,'" he replied with commendable modesty. "A blend of our finest eaux-de-vie, some dating back to the reigns of Louis XVI and the Emperor Napoleon I. And if you are wondering where you could buy more, I would have to reply that it cannot be bought, only shared with a discerning few, among whom may I now include yourself?" Baxter raised his glass in salute.

I am enough of a fisherman to recognise a baited hook, though what he was angling for, I had no idea. At such moments I find it's best to get on the front foot and, to mix sporting metaphors, bat the conversation where I want it to go. Frowning, I leaned forward. "So, what's the connexion between an old inn, this blissful brandy, and sharing it with me?"

"Does there have to be one?" Baxter replied, eyebrows cocked. "Cannot two colleagues relax and converse in a civilised manner?"

"No." I shook my head. "You've never struck me as the sort of bloke who wastes words. Words have value. Words have purpose. Words count when time is of the essence, and one has 'just popped over from France.'" At which point I shut up, sat back, and resumed sipping his sublime cognac.

"Are all Australians this gruff?" Said with an irritable frown.

"'Don't know," I replied, still playing the plainspoken Colonial, a ruse designed to keep him off-balance while I kept bowling verbal spinners to break through his guard. "'Haven't met 'em all yet."

He took a thoughtful nip of the world's finest spirits and considered his options. "Very well. I had intended we speak after dinner. But as you say, time is of the essence, and I must return to Hendon early tomorrow morning." It was his turn to lean forward. "Lord Nobury visited you in hospital. Doubtless you spoke of family matters, but did he then have anything to say about General Monash that might indicate how Cabinet is leaning *vis-à-vis* command of the Australian Corps?"

I shook my head. "No. But from his questioning, I'd say it is still in the balance."

"What did he want to know?"

"My frank opinion of Mr Monash, upon those occasions we met in peacetime, and of General Monash since then."

"How did you reply?"

"With strict impartiality." I had a feeling that Baxter already knew more than he was saying.

"For instance?"

"I did not gloss over the fact that, viewed though a young lad's eyes, he was an outrageous flirt, always needing to be the centre of attention. And if he wasn't, would soon make sure he was by blowing his trumpet at full blast."

"And how does he seem now, viewed through adult eyes?"

"Much the same. He is still a shameless charmer, as we saw when he met the Countess at Clermont-Tonnerre," I replied, with some reservation. "But when lesser men are chasing around like chooks with their heads chopped off - as they were at Doullens - I could not imagine anyone better equipped to get a grip, quick smart. Later, at Franvillers, I took his dictation and transcribed the Ancre's Order of Battle in clear, concise, plain English that any private could execute without question." I paused, eyeing Baxter, closely. "But you know this already, don't you?"

"Yes, but until now I was not sure that Nobury knew it as well. Thank you for telling me." He stood as Mrs Williams approached to announce that our meal was ready. "His Lordship has considerable, albeit invisible influence; we might yet beat Messrs Be'an & Murdoch at their own game…"

As if sealing an unspoken agreement, we clinked glasses, finished our drinks, and went inside.

145

The meal was a simple affair of vegetables from the garden and braised rabbit that had, until earlier today, enjoyed a carefree life of kitchen scraps and garden weeds in its backyard hutch; to waste even a morsel of food, was rightly considered treason when nearly one million tons of Britain's merchant fleet were being torpedoed on the Atlantic's Western Approaches, every month.

The average private soldier was better fed, in France, than his civilian relatives in the United Kingdom and the hungry joy in their eyes when Dad, or Brother, or Son came home on leave and displayed a tin of corned beef or a few ounces of canteen chocolate from his haversack, can well be imagined

After thanking Mrs Williams, Baxter and I went into the study and shut its horsehair and leather padded doors, separated by an airlock sufficiently deep for two standing men. There was no need for him to remind me that what was said in here, stayed in here as he took one of the upholstered easy chairs beside the unlit fireplace. I took the other and waited for his next move.

"Concerning General Monash," Baxter began, without preamble, "I'm glad you've identified the potentially fatal chink in his armour. It saves me mentioning that he's an habitual womaniser, with racy appetites and a collection of erotica I prefer not to describe, since at least the time when his business partner thrashed him for seducing said partner's wife when their firm was on the brink of bankruptcy. Thirty years later, with the newly-elevated Lady Monash confined to barracks in Australia, Sir John is fooling around with a Miss Lizette Bentwich, whose correspondence is recklessly explicit –"

"How the devil d'you know that?!"

He shook his head sadly. "How often must I remind you that 'not a sparrow falls...'?"

"You're reading her letters?!"

"Of course." He feigned surprise that I should think otherwise. "How else am I, and those I serve, to ensure that nothing compromising is read by our enemies, domestic and foreign?" He paused, waiting for an answer that never came.

"Not a whiff of this must reach the Palace," he continued, perhaps disappointed that I declined to comment, or maybe glad that I chose to remain silent. "HM is a former naval officer and correspondingly broadminded, but the Queen, who exerts considerable influence over her more amiable husband, is a very straitlaced German princess whose stern disapproval of their sons' louche conduct extends to all others who fail to toe the *Korrekt* line..."

"This sounds disgustingly underhand to me!" I still had much to learn.

"Agreed, but we cannot afford to be squeamish in our Defence of the Realm," Baxter retorted, with a curt sniff. "Namely, frustrating Be'an & Murdoch's plans to undermine Monash's acting command of the Australian Corps, by conspiring to promote Brudenell-White in his place. As you can well imagine, if Miss Bentwich's *billets-doux* were to fall into the wrong hands it would be, as I believe you Australians say: 'All over, Red Rover...'?"

I still said nothing.

"Personally, I applaud their choice," Baxter resumed his monologue. "BW has a brilliant military mind, as one would expect of the first of your countrymen to pass at the Imperial Staff College, since when he has distinguished himself in all that he's put his hand to. Additionally, he is courteous, urbane, modest, kindly, loyal, and steadfast. So, you may very well ask, 'what's the problem?' Why struggle to advance the interests of a vain, bombastic, self-promoting, indiscreet fellow who, to put it crudely, can't keep his mouth shut or his breeches buttoned up?"

"Deuced if I know!"

"Then ask yourself this: does the Empire need a kindly, urbane, modest chap politely leading its finest shock troops at a time of extreme peril? Or do we need an ambitious, ruthless outsider with nothing to lose and everything to gain as he shows the world what a splendid chap he is, by smashing the Hun...?"

"The latter."

"Correct. Sir John, for all his faults, is the right man, in the right place, at the right time. Therefore, our duty is to ensure he secures the job, and then shield him until it is well and truly done."

"But surely others can see it too? Without all this slimy intrigue?!"

"No." Baxter shook his head. "Be'an told you himself that he means to write a history of the Great War, as your nation's *Illiad*, 'to inspire generations of Australians unborn.'"

"Yes, but -?"

"It is no part of his grand design that a German Jew, once removed, shall get the credit," Baxter ignored my interruption. "He will use every stratagem at his disposal to ensure that a Protestant, Anglo-Australian country gentleman wears the victor's laurels, always assuming there are any. But what of our vengeful son o' the kirk, you may ask?"

"Enlighten me."

Baxter sat back, the better to read my face as he answered his own question: "Murdoch has never forgotten that, during his pre-war search for employment on Fleet Street, he was reduced to trying his luck with the *Law Journal* owned by one Herbert Bentwich, a Jewish gentleman who made it abundantly clear that he had no use for a stammering gentile from a recently emancipated convict colony..."

"Then it's a grudge fight?"

"Like many another, ever since Cain ambushed Abel in *Genesis 4: 1-18*."

"Why are you telling me this?" I frowned.

"Because, as soon as 3 Division can be safely left in others' hands for a few days, 'Mr Knight' will arrive at the Savoy, where nice people have gone to be naughty ever since Oscar Wilde and Lord Alfred Douglas led the way, and once there, hop into bed with 'Mrs Knight' née Bentwich. Such being the case," Baxter concluded, "it would never do if his authentic wife's nephews, Captains Moss and Simonson, discovered what larks uncle got up to, when let off the leash. Hence our need for a discreet go-between with whom we can maintain contact, should it be necessary to summon Sir John back to HQ post haste."

"And I'm that one?"

"Correct." Baxter briefly read his wristlet watch to check the time. "'Mr Knight' is a prosperous businessman dealing in hush-hush government contracts. It is not unreasonable for him to employ a slightly disabled young personal secretary to guard the gate. I consider you are the best man for such a sensitive post."

"That may be so, but what does General Monash think?!" I snapped back.

"He approved of my plan."

"Oh."

"I'm not sure how to put this tactfully," Baxter continued, choosing his next words with care, "Sir John knows of your connexion with the Noburys."

"It was. Reported. In the *Times*. As I recall!"

"Indeed." We both fell silent until Baxter cleared his throat and resumed speaking. "Anyhow, Ian, don't be surprised if he asks for a meeting with His Lordship..."

"You think he might?"

"You may very well ask yourself: 'Will such an agile social acrobat miss this golden opportunity to perform in front of a senior member of those great families who direct the invisible ebb and flow of history?"

"Point taken." Said reluctantly, for I did not like this scheme at all. "Assuming he does ask, what's my response?"

"Indulge him. Nobury is a shrewd judge of character. He'll see through the pushy bravado and recognise that Monash brings a unique set of skills to a new form of warfare that is being readied even as we speak. But that's a story for another day -"

"Why not now?" I queried, by no means certain I was hearing the whole story.

"'Unto all things there is a season, and a time to every purpose under the heaven,'" he replied with an arch smile. "*Ecclesiastes, 3:1*. But to satisfy your curiosity, contrast and compare the battles you fought on the Dardanelles, with those in the Ancre Valley and Villers-Bretonneux. Then, assuming by God's Grace we avert imminent defeat, project your imagination on the final battlefield and be ready for a summons to the Savoy as 'Mr Page,' with a room on the same floor as 'Mr Knight.' All communications from 3 Division telegraphed to Geoffrey Clarke at the War Office, who will courier the decrypts to you, as they come in."

"Does Clarke know what's going on?"

"No. This is 'Eyes Only,' like your incisive analysis of that Dutch sand and gravel business. So far as Clarke and everyone else is concerned, we're running a counterintelligence exercise." He stood. "Anyhow, enough of that. There's a staff conference at Bertangles tomorrow afternoon and I have a brief to prepare beforehand. So, you won't mind if I leave you to make yourself at home?"

"Not in the least."

"Good man. Good night."

We shook hands and I let myself out through the airlock as Baxter moved behind his desk and set to work.

146

I overslept. By the time I'd bathed, shaved, and gone down to breakfast, Baxter was probably three thousand feet above the English Channel, flying due south. However, before leaving, he'd made time to compose a handwritten note propped against the salt cruet.

> *Ian*
>
> *My study and library are kept locked for*
> *reasons of professional confidentiality,*
> *but in all other respects this house is yours*
> *for as long as you need to rest and*
> *recuperate on your own.*
>
> *Jeanne assures me that she does not mind*
> *you using her studio (behind the green-*
> *house) provided "he clean my brushes and*
> *leave everything exactement he find it." Brrr!*
>
> *The children are at boarding school during*
> *the week but return home for the weekend*
> *unless on a supervised excursion or engaged*
> *in supplementary studies. They have been*
> *instructed not to pester you with questions*
> *about the nature of our work in France, should*
> *you meet them.*
>
> *There are several excellent walks on and around*
> *the Heath, and Highgate Cemetery is within*
> *easy distance. Find Comrade Marx' grave and*
> *ponder the impact his life had, and continues*
> *to have, upon countless others...*
>
> *S.B.*

I replaced the note in its envelope, wondering what the unspoken purpose of that final paragraph was, and spent the next half-hour or so reconnoitring my new quarters by tracing a mental map of the house and its surrounds.

The overall impression was of a cultivated family home, its music room smaller than the one at Hochheim - the Shusters' mansion in Melbourne - but with a larger range of instruments than the obligatory grand piano; someone here played the cello and viola, and perhaps someone else was a flautist, there was no way of telling. And yet there was an odd feeling of stasis, as if the furniture had not moved an inch since its arrival, possibly delivered by a Liberty & Co horse drawn pantechnicon earlier in the century and set down in dead straight lines from door to door.

Happily, the outside garden was less inflexible, with aromatic shrubs of lavender and rosemary lining the pebbled pathways, one of which led to Jeanne Baxter's studio. Borrowing the key from Mrs Williams, I unlocked its door and peered around inside. Disused since 1914, this dusty, musty shed was still very much an artist's studio as I swung open its hopper windows to let in the fresh air and began bringing it back to life.

One phrase in Baxter's note had struck a responsive chord; his invitation for me to recuperate on my own. The man was psychic! For the more I thought about it, the more I realised that I had hardly spent a moment by myself since enlistment. Instead of which, swept along on the torrents of war, I had become just another faceless number on a battalion's "mustard roll," as we nicknamed our muster rolls. And in the process an independently minded young Ian Cribdon had been supplanted by an obedient automaton who took and gave orders with as much thought as a railway station ticket machine.

There was much else to reflect upon, as I cleared the stray leaves that had drifted into this shed and dusted its shelves before re-arranging their contents to my satisfaction. That done, I selected a pad of cartridge paper, sharpened a selection of pencils, and began transcribing some previous sketches into saleable artwork for *Punch*.

In one, the spike on the Kaiser's *Pickelhelm* had melted like candle wax. His usually upturned moustache drooped, making him look like a sad walrus. His shoulders were slumped, the crumpled uniform encasing them, sizes too large. And the new caption read "Alas my poor people!" as heaped skulls glared back through empty eye sockets. I also considered my *Comrades in Arms!* worth development, the pair of them easily covering the cost of my new civvies, when Mr Henderson presented his bill a few days later.

Not that I needed the money. There was more than enough in my army account at Coutts' Bank, plus what I was making on the side in cash, even without the quarterly dividends from Aunt Lucinda's trust fund. But I've had a holy horror of debt ever since my earliest memories of moonlight flits between squalid lodgings, Papa one stumble ahead of the rent collectors and bum-bailiffs.

Summoned for lunch, I left *Comrades* and went indoors to scoff a hearty vegetable broth thickened with leftovers from yesterday's meal. Convalescent and easily tired, I went upstairs to my bedroom for a nap that lasted until Mrs Williams tactfully knocked and delivered my share of the afternoon post.

Puzzled, unaware that anyone knew of my present whereabouts, I slit the envelope and unfolded a handwritten note:

Royal Military Academy
Woolwich

My Dear Cribdon.

The Hon' Caro' has kept me informed of your progress.

*I would have called at KE's earlier except that,
until yesterday, I was umpiring field exercises
in Norfolk.*

*The Hon' recorded your new destination
and I would very much like to catch up, when
convenient &c.*

P. Grenville

As my wife had ofttimes reminded me: "Letters are more than the sum of their parts…" and this one's clipped phrases echoed my weeks at Wandsworth helping a stiff-upper-lipped Englishmen prepare for his Selection Board. And, later, his hospitality in the centuries' old surrounds of Hampton Rise. But even so, I was in no hurry to respond.

As previously noted, this was the first time I'd been truly alone in almost four years and too many unresolved questions were now free to torment my bruised and battered mind; I could ill-afford the distraction of company until I'd got myself sorted out. The housekeeper and her husband, the gardener, sensed this and although attentive to my needs, tacitly left me in peace, for which I was most grateful.

I shall skip this episode in my tape-recordings for Frances, not wishing to explain the many sketches of Sandra's belovéd face, made from memory while pleading with her to return, as if by ancient cavemen's wall-painted magick I could raise her whole and well again from the Channel's tidal depths. Mercifully, no one overheard my sobs or saw the tears as morning folded into afternoon into night into next morning. Next afternoon. Next night. Next morning. During which time I clung to the vain hope that my wife had miraculously survived machine gunfire; had been washed ashore in Normandy without identification; and was now in some provincial hospice or asylum, recovering her memory.

All the evidence suggests that I went more than a little mad during my stay at Merton Lane and was by no means recovered when Jenkins returned with the Rolls for my check-up at King Edward's. However, instead of "the Hon'" as Grenville called his formidable cousin-in-law, a sweet young thing ushered me into the presence of today's duty consultant who happened to be the King's Physician in Ordinary doing-his-bit for the War Effort.

"Ah! Captain Cribdon." Sir Andrew Crawford glanced up from his clinical notes. "Baxter's told me a lot about ye." His stern, Scottish manner softened a fraction. "There's nae need to traipse into Town when I c'n hop o'er the garden stile. But since ye're here, strip off and let's see how ye're farin'."

Another morale lifter had been the delivery of my new civvies; now I could get rid of the Hospital Blues and wear-in the suit and shoes, ready to impersonate a civilian clerk whenever Baxter directed me to the Savoy.

I was sufficiently settled to uncap my fountain pen and reply to Grenville's note in a similarly brisk, no-nonsense vein:

*2 Merton Lane
Hampstead*

Dear Grenville.

Apologies for not replying sooner but am
still not 100% after crashing a mo'bike and
cracking a few ribs.

Your company will be a welcome tonic any
time you're free to visit me here.

I.Cribdon

Undated, for I'd lost track of time at King Edward's and had no subsequent reason to concern myself with such matters, I sealed an envelope addressed to RMA Woolwich, took it up the road to Hampstead Village and joined the queue at the local Post Office where I bought a penny stamp, before dropping Grenville's letter in the adjacent pillar box.

It was here that I experienced an iconic incident of the Great War when an agitated, middle-aged woman demanded to know why I was not in uniform and, without waiting for a reply, presented me with a white feather before storming off to hunt down another cowardly young man.

My first impulse was to unleash Sarn't Cribdon's Wrath of God, a terrifying experience for all but the most hardened soldier, but wisely thought better of it. For aught I knew, the poor woman had just received an even more terrifying telegram that began: "It is my painful duty to inform you…" Ending with: "The Army Council expresses its sympathy and regret at your loss." So, instead, I politely thanked her for the unwanted gift and continued on my way.

The following morning, by now changed back into uniform to prevent my civvies from becoming soiled on the Heath's dusty tracks between wartime cattle pastures and sheep folds, the same woman happened to be coming towards me, towed along by a cocker spaniel. Her embarrassment was painful to behold as I switched my cane to the other hand, touched the peak of my cap, added a polite nod of recognition, and continued around Millfield Pond.

What else could I do? As Aunt Lucinda had never failed to impress upon me during my sulky, petulant moments at Tralee House; "'To err is human, to forgive divine.' And don't you forget it, young fella'm'lad!" Though, of course, I often did and shamefully still do, from time to time.

Meanwhile, Grenville had received my note, telegraphed his intention to visit the following day, and duly drove up in a Humber staff car befitting a two-pip colonel as he now was, with scarlet and gold thread collar-patches, as well as the cherry red ribbon of a CB worn in pride of place on his tunic.

"My! You have gone up in the world!" he laughed, inspecting me as much as I was inspecting him, for the last time we'd met I had still been a newly fledged one-pip RFC observer/air gunner, but was now an Intelligence Corps Captain on the Staff.

We moved into the conservatory where Mrs Williams served nettle tea and grey, wartime economy scones split with homemade, homegrown plum jam, before bustling off to feed the army driver, comfortably seated at her kitchen table.

Grenville waited until she was safely out of earshot before giving me an enquiring look. "So, how are you keeping…?"

I sensed what he was alluding to. He had been quick to congratulate me when the *Times* announced my wedding to Sandra Nobury and was the very first to send a letter of condolence - as a good friend would - when the same newspaper reported her death in action.

"Oh, you know how it is?" I shrugged. "Some days are better than others, but what's with these field exercises in Norfolk?" I was determined to steer the conversation onto neutral ground, to spare him the embarrassment of reporting a happier marriage than his first one. "Weren't you supposed to be training young sappers…?"

"That didn't last long. We'll need all the field engineers we can muster, paired with the Tank Regiment, to consolidate the gains that RAF machines will bomb ahead of our mechanised thrusts."

"Oh?" I let my unspoken question linger while he decided how much to reveal, how much to conceal.

The laurel green collar tabs tipped the balance in my favour. "Anyhow, you must know more about *Harvester* than I do," he continued "so will have already seen how, instead of throwing thousands of men and millions of shells at entrenched barbed wire, our synchronised, all-arms attacks are about to punch the Kaiser clean out of the ring…!"

This was news to me and, I thought, improbably optimistic with Oskar von Hutier's storm troops within grasp of Amiens' railway yards and workshops, but I didn't have the heart to say so as Grenville sat back and shared his usual, kindly smile. "Anyhow, let's speak of happier days to come. You made quite an impression on the Godwins, bless 'em! 'That young lad from Horse Strayuh, knowed a thing or two!' High praise indeed! They're looking forward to your return as much as I am…"

And for the next hour or so we swapped fishermen's tales of memorable days on Victoria and Tasmania's dashing forest streams and icy mountain tarns versus the Itchen and Test's slower, more mysteriously moving waters.

I think it fair to say that my older friend was as sad as I was to part company when he finally rose, shook hands, and drove off to resume his part in whatever *Harvester* was.

147

My return to duty came sooner than expected, when a War Office despatch rider delivered Baxter's decrypted telegram alerting me to Mr Knight's arrival at the Savoy, tomorrow afternoon, for which I must be ready beforehand.

Now, instead of spending the day fossicking around Highgate Cemetery, looking for Karl Marx's grave – as suggested in Baxter's earlier note - I could focus on more immediate matters than the dead author of some badly printed, poorly translated pamphlets left on my bedside table.

How anyone hoped to ignite a world revolution with flabby stuff like: "Religion is the sigh of the oppressed creature, the heart of a heartless world, and the soul of soulless conditions. It is the opium of the masses," was beyond my understanding. Far more incendiary was *La Marseillaise* that Aunt Lucinda would chant to demonstrate the power of words to rouse the spirit with its stirring call to arms against invading tyrants, and roaring threats to irrigate the fields of France with their foul blood!

Rouget de Lille's immortal anthem had been a demolition charge under *le Ancien Régime*, whereas Karl Marx's Germanic philosophising was not even a damp squib in our modern world. Or so it seemed to me at the time, clear evidence of how much I still had to learn as I packed my bag while Mrs Williams telephoned for a taxi to Hampstead Village railway station.

The Tube, as Londoners call their network of underground railway lines, delivered me to Charing Cross about twenty minutes later. Then, bag in one fist, cane in the other, I climbed up to ground level and turned left onto the Strand, limping a short distance to Coutts Bank where I withdrew ten pounds from my army account, there being no way an hotel would honour my cheques signed by a civilian clerk.

I set off with a leaden heart towards the Savoy on the other side of the road, glumly wishing that General Monash had chosen some other address for his illicit romp. Sandra's spirit, forever present, would be doubly so at the place where we should have celebrated our wedding breakfast, not her wake. Accordingly, it was a morose young man who wrote *Mr Ian Page, 2 Merton Lane, Hampstead* in the Reception Desk register.

Baxter had ensured I was expected and that everything was in order as a real page carried my bag to the lift, then to a top floor room which, by eerie coincidence either was, or very nearly was the one that Claude Monet chose to set up his easel on foggy afternoons overlooking the Thames.

This I deduced by comparing the actual views, from my window, with memories of those on display at Tralee House; further instances of Aunt Lucinda's shrewd partnership with Richard d'Oyly Carte, William Gilbert, and Arthur Sullivan when they pooled their funds to build the Savoy Hôtel and its adjacent theatre. An arrangement that empowered her to settle Monet's accommodation account by acquiring a good selection of his canvases for her future Australian home.

A veil will be drawn over the next few days when I resume my recordings for Frances. What General Monash may or may not have done in the privacy of his room, five doors along the corridor from mine, was nobody's business but his. Nowadays, he enjoys a posthumous reputation as Australia's greatest military leader, and if revisionist historians or prurient biographers wish to exhume his darker side for public fun and private profit, they will get no help from me!

Instead, my first task was to inform Geoffrey Clarke that I would either be resting up in my room, for I was still not fully recovered after the motorbike crash, or downstairs with my sketchbook. A young man seated alone in a public space, imagining he was the THL whose monogrammed crayon drawings of *le Moulin Rouge* decorated the dining room at Tralee House, was bound to attract the attention of young women with too much lipstick and too little clothing under their fake fur coats.

I was polite in my refusals, much as Henri de Toulouse-Lautrec would have been had the Savoy's American Bar been *le Divan Japonais Café-Concert*. Earning a crust on London's cruel streets was hard enough without the cuffs and rebuffs of those more comfortably situated than these poor souls. However, none of them was selling anything I wanted. The enshrined memories of Alexandria were sufficient for my needs and would remain so for many a long and lonely year to come.

In the event, my only female company during that stay was "Mrs Knight," when "Mr Knight" invited me to share luncheon with them. I shall leave it for others to comment upon Lizette Bentwich's minor role in the Great War, but what I can say is that she had the gift of laughter and light-hearted teasing that General Monash needed at a time of great stress and uncertainty, both in his private life and military one.

The promotion to temporary command of the Australian Corps was based upon seniority, but with so many enemies undermining his reputation, and a prime minister *en route* to London with a letter of dismissal, he was on borrowed time.

Clearly there was more to this luncheon than her amiable banter and *sole meunière* cooked to perfection, with a glass of excellent Chablis to cleanse the palate before raspberry tart and cream. However, Monash tactfully waited until Miss Bentwich went off to do some shopping at Selfridges' before getting down to business.

"Tell me, Ian, have you maintained contact with Lord Nobury?"

"Yes sir."

"Sufficient to arrange a meeting at short notice?" He continued, coming straight to the point.

"I believe so."

"Then kindly inform His Lordship there are matters that Cabinet needs to be made aware of, but which are being deliberately withheld from them." He hesitated. "You understand?"

"Yes sir." I paused, carefully weighing my next few words. "There's reason to think he will welcome the opportunity to speak with you..."

"Oh?" Monash could hardly contain his excitement. "Why is that?"

"During a visit to King Edward's, to discuss family business, he was curious to know what others thought of you, in Melbourne, 'before his true character was cloaked in khaki and gold braid...'"

"How did you reply?"

"I said, I thought it was bad form for one gentleman to gossip about another, behind his back."

"Well done."

Shortly afterwards, I went up to my room, took a quarto sheet of headed notepaper from the writing desk, and uncapped my fountain pen again:

The Savoy Hôtel
London

My Lord.

Major General Sir John Monash is presently at this address, incognito, and would value the opportunity of speaking with you in private.

If there is a convenient time, kindly inform me by leaving a message for "Mr Page" and I shall make the necessary arrangements.

I have the honour to be Your Lordship's attentive servant.

Ian Cribdon.

I sealed it in a matching envelope, went down to the Concierge and asked that it be immediately despatched by messenger. One glance at the handwritten address - *The Right Honourable Earl Nobury KStP, GCStJ, PC, Berkeley Square* – earned me a bow that bordered on an obsequious crouch.

There was no reason to expect a reply within the next day or so, given the gravity of Cabinet's concerns at this stage of the Great War, so I was astonished when a hurriedly scribbled note, on a sheet torn from a jotting pad, was delivered to my door, two hours later:

My Dear Ian.

Kindly accompany Sir John to dinner at 8 o'clock tonight, en famille, where I shall be pleased to hear what he wishes to impart.

Nobury.

I phoned through to General Monash's room where, to judge from his grumpy tone, I had just interrupted whatever he and Miss Bentwich were enjoying. However, his attitude brightened when I told him where and with whom he would be dining tonight. True to form, his first thoughts were to hire a full evening dress with silk top hat and opera cloak, but I insisted that the meeting would be informal and therefore a plain business suit was quite sufficient.

I am not sure he entirely believed it, being too much of a showman not to want to display his medals and order of knighthood, until he saw me in my clerk's civvies, holding the taxi door open for him to get aboard first. During our short drive to Berkeley Square, I sensed an outsiders' hunger for acceptance and suspected that, in imagination, he was once again Dux of Scotch College, being summoned to the headmaster's study to receive an accolade or reward.

Custom required we arrived five minutes before the hour and were shown past the Gainsboroughs, into the room where I first confronted what I'd thought was a hostile reception. It was a similar scene now, except that James was in France, and it was my responsibility to introduce General Monash to the Earl and Countess, both of whom were the embodiment of gracious dignity as we lightly conversed until dinner was served.

I would bet a pound to a penny that he never expected to share a frugal, wartime rationed meal of potatoes, cabbage, and corned brisket at a nobleman's table – especially after dining on the Savoy's relative abundance – but I'd say it set the tone for more serious matters, upstairs, while the Countess and I took nettle tea in the withdrawing room, downstairs.

This was the first time that she and I had been alone together, and it was a strained experience for both of us. After a brief enquiry about my treatment at King Edward's, which I could not praise highly enough, she fixed me with a sad, enquiring smile: "Tell me, Ian, were you and Sandra lovers? And I don't just mean 'in love'?"

"Yes, ma'am." I surprised myself with the speed and frankness of this proud reply. "We were."

To my even greater surprise, instead of berating me for seducing her eldest daughter, she simply replied: "I'm glad."

148

That evening's encounter was probably as far up the social ladder as my GOC had climbed, thus far, and was clearly astonished to discover that a British noble had brains; unsurprising, given the average Australian's opinion of those we jealously imagine are inbred Chinless Chumleigh chumps.

"He understood every move I made," Monash continued expansively as we drove back to the Savoy, "and required to hear, in detail, why I chose certain options during my attack on Messines Ridge. But when he got out the Ancre Valley map, I swear he pinpointed every artillery piece. I told him straight; I could've used him on my staff! To which he replied that he must've acquired the knack on Kitchener's, during their Soudan Campaign -!"

My hope was that Monash had not overplayed his hand, for I wished him every success and got no joy from seeing an old family friend sabotage his chances of securing the highest Australian command. My other hope was that Baxter had been right when he said that Lord Nobury would see through the brassy self-promotion that was a protective shell around an otherwise brilliantly ordered mind and penetrating intellect.

Upon arrival at our hotel, Monash gave me a firm handshake for arranging this meeting at such short notice, then bounded upstairs to replay it with Miss Bentwich while I went into the American Bar to order a whiskey sour, a cocktail I was keen to explore after the unimaginative drinks list of a frontline officers' mess.

By now I was sufficiently self-aware to recognise alcoholism at a time when many hundreds of thousands of other young men were in a similar plight, for one easily became addicted to SDR rum when about to clamber up a trench ladder into No Man's Land or needed to settle the nerves with a glug of Scotch before taking-off to fight the swooping rattle of enemy fire above the Western Front.

However, I had succeeded in deluding myself that cocktails were comparatively benign, containing less alcohol, more fruit juice, and a dash of harmless flavourings. Which was true enough, provided one kept to a single glass, or maybe two, but the third, fourth, fifth, and sixth were never more than clicked fingers away in the American Bar.

Opened during the last years of Queen Victoria's reign, for visiting millionaires with marriageable daughters on the prowl for an aristocratic title, it soon became The Place where The Young Crowd shimmied to the latest ragtime tunes from across the Atlantic, while their parents sedately fox-trotted around the adjacent ballroom. An historical aside sure to amuse Frances, it was here that Bertangles' chatelaine, the then-young *Comtesse de Clermont-Tonnerre*, scandalised London's High Society by becoming the first lady of rank to puff a cigarette in public. *Quelle horreur!*

That was twenty-odd years before my time and the air was now thick with aromatic smoke, much of it from boisterous US Army officers on leave – or furlough, as they called it – in England. One of them had commandeered the piano and was entertaining us with a selection of Broadway melodies, including

Over There, which declared that the Yanks were coming, and that the war would not be over till they were over here in Europe. Their innocent exuberance reminded me a lot of my own people's high spirits before Gallipoli, the Somme, and Flanders sobered us up.

Settling into a corner seat, prepared to blind-sketch interesting faces on a cartridge paper block held in my lap, I still could not help fearing that Monash had overplayed his hand with Lord Nobury.

For the more I pondered, the more I wondered if he was being tested for something other than command of the Australian Army Corps. Whether he passed muster or not would largely depend on how well he controlled his urge to puff his opinions with men who instinctively recoil from brash behaviour, preferring instead to wrap their thoughts inside the foggy speech that so infuriated my wife whenever she compared it with German's logical grammar and orderly syntax.

Not for the first or last time, I was reminded how lovingly Sandra had coached me in the understated nuances of the British Upper Class, and how easily an outsider could mistake their restraint for dim-witted disinterest. It was a timely warning not to mistake politeness for weakness, but to recognise it as a "cultural safety-catch" - her description, not mine – on a loaded magazine of coldblooded Anglo-Norman violence that more excitable races often failed to recognise until it was too late to avert the consequences.

As she'd reminded me in Alex': "We did not keep our heads off the Tower of London's chopping block during the Tudor Terror; emerge on the winning side of the English Civil War; overthrow one king and put another on the throne; master political intrigue during an Age of Revolutions; all the while acquiring the largest empire the world has ever known, just by luck alone, Darling..."

However, this evening, General Monash was of more immediate concern as I signalled a third whiskey sour. I took my duties seriously as his Praetorian Guard - Baxter's description, not mine – because, upon closer acquaintance, I recognised a risky embodiment of contradictions, not the least his hunger for acceptance by the British Officer Corps.

A yearning that shaped his every move, from the fiercely trimmed military moustache to the ruthless dieting that stripped nearly two stone off his waistline, the better to fit-in at staff conferences where an appraising glance could make or break a reputation.

And yet, at heart he remained a tough, practical, Australian civil engineer who had overseen gangs of railway navvies blasting tunnels, building viaducts, laying track across Victoria's High Country.

There was no way a pukka British major general would have loaned his bedroll to an exhausted three-pip, with orders to get some rest, whereas Monash had done that for me without a moment's hesitation, at Franvillers. This one simple act illuminated his true character more than anything else and I'd made an especial point of emphasising it when speaking with Lord Nobury at King Edward's Hospital.

I had also added that the secret of the Monash Touch was his common touch, one that 3 Division's troops intuitively recognised, confident that their lives were in the steady hands of a commander who would never sacrifice them on showy, futile stunts.

Concerned and thoughtful I eventually retired for the night, awakening somewhat later than usual before going down to the Savoy Grill for whatever their Full English Breakfast amounted to in wartime.

I was about to tuck into a grilled mock-pork sausage when one of the staff approached me with a handwritten note:

My Dear Cribdon.

*I shall be attending to personal
business for the rest of today.*

*Feel free to amuse yourself as best
you please.*

J.M.

I enquired if Mr Knight had gone out alone or been accompanied by Mrs Knight? The answer confirmed my suspicion that General Monash's private business most likely included a visit to Selfridges' department store, where Miss Bentwich had her eye on a couple of new dresses, and tickets to the Alhambra Theatre, Leicester Square, for a matinee performance of *The Bing Boys*. This I inferred from the wistful way in which she had teased her married lover over lunch, humming that show's hit-song, *If You Were the Only Girl in the World*, with her own refrain: "If I were the only girl in your world…"

Two slices of Victory Loaf toast, a smear of crab apple marmalade, and I now had the rest of the day to do as much or as little as I pleased. For a short while I considered another visit to the National Gallery, but its associations were too painful, as they were for the rest of London's West End, between the Savoy and Berkeley Square.

However, I had long been intrigued by the colourful tales Mama told of life in London's East End: "Wot larks we yewster get up to! Fings was allus such fun in them dayz…!" she would say with mingled tears of joy and sadness, reliving her modest ascent from *Marvo the Magician*'s sawn-in-half assistant, at Nutley's Music Hall, to leader of *Six Saucy Cyclettes*, an all-female troupe of trick bicyclists on tour with Fitzgerald's Circus in the Australasian Colonies, a frugal career that ended when she was wooed and won by "Champagne Charley" Braithwaite, the ne'er do well scion of a New South Wales' pastoral dynasty.

"Lun'nen's such fun! Wiv'orl them nice stalls in the Shadwell Market, lit up a'nights, where thru'pence buys wha'ever tickles yer fancy!" Wistful memories relived during one of Sydney's summer heatwaves, when Circular Quay bubbled with fermenting filth and pockets of methane gas sporadically exploded in neglected cesspits, often demolishing the rickety dunnies built above them.

Maggie Stubbs, exiled half the world away from Home, and bright enough to know what a mess she'd made of her crumpled little life, mercifully never knew how short it would be.

Recalling those early years, I believe she saw in her only child a return ticket to the bright lights and imagined splendours of Theatrical London. This she strove to attain by coaching me as a trick-cyclist, with limited success as I kept wobbling off the handlebars.

Nor was I much use as the straight man in a comedy duo entitled *Maggsy & Bill* with Mama using me as the foil for wheezers like: "'Ow many tickles it takes t'make an octopus larf?" Answer: "Ten-tickles!" And: "Why's a dog like a tree?" Answer: "Becozz they both loses their bark when they's dead!" However,

I did show promise as what used to be called a Recitationist, declaiming topical ditties like: "You's prob'ly wonderin' who I iz! And at my slim figure you giggle an' squiz! At once yor doubts I'll gladly destroy! I'm Poor Bob, the Charity Boy!" Then, ever onward and downward through the hulks to a convict's fate in Van Diemen's Land: "Fer nickin' a shillin' -!"

These, and many another sad memory, accompanied me as I caught a crowded electric tram to the Tower of London, the easternmost bastion of the old Medieval City beyond which sprawled the festering slums and thieves' kitchens of more recent centuries.

It would not have surprised me to find a customs barrier and passport control waiting for us, so real was the sense of passing from one land to another as I changed lines at St Katharine's Docks and, steel wheels squealing along iron rails, shuddered and shook into the East End along the notorious Ratcliffe Highway to Limehouse, a location familiar to every reader of Sherlock Holmes' adventures with their descriptions of foggy streets, clattering Hansom cabs, and Oriental opium dens.

Like Conan Doyle's evocative word-pictures, it required no great power of the imagination to realise that I was in another world as the tram growled past towering warehouses serving Tobacco Wharf and Newlands Quay, Atlantic Wharf and Free Trade Dock, with intermittent glimpses of the River Thames fringed by crane jibs nodding over moored tiers of rusty tramp steamers and quite a few three-masted schooners, each having woven its way through the U-boat blockade, and must do so again, and again, until its luck ran out.

As a soldier I gave scant thought to the ordeals "those who go down to the sea in ships and do their business upon great waters" - as one of King David's Psalms proclaims – had to stoically endure if we were to be kept supplied with rations and reinforcements.

A high proportion of the tramps' crews were Lascar stokers from the Indian Ocean and Bay of Bengal. Slender brown men whose devotion to duty - shovelling coal into hellish engine room furnaces, aware who would be the first to drown when their ship hit a mine or was torpedoed – never rated a mention in the Great War's official histories, an omission I still find impossible to condone.

However, what most forcefully struck me as I got off the tram at Limehouse Basin, was how very much like Gulliver in Lilliput I must have seemed to the grimy midgets jostling past. Not that I am tall by Australian standards but here, in the East End of the Empire's capital, I stood head and shoulders above its malnourished denizens. For whereas London's well-to-do citizens were strolling about in the West End's bright sunshine, enjoying a balmy summer's day, five miles downstream a permanent pall of coalsmoke and industrial haze had turned that sun into a dull orange ball that gave neither light, nor warmth, nor health to those forced to scratch their meagre livings below it.

This was another scene reminiscent of those other Impressionist paintings at Tralee House. Especially the Pissarro depicting London street-urchins of the 1870s, playing hopscotch while a moustachioed Italian barrel organist ground out a tinkly tune, the grinder's captive monkey in its tight red jacket and black fez cap, outstretched paw gripping a tin mug, begging for farthings and ha'pence, a look of sad bewilderment on its wizened little face as carefree young humans capered about in the pallid sunlight.

A generation or so later, those young East Enders who'd survived its sporadic outbreaks of typhoid, and cholera, and chronic malnourishment, were now stunted adults in the fourth year of a Great War where few had reason to dance or laugh.

I never learned if Maggie Stubb's fond memories of Cockney costermongers gaily ribbing each other in street markets lit by the glare of carbide lamps or singing perky ditties in ale houses like Wapping's *Prospect of Whitby*, ever returned after the Armistice, for this was to be my first and last visit to the maternal homeland.

During the next few hours, I limped along filthy pavements that reminded me of Cairo without its vibrant, sunlit chaos. Past sordid lodgings that rented by the hour, and garish gin palaces overflowing with drunks. Never once seeing Stubbs on a shopfront or billboard. Several times I asked, but although my questions were clearly understood, I was unable to understand the plaintive yowls, swallowed vowels, and snotty snuffles of their replies. For aught I knew, these grimy little Britons were speaking Chaucer's English.

Bursting for a leak, with no public urinals to be found, I did what other men were doing and faced a corner wall near *Jamrach's Animal Emporium*, where newly arrived sailors sold their tropical birds and reptiles for the price of a booze-up and tried not to get my shoes wet; how the local womenfolk fared, I cannot imagine, nor do I wish to.

Hungry, in need of a sit down to rest my leg, I paid sixpence to enter the music hall annexe of a pub called *The Grapes* - pronounced *The Gripes* - where I lunched on half a pint of bitter and a bowl of jellied eels, both of which I enjoyed immensely.

Meanwhile, on a bare wooden scaffold that doubled as a stage, a rosy nosed comedian in a flashy, bookmakers' suit and bright green bowler hat, raised gusts of coarse laughter with threadbare jokes like: "There's a posh geezer up the West End so fat you could looberkate yer cart's wheels wiv 'is shadder!" And: "Didja 'ear about the Irishman wot entered the scrapyard an' sed, 'Begorrah! Does yez buy rags and bones?' To which the yardman arnserd, 'Indeed I do!' To which Paddy sez, 'Then be puttin' me up on the scales -!'"

I understood the dark fears that prompted such cruel humour when dodging a policeman's truncheon, or a debt collector's cosh, or both.

It was inevitable that I would catch the eye of a flower girl, the polite name for a prostitute who could not be arrested for soliciting when all she had done was offer a bunch of tatty blooms for a few pence, albeit hinting at what other delights a florin could buy; an unsavoury detail that Mr Shaw glossed over when writing Eliza Doolittle into his implausible stage play *Pygmalion*.

I paid a fair price for the freshest bunch of violets but declined her other wares and limped a short distance westward along Shadwell Road to St Paul's church and, inside its dimly lit space, found memorials to, and thank-offerings from, long-dead sea captains who had survived their perilous voyages to safely berth on Shadwell Basin.

Approaching the altar, I placed my flowers at the foot of a polished brass crucifix, bowed my head, and–

"May I ask why you're doing that?"

I turned sharply, not having noticed the Sacristan standing in his Vestry door. "It's the best I can do for her now," I replied simply.

"Who?"

"My Mum."

"Oh?"

"She came from somewhere near here."

"But not you?"

"No. Melbourne. Australia."

"A soldier?"

"Yes."

He sensed my reluctance to elaborate any further and wished me Godspeed as I left, only pausing to fold a ten-shilling note into the Poor Box.

The tram ride back to the Tower allowed me ample time to review the ingrained squalor and despair I had seen, and felt, and smelt.

Even at our worst moments, skulking among the Rocks that overlook Sydney Cove, there was always a hope of better things to come, provided we kept our wits sharp at a time when a likely lad could sign aboard a trading schooner and start anew in the South Sea Islands, or hop the rattler to seek his fortune along the Outback's railway tracks.

Australia was still a land of opportunity for those willing to give life a go and learn from their mistakes. The chances were fair to middling that Poor Bob the Charity Boy, having done his time and kept his nose clean in what is nowadays Tasmania, died a comparatively prosperous free citizen, worth far more than the stolen shilling that sent him halfway around the world to a brighter future than he would have ever known, mired in the East End's dispiriting poverty.

149

Emotionally exhausted after visiting an England I'd read about in novels, but had never really believed existed until now, I retired early to bed and fell into deep, dreamless void for the first time in many a long while until the Night Porter telephoned from Reception.

Cursing fluently, for dawn was barely a glow on the horizon as a million less fortunate men stood-to in their trenches on both sides of the Western Front, I learned that a priority telegram was on its way up to my room.

Waiting at the door, I tipped the page and returned to the small writing desk where I slashed open a buff-coloured envelope and flicked out a flimsy:

> PROCEED WITH JM TO GHQ
> MONTREUIL FOR CONFERENCE
> 1800HRS THIS EVENING STOP
> CLARKE TO SUPPLY REQUIRED
> PAPERS 0800HRS ENDIT BAXTER

My wristlet watch read 0510 hours, far too early to disturb General Monash and his bedmate so, instead, I tackled yesterday's *Times* crossword to stay awake until it was time to inform him that he had an appointment with Field Marshal Haig's staff at six o'clock this afternoon, on the other side of the English Channel.

I braced for verbal fireworks when he sleepily answered the telephone, but I'd misjudged the man; he was fine spirits when we met in the Grill for an early breakfast, both in uniform now.

"Good morning, gentlemen." Clarke clicked to a halt and saluted, spot on 0800 hours as we finished our coffee.

"'Morning."

"These are your orders for transport to Folkestone where you will join the official party aboard *HMS Afridi*." He handed over a packet of travel warrants and passes that Monash motioned for me to carry. "Upon arrival at Boulogne you will be conveyed directly to GHQ, arriving no later than 1730 for the preparatory briefing. Sir."

"Thank you, Mr Clarke. Is there anything else I need to be appraised of?"

"No sir. Mr Baxter has everything in hand."

"Very well. Proceed."

"Yes sir. This way gentlemen."

As General Monash's aide-de-camp, I had already settled our accounts and filed their receipts for the Divisional Paymaster, so there was nothing more to be done as we marched across the foyer, acknowledged the doorman's doffed top hat, and got aboard a Vauxhall staff car parked at the kerb, after taking our leave of Captain Clarke.

"What d'you make of this summons?" Monash enquired as we set off through heavy traffic towards London Bridge, a major general's red pennant fluttering urgently on our offside mudguard.

"Hard to tell, sir," I replied, stifling a yawn. "There's been no indication that any of our brigades are under attack. And if they were, would you not have been recalled directly to Bertangles?"

"Quite."

We fell silent, each alone with our thoughts and conjectures about what the next several hours held in store as we crossed the Thames and sped southeastwards through London's increasingly leafier suburbs.

Our driver had done this trip before and there was no need for him to consult a map or gazetteer to find his way into the Kentish countryside I remembered from a previous journey. Not so many months ago. When I still envisaged myself as a happily married landscape artist. With his studio in a quaint farmhouse. Among the hop fields. Or as a banker. With a country manor. For his family's weekend escapes. Teaching our children how to shoot. And trap. And cook. Wild game -

I suppressed these and other raw memories as we hurried through Maidstone, crossed the Downs at Ashford, and motored into Folkestone Docks, a fortified camp since 1914. An MP sergeant bawled out the guard as our two-star pennant fluttered to a stop on the hardstanding. Monash coolly acknowledged the synchronised smack of open palms on rifle butts while I displayed our papers authorising us to proceed through the barbed wire to where *HMS Afridi* of the Dover Patrol was readying for another cross-Channel dash.

One of the Royal Navy's new, Tribal Class destroyers, *Afridi*'s steam turbines could raise 33 knots, just enough to outpace the Imperial German Navy's G/6D torpedo, making her an ideal vessel for the VIP shuttle service between England and France.

Going aboard, I was politely but firmly detached from General Monash who alone was allowed into the wardroom where senior brass hats, and a gaggle of politicians were being hosted by the Royal Navy. Instead, we Joes were shooed down to the midshipmen's overcrowded gunroom and offered tots of pink gin to settle our stomachs before the destroyer cast off and charged from behind Folkestone's anti-torpedo netting, out onto the Channel's choppy waves.

In an historical aside for Frances, this was my first glimpse of the British Prime Minister, and I was not greatly impressed by what little I saw of him. There was something about the fellow that reminded me of "Champagne Charley's" ruinous betting schemes and shabby confidence tricks. Later events substantiated this opinion when Lloyd-George published his *War Memoirs*, by which time Field Marshal Haig was safely dead and unable to refute the PM's venomous slanders or counter his faint praise for our armies' epic achievements during the last hundred days of victorious battles before the Armistice on 11th November 1918.

The gin seemed to work, for only a few of us needed the galvanised buckets stationed around the gunroom as *Afridi* zig-zagged across the Narrows to Boulogne, where a French military band played the English notables ashore with *Le Regiment de Sambre et Meuse*, bugles, and drums defiantly loud and proud.

Lloyd-George and his political henchmen scurried aboard their limousines and shot off, leaving the rest of us to muddle along as best we could. Fortunately, Clarke was right, Baxter had organised transport for the last leg of today's magical mystery tour - as it seemed to me - on our way to Montreuil sur Mer, an odd name for a place several miles inland from the Channel coast.

This was my first visit to GHQ since its relocation from St Omer to a town halfway along the telegraph line between London and Paris where Marshal Foch was having to balance the competing interests of two traditional enemies, Britain, and France.

Montreuil must have been a neat little town in peacetime, but since 1916 every square inch of its available space was crowded with Nissen huts, mechanical workshops, supply dumps and tented cantonments, inside and outside its sturdy brick ramparts built during the 1500s, when this was the turbulent frontier between the Kingdom of France and the Hapsburg Empire's Netherlands. Strengthened a century later by the Sun King's military engineering genius, Marshal Vauban, his bastions, and outworks were still giving good service in 1918, as emplacements for ack-ack batteries and searchlight units on high alert against Gotha bombers based in Belgium.

Baxter was anxiously awaiting our arrival on the forecourt of an old military academy, now the central nervous system for one million British and Imperial troops manning our northern stretch of the Western Front.

He snapped a crisp salute at Monash and then faced me: "Good to see you back, Ian. We'll catch up later. Billeting's a bit tight but I've arranged a bed. Sign in at the Mess and they'll show you where to go." This was his politely oblique way of saying that my services were not required yet, as he and the acting-GOC Australian Corps marched off towards GHQ, deep in discussion.

I presented my card to the Mess Secretary, a pre-war custom that was still viewed favourably although no longer insisted upon, mostly because not all newly commissioned officers lived long enough to get their cards engraved and printed.

A mess steward took my valise and led the way across the main building's rear yard towards a nearby stable block; I did not realise it yet, but this was deluxe accommodation at General Head Quarters where most others of my rank had to make do with a cramped tin hut or tent.

"'Ere you go sir!" We halted at the solid oak door of what had been one of the stable's feed stores until commandeered by the British Army. "Ta ever so much -!" He palmed my sixpence while I read a plain white card thumbtacked to the door:

Captain the Honorable James Nobury MC
Royal Dublin Fusiliers

"Er, I 'ope it's a'right, sir! Um, you know 'im...?"
"He's my brother-in-law."
"Blimey!"

I went in and looked around at the rustic timberwork, the swept cobbled floor, the antique wooden mangers now serving as improvised wardrobes for our uniforms and kit. Also, two made-up camp beds, one with a handwritten note on its pillow:

> *Baxter says you need a billet.*
> *If you don't mind sharing mine*
> *I'd be glad of your company.*
>
> *J.*

As I would be glad of his, I thought, kicking off my boots and stretching out for a short doze after a long day's travel. Instead, I must have fallen fast asleep for the next thing I can remember was James giving my shoulder an insistent shake. "Wakey-wakey, rise and shine!"

"Gnnh?" I blinked blearily. "Whu'zup?"

"Mess Call."

"Hnnph." I wearily half-rolled off the bed, laced my boots, and stood to shake hands. "Good to see you mate."

"You, too. Mate." He meant it and I could tell he was secretly pleased to be addressed as if he were one of our more egalitarian Australian Army Corps, for I had not forgotten his description of privileged birth as a golden ball and chain that limited his choices and chances in life. But, by addressing him in our breezy, informal manner, I was in effect appointing him an honorary Digger, a title to be treasured far more his unearned Honourable.

With the innate kindness I associated with memories of his sister, he adjusted his pace to my slower tread across the stable yard towards the main building, as dusk settled over Northern France and a stiff breeze carried the persistent grumble of distant artillery fire.

"So, what's it like in the Gilded Cage?" I quipped, pausing to glance up at the citadel's silhouetted turrets and steeply pitched rooflines.

"I'll let you know when I've been here long enough to form an opinion," he replied.

"Oh?"

"Most of my time is spent shuttling between Montreuil and Chaumont, *en liaison avec* the American Expeditionary Force," he explained.

"Strewth! How did you jag that one?"

"Not the slightest idea!" he chuckled. "But having a cousin married to the daughter of a toothpaste millionaire, probably made someone imagine I was an authority on Anglo-American relations."

"And are you…?"

"Hardly!" He shook his head. "They're an odd lot. On the one hand, rabid anti-monarchists who refer to the 'Royal British Army' as 'Redcoats.' On the other hand," his voice darkened, "swift to put 'Lord Nobury' on display as if I were their regimental mascot."

I let the subject drop as we entered GHQ's Officers' Mess, a collegial dining hall that had long since outgrown the pre-war military academy's requirements.

Field Marshal Haig dined in solitary splendour, or with visiting grandees, at Beaurepaire his personal château a short distance away. Below him dined the senior brass hats, served by their own domestic staff in a suite of rooms adjacent to Montreuil's main hall. The rest of us, Joes and middle ranks alike, lined up at the buffet before competing for vacant seats at crowded trestle tables.

James and I joined the queue and were soon in conversation with several other young men, mostly red-tabbed staffers who seemed genuinely delighted to see him, which told me a great deal about the man I'd instinctively liked from the moment we first met at Berkeley Square, but only now was getting to know better.

He had no hesitation introducing me as family, doubtless raising a few eyebrows as his friends shook hands of this strange hybrid who wore a British tunic with green collar tabs, but Australian corduroy breeches and khaki puttees over beetle crusher boots. The half-wing and MC, DCM ribbons added to their confusion as they made room for me to go first and load my tray with a bowl of Brown Windsor soup, a bread roll, steamed vegetables, and a slim cut of roast beef; better fare than we got in the trenches but well below our jealous imaginings of high life at GHQ, as I found a place on the bench opposite James.

"Baxter tells me you took a bit of a tumble," he remarked, between considered mouthfuls. "I do hope you were not too badly hurt?"

"Just a few bruises and cracked ribs."

"What happened?"

"What looked like a shallow puddle turned out to be somewhat deeper," I replied, forking a broad bean. "The mo'bike came off worst, though. But speaking of dramatic adventures," I continued, eyeing the new purple and white ribbon above his left breast pocket, "That never popped out of a Christmas cracker. Congratulations!"

"Thank you," and I swear he nearly blushed. "It is real," he added defensively, "not a 'Prince of Wales.'"

"'Never thought it was," I reassured him, aware of the widespread resentment when HRH got a Military Cross that others shed blood for, but which had been awarded to the King's eldest son for motoring up to the Front and graciously mingling with mud-bespattered troops while a Pathé kinematographer cranked film for next week's newsreel.

"A pillbox caused us a spot of bother at Poelcapelle," James explained simply. "Someone had to sort it out."

I have never destroyed a machine gun nest, armed only with a Mills' bomb and my service revolver, but I do have enough experience to picture the moment when the next Earl of Nobury crawled forward under daisy cutter bursts from a Zero Eight, and cleared the way for his men to resume their attack.

He may have said more but instead looked straight past me. I turned sharply and saw Baxter threading through the crowd, scanning left and right. James raised his hand: "Over here!"

Baxter glimpsed it, changed course, and steered towards us. "Well met, gentlemen!" He halted beside me. "Is there a chance we shall find three spare glasses in your quarters, Mr Nobury?"

"I'm certain we shall, sir."

"Splendid." I could feel Baxter's restrained excitement. "When you've finished your meal, let's put them to good use."

150

James led the way to our billet with his electric torch before striking a match to light the hurricane lantern on a table improvised from packing case lids and upended mortar bomb crates; the imagined luxuries of life at GHQ continued to prove less lavish than I'd previously thought.

"'Midst pleasures and palaces we may roam, be it ever so humble, there's no-o-o place like home...'" he announced with wry humour, trimming the lamp's wick to coax a flame while Baxter took a chilled Veuve Cliquot from his haversack, popped its cork and waited for our host to assemble three trench-raid trophy Pilsner glasses.

Baxter raised his. "Fallen comrades."

We clinked and drank.

James broke the silence after a reflective pause. "May I ask what we're celebrating, sir?"

"Is not the delight of your company sufficient?" the older man responded.

"I don't wish to imply an ulterior motive, but – !"

"No offence taken," Baxter cut the younger man short, with an understanding smile, "but allow me to mark the satisfactory conclusion of a devilish hard brief, during which there have been moments when it felt as if I were leading for the Crown with the Lord Chief Justice - in this matter Sir Douglas Haig – presiding over a testy court!" Baxter chuckled as the bubbly worked its subtle magic. "And yet, despite many a persuasive rebuttal and persistent denial, we have gained a favourable summary judgement..."

He perched himself at the end of my camp bed, raised his glass to the lamp flame, and studied beady threads of carbonic acid gas racing upwards behind a screen-printed image of Kaiser Bill superimposed on an Iron Cross and *Gott Mitt Uns* in red and black Gothic lettering. "Passing strange, is it not?" he continued, still thinking aloud. "When historians come to write their accounts of the Great War, few if any will record one of its most decisive victories."

James blinked uncertainly. "When and where was that?"

"A short while ago, in the C-in-C's study." Baxter cocked his other eyebrow. "You seem surprised?"

"I'm lost for words!"

"Not to worry. Suffice to say, General Rawlinson can now proceed with *Harvester*, albeit on a reduced scale, to appease its fretful nay-sayers."

My ears pricked up. "'*Harvester*'?"

"You've heard of it?"

"Phillip Grenville made a brief reference when he visited me at Hampstead. Nothing indiscreet," I added, quick to defend a friend's reputation, "just something about his sappers advancing with tanks and armoured cars, under air cover, while infantry mopped up and consolidated."

"A welcome reversal of your usual roles," Baxter observed drily.

"Indeed," I replied, "assuming it ever happens!"

"It will," he insisted, quietly, "despite stiff opposition from those more traditionally minded, to the idea of a 'new-fangled Air Force thing' stopping enemy reinforcements from reaching the battle, in time to affect its outcome."

"A not unreasonable concern." My restraint relaxed as the alcohol took effect and I visualised inevitable muddle and mistakes a thousand or more feet above the Front. "I wouldn't put too much reliance on observer/air gunners reading maps, shouting directions at their pilots, all the while fighting-off swarms of Fokkers…"

I sensed my brother-in-law's shock at what was probably his first exposure to the notorious Australian talent for voicing blunt opinions in polite company, with the added possibility that he'd misheard Anthony Fokker's surname. However, if either of us expected our superior officer to protest, we were disappointed. Instead, Baxter shared another of his imperturbable smiles. "Well said. But why d'you imagine such a combined operation has not been attempted before now? And why have we persisted with tactics the Duke of Wellington would have recognised, absent the poisonous gas, the barbed wire, the machine guns, the trenches?"

"No idea." I was defensively brief as this shrewd man unrolled his tobacco pouch.

"Be patient," he smiled again, seeming to read my mind, "first things first. Starting with two rival interests. On the one hand, a coalition of political cronies promoting peripheral campaigns in Bulgaria and Palestine until the American Expeditionary Force is ready to spearhead an Allied offensive next year in France, thus securing victory for the United States, with all that implies for our post-war loan repayments. To which end the PM has been instructed to tell his arch-nemesis, Sir Douglas, that the four reserve divisions currently in Britain, will not be going into action until the 1919 Spring Offensive."

"I didn't know that!" James, who was more politically astute than I at the time, sat bolt upright.

"You do now," Baxter remarked, loading his briar pipe, "and understand why you must be doubly alert to what our Transatlantic Cousins are doing, and saying, and plotting behind our backs at Chaumont…" This was the first inkling that my brother-in-law and I were both working for Intelligence and explained why he had been seconded to the AEF's Headquarters.

"On the other hand, there are those who believe we have sufficiently marked, learned, and inwardly digested the Somme's lessons to break the German Army before this winter -"

"Seriously?!" I interrupted, unable to believe what I was hearing.

"Why the doubts, Mr Cribdon?"

"It's bloody obvious," I frowned back. "If Fritz takes Amiens, we'll be suing for peace, not celebrating victory!"

"'If'," Baxter observed laconically, "as the Spartans, famed for their brevity of speech, told Phillip of Macedon when he thundered: 'If I conquer Lakonia, you will be destroyed, never to rise again!'"

"So?" I responded, for when push comes to shove, a modern Australian can be just as laconic and thrifty with words as were those Ancient Greeks.

"Be patient." Nothing one could say or do could dent this man's imperturbable composure. "General Rawlinson has been planning an all-arms battle ever since Birdwood took command of the Fifth Army. For despite deep differences of opinion, those at the highest levels of command are agreed upon one thing: the Empire will not stomach another Passchendaele.

"Equally, we must not allow General Pershing to claim that he won the Great War for the United States, with some trifling assistance from Britain and France, with all this would signify for Europe's future political map. Therefore, to be of any value, the fruits of victory must be harvested before this winter, not next spring, an interval of six months that will affect the next one hundred years." Baxter leaned forward to light his pipe by raising the lantern's chimney glass and drawing the flame across the briar's bowl. "Because." Puff. "1919." Puff. "Will be too dashed late."

"Too late for what?" James wondered aloud, stroking his chin.

"Consider this," Baxter replied, sitting back to draw on his pipe. "Barely a century ago, in 1815, after a coalition of European allies defeated Napoleon's ephemeral empire at Waterloo and set about recalibrating the Balance of Power —"

"Ah ha!" James clicked fingers, making mental connections I was unable to follow. "That's what's at stake?!"

"Quite so, Mr Nobury." Our mentor nodded his approval. "What happened shortly thereafter, at the Congress of Vienna, will happen again with temper tantrums, broken promises, backstairs intrigues aplenty as former-allies squabble over the spoils of war. Therefore, our task is to ensure that the British Empire wins the lion's share at the next peace conference, in much the same manner as your illustrious forefather the Third Earl did when he outfoxed Metternich over the 'Ionian Question,' at that previous collision of ambitions."

"Say again?" I queried, always uneasy whenever this cunning man spoke in riddles.

"It is no exaggeration to say that everything hinges upon how well the next two or three weeks play out for us," Baxter continued, ignoring my second interruption. "Until an hour ago, Rawlinson's masterplan still lacked a sufficiently meticulous, judicious, ruthless divisional commander to implement such 'recklessly experimental warfare,' as some have described our mechanised response to *Sturmtruppenkrieg*, absent General von Hutier's presiding genius.

"A short list of senior officers was considered to make good that deficiency, but only one embodies the necessary leadership qualities combined with proven experience of building railway viaducts, excavating dams, blasting tunnels through bedrock. Complex operations that resemble *Harvester* in that nothing can be left to chance, and everything must be done with mathematical exactitude. On time. On budget."

Baxter gestured with the pipestem for James and me to finish off the champagne as he stood to take his leave. "Sir John will soon require your services, Ian, pencil and notebook at the ready. Good luck and, ah, keep me posted…"

151

Which happened sooner than expected when an HQ runner delivered a short note from our General Officer Commanding, early next morning, ordering me to standby with a staff car at 0900 hours; this meant skipping breakfast if I was to get the Transport Pool's paperwork sorted and our petrol coupons issued in time.

Forewarned by Baxter's parting remark, I raided the stationery cupboard for a stock of shorthand notebooks, a fistful of HB pencils, and a nifty little sharpener that gave a much better writing point than one whittled with a jack knife.

My final stop was the Q-Store where I indented for a despatch rider's leather satchel, similar to the one lost between crashing Trusty and being lugged into a dressing station's dugout, to improvise a portable desk in the days ahead.

General Monash strode onto the forecourt as the Military Academy's clock struck nine, returned my salute and nodded for me to follow aboard a green camouflaged Crossley tourer, its canvas hood buckled down against unseasonably cool, showery weather. "Bertangles."

"S'uh!" Our WAAC driver stooped, cranked the motor, and set off through Hesdin and Bernaville towards the Australian Corps' HQ north of Amiens. In normal times, a journey that would have taken her a couple of hours to complete, but these times were anything but normal.

Fortunately, I had remembered to loop a corps commander's three-star pennon around the Crossley's stumpy metal flagstaff. This, plus our driver's insistently honk-honking horn, got us past the convoys of laden GS wagons, the sullen glares of tramping infantry, the clattering batteries of horse-drawn artillery, every man, every draught animal, every vehicle, every item of equipment, heading to the Front.

Neither General Monash nor I said much. In his case it was not hard to imagine what was on his mind. The planning and execution of an experimental, all-arms battle at this crucial juncture in the war, must have been a daunting prospect, even for a man of such prodigious self-confidence as the acting-GOC Australian Corps. Perhaps needing a distraction, he cleared his throat and glanced sideways: "I owe you belated condolences."

"Sir?"

"A recent letter, from home, described your great-aunt's funeral. A splendid affair, befitting a remarkable lady."

"Thank you, sir."

He hesitated before adding: "She intervened when my partner lost a large sum of the firm's money. Bankruptcy and dishonour were inevitable had not our doctor, yours too, brought the matter to her notice. Others extended loans at usurious rates of interest; her terms were a simple repayment of the principal within twelve months." He gave a dry cough. "One never forgets such generosity and trust."

I sensed that the subtext of these last few words was another reason why I had played "Mr Page" and now was about to become his Military Secretary. This struck me as a puzzling arrangement, given that Corps' HQ already had a fully manned Admin' Department, and could see no point giving the more jealous and conspiratorial staffers further reason to gossip about their nepotistic chief. Not that I lost any sleep over their sly whispers and covert glances, having learned early in life to restrict my friendships to a trusted handful while keeping everyone else at a polite arm's length.

The Crossley sped up the Château's gravelled drive and braked at the main entrance where we dismounted. General Monash paused to acknowledge the bark of command, the crunch of heel irons, the slap of sentries' rifle butts, before we continued indoors and ascended the grand staircase together.

I felt stares of suspicious interest as the GOC and I kept step through a labyrinth of partitioned outer offices, all ranks springing to attention as we marched past and entered his study on the third floor overlooking Clermont-Tonnerre's forecourt.

I shut the door as Monash tossed his forage cap, gloves, and swagger stick onto a side table, then turned, unbuttoning his Crombie. "Major Baxter spoke with you last night."

"Yes sir."

"A first-rate legal practitioner. Sound of judgment, keen of mind." He continued, shrugging out of his greatcoat, and draping it across a chairback before sitting down at the scrupulously organised desk. "However," he continued, glancing up, "take heed. His loyalty is to England whereas ours is to Australia. For as long as the two coincide, there is no cause for concern. But should a situation arise when he must choose between Us and Them, we shall be cut adrift without a moment's hesitation." Monash stopped short, eyeing me closely. "You doubt it?"

"With respect, yes, I do."

"Oh?"

"Major Baxter spoke of a related matter some weeks ago, during which he happened to describe himself as 'a son of the vicarage,' where not only the 'church mice were poor and needy.'"

"'Happened'?" Monash almost laughed as reached towards his pipe rack and tobacco jar. "Be wary! My redoubtable spymaster never utters a single syllable without there being a deeper reason for doing so," he continued, loading his briar. "So why did you 'happen' to be speaking about poor church mice?"

"Well, sir, he informed me that Cecil Rhodes was also a vicar's son, was also from Hertfordshire, was also determined to make a go of life. Therefore, they had much in common when they met at Oxford, where Major Baxter was still a student and Rhodes was on a recruiting drive for an imperial secret society of some kind," I replied cautiously. "Both continued to correspond until Mr Rhodes' death, since when Major Baxter has taken upon himself to continue the missionary work, so to speak."

"How?" Monash struck a match and slowly waved its flame across his pipe's bowl, eyelids hooded. "Why?"

"I think the nub of both questions is something else that Rhodes allegedly told his young listeners," I replied, with studied caution. "According to him, since the Babylonian times, all empires have only lasted ten generations, or roughly two hundred and fifty years from go to whoa, at which point they've degenerated and become easy prey for more virile enemies."

"Hm." Monash seemed to be looking inwardly at something or someone unseen. "And what did Messrs Rhodes & Baxter propose should be done about rectifying this dire condition?"

I hesitated, before replying. "To paraphrase what I can remember of our conversation, the future leadership of a rejuvenated British Empire lies not with 'poodle faking loafers and pudding-faced parliamentarians in the City of London,' but with those Overseas Britons who had the gumption to emigrate to Canada and South Africa, Australia, and New Zealand. Men who may not have lived blameless lives in the Old Country, but who had the grit to roll up their sleeves and build a new future for themselves, and the Empire…"

Monash aimed a slow trickle of smoke at the ceiling. "Any idea where he sees you fitting into his grand design?"

"Not the foggiest," I replied candidly. "But to answer your original question, I'd say his loyalties are on a higher plane than a simple Us versus Them ding-dong between Diggers and Poms."

Monash removed his pipe and eased forward, elbows on desk. "You've given me much to think about. But of more immediate interest, what did he tell you about our present operations and personnel?"

"I-I'm not sure I am at liberty to discuss -"

"Nonsense! Just the facts; the opinions you may keep to yourself."

"Very well, sir," I replied cagily. "He spoke of General Rawlinson's all-arms' battle as the Allies' response to von Hutier's infiltration tactics, and -"

"The damn' cheek!"

"Sir?"

"I'm the one who's been agitating for *Harvester*, ever since I captured Messines Ridge, thus proving it could be done!" Monash regained his composure. "Proceed."

"There's not much else to say," I replied tactfully. "According to Mr Baxter, several divisional commanders were considered before you were chosen because of your engineering skills and organisational experience."

"And because, should anything go wrong, an upstart military amateur from the colonies is available to take the blame."

"That's not how it sounded to me," I replied sharply.

"Of course not! King's Counsels of Baxter's calibre are not paid hundreds of guineas *per diem* to appear in court and perform like dithering dimwits!"

"That I cannot say, sir," I announced, rather stiffly.

"Then what can you say?"

I straightened. "Despite his initial misgivings, and my displeasure for being taken off flying duties, Mr Baxter has always treated me fairly. I have twice been his family guest and, as it were, partaken of his bread and wine." This must have sounded insufferably pompous although the Biblical allusion would not have been lost on my listener as I concluded: "I will not betray his confidence any more than you would have betrayed Aunt Lucinda's when she bailed out your firm. Sir."

"Which is the very least I expect of a gentleman," he snapped back. "However, I am also very much aware of your secret correspondence with Messrs Bean & Murdoch –"

"Never!"

"Enough." He raised a cautionary finger. "I authorised it. *Operation Porridge* will continue feeding *Vegetable*'s fertile imagination with fresh manure, based upon your experiences as my nominal liaison with 3 AFC -"

"Thank you, sir!" I was unable to restrain a sudden grin. "It'll be great to be back on the squadron."

"Pay attention! I said 'nominal.'"

"Oh."

"In truth, you will be Stephen Baxter's junior, a term both he and I are familiar with, at top-level briefings about to begin. Understood?"

"Yes. Sir."

He reached for the topmost file on his in-tray, a sign that our meeting was at an end, as he added an enigmatic: "Be grateful. Few men are privileged to witness history in the making."

I failed to think so at the time, but with the wisdom of maturity, I can see that he was right. Despite many a close call and my share of discomfort, I'd had a lucky war and was actively engaged, right up to the end. Millions of other men – and women - were never that fortunate.

152

My shorthand notes of those briefings were probably tossed into HQ's incinerator after I went north to Scotland, for they would not have seemed worth keeping, although in retrospect their hurried squiggles and scribbled marginalia were a unique record of the angry exchanges and murky politics that prefaced the Battle of Le Hamel. Instead of which, historians like Frances Baxter will have to make do with what I can remember of 4 Division's training with the Tank Corps, the Australian Flying Corps, the newly raised Royal Air Force, and initially a battalion of American infantry, as we set about redefining modern warfare.

By the standards of that time and place, Le Hamel was a sideshow. One million shells never pounded the enemy's lines; five hundred tons of Amatol never exploded under his trenches; there was not even a multiple-page casualty list. Most astonishing of all, the objectives that the Allied High Command said were impossible to capture in ninety minutes, predicted by General Monash, only took three minutes more to deliver a stunning victory. Thus, it was not only what took place at dawn on the 4th of July 1918, that excited Allied planning staffs, but the elegant and economical means by which it was executed with minimum loss and maximum gain.

When I tape-record this episode for Frances, I shall begin by suggesting that she imagines herself in the observer's cockpit of an RE8 above the battlefield. Directly below, from right to left, the Somme languidly loops and curls its way from the limestone escarpment east of Péronne, westwards to St Valery on the Channel coast, though to describe it as a river is a bit of a stretch; in Australia its lagoons and marshes would barely rate as a billabong.

That had not always been the case. Roman barges navigated as far inland as Corbie, trading Mediterranean wine and luxury goods for the Gauls' honey, leather, and grain, but centuries of digging out the riverbanks for brick clay and impounding hundreds of acres of *hortillonages*, or raised vegetable garden beds accessible only by shallow punts, caused it to silt up during the Middle Ages.

Seen on our 1:40,000 military maps, the Somme-Ancre valley systems resembled the top and bottom sides of a roughly sawn wooden wedge, pointed at Amiens where the Avre adds its dribble to the other two rivers' lethargic flows. This topographical chokepoint made Picardy's provincial capital the hub of every mainline railway in Northern France during the sixty-odd years prior to 1914, and the target of relentless German attacks during the next four.

By now the *Reich*'s men and munitions were almost spent. To win one last throw of war's iron dice - an apt phrase coined when the civilian *Reichstag* voted itself into irrelevance by ceding its powers to the generals in 1914 - Ludendorff had to capture Villers-Bretonneaux, and came perilously close to success in April, before 13 and 15 Brigades AIF derailed his plan to cut the Franco-British supply lines.

Two months' later, reinforced by fresh drafts of troops and artillery across the pontoon bridges at Corbie and Vaux, the tiny village of Le Hamel became his springboard for a second attack on Veeb, from which to shell Amiens into submission.

Thwarting this mortal threat was now the responsibility of Australian Army Corps' acting-GOC. My task largely consisted of shadowing General Monash, despatch bag slung over one shoulder, pencil and notebook jotting down his lucid orders before transcribing them on the nearest available typewriter.

My draft copies were then edited and duplicated for circulation down the chain of command from division, through brigade, and battalion, to company and specialist platoon levels, so that by the end, every man knew exactly what he had to do and understood why it had to be done.

In hindsight, the preparations for Le Hamel were what one would expect with a civil engineer as its project manager. A more constricted military mind would have demanded strict obedience, but General Monash was astute enough to leave sufficient leeway for initiative in a volunteer army where private soldiers were expected to take command whenever the situation required immediate action. As happened on several occasions when hapless gaggles of Tommies were rounded up by a single Digger, who then led them into battle until a British unit could be found to take them off his hands.

It was not always that easy. Our faith in the ability of the Tank Corps to flatten wire and crush machine gun nests was badly shaken at Bullecourt the previous year, when the best that can be said of the Mark-I tank was that it failed to deliver on its promises. However, twelve months later, it was a different game when two brigades of the faster, greatly improved Mark-V were detailed to lead the attack on Le Hamel.

Even so, 4 Divvy's troops were notably hesitant until our GOC drove down from Bertangles. It did not take him long to assess the situation and order the lads be given the rest of the day to joy ride on the tanks and make friends with their crews. By nightfall, confidence was fully restored, and I had witnessed another example of the Monash Touch working its magic.

The only time that I saw him close to despair was when the American general, Pershing, ordered his contribution to the Australian attack be withdrawn less than a day before Z Hour. As often the case, politics and personal pique were behind this sudden change of plan, there being no way Pershing was going to share the glory of his troops going into battle under another general's flag, especially when that other commander was a despised Redcoat.

Eventually, after stormy telephone calls between Bertangles, Montreuil, and Chaumont, a token American contingent was grudgingly allowed to remain as dawn broke on July the 4th, but only after Monash threatened to cancel an already undermanned attack rather than risk another massacre like Bullecourt.

Thinking back on it, I suspect the only reason that Pershing allowed this meagre concession to Allied solidarity, was to claim an American Independence Day victory for hometown newspapers to trumpet his name and fame on the other side of the Atlantic.

None of which was helped by the unwelcome arrival of Australia's deaf, cantankerous weasel of a Prime Minister at the Château. His was one distraction that nobody needed as he poked around HQ, yapping vapid questions, fishing for snide remarks he could use to justify replacing Monash with Brudenell-White. To their credit, even the GOC's critics - of whom there were more than a few - closed ranks and supported him rather than sabotage the impending battle.

I, meanwhile, had been detailed to liaise with the Royal Air Force who were tasked with providing sound cover by flying their Handley Page night bombers, up and down the valley, muffling the Tank Corps' softly chug-chug-chugging engines as their ponderous machines crept forward, following the white tapes laid in the dank, pre-dawn darkness.

Something else I assisted with, and identified with closely, was the supply of ammunition for our Lewis gunners. In the normal course of events, we needed at least two bearers to go back and bring up a couple of buckets of 0.303 Ball apiece, often over a combined distance of a mile or more, for just a few minutes' firing.

However, Larry Wackett - a 3 Squadron pilot from Queensland - was experimenting with the idea of dropping individual loads of ammo to our advancing troops. I immediately saw the point of it and, like the bush mechanic I'd become, thanks to Karl Steiner's tuition on the Westralian Goldfields, modified the RE8's bomb racks to carry four padded sandbag loads of 0.303 Ball apiece.

Each was then attached to a static line and parachute drogue that cushioned their landings near equally makeshift ground markers. These were mostly torn-up strips of bedding scrounged from abandoned civvy homes - dyed yellow with explosive picric acid boiled from unprimed grenades – that I instructed our gunners to display as X'd bullseyes for aerial cargo drops.

The previous several weeks had worn me down more than I cared to admit, evidenced by my frequent flashes of temper and moody silences. However, as at Franvillers nothing escaped Monash's attention for long and I was given immediate orders to stand aside, pop a pill, and get some zeds.

They must've been needed for I never felt the thunderous crash of our opening barrage; or saw massed tanks crushing barbed wire and machine gun nests; or heard squadrons of warplanes strafing and bombing the way ahead for 4 Division's troops, as they mopped up the enemy's shattered resistance.

Le Hamel was one lesson Fritz never forgot and two decades later would assess, adapt, and adopt as *Der Blitzkrieg*.

Meanwhile, congratulations flowed in from all over but not everyone was happy. Australia's Prime Minister looked as if he had bitten on a bad tooth when Monash flourished a telegram from Marshal Foch, praising Australian Corp's victory in the most extravagant terms. Field Marshal Haig's signal was more restrained, as one would expect of a Scotsman, but no less heartfelt as he confirmed Monash's promotion to Lieutenant General i/c the Australian Army Corps.

Frustrated by success rather than buoyed by failure, Mr Hughes tore up the letter that he and the Bean-Murdoch cabal had been planning to deliver and stormed off to begin a whirlwind tour of Australian units, speechifying for overseas' votes in the forthcoming Federal General Election. One of the self-styled Little Digger's stage props was a borrowed slouch hat that shaded but failed to conceal his toothy, rat-like grin.

Le Hamel was widely regarded as the Western Front's breakthrough battle and Monash lost no time dictating a training pamphlet to showcase his achievement, which I transcribed and edited for distribution across all commands, including the AEF at Chaumont. It was while doing so that I became acquainted with Captain Thomas P. Winthrop, a newly appointed US Army liaison officer.

I naturally assumed that his duties, with us, were the same as James Nobury's at the American HQ. In other words, spying on an ally, for it was

James who introduced us during a quick visit to Bertangles. This was not an auspicious moment. Helping the Army Survey Corps' compositors to set dense statistical tables and columns of figures, had exhausted my depleted stock of goodwill to all men. The very last person I needed to meet was an animated youth, frothing with joy at finally taking part in the Great War's Big Adventure.

Things failed to improve when James announced that I was his brother-in-law. Captain Winthrop's eyes opened wide with excitement as he gave me an ingenuous grin: "Are you also a lord?!"

"Nuh," I scowled back. "Big Chief Kanga of Rooly Dooly Land."

"Wow!"

"Ian is Australian," James intervened with his customary tact, "they have a distinctive sense of humour."

"Gosh…"

Later, when we were alone again, James gave me a concerned frown: "It's unlike you to be so rude, Ian. Whatever is the matter?"

"Buggered if I know." Shoulders slumped I stared upward into space.

His concern deepened. "We'd better wangle you a few days at Chaumont. They really know how to look after a chap and are frightfully keen to learn from our experiences. You'll be a great 'hit'!"

"Maybe." I was far from convinced that whatever knowledge I had to impart could put into words these newcomers would understand, despite Captain Winthrop's persistent, nagging friendliness after James returned to AEF Headquarters. It did not help that I sensed an unwanted hero-worship after he learned that I'd been in uniform since 1914 and had served in Egypt and the Dardanelles as well as in France.

Matters failed to improve when Lieutenant Colonel Harry Murray VC visited Bertangles as a reluctant exhibit in the Prime Minister's travelling political circus. Glum at being led around like Jumbo the Elephant and put on display as Australia's most highly decorated soldier. Harry's face lit up when he saw me, and urgently pointed to a vacant table in a far corner of the Mess. "It's a tonic to see you again, mate!"

"Ditto," I replied, as we shook hands before sitting down and beckoning a steward to come and take our orders.

It was as if the previous four years had dissolved like a sunny morn's mist and we were once again seated on a park bench outside Perth Library & Art Gallery, he trying to excite me with Ancient Greek legends, and me working equally hard to get him – and Percy - to come and see the painting of an itinerant swagman moodily contemplating his campfire. Three carefree Diggers enjoying a few hours' freedom away from the army.

Harry must've guessed what was on my mind when he asked: "D'you remember how we worried the war would be over before we had a chance to see France…?"

"Yeah." I pondered his question. "Perce' got quite shirty. Something to do with crossbow triggers, wasn't it…?"

"Uh."

"Did you, ever find him…?"

Harry shook his head. "Not even a coat button, after the Minnies plastered us with HE and gas…"

We fell silent, each with our private memories of No Man's Land's vile, swampy wilderness of flung-open shell craters and splattered bits of soldier.

The steward delivered our drinks, two pints of best bitter. Waiting until he had gone, Harry raised his glass. "Percy Black. Our Ulysses..."

"A prince among men," I responded, saluting an older man who'd thumped a callow young fellow into adult shape, that first morning at Blackboy Camp.

Later, Captain Winthrop sought me out, keen to learn how I came to be on such good terms with "a real he-man like Colonel Murray!" To which I snapped that it was none of his bloody business and stormed off, determined to keep a safe distance from this nosy twerp.

There's no telling what else I might have said and done but for Stephen Baxter's post-haste return from Montreuil, one morning at the end of the first week of August. "Kit up. Chop-chop!"

"Why?" I snapped suspiciously.

"To observe what I'll bet you never thought we'd see."

"Like, what?"

"Come along. Hurry up!"

I collected my gasmask and steel helmet and followed onto the main courtyard where a staff car was parked, engine running, waiting for us to hop aboard.

"Le Querrieu."

"Yes sir!" Our WAAC toed the accelerator and off we sped, weaving past columns of mud bespattered infantry tramping forward in battle order; past trotting batteries of horse artillery, offsiders astride their mounts, whips cracking; past convoys of GS wagons and motor lorries laden with supplies and munitions for a frontline that was now advancing yard-by-yard, furlong-by-furlong, mile-by-mile, day-by-day gaining irresistible strength and momentum as it went forward.

Slumped on my seat, I was dimly reminded that whereas infantry dash and determination may win a single action, it was these anonymous ASC waggoneers and lorry drivers who were winning the war. Without their devotion to duty, in all weathers, by night and day, often under fire themselves, we who manned the trenches could never have done what we did. When we did. For as long as we -

"A penny for your thoughts?"

I shrugged, in no mood for small talk as we crested a low escarpment and halted overlooking a panoramic view of the Somme's haunted barbed wire thickets of 1916. I'd seen them countless times before, on the ground, from the sky, in my nightmares, but never like this. The incessant boom and crump of gunfire was quickening and everywhere there was movement, as if a giant's boot had kicked over a monstrous ants' nest.

Seemingly miniature cavalry patrols and formations of tanks were probing the way ahead for toy-like khaki infantry and field gun batteries to follow, even as straggles of gaunt prisoners, many supporting a wounded comrade or shouldering one corner of a laden stretcher, trudged the other way escorted by a single Tommy, rifle slung, cheerily puffing a Woodbine and quite often lending a hand to an exhausted Fritz.

Squadrons of warplanes kept roaring overhead, eastward-bound to strafe, and bomb the enemy's lines of communication; this was Le Hamel scaled-up from a few thousand to hundreds of thousands of men and machines inexorably rolling onward.

It was later revealed that Ludendorff was about to inform the Kaiser that 8th August 1918 was The Black Day of the German Army, and that His

Imperial Majesty's only hope of staying on the throne was for his troops to fight stubborn rear-guard actions while his previously disdained civilian ministers tried to negotiate with London, and Paris, and Washington, and Rome, from positions of ebbing strength.

Germany's boy conscripts never stood a chance, driven backwards with hammer-blow attacks that rarely paused but never stopped, during the next one hundred days of unbroken contact.

"Well?" Baxter enquired, closely watching my face. "What do you think?"

Unable to answer, choked by the bitterest of sorrows that I had lived to see this day, but that Sandra had not, I crumpled onto the Ford's warm engine bonnet and wept.

"Take it easy, old chap." Baxter laid a comforting arm, I thought was hers, across my quaking shoulders. "You've more than done your bit..."

153

The High Kirk of St Giles' bells were clanging the latest Allied victory as our hospital train shunted into Edinburgh's Waverley Street Station. How I came to be aboard it with a dozen other officers, all British except for one Canadian and myself, began when Baxter telephoned the Divisional MO, requesting an immediate examination.

Despite my protestations that I was feeling fine, just a bit wonky, he was not fooled and within five minutes had stamped my AF-1220 medical record card CFG – *Comburo Foras Gravis* – dog Latin for Severe Burn Out, a bogus condition diagnosed by sympathetic doctors at this late stage of the war, for soldiers of my experience and length of service.

Three days later found me back at 3LGH, sharing a ward with men whose condition ranged from jerky tremors, through frightened upward stares, to one lost soul who kept repeating his name, number, and rank, like a stuck gramophone needle. By contrast, I had folded inwards, becoming a self-contained melancholic who bothered no one and asked nothing of anyone. Had I been a clock, the staff at Wandsworth Military Hospital would have said that my spring was broken.

The journey from London to Scotland was normal by wartime standards, with frequent stops to let troop trains bypass us, hurrying south to the embarkation ports, now that victory on the Western Front seemed increasingly possible before winter set in.

Our VAD attendants treated us kindly and the only trouble we gave them was when one young fellow jumped off the lavatory pedestal and hanged himself with his necktie. After that, our escorts kept a much closer watch until we reached Edinburgh where a civilian omnibus – probably chosen for its easily locked door, and windows that were hard to open at the best of times – was waiting to take us and our bags to a commandeered hydrotherapy hotel at Craiglockhart in the city's outer suburbs.

Nicknamed "Dottyville" by my later acquaintance the poet and novelist Siegfried Sassoon, when he was a patient here in '17 and saw that its chaotic treatments were even more insane than most of its patients. However, by the time I arrived, its third and final Medical Director had instituted a more rational regime.

Drawing upon his experience treating shell shock in France, Professor William Brown interviewed each newcomer over tea and biscuits in a conservatory with stunning views across an expansive, expensive golf course, towards the city skyline and distant Forth estuary. The Merchants of Edinburgh had, earlier, made the Hydro's patients honorary members of their club not that I ever availed myself of their generous offer; swatting a small white ball around a manicured paddock was never my idea of a fair day's play.

Bertangles' CFG diagnosis was the Prof's assurance that I would be no trouble and might even be useful once he discovered that I could sketch, paint, and write up a newspaper column. The Hydro's in-house magazine, *Hydra* - a punning reference to the many-headed monster whose defeat was the most onerous of Hercules' labours – always needed fresh copy and illustrations. It also needed someone who understood machine rooms and photo-engraving studios, a job that fell to me.

In hindsight there was more to his treatment plan than I realised at the time. Mitigating traumatic neuroses was still an imprecise art whose origins, in Germany and Austria, made it even more suspect in a conservative profession that equated psychoanalysis with cartomancy and palm reading.

Professor Brown's assistant, Dr Arthur Brock, was an enlightened exception. Instead of the previous regime's ice baths and electric shocks, he promoted Ergotherapy, the idea that a nervous system could be encouraged to repair itself by progressively reintroducing the activities it enjoyed in peacetime. Thus, a man who had been keen on woodwork might soon find himself helping at a cabinetmaker's workshop, or if a gentleman landowner, working alongside a local farmer, tossing hay, and digging spuds, to reconnect with the soil.

In my case, he crafted a situation which forced me to inch out of my shell and monosyllabically converse with strangers, for I could hardly use sign language or chalked diagrams on a concrete floor, when assisting the compositors to lock-up a chase or telling the engravers where to crop a picture.

However, an even more subtle therapy was at work in the printers' Dickensian factory near a canal whose barges brought fuel from the Lanarkshire coalfield to thousands of Auld Reekie's open cooking fires and industrial boilers. It was here that I would sit outside in the yard with the workers, during lunch break, listening to their homely Scots' burr.

All were elderly, their apprentices conscripted into the Army, and three wore black armbands for those who had also been sons. The firm's management had previously told its staff where I'd been these past four years, and the reason why I was currently at the Hydro, so out of courtesy and respect they avoided talking about the war in France.

Instead, they were more interested to hear about Australia, and seemed quite perplexed that I had never met Andy McPhee, or Bobby Muir, or young Gordon Smith who, with many another friend or family member, had emigrated to Sydney. Or was that Melbourne? No, Perth! Fifteen years ago. "No-o-o, twenty-one! The Queen's Diamond Jubilee Year, ye ken?"

They found it impossible to believe that the vast emptiness between Perth and Sydney is about the same distance as that across Europe from Madrid to Moscow, not that any of them had much idea where those places were on the map, despite Scotland's generally higher standards of public education.

Other times, weather permitting, Dr Brock would tap the Amenities' Fund and hire a *char à banc*, a light horse-drawn bus pronounced "sharrabang," that took us for picnics on the nearby Pentland Hills, their slopes ablaze with purple heather at this time of year.

These excursions became less frequent as the hours of daylight rapidly shrank, as they do when fifty-five degrees north of the Equator, and autumnal rains fall more frequently. On such grim and gloomy days, Dr Brock encouraged me to play exhibition games of billiards in the Recreation Room, with masterclasses afterwards for those keen to improve their cue work.

The Hydro's library subscribed to a good selection of national dailies, which allowed us to keep tabs on the victories that St Giles' bells were joyfully proclaiming at closer intervals.

I cannot speak for other patients, but although the placenames were familiar – Bapaume, Péronne, Armentières, and so on – none of them made much impression on a mind that no longer cared what happened beyond the comparatively sane confines of our genteel lunatic asylum.

Of more immediate concern was an outbreak of influenza that soon ceased being just a filthy headache and sweaty chills, which is how it hit me. Quite a few locals got bowled over, but the civilian casualty lists were rarely as long or as regular as those from France and Italy, Salonika, Palestine, and Mesopotamia, which explains why the Spanish Flu' faded so quickly from the public's memory. As I discovered quite recently, when speaking to a young member of the Mac's staff who had never heard of it; so far as she was concerned, I was describing a Medieval visitation of the Black Death.

Even though the only treatments available in 1918 were Aspirin tablets, carbolic acid vaporisers, camphorated oil chest rubs, and gelatine capsules of cinnamon powder, I still managed to get back on my feet by the time news came through that an Armistice had been signed and that all fighting would stop at 1100 hours GMT, of the eleventh day, of the eleventh month of 1918.

It was already 0930 at Craiglockhart; only another ninety minutes for a sniper to stalk his prey and thereafter brag he'd bagged the Great War's last casualty; only another ninety minutes for a machine gunner to rip through his remaining belts of ammo; only another ninety minutes for a gun battery to shoot off its HE and Shrapnel by bombarding an imagined enemy attack. Had we been officially sane and back in the trenches, we would most likely have taken part in this collective madness.

Instead, our muted cheers sounded more like sardonic jeers when the Hydro's clock finally struck eleven and St Giles' clanged a triumphant Victory Peal across the valley. All that our broken brains could feel was an aching void, as if our sole reason for living had been abruptly switched off and replaced by, nothing.

It was inevitable that men in our sorry plight would feel this way. My whole adult life had been spent in uniform, one small cog in a vast, impersonal mechanism. With rare exceptions I had obeyed my superiors and passed their orders to my subordinates with impersonal efficiency. Now, confronted by the doubts and uncertainties of civilian life, I felt the first tremors of a fear unlike any known under fire. Not that I had material reasons for concern.

My share of Aunt Lucinda's trust fund was more than sufficient - now or in any foreseeable future - and Sir Arthur Stanhope's offer of a place in his investment bank had the potential to grow my small fortune so that, by middle age I could be a millionaire, but to what end?

All the money in the world was never going to revive my wistful daydream of a small country estate where Sandra and I could take the children for family weekends, and fondly watch them grow into sturdy, confident young adults.

The hospital staff did their best to lighten the mood by laying on a celebratory luncheon from their hoarded stock of rations while a local school choir serenaded us with patriotic songs. We did our best to look happy and glad for their kindly presence.

After the school choir had packed up and gone home with their bars of canteen chocolate, I found a quiet corner of the Reading Room where there was a desk, and writing paper, and I could uncap my fountain pen without being disturbed:

11th November 1918

My Dearest,

*I wish you were here to share the day for which we have
both given much, you most of all.*

*A short while ago I imagined us taking the kids to our
country home in Kent; I'd had a hard week in the City,
managing others' money, and needed to rest and regroup.*

*You were getting ready for a meeting of the Anglo-German
Friendship League, and I was glad to be helping you
make that Better World of which we often spoke. We both
knew it would take time and patience but were resolved to
give it a go! Ist das nicht wahr, Liebling?*

*Whether or not it will come to pass is impossible to say.
Peace is barely a few hours old, and I very much doubt
if Fritz will respond kindly to an Aussie machine
gunner extending the cordial right hand of mateship,
nor we to his, but we must never give up hoping for
better times to come, or else what were the past four
years all about?*

*I cannot tell what the future holds in store for anyone,
least of all myself, but come what may, I shall strive to
uphold our family's Gravitas, Dignitas, Integritas,
sustained by your gentle presence, for I often catch a
glimpse of your smiling face, from the corner of my eye.*

Rest well my eternal wife. Until we meet again.

Ian.

I would bet any sum of money that my letter – and those others written during the small hours of many a lonely night thereafter – was not unique. Spiritualism attracted a considerable following as a generation of widows and orphans strove to connect with husbands and fathers on the Other Side. Sadly, it never worked for me, having formed a rather sceptical view of jigging tables and husky, disembodied voices, while eavesdropping on Aunt Lucinda's séances at Tralee House.

Instead, I devised my own ritual of comfort and reassurance by taking Sandra's letter up West Hill, on the far side of Glenlockhart Road, where I solemnly burned it in the shelter of a rock. Then, standing tall and proud, scattered its ashes, willing a stiff nor'easterly to bear my message to that blesséd place where matrons never grumble, and colonels never pry.

154

As well as designing and illustrating a combined Victory & Christmas edition of *Hydra*, there were other letters to write and respond to as Dottyville began discharging its inmates.

There was one I had a premonition would eventually arrive, not having heard from David's parents for over two months, reporting that both were sorely missed by their many friends in Melbourne's Jewish Community, after the Spanish Flu' killed them both within a day of each other.

The factory and retail premises of L. Shuster & Son were being merged with another chain of bootmakers and, after various bequests and settlements, the residual sum would be divided between Melbourne University to establish a scholarship in the Natural Sciences, and Central Synagogue's *Zedakah* or Benevolent Fund. Additionally, one thousand pounds were being set aside as a token of Leon & Hannah Shuster's love for their dead son's oldest friend. Details of my account with the National Bank of Australasia were therefore required. Signed: Dr Nathan Krass.

Saddened but not surprised, I then opened today's other letter:

13th November 1918

My Dear Cribdon.

With the cessation of hostilities, I take this opportunity to give thanks for your steadfast service during recent times of great peril and uncertainty.

That the AIF succeeded in vanquishing the enemy is due in large part to the devotion to duty of my Staff Corps among whom you served with notable loyalty and attention to detail, for which I am most grateful.

John Monash
Lieutenant General

As one would expect of such a man there was no sentimental tosh, and the fact that it was handwritten rather than a signed duplicate, made me feel especially privileged. Others had not forgotten me, either.

Elspeth McCracken (Miss) still corresponded quite regularly although she was no longer at Toorak Primary School but was in her first year at Presbyterian Ladies' College, in nearby East Melbourne. Her artwork was becoming more individual and less derivative, as evidenced by the quirky little sketches and occasional cartoon figures that decorated her thank'ee notes for my hand-drawn postcards from France, and England, and Scotland.

One letter that really surprised me, though, arrived towards the end of the month:

Headquarters
American Expeditionary Force
Chaumont
France

November 20, 1918

Dear Captain Cribdon.

I trust you are in good recovery and will soon be convalescent.

Although ours was only a brief acquaintance, it was enough to prove that Australians were the finest allies and bravest fighters it was my honor to meet on the Western Front.

Should you ever visit the United States and find your self in Boston, don't hesitate to look me up. A note to our firm's office on Atlantic Avenue will ensure you will be hosted in true, Bostonian style.

Sincerely yours.

T. Winthrop

I gave a quiet chuckle and tucked the letter back into its envelope; I had been right in my assessment of seemingly innocent, wide-eyed Captain Thomas P. Winthrop, after all! The man who wrote these few lines was innately shrewd and poised, not at all the cartoon-Yank he'd bluffed us with at Bertangles.

A few days later, a note arrived from Phillip Grenville, inviting me to spend Christmas at Hampton Rise with himself and his new wife, and I was strongly tempted to accept. However, Stephen Baxter had already made a similar offer and to complicate matters there was the Noburys' invitation to be their guest at Berkeley Square.

One of the traits that distinguished we Edwardians from subsequent generations was our adherence to an unwritten code of conduct that expected us to be considerate of others' feelings. For instance, it was the "Done Thing" to always step aside, hold the door open, and raise one's hat for a lady, as all women were regarded, irrespective of their occupation or class.

Not everyone did so, of course, but it was one of the expected standards of behaviour that encouraged men to refine their manners and be aware of others' needs before their own, which is an oblique way of explaining why I accepted the Noburys' invitation despite grave personal misgivings.

Truth be told, Berkeley Square was the last place on earth I wanted to visit, but I had read more into their gracious invitation than the words themselves conveyed. There was within them a heartache, a loneliness, a need for young company, James having told me in a quick note that he would be on duty over Christmas, as GHQ dismantled and dispersed lorryloads of records and tons of office equipment.

My discharge finally came through two days before Christmas. Professor Brown warmly thanked me for my help with *Hydra* and waved goodbye as the taxi drove off into town, dropping me at Waverley Street Station as a leaden sky dumped rain across the concourse. I was still in uniform, already a less frequent sight than even a couple of months ago, which entitled me to sit up overnight in an officers' carriage, on the way south.

I don't remember much about the journey and kept to myself while others chattered about friends, and family, and their post-war plans, occasionally casting furtive glances at the green tabs on my tunic, the Intelligence Corps having earned a reputation for stealth and intrigue during the war, which inevitably attracted jealousy and suspicion among non-specialist personnel.

The sky was still wet and sorrowful when our train panted to a halt at Kings Cross Station on the morning of Christmas Eve 1918. The mood was markedly different from my last visit. There were still troops milling about, returning home on leave, but these were spruced up and clean compared with the mud bespattered trench fighters of '16 and '17, and none of them would be returning to an uncertain future in Picardy or Flanders.

I caught a taxi to Berkeley Square, gave my cap to the maid Doris who gave me a sad smile in return, and was respectfully greeted by Mrs Simpkins the housekeeper who informed me that the Earl and Countess were presently Out, but had left instructions that I be invited to take a rest after a long and tiring journey.

This I duly did in my old bedroom, and slept through to mid-afternoon, after which I shaved and made myself presentable before coming downstairs to find my hosts helping their domestic staff put up coloured paper chains and scraps of pre-war tinsel in a doomed attempt to be jolly and bright. Lord and Lady Nobury were leading by example, sharing smiles, and encouraging others to do the same, but I could tell their hearts were not in it. Nor was mine.

Both were attentive over dinner and kindly invited me to accompany them to the Christmas Eve Service at St George's in nearby Hanover Square. I could hardly refuse and, as it happened, was glad that I had not wriggled-out. For instead of what I dreaded would be an interminable sermon raking over the war's hot embers, a small choir accompanied by brass and strings from the Royal Academy of Music, performed a parlour version of *The Messiah* in Handel's own parish church, composed when he was living a short distance away by sedan chair, in Brook Street.

Spiritually refreshed, or in my case humming the *Hallelujah Chorus*, parishioners of all classes wished each other a Merry Christmas - for it was already past midnight - after which we returned to Berkeley Square where the Noburys insisted that I join them for a light supper and nightcap. Both were clearly working up to say something but seemed unsure how to go about it. Finally, I took the initiative and simply asked: "What is it you wish to tell me, sir?"

I think he was relieved that I had created an opening, when he replied: "We have no desire to intrude into your personal life, and greatly value the symbolic act, you performed, at our daughter's memorial service," said with a pointed look at my left hand, "but…"

"'But'?" I stiffened, resolved to accept my marching orders with the same Stoical dignity as, I am sure David had, when ordered to leave his Mary's ducal home and never darken its doorstep again, the Fifth Earl having finally learned of my sordid parentage.

"You are a young man, with bright prospects," His Lordship continued, feeling his way, word by word. "One who will, in the natural course of events, wish to raise a family." He cleared his throat. "The memory of your love for our daughter must never interfere with your future plans." He trapped a dry cough in his clenched fist. "We shan't think any the less of you, when the time comes, to introduce, your new wife."

I recovered my composure. "That is most generous, but I am not sure, you understand."

"Understand, what?"

"That some memories, are too sacred, ever to be supplanted, by others."

"But -?"

"Sandra is my eternal wife," I continued, in an increasingly choked and husky voice. "I feel her kindly presence, beside me, wherever we go. She was always with me, in war. She still is, in peacetime. And I know she always will be. Until we are one again."

Lord Nobury composed himself before looking up again. "Thank you, Ian. Good night m'boy. God bless."

"Good night, sir." I turned and gave another short bow. "Ma'am."

155

I slept in late and came downstairs through the formal dining area where preparations were underway for the domestic staff's own Christmas luncheon, traditionally served and waited upon by their master and mistress.

His Lordship was seated alone in the breakfast room, moodily stirring a cup of tea while the other hand flicked through the *Times*.

"Good morning, sir."

Distracted, he glanced up and peered over his reading glasses. "Let us devoutly hope so, for this one Holy Day of the year, at least."

"Amen to that." I lifted the chafing dish lid to see if my share of the fried potatoes and macon – a substitute bacon sliced from smoked mutton - was still warm.

"Baxter tells me you speak Russian."

"A little," I replied, selecting a plate.

"Strange people," he observed in an unusually withdrawn tone of voice. "I met them at the Coronation. Flawless manners. Charming French. But one had a feeling that something wild and unpredictable was always about to erupt in their company. As if a Cossack horde was going to gallop from the Steppes, overturning everything and everyone in their unruly path." His forefinger tapped an item in the *Times*. "It seems like nothing much has changed."

"How so?" I enquired cautiously.

"A Red Army, commanded by Bolshy bomb-throwers, is battling a White Army, led by an admiral, while an anarchic Green Army of peasants is at war with all and sundry," he replied. "Adding to their chromatic confusion are the British, the French, the American, the Japanese armies, hoping to stop the munitions we supplied to the Imperial Russian Army falling into the wrong hands, as if anyone knows who's those are now!" He gave a baffled shrug. "Small wonder Cabinet is so concerned by the actions, reactions, inactions of that unhappy country..."

I began paying closer attention. This was the first time he had included me in a conversational reference to his ministerial duties, as he continued thinking aloud. "To paraphrase Victor Hugo's '*On résiste à l'invasion des armées; on ne résiste pas à l'invasion des idées.*' Or, in our present situation, we may succeed in resisting a revolutionary army, but how does one resist a revolutionary idea?"

"I don't know, sir."

"That's the point, nobody does," he smiled ruefully. "For the moment, Bolshevism is a localised political infection, but we ignore at our peril its potential to leap from mind to mind, from country to country, continent to continent, like this influenza thing that's such a nuisance. However, at least while the Bolshies restrict themselves to murdering each other, we shall be spared having to deal with the Russian Question at this Peace Conference. Unlike the previous one in Vienna, when the Third Earl had to contend with Czar Alexander's fantastical 'Holy Alliance.'"

"I, I'm sorry sir, you've lost me," I replied, baffled by his brooding tone.

"Not to worry." He shared a sad half-smile. "Of more immediate concern, in Paris, will be whether we 'Men of 1919' can secure a peace as lasting as those 'Men of 1815' did, in Vienna, at the end of their war."

"Then may I wish you every success?" Spoken from the heart. "There has to be a better way of running the world than by blowing it to bits."

"Agreed." He pushed away from the table and stood. "For which purpose we are paying close attention to President Wilson's Fourteen Points and his proposed League of Nations." I leaned forward, hearing in his voice an echo of Sandra's Anglo-German Friendship League. "How would that work?"

"Broadly speaking, a Permanent Oversight Committee based at a central location – probably neutral Switzerland – where international disputes can be settled in an open, orderly, civilised manner."

I waited for him to leave the room, then sat down at my place and reached for his newspaper, flicking through it with one hand while forking up the potatoes and mock bacon with the other.

Our hopes and prayers for a more enlightened, more peaceful world after the previous fifty months were not encouraged by column inches reporting a Russian Civil War from the Baltic to the Pacific, as the murdered Czar's empire tore itself apart. And street battles in Germany, after the Kaiser's abdication, between embittered soldiers and Communist agitators accused of sabotaging the *Reich*'s War Effort.

And unrest in Italy, incensed by the high price paid in dead and war taxes for a few Alpine valleys and scraps of Austrian territory along the Adriatic, Rome's paltry reward for signing the secret Treaty of London that switched the Kingdom of Italy against their former allies of the Triple Alliance.

And turmoil in the defeated Ottoman Empire, currently misruled by Sultan Mehmet VI, though for how longer his ramshackle inheritance could hold out against Anglo-French designs on its Middle Eastern oilfields, was doubtful.

Eventually it was time for the staff's luncheon to be served by the Earl and Countess, clad in striped blue and white aprons, waiting on their retainers with soup, roast goose with all the trimmings, and plum pudding bathed in brandy flames that were a sad reminder of my last peacetime Christmas, at Pat and Dulcie Donovan's home in Kalgoorlie.

Afterwards, crackers snapped, and everyone got a small silver charm struck for the occasion by Mappin & Webb. The young boot boy rummaged around under the Christmas Tree, handing out wrapped presents, including one for myself which he brought into the kitchen where I was up to my elbows in soapsuds, washing plates and dishes.

Wiping my hands dry, I opened a small, carefully wrapped packet to reveal an elegantly tooled leather wallet that opens to become the two picture frames I stand on the bedside table wherever I'm staying for the night. In the left-hand panel is a sepia-toned family photograph of the Earl and Countess with their three children, smiling at the camera on a country manor croquet lawn during that last golden summer of 1914. In the righthand panel, a coronet-embossed card that simply reads, in by-now faded black ink:

With deep affection and regard for our Ian.
Lionel & Claire Nobury.
Christmas 1918

Both of whom helped me to clear the table and finish putting away the silverware after wishing every member of staff a safe journey to their families - mostly in the East End of London - for the next two days.

Each servant took with him or her a bonus that, before the war would have been a golden sovereign but today was a paper ten-shilling note, Emergency War Taxes being so high and the rents from Irish agriculture so low, even without a Fenian Rebellion about to convulse that unhappy land.

Only the housekeeper and her husband, the butler, were staying on-duty for the Festive Season although it was effectively a holiday for them as well, Lord and Lady Nobury having a full diary of engagements the first of which was booked for later that same afternoon, at Viscount Alwyn's residence in nearby Curzon Street. On the way there I learned that Alwyn was Claire Nobury's cousin by marriage, though I sensed that he was not a favoured relative, which left me wondering why we were making this visit at all. Family tradition, I suppose.

Before 1914 we would most likely have arrived by landau and pair, but with horses commandeered by the Army, and coachmen driving GS wagons in France, a taxi delivered us to a terraced Georgian town residence where a porter – in the original sense of a servant who minded the main door – took my greatcoat and cap.

The initial impression was of how pleasantly warm the place was, compared with the inadequate heat of rationed coal at Berkeley Square, but the reception was anything but warm when my turn came to shake Lord Alwyn's hand. I was unaware of it at the time, but there had been high hopes of a marriage between the Honourable Gerald Alwyn and the Honourable Lady Sandra Nobury, not that I was unduly troubled, being quite able to give as good as I get in the frosty smiles department.

It was somewhat later that I learned how Fitzgibbon Alwyn – "Fizzy All Wins" to his chums – had been the Prince of Wales' pimp whenever the future King Edward VII graced a stately home that had good shooting, an excellent cellar, and a regal bed into which Alwyn could steer an available daughter of the loyally compliant family. One of the few occasions on which this self-appointed Procurer Royal failed to deliver the goods was with Claire Fortescue, who preferred the more sober courtship of Captain the Honourable Lionel Nobury, a snub that still clearly rankled.

Not that it dimmed All Wins' shady reputation on the turf where it was believed that, not by luck alone did he know which jockey would cross the finishing line first in any given race. A less well-connected punter would have been barred from the betting ring, but Fizzy always knew how and when to lose a sufficiently large sum to keep the bookies sweet and retain his stall in Tum Tum's stable of aristocratic rakes, as Queen Victoria disapprovingly referred to her fat son's racy companions.

Lord Alwyn was assisted in this noble endeavour by another winning bet, marriage to the only child of a Denver mining promoter whose schemes occasionally profited their shareholders, but which never failed to augment his personal fortune; the American father and his English son-in-law were a matched pair of rogues.

By the time we met, Miss Daisy Suggers had blossomed into Fleur, Viscountess Alwyn, a prominent identity among the expatriate heiresses who were reinvigorating as well as refinancing the British aristocracy. By now a handsomely preserved woman of a certain age, with a knowing twinkle in her eye, it was not hard to see why men fell so readily under her spell.

Lady Alwyn had heard much snooty gossip about Sandra Nobury's Aw-stray-yun fiancé, which made us comrades-in-arms on the frigidly polite battlefield of England's Class War. Not that it was ever said as such. There was no need to. We were both cut from the same rough cloth. Besides, she relished conversing with a young man whose life on the Westralian Goldfields echoed her own early years, wild and free in the mining camps of Colorado and Nevada.

Even allowing for the natural human tendency to embellish a good yarn, I could tell that she'd ridden the sort of horses that never ran at Ascot; had been on first-name terms with the madam of many a frontier bordello; and could handle firearms as well as any man, as at least one discovered when she dropped him with her Remington 0.44 revolver, abruptly ending their disagreement on the main street of a shantytown appropriately named Last Chance.

Dinner was a more sedate affair and reflected Fizzy's connexions on the black-market as well as at Newmarket, making our Berkeley Square meals rather drab by comparison. This was partly because the Noburys believed that wartime rations must be shared equally, and partly because Blackjack Suggers had endowed his daughter with ten and three-quarter million dollars from which she kept her spendthrift husband on rations of a different sort.

Throughout all their lordly waltzing around, I was conscious of social crosscurrents and encoded messages that a plain Australian outsider was not required to understand, nor would ever want to. This did not worry me unduly, being by choice the attentive guest who knows when to insert a mild enquiry or make an apt quip to ease the conversation along.

But no matter how often I smiled and nodded, and how hard I listened, I still could not fathom the purpose of this awkward family gathering, for it was painfully obvious there was no love lost between the two cousins. As for their respective spouses - Nobury and the American heiress – they might as well have been trying to communicate by sign language across Grand Canyon.

The scene only began to clear when the earl and the viscount prepared to go into the Smoking Room while their wives withdrew to discuss matters pertaining to the American Red Cross, of which Lady Alwyn was a prominent public figure, like Claire Nobury's equally powerful though less evident position in the St John's Ambulance.

Lord Alwyn ordered me to toddle off and amuse the ladies while We Chaps got down to business, but Lionel Nobury shook his head: "That won't do, Fitz'."

"Ay? Wot?!"

"I trust Ian's discretion and value his judgment." Announced with a firm smile. "We are together."

"Hmph!" Alwyn gave a dyspeptic scowl. "Oh, very well, if you insist." Then, with a glare in my direction: "Come along young felluh!"

156

I followed through a nearby set of doors and, with a sketcher's eye froze the scene for future reference. Whereas Lord Nobury's library told of a studious man engaged in high matters of state, Alwyn's room was an overstuffed gallery of racehorse portraits and photographs of himself when young and bewhiskered, standing attentively behind Edward, Prince of Wales whose burly bottom sat centre stage with the Czarevitch, or the German Crown Prince, or whichever ill-fated Archduke was currently the Hapsburg's Heir Apparent, in a Victorian courtier's scrapbook of Life at the Top.

I waited for permission to sit, but after a while took matters into my own hands and chose a seat to the left of Alwyn's line-of-sight as he lit a lonely cigar, doubtless aware that Nobury disliked the habit, and never thinking to offer me one to decline.

"We've read your memorandum," he boomed though a gust of smoke, "and emphatically reject it!"

"May one ask why?"

"Reparations must squeeze the German Lemon till its pips squeak!" our ungracious host replied with a tediously unoriginal figure of speech. "The Huns must be left in no doubt they've lost the war and will pay for it!" Alwyn heaved a wheezy breath. "Once a Hun, always a Hun! Either at our neck or at our knees! Now's the time to keep 'em under our feet!"

"And how, pray, do you propose doing that?"

"Military occupation!" Alwyn replied. "Blow up their factories and coalmines so they never trouble us again! Tighten the naval blockade! And if another million starve, sicken, die, so much the better!"

"This is what your colleagues in Birmingham, and Sheffield, and the Durham coalfields want?"

"Abso! Lutely!" he coughed. "The Royal Navy no longer needs our coal for its battleships! Profits are down! Collieries will close! At a time when Treasury is instructing me, to award, no more, cost-plus c-c-contracts!"

"As one would expect," Nobury thought aloud, with mild surprise, "given that the war is effectively over?"

"You're, missing, the point!" Alwyn thumped his chest to dislodge a clot of phlegm. "There'll be anger! When I do cancel 'em!" Gasp. "Restoring peacetime production won't be easy!" Wheeze "Unless we crush the Huns' ability to compete on the free market!" Gag. "By raising Imperial Tariffs! To safeguard British industries! British interests -!"

"You surely don't believe that?"

Recovering his breath, Alwyn looked up from the carpeted floor. "I dashed well do! As do all men of substance! And you had better believe so, too! Or they'll make their displeasure known -!"

"How?"

Alwyn sucked more hot smoke. "Northcliffe and his army of readers stand foursquare behind us! Can you say as much for your 'Peace Initiative' and 'League of Nations' twaddle?!"

"No."

"Well then!"

Nobury flinched as another gust of fusty breath wafted past before regaining his composure. "Come off it, Fitz! You must've gained some political *nous*, chairing the Munitions & Materiel Procurement Board," he thought aloud. "Pray tell me, what is the essential difference between a politician and a statesman?"

Our host blinked, suspecting a trap set by this shrewd, unelected cabinet minister. "None! Vote-grubbing commoners! The whole dashed lot of 'em!"

"And there we must agree to disagree," Nobury replied with a reproving shake of the head.

"Ay? Wot?!"

"Politicians must, by the very nature of their work, pander to the daily newspapers' headlines and trim their sails accordingly," Nobury continued, ignoring Alwyn's choleric interruption. "Statesmen, by contrast, have sufficient moral strength and wisdom and means to act independently whenever they see that a popular, short-term gain must end in long-term loss."

"I don't care for puzzles!" Alwyn coughed again, showering sparks from his cigar. "Plain and simple! Only way to run the Empire!"

"Then I shall trouble you no more," Nobury said with a distant smile, "except to observe that in these dangerously unstable times, we must unite behind and support our statesmen while restraining their politically myopic brethren, like your Durham coal barons –"

"Now look'ee here -!"

"Or else Red Revolution will overwhelm everyone, high and low, rich and poor, without distinction and without mercy," Nobury concluded, unfazed by Alwyn's splutter.

"An' what's that got to do, with your namby-pamby, 'Peace Initiative!' And 'League of Nations' nonsense! Ay?!"

"A very great deal. Perhaps, everything?"

"Piffle!" Alwyn thought he saw a flaw in his adversary's argument. "You're not the only chap watching the world! Every week, more and more 'nations' keep popping up like blasted toadstools! If it was hard enough managing the peace with only two Triple-whatsernames to play off against each other, how's it going to be once ancient relics like Poland, and Lithuania, and the Balkans resume their ancestral squabbles at your international tea party!"

"What would you have us do instead?"

"Keep 'em down, keep 'em out, and leave the Bank of England to do what it does best. With some help from the French."

"And the Americans."

"What of 'em?"

"Really Fitz'!" Nobury chuckled. "I'd have thought that Fleur had, by now, taught you that when it comes to bare-knuckle business, your in-laws have little to learn from us. That aside," he continued, no longer smiling, "until recently they were chorusing a popular song entitled *Over There*. Now they're Over Here, in considerable numbers. Not quite an Army of Occupation, *per se*, but still sufficiently strong to enforce another inconvenient set of numbers, if required..."

"What damn' numbers?!"

"Wilson's Fourteen Points, which have promised your 'ancient relics' an equal voice in world affairs."

"A pox on the whole damn' lot, I say!" Alwyn grunted dyspeptically.

"Most constructive." Nobury flapped a hand to disperse the stale smoke. "Anyhow, you may tell your people that HMG notes their concern –"

"And you may tell Cabinet we're not buying any more of 'His Majesty's Government' soft soap!'" Alwyn interrupted, with an audible twang of his wife's Transatlantic slang in his voice now. "When you get to Paris with Milner, and Bonar Law, and the rest, you'd better keep British commerce front and centre, or else there'll be big trouble!"

"Is that a threat?"

"Only if you make it so," Alwyn stubbed out the greater part of his cigar. "Consider this a timely reminder that the bankers took our arms' contracts - not the Kaiser's - as collateral for their War Loans. But only after your precious 'HMG' guaranteed a five percent return, plus principal, in gold- backed paper! So, default is not an option…"

"Is not Victory sufficient?" Lord Nobury enquired mildly.

"Hah!" Our host's florid, puffy face seemed to deflate as he hunched around his failing lungs. "The way they see it, 'Armistice' means 'Draw,' not 'Win.' The Huns can still pull the wool over our eyes! One against four? It won't be hard playing Britain against France; France against America; the Italians against themselves; and Japan against China now that we've promised 'em the German naval base at Tsingtao. You lot had better deliver the goods, pronto, while we still hold a winning hand!"

I eased forward and began paying much closer attention; Fitzgibbon Alwyn was not such a fool after all.

Thereafter, the conversation steered into less-choppy waters of Family, Friends, and Finance, until it was time to leave. Lord Nobury remained deep in thought during our return journey to Berkeley Square. Lady Nobury sensed her husband's sombre mood and took up the conversational slack by telling me of her plans to launch an Anglo-American Red Cross Famine Relief for Eastern Europe, not that I understood much of what she was describing but courtesy required that I offer to help in whatever way I could.

Having paid off the taxi and let Mrs Simpkins take our coats, Nobury beckoned me to follow upstairs to the study where the portrait of Lady Caroline Fyffe did nothing to ease my abiding sense of loss. "Sherry?" He un-stoppered a decanter and glanced enquiringly in my direction.

"Yes, thank you sir." I waited until his glass was also charged before taking mine and returning a silent toast.

He gestured for me to one of a pair of high-backed chairs, facing each other across an unlit fireplace, while he took the other. "So, Ian, what do you make of that meeting?"

I made time for a considered response by taking a sip of the elegantly dry, straw-coloured *fino*. "Well sir, if you are referring to the conversation at Lord Alwyn's, I must confess that most of what I overheard was in Commercial Code, so to speak, and I don't have its decryption key. However, I could not help agreeing when he said that the Armistice is little more than an exhausted pause, not a decisive victory. Or words to that effect."

"Does it substantially matter?"

"Not to our troops at the Front, for whom any excuse not to kill or be killed is sufficient reason to be glad." I took another pensive sip. "But I can't buy his 'military occupation,' and 'blowing up factories' stunt."

"Why not?"

"Because, unless he's going to do the dirty work himself, he'll need soldiers, and all they want to do now is go home."

"But surely they'll obey their superiors' orders?"

"Like they did the other day at Le Havre, when the Gunners burned down their barracks?" I enquired neutrally. "Lord Northcliffe's editors could not believe their luck if more ringleaders were shot, in peacetime, like those poor devils were at Étaples, last year. Frankly, I concluded, "the quicker we're disarmed and dispersed, the better for all concerned."

"Why?"

"Because His Lordship won't find many volunteering to stay on and blow-up coalmines when the alternative is going home to the missus and kids. Besides," I concluded, "even if he did destroy Germany and starve its population to death, is that really such a good idea?"

"Go on..."

"Well, sir, and this is hard to put into words," I replied, with some hesitation, "but it's something Sandra and I often discussed when we spoke of going to Germany, after the war, as 'goodwill emissaries -'"

He leaned forward. "I never knew that."

"There was no reason why you should. At the time, it was only one of several plans. Anyhow," I continued, with increasing difficulty, for this was sacred ground, "she often told me how Prussia recovered after their defeat at Jena and subsequent occupation of Berlin by the French. And yet, so strong was the Prussians' resilience, that within seven years their army had remodelled itself, funded by a civilian population who gave up their gold and silver jewellery to fund arms and equipment in exchange for a simple iron ring, worn with patriotic pride."

"Hence the Iron Cross?"

"Yes, I believe so. But crucially," I added, "it was this new Prussian Army that sapped Napoleon's forces in the days before Waterloo and showed the world what *Kriegschule* staff work can achieve, when directed by generals like Gerhard von Scharnhorst."

"And the moral of her story is?" Nobury enquired, quietly. "Or was."

"Not one, but two." I replied, steadying my voice as best I could.

"Go on..."

"Firstly: that it would be a grave mistake to provoke a similar reaction by imposing the humiliation of a 'Carthaginian Peace' on Germany and its people, after this, their latest defeat. Or else risk a similar national resurgence."

"And secondly?"

"That Bismarck made a fatal error when he encouraged his generals to build their magnificent professional army without, at the same time, raising a parallel Diplomatic General Staff – *Diplomatischer Generalstab* is how she described it – with equivalent status and authority, to counterbalance the iron fist of 'Prussian Militarism' with the open hand of 'Prussian Pragmatism' or *Realpolitik*. A curious oversight," I concluded sombrely, "for in her opinion he was 'the consummate diplomat...'"

"Heavens!" Lord Nobury exclaimed. "And all we thought she was doing in Berlin was improving her Conversational German -!"

"Believe me, sir, Sandra's enquiring intellect went much, much deeper than shallow, social chit chat..."

Shaking his head, he stared into the cold fireplace. "How little we know of our children until it's too late." Adding, with real anguish in his voice: "Dear God Almighty. If only we had more like her, informing our policies, instead of vindictive swine like Alwyn. And reptiles like Northcliffe, the former Alfred

Harmsworth," deliberately misspoken as Harm's Worth, "poisoning the minds of his one million newspaper readers, every day -!"

I said nothing. There was nothing to say. Rarely have I seen a more despairing look on another man's face as a grieving father gathered up his strength and belief in humanity's better angels, determined to keep the faith with his murdered daughter. "Ours will be a long, hard struggle, Ian. Restoring a world where international disputes are settled in a civil, civilised, civilising manner, won't be quick or easy. But done it must be. For the alternatives are too dreadful to contemplate -!"

157

During the next few days, after courtesy calls on other relatives and friends, His Lordship and I would retire to his study and, with growing regard and mutual respect, explore a wide range of topics. Some were private, family matters, while others touched upon his plans to make the British Empire a cornerstone of the League of Nations.

It might be wondered why a senior Cabinet Minister would confide in a relatively unknown young man from the other side of the globe, but as he had already said, he trusted my discretion and needed an attentive listener while dissecting complex issues on the agenda at 10 Downing Street.

I shall not betray his trust now by revealing what they were then, even though the empire we both served has long since done what Rudyard Kipling eerily foretold at the height of Britain's imperial pride in 1897:

> Far called, our navies melt away
> On dune and headland sinks the fire
> Lo, all our pomp of yesterday
> Is one with Nineveh and Tyre!

I am quite sure that a man of Lord Nobury's intellect and understanding would have been aware of our inevitable decline and fall, long before it became apparent to that useful legal fiction: "The man on the Clapham omnibus."

I am equally certain it underpinned his belief that the English-speaking nations, principally Britain and the United States, should form a voting *bloc* of common-sense interests within the League of Nations, and by so doing continue what the Third Earl did when Europe began ninety-nine years of comparative peace and prosperity at the Congress of Vienna, in 1815. Or so we hoped in 1919.

I was sad when the time came to accept Baxter's invitation of New Year at Hampstead. Lionel Nobury was a decent, kindly husband and father who very much reminded me of his eldest daughter. If only the same could have been said of his youngest! Though hardly more than a schoolgirl, Meg was already a pert, opinionated little minx whenever I happened to be nearby.

I charitably ascribed these attacks of the vapours to the fact that she had qualified as a Probationary VAD just in time for there to be no further need for her services. And this, by some twisted female logic, made me the target of her petulant displays of temperament, which reached a crescendo when her father telephoned for a taxi to Hampstead.

During the short drive through North London's rainy streets, I tried to recall what I'd been doing a year ago, on the last day of 1917, but failed to remember. Worse still, I could not be bothered trying to remember. Getting from dawn to dusk, one numb day at a time, was as much as I could handle.

The taxi turned into Merton Lane. Baxter heard it coming up his gravelled drive and hurried down the front steps, holding an opened umbrella, for by now the rain was fairly pelting down. "I'm so awfully glad you could come, Ian," he said, sharing the brolly. "Here, let me help you with that," and insisted on taking my valise while I paid off the driver, then led the way indoors where nothing had changed, the furniture still running in mathematically exact lines from door to door, as if frozen in time and space.

A delighted Jeanne Baxter welcomed me, no longer the fierce *Mme le Médecin* of our initial acquaintance. Gone was the dowdy black dress now that Alsace-Lorraine was freed from German occupation, instead I shook hands with *une trés chic* French lady who proudly introduced me to her pigeon pair children, both of whom stood head and shoulders above their diminutive mother.

Georges was living proof of genetic crossover, a dark haired, dark eyed, smoulderingly intense Celt. By contrast, his sister Cécile was a tall, graceful blonde who just as clearly harked back to her father's Anglo-Saxon ancestors. Then I noticed her eyes. They were blank. She was blind. Not that it seemed to trouble her, hand extended, smiling towards my voice. And in that moment, I understood the linear furniture that enabled her to walk about freely, using soft clicks of the tongue to bounce barely audible echoes off doors, walls, and cavities.

This became apparent as we got to know each other better, but first I was shown upstairs to the guest room and advised to get some rest, ready to celebrate *le Réveillon* - or New Year's Eve - in the French manner, with as rich a feast as wartime rationing allowed, culminating with rowdy cheers, fists pounding the table and shouts of *"bonne année!"* to drive away lurking hobgoblins, when the clock struck midnight.

I had heard about this in France, of course, so none of it came as a surprise when about twenty of Jeanne and Stephen Baxter's expatriate friends arrived, full of fun and laughter, but what pulled me up with a jolt – between the main course and *le dessert* – was a musical intermission of sprightly 18th-century *gigues* played on the flute and violin.

Georges was a talented flautist, but his sister had that indefinable something extra that divides mere technical brilliance from sheer genius. Sounds were her way of seeing, aided by a phenomenal memory. She only had to hear a piece of music once, no matter how intricate, for her to transcribe it to strings.

I was awestruck and correspondingly warm in my praise, for although I can barely play *Pop goes the Weasel* on a comb and paper, I was not a musical illiterate after much exposure to Aunt Lucinda's romantic nostalgia for Franz Liszt, the Shusters' amateur concerts, and James Nobury's technical analysis of Beethoven's piano sonatas.

"Merci, M'sieur Cribdon," Cécile replied in, as one would expect, a pleasantly modulated voice. "I hear you mean it. Papa says you have artistry of your own, drawing pictures I cannot share, but instead let us be friends in music." An astonishingly mature statement from a young girl of about the same age as the one I'd gladly left behind at Berkeley Square.

"Cela me donnerait le plus grand plaisir," and I meant it. To be her musical friend would indeed give me the greatest pleasure, as she would in due course give to the world, touring it with her husband the equally celebrated pianist Jacques Lebrun.

After such a night I overslept and eventually went downstairs to find Baxter doing the *Times* crossword. "'Centaur in woollen headgear under fire. Seven letters.' Any ideas?" he asked, glancing up as I came into the room.

A mental picture sprang to mind of a half man, half horse, mown down by Russian grape shot at Balaklava, immortalised in Lord Tennyson's *Charge of the Light Brigade*. I ticked letters on my fingertips. "'Cavalry.'"

"Ah!" He pencilled squares and nodded his approval. "Thank you."

I was not fooled. He had not needed my help to solve such a simple clue, I thought, taking my share of fried vegetable patties from the chafing dish, plus one of the rationed eggs, and awaited his next move

"How are things at Berkeley Square?" he enquired with a light smile that further alerted me to General Monash's warning that his spymaster never uttered a single syllable without there being a deeper reason for doing so.

"Not too bad." My reply was deliberately non-committal. "I'd hoped to catch up with James, but he's still in France, helping to dismantle GHQ."

"Ah yes," Baxter nodded, "we need a man of his integrity and discretion to oversee the 'burn bags.'"

"Uh huh." I thumped dollops of HP Sauce over the patties.

Baxter removed his reading glasses, the better to observe me. "Although this present war is not yet officially over, we have a duty to ensure that future historians don't get the wrong idea concerning our motives, means, and methods chosen to achieve such a desired end. Speaking of which," he added, as if the idea had just struck him, "what did you make of Alwyn's post-war plans?"

"How the devil -!"

"Ian?" He gave a disappointed frown. "How often must I remind you: 'Matthew 10:29'?"

"You and those blasted sparrows!" I snapped, the bonds of military discipline continuing to slip with the realisation that my time in uniform was fast coming to an end. "Do you have an ear at every keyhole?!"

"Only those that matter." His steely grey eyes never wavered in their piercing gaze. "And spare me the 'gentlemen never gossip about gentleman behind their backs' lecture, for of course we do, even as we strive to pretend otherwise. However," he continued drily, "our womenfolk are more forthright, and it behoves us to winnow the wheat from their chit-chat's chaff." He paused, watching my response. "So, a precis of the conversation at Curzon Street, if you please."

"A pound to a penny says you already know!"

"Pay attention." He eased back in his chair, fingertips steepled. "By now I had hoped you'd grasped that there is always more at stake, in our peculiar business, than at first meets the eye. The analyses we make, the reports we submit, the decisions we affect, shape the fate of nations and the lives of millions. Hence the need to take multiple readings of matters-that-matter, testing each component part by applying the Rules of Evidence that guard against hasty verdicts and flawed judgments." He paused again, watching me even more closely. "So, your precis of the Curzon Street meeting."

I could not be bothered arguing any further. Instead, I dabbed piquant sauce on a forked morsel of fried vegetable mash. "Lord Alwyn wants 'the German lemon squeezed until its pips squeak,' by imposing ruinous reparations to pay for the war." I finished chewing and reached for the teacup. "And before you ask, he failed to explain how that could be done after 'blowing up their factories and coalmines,' and starving another million civilians to death."

"What did Nobury say?"

I sipped tea. "He asked if this was the preferred policy of the Durham coal barons, to which Alwyn said that it was, and unless their interests were kept 'front and centre' at the Peace Conference, there would be 'big trouble' from the banks holding munitions contracts as collateral for War Loans at five percent, plus principal, in gold-backed paper."

"Names?"

"None."

"Proceed." The tone of voice told me that Baxter KC was cross-examining a witness at the Old Bailey.

"His Lordship protested by arguing for a more lenient policy, based upon a League of Nations rather than Northcliffe's venomous editorials," I replied. "Alwyn threw cold water over that one by saying, with new countries like Lithuania and Poland 'popping up like toadstools,' international affairs will be even more unmanageable than they were when it was just a question of balancing the Triple Entente's interests against those of the Triple Alliance."

"To which His Lordship said…?"

"That the British Empire and America must combine as a voting *bloc*, to manage the League's agenda and avert further conflict."

"How do they propose doing that?"

"'No idea." I dabbed more sauce.

Baxter fell silent and remained so for quite a while before looking up again. "What are your thoughts, *vis á vis* Alwyn's squeezed lemons…?"

"Who says I have any?"

"I do."

"Right question, wrong person." I laid my knife and fork aside. "It was my wife, not I, who spoke of German 'geography as destiny,' and proposed that we go as 'goodwill emissaries' from her Anglo-German Friendship League, after the war, to ameliorate a 'Carthaginian Peace' and avert a 'resurgent *Reich*.'

"How prescient." Baxter got ready to stand and tactfully leave me alone. "The loss of Lady Sandra's wisdom and compassion is a dreadful tragedy for you, I can see, but her death is an equally great loss for the Empire. And before you protest," he raised a quick hand to stop me interjecting, "the last four years have shaken the Social & Political Kaleidoscope in ways previously impossible to imagine. In such dangerous times as ours, the Empire, and Civilisation itself, will need all the wisdom and compassion they can muster, if we are to navigate the tempest-tossed seas of a worldwide revolution -"

"Meh!" I was angered to hear such hackneyed imagery spoken in the same breath as Sandra's sacred name.

He read my face and finished standing. "Let's take a stroll to blow away the cobwebs. Finish your breakfast. I shall be back shortly."

158

I buttoned into my uniform and pulled on the Crombie, a much warmer combination than the clerk's suit that was still my only set of civvies and accompanied Baxter down the gravel drive towards his gateway, he dressed in Harris tweeds, Ulster overcoat, and Donegal bucket hat. However, instead of turning right and crossing Millfield Road to reach Hampstead Heath, as I imagined we would, he turned left up Merton Lane, bespoke brogues scuffing through drifts of fallen leaves from the overhanging oaks and chestnut trees.

"Not much longer," he observed with a shrewd, sideways glance, adjusting his pace to my slower tread, "then you'll be free to return home to a sunnier land than our damp little island. But when you do, please don't think too harshly of your former 'Pommy mates.' Concerning which," he continued in that obliquely English way I find so irritating, "what are your post-war plans? Will you continue to paint and draw? Or have you considered a profession?" Said with another sideways glance. "You'd make a good barrister, one who would do well in our chambers…"

I shook my head. "No thanks."

"Why not?"

"I'm going to Sweden."

"Well, I'll be dashed! You never cease to surprise!" Baxter recovered his poise. "May one ask why you wish to go there, of all places on earth?"

"You may." I did not mean to be brusque, but last night's festivities by happy couples with much kissing and laughter under the mistletoe - more of a French custom than most Britons imagine - had further depressed my spirits. "Firstly: I no longer have a home in Australia. Secondly: the few friends I once had are now mostly dead. Thirdly: The Swedes make Primuses."

And for the first time in our acquaintance Baxter looked genuinely bemused. "What in Heaven's name is so special about a paraffin stove?"

"I bought one in Perth, shortly before embarkation, to heat my rations," I replied, slightly short of breath as we tramped along. "With instructions, in six foreign languages, engraved around the fuel tank, it became a lucky charm. Whenever Fritz strafed us, hot and hard, I'd give it a quick rub, like Aladdin's lamp, and imagine flying his magic carpet, to those distant lands."

"With Sweden top of the list?"

"Yes." I hesitated before concluding: "It seemed to me then, like it seems to me now, that any nation able to design and make something as functionally elegant as a Primus stove, and yet stay out of the war while the rest of the world went mad, is worth taking a closer look." This was the first time in a long time that I had spoken to anyone else of life beyond the immediate present. "I'll try for a job on the factory floor. And start doing something useful with my hands. Instead of, whatever."

We continued uphill in silence, after my impromptu confessional, until Merton Lane joined West Highgate Road.

A horse-drawn Express Dairy milk cart clopped into view, galvanised steel churns and cream cans clanging alongside the driver. He, proudly erect in white smock coat and peaked cap, leather cash satchel slung across his chest. Reins in one hand, whip in the other, perhaps imagining himself as Ben Hur about to thunder around the Circus Maximus, cheered on by a crowd of thousands. If so, it was a more heroic daydream than the reality of his daily deliveries to the tradesmen's entrances of posh middle-class homes, not yet displaced by ugly blocks of flats.

I gave him a relaxed wave, as one does when seeing another bush worker tramping the Wallaby Track. This unsettled the poor old blighter until he saw that I was one o' them there peculiar Ozzies much in the news, recent like, and raised a furtive hand by way of a shy reply.

This simple act of informal mateship broke Baxter's introspective silence as he shot me a quizzical look. "And after Sweden, what then?"

I gave another shrug. "Stick a world map on the wall. Chuck a dart over one shoulder. Go wherever it sticks."

"But what will you do for money?"

"There's plenty in my accounts. But if I need more, I turn pavement artist, selling character sketches. Sixpence plain. One shilling coloured."

"You really are serious then?!"

I ignored his incredulous tone and revisited fond memories of depicting a semi-nude on a Kalgoorlie hotel wall, to earn my keep after a gang of pickpockets dipped me on Kalgoorlie's crowded railway platform.

Baxter had sufficient tact not to enquire any further as we continued plodding uphill before changing direction, past a church and down a laneway into Highgate Cemetery, the last place on earth I would choose to be on such a horrible day. So far as I could tell, everyone else in the neighbourhood was sensibly staying indoors rather than risking a cold - or worse – by visiting this gloomy Gothic necropolis, with its deserted avenues of family sepulchres overgrown by creeping ivy and weeping willows.

It says much about my state of mind that an inverted rifle, bayonet stabbed in the ground, gashed steel helmet hung on the butt, was more authentic than anything else among these acres of extravagant memorials to modest lives soon forgotten, as my guide continued leading the way between sorrowing angels, intricately woven Celtic crosses, and shrouded urns.

At the time of which I shall speak to Baxter's granddaughter-in-law, Karl Marx's grave was a very ordinary affair, as one would expect of a man who was still no more than an historical footnote for all but the most fervent Radical. It was only later, after the Soviet Union had used his words and works to justify the murder of millions, that the British Communist Party reburied him and his family under a monstrously ugly plinth crowned by an equally Stalinist bearded bust.

When I eventually read about it in *La Prensa,* seated at the bar of a Buenos Aires' *bodegón* sometime in the mid-1950s, I could not help thinking that seven tons of granite and concrete were a reasonable alternative to a sharpened wooden stake hammered through Karl Marx' heart, and quite enough to prevent the loathsome creature escaping to inflict more misery upon our world.

That was clearly not the Comrades' intention at the time, gathered around his new gravesite, clenched fists raised high, swearing allegiance to their prophet's World Revolution, a scene unimaginable on the first day of 1919 as I caught Baxter's attention with a sharp cough. "Is this what you wanted me to find, when you left that note?"

"Yes."

"Why?"

"To stimulate your curiosity. Tell me." He unrolled his tobacco pouch. "Who wrote: 'The Bourgeois believes in cowardly compromise, declaring that half a loaf is better than none; the Communist demands the whole loaf, and its means of production! To settle for less is to betray the masses! There can be no compromise in the struggle against the Ruling Class! The Dictatorship of the Proletariat must and will prevail on the Long March of History!'" He shot me another penetrating look. "Well?"

"From its context, this cove." Said with a downward glance as Baxter knocked his pipe on the headstone, dislodging a plug of grey ash that he deliberately ground into the dirt with his heel.

"Correct." He took a pinch of Signature Blend and thumbed it into his briar. "So, why are we discussing it now, above the mortal remains of the bitter, vindictive, spiteful, slovenly, diseased, self-pitying, frequently drunk *Herr Doktor* Marx?"

"No idea!"

"Then consider this. Assuming Lord Nobury's idealists succeed in establishing a League of Nations. And assuming delegates from hither and yon gather around the conference table, bickering and babbling, lying and cheating as is their wont. And assuming the Bolsheviks succeed in conquering much of Eurasia's landmass; admittedly remote at present, but not impossible the way things could go. What are our chances of negotiating World Peace with a fanatical sect sworn to overthrow a civil, civilised, civilising society founded upon the Laws of Tort and Contract, Trial by Jury, and Presumption of Innocence? Thereafter supplanting it with a Jacobin Reign of Terror that will slaughter all who dare question their Satanic rule…?"

He struck a match, drew its flame into his loaded pipe, and left me to ponder this conundrum. "Not much," I replied, after a short, moody, silence.

"Not any!" Baxter corrected, speaking around the pipestem. "It therefore follows, if your dart fails to hit a suitable mark and you decide to practice Law instead, you will discover that for negotiation to succeed, there must be reciprocity with a concomitant readiness - by all parties - to find the middle ground. In other words, a willingness to give as well as take. However! With Dr Marx' demonic disciples, it will always be 'take!' And regardless of how much is taken, it will never be enough to satisfy their greed for absolute control of 'the Masses' they profess to serve, but secretly despise as an éé 'Lumpenproletariat'!"

"Plain English, f'God's sake!" I did not mean to be so offensive, but on such a dreadful day as this, hemmed in by countless thousands of mute memorials to little lives briefly led, it was inevitable that the Hydro's improvised psychotherapies were losing their power to subdue my increasingly frequent angry outbursts.

"Very well." Baxter remained infuriatingly unruffled. "The recent shooting war has paused for the moment but, as 'this cove' rightly predicted with his 'Long March of History,' there is another that will never end -"

"Meaning, what?!"

"Meaning, the cosmic struggle between Light and Dark, Good and Evil, God and the Devil. A war in which, unlike Sweden's recent, highly selective neutrality, there can be no waiting to see which way the cat jumps…"

"Like that Mani-whatsit stuff, you spoke of on the train?" I scowled.

"Ah. You remember." He gave an appraising nod. "Good."

159

Lowering clouds spat sleety rain as we hurried back to Merton Lane where a chauffeured Sunbeam Tourer had driven up while we were away and was now parked at the main entrance.

"Well, I'll be dashed!" Baxter exclaimed. "I thought they were still in Sussex!"

"Who?" I asked, more to be polite than with any urge to know the answer, there being much else on my mind.

"Sir Edward and his wife. Lady Alice probably wants a consultation with Jeanne, about some woman thing or another. Here, let me introduce you."

I dawdled after him, handed over my slouch hat and Crombie for Mrs Williams to dry in her warm kitchen, and trod into the music room where Baxter was conversing with an elderly man wearing a Kitchener moustache below a hawk nose, much like the one Goya depicted in his portrait of the Duke of Wellington.

"Ah! Ian. Allow me to introduce Sir Edward Elgar. Sir Edward? This is Captain Cribdon, a dear friend and colleague of ours."

We shook hands and sized each other up and down, as men do when meeting for the first time. I have no way of telling what he thought of this odd hybrid of soldier, airman, and Intelligence officer, but fortunately he could not see inside my head where his name immediately triggered echoes of chanting *Land of Mud & Whizz Bangs* - a coarse parody of his noble *Land of Hope & Glory* - with my ghostly cobbers of 48 Battalion, as we slogged up the line to Moo Cow Farm.

"Do you play music, Captain?"

I returned to the present, with effort, and realised that a quip about playing *Pop Goes the Weasel* on comb and paper would not go down well in present company. "No sir."

"A pity."

And that was the extent of my conversation with the Empire's most eminent composer as he resumed speaking with the Baxters, for Cécile was also present. "Your girl's been asking when I'm going to complete my Second Violin Concerto," he announced in the bluff, assertive accents of an English country squire that, I suspected, were his camouflage in bluff, assertive English company; we social chameleons are quick to identify others of similar hue.

"It's not that easy anymore," he continued. "Tempi, key signatures, notations, flowed so melodiously in '09. Audiences loved what I did! But something's broken. Nothing feels right anymore. It's all different. Modern music is an affront to the ear. They call me *passé*, but at least an errand boy can still whistle my tunes, which is more than anyone can say of this blasted jungle noise 'jazz' from America!"

I heard an elderly man striving to justify his life's work in a strange new world of manic, discordant sounds that mirrored a strange new world no longer sure of itself or of its purpose. And intuitively felt what a challenge this must be for someone - I later learned - born into a rural cottage family not long after Queen Victoria ascended the throne in faraway London Town. Effectively a foreign land for those few who had the reason, and could afford the fare, to go there by mail coach.

"Nothing feels right anymore," he repeated, still trying to excuse his fading reputation since the time when *Enigma Variations*, and *Pomp & Circumstance* defined the self-confident strut of our imperial noon before the catastrophe of '14-'18 overwhelmed everything we'd imagined would last forever. "This wretched war has destroyed so much more than men and machinery -!"

"How do you mean, sir?" Cécile was listening intently.

"Well, m'dear, it's not easily put into words," he replied kindly, for he had a daughter of his own. 'Maybe I can explain it better if you'd allow me to borrow your instrument for a few moments?"

"Of course." She walked straight to where her violin was kept between practice sessions, returned, and handed it over in a remarkable display of assurance for one so disabled.

Elgar made a slight adjustment to the tuning, lifted the bow, and tried to strike a beguiling theme that could be developed as the first movement of his next violin concerto, but even with my limited understanding I could tell this was no more than a shallow ripple of sounds. At best it was a trifling little piece for a Palm Court Orchestra to play while Society ladies took afternoon tea. Except that their decorous world had just been massacred on the Western Front and was never coming back. All of which made his tepid tune sound even more drained of hope or glory. His critics were right; he was *passé*.

"Well, my dear?" Elgar asked, lowering her violin, his tone-of-voice pleading for another creative artist to throw him a supportive lifeline.

Cécile said nothing. Instead, frowning inwardly, she fingered imaginary chords. "It might work better on the cello, if you will allow me to show what I mean?"

I heard Baxter's sharp intake of breath. A teenage girl, telling England's Greatest Living Composer how to write his music, was not an everyday event in this household, even if their children were friends and he himself gave Cécile informal masterclasses on the violin, whenever Lady Elgar needed to visit Merton Lane's consulting room.

"Of course, m'dear," he replied affably, one musician to another.

With the same aplomb as before, she went over to the larger stringed instrument, sat down, and tucked it between her knees. Then, reaching for the bow on its table alongside her chair, struck an extended chord in B minor and began repainting his tune from the cello's richer palette of colours.

It was an improvement but nothing special until she switched keys to E minor in a manner that froze the marrow of my bones. Developing it with melancholy sweeps and swoops of the bow. Fingers pacing the fretboard with the sombre tread of a bearer party carrying their flag-draped coffin on stooped and sorrowing shoulders. This was not music for afternoon tea parties. This spoke for David, for Percy, for Pat Donovan, for Sandra. For an entire generation cut down in its prime -

"Stop!" Elgar took an abrupt step forward.

Gutted by what I had just heard and felt, I failed to understand what he meant by interrupting in such an agitated manner but was mercifully excused from commenting when Jeanne Baxter and her patient chose that moment to appear. Hands were shaken all round in the French manner, compliments exchanged, and the Elgars left for the short drive to their home in Netherhall Gardens, on the other side of Hampstead Heath.

Cécile took my arm as we dispersed and guided me back to the Music Room, to help put away the instruments, then faced me again with her disturbingly blank eyes. "Thank you, Mr Cribdon. For proving I was right."

"How?" My voice quaked.

"Your tears told me."

"That's impossible -!"

"How would you know?" she demanded with a confident flick of the chin. "Blindness has its compensations! One of which is an acute ear. I heard your gasp of pain and also wanted to weep." She steadied her voice. "Do you think Sir Edward, might be able to do something with it, one day?"

I shrugged helplessly, unable to speak. However, if I do retell this encounter for Frances, I shall suggest that she buys a gramophone recording of Elgar's *Cello Concerto* of which there are now several good readings despite its disastrous first performance. Then find somewhere secluded to lower the needle onto its spinning groove and feel the first movement's sobbing melancholy that speaks of the drenching grief that affected everyone, in the aftermath of a Great War that corrupted old men had promised us would end all war.

160

Taking a long walk in dank, cold weather while still convalescent, had its inevitable consequence. Those former, comparatively swift recoveries after Gallipoli, and the Somme, had overdrawn my account with the Bank of Good Health & Wellbeing. Forced to take up residence in the Baxter's Sick Room - similar in style to the one at Aunt Lucinda's mansion on Grange Road – it was not long before Sir Andrew Crawford hopped over the neighbouring fence to take my pulse, listen intently to his stethoscope, and sign the paperwork for sick leave from the AIF. Not that I was ungrateful for this opportunity to rest and regroup after a rough trot, a condition the family responded to by rallying around their involuntary patient.

Jeanne Baxter donned her white lab' coat and plied me with pills, powders, and potions, morning, noon, and night, becoming better acquainted as I glimpsed the secret pain of an obstetrician who gave birth to a blind child, and from that, sensed how much it had subsequently affected her manner.

Reminded of 15AGH in Alexandria, where and when I'd cheeked and chaffed the beautiful young VAD who became my eternal wife, I now employed a similar stratagem to gain a better understanding of *Mme le Médecin* and it was not long before she was chatting about her family and discussing current affairs, now that Stephen Baxter was back on duty at the War Office.

Even so, I was sufficiently attuned to the man and his methods to imagine him at breakfast, arming her with a list of questions she would later put to me with a charming smile and tilt of the head, for Mlle Martell must have been a winsome young woman in her day. I was therefore careful to stick to my legend, as we later called our background stories during the Second World War, and only once briefly mentioned my fictitious tea planter parents, both allegedly stricken by fever when I was too young to remember them clearly.

Baxter always popped upstairs after returning home from Whitehall, to see how I was getting along and to discuss the day's news. Recently appointed an Officer in the Most Excellent Order of the British Empire on the Victory Honours List, I'm sure he also wanted to show-off the OBE's purple and red-striped ribbon above his left breast-pocket while pretending not to notice, of course.

Lazing in bed, staring at the Sick Room's ceiling, gave me ample time to review his artful comments over the past several months. From the very beginning I'd known they were not as innocent as he wished me to think they were, but it was his spontaneous "Now you see, now you don't!" conjuring trick with Charles Bean's visiting card, and the description of how he met Cecil Rhodes at Oxford, that finally revealed his hand.

The millionaire miner's vision of a secret society pulling the invisible levers of Anglo-American imperial power - benevolent or not, depending upon one's viewpoint – must have resonated strongly with a threadbare young student bereft of family influence, subsisting on his scholarship's meagre stipend and the few extra shillings earned as a private tutor.

It was not hard to imagine how Baxter saw this chance encounter at Oriel College as his Big Chance, and grabbed It with both fists, remaining a loyal disciple even after Rhodes' premature death in 1902. That he was eyeing me as a potential member of whatever they called themselves nowadays, was clear, but he was much mistaken if he thought that I shared his appetite for secrecy; I had my fill of secrets without becoming the custodian of others' as well.

No way was he going to lure me into his *Boys' Own Annual* spy game, like some latter-day Kim in Kipling's novel of that title. Not that I minded plying him with ambiguous answers and edited slips of the tongue in exchange for the generosity and attention I was receiving under his roof, but nonetheless I never let my guard down.

Experience of a wider world, since enlistment, had taught me that men like Stephen Baxter KC expect to profit from every minute spent talking with strangers. Such being the case, there had to be a compelling reason why he'd invested hours, days, weeks upon a previously unknown, unremarkable Australian...

This puzzling thought was interrupted when *Mme le Médecin* - as I still thought of her, not wishing to get too friendly in case she got too close and discovered too much - escorted Claire, Countess Nobury into the Sick Room.

"Good morning, Ian," Her Excellency smiled, graciously depositing a fresh basket of hothouse grapes on my bedside table, "I'm delighted to see you looking so well."

"How could it be otherwise?" I replied with a grateful smile in Jeanne Baxter's direction as she turned away and tactfully left us alone. Not that we had anything particularly confidential to discuss, Lord Nobury having left for Paris on the morning train, with others of the British delegation to the Peace Conference. The Countess would soon be going there herself, to re-join him and be nearer their son at GHQ Montreuil. Accordingly, their London home would be vacant, except for a skeleton staff, and I was welcome to use it as my base while the Australian Corps demobilised from our Horseferry Road HQ, no great distance away from Berkeley Square.

I thanked her warmly, quite overwhelmed to have such a fine London address at my disposal, and sent my regards to Lord Nobury, with an assurance that I was mindful of our conversations about the need for a League of Nations to secure the peace; I saw no point in adding Baxter's gloomier prediction.

Another, more regular visitor was Cécile, who gave me private concerts that counted as practice sessions for her studies at the Royal College of Music in Kensington. As thanks for widening my musical education, I whistled several bush melodies heard on Westralia's Goldfields. Her counterpoint of *Waltzing Matilda* and *Click go the Shears* became a popular encore piece, touring Australia with her husband for J.C.Williamson & Co in the late-1920s and early-30s, and never once failed to delight their audiences. It was rare in those years for visiting European *artistes* to recognise that we had a cultural identity other than Don Bradman's dazzling Test Cricket scores.

The only Baxter I did not see much of at first was Georges. He kept avoiding me, being either too busy preparing for his matriculation exam or visiting friends, until I'm sure his mother gave him a verbal cuffing and ordered him upstairs with recent copies of *Le Temps* and *Berliner Zeitung*.

"Pa' says these are for you, sir." His words were for me, but his eyes were fixed longingly on my tunic, slung over the back of a chair.

I remembered Baxter reading a letter on the terrace of *Hôpital Militaire 731*, in which this young lad spoke of doing well in the Officers' Training Corps at Westminster School, and of his eagerness to see active service in 1919. Instead of which, like Meg Nobury's frustrated VAD hopes, the Armistice had cheated him of a part in his generation's defining experience.

Small wonder he was ill-at-ease with a decorated veteran only a few years older than himself. However, toughening recruits who were no longer boys but not yet men, had given me a fair idea of what was frothing inside his head. "Sit!" I pointed to the chair. Delivered in a tone that only those of us who've earned the ancient and honourable rank of sergeant are entitled to use.

He sat to attention as I swung pyjamaed legs over the side of the bed, facing each other at eye-level. Then, without preamble: "I envy your luck."

"Sir?"

"You have a bright future. Don't waste it on futile regrets."

"S-Sir?!"

"Blokes like me have a brutal past that will dog us until our dying breath," I continued grimly. "The ribbons and badges and pips you envy will soon count for bugger-all on Civvy Street –"

"But sir! You don't understand!"

"Wrong," I snapped back, much reminded of myself at eighteen years of age, about to be kicked out of home and into two years of sweat and grime on the Goldfields, followed by four years of war, "I understand only too well. You've hit a rough patch. It's one we must all get through if we are to properly grow up."

"But -!"

"Tormented by dark fears and strange urges," I ignored his interruptions, "and the only cure, you think, is a smart uniform that bestows an adult identity. Odds are," I added, "there's a girl somewhere who will, you hope, swoon when she sees your picture in the local newspaper."

"It's not like that!"

"My bloody oath it is!" I was deliberately roughening my speech to jolt him awake to the reality of his condition. "You're stuck with being a civvy in a post-war world, one where I'll bet you a pound to a kick up the bum, limbless ex-service beggars will be watching enviously as carefree youngsters stroll past! So, thank your lucky stars and never look back. Because, as someone smarter than I once said: 'Peace hath her victories no less renowned than war'!"

I stopped short. The last time I'd used this quotation from a letter that John Milton - the author of *Paradise Lost* - wrote to Oliver Cromwell, was in a note to David, hoping to dissuade him from enlistment. Not that it had done much good then, and there was no reason to think I would be any luckier with Georges Baxter.

"But I don't know what to do, now it's all over!" he exclaimed in a voice bereft of hope or purpose.

"Watch and wait," I advised. "You're not alone. Nobody knows what the hell to do with the hash we've made of things. His Majesty once told me that he wished he could return to the world before the war but confessed that even if he gave everything a king could, it would not make a skerrick of difference. What's done is done and we're stuck with making the best of a bad job."

"Um." Georges groped for words before settling on a simple: "Is that what you see happening?"

I gave a rueful shrug. "My crystal ball went on the blink yonks ago; I'm hoping the Swedes can fix it. As for yours," I continued, "look into it deeply enough and you'll see a strong and confident young man making his way amidst great change and immense challenge." I paused, distracted by memories of myself at about the same age. "As a wise old lady oft reminded me, drawing upon her own considerable experience of challenge and change: *"Dans l'adversité, c'est l'opportunité!"*

"Was she French?" I had deliberately quickened Georges' interest and distracted him from the pride, pomp, and circumstance of inglorious war on the tunic he was sitting against.

"No. Australian. An actress and performer of high renown in her day. One who knew everybody who was anybody during the Second Napoleonic Empire. A pioneer of women's education in France. *Une dame d'honneur* when the Empress Eugénie opened the Suez Canal. A dauntless organiser of medical services during the Siege of Paris. And when it was all over, the one chosen to present a petition to Bismarck, on behalf of three hundred orphaned girls about to be evicted from their asylum to make room for his Prussian officers."

"What happened?!"

"They camped with their men, on the racecourse at Auteuil."

"Gosh! I'd love to hear more!"

"Later, maybe, but I'm still not tickety-boo and need more zeds," I replied, choosing a Hindi slang phrase that roughly translates as "ready for action," often heard among our Indian Army mates on Gallipoli. I then swung my legs back onto the bed, rolled over, and faced the wall.

After our initial encounter, we enjoyed another couple of lengthy conversations during my last few days of convalescent leave; Georges was bright, and inquisitive, and there was much in him that reminded me of David Shuster.

Inevitably he wanted to hear about the war; just as inevitably I did not. Instead, I told breezy tales of how Percy, Harry, and I climbed the Great Pyramid; of the discoveries we made in the Cairo Museum; of our mad *gharri* ride through the backstreets, omitting the Wozza's squalid brothels, of course. I also ducked Gallipoli and the Somme by yarning about life in the Outback. Describing, instead, how we fossicked for gold and pulled sandalwood for cash; shot 'roos and trapped rabbits for tucker; swapped yarns and told jokes around the campfire, for our entertainment. Great Outdoors imagery that any normal, healthy young lad with even a drop of adventure in his veins, wants to hear about and learn from.

There was more to this than an amiable passage of time. Not only was I telling his father what I wanted him to know and think, I felt it was my duty to advise and encourage a young man at this crucial juncture of his life. In a way, I was passing the torch that Lieutenant Commander Shaw handed to me during our star-strewn night watches in Westralia's Never-Never Country.

It was not an altogether one-sided arrangement. I gained useful insights into what it was like to be a young Anglo-Frenchman, or Franco-Englishman depending upon how Georges felt on any given day at Westminster School, arguably the oldest and most selective of all England's seven great public schools, dating back as it does to the Norman Conquest.

His one constant in life was the worship of a girl at St Paul's School, so I was right after all! The way he spoke of her reminded me of David's adoration of Lady Mary Strathallan, though this romance was unlikely to end badly, both families being of a similar caste, with similar tastes, similar friends, and similar ambitions for their children.

It was inevitable that he would awkwardly nudge our talk around to You Know What, having deduced from the gold ring on my finger, that I was a full bottle on Those Things That Cannot Be Spoken Of.

Better than he could possibly imagine, I recognised an unexploded booby trap of raw passions, much like the enticing *Sprengfallen* that retreating German troops had planted for the unwary to pick up and blow up. There was a great deal that could cripple him for life unless defused with tact and knowledge of how fragile young men are behind their defensive bluster.

The crude mechanics of sex were bound to be a commonplace subject of smutty jokes among these aspiring rulers of the British Empire, so I took a different tack by summarising what I'd told Sandra about my theory that men and women are created equal halves of a better, greater whole. Concluding that our most sacred purpose in life is to search for and cherish that other half who most completes our incomplete selves, for only then will You Know What attain its fullest splendour and radiance and beauty...

"Um. Is that what you did, sir?"

"Yes."

"And?" he persisted eagerly.

"And, as your dad would likely say: 'Here endeth the lesson.'" Or so I thought. Instead, Georges was present the following day as I got ready to board a taxi to AIF Headquarters, stepping forward to shake hands with unusual sincerity for one so young. "Thank you, sir. That, uh, thing you told me, is a big help."

"Glad to hear it. But don't forget, one day it'll be your turn to share the knowledge." I dipped a conspiratorial wink. "Meanwhile, give the young lady my best wishes. Tell her I know she's backed a winner..."

"Gosh."

I turned away, chucked my valise and cane onto the rear seat, and hopped up beside the driver: "Horseferry Road."

"Yuss Guv' -!"

161

This commandeered warehouse had been the engine room of Australia's war effort in Europe for the past three years, its plywood cubicles and offices pulsating with energy and purpose whenever I'd visited in the past, but no longer. The typewriters still clacked but the messengers no longer had a spring in their step as they pushed laden trolleys of documents to and from the Registry, dawdling and gossiping while they did so.

The war was over in all but name. No way could Lord Northcliffe's venomous editorials gee-up the exhausted Allied armies against Germany's starving, mutinous boy conscripts, even if the Peace Conference failed to deliver what the victors were demanding from a surly, resentful, technically unbeaten enemy.

The machine was running down. Soon it would slump to a halt when the last Digger shouldered his kitbag aboard the last troopship and began the long voyage home to a family that would have changed as much as he had during their years apart.

Accordingly, we of the Repatriation Department had our work cut out organising trade training in British factories, agricultural skills on British farms, advanced studies at British colleges, and basic schooling for those many who'd signed their attestation papers with a squiggle or witnessed cross.

This was the substance of my briefing when General Monash welcomed me back to light duties as his personal aide. Though nobody in command was saying so in public, there was a palpable fear that our bored and restless troops would become a breeding ground for Bolshevik agitators unless diverted with sports, and concerts, and conducted tours of famous landmarks they had heard about but never seen before.

That there was every prospect of discontent was evident when units of the usually stolid and compliant British Army began chucking away their kit and going home to mum and the kids. Outright mutiny and desertion, of course, the most serious of all military crimes, but nobody in authority was game to risk a repeat of the Étaples revolt, on British soil, not with rebellion inflaming Ireland, and civil wars convulsing the former Russian, and German, Austro-Hungarian, and Turkish empires.

As Monash elaborated - after inviting me to sit while he paced up and down his office - if the normally obedient Poms were getting Bolshy, he never wanted to see what our troops were capable of doing once the novelty of not being shot at wore off! The destruction of Cairo's red-light district was a foretaste of what could happen to Central London once the weather improved, and larger numbers of bored Australians began prowling Soho's clubs and pubs.

It only needed one officious Bobby to arrest a tipsy veteran of the Western Front, for every other Digger within cooee! to pile-on and free their mate; the policeman would be lucky if he only got thrown in the nearest horse trough, his helmet and truncheon souvenired by jeering Aussies.

I could only nod in agreement, having voiced similar thoughts earlier, to Baxter and Lord Nobury. "Then what's our plan, sir?"

"That depends upon our SNCO's keeping a firm grip without becoming heavy-handed. The Education Scheme is running well, here and in France," he elaborated. "The *Anzac Bulletin* is doing a fine job of publishing good news from home while informing the men how fast their demobilisation is coming along. Speaking of which, pop over to the High Commission in the Strand, introduce yourself to Captain Smart the *Bulletin*'s editor, find out what else he needs to keep up the good work."

"Sir." I jotted an entry in my notebook.

"Additionally, those with family in Britain, are being issued with leave passes and a fortnight's rations, to spend time with their relatives."

"Good idea," I nodded, "the more widely they're dispersed, the less chance of barrack room Bolshies infecting them."

"Quite." He resumed his seat behind the desk. "Speaking of matters personal, you are long overdue for repatriation. I shall be sorry to lose your support, but you've done more than enough." He looked pointedly at the gilded brass A's we both wore on our shoulder flashes, and then at the wound stripes on my cuff. "Go downstairs, see Conroy, tell him I want you on the next draft home."

"Thank you, sir," I replied, after a moment's reflection, "but I'd rather that berth went to someone who needs it more than I."

"How do you mean?" Monash frowned.

"Aunt Lucinda's estate has been sold and I have nowhere else to go in Australia," I replied. "I might as well remain here for as long as I'm needed."

"And then what?" He sat forward, hands together on the blotter. "We'll be done and dusted by midyear."

"That sounds like the right time to visit Sweden."

"'Sweden'?" He sat back sharply. "May one ask why?"

"I intend to see where they make Primus stoves. I've had one in my kit since embarking for Egypt. It's never let me down."

"Hm. Each to his own." Monash sat forward again. "Very well, familiarise yourself with our procedures, and if you do change your mind, say the word."

"Thank you, sir."

And so began arguably the most intensely varied period of my service in uniform, assisting with the repatriation of one hundred and forty thousand troops and their twenty thousand dependants, many of our lads having married British, French, and Belgian girls. These were now assembled in Salisbury Plain's vacant military camps, awaiting their travel warrants to Tilbury or Southampton and the start of a two months' voyage to uncertain futures on the far side of the globe.

Given the complexity of this operation, things went astonishingly well, for which all credit must be given to General Monash and his senior staff under whom I worked, along with other junior officers who could be relied upon to deal with minor concerns before they became major problems higher up the chain of command.

We worked long and hard to project an impression of bright, brisk, cheerful efficiency but inevitably there was a dark side to dismantling an army, starting with the disposal of its vast stocks of arms and equipment. Some could be returned to Australia for peacetime garrison duties, but what does one do with a rusting hillock of steel helmets on a disused parade ground? Or five Nissen huts stacked to the rafters with discarded webbing, mess kits, and entrenching tools? Or acre lots of lorries and ambulances parked on French fields behind the old Front Line? Or thousands of GS wagons and tens of thousands of mules and horses?

The official policy was to auction everything for whatever it would fetch and let the Pay Corps credit Treasury's account with the sums raised. The unofficial reality was somewhat different after shady characters of all persuasions slithered from the shadows, clutching wads of pounds, and dollars, and Swiss francs.

Seriously large sums of money changed hands as factory-new machinery, tools, and spare parts were struck off Service Corps' inventories and bought by fictitious scrap merchants, none of which went anywhere near a blast furnace. At the same time, huge quantities of clothes and bedding, food and household goods were snapped up by black-marketeers or, if military equipment, sold to the illicit arms' dealers who were fuelling Europe's civil wars.

I could have easily exploited these chancers had I so wished; that I didn't was not because of any moral qualms about swindling a remote and impersonal Australian Government, but simply because I had no need for their tainted money.

As I'd told Baxter on our way back from Highgate Cemetery, Sandra's death meant that from now onwards I would be traveling alone, and there were ample funds for that in my bank accounts.

Another one hundred, or one thousand, or one million pounds, or all the money in the world, would never bring her back to life, so what was the point of having more than was needed for my daily keep?

I'm not sure he understood. Instead, he kept hoping I would find purpose in life as a family man, ideally as a barrister, for he had not given up trying to recruit me into his law firm.

Thankfully, there was one person for whom family life still mattered. Phillip Grenville was about to take early retirement, now that the army was retrenching its numbers, and return to his flock at Hampton Rise where, in the fulness of time, he would sit on the bench of magistrates as a Justice of the Peace and be commissioned a Deputy Lieutenant of Hampshire.

None of this was yet apparent when we met for dinner at the Shaftsbury Hôtel where I'd taken digs at five shillings and sixpence a night, all found, leaving me a couple of bob subsistence allowance *per diem*, sufficient for the odd snack and drink at the War Chest Club before it packed up and went home to Australia.

He and the former Miss Pamela Gore-Stanley were in Town to see *Chu Chin Chow*. When asked if I had seen it yet, I shook my head, the truth being too painful to admit, not that they noticed my distress.

It was easy to see why the Hon' Caro' at King Edward's had been so keen on this match. The second Mrs Grenville was indeed a fine specimen of an English county girl. Good stock. Good breeding. Good pick. Clad in a stylish maternity frock, Thomas de Grenouille's bloodline was clearly good to go for another generation.

That they were very fond of each other was also plain to see, despite some difference in ages, and I was warm in my congratulations for I liked them both. Rather more restrained was my promise to "show us around Australia," as Grenville expressed their wish, clearly imagining a sunnier, more expansive Hampshire that we could picnic tour, motoring from village to village, visiting sheep studs much like his own.

162

Upon reflection, it is easy to see why I warmed to Phillip Grenville. As we say in Australia, he had "no tickets on him," which was quite astonishing for those who imagine such men as boozy, bigoted Colonels Blimp. Rather, he had the natural grace of a man who felt no need to affect the pompous airs of less secure city folk. His friendship was true, his loyalty firm, and there was always a place for me at his dinner table whenever I revisited England during the years ahead.

Almost the same could be said of my welcomes at Hampstead or on the French Riviera, where the Baxters were equally keen to hear of my adventures in less-frequented parts of the world. As a couple, they were always glad of my company, but I could never entirely relax in his, or he in mine, and was frequently reminded of two fencers warily touching steel in a *salle d'armes*.

The reason was not hard to find. Men are naturally competitive creatures, viewing each new acquaintance as a potential ally, or potential rival, or potential enemy. Openhearted friendship, such as David and I once shared, is never given lightly. These responses are in our blood, in our bones, in ancestral memories of defending our caves and campsites during dark ages past.

I therefore understood Baxter's caution with a disturbingly different young man like myself. On the face of it, an educated Old Melburnian from a cultivated family background, but also - in his own words – one he would not care to meet up a dark alley. My prank with Commandant Moreau must have sown a rich crop of doubts in such an upright and principled Englishman, although he himself had been notably quick when called upon to play the fictitious Duke of London...

This ability to switch masks in the blink of an eye was probably honed and polished at Oxford during the 1890s, a time and place where those with noble ancestors must have viewed a shabby, penny-pinching scholarship boy as amusing sport in their academic bullring. Still guessing, I'd say it was not only Charles Bean's expatriate Australians who strove to camouflage themselves by becoming more English than the English.

I may develop this theme in my next recorded conversation with his granddaughter-in-law, for it might cast further light on the enigma who became Sir Stephen Baxter KCMG, OBE, KC, MA (Oxon) with a full column of public achievements in *Who's Who*, but a husband and father who left barely a trace of himself in the family photo album. It might also account for why he was so quick with the Latin tag and Biblical verse, his "cuttlefish ink," as he'd cheerfully confessed when his wife scolded him for speaking in riddles at *Hôpital Militaire 731*.

By contrast, she had no need for, or patience with social camouflage. Born into wealth, Jeanne Martel Baxter could afford the luxury of plain speech. Besides, hers was a profession that dealt in hard, verifiable, scientific facts, unlike her barrister husband's grammatical gymnastics and verbal ambushes. Theirs was an attraction of opposites, rather like the snapped-together North and South Poles of adjacent magnets.

Mlle Martell would have brought a substantial dowry into their marriage, and with it a measure of influence hinted at by the children's French forenames, most likely those of her *haut bourgeois* parents, not those of her husband's village vicar father and primary schoolteacher mother.

Stephen Baxter's share in their joint venture was, I'm sure, his growing eminence at the Bar and the invisible powers that Cecil Rhodes' secret society conferred upon its handpicked membership, a gift that would have given much satisfaction to those with old scores to settle, as he himself had hinted at when he reminded me that "revenge is a dish best eaten cold." Apropos of which, I would not mind betting that quite a few of his scornful Oxford contemporaries had reason to wonder why their luck turned so consistently bad in later life.

Meanwhile, signals, requisitions, and memoranda kept shuttling between my In and Out trays. A period when, if I was not putting in a full day's work at AIF HQ, I'd be hitching courier flights across the Channel to deal with problems that ranged from the disposal of miles of uncleared barbed wire, to pacifying angry French fathers whose daughters had been left holding the baby when their Aussie boyfriends skipped town.

Consequently, I had neither the time nor the inclination to stay in touch with Baxter after his return to civilian life. Thus, it came as quite a surprise when a Corps of Commissionaires' messenger delivered an ivory bond envelope addressed to me at Horseferry Road, an intaglio-engraved globe of the world and The Garrick Club where there would normally be a postage stamp with the King's head in profile. No return address. No telegraphic code. Nothing. And the handwritten note inside was equally aloof:

Ian

It will be greatly appreciated if you can spare the
time to take luncheon with me, tomorrow,1pm.

S.B.

I was naturally irritated by the assumption that if one had business with him, or with it, one would know where to find them. Scowling at their thinly veiled insolence, I was about to give the messenger – patiently waiting outside for a reply - an equally curt note, citing a prior engagement, when General Monash, whose office abutted my cubicle, glanced up from the minutes of yesterday's staff meeting and sensed my darkening mood. "Problems, Ian?"

"Mr Baxter has invited me to lunch tomorrow."

"Any special reason?"

"None that I can see."

"Hm. Let me take a look."

I went across to his desk and laid Baxter's note on my current chief's blotter, adding an exasperated: "He must think I've got nothing better to do than to come running whenever he snaps his fingers!"

"And have you?"

"Of course," I replied stiffly. "The 'Gazers are forecasting three-tenths alto cirrus, and a fifteen knot sou'westerly, for tomorrow's flight to Cologne with 3ACCS's demob' schedule." This referred to an Australian Casualty Clearing Station that was our element in the British Army of Occupation of the Rhine.

"True," he nodded, "but do you not remember me saying how my worthy spymaster never utters a single syllable without there being an ulterior motive, or words to that effect?"

"Frequently, sir."

Monash, a practicing lawyer himself, resumed a close examination of Baxter's note before glancing up again. "By the same token, we may be sure he never sets pen to paper without weighing every comma, every full stop. And notice his choice of location for your meeting."

"It matters?" I frowned.

"Oh yes." Said with a cryptic smile. "Membership of the Garrick is restricted to leading King's Counsels and Senior Judiciary, with a leavening of distinguished actors, authors, and prominent journalists. A Bohemian cabal that meets and mingles, plans, and plots, without lesser mortals being any the wiser."

"Well, as I'm none of those, I see no reason why I should comply with his peremptory summons!"

"Quite the reverse. You will accept his generous invitation -"

"But what about 3ACCS, sir?"

"Conroy can handle that. I need to know what part our Mr B is playing in the aforesaid planning and plotting. Because, of one thing we may be sure, this leopard will never change his spots…"

"Yes. Sir."

The following day, I took a taxi to the top of St Martin's Lane, a stone's throw from Covent Garden Opera House in the heart of London's Theatreland. From there I took a right-hand turn down Garrick Street; pacing towards Number 15, twenty minutes before the appointed time; in appearance just another colonial soldier exploring the Empire's capital city before going home with a lifetime of stories to tell, retell, and embellish.

Pausing where Floral Street enters from Covent Garden market, I propped against one of those black-painted stanchions that look as if someone had repurposed old cannon when breech-loading artillery entered service during the previous century and took out the pocket guidebook that all AIF troops were issued with, before going on leave in Britain.

I flipped pages, a sightseeing Australian wondering where to go next, natural cover that gave me ample time to study the club's three storey, Italianate façade on the other side of the street. What I was looking for, but failed to see, was its service laneway. There had to be one, for I could not imagine such an establishment allowing provision merchants to traipse through the front door with their baskets of vegetables, boxes of fish, and sides of meat.

The chances were good that I had passed a rear entrance when my taxi drove up St Martin's Lane. Not that I had reason to imagine it would be needed in London, but my apprenticeship as a Sydney barrow thief had trained me to locate at least one alternative escape route before entering an unknown space or place.

Recce completed to the best of my ability, I pocketed the guidebook and continued down Garrick Street to New Row, where I crossed over and approached the club from the opposite direction, arriving at 1 pm on the dot.

This was my first experience of London's fabled men's clubs. To be frank, I failed to see what all the fuss was about as I climbed a short flight of steps and entered the vestibule, my sketcher's eye noting its richly hued Victorian decor and polychrome tesserae pavement adjoining a chequerboard tiled floor at the foot of an ornately carved oaken staircase.

"How may We assist you, sir?" A uniformed servant emerged and barred my way.

His regal "We" raised my hackles. "You've got a bloke here called 'Baxter.'" Announced in the menacing growl that Sarn't Cribdon kept for unlucky soldiers.

"Er. Um. Mr Stephen Baxter -?"

"The same. We're having lunch. Where is he?"

"Upstairs. In the Library. This way sir!"

"Stand. Guard the gate. I'll find him."

"But -!"

Ignoring the fellow's anguished squeak, I began ascending the carpeted staircase alone, pausing now and again to admire several choice portraits of eighteenth-century actors and actresses, contemporaries of the Club's namesake, David Garrick, actor manager of Drury Lane Theatre during the 1750s.

Two elderly members, descending from the second floor, were visibly alarmed by the sight of an unaccompanied Australian examining their prized art collection, and probably imagined I was about to souvenir the lot, for such was the AIF's reputation as a gang of freebooting vagabonds. Proving that discretion being the better part of valour, they decided against challenging me and, instead, hurried downstairs muttering angrily.

Several images I recognised from a volume of etchings in Aunt Lucinda's library, including Harlow's *Sarah Siddons as Lady Macbeth*; Lawrence's portrait of her younger brother, Phillip Kemble; and Hogarth's portrayal of Garrick himself as Shakespeare's *Richard the Third* awakening from a nightmare on the eve of battle. But what really stopped me in my tracks was an elegant Romney entitled:

Miss Kitty Brandon of Smock Lane Theatre Dublin
as
Fanny Flounce in The World Aghast, or The Truth Will Out

Had I not known better, I could have sworn that a radiantly youthful Aunt Lucinda had posed for England's most eminent theatrical portraitist. Impossible, of course, George Romney having died in Northern England twenty-odd years before Lucinda Cribdon was born in a convict colony on the West Coast of the Pacific Ocean. And yet, despite all, the resemblance was astonishing. Whoever this unknown actress was had the same fine features, the same exuberantly auburn hair, the same confident tilt of the chin, the same sprightly twinkle in her eye as she glanced over her right shoulder, artfully twitching the hem of her petticoat to display trim, white stockinged ankles –

"Stop! Please!!" The porter was panting upstairs after me. Still puzzled by what I had just seen, I allowed myself to be chivvied the rest of the way to the second floor by an understandably nervous club servant, for no doubt those two members had just strafed him for allowing an unsupervised visitor to roam their premises.

Stephen Baxter was ticking clues on today's *Times* crossword. He glanced up, saw us approach, tucked his propelling pencil into its waistcoat pocket, folded the newspaper and stood. "Compose yourself, Mr Burns. Captain Cribdon is an old colleague and most welcome guest."

"Yesser! Thenk'ew'ser!"

Baxter consulted his fob watch, secured by a slim gold chain strung from left to right across the immaculately tailored dark grey waistcoat, "I've booked a table for one-thirty. Sufficient time to share our news and compare our views. Come." He began gently steering me towards the Members' Bar, like the rest of this rummy establishment a crowded gallery of etchings, engravings, and portrait busts of everyone who was anyone during the previous two centuries of English theatrical life and letters. "Now. Refresh my memory. Did you not take Scotch & Soda at *le Réveillon*...?"

"Too early in the day. Water will do fine."

Baxter caught the waiter's eye: "One Seltzer. One G&T." Then, as we settled into one of the discreet corner tables: "It's awfully good of you to accept my invitation at short notice. I know how busy you chaps are at HQ, but things are no less hectic in civilian life. Especially with Jeanne dismantling the hospital in Nice, and me booked aboard this evening's Cross-Channel Ferry."

"Then it is I who should be thanking you for making time to shout me a meal." I had decided to play the slangy, irreverent Australian in these dignified surroundings, a pose crafted to keep Baxter lightly off-balance in our latest duel of wits.

"*Au contraire,*" he smiled, pleasantly enough, though I'm pretty sure he had my measure, "but by the time I'm done with the Peace Conference, you'll be off on your travels, and I would not wish you to leave England without saying goodbye."

"Is this my cue to enquire what you'll be doing in Paris?"

"I'd be most disappointed if you did not," he replied. "As previously observed, our business requires a lively, albeit discreet curiosity. But to answer your question directly," he continued, glancing up to acknowledge the drinks waiter, "Nobury is having a spot of bother with the French over Syria and Lebanon. None of which is helped by a chap from the Arab Bureau, for whom the prospect of two new kingdoms – Iraq and Trans Jordan – is still not enough. He now wishes to revoke Sykes-Picot and, in its place, stitch together a third Arab kingdom from that ragbag of ancient animosities, Palestine..."

"Bloody Gyppo Land!" I had settled into my role as the rough soldier who believes he is an authority on the Middle East after a brief exposure to its garish sights and pungent smells.

"Too far west," Baxter corrected with a disapproving frown. "The Canal remains pivotal but there's a zone of equal importance around Kirkuk on the Mosul oilfield, in what is still nominally the Ottoman Empire, though for how much longer is anyone's guess. Then what?"

"No idea," I shrugged. "But from what I've seen of the place, when God gives the world its next Noah's Flood enema, Egg Whipped is where He'll shove the fire hose."

"Very expressive," said with a curt sniff, "however I would prefer you to focus your quickness of mind, rather than glibness of tongue, on matters- that-matter!"

"Which are?"

"The imminent break-up of the Turkish Empire."

"Is that such a bad idea?" Said by a young man with vivid memories of being shot at and shelled by the Turks.

"No. Worse."

"How so?"

"Because we risk dismantling six centuries of despotic rule, thereby uncaging millennia of tribal hatreds that will render the Middle East ungovernable for as far ahead as one can see," he replied with a sharp, sideways glance to read my expression. "And the tragedy of it all is that a more adroit

Foreign Policy in Whitehall, one more sensitive to Ottoman pride and greed in Constantinople, could have kept Turkey a viable neutral power!"

"How?" I blinked incredulously, for I still had much to learn.

"By recognising the Levant's Golden Rule," Baxter replied drily. "Plump bags of sovereigns, discreetly distributed, would have done much to modify Mehmet Pasha's pro-German stance -"

"You're not suggesting we could've bought them off, before Gallipoli?" I interrupted, not yet aware of *Realpolitik*'s cruel indifference to life, love, and liberty.

"Of course." Baxter shot me another shrewd, sideways glance. "An additional two million pounds, with a gracious note of apology, would have been a bargain price to pay for that pair of battleships stolen by a recklessly arrogant First Lord of the Admiralty, and checkmated those two battlecruisers the Kaiser replaced them with, free of charge. Instead, we've squandered tens of millions more in Mesopotamia and Palestine, fighting the Ottomans, and in the process done incalculable harm to our long-term interests..."

"That's as maybe," I scowled, "but what's the connexion between Lord Nobury, the French, two stolen ships, and whatever the hell an 'Arab Bureau' is?"

"Thank you for reminding me." Baxter was too old a fox to be fazed by my rough manner. "Colonel Lawrence has an appointment with us at Hôtel Crillon tomorrow afternoon, during which we shall curb his romantic enthusiasm for Arabia and, instead, focus it on a more immediate concern -"

"Which is?"

"Crude petroleum," my host and mentor replied simply. "We shall need an overland pipeline from Mosul to a Mediterranean port, either Haifa or Tripoli, to limit our reliance upon seaborne tankers from the Persian Gulf. However," Baxter concluded, "before certain interests commit their funds to such an ambitious project, HMG and the French Government must be sure of political stability in a region notorious for its instability. Especially now, with Bolsheviks agitating the Trans-Caucasian oilfields..."

"And you think this Colonel Whatsisname can deliver?"

"He unified disunited tribes against the Turks. Let's see if he can perform a similar trick by safeguarding a pipeline of inestimable strategic value, best imagined as our aboveground equivalent of the Suez Canal..."

"How does that work?" I frowned.

"'Think about it and report when you have the answer,'" Baxter was reading his watch to check the time. "But here's a clue," he continued, looking up again. "The Royal Navy has decommissioned its last coal-fired warship and is now wholly dependent upon the kindness of strangers for its imported fuel oil, rather than the brawny muscles of Durham or Welsh coal miners..."

"So?" It says much about my lack of understanding that I failed to see what is, nowadays, commonplace knowledge.

"Ask yourself this." Baxter countered. "If, as has been claimed: 'No nation has permanent allies, or permanent enemies, only permanent interests.' What is the Empire's supreme 'permanent interest'?"

I remained silent, reminded of a similar phase during David's shrewd analysis of Australia's need for Blood Debt - on land, at sea, in the air – to counterbalance Japan's ambitions for German New Guinea.

"Well?"

"No idea."

"Then ask yourself this: how come a pair of rainy islands imposed their rule on one quarter of the planet's landmass? And what is it that sustains such extraordinarily good fortune…?"

"Still no idea, but I'm sure you're about to enlighten me."

"Trade," he replied simply. "Raw materials 'In'; manufactured goods 'Out'; every ton carried on 'British bottoms,' as London's insurance brokers quaintly describe our Merchant Marine. Thus, the wealth of five continents passes over the counter and through the cash box of our 'Nation of Shopkeepers.' But, and here's the rub, this good fortune can only continue for so long as the Royal Navy patrols and controls our shipping lanes…"

"Hence the need for that oil pipeline thing?" I was beginning to discern a cobweb of global power radiating from the Bank of England in nearby Threadneedle Street.

"Correct." He hesitated before concluding: "If this war, just paused, has taught us anything, it is that petroleum, in its many forms, will decide the next one -"

"'Next one'?" I interrupted with all the righteous indignation of a young man who'd had his fill of war. "The League of Nations will damn' soon have something to say about that!"

"You and I both hope so," Baxter agreed with an imperturbable smile. But to wager everything on Peace Everlasting is to bet, at devilish long odds, against five thousand years of recorded human history. And before you interrupt me again, recall what I said when we visited Dr Marx's grave: an existential struggle is underway in Russia and gaining ground in the borderlands of Europe and Asia. High hopes and pious principles will never nail the lid shut on that Pandora's Box of evil spirits."

He forbore from mentioning Lord Nobury's name, but I knew of whom he was thinking as he continued in the same brooding tone: "America's president should never have promised the world a League of Nations in his Fourteen Points – four more than God allowed Moses on Mount Sinai - without first squaring the Isolationists in Congress."

"Why not?"

"Because those pragmatic, hard-headed New World businessmen have no further need to concern themselves with the Old World's cares and woes," Baxter replied simply. "By intervening as and when they did, 'to save Freedom & Democracy,' they ensured that their War Loans will eventually be repaid in full. Unlike what would have happened had Ludendorff won at Amiens."

"So, you're saying, the League doesn't have a future?!"

"I'm sure it has," he shrugged, "but for how long, once America reneges, as she surely will?"

"Then, these past four years, have been, for nothing?!"

"That is not for me to say," he shrugged again. "I merely present Evidence for the Prosecution; juries of historians will decide the verdict. But of one thing we can be sure," he continued, "the world is entering a time of dangerous uncertainties, unlike anything we knew as recently as four years ago, as Sir Edward sensed when you met him at our place and as you're about to discover in Sweden. Something to do with Primus stoves, is it not…?"

"And much else."

"Like?"

"Nothing you'd understand."

"Try me…"

"It's private."

"Very well." Baxter finished his drink, read his watch, and looked up again. "There being no more on the agenda, let's adjourn to the Dining Room. Our Beef Wellington is the best in London, and I've taken the liberty of ordering in advance; it should be about ready."

In these exalted circles one may discuss business before a meal, and after a meal, but never during a meal for to do so would disrespect the chef's skills and artistry. Not that I had much to say after our conversation ended somewhat abruptly. Baxter was corresponding withdrawn as we shook hands while the porter loaded bags into a waiting taxicab. "Good luck, Ian. Stay in touch."

"That will depend on where the dart sticks," I replied cagily.

Later that same afternoon, General Monash quizzed me about our meeting and seemed as baffled as I was when I described its inconclusive nature. "But you say there was mention of an 'Arab Bureau,' and talk of revoking Sykes-Picot?"

"Yes. Whatever the hell those mean."

"They could mean that London's agreement with Lord Rothschild requires closer attention."

"Sir?"

Monash glanced up and shook his head. "Nothing."

Baxter's next communication was just as opaque as General Monash's cryptic remark when, two days later, I received a well-worn copy of:

His Majesty's Consular Service
Briefing Notes (Sweden)
1913

Its loose-leaf pages laced together between blue, gold-embossed cardboard covers, addenda, and corrections cut and pasted over previously annotated entries. On its title sheet a neatly handwritten:

Read, mark, and inwardly digest.

S.B.

163

By now, our original one hundred and forty thousand AIF troops had shrunk to fewer than ten thousand, prompting the realisation that unless we staged their Victory Parade soon, it would be a paltry affair indeed. Accordingly, one was scheduled on Saturday May 3rd for all departing Dominion troops.

Contingents from Canada and Australia, New Zealand, South Africa, and Newfoundland - in that order - were detailed to lead British cavalry and infantry, sailors, and nurses, plus war trophies like the dreaded "Minnie" *Minnenwerfer*, and a crumpled Fokker Dr-1, mounted on motor lorry trailers. Not quite a Roman Triumph, after His Majesty quashed the bizarre idea of including German prisoners of war under armed guard, but not a bad shot given the limited time we had to organise it.

One contingent, noticeable by its absence, was the Indian Army's. I thought then and still think this was a disgraceful omission. India's professional army had served with the utmost courage and devotion to duty on every battlefield of the Great War and ought to have marched alongside us. I can only hope that someone in authority spotted the oversight and made certain that an Indian contingent had pride of place in the main parade – ideally the Bikaner Camel Corps' mounted infantry in all their buccaneering glory, followed by marching ranks of Gurkhas and Sikhs, Dogras and Garhwalis, among others - when Peace was officially declared six weeks later.

Meanwhile, my duties largely consisted of seeing that our men did not stray too far from an encampment the Royal Engineers had built in Hyde Park by erecting hundreds of tents and marquees, strung together by electrical cables and a network of temporary water mains. Then, just as smartly, erecting mess huts and latrines for the five thousand men and women who would form-up on the road near the Wellington Memorial at 0930 hours.

My greatest concern was that some hooligan in our ranks would pull a memorable prank as we marched down Constitution Hill and left-wheeled past the royal saluting base outside Buckingham Palace. Accordingly, I had a word with our NCOs and reminded them that they were not only marching for themselves but also for tens of thousands of dead mates.

They got the message and behaved impeccably, with General Sir John Monash and our other corps commander, General Sir Harry Chauvel, riding at the head of the AIF's contingent. Of the two it was clear who had led the Desert Mounted Corps to victory at Beersheba and Nazareth before storming across the Golan Heights to capture Damascus.

By contrast, Monash the infantryman was never at ease in the saddle and, despite my best efforts to pick a quiet mare, and a veterinary officer's mildly doped oats, his mount became skittish whenever the Canadians' brass band banged and blared at the head of our procession.

This I only learned later, after the parade returned to our starting point, each contingent having saluted the royal party before marching down Buckingham Gate, along Victoria Street, up Whitehall to Trafalgar Square, Haymarket, Piccadilly, and back again to the Wellington Memorial, cheered every yard of the way by crowds of flag-waving Londoners, despite an unseasonably light drizzle and the threat of heavier rain.

Not that I witnessed these events. Marble Arch, Hyde Park, the Serpentine were hallowed ground as I trod past the silent bandstand where Sandra and I had waltzed *Any Time is Kissing Time*, until reaching the wooden jetty. Head bared and bowed, I stood alone, looking down at our little rowing boat, moored with others awaiting hire.

Returning to my post, I watched the parade fall out to spend the rest of the day sightseeing or flirting with the nurses or service women from the Army, Navy, and Air Force. After checking with my NCOs, I typed a positive report which I delivered to Monash's office the following day.

He paused from emptying his desk drawers, flicked through the foolscap file, and looked up again. "Thank you, Ian. Well done."

"Thank you, sir." Then, aware of the echoing, deserted office space at ground floor level, for it was Sunday morning, I added: "Strange to think, when the next draft embarks, it'll all be over..."

"No." He shook his head. "It won't."

I blinked with surprise: "How do you mean, sir?"

"We have one last duty to perform."

"And what might that be?" I queried, surprised by his sombre tone.

"Take the blame." Monash composed his features before looking back at me. "Political reptiles by their very nature lie, and cheat, and obfuscate. Such being the case, you surely don't imagine that the likes of Billy Hughes and his Gory Bleeders will ever admit to creating the conditions, in peacetime, that widowed and orphaned so many tens of thousands of voters, in wartime?"

"It seems unlikely!"

"You always were a master of understatement," my chief observed drily. "So, whom to denigrate and accuse of mishandling the war? Why, the Officer Corps, of course! Easy prey for newspapers to depict as gin-swilling butchers who bungled what politicians fomented, on terrain that politicians chose, with means that politicians begrudgingly gave us to do their filthy political work -"

"That's a bit harsh!"

"Not harsh enough." He got ready to resume his packing. "I expect a lukewarm reception, at best, when Lady Monash and I return home."

"I still think that's unduly pessimistic," I insisted, uncomfortable with the sight of a man I admired, so downcast, as I imagined, unnecessarily.

"I think not." He straightened. "Concerning other matters, I've looked at your papers. To my surprise, you were still only a substantive second lieutenant although having more than fulfilled your duties as an acting-captain."

"Thank you, sir."

"I've confirmed your captaincy and backdated it six months on full pay. This should be more than enough for a well-earned rest in Sweden."

"Thank you, sir!"

"I look forward to hearing of your adventures when you return to Melbourne." He shared a wry smile. "By then we'll qualify as old comrades. Meeting on anniversaries. Reminiscing about times and places that no one else cares about anymore."

"I suppose so..."

"You suppose rightly." He straightened. "Anyhow, I had better not detain you any longer." He put out a hand for me to shake. "I'm going on leave. Lady M wants to view the battlefields she's only seen as maps and kinema newsreel pictures. I don't suppose you'll still be here when I return in a month's time. As you say, 'it's all over now.'" He almost smiled. "I'm sure a man of your resourceful nature will choose the right moment for his departure."

He was right. I did choose my time to leave the AIF, but not before taking delivery of a bespoke tweed Norfolk jacket and plus fours by Huntsman of Saville Row, and a matching a pair of brogues from the royal bootmaker, John Lobb in St James Street. New shirts, stockings, and underwear of the same quality completed my escape kit, as I called it. Having read how variable the weather can be in Sweden at this time of year, I kept my Burberry trench coat, the three pips stripped from its epaulettes.

My last day in uniform, or so I imagined at the time, was the Thursday morning I reported to Horseferry Road, now an empty shell awaiting a demolition crew to rip out the plywood partitions and internal walls, prior to restoring it as a warehouse.

There was nobody at Reception. There was hardly anyone inside the place at all. Only a couple of civvy contractors with tape measures, estimating the salvage value of its wood and fittings. One of them heard my footsteps and glanced up with surprise. "Gor! We thort yous woz'orl gon!"

"I'm the lucky last." As I probably was, now that our final draft was heading into the Bay of Biscay, after embarkation at Southampton. "'I've come to say cheerio to the ghosts."

"There'll be a few o' them…"

"Uh huh."

"Well. Anyfink we c'n'do, jus'arsk."

"Thanks." I turned away and went into the Registry, its shelves cleared of indexed files and boxed papers the previous week. Shutting the door firmly behind me, I recovered a cache of blank forms and rubber stamps hidden deep under the countertop.

I then authenticated my name, number, and rank with illegible signatures and thumps of green ink, reminded of the time I'd bluffed the French railway authorities into issuing Baxter and myself with their highest priority travel pass a lifetime ago, or now it seemed.

That done, I took my discharge papers around to the Paymasters' Department and oversaw the banking of my accumulated pay before stepping into the Strand to hail a passing taxi: "The Shaftsbury."

"Ri'oh Guv'!" The slouch hat promised and got a good tip, for I was feeling increasingly buoyant as I cut ties with the past, having taken my leave of the Noburys en famille the previous night, during which Meg had been sharply rebuked by His Lordship for her petulant misbehaviour.

There was also growing sense of anticipation and excitement - not unlike the splash of Ascanius' mooring lines when we inched away from Fremantle's quayside - as I took the lift to my room where I stripped off before changing into civvies, quite impressed by the trim, weathered figure in the wardrobe mirror; only the cropped scalp marking me as an ex-soldier.

My dress uniform, flying helmet, goggles and logbook, revolver, correspondence, and various souvenirs were already on their way to my aunt's firm of solicitors in Melbourne – stowed inside an empty Lewis gun chest To Be Collected – though by whom, or when, or how was as unknowable as everything else ahead of me.

The barracks uniform I hung up on the wardrobe door and, using my pocketknife to unpick the Winged-O brevet, carefully recovered the silver sixpence tucked behind it, a lucky charm that had clearly worked against the Fokkers' Evil Eye. Then my MC and DCM ribbons, wound stripes, overseas' service chevrons, Anzac-A, Intelligence Corps' laurel green collar tabs, and finally my captain's pips. These I rolled in a spare khaki handkerchief and tucked alongside *Briefing Notes* in my valise.

I'd found them quite useful, sitting up in bed at night, reading a page or two while the Veronal wove its magic spell. Not that I had reason to memorise the 67,938 tons of newsprint exported in 1913, milled from forests that covered more than half of Sweden's 174,000 square miles.

Or be concerned that this narrow country - sandwiched between a newly independent Norway and a recently liberated Finland - extended 978 miles from the Arctic Circle to within sight of Denmark.

Or wonder why Sweden's 5.7 million inhabitants mostly lived, worked, and farmed within a triangular area bounded by Stockholm, Malmö, and Gothenburg

That I did so was the curse of a flypaper memory for statistics and data, useful or trivial, it made no difference. In the former category I filed the discovery that Sweden had been a Great European Power until a century ago, after which it shrank within itself, cultivating a national mood called *Lagom* in which everyone competed to be more modest and self-effacing than his neighbour. That a brash young Australian might find this hard to swallow and follow had occurred to Baxter, whose pencilled *Nota Bene! S.B.* in the margin was a timely warning. As was a similar note on a recent addendum, reporting Sweden's pro-German sympathies, despite an official policy of neutrality during the recent war.

HM's Consular Service had no interest in the progressive social policies that Sandra had intended to assess, adapt, and adopt for our Anglo-German Friendship League, after I'd explained to her how a pocket Primus stove symbolised sanity in a world gone mad. This was the private business I'd blocked Baxter's enquiry with, at the Garrick, and her unspoken bequest to me now as I packed the last of my kit before buckling the valise's straps and hefting its German leather rifle sling.

Finally, I uncapped my fountain pen and composed a brief message to the chambermaid:

> *Permission granted to sell my uniform*
> *for whatever it will fetch in Petticoat*
> *Lane second-hand clothes' market.*

> *Wm Braithwaite*

I have no idea why I chose my true name as I poked this note into the tunic's top buttonhole; perhaps to further cover my tracks, before addressing a plain postcard to:

> *Mr & Mrs Stephen Baxter*
> *2 Merton Lane*
> *Hampstead N6*

On the reverse side, an unsigned:

> Job 20:9

It would take them far less time to decode my laconic farewell than I had needed to discover an apt verse in the hotel's *Gideon Bible*.

One final inspection to check that nothing but memories was being left behind, then downstairs to settle my account and buy a ha'penny stamp for the card, dropped into the Shaftsbury's polished brass letterbox as I strode out into a delightful sunny day.

Halting at the head of the steps, I inhaled the heady air of freedom and read my silver wristlet watch, the RFC's *pheon* broad-arrow mark on its luminous dial; only another hour and a quarter to go before taking a reserved seat on the Newcastle-Gothenburg Ferry Express.

A cabby spotted my raised cane and braked hard. "Where to Guv'nor?!"

"King's Cross Station."

The End

The Book

Typography and interior design and are by Katharine Kempton of inkboxgraphics.com.au who selected 10point Palatino, a font that celebrates the sixteenth century Italian master of calligraphy Giambattista Palatino and is now among the world's most widely read typefaces.

Front cover design, map illustration and photography; back cover image montage and artwork by Michael Cannon of designeyecreative.com.au

Text by James Patrick Talbot @ jptalbot.com.au

Made in the USA
Las Vegas, NV
11 November 2023

80648214R10393